TOUCHSTONE

THE ODYSSEY
A MODERN SEQUEL

by Nikos Kazantzakis

TRANSLATION INTO ENGLISH VERSE,
INTRODUCTION, SYNOPSIS, AND NOTES

by Kimon Friar

Illustrations by Ghika

A TOUCHSTONE BOOK

PUBLISHED BY SIMON AND SCHUSTER

A TOUCHSTONE BOOK
PUBLISHED BY SIMON AND SCHUSTER
A DIVISION OF GULF & WESTERN CORPORATION
SIMON & SCHUSTER BUILDING
ROCKEFELLER CENTER, 1230 AVENUE OF THE AMERICAS
NEW YORK, NEW YORK 10020

ISBN 0-671-20247-2
LIBRARY OF CONGRESS CATALOG CARD NUMBER: 58-9048
MANUFACTURED IN THE UNITED STATES OF AMERICA
PRINTED BY THE MURRAY PRINTING CO., FORGE VILLAGE, MASS.
12 13 14 15

This translation is
for James Merrill

CONTENTS

INTRODUCTION

I. A MODERN SEQUEL TO HOMER

When in the winter of 1938, at the age of fifty-five, Nikos Kazantzakis first published his *Odyssey* in Athens, it had long been awaited with intense anticipation, and was received with confused bewilderment. Expectation had run high during the twelve years since 1925 when he had worked and reworked through seven complex versions of what he hoped would be the final and best summation of his life and thought. Already he had taken his place among the greatest of modern Greek authors with his many prose and poetic dramas,* his novels,† his books of travel and philosophy, and his invaluable translations, including Dante's *Divine Comedy* and Goethe's *Faust.* Later, he was also to publish his translations into modern Greek of Homer's *Iliad* and *Odyssey,* but now he had dared to challenge, or so it seemed, the most sacrosanct of all poets not only by grafting his own epic firmly on Homer's poem, but also by giving it the same title and by continuing "the sufferings and torments of renowned Odysseus" in a modern sequel three times the size of his predecessor's original. He had even dared to attempt this in an age in which, all scholars were agreed, it was no longer possible to compose a long narrative poem based on myth. The critics now found themselves confronted by a huge tome of 835 pages (subsidized by an American patron, Miss Joe Mac Leod), 10 by 15 inches in size, handsomely printed in a special type, limited to an edition of 300 copies, written in 24 books (one for each letter of the Greek alphabet), and in 33,333 lines of an extremely unfamiliar seventeen-syllable unrhymed iambic measure of eight beats.

Furthermore, the poem was filled with disturbing innovations and seemed to depart from tradition in every conceivable way, for the poet had chosen to publish it in a form of simplified spelling and syntax which he had long advocated, analogous in English to the experiments of Robert Bridges in *The Testament of Beauty.* Worse, he had ruthlessly cut away the atrophied yet hallowed accentual marks imposed on ancient Greek by Byzantine scholars, retaining only the acute accent for certain syllables in order to indicate stress, much as in Spanish. Blood had been spilled and scholars deposed from their chairs at the University of Athens for proposing similar linguistic simplifications. But most distressing of all to

* Of interest to readers of the *Odyssey* are *Odysseus, Theseus, Christ, Buddha,* and *Prometheus,* a trilogy.

† In the United States and in England Kazantzakis is best known by his novels *Zorba the Greek, Freedom or Death,* and *The Greek Passion* (entitled *Christ Recrucified* in England).

Athenian intellectuals was to be confronted with a special lexicon of almost 2,000 words appended to the poem and meant to elucidate a diction and an idiom with which they found themselves disconcertingly unfamiliar, although (as I was later to attest) these words and phrases were in daily and familiar use by shepherds and fishermen throughout the islands and villages of Greece, or imbedded in their folk songs and legends. Even then, however, there were many who hailed the book for what it was—the greatest of modern Greek poems and a masterpiece of the modern world. Yet it was inevitable that most critics, confronted with a work of such scope, should shy away from considerations of its meaning and its poetic worth and preoccupy themselves with its exterior manifestations, its strange spelling, its unfamiliar diction, its lack of accentual marks, its unusual measure, and primarily with its "anti-classical" style and structure.

The appearance of Kazantzakis' *Odyssey,* in short, created as much furor in Greek circles as the publication in English circles of another epic of comparable proportions and intent, the *Ulysses* of James Joyce. Both works are concerned with the modern man in search of a soul, and both utilize the framework of Homer's *Odyssey* as reference, though in strikingly different ways. In a recent work, *The Ulysses Theme,* Dr. W. B. Stanford, Regius Professor of Greek at the University of Dublin, traces the permutations of Odysseus in literature from Greek, Hellenic, Alexandrian, Roman, Renaissance, Medieval and Modern times through almost three thousand years of changing development, and then devotes his last chapter to a consideration of Kazantzakis' *Odyssey* and Joyce's *Ulysses* as "the most elaborate portraits of Odysseus in the whole post-Homeric tradition," as "unusually comprehensive symbols of contemporary aspirations and perplexities," and concludes that Kazantzakis' *Odyssey* "offers as much scope for ethical, theological, and artistic controversy as Joyce's *Ulysses.*" He asserts that both works justify their bulk by their complex development of the theme's content and symbolism, and that it says much for the vitality of the myth that its greatest extensions should have emerged almost three thousand years after its first appearance in literature. Kazantzakis, Dr. Stanford continues, "has found many new ways of understanding Odysseus in terms of modern thought," and has presented "a fully integrated portrait of the hero—as wanderer and politician, as destroyer and preserver, as sensualist and ascetic, as soldier and philosopher, as pragmatist and idealist, as legislator and humorist," combining many scattered elements in both ancient and modern traditions until the episodic and spatial enrichments of the myth "are augmented on a scale, both physical and imaginative, far beyond any contributions since Homer's."

In his characterization of Odysseus, Kazantzakis has, of course, derived many of his hero's qualities and adventures from the early Greek epic, but in essence, Dr. Stanford believes, "his Odysseus is an avatar of Dante's centrifugal hero, and derives from the tradition which leads from Dante through Tennyson and Pascoli to the present day." In the twenty-sixth canto of Dante's *Inferno,* Odysseus speaks from a two-forked tongue of flame: "Neither fondness for my son, nor reverence for my aged father, nor due love that should have cheered Penelope could conquer in me the ardor that I had to gain experience of the world and of human vice and worth; I put forth on the deep sea, with but one ship, and with that small company which had not deserted me. . . . 'O brothers,' I said, . . . 'deny not experience of the unpeopled world beyond the Sun. Consider your origins: ye were not formed to live like brutes, but to follow virtue and knowledge.' " Dr. Stanford finds that Kazantzakis' Odysseus is closer to Tennyson's in essence, "for though Tennyson makes his hero's expressed desire 'To follow knowledge, like a sinking star, / Beyond the utmost bound of human thought,' yet his immediate motive is to free himself from his domestic environment in Ithaca." This is similar to the thought of the great Greek-Alexandrine poet Constantine Cavafis, who in his poem *Ithaca* wrote that what was meaningful for Odysseus was not the arrival in Ithaca but the enriching experiences of the voyage itself, for when the mariner comes to understand that Ithaca has given him the beautiful voyage, that without her in mind he would never have set out on his way, and that she has nothing more to give him now, then he will have understood "what an Ithaca means." And in Book XVI of Kazantzakis' poem, Odysseus exclaims: "My soul, your voyages have been your native land!"

Dr. Stanford believes that "Kazantzakis has singled out the wish to be free as the dominant passion of his hero. In fact, psychologically, his epic is an exploration of the meaning of freedom." Throughout his poem Kazantzakis explores the meaning of freedom in all its implications of liberation, redemption, deliverance, and salvation. "Odysseus," he once said in a newspaper interview, "is the man who has freed himself from everything—religions, philosophies, political systems—one who has cut away all the strings. He wants to try all the forms of life, freely, beyond plans and systems, keeping the thought of death before him as a stimulant, not to make every pleasure more acrid or every ephemeral moment more sharply enjoyable in its brevity, but to whet his appetites in life, to make them more capable of embracing and of exhausting all things so that, when death finally came, it would find nothing to take from him, for it would find an entirely squandered Odysseus." Kazantzakis has expressed the last part of this thought in verse in the beautiful opening to Book XXIII, lines 27-37, and in these courageous ten lines he has written his own best epitaph.

After considering the development of Odysseus in vernacular plays, lyrics, novels, and moral discourses, Dr. Stanford concludes that "Joyce's prose narrative and Kazantzakis' poem are nearer to heroic epic than to any of these genres. This epic quality enables these authors to treat of Odysseus with a greater objectivity than in drama, and a greater weight of heroic symbolism than in a novel. Here, in fact, we return after a long interval to the heroic-romantic atmosphere of the *Odyssey*, an atmosphere less strictly epical than that of the *Iliad*, but closer to it than to any other genre of classical literature, and an atmosphere especially congenial to the versatile and often unorthodox heroism of Odysseus." Yet for Kazantzakis the question of whether or not his poem was an epic seemed of little importance. "Nothing, in truth, is more superficial or more barren," he wrote in answer to a young Greek scholar, "than the discussion as to whether or not the *Odyssey* is an epic poem and whether the epic is a contemporary art form. Historians of literature come only after the artist has passed; they hold measuring rods, they take measurements and construct useful laws for their science, but these are useless for the creator because he has the right and the strength—this is what creation means—to break them by creating new ones. When a vital soul feels, without previous aesthetic theories, the necessity to create, then whatever shape his creations take cannot help but be alive. Form and Substance are one. So far as I am concerned, there has been no age more epical than ours. It is in such ages which come between two cultures—when one Myth dissolves and another struggles to be born—that epic poems are created. For me, the *Odyssey* is a new epical-dramatic attempt of the modern man to find deliverance by passing through all the stages of contemporary anxieties and by pursuing the most daring hopes. What deliverance? He does not know as he starts out, but he creates it constantly with his joys and sorrows, with his successes and failures, with his disappointments, fighting always. This, I am certain, is the anguished struggle, whether conscious or subconscious, of the true modern man. In such intermediate periods, a spiritual endeavor can either look back to justify and judge the old civilization which is disintegrating, or it can look ahead and struggle to prophesy and formulate the new one. Odysseus struggles by looking ahead unceasingly, his neck stretched forward like the leader of birds migrating." In Book III, as Odysseus watches the tribes of blond barbarians slowly seeping into Greece from the North, he exclaims: "Blessed be that hour that gave me birth between two eras!"

Nor was it ever Kazantzakis' intention to emulate or to imitate Homer. Although he has grafted his poem directly on the main trunk of Homer's *Odyssey,* by lopping off the last two books and wedging his opening firmly in Book XXII, it does not continue in a direct line of ascent but swerves almost immediately into its own directional growth, into the modern world and its problems, ruthlessly abandoning what it does not need, yet plunging its own veins deep in the main trunk to drink up vast primordial sources overlaid with the parasitical growth of almost thirty centuries. Odysseus completely ignores Penelope, as though her image had vanished after nineteen years of longing; a new relationship between himself, his son, his father, and his people is formulated; the Olympian gods are almost entirely abandoned to make way for the slow appearance of a new agonized deity, and the turbulent quest of the modern man for new questions and new answers almost immediately begins.

II. THE PHILOSOPHY

Just before Kazantzakis began to write the *Odyssey,* he completed a small book, perhaps best titled *The Saviors of God* and subtitled *Spiritual Exercises,* where in a passionate and poetic style, yet in systematic fashion, he set down the philosophy embodied not only in the *Odyssey* but in everything he has written, for he was a man of one overwhelming vision, striving to give it shape in all the forms he could master, in epic, drama, novel, travelogue, criticism, translation, and even political action. A brief summary of the skeletal ideas of that book will place in a more comprehensible order the same vision which is scattered and intermingled with narrative and incident in the *Odyssey,* primarily in Books XIV, XVI, and in those following when Odysseus meets various representative types of mankind such as Prince Motherth (of Buddha), Margaro (of the Courtesan), the Hermit (of Faust), Captain Sole (of Don Quixote), the Lord of the Tower (of the Hedonist), and the Negro Fisher-lad (of Christ). I have appended a complete synopsis of the poem at the back of this book, but a reading at this moment of the brief summaries of Book XIV and XVI will help the reader toward a better understanding of the exposition which follows.

A man, writes Kazantzakis, has three duties. His first duty is to the mind which imposes order on disorder, formulates laws, builds bridges over the unfathomable abyss, and sets up rational boundaries beyond which man does not dare to go. But his second duty is to the heart, which admits of no boundaries, which yearns to pierce beyond phenomena and to merge with something beyond mind and matter. His third duty is to free himself from both mind and heart, from the great temptation of the hope which both offer of subduing phenomena or of finding the essence of things. A man must then embrace the annihilating abyss without any hope, he must say that nothing exists, neither life nor death, and must accept this necessity bravely, with exultation and song. He may then build the affirmative structure of his life over this abyss in an ecstasy of tragic joy.

A man is now prepared to undertake a pilgrimage of four stages. At the start of his journey, he hears an agonized cry within him shouting for help. His first step is to plunge into his own ego until he discovers that it is the endangered spirit (or "God") locked within each man that is crying out for liberation. In order to free it, each man must consider himself solely responsible for the salvation of the world, because when a man dies, that aspect of the universe which is his own particular vision and the unique play of his mind also crashes in ruins forever. In the second step, a man must plunge beyond his ego and into his racial origins; yet among his forefathers he must choose only those who can help him toward greater refinement of spirit, that he may in turn pass on his task to a son who may also surpass him. The third step for a man is to plunge beyond his own particular race into the races of all mankind and to suffer their composite agony in the struggle to liberate God within themselves. The fourth step is to plunge beyond mankind and to become identified with all the universe, with animate and inanimate matter, with earth, stones, sea, plants, animals, insects, and birds, with the vital impulse of creation in all phenomena. Each man is a fathomless composite of atavistic roots plunging down to the primordial origin of things. A man is now prepared to go beyond the mind, the heart, and hope, beyond his ego, his race, and mankind even, beyond all phenomena and plunge further into a vision of the Invisible permeating all things and forever ascending.

The essence of the Invisible is an agonized ascent toward more and more purity of spirit, toward light. The goal is the struggle itself, since the ascent is endless. God is not a perfect being toward which man proceeds, but a spiritual concept which evolves toward purity as man himself evolves on earth. He is not Almighty, for he is in constant danger, filled with wounds, struggling to survive; he is not All-holy, for he is pitiless in the cruel choice he makes to survive, caring neither for men nor animals, neither for virtues nor ideas, but making use of them all in an attempt to pass through them and shake himself free; he is not All-knowing, for his head is a confused jumble of dark and light. He cries out to man for help because man is his highest spiritual reach in the present stage of his evolution. He cannot be saved unless man tries to save him by struggling with him, nor can man be saved unless God is saved. On the whole, it is rather man who must save God. When a man has had this vision of the ceaselessly unsated and struggling spirit, he must then attempt to give it body in deeds, in political action, in works of every nature, realizing, of course, that any embodiment must of necessity pollute the vision, yet accepting and utilizing such imperfect instruments in the never-ending struggle.

The essence of God is to find freedom, salvation. Our duty is to aid him in this ascent, and to save ourselves at last from our final hope of salvation, to say to ourselves that not even salvation exists, and to accept this with tragic joy. Love is the force which urges us on and which descends on us as a dance, a rhythm. Injustice, cruelty, longing, hunger and war are leaders that push us on. God is never created out of happiness and comfort, but out of tragedy and strife. The greatest virtue is not to be free, but to struggle ceaselessly for freedom. The universe is a creation in the meeting of two opposite streams, one male and the other female, one ascending toward integration, toward life, toward immortality, the other descending toward disintegration, toward matter, toward death. It becomes a blossoming Tree of Fire whose summit bears the final fruit of light. Fire is the first and ultimate mask of God. One day it will vanish into the deepest and most distilled essence of the spirit, that of silence, where all contraries at last will be resolved.

In his early youth Kazantzakis wrote two treatises, one on Nietzsche and one on Bergson, and though scholars may later trace in his thoughts pervading influences of such diverse and contrary strains as Buddha, Lenin, Christ, Spinoza, Spengler, Darwin, Homer, Frazer and Dante, they will discover, I believe, that the earliest influences were the deepest. Nietzsche confirmed him in his predilection for the Dionysian as opposed to the Apollonian vision of life: for Dionysus, the god of wine and revelry, of ascending life, of joy in action, of ecstatic motion and inspiration, of instinct and adventure and dauntless suffering, the god of song and music and dance; as opposed to Apollo, the god of peace, of leisure and repose, of aesthetic emotion and intellectual contemplation, of logical order and philosophical calm, the god of painting and sculpture and epic poetry. We shall see, however, that though this was for him a decided predilection and a biased emphasis, it was not at all a rejection, but rather an assimilation of the Apollonian vision of life. He had always strongly felt the opposing attraction of Apollonian clarity. Once, as he stood before an elaborate baroque church in Spain, lost in its intricacies, Kazantzakis felt a distaste for so much complication and lack of clarity. "Surely," he wrote in his travel book on that country, "the highest art lies in the restraint of passion, in imposing order on disorder, serenity on joy and pain. . . . A man must not be seduced by superfluous beauties, he must not be misled to think that by filling up space he has conquered time." He then recounts how Dionysus came out of India clad in multicolored silks, laden with bracelets and rings, his eyes ringed with black, his fingernails painted crimson. But as the god proceeded into Greece, his adornments fell from him one by one until he stood naked on a hill at Eleusis. Dionysus, the god of ecstatic and visionary drunkenness, had turned into Apollo, the god of serene beauty. Such, wrote Kazantzakis, is the progress of art. Ultimately Kazantzakis wished to combine the two in what he called the "Cretan Glance," to remind scholars that Dionysus as well as Apollo was a god of the Greeks, and that the noblest of Greek arts was a synthesis of the two ideals. He may be compared to Yeats who in his philosophical work *A Vision* describes human character and human history as a conflicting war between subjective and objective elements, yet who had a decided predilection in his own work and in that of others for those of subjective, or what he called "antithetical" temperament.

From Nietzsche, Kazantzakis also took the exaltation of tragedy as the joy of life, a certain "tragic optimism" of the strong man who delights to discover that strife is the pervading law of life, the "melancholy joy" which Wagner discerned in the last quartets of Beethoven. Innumerable epigrams from *Thus Spake Zarathustra* may illustrate various sections of the *Odyssey*: "Live dangerously. Erect your cities beside Vesuvius. Send out your ships to unexplored seas. Live in a state of war." "My formula for greatness is *Amor fati* . . . not only to bear up under every necessity, but to love it." "Thou shalt build beyond thyself . . . Thou shalt not only propagate thyself, but propagate thyself upwards." "He who strideth across the highest mountain laugheth at all tragedies." But in contrast to Nietzsche, Kazantzakis had an intense love for the common man and a belief in socialistic orders which try to alleviate poverty and lift oppression. Though he distrusted the purely "intellectual" men, he accepted certain aspects of Nietzsche's superman, and depicted Odysseus as a type of those superior beings in humanity who must ruthlessly take the vanguard and lead mankind toward spiritual fulfillment. It was Kazantzakis' vain dream, perhaps, as it was that of Odysseus and Moses, to make all individuals into superior beings, to lead them toward the Promised Land and to test them to the breaking point. Nietzsche and Spengler also confirmed him in his belief that civilizations flourish and then are destroyed by some more primitive force, as the Doric barbarians in his poem overrun Greece, Knossos, and Egypt; as the Romans overran Greece; as the Teutons overran Europe; and as the Russians today threaten to overrun the vacillating democracies of both hemispheres.

Perhaps the deepest influence on Kazantzakis' thought has been that of Bergson. The relationship which Aristotle and Thomas Aquinas bore to the thought and structure of Dante, Bergson bears to the thought and structure of Kazantzakis, and it is not without significance that he studied with Bergson at the Collège de France during his formative years. At the core of Kazantzakis' thought and his Dionysian method lies Bergson's concept of life as the expression of an *élan vital,* a vital or creative impulse, a fluid and persistent creation that flows eternally and manifests itself in ever-changing eruptive phenomena. "According to Bergson," Kazantzakis wrote in his treatise on his former teacher, "life is an unceasing creation, a leap upwards, a vital outburst, an *élan vital.* . . . All the history of life up to man is a gigantic endeavor of the vital impulse to elevate matter, to create a being which would be free of the inflexible mechanism of inertia. . . . Two streams, that of life and that of matter, are in motion, though in opposite directions: one toward integration and the other toward disintegration. Bergson thinks of the *élan vital* as a seething stream which in its ebullition distills into falling drops. It is these drops which constitute matter." Life, as Bergson describes it in his *Creative Evolution,* is more a matter of time than of space; it is not position, but change; it is not quantity so much as quality; it is not a mere redistribution of matter and motion. The emphasis lies not on matter but on mind; not on space but on time; not on passivity but on action; not on mechanism, but on choice. Life is "always and always the procreative urge of the world." The shape of things is not imposed from without, but impelled from within. Although life abandons the individual to disintegration, it conquers death through reproduction and an unceasing creative evolution.

The impulse of life, according to Bergson, has manifested itself in three stages in its effort toward more and more freedom. In the first stage life was rooted in the dark torpidity of plants and in the security it found there; in the second stage it froze in the mechanical instinct of such automatons as the ant and the bee; in the third stage, through vertebrates, through intelligence and will, it cast off routine instinct and plunged into "the endless risks of thought." For Kazantzakis, as for Bergson, intuition (allied to instinct) is a more penetrating and more Dionysian vision which seeks the essence of things, but both based their ultimate hope on the intellect which, as it grows stronger and bolder in evolutionary growth, seems to embody best the highest forms through which the *élan vital* may find its supreme expression. Yet it must be stressed that both intuition and intellect have a common ancestry, that they are yoked bifurcations of the same body. "They are not successive degrees of evolution," Kazantzakis writes; "they are simply directions which the same fermentation took. Difference of quality and not of quantity exists between instinct and intellect. Instinct knows things, intellect the relationship between things. Both are cognitive faculties. . . . Intuition has the advantage of entering into the very essence of life, of feeling its movement, its creation. But it has one great disadvantage: it cannot express itself." Language is an instrument of the intellect. That philosophy which wants to interpret experience and to understand the essence of things cannot do it with the intellect alone. "Intellect must therefore work hand in hand with instinct. 'Only the intellect,' says Bergson, 'can seek to solve some problems, though it will never solve them; only the instinct can solve them, though it will never seek them.' There is need, therefore, of absolute collaboration."

"Life," writes Kazantzakis, stressing his words by underlining them, *"is what inspiration is to a poem.* Words obstruct the flow of inspiration, but nevertheless they express it as best they can. Only the human intellect can dissect words, or unite them, or delineate them grammatically; but if we are to comprehend the poem, something else is needed; we must plunge into its heart, we must live in its inspiration, we must enter into a rhythmical harmony with the poet himself, for only then may the words lose their rigidity and inflexibility or may the current rush on its way once more and the poem seethe in us with its true essence, and which a grammatical analysis can never discover. Similarly, in order to comprehend the *élan vital,* the human intellect is necessary, the examination of created things, the history of our earth as our scientific researches show them; but this is not enough, just as words are not enough by which to comprehend a poem. Both elements are indispensable."

The unceasing creativity of life, casting up and discarding individuals and species as experiments on its way toward more and more liberation, is what Bergson and Kazantzakis both meant by God. For both men God is not omnipotent, but infinite; he is not omniscient, but struggles and stumbles, impeded by matter, toward more and more consciousness, toward light. "God, thus defined," writes Bergson, "has nothing of the ready-made; He is unceasing life, action, freedom. Creation so conceived is not a mystery; we experience it in ourselves when we act freely." All the impulses in man toward further strength and betterment are the voices and the surge of the creative force within him pushing him onward and upward in an unending stream of creation and re-creation. Finally, what appears but darkly, hesitatingly, tentatively in Kazantzakis (especially in the last encounters of Odysseus with Heracles and Prometheus) is enunciated clearly by Bergson: the final hope that life in its struggle with matter might in time learn how to elude mortality. "The animal," writes Bergson, "takes its stand on the plant, man bestrides animality, and the whole of humanity, in space and time, is one army galloping beside and before and behind each of us in an overwhelming charge able to beat down every resistance and clear the most formidable obstacles, perhaps even death." *

Like all poets, Kazantzakis is not so much a systematic philosopher as one who, reaching out the tentacles of his mind and spirit, and grasping whatever might bring him nourishment, sucks up all into the third inner

* I am indebted to the section on Bergson in Will Durant's *The Story of Philosophy.*

eye of vision peculiar to himself alone, and moves the reader with an imaginative view of life so intense as to be, in truth, a new apprehension. Basic to all of Kazantzakis' vision, as to that of Yeats, has been the attempt to synthesize what seem to be contraries, antitheses, antinomies. His own life and personality would seem to be a battleground of contradictions unless one looked upon them with the third inner eye, and from a higher peak, as on an unceasing battle for a harmony never resolved. This eye, this glance, between the eye of the Orient (or Dionysus, who came from India or Asia Minor) and the eye of Hellenic Greece (or Apollo), Kazantzakis called the "Cretan Glance," for he was born on the island of Crete, at the crossroads between Africa, Asia, and Europe. In replying to a young Greek scholar who accused him of being "anti-classical" in his *Odyssey*, Kazantzakis answered that the streams which created the ancient Greek civilization were two: the dark underground stream of Dionysus, and the upper lustrous one of Apollo. The underground stream watered and nourished the fruits of the upper world; if Dionysus had not existed, Apollo would have become anemic. Both were primitive and fertile Greek roots, but in the three thousand years that have passed, much new blood has entered into Greek veins and enriched them. A creator might take either one of two roads: he might deny anything that was not part of "classical Greece," and of that accept the Apollonian vision only; or he might try, as the incurable descendants of an abundant richness, to create the synthesis of all these bloods, to find the expressions of a hyper-hellenic wealth. "You," wrote Kazantzakis to the young scholar, "prefer the first road, that of ancient classical Hellenism, and I the second. In my *Odyssey*, I attempted to make this synthesis and to find this expression. Odysseus is not only a general sketch of the newer man who longs for a new and superior form of life, but he is also, in particular, the Greek who has to solve a most fundamental dilemma of his destiny; Odysseus chooses and lives the solution which seems to him the most true; he does not seek to prune his life, he denies nothing, he seeks the synthesis."

Kazantzakis then makes two distinctions between Greece and the Orient. The chief characteristic of Greece is to erect the secure fortress of the ego, the fixed outline which subdues disorderly drives and primitive demons to the dictates of the enlightened and disciplined will. The supreme ideal of Greece is to save the ego from anarchy and chaos. The supreme ideal of the Orient is to dissolve the ego into the infinite and to become one with it. Passive contemplation, the bliss of renunciation, an utterly trustful abandonment to mysterious and impersonal powers—such is the essence of the Orient. "There is nothing so contrary to the spirit and practice of Odysseus as this Oriental conception of life," Kazantzakis wrote to his young critic. "Of course he does not, like the Greeks, cast a veil over chaos, for he prefers, instead, to keep a sleepless vigil and to increase his strength by gazing into it; yet he never abandons himself to chaos, for on the contrary, until the very last moment, when Death appears, he stands erect before chaos and looks upon it with undimmed eyes." This attitude toward life and death is not Greek, nor is it Oriental;

it is something else: "Crete, for me (and not, naturally, for all Cretans), is the synthesis which I always pursue, the synthesis of Greece and the Orient. I neither feel Europe in me nor a clear and distilled classical Greece; nor do I at all feel the anarchic chaos and the will-less perseverance of the Orient. I feel something else, a synthesis, a being that not only gazes on the abyss without disintegrating, but which, on the contrary, is filled with coherence, pride, and manliness by such a vision. This glance which confronts life and death so bravely, I call Cretan."

Kazantzakis then goes on to trace the Cretan Glance to its origins in the old pre-classical Minoan civilization of Crete. Minoan Crete, with its dreadful earthquakes symbolized by the Bull-God, and with the acrobatic games which the Cretans played with this same Bull, was a true realization of what Kazantzakis considered to be the superior vision: the Synthesis. The Cretan bull-rituals had no relationship to the bullfights of modern Spain. The Cretans confronted the Bull—the Titan-Earthquake—without fear, with undimmed eyes, nor killed him in order to unite with him (the Orient) or to be released from his presence (Greece), but played with him at their ease. "This direct contact with the Bull honed the strength of the Cretan, cultivated the flexibility and charm of his body, the flaming yet cool exactness of movement, the discipline of desire, and the hard-won virility to measure himself against the dark and powerful Bull-Titan. And thus the Cretan transformed terror into a high game wherein man's virtue, in a direct contact with the beast, became tempered, and triumphed. The Cretan triumphed without killing the abominable bull because he did not think of it as an enemy but as a collaborator; without it his body would not have become so strong and charming or his spirit so manly. Of course, to endure and to play such a dangerous game, one needs great bodily and spiritual training and a sleepless discipline of nerves; but if a man once trains himself and becomes skillful in the game, then every one of his movements becomes simple, certain, and graceful. The heroic and playful eyes, without hope yet without fear, which so confront the Bull, the Abyss, I call the Cretan Glance."

Kazantzakis was well aware that throughout the world and in contemporary Greece other clear glances existed, filled with light and nobility, which looked on the world with greater composure and did not inflame it with tension. He respected and rejoiced in the Apollonian or classical ordered vision of life, he was drawn to it and influenced by it even more than he realized, but he did not consider it to be either his own particular view or the one which could best gaze upon and understand the violent transitions of the modern world. "The epoch through which we are passing," he wrote, "seems to me decidedly anti-classical. It seems to break the molds in political, economic, and social life, in thought and in action in order to achieve a new balance—a new classical age—on a higher plane; to create that which we have called a new Myth, and which might give a new and synchronized meaning to the world at last. Our age is a savage one; the Bull, the underground Dionysian powers, has been unleashed; the Apollonian crust of the earth is cracking. ["And what rough beast," wrote Yeats in *The Second Coming,* "slouches toward Bethlehem to be born?"] Nobility, harmony, balance, the sweetness of life, happiness, are all virtues and graces which we must have the courage to bid goodbye. They belong to another age, either past or future. Every age has its own face; the face of ours is a savage one; delicate spirits cannot confront it; they swerve their eyes in terror; they invoke the noble and ancient prototypes; they cannot look directly at the contemporary, prodigious, and dreadful spectacle of a world in painful birth. They want an art work cut in the pattern of their desires and their fears. They watch contemporary life exploding before them every minute with a world-destroying demonic power, and yet they do not see it; if they had seen it, indeed, they would have sought for its reflection, its mirror-image, in contemporary art."

The Cretan Glance for Kazantzakis, therefore, was an attempted synthesis of those contraries which he believed underlie all human and natural endeavor, but a synthesis not so much of permanent as of momentary harmony, which in turn builds into a greater tension and explodes toward a higher and more inclusive synthesis in an ever upward and spiraling onrush, leaving behind it the bloodstained path of man's and nature's endeavors. This may explain much that, from a more restricted point of view, seems contradictory in his life and thought, but which takes on another value when seen as the ever-shifting sections of larger and, in themselves, ever-changing unities. The emphasis here is more on the constant tension and flux of the *élan vital,* the creative impulse, than on any momentary object which it has cast up along its way in its onward rush—whether plant, or animal, or man, or star. It is a double vision between whose dual tensions rises the third inner eye that soars on the balancing wings of good and evil, that no sooner creates a new law than it begins immediately to conceive of an opposed and contrary law with which to knock it down. In Book X, Odysseus exclaims: "If only I could fight with both my friends and foes, / join in my heart God, anti-God, both yes and no, / like that round fruit which two lips make when they are kissing!" In Book XI he says: "God spreads the enormous wing of good from his right side, / the wing of evil from his left, then springs and soars. / If only I could be like God, to fly with wayward wings!" And in Book XII: "To all laws I'll erect contrary, secret laws / that must deny with scorn and smash all former laws."

Two aspects of Kazantzakis' thought, which have been most misrepresented in Greece, should receive clarification here. The first is his attitude toward despair. Readers are often so impressed, so overwhelmed by his insistence that man must gaze open-eyed and without illusion on the dark Abyss which eventually must swallow all, that he has been termed an anarchist and a nihilist, whereas his entire life and thought emphasized the exact contrary. He insists, simply, that it is precisely on this abyss that man must erect the structure of his life and work; that the great affirmation of life has meaning and value only when it accepts and rises above the great negation; that such is the double vision necessary to a realistic apprehension of life. In a letter to a critic who had written of him as the completely despairing man, Kazantzakis answered, "Only beyond absolute despair is the door of absolute hope found. Alas to that man who cannot mount the final dreadful step which rises above absolute despair; such a man is necessarily incurably despairing. Only that other man who can mount that step can know what is meant by impregnable joy and immortality." In man's world, the success or defeat of the spirit depends on man himself, and the upward path is one of unceasing, ruthless, and bloody strife. To the man who erects his home on the Abyss, this challenge does not lead to despair or suicide but to acceptance of necessity in joy, to laughter on the highest peaks of existence, and finally to a creative "play" with tragic elements in an ecstasy of joy which is the chief characteristic of Kazantzakis' style, and is especially embodied in the divertissement of Book XVII. His laughter, therefore, is not the ironic wit or subtle interplay of mind of our modern metaphysical poets, but has affinities rather to the *saeva indignatio* of that Jonathan Swift who wrote *A Modest Proposal,* and to the broader bite of an Aristophanes or a Rabelais.

The second point to be elucidated is Kazantzakis' use of the word "God." God, for him, is identical with the *élan vital,* the onrushing force throughout all of creation which strives for purer and more rarefied freedom. He prefers this appellation because it has become saturated and battered with man's historical endeavor, ever since his dim origins, to struggle above his atavistic and bestial nature. In the first half of the *Odyssey,* God is apprehended as an anthropomorphic being, yet he is not projected as a concrete object, thing, person or goal *toward* which man proceeds, as in much of Christian theology, but as concomitant and identical with man himself, as part of the struggling spirit in all nature which has found, thus far, its purest co-worker in man, and which now strives to find an even purer embodiment, perhaps even its own immortality. After the destruction of his Ideal City in Book XVI, Odysseus turns away, more and more, from attempts to free the struggling divine spirit within him, abandons the last hope of an Elysium, Paradise, or divine Justice whether on earth or the hereafter, and concerns himself more and more with the outer world, with the ever-spiraling evolutionary process upward of the universe from inorganic matter, from the emergence of organic matter and its highest development in man, to the continuous disappearance of every individual, and even of species, as the *élan vital* finds other modes of expression. "This unbelievable man has a terrifying impulse toward creation," Kazantzakis wrote, "until that moment when an earthquake crumbles to its foundation the city he had built. . . . From then on his fall begins, a fall which he does nothing to stop." Yet it is this fall, as has often been remarked of Adam and Eve's fall from grace in the Garden of Eden, that leads to the true rise of Odysseus toward his full stature.

In the first half of the poem, God is Odysseus' constant companion, locked within his body, crying to be released; in the second half of the poem, Death is the very flesh and bones of Odysseus himself, tagging always at his heels like his shadow or faithful dog, the mirror-image of his own identity. In the first half of the poem, when Odysseus is purely a man of action, his struggles are deeply spiritual in an anguished effort to purify his vision of God; in the second half of the poem, after Odysseus sinks into an intuitive contemplation, he no longer seeks God, or the Spirit, but turns his attention outward, to the senses, to earth, to the Spirit's humanistic manifestations in various representative types of man. "After the catastrophe," writes Dr. Stanford, "he abandons the cult of doing for the cult of being. . . . He now seeks self-knowledge and self-improvement in asceticism and in the exploration of personal relationships with people who are also seekers after the inner secret of being and non-being." He now becomes the Lone Man. It is when he turns ascetic that Odysseus becomes most materialistic.

In the complete acceptance of nature and its unmoral laws, all dualisms are resolved in a dynamic monism as equally real aspects of the same thing. Evolution means not merely change or increased complexity, but an always upward movement toward higher, more valued forms. Man is a creature in nature which, for the first time, by the exercise of a unique consciousness, purpose, mind, will, and choice, can intervene purposefully in a process which, of its own accord, though with an infinite indifference, unwinds toward more and more perfectibility. Man's mind, his will and powers of choice, though limited and conditioned by the materials through which they manifest themselves, by his heritage and his environment, are part of that "blind," seemingly purposeless creative impulse toward perfectibility. If such value-judgments are purposeless *for* Nature, they are nevertheless purposeful for man himself, who is a portion of Nature, and *in* Nature. If man and his powers are not necessarily the highest perfectible reach of Nature *for* Nature, man can nevertheless rise beyond the limits of his heritage and environment to intervene and redirect the very forces which created him and which push him onward. He sails an unlimited and shoreless sea, his ship swept swiftly by dark and powerful currents, a moribund God for companion, but his hands on the helm or the tiller allow him to become, to some extent, the master of his own fate. In his own world within the world of Nature, man is the arbiter of his own destiny, though he is himself directed by invisible forces. His glory lies in the modicum of purpose or direction which his hands might command. From the biological viewpoint of Sir Julian Huxley, "Man's most sacred duty and, at the same time his most glorious opportunity, is to promote the maximum fulfillment of the evolutionary process on the earth; and this includes the fullest realization of his own inherent possibilities." * When Menelaus tells Odysseus that man, and even the gods, must "follow their own road like banked-in streams," Odysseus exclaims: "I think man's greatest duty on earth is to fight his fate,/to give no quarter and blot out his written doom./This is how mortal man can even surpass his god!"

In the summer of 1954 in Antibes, when Kazantzakis and I were slowly reading his poem together in Greek for the first time, he was asked to

* *See* "Business of Evolution," by Joseph Wood Krutch, in *The Saturday Review*, March 15, 1958.

write a "Credo" for a proposed third volume of *This I Believe*. It contains the last summation which Kazantzakis was to make of his life and work:

From early youth my fundamental struggle and the source of all my joys and sorrows has been the unceasing and pitiless battle within me between the flesh and the spirit. Within me are the most ancient, prehuman dark and lustrous powers, and my spirit is the arena where these two armies have met and fought. I felt that if only one of these two conquered and annihilated the other, I would be lost, because I loved my body and did not want it to vanish, yet I loved my soul and did not want it to decline. I struggled, therefore, to unite in friendship these two antithetical and universal powers until they should realize they were not enemies but co-workers, until they should rejoice so that I also might rejoice with them in their harmony.

This struggle lasted for many years. I tried many different roads by which to reach my salvation: the road of love, of scientific curiosity, of philosophical inquiry, of social rebirth, and finally the difficult and solitary path of poetry. But when I saw that all these led to the Abyss, fear would seize me, and I would turn back and take another road. This wandering and this martyrdom lasted for many years. Finally, in despair, I sought refuge on Athos, the holy mountain of Greece where no woman has ever set foot, and where for a thousand years thousands of monks have dedicated their lives to prayer and chastity. There, in the solitude of the Holy Mountain, in an old hermit's retreat above the sea, I began a new struggle. First of all I exercised my body in obedience to the spirit. For many months I taught it to endure cold, hunger, thirst, sleeplessness, and every privation. Then I turned to the spirit; sunk in painful concentration, I sought to conquer within me the minor passions, the easy virtues, the cheap spiritual joys, the convenient hopes. Finally one night I started up in great joy, for I had seen the red ribbon left behind him in his ascent—within us and in all the universe—by a certain Combatant; I clearly saw his bloody footprints ascending from inorganic matter into life and from life into spirit.

Then suddenly a great light was born within me: the transmutation of matter into spirit. Here was the great secret, the red ribbon followed by the Combatant. Though he had freed himself from inorganic matter and leaped into the living organism of plants, he felt himself smothering, and therefore leaped into the life of animals, continually transmuting more and more matter into spirit. But again he suffocated, then leaped into the contemporary Apeman whom we have named "man" too soon, and now he struggles to escape from the Apeman and to be transmuted truly into Man. I now clearly saw the progress of the Invisible, and suddenly I knew what my duty was to be: to work in harmony together with that Combatant; to transmute, even I, in my own small capacity, matter into spirit, for only then might I try to reach the highest endeavor of man—a harmony with the universe.

I felt deeply, and I was freed. I did not change the world—this I could not do—but I changed the vision with which I looked out upon the world. And since then, I have struggled—at first consciously and with anguish, then bit by bit unconsciously and without tiring—not to do anything which might find itself in disharmony with the rhythm of the Great Combatant. Since then I have felt ashamed to commit any vulgar act, to lie, to be overcome by fears, because I know that I also have a great responsibility in the progress of the world. I work and think now with certainty, for I know that my contribution, because it follows the profound depths of the universe, will not go lost. Even I, a mortal, may work with One who is immortal, and my spirit—as much as is possible—may become more and more immortal. This harmony, which is not at all passive, but an unceasing and renewing reconciliation and co-operation with antithetical powers, has remained for me my freedom and my redemption.

III. THE MAN

Nikos Kazantzakis was born in Herakleion, Crete, on February 18, 1883 and died in Freiburg, Germany, on October 26, 1957, four months before his seventy-fifth birthday. He received his early schooling in his native island and in Naxos, took his degree in law from the University of Athens, then spent five years in travel throughout Europe, mastering five modern languages in addition to Latin and ancient and modern Greek. During various periods in his life he also traveled in Palestine, Egypt, China and Japan, spent two years in Russia, a few months of contemplation on Mount Athos. In 1919 he was appointed Director General of the Ministry of Public Welfare in the government of Venizelos, and in this capacity directed a mission to the Caucasus and South Russia for the transportation and immigration of 150,000 Greeks to Macedonia and Thrace. During the German-Italian occupation of Greece he lived in near-starvation on the island of Aegina. For a short time in 1946 he acted as Minister of National Education, without portfolio, in the government of Sophoulis, and in 1947 he was appointed Director of Translations from the Classics for UNESCO, but withdrew after a year in order to devote himself exclusively to his literary work, and settled in the ancient Greek city of Antibes (Antipolis) on the French Riviera. He was married twice, first to Galatea Alexíou, then to Helen Samíou. There were no children.

In June of 1957 he wrote me from his home in Antibes: "Again I am taking the road of insanity [that is, of Dionysian ecstasy, of spiritual adventure] which has always remained for me the road toward the highest wisdom." He was on his way to China on the invitation of the Chinese government. In 1935 he had visited that country and Japan and soon after published a travelogue of his impressions, and though he had now been suffering from lymphoid leukemia for the past few years and was seventy-four years old, he was eager to see the changes opposing ideologies had wrought. From Peking he sent me a card of a bird perched on a blossoming cherry bough, and wrote, "I force my body to obey my soul, and thus I never tire. We shall return to Europe via the North Pole." In preparation for his visit to Hong Kong, he had inadvertently been given a smallpox inoculation, and as he flew on to Tokyo and then past the Arctic regions on the North Pole route, the vaccination puncture on his right arm developed a deadly infection. Though he passed this immediate peril in a hospital in Copenhagen, and then at the University Clinic in Freiburg, he was unable to resist the subsequent ravages of influenza, and died at 10:20 on the evening of October 26. His last days had been made happy by a visit from the man he most admired in the living world, Albert Schweitzer, who had long proposed him for the Nobel Prize in literature. His body was taken to his birthplace, Herakleion in Crete, and with great national mourning placed in the Martinengo Bastion of the old Venetian Wall which surrounds the city. The grounds will be made into a public park, including a museum housing the furniture of his workshop, his library, and his manuscripts. By one of those astounding coincidences which topple rational thought, yet seem somehow designed by the subconscious will, Kazantzakis in old age had flown to the northernmost extremity of the earth to meet his death there, exactly as his autobiographical hero in the *Odyssey* had confronted death in Antarctic regions. Thus the two embraced between them the whole world from each of its two extremities, and thus harmony had been preserved in frozen and antipodal balance.

I have never felt so immediately and persistently in the presence of greatness as before him in day after day of close collaboration and discussion when souls are tried, tested, and revealed. In aspect he was arresting, tall and thin, of a bony and ascetic angularity, with shaggy tawny-gray eyebrows, and the only eyes I have ever seen which made credible for me those old clichés "piercing" and "eagle-eyed." His greatness was lambent and transparent with the simplicity which one always posits for true greatness yet rarely expects to find, a serenity that accepted all and dwelt in a higher tension beyond trivialities. Extremely shy, he dressed simply, ate sparingly, and was by temperament an ascetic. And yet, like Yeats, he had a passionate admiration for violent men of action like Zorba (an actual friend) who reveled in deliriums of flesh and freedom. Like Yeats, also, he belongs to Phase 18 of the Irish poet's lunar philosophy, the phase of the Antithetical Man (with Dante), for his own life and thought were formed in a double vision of tension between opposites, an explosive conflict which ascended unceasingly upward toward higher and higher spiritual reaches over an abyss of nothingness. Though he ate little, he always described men of voracious appetites; though he was sensitive in his relations with women, his heroes are often brash and bold in their approach; though he delighted in describing grandfathers with their multitudes of great-grandchildren, he was childless after two marriages; though he roamed about the world, he was drawn again and again to a hermit's retreat; though he loved Greece, and Crete in particular, he lived much of his life abroad; though he had an infinite compassion for humanity in general, he found it difficult to approach individuals or to like many of them; though he admired the self-sacrifice of a Christ or the abnegation of a Buddha, he accepted cruelty, injustice, and barbarity as part of the necessary elements of life.

Much of the ambivalence of his character, as in that of his autobiographical hero, Odysseus, stemmed, I believe, from his endeavor to synthesize these dualities in himself, in his action and his work, to accept all the antinomies in nature which are neither good nor evil, moral nor immoral in themselves, and to fuse them in the fire of a mystical vision which arose, nevertheless, from a realistic view of nature as microcosm and macrocosm both. In the traditionally ambivalent character of Odysseus, amplified and enriched through almost thirty centuries of additional accretion and interpretation, Kazantzakis found a sufficiently complex character to depict not only his own temperament but also that of the entire Greek nation for whom Odysseus is still the ideal character, the admired pattern. In an early novel, *Toda Raba,* composed in 1929, he wrote: "You know that my particular leader is not one of the three leaders of the human spirit; neither Faust, nor Hamlet, nor Don Quixote, but only Don Odysseus. . . . I have not the unquenchable thirst of the occidental mind, nor do I sway between yes and no to no end in immobility, nor do I any longer possess the sublimely ludicrous urge of the noble battler of windmills. I am a mariner of Odysseus with heart afire but with mind ruthless and clear; not, however, of that Odysseus who returned to Ithaca and stayed there, but of that other Odysseus who returned, killed his enemies and, stifled in his native land, put out to sea once more."

Odysseus is the "man of many turns," which for Homer probably meant the much-traveled man, for his enemies the man of chameleon duplicity, unstable and unscrupulous, and for his friends the resourceful and versatile man, ready for all emergencies. He is cruel yet compassionate, modest yet boastful, cunning yet straightforward, heavy-handed yet gentle, affectionate yet harsh, aristocratic yet public-spirited, sensual yet ascetic, a man of mixed motives in a constant state of ethical tension. Only such a complex and contradictory character could hope to give the Greeks, from ancient days to the present, a sufficiently satisfying pattern of their lives and aspirations, and this is why his myth is no less living today than it was almost three thousand years ago. Only one of the twelve Olympian deities had a character equally complex—she who in Homer was Odysseus' constant companion and protector, and for whom the Athenians named their city as a tribute to both their involved temperaments: Athena. Kazantzakis and Odysseus are creatures of double vision, of the third inner eye, of the "Cretan Glance" which, caught between two conflicting currents—one ever ascending toward composition, toward life, toward immortality, and the other ever descending toward decomposition, toward matter, toward death—glimpses the ideal synthesis and yearns for its almost impossible embodiment in life and in work.

IV. THE PROSODY, THE DICTION, THE STYLE AND STRUCTURE

The Prosody. The traditional meter in which most of modern Greek folk songs and long narrative poems are written, comparable in English to blank verse (the ten-syllable unrhymed iambic line of five beats), is the fifteen-syllable iambic line of seven beats. To the educated Greek Kazantzakis' abandonment of the traditional meter, and his use of an extremely rare measure for the *Odyssey,* that of the seventeen-syllable unrhymed verse of eight beats, came as an unexpected and shocking disturbance. A comparable effect would be obtained (though not so violent) if an English poet today were to write an equally long poem not in the traditional blank verse of ten syllables but in the less-known measure of twelve syllables. In both cases there would be the addition of an added iambic foot to the traditional measure of both countries, an addition of two syllables; in English recently we have had somewhat of a precedent in Robert Bridges' *The Testament of Beauty*. To the English or American, however, attuned to more experimentation in meter during the past fifty years than in all of his previous history, the six-foot line would not seem too daring a novelty for a long poem. Indeed, our now popular "sprung rhythm" measure has already added more syllables to lines which still retain a traditional number of accents (as in the plays of Eliot and MacLeish), and discontent has often been voiced with blank verse as too stately and too exhausted a measure to carry the more speedy, more nervous rhythms of modern speech. I have often thought that a hexameter today (among traditional measures) might be equivalent to yesterday's pentameter, and might more fittingly enclose the rhythms and breath-groupings of modern speech, if one wishes to retain, that is, the iambic measure and not the measurement of sprung rhythm. For a while I experimented with the seven-beat and fourteen-syllable line Chapman used in his translation of Homer's *Iliad*, but I soon discovered that the monosyllabic character of the English language permitted so much condensation that the six-beat line, for which I had a predilection, allowed me to cut away five syllables from every line of the original, and that instead of being forced to pad a line, I was sometimes forced to delete.

Kazantzakis' explanation to his critics of why he used the seventeen-syllable line is characteristic: "I wrote in the seventeen-syllable line because this followed more truly the rhythm of my blood when I lived the *Odyssey*. A verse is not a garment with which one dresses one's emotion in order to create song; both verse and emotion are created in a momentary flash, inseparably, just as a man himself is created, body and soul, as one being." It is of interest, also, to point out that though Homer's own line is composed of six beats only, it is written in dactylic feet of three syllables each (though the sixth foot is always disyllabic) and therefore contains about seventeeen syllables, so that Kazantzakis' measure of seventeen syllables and eight beats is a more exact approximation, at least in number of syllables, than the traditional modern Greek measure of seven beats and fifteen syllables. It is perhaps no accident that in his own versions, Kazantzakis translated Homer's *Iliad* and *Odyssey* in the same measure as that in which he wrote his own epic poem. For better flexibility, I have interspersed my iambics with occasional anapests (also to simulate at times the frequent extra though elided syllables characteristic of Greek), and I have almost always ended each section within a book with a seven-beat line to effect a more definite close, much as in the last line of a Spenserian stanza. Occasionally, for the sake of rhythm or verisimilitude, I have interspersed a seven-beat line in the running narrative. Those who wish to inquire further will find a more technical analysis of meter in the Appendix.

The Diction. When after almost one thousand years of subjection under Romans, Franks, Venetians, and Turks, the Greek nation obtained its independence about 1829, it immediately set about purifying its language of foreign influences. Several scholars constructed an artificial language called "purist," based primarily on the diction and syntax of ancient Greek. A more demotic, a people's language, had been forming, however, ever since Hellenistic times, surviving the many centuries of occupation, retaining a certain purity of its own in the remote mountain fastnesses and islands throughout Greece, changing in grammar and syntax, assimilating many foreign words and then rejecting most of them, and retaining still the strength, flavor, and even many words of Homeric times, much as some Shakespearean words may still be found in the Tennessee hills. There is no other language, certainly not in the Occident, which has so retained an unbroken, living though changing tradition for some three thousand years. Though the gap is wide, there are, nevertheless, fewer differences today between ancient and modern Greek than between Chaucer's Middle English and the present state of the American language.

Since the birth of the modern Greek nation, a passionate battle has raged between scholars and academicians on the one hand, who have tried to impose the purist tongue from above, and most authors—poets, novelists, dramatists—who, equally proud of their long tradition, have found themselves unable to express their emotions in an artificial and bloodless tongue whose textual roots go so deep as to evolve into no living blossom. Fifty years ago Athenians rioted in the streets when a troupe tried to stage the *Oresteia* in modern translation, and several students were killed in an attempt to keep *The New Testament* from being translated into the demotic tongue. But as in every other nation where such a problem existed, authors have always been impelled to use the daily vulgar tongue which their tears and laughter had drenched during their unfolding growth as they spoke it at home and in the streets of their cities from childhood on. The demotic tongue is rich in concrete nouns, adjectives, verbs, and idioms to express the direct, passionate, metaphorical and lyrical emotions of daily life, as the folk songs and legends of all nations will testify, but it is lacking in the abstract words necessary for more metaphysical introversion and analysis. The demotic tongue, as always, has of course won the battle, though in the years to come (for the Greek language is at once very old and very young) it must slowly borrow, assimilate, and invent many abstract and scientific terms for which there has never been a lack of roots or precedents in the Greek language from Homer to the present day. Indeed, for centuries, Greek roots have been borrowed avidly by the languages of all the world to express new concepts in science and philosophy.

It is curious and ironic, therefore, that in Greece Kazantzakis should have been criticized not only by the proponents of the purist tongue, but even more violently by many of those who have fought on the side of demotic usage. The charge levied against him is that he has in every way exaggerated the demotic peculiarities and idiomatic richness of the people's tongue, in syntax, grammar, in pronunciation, and especially in choice of words. They point out that his poem, with an appended lexicon of almost 2,000 words, contains many words and idioms unknown to the well-educated Greek, seemingly unaware that the majority of these terms (as I have myself attested) are in daily and familiar use by fisherman and peasant, though often not simultaneously in the same part of Greece. Kazantzakis wandered over the length and breadth of Greece, throughout her numerous islands, and with great love and care collected notebook after notebook of words from every occupation and region until he had prepared a large dictionary of the demotic tongue, which no publisher, however, has yet printed. It is indicative that even to this day no adequate dictionary of the demotic tongue exists.

To any historian of the development and changes of language, Kazantzakis' predicament is a familiar one. The same outcry was raised when Dante dared to write in the common Florentine parlance of his native city, when Chaucer wrote in the Middle English idiom of London, when Gonzalo de Berceo translated the lives of the saints from the Latin into the newly formed Castilian tongue. "In the critical evolutionary stage through which our demotic language is passing," Kazantzakis wrote, "it is natural, essential—and extremely useful—for a creator to treasure avidly and to save as much linguistic wealth as he can, as in similar periods of Dante, Rabelais, and Luther. Our tongue, because of the laziness and linguistic ignorance of the 'intellectuals,' and because of the linguistic corruption of the people subjected to faulty schooling and newspaper jargon, is in danger of being deformed and impoverished. The creator is more anguished by this danger than anyone else, and because for him every word is a part of the spirit, because he knows that the greatest responsibility falls to him, he opens the doors of his works wide in order that the nouns and adjectives may find a refuge there. This is how it has always been; the creator, in these endangering periods, even though he knows that his vocabulary may become overladen, wants to receive under his roof (he cannot, he must not resist) all the homeless linguistic refugees who are in danger of dying. Only in this way can the constantly increasing linguistic wealth be saved, that is to say, spiritually." Kazantzakis would have found enthusiastic and cantankerous support in Ezra Pound and H. L. Mencken.

An interesting and contrasting parallel may be drawn between Milton's and Kazantzakis' use of their respective native tongues. Milton forced the natural resilience of English into the elaborate constructions and borrowed diction of his beloved Latin and Greek, yet with the stamp of his genius, his complete immersion in his vision, his identification and sincere belief in his method, created a poetic parlance which, though unique, is indisputably one of the glories of the "English" language. Conversely, Kazantzakis reached deep into the demotic roots and practice of modern Greek, saved from dissipation the syntax, diction and idioms of the common people throughout Greece, without distinction of regions, and in words and rhythms as simple, uncomplex and lilting as folk song, achieved for the Athenian intellectual a style almost as foreign to him as that of Milton's for the tolerably educated Englishman.

Of course this tension and this problem in language disappear—perhaps fortunately, or perhaps unfortunately—in an English or American version, for we do not have the extreme dichotomy in language which exists in modern Greek. What remains, and what I have tried to capture, is the racy, idiomatic, highly colloquial flow of the original. The borderline between colloquial and slang is often hard to draw, and I would have felt untrue to my original had I attempted to reproduce it in such idioms as those used by Ezra Pound in his recent translation of Sophocles' *Women of Trachis,* which seems to me a *tour de force,* a parody in extreme American colloquialism and slang which has no parallel in the original diction of the central characters of the play. Instead, I have used the simplest and strongest words I could find to capture the zest and swing of the language, the playful juggling even of serious and tragic moods, the liveliness and the strength. Although the Greek original is more supple and flowing with liquid polysyllables and easily formed compound words, the English version is perhaps stronger, due to the more condensed line I have used and the greater prevalence of monosyllables in a tongue based on Anglo-Saxon roots. This aspect of the translation pleased Kazantzakis more than any other, and he would pound the table with delight as he declaimed in a loud voice: "And thick black blood dripped down from both his murderous palms!" As often as I could, I preferred to discard a word in English derived from the Greek word which I was translating, and to substitute for it a synonymous word derived from Anglo-Saxon roots. I have tried, as much as possible and with very few liberties indeed, to make this poem sound and read as if it were written originally in English (or perhaps *American* would be truer to the mark) though I have also deliberately retained certain epithets, expressions, and many compound words in order to link it with its Homeric prototype.

The Style and Structure. The most disconcerting adjustment the reader of any nationality must make in reading Kazantzakis' *Odyssey* is toward an utterly unexpected style and structure. Whether he is conscious of it or not, the educated as well as the common reader expects a style which, in truth, is far removed even from Homer's rather colorful, adjectival, and epithet-laden diction. He has come to think of Homer as a "classical" writer and to confuse him with the stylistic characteristics of a much later period, to expect the leanness and simplicity of a Doric column, a style more Hellenic than Homeric—orderly, composed, controlled, and without digressions. Instead, he will fall headlong into an adjectival cataract of rich epithets, a gothic profusion of metaphors and similes, of allegorical and symbolistic characters and episodes, of fables and legends that seem to digress and never to return. He will be confronted, in short, not only with a work which is not "classical," but which, in fact, is anti-classical, anti-Hellenic, and most definitely romantic and baroque. "What would one of the builders of the Parthenon say," Kazantzakis wrote to his young academic critic, "if he saw a gothic cathedral? He would exclaim that it is overladen with gods, men, beasts, and chimeras, filled with alarming mystical battles between darkness and light, incongruous, disquieting, barbarous." If the modern reader would seek touchstones by which to interpret the *Odyssey,* he will find much to aid him in Homer's own poem, but he would do well, also, to turn to other sources for style and structure: to folk songs and legends, to the picaresque novel, to Cervantes and Rabelais, to Aristophanes, to the Euripides of *The Bacchanals,* to Paul Bunyan, to all tall tales, fairy stories, and incredible adventures. A song, a dream, a story in the *Odyssey,* Kazantzakis wrote, will not then seem like rhetoric or manufacture, for if the reader will gaze from within he will find the esoteric necessity for each detail, he will live through "the spiritual transitions from one situation to another as though through a natural passage. Whoever lives these metamorphoses inwardly feels them to be as natural, as simple, and as indispensable as the ripening of a fruit—of a grape, let us say: from the dry twig to the sprout, from the sprout to the flowering cluster, from there to the sour pip, then to the sweet grape, to the wine, and finally to the song." If he does so, the reader will find beneath this gothic façade a skeletal clarity of line, a structure of noble proportion and thought, a development of ultimate simplicity which betray an Apollonian counterbalance.

Perhaps the aspect of diction in Kazantzakis which might be most disconcerting to American or English readers, trained in the leaner diction of a Hemingway or an Eliot, is his evident love and use of adjectives. The translator here is at a disadvantage because, as in all inflected languages, an adjective in the Greek can as easily follow as precede a noun, often in a flanking balance, whereas a translator in English is forced to rank both adjectives before the noun. Also, the polysyllabic character of Greek permits the easy formulation of many compound words (in which the *Odyssey* is especially rich) where two or sometimes three adjectival roots are fused into one word. An exact translation into English, however, though sometimes effective, would more than likely be cumbersome, for a long poem cannot sustain such compressed neologisms as Hopkins' famed and beautiful "dapple-dawn-drawn falcon." I have often been forced, therefore, to break down such a compound word into its component parts, and then, more often than not, to choose the more striking or precise adjective and to delete the second or third. Nevertheless, an adjectival abundance remains, to which perhaps the experiments of a Gerard Manley Hopkins and the richness of a Dylan Thomas may again make us attuned. Many other compound words must be decompounded in English, as in the following three words describing the beauteous Helen: *μυγδαλογελάστρα,* "she whose laugh is like an almond tree," *ροδοστάλαχτη,* "she on whom roses fall," *ποθογλίστρες πλάτες,* "shoulders on which desire glides." Every translator is filled with envy to find words in a language which denote a certain phenomenon for which there is no equivalent word in his. Such are two words which Kazantzakis found among the peasantry but which are unknown to most Greek intellectuals: the expressive word γιορτόπιασμα, a contemptuous expression used to denote a child conceived by its parents during the lax gaieties of a fiesta, and λιόκρουσι, describing that moment when the full moon, rising in the east, is struck by the rays of the setting sun.

For Kazantzakis, however, the adjective had further and more dialectical significance. "I love adjectives," he wrote, "but not simply as decoration. I feel the necessity of expressing my emotion from all sides, spherically; and because my emotion is never simple, never positive or negative only, but both together and something even more, it is impossible for me to restrict myself to one adjective. One such adjective, whatever it might be, would cripple my emotion, and I am obliged, in order to remain faithful to my emotion and not betray it, to invite another adjective, often opposed to the previous one, always with a different meaning, in order that I may see the noun from its other equally lawful and existent side. Only thus, by besieging a meaning from all sides, may I conquer it, that is, may I express it. The wealth and variety of my love for the adjective, and often for its crudity, is an imperative necessity for my complex inner vision, and not at all decorative. Nothing for me exists more substantial than the adjective. The attempt to find the exact adjective and to enclose within it an essence that might not go lost, is almost always painful; and the longing to express all co-existent, antithetical attributes of a noun, and not condemn to death any one essence, is indeed tragic; nor has this any relationship to the often careless, playful, and pleasant coloring of a decorative disposition."

The effect of rhetorical richness in Kazantzakis is further enhanced by his astonishing fertility in the invention of metaphor and simile, especially in those tropes where the two component parts are rooted in a loving observation of nature. Just as he often "invited" not simply another but even an opposing adjective to express his complex inner vision and "the antithetical richness of a noun," so Kazantzakis saw metaphor and simile as technical manifestations where two opposites are caught in a hovering balance in which each part, in thesis and antithesis, retains its identity yet evokes an imaginative synthesis. A catalogue only of his various tropes to describe the sun would give an astonishing indication of his range here. The sun, flame, fire, and light compose the chief imagery of the *Odyssey*, flowing in a dazzling current throughout the poem just as the sun in Greece itself constantly pulses throughout the clarity of its azure atmosphere, blazing on rocks, mountains, and the deviously tortured coastline and islands of that sun-washed country. According to the occasion, the mental or emotional condition of the observer, and the geography (whether, for instance, on the sands of the Sahara or on the horizon of the Antarctic icefields), the sun revolves around the *Odyssey* in a protean metamorphosis. It stalks like a great Oriental prince, it strides like a stalwart youth on the Nile and cracks its mud banks, or like a drunken red-faced lord it stumbles and staggers up the clouds with glazed eyes. Sometimes it is a child of the granite gods of Egypt, falling into the stone cupped hands of his great forefathers; sometimes it is a god who wedges his golden horns under the horizon, lifts the clouds and slowly frees his forehead, his eyes and mouth; or at times it is a god whose rays are five-fingered hands caressing the world and revivifying the dead. It is a spearsman; it is an expert archer who kneels on mountain summits and stretches his bow taut to shoot with arrows of flame; it is a caparisoned warrior slashing at the horizon impassionedly; it is an unsleeping sentry who leaps up and warns of the approaching enemy; it is a melting bronze hanging in mid-sky, a flaming armor, a pouring honey. But it is also an infant with golden bonnet and swaddling clothes of azure smoke whimpering in the arms of Mother Night; a baby suckling at the nipples of conflagration; a plump boy fondling the world with fat, small hands. It is a golden lover sitting on a sunflower and gazing, lovesick, at the earth; a peddler roaming the villages with a golden sack and selling his goods of musk-deer, blue-furred fox, fishes, and eggs; a charioteer with snow-white steeds; someone flinging roses on snows, waters, and mountain peaks. It is a smith's hammer beating on the anvil of an iron mountain summit that blazes and floods with fire; a golden sphere wedged between the horns of plowing oxen; a gold-rimmed heavy wheel bogged down in the mind's mud; a vermilion quoit hurled along the sky's rim by dawn, the discus-thrower; a flame-eyed disk rolled along the sky by Yesterday and Tomorrow; a bursting sphere that roars down the heavens and beats and rebounds on earth's drum-taut hide. It is a celestial tambourine made of crimson hides, a frightening and booming drum stretched tight with lion pelts, a resounding golden war-shield held aloft. It is the golden cap of the mind, a quick and coquetting eye, a charm hanging on the pulsing throat of a singing bird, a round breadloaf issuing from the oven of the sky, a fruit hanging amid tree branches and pecked by birds, a pomegranate tree weighed down with fruit and flowers on which a drunken skylark hops and sings; a rose which has shed all its petals until only the pollened stamen remains. It is a flickering lamp hanging in Hades with gentle and compassionate flame, the golden lantern of a bridegroom seeking his bride, a blazing kiln that shoots savage spears of flame to earth, a golden tassel hanging from the fox-fur cap of Death. It is a mansion with double doors that open to the East and West and through which birds, ghosts, thoughts, and the imagination's fancies pour.

In its more terrifying aspects the sun is a slain head slowly tumbling down the burning sands, the head of a pale phantom rolling from mountain peak to peak, a lord wading in deep pits of blood, a blood-drenched body splattering a city, a pallid mourner sitting by a deathbed and caressing the coffin, a maker of coffin-candles and flaming funeral wreaths, a drowning cadaver, the Black Sun of Death. Among animals, it is a lobster with crimson claws, a russet hound, a lean leopard pouncing on wheat fields and olive groves, a bellowing bullock dragged to the slaughterhouse in the West, a drained black ram with shrunken bags after it has just tupped row on row of buxom ewes, a bear cub whose face is being licked away by its mother, a white polar bear. Among birds, it is an obedient falcon with fine golden chains tossed into the sky by a falconer; a gaudy and spurred cock-pheasant with gilded cockscomb; a rooster crowing on the rooftops; an early-morning sky-cock flapping its wings; a pallid cock with plucked and molted wings limping on the sky's rim; an old hen sprouting a crest and crowing hoarsely on the terraces. It is a golden egg hatched by night in darkness to spring like a crimson-crested cock; it is the golden egg from which day is hatched.

The entire Prologue is an invocation to the Sun as the fecund principle, as the ultimate symbolic goal of a time when "stones, water, fire, and earth shall be transformed to spirit, / and the mud-winged and heavy soul, freed of its flesh, / shall like a flame serene ascend and fade in sun." The Epilogue is a depiction of the sun as a great Eastern prince sinking to his palace in the West, lamenting the death of Odysseus and refusing, in his sorrow, the food, wine, and women his mother, Earth, had prepared him for consolation. Thus the poem begins and ends with the Sun as image and symbol of the entire narrative. Throughout Book XXIII the Sun becomes one of the protagonists, hovering above Odysseus' head in constant apprehension and lament during the long Antarctic summer, and the climax of Kazantzakis' dialectical use of metaphor is marshaled in the opening of this book where the Sun is apostrophized as a Holy Trinity: as the fructifying Father, as the breeding Mother who gives the world suck from her dazzling breasts of light, and as the Son who gambols on the grasses and waters of the world with joy. Finally, in a magnificent passage where Odysseus says farewell to his five elements, Earth, Water, Fire, Air, and Mind, he cries:

Fire will surely come one day to cleanse the earth,
fire will surely come one day to make mind ash,
Fate is a fiery tongue that eats up earth and sky.
The womb of life is fire, and fire the last tomb,
and there between two lofty flames we dance and weep;
in this blue lightning flash of mine where my life burns,
all time and all space disappear, and the mind sinks,
and all—hearts, birds, beasts, brain, and loam—break into dance,
though it's no dance now, for they blaze up, fade, and spin,
are suddenly freed to exist no more, nor have they ever lived!

Perhaps the most beautiful metaphor in the entire poem is that in which the poet likens Odysseus' last conscious moment to a flame that leaps from its wick and hangs for an instant disembodied in air before it vanishes forever:

As a low lantern's flame flicks in its final blaze
then leaps above its shriveled wick and mounts aloft,
brimming with light, and soars toward death with dazzling joy,
so did his fierce soul leap before it vanished in air.

It is in this eternal moment of the suspended flame, when only Love and Memory remain, that the entire action of the twenty-fourth and final book takes place.

Much curiosity has been aroused by the round (or rather unevenly round) number of verses of which the entire poem is composed: 33,333. Some have thought that Kazantzakis deliberately padded his poem in order to arrive at such an impressive and mystifying summation, but the poet once wryly informed me that, on the contrary, his sixth and next-to-the-last draft of the poem numbered 42,500 verses, and that he suffered as though cutting into living flesh when he carved it into leaner proportions. Those who thought the number three might have for Kazantzakis a symbolical, a mystical (and not mystifying) significance, came to closer understanding, though his own explanation has more metaphysical import: "The number three is a holy number simply because it is the mathematical expression of the dialectical progression of the mind from thesis to antithesis and finally to the summit of every endeavor, synthesis. I can never think of or accept an A without at the same time thinking of and accepting an A—, and to want at once, in order to free myself from this antinomy, to unite them both in a synthesis, into an A+. The A always seems to me a miserable thing, no matter how useful it may be in practical life; the A— seems to me scant and infertile, and only the A+ succeeds in making firm, in fertilizing, and in disburdening my thought. This triple rhythm, transferred from dialectical thought into a metaphysical and mystical vision, gave birth to all the Holy Trinities in many religions. Father, Mother, and Son form such an evident completeness that from the first awakening of human thought it was evident the Trinity would be made divine. This is why, from every consideration, the number three can be thought of as sacred; in the case of the *Odyssey*, however, it is not necessary to seek recourse to mysticism or orientalism; the number three is holy because it symbolizes the dialectical progression which the thought and diction of the *Odyssey* follow." Kazantzakis was delighted when I informed him of an antithesis to this thesis, one of which he was unaware: that throughout the peasantry in Greece, the number three, in innumerable jokes and anecdotes, represents the male genitalia.

Although the rhythm and scope of the *Odyssey* are epical, the psychological insight and development dramatical, the structure mystical and symbolical, the narrative method is often lyrical, essentially that of Greek folk songs and legends. The diction is direct, simple, strong, and completely demotic; there is an unceasing delight in the formation of epithets and compound words (though Kazantzakis *invented* only about five or six entirely new words), and there are the same exaggerations and tautologies, the same lack of strong run-on lines, the same simple sentence structure and lack of subordination, the same lyrical repetitions of phrases, the essential bardic approach to narration. Indeed, throughout his poem Kazantzakis has embedded many lines taken directly from the folk poetry of his nation, many of which I have indicated in the Appendix. He has also lovingly culled this literature for words and phrases to enrich his own demotic texture. His approach to his materials and method has always been so direct, simple, and passionate that he has never considered any of his work to be a constructed form of "literature," but more as the inspired vision of a minstrel who by the fireside day after day unfolds his narration as the moment inspires, drawing on the richness of a memory replete with many songs and legends, of his many wanderings, and of a philosophy and a technique which unfold naturally, like a flower, intuitively, from within. "When an African witch doctor," he wrote, "with his paints, woods, feathers, seashells, and often with his father's skull, creates a mask to wear in the sacred dances of marriage or death of his tribe, he is not deliberately creating 'art.' Technique is the outward expression of vision, in order to embody, to control, or to exorcise."

His approach to life and literature both was primarily Dionysian, although it was tempered with Apollonian clarity. He would have agreed with Zarathustra: "Write with your heart's blood, and you will see that the blood is spirit." Every morning when he sat down at his table to write the *Odyssey,* he was without plan, nor did he know where his poem or his characters might lead him. When I objected sometimes to a statement or an action of one of his characters, he would sigh and tell me there was nothing he could have done, because the character in question insisted on behaving in just that way, as though it were a living person with a will beyond the control of its creator. He felt within himself, he said, certain "musical states," and his poem unfolded as the musical conditions of his spirit directed. In just this way Odysseus went to Sparta, to Crete, to Egypt, and in this way plunged into all his adventures. Essentially, artistic creation was for Kazantzakis a superior and more faithful form of confession, the witness of man before the world of his struggle to understand his condition and to give it meaning. He believed in Goethe's dictate: "If you wish to leave something useful to future generations, this cannot but be confession," and his last book, one of spiritual memoirs, which he left to be published after his death, carries the title *Report to Greco,* in which he gives an accounting of his inmost life.

V. ACKNOWLEDGMENTS

It was Nicholas Hadji-Kyriaco Ghika who first spoke to me with enthusiasm of the *Odyssey* and showed me the twenty or so illustrations he had already completed for the poem, waiting to be assured of reproduction before he undertook to complete his project. It gives me great pleasure to know that my translation into English has spurred him on to complete his plan and has made possible the first printing of his magnificent drawings. At his ancestral villa on the island of Hydra in the summer of 1950, and with his patient assistance, I first essayed to translate, into prose, those lines which he had chosen to illustrate. Some of these prose translations were later published in several American periodicals and anthologies with some of his drawings.

I first met Nikos Kazantzakis and his wife, Helen, in a students' hostel in Florence in the summer of 1951. After the first half hour of flurried talk, he exclaimed that surely I must have read all of his work because, with the exception of his boyhood friend, Mr. Pandelís Prevelákis, he felt he had met no one who seemed to understand his thought so well. At that time, however, I had read only those sections of the *Odyssey* which I had translated for Ghika's illustrations, but our future collaboration confirmed both of us in the rapport which each felt for the other in personality and thought. I spent four months with Kazantzakis and his wife in the summer and fall of 1954 at his home in Antibes on the French Riviera, reading his poem with him carefully, word by word, as I filled notebook after notebook with commentary on diction, meter, interpretation, and the significance of allegories and symbols. Because he could read English well and had himself translated many of the great epics of the world, he understood the problems of translation thoroughly, and was therefore the perfect collaborator. From the beginning, feeling certain that I understood his meaning and his method, he gave me complete freedom to work in my own medium of the English language as I thought best. When I had half-finished the poem, we met for a month, in August of 1956, in the Yugoslavian Alps above Ljubljana, and then again for another month, in May of 1957, for the final checking, when I had finished the third draft of the poem and was on my way to the United States. From various parts of Greece where I had been living during this period, from mid-October of 1954 through April of 1957, I sent him each book as I completed it, with a list of questions, and he would reply immediately from Antibes with full answers.

My translation has involved a circuitous Odyssey of my own, for I have worked on the poem in Duluth, Chicago, and New York; in many ships and airplanes on and over several seas and oceans; in Antibes, Cannes, and Nice; in Athens and Sparta; in various parts of the Arcadian Peloponnesus; in Thessaly, Thrace, and Macedonia; in the whitewashed rooms of many waterfront hotels in the Mediterranean islands of Aegina, Poros, Hydra, Andros, Ithaca, Cercyra, Crete, Chios, Lesbos, Limnos, Samothrace, and Thasos; in the Yugoslavian Alps; and now finally here, at the other side of the world, in Antofagasta, Chile; and I shall be making revisions and correcting proofs in Santiago, Puerto Montt, Aisén, Coyhaique, Buenos Aires, Montevideo, São Paulo, and Rio de Janeiro.

I am greatly indebted to Mrs. Helen Kazantzakis for the patience, kindness, and loving care with which she saw to my comfort when I was living in Antibes, for her perceptive answers to all my questions, for her assistance with many tedious details, and for her revealing discussions with me of her husband's work and character. Since her husband's death, she has diligently sent me much needed information from Athens and Antibes. I am particularly obligated to Dr. W. B. Stanford who read each book as I finished it and who sent me promptly, from his chair at the University of Dublin, many suggestions and illuminating comments, all of which I have gratefully used. To Mr. Justin D. Kaplan of Simon and Schuster I am similarly obligated. To Kazantzakis' nephew, Mr. Manolis Banis, I am particularly indebted for many hours of technical and philosophical discussions in Athens over a period of more than a year, for his careful consideration with me of many problems before the final questions were formulated and sent to his uncle in Antibes. To him, also, I am obligated for further information sent me from Athens. During most of a year when I was hospitalized and then confined to my apartment in Athens, I owed a great deal to my dear friends, Mrs. Marguerita and Mr. John Goudélis (the Greek publishers of Kazantzakis), to Mr. Alcibiades Kotzámbasis, and to Mr. Stratis Haviarás for their tireless care, their loving considerations and their many thoughtful solicitudes which helped bring my work to a happy conclusion in Greece. To the novelist, poet, and dramatist, Mr. Pandelís Prevelákis, to whom the poet had given several drafts of the *Odyssey*, I owe particular thanks for the clarification of various knotty passages and the resolution of those final questions which still remained after the death of his cherished friend.

Here, in Antofagasta, I wish to thank my uncles and aunts for the warm hospitality which they have extended over a period of several months to a nephew they had not seen since he was two years old: Miss Merope Politis, Mr. Gabriel Politis, Mr. Phótis Politis, and in particular Mrs. Pulhería Farandáto, her husband, and my first cousin, Miss Ketty Farandáto in whose home I made many revisions of the poem, wrote the Introduction and the Appendix, and who with loving attention saw to it that I was always freed from any inconvenience. For similar considerations I am indebted to my first cousin Mrs. Ketty de Opazo and her husband Mario, to my cousin Mr. Constantine Boudózis and his wife Aphrodite, and to my Homeric uncles, Mr. Agamemnon Politis and his wife Trudy of Santiago, and Mr. Heracles Politis of Neuva Imperial.

I owe thanks to the Fulbright Committee who made it possible for me to spend the academic year of 1954-55 as a Research Scholar in Modern Greek Literature at the University of Athens. To Archibald MacLeish, Allen Tate, Conrad Aiken, Theodore Weiss, John Malcolm Brinnin, James Laughlin, Seymour Lawrence, and Lawrence Durrell I am grateful for the encouragement they gave me in my various translations from modern Greek poetry to their culmination in this work. In particular I am grateful to Sir Cecil Maurice Bowra, Arthur Miller, Gore Vidal, Karl Shapiro, John Ciardi, James Merrill, Ronald Freelander, Anthony Decavalles, and Dean Moody Prior of Northwestern University, all of whom read my first tentative experiments with the *Odyssey* in both prose and poetry and encouraged me to attempt the more arduous but more rewarding metrical version. T. S. Eliot wrote me of his pleased astonishment that any publisher today would be willing to gamble on the publication of so long a poem, and in verse translation. I owe this to the initial inspiration of Mr. M. Lincoln Schuster, who first sent me to Antibes to collaborate with Kazantzakis, and to whom I have been most grateful during these past four years for his continuous support and unfailing enthusiasm.

Antofagasta, Chile
April 1958

Prologue

O Sun, great Oriental, my proud mind's golden cap,
I love to wear you cocked askew, to play and burst
in song throughout our lives, and so rejoice our hearts.
Good is this earth, it suits us! Like the global grape
it hangs, dear God, in the blue air and sways in the gale,
nibbled by all the birds and spirits of the four winds.
Come, let's start nibbling too and so refresh our minds!
Between two throbbing temples in the mind's great wine vats
I tread on the crisp grapes until the wild must boils
and my mind laughs and steams within the upright day.
Has the earth sprouted wings and sails, has my mind swayed
until black-eyed Necessity got drunk and burst in song?
Above me spreads the raging sky, below me swoops
my belly, a white gull that breasts the cooling waves;
my nostrils fill with salty spray, the billows burst
swiftly against my back, rush on, and I rush after.
Great Sun, who pass on high yet watch all things below,
I see the sun-drenched cap of the great castle-wrecker:
let's kick and scuff it round to see where it will take us!
Learn, lads, that Time has cycles and that Fate has wheels
and that the mind of man sits high and twirls them round;
come quick, let's spin the world about and send it tumbling!
O Sun, my quick coquetting eye, my red-haired hound,
sniff out all quarries that I love, give them swift chase,
tell me all that you've seen on earth, all that you've heard,
and I shall pass them through my entrails' secret forge
till slowly, with profound caresses, play and laughter,
stones, water, fire, and earth shall be transformed to spirit,
and the mud-winged and heavy soul, freed of its flesh,
shall like a flame serene ascend and fade in sun.
You've drunk and eaten well, my lads, on festive shores,
until the feast within you turned to dance and laughter,
love-bites and idle chatter that dissolved in flesh;
but in myself the meat turned monstrous, the wine rose,
a sea-chant leapt within me, rushed to knock me down,
until I longed to sing this song—make way, my brothers!

Oho, the festival lasts long, the place is small;
make way, let me have air, give me a ring to stretch in,
a place to spread my shinbones, to kick up my heels,
so that my giddiness won't wound your wives and children.
As soon as I let loose my words along the shore
to hunt all mankind down, I know they'll choke my throat,
and when my full neck smothers and my pain grows vast
I shall rise up—make way!—to dance on raging shores.
Snatch prudence from me, God, burst my brows wide, fling far
the trap doors of my mind, let the world breathe awhile.
Ho, workers, peasants, you ant-swarms, carters of grain,
I fling red poppies down, may the world burst in flames!
Maidens, with wild doves fluttering in your soothing breasts,
brave lads, with your black-hilted swords thrust in your belts,
no matter how you strive, earth's but a barren tree,
but I, ahoy, with my salt songs shall force the flower!
Fold up your aprons, craftsmen, cast your tools away,
fling off Necessity's firm yoke, for Freedom calls.
Freedom, my lads, is neither wine nor a sweet maid,
not goods stacked in vast cellars, no, nor sons in cradles;
it's but a scornful, lonely song the wind has taken . . .
Come, drink of Lethe's brackish spring to cleanse your minds,
forget your cares, your poisons, your ignoble profits,
and make your hearts as babes, unburdened, pure and light.
O brain, be flowers that nightingales may come to sing!
Old men, howl all you can to bring your white teeth back,
to make your hair crow-black, your youthful wits go wild,
for by our Lady Moon and our Lord Sun, I swear
old age is a false dream and Death but fantasy,
all playthings of the brain and the soul's affectations,
all but a mistral's blast that blows the temples wide;
the dream was lightly dreamt and thus the earth was made;
let's take possession of the world with song, my lads!
Aye, fellow craftsmen, seize your oars, the Captain comes;
and mothers, give your sweet babes suck to stop their wailing!
Ahoy, cast wretched sorrow out, prick up your ears—
I sing the sufferings and the torments of renowned Odysseus!

I

And when in his wide courtyards Odysseus had cut down
the insolent youths, he hung on high his sated bow
and strode to the warm bath to cleanse his bloodstained body.
Two slaves prepared his bath, but when they saw their lord
they shrieked with terror, for his loins and belly steamed
and thick black blood dripped down from both his murderous palms;
their copper jugs rolled clanging on the marble tiles.
The wandering man smiled gently in his thorny beard
and with his eyebrows signed the frightened girls to go.
For hours he washed himself in the warm water, his veins
spread out like rivers in his body, his loins cooled,
and his great mind was in the waters cleansed and calmed.
Then softly sweet with aromatic oils he smoothed
his long coarse hair, his body hardened by black brine,
till youthfulness awoke his wintry flesh with flowers.
On golden-studded nails in fragrant shadows flashed
row upon row the robes his faithful wife had woven,
adorned with hurrying winds and gods and swift triremes,
and stretching out a sunburnt hand, he quickly chose
the one most flaming, flung it flat across his back,
and steaming still, shot back the bolt and crossed the threshold.
His slaves in shade were dazzled till the huge smoked beams
of his ancestral home flashed with reflected light,
and as she waited by the throne in pallid, speechless dread,
Penelope turned to look, and her knees shook with fright:
"That's not the man I've awaited year on year, O Gods,
this forty-footed dragon that stalks my quaking house!"
But the mind-archer quickly sensed the obscure dread
of his poor wife and to his swelling breast replied:
"O heart, she who for years has awaited you to force
her bolted knees and join you in rejoicing cries,
she is that one you've longed for, battling the far seas,
the cruel gods and deep voices of your deathless mind."
He spoke, but still his heart leapt not in his wild chest,
still in his nostrils steamed the blood of newly slain;
he saw his wife still tangled in their naked forms,

and as he watched her sideways, his eyes glazed, almost
in slaughter's seething wrath he might have pierced her through.
Swiftly he passed and mutely stood on his wide sill;
the burning sun in splendor sank and filled all nooks
and every vaulted cell with rose and azure shade.
Athena's altar in the court still smoked, replete,
while in the long arcades in cool night air there swung
the new-hung slaves, their eyes and swollen tongues protruding.
His own eyes calmly gazed in the starry eyes of night,
who from the mountains with her curly flocks descended,
till all his murderous work and whir of arrows sank
within his heart in peace, distilled like mist or dream,
and his wild tiger heart in darkness licked its lips.
After the joy of bathing, his mind grew serene,
nor did he once glance backward toward the splattered blood,
nor in its cunning coils once scheme for ways to save
his dreadful head from dangers that besieged it now.
Thus in this holy hour Odysseus basked in peace,
on his ancestral threshold standing, bathed and shorn of care.

Meanwhile in every courtyard the swift news had spread
how slyly their king had stolen to his ancestral land
and slain the suitors round the feasting boards like bulls.
Leaning on their oak staffs, the slain men's fathers shrieked
and knocked on each town door to rouse the angry crowd;
the common workmen threw their rough tools to the ground,
the craftsmen closed their shops, and from the seaside pubs
the drunken oarsmen lurched, climbing the winding paths.
Cluster by cluster in the market place all swarmed
like angry bees when wasps have robbed their hives of honey.
A woman who had lost her man on Trojan shores
for Helen's sake raised her love-aching arms, and cried:
"We've welcomed him too well, my lads, that barbarous butcher!
Behold his gifts: a sword, a shield, three flasks of poison:
one to be drunk at dawn, one at high noon, the third
most bitter one, dear Gods, to be drunk in bed, alone!"
Shrilly from doors, roofs, terraces, the widows swarmed,
flinging black kerchiefs round their heads, and yelled with rage:
"May Zeus curse him who scorched us now in our first bloom!
Our beds are filmed with mold, our honest homes are ruined,
and all for the sake of a man-luring, shameless slut!"
They beat their sterile breasts, for lack of children shrunk,
and one, swept by her grief, wailed in a wild lament:
"I weep less for my good man's death or widowed arms
than for my fallen breasts, my teats that shrank and dried
for lack of milk and a stout son to bite them sweetly."

Secret and ancient wounds in their hearts bled again,
their eyes grew dim, and the sun's little light grew faint
as on black floating clouds astride, dark shades of men,
stranded on hopeless shores, came slowly drifting in.
They passed through desolate dusk in silence, wrapped in webs,
and swiftly gliding along high walls, vanished in doorways.
One lightly touched his father, and the old man shivered,
one let his shadow fall on his home's scattered stones,
one on the shriveled apples of his wife's worn breasts.
The fondled shoulders quivered, knees gave way with fright,
the air with dead men thickened, and the stifling widows
tightly embraced the empty air with grief, and moaned.
An armless man, whose hands the Trojan shores devoured,
leapt on a rock, and soon there huddled thickly round him
the maimed, blind, warped and crippled of man-eating War.
"Comrades," he yelled, and flailed the air with his arm-stumps,
"our king's come back and brought *his* body whole, unharmed,
both of *his* hands, his feet, his eyes, his wily brain;
but we're now crawling beasts that grovel on the ground;
we grasp, but with no hands, we leap, but with no feet,
and with our blank eyesockets knock on the archons' doors."
Then his voice stopped, his head thrust back in hollow shoulders,
and his friends cheered him wildly and embraced him tight;
the widows rushed into the streets bareheaded, bold,
grabbed torches, scattered through the town and spurred the men:
"Ho! look at these brave lads that drip tears and saliva!
Take up our spindles, bind your heads with our black kerchiefs!
Women, raise high your torches, fire that murderous man,
burn down his palace tonight and strew the ashes to the four winds!"

And you, in the quiet of night, you felt, O harsh sea-battler,
the tumult of the insolent crowd, the flaming torches,
and as you stretched your neck to listen, your heart flared:
"Even my isle moves under my feet like angry seas,
and here I thought to find firm earth, to plant deep roots!
The armature of earth is rent, the hull gapes open;
the mob roars to my left, the archons crowd my right;
how heavy the cargo grows; I'll heave to, and unballast!"
He spoke, then with great strides sped to his central court,
his ears, lips, temples quivering like a slender hound,
and as he groped his body stealthily, he seized
his wide, two-bladed sword, in many slaughters steeped,
and all at once his heart grew whole again and calm.
From the high roofs his slaves discerned the seething mob,
unloosed their locks and filled their rooms with lamentation;
the queen took courage, rushed to where her husband stood

and mutely flung her arms about his ruthless knees,
but he commanded all to lock themselves in the high towers,
then bellowed for his son till all the palace rang.
The young man, lolling in his bath, leapt at the cry,
thrust through the frightened slaves who washed his chest of gore,
strode out and firmly stood by his dread father's side.
His naked body, flushed, still steamed in darkling air
and like a bronze sword, slaked with slaughter, glowed and glittered.
He who has borne a son dies not; the father turned,
and his sea-battered vagrant heart swelled up with pride.
Good seemed to him his young son's neck, his chest and sides,
the swift articulation of his joints, his royal veins
that from tall temples down to lithesome ankles throbbed.
Like a horse-buyer, with swift glances he enclosed
with joy his son's well-planted and keen-bladed form.
"It's I who stand before my own discarded husk,
my lip unshaven, my heart still covered with soft down,
all my calamities still buds, my wars, carnations,
and my far journeys still faint flutterings on my brow."
Not to betray his joy, he lowered his eyes, and frowned:
"Tall tower of our tribe's fort, my son, my only son,
take heed: the knavish mob now rears and tries its wings,
the maimed have taken arms, slaves have cast off their yoke,
the ballast, risen to foam, now tries to guide the prow.
Pretend I've not returned, that waves have gulped me down,
and come, tell me how *you* would crush this crude revolt."
A mild breeze blew on ringlets of a fallow brow,
somewhere amid an olive tree a nightbird sighed,
soft seawaves far away on the smooth shingle murmured
and happy night in her first sleep mumbled in dream.
Telemachus then turned to his harsh-speaking lord:
"Father, your eyes are brimmed with blood, your fists are smoking!"
The cruel man-slayer grabbed his son and roared with laughter;
two crows on two black branches shook with fright, and fled,
and in the court an old oak swayed with all its stars.
"Hold firm, my son, or my strong laugh will knock you down!"
But the young man shook free from his strong father's grasp:
"At your side, sire, I think I bent the bow well, too.
Are not our hands now slaked and satisfied with murder?"
The eyebrows of his ruthless parent scowled in storm:
"My son, on shores and islands far away still smoke
luxurious palaces, still groan their slaughtered kings;
our people have grown haughty, wars have smudged their hearts,
they rage to cut down man's most venerated peaks;
I see the scales of fate now tottering in the balance."
But raising his eyes boldly, the brave youth replied:

"If I were king I'd sit beneath our plane tree's shade
and listen like a father to all my people's cares,
dispensing bread and freedom justly to all men;
I mean to follow in the path of our old kings."
His father laughed and his eyes flashed. "My son," he mocked,
"those follow old kings best who leave them far behind."
The young man, struck with fright, stepped back and thought: "This man
is like the cruel male hare that kills its newborn sons.
O Gods, I'd seize him if I dared, bind both his hands,
nail him to my most winged prow and send him far
beyond the sun's returning, to return no more!"
The lightning-minded man divined at once his son's
dark thoughts, and his clear heart was wrapped in sudden clouds:
"You haste my going too soon, my only son. It's said:
'Die, dear, that I may love you; live, and be my foe.' "
The young man stood abashed and dropped his silent glance,
but his voracious father shuddered, for he recalled
how as a still unshaven lad, in youthful rage,
he too had raised a mailed fist once against his father.
One day while hunting wild game in a black ravine
they found in a deep pit a wounded rutting boar
that snarled with rage and plowed the earth with its sharp tusks.
As both rushed panting, the son sprang with ready spear
but, in his father's feet entangled, tripped and fell.
He leapt at once erect, frothing with seething rage,
his blood rose high and turned his brain to mud, but as
he roared and flung himself on his father, just in time
their hunting hounds dashed in the breach to part them. Ah,
now in his own son's eyes he saw that black ravine.
Gently he touched with love his son's mane, raven-black:
"Ah, lad, I feel your pain, and I love your sharp impatience,
but hold your wrath: all things shall come, all in their turn.
I've done my duty as a son, surpassed my father,
now in your turn surpass me both in brain and spear,
a difficult task, but if you can't, our race must perish,
and then our turn shall come to fall prey to the mob."
He spoke, then set the gate ajar to catch the hubbub,
and in the wind his ears flashed like long pointed flames.
The clamor heaved and swelled as tramp of feet rang out
on the stone royal road that mounted toward the palace,
and torches flared and vanished at each winding turn.
The sly man turned then to his son with mocking laughter:
"Ah, you were born too late, for grim times crush, and soon
your peaceful plane tree shall be hung with gruesome fruit—
either with our slaves' heads, my son, or our own heads!
Run quickly, gird your sword, and if we live, we both

may sit serenely by our plane tree's shade one day,
but at this moment, arms, I think, are a man's first duty."
The young man dashed in quickly, on his shoulders cast
a blue embroidered cloak with silver clasps engraved
with swallows, shod his wing-swift feet with fretted sandals,
and from the smoke-black column seized and buckled tight
his gold-emblazoned leather belt with its bronze sword.

Father and son unbarred the outer gate and sped
stealthily down the road, treading the earth like leopards.
It was a sweet spring night, in blue-black heavens hung
the dewy stars enwrapped in a soft down, and trembled
like early almond flowers swung by evening breezes.
"My son," Odysseus said, as blue shores swept his eyes,
"I bring to mind a brilliant shore where waves once cast me;
my sturdy boat was wrecked one evening on sharp rocks
and all night long I fought with Death in frothing tombs;
sometimes the Sea-God smashed my sides, sometimes, in turn,
with seaweed hands I smashed his murderous three-pronged fork.
I held my stubborn soul between my teeth, like meat,
and when day broke, stretched out my hands, grabbed at the world,
hung to an osier branch, and dragged myself ashore;
at once the almighty and pain-easing god of sleep
poured on my salt-cracked battered flesh his tender down.
Next morning in my sleep the roaring pebbles rang
with rowdy laughter till I heard my brain resound
like festive shores with female cries and wooden clogs.
For a long time I held my eyelids closed and joyed
in earth and in man's life as in a thrush's song;
but my brains longed for sight, so through half-opened lids
I spied on maids with flowing hair playing by the shore,
tossing their flame-red apples in light, and with long strides
catching them still in flight, their flushed necks glittering in air.
In the maids' midst a nude, cool-bodied princess stood,
with hair of honey-gold piled on her new-washed head,
and watched her playmates gamboling on the golden sands.
I swear that these world-wandering, glutted eyes of mine,
blessed to have seen nude goddesses on deathless shores,
never before rejoiced in such reed-supple form;
when she was but fourteen so must have flowered, I know,
amid cool oleander blooms, fair Helen's body,
and I said longingly within my salt-caked heart:
'Just such a maid as this must suckle my son's children.' "
Suddenly startled, his son blushed, his temples throbbed.
"Tall lily on far shores, and see, my son's mind dazzles!
Soft silver laughter, gleaming throats, and fragrant apples,

hands that resist, then open, then softly close again—
O may the night not drain its hours, may dawns be dark,
and may he hear those flaming apple trees asway
in lush warm gardens far away, their sweet fruit falling!"
Suddenly through the mind of the mute quivering youth
a pure love flowed for that rapacious man, his father.
Thus did the two lords speak as they lunged down the slope;
a breeze blew freshly, earth was fragrant as after rain,
and perched in ancient olive groves, the lovebirds sighed.
Somewhere high up in heaven's gorges, in the wind's blast,
the stars like molting pure-white flowers in darkness fell;
low on the grass, like constellations, houses gleamed;
lamps stood in doorways suddenly to watch with stealth
the two night prowlers plunging headlong from the palace.
But doors were bolted quickly, clanging in the strange hush;
old women spat thrice past their breasts to ward off evil;
and black dogs thrust their tails between their thighs, and whined.
The stooped house-wrecker in his brine-black heart drank in
the uncivil poisoned welcome of his shameless people
and in his wrathful heart a lightning longing seized him
to fall on his isle ruthlessly and put to the sword
men, women, and gods, and on the flaming shores of dawn
scatter to the wide winds the ashes of his own homeland.
Such were the thoughts that whirled in his blood-lapping brain;
his son watched him askance and guessed with dread what thoughts
swirled in this ruthless stranger who so suddenly swooped,
flung into seething uproar palace, mother, and slaves,
then from his own long locks snatched off the royal crown.
Who was he? His own blood leapt not when he first saw
this grimy stranger crouched in rags, hunched on his threshold;
nor had his mother flung herself on his breast for haven
but in the women's quarter had crouched in speechless dread.
"Speak now with kindness to your loved subjects, father, repress
your rage like a great lord, consider that they too
possess a soul, are even a god, but know it not."
Thus spoke the son and looked straight in his father's eyes;
but as Odysseus neared the shore and breathed the sea,
his mind grew cool, and soon within his pulsing heart
a white gull soared from far-off seas and flapped its wings.

Meanwhile the widows waved their flaming torches high
though they would not confess how deeply their hearts quaked,
then they all joined in rousing songs, and with hoarse throat,
alas, roared out a tune to give their weak hearts strength:
"Comrades, unsheath your bosom-knives, let come what may,
we'll either finish the job tonight or fall on ruin!"

But all stood still at once and trembled with choked voice
for in the shifting light they suddenly sensed a head
held high, the long peaked cap, the coarse mustache gone gray
by many sunlit shores, their master's swirling glance.
All turned to stone, the young men hid behind the women,
the old men wrenched their necks, the maimed grew hollow-kneed—
only the sound of dripping resin broke the hush.
The murderer glared into his people's eyes, but spoke not;
two roads within him opened up for possible action:
should he unleash on the coarse herd his lion-mind
that men and demigods and even gods disdained,
or pity his poor people, open his arms wide,
and merge serenely with his flock like a good shepherd?
He weighed both well, and finding pity to his advantage,
opened his arms and hailed his people with feigned joy:
"A thousand thousand welcomes, old and tender shoots
of my fruit-bearing, many-branching regal rod!
I came with justice and revenge held in both hands;
first I set straight my shaken castle ruthlessly
and now descend to greet my long-loved island too;
it does me good to see you mount with your town elders
to bow down low before your loved much-wandering lord."
His head like a bellwether's glowed among the sheep,
and the crowd shuddered, tossed between two scorching fires;
from ancient times their backs had bent to the cruel yoke,
much bitter gall, dark horrors, hands made stiff and tough
at their lord's rowbench sometimes, then at the hard plow—
how might the enslaved soul ever raise its head in pride?
But now among downtrodden hearts a cry burst out
as frightened freedom opened her still tender mouth
because an armless man dared speak, because the first
bold voice was heard opposing the soul-grabbing king:
"No! we shall not bow down! Our turn has come, man-slayer!"
His hollow shoulders shook, his dull eyes flashed with fire
though the crowd rushed to choke the newborn cry of freedom;
then an old townsman tried to soothe his master's wrath,
but he shook off the elder, grabbed a torch and thrust
his way amid the crowd, holding the blaze aloft,
and one by one he searched them, cowed them one by one.
An unexpected joy blazed through his heart, for he
had heard a free soul dare speak out, dare to withstand him.
"Who spoke?" he cried, and searched all faces with his torch,
but cheeks turned sallow-green, eyes glazed, and all
stepped backward stealthily and vanished one by one.
Then the tart man laughed bitterly and said: "O heart,
you hoped in vain to find one like yourself to fight with,

you on the right, he on the left, your isle between!"
He gave the torch to his young son and his voice rang:
"Who among all of you dared open his mouth to curse me?
Who had a word to say, who dared to answer back?"
But no one spoke, all blinked their eyes and watched with fright
how in the smoke an owl's full round yellow eyes
were slowly mounting up their master's pointed cap.
The young blades thrust their reckless knives into their belts,
and in the torches' fluttering light a swarming host
of Trojan dead appeared and disembarked from ships;
with rotted cobwebbed spears and dirty unkempt beards
they rushed in silence through the air and fell in line
to right and left of their king's back, like wings of night.
The pallid mortals backed in fear, their hair stood straight,
until the boldest elder touched his master's knees
with reverential fear, and finally bid him welcome:
"May the Immortals guard and bless this longed-for hour
when you once more stepped on your orphaned island, sire;
now earth shall bloom once more and the stones sprout with grass.
We kiss the hand that knows both how to kill its foes
and to bestow rich gifts on friends; and I, true friend,
bow down and kiss your footprints; welcome, and thrice welcome."
But still their master's mind was filled with seething rage:
"Who runs, drinks, fights, or makes love better than I?
What other mind can think up truths or lies like mine?
I can in a brief moment snatch the royal crown
from my own head, then gain it by myself once more;
I've held it neither from my own father nor from you!"
The elders stooped and mutely touched his ruthless knees,
and though he suffered all their slavish strokes with scorn,
his anger beat against him still like battering waves.
"When I returned, I should have punished you at once!
How could your hearts endure to watch my wealth for years
devoured by spongers that like dogs gaped for my bed?
Not one was found among you to rise and to speak out.
Don't fear—though I've returned from the earth's ends, I find
I'm full of pity, my heart aches for mankind's pains,
my memory blots out evil and retains good only.
Don't quake, I've not forgotten I'm my people's father;
the sun shall also rise tomorrow, our talks resume.
Raise high your torches, slaves, it's time I left. This day
has also passed, we have well earned our daily bread together."

All took the steep ascent, the widows rushed ahead
with torches held aloft to light their master's way;
behind them poured the living, far behind the dead,

and further back the dead dogs, horses, ox and cows
that even in Hades long for yokes and goading prongs.
The double shepherd led like a bellwether and heard
behind him the mob flooding like a rumbling herd,
and suddenly felt his body dead and living both,
a sunburnt, many-breasted, many-souled thing full
of eyes and mouths and tentacles that seized his isle
and growled, a shepherd, sheep, sheep dog and wolf all told.
Absurd, contrary longings leapt within his breast,
but he held firm the reins of his capricious soul
and when he reached his castle, passed in silence through
the blood-drenched threshold with its two stone lion guards,
and his son followed boldly like a lion's whelp.
The torches choked in embers and the stars leapt low
like hungry glaring eyes of wolves in a dark wood;
Odysseus reached his hairy hands in his wild court
and double-barred his copper-banded groaning gates.
The gardens moaned like caverns and the palace roared
till the crowd backed in terror, for in the star's light
it seemed the guardian lions moved their stony jaws.
Father and son then parted mutely in the large hall;
the lone man climbed the tower to calm his seething mind
while the young man lay restless on his bed and heard
his wingless temples creak and open wide to hold
the many-branched audacious brain of his rash father.
"Dear God, he swoops and ravages in every soul,
he stands erect on the earth's threshing floor and rakes
and winnows worthless chaff from wheat in a full wind,
throws half to the livestock and casts the other half
in his mind's silent millstones and slowly grinds it fine."
Longing to exorcise his father and make him fade
once more like spinning foam on the night-wandering wave,
the young man wove and unwove sly snares in his mind's loom
until he wearied and curled tight in soothing sleep;
but as his eyes grew glazed and his mind dimmed, a dream
swooped like a vulture and perched high on his skull's back.
He dreamt he stood on a tall rock by the sea's rim
and longed for his great father to rise from distant waves,
but as he wept, he heard enormous wings sweep down,
and when he raised his eyes a wind-swift eagle swooped
and plunged its claws deep in his head unpityingly,
then, shrieking thrice, soared swiftly to the wind's high peak.
The youth clung to the eagle's neck in dread and closed
his eyes, fearing to watch the downward-plunging earth.
"Where are we flying, Father? Stop! My head spins round!"
But as they mounted higher, he felt his shoulder blades

sprout wings of curly down till to his startled eyes
the earth seemed like a tiny hare that browsed on wind;
an eagle's heart rose in his chest, his claws grew hard,
and on the ancient eagle's neck he swayed with pride.
"Father, my wings are strong now, drop me from your claws!"
The ancient eagle shrieked with maniac rage and joy,
beat his enormous wings, opened his branch-thick feet
and hurled his young son headlong through star-burning air.
The young man shrieked in terror, leapt from his low bed,
groped in the dark, and then grew calm: all seemed a dream,
a crazy thought new-hatched in the deceiving night.
But wild sleep now escaped him: all night long he heard
two monstrous eagle wings that beat above his head.
Meanwhile the castle's lord had passed to a far room,
and when he'd loosed his belt and hung his crimson robe,
his black and hairy chest blazed in the lantern's light,
his thighs were ringed with flame till the whole house caught fire.
Amid thick hair, his face, his eyebrows, his coarse beard
darkened, and in his blackened flesh his soul flashed fire.
Like a swift agile youth, he leapt, and his chaste bed,
long-suffering and unsoiled, joined to an olive tree,
trembled and groaned. Penelope then, new-bathed and mute,
raised her long lashes stealthily and gazed on him with fear.

Waking in early dawn, he stole like a thief downstairs,
unhooked a four-flamed oil-lamp and with caution searched
his house like a sly landlord counting all his goods.
He passed through his deep vaulted cells, uncovered all
his huge embellished jars and in his mind summed up
what oil, wine, grain the revelers had left untouched.
Then he knelt down and quickly broke the double locks,
uncovered his stone caskets buried deep in earth,
and in his raging mind recalled what golden cups,
what brooches, necklaces, what precious stones and rings,
how many golden crowns were missing or still safe.
He raised his lamp and to his secret armory passed
where all his pointed lances shone, his broad shields smiled,
and plumes on his bronze helmets swayed like living manes.
He passed beyond to further cells and with his glance
grasped looms and caldrons, brazen lampsteads, earthen jars,
counting and adding all, then shook his head in wrath.
Like a slim hunting hound he sniffed the pungent air,
his nostrils quivering at fat sheepskins and soft beds
to nose out all the shameful secrets of his house.
He passed by slowly and held his lamp aloft so that
his tall and flickering shadow leapt from wall to roof,

and his worn slaves, still sleeping on their humble pelts,
hearing a noise, half-opened their thick-lidded eyes,
but quickly cowered, and covered themselves in silent fear.
He passed the women's quarter, sniffed the holy blood
of all the new-slain youths till murder bloomed once more
within his heart like a rose garden drenched with sun.
Stark naked on a sheepskin, his old father lay
in a far corner, raised his pate, looked at his son,
and his blank eyeballs, wounded by the lantern's light,
brimmed with quick tears and blinked like bats in a dark cave.

His son stooped over him and gazed without compassion
on the old rotting hulk that in youth's flower one night
embraced his bride and sowed the sperms of his son's birth;
now to what state reduced, for shame, filth on the earth!
He grunted, crossed the sill and stepped into his court
where under roofed arcades his slavehands slept and snored
and in their sleep smiled quietly and dreamt, perhaps,
that their fierce lord had drowned at sea, not to return.
But he was gliding from his wine to his oil vats,
rejoicing to caress the old friends of his youth;
he bent and stroked the shafts, the mangles and worn wheels,
and talked with them as though they were old warriors, joked
about their spilled intestines, their worn broken teeth,
and they guffawed and creaked at their old master's banter.
At last he entered his ox-stables, his warm stalls
where frightened mares reared up, alarmed, with flashing eyes,
but his ox slowly moved their necks and chewed their cud,
and the man-slayer drew back so that his cutting glance
might not disturb the passive beasts' contented calm.
Thus, landlord, did you hold your lamp aloft to count
your goods with care and stack them in your storied mind.
The cocks on the dungheaps had now begun to crow,
and the thick-headed sparrows in the eaves awoke,
for rose-lipped azure day laughed in the opaque sky.
The man of many sorrows joyed to hear once more
his cocks bring in the sun in his own native land,
blew out his lamp and leant against Athena's feet.
His past whirled in his mind; old sorrows and old joys,
all seas he'd ever sailed flashed in his eyes, green shores
twined crimson in the sun, and snow-white mountain summits.
His mind, round like the sun, shone in the first rays,
holy and good, a ripe fruit filled with fertile seed.
His eyebrows leapt and zoned his voyages like lightning,
waves roared and beat against his temples, garden-mint
and honeysuckle blossomed in Calypso's cave,
and amber scrolls like honey wound round Circe's bed.
He felt his hands with poisoned heavy lotus brim,
alluring lethal songs rang in his ears once more,
but he heard all, rejoiced in all, set sail, and no
excessive sweetness turned his brain from his true course.
He wished to fight with no gods, but when fate decreed,
he'd fought a lethal battle with the sea's great lord
and with the ungirdled goddess and her pubic whirlwind.
All dangers he had passed now crossed his silent mind,
and in that hour, on Troy's far-distant azure shores,
the dawn broke sweetly: hungry vines with berries weighed

climbed through the jagged ruins and browsed on broken stones;
charred embers choked with flowers, and tall grasses rose
from the cracked skulls of princes, lizards strolled in sun
and with their flickering tails crumbled the famous walls.
As the man-slayer smiled and tenderly caressed
Athena's slender ankles, her bronze feet, he joyed
to feel the goddess was his faithful comrade still.
His claw-tipped brain grew crimson as he stooped with calm
above black pits that brimmed with blood of new-slain throats
and filled his fists, then slowly laved the Immortal's breasts,
her thighs and knees, as though he stroked a mortal maid,
until the wisdom goddess laughed in sunlight, smeared with blood.

His tenant farmers, meanwhile, from far hills and fields
swarmed round his outer gate and wondered in mistrust
how to address him, what to say, how touch his knees,
and as they waited, addle-brained, with humbled heads,
Odysseus slowly came and stood before them calmly,
and all knelt down and kissed the sly man-slayer's hand.
An ancient shepherd leaned on his oak staff and wailed,
some touched their master's knees, his chest and shoulder blades,
until emboldened by his calm all touched his body
that in the light unmoving stood with a bull's splendor.
When they had wept and laughed their fill, they huddled close
and joined their heads to answer their lord prudently.
He asked his shepherds first about his flocks, how many
the leeching suitors in their orgies had gulped down;
next with his mud-brained farmhands he discussed his vineyards,
his ancient unpruned olive trees, his unsown fields,
then asked his slaves how much ripe fruit their wives produced,
how many male and female slaves to his increase.
On two wax tablets he set down in ordered rows
his heavy losses, left, his meager profits, right,
till squandered chattel and real property rose up
unwinding from his rapid hands and climbed his brain;
then he stood up and portioned jobs to every hand:
"I want all of my vineyards, olive trees, my farms,
my horses, sheep, my ox, to know their landlord's come!"
Stooping with joy, the elders kissed their master's knees,
then, young again and light of heart, sped to their work.
Odysseus called to all his heralds and cried out:
"Runners, speed with your myriad mouths and lengthy strides,
swarm through my villages and towns and thunder out:
'Your lord invites you to a great feast at the full moon;
wash and bedeck yourselves, hasten to grace his boards.
He's come! Let his land welcome him with blood and wine!' "

His heralds bound their hair with leaves of the wild olive,
then seized their staffs of ilex wood, puffed up their brains,
and rumbled downward toward the fields like swift cascades.

Day like a shepherdess awoke, the world was filled
with wings and birdsong, clamorous noise of man and beast,
and in the ancient olive trees, the early cuckoo's song.
As he pricked up his ears to catch the sounds of spring,
his mind like frothy loam was covered with new grass
and his much-traveled heart dissolved in mist; sounds rose
most sweet out of the earth and now allured him: "Come,
come grandchild, O great grandson, bring your brimming jug."
The great man-slayer shook to smell his dread forebears,
his hairy nostrils filled with deadly camomile,
and leaping up, he glanced about him, chose a jug
whose copper belly had once borne the reveler's wine,
and with a double-handled crater scooped blood from the pit
and filled his brimming jug to water his forefathers,
then plugged its bubbling mouth with aromatic thyme
and took the ancient crooked path to the moldering graves.
All of his dead leapt on his chest like crabs and spread
their sallow bellies and pale claws till he yelled out:
"Oho, how have the dead increased! They'll knock me down!"
But when the mountain's fresh breeze struck him, he took heart;
the gorse was fragrant, honeybees on savory browsed,
swift swallows cut the light, and their white bellies, warm
and starry-downed, filled the tree-flowering air with love.
His nostrils quivered and breathed in his isle far down
to the musk-odorous shore with its thick salty seaweed.
"How good earth is, dear God," he murmured; "nostrils, eyes,
hands, tongue, and ears here browse unbridled on good soil."
But his forefathers growled until once more he took
the sacred road to water earth's unbreathing throats.
For ages on their stony beds, swords at their sides,
with gaping jaws unlocked, they'd waited for their grandson,
and now the traveler quaked for fear he'd come too late
and find his own dead vanished, in rank grasses smothered.
But soon the rugged wall came into view, well built
and well matched with smooth cornerblocks like a skull's bones.
Black souls like ravens perched on it in a long row,
and when they saw their son ascend with brimming jug
they opened wide their bottomless thick beaks, and some
perched on the fat fig tree that browsed on women's flesh,
some by the oak that sucked up male ancestral strength.
The mute world-wanderer on the destined threshold stood,
pushed to one side a rock that blocked the gate, and entered.

The tombs were softly melting in the sun's fierce blaze,
audacious ivy struck deep roots in the rock clefts,
—great sweetness, fragrance, happiness—and bees buzzed round
the camomile that like star-clusters filled the ground.
Chiseled upon the lintel's huge stone block on high
an ancient crane stretched out his slim long-voyaged wings,
lean carter of the sky who on his bony back
and the deep hollows of his neck brings back the swallows
then fans them jocundly throughout the warm spring air.
Suddenly on his skull the rugged grandson felt
the secret archon of his dread tribe watching him.
"Welcome, grandfather crane, old swallow-mount, thrice welcome,"
he cried, then cast aside the thorny thyme and flung
fistfuls of brimming blood to give his forebears life.
The man of seven souls rose like a crane, his head
grew wings, his blood-drenched palms and his knees quaked to feel
invisible blind souls that groped to find out what
he sought, if friend or foe, and what his shoulders held,
till the jug rang as though pecked by a thousand beaks.
Like a bird-hunter that bestrews the ground with barley
he cast thick drops of blood on the tombstones and called
with throaty clucking sounds on all the souls to eat,
then knelt amidst the tombs, uncovered the dark pit
that brings together dead jaws with warm living breath
and poured out all the jug like a fresh-slaughtered throat
till blood in fountain-falls plunged gurgling down to Hades.
Pressed tight like mud-soaked and lethargic beasts, the dead
lay rotting on their backs, their white skulls packed with earth;
then the world-traveler hung above the deadly pit,
laid his ears close to earth and heard far down in Hades
firm necks knit straight again and whole, bones creak and stretch,
fists clasp with savage strength at swords deep in the earth
till the tombs rang like battle bivouacs far away.
They lapped the human blood, grew strong and licked their lips,
then slowly lifted toward the light their muddy heads
like snakes that thaw out and uncoil in the sun's blaze.
Their grandson's soul grew strong as they grew strong, he groaned,
leapt up, and with his thick soles swiftly thrust aside
the gravel round the graves, charred bones of bulls, clay shards,
and on Death's threshing floor spread out a dancing ring.
He flung his coat far from his back, and in the sun
his well-knit sturdy body gleamed with many wounds.
Dancing around his sunburnt loins, tattooed in blue,
the twelve signs of the zodiac glowed like living beasts:
the scorpion spread its claws, the lion leapt for prey,
fishes in pairs sailed undulating round his belly,

and the scales tipped in balance just above his navel.
As though it lived, he touched the earth with quivering feet
and slowly on Death's threshing floor began to dance.
He called first to the men, and his grandfathers leapt
with their bronze moldy armor, grasped each other's arms,
and from their beards shook off the still voracious worms;
he walked then to the women's side and hailed with awe
deep in the earth his tribe's milk-bearing ancient roots.
Like pomegranates, the tombs burst and cast their seed,
and mothers grasped their grandson's still warm living hand,
then beat the earth like strutting partridges and stepped
in stately measure with their naked incensed feet.
Mortal Odysseus led the dance and hoarsely yelled:
"Hey, mothers, hey, straight-backed like candles, grassy-haired,
your rhythmic heels glint in the sun like crimson apples!
Go to it, grandpap, air has once more filled your lungs,
and I, your grandson, rush in the lead and start the song!
Never before, I swear, have I wished to praise the tombs,
but now, for your sakes only, I'll adorn them richly.
O tombstones, wings, O brooding wings spread on the ground
to hatch your huge eggs and to warm your sturdy eaglets,
ah mother eagles, all of your eggs hatch in my mind!"
Thus the soul-snatcher danced and woke his great forefathers;
some seized him by the arm, some grasped his dancing feet,
others, like falcon-bells, hung round his swinging throat,
and thus for hours he danced with his ancestral ghosts,
swift in the lead sometimes or at the tail's slow end,
bursting with song like swallows that return in April.
But soon the noon at zenith dripped heat drop by drop
and he stopped dancing, sated, bid his flock farewell
then took the goatpath hurriedly to reach the peak,
for his eye longed to take in all his isle once more.
In tingling air the mountain blurred in the heat-haze
and the armed insects plunged like pirates on first flowers
of fragrant golden gorse, wild thyme, and sweet whitethorn.
Amid the first betrothals, before nest-building cares
oppress, and bodies meet and passion vanishes,
the small birds flit from branch to branch in joyous ease.
A gray hawk in the sky wove swift wreaths silently
and sought no prey, but flexed his overbrimming strength
before the female hawk should call and drain him dry.
The man of many travels climbed, and his heart filled
with myriad wings and playful thoughts and fragrant herbs.
He climbed, his country's threshing floor in splendor spread,
and when he stepped at length on the bald mountain's peak
and saw his poor isle's slender body far below,

he blinked his eyelids to hold back his brimming tears.
"This is the rock, the bare dry rock I've loved and longed for,"
he murmured then, and teardrops on his lashes gleamed.
His mind, a hovering hawk, spied out the world below:
gold sunburnt beaches bathed like athletes by the sea,
all huts were drowned in light, and on the sun-drenched fields
the sluggish oxen cut the earth's fruit-bearing womb.
But suddenly the earth and seashores shook, farms swayed,
and the whole island, trembling like a mist, rose high
and vanished like a cloud dispersed by the sun's stroke.
Odysseus felt his heart fill up with freshening sea;
for hours he gleaned his country's sweetness from the summit,
then feeling hungry, turned to his body, laughed, and said:
"Ah, comrade workhorse, let the long day's labor cease.
We woke before cock crow, worked hard by the lamp's light,
gave orders to the wretched living, and fed the shades;
now it's high time to feed you also, faithful beast."
He spoke, and then with haste plunged down the burning stones;
a bitter sea-chant rose and throbbed, beyond his will,
and beat between his towering temples like resounding waves.

He lunged down the descent, and with his salty songs
his solitude rose like the sea and bathed him whole
till dead and living turned to waves within his mind.
But all at once Odysseus stopped, his wild song broke,
for in an olive grove he saw blue smoke ascending;
a humble hut, nestling among the trees, stood guard
over a mortal's goods: a jug of water, a bowl of clay,
the poor and holy tools of work, an earthen god.
Before the hut there crouched a bent old man who slit
fresh reeds and wove them in a basket skillfully.
"Good day, old man, I marvel at your crimson cheeks,
your supple fingers and your green old age. I'm hungry!
God is most great and swift repays a good deed done."
The old man rose, and in the outstretched palms he placed
a bowl of water and a dry crust of barley bun:
"The crab, though poor, is thought a king in his own lair;
bread, water, a good heart, are kingly presents, stranger."
He spoke, then stooped again to his reed-weaving task.
Squatting upon the ground under an old tree's shade,
the beggar, like a guileless beast, chewed on his bun,
and when he finished, turned and smiled at the old man:
"The bread was good, grandpap, it knit my weary bones,
good was the water too, it cooled my heart to the root,
but I have never taken gifts unpaid for, and now
I shall not rise till I've repaid you with good news.

Old granddad, prick your ears on high, do not be frightened:
renowned Odysseus moored in his native land last night!"
But the old man only shook his sun-devoured head:
"We who must work day after day to eat, dear God,
what do we care if kings return or drown in exile?
We care about the rain, our vegetable plots, our lambs,
the holy bread the Immortals feed us with our own sweat;
kings are uncapturable birds, clouds blown by winds."
The border-guard disliked these wry complaining words:
"For shame, old man, raise your head high above all need.
He's come, and bears in his strong hands a vengeful bow
whose god perched like a black crow on his shoulder blade
and for whose sake he's strewn the ground with young men's corpses."
Between dry fingers the old man crunched a bit of earth:
"I pity not the idle and scented youths he slew,
nor was the queen worth all the lads slain for her sake;
the lady passed her time well, weaving and unweaving,
shuttling with craft her yes and no from warp to woof.
Our master from a babe showed brashness—all his journeys,
his myriad cares and slaughters, have not sweetened his mind,
but forty millstones grind in his tempestuous head."
The self-willed solitary glared at the old wretch:
"The mind was not created to grow soft by grinding
nor to be bent and yoked like cattle for men's comforts;
the more the soul grows old the more it fights its fate!"
The old man sighed and answered with great sweetness then:
"The soul was made not to deny or shout in vain
but to stoop low and merge with the bread-giving earth.
Behold me, son: I was begotten, sprang to youth,
and when a light mustache bedewed my upper lip
I longed to see long braids beside me on the pillow
and sold the two lone ox I had and bought a wife,
for I could sleep alone no longer, nor eat nor drink.
When we had lain together, sons and daughters came;
I ate bread, worked the earth, but tax-collecting Death
passed, and we shared the children half and half, like brothers.
Lately he's passed by with his mule and snatched my wife.
I've seen and taken count: there is no greater good
than holy mute obedience to man-eating earth."
Odysseus rose with arrogance and boasted proudly:
"I've also taken count: there is no greater good
than when the earth says 'Yes' and man with wrath shouts 'No!'
And I'm acquainted with *one* soul that never deigned
to stoop under the yoke of demon, man, or god,
but sailed and traveled till his heart became a wineskin
for all four good and evil elemental winds;

he scorned the comfortable virtues, nor made friends
with wealthy shepherds or with lambs or honest dogs
but outside his own sheepfold howled like a wild wolf.
People called him a beast, a god, and he but laughed,
for he knew well, quite well, he was not god or beast
but only a light drifting smoke, a passing crane.
I'd give him my one son to walk by his proud side."
He spoke, then grasped the old man's knees in deep regret:
"Grandpap, forgive me this ungrateful pay for bread;
by God, I measure often but find no measurement;
just like the two-faced queen, I ply the crafty shuttle;
now learn, old man, my warp is No, my woof is Yes,
and what I weave all day I swift unweave by night.
But why cast words into the wind? All roads are good
and blessed on earth, and your own road is holy too;
I kiss with reverence, grandpap, your exhausted knees."
"Good journey, stranger; may God sweeten your proud mind."
Through silver-branching olive trees, in azure dusk,
the old man watched the sturdy body plunge in fields
and vanish without trace, as though the wind had snatched it.
The slit reeds fell and scattered from his puckered hands,
his light dimmed as though lightning bolts had split his brain:
"That's not the stature nor the tread of mortal man;
either a god's descended to my hut to tease me
or my decrepit eyes have looked upon the dread Odysseus!"

While the proud archer chased the empty air and played,
his ancient father crawled across the bloody threshold.
He crept to a hot windless pit amid the fields
and lay down without speaking, merged his back and hips
with the warm earth and the green clover flecked with flowers;
like an old scarab, battle-scarred, with broken wings,
that eats, works, spills its seed, then crawls in a dark pit
and has no will to live since all its guts have drained,
thus did Laertes crawl and thrust himself in earth.
He smelled the loam and softly smiled, caressed the grass,
stretched all his bony limbs and yawned, then wryly sighed;
a thick black swarm of ants crawled up his withered shanks,
but like an ancient tree he suffered the dark mites
to roam his flesh, nor felt their sharp exploring bites.
Only one dark and secret wish perturbed him still
like baby's whimpering or water's murmuring
or dry reed's moaning by the lake when the wind blows.
One prayer, one sole entreaty chirped in his mind still;
he gazed on earth, his lips moved and his words arose
like water lilies in his mind's warm murky pools.

"O earth, dear wife, I've tilled you like a humble plowman,
I was your faithful king, the oxen my mute brothers,
I was your glowworm, crawling through your herbs at night,
delighting in your rain-soaked soil with my bright belly.
I passed above you, Dame Bread-Giver, and sowed my seed,
and you received it mutely in your guts, and slowly
and patiently we stooped and waited for the first rains.
I'm through with tilling the earth now, I want my wages;
make my old body young again to breed me grandsons!
Like a great warrior who adorns himself for Hades

and girds the sharp sword to his side, and grasps his spear,
and paints his old scars red, and thus descends and slides,
so shall I grasp my scythe, my hoe, my prodding goad,
a jug of water, my two brothers the dumb ox,
and like a bridegroom steal into your house at night;
the tender meadow grass shall cover up our bed
that I may lie, dear Earth, sweet wife, at your cool side;
make my old body young again to breed me grandsons!
I'll not have them resemble my one faithless son
who spurned you; they'll become field workers, worms of earth,
their minds shall gently steam with grass and soil and rain.
Lady Bread-Giver, I'm tired! Take me, but don't cast me
on sands of disavowal or in Lethe's well;
make my old body young again to breed me grandsons!"
The temples of the old man sank, he closed his lids,
his whole life seemed like a far buzz of honeybees
that slowly, sweetly fades away on flowering fields,
and he a stingless drone that lies supine, and dies.
He smiled, spread out his hands and touched the fragrant herbs,
leant back his head on the good earth and called on sleep,
and the god came like a light, downy death, and took him.

Three days the heralds, olive-crowned, beat on all doors:
"Elders, take up your staffs; young men, gird on your arms;
women, unlock your bridal chests of scented wood,
choose from your dearest dowry, your best panoply!
Minstrels, take down your lyres hung with ringing bells
and beat your brains like trees for the ripe songs to fall!
Let empty stomachs laugh and all dry throats rejoice—
brothers, our king invites you all to a rich feast!"
Under ancestral plane trees, still new-leaved and green,
row upon row the tables sagged with food and drink;
a savage lowing rose from beasts slain on the grass,
from the crowd's helter-skelter and its husky laughter.
The furrows round the plane grove flowed with the beasts' blood
and girdled the whole town with a red steaming belt.
It was a cool late afternoon, the evening's dusk,
and as the mules descended with their copper bells,
the azure mountain with its white paths heaved and swayed
and roared as though cascades plunged down its pebbly sides.
The new-bathed women with their snowy kerchiefs shone
like constellations on the dusk-strewn mountain slopes;
behind them clanged young men in arms with pulsing hearts,
pounding their feet to see at last renowned Odysseus;
the old men with their crooked staffs came hobbling last.
As the re-echoing mountain rumbled downward toward the town,

and young men longed to see him, and the old recalled
his fierce glance, his proud bearing and his body's swing,
the full round moon rose flaming in nocturnal air,
and as it rose the birds stopped singing, the old men screamed,
for as it swayed and dripped with blood, it forecast wars;
but the youths laughed and sped their pace, their nostrils flared
to smell thick greasy odors slowly mounting high
from slaughtered beasts that shepherds roasted on long spits.
On the white pebbled shores the town burst like a rose,
the soul of every peasant leapt high in his breast,
mules slipped and stumbled on the paths, the gravel sparked,
and window shutters everywhere were flung wide open
to watch the spangled peasants flooding toward the fair.
But as maids neared the feast under the plane trees' shade,
stooped in their headbands, all dismounted silently,
though on the road they'd cackled like gay partridges
or like swift fountains babbling in a fall of waters;
but in the town now they felt shy and lowered their eyes.
The people swarmed, old country loves met once again,
old friends walked arm in arm and talked their hearts out, here
young men could stroll and eye the girls and wink their full.
Death pulls a long ill-tempered face when music comes,
and from the mountains plunged the minstrels, lords of song,
their sonorous heads adorned with berry-laden ivy.
Songs heaved and foamed inside their heads like heavy seas.
What should they choose to sing? All manner of songs are theirs.
They cultivate their flower beds in rows where bloom
in separate plots food's wine-flushed songs, blue exile songs,
gray songs of the open road, rose-crimson wedding songs,
all fenced with the black songs of grief like cypress trees.
They sat on walls like a long row of spouting springs,
but one with a lean cricket's shape and pointed head,
his reed pipe stuck under his arm, strolled by and laughed:
"Hey, Kentaur, hold on tight; don't faint with the food's fumes!
Take heart, my heart, we're moored in the port of eat and drink!"
The grove of plane trees shook, for in the moon's glow rose
a mountain of meat, three floors of belly and underbelly,
grunting and panting, heaving, drenched with streams of sweat.
"Orpheus, we'll stuff our guts full at our master's feast;
let's make the rounds, my friend, let's grab leftover meats,
for see, my bellies droop in folds, my thighs have shrunk."
The squint-eyed piper laughed, swallowed his spittle, and sighed:
"Oho, the smells bash in my nose, I'll faint and fall!
If only men had bodies like humped camels, friend,
then food and drink could flow in floods down two forked roads;
some could plunge downward toward the belly and others spout

high up the hump and there be stored till the back bursts;
then when you're famished, the huge hump would slowly melt
while you sit idly like a king and eat it all away!
Brother, what humps the both of us shall raise tonight!"
Kentaur, that splayfoot, bellowed like a hollow pot:
"Hey, chum, your pointed pumpkin head is stuffed with brains!
If I were God, I'd change the seas to muscatel
and all our ships to goblets, beaches to red meat,
our bodies to barrels that sail ashore to eat and drink!"
The two friends sighed and talked, greedily slunk about
the wineskins and the piled roast meat, and gulped with hunger.
At last the conches blared and all the heralds cried:
"Immortal gods, may you enjoy our food's rich odor!
Welcome, O mighty archons, welcome, O great kings!
People, unloose your belts, reach out your hungry hands,
let the great feast of our thrice-welcomed king begin!"
First to appear and seat himself on the highest throne
was golden-crowned Odysseus, their much-traveled lord.
All voices hushed, and old men stooped and hunched their backs:
dear God, he'd grown to forty foot! How his eyes sparked
and swiftly pounced like two wild beasts on the poor crowd!
His long stride and his body's lithesome undulation—
how like a leopard who slinks out to prowl at night!
This man was not a king or shepherd of his people
but a huge hungry dragon that sniffed human flesh.
The good and sweet-faced son sat on his father's left
and like a lily gleamed on his rough parent's cliff;
his curly locks swung gently down his sunburnt back,
around him his lean hounds like dolphins leapt and played
then leant their gleaming necks on their kind master's knees
and the youth placed his hands on their quick-witted heads.
Two slaves upheld the body of the archer's father
and carried it with care, like smelling meat gone bad;
his eyes and ears were dulled, his mind a stagnant marsh,
and he stooped low toward earth as though he knocked to enter.
Odysseus shuddered at the sight, lowered his eyes,
looked on the ground and cursed the rotting fate of man;
his sturdy body, wedged between his son and father,
suddenly rotted on the right, bloomed on the left,
and for a lightning flash he choked and gasped for air
then jumped up to shake off the oppressive company
but drew his heart's reins tight and stopped at the cliff's edge.
Goblets made of the purest gold, with gods embossed,
heavy and double-handled, glittered before the kings,
and the plates steamed with double portions of choice meat.
Town elders lay stretched out in pride on fat sheepskins;

with pale, exhausted faces and with bloodshot eyes,
some looked like dogs or foxes, some like bony mules.
Holding their lyres straight on their knees, the mighty bards
grasped them by both curved horns like bucking animals
and led the old and new tunes in their heads like flocks
as their minds picked and chose amid the noisy fold.
The people cast themselves down by the fuming boards
while servants cut the roast, mixed jars of wine and water,
and all the gods flew past like the night-breaths of spring.
The chattering female flocks sat down by farther tables,
their fresh prismatic garments gleaming in the moon
as though a crowd of haughty peacocks played in moonlight.
The queen's throne, softly spread with the white furs of fox,
gaped desolate and bare, for Penelope felt ashamed
to come before her people after so much murder.
Though all the guests were ravenous, they still refrained,
turning their eyes upon their silent watchful lord
till he should spill wine in libation for the Immortals.
The king then filled a brimming cup, stood up and raised
it high till in the moon the embossed adornments gleamed:
Athena, dwarfed and slender, wrought in purest gold,
pursued around the cup, with double-pointed spear,
dark lowering herds of angry gods and hairy demons;
she smiled, and the sad tenderness of her lean face,
and her embittered fearless glance, seemed almost human.
Star-eyed Odysseus raised Athena's goblet high
and greeted all, but spoke in a beclouded mood:
"In all my wandering voyages and torturous strife,
the earth, the seas, the winds fought me with frenzied rage;
I was in danger often, both through joy and grief,
of losing priceless goodness, man's most worthy face.
I raised my arms to the high heavens and cried for help,
but on my head gods hurled their lightning bolts, and laughed.
I then clasped Mother Earth, but she changed many shapes,
and whether as earthquake, beast, or woman, rushed to eat me;
then like a child I gave my hopes to the sea in trust,
piled on my ship my stubbornness, my cares, my virtues,
the poor remaining plunder of god-fighting man,
and then set sail, but suddenly a wild storm burst,
and when I raised my eyes, the sea was strewn with wreckage.
As I swam on, alone between the sea and sky,
with but my crooked heart for dog and company,
I heard my mind, upon the crumpling battlements
about my head, yelling with flailing crimson spear.
Earth, sea, and sky rushed backward; I remained alone
with a horned bow slung down my shoulder, shorn of gods

and hopes, a free man standing in the wilderness.
Old comrades, O young men, my island's newest sprouts,
I drink not to the gods but to man's dauntless mind!"
All shuddered, for the daring toast seemed sacrilege,
and suddenly the hungry people shrank in spirit;
they did not fully understand the impious words
but saw flames lick like red curls round his savage head.
The smell of roast was overpowering, choice meats steamed,
and his bold speech was soon forgotten in hunger's pangs;
all fell to eating ravenously till their brains reeled.
Under his lowering eyebrows Odysseus watched them sharply:
"This is my people, a mess of bellies and stinking breath!
These are my own minds, hands, and thighs, my loins and necks!"
He muttered in his thorny beard, held back his hunger
far from the feast and licked none of the steaming food.
Soon from the abundant meat and the unwatered wine
a sweet mist crept upon the crowd and dulled their brains
so that the armless sprouted arms, the crippled legs,
and eyes sank secretly into their hollow sockets.
The moon slid like a man between each woman's thighs,
sat on the knees of each youth like a lustful wench
and sailed with laughing face within the purple wine.
In heat that night for the first time, a young girl felt
her small breasts rising in her open blouse amid
the fragrant shade, and eyed the young men secretly;
a sweet knife cut her heart remorselessly in two.
Kentaur, big-bellied dragon with a twisted tail,
turned up his wineskin to gulp down the final dregs,
and Orpheus rode astride his huge friend's fatfold nape
and with his thickly smudged and wine-besplattered face,
his shameless, mindless mind, his spluttering, stuttering tongue,
talked grossly with old men and teased the ripening girls;
all necks turned backward toward the sky like gurgling flasks.
But suddenly the piper stopped his stuttering squeaks
and his loud-mouthed and impish throat dared mock and prod
the palace bronzesmith who with his long golden curls
sat feasting by himself apart, bolting his food.
He pointed to the blond curls round the sooty face:
"Hey, here's a riddle! the reward's two salted herrings:
even the charcoal pit's brought forth pure golden earrings!"
The bronzesmith leapt with wrath, reached with his calloused hands,
and as a cricket splutters in a wildcat's paws
so did the cross-eyed singer shriek in his black grip.
Fat-buttocked Kentaur bawled with rage and raised his fist;
blood would have flowed had not the elders filled the breach
and soothed the crude beasts in the grove with gentle words,

but then the piper had lost heart and his voice choked.
All overate and overdrank, brains reeled in air,
men felt their black-fringed kerchiefs tightening round their heads,
the women's headbands tumbled down, slid on their backs,
till their smeared hair with oil of laurel berries glowed.
An old man eyed his wife: she shone as on that night
when he'd besieged and first torn off her breast's thin veil;
the young men eyed the girls and could not breathe for longing;
a heavy suffocation weighed on the rich feast,
maidens and adolescents, like two armies, paled,
and the men's pointed dogteeth gleamed with lust in the pale moon.

Then the chief minstrel rose, the oldest in the land,
who in the cradle had sung the archer lullabies,
and every throat grew sweet at once, all hearts grew light,
all ears pricked up with greed to hear a new refrain.
He leant his body on a plane tree, and his beard
shone in the limpid moon like a tumbling waterfall;
then slowly he began to sing of their courageous king's
far childhood years, and the dumb crowd gaped rapturously.
"Friends, a deep longing seized me, lest I suffocate,
to sing a rousing wine-song and adorn this feast
and welcome thus our king, new-come from foreign shores.
Like a great master-shepherd, owner of many flocks,
who stands straight by his sheepfold and selects with care
his fattest ram to slay at his best friend's reception,
so did my mind rise up to count its flocks of song.
Our minds rejoice in admiration of a good man
when his full-flowering body knits and first bears fruit,
or when, grown old, he sits like God in the market place,
his head a heavy honeycomb that brims with honey.
Lads, there's no greater joy upon this desolate earth
than that of the minutest seed the plant lets fall
which with its roots grasps earth and with its head grasps light
and in its passing crumbles rocks and cracks the hills,
and I shall sing this night of that most small, small seed.
The king's grandfather and I, stretched out on lion-pelts,
enjoyed the setting sun from the high palace terrace,
and like the ancient gods grown old, we reached our hands
and drank sweet wine, and watched the sea to its far rim.
Just as the sun in blood-red waves stooped to expire,
a pain unbearable began to crush the old man's chest,
and nurses ran and brought, wrapped in gold swaddling clothes,
his precious grandson, lone support and consolation.
O king, he raised you like a burning coal in light
and said: 'Your plowman father wants you to plow land,

and sings you lullabies in fields, rolls you in ruts,
but I plunge you in waves: may you become a pirate!
Your father gives you toys of plows and earthen ox,
but I give you bronze armies and two-bladed swords
and six toy pairs of deathless dwarfish gods to play with.
Ahoy, my grandson, grow up quick and resurrect me!'
Then your old grandsire laughed, jounced you on his right knee
and on his left struck at the savage lyre and sang
the monstrous troubles and vast joys of all mankind;
and you, clinging with your plump hands about his neck,
listened, and in your mind bloomed azure foreign shores
till your still tender loins were drenched with sea-swept brine.
One night on a high tower your old grandsire and I
sat sipping wine, bidding farewell to the afterglow,
and our four temples burst their bolts from too much wine;
our souls soared from our bodies, shadows reeled, rooms shook.
Then arm in arm we dashed and reached the women's quarter;
I've not entrusted this to any man: tonight I tell
a deep dark secret of the three great Fates that blessed you.
The lampsteads in the corners dimly glowed, and all
the nurses slept upon their soft warm mattresses;
your old grandfather rushed ahead, his beard flashed fire,
and his white hair fell down his back in waves of light.
He longed to see and touch you with his rugged hands,
for as we'd perched like two humped eagles on the tower,
we'd seen three shadows swiftly dash into the palace:
'Surely those are the Fates,' he cried, 'the Three Great Graces!
Quick, let's defend the royal seed asleep in its cradle!'
But as our eyes discerned your small shape in the dusk,
our hollow knees, O king, gave way and shook with fright:
three savage dragons hung, like swords, over your head!
And I, who night and day consort with gods and demons,
whose mind like a high threshing floor corrals the winds,
I saw in the dark and recognized those three great dragons.
First, like a topless cedar tree by lightning seared,
Tantalus stood, forefather of despairing mankind;
with vulturous claws he tore at his voracious chest,
uprooted his abysmal heavy heart, stooped low,
and wedged the graft deep in your own still tender breast;
your cradle blazed as though your entrails had caught fire.
The middle Fate then raised its awesome brow, and I
with trembling recognized Prometheus, the mind's master,
who in his wounded hands, that softly glowed, now held
the seed of a great light, and stooping over your skull
gently unstitched the tender threads, and sowed the seed.
Then the third dragon lit a fire and threw for kindling

huge looms and thrones and gods to swell the unsated blaze.
Your grandsire roared and rushed up with his spear, but I
seized him in time, held tight, and whispered in his ear:
'Hold on! These three great Fates are gifting your great grandson!
That dragon with the red locks of a lion's mane
is Heracles, that iron sword, that famous athlete.'
Stumbling, the old man grabbed a column, mute with awe;
and when the soaring conflagration licked the roof,
the dragon seized your infant form, flung it in flames,
and you flushed crimson, rose like flickering tongues and leapt
to the gilt beams and fluted with the singing blaze.
The whole night through you laughed and played, refreshed in fire,
and we, struck dumb, rejoiced in your salvation's wonder,
embraced each other tight as our tears flowed in streams.
The first cocks suddenly crowed in courts, and the great dragons
scattered like clouds and vanished in the downy air of dawn."

Silent and stooped, Odysseus listened and bit his lips;
his mind was far away on desolate seas and caves,
and when the bard had closed his skillful lips, at once
the archer leapt up, dug his nails into his seat
till the gold goblets on the table tipped and spilled.
His voice roared out with heavy mockery and hot rage:
"To my great shame my hair has whitened, my teeth loosened,
but I still squander my soul's strength on worthless works!
You'd think I'd plundered the whole world with sated fists,
nor knew of further seas to cross or men to meet,
and, full of pride, moored in my native land to rot!"
He spoke, sat down, then cast his baleful eyes about
as though the whole crowd were a nightmare, a bad dream.
The people turned to stone, their cups hung in the air,
and the old archons, sitting by their angry king,
felt his hot breath like sulphur flowing through his nostrils.
The guests thrust frightened heads between their shoulder blades,
and the carousers cowered, smothering in the plane-tree grove,
but as the hawk of anger passed, they raised their heads
and filled their winecups and their empty veins once more.
Big-bellied Kentaur laughed and roused their fallen spirits:
"Turn poisonous cares away, let fate bring what it may!
Eat all your oxen to the bone, gulp down your wine,
and steal a breast stroke on the girls, for life is short.
The black cock soon shall crow, and death shall dawn too soon."
The piper then took heart and stuck his oar in too:
"My friends, now here's an elegant verse for you to hear:
'To eat, drink, sleep, and love: this is the life of man!' "
Then the much-suffering man fell on the meat and wine

and like a starving giant began to eat and drink;
his bloodshot eyes grew small as in his mind he raved:
"Wise bard, you don't know who my oldest forebear is!"
Within his bowels he felt his wild forefather move,
a monstrous hippopotamus who step by heavy step
rose from thick mud to sun himself high in the heart.
The revelry continued till the break of day,
the stars grew milky in the sky, the torches paled,
the light trees rustled in the early breeze of dawn,
and in their nests the fledglings flicked their wings and raised
their small round eyes to see if the red sun had risen.
Then the king rose, the people scattered, the lyres ceased,
packsaddle mules were spread with brilliant woolen rugs
on which the giddy peasant women sat and swayed.
The old men took the road, bent on their crooked sticks,
but had no heart to sleep now, for their tipsy minds,
carried away by too much food and drink, gave birth
to lies and truths indifferently, just as they chanced
to fall from rosy clouds of dawn and roadside trees,
and thus the fabled myths of fabulous Odysseus
were born and grew like dragons in the daze of dream.
Far up the road the green youths cackled like hoarse cocks,
for each held secretly within his wine-drenched arms
rose-breasted Helen in a downy cloud of dawn.
They were all young and beardless, ignorant of love,
and sang sweet, sentimental, amatory songs:
"Strike me, my brother, and I'll strike back, fight and I'll fight!
I've lost my wits to a white breast, to black black eyes.
Mother, O Mother, the bitten apple, my sweet bride,
I saw her by the seashore, gazing far out at sea,
and her breasts shared a foreign air on foreign waves—
they're snow without the snow, and rain without the rain!"
As, like a silken thread, the crowd climbed twisted paths,
Telemachus in wrath stalked toward the castle keep
with his two snake-slim hounds to right and left, alone,
and thus provoked his father in his guileless soul:
"My eyes once smarted, sire, to watch the barren waves;
ah, had my fate decreed that you should *not* appear!
Now that you've come, may you be cursed, may other waves
soon sweep you to the world's far ends of no return.
You set all minds on fire, you plague man's simple heart,
you drive the craftsman from his shop, uproot the plow,
until the country bridegroom wants his bride no more
but longs for travel and immortal Helen's arms."
The archer meanwhile passed the plane grove, slowly sloped
down toward the morning shore and breathed the salty sea.

Gliding along the harbor with its slim caïques,
he passed the rowboats that with oars crossed on their chests
slept like poor workers calmly by the white shore's foam.
He crunched sand underfoot and skirting the curved coast,
leapt on the jagged boulders, put the cape behind him,
and like a tranquil seabird skimmed between the rocks.
His fevered eyes grew cool amid dawn's freshening breeze,
his burning feet grew cool, with splattering water drenched,
and the Evening Star shone in his beard, a drop of dew.
Long, long he gazed far out at sea in a sweet languor;
this was not he who'd fought with gods, embraced sea-sprites,
laid out the grooms like slaughtered beasts and choked his courts;
his mind was now a virgin boy, his hands white roses,
and his old longing shone like mother-of-pearl deep down,
far down in the sea's depths as he, above it stooped,
smiled and with slow caresses combed his star-washed hair.
Calmly his crude soul, star and water now, dissolved;
his memory, like a female gull in a dark cave,
slept in his breast, and his serene mind rose and sank,
a silent male gull floating on the foaming azure waves.

II

The next night by the fireside, when the great bronze
gates of the castle closed, and slaves and cattle slept,
Odysseus told the long tale of his sufferings slowly.
He sat upon his lion-throne and gently eased
his sea-embattled body softly on fine cushions.
The queen sat on a low throne, and with tearstained eyes
shook like a bobbin or thin thread ready to snap;
waves were already beating on her battened heart.
She stooped and with skilled fingers spun an azure yarn
of purest wool to weave Athena's brilliant mantle,
and planned to stitch a black ship on the rolling waves
and round its hem the toils and troubles of her famed husband.
Laertes on a sheepskin in a far corner crouched,
his chin thrust in his knees, his thin arms crossed about him—
an infant waiting for his mother's womb to open,
or corpse returned to earth, the greatest womb of all.
Telemachus stood upright by the hearth and watched
with wary eyes in the flames' light his father's mouth
that rumbled and prepared to speak with subtle craft.
His words were sonorous bees that buzzed with stings and honey,
contending in the beehive for the first flight out;
and the young man spied on the swarming mouth with wrath.
The household snake-god came and coiled himself in rings
in a far corner of the fireplace and flicked
his two-pronged tongue to listen to his master's cares.
Odysseus placed his hand over his mouth in thought;
seas swelled within his mind, far seashores tinged with rose,
clamorous weeping, laughter, joys, and burning towers;
his harsh throat choked and overbrimmed, he could not speak.
The azure trap door of his sea-swept memory burst:
whom should he first remember and whom cast in darkness?
Dim shades of loved friends rushed into his heart's deep pit:
"Give us your blood to drink that we may live an hour!"
But he chose ruthlessly among the shades, gazed long
at the fierce flames, then dredged his wandering voyages
from his resounding memory's well, and told his fabulous tales.

"At the far ends of the world, on noble feasting boards
the lyre rises, greets the lords, and sings to the wind.
Ten years we stormed the castle, ten wide rivers rolled
our steaming blood down toward the sea, and slowly vanished,
for the gods on high secured those lawless battlements.
One morning when I woke, and my brain brimmed with thought,
I seized an ax and felled white poplars, built with skill
a lifelike and gigantic mare with swollen belly
and as a votive gift to Zeus leant it against the walls,
but its huge pregnant womb was filled with gallant troops;
thus did my sly mind set the trap, and in the night
the untaken walls and the Immortals crashed in ruin.
Besmirched by the thick smoke, wounded in forty places,
the fearful gods at dawn rushed from the ruthless flames,
plunged deep into the heavens and cursed the insolent earth;
but when their jaws had once more knit, they laughed, unshamed,
drank of oblivion's deathless wine, and soon forgot.
But the chief god, wrapped up with savage wrath in clouds,
would not permit his mind to drink and thus forget;
stooping above the gold-lipped rim of heaven, he sighed:
'The scales of fate tilt upside-down, earth's at our heels!
I see the archer's wily head stuffed full of brains
and brashness, leaning even on our Olympian walls!'
He spoke, then summoned Death to come before him swiftly,
and he, black crow who browsed replete on Trojan corpses,
flew up to heaven and perched upon the god's right hand.
Then murderous Zeus rejoiced to hold his strapping son:
'Good bird, my faithful thought, swoop down and fix your claws
deep in the brazen skull of unabashed Odysseus;
become flame, woman, sea, grind his brash brains to powder!'
He spoke, then in my skull thrust Death like a sharp sword."
The martyr's eyes flashed fire, and deep in their dark pools
the great death-battle raged, on land, sea, air, and fire,
of one despairing man with all the omnipotent gods.
The cunning voyager fell silent and cast to see
how skillfully to dress the truth with subterfuge,
but felt ashamed before his wife and son, lost courage,
and thrusting tempting wiles aside, shook his proud head
and sailed unhindered on his sea-swept memory.
"Three were the worse most deadly forms which Death assumed
to strip me of my weapons and uncoil my brains.
In cool Calypso's cave he came with laughing wiles
and twined himself about my knees like a plump wench
till in my mortal arms I took the immortal maid
and hugged her like a sweet dream on the sandy shores.
The blond-tressed goddess bathed my muddy feet each night

in a gold basin filled with cold and crystal water
that her gold-woven bridal sheets might not be soiled,
and I would laugh with joy to see man's muddy feet
entwined in bed with such unwithering deathless calves.
For the first time I joyed in flesh as it were spirit,
heaven and earth merged on the beaches, deep within me
I laughed to feel my muddy entrails sprouting wings.
Heaven and its foundations swerved to serve us both,
stars vanished in the sea but others blazed with smiles,
and we, two glowworms merged as one, gleamed on the sands.
Like a night sun, misleading Zeus's star first leapt
on the sky's rim and joyed to watch with admiration
the blond-haired goddess on the desolate beaches quake
within a mortal's earthen arms and bear him fruit.
Blood-lapping Ares strode behind him, fully armed,
rolling between the mountain peaks, bursting on rocks,
twisting and turning like a crab caught in the fire,
and we on slippery pebbles lay and laughed with joy.
Then last of all at daybreak, with her white seabirds,
passing with dance and laughter through the rosy mist,
great gracious Aphrodite would caress on earth
our bodies by the shores at rest, now merged in one.
Like the swift beating of an eagle's wings, our days
and nights of love vanished in empty skies above us,
and as I held the Immortal tightly in my arms
I suddenly felt at dusk one day, with speechless dread,
that God had spread his tentacles and choked my heart.
The world then seemed a legend, life a passing dream,
the soul of man a spiraling smoke that rose in air;
in my clear head gods suddenly were born, blazed up,
as suddenly were lost, and others rose instead
like clouds and fell in raindrops on my sun-scorched mind.
Only my dreams seemed to be living still—they crawled
like many-colored snakes and mutely licked my lids;
seas then unfolded in my brain, rooted in pearls;
within thick waters gold fish gazed upon me sadly,
and from blue depths the sweetest, sweetest voices rose.
My body stretched in length, my arches curved in height,
my head cut through high waves like a curved figurehead
where the road-pointing North Star hung like dangling dew.
My body like a pirate's galley sped nightlong
and all my hold was filled with the earth's fragrant smells.
But my dream swiftly emptied, snakes grew numb with cold,
and my free heart, that could unshape or shape the world,
turned sterile, dead in a divine tranquillity.
Man's passions in my heart were purged and drained away,

my native land was drowned, and shone in Lethe's depths,
till like a play of light and cloud that swayed in wind
my father, wife, and son met, parted, and were lost;
Death rose in a god's shape and wrecked my mortal heart.
Unlaughing, painless, mute, I skimmed over the rocks,
for my transparent body cast no shade on earth
and seabirds swiftly darted through my legs, unfearing,
as though a god walked on the shores invisibly.
One morning on the barren stones I chanced to trip
on a long piece of wreckage cast up by the waves,
and raised it slowly and strove to think what it might be:
bone of a monstrous fish, leg of a mammoth bird,
or staff of some sea demon, branch of a huge sea tree?
Light slowly filled my mind till in my feeble hands
I saw I held a much-beloved and long-stemmed oar,
and as I stroked it tenderly, my dull eyes cleared:
I saw at the oar's end the sunburnt hand that held it,
I saw the foaming keel and sails of a tall mast,
old comrades came with peeling limbs and crowded round me,
the sea flung in a burst upon me and shook my brains,
and I recalled from where I had come and where I longed to go.
Ah, I too was a mortal soul, my heart was dancing,
I had a country, wife, and child, and a swift ship,
but my poor soul was wrecked and lost in a great goddess.
I quaked in fear of being made a deathless god
without man's springing heart, without man's joys or griefs,
then turned and plunged my wasted face in the cool waves,
cast water on my withered lashes to revive them,
smelled the salt seaweed on the shore as my brows burst,
and my head brimmed with light and water, fire and earth,
till my blood flowed, my royal veins began to thaw.
Seizing a cleaving ax, I plunged into the woods,
cut down huge trees and split them, matched them, chose a cypress,
fit planks together, carved long oars, raised up the mast,
—all in a rage of joy—you'd think I hewed and carved
backbone and hands and feet, head, belly, breast and thighs,
as though I built again my god-smashed, ravened body.
And when my shape had spread at length from stern to prow
and I had stretched Calypso's blue cloak for a mainsail,
O new-carved ship, you sang then like my warbling heart.
What joy to unfurl sail suddenly in the buffeting winds
and, scudding swiftly, shout farewell to your belovèd:
'Much do I love and want you, dear, but let me first
mount on my plunging ship, pay out my billowing sails,
as with one hand I hold the tiller for open seas
and with the other wipe departure's tears away.'

New-washed and fragrant by her holy water's well,
the goddess combed her long immortal hair and sang:
'For the first time I felt my marble thighs aglow
when once they leant against your warm and mortal thighs.
My stone mind softened, my heart beat, and my knees quaked,
my veins brimmed full of milk, I laughed and turned to woman
and held the whole world on my bosom like a baby.'
Her song could cleave a rock in two; it cracked my heart:
'Be still, my heart, I know, but the mind aims elsewhere.'
Then as I sped like arrows on the foam-peaked waves

and her song dwindled sadly in the twilight's mist,
my ship, grown heavy, slowly sank to its low rim,
for loved shades crushed it, weighed with country, son, and wife,
till I set free my heart to follow as it wished
and it broke down in tears and turned human again!"
Odysseus spoke no more and gazed into the fire,
but in his heart he voyaged still without a word:
islands sprang up in his far mind, moons glowed and swayed,
the rigging in his memory creaked, and his dark head
thundered above the waves like a wild mountain's peak.
The spindle fell from his wife's golden-fingered hands,
her knees shook secretly, and in her pulsing throat
she choked back bitter sobs and bit her trembling lip;
and his son, shuddering, spied on the hard knees and thighs,
the hands that could choke virtue, that on savage shores
brashly could seize yet cast aside the dread Immortals.
Squeezing his tender palms into a fist, he thought:
"This man breaks through all bounds, confounds men with the gods,
smashes the sacred laws that hold the toppling world!"
Laertes, crouched in sleep in a far corner, dreamt
how as a youth not yet turned twenty, he'd built a ship
with three long tiers of oars and sailed to steal a wife,
but at the harbor's narrow strait a crab sat crouched,
bending a fresh green reed to form a curving bow,
and blocked the bridegroom's passage and the vessel's sailing.
Then the world-traveler rose and in the fire cast
an olive log, and poked the glowing embers slowly.
He watched abstractedly the nude flames as they danced
whistling and licking round the logs, stabbing the walls,
and heard choked lamentations, shouts, and burning towns,
welcoming cries, coarse laughs, and distant threnodies.
With ruthless justice, nonetheless, he winnowed wheat
from the crude chaff, then turned serenely toward his throne,
leapt on his vessel's prow and voyaged on once more:
"Hunger thrashed at my guts, my throat was parched with thirst,
for days I licked dew only, on my oars distilled,
and raised my eyes toward heaven—not even one small cloud
passed by to bring a cup of air and puff my sails.
My mind swayed in delirium while a honeyed swoon
wrapped softly round my breathless body like a spell,
and as I hung my heavy head, prepared to fall,
I saw on the sea's rim, like a dawn's glowing cloud,
the sun-washed, rock-strewn body of my longed-for land.
Her capes were foaming, her towns gleamed on mountain slopes,
my sheep flashed white on greenest grass, the cattle lowed,
I heard a shepherd's flute, a cascade's tumbling song,

and twittering landbirds came and perched high on my masts.
My son, you stood on shore with shaded eyes, and watched,
your tongue grown sore with questioning sailors year on year;
then on my palace roof a woman stood and glowed.
'My harbor, ho!' I yelled, then leapt, close-reefed my sails
and skimmed down toward my country mutely, plunged in dream.
But lo, harsh laughter smote the spume, the wild waves beat
my wretched prow with mockery, the divine shore swayed,
a brilliant gauze on the horizon's mist, and vanished.
With gaping eyes I saw my land dissolve from sight;
the seams of my skull creaked and cracked with seething rage
for everywhere I saw the lawless gods that mocked me.
I seized the tiller and swore to make them choke with wrath
nor ever surrender my ship or soul to their caprice.
Sleep seized me in light snatches, and half-dazed once more
I shook my head to chase away that deadly nightbird,
until, behold, as I stared on the sea's face mutely,
I saw snow-clad Olympus blaze in brilliant light
and its divine gigantic nest shine gold on top.
I felt my vapid body soar like a light cloud
high up the lambent god-trod peak, and both my oars
flapped quickly from my sides like wings that cut the waves.
I reached at last and stood upon that deathless threshold,
and as the shadow of my peaked cap fell upon it,
the gates at once sprang open like two human arms
and showed the whirlpool sea-god, calm and tranquil now.
He seized and pressed me to his bosom and cried out:
'My son, we've played like dolphins on the frothing waves;
spiteful and stubborn each in turn, we fought like men,
and like two gallant warriors tumbled on the sands.
Now let the contest end, let endless friendship start;
forgive me, friend, and may you also be forgiven.'
Thus did the wave-brained god address me and embrace me,
and like two dolphins we caressed in azure air.
Joyfully then tall wisdom's goddess came and placed
her spear-delighting hand on my wave-whitened hair:
'Dear friend, the nights of the Immortals have no dawn,
and we have longed for you to come and cheer our hearts.
Much-suffering man, sit by my right on the high throne
and open wide your heart, your brains, and your thick lips,
for we gods long to hear of man's cares and ordeals.'
Athena spoke, and the gods came from their high thrones
and pressed about me to admire my aging body,
my puckered hands and feet devoured by sun and brine.
They treated me to deathless wine, and the small-waisted
goddess of youth knelt down and loosed my sandal straps,

but as I gazed between the golden columns down
on the blue sea that spread and laughed in blazing sun,
I suddenly felt that dreams had snatched my giddy brain,
and with great rage I shook my empty head from sleep
until the sacred mountain swayed like dazzling mist, and vanished.

"It seems that hunger must have driven my poor wits crazy;
the gods had found me stripped of weapons, ready to hand,
and mocked my mind with shifting visions of firm land;
ah, had I but one bite of bread, one sip of water!
As I blasphemed, it seemed to me I heard before me
in the sea-fog a bestial cry, a woman's laughter,
and my keel gliding, skidding gently on smooth sand.
I rushed to the prow headlong, tried to pierce the fog,
and saw a thickly wooded isle, a snaky path,
a beach of yellow sand that spread like scattered wheat,
and on the shore a young girl stood and held her breasts,
and all her blue-black body steamed as poured from bronze.
Two slender jet-black leopards leapt and danced about her,
licking her rounded belly and her small-shaped feet
while she smiled broadly with her thick black hair unbraided,
and her man-eating teeth like stars flashed in the fog.
Her breasts leapt high like two wild beasts to welcome me,
and I said, trembling, 'I've not seen a deeper face of death!
My soul, do not betray man's narrow pass to virtue!'
But when I'd washed myself within her golden rooms
and food was spread in the cool grove, and winecups foamed,
and heard her sweet voice, then my duty was all forgotten.
'My dear, you've washed and eaten till your veins flow free,
your sturdy body glows like a crisp youth of twenty;
welcome, beloved, let's play in bed with fun and frolic.'
She spread a layer of marjoram, a layer of basil,
and like a thousand-year-old cave, her bed resounded.
The sun stood still, the soul rolled down her curly pit
and vanished, man's bright face became pig-snouted till
the sleepless flame that trembles high between man's brows
went out, for fragrant flowers, virtues, shames, and love,
alas, grow on the surface only, wither in haste away,
and Mother Mud grips firmly in our deepest roots.
How to forget, dear God, the joy that shook my loins
when I saw virtue, light, and soul all disappearing!
With twisted hands and thighs we rolled on burning sands,
a hanging mess of hissing vipers glued in sun!
Slowly my speech turned mute within me, hearth-flames choked,
the infected mind, weighed down with flesh, plunged in my guts,
for just as insects slowly sink and drown in amber,

so in my turbid mind beasts, trees, and mortals sank.
In time my heart was battered to a mess of fat
where passions flared and vanished in a torpid daze
till we plunged, grunting, deep into a bestial pit.
I lay well fitted in foul flesh, while man's great cares,
his hopes, flames and ascensions flew in scattering air.
Farewell the brilliant voyage, ended! Prow and soul
moored in the muddy port of the contented beast!
O prodigal, much-traveled soul, is *this* your country?"
Then the world-wandering athlete sighed and scowled with wrath;
for a long time he gazed upon the flames in silence
but all at once a jolting laughter brimmed his throat:
"God, if this *is* our country, the mind has many skills
to rip it up with all its roots and build a prow!"
He spoke, then twirled the spindle of his mind once more:
"One day as I lay grunting in my fleshly sty,
I saw a light smoke rising on the shore, a fire,
and round it squatted men who with slit rushes pierced
a row of fish and roasted them on glowing coals.
A woman with a baby at her bosom stooped,
unbared her breasts till her son grasped her nipples tight,
and she refreshed him like a fountain of pure milk.
As the fish reddened and their fragrance smote the nostrils,
the fishermen pressed round the fire and sat cross-legged,
and when the mother came with outstretched hands, they filled
her palms with double portions of black bread and fish.
They ate with greed, munched silently, and watched the sea,
then wiped their long mustaches, tipped their flasks of wine,
drank deep, passed it from man to man, last to the mother.
O poor immortal comforts: fish, some bread and wine,
the blue sea stretched before you as you slowly munch
and feel your spirit fortified, your flesh renewed!
I felt, dear God, that I myself once knew such joy.
After the meal, they raised their hands to burning skies
and the glad mother swayed her torso right and left
and poured into the air a slow sweet lullaby.
The words fell emptily and sank in my mind's marsh
but I received the sweet sounds in my breast, and there
the parched and thick-skinned leaves of my heart trembled.
With pain I struggled to recall as my chest heaved:
great courtyards, vineyards, ancient olive trees and fig,
a marble-throated woman that suckled my only son—
oho, to climb a mountain peak, to shout and yell!
Then all at once my throat swelled and my neck veins burst;
tears brought me near you once again, O race of man.
Once more I hewed the forest, carved out new-shaped wings,

oars, sails and masts so that the soul might rise for flight;
once more, O joy, winds blessed my sails, and I swept free!
The man-enflaming, high-rumped maid screamed on the shore,
the leopards leapt like flames about her, flicked their tails,
and all the sun-washed bodies called from burning sands:
'Where are you going, to the crags of man, to the cliffs of his mind?
Where are you going, beautiful body, smashed like a jug?
My breast is your native land, for no matter where you go,
you'll not find such a tranquil port, such sweet oblivion.
The soul of woman is very sweet, for it is filled with flesh!'

"Shrill sounds and passion's exclamations slowly faded
as in the fiery sunlight the sandy harbor vanished.
All day I sailed to windward, and my vessel beat
like a poor human heart escaped from the jaws of death;
at night the heavens glowered and filled with lightning bolts,
the sea clutched at the sky, sea-demons danced on billows,
and their harsh laughter burst about my head and roared.
I heard them quarreling how to seize and share amongst them
like vultures, my strong ribs, my brains, my eyes, my entrails,
but with my ship for shield, I fought them breast to breast
and held on tightly to keep flesh and bone together.
But in the frenzied dawn the searing lightning smashed
my sails and planking, and I plunged in roaring waves
and grit my teeth to keep my fainting soul from drowning.
I cut through all the flooding waves with wide breast strokes
until my hands at daybreak hooked on jagged rocks.
Oho, firm land, I've seized you and plant roots once more!
Laughing and crying, I kissed the earth and stretched on stones,
and it was then Death's sweetest face rose to confront me."
The seven-souled man ceased, knelt down and fed the flames
with stacks of laurel boughs until the crackling fire
sent a sweet fragrance spreading through the dazzled house.
For a long time he stooped to admire, wrapped in thought,
how the flames slowly licked the boughs caressingly,
crawled up to their dark tips and tightly bound them round
while they burned on, uncaring, all their twigs ablaze.
The man of many cares laughed secretly and stroked his beard:
"Death masqueraded like the virgin of a noble tribe
who on the beach smiled softly at a shipwrecked man,
and my much-suffering heart rejoiced to smell the ripe
and mortal body, the humble holy warmth of man.
She was not a divine, tall crystal peak, nor yet
a smoking, hungry blaze confined in a beast's loins;
I marveled now at man himself on earth, and joyed
to see myself reflected wholly in her eyes.
She neither raised me to the empty sky nor hurled
me down to Hades, but we walked on earth together,
and my wild backbone trilled with sweetest fluting sounds:
'Lucky that worthy man who sleeps with her as bridegroom!
This is the sweetest siren of all, see how she waves!
See how her holy bosom yearns to suckle men!
Dear God, to build a home at length, to smash my ship,
to make a crossbeam of its mast, its hull a bed,
and its old, sea-embattled prow my own son's cradle!'
But I made my heart stone, precisely weighed all things
between my just mid-brow till Reason stood erect:

'When in my native land one day I've moored for good,
then I shall load a many-oared, tall bridal galley
with fragrant honey, wheat, and wine to sail and buy
this sun-washed nest of children for my only son.'
My heart had never gleaned such rooted Victory."
Odysseus sealed his bitter lips and spoke no more,
but watched the glowering fire fade, the withering flames,
the ash that spread like powder on the dying coals,
then turned, glanced at his wife, gazed on his son and father,
and suddenly shook with fear, and sighed, for now he knew
that even his native land was a sweet mask of Death.
Like a wild beast snared in a net, his eyes rolled round
and tumbled down his deep eye-sockets, green and bloodshot.
His tribal palace seemed a narrow shepherd's pen,
his wife a small and wrinkled old housekeeping crone,
his son an eighty-year-old drudge who, trembling, weighed
with care to find what's just, unjust, dishonest, honest,
as though all life were prudence, as though fire were just,
and logic the highest good of eagle-mounting man!
The heart-embattled athlete laughed, dashed to his feet,
and his home's sweetness, suddenly, his longed-for land,
the twelve gods, ancient virtue by his honored hearth,
his son—all seemed opposed now to his high descent.
The fire dwindled and died away, and the four heads
and his son's smooth-skinned calves with tender softness glowed
till in the trembling hush Penelope's wan cries
broke in despair like water flowing down a wall.
Her son dashed and stood upright by his mother's throne,
touched gently with a mute compassion her white arm,
then gazed upon his father in the dim light, and shuddered,
for in the last resplendence of the falling fire
he could discern the unmoving eyes flash yellow, blue,
and crimson, though the dark had swallowed the wild body.
With silent strides Odysseus then shot back the bolt,
passed lightly through the courtyard and sped down the street.
Some saw him take the graveyard's zigzag mountain path,
some saw him leap on rocks that edged the savage shore,
some visionaries saw him in the dead of night
swimming and talking secretly with the sea-demons,
but only a small boy saw him in a lonely dream
sit crouched and weeping by the dark sea's foaming edge.

Death is a skillful pruner, trims the trees and knows
what bough shall wither and what flower will turn to fruit.
At cock crow once when old Laertes could not sleep
he crawled to the main court and poked his agèd nurse.

When he was young he'd slept with her in joy one night
then left her all her life to weave in his dank vaults;
but now that he hung drooping like a rotting fig,
he'd brought her back to care for him in his old age;
this was the ancient crone whom he now prod at dawn.
The old nurse opened startled eyes and in the dusk
perceived the bald pate of her master softly gleam
as over it two black, enormous, wide wings fell.
"The poor man knows he's lying in Death's shadow now."
Thus did she think, then tied her kerchief silently,
lit up the fire and put some fragrant mint to boil
so that the infirm old man might drink and brace his heart,
but he stood by the door for fear he'd leave too late.
Guessing he wished to hasten to his loved grove and there
give up his soul at last to the trees' holy roots,
she wrapped him tight in a warm mantle, took his arm,
and both together crossed the court, unbarred the gate
with shaking hands, and stumbled up the farmhouse path.
The cloudy dawn hung trembling on the verge of tears,
earth smelled of musk, the olive trees still dripped with dew,
and misty morn cried in its cradle like a child.
A fat crow passed them to the right with whistling wings
and the old woman cursed it with the curse of death;
but others came and cawed in chorus joyously
and played and coupled lovingly in the dim air
nor smelled an old man's corpse nor heard the frail crone's cry.
When finally they reached the orchard's matted fence,
light broke, the slaves had wakened and were hard at work,
and in the moist air cocks thrust out their necks and crowed.
As the old man grew tired, she made him lean against
the ancestral hollow olive tree that kept the gate,
gave him a gourd of old wine that his knees might knit,
and he with both hands grasped the dripping wine-bowl fast
and drank deep gulps to strengthen his exhausted heart.
He felt the warmth spread down his vitals, his eyes shone,
till in his darkening head his mind cast its last beams.
He saw then his loved orchard, spread his joyful hands
and slowly greeted all his trees, each by its name:
"O my sweet apple tree with apples hung, O loved
and honeyed fig tree, thin-shelled almond, musk-grape vines,
farewell, I fall to earth. Eat me, O mother-roots!
I, too, am the earth's fruit, and rot; dry leaf, and fall!"
Wagging their tails, his two white hounds rushed up and barked,
then leapt upon him lovingly and whined with joy
as their old master leant his hands on their thin ribs
and drank deep of his dogs' warmth and the earth's odor.

The flower-laden trees glowed softly, cloaked with mist,
honeybees buzzed and swarmed till leaves and branches swayed,
and two old ewes, which the old man had raised, came bleating
and sought to lick his warped, beloved, familiar hands.
A musk-roe gently raised with pride his clever head,
recognized his old master, his eyes shone with joy,
and like a prince approached to greet the frail old man
who gathered all beasts in his shade now like a tree.
His nurse stood by his side and wept, for she knew well
the mind was but a lamp that flares and fades forever
and that Laertes hailed the world for the last time.
When a fat ancient crow he once had nourished came,
brimming with joy, and perched on his right shoulder blade,
he shook with fear to feel the harsh beak in his ear
and closed his eyes as heavy sweat poured down his body.
The nurse cried bitterly, the servants gathered close,
the faithful cowherds came, taking the cows to pasture,
and shepherd boys approached, holding their crooked sticks.
The slaves pressed round their master, grasped his withered knees
and his damp hands and begged him not to leave them now,
but he, far from his living friends, with empty gaze,
blinked his dim eyes and leant on the old olive tree;
he stood on Hades' threshold mutely, eased of care,
and turned his pale face round and bid the world farewell.
Kneeling before the death-doomed man, his nurse cried out:
"Dear master, let me send a slave to fetch your son."
But when Laertes heard her, he stared and bit his tongue,
then with numb fingers grasped his nurse and held her back.
Now on the blossomed trees a drizzling shower fell,
flowers grew dim and the earth odorous, cuckoo birds
perched on the olive boughs and shook their watery wings.
Bending his head, the old man smelled the steaming sod;
his brains, like mud-balls in a sudden shower, crumbled,
and sluggish oxen in his mind began to plow.
He held the plowshare tightly, his feet sank in furrows,
and skylarks, swallows, storks and cranes flew low and cried:
"Grandfather, plow the loam, open the earth to feed us!"
He heard and prod the beasts until his entrails burst
like earth, and birds flew back and forth and ate of him.
Such were the joys and memories that now brimmed his mind,
and slowly stuttering, back and forth he swung his arms
in a wide sweep, like a good farmer who sows his seed,
and his old nurse, guessing the plowman's secret wish,
poured grain into her kerchief from a storage jar
and spilled it in her dreaming master's lap, and he,
feeling the holy seed within his trembling palms,

took on new vigor, smiled in silence, and stood erect.
Earth softened in the drizzling rain, and from deep pits
of moldering soft manure came odors of plowed fields.
The old man swayed and staggered as he raised his hands
to cast the fruitful seed in earth, but tripped and fell,
then on his belly dragged himself on shaking knees
and sowed with open arms, as though he blessed the seed,
but fell face forward, raised himself, clawed at the ground,
and fell again, until his beard was caked with mud.
Pecking the earth, the sparrows zoned him happily,
the old crow came and hopped upon his master's back,
and his white hounds preceded him in the thin rain.
Then all at once the rainbow sank its feet in grass
and hung in mid-air, blazing bright with sweetest joy;
heaven and earth were bridged, and the slow drizzle ceased.
But the old man, engrossed in sowing, ignored the sky,
struggled to cast his last fistful, but fell face down,
and his head thrust into the rain-soaked soil like final seed.

When the long-suffering man heard of his father's death
he felt his entrails pull apart and fall to earth
as if a huge part of his famous bronze-hewn body
had rotted suddenly and dropped in an open grave.
Holding his father's still warm body in his arms,
he mounted toward their moldering, old ancestral tombs,
slew oxen on the grave and sent them down to Hades
so that his father's ghost might plow the shades, sow deep,
and glean Elysian wheat with his dead, reedy hands.
He placed a sharp goad by his father's side, a scythe,
a bronze jar of cool water, a warm loaf of bread,
then last of all he masked his father's holy face
with pure gold leaf, marked out his lashless eyes, his mouth,
his thorny eyebrows, long mustaches, cheeks and chin,
and bending over the tomb cried thrice his father's name,
but it went lost, and no loved echo rose from earth.
Odysseus smoothed the grave's light soil and planted there,
to suck and drain his father's flesh, an olive sprout
under whose shade in time grandsons might come to play.
The fruit rots blessed in earth, for it has cast its seed,
and that same night Odysseus ordered a swift ship
full-armed with crimson sails, loaded with amphoras
of old rich wine, with wheat, with copper kegs of honey,
a marriage god nailed to the prow for figurehead
holding the mystic, many-seeded pomegranate.
He summoned two town elders and his lustrous bard:
"My castle's worthy chiefs, go as my marriage brokers

due north to a deep-gardened and green-wooded isle.
With vine leaves on your heads, with your tall staffs in hand,
ascend with pomp the wealthy palace, pass the threshold,
and bending low before the old king, hail him thus:
'Greetings! Our king, the famous castle-battler, sends us.
We bring a dowry-ship of honey, wheat, and wine,
the rich gifts of our master's son, to take for bride,
with your permission, Sire, your daughter nobly bred.
Since that dawn when our master saw her play on shore
he longed for her to rule his home and breed him grandsons.' "

He spoke; at once his words became a laden ship,
and the three marriage brokers sailed and searched their brains
to find what artful words might bring the wished agreement.
Odysseus stood upon the shore and watched the ship
scudding ahead, its red sails filled with the South Wind.
Watching his son before him run to find a bride,
feeling his father's body rot in the grave behind him,
and he at the dead center, bridegroom both and corpse,
he shuddered, for his life now seemed the briefest lightning flash.

He turned and looked about him: all his streets seemed narrow,
strange generations trod the roads, new boys and girls
seeded when he was flinging spears on foreign shores;
his isle had bloomed and borne fruit like a tree in season.
The sun had set but on the mountains dragged its light
slowly, as though it had no wish to leave the earth.
Sitting on low stone walls, old men of the first rank,
their chins upon their staffs, chattered in low tones,
weighing each word with prudent craft before they cast it,
flinging each other hints, hiding their secret thoughts.
Yet but one secret thought pierced through the elders' hearts,
and though it burned their lips, could find no passage out.
They suddenly ceased like crickets when man's shadow falls,
for far away in twilight they discerned their king
pacing with lion strides, nearing the plane-tree grove,
till he approached and stood before their shriveled forms
and all bowed low with great esteem and wished him well.
The sea-wolf looked with scorn on his town's elder chiefs
and thrust their rotting forms aside, struggling to find
their manly bodies that on earth once prowled like lions,
how sagging now, as though earth clutched and dragged them down!
Odysseus grabbed an old sea-churl with battered ears:
"Ah, famed man-slaying pirate of storm-battered seas,
remember how your native harbor laughed and flashed
when you returned and piled your loot high on the quays?
Once in my early youth I watched in admiration
how you tread groaning earth as you flung out at me:
'Your earth is narrow, prince, your quays can't hold me now,
I shall enthrone myself amid rich ships in ambush!'
You spoke, and suddenly in my heart my land grew small,
but now, for shame, you lick earth's filth like a dung-beetle!"
The codger glanced with spite on his king's jeering mouth:
"When I was young I spurned all shores and gleaned the waves,
but in mid-sea I'd raise a shout that stopped my ships:
Ah for cool water from my well, fruit from my trees!
Dear God, had I my woman now upon my knee!' "

The foxy-minded man then laughed till the earth shook:
"Strange fruits are sweetest and strange breasts smell best of all!
O rotting hull, my native land, you rise and fall
between my brows and break on the mind's jagged cliffs!"
He poked his neighbor and heaped the sea-wolf with scorn:
"This man once rivaled me in cunning wiles, his mind
turned to a small, white fox when he tread whitest snow,
turned to a yellow-crimson hare on sun-hot sand,
an emerald locust lost amid the greenest grass;
and when he rose in council, all our giddy thoughts
would fall in his words' lovely snares like partridges:
now he chews pumpkin seed and plucks his hair of fleas!"
But then the old fox curled his lips and bared his teeth:
"Aye, king, beasts of the wood grow old, and gods grow old,
and old age with its cares strikes even the soul of man;
you, too, will pay the price, whether you will or not!"
The man of stone heart laughed with spite and the men quaked:
"Learn that the soul sprouts twice with youthful fruit and flower
from rooted, ancient trees, nor pays the slavish tithe;
no matter how old I grow, I'll fight toward youth renewed!"
He spoke, and to his left seized a distinguished chief
with gleaming flesh and five-fold fat, with curled white locks
who pursed his painted lips with girlish coquetry.
Odysseus looked him up and down with scorn, then spoke:
"Behind your fat make-up I still make out your mug:
you are that famous bard who one warm evening sang
so well amid our feast that my great father rose
and pinned upon your warbling chest a golden cricket.
That sacred cricket now is dead—behold its husk!
By God, now in this twilight's murky glow you seem
like a bald peacock plucked by scurf to an old hen,
or like a shameless fat-assed goddess smeared with grease
who, naked on the crossroads, spreads her thighs for hire."
The lickerish old man with a coy wink replied:
"My king, here is a proverb said of two-faced life:
'It's good to change at times from male to female hare.' "
The old men plucked their chins and giggled in their beards,
but sorrow crushed the manly chest of the world-traveler
for he recalled how when waves tore his prow he longed
to reach his rocky isle and to hold council here
under this plane-tree grove with his town elders round him—
was this, by God, the foul fistful his soul desired?
For a long time he watched them with a mute compassion
and they took courage from his silence and soon began
to speak their minds and give him prudent, sound advice:
"Aye, king, your eyes, ears, fists are surely sated now.

They say you've plundered cities, crossed far-distant seas,
fought with great gods and slept with goddesses in caves,
even that you flew to heaven and plunged down to Hades.
Words swiftly flew in flocks over our isle like birds
in spring and fall, bringing us news of your great deeds;
don't vanish now, your soul has done all it has wished,
but beach your idle ship upon your sands at last.
The risks of youth are good, but when time's firm foundations
steady a man at length, it's time he put to port;
boundaries are sacred: woe to the mind that crowds them close!"
But the sea-battler rose and left without a word;
his feet, like a wild beast's, tread softly rock on rock
until he took the stone-paved path to his high castle.
The elders locked their minds, leant on their staffs once more
and gabbed about their vineyards, their new-planted greens,
to chase away their master's ponderous and crushing shade.

Many the silver moons that rose and fell and played
in changing skies like round full suns or slender scythes.
Grapes in the vineyards reddened, stalks of wheat grew golden,
ripe figs at noon dripped with sweet honey on the earth,
heat swelled, young girls grew pale, their armpits smelled of musk,
and the mind-spinner held time in his salty hands
like fruit, like pomegranates or green grapes, and waited.
He stood by his bronze gate and listened to the sea
as in his mind his vessel leapt like shoals of fish;
his wretched wife urged all her frightened slaves to sing
their sweetest songs and drown the roar of beckoning seas,
but he already stood by sails and watched the waves;
his feasting boards were spread with air, sea, birds, and sounds.
One day close by the shore he stood near a poor hut
with swelling osiers, oleanders, low stone walls,
and a worm-eaten hull that, flat on sand, was now
a washing tub where an old woman scrubbed her clothes.
But the ship's figurehead still stood upon the sand,
leprous and mangled, breast and throat devoured and maimed;
only its dark blue eyes were cool and deathless still,
gazing on seas with rapture still, longing to leave.
Here Captain Clam, a shaggy, battered old sea-wolf
sat with his grandchild on the shore and chewed his lunch.
"Good hour, Captain Clam, I'm thirsty for cool water;
rise up, and may your famous hands refresh me now."
The ancient sailor wiped his hanging white mustache
then washed his hands at the sea's edge, welcomed his king,
and, smiling, brought a bowl of cool, refreshing water.
Then the two old sea-eagles squatted on the sand,

and the archer placed his palm on the old boatman's back:
"Aye, Captain Clam, how glad I am to touch your body!
I bring to mind your daring deeds on sea and land:
what shame that such a body now should waste away.
By God, let's kick our flagship in the sea, old friend,
until the sails stretch taut and our minds fill with brine!
Ahoy! new voyages rise in my heart once more!
You've only one life, Captain Clam; don't let it rot.
All others age and slump, but we'll mount upward still!
Leave women and your grandchild now and come with me."
Crouched on the sand, old Captain Clam began to growl
like a ship's dog just freed from his confining leash.
His steady and sun-battered head with its gray hair
flooded with waves and thundered like a seagull's cave,
but he said nothing as he watched his grandchild play,
then gazed far off and deeply breathed the sea's wild spume.
The great soul-snatcher softened his harsh voice and spoke
as when a lover wishes to persuade his loved one,
and then he rose and took his way along the beach,
but from the corner of his eye he saw the boatman
plodding within his footsteps down the sandy shore.
The cunning rogue then laughed and sighed, rejoiced, and thought:
"The soul is like a woman who not even *can* not,
but *will* not resist warm words that lure her like a man."

He leant next evening slyly by the bronzesmith's door
and marveled at the red-haired smith, the savage stranger
who stooped and struggled by the flames, a soot-smirched god
come down from the high mountain tops and their dense woods,
crude in his speech, his fair locks flowing down his back,
with neither wife nor child, a heavy and secluded wolf.
A stain spread on his right cheek like an octopus,
for in her pregnancy his mother had seen flames
and burning castles shining on her blazing son.
Odysseus gazed with wonder on that hulking body,
and when he'd had his fill, his harsh voice mocked and jeered:
"Hey, Hardihood, you've a firm back and breast and arms,
but it's a shame, I say, that you still deign to battle
with unresisting bronze, that gummy, waxen god.
Know that a newborn god now leaps and shouts in flames!"
The red stain on the bronzesmith turned to blue, his breast
throbbed, but he knew the wanderer's words, though harsh, were true.
Odysseus crossed the soot-black threshold then and thought:
"I'd like to have this blond beast for my traveling comrade."
He closed the door, and when both stood before the fire,
out of his heavy belt he drew a glittering sword

made of the purest iron, blue-black and double-edged.
The bronzesmith leapt and rushed to touch the dread new god,
but the fox-minded man stopped him with outstretched hand:
"One night, walking along a barbarous coast alone,
I mounted toward a temple perched on some high rocks
and broke the door down till the walls thundered and groaned,
and as I groped in darkness my hands fell with greed
on a new god who wore this iron thrust through his belt,
and then I heard the almighty one sob chokingly.
But my heart, overbrimmed with tears of men and gods,
no longer feared what secret cries might come from darkness,
and I flung out my hand unfearing, ripped the belt,
and thus the god's sword passed into my mortal hands."
The proud thief spoke no more, but in the flaming blaze
he grasped the bronzesmith by his lion's mane and showed,
upon the sword's black hilt engraved, the new god's sign:
a cross with grasping hooks that whirled like a swift wheel.
The bronzesmith's chest became a bellows, and he roared:
"Oho! What shame to live like moles, far from the light!"
He spoke, dashed down his leathern apron to the ground,
then thrashed about with open arms as though he choked.
Odysseus smiled, contented, for his iron hooks
had caught this mullet's entrails and could not be snapped;
with joy he crossed the door and soon was swallowed up in darkness.

After three days, he sought to hunt some other soul,
and found broad-buttocked Kentaur rolling in the street.
Returning from the beach at break of day, he saw
sprawled in the middle of the road a monstrous beast
whose hairy chest dripped with a mess of wine and food,
whose belly in the dawn's light shone like a holm oak.
When glutton saw his master mounting up the slope,
he did not rise, but rolled aside to clear the road,
and then Odysseus kicked the drunken pig with scorn:
"I like this mountain of fat meat your soul lugs round
like a gold scarab rolling its black ball of dung!
What shame to eat and drink but be unsaved and useless!
Both bread and wine are good, abundant meat is good,
when in your guts they turn not into dung, but spirit."
Broad-buttocks thundered like a cave till the streets shook:
"They've named me Kentaur well, for in my greasy loins
I feel two monstrous rivers clash, then swirl and roar;
the one's called God, the other Beast, and I dead center."
The unsated fisher laughed, then threw his sharp harpoon:
"Follow me then, broad beast, come board my feathery craft for ballast!"

Somewhere it flashed and thundered, somewhere the hail fell!
No lightning flashed, no thunder roared, no hard hail fell,
but in a distant cave four dragons ate and drank!
Bakers brought loaves of wheat bread, slaves brought skins of wine,
shepherds at dawn brought fat lambs slung across their backs
and still the dragons feasted till frontiers of heaven
and earth swayed wildly and all life like sea-flies swooped
amid their wine-drenched beards and salty long mustaches.
The more they drank the more they splashed in seas that part
men from their wives, till from great longing their eyes glazed
as distant countries rose on waves to lure them on.
How many vessels sail the seas, how many arrows,
how much rich merchandise lies in the hold supine—
souls, bodies, wines—and the swift wind commands the helm!
Laughter and shouting, sailors munch, and shores appear:
"A thousand welcome, lads, with your good merchandise!"
The harbors smell of pitch, the hoarse-voiced port-girls laugh,
night sprawls with open thighs, and the lighthouses blaze.
"That's not a crimson apple, boys, it's a bright castle!"
Bound and unmoving on the beach, with drunken ears
brimming with sound, eyes filled with tears, the dragon pairs
went wandering off in fantasy to foreign shores
and groaned against each other like four dreaming triremes.
One day a flying fish leapt to a man's height,
and Kentaur, jealous of the fish's yearning, sighed:
"Master, I've but one word to say, don't get me wrong:
Ahoy! It's time our hearts leapt high like flying fish!
I still recall those words you cast in the street once:
'Both food and wine are good if they're transformed to travel!' "
Then the much-traveled man laughed long and teased his friend:
"How would your dull brain know I'm in full sail already?
Deep in the hold you lie like ballast, a dog on dung;
wine spins your head until you only dream of land!"
Then Captain Clam grabbed at his seaweed beard and said:
"Aye, by the sea! we've set full sail in our minds only;
I say it's time we built our ship's keel high on rocks
for I'm the kind who likes to grasp his dream like flesh."
In Hardihood's beclouded eyes mute fires burned,
the beach became a bronzesmith's shop, and the rocks sparked.
Cunning Odysseus raised his heavy hands on high:
"Free souls, agreed! I've waited only for you to speak.
Let's sacrifice a three-combed cock to bless our keel,
then drench our trees with wine before we cut them down
that the wood-demons with branch beards may harm us not.
Up, lads, the mind of seven-souled mankind will help us now!"

At the new moon, all four began to build their keel;
they cut down pine and oak, then matched and trimmed the planks
and on the beach lit blazing bonfires row on row.
They worked with all their strength, but when the sun would set
they'd fall on food and drink and thus carouse all night.
The piper watched, on tenterhooks, a short ways off;
his heart would yell "Ahoy!" his timid mind, "Draw back!"
till he could bear the smell of spitted meat no longer.
The hungry beggar opened his lean shanks and perched
on a high rock like a reed-slender stork, then stooped
to spy with his cross-eyes on the carousers' cave,
but when Odysseus saw him with swift eyes, he yelled:
"Hey, welcome to the mermaid-taken fool, the screw-loose!
All hail to the fool's cap of God with dirty tassel!"
But still the bony body quaked and feared to approach:
"Master, I'm scared, and bring to mind the fox's story:
many the beasts he saw go in the lion's den alive . . ."
But all at once his speech stopped short, his cross-eyes saw
on sand the glutton's naked bellies three floors high.
Stretching his bony hands, the coward steeled his heart,
leapt down amid the savage pack and stuttered out:
"Hullo, you forty-footer! My poor heart's grown lean
to watch the turning spit night after day from far!
I've come now with my songs to give it an extra twirl!"
Odysseus lightly laughed, fearing to scare the fool:
"They say that when the cricket's gone, the grapes won't ripen,
and that the roast without a song will lose its flavor;
sit down to eat and drink, cross-eyes, give your heart strength."
He ate and drank to bursting, till his veins swelled up
and his dream-taken brainpan spilled with whistling winds
so that he seized his flute and struck a lively tune.
And thus with banqueting and work, with planks and dream,
the ship's hull slowly rose upon the finished frame,
and many-willed Odysseus marveled at man's strength:
man sighs on earth while his desires fly above him
like nymphs with kerchiefs woven of the finest air,
and when he grabs one, she turns flesh, follows him home,
his wife and sweet companion, mother of many children;
sighs turn to splendid sons, and drunkenness to ears of corn.

At length the burning summer passed, the leaves caught fire,
the last grape-clusters in the vineyards hung and swayed,
night-birds cried out for dryness, cuckoo-birds for rain,
cranes flapped their slender wings and danced upon the wind,
and all migrating birds assembled in the trees,
fluttering and balancing their wings, swelling their throats,

and felt the sky to be an endless road, and trembled.
Down in the cave at dusk the master's voice rang out:
"We have worked well again today, my friends, and now
it's time to quit, for we are free to play awhile;
kisses and wine belong by right to the hard worker."
They all lay down to supper, and the piper played
softly until the minds of his companions swayed
with dizzy catches, songs resung, and short sweet tunes.
One day, as she scooped sea salt out of coastal pits,
a young girl had strayed far from her stern mother's eyes,
and Kentaur saw her, grabbed her like a frightened doe
and gave her, singing, to his comrades' hairy arms:
"Give me, dear God, but brains enough to eat and drink,
to spend my whole life nibbling at all lovely maids!"
The girl cried out demurely, but in time got used
to their wine-smelling breaths and skilled, caressing hands.
Time and again at midnight they would disappear,
don bullhides, paint themselves like gods, then hug the walls
and poke themselves into the homes of mortal men.
They'd find the lonely widows, girls in their first sleep,
lower their voices, flap their wings and spread their pelts,
pretending to be gods who deigned descend to earth
and plant immortal children deep in thankful mortal wombs.

Thus did the days roll by in work, the nights in play.
A rumor spread from town to town that demons lashed
their king who all night long danced naked in the moon,
assumed a thousand dragon shapes, turned to a ghoul
and ravaged lambs, or fell on babes and ate them whole,
or laughed with sirens by the shore, changed to a sprite.
"Witches with your strong brews, your spells, your charms, your arts,
come heal our pain, enchant that choking dog, alas,
that leaps on all our flocks! Bind him with cricks and cramps!"
Thus did the shepherds cry, and brought the witches herbs,
thus did the landlords cry, and brought the witches bread,
thus did the women cry and beat their plundered breasts.
And then one crystal moonlit night the witches left,
taking their charms and sorceries and their salty buns,
taking a small dwarf made of wood, dipped in strong spells,
dressed in full royal garb, with peaked sea-demon's cap
and a sharp, thickset, poisonous knife thrust in his heart.
Grasping their charms, they wakened gnomes and star-struck ghosts,
lamias and leprous Nereids from the frothy waves,
till triple-eyed and one-eyed dragons trod the sands
and the whole seashore roared with drums and spooky laughter.
Naked, with streaming hair, the witches danced and poked

small nails into the dwarf and mumbled magic spells:
"As sways the sea so may your guts sway night and day,
as throb the hearts of frightened birds, so throb your heart;
feel in your flesh these nails we thrust in this wood now!"
They groaned, then threw the dwarf far out at sea, and stoned it.
Next day when the drunk dragons saw the bobbing dwarf
sail on its back on foaming waves, its hands crisscrossed,
the piper swam out, grabbed it, brought it to his master
who read the magic signs at once and burst in laughter:
"It seems this sea-dwarf looks a bit like me, my lads,
but I'm no easy prey for spells, I come of dragon root,
and I shall sprout a wing for every hammered nail!"
He spoke, then threw it in the embers for a bit of kindling.

One day a slender stranger passed as they sat eating,
and his proud eagle glance was glazed with savage grief.
He stopped as though, if they should give him wine and meat,
he might consent to join them, like a gracious king.
Odysseus joyed to feel the man's nobility:
"Sit down, and welcome, stranger, drink some wine with us.
If, as they say, the soul shows through the flesh's garb,
I see a great and saddened eagle perched on crags."
The regal-looking man with his clean glance replied:
"I know that the great mouth of the world-wanderer speaks
and what a shame it is to hide before his gaze.
They call me Granite, and I come from a great mountain.
A mighty lord's white tower shines between two peaks
and there the ancient chief gave up his soul on earth
and left behind two sons and a young, lovely maid.
The brains of the youths blazed, their eyes were whipped with blood,
both burned for the maid's body and grew pale as almonds.
They met on a high threshing floor, unsheathed their knives,
and in the center placed the maid dressed like a bride.
The bearded son there killed the fledgling, and the bride
flung herself on the slayer's knees and cried with joy:
'It's you I've always longed for, take me in my first flower!'
But he, instead of looting her cool flesh and lips,
strode past the bloody threshing floor, rushed to the shore,
and in the sea washed and rewashed and scrubbed the blood
until the whole shore reddened; then he sailed away,
and now see where he lies before your feet, Odysseus."
The suffering man flung out his hands to the four winds:
"A woman's body is a dark and monstrous mystery;
between her supple thighs a heavy whirlpool swirls,
two rivers crash, and woe to him who slips and falls!"
He spoke, then filled the tall newcomer's cup with wine:

"A thousand welcomes, Granite, a thousand and two thousand!"
As the new friend threw back his throat to quench his thirst
he saw the sun sail in his goblet like a ship,
he saw long voyages and rivers, cares and castles,
he even saw brave Granite sailing in the purple wine.

Thus hands were multiplied until the tall ship swayed
as though it were the South Wind's sandal flung on sand,
until the proud stern crowed, the prow raised its head high
and all the master-dragons measured and built with speed.
Rains pelted down, clouds laughed in the clear sky once more,
the winter's sun shone gently on a sleeping world,
old crones bent down from hedge to hedge to gather snails,
girls picked the best remaining olives from the trees,
and still the dragons worked with hammer, wood, and brain.
Alas, how swift time flies, how quickly earth's wheel turns
when hands and brain set out to build a mighty work!
The whole world drowned, the cuckoo chirped in olive trees,
black earth once more turned green, the ilex sprouts turned red,
and swallows soon returned in South Wind's warming hands.
On distant foreign shores, abandoned mothers heard
that their seducer walked his native land once more
and brought great wealth to raise whole flocks of sons and daughters.
From all sides, sailing in swift ships, his bastards came:
all those he'd sown full measure on his fruitful trips,
for always in his tent at night, stretched out on pelts,
he liked to sport with women when he came from battle;
or when he anchored as a merchant on strange shores
he liked to spread on sand seductive merchandise
and watch the savage maids run down from mountain slopes
with hides of wild beasts, wares of brass, and brawny ox,
and come down trembling to the sands to give and take.
The crafty man would choose the loveliest girl and meet
amid the osiers, in cool caves, or the ship's deep hold.
What joy to hear a girl cry out in the dark night
like a rich plundered town when it unbolts its gates
till in the hush its windows, doors and streets resound.
Now like a lord's rich harvest, he received his bastards:
the down had spread already on the young men's cheeks,
the girls' small breasts had grown to be as hard as walnuts.
Sometimes their eyes, like emeralds, flashed with greenest light,
blue like the sea sometimes, or pitch-black like his own,
and in their eyes and features, tender tone of voice,
the woman-chaser struggled to recall each mother.
He welcomed all, shared out his sons throughout his land
and made them foremen, plowmen, shepherds, fishermen,

and placed his daughters with his cellar's busy looms.
As they were shared and scattered, their sly father smiled:
"If they're not pleased with their day's wages, let them sail,
and let them, like their father, take the road of exile;
if they adapt themselves, then may their toil be blessed,
and may they plant strong sons to cast deep roots in earth."
One evening on the beach when the friends stopped their work
and turned the spit or dragged the wineskins from the shade,
a blond-haired girl came slowly and stood before their cave.
The archer turned, then paled to see her sapphire eyes,
and knew at once Calypso's godly form and sea-blue gaze.
Startled, he stroked her soft wheat-golden locks, and spoke:
"From what high, holy summit have you come, my child?"
She looked serenely in her father's eyes, and said:
"If you are truly the much-wandering, racked Odysseus,
I kiss, my father, your renowned and sated knees;
a blond-haired goddess gave me birth in a deep cave."
His flaming hands reached out and seized the firm-shaped girl,
devoured with greed, caressed with love her tender flesh,
and like a heavy beast that licks its cub, he lowed,
till tickled by his thorny beard, the maiden laughed.
He ached, and laid his much-loved booty on the sand,
but hid his features in his hands and softly wept.
O azure shores, gorged honeycombs, thick cloying hours,
crystal unsleeping bosom with your double guardians,
stars that rolled down and twined themselves in golden locks,
and the warm night that smelled of woman's thick-haired armpits!
What joy to anchor in the deathless deeps of myth
until both time and place roll on like twin slow streams
and Death comes in the likeness of an ancient blackbird
and dips his beak and cools himself in the calm current.
The North Wind blew, and memories fell like almond flowers
before fruit comes, and whitened all the archer's hair
as round him his untroubled comrades feasted well
and listened to their master's heavy sighs that mingled
with the erotic lamentation of the blue-eyed sea.

The future hour lies shut like an unopened rose,
and while departure's arrow on the shore was aimed,
the son was plotting the destruction of his father;
both precious souls thus tilted on the scales of fate.
Telemachus would leave the side door open at night
through which the armless leader slipped for secret talks;
prudent Penelope in silence felt the noose
grow tighter round her husband's neck, but locked her mouth,
for her most faithful heart was scorched by myriad bastards

who trooped in long rows from the shore and filled her home.
Carousing all night long upon the beach with tramps,
he shamed his son and house and all his noble stock:
"If only he still roamed on distant shores and longed
to see smoke rising from his roof, but found his hands
unworthy still, O Gods, to touch his native land!"
O heavy-fated wife, such were your sad complaints
as in the night, alone, you tore your hair in silence.
The trickster felt the sting and guessed what treacherous nets
his son was spreading round his feet to trip him up,
but his resplendent head reared with unfearing scorn:
"Dear Gods, I'm sorry for my wretched, well-bred son;
he stoops to drink but shies at shadows, eats and quakes,
falls on his bed to sleep, but nightmares crush him flat.
Sleep or awake, I crowd him thickly round and choke him!
Be patient! On that night when I shall lock you fast
within your nuptial chamber that our race may flourish,
I shall unfurl my sails to windward, grasp a stone,
and chortling on the deck, throw it across my shoulder.
Exile's my country, and my son but froth on foaming sea."

When summer came, the mistrals fell upon the land
and all the wide sea smelled like a fresh fruit broke open.
The great grain-grinding then began for the son's wedding
to bake the five-rayed ring-cakes in the bustling palace;
nine women, but once married, sewed new mattresses,
for the red sail had now been seen far out at sea.
Felicitating sentries ran from the cape in joy
and spread the happy news from village house to house;
windows and doors opened and shut, stairs groaned and creaked,
red quilts were hung down from the roofs, rugs were unrolled,
mules bore huge loads of berried laurel and myrtle boughs,
and the steep palace road was strewn with fragrant leaves.
Craftsmen untied their aprons and shut up their shops,
town elders with their clean white linen and tall staffs
descended to the beach in haste to greet the bride;
the face of each man glowed as though he were the groom.
Then the gates opened, father and proud son appeared,
and people, turning, saw two lions descend in haste
and tread on stones that rumbled down and swept the road.
The crowd made way with fear, and when Odysseus stood
alone, apart, an empty ring spread round about him.
But he, his eyes on the red sail, smiled secretly,
for there, fast in her scaffold locked, far up the beach,
his new-built vessel creaked and longed to sail—so might
his soul one day flee scaffolds of wife, son, and country!

Standing erect, he glued his eyes on the bride's ship
to lure it swiftly, that his bitterness might end.
Telemachus walked with joy and hailed the ancient archons,
then turned, smiled on the workers, and all the girls caught fire
and longed in secret to embrace his noble form.
The bridal ship now hugged the shore in twists and turns
and sought the help of every wind to make the port.
Crowded about the gunwale's rim, shining like doves,
the well-born foreign ladies-in-waiting hailed the town;
then red sails fell down fluttering like a woman's veil
and all the ladies prinked and pranked, swaggered and swayed,
and when they leapt to earth, the harbor towers glowed.
The standard-bearer raised on high the bridal banner:
a long oar twined with pure white roses, on whose tip
the still unbitten virgin's apple flamed and flashed.
Behind the maidens came the bride's old trusted lords
with their tall, gold-tipped staffs and their long, flowing beards,
and in their midst the Cretan minstrel loomed and glowed.
When he was young he'd slaked himself with spoils and wars,
but now in his old age's honeyed afterglow
he held his bell-hung lyre and sang his joys and toils.
To him her father had entrusted the young bride,
to stand beside her and console her in dark exile;
his head was a rich vessel filled with many toys,
with shoals of sirens, riddles, prophecies and songs
with which to cheer the darling daughter wed afar
until she swelled with child and could forget her country.
Like a deep river, slaves behind them dragged the dowry:
unliftable brass kettles, gold cloaks, amber beads,
and seven peacocks strutting like coquetting dames.
Suddenly in the prow the bride blazed like a candle,
trembling and throwing timid looks on her new land;
and standing on the beach, the bridegroom shook with longing
to see what godly shape he'd hold that night in darkness,
then felt ashamed and turned his glowing eyes to the ground.
When worldly-wise Odysseus saw the trembling bride
treading with slow and timid steps upon his land,
his heart, like that of a good man's, was moved with joy,
for he remembered with what ache in his green youth
he'd stroked and touched for the first time a maid in darkness.
He pitied youth and felt the unspeakable deep grief
of maids, and like a god spread out his hands and blessed them:
"It's time that love and tranquil peace should rule on earth.
The greatest dowries are the sun, rain, trees, and soil;
now let the loving pair play a brief hour on earth."
The bride stepped lightly on the ground, and all the world

was dazed, for on her breast she wore the sun and moon,
her lips smiled like the dawn, her eyes were peaceful ports.
Kneeling, she kissed the knees of her father-in-law, then glanced
at her groom shyly, but quickly lowered her eyes in shame
for her heart throbbed to glimpse his bearing, his slim form.
The bridal pomp passed on, all streets spread wide in welcome,
and two young sailors, crowned with flowing seaweed wreaths,
drew breath and blew their conches till the whole town shook.
High up on festive roofs a shower of women yelled,
seashells and magic charms gleamed in their tinkling hair,
and when the bride passed by, rained her with grain and flowers.
Girls hung from the high terraces and shrilly sang:
"Like the green vine that climbs a tree and takes firm root,
so may the bride spread roots about the bridegroom's thighs!"
Below, old crones winked at the bride and screamed with laughter:
"Red pomegranates hang from the groom's savage belt
and in the center hangs, shy bride, his cool grape-cluster!"
Then when the pomp had reached the lion-guarded gate,
a rose-cheeked boy of living parents slowly paced
and gave the bashful couple gifts of nuts and honey.
The bride then fed the bridegroom, and the youth his mate,
that both might pass the dreadful sill with sweetened breath.
She dipped her finger in the honey, leant by the door,
and on its upper panel drew a crescent moon;
the youth unsheathed his sword and with untrembling stroke
and deep desire carved on the door a large round sun.
The bronze gates of the castle opened, and the world-sung
form of her mother-in-law appeared with open arms:
"My bride, my noble bride, welcome a thousand times
with wedding wreath around your head, sons in your womb;
our house shall ring again with children's laughter soon."
The virgin knelt with awe to kiss the careworn knees
and the pale hands devoured by looms and scorched by pain,
and when her mother-in-law had kissed her on both cheeks
they raised their right feet high and crossed the sill together.
Odysseus watched his son who now with a strange girl
broke down his savage door, possessed his spacious courts
and occupied with firm tread all his floors and vaults.
His father's home was being uprooted from his heart,
his land was being uprooted, and the bitter sea
flooded his rooted feet and crumbled them away.
The bride within the courtyard, meanwhile, stooped above
the sonorous household well and bowed with reverence thrice.
Bending with fear, she watched her face sail on the water,
then thrice called to the household guardian spirit, and said:
"I bow down low and greet you, grandsire! Good health and joy!"

The grandfather's groan and the well's rumbling sound were heard
so that the bride rejoiced and rose with cool, quenched throat
because the guardian ghost coursed through her bones like water.
A mother, whose twelve sons were still untouched by death,
from her breast gave the bride a flaming pomegranate
and she flung it against the tiles with all her strength
so that its rubies in the sunlight danced and glowed
and all the bridesmaids raised their arms and cried with joy:
"May your womb soon become a swelling pomegranate
to burst and fill these spacious courts with sons and daughters!"
They threw grain in her lap and she clucked at her hens,
greeted the oxen and the horses in their stalls
and fed the dogs who licked her hands of honey-bread.
She passed the inner door with awe to the men's quarter
and by the smoked hearth where two logs of fir and oak
burned slowly, opened her arms wide and bowed with awe:
"O Fire, great household spirit, mistress of the world,
who sit in vigil by the hearthstones all night long,
I bend and bow low to your grace, O grieved grandmother."
Then in the hearth she cast large stacks of laurel leaves
till flames between the oak and fir logs leapt and crackled
and Grandma Fire laughed with pride as though she bounced
a babe already on her knees and the house had filled
with infant laughter, lullabies, and bonnet bells.
The shy bride crimsoned, then sat down next to the hearth
and like a mistress clapped her hands and gave her orders.
Servants and slaves assembled, nurses and mammies swarmed,
and to these good souls she threw armfuls of fine gifts,
brooches, embroidered kerchiefs, earrings, and bronze bracelets,
and all stooped low and kissed her knees and stretched their arms:
"May you stand upright in your husband's courtyard, Lady,
like a tall cypress tree, or plunge roots like an oak,
or like an apple tree bear flower and fruit, and drop
one daughter and eleven sons round you like apples."
When she had finished with her wedding salutations,
she raised a jug and slowly went to the deep well
to fetch some speechless water for her bridal bath that evening.

Night, woman of easy virtue with her many beads,
walked with slow strutting steps, passed through the palace courts
where the king's wedding guests had come in his son's honor.
The lords and the great chieftains sat on stools apart,
the poor and all their kind lay on the ground apart,
and in a place apart the fresh pair shone like stars.
The youth felt secretly aroused in the warm night,
his strength swelled like a tree with bursting buds and flowers,

and the bride acted like a bride and veiled her eyes,
but in the shade her heart leapt like a frightened hare.
Odysseus, standing, watched his son and lords with stealth,
caught the sly looks between them, saw their armored belts,
and heard from dimlit corners choked and breathless whispers;
he felt their cunning in his heart, suspected all,
for treachery in his courts like snakes uncoiled and crawled.
His five boon brothers mingled with the wedding guests,
followed his cares and watched him, waiting for a sign,
and he rejoiced to feel roads spread in him once more,
though he was late in choosing, since all roads seemed good.
But suddenly when he saw the ancient Cretan bard
rise in the night, his heart throbbed, for the minstrel held
pressed tightly to his chest, as though he battled with it,
a lyre made of two curved bull-horns hung with bells.
Bronze dog-faced demons, golden gods, and echoing shells
glittered around it like clusters of ripe grapes, and tinkled.
The small eyes of the minstrel gleamed like a wild beast's,
and as the flames' reflection flickered round his body
and the resounding lyre's horns flashed on his shoulders
he reared like a tall bull-god amid the feasting boards.
His eyes flashed, and his voice burst like a battlecry:
"The world throws stones at the fruit-bearing giant tree,
and I shall cast a word, O king, at your high peak!
Good is your lean and meager coast with its cheap gods,
with all its sluggish windmills and its wretched lords,
and with its fertile gossip by each door at dusk.
I've wandered all the world, no narrow street can hold me,
I've circled round all apple trees, I've eaten their fruit,
sweet taste within the throat, most bitter in the mind,
and my eyes brimmed with gods, grew weary of all men
till horses with red wings swooped down and swept me off
past every boundary till we stopped at Lord Death's door.
Then Death and I went trotting with our gallant steeds—
all things were ours, and we admired the unnumbered flocks,
and passed through villages and towns, counting each man,
counting the great gods in the sky, the spirits of air,
just as the shepherd every morning counts his flock."
But the impatient king broke in upon the songster:
"I also have roamed foreign shores, fought gods and men,
I've even mounted, it seems to me, your crimson steeds.
Now, by the sword I wear, I too concede no boundaries!"
The old bard turned his head and spoke with bitterness:
"The world is wider than Calypso's cave, Odysseus,
and deeper than black Circe's dense and curly pit.
Athena's helmet, boys, has now been smashed to bits

nor can it ever again contain the whole world's head.
All the strong gods you met on your slight voyages
are smoke that rises from a lord's contented roof
or the long shadow of a startled slave at nightfall.
I know a living land whose entrails are still burning,
where still the bull-sun mounts her like a cow each dawn;
her god is well knit, formed of sturdy flesh and bone
and stands guard at his boundaries with black, iron swords.
He hungers, and when meat is scarce, invents new wars
and beats on iron pans to marshal all his tribes;
he feeds his buffaloes and stallions all alone,
and all alone smears his pronged arrowheads with poison,
and by himself keeps sentry duty all night long.
He's not a god to place his trust in rotting man;
he knows men well, they can't hold out, they fret and fall.
Like soldiers, maids and youths stand by their tents in fear
as he inspects them like a general every dawn,
prodding them silently in shoulders, knees, and loins,
and when he finds one profitless for war or plow,
with his mute sword he slits that useless throat at once;
hold your mind high, O king, this cruel god suits you well!
Forgive me, friends; heavy's the speech I've flung tonight;
my lips had longed to deck you with gay wedding songs,
to wish this loving couple life and ripe old age
that in their hands life's withered branch might bloom and bear,
but suddenly on the threshold bent, ablaze with light,
I saw the still unsated bow of cruelty aimed!
Aye, hunter, do not waste your time on scraggly birds
but keep your spirit unspent for great Necessity!"
He spoke, and when he set his heavy lyre down,
a bellowing rose as though a bull had crashed on tiles.
The pale king leant against the doorjamb, lest he fall,
and felt ashamed before the bard, for the world swelled,
and in the dark his wild brows creaked and grew immense.
The son discerned his father's dizziness, leapt up
and slid along the porch to buckle on his sword;
the armless man rose, too, and in the flame-lit courts
began to rouse up secretly the drunken workmen.
But the man-slayer guessed the plot, shook off his swoon
and dashed to the men's quarter where his son was arming,
then doubled up his fists, held back his wrath, nor seized
the columns there to shake the palace to its roots.
"Son of Penelope!" he cried, but his voice choked.
His son stood still at once, and his chin shook with fear.
"Lay down your futile arms, turn back and take your bride,
it's time you climbed the nuptial couch and slept embraced;

I should not like to stain your marriage wreaths with blood."
His son frowned wrathfully, then tensed his knees and yelled:
"I won't live in your shade—do you hear?—to rot and wither!"
The startled father seized his angry son with joy:
"My son, flare up again that I may see you well!
In our black parting now, this is my greatest joy:
your eyebrows flame with rage, your flesh is still my flesh!"
The son then looked unfearing in his father's eyes:
how they flashed fire and laughter! deep in their irises
he saw a rearing lion that licked its whelp with love.
His mind's foundations shook; for the first time his heart
leapt up before this man to acknowledge him as father,
but he restrained his joy nor reached a hand to touch him.
Odysseus placed both hands on his son's shoulder blades:
"Forward, my son; this is a good time for us to part.
At daybreak I'll set sail and leave my native land;
take all my island with its flocks of sheep and men,
it's yours, and wear it in your hair, a crown of stone.
I'd like to leave you now a final testament,
but, by my soul, I can't find what fine words to say!
What should I wish you? That you stifle here on stone
and gaze with longing on far waves while your heart burns,
or that you plant roots here thrice-deep and never move?
What shame to give you blessing now or sound advice!
Let your soul fly with freedom, and let come what may!"
He spoke no more, and in his fists, as in farewell,
clasped tight his deeply moved son firmly by the arm.
But all at once the archer's mocking laughter broke:
"It seems I'll never look on your face again, my son;
now see if you can't spread your hands to blot me out,
an ancient debt all sons discharge to ease their hearts."
He spoke, then from the wall took down his heavy bow
for he already had set sail on his new voyage.
His son returned to the courts and said good night with grace
to gentry and lowborn to end the wedding feast,
and then approached and touched his wife's sun-lily hand
and helped her tenderly to mount the holy stairs.
But when they reached their bridal-decked and fertile bed
they found three wreaths that glowed in the lamp's light: the first
was woven of thorns, the second of myrtles, the third of roses,
and then the groom put out the lamp, to spare his bride.
While the wide courtyards emptied and the torches smoked
in their bronze heavy holders, and over the silent palace
the heavens streamed with stars and filled with sudden sparks,
the five rogues prowled about the palace to find out
what halls led to the armory or to deep wine cellars.

Odysseus took them to his castle's secret rooms:
"Fill your sacks full with flour and wine, plunder my weapons,
grab what we need, better or worse, for a long voyage."
He spoke, and cast his eyes round his own house to rob it.
When at long last the plundering ceased, he gave commands:
"Before day breaks, let's place our ship on rollers, lads,
uproot our country from our hearts, and say farewell;
let those who can, throw her behind them like a stone,
let those who can't, hang her about them like a charm;
at dawn we sail for the last voyage of no return."
He spoke, then all, weighed down with skins of flour and wine,
with rich wares from the cellars and bronze-plated arms,
slunk stealthily out in silence past the palace gates
and in dark midnight took the steep descent to their new ship.

Unmoved, Odysseus mounted to his lofty bed
and for the last time lay beside his luckless wife.
A sweet and satisfying sleep relaxed his brain,
but just before cock crow his crimson rooster leapt
and shrilled in the large courtyard by the well's dark rim.
The archer heard in sleep his glad three-crested cock,
dashed to his feet and buckled on his iron sword,
then hung his twisted hornbow down his sunburnt back
and drew the door bolt softly, not to wake his wife.
But she had lain all night unsleeping, with closed eyes,
her mute, incurably pale lips drawn tight with pain,
and when the bronze bolt creaked, she slightly raised her lids
and saw in dawn's dim light her husband stealing off.
She did not move nor fall on his stern knees to weep,
for the grieved woman knew the time for hope had passed,
yet when she heard the creaking stairs, she rose and rushed
in time to see her husband in the azure moon
treading on tiptoe through the court, and like a thief
grasp and slide back with stealth the outer gate's bronze bolt,
and, without looking back, stride swiftly past the sill;
then the poor woman tore her hair and shrieked with grief.
But the lone wanderer of rough roads opened his arms,
drank deep to his parched entrails the cool morning breeze
and lunged down the path swiftly to the shadowy shore.
His dragon crew were hard at work, pushing with pride
their new ship slowly down the heating logs with care
while the scared piper drenched them to prohibit fire.
Just as they braced their shoulders for the final heave,
their captain rushed in time to join them, spread his hands,
shoved hard, pushed off the virgin keel into the waves
and from his isle's belovèd body thus cut the navel cord.

In the dull, somber, morning air, as the earth steamed,
Granite appeared on the steep sheepfold's winding path,
dragging a huge white ram behind him that the crew
might eat, drink, and take heart in their departure's hour.
The archer laughed and grinned from ear to ear, then rose,
rolled up his sleeves and lit a fire, then slew the ram
and hung the hairy head with its curved, twisted horns
high on the topmost mast to serve for luck and lookout.
At last when the meat reddened on the spit and gleamed,
they washed their hands in the salt sea, stretched on the sand,
and glutton spoke as the fat grease dripped down his neck:
"Brothers, I'm seized with heartfelt pity, so hear me out:
whatever man won't eat—dung, bone, meat-smoke, and hair—
let's throw to the great gods for alms, who faint with hunger!"
The dragons laughed till their necks swelled, then called the gods
to stand about their feast like dogs and lick the bones;
but their dark master rose, his fists weighed down and sagging
with the great ram's soft brains and fertile testicles;
with throbbing heart he plunged his gaze deep in the earth
then cried out till his dread grandfather stirred in his guts:
"Potent forefather, come alive once more, rise up and eat!"

III

God sent a gentle shower on earth to cool with balm
the hairy fists that pulled at oars in the open sea.
All kept their silent faces turned toward their loved island;
fragrance of wild thyme drifted down the mountain slopes,
odor of vines and ripening grain, and smothered their minds;
the mountain partridges came down to drink, and all
the glimmering valley glades soon rang with their harsh cackling.
Amid the hazy light of dawn, its feet wrapped up in mist,
their sacred island softly smiled, a babe awakening.
Perched on the mountain slopes, the hamlets gleamed with light,
bells softly sang like birds or cool cascading waters,
and suddenly unrestrained, with patient threnody,
as though the whole earth sighed, a cow's deep lowing rang.
A smooth land breeze blew softly, and the mainsail flapped
until the pointed ship leapt like a huge dolphin
with two enormous eyes that stared from the wet prow,
and the azure-painted tail rose proudly over the billows.
But when the cape was finally rounded, the sweet sounds
of women singing rang like bells from rose-lit caves;
they sang, and all the seashore wailed like widowed maids
swept up by saddening memories as they watched the waves.
Then Captain Clam shaded his eyes with his rough hands
and gazed with dancing heart far out upon the crags.
Once in his youth at sea he'd heard a tune like this
when he was bringing home his bride for the first time.
God laughed then over the waves, and all the pebbles laughed,
the sails swelled like the groom's own heart, and the new bride
beside the festooned prow sang gentle lullabies
to greet her husband's native land that loomed so strangely.
Then Captain Clam, the new-wed groom, twirled his mustache:
"Ahoy, blow wind, churn up the sea, and make for port! . . .
Ah, to come home again, dear God, and bolt the door!"
But when he heard the same sweet tune, his wits spun round.
And when a shepherdess hailed Kentaur from her sheepfold,
his ever-willing phallus woke, and he, perplexed,
wished both to make for land and yet play deaf and dumb

for sweeter, younger cowgirls found on foreign shores.
But Hardihood saw flames, and Granite, unicorns,
and the dream-taken piper heard his native land
that whimpered like a woman on the sands abandoned,
stoning the veering waves with bitter lamentation.
Drawing his pipe, he played a sprightly dancing tune,
blew hard and puffed away his sun-drenched native land
as though it were a tallow-faced and cobwebbed ghost.
Steering his rudder far from land, without a word,
Odysseus wound his island slowly about his brain,
uprooting houses, mountains, sheepfolds, harbors, trees,
till all rolled tumbling down the funnel of his mind
as memory tore them up and swallowed his whole island.
But when his shore and native land fled from his eyes,
his heart contracted and a bitter sorrow crushed him:
"Comrades, our eyes shall never look on her again!
She was a small, small bird that passed, a toy that broke,
a sprig of curly basil fallen from over our ears."
Hardihood scowled with wrath—he'd have no truck with such
unmanly caresses in the hour of separation,
but he recalled wide rivers with their shoals of fish,
the hamlets hushed on slopes with snow as huge as rocks,
the strapping lads that steamed like stallions in hoarfrost,
the blond and manly women with their sturdy hips,
and that mist-laden morning when he'd chosen to leave.
He'd wrapped his calves in sheepskins tightly, strapped his feet
with roughhewn snowshoes like round leathern pans,
slung his sack down his back, his hatchet in his belt,
and on!—without one glance at children, dog, or country;
if his heart then was heavy, other cares had crushed it.
The comrades rowed in silence till the sun awoke,
shone on their backs and thighs, dripped down their glistening beards,
until the voice of the deep-sighted man rang out:
"Hey there, you piebald ship's bird, clutch the heaving prow,
scatter the heavy fog that threatens to drown our ship,
swell up your supple throat with song and wring your brains,
sing lively and transform our pain to nightingales!"
The siren-taken songster crouched near the prow in sweat,
wrung his unripe resounding brain with labor-pains
and struggled till his neck veins burst, like a thawed snake
that writhes amid dry thorns to shed its withered skin.
Then Kentaur laughed until the whole ship shook, and yelled:
"Hold tight, you pregnant bitch, give us no stillborn freak!"
The piper sighed, then wedged his flute between his lips,
trilled twice or thrice in air, summoned his wandering mind
till his small cross-eyes were with distant rapture glazed.

His hollow chest flapped like a vessel's windless sails,
then he leapt up, his brains puffed, his chest heaved and swelled,
and God! his thin voice broke out suddenly in a roaring gale!

"Go to it, piper, snatch your tune, kick it about,"
he sang, "strike sparks on the hard ground till rocks fling fire,
shut your poor squint-eyes tight and sing all that you see!
Empty are land and sea and crystal clear the air
that neither smoke of chimney dulls nor man's breath sways;
nor has the mind appeared as yet to send it tempest-tossed.
Like two twin, groping moles, my eyes dug deep in earth
and to their sockets in the dead of night returned:
'Master, the world is waste, not a soul or worm's abroad.'
But from my heart I heard a murmuring in the grass
and two small palpitating hearts dared answer me,
ah, two green worms poked through the crust of the upper world!
My heart cried out and fluttered, then sank low to earth
and joined the crawling friends that we might trudge together.
In waste, in desolate waste, even a worm's shade is good.
I walked the river bank in stealth, crept in the weeds,
my eyes and ears perked up with awe, my nostrils flared:
these were not worms, dear friends! I knelt and bowed down low,
much-suffering Lord and Mother, forebears of all mankind!
When day appeared, the worms stood in the sun for warmth,
but God discerned them from on high and his eyes flashed:
'I see two worms! Who cast them in my fruitful vineyards?
Rise out of snow, O frigid Frost, freeze them to ice!'
Then Frost fell silently on earth in soft snowfalls,
unwound a thick white shroud and pallid dead man's sheet,
then grasped and smothered the high peaks and swept the fields.
The poor worms shook with fear and crawled in a deep cave,
and when he saw his small wife weep, the male worm said:
'I will not let the snow take you from me, beloved.
Lean on me, dear, and press your body to my warm chest;
a murderer rules the sky, jealous of Mother Earth,
and from his white lips drip nine kinds of deadly poison;
but I shall rear my head against him, Lady, for love of you.'
The words hung on his lips still when the twisted brain
of God Almighty flung in the cave his lightning-flash;
but the worm rushed to the holy fire and lit his torch,
piled heap on heap of dry leaves till the bonfire rose
to highest heaven and singed the grisly beard of God.
Then the child-eating Father stormed and yelled for the hag
with hanging dugs and face of plague to come before him:
'O Hunger, thin lean daughter with your slender scythe,
fall on the earth and thresh it well, fall in their guts,

tear up each overweening root, body and all!
I won't allow a soul on earth to rear its head!'
Then bony Hunger crawled to earth, mowed down the grass,
mowed down the pregnant bowels, and like a lean hyena
licked with her scabrous tongue both bones and meager meat.
The two souls were drained hollow, their eyes dulled and glazed,
and the male worm crawled slowly to his fainting mate:
'Dear wife, don't let the fire go out, crawl near the hearth,
blow with your breath upon it, feed and tend it well,
for I have carved myself a bow to hunt the stag.'
The livelong day and night the female fed the fire
and in her husband kept her faith and mocked at God:
'Keep thundering on, you slayer, and do whatever you dare!
My husband's a stout hunter and he'll fetch me game!'
Her lips were twitching still when she heard manly strides
and saw the male worm gladly burdened with wild game;
the fire blazed till the whole cavern leapt and laughed;
the female carved a lean long stick, and singing shrilly
her stubborn, scornful tune, she twirled the spitted meat.
When they had eaten and revived, they sat by the hearth
and the male worm turned round and spoke to his brave spouse:
'Dear wife, if only God would let us rest a while
to fix the heart firm in its breast and to stop trembling!
How good to sit in the cool evening after meals
and spend the night, beloved, in sweet and gentle talk.'
But the meat's odor rose and stuck in God's wild nostrils
so that he grabbed with rage the rain's black hanging dugs:
'Burst open, you cataracts of heaven, deluge the world!
I scorn to share the earth with others, it's all mine!'
The unceasing waters fell and flooded the upper world,
the land was drowned, the mountains' snowy peaks sank under,
and God rolled choked in laughter above the deluged earth.
'The world's all mine to flood or fire as I well please!
I'm not a fool to let the dust rear up its head!'
He roared until a whirlwind whipped the waves to froth.
But in a high ship then, at the world's edge, there loomed
the great worm scudding swiftly by with swelling sails.
The oldest Murderer shook and crawled in his blue cave
then roared and called his first-born son and greatest heir:
'Help me, dear faithful Death, help me, my life's imperiled!
Two small worms rear their heads on earth and threat to eat me!'
Death took his sharpest knives, crawled down into the cave,
crept close beside the two small worms and spread his feet
to warm himself by the hearthstones and spy with greed
on the pair's simple and calm gossip around the fire.
And when the male worm saw him there, his small heart froze,

but he said nothing, for fear his wife might faint with fright,
and when night fell at length and they lay down to sleep
the worm crawled slowly, careful not to waken Death,
and in the darkness hugged his mate in tight embrace.
Death's dry bones glowed with light in the erotic dark
but he woke not nor felt the two warm bodies merge;
the male worm then took heart and in his wife's ear whispered:
'With one sweet kiss, dear wife, we've conquered conquering Death!' "

The piper's shrill voice broke, but still his lips flashed fire
and every hair on his head steamed with drops of sweat.
His squint eyes laughed and brimmed at the same time with tears
and his thin voice returned to his lean throat once more:
"Ah lads, the song's a heavy and devouring beast;
by God, the mind itself has sown this song to play with,
my pipe begot it then in fantasy's high nest,
but made of reed, air, brain, and cloud it passed and vanished,
and yet, dear God, it hurt my heart like a live thing,
as though, in fact, both worms had hatched within my heart."
The bosom friends fell silent, their hands froze at the oars,
till Granite tossed with pride his handsome head and spoke:
"Piper, the murder in my heart turned song to hear you;
somewhere afar the mountains quarrel and stars collide,
brother kills brother somewhere far in fabulous tales."
Then Captain Clam, lover of kin, sighed secretly:
"Now I recall how once I teased my grandson thus:
'Youngster, good luck! May you live long, may you grow strong
and take the same sea-road and sow a slew of children,
and may God grant that we both meet at the sea's bottom!' "
Oakheaded Hardihood spoke not a word, for still
within his heart the worm prolonged its writhing war
and like a scorpion flung its tail against the heavens.
But Kentaur could hold out no longer now, and howled:
"You've snatched away the song and left us high and dry!
I've waited for the two, God and the worm, to come
to grips on the firm ground, and let Death take the hindmost!"
The gap-toothed piper laughed and called a fig a fig:
"I trotted hard behind their fate but lacked their strength.
My friend, the heart, no, nor the throat, may go much further."
Then their sagacious leader raised his hand and spoke:
"Ahoy, my lads, heave at the oars, don't worry now,
one day I too may suddenly call on memory's help
to end this song that had no end but hung in air,
because, my lads—don't laugh!—believe all that I say:
I, too, lay stretched in that dark cave when Lord Death came!"
He spoke, then turning to the sky with searching glance

he sought to find which of the swirling winds to take
and cleave a road—all roads are good—on which his soul might sail.

Dusk fell, the foaming waters to the sky's far rim
reddened like coppery wine, and tipsy Hesperus
rose up to dance upon the gold and crimson waves.
Helen strolled slowly by Eurotas's rose-laurels,
raised her assassinating eyes to the swank star
and smelled a small rose-laurel blossom as her mind
turned back and wandered on Troy's old blood-splattered shores;
she saw the bodies glittering in the burning fields,
admired the chests of friends and enemies alike,
blood-clotted beards and hairy shoulder blades and thighs,
and joyed to know they killed each other to win her smile.
Now as she withered here in idleness alone
and walked the desolate bank and smelled the bitter blooms,
a lawless lamentation choked her burning throat:
"I cannot bear this life, my tight and curly basil
withers and dries without the stroke of manly hands.
I was not made for solitude and household cares!
Dear God, make me an apple tree that shades the road
and load me with sweet fruit to feed all passers-by!"
She raised her hands to the bright star at night's dark gate:
"If only a swift pirate's ship swooped down once more!"
Meanwhile, five oarsmen, watching the same star, reached out
to eat with longing moldy meat and black wheat bread,
then drank from copper beakers sweet yet tangy wine.
They stooped above their holy meal with deepest joy
and felt their flesh and soul merge tightly and plunge roots
until their hollow bones were crammed with manly marrow.
When they had eaten, they turned for water, but laughed long,
for all their sheepskins burst with wine, and none held water!
Sprawled at the prow, the piper played a warbling tune
like rivers flowing, till thirst passed and their brains cooled,
and then their captain wiped his mouth and cried with joy:
"What does my heart care where it's going? Row on, my friends!
The billows race and flow, and I, in the sea's center,
gaze on our islands, right, while to my left the land
sprawls like a high-rumped whore and longs for us to rape her;
our country's vanished in our mind's rough rocky crags!
I look ahead, and like an old ringleader of quail
rejoice to feel warm Africa's full fragrant wind.
I've let fate loose to feed with freedom in my heart:
slowly, with rowing, laughter, thoughts, and song, we'll find
in time exactly where to head our prow, my friends.
Forward! Heave at the oars and make your minds a blank!"

Their captain spoke, the oarlocks creaked, and all their brains
filled far and wide with purposeless and shoreless sea.
The mountain winds came down and swelled the sails until
the ship leapt like a male beast on the bucking waves.
Night fell, stars hung aloft in the dark heavens and gleamed,
and over the waves the man of craggy mind cried out:
"The wind's our captain, Captain Clam, blow where it may,
and I shall give my body's hull to calker sleep."
He spoke, and the ship brimmed with his calm breath and body;
but when his eyes shut tight, Dream came like a white bird
from lofty mountain peaks and stood straight by the prow,
and when dawn on his lashes spilled, his mind turned rose,
and he saw Helen hovering in the upper air!
Her lily-face like dew-wet ivory gleamed in light
as though a beating rain or tears had drenched it through;
her white veils flapped and fluttered like tempestuous wings,
and both her armpits shone with clots of thickening blood.
"Helen!" the archer cried, and swift of hand he seized
his large ancestral bow and knelt by the ship's prow,
glancing toward land and sea, prepared to guard her beauty.
And Helen looked upon the man's deep wrath with joy,
forgot her pain, smiled wanly till, as her tears gleamed,
a glittering rainbow flashed and curved about the ship.
Then the much-suffering man smiled sweetly in his dream
and dreamt himself grown suddenly young, the earth refreshed,
that friends at dawn had walked with him to a high mountain
where he bid all farewell, plunged like a groom to his bride,
then laughed and wrapped the dazzling rainbow round his waist.
"Helen!" he sighed once more, as though he hunted her
through reeds in a dark place, and like a nightmare moaned.
But all at once the woman's white veils swirled and scattered
as though a strong wind rose and blew from his burnt chest.
Odysseus screamed and fell down, huddling by the prow;
her nude and sacred body gleamed still in his eyes
and from her armpits the blood dripped like warm rose petals.
Her shoulders twitched and shuddered still, as though they longed
to rise, though with no hands, to clasp, though with no arms,
and her despairing cry pierced through his heart: "Help, help me!"
The archer leapt up frothing, gripped the mainmast tight,
and while his helpless crew with anguish watched him writhe,
convulsed with dream, as his mouth twitched and his teeth gleamed,
his dazed eyes fell on his scared wolf-pack, and at once
he grew serene and turned with joy to his old helmsman:
"Head due south, Captain Clam, take bearings by the stars,
a phantom stands at our ship's prow and gives the orders:
'Blow North Wind, swell the sails, for Sparta far away

awaits you like a maiden lodged in bitter laurel!' "
He spoke, the North Wind blew, the sails puffed up replete,
and then a clear mirage flashed in their savage heads:
air, mountain, sea, and earth swayed in the blazing sun;
a castle, like a dragon's nest, loomed high in dust,
and on the castle's top a tall flame beat the dazzled air.

On the next day a deep thirst wrung their sun-parched throats,
and as the North Wind failed and their sails slacked, the friends
grasped their unliftable long oars and rowed, exhausted.

Then Orpheus told old nurses' fables, shocking tales,
and coarse jokes hour on hour to make the parched crew laugh,
but galled with thirst, they growled with pain and weariness.
Then from the high dark garret of his head, the great
voyager brought the male worm down to his ship's prow
to give his dragons courage and feed their flagging fires:
"Take heart, my lads, heave at the oars, I shall sing on
from where our piper's mouth abandoned song and myth;
I shall unwind the tale to its end for your dear sakes.
The land is vast, my friends, our heads can't hold it all,
but vaster still the sea, for which there is no ending.
Our brave worm grew more stubborn still and sailed straight out,
due north, sheer north, and swore not to stop rowing ever
until his prow had drunk the sea to its far verge,
because his heavy heart cried out and mourned his wife
whom the invisible Murderer slew with wiles one evening.
He passed through straits and islands, rowed through misty seas
till fogs rolled down, and clouds like frigates drifted by,
and seals from his deserted bulwarks hung and screamed,
and all the sterile sea-mud stank of fat and grease.
The worm's feet turned to ice, his joints froze to the bone,
and crystal icicles dripped down his snowy hair,
but he'd sworn never to stop and never forswear his vow.
Two months passed by and still he sailed, three moons slid past,
and on the fourth and waning moon at length the sea
ended, and the god-battling worm leapt out on snow:
'O sea, my throat has drained you dry like a wine flask.
Now that I've slaked my thirst, I'm hungry to eat land!'
He swiftly strode upon the desolate, frozen wastes,
his two long oars like wings flapped on his shoulder blades
and in his chest he clasped a warming heart of flame.
Close at his heels there howled a pack of hungry wolves
whose burning eyes flashed like noctural towns with lights.
Swaddled in crystal ice, the numb trees creaked and cracked,
and in their branches Night and Day, two lean birds, wailed
like babies and with green eyes watched the traveler pass.
He crawled through frozen wastes and left trees far behind,
the pale sun grew consumptive, as though from a long illness,
the moon spilled out on snow as from a tilted milkpail,
but the male worm drove onward toward the world's end still.
One evening in a funneled glade he saw some lights
that gleamed from thatched huts huddled close, deep in the snow,
and smoke rose calmly like a man's breath, thick and blue.
The worm's heart melted, for man's holy odor warmed
his widowed heart and tamed his grief-struck savage mind:
'Here by my brothers in snow I'll warm myself a while.'

He spoke, then lurched with joy down toward the distant mortals,
but as he plunged, a burning meteor burst and fell
and like a flaming ax split all the roofs in two.
The narrow valley flashed with fire and the snows laughed;
they say sardonic sneers and footsteps rang on high
as though a fiery dragon had cast his quoit from far.
Men rushed out from their cloven huts, the mothers wailed
and gathered what remained of their charred children's bones;
the braves flung arrows at the sky and cursed with rage:
'Come to grips here on snow, you murderous ghoul! We dare you!
You owe men blood! Whether you will or not, you'll pay it!'
But God on high laughed long and cast his thunderbolts.
The worm felt pity for this bitter breed of men
and soothed the frenzied mothers, dressed their wounds with skill
till hearts grew calm, and the scorched widows knelt and clasped
his frozen knees and begged him humbly not to leave them.
He stayed and built a hut, sent tall smoke belching out,
a wild and warlike banner, took himself a wife,
stretched on the ground, spawned children, and struck roots in snow.
One day when he was drunk, he cocked his cap askew
and fell on the black meteor with his thick sledge hammer.
Then the emboldened townsmen also quickly struck
God's dark man-cleaving ax, and swiftly gathering up
the splintered fragments, smelted them in blazing kilns.
This was the black bronze, iron, which rules the world now, lads!
They wrought and hammered trivets, hammered out new plows,
the young men forged their spearheads, maids their wedding rings,
the old men hung shards on their chests to ward off evil,
and the male worm forged in the fire a lean, strong sword;
thus the sky's thunderstone passed through the hands of man.
But lean years came when Death swooped down on the worm's home
and grabbed his sons, swooped down again and grabbed his daughters,
then swooped once more to seize his last small son, and vanished.
But the worm skinned his son and stretched the still-warm hide
over a hallowed plane-tree trunk and made a drum.
He painted his hair sapphire-blue, his eyes ink-black,
dressed like a groom who goes to a fair to buy a bride,
and every midnight stood erect on a mountain top
and beat his drum at the high stars till the dawn broke:
'You've matched all well on earth, wine, women, bread, and song,
but why, you Murderer, must you slay our children? Why?'
He beat and yelled until the funneled valley roared.
God couldn't sleep a wink that night, then cast with wrath
the Black Ant down to earth and bade him seize and fetch
that insolent worm who yelled on the high mountain top.
The Black Ant swooped and ate his way both right and left,

he crawled and groped and munched with stealth to the snow town
and came on the sad weary worm returning home
at break of day, his pale throat torn with savage shouts.
'Good day to you, great worm. God sent me down to fetch you.'
'Aha! Good day to you, Black Ant, our Lord's great headsman!
Wait till I smarten up and gird my weapons well,
wait till I curl my graying hair to face my master.'
He cocked his cap askew and buckled on his sword,
then slung his drum across his back and made for God.
When the cruel Slayer saw the worm, he thundered out:
'Worm, is it you who spoil my sleep all night and shout:
"You've matched all well on earth, wine, women, bread, and song,
but why, you Murderer, must you slay our children? Why?" '
The worm stood straight on God's blood-splattered threshold then
and beat his drum, beat it again, and raised his throat:
'You've matched all well on earth, wine, women, bread, and song,
but why, you Murderer, must you slay our children? Why?'
God foamed with rage and raised his sword to pierce that throat,
but his old copper sword, my lads, stuck at the bone.
Then from his belt the worm drew his black-hilted sword,
rushed up and slew that old decrepit god in heaven!
And now, my gallant lads—I don't know when or how—
that worm's god-slaying sword has fallen into my hands;
I swear that from its topmost iron tip the blood still drips!"

Then the god-slayer closed his huge myth-making mouth
and quickly wiped his sweating brow with his coarse hands,
and all forgot their thirst, and rowlocks creaked and swayed
as though the worm himself had come and seized the oars.
The piper sighed and thrust his reed back in his belt:
"Oho, I'll stop my singing and I'll break my weapons;
my skull is much too small and my heart much too weak
to grip and hold complete the brave worm's monstrous bulk!
It's shameful to climb the high crags and cliffs of song
if you can't make the summit and your knuckles break."
Then bulldog Hardihood turned with a laugh and mocked:
"Hey, hey! In every braggart shall be found an ass!"
All laughed, and the poor piper hung his head in shame.
Thirst gripped the boatmen as they strained against the oars,
their prow could not cut through the sea's unmelting lead
but suddenly from the mast they heard their chief mate cry:
"Courage, my lads, just two more heaves and we moor on sand!"
A thick green-foliaged sandy shore loomed to their right,
fig trees hung high on cliffs above the sea and swayed,
weighed down with fruit, and clove the rocks with twisting roots;
a land-breeze lightly brought the scent of mountain thyme,

their nostrils quivered and their hands gripped at the oars
till like a thirsty seagull their prow skimmed on sand.
With Hardihood, gaunt Granite, and some empty wineskins,
Odysseus thrust through osier trees and mastic shrubs
to find that antidote to thirst, cool running water.
"Fellows, let's all take different paths," the archer said,
"and may the best man win!" The water-hunters scattered,
and the archer thrust through shrubs to find life-giving wells.
As with his head erect he sniffed the blazing air,
a secret song beat its soft birdwings in his mind
and cool-voiced fountains spouted in his thirsty heart.
He pushed on with a sated and rejoicing head:
the old worm, water, Helen, all mingled in his mind,
and like a woman's tender rustling, wings, or birdsong,
God drifted through the air and ruffled his gray locks.
This god was not a murderer, wrapped in swirling clouds,
he held no thunderbolt in mind, no sword in hand,
but blew about Odysseus now with sweetest breath.
God was a fair and helping wind that swelled the heart.
And though he sought life-giving water, his mind surpassed
the body's narrow need and in the desert chirped:
"God is a song in azure air and no one knows
from whence he comes or what the meaning of his words;
only the heart, a female bird, listens and trembles."
Singing, he pushed on quickly till he suddenly heard
fresh water warbling in a vale of green plane trees.
He stooped and saw a sunburnt, black-haired maiden there
pushing a curly bull-calf in the stream to cool it,
and he rejoiced because earth gave him now all three
of man's most basic treasures—water, woman, food.
He came up slowly, sweetening his face as best he could,
but when the maiden saw the stranger, she drew back,
for he seemed like a god who'd come to earth for water.
"When I first stepped on sand, I sought three joys from earth,"
thus sweetly spoke the sly beguiler of men and gods,
"I asked her for a curly bull to feed my crew,
for gurgling water that their guts might not go dry,
a lass of twenty or so to play with on the grass,
and see! the earth has crammed my fists with all her treasures!"
The supple and compliant girl crouched in the shrubs
and her breasts ached and fluttered like two timid doves.
"A god has chanced to find me by this spring," she thought;
"I bend and bow low to his grace, his will be done."
The swift mind-reader felt the maiden's fear and joy:
"Yes, you've divined it, lovely lass, I'm a sea-god
who saw you far off from the waves and leapt ashore

so that the thighs of god and man might meet in love."
The maiden hid her flushed face in the tender leaves,
then tied her bull-calf tightly to a plane tree's root
and waited, trembling on the grass, nor moved, nor spoke.
Fierce heat! The sweating bull steamed in the blazing sun
and the young girl smelled strongly like a rutting beast.
The cunning man fell on his knees to Mother Earth
and drank till his parched flesh rejoiced from head to heel,
then spread his hands and bent the maiden to the grass.
The young girl felt as though a god embraced her sweetly,
as though her earthen womb had brimmed with deathless seed.
She hid her face then in his briny beard, laughed, wept,
heard the whole dancing sea crash wave on foaming wave
and wash her body wholly in a cooling flood.
A sweet compassion glazed the man's discerning eyes,
and as she knelt and clasped his knees and kissed his hand,
he stroked in ravishment the girl's disheveled hair.
Then he leapt up, filled his skins full, tucked up his sleeves
and seized the callow bull-calf, stabbed it through the throat
until the handsome beast fell to the grass and groaned.
The maiden helped the slayer, then knelt and washed his hands;
and as she marveled at his godly strength in stealth,
the water's sound danced in her womb like a new son.
The foxy man then wedged his fingers in his mouth
and whistled like a shepherd for his two lean hounds.
When the friends heard and rushed to find him, maddening thoughts
raced pellmell through their heads, a thousand fears—perhaps
cutthroats had seized him, some dread god or local demon,
but when they saw him wave with laughter, their hearts calmed.
"You wily hunter," Granite yelled, "I see you've flushed
your pretty prey while we, for shame, come empty-handed!"
The prowler laughed, shrugged his burnt shoulders and replied:
"Don't growl, it's your own fault! Don't you know God needs scaring?
The more you ask of him the more he gives you, lads.
You asked for water only, nothing more, but I
demanded springs and kisses, nor could my wants fit
in empty wineskins and this short-breathed flesh I lug,
and that's why God got scared and gave me all he had."
They slung the bull and waterskins about their backs
and trod on, while the maiden hid her breasts and followed;
flowers sprang up from sterile sands wherever she passed.
Soon, when they reached the seashore, the seducer turned
and stroked her shoulders longingly in sweet farewell:
"Dearly betrothed, don't weep; in nine month's time, I swear,
I'll lie upon your lap once more and touch your lips;
an infant god shall suck your breasts, your house shall shine."

He waded to his curly loins in the cool sea and seized
the gunwale, leapt into his tossing vessel lightly,
and his friends laughed and eyed the maid so slyly kissed;
then they rigged sail, rowed hurriedly, and skimmed the sea.
The pregnant maiden stretched her hands toward the far waves,
and her tears gently flowed, her eyes gleamed in the sun,
but good winds freshly blew, the earth swayed like a dream,
and soon the fruitful maiden vanished in the fluttering air.

Two days and nights they sailed, backed by the wind's breath.
Water they had, and wine, and meat stacked in the hold;
their souls grew strong nor from their flesh could be dislodged
and scorned now to look back, nor feared what loomed ahead,
but as the wasp clings to the grape and sucks it dry,
so did the comrades seize and glean each fleeting hour.
Where they were going or toward what goal or what they wished
and what sword hung above them ready to cut them down
they scorned to ask themselves a moment even in thought.
The first day and its night passed on, its sun and moon,
a second day and night flashed like a double flame,
and in the third night's dawn they skimmed in the wished haven,
gathered their sails, rowed quickly, then crossed idle oars
The village wakened in rose light, the rooms resounded
with laughing girls who flung their window-shutters wide
on purple-spotted violets and curled basil leaves.
Fishermen cast their dragnets by the sounding shore,
and when they saw the scudding ship, they yelled in welcome,
and six glad greetings came from the deck in swift reply.
The captain marshaled all his crew and gave strict orders:
"I'm going, lads, to Sparta, but I still don't know
what fate may have in store nor what my own mind wants;
slowly, by what I see and do, I'll work things out.
Keep all your wits about you, don't roam far from shore,
don't let fat oxen, wine, or maids lead you astray;
earth is a baited hook, and here's the trick, my lads:
let's see you snap up all the bait and not get hooked!
But you're mature men all and need no advice from me."
He turned toward Kentaur then and slapped him on the back:
"You hangdog, you and your meat-mountain shall go with me!
I'd like to see your thick fists hold the heavy reins
of my bronze chariot as my steeds eat up the road
and we ascend to Beauty's castle in afterglow."
Glutton then grabbed his monstrous paunches, laughed, and roared:
"I see no chariot here! It won't be easy dragging
these folds of greasy fat through fields in dust and sun;
take thin-assed Orpheus in my stead, he's lightly laden!"

The piper's blood ran cold, his heart skipped twice or thrice,
and he crept low and crouched between the paunch's thighs,
but the archer frowned and flung his words sharp as a shaft:
"Few words are best, do you hear? Push on! I see a field
so wide it'll yield us many chariots, many steeds.
Let's go! All that a great mind wants will cross his path."
Then from the hold he brought a precious ivory box,
a mortal's godly present for sun-loving Helen,
and there a crystal ball flashed, a miraculous eye
through whose clear waters countries, seas, and persons passed;
all houses were unroofed and all their shames exposed,
all heads, transparent, empty, rose like lotuses
in that eye's glare, and every secret thought passed by
like small distended goldfish in a crystal bowl.
Battalions moved like phantoms at the world's far ends,
kingdoms rose up from every seashore's rim like clouds,
scattered once more, and others loomed in storm behind
as though the life of earth and man's black fate were all
a tiny plaything made of water, light, and air.
This godly eye Calypso once had given him to recall
that first sweet night when in her cave they'd slept together.
He'd gazed in it for seven lightning years that passed
and seen his native land, his father, son, and wife;
he'd seen his treasures squandered on his courtyard's tiles,
but, like a god, disdained to be distressed in spirit.
Through every joy and grief he'd kept this magic eye
hung on his sunburnt bosom like a heavy charm;
but now he had no need of it and thought to hang it,
a star, a flame, a blazing fire, on Helen's gleaming throat.

The two friends trudged at daybreak in the early fields;
clouds eastward flushed with rose, the fields with golden grain,
and leaf by leaf light poured like oil on sunshot trees.
In a deep silence the two friends trudged down the fields;
the first felt Helen in the gentle rose-red light
rise like the crescent moon in day to fade in sun;
the second scurried right and left to find a chariot.
Soon in a darkling copse they saw a farmhouse gleam,
and drawing near, found slaves and yards still drowned in sleep;
only an old man in the stables groomed the horses,
and in the courtyard shone a smart bronze-armored car.
Holding their breath, they slunk in slyly like night beasts,
and when they rushed the slave, he screamed like scalded hens,
for in their flaming eyes he guessed their pitiless purpose
and dashed to escape them through the narrow stable door,
but Kentaur seized and gagged him with a horse's reins

and bound him to the bronze rings of the feeding trough.
Meanwhile the archer bound the steeds to the car-yoke
then saw and seized a whip that lay on the well's rim
and, clucking softly, led the steeds to the main road.
"Be quick, get in," he whispered, and his splayfoot friend
lurched in, grabbed at the reins, till all the chariot creaked;
then like a lightning flash they pierced through rising dust,
and when the farmhouse vanished in the twisting road,
the sharpster nudged his sudden charioteer and chuckled:
"Hey, I forgot to tell the old man I'm a god
that he might be consoled for his poor plundered stalls!"
Bold Kentaur laughed, twisted his grimy neck, and yelled:
"Let's turn the horses round to tell him then, by God!"
The shrewd man secretly admired his fearless friend
and through his mind there flashed a wild caprice: to turn
and watch the landlord howl and all the poor slaves yelp,
but he reined in his senseless whim and spoke with calm:
"Sit on your eggs, O seven-floored beast! Don't overdo it!
I'm all for playing with danger, too, on the cliff's edge,
but even prudence suits the brave man well at times.
Speed on! Let's see the face of Helen before light fades."
He ceased, then turned in his wild mind what fate writes down:
how to pass Menelaus' threshold, with what wiles
and what sly glance to shoot at Helen at their first meeting.
Although he longed for Menelaus, his old friend,
he hated loves like stagnant bogs with their fat blooms,
and trailed with fear the lofty flame that seared his heart.
The swan-god's daughter rose once more in his mind's prow,
blood sprang like fountains from her amputated wings,
and his contentious heart dissolved to watch such grace
allure weak man with blood and tears and smiles until
his weapons fell disused before her nakedness.
But he had never longed to embrace lascivious Helen,
for this seductress drew him far from carnal wars
to the high valor of the mind, the peaks of passion;
the North Star shown between his brow and lit a long,
long road beyond the raptures of love's spreading thighs,
beyond the flesh's shame, its sticky, slimy kisses.
Kentaur fell silent, for he guessed his master's mind
was weaving cunning wiles once more since his dark face
showed not the slightest smile, nor did his glance gaze out,
but plunged profoundly in his breast and inmost thoughts.

When the sun rose, the threshers scattered to far fields,
and coarse-mouthed Kentaur whipped his steeds to a swift pace.
His eyes rejoiced to see in fields the monstrous grass

with ripe and bearded heads that billowed in wide whorls,
and the old river by his side that through thick laurel
coursed sluggishly down to sea in slow and shallow falls.
Women and men bent low and flung their arms out wide
till their bronze scythes like lightning in the grainfields flashed.
They grabbed armfuls of wheat, gathered them up in shocks
and stacked them in straight rows on blazing threshing floors
where with their pitchforks in the light-blown breeze, they fanned
and winnowed the full-seeded and abundant fruit.
"Good is the earth and good her womb; it's a great joy
to live like man and wife together, to eat, make love,
and work hard side by side like mates in scorching sun.
The earth's our faithful and hard-working wife, unlike
the brainless, giggling sea, and gives our children suck."
Thus Kentaur spoke to his own heart and called to mind
how he had lived with earth in joy as a young plowman
far off amid his father's fields on eastern shores,
and now, by God, see where the wheel of exile flung him!
Kentaur whipped up his steeds while his enchanted mind
flew like a hungry beetle to reap memory's harvest:
deep gardens and well-dowried girls in their full bloom
who would come down to watermills, set up their poles
with wool for washing, and fluff their clothes till the dale rang.
Broad-buttocked Kentaur marveled how the years had fled,
how, wounded by the maidens' charms, he'd hailed them blithely,
"Don't tire yourselves, my dears, I don't want any clothes,
give me but fertile thighs for dowry, night-long kisses;
ah! even your feathery blouse will do, and that's too much!"
A maiden then, sweet God, threw him a bitten apple:
"Go on, splayfoot! Stop twirling your mustache! Don't moan!
Our curved breasts are encircled by a thousand guards!"
Alas, where was she now? A rotted apple, lost!
"Fellows, she had a small mole on her olive cheek,
and on her throat—it drove me wild—a small, small lovebite."
Both neck and cheek rose vivid in the empty air
but suddenly his monstrous flesh, that sped far off,
flung itself from the dream, drew in its reins, and stopped.
A jostling troop of children, maids, and blond-haired braves,
cartload on cartload, some on horseback, some on foot,
poured through the valley's narrow pass like hairy demons.
Odysseus suddenly stopped and bent his body in two;
thick droves of wild-faced women passed, big-bodied maids
whose wide loins could contain whole yards of noisy children,
and young men trotted by their side with iron swords
flashing in air, and raised thick clouds of swirling dust.
The grainfields shook with thunder, and the gleaning stopped.

"New salty blood comes pouring into withered veins,
our homes have fallen in ruin, our towns have lost their men,
for see, these blond-haired roundheads burst from the far North!"
Deep in his mind the dexterous man confessed the truth:
"Their undistilled and turgid blood still seethes like must,
firm lands and islands boil and burst, the world's renewed;
though my left foot is rooted deep in earth, the right
shakes high beyond the chasm's edge and longs to dance."
He watched the strangers pass until his fingers itched
to grab their bodies, plunge in their blond hair and feel
their warmth and fierce resistance, to rejoice in wars.
But when the mob had passed and only horseflesh stench
still choked the valley, then the devious man growled out,
"Blessed be that hour that gave me birth between two eras!
Hey, glutton, gird your barrel-bellies round with iron,
I see deep cliffs before us and dark streams behind;
we'll leap in darkness soon, and who knows where we'll land?"
But glutton grabbed in haste his twisting reins, and yelled:
"Don't worry, I know well that all who steel their hearts
with you in friendship must soon learn to shuttle back
and forth from thirst to hunger swiftly, life and death."
The sun now stood at zenith and deep shadows fell
in a black heap and huddled round the roots of trees.
"Make for that thick-leaved plane tree by the riverbank,
unyoke the horses there, it's time we all four ate."
The master spoke, then both jumped down, unyoked the horses,
let them run loose in the cut stubble and lay down
under the plane tree's heavy shade to eat their bread.
They spoke no word but bent to earth and ate with greed,
though in his mind the devious man chewed up like cud
blond hair and iron, sturdy swords and gaudy tents;
he bent his long bow taut and fixed the arrow's nock
firmly against the gut, though undecided yet
whom to mark out for friend or foe, and where to shoot.
The heavy-hearted man then frowned, leapt to his feet,
and glutton also leapt, food in his mouth, and thought:
"By God, better to live in the teeth of a wild beast
than be storm-tossed against this man's dark ebb and flow.
I want to flee, but can't; I want to stay, but quake."
He yoked and whipped the horses till they leapt with fear
and with their lean hooves swiftly wound the world as on a reel.

Soon the five-fingered mountain rose and blocked the air;
its five peaks stood up proudly in the sun and vanished
like five thoughts in an archon's subtle, scornful head.
"Just such a mountain should have stood beside my cradle

and hung my life long like a sword above my head!
I know it now: I've never in my life loved man
nor deigned to let him build his home on my rough crags,
nor browse nor breed his cattle on my mountain slopes;
but I, too, like Five-Fingers here, cliffs clean of men,
thrust to the sky my naked form and fade in sun!"
Odysseus clasped the mountain close and brooded long;
the river rolled in sluggish twists and turns through reeds;
rush-slender maidens, bearing on thick shoulder-pads
their cooling pitchers, walked with grace to wishing-wells
and preened as though, even now, their wombs were filled with sons.
Kentaur in admiration thought: "This field produces
fine mares and finer women," but he dared not speak,
for he was startled by the archer, coiled and writhing,
who like an angry viper hissed with bloated throat.
A roadway shrine of Aphrodite suddenly shone,
cut in a crimson rock thrust deep in myrtle shrubs,
round which the goddess's erotic doves were sighing.
Amid the myrtle boughs the nude bronze body smiled
of the sweet yielding Lady and lured the passers-by;
in her cupped hands she held her fat and fertile dugs
that swelled and pained her, rigid with congested milk.
Lovers had hung small hearts of clay about her feet,
pair after pair, that she might grant surcease of passion.
"It's time the castle came to view, let's stop an hour
and in this water cleanse our bodies till they glow;
we must not pass that deathless threshold still unwashed."
Odysseus spoke, and both plunged in the freshening stream.
Like a big-bellied buffalo his friend rejoiced
to feel the water flow along his hairy thighs,
and when he'd had enough and scrambled up the bank
he saw the archer sprawled like flame so that around him,
far round about him, all the ground was rimmed with fire.
Then the compliant goddess like a humble beggar
stooped down and spread her hands above his blazing head;
but the man's mortal eyes were thrust deep in their sockets
and, filled with longing, sauntered through an inner grove.
In truth, he saw a garden opening in his heart
on a shore's rim with almond trees in their first bloom,
but couldn't remember where, on what large land or island.
He only could recall a slow, warm drizzle falling
that robed the flowers with a transparent veil until
the almond branches seemed to laugh and gently weep.
He'd risen on tiptoe longingly to break a small,
wet twig, for his heart shook with passion unrestrained,
and as the tree with all its flowers swayed, cool drops

rained down on his dark head, his lips, his chest, until
he blenched, and in a lightning flash remembered Helen!
Once, he recalled, she'd smiled at him behind her veil;
her husband's ship had set its sails for their far land
and she had raised her crystal arms by the ship's prow
to say farewell to shores in silence, right and left;
she hailed the still warm ashes of the toppled towers
and hailed the gallant lads who glowed far up the beach,
then turned and saw him with his peaked cap standing there,
and slowly, deeply smiled until her white veils flashed
and light poured through his mind as though sweet day had dawned.
Thus, in a joy complete, in a blind, dazzling silence,
he held between his wet thick lashes all her beauty.
Like travelers who shut weary eyes and lose themselves
in scent of jasmine flowers blooming far away,
Odysseus breathed in the atmosphere a phantom Helen.
Her features changed and winked in air, gleamed like a star,
for still the mind of man had not yet brought to proof
whether her flesh had truly blossomed in Troy's walls
or whether friend and foe had fought for an empty shade.
But now with lucid head he dashed to see her, touch her,
and if she would not flee his hand like airy clouds
he'd lure her with seductive speech and dark caresses.
Just as the Eurotas ran to sea with dance and smiles
and she had watched by day and heard it all night long
until she sighed one day and rose to follow after,
so would his mind roll round her like alluring streams.
The secret purpose of his voyage burst upon him
and he laughed loud, then clapped his hands and called his friend:
"Hey, muddy beast, come close, let's bandy words about!"
Kentaur rose steaming like a river ghost, approached,
and the archer slowly stroked his friend's fat shoulder blades
for fear his words might hurt or wound that guileless heart:
"Brother, we're now quite close to that world-famous castle
and soon your manly heart shall look on star-eyed Helen.
Your flesh hangs heavy and your words spring out unleashed
and fall to earth like birds that couple shamelessly;
hold back your wits and do not shame us, check your tongue,
open your eyes, gape on that marvel silently,
and say within you, 'I never hoped for this good fortune.' "
The big-boned man then hung his face, choked back his wrath,
but uttered not one word, for what his friend had said was true.

When they had dried at length in the tame sun of evening,
Odysseus rose and prayed alone amid the myrtles
to that brash Lady with a sow's long tier of dugs.

"Lady, I don't fall at your feet, a swooning boy,
for my dull loins are cleansed, my needs are tamed, and now
I hold you like a mortal and well-bedded maid.
But I know well, nude form, that you still rule the world.
I beg you: come with me today, abet my purpose;
storm through my blood, dear Lady, that my ship may sail,
let loose the alluring thought that will abduct fair Helen."
But you, O Lady of Myrtles, you had your mind elsewhere,
and with your small lips still unslaked you smiled with craft
and watched the body of the arch-eyed lady lying
on distant sheepskins, sauntering by tall dappled tents,
the archer lost in her deep mind where all men quarter.
He did not hear, however, the unfaithful goddess laugh,
and leapt with joy into his chariot, cleansed and pure.
Field after wheatfield passed, and a new fragrance poured
from tufted rose-bays by the banks and slopes of thyme;
old women seemed more sturdy, girls as lean as candles,
for the whole world seemed cleansed to glance of new-washed eyes.
The castle suddenly loomed in twilight's azure dusk,
light fell like mist between the toothless battlements,
long, bearded ivy shadowed all its cracking towers
and owls hooted in its ruined foundations now.
Pressed tight about the castle walls, dark row on row,
huddled the humble huts of the day-laboring poor;
the smoke of evening had begun to rise from roofs
until Odysseus' hairy nostrils quivered with greed
to sniff the holy odors of burnt, fragrant pine.
Rejoicing in the downy mist of peaceful night,
he suddenly heard hoarse cries and scuffling, peasants shout
and swarm in tumult round their grain on threshing floors
while women ran like panting dogs and prod the brawlers;
then all dashed toward the castle gates with flailing scythes.
An ancient plowman crossed their path. "Grandfather, stop!
What's all the shouting?" Kentaur bawled above the clamor.
"The people roar and want to take their harvest home!"
Then the man-slayer ground his teeth in holy rage:
"Whip up the horses! We've reached the castle just in time!"
Bold Kentaur snapped his flickering whip until the streets
flashed fire as the mad and frothing horses raced far up
the steep ascent and stopped like lightning by the castle's gate.

The wrathful man leapt down, thrust through the crowd in haste
and strode through the bronze threshold with its rampant lions.
The mob swarmed clamoring in the central courtyard, armed
with their sharp tools of work, hoes, pitchforks, sickles, scythes.
A long-haired peasant leapt on an ox-cart and yelled:

"We are the ones who plow and sow, who thresh and sieve!
It's we who bear male children; the grain is ours by right!
Why should the fat-assed lords devour the workers' honey?"
Their souls at once caught fire, their strong bodies blazed,
and all turned back their laden ox-carts toward the town;
but high above the workers' heads on the sun-roof
the daughter of the swan appeared and stood with calm.
Their hearts throbbed as though each had seen his dark desire,
their wrath subsided for a moment, and their quelled minds
felt a light breeze that blew beyond revenge or need.
But in that breathless silence a voice roared out: "Hunger!"
and all at once the sweating mob burst out in rage
and surged up arm in arm to crash the quivering doors.
But the bronze gates groaned open, and lo, their king appeared,
short-bodied, stout, with rose-red cheeks, and fat with age.
He wore a short sword at his side, a lance in hand,
and on his helmet reared a tall and threatening plume.
As the sun's final rays gleamed on his flashing form
it seemed his golden shield and spear burst in loud laughter.
He rolled his eyes in rage and glared on the cowed mob
until the cowards trembled, old men shook for fear
the stone beasts of the castle gate might leap alive.
Once long ago in ancient times, their grandfathers said,
the slaves had reared in strong revolt and rushed the castle,
but the stone lions roared, earth shook, the town was smashed.
The elders paled with memory, shook their staffs and pled
with the wild mob to calm down and disperse in silence,
but then harsh laughter broke—a worker, warped by hunger,
goaded the threshers with his coarse and mocking talk:
"Hey, comrades, make way there, his cuckold horns might hurt you!"
Then the whole palace shook with their lewd laughs,
and the king roared in rage till all fell suddenly silent:
"Slaves, all this earth's been mine from father to father down!
When you crawled on all fours like bears and browsed on acorns,
either your foes' swords pierced your bent and haltered necks
or my forefathers herded you from your dark caves,
showed you how to build fires, gave you swords, walled round
your goods and taught you to walk upright like true men!
Scum! Slaves! You owe your bodies and souls to us, your kings!
The sky and earth's our ancient field held from our fathers."
But an old codger, rag and bones, shot back and mocked:
"Now don't get sore, my king; let's share and share alike:
why don't you take that high patrician sky for *your* share
and leave the wretched earth for us, your slavish workers?"
Then the mob leapt and seized the reins until the wheels,
heavy and muddy, groaned laboriously toward the town;

but the king ordered that the castle doors be barred,
that all the guards kneel down beside the battlements
to fling their murderous arrows at the mob's thick hide.
Hearing the order, the strong harvesters went wild
and rushed to seize their silver-horned, cuckolded king;
murder had broken loose, the piglet drowned in blood,
had not Odysseus leapt at once on a high cart
and flung his arms above the mob, hands steeped in slaughter's ways.

In a far corner crouched, he'd heard the whole revolt
and the mob's savage rage that shook the palace walls;
he'd seen the pitiful king stand in the azure dusk
and with his vulgar voice, his round pot-belly, howl
to his great forebears and denounce the ungrateful mob.
His soul had swayed between them like a flickering flame
until he pitied his old friend and sprang on the cart;
he knew well how to make lies stick, none could outtalk him:
"Put down your arms, don't shout, listen to me, you fools!
I bring news of great danger to your lives and wealth!"
The mob drew back and raised their brands to see him well,
but he with flashing eyes lowered his pointed cap
and swayed the mob with blows and flattery, hot and cold:
"I've worn my feet out trying to reach your king in time
and with great danger pay the debt of an old friendship:
King, there's a blond and barbarous army that swarms close!
They grasp swords made of iron, their gods are made of meat,
they bear their infants on their backs, they're threshed by hunger,
they've learned your harvest's good, that your barns burst with grain,
and soon, this day or next, they'll swarm to kill and loot!"
A deadly terror choked the mob, they gasped and gaped,
and all the wealthy landlords pressed about their king
to seek salvation for their rich, endangered world;
but he was striving to discern amid the flames
the sudden herald's face; his mind strove to recall
that noble bearing and that once familiar voice.
Meanwhile the mob's blind vacillating wishes swung
to right and left, young men and old brawled in dispute
until the sly voice cut through all and showed the way:
"Ah, if those slow barbarians could but see you now,
gobbling each other up like wolf-cubs in this castle!
For shame! Hurry and drag your goods and grain at once
to your king's bins and crouch like herds in your king's shadow!"
But when he saw the mob perplexed, he laughed and flung
his words like armored hooks amid that sea of men:
"You oafs, first save your hides, then later we'll provide
how to preserve your fields and vines, by hook or crook.

And you, Great Shepherd King, quick, bring your treasures here
to tempt the dull barbarians with gold dazzling gifts;
the king should in great danger give up all his wealth,
and even his life! His people hang about his neck!"
Fat Menelaus at last recalled that cunning glance:
"Ho-ho! Zeus must have whistled in his crafty ear,
and here he is, with all his nets and barbed harpoons!"
His heart fell into place so that he rose with wrath
and raised his golden staff above his frightened herd:
"Hear me! This whole night through my castle's brazen gates
shall be flung wide to safeguard all your precious goods;
at dawn when they clang shut, I'll swoop to fight the foe!"
He spoke, and the crowd dashed like moles to heap their goods;
the cellar guards unloaded grain from all the carts
until the palace storage jars brimmed row on row.
Fat, sweating Menelaus followed and held tight
his tower-tiered ancestral ring of gleaming gold,
and as the jars were closed, he pressed hard on each lid
and on the soft clay set his sacred, regal seal
that in a proud relief raised high this lyric scene:
A lean bare-breasted maid stood on a mountain top
and coldly aimed her tautened bow at a crouched man
who clapped his hands on his dazed eyes for fear his wits
might suddenly burst from so much splendor, so much joy,
and two fierce lions knelt and licked her oval heels;
this was the stamp with which the king sealed all his wealth.
He finished hurriedly, then hastened from his vaults
and in the courtyard sought his friend with happy heart,
but that notorious form was nowhere to be seen.
"A friendly god," he grieved, "must have assumed his shape
and vanished, but in morning's light I'll slay a calf,
and may the rising smoke soon find him and refresh his throat."

The cunning trickster, meanwhile, stole through palace rooms
where torches had not yet been lit in scented halls,
and like a stealthy thief groped columns and dim walls
In misty darkness, gold-wrought inlays gleamed like snakes,
mother-of-pearl glowed softly like fine, human flesh,
and as his fingers suddenly touched an amber's gloss,
he started back, as though he'd touched fair Helen's arms.
Trailing their languorous blazing tails, the peacocks screamed
like strutting ladies of the court, as in dark night
Odysseus passed and trembled like a still green youth
who fumbles through his sweetheart's house for the first time.
And as the burning doves above him sighed with love,
and fountaining waters fell within the fragrant night,

and one bird warbled in the garden close, he felt
suddenly sheathed and lost in Helen's enclosing flesh.
In truth, a slender lady loomed there by the threshold;
her motionless white hands, her face and throat were bathed
in misty moonlike glow by the door's golden mouth.
The savage solitary's temples throbbed like wings
for Helen stood awaiting him on the deathless threshold.
For a long time they held each other's hand, nor spoke,
but tasted the fine flavor of unhoped reunion,

till like a tree's soft rustling Helen spoke at last:
"Good is the earth, life in this world is sweet, most sweet.
Dear God, I hold Odysseus' hands in both my hands!"
"I love earth, too, for now I hold your hands in mine,"
and as he spoke his keen eyes strove in dark to see
if her black hair had grayed, her flashing eyes grown dull.
"Do you recall that night you saved me, dear, when all,
mortals and gods, had cast me off before death's door?
Blond Menelaus had drawn his sword to pierce my throat."
On her full lips, round as a ring, the stars rained down,
but the heart's tempter had already spread his nets:
"The past has fled, all totally vanished, sunk in earth,
and in this holy hour, complete and stripped of evil,
I'm blessed to stand with my gray hairs in this famed court
and hold within my mortal palms the immortal moon.
I swear—I see and touch you for the first time, Helen!"
Then both fell silent; time stood still above their heads
like a gray eagle hovering on the air's high peak.
Perhaps a lightning moment passed, perhaps ten years,
those ten years that had flashed to take those toppling towers;
all things now turned to stone and in the heart lay still,
and dull life burst with stars and turned to fabled myth.
This was not gore and conflagration, no grand castle,
no brash young blade had seized the swan-born maiden yet;
a rich field of red lilies, reed-pipe of a small
and lovesick shepherd had softly swept their brains like clouds
and set them gently on far-distant mountain tops.
But the spell vanished, time turned in its rut once more,
the peacocks closed their brilliant tails in fright, and fled,
for the king came, and slaves lit torches row on row.
As the ground flashed with light, the stars of heaven grew dull,
and the king threw himself in his friend's arms, and wailed:
"Dear friend, I thought you were a god, and my soul quaked,
but now I feel your warm flesh, smell your savage odor,
and recognize the deep scar on your knee, Odysseus."
For hours on the bronze threshold there the two great kings
talked arm in arm about their old strong joys and griefs
and would have walked on air the whole night long, nor eaten,
had not the queen, reminding them of mortal duties,
brought them to firm earth once again and its sweet needs.
"I know the soul is never slaked to hear and question
and tightly hold the flesh it loved and longed to clasp,
but come, a feast awaits us on the great sun-terrace.
It's good to sit with friends after great perils passed
and share the bread of happiness with long talks all night through."

Thus Helen spoke, then like a partridge proudly stepped,
rustling in her black linen gown stitched with long flames,
and strode through the hushed courtyard, gleaming like the night.
They walked up marble stairways where young handsome boys
in every nook held torches high to light the way.
Odysseus in the wild glare saw the wealth about him
and stealthily spied the murals with rapacious greed:
shameless nude goddesses that merged with men, and swans
that lunged with reared necks lustfully on women's thighs.
"These are no longer his," the castle-wrecker raged,
"nor tripods, lampsteads, golden swords, nor handsome boys,
nor marble stairs I tread, for he's no longer fit
to fight for them each moment with his blazing sword."
On altars strewn with flowers, close by erotic rooms,
he saw the gold, ungirdled form of a nude goddess
who cupped her breasts and with her right teat suckled all
the immortal gods, and with her left both men and beasts.
A sweet shade fell upon him, and his eyes refreshed:
"Cleaver of men and women, hail on Helen's threshold!"
And when they reached at length the terrace where stars flamed,
Odysseus breathed in deeply the night's moist aroma
and like a sea held in his heart the foaming sky.
All three reclined with joy around the rich repast;
a former blue-eyed princess, now their slave, poured out
the wine in golden goblets while bronze tiny gods
tinkled with cooling sound about her neck and hair.
As the harsh voyager drank deep, he felt his head
armed tight with deathless rage and supple tentacles;
he heard the rushes' gentle rustling far away,
the nightbirds sighing in dark caves, seduced with love,
and took great joy in hordes of boreworms and blind moles
that dug deep mines in earth and munched the world's foundations.
Slowly he turned his glance to brood on Helen's form
and raised her veils and hair in silence ruthlessly
to sum her with his eyes like a rapacious butcher
who grabs a fat ewe by the loins and weighs her well.
And Helen, bent above her golden cup, rejoiced
in his dread glance, abandoned to his rude caresses.
After their feast was finished, two dance-slaves rushed out
and whirled beneath the stars of the unexhausted sky;
a slender white-haired minstrel sat cross-legged
at the stair's head and played on a long slender flute
so that the naked feet kept tune and gently pecked
the terrace joyfully like wild erotic doves.
In a sweet stupor, drugged with so much food and drink,
fat Menelaus watched with heavy-lidded eyes,

but the great castle-wrecker's heart beat far away:
"We have both much to say, and I don't think it suits
old warriors such as we to watch such silly jigs!"
He spoke, and his old friend was shocked and deeply shaken;
the dancers teetered on their tiptoes, quaked with fear,
lifted their long transparent veils to hide with shame
their slender loins, their breasts, their lovely necks and lips,
then slithered back along the walls, and suddenly vanished;
the old bard also thrust his flute beneath his arm,
slid noiselessly down the stairs and disappeared in darkness.
The pitiless man then turned and pierced his comrade's heart:
"Old friend, I can't bear now to see your radiant eyes
grown dull and turbid, given up to easy joys;
take care, my king, old age will snag you from behind!
When we were young, this black earth shone with our resplendence—
how shameful now if our souls fall to food and lust!"
But the soft-hearted lord replied in frail complaint:
"Your heart is truly made of iron or sturdy oak,
you bear arms still, and still resist all sacred law.
Old age is good and dowered by gods with sacred gifts;
joy to that man who like the good fruit-bearing tree
completes life's cycle wholly, flower, fruit, and seed.
It's only now that I've begun to know the taste
of good wheat bread, refreshment of cool running springs,
and all the holy warmth in bed of lovely woman.
Yes, I've begotten children, conquered towns and cities;
my life, like a strong arrow, mounted toward the sky,
but now the earth allures it to a sweet descent;
man is a weather vane, his life an arrow's flight."
The archer's taut throat laughed with malice unrestrained
and sang out to his friend, blowing now hot, now cold:
"I don't think you'll enjoy the gifts of age in peace!
The news I let loose in your courtyard, Menelaus,
was not a cunning ruse alone to save your skin:
hungry barbarians have in truth sniffed out your bins,
they've heard your concubines complaining in your palace
because your loins are drained, O king, your heart has shrunk,
and now new hearts and loins shall inundate the earth.
I see, even now, your sacred, amputated head
high on a palace column blink with bloodshut eyes!"
Helen's pale shoulders broke in the cold sweat of fear
and all her swan-begotten flesh with roses flushed;
the king turned pale as wax and cold beads drenched his head:
"What a fine way to requite your dinner, friend, to caw
your prophecies like a black crow here at my feast!"
"I'm not a cuckoo to proclaim the sun in snow;

you've guessed it, friend, I perch here on the laden feast
like a black crow and patiently wait my turn to come."
Giddy with wine, he talked and heard his heart cry out,
disdaining now to sit on earth amid mere mortals.
Helen knew how to cast love-herbs into their wine
so that the men's harsh hearts would grow serene at once,
but she rejoiced to hear them clash in rage before her.
The archer understood, and with raised, mocking brows
turned round and struck her ruthlessly with brazen words:
"The lovely queen dawned on the terrace like a star
to tame the people's hunger and their savage hearts,
but now man's soul has soared above your beauty, Helen!"
But she had never observed the words of any man;
she was delighted only when their eyes lit up
and when their veins swelled savagely between their brows.
Good-natured Menelaus shuddered, and then sighed:
"I never thought you'd storm my castle like a lion,
but longed to see you come with pomp's rich retinue
that I might spread red carpets for your regal tread;
I dreamt of killing gold-horned bulls, that all my land
might feast and drink and toast your health a thousand times
while we, two old men sitting by the hearth embraced,
would tell each other of old passions, joys, and crimes.
Time would pass swiftly by, days open and nights close,
and we would slowly talk like sated, sleepy gods,
our souls spread out like an unrippling, endless sea."
Then sage Odysseus touched his friend's knee in reply:
"These thoughts you had for your old friend were good, all good;
I too would want to make my friend's reception glow
at my own castle gate with contests, wine, and steeds,
whether from love, or lordly airs, or sense of honor.
But times have changed, the earth is crushed by cruelest need,
and all these joys and these embracements by the hearth
cannot delight our weary bones here, Menelaus:
a new god mounts from the soil now and rules the earth!"
The slayer spoke and gazed intently in Helen's eyes,
but she in fear clung to a column as though thieves
had dashed into the palace, twined their impious hands
about her coal-black hair and tried to drag her off.
"What kind of god?" the king asked, with wry, trembling mouth.
But the sly man rolled up his mind like a closed hedgehog.
The hovels softly twinkled in the village still,
clay lamps still swayed and sputtered in the tiny yards
and all earth quivered like a star's weak, fading rays.
Once more Odysseus' mind heard boreworms and blind moles
eating away in fields at the world's worn foundations,

and gently, with no wrath, but ruthlessly, he answered:
"I shall not be here when your slaves once more revolt
and, fierce with hunger, cast new flames in your rich vaults,
and if I were here—then, who knows?—I might not raise
my hand to save you from the serpent's mouth, dear friend,
for my soul forges forward, spurning loves and virtues."
Choking his tears back painfully in his harsh throat,
he turned his eyes and marveled at man's precious wealth;
his eyes caressed the lovely woman languidly,
though not consoled, as though he bid all things farewell.
A hush fell, and the crackling torches dripped on tiles,
the nightbirds still sighed lovingly in olive trees
until a woman's voice fell through the tranquil hush:
"O sly, resourceful man, I'd stay awake the whole
night through, though stooped and shuddering, just to hear your tales;
I never knew an archon who so matched the sea
with her smooth beaches and her myriad bitter waves
as you, my dear, with your strange, vacillating soul.
But sleep is also good, a vast sea and a god;
this day has ended well; tomorrow, when day breaks
with brilliance, choose whatever joys your heart desires—
sweet conversation, wine, or noble games of skill;
the guileless gods grant freedom only to earth's masters."
Slim-waisted Helen, from whom roses poured, stood up,
and slave boys ran and seized the torches, lined the stairs,
stood motionless and lit their masters' regal way.
A strutting peacock with a long and glittering tail,
thrice-noble Helen slowly paced the marble stairs,
and her large black eyes, tinted to her eyebrows' verge,
gleamed velvetly and mystically like cool dark wells
of peril in a wood where beasts come down to drink.
All stopped to part before the many-breasted goddess
where the sly man took from his chest an ivory box
that like an eyelid hid the magic crystal ball
of myriad eyes, and placed it in her startled hands.
And Helen shuddered, as though she held a living head,
as though she touched the soft and tender hair of Paris.
"I greatly fear the gifts you bring, soul-snatching friend,"
she said, but laughter boiled like water in her throat,
and on her deathless breast she hung the ivory box.
They parted, Helen led the way, the old king followed,
and soon both vanished in the labyrinthine women's quarters.

The archer passed to the great hall where slaves had strewn
the ground with red-gold woolen rugs on which to sleep,
but his dark lids would not shut like a tight trap door

to blot the world out and make fast the lambent brain;
day hung between his eyebrows like a jocund star
and shone with brilliance and with no desire to set.
The crossbeams of his room smelled of sweet cypress wood,
and the world-wanderer rose in bed with beating heart;
light poured through the low casement like an azure sea,
apples were somewhere ripening, gardens somewhere swaying,
until his hands and the night smelled of apple trees.
Then the man-slayer's mind was wounded and unhinged:
"So must her coffers smell of apples now," he thought,
"her clothes, her hair, her breasts kissed by so many men."
He leapt up from his mattress and rebuked his mind:
"What! Have you not yet learned to come and go uncaught
yet eat within the snares of flesh, or walk in hunger
under that tempting bait and mock your own starvation?"
He spoke, his great mind blushed with shame, and then he laughed
and like a thief began to prowl the palace halls.
Deep stone lamps filled with oil burnt with full upright flames,
gods smiled from every corner, all the bronze-work gleamed,
and row on row the embellished jars stood brimmed with grain;
carpets and woolen rugs lay heaped to the domed roofs.
"All very fine and lavish! What brazen opulence!
Hey, all you hungry hordes, come kill and plunder us!"
These were the devious thoughts in the night-prowler's mind
as he passed by and marveled at his friend's great wealth.
And just as Victory, that winged bird with bloody beak,
wavers and sways between two vast, contending hosts,
so did his vacillating spirit flap and hover.
"Farewell, O aromatic coffers, fruit-filled jugs,
rude, shameless murals, goddesses, and noble feasts!
Blaze with light, lamps, that I may see and bid farewell."
Thus did he speak and gaze on all that vested wealth,
and as he wandered slowly in the lamps' bright glow
his soul turned peaceful drop by drop, his eyes grew heavy,
till not a single thought obscured his lambent mind.
But as he turned to his soft bed to rest, he thought
of Kentaur who had sprawled amid the storage jars
nor shown his barrel-bellied body at the feast,
and wondered idly where they'd stretched his humble bed.
But Kentaur lay in a long hall by huge wine-jars,
drank from big-bellied jugs and ate from laden trays;
the slaves took heart until slave-girls approached with fear
and wandered round his thighs that spread like castle gates,
and soon a small maid, growing bold, laughed long and crowned
his hippopotamus's head with fresh vine leaves.
The glutton ate a whole young lamb down to the bone,

and then, dead drunk, watched the slave-girls with their short robes
running in haste and jostling on the stairs to bring
their lordly masters fine rich foods and cooling drinks.
He strained his ears to listen to the hurried news
brought from the upper terrace by the panting slaves:
"The stranger laughs and holds his golden goblet out,
and the wine-steward brims it over and over again."
"He talks now, and his head flings flames as though his hair
caught fire, and the night burns, and the sun-terrace shines."
"He's silent now and cleans his hands in a gold bowl
and contemplates with calm our mountain's darkening bulk."
The guzzler then held out no longer and burst out:
"That man, my lads, is a great demon of the sea!
His nostrils smell of crabs, his lips of cuttlefish,
his brain's an armored lobster thrashing in its lair,
his beard's of sea-thorn made—beware its deadly sting!
One day he chanced to quarrel with the sea's booming god
about which of the two should hold the three-pronged spear.
They fought for years like lions, the god with all sixteen
strong, elemental winds on his proud seaweed chest;
but my sea-captain, mounted on a frail plank, clasped
his heart alone for helpmate, woman, friend, and god.
At length he set foot on dry land, looked round and chose
a new crew for his ship and a brief lethal trip;
that's how he hooked even me, my lads, one fine false morning!
But in his hands all souls are soon drained dry, and then
he throws them in the sea again and harpoons others!
Farewell, my lads! I too shall melt in his hands soon!"
He spoke, then seized the jestful wine and gulped it down
and sent it gurgling to his bellies' bottomless pits;
it was a sweet old wine—his eyes, as round as eggs,
grew groggy, but he chased dull sleep away that sat
upon his eyes like night-moths and caressed them gently.
A red-haired lad dashed from a column then, and said,
"When he had washed his hands well in a golden bowl,
the dread guest spoke with calm these strange and startling words:
'A new god mounts from the soil now and rules the earth!'
Confess, dear comrade, you must know what god he means."
Then Captain Sot, who from his wine-soaked mind now saw
all things like a great god, beyond man's meager bounds,
spoke up, and raving in that dungeon, shaped a god:
"One day when we sat drinking by a sandy shore
and talked of voyages and past heroic deeds,
I saw a god in starfire pass through mounting waves.
He sat astride a long-tailed ship, blazed through the sea,
shot piercing glances round, stooped down, bit his lips hard,

then gripped a heavy spear made of black bronze, the length
of two tall men, to which a long-haired race bow down
high up in the far North, and secretly name it 'iron.'
God passed; the sea turned spume and all the seashores shook!
I fell down trembling, fearful that the god would spear me,
but my bold master leapt erect, reached for the waves,
and his eyes harrowed all the sea with piercing glances.
The sky hung down pitch-black, the sea boiled up like tar,
between them both the iron spear like pure flame leapt,
and straight, inflexible, it held the sky from falling.
'He's waved to us!' my master yelled, and his proud eyes
shone from the iron. 'He, too, raised his hand high in air!'
Thus arm in arm we looked afar at our salvation,
but in a flash god vanished, and our vision passed."
Kentaur fell silent then, and his huge tears rolled down,
but his vast mouth, deep as a well, stretched wide with joy,
and flinging out his arms to all the slaves, he bellowed:
"This flash on the sea's waves is God, dear souls! Beware!"
He roared, and all the storage jars rang out with his harsh cackling.

And in that very hour Odysseus wondered where
the servants had laid down his sottish friend to sleep,
but when he heard the reveler laugh, his heart leapt up,
and he crept softly down the cellar steps and stood
and filled the door's huge mouth with all his shining length;
it seemed as if his head flashed with long, azure rays.
With piercing cries, the slaves crawled back into the dark
for fear this was the guzzler's god new-risen from waves;
but when the cunning man walked in that room with calm,
the gross man stumbled up, holding his bulging bellies:
"Forgive me, Cap, I found their food and wine so fine,
their company so good, I clean forgot your worship!"
His master shot a hand out, seized the blue, grimed cloak
of his intoxicated friend and ripped it off
so that his body stood stark naked as a wine-jar,
and the sea-eagle marveled at this ballast made
of lard and fat that kept his craft in proper balance.
Shrieking, the slaves thrust their flushed faces in their hands
yet looked with longing through their fingers on that huge
and shaggy bulk that stumbled up the creaking stairs;
his master followed after with his high peaked cap
and with both hands held up those monstrous bulging sides.
Thus like one flesh they mounted to the great bedchamber
where with a mother's care Odysseus tucked the drunk
in bed, the crown of vine leaves fallen about his neck
as greasy drops of sweat dripped from his hanging teats.

He covered Kentaur with a scented sheet, then stood
and watched the myriad folds of flesh sink down in sleep,
and when the wine-soaked breasts, immersed in a deep calm,
swelled up and down in rhythm like a halcyon sea,
the man of many passions slept near by on royal rugs.
An unexpected love, huge, harsh, now crushed his breast:
he pitied all men, foe and friend embraced within him,
and he recalled his home, his son, his peaceful shores,
and sighed, for now his heavy soul denied them all.
He brought to mind those faithful friends who by tall waves
awaited him, though all knew well no soul could flee him,
yet followed, though they knew none would return.
Where were they heading now? Why leave their rich good times
on sandy shores, their high thrones by the plane tree's shade?
At midnight still his mind was roaming round the world;
the deep sea fell asleep, all brains dozed on, and dreams
flung wide their fabled casements on close-lidded eyes;
like dappled beasts who ate their fill, the cities slept,
and sleepless owls perched in olive trees, and wept.
The archer's wide eyes flashed with fire in the dark,
his ears perked up and hearkened to night's muffled sounds:
the beasts slept fitfully by their troughs and softly sighed,
from the arcaded courtyard round he heard the slaves
snore deeply as they sailed unfettered in their sleep,
and now, for the first time, he felt he loved all men:
he loved their eyes, their bodies and their clay souls, all—
loved the whole wretched earth and all its precious cargo,
and as he lay stretched out on Helen's luxurious rugs,
his eyes and brain filled up and brimmed with all mankind.
His mind flew far away while dawn burst on the world
and trees in the warm night cast pearl-drops on the ground;
earth worked with patience darkly in the boughs of time
to turn the hanging, acrid grapes to drops of honey;
so did his thorn-pierced heart, he felt, deep in his breast
hang crude and heavily in the night to ripen slowly;
thus clusters turn to honey soon, bark into fruit,
sun, air, and water merge, the good soil bursts, and all
our shaggy forebears in their grandsons sprout with wings.
The suffering man, the pirate of the sea and brain,
grew tranquil now between the embroidered linen sheets
woven by Helen, until his seething simmered down,
and his voracious mind, that whirlpool, lay becalmed.
The daughter of the swan, no doubt, had slipped him herbs
so that the mistral strengthened, his brain opened sail,
and his soul vanished in the deep blue sea of tranquil sleep.

IV

Dark night shook loose her glaucous hair then slowly turned
and took off her old ivory comb, the crescent moon;
stars browsed for salt like white lambs on the foaming waves,
and the black rooster shook his wings, though night still reigned,
for he had dreamt of suns, and rose to crow in darkness.
He'd roosted in a spacious pine in the king's court
and now half-raised his wings and skimmed from the low boughs.
Old Menelaus' sleep came dear that night, his eyes
at dawn were open still, for still his mind could smell,
with fear and joy, the lion-stench of his old comrade.
But as the red cock raised his heavy wings to crow
at crack of dawn, sleep fell on the old king like lightning;
and as one sprawled beneath a flowering tree when strong
winds blow feels in his lap the flowers fall like petals,
so dreams in a deep hush fell thick and fast on the king's chest.

He dreamt they both had mounted two white steeds and shone
in the dark night like stars, like wings, with brimming minds:
"This is not earth, dear friend, nor do we tread on land,
for my heart opens, my chest soars with flapping wings
until the worms of misery turn to butterflies.
It's not the mind which squats now in my brittle head
and, stooped with cares, counts and recounts the world's dismays—
a nightingale with full throat sings in my skull's cage! . . .
'Farewell, dear wife; we're on our way. Go to your loom,
weave a firm cloth of two fine strands, embroider there
your husband on a pure white horse, his friend beside him
with his seafaring cap, and in his huge hands place
the four winds like four birds of multicolored plumage.
Then place the red sun right, the white moon left, and let
them run behind their masters like two faithful hounds . . .'
I ordered it from my poor wife, remember, friend,
while she filled and refilled with wine our golden cups.
'Sweet love,' she wailed, 'take me with you to hold the taper
while you wash in gold bowls or change your handsome robes;
my lord, I'll be the earth you tread, the cup you sip,

let me but sail, dear love, within the wine you drink!'
We laughed, leapt on our steeds, and then I said, remember:
'My wife, you speak a thousand truths, but we ride far;
the world's too small even for one, and two's too many;
listen: the past is past, swept clean by the four winds;
we ride like two blood-brothers, and there's no returning.'
We whipped our horses, and her black eyes vanished soon."
He spoke, then spread his arms to touch his silent friend:
"Brother, give me your hand, this is what great joy means:
two friends that ride embraced and drain their hearts with talk."

The archer reached his hand, huge as a dragon's paw,
and horsemen and their horses, sun and moon passed through
tall mountain ranges till they came to a green field:
"The trees have blossomed, brother, or is this a dream?
Look at the loving pairs that pass in light and flowers,
all woven of swoons and sorrows, tears and trembling air,
each pierced like swords by cruel, invisible sons they long for."
Then in his saddle the proud man with peaked cap rose,
snapped a tall flowering branch, then gave it to his friend,
when lo! the branch became a wing, the wing a sword,
until the king's mind reeled and his sleep blazed with light.
A mild wind blew, roads opened everywhere like roses,
and he rejoiced at the road left, at the road right,
yet longed to whip his horses and drive straight ahead.
He stood thus at the great crossroads where freedom blew
like a sweet breeze toward all four corners of his head,
for earth was good, the mind ran everywhere and sought all roads.

His soul profoundly plunged in freedom's deep delight;
dear God, his youth revived, the cypress tree bore flowers,
and memory stripped and lightly danced like fantasy
till even the worm that crawls from far to eat each man
sprouted its gaudy wings and soon forgot in flowers.
And when in freedom's gentle breeze the strange dream faded
—it was but a brief lightning flash—at that same hour
the cock was falling toward the courtyard tiles, and there
closed its red wings, swelled its long throat, and crowed
until the coward king in his dream's dazzling fog
heard the cry strike his mind like the sun's radiant spear.
He leapt and smiled as though he'd seen some lovely dream,
but he'd forgotten the wonders of that flowering night
and only in his heart still held a drop of honey.
Striding with haste to his large yard, he ordered slaves
to yoke his costly chariot with two pure-white steeds,
fill his engraved wine-gourds with thrice-old mellow wine,
and bring a spitted lamb, warm bread, and fresh-plucked fruit.
His proud soul longed to ride his friend about the grounds
and show off his abundant wealth and strike him dumb;
already he rejoiced to guess his friend's surprise.
When many-willed Odysseus stood before the door,
the king approached him happily and spoke with joy:
"I can't believe you're still here in my house, dear friend;
I couldn't sleep all night for fear you'd fade away,
and now in day my heart beats like a hawk to see you;
come mount, dear friend, let's gallop through the upper world,
I like to feel you close beside me, knee to knee."

The archer, who at morning kept his spirit locked
till the sun pried it open to speak in human tones,
climbed close-mouthed in the chariot but rejoiced in heart
to reach the mountains soon and breathe the crystal air.
Slowly they rumbled down the crooked path to town
where crowds at daybreak swarmed with lifted arms around
their two ancestral altars raised to Fear and Laughter,
meek gods of poverty that shone in the dawn's light;
but the offerings hung in air, for no one yet could tell
which of the gods would seal their fate and fortune soon.
When the town elders saw the white steeds gleam, they ran,
pressed round their king with questions, hung on his fat lips,
till he smiled graciously and raised his hand aloft:
"Give votive gifts of honey to your good god Laughter,
for I stood sleepless guard above you all night long
then sent my men on foot and horse with laden mules
to fetch the foe full wineskins, sacks of grain and gold.
I didn't spare my wealth or goods to save my country!
Choose from my fat flocks now the best of all my calves,
slay it on Laughter's altar, and let my people spread
a feast to drink their king's good health who like a father
kept vigil night and day to guard earth's happiness.
And now, my faithful councilmen, hear this good word:
Let all young men tomorrow prepare for games of skill.
Let them adorn their bodies and bedeck the fields
for we must try to please our guest, our glorious savior."
He spoke, then flicked the horses with his golden whip,
and the town elders scattered through the crowd, held high
their king's word like a ripe and downy dandelion
and scattered the frail seeds with shouts along the morning air.

Then both kings, shining like two flaming stars, swept off
toward the far fields, leaving behind a star's lean trail.
After long silence, Menelaus suddenly touched
his comrade's knees and with great anguish thus confessed:
"Old friend, my heart's ashamed and does not condescend
to fool and bait my people to retain my realm;
my soul longed, for a moment, to tell the entire truth,
but when I caught your glowering glance, I stopped in fear."
The weaver of minds smiled bitterly and mutely scorned
a mind that had not learned as yet how the world's governed
and what a cruel and crafty heart a leader must have;
his mother had made this king a lamb, fate made him shepherd.
"Old friend, though your lips smile, yet you don't say a word."
The sly man opened his mouth as though his flesh had ripped:
"My mind was far away on shepherds, lambs, and gods."

He spoke, and his wound closed, his mind engulfed his tongue.
Silent, he hailed the holy field, the new-cut stubble,
the crocus-colored soil of summer's blazing heat;
earth lay in downy haze like a child-bedded woman
threshed by dark pains of late but who, exhausted now,
released and tranquil, turns to smile on her son gently.
The strange, rapacious man sighed in his stifled heart;
his mind had never been yoked or broken to the plow,
nor had he longed to live like his field-working father,
but sometimes, when he'd watched the ripe corn from his prow,
vineyards and olive trees and peasants stooped to earth,
he'd sighed with sadness softly, fearful his crew might hear him;
you'd say that some old plowman still plowed through his blood.
He saw, in a poor hamlet, bone-warped women working,
flat-chested, hairy-armed, voices most crude and harsh,
whose husbands, lost in distant wars and distant seas,
left them with bodies uncaressed, untilled, unwatered.
The mind bends down to female earth, both merge as one
and join as wife and husband, swarm with offspring soon,
with hogs and grain and girls and dreams composed of clouds,
and the great couple in the sun caress and fructify.
But at his side his wealthy friend weighed all things well,
and in his anxious landlord's eyes could only see
in the whole world but gain and grain, what's yours, what's mine.
The king stood straight in his chariot, unrestrained, and spoke:
"As far as your eye sees, dear brother, mountains, vales,
fields tilled or fields unplowed, fat meadows, all are mine.
My vineyards flood my fields with wine and make them harbors,
my olive trees turn to green seas until I hear
their cool smoke-silver waves at dusk from my sun roof,
and when my bees swarm up in clouds, the sun's eclipsed."
The landlord's mouth filled to the brim, his chest puffed wide,
and his soul turned to a deep jug that gulped his fields.
But as he spoke, his face's threshing floor grew dark,
for blue-eyed men in rags, with hatchets in their belts,
scattered like thieves in the blond fields to glean the stubble,
and manlike women, whinnying, gave their babies suck.
Sighing, the landlord turned to his fox-minded friend:
"Like blond ants, brother, these bread-hungry people fly
to glean poor scraps from harvest, olive crop, and vintage.
All day they rage and raven, all night long in rut
they couple shamelessly on grass about their fires.
They stomp like giants on my ancestral soil! I fear them!"
The snake-man bared his fangs, laughed long, and shot his sting:
"All the old legends will one day come true, my friend;
these are the dragons now; it's time for us, the dwarfs,

to scramble up the chick-pea bush and eat chick-peas!"
The king gulped down his secret wrath, and whipped his steeds;
he could not stomach talk of poverty and downfalls.
Then soon they came to olive groves within whose shade
they cooled their eyes and brains scorched by the burning fields;
that year the olive trees were blessed with fertile fruit
so that the king crowed with delight: oil brimmed his brain,
oil presses ground within him, oil jars rose in heaps,
crude oil poured tumbling in huge vats while oil soup steamed,
and deep jars, smeared with oil, shone glittering in long rows
until from too much grinding and from too much joy
the king in light stood shimmering like an oil-drowned mouse.
But he soon wearied and spread his arms toward the cool shade:
"I'm scorched with heat, let's lie down by an olive's root
and have a bite or two to rally our tired flesh;
it's gone through much, poor thing, and needs a little rest."
The archer then dismounted, grunting, bit his lips
so that no scornful word might heedlessly escape him,
and when both stretched in the thick shade, reapers at once
ran up with brimming jugs to quench their master's thirst.
The king, sprawled on the grass, recounted all his gain,
his honey, wine and oil of a fine and fertile year,
while the unyoked mute slayer of men beside him thought
how fat his comrade's nape had grown on the lean earth.
They drank the undiluted wine till their brains blazed
and all the olive trees lit up, each branch a lamp,
each tree a candelabrum filled with brimming oil.
The lizard glued its belly to the earth in bliss,
the cypress raised its slender length from the white ground,
and in the cricket's careless head the whole field burned;
the sun, like a lean leopard pounced and prowled around
the ripe grain, olive groves, the two friends sprawled in shade,
till suddenly the archer turned to his friend with love:
"O Menelaus," he cried with throbbing voice and heart,
"let's leave at once! Abandon all these vines and fields!
Youth blooms upon our temples twice! Death comes once more
to take the lead—let's follow him no matter where!
Though no sweet woman's body waits where Death's road ends,
new higher castles rise, my friend, new higher cares!"
He spoke, then leaning closer, gripped his comrade's knees,
and he but turned his wine-dazed head toward the tree's bole:
"I'm tired; I'd like to rest a moment on the grass."
But the home-wrecker crouched like a mad, snapping dog
and growled between his teeth in rage, "Then I'll snatch Helen!"
Yet, as he spoke, he wryly smiled and swept the field:
"I was born yesterday, by God, and I shall die today;

the earth has time enough to stand and chew her cud:
with eons before her and behind, what does she care?
We come and go like flames: 'Good morning' and 'Good night.'
Great joy to him who grasps the lightning flash in time!"
He spoke, then shook his spirit free from dizziness
and leant against the olive tree to plan the seizure;
but all at once he lay stark still with staring eyes
and gazed on the tree's bark where a cocooned cicada
struggled and slowly squirmed to pierce through into light.
Stretched on the ground, Odysseus watched and held his breath.
Like a warm body buried alive, wrapped up in shrouds,
the poor worm twitched to pierce through its translucent tomb
in a mute, heavy war with death, till the archer stooped
and with his warm breath tried to help the writhing soul.
Then lo! a small nape suddenly slit the shroud in two,
and like a budded vine leaf, soft and curly, poked
a blind, unhardened head in light, swayed gropingly,
then strengthened soon in sun and took on form and color.
It stretched its neck and struggled, crawled from its white sheath,
unglued its soft feet from its belly, clutched with bliss
the tree's gray bark, then slowly stretched its body taut
until its fledgling wings unfurled and shimmered in air.
The honey-pale cicada basked in the simmering sun,
and the three rubies on its brow burst in three flames
as it plunged deeper still in the world's warmth and scent.
Fixing its glassy, greedy eyes on the tree's foliage,
its soft smoke-silver body overbrimmed with song
yet made no sound, enraptured still by sun and light
and the huge joy of birth as on earth's sill it stood
before it entered, speechless, numb with the world's wonders.
The man of many passions quaked and mutely watched
how the soul pokes through earth and squirms out of its shroud;
and thus the world, he thought, crawls like a worm to sun,
and thus the mind, in time, bursts like a withered husk
from which there spring, time after time, new finer thoughts
until the ultimate great thought leaps forward: Death.

Then as the subtle man lay on the ground and brooded,
he heard the king scream in his sleep and leap awake:
"As I slept here on grass, a dread dream crushed me, brother:
I dreamt we sauntered on the earth together, arm in arm;
crimson carnations sprang up from our steaming steps,
our words soared high like eagles in the crystal air,
but my eyes turned to clay and suddenly spilled on grass."
The murderer shivered and his heart was clogged with blood,
but he restrained himself and gently touched his friend:

"The lances of the sun were hot and heavy this noon;
let's rise and cool our hearts high on the mountain's ridge."
Then they set out, passed olive groves and distant vineyards,
fresh fields where horses grazed, wild wastelands where bulls browsed,
and slowly climbed the mountain slope's steep, sunlit paths
until the highlands gaped with wide mouth and devoured
horses and kings, then once again closed tight behind them.
At length they stepped on Mount Five-Fingers' breast and rode
through a smooth pass between two cliffs by cool winds tossed.
Hornbeam and ash grew thick, fat fir cones puffed and swelled
till their hard kernels burst with heat in the sun's rays;
high up, at all the firs' forked peaks, new tips sprang up
and like green thirsty tongues stood straight and drank the light.
They saw a wretched mother hang her sickly son
in clefts of blasted rock to take the lightning's strength,
whose bolt had cloven the earth like a two-bladed ax.
She pummeled the hard rock and yelled in the deep chasm:
"Dame Fire, rise up and lick my son's consumptive cheeks!
Ax, seize and heave him by his arms, give him your strength!
Flame, I don't want a sickly son! Sharp ax, decide!"
When the archer heard the mother, his heart leapt with gladness:
"Mother, good health and joy!" he cried. "I stand amazed
and praise your scorn not to give suck to a sickly son!
If only Mother Earth chose with such care as you!"
He turned to share his wild joy with his bosom friend,
but he was standing straight to admire with sated eyes
how white amid the tufted pines gleamed row on row
his sheepcots, barns, thatched huts, dairy and cattle pens,
and how as far as high plateaus, on rocky crags,
his flocks shone in the sun and rang with silvery peals
so that the highlands seemed to sway with black-white wool.
The landlord spoke then in a loud and boastful voice:
"Brother, lift up your eyes, for the world's face has changed;
in the low meadows moisture eats the jocund bells,
but here goat-bells and ram-bells peal in well-tuned sounds,
and when you lie in my thick groves of pine beneath
my penfolds, you'll forget your cares and fitful passions;
the mind's a sheep and grazes on green pastures, too."
He spoke, dismounted from his chariot, and with short legs
stippled with sweat, trudged slowly up the high plateau.
The shepherd dogs smelled their approaching master's scent
and jumped on his belovèd breast, barking with joy;
from the steep crags his old familiar shepherds plunged
and welcomed to their cool greensward their visiting king.
"Tonight we'll sleep close by the croft; spread sheepskins there,
and bring us pailfuls of fat milk to quench the flesh."

Thus did the king command, then lay in a pine's shade
and the old pine rejoiced to give its shade like fruit.
The shepherds ran and brought full frothing jugs of milk:
"Though there's small milk at season's end, it's thick as curds,"
they said, and taking heart sat cross-legged on the stones
to marvel how divine flesh, too, must eat and drink.
But as the archons gulped the milk to feed their minds,
they heard on high tumult of wings, shrill vulture cries,
and saw enormous flames that flashed on the far crags.
The shepherds leapt erect and shouted with great joy:
"It's Rocky! He's climbed and set the eagles' nests on fire!
Those wild birds plunder all our flocks! At the blaze of noon
they swoop with sharp claws on our lambs and carry them off.
The crags are swarming with their young, and Rocky swore
he'd wipe out all that lawless tribe with raging fire.
See how he grills them now like lambs on glowing coals!"
Then both kings raised their eyes to the high crags and watched
the eagles plunge in flames and shriek with agony;
some with scorched wings fell sizzling headlong down to earth,
some seized their fledglings in their claws and fled far off.
They saw a slim form lightly leap from rock to rock
and soon stand sweating by the king to pay him homage.
The young man stood erect in the sun's blaze and stank
like a wild bull; his wedge-shaped beard, black as a crow,
dripped laudanum and sage-sap, glowed and steamed until
the archer marveled at the godly race of man,
at this sharp, swordlike body fed with rain and sun
that rose with raging wrath to storm the blazing air.
"Old friend, I like this gallant youth, he strikes the eye;
that broad back should wear bronze, those hands should hurl the quoit.
Give him to me! Now spread your hand in regal gesture!"
Then the king's generous heart rejoiced to make the gift:
"You give me great joy in this hour, my brother! Take him!
I'll not say no to spoil your mood; we two are one."
The landlord raised his voice and called his shepherd then:
"I here renounce my vested rights and give you all,
tough body and proud soul, to my world-famous friend,
for in his service, lad, you'll find your heart's desire."
The shepherd scowled, displeased, for on the hands and face
of his new master he could smell the sea's sharp brine,
and though he spoke not, schemed how to escape him soon.
He roamed his pastures round and bid his beasts goodbye:
"Farewell, high mountains! Ah, farewell, my prize milch cows,
don't weep, I'll come back soon, my oars across my back,
and turn them into ladles then to stir your milk;

I'll bring you sea-salt in my fists, dear lady lambs,
I go to sea like a black ram to browse on the sea's salt!"

The king's thick flocks were herded soon into their pens;
the sheep rolled down in rows, ram-bells and sheep-bells rang
and tumbled down the mountain slopes like cataracts.
Goats with thin silvery bells leapt down; their varied horns
—curved kissing half-moons, spreading boughs, or taper-straight—
flashed in the sun; the he-goat with his haughty tread
led like a lowering god and clanged his clamorous bell.
Last came a shaggy ram with twisted horns, blear-eyed,
who dragged himself with pain, drained out by too much lust,
for all day long he'd leapt and tupped his rutting ewes.
A few goat-boys lagged in the rear to pry out some
stray kids who'd fallen in crevices or craggy clefts.
The king stood up to watch and revel in his great wealth
and looked like a stout gelded ram with twisted horns.
"How swiftly beasts increase in the charmed man's enclosures,"
he murmured with great pride, and then lay down once more.
On low round stones before the penfolds, milkers sat
and filled their caldrons and clay pots with frothing milk,
while Rocky in a corner penned a herd of goats
and chose a tender kid to slay for the king's welcome.
A shepherd's supper soon was spread on the grassy lawns
round which their lords reclined, and peasants sat cross-legged,
while in the quickset hedge lambs bleated and goats brayed,
and like a master shepherd the good king rejoiced
to talk with the young goat-boys condescendingly.
He bent his mouth close to his friend's ear and whispered:
"If God had not predestined me to rule my people,
I'd be a shepherd browsing herds on these far hills."
The demon-driven man laughed low, and boldly answered:
"If God predestined me as shepherd on these high crags
I'd give my lambs to wolves, plunge to the fields, round up
brave lads and be wolf-leader of a fierce wolf-pack.
And if God chanced to make me a leader of a people,
again I should cast off my crown with proud contempt
and sail away, stripped bare, alone on a small raft.
It suits me, brother, to fight fate with lance and spear!"
The sweet-faced landlord did not like these brazen boasts:
"Brother, do not blaspheme, for it's man's sacred duty
to tag with calm behind whatever his fate ordains
and trudge her road to the far verge his whole life long.
This is the only way that we can match the gods,
for they, too, follow their own road like banked-in streams.

May God forgive me for this weighted word I fling:
he is a god who follows his fate to its far end."
But the bold captain disagreed, and his hair flamed:
"I think man's greatest duty on earth is to fight his fate,
to give no quarter and blot out his written doom.
This is how mortal man may even surpass his god!"
The startled king moved from his place as though he feared
both might be struck beneath the pine by a just bolt:
"His mind's decayed, his heart's grown bold, his doom stalks close,"
he thought, then closed his eyelids, shuddered fitfully,
and flattered sleep with secret wiles to come and take him.
The sleepless archer stretched on quilts beneath the pine
and marveled how the stars in the pine needles swayed
slightly and fell amid night boughs like plundered petals.
His eyes were still unsated with that rich-wrought field
where stars gleamed town on town and whitened nest on nest;
Zeus, that deceiving star, and Sirius, the night-prowler,
blazed as the great Star-River rolled and drowned the night.
He closed his eyes and thought that he had lain with joy
to sleep at the sky's roots, that the vast tree had bloomed,
that pure-white blossoms fell and fell and showered his brain
until his mind plunged down to sleep like flowering constellations.

While the two kings slept on beside the hedgerow paling,
Helen afar lay sleepless in her golden room
attended by the chattering slaves she'd brought from Troy:
ladies of noble birth who had once gleamed in courts
but in black exile now had withered away with weeping.
"Dear waiting-maids, good ladies, in my heart there rears
that toppled tower, alas, and that far, fleeting joy.
I hold in my hands like a white rose that limpid moon
which for the last time shed its glow on your dear homes
that now lie threshed and ruined on the plundered sands.
Somewhere a sweet wind blows, memory grows fresh, and what
was lost on earth returns immortal to the mind;
last night my old wounds swelled, my old desires returned,
for in this palace stalked that murderous man whose snares
toppled the famous walls of your far-distant land."
Thus the swan-seeded lady spoke, and threnodies
fell like spring showers in a wooded valley glade.
Their famous castle towered again, their houses gleamed,
their chambers teemed with children, feasting boards were spread,
soft beds were readied and the sweet strokes of hands began
until the oil flames reared like wide-eyed witnesses.
Then their heart's threnody became a bitter song:
"O swift bird fleeting through the sky, let down your wings

that I might hang from your white neck and fly the fields,
that my dry throat may be refreshed and smell of brine;
then like the wild rock-partridge who has lost her young
I'll take my eyes alone with me, drink water only,
roll in my country's ashes wherever I may find them,
and wail wherever I find my lone son's cradle hung."
The sad tune broke in uncaressed and hopeless throats,
for in the gray or black hair of each noble lady
her precious castle shone, a bloodstained golden crown;
Paris still rolled his curly head in Helen's lap,
and all, queen and her slave-girls, sighed, made kindred all
by aching passion for that far-off, bygone joy.
While the sad slaves lamented, far in distant woods,
in mingled moon and setting sun, cock-pheasants stepped
and strutted round their females till their cockscombs swayed
in all the erotic dance's dizzying vertigo,
and feathers molted till the female chose that male
to crow in victory last who leapt the highest in light,
then raised her tail and took the chosen seed deep down
in her small flaming body and made it ever immortal.
Amid old ruins, female spiders armed themselves,
slung poison in their tails, stored venom in their veins,
swelled up with lust and crawled to pounce upon a mate.
In the sea's glaucous depths the female cuttlefish
lay on soft sand like a white bride, her belly trembling,
and ink-black bridegrooms, struck with longing, swarmed close by,
while emerald nights and days passed far above, and yet
not one dared spread a tentacle to touch the bride.
A fisher in his torch's blaze threw soothing oil
until the sea spread smooth and he could spy far down
the erotic gathering as he cast his spear, and then
slowly drew up the female cuttlefish with craft
and scooped in nets the following and lascivious wooers.
Air, sea, and land burst with lust's frenzied vertigo,
the mind, even like the heart, got drunk, and the queen sighed,
dismissed her maids, and on her mother-of-pearl divan
bent over the magic crystal eye to watch her fate.
At first she could discern but a dark bubbling stream,
then traced the water longingly from bank to bank
till slowly in the flowing pool her eye discerned
a small ship scudding, filled with hairy-chested men,
and at the prow a pointed cap like a tall flame.
But then she tossed her black locks, and the crystal moved,
the murky waters rolled again and the ship vanished.
Then slowly new signs etched themselves on the swift stream:
bull-horns and golden palaces, full suns and moons,

a bent old man who counted pearl-strings, bead by bead. . . .
But misted by the warm sun-lovely lady's breath,
the holy crystal drained, the pearled immortal pool
rolled sluggishly as a white swan sailed on its stream
with straight, mute throat and vanished in her open bosom.
All night she stooped above that crystal eye, entranced,
and watched the swan pass like a dream through her dimmed brain;
and thus her maidens found her stooped in heavy sleep,
at daybreak, when they softly slipped into her golden chamber.

But far in the high hills the Day Star leapt with fire
and struck all rested eyelids, woke the dreaming kings,
for mountain sleep had filled their weary bones with joy.
They gorged themselves on goat's milk, and in the young day
hailed mountains, shepherds, sheep, then followed close behind
by reed-slim Rocky, at whose tread the whole earth shook,
plunged down the beetling mountain paths and slippery stones.
A fierce sirocco rose and the olive trees turned silver,
struggled and howled as if to uproot themselves from earth;
the grainfields, still uncut, tossed like a troubled sea,
and raging clouds of thickening dust eclipsed the sun.
"A wrathful god swoops through my fields and stalks my wealth!"
So thought the regal landlord as he whipped his steeds;
they tossed their necks and snorted, tore through the far fields,
shot through the vineyards, groves, and grain like lightning bolts,
swept up the palace's steep road at drop of noon
and beat on the great castle gates with foaming breasts.
Helen was standing on the tower with rapturous joy
as the wind's savage tumult struck and swept her mind.
She wore a rose-flame gown embroidered with gold wheat,
a silver-winged cicada kept an ardent guard
on one pale shoulder while an ivory half-moon sank
with deep fear in her bosom's dark and downy cleft.
Her blue-black hair, new-washed with magic perfumed balms,
coiled like a castle round her head in three tall tiers,
and as the great gale struck her by the tower, she seemed
like a long flame that licked the battlements with greed.
Her black eyes gazed far out beyond the fruited fields
and broad Eurotas that rolled on to the far sea,
laden with laurel, myrtle, osier and rose-bay.
Suddenly on the reed-glad bank far off, the two
great kings shone like two insects, like two golden scarabs,
and Helen sent her slaves to the high tower to call them.
After the tiring journey, Menelaus longed
to sink in lukewarm water and ease his weary flesh
that he might come before his people cooled, refreshed,

and watch his young men playing at their skillful games.
But the home-wrecker lightly leapt the tower stairs
two at a time, shining with youth, to talk with Helen,
and the seductress felt her soul, like a small bird,
leap, too, in her notorious body, and flap its wings,
but she reined back her fright, gazed at the ground, and smiled.
Then the soul-snatcher slowly stalked his tender prey,
a lion who in the water's glitter spies a doe,
but when he could have stretched his hand and seized her throat
he stood before her heavily and held back his strength.
Slowly the god-born lady raised her downy eyes,
looked in the sly abductor's face and boldly spoke:
"In that strange eye you gave me once to watch my soul,
I stood by a black prow beneath your shade, Odysseus!"
Before the seaman's eyes there flashed his bloodstained dream
—the godlike amputated flesh—and his heart softened:
"I heard your cry borne on the wind, and I've come, Helen.
Your soul must not go lost and leave no trace behind."
She moved her black arched eyebrows and her painted lips:
"One night when I felt choked with restlessness, I strolled
on the sun-terrace, raised my arms and called you twice.
I've never called but that the air's become a man;
now here you stand full in the sun, and just behind you
I see a ship with hoisted sail, a sunburnt crew,
and all my future tossing on the endless waves."
Then she fell silent, watching the far fields, the hills
and the old river that cut through earth like a slim snake.
She smiled, and in her smile the whole world suddenly seemed
to be a deep, round, miracle-working crystal sphere
in which her shadow slowly passed like a black swan,
but when she turned, no tremor shook her crystal voice:
"When will you come to take me, midnight or break of day?"
The heart-seducer touched her sun-bright shoulder gently:
"At break of day; we'll stand by my ship's prow by dusk."
Then they fell silent, and Helen left the tower serenely
to gather her rich garments and her precious gems,
for none should go to war without their proper weapons.
As the home-wrecker from the watchtower cast his eyes
on the far fields, a trenchant longing suddenly seized him
to shriek out shrilly like a hunting hawk high in the air.

At length the people left their threshing joyfully,
descended to the river, washed themselves, then climbed
to sit at ease on the palaestra's shady stairs.
The workers' faces glittered as at length they stretched

their scraggly bodies on stone seats, worn smooth by time,
and gaped at archons dressed in white who sat on thrones
and held tall gold-tipped staffs, like tribal chiefs or kings.
Far down, on sandy stretches fenced by river reeds,
the young men chafed with longing for the games to start,
and like crisp water-sprites shone in the sun's refulgence.
The callow youths were parted in three warring camps.
At one side, an old gymnast talked to the workers' sons
to put them on their mettle and whip up their pride:
"Boys, when you flood the field with your lean bodies soon,
scorn life and death; victory alone counts here on earth.
Don't let the youths of noble blood mock at your fall
or shout that you were born for work and slavery only.
May earth on such a day gape wide and swallow us all!"
In their midst stood a humble altar raised to Hunger,
and the old gymnast snapped his three-lashed leathern whip
as round the unlaughing goddess with her empty dugs
the young men ran and cooled her flesh with their warm blood.
Meanwhile the well-fed noble youths stretched on the sands
and vied in praising the fine lines of each one's body,
to demonstrate whose tight thighs, shoulder blades, or chest
bore witness that a god once bred with his ancestress.
But their own gymnast goaded them with stubborn words:
"O well-born lads, I think that poverty's pale offspring,
who mock at pain and take their lashings silently,
shall shame your god-bred bodies in the ring today.
Forget the immortal blood that flows through all your tribe:
victors alone clasp gods, or from gods take their seed!"
The youthful bodies then like well-bred horses tossed
their heads and held their strength in check like noble lords;
they longed impatiently for that one moment in light
when they might prove their god-descended seed and grace.
Further away, on the low ground by the river's edge,
played boys of myriad seed, those spawned by secret stealth.
When wars had dragged the Spartan men to far-off strands,
blond-bearded chieftains from the North descended south
and spied lone women stooped and tilling the hard soil:
"Madam, the farm work's heavy; let me help you sow."
"Stranger, that's true; what wages shall you want this day?"
"A bit of bread; then, if you like, a kiss besides."
Since the maids wished that, too, they closed the bargain soon,
the men bent to the yoke, plowed up the barren soil
and sowed, plowed in good measure the maids' barren wombs,
till all together, farms and flesh, burgeoned with fruit.
A slender blue-eyed trainer set these youths on fire:
"Boys, I've a fine speech; chew it well, turn it to meat:

Our god's a drunkard, a man-slayer, an eater of steak!
He bridges and unbridges rivers, roots up rocks,
grows thirsty and spies vineyards, hungers and spies grain,
turns to a mill and grinds, to a press and crushes grapes.
Come close, my lads, for now I'll tell you a great secret:
Cast your eyes round: all that you see we'll burn one day!"
Meanwhile the two kings came to view on a high mound,
Helen between them swayed like a tall lily's stem,
and earth turned to a vase to hold its precious bloom;
the air was drenched with fragrance, and the people hushed
as all three gods enthroned themselves on lionskins.
The king gazed proudly on his people, his fat fields,
his ancient river, the bright youths grouped round the reeds,
then with glad heart and sated loins he raised his staff
and all the conches blared and the brave games of skill began.

When a poor shepherd's flute was heard, the rushes moved,
and the first group of young men dashed into the ring,
their bodies scooped by hunger and devoured by toil,
but who still trod the earth with stubbornness and pride.
Their gymnast then approached the king and spoke out frankly:
"Great lord, we're not of noble blood nor sport all day
to shape in these arenas, with untroubled calm,
the bodies given by earth, and turn them into spirit.
Forgive our lean flesh, king, devoured by heavy toil;
but we resist cruel need as much as man's soul can,
and fight with stubborn wrath to turn it into freedom.
Now condescend, great king! Gaze on our liberation!"
He spoke, turned to his boys, raised his flute to his lips,
and their lean bodies listened to the reed's shrill sound
until sound was transformed to spirit and air to storm
as their lean bodies swayed to the flute's will in rhythm.
The threshers first fanned out across the field in pairs,
and with wide swinging curves, throwing their bronzed arms wide,
they cut invisible grain to the tuned air's injunction.
For a long time they threshed to the shrill music's beat
like nobles to whom workers' toil seems sweet in dream
till you, brute work, become a god's intoxication.
But then the tune changed suddenly as the flute grew bold,
their thighs stretched wide, legs gripped the ground, arms reached up high
then struck toward earth and struck again, glittering in light
as though woodcutters flailed their axes on far banks
and hewed down huge invisible forests silently.
And as they worked and shadow-hewed their woods of air,
a song of freedom burst from their enkindled chests
until the stooped soul of the workers leapt in sun.

This was no fancied game, nor no mere cutting of wood—
their eyes grew wild, froth edged their lips, and their necks swelled,
until the king leapt up in terror, shook his staff
and choked the bold song in the young men's flaming throats.
Then with great wrath he waved the workers' sons aside.
A throttled muttering sound rose from the seats below,
but the storm smothered and flicked out, a shuddering only
flashed like mute lightning in the workers' simmering breasts.
A lyre emerged then, wreathed with pure-white lily blooms,
and in the air re-echoed with high, tranquil tunes.
Archons puffed up like adders, the king leapt to his feet
to admire the noble bodies decked with flowers. He sighed,
remembering how in youth he, too, once shone in sun.
The sullen crowd looked on and whispered to each other:
"Their bodies are well fed, they shine and gleam, we know,
because they're not worn out by toil nor drained by hunger."
But who has ever heeded the poor workers' words?
No god or noble has ever listened to their complaint.
Their arms twined round each other's shoulders, the noble lads
advanced in a round wreath before the triple thrones,
and the swan's daughter craved their unexhausted youth.
The earth rejoiced in pride, and even the sun stood still
as their old gymnast led and held his lyre aloft
with fingers white as lilies, then addressed the throne:
"I know of only one great joy on earth, O king:
to sit well washed and watch the beauty of noble youth."
He spoke and struck his lyre, the handsome bodies swayed
then spread their hands so that their rosy fingers met
until a light-winged dance bent the lads slenderly
as though they were slim water plants in the sea's depths.
The dance swirled on, the tune grew shrill, the bodies swayed
in the slant sun like fresh green reeds by the riverbank.
They whirled and reached the highest peak of their contending,
but just before the storm could break, the lyre grew calm
and balanced pure joy nobly with the body's grace.
The king's eyes filled with tears to think of his own youth.
Oho, when he was still but a green lad of twelve,
how crossroads flamed, how the earth flowered wherever he walked!
One day a bearded man stole him and took him far
to the five springs of Mount Five-Fingers; in a thatched hut
they drank sweet wine till their minds swam, till mountains swayed
and a full vaporous moon rose crimson in the sky
like an enormous tom-tom thumped by wedding guests.
When their sweet honeymoon had ended, the man gave
the young boy gleaming armor, a strong lusty bull,
a large two-handled winecup to carouse with friends,

and when the boy plunged to his town from the high slopes,
all, kin and strangers, marveled at his hoarse new voice
and how he stalked his house like the one master there.
How fast the years had sped to where there's no returning!
He turned to his old comrade to unburden his mind
but drew back, startled, when he saw his savage guest
leap to his feet and lash out at the youths with rage:
"Great is the gift of body's grace here on this earth,
but I cry shame to that weak man who lives and dies
without great mental cares or burdensome grief of heart.
I've been devoured by great spite, joys, brine, and gods,
but gaze on my gray head, O well-born sons of nobles—
it thrusts to pierce beyond nobility and beauty!"
The noble lads drew back in fear and stopped their dance,
the king grew red with wrath, scowled at his friend and thought:
"Fate has in him grown proud, the holy measure is smashed
that balances the good and evil powers within us.
May God grant that he go away from my side quickly!"
His thought was drowned in the great noise that filled the field,
for youths of unknown fathers rushed out brandishing high,
like flaming demons, swords and shields of glittering bronze.
Their chieftain, dragon-fierce, beat on a brazen tray
and ruled their bodies with a swift but heavy beat.
They broke in ranks and then ran shouting in mock battle;
they played and seized each other, embraced and disengaged,
but more and more their blood boiled and their eyes grew wild
until, behold, the play turned real, the battle swelled,
till a slim youth rolled on the ground with shattered chin
and all went wild at smell of blood, for slaughter leapt
in veins, old, atavistic, and all flailed their swords.
Ah, what great joy to die in the games' swift vertigo,
until your blood mounts to the boiling point and bursts
your narrow body nor longs to flow through idle veins!
Many strong bodies had fallen in the blood-red riot
and in the brimming froth of power, had not the king
risen in rage and ordered all disbanded swiftly
in shame, for they had stained that holy day with blood.
But the archer looked with longing on the burgeoning youths
and thought, "If only these wild bodies were all mine!
God, I'd let loose my lion-soul on them to do
all that I've left undone on land or sea or mind.
How can one withered body do all the heart desires?"
The flaming Evening Star flailed at the gathering dark,
the conches blared, and then the king rose and proclaimed:
"My people! I crown the noble youths victors in beauty
and in the stable governance of wrath and passion.

They kept their rhythm, scorned intoxication's lust,
their bodies were obedient swords to their calm souls;
it gives me joy to wreathe their heads with the wild olive."
He spoke, but the crowd seethed with uproar and yelled boldly:
"The victor's crown belongs by right to the workers' sons!
They mixed with skill their own strength and their country's good,
each move they made surpassed an empty, formal grace.
We'll raise an altar to these lads and rear in bronze
the one most handsome, zone it then with low wide walls
where pregnant maids may sit in rows and gape at dusk."
But the king struck his throne in wrath with his gold staff:
"Who said the people could judge? When have they ever been heard?"
A mass of heads swayed, torsos writhed in stormy air,
the wretched workers like a foaming hollow sea
thundered, and slowly pressed hard on their master, growling.
But suddenly there, between the mob and angry king,
the castle-wrecker's arm stretched like a heavy wall:
"Great king, give me the right to grant the olive crown! . . .
I give this bitter wreath of manliness and freedom
not to the poor who thunder idly and spout words,
nor to the lustrous noble youths who strut and crow
as though all earth were a dancing floor and mind a garden—
I crown instead those heads that were blood-broken in battle!"
He spoke, and the games ended. Mob and archons fled
and took their several roads in swarms, but their hearts roared
of bad news, earth turned off its course, of law unsaddled,
of strangers who had burdened them with strange new gods,
all dark and evil signs of the world's imminent end!

The queen leant forward in her white-horsed chariot, hushed,
while her belovèd handmaid held the golden reins;
her mind had flown far off to distant lands and peoples.
As in a cloud of light she rode to the castle's crown,
her large nostalgic eyes caressed the sweating lads,
the reeds and ancient river, like a wandering dream.
In silence the two friends strolled by the river's edge;
the torrid sun had sunk to rest, from the cool ground
the first sweet, quiet sounds of night began to rise.
Ah, sorrow makes strong knees grow weak, and the king walked
yet felt untimely old, for the mob speeds and casts
its kings like empty rinds on the road ruthlessly.
What conflagrations scorched his heart when he was young
and his flock followed, trembling, his bold spirited lead!
When he became a man, his heart merged with his people,
unnumbered brains spoke in his words whenever he thought,
and when he raised his hand, unnumbered hands rose too.

Sparta was a huge body then: men, beasts and tombs
that sprawled along the riverbank, and he its soul.
But now he dragged behind, his soul a mouthful of spoiled meat.
The stumbling king sighed heavily and stood stock-still,
and the heart-reader guessed his pain unerringly
but lashed out at his friend nor spared him in frank talk:
"Only the strongest spirit has the firm right to rule!
If you want to hold Sparta, then your mind and strength
must far surpass all other Spartan minds and strengths.
If you but crack, then give your throne at once to your betters!"
The pallid king complained to his ungentle friend:
"Only a god may utter such unmerciful words,
for only the Immortals know not downfall or old age.
Aren't you afraid that soon one day your mind and knees
will suddenly buckle, too, and fall to earth decayed?
Then a young man shall come and make you eat your words!"
The savage athlete's mouth turned to a bitter smile:
"Old friend, I battle night and day never to fall;
I look on youth as on my strongest sons and foes,
and they watch me impatiently with greed and search
my eyes for signs of dullness and my teeth for rot
and if my mind still stands erect on battle's peak.
But if a young man ever should come and make me quail,
then I'll rise up at once myself, give him my throne,
and like a moribund old octopus drag down
my tentacles to the sea's deepest pit, and croak there!"
The king was struck with terror, and all at once his flesh
and old bones melted in the slant sun's spidery snares.
Night brimmed with soft caresses, waters filled with shade,
the first faint stars struck fire, and the slender moon
hung from night's collar like a sacred amulet.
The lion stalked its prey and yawned with rumbling growls,
and far away on snowy peaks, in lichened woods,
knock-kneed and shaggy bears swirled in lightfooted dance.
Hunger and Eros prowled through mountain passes then
and softly slunk in hamlets, knocked on every door,
till boys and girls met slyly in delirious night
to tell each other lovers' tales, and shadows rolled
entangled on the ground, by lickerish night devoured.
Wide riverbanks of honeysuckle shook the mind,
and soon the two great kings, old friends in joy and war,
hurried their pace, and arm in arm climbed toward the castle,
longing to see that godly form and calm their minds.
But when they reached the castle gate, from the black night
leapt seven monstrous women, seven towering men.
Rude leggings bound their shin-bones, sheepskins wound their flanks,

their coarse blond hair like hawsers tumbled down their backs,
and from their belts of rush hung pitch-black double-axes.
Glaring with blue eyes boldly on the king, they said:
"We bow low to your crown, O mighty Crown of Earth!
Our tribe sends us as heralds to your majesty;
we hunger and need earth to sow, good ground to grasp;
our starving race rolls down from the cold, craggy hills,
and here the fields turn green, the weather is sweetly warm
till now we haven't the heart to rise and go elsewhere.
Give us your untilled fields, Great King, let us take root!"
The fourteen bodies reared and spread their roots like trees
till the pale king turned to consult his friend in fear:
"Help me, dear friend! What shall I do, for my heart quakes?"
But the lone man rejoiced to touch the iron barbs
of magic charms that jangled in the sun-blond braids.
He then recalled the old male worm, and his mind reeled.
The abject king asked him again, and gasped for breath:
"Help me, dear friend! What shall I do, for my heart quakes?"
The archer turned, gazed on him well, then flung his shaft:
"Your loins are shrunk and dry! Now that new blood pours down,
open your veins and graft them! Let fate's will be done!"
The king puffed up his chest, and his heart heaved with pride:
"My strength is like a lioness who has given birth!
Welcome, blond beasts, come step into my yawning mouth!
Take fields, plow hard, but I shall gather the gold grain!
Take slopes and plant the vineyards, but the wine is mine!
Take women to your beds, take men, may your wombs bulge,
but I, your Great Chief, shall corral your children yearly!
If you're agreed, we'll slay a he-goat and swear oaths."
A strapping red-haired woman raised her hands on high:
"God shouts and asks for earth, he likes your flocks and fields.
Forward! Let's slay black he-goats and exchange great oaths!"
Odysseus smiled and winked to an old barbarian chief:
"I know what god rolls down on wheels with grappling irons
and from the high snow-covered peaks sweeps through these fields!"
The old chief turned till blue and black eyes merged in stealth
and for a long time their crossed glances sparked with fire.
The lion had pounced upon his prey, devoured it whole,
and soon, with his rude tongue had wiped his bloodstained chops;
the lovesick sweating bear had finished his slow dance
and in the moonlight licked his bandy paws like honey;
so did the archer caress the old barbarian chief
who licked his lips as though they dripped with blood and honey
when he first heard the foolish king give up his fields.
The bearers of good news set forth, grinning with glee,
and the sharp-eyebrowed evening with her new moon smiled.

Then the two kings, sunk deep in thought, stepped silently
beyond the brazen threshold guarded by two aging lions.

Tall, gracious Helen welcomed them in the great chamber,
and when Odysseus raised his eyes, his heart rejoiced
because the dress she wore spoke of their secret flight:
a lengthy sea-blue mantle stitched with shells and stars,
pale pearly nautili that sailed around the hem,
two rows of oars that plied the waves about her waist,
and when she moved, the house was drowned in shining sea.
A conch resounded sweetly in the boatman's breast,
but he choked down his joy, and through the skylight watched
how night like a black panther prowled the royal groves.
That night the famed seductress ordered the rich feast
of their great secret flight spread in the men's quarters.
They sat on thrones and ate of the fine food in silence,
and as the undiluted wine snaked through their brains
the hypocrite raised high his brimming golden cup:
"I drink this vineyard's blood to your good health, dear friend!
My words are salt and water, yet friendship stands like rock;
our lips pour out a stream of uncontrollable words—
the mindless wine spills some, and some our wretched need,
and some the mad wind that sweeps by and knocks us giddy,
but the heart's words are deep, dear friend, they need sea-divers.
I speak now from the heart in separation's hour:
whenever I recall your eyes, the world grows sweet!"
Tears suddenly blurred the king's dark eyes as he replied:
"Brother, a piercing voice of sorrow tears my heart:
'Open your eyes and gaze your fill for the last time,
O soul, for you shall never again look on Odysseus!' "
The double-minded man's voice choked, his throat drew tight:
"Dear friend, I hear the same sad voice tear through my heart,
but the tough mind won't stoop to tears and soft caresses—
I freely mold my fate as though it were my will;
I bless, dear friend, the destiny that joined us both
to see strange peoples, shores, and towns, that on a night
like this we may sit drinking in your palace here
and gaze with marveling dread on our dissembling Helen.
But we have said enough, and our eyes overflow."
The king, however, was not consoled, and sadly thought:
"The heart is not enough, it's an unbrimming sieve
poured full of joy both night and day, yet never full."
The subtle man then turned and smiled on arch-eyed Helen:
"I drink your health, O deathless daughter of the swan!
You merge both god and beast, and on your eyebrows weigh
earth's savage passions and the sky's high holy grace.

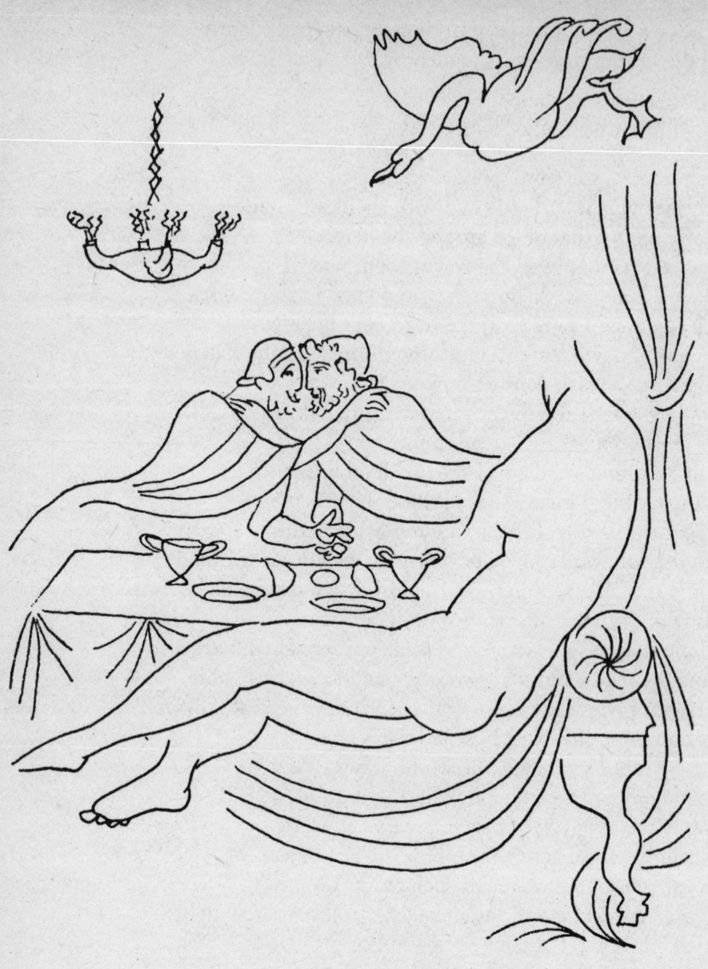

May you be blessed because you lit in slothful souls
a raging war that opened minds and widened seas
till in our crude heads victory rose and sat enthroned—
a small bird of sweet song and blood-bedabbled wings.
May you be blessed on green earth and the glaucous waves;
you burst in the unflowering grass like a great rose,
like a great thought, all curly, flaming, many-leaved,
O rose of earth, loved of all eyes, the black air's joy!
The soil blooms for your sake, poor brides grow beautiful,
for every groom in darkness kisses his own Helen.

We weep and cry till in our minds the swan's child smiles
and on the peak of darkness shines like mother's bosom
till the distracted mind laughs like a suckling babe.
The flower of Lethe, Lady, blooms between your breasts."
Helen laughed silverly to hear her praises sung:
"The great all-knowing goddesses on their cool beds
taught you nightlong your many blandishments, your spells,
and how to unlock the double-bolted woman's heart,
till now, in truth, you hold us like a full-blown rose,
and when you talk, I'm deeply glad to be alive!
A woman's beauties are her gifts and dear adornments,
but only when a great man's hands enjoy them and caress them."

The king then raised his tearstained face and softly touched
his comrade's knees and smiled upon him tenderly:
"My heart bids me give you a precious, parting gift
to hold deep in your heart and to recall your friend,
for if I fade from your bright mind, I shall soon perish!"
He spoke, then left to open his huge treasure chests.
With cunning craft the archer watched him fade in dark
and vanish in the labyrinthine palace vaults,
then turned in time to catch the smile on Helen's lips
and in a sudden shock his heart ached for his friend:
"Doesn't your marble heart feel for him, Lady, now?"
But the uncompassionate seed of god and beast replied:
"My marble heart feels no compassion, for that's gone;
life can create with him nor fruit nor flower now."
He sighed with heavy heart, for in the woman's eyes
he saw man lying supine, decked out with funeral gifts,
and shuddered, for he felt he too might one day lie
like a dead man in both her starry, nightborn eyes,
for woman's breast is a sweet refuge, a safe harbor.
He shook his still ungiddy head from her sweet glance:
"My own heart throbs to fall in his good arms with love;
I hold his body in my hands, and my heart breaks
as though I grasped sand slipping slowly down to earth."
Meanwhile the king bent low and soon ransacked his chests
till his deep palms with gold and silver treasure brimmed
and with ecstatic greed and joy caressed the wealth
his crude forebears had heaped with so much blood and war.
He chose at length his most illustrious prize and raised
it high in the lamp's spluttering flame to glut his eyes.
Within his hands there flashed the small yet golden form
of that trustworthy god who screens and safeguards friendship:
in his right hand he held the lightning bolt of vengeance,
and in his left a flaming ruby, man's own heart.

Trembling, the king caressed the god and begged with fervor:
"Keep well, almighty dreadful God, in my friend's heart,
keep there my memory green, let not my shadow fade;
I have none better on earth to whom my soul may cleave."
Still praying to the god, he placed him for remembrance,
and his last hope, in his friend's double-dealing palms:
"Dear friend, there's no more lustrous gift in all my chests.
That night when God embraced my lovely mother-in-law,
he flapped his wings like a great swan, and fled forever.
The god-kissed bride tore at her hair and begged a sign
for solace that a god had taken her first flower,
and as she wailed, she felt this gold shape lie in her lap.
On my blessed wedding night, the Swan's celestial mate
placed it upon my hearth that the dread god might guard me.
Now I rejoice to place it in your palm, Odysseus."
Then the arch-cunning merchant, learned in all merchandise
of heaven and earth, weighed in his palm the gift with skill:
"Brother, I love the goldsmith's hands that fashioned this;
it must be worth a huge shipload of wine and grain.
May God who holds the keys to man's heart witness this,
and may I never again know joy nor my own land,
but may my entrails heave and sway like the sea's waves
if my mind ever lets you fall in Lethe's well.
I call on you, pure patron of great friendship, hear me!"
Thus did the perjurer speak, and the god squirmed in dark
until a voice buzzed in the heart-seducer's ears:
"Ah, cunning, sly, perfidious fox, have you no shame?
If I should rise to tell all that I know of you,
mocker of gods, the stones of earth would rise to stone you!"
The treacherous man scowled angrily and shouted back:
"Sit on your eggs, you deathless scarecrow; don't get smart!
If I should rise and to the quaking mob disclose
all that I know of *you*, O fool, you're a lost wretch!"
A quivering voice pled secretly in whispers then:
"Swallow your tongue, dear friend, hold our old secret fast;
don't let the fools get wind of us, keep all your wits!"
The arrogant man laughed loudly, and in calloused hands
tossed high the terror-stricken god like burning coals.
The king was startled to hear the loud indecent laughs,
but the sly man embraced his friend with feigned concern
and for the second time swore friendship's deathless oath:
"I'll not forget you, friend, even though my dust turn dust;
all my life long you'll live, too, in my memory
until my body stoops and spills its brains in mud
and you and I descend like moles or shades to Hades."
But the king groaned, for such need seemed but bitter balm:

"Alas, my mind rejects the thought, my heart can't bear
to touch and talk with its old friend and then to turn
and find him suddenly vanished in the empty air."
The demigod then pitied his ill-fated friend:
"Brother, all life's a dream; don't let your heart grow bitter.
Troy rose once in our brains like a resplendent toy
fashioned of mud and women, slaughters and far shores
that we gulped down like a deep cup of maddening wine
till our minds reeled and set their sails for open seas.
Don't let the mocking spirit of wine deceive you, friend;
it's not true that we once set out with our swift ships,
that for ten years we fought to take that famous town
or that one night its dust was strewn in air like smoke;
all these were monstrous phantoms, playthings of the brain.
The mind of giddy man sways but in slight commotion
and fashions shores and castles, gods, sweet bodies, ships,
and on the highest peak of all its wealth enthrones its Helen.
These creatures shine like mist a moment in our minds
then fade from sight abruptly when a small breath blows."
Thus did the double-dealing man attempt with craft
to calm his friend who soon would lose his light, his Helen.
The exhausted king was startled, as though his life had drained,
but memory swiftly reared and flared high in his head:
"Though all life were but dream and empty shadow, yet
I held embraced the holy truth, dear friend, that day
when all the castle burned and from the savage flames
I crushed full-fragrant cooling Helen within my arms."
Then Menelaus smiled with sorrow as he recalled
how he had raised her in his arms, a fainting fawn,
and plunged in sea up to his loins, parting the waves.
The armies were all dazzled, and at once the ten
long years flared like blue thunder in their heads, and vanished.
If only Zeus had crashed like lightning in that hour,
the high peak of his life, and scorched him into cinders!
He closed his eyes and secretly deplored his fate,
but slow, unwilling, step by step, his drowsy mind
slid down and fell, a lump of muddy earth, to torpid sleep.

And when the two remained alone in the men's quarters,
the brains of the maid-snatcher gleamed like mountain peaks.
"Helen, for ten long years, they say, we fought in vain
to save your god-born body from inglorious shame
the while you sat, untouched, high in a cooling cloud
and sent, they say, your shade alone to both armed camps."
Helen sat silent in the night, rejoiced to hear
how swift her legend spun on fantasy's fast spindle,

for it had been no shade that stretched on soft divans,
no shade that cried out with delight in tight embrace;
but she said nothing, for she loved to hear how men
bandied her name about with words dispersed by winds;
her eyes burned with black flames and speared the archer's eyes
and her fine features played like the seductive sea.
But the bird-catcher frowned and came to stand beside her:
"Today when my brain sees you through a mist of wine
you seem the variable morning star of shifting face;
yet, by my body and the soul which it enfolds,
I want to sunder truth from dream today, fair Helen."
The eyes of the seductress gleamed like showering lights:
"How can the shallow brain of mortals, O sage man,
separate vapid truth from dream, or mist from mist?
Both life and death are rich, intoxicating wines.
Was it then I who laughed and wept on Trojan shores,
or but my empty shade, and I in my husband's bed
dreaming of seizures, handsome youths, and gallant deeds?
Even now, as we sit here beside our peaceful hearth,
the mind grows blurred, the dream blows and the palace creaks
like a full-masted sloop and sails in the wind's arms."
Then both fell silent, a sweet dizziness drenched the air,
Helen's faint breathing smelled like cool refreshing sea,
a water's whispering susurration lisped far off,
and sails sprang suddenly from their breasts, from cups of wine,
and from the cobwebbed armor and dull mother-of-pearl
that decked the erotic swans' wide wings from wall to wall.
The palace rose in dance, the corner towers swayed,
the cypress trees, tall in the courts, like rigging swished,
and suddenly peacocks screamed like seagulls in the night.
Odysseus rose, and his head throbbed with miracle;
he wanted to shout, "Set sail!" but he restrained his cry
for fear the wonder might fly out like frightened birds.
In hovering silence then they heard the king laugh low,
for he was dreaming in sweet sleep how as a youth
he'd played at hide-and-seek with Helen secretly.
But they moved on nor turned their heads to look at him
and took the long unending voyage of departure.
Again her firm-shaped lips, round as a ring, sang out:
"I'm not a goddess, and I hate the empty skies;
I love the earth, my heart is filled with loam and roses.
This house constrains me now, my spirit spreads to clasp
fierce conflagrations, open seas, and wild men's knees.
But if I leave with you at dawn for your black ship,
I won't rush to the cliff's embrace like a green girl.
Paris passed once through the great gaping sea, and vanished!

I, even as you, refuse to let my soul decay."
The mind of the quick-tempered man spun like a whirlwind
and flung her swiftly round its apex like a rose leaf.
But he stood still, for his cup suddenly brimmed with joy
to watch her whose laugh bloomed like almond trees, and said:
"My thousand-year-old memory plunges roots and twines
my thick bones like wild ivy in a savage growth.
When I sit idle and serene, with tranquil heart,
then God seems like a dream, or my mind's misty shadow;
but when abruptly I get drunk with cares or wine
then memory rises in my heart like a dark beast
and God mounts like a buffalo in my muddy guts.
This is the man who guides my black ship, Helen! Choose!"
The queen fell silent then, and though she frowned, she thought:
"Ah, I shall never escape alive from his cruel claws!"
Then for a lightning moment she wanted to cry out,
to scream and wake her husband, the archons, the guards, the slaves.
Her soul cried out for help, but her heart felt ashamed
although she watched the lawless pirate with mute fear.
And as by a deep shore we watch an old town's ruins
where silent fishes come and go and spawn in pits
and waves laugh murmuring high above the castle doors,
so large-eyed Helen gazed into the pirate's eyes
and saw her life entwined in poisonous green roots.
Cunning Odysseus felt her fear, laughed long, and mocked:
"Ah, I've a tough hide, Lady! I'm not at all like Paris,
and you'll not slip alive from these sharp claws of mine.
I give you leave: you still have time to shout for help!"
"Yes, I have time, but choose to follow my fate freely!"
The great abductor stood erect and his heart throbbed:
"O free soul, welcome to my ship a thousand times!"
They spoke no more, and as they looked at open doors,
at courtyards, fragrant gardens, and bronze outer gates,
they took, in thought, the riverbank to the far sea
as the day broke and bodies flushed with flaming beards,
and comrades seized their oars and beat the sluggish waves.
The guileless king woke in this noisy hush and said:
"I slept, and your sweet conversation lulled me softly
as though I heard seas breaking on far-distant strands
and pebbles gurgling on the seashore's shingle there;
you spoke of visions, dreams, and distant voyages."
Then Helen arched her brows and rose to leave her throne,
but false Odysseus seized his poor friend in his arms
and his heart burst in shrill wails like a bell-hung lyre
so that a lump rose in the king's throat, and he, too, wept.
And thus the two great kings clasped by the lapsing hearth

and wailed till their eyes ran like gutters down their cheeks.
But then arch-eyebrowed Helen shot a spiteful word:
"How shameful for great warriors to lament like widows!
A thousand times you've tasted separation's grief
with mortals and immortals in your crime-packed lives."
She spoke, and the kings disengaged themselves with shame,
and smiled, so that it seemed as if the rainbow's arch
shone with its seven smiles of light on their thick lashes.
Then with no further word the two old friends parted forever.

Odysseus went to find his soft bed and to sleep,
but in the lamp's dim light he glimpsed his splayfoot friend,
stark naked, sprawled near Rocky, whispering happily;
but both were unaware, their backs turned toward the door,
that their sly leader crouched and listened to all they said.
They had become fast friends, and the broad-shouldered man
was telling his new comrade of the sea's seductions:
"Don't be so sad, my friend; I've no doubt earth is good,
but the sly giggling sea can snatch your wits away!
I, too, once plowed and sowed the earth; I, too, grazed sheep,
but when the waves burst on my chest—God curse them all—
and my hands gripped the oars, then surely I went daft,
for then—I swear by wine!—I scorned earth like a mule!
For us the wind's a shepherd, waves are sheep and goats,
our prow's a pointed plow, we sow the empty air.
The sea's a monstrous vineyard of unending harvest!"
The shepherd listened to the blue sea's sonorous myth
and once was swept like seagulls on the savage foam,
and once allured by the green-haired seductress, earth.
Then glutton laid his hands on his friend's hill-born back:
"Three seas rage in me: women, wine, and a sea-captain;
the wine's a heavy beast, but heavier still is woman,
and a still heavier greedy beast is my sea-captain.
You know he'll crunch you sure one day, dry bones and all;
and if you work for him, then let the world go hang,
let loose the wings of life and death on yawning cliffs!"
The sea-enraptured man laughed low and then went on:
"One day I'll show you, Rocky, when he stands in sun,
how many shadows his seven souls, his body casts;
he casts as many shadows as his crew of friends,
stands like an axle in our midst and twines us round."
Odysseus burst out coughing then and laughed with joy:
"Ho, what unswallowable lies, huge as your monstrous bulk!
Ah, Rocky, don't believe him—I've one spirit only,
one body, one light shade for a brief while on earth.
I hunger, I thirst, and surely I shall die one day;

meanwhile, I play, and keep my soul and body well."
Big-bellied glutton leapt and grabbed his master's arms:
"By God, I get all twisted with what's true or false!
When you're before me, then I think you're meat and bones,
chock-full of blood and tears, a mortal just like me;
but when I see you from afar, in memory's mist,
then you grow monstrous like a god, and I go daft!"
Odysseus then rejoiced to feel how his friend's hands
licked at his brawny body like a lion's tongue,
but when he'd had his fill, he moved off toward his bed:
"It's time, lads, to resign our bodies to calm sleep;
they've fed and overfed us in this wealthy place,
our flesh has brimmed with strength, our veins have overswelled,
and in the morning all this dammed up, aching strength
shall burst in difficult works and thus not go to waste;
the day's gone well, an apple tree with ripe fruit laden."
The two mind-slaves without a single dream set sail
with crossed hands on night's ancient sea, mother of sleep,
but the uncompassionate fisher hooked a mammoth shark:
deep in the dead of night, before the crack of dawn,
the fearful patron of pure friendship, Zeus, came down
and stood with flashing flame before the archer's bed.
He foamed with fury at the lips, his thunderbolts
twisted and turned like scorpions in his monstrous hands,
but the archer yelled: "Unhappy creature of our hearts,
I pity your sad doom and harmless thunderbolts.
Should I but bend or move a little, or open my eyes,
poor orphaned child born of our fear, you'd fade in air!"
He spoke, then raised his lashes slightly, and the god vanished.
When day's face in the light shaft whitely shone at last,
the wry, fox-minded man thus hailed it with a smile:
"The awesome ancient gods are now but poor bugbears
who roam with secret stealth the unguarded brain at night.
Welcome, O light, O sacred rooster of man's awakening mind!"

He rose, belted his knife, then prodded with his foot
the two bright bodies that still sailed in sleep close by:
"Get up, my lads, it's daybreak, and a long road's before us."
The two shook from their heads the heavy foam of sleep,
looked at the light, leapt up and thrust knives in their belts,
their full hearts brimming with the abundant strength of night.
Then their quick-witted leader portioned out each task:
"You, Kentaur, speed at once to the great stable stalls,
and to the finest chariot yoke the finest steeds,
for I know well how good you are at chariot-stealing!
Rocky, glide up the tower on tiptoe, then swoop down

and kill the guards there stealthily, and make no noise.
Our minds and arms must make no errors this heavy day."
He spoke, and the two pirates sped, each to his task,
while the light-footed archer prowled the zigzag palace.
The flames still dimly shone high in the brazen lamps
and oily smells hung heavily in the blue-black halls.
He climbed the staircase softly to the women's rooms
and smiled with cunning pride at his own shifting will,
for he was free, he knew, to change fast fortune's wheel
at the last moment even, or stop at any stair,
and as he joyed in his deep freedom step by step,
a monstrous shadow leapt in the lamp's light beside him.
He drew back, startled, thinking great Athena loomed,
then laughed to see his own tall shadow with peaked cap
leaping and dancing on the wall in the lamp's light.
Like a huge beetle thrusting through a fragrant rose,
Odysseus softly stole into the women's rooms;
the swans gleamed mistily once more, the great gold birds
in the lamplight's reflection spread their wings for flight,
and foaming azure waves rolled round from wall to wall
till from the shrine of the gold brainless goddess, lo,
the graceful, godlike body of the swan-born loomed,
a rosy finger placed against her warning lips.
The devious man turned toward her shade like a black swan
and in the dark the whites of his large eyeballs flashed
as he discerned between her breasts the crystal ball
that rolled like darkling waters where fate's frigates sailed.
The hairy nostrils, beard, and brains of the man-slayer
smelled sweet as though in truth he'd thrust in a blown rose,
as though he held in his embrace all women on earth.
The decoy bird went first and the bird-catcher followed,
and when they reached the bottom stair, they heard a shriek
from the top tower as though a strident hawk were slain.
Then Helen paled and to her abductor turned with fright:
"That's a bad sign," she murmured through clenched, trembling teeth;
but the man-slayer laughed and with no haste replied:
"That's a good sign; a trusted guard will speak no more."
Helen turned calm and draped her head with a thin veil
as in the courtyard they saw Kentaur yoke his steeds;
he steamed and laughed like some huge shaggy stable-god
with regal reins and trappings flung across his back.
Then Rocky suddenly loomed with stealth, his vulturous eyes
and black beard gleaming gently in the rosy light,
and when his master questioned him with a sly wink,
he signaled softly how he'd slit the sentry's throat.
When in the courtyards all the cocks had risen to crow

and the poor slaves in dungeons stretched their limbs and yawned,
Odysseus strongly seized the outer gate's bronze bolt,
and though he dragged it from its ring with artful skill
the opening hinges shrieked as though they wept with pain.
Snow-ankled Helen laughed and cried, then raised her foot,
but her gold-broidered sandal tripped on the bronze sill,
and thus in its first step toward freedom, her soul staggered.
At once the man of fleet foot reached with his strong arms
and seized the pure-white bird, raised it aloft with grace
and in the fragrant chariot placed it with closed wings.
As Kentaur turned, he suddenly saw his master's teeth
gleam white and pointed in the courtyard's early light;
the stars still hung in necklaces of clustered pearls,
on the horizon's furthest verge day wanly smiled,
and from mist-laden mountains frosty breezes blew.
Gripping his three-lashed whip, the charioteer struck hard
until the horses tossed their haughty heads with wrath
and dashed along the banks where streams through myrtles snaked
and rolled the crimson-golden dawn down toward the sea.
The heart-seducer stooped, and with a soft caress
covered with warm fur Helen's trembling crystal arms
and on her soft thighs placed a long-haired tiger-skin;
the swan-born shuddered with joy to feel his dreaded hands.
Her eyebrows glittered like two moons but two days old,
she wore a pure-white mantle clear as lucid light,
the hand she carried to her throat, her curling mouth,
and her large eyes, like almonds, slender-shaped and long,
glimmered with spikes of flame in the dawn's red-rose dusk.
Far off, cock pheasants stopped in their erotic swagger,
and the victorious dancer like a bridegroom leapt
at daybreak on the multicolored female's back, and crowed.
Low in the East, still-wakeful Aphrodite winked
like a night-prowling woman who returns replete,
pallid with too much love in oriental skies;
the rosy mountain peaks laughed like high lustrous thoughts,
and Helen, speechless, raised her pale hands toward the sun
and joyed to feel its warm rays falling on her frozen palms.

V

The sun turned toward his mother, and his mother, frightened,
rushed to light all her ovens at the sky's foundations
and cast in forty loaves of bread to feed him well.
When the crew saw the sun dip down, they lit a fire
hard by the coastal rocks, then broiled a spitted kid
found wedged between a rocky cleft and swiftly roped.
The half-baked piper sat cross-legged on stones and turned
the spit, and as his cross-eyes blinked with smoke, he laughed,
nibbled with secret glee, and licked the luscious meat.
All watched the reddening kid on the hot coals and yearned
to eat at last, for hunger threshed their entrails cruelly
until for solace they, too, nibbled and sipped wine.
Thorn-bearded Captain Clam, nostalgic for the sea,
sighed heavily and began to sing a plaintive ditty:
"Ah, Mistress Captain Sea, with all your teeming ships,
you swish and sway and saunter on the rosy sands,
you swagger on the beach and fill young men with longing.
The wretched mothers in their rooms, the wretched sisters,
the wretched sweethearts by their looms all raise their hands:
'May you be cursed, O bitter sea! You drive men daft!
You strut upon the sands and your white ankles laugh,
your eyes and your teeth laugh, and all your beaches laugh,
till young men laugh and sigh and come down to your sands:
"Hi, Mistress Captain Sea, what wages will you give me?"
"The four winds for a blanket and the waves for pillow,
and a small seagull that will bring the sad news quickly
to mother and to sister and to coddled sweetheart." ' "
Thus Captain Clam with his hoarse voice sang bitterly
while the spit swiftly turned and broiled the fragrant roast.
Hardihood then spoke roughly and spread his grasping hands:
"Well spoken, Captain Clam, well said, but I'm still starved!"
Bush-bearded Captain Clam laughed loud and stuffed his mouth:
"Let that cantankerous song go bawl and babble! Oho!
If you're in love, give bones and body to the crows!
Lads, I'm a toady toad-fish and a perching perch-fish!"
The wine-companions laughed, cut up the kid in shares,

and fell upon it greedily, gleaming tooth and nail;
only the munching of their sturdy jaws was heard
and clean-picked kid-bones falling on the pebbly beach
and tipped-up wine-gourds gurgling on their greasy lips.
When they had eaten well and washed their hands in sea,
the comrades broke their silence and began to talk:
"If only our fierce captain were to loom up now,
bearing in his embrace the lady of arched eyebrows!"
These words of hope still hung upon the piper's lips
when hawk-eyed Granite leapt and thundered through the hush:
"Fellows, is that his seacap gleaming not far off?"
The crew leapt to their feet, made out a chariot's shape,
picked out their captain's cap, and saw a pure-white dove
that flew as harbinger ahead and showed the way.
The five brave gallants dashed like savage lion-cubs
who spy their father with wild game between his teeth.
They raised huge dust clouds, and the piper, panting, last,
ran stumbling on his pigeon-toes, stuttering with yells:
"Fellows, I see two white wings in the chariot there!
Ahoy! We'll sleep tonight beside man-loving Helen!"
Then Captain Clam ran forward and held the foaming steeds;
with shouts and laughter the smith seized in brawny arms
the world-famed woman, gently put her down to earth,
then turned his fevered face toward hers as though just then
he'd carried to his forge and on his anvil placed
bronze metal white-hot from the fire for murderous swords.
"Quick, fellows, rig the sails, and off! Our task is done!"
Their Captain roared, and all, wing-footed, rushed down toward the beach.

Evening had not yet faded, as on mountain slopes
night stepped with crimson feet like a wild partridge, slowly.
The tranquil evening veiled the world with sweet delight,
each heart in the breast's branches perched like a calm bird
and sang night-long all it had feared to sing by day.
A girl sighed in her loneliness, and all leaves swayed,
a widow sent her longings out to browse at night,
and old king Menelaus fell on his terraced roof
and slowly shook his head like an exhausted hare.
He turned his crown in his pale hands and played with it
for many speechless hours while his mind raced far
on desolate shores, on steeds, on laughter, on white roads.
His motionless dry eyes looked southward steadily
as though they followed an unceasing falling star.
At that same hour the comrades leapt into their ship
and placed star-breasted Helen gently by the prow.
"Welcome, foam-born, our vessel's gorgon figurehead

with your fate-written crystal on your warring breasts!"
Thus spoke the enduring archer, and his heart rejoiced
because the unknown far future always stormed and tossed him;
he never wanted earth to lose her virtue, raped by mind.
The sails and rigging creaked, the painted prow's eyes glared,
till like a swimming steed the vessel plunged in foam
and reared with upright haunches in the streaming sea.
Astride the bowsprit, the light-headed piper yelled:
"Hey, fellows, may this holy voyage never end!
Ho, for a slender ship, for Helen at your side,
to sail the seas without a country endlessly!"
But Helen watched in silence the sea's emerald wash,
the curly momentary foam, and joyed to feel
the seawind thrusting at her breasts like a man's hands
and cool her deep down to her foam-smooth rosy heels,
nor turned her head at the port's mouth to see that isle
which sweetly spread its shade and flowering grass for her
when once she twined limbs lovingly with handsome Paris
and shamed her household gods in an erotic swoon.
As the world-wanderer held the tiller, he recalled
far-distant shores, and wondered where to set his course.
Then as the warm stars glowed and thickened round the masts,
the men pressed close about the narrow deck to eat,
and the brave crew had never tasted bread more sweet
nor had a cooler mistral ever flicked their brows.
Man-loving Helen sighed with joy, for once again
men's heavy odors rose, great cities shook once more,
and freedom's wind blew once again about her brow.
She had not tasted such sweet bread for many years,
for many years no wind so sweet had touched her brow.
Strengthened with food, the gallants sat astride the thwarts
and all life in their entrails laughed like cooling wells
till in their minds fate blossomed like a crimson rose
and they, like scarabs, plundered all its golden honey.
These were not waves, nor this a scudding ship they rowed,
but they were wandering leaf by leaf a fragrant rose
till all their thighs and bellies filled with pollened gold.
Their minds shook in their haughty heads, the wide world shook,
though life was not a cooling waterdrop, nor fate a rose,
but they breathed Helen's misty breath, and their minds shook.
Then Kentaur stroked his beard, opened his he-goat lips,
and with a wily voice spun truths and shameless lies
in a close web of slaves, rich wine, and golden castles,
and as he talked life turned to legend in his mind:
how slaves caressed him as he sprawled amid the wine-jugs,
how from the tower's roof their master's laughter plunged

and ate the strong foundations like a river's rush,
then how he swooped on Helen with his eagle claws.
The horses scattered in the fields, doves in the courts,
until his comrades' skulls struck sparks, echoed like stones,
so much had their blood-brother swept them with his guile.
But Rocky stood apart, leaning above the gunwale,
admiring flocks of black-white sheep, the goats that ran,
and other curly herds that pushed behind: a sea
packed full of sheep, the penfold of a Shepherd King.
Meanwhile their skipper spun strange cities in his mind;
he thought of sailing through waste seas of the far North
and like the male worm hang his beard with crystal ice;
of turning his prow boldly toward the distant South,
toward that dark land of savage beasts and crinkly men
for which the Cretan bard once opened the iron doors.
He longed for the black, aromatic shores of Africa,
land where the sun bakes bread and the full moon is milked.
"Welcome and hail, black brothers! I did not want to fall
and vanish beyond the waves before I bade goodbye.
I've heard that earth hangs down your neck like a huge drum;
now raise your hands, my brothers, beat it until it bursts!"
Thus murmured the deceiving mind of the world-roamer;
all things seemed beautiful, earth spread before his eyes,
a hand with five roads, luring onward toward the waves.
He bent above the black eyes of the swan-born mutely
to see where fate would moor them, but the godly one,
leaning upon her crystal arms, was idly dreaming:
a vine of thick grape-clusters grew above her head,
a cool and gentle wind through azure shadows blew,
and she, stark-naked on a black bull, ambled by . . .
As the all-knowing man hung on her bosom's cliff,
his great mind dimmed, his castle-skull began to shake,
and he yearned suddenly to cast his friends mid-sea
like dolphins, and to sail alone with Helen there;
meanwhile his masts would sprout with clusters of crisp grapes
and he would lie on vine leaves, fondle her with pride,
and in her womb entrust a son that one day would surpass him.

But as the archer horsewhipped man's unruly passions,
Captain Clam climbed the mast to spy with careful watch
on wind and weather both amid the starry dark,
till on the deck abruptly his wild cry rang out:
"Fellows, take in the sails! A fierce North Wind comes plunging!"
The archer raised his eyes and like a dragon scanned
the lowering, wrathful clouds that on the billows cast
their savage claws and blindly dragged the heaving waves.

The hollow sound of thunder broke, and earth and sea
was zoned with lightning as though God flashed wrathful eyes
with fiery strokes for fear the new ship might escape,
that now sighed, bitter and profound, like man's own heart.
Then the quick-tempered skipper bit his lips and yelled:
"You murderer, you! How long will you breathe down my back
or cleave my skull with your sharp ax of lightning bolts?
For shame! Go hide your head! Have you no honor, God,
to take it out on man's small nutshell of a ship?
I hoped you wouldn't come just now because I feared
this flowering body that sails beside me here would drown;
you know I don't care for myself or my harsh hounds,
but since you've deigned to come, hail then a thousand times!"
This sharp arraignment hung still on his bitter lips
when an enormous wave crashed on his battered head
till all his body, fingers, lips, and nostrils stung
as though unnumbered fiery sparks flared up and died.
Odysseus bit his flaming mustache hard, and mocked:
"That violent squall came close enough to prick me then!"
Poor Rocky tripped and staggered, grabbed at the rail with fear
as his proud body buckled, for these storm-tossed fields
made his young shinbones stagger till with shame he thrust
his face within his arms that smelled of savory still.
Waves kicked and struck the piper by the mizzenmast
and when salt blood ran from his gap-toothed mouth, he shrieked:
"Oho! I'm for the fishes now and a watery grave!
Spread out your hands, dear God, and save your silly songster;
I'll bring you first-grade oil in monstrous buffalo skins!"
The coward vowed and whined, then plunged into the hold.
Waves rose like cutting scythes, swooped down and threshed the hull
until it buckled at the knees, reared high, plunged down,
sighed deeply, and like light foam danced on thundering foam.
The winds threshed at the sleepless crew all night till God
at daybreak hurled the dark sun like an iron quoit,
but still strong-souled Odysseus scoffed and gripped the tiller:
"Blow, foam-brained blabber-lips, choke in your own rage,
but get this through your head: you won't eat our poor plank—
it grips its soul between its teeth and won't give way!"
Two days and nights they fought with death, lunged down in waves
and then shot hurtling upward, and again crashed down.
On the third day the solid waves smashed the frail rudder
and all the dread gods of the sea with snarling roared
and shared with howls and laughter the still-living craft.
The South Wind claimed the archer, the Northeaster Helen,
and scornful Captain North Wind mocked at Captain Clam:
"What a fine curly beard! I'll thrust it full of weeds

that eels and gudgeons may skid through and squirt their milt.
You've got my dander up, and I'm out for vengeance now!"
But Captain Clam flung back the words in North Wind's teeth:
"You dolt! I've yet to eat much bread and gulp much wine
before my bones fall to your claws to be licked clean.
Come butt our hull in vain and break your puny horns!"
But Kentaur felt already through his hairy thighs
the stinging jellyfish and the black scuttling crabs.
Flat on his back in the drenched hold, he growled like a bull:
"Damned if I let you gulp me down without a fight!
When my time comes to croak, it'll be on good firm earth!
Ah for a fresh green branch to whittle a small switch;
you'd see then, Master Charon, how I'd lay about you!"
Granite and the slim shepherd, that landlubbery pair,
grabbed at each other, bit their lips, and then fell flat
lest fear—what shame!—should slip and pass their quaking throats.
On the third day a pointed head poked through the wineskins
like a whipped short-winded dog and whined in a shrill voice:
"Brothers, not one soul shall escape from pitch-black death;
our crime hangs heavily like a millstone round our necks.
God roars with thunderbolts and flashes through my head:
'Give the waves sacrifice to expiate your crime!' "
The shrill voice finished and the pointed head at once
plunged in the hold and left a drenched and shaken crew;
all glared in silence toward the savage, tossing stern
where godly Helen lay amid the ropes entangled,
and Helen felt their furtive looks and shook with dread,
but scorned in her great pride to wail or weep or plead
or lean her breasts as suppliant on the men's hard knees.
She had surpassed the common lot of women, and felt ashamed.
Hardihood rose in silence and his red stain swelled
and thrashed his savage face like a live octopus.
He strode across the thwarts toward the all-holy form
and for a flash the weather cleared and North Wind paused.
The great-graced lady thrust her face between her hands
and all life passed before her like an oar-winged dream,
a gold bird flown, a dulcet dizziness that vanished.
But as the bronzesmith lunged to seize those famous locks,
he suddenly clenched his fists and slowly turned away
and bit his red mustache with an ill-tempered shame.
Swift-eyed Odysseus, who ruled fate with sleepless eyes
and weighed the souls of his ship's crew, yelled out with joy:
"Your health, O Hardihood, for in this difficult hour
you rose up proudly like a king and flouted Death!
Now, by the brand-new God I bear, I swear this oath:
on the first land where we shall moor, I'll crown you king!"

But the boar-bristled boatman laughed with bitterness:
"Man, don't you fret! We'll never see dry land again!
But, even so, your words have wreathed my carrot-top
with a gold crown, and I shall drown like a true upright king!"

But then, as Granite seized the prow, flat on his face,
he spied an azure peak amid the spuming waves
tossing and gleaming on the heaving sea's horizon.
"Ho! Land ahead!" he yelled, and all eyes pierced the spume.
Captain Clam tried for a long time to see earth's face,

and the world-wanderer questioned in his laughing heart
where of all places the four winds had slung him now.
All strands seemed equally good to him to test man's soul.
Then with great joy the old salt-tar yelled out: "It's Crete!"
All hearts leapt up and tossed toward the all-holy mother,
and the sagacious man laughed low and said to his god:
"I begged for one breadloaf: you cast me ovens full;
one sip of wine: you gave me casks big as my body;
I begged for a small belt of land, a branch to grasp:
and lo, from waves you hand me Crete on a gold platter!
Thanks for the bite, it just exactly suits my hunger!"
Meanwhile the weather slowly cleared, the squalls calmed down,
and the storm-battered vessel raised its prow and sailed.
They tied their long oars to the rowlocks, the tholes creaked,
and keeping the isle in sight, plunged toward it, oar and sail.
Helen smiled thinly through her tears like the pale dawn;
the black locks round her temples tossed in the land breeze
as with drenched hair she gently touched the archer's knees:
"I have some words to say, my dear, but my voice chokes."
Yet as the sweet-voiced lady rose and saw his eyes,
she paled with fear and leant her head on his soaked chest.
Deep in his bottomless eyes she saw Crete rise and fall
and break between his eyebrows like a foundering ship.
The leader of souls then stroked his beard in silent thought
and his sharp smile rose in a curve to his thick ears,
for, many-breasted, shameless, nude, Crete's body spread
her practiced thighs amid the waves, swarming with merchants.
He'd often met their wealthy barques on distant shores
and marveled as they sauntered on the quays adorned
like birds with peacock plumes and bracelets of pure gold.
These acrid captains ate and drank till their guts burst,
they'd seen all, kissed and drained their bodies dry with lust,
till drenched in fine perfumes, fluttering their feathery fans,
they swooned now in the firm embrace of their black slaves.
Their fingers were all rotted, but their rings remained,
their empty loins were withered, but their thin skulls shone
with wide-eyed sophistry and brimmed with mocking smiles.
In their plush homes, the gods, demeaned to bric-a-brac,
cooped up like parrots in their cages of gold bars,
were hung in windows where with human voice they squawked
and cackled back those words which they were taught to say.
The archer nailed his eyes on the great, regal island,
and saw Crete stormed and tossed amid the heavy waves
like a rich galley overstuffed with precious wares.
They skimmed close till the peaks of Ida flashed serene
and towns shone white like dragon-eggs wedged in the clefts.

When Rocky smelled the earth, his soul filled up with loam;
he saw far off, high in the sun, the verdant fields
and longed to clamber up and hear the jangling goat-bells,
until his wedge-shaped beard perked up like a he-goat's.
The two landlubbers broke in song, like partridges,
like cool cascading waters in a wooded gorge:
"God, to climb hills again, to clear our heads with air,
where blooms the haughty asphodel, where pine trees drip
with resin, where the dappled partridge spreads its wing!
Ah, that the girl I love might hear and bolt her door
with a thick spray of basil, fresh mint on her breast
for lookout, and the curled carnation for her sentry."
Thus did the mountain lads pour out their hearts in song,
and rocks grew huge and savage, seashores opened wide
their arms like a crab's claw until the battered prow
plunged groaning, like a bolting colt, in the port's mouth.
All Crete jounced over them and swayed with upright teats,
till Helen suddenly shuddered and grew pale as wax,
for as she watched the famous island gleam on the waves
there rose high in her memory ancient dragon tales
that her old nurse had crooned to make her fall asleep:
"Far, in the far strands of Crete—may she be cursed!—
a hornèd dragon roars and feeds on mortal men.
Crete like a lamia sits on the all-sucking waves,
laughs lightly, braids her hair, then sinks all passing ships.
Ah, may your foam-feet, Helen, never tread on Crete."
Now she was rushing headlong—who could stay his fate?—
in the man-eating mouth of the bull-snouted god.
But you, O Captain Clam, pulled on your oars like wings,
nor were you seized with fear, nor with old midwives' tales,
and if fate doomed your salt-caked flesh to be devoured
by this world-famous island where you plunge full sail,
you neither broke in sweat, nor gave a salt-tar's damn!
You pulled the toughest oar, your lips gave you no rest,
until you decked the sea's Dame with a thousand gems:
"The sea is a huge loom where Crete sits down and weaves;
lucky those eyes who've seen her shuttling on the waves.
If you're sick, you sprout wings, if sluggish, you grow wild,
and if cares crush you, your dazed mind glows like the moon,
and you forget black pain and raise your arms on high
and bless your happy parents who once gave you birth."
Odysseus opened his brains wide, his eyes and ears,
till odors, Crete, and castles plunged in his deep wells.
A sentry from the headland yelled: "A ship, ahoy!"
A sentry from the seashore yelled: "It's made the harbor!"
The archer leapt on shore and cried: "Well met, O longed-for Crete!"

Upon the summit of great joy Dread holds his throne,
and comrades, masts and oars, women, and high waves,
unshaven lips and laughing eyes and gaudy wings
pass by as though they swam through harsh nightmarish dreams.
A stout coastguard approached to ask about their tribe,
and his mouth gurgled in the sun like a tipped jug;
he held a wax plaque and bronze style to etch their words,
but the bold archer laughed and stroked his curly beard:
"Let us alone to sleep a while, and when our souls
distill once more, we'll tell you from what land we come;
now set us down as tattered sails and seals of the sea."
He spoke, and all slid through a shadowy cool arcade,
fell on the tiles as dead, while from the fragrant earth
sleep rose like moss and covered up their curly brows.
Night fell, and the green bellies of the glowworms shone,
the high stars leapt, the breasts of Helen swayed and burned
within the lustrous night like two matched crystal pears,
and sleep crouched like a fisherman on the crew's eyes,
patched up their tattered nets, stitched all their fishing hooks,
and calked again the battered planking of their bodies.
But that beast, Hunger, conquered sleep at drop of noon,
and first to raise his eyes and cluck his tongue was glutton:
"I'm starved! O for a bite of meat, a hunk of bread!"
And then the whistling voice of cricket-face piped up:
"Glutton, rise up and shine with health! You'll eat, don't fear!
Friends, are my eyes flickering, or do I see, even now,
the crown of Crete shine on the locks of our brave smith?
Rise up, great King, command us women, food, and wine!"
Then Granite stretched his haughty body above the ground:
"By God, my soul has longed to stroll on this good earth
more than it longed for women, bread, or finest wine!"
Then Rocky lightly leapt and stood by his friend's side,
but the archer's mind had gone to work before the dawn:
"It's only just to care for our bruised bodies first.
Let's go! The hunter Mind has flushed a hare in harbor."
When the three vanished in the harbor's jostling crowd,
fair Helen from her bosom's secret cleft brought up
the prophesying globe to see her soul's new road.
She bent above the god's eye, but saw nothing more
than all her hairy comrades round her like adornments;
with their crude hanging beards they seemed sea-battered seals
cast by the raging sea on some far-distant strand,
and in the seals' nest she discerned a pure-white swan.
Stooped low in silence thus, the sun-born sniffed her fate
and strove in foggy inner woods to see her way.
But the clear crystal suddenly dimmed, its riches vanished,

until a peaked cap rose and covered all its globe,
and Helen, trembling, thrust the eye back in her breast.
Their leader's voice was heard then, full of cheer and joy:
"Come, dear blood brothers, stuff your bodies, eat and drink!"
He spoke, then broke a basket open and filled their hands.
All fell to eating headlong, and their dreadful jaws
ground round like millstones till the archway shook and swayed:
when they grabbed bread, their fists were filled with plunging swords,
when they drank wine, it thunderously plunged at once
like armored mail and wrapped them round with brazen shields;
wine turned to crimson blood, meat turned to sturdy flesh,
and when they'd eaten, the port stopped swaying, earth grew firm.
The piper then, wine-dreg of God, laughed loud and long:
"O God," he roared, "patron of friends, bread, wine, and meat,
how you've declined and poked yourself in our wide guts!"
The heaven-baiter laughed and thrust his hardened hands
to cool them in the wine-flasks and the luscious fruit.
"Brothers, I've roamed the world, my eyes have joyed in much,
yet never have I seen bazaars where gods are sold;
but it was foreordained that I should gape at gods
spitted like crabs on reeds and sold in clustered groups.
Here mortals may choose gods for every single need:
gods of the sea, gods of the earth, gods of good health,
one to cure goiters, belly-aches, or falling-sickness,
another to cure jaundice, sore throat, fever, dropsy.
Here gods are sold in rows, nostrums of every kind.
I dragged my god there by his feet, a votive beast:
'Merchants, your health! I bring this miracle-working god,
defender of fine friendship with his bolts and lightnings.'
An old man turned and whistled through his hairless lips:
'How nice of him to come, too. Drag him out, let's see him.'
He rubbed him with a touchstone, weighed him well on scales:
'Great is his grace, by God! He's true, pure, solid gold!'
He yelled, and from great joy his ears broke in a sweat;
then we began to bargain, and closed the deal with skill.
Now, lads, your brains shall grow huge, for you've eaten God,
but still be patient, for the wonders have not ceased."
Then sly Odysseus turned and winked his eye at Granite,
and he with chuckles overturned a monstrous tub
from which at once poured sheepskins, sandals, vests and belts
which the great captain portioned out in equal shares:
"God has arranged for everything, for he's all-knowing;
let's dress like native Cretans; I'd be filled with shame
to face great King Idomeneus clad in rags;
and fellows, look, I've bought the starry sky for Helen."
He then unfolded in the light a woman's robe

that shone with rich adornments and with sparkling gems,
and she, who was love's face, rejoiced and spread her arms:
"O skilled in many crafts, you rule the heart of woman
as if it, too, were but a heavy storm-tossed sea,
for headcoins, feathers, silver chains and frills delight
the godly, gaudy bird caged in a woman's skull."
She spoke, then gathering her brocaded armor, vanished.
The men then quickly armed themselves in their brave robes:
"Ahoy, we too shall walk tight-assed and scissor-stepped!"
they shouted gaily, and their mocking laughter rang.
But when they saw the lean-branched lady turn a corner,
they cupped their hands against their eyes to bear the dazzle:
her firm voluptuous breasts shone naked in the dark,
high sandy rose-red hills in the world's desolation,
and her dress flowered like the wealthy frills of spring.
Their leader's eyes flashed fire, his gray hair stood on end:
"Fellows, I once saw fierce War firmly plant his feet
on two high peaks, then stoop and drink the rolling river,
and the deep water boiled with rage and turned to blood,
yet I feared not, as now I fear the sight of Helen!"
And Granite suddenly shuddered and recalled his brother:
"I've often thought, O Captain, to my heart's great shame,
that you and I, body and soul, like black lambs follow
the woman warrior with her nude milk-laden breasts."
Then the great-masted mind fell silent and refused
to show his most precipitous hope, his deepest grief,
but gathered his old friends and told them what to do:
"Scatter throughout this famous port, poke everywhere
and open your eyes wide, your nostrils, ears, your hearts,
because this earth, though beautiful, does not last long,
and then let's meet for council when the twilight falls."
He spoke, and each one scattered where his own heart wished.
Hardihood went alone and poked about the workshops.
Broad-shouldered Kentaur grabbed the piper by the nape
and climbed the crooked alleys of the harbor town
in search of good red wine and good full-bodied maids.
The mountain pair strolled arm in arm about the wharfs
where heavily-scented harbor girls winked playfully
with hanging hair and tinkling gods between their breasts;
but they, in the sweet snare of friendship soon forgot
to care for food and drink or even a girl's kiss.
And knotty Captain Clam, like a ship's dog let loose,
leapt every anchored prow to nose out his old friends;
his salt seafaring mind rejoiced to stroke the ships
with their swift-voyaged demons painted on the prows,
but all at once a shrill voice seized and cast him ashore:

"Aye, Captain Clam, your eyes are welcome as snow in heat!"
He turned and saw an old friend, a thin-haired shipmaster
with narrow skull and white hair flowing down his back,
and the old friends fell moaning in each other's arms.
They talked for hours of the sea, that wild horse-maid,
and like two oysters closed and opened their old entrails
while all the raging sea broke over them and dragged them down.

Meanwhile Odysseus and arch-eyebrowed Helen gaped
at the great wealth unstacked and heaped upon the piers
from the long-voyaged, many-oared, far foreign ships.
Crete in the harbor tower sat on her high throne
and from the far ends of the earth her four wind-lovers
brought her sea-caravans brimmed with many precious gifts.
First always came the harsh North Wind with his blond beard
and at the briny wheat-brown feet of his belovèd
he spread the hides of wild beasts, wools, and fertile slaves,
and on her hot stones cast his honey-colored amber.
Then blowing from the shady side, the West Wind came
with his upturned mustache, his anklets of fine bronze,
and brought her gifts of tin and silver huge as loaves.
Then from the sunny side there came the withered, sly,
and winking lover of the sweet-breasted ancient East
with his bright silver rings and painted pouting lips,
and in her open hands and garnished lap heaped high
most precious spices, golden birds, and magic balms.
And Lord South Wind, that famous lover with moist locks,
brought her close-woven colored baskets, ivory gifts,
miracle-working letters, demons, monkeys, charms,
and Crete sat on her lofty throne, with naked breasts,
and held the scales above her seas and weighed each kiss.
Helen, unspeaking, felt the four winds blow about her
with hot erotic breath, whistling between her thighs,
and wished she were that robust isle in the sea's midst
hard-beaten by her lovers, the four Captain Winds.
But woman's flesh is an unable, transient thing,
and then lip-closing Charon grabs it by both braids
before it can rejoice an hour in man's embrace.
The multicolored, raucous, crowded harbor swayed,
and in the woman's towering, full, and famished throat
the suffocating wild dove secretly complained.
Then a slim peddler, smelling of rank musk and goat,
slid near the arch-eyed lady, and slowly in the sun
unwrapped in waves a rich-embroidered magic robe.
Black, white, and crimson horses dashed about its field,
and kings astride them bent their bows with golden darts

and shot slim green-blue beasts amid wild cypress groves,
and all around its hem rolled cool cascading waves.
Helen was dazzled like a quail, and shut her eyes,
but the old corsair bowed and said with lilting voice:
"I've traveled round the tree of earth, and yet I swear
I've never seen such beauty in a mortal maid.
Oho, who lies beside you longs for sleep in vain!"
He spoke with lowered head, but glanced with snaky eyes
and measured well the stanch man by the rose-drenched maid.
Odysseus laughed and seized the peddler's hairy arms:
"By God, if she were all alone on distant shores
we'd fling her on our backs and make for our swift ship!"
The peddler's thick lips cackled and his small eyes flashed:
"By God, if only all you say were true, my friend!
But God has sent her near me in a jostling port
and placed a true man by her side, a rampant lion.
You must have come as pilgrims for this holy feast day."
His tongue began to wag around his lilting mouth
about the island's withered souls, its barren maids,
its animals diseased and sterile, its drowned fleet.
"And all this, sire, because old age has crushed our king;
his strength has drained away, his rotted loins have shrunk,
and Crete, his flesh and blood, grows old as he grows old.
Today he climbs to God to snatch at youth renewed,
that strength might once more crackle in his empty bones
and he descend at dawn with strong loins and new laws.
But if our Bull-God scorns to fill that putrid flesh,
our foul-lunged king will vanish in the cave and never
from out that labyrinthine darkness find the light.
The simple-hearted people fall on palace tiles
and all night long with holy water and love-making
try to assist our shrunk king to regain his strength."
The shoulders then of sun-born Helen began to shake
until the old oriental codger stooped and smiled:
"Don't let your lips, those red carnations, tremble, lady;
the Bull-God gulped our kings only in ancient times,
for now they've learned to be on good terms with the gods
and climb unruffled toward them, bearing golden towers,
for learn, the gods are merchants now and strike hard bargains."
He spoke, then from his bosom dragged an ivory god
with seven towering heads piled on each other, worn
by myriads of caressing hands and pilgrim lips.
Odysseus grabbed at the ivory wonder eagerly;
the seven heads all swayed, and seven-colored flames
rose in his mind as with his finger tips he stroked
and gently licked with slow caresses each strange head.

Time shut its wings for a brief moment and stood still
so that the lone mind could have ample time to climb
with skillful fingers all the rungs of mortal virtues.
Below, the most coarse head, a brutal base of flesh,
swelled like a bloated beast bristling with large boar-tusks,
and it was fortified with veins as thick as horns.
Above it, like a warrior's crest, the second head
clenched its sharp teeth and frowned with hesitating brows
like one who scans his danger, quakes before death's door,
but in his haughty pride still feels ashamed to flee.
The third head gleamed like honey with voluptuous eyes,

its pale cheeks hallowed by the flesh's candied kisses,
and a dark lovebite scarred its he-goat lips with blood.
The fourth head lightly rose, its mouth a whetted blade,
its neck grew slender and its brow rose tall as though
its roots had turned to flower, its meat to purest mind.
The fifth head's towering brow was crushed with bitter grief,
deep trenches grooved it, and its flaming cheeks were gripped
with torturous arms as by a savage octopus;
it bit its thin lips hopelessly to keep from howling.
Above it shone serenely the last head but one,
and steadfast weighed all things, beyond all joy or grief,
like an all-holy, peaceful, full-fed, buoyant spirit.
It gazed on Tartarus and the sky, a slight smile bloomed
like the sun's subtle afterglow on faded lips;
it sauntered on the highest creviced peaks of air
where all things seem but passing dream and dappled mist;
and from its balding crown, that shone like a smooth stone
battered by many flooding seas and licked by cares,
there leapt up like unmoving flame the final head,
as if it were a crimson thread that strung the heads
like amber beads in rows and hung them high in air.
The final head shone, crystal-clear, translucent, light,
and had no ears or eyes, no nostrils, mouth, or brow,
for all its flesh had turned to soul, and soul to air!
Odysseus fondled all the demon's seven souls
as he had never fondled woman, son, or native land.
"Ah, my dear God, if only my dark soul could mount
the seven stories step by step and fade in flame,
but I'm devoured by beasts and filled with mud and brain!"
The wily peddler smiled in secret satisfaction,
feeling his dangling hooks had caught the octopus,
and then Odysseus filled the peddler's hands with gold:
"O cunning fisherman, you snare the mind with skill;
here, fill your itching palms with gold, heal my desire,
give me that seven-headed demon, that bright robe."
The greedy palms sprang open and devoured the gold,
and then the roguish stranger caught the crystal hand
of the world-famous lady, stooped, and scanned her palm:
"My grandsire, a great sorcerer, could read the fates;
they say his hollow shoulders held two monstrous heads;
the one, with eyes wide open, could expound the past,
the other, blind, could scrutinize the foggy future,
and his great power still reigns within his grandson, Lady."
He studied then her rosy palm and spoke with awe:
"O godly woman, stars and swords flash in your hands!
I see a mountain-heap of bodies and red streams

amid deep gardens of thick smoke and blind canaries."
He spoke, then vanished like a snake in the town's streets.
The archer covered Helen's quivering shoulders gently
with the resplendent gold-stitched robe so that it gleamed
on her seductive back with waters, steeds, and kings;
and as the proud stag leaps with lighting on the doe
so did the impetuous archer seize her by the waist:
"You hold the scales of Fate deep in your bosom's cleft,
and if it's true that you're ordained to burn the palace,
I ask this boon: grant me for wage and recompense
a small, small pointed ship on which to flee one dawn."
Then hurriedly he unclasped that man-bewitching waist
and his slight smile's reflection vanished from his brow:
"Lady, it's time we climbed to the bull-fighting castle;
our words were playthings of the brain and the wind's whistle."
The comrades from their rambles had returned replete,
and when the archer marshaled them, he gave commands:
"Helen and I today shall mount to the king's court;
he's an old comrade, strong in war, and when he sees
and touches Helen, his thin backbone will rejoice.
But you must calk our battered ship with skill and strength,
arm it with sails and rigging, spread it with thick grease,
for when God comes to snatch our tiller, he swoops swiftly.
Kentaur, take care, don't fall to wine and kisses now,
for lads, at any moment we may need our souls,
so keep them far from wine and women, safe and sober.
I speak to all, and not to Kentaur only, friends,
so hang my words like earrings from attentive ears.
But Hardihood, you'll come with me; who knows what work
a bronzesmith's sooty hands may find in palace walls?
My breast's a buzzing beehive of unruly bees,
and I don't know as yet just when the bees will swarm;
all have unsheathed their sting, but hold their honey still.
Nor enmity nor friendship pulls me toward the castle;
my vacillating spirit is armed to right and left
for a sweet friendly feast or the red sword of war.
Whatever that holy pair begets—fate and man's mind—
is welcome! We'll unswaddle it with ready hands!
Bronzesmith, push on, the anvil yearns for the hammer's stroke!"
Rocky grew sullen then and flung out, bold and rash:
"We, too, have souls and strength—not that you seem to care!"
He spoke, then suddenly felt ashamed and dropped his eyes.
The archer sank his hands in his friend's curly locks:
"Don't rush yourself, green lad! I won't forget! I know
quite well your soul's prepared and chafes to take its turn."
But as he spoke and stroked with love the warm gnarled head,

a dark thought struck him: the black earth—may it be cursed!—
would one day gape and swallow whole this brawny man!
He felt like shrieking out a great blaspheming curse
but held his blind wish back and swallowed his wild wrath:
"Rocky, don't hold a grudge against me, don't be vexed,
I swear to throw your way one day the heaviest mortal duty."

Thus the three friends of fate, their destiny unknown,
on a huge heavy ox-cart climbed the palace road
and the day gleamed and glittered like a bright bronze cow.
A sweet breeze rose to cool the earth at afterglow,
olive trees swelled with wind, and the admired light
rose stone by stone on the green mountain slopes, and faded.
A girl stood in the vineyards all alone and sighed
as all the vine-leaves round her withered with her pain
till the compassionate man felt deeply the girl's ache:
"Helen, earth sighs, it seems to me, and my heart breaks."
But Helen smiled at man's fantastic lunacies:
"Ah, lover of the bow, don't grieve; it was not earth
but some green girl who smelled man pass, and her loins flamed."
The knowing man laughed wryly but did not reply;
there was but one short phallic bridge between the sexes,
and then deep Chaos where even a bird's wing might not pass,
for man's soul perched, an eagle's nest, high in the head,
and woman's soul lay brooding deep between two breasts.
The silent archer tasted thus dusk's bitterness
while all of Mother Earth's serene, sad tenderness,
the mountains round, vineyards and trees, were drowned in light,
as though Odysseus gazed on ruins in deep water,
a swordfish sailing in the sea's dark azure depths.
A swarming crowd climbed slowly the white palace road,
all who had vowed this pilgrimage, and tightly clutched
clay miniatures of poppies, pigeons, calves and hearts,
their humble gifts to the dread Mother of men and beasts;
and the sea-chested pilgrim climbed with the great crowd
to proffer Helen to the myriad-breasted goddess.
He listened to his sparse-haired cunning wagoner
who, starved for talk, unfolded to the smith the shames
of their old king, the secrets of their holy rites:
"He shall return renewed today from the high mountains,
and next day bulls shall dance within the ritual ring
like wedding guests who bring the bridegroom to the bride."
Then the ox-driver laughed and winked his eyes with craft:
"In the ring stands the bride, a hollow cow of bronze,
on which the Bull-King swoops until both merge in lust.
Don't let them fool you, friend, for here's the mystic secret:

in the bronze belly of the cow a real girl lies!"
The driver's flickering tongue wagged on, and his eyes sparkled:
"And yet, my friend, take lightly what I'll tell you now:
our doomed king lusts to take for bride his virgin daughter!
In all the caves he's set loose bands of wild-game hunters,
for Krino, still unmounted, hates all mortal men.
Alas, though born of dragon seed, she'll not escape."
The beardless driver laughed and goaded his dull oxen,
but the hunched, silent bronzesmith felt his heart leap up
like a dark beast who hears a rustling in the leaves.
The dark blue twilight spread on the respiring soil,
fuzz-breasted insects fell embraced on lily leaves,
and when a shepherd rose and leant on his lean stick,
the mountain slopes swayed with the sound of silver bells.
Then the arch-eyebrowed lady longed for cooling water.
Within a garden of plump water-nourished leaves
a blond-haired gardener turned his chain-pump like a horse
until the buckets overbrimmed with gurgling sound;
there tall sunflowers shone like princes by stone walls
and marigold and balsam filled the dusk with scent.
When the cart stopped, Odysseus gave his sharp command,
and the tall gardener seized a bowl, brimmed it with water,
and proffered it on muddy knees to the arch-eyed lady.
Her rose-red palms refreshed, her godly throat grew cool,
her veins swelled and rejoiced as though a man passed through them
till the sun-bearded gardener steamed with joy to gaze
on the tall-throated beauty sipping like a bird,
and her alluring glances struck him like the sun's rays.
The archer glowered to see how her nostalgic eyes,
smothered with passion, loitered on the young man's chest,
and he was suddenly seized with wrath and clenched his fists:
"Drive on! Night falls, and little time hangs in the scales!"
They moved on, but her soul still lingered on the road.
Just as an eagle hunts the misty fields for hare,
the castle-wrecker's mind gazed on his muddy entrails:
"You driveler, when will you stop groaning, muddy guts?
And you, wolf-dancing heart, when will you ever find rest?"
The fertile-minded man thus scolded his dark roots.
A bull growled deep in earth, and the ox-driver stopped:
"O master, raise your hands on high, open your eyes,
for the great palace soon will suddenly come to view."
Then the world-rambler deeply felt his chest swell up:
"Life is a hunt, we dash with arrows at early dawn,
and God, how many pheasants and slim deer to kill,
how many trysting-places on the crinkly grass!
O keep your gut-string taut, dear bow, do not snap now!"

He turned and reared his neck high like a greedy snake,
then opened his eyes wide to catch the lightning flash.
His temples creaked, rejoiced, and all the city spilled
like gurgling wine and cooled him to his thirsty guts:
bronze columns, towers, gardens, gods, men, terraces
enriched his white-haired mind, till like a partridge cloth
the wealthy, gaudy town swayed in the darkling air
until his deep unsated brain with satiation smiled.

A high joy seized their minds, their bones felt light as air,
and as they slowly climbed the palace's long stairs
they felt their shoulders sprout with downy, curly wings.
The lone man turned to admire the famed decoy of men
as step by step she breached the palace like a flame.
It was just such an hour as this when the bright star
of the nude wagtail goddess laughed, shadows embraced,
as by Troy's battlements he'd placed the pregnant mare;
the azure darkness dimly shone like this when once
he stood, new-washed and mute on his ancestral threshold,
and held the wages of just slaughter in firm hands.
Odysseus moved his lips and hailed the coming night:
"O dark-eyed lady, this is a pure and lucky hour."
In dusk the crowd shone faintly in the central court,
and from the terrace of the women's quarter stooped
bare-breasted, golden-feathered ladies, budded flowers,
and laughed with wonder at earth's multicolored ants.
The Serpent Sisters, consecrated maids who served
the many-dugged old dame of earth, in joy adorned
the squat round columns with white lilies and green palms,
and decked the king's courts to receive the miracle.
But suddenly as the inner gate swung wide, there loomed
three monstrous-bodied Negroes with thick brazen spears;
between their savage thighs two slender leopards slunk.
Then a wasp-waisted Cretan sniggered to the bronzesmith:
"All joy to these black lovers of lush Diktena!
Evil tongues say that our good-natured princess now
cries out in bed with these three blacks the whole night through."
He was still speaking when the gold jambs shone like stars;
Diktena's soft and tender body stood revealed
and her breasts swayed like two newborn and curly beasts.
She slowly lifted heavy-lidded, painted eyes,
harrowed the courtyards, the men's bodies, festive dames,
then smiled and slowly vanished in the night once more.
Arch-eyebrowed Helen sank her face in her cupped hands:
"My eyes are tired of gazing and my ears of hearing.
Ah God, to lie down in a nook till the world cools!"

The archer's heart then ached for that celestial body:
"Helen, I'll tell the guards of our renowned descent;
the gates shall open then, you'll lie on golden beds,
for our renown has surely reached these distant shores."
He spoke, pushed through the milling crowd, and vanished soon.
Hardihood, meanwhile, gaped with silent envious awe
on adamant embellished armor highly wrought
with rampant rushing lions, lilies in full bloom,
and girls that played and tumbled with ferocious bulls:
you'd think that each sword cried with its own special pain.
The Evening Star had vanished in the sea like flame,
and honeysuckle, tangled in the hair of night,
burst, till the curled locks in the courtyards smelled of musk.
And Helen, leaning on a sea-blue column, watched
the pert court ladies with their flouncing furbelows
who bent and wriggled their wide loins with swaggering sways
and kept the double treasure of their bosoms open.
Deep in her mind, the crystal-breasted woman scolded:
"It's best that women keep their breasts well hidden, clothed,
to veil them like wild flames and so preserve their strength;
that which you wish to give, keep hidden and unspent."
Then as all-knowing Helen appraised the women's armor,
and saw with sidelong glance the blond-haired gardener come
and stand beside her like a chaste and guileless bull,
naked, with but a sheepskin round his sunburnt loins,
she looked on his strong sturdy knees with stooped submission.
The snow-white swan-god suddenly passed through her dazed mind,
he who had swooped and cast her mother supine on grass,
and now, dear God, he'd come again to seek her out
with wine-drenched beard, mud-splattered feet, and heavy flesh!
Thus, stooped, she felt his panting stallion breath above her
entering her brimming neck and coursing down to her loins
until she felt the old sweet dread that seized her mother.
He reached his calloused hand in silence, filled her palm
with a grape-cluster, his first fruit, huge as an infant,
and then the swan-born heard his steps withdraw, and sighed
with soft desire as she watched his firm calves vanish.
She raised her head and ate with greed the luscious grapes;
three-headed time was conquered: in one lightning flash
loam, grapes, and wine had merged, intoxication spread
like a tall vine and twined about her famous thighs.
And thus the lone man found her, sunk in hidden thought,
the bittersweet grape-cluster in her rose palms still.
He saw her eyes brim sweetly with a blond-haired man
and mocked her gently as he spoke with slant allusion:
"Lady, good weather at your prow, wind in your sails!

You're scudding swiftly on deep seas to distant shores!"
He laughed without much heart, then with great anger said:
"Tonight we three must lie here in a courtyard nook
and sleep with the remaining pilgrims till day dawns,
but when the king finds out tomorrow who we are
we'll enter his great palace as befits our rank."
The bulldog bronzesmith then appeared with sullen glance
and all three lay amid the columns on myrtle boughs.
The people swarmed about them, and the stars dripped dew,
the women tucked their rich-embroidered wings like birds,
girls giggled in the shade, the young men strolled and swaggered,
all waited for the holy moon to rise and light the world.
Fires in every town and hamlet were put out, and flame
still lingered only on the Bull-God's steaming wicks;
all looked toward dawn when the new fire would light their hearths.
A golden lamp within the courtyard's smoking shrine
shone softly flickering and caressed the fertile Mother
who held her swelling breasts as votive offering high,
while the male double-ax hung over her, and swung.
Then white-winged Helen reposed at last like soil on earth,
and shut her gracious eyes, but in her mind still saw
the fat, rotund great goddess with her spreading flanks;
her eyes dimmed and her mind spun till there rose from earth
the holy fruitful tree of the dark goddess—sleep.
Gold votive offerings hung like apples from its boughs,
and with a mother's sleep-alluring languid lullaby
the votive tree kept rustling till the seductress slept;
but then with a light twist of her unguarded mind
the full tree vanished, and above her bosom hung
a cluster of firm grapes, a bloodstained double-ax.
She laughed and raised both breasts on high as votive gifts.
Thus did the famous beauty dream on palace tiles,
but at her side the sleepless archer fought his heart
and gripped it like a snapping bitch to choke its yelping.
The door guard had not quaked to hear his dreaded name
but spurned him with no fear or reverence, barred the door,
so that his savage flame-filled heart had rushed at once
to fall on that pigheaded guard, break down the doors,
and, by a hair, had almost dragged the body with it.
Now sleepless and distressed, he took his heart to task:
"Bitch, will you still resist and bite your chains with rage?
You're not the master at my castle's brazen doors,
nor can you shut out or invite all those you please!
And when the sentry thwacked us with his heavy spear,
didn't you hear me cry to swallow your tongue, you bitch?
But you howled on nor stopped until I called you thrice.

Don't hurry, you poor wretch. Be patient, our time will come."
Thus did the great heart-battler argue all night long;
he clenched and then unclenched his fists to grip his thoughts
as though composed of bodies, spears, or kindling wood.
The air blew like a sweet and cooling summer breeze,
lilies and myrtles swayed, and in the lofty cornice
the royal banners flapped, the double-axes gleamed,
till suddenly in the frenzied mind of the sea-battler
the night-drenched palace rose like a great-masted ship.
Oho! See how it proudly scuds with open sails
loaded with all the riches of earth, sea and mind;
but all the foaming waves are full of reefs, the pilot drunk,
and God sits in the laden hold and rips the heavy planking!

Then the light sleeper rose and cocked his subtle ears,
for far in the high mountains, in God's twisting gullet
the king groped toward the cavern to regain his youth.
The Serpent Sisters slowly in the waning moon
began to sway with naked feet on the courtyard tiles
that their shrill cries and dancing might sustain their king
who walked the perilous verge now of the Bull-God's path.
They leapt like slender tiger-cubs in the moon's light,
and their unmounted bodies were coiled tight with power;
looped thrice about their arms, or hissing from their hair,
the sacred snakes of ritual slid in smooth contortions.
Raising their hands toward the high hills, the maidens cried:
"O Mother, Mother, mistress of mountains, sea, and air,
whose gorged breasts burst with anguish of redundant milk,
Crete weeps and starves! Come to her shores now, give her suck!
Ah, Mother, may the exhausted earth revive once more
that our great seed may sprout, our trees bear flower and fruit,
our headlong herds increase, our green ravines and vales
wabble with newborn lambs of white wool, black, and gray;
and may our ships sail always with fair winds once more
while you, a gorgon at their prow with savage eyes,
cut new roads in the waves for Crete to spread her claws.
Strengthen the loins of our pale men, pity our maids
and give them swelling breasts that flow with milk and honey!
Crete calls with all her loam! Dear Mother, fill her womb!
Crete calls with all her horses, Mother, her sheep and ox,
Crete calls with all her men, her women beg and wail,
come spread your holy hands above our old king, Mother!"
Thus did the Serpent Sisters cry in whirling dance,
swaying on high their snake-kissed arms in the moon's light
till the crowd surged and men and maids struck up a dance
then raised their hands on high and shouted toward the hills:

"O Mother-Mistress, Huntress, Priestess, Captain, come,
come to this court, come down and take the lead, come kick
this earth and whirl it like a spinning top anew!"
The people shouted till their temples creaked like gates,
their brains spilled from their skulls and boiled like seething must,
their minds grew savage as all former boundaries broke,
and when a shadow suddenly leapt on tiles, they gasped—
wild hair, bow stained with blood, shrill twang of speeding arrow!
It leapt high, seized the lead and swirled the dancers round;
the bridegroom lost his bride, the young girl her betrothed,
the dancers wept and whined and howled for their return,
but Death, their Leader, raged and threshed them like a whirlpool
till all, with throats caught in the lime-nets of the moon,
burst out in joyous and bold song like nightingales
who vanish, lovesick, carefree, lost in flowering shrubs.
But all at once the swift dance broke and all sides scattered;
a vulture's shrill cry sounded from the palace stairs
and all with terror hid themselves near the squat columns.
The women screamed, and pressed their hands against their ears:
"It's Phida, shrill-voiced, first-born daughter of our king!
God's heavy hand has felled her once again, she's moonstruck!"
Leaning against the sacred double-axes by the stairhead,
a young ecstatic girl with red rags round her waist
flung her pale hands on high with rage and beat her breasts:
"Great God, for years I've torn my heart out calling you!
Rise from the earth, you slayer, gird on your iron armor,
spew fire and burn our ships to coal, scorch Crete to ash!"
She screamed, foamed at the mouth until her pale throat choked,
and then she tumbled headlong down the darkened stairs.
In terror of the moonstruck girl the people fled,
but through the scattering crowd the archer strode and knelt
above the shriveled form convulsed in the sallow moon.
A dread bloodthirsty god sucked at the young girl's brains
and she like a hooked fish thrashed wildly to cast off
the curved iron hook that jabbed deep in her choking throat.
Then the much-suffering archer gently raised her head
so that she might not break her skull on the hard stones,
and watched in silent fear the whites of her wild eyes
turned upward, glazed, or rolling round in bloodstained sockets.
But as he reached to wipe the sweat from her damp lobes,
the gates were suddenly flung wide, bald eunuchs dashed,
stooped down, then from the earth scooped up the girl like rags,
and vanished, fleeting down the palace corridors.
Odysseus, deeply wounded, stretched on myrtle boughs
and brooded on the weak and pallid soul of man:
a small sail on a small boat by all four winds thrashed.

He leant his harsh head gently by a column's base
till the flesh-healing god of sleep leant mutely down
and all night stitched with care the cracked seams of his skull.

Thus did the spacious courtyards shrill in the sick moon,
but pairs of dancers in four rounds rose quickly again
as all strained to enkindle and sustain their king.
Meanwhile, Idomeneus crawled on craggy cliffs
and wanly smiled with hairless lips as his flat pate
shone dimly in the silver moon like a bleached skull.
At length he crawled close to God's mouth, a deep dark pit,
and stood near, panting, gasping long to get his breath.
A cool wind gently blew, and all the stars marked out
with mystic characters what fate had foreordained.
He cackled dryly with his withered, toothless gums:
"My wretched forebears scanned the stars at night with fear
and yearned for a good sign before they dared to thrust
their noses in God's cave to see the Holy Mother;
but now I bring them gold—that is, both sky and stars!"
He spoke, then boldly thrust himself through the low entrance
and squirmed upon the cavern's glooming slippery stones.
The cavern's arches spread until God's monstrous mouth
gaped open slowly, high and wide, and darkly gleamed.
Long rows of hanging stalactites dripped in the gloom
and rose like thick round phalli twined with maidenhair
and red rags tied by women in their votive rites.
The winding pathways broadened in wide whorls and twists
until the thick black gore distilled in murky pits
as the king slipped and slithered in God's bloody entrails.
Huge startled bats sped by his ears without a sound,
and suddenly torches blazed, shrieks rang, and maidens masked
like cows, bare-bosomed and one-breasted, sprang from clefts,
bellowed with rage and butted their old king to leave.
A woman's cry in birthpang suddenly split the air
and all the women rushed about a rutting bull
poured of pure bronze that in the savage torchlight flashed;
a tall black double-ax gleamed on its golden horns.
Then slowly from its loins a dragon-woman rose
holding in both her hands her two milk-laden dugs.
The king fell on the earth face down and shouted, "Mother!
Help me, thrice-Mother, who begets gods, men, and beasts!
All think I'm a great monarch, for one night you placed
your hands on my bald pate till God's soul boiled and rose,
and from your tenfold fingers strength poured through my heart.
That sacred sperm you planted in my split head, Mother,
has sprouted and borne fruit: ships, laws, and famous wars;

but Mother, it's all withered now and casts no sprouts.
I've squandered all that spirit, my loins are drained dry.
Look, I've brought back my body. Fill it with God again!'
The Mother-Dragon mutely weighed the old man well
then slowly her loud cavern-roar rang mockingly:
"Old king, I don't think you can bear the Bull-God now!
If I should place my dreadful hands on you, old man,
you'd burst in fragments like a sheepskin filled with flames."
She roared, then gave commands for all her maids to leave,
and the young cows scattered in rings and hid in rocks.
No sooner were the two alone than their eyes met
and merged with laughter like two wily beasts in darkness.
Slowly the Mother spread her plump and painted hands
and in one palm the king heaped high thick towering pearls
and in the other poured, with sweet seduction, gold and gems.
When the she-dragon cast these gifts in the Bull's belly,
she reached out both her hands with ravening greed once more.
"I give you also, unslaked Mother, three large towns:
one in the fields for grain and all your flaxen robes,
one in the harbor to enjoy the sea's great wealth,
the third and best is planted on a high plateau
where your bull-calves may browse and your male children breed."
The Mother laughed, full-satisfied, then crossed her hands,
uttered shrill cries of joy until the young cows dashed
and carried in their hands the sacred, regal dress:
tall peacock feathers, three-peaked golden-lilied crown,
an ivory tray with mystic, thousand-spiraled signs
where in the center God's great eye turned savagely
as round it hearts and human heads danced arm in arm
in a wide belt adorned with women, beasts, and snakes,
and on the disk's rim, tall and straight, nine galleys sailed,
all mystic signs that etched upon the precious ivory
the great commands and cares of their most dreaded God.
The cunning king stooped low and then the Mother placed
her hands on his bald shining pate and shrilled aloud:
"I've watched and weighed you like a hawk, then swooped and seized you!
I'll raise my double-ax now high and split your brains!
Descend from horns, O Strength, and make his weak mind firm!
Ascend from the new phallus, Strength, and rouse his loins!
Rise up, O Mystic Snake, and nine times zone him round,
God fills his heart now with nine winter-summer seasons."
She spoke, then from the cavern mouth a flame leapt out,
tall as two men, and heralded the newborn news.
The flame then leapt with joy on high Mount Dikte's peaks,
dashed downward like a flashing star to Mount Selena
and rooted in its craggy rocks where round it leapt

goatherds and shepherds in a savage Cretan dance.
High above Knossos the tall peak of Grouhla flamed,
and shepherds beat bronze pans, cast trees into the hearth,
till like an eagle beating his red blazing wings
the flame leapt on the palace roof, fluttered, and lit
all upper windows swiftly with its burning beak.
Then it fell lightly to the royal courts, sped toward the town,
leapt in and huddled swiftly in the flameless hearths
and hatched a burning coal for egg wherever it stayed.
The king passed through the fields, his nuptial chariot drawn
by four pure snowy bulls with horns of gleaming gold.
The largest stars still wanly burned high in the heavens,
and all the nearby villagers dashed out with palms
and bowed with reverence low before their potent king.
Young women spread the ground with their embroidered dowries,
for the king now so brimmed with God that his new strength
would pass through chariot, bulls, and wheels, spill on the ground,
where scooped by garments, it would pass to hopeful bodies.
Clutching his seed, the king rode all day long in state
while the three comrades sauntered through the lower town.
Taverns at every corner opened, doors were decked,
sills flashed with new-washed garments, and young maidens drenched
with water their slim lilies, basil, and green mint.
They turned their festive faces suddenly toward the East:
was it a golden cloud that rose on mountain passes
or did a thunderbolt split the exhausted fields,
or could it be the king who dashed down from the mountain slopes?

Drums beat at sunset in the spacious palace courtyards;
and all at once the whole town thundered, palm leaves swayed,
and black eyes filled the air to gaze on the healed king,
but he fled down the labyrinthine halls in rage,
for all his hunters had failed to seize his daughter-bride
and had returned with empty hands and empty nets.
In frenzied wrath he ordered the three hunter-chiefs
first slain with double axes and then meshed in nets
which they had long borne on their shoulders all in vain.
All shook to see the godly strength that filled their king,
untamed as yet by mankind's gentleness and patience.
Odysseus waited for the monarch's wrath to cool
and then sent word that he'd been waiting by the gate
with world-famed, wondrous-eyebrowed Helen at his side.
For hours they waited by the gate for the king's word
until the archer's head boiled like a seething caldron
fed by the bronzesmith's spiteful words as by hot flame:
"I can't believe my eyes, nor get it through my head

that the great archer stands and begs at the king's door!"
But though the rash man's blood now boiled, he bit his fist:
"O heart, keep vengeance deep, caress her secretly,
for there's no bride with greater dowry in all this world;
she carries ashes in her chests, blood in her jugs,
and brings a long black-hilted sword as the groom's gift!"
A warm and heavy South Wind rose, the far seas rippled,
and like white, silent, sailing ghosts, with shrouds for sail,
fishing-boats, triremes, galleys, slowly, slowly sailed
into the ponderous azure dreams of slumbering Crete.
Crete slept on like a silent sea-beast that once rose
from time's deep pitch-black mire to get a little air;
for a short while, then, plants and beasts and men had time
to stretch their carefree legs and raise a bit of crust
until on her thick hide she felt with mild annoyance
the myriad lice-race softly crawl and saunter by;
but when she scratched herself, all fell in tangled heaps,
and when she yawned, swift earthquakes gulped the towns
till she could get some air and sink in seas again.
But just before she sank in waves or plunged in mire
the archer grasped one of her columns tight, and roared:
"Dame Crete, don't sink again before my mind's revenged!"
The slayer was growling still when footsteps sounded near
as the gate suddenly opened and two gold-plumed lords,
as squat as jars, spoke greetings in a shrilling voice:
"The true son of the Bull-God, the sea's unconquered king,
has with great royal kindness deigned to let you see him!"
With golden staffs, they showed the way through the dark halls;
long rows of empty cellars, old worm-eaten stairs,
moss-covered gaping towers, and balconies half-fallen—
as though the palace once had been a dragon's armor
where now his thin debilitated grandson sailed.
In the black wall a secret door gaped suddenly
and a great golden room spread to their startled eyes.
Between tall double-axes on a high throne, the prow
of a great sea-battling ship, the monarch proudly sat
like a majestic sea-god carved from a huge pearl
and leant upon a coral tree that rose to his right.
On low thrones round him, old sea-skippers sat and stank
like withered apples with their hairless senile flesh;
behind them sat plump eunuchs, guards of God and maids,
sly dream-interpreters, and bath-attending lords.
Naked young pages, all adorned with peacock plumes,
some holding incense-burners, others long-stemmed lilies,
bedecked the throne like rich festoons and shone like snakes.
Idomeneus placed then in a goldsmith's hand

a ball of solid gold, large as an infant's head,
to carve God's blessing richly on a holy rhyton.
He ordered the skilled goldsmith to remember all:
"God stood on high and I stood straight on earth before him,
the great sun hung low to my right, the full moon left,
so that their double beams met in my dazzled eyes.
God spread his hands and gave into my trust the firm
round disk of earth with all its souls and mighty laws.
I did not move, and held the whole world in my palms;
God questioned, and I stared straight in his eyes and answered.

I questioned too, and he replied like a true friend.
Gather your wits, O goldsmith, teach your crafty hands
how to immortalize this meeting in pure gold.
Make infinite what lasted but a lightning flash on earth!"

He spoke, dismissed the goldsmith with a regal gesture,
then turning slowly with his half-shut snaky eyes,
suddenly hissed, and hailed the royal pair before him:
"Great is the Bull-God's joy this holy night to take
and taste in his wide mouth sun-lovely radiant Helen;
even though Chance is blind, God leads her by the hand.
Welcome, tall lily of the air, immaculate flower,
that you may also hang from the god's golden horns."
His mocking eyes gazed downward on the cunning man
but his soul trembled, for his mind divined some evil:
"Quite well do I recall your slanting sea-capped head;
somewhere on neighboring beaches once we met by fate—
you were a common shepherd, then, in a poor farm;
yet got to be the frequent comrade of great kings
because your crafty brains gave birth to wiles and tricks."
But the quick-tempered man reined in his heart and brain
and soothed his mind, recalling how in the dread cave
he stood erect before the one-eyed monster, Cyclops,
and in clay basins poured out wine for that tricked brute.
"Hold tight your miseries, O my heart, and lick your leash,
put on a pleasing face, smile now and pour with skill
the new bright wine you bear here: Helen's wanton eyes."
The nimble-fingered weaver chose what woof to weave
and signaled with his eyes to her for whom Troy fell,
and she with fear ascended the throne's golden steps,
and with her rose and flickered that great lady, Fire.
Then the decrepit king sank his exhausted hands
in her bright hair till its perfumes unhinged his brain:
"Warm is the earth, the hills are fragrant, and horns sway.
O heifer Helen, the Bull-God roars deep in my loins!"
The eunuchs smiled with pallid lips and swung their necks
so that their golden earrings tinkled jauntily.
The king spread out his hands, his wily eyes grew glazed:
"Dear Bull-God, large-eyed father, when on the great waves
you saw this new bride coming with her naked breasts,
you bellowed as you licked your lustful, lustrous thighs.
Your grace is double, double your mind, and your horns double!
I know now why in my thick nets you would not snare
my virgin daughter whom nine hunted night and day.
Let heralds with their conches blare in towns and hills
that God has found his bride, let Krino and her troop

dance with no fear now on the sacred threshing floor."
Thus spoke the senile king and shook with smothered passion
as the sly weaver watched the old man swirl in rings
and vanish in the whirlpools of his spinning mind.
Though frightened Helen signaled with her eyes for help,
feeling the beast's deep breath already on her back,
bespurred Odysseus saw her quake, and was not moved:
"Many think she's a goddess and bow to her great power,
others embrace her as a woman and lose their wits,
for me she's but a singing decoy-bird in my god's hands."
He brooded in his brain, then set the king a snare:
"With hand on heart, I bow low and salute the Bull!
He stood a fisher on Crete's shores, and pulled me in
with all my ships, deep in his bloody nets of love;
we sail now in his holy mouth—his will be done!
Helen, how fortunate! You'll lie in the bronze cow,
for God is good and loves the fragrant smell of man."
But bitter gall rose in the king's suspicious eyes:
"O treacherous man, even as you spoke, I knew quite well
what crafty trap you leant against my castle walls.
I loathe that man with blinders on who his life long
turns like a beast the slippery well-pump of his brain
and, like a sterile mule, breaks no untrodden road.
And now you place the same snare by my castle walls:
a bronze cow with a white flame in its womb—fair Helen!
But my ax-bearing heavy God can smash all wills,
and you've come vainly to my house with torch in hand;
O crafty fox, you're caught now in my own god's snare!"
Odysseus cast his piercing glances round him then
and reckoned that their skulls encased but thinner brains
and that God never thrusts his strength in double-axes
but in the muscular strong hands that hold them tight.
Idomeneus watched the archer's glances thrust
like swelling firebrands amid his myriad wealth
and said, as though his crooked brain decided then:
"I hold earth on my back, life is my heavy duty,
it's only just that with my heels I crush this flame
that rears its tongue, or it will swell and burn me down,
because, O evil-footed man, in every home you've stepped
you came with torch to set a conflagration blazing."
Then the flame-sower felt deep fear, yet held his dread:
"There is a god of friendship who defends pure love.
I came like an old friend to knock on your bronze gate,
and hold no blazing torch but only friendship's apple."
The king then turned to his plump eunuchs mockingly:
"This man who passed and stole his trusting best friend's wife

dares talk of friendship! Why has the earth not swallowed him?"
"A God commanded! I swear I wept till my heart broke!"
"And God was wise to thrust you deep in the Bull's belly.
Try to escape now from his twisting, torturous guts!"
He spoke, and all the eunuchs laughed, till once again
their golden earrings tinkled in their downy ears.
Helen then placed her suppliant hands on the king's knees,
and round her neck a vixen's blazing colors flashed:
"I swear I left my happy hearth of my free will.
A great god seized me and I followed joyously;
he came to play with me on grass like a white bull,
then suddenly bellowed, shook himself, plunged in the waves
and placed me at your golden feet, still drenched with foam.
Now I rejoice to know you are the Bull-God truly."
The king closed both his eyes, her voice seemed honey-sweet,
and she rejoiced, whose speech was cool as fragrant flowers,
and her much-kissed and ruby mouth sang out once more:
"I ask one favor only for my wedding gift:
dear bridegroom, do not touch my sorrow-laden friend."
Her body's crackling warmth rose in the old king's brain:
"For your dear sake, my bride, I shall protect his head
though God within me shouts it's high time, Helen, now,
that his sly brains and eyes should vanish from the earth."
He turned then to the archons of the women's quarters:
"Go tell my Serpent Sisters to lave Helen's body
with thick balms and aromas, and to teach her how,
in seven days and nights, to mingle with God sweetly.
Let her lie on my daughter Diktena's divan
but let not my cursed daughter Phida touch her ever.
Her friends shall be our guests in the rich archons' room,
to eat and sleep as it befits a monarch's wealth;
their hated heads are guarded by the hand of Helen.
But never let them once take wing to flee the palace,
but keep them locked like eagles in a golden cage
so they won't fly in light or their souls slip my claws.
Let the page boys remain; it's time I bathed my body
to give my flesh new strength and grace, to cool my mind,
for all night long I've battled with my heavy God."
He spoke, the drowsy noblemen and eunuchs rose,
slaves ran from everywhere with torches, some bent low
and raised the heavy-laden, gold-decked king on high.
The naked page boys, shaking golden perfume flasks
ran on ahead, sprinkling the way with flower-water,
and last of all the castle-wrecker strode: his soul
flashed fire from his twenty finger tips and toes,
and his gaunt head, all seven stories high, swayed in the air.

❧ VI ❧

The cocks had not yet crowed, the shimmering stars still burned,
and earth, filled with closed eyelids and crossed hands, slept on
within an azure, cooling darkness flooded with fine mist
and sweetly dreamt that the great sun had risen already.
The Serpent Sisters raised their hands to the high hills,
their arms still tingling in the frosty breath of night,
and with their painted mouths sought to allure their god
to plunge to earth now in the guise of a strong bull.
"Descend, Bull-God! We've brought you cooling water here,
the feeding trough of earth now brims with meadow grass
and an unmounted calf shines in the greening pastures.
Come down to earth, male god, if it should please you now!
The wine vats seethe with wine, and the old crones have baked
you bread to tame your mind and sweeten your wild flesh.
By the great gate a pale unmounted virgin waits
and trembles, and her breasts are bare to the four winds;
she waits for you to come like a groom with his sweet knife.
Descend, Bull-God, on Mother Earth, and mount her now!
She lifts her tail like a young cow and moos and moans;
when shall your gilded horns shine from the high mountains?"
The Serpent Sisters shrieked and raised their gleaming throats
and crystal hands toward the high hills and waited, trembling.
The dew descended from the mountains, light, cool-plumed;
and like a white dove in smoke-silver olive groves
the Morning Star came down and played, blazing with light.
A tiny hoarse-voiced cock leapt on a roof and turned
his callow and inexpert neck to hail the sun
—that gaudy, spurred cock-pheasant with his gilded cockscomb—
and the sun, listening to his grandchild, leapt and shone.
A downy, milky light licked all the mountain rims,
spilled gurgling down the gleaming slopes, stone after stone,
and when a cypress tree saw it afar, it smiled
as though red roses climbed its peak and blossomed there;
a bent old shepherd led his flock, and his white beard
kindled like brushwood when he turned toward the bright slopes,
and his stout shepherd's staff was splattered with fine gold.

The palace roofs then laughed, the double-axes woke,
the sacred snakes woke also and uncoiled in light,
and all the twisted bull-horns shone like crescent moons.
What joy the sun's hot eye must feel, dear God, to watch
the world each morning hatch in light like a huge egg!
The brazen castle gates of day creaked open slowly,
the brains of men cracked wide, and thoughts like dithering larks
awoke and soared straight in the light, all wing and song.
Men wrapped their sashes round their waists, maids combed their hair,
girls opened their black eyes enwreathed with violet paint,
and dressed like stars for festival—this was a rare day!
All climbed up chattering to the highest tiers of stone
where the poor sat and watched the archons' ritual ring.
The sunburnt heads of males in wheatfields waved like grain,
their gleaming eyes burned in the misty light, the shells
worn round their necks and their brass bracelets laughed and tinkled.
Young girls then turned their eyes with stealth toward the great palace—
when would the bronze gates open, God, and spew forth all
the haughty palace dames with their patrician bearing?
The ancient gossips babbled on and on, their tongues
clacked on like spinning wheels from morn to night, nor stopped;
the married matrons roared with laughter, maidens blushed,
and in the increasing rose of dawn all came to light—
chins, bosoms and cosmetics—till each maiden sighed:
"O strong Bull-God, grant that your grace may fall on *me!*"
But all at once all faces glowed, then chitchat stopped,
the palace gates sprang open and the hallways gleamed;
painted, bare-breasted, newly bathed with flaming graces,
the curly-haired and carefully decked grand dames appeared,
swaying and strutting step by step, ruffling their plumes
like wriggling wagtails, and perched, slow-winged, on the stone stairs.
Flickering in early morning mist like lustrous stars,
their earrings, bracelets, their ancestral neckwear gleamed,
and a sweet scent of musk flowed through the ritual ring.
Behind them toddled their pale-faced and wrinkled lords,
tall tufts of feathers on their heads, gold staves in hand,
with narrow painted lips like wounds that would not close.
Then the mob hushed, gaping like babes on wealth and lords,
and thus forgot their griefs, swept far by gold and glitter.
Scornful Odysseus sat among the sallow archons
and with his grappling glance cut through and scanned their heads:
"So this is Mother Earth," he thought, "and these her children,
painted and pallid, a foot in the grave, awaiting the sun!"
He turned then to his glowering friend who crouched beside him:
"Hardihood, aren't you pleased now with the upper world,
the handsome men that walk the earth, and their sweet maids

whose hair, new-washed, still smells of fragrant laurel oil?"
But his friend growled like a ship's dog and would not answer.
The myriad-willed man harrowed with his gripping glance
the ladies, lords, and the vapid antheaps seated high
until an unforeseen compassion blurred his mind.
He turned once more with hushed voice to his stubborn friend:
"I never tire of watching how they walk on stone,
blossom like trees, and bare their throats like radiant stars.
They open earthen eyes, and all the world is born,
their earthen breasts become immortal spurting springs,
and I smell deeply now their sweat and their sweet breathing.
The hot brief flash is good where all earth's creatures move,
live, laugh, and weep, and sun themselves on fragrant soil.
Joy to that worthy mind that fondles them in passing!"
But his dour friend mocked at his now compassionate master:
"O man of many wiles, I know you well, nor does my mind
draw back from the earth's sweet seductions you spread here.
Like a lone lion whom hunger has not pinched as yet,
you hold the fawn between your teeth with marveling glance,
caress your quarry first, and then you pounce, and eat!"
Before the man of seven souls could even reply,
the Serpent Sisters in the ritual ring all shrieked
and then stretched toward the sky their pale night-frozen arms.
Behold, the sun's first rays had leapt and smeared with rose
the crisp and rigid teats of Crete, then with slow strokes
her famous, fabulous lover with his golden hands
caressed her haughty breasts and rolled down toward her belly.
The crowd glowed in the light and their hearts frisked like calves;
with their deep krytons then, the Serpent Sisters paced,
sprinkling the earth with milk and honey, and invoked
the sacred Bull-God's secret, most erotic names.
Gold as a wedding ring, the holy moment hung
with heaviness, while mortals quaked, poor rustling reeds
that God adjusted to his lips and played like flutes.
The king then mounted his high throne, a monstrous beast;
he wore the skull of a black bull with shining snout
on which two golden horns stood stiff and flashed in light.
Leaping about him with shrill cries, the Serpent Sisters
broke in a swirling dance and screamed like hawks at dawn
that from the mountain tops fly out to greet the sun.
The king then raised his fist on high, the hubbub ceased,
and from his heavy mask his bellowing voice rang out:
"Welcome, O Bridegroom Bull, twin spear of piercing light!"
He spoke, then gave the ceremony's secret sign,
and Diktena's three Negro lovers raised on high
their sea-resounding conches, took deep breath, and blew

until the twisting valleys roared like slaughtered bulls.
Then suddenly on the riverbank appeared in dance
the sacred combat's curly-templed, new-washed bulls
pushed by the plump bucolic girls that tend the cows.
The crowd leant forward, hushed, the palace dames rejoiced,
fluttering their painted lashes, and in secret yearned
to see warm human blood shine on those murderous horns.
And when they raised their eyes, their hearts began to throb,
for in the light of dawn at length, in the blessed ring,
the perilous games and passion of the suffering God began.

Body and soul, two kindred cows, mooed amorously,
and on a white bull's hide beside a brazen cow,
trembling on the low ground, a votive beast, a bride,
the holy body of Helen wailed, with hair unbound.
Naked, she held a pure-white lily in her hands,
her new-washed hair was clothed in mist of saffron dust,
and as the rites decreed, she wept, tore at her hair,
then stooped to earth, let her locks fall, and pressed her mouth
to the black soil and thrice in dread cried out for help.
At her first cry the shadows in the sunlight spluttered,
but at her second cry drums beat and the earth rang
as though battalions broke far off, as though steeds sped,
and earth's hide like a tom-tom beat to trampling hooves.
At her third cry tall, sturdy Mountain Maids took wing
and wheeled about her in a swift-paced swirling dance
as virgin Krino leapt and led the group with throat
held high, a slender cypress, royal branch unplucked.
They danced, and with their javelins beat their brazen drums
as their nude thighs now swiftly gleamed in light, now darkened.
Krino first raised the cry to strengthen Helen's heart:
"Spirit, you cried for help! We've rushed to your defense!
The dark and burning bull-beast roars and longs to eat you!
Rise up in light, Dame Soul! Don't cry; take up your weapons!"
But the voluptuous body raised its eyes and sighed:
"Dear God, I fear all weapons, nor was my flesh made
for wars, but to bear babies and to give them suck.
I fear and weep but I can't fight the Bull-God's will."
The voice then of the crystal virgin shook with pride:
"I can admit the great male God as spirit only,
but you, for shame, wait for a bull to come and mount you!"
Then Helen's mouth became an open, slow complaint:
"I wail, and long for God to come more tenderly,
but I'm a woman still and love his masculine odor."
Then the bold chorus stamped on earth with wrath and yelled:
"We shall rush out to fight him, whether you will or not!"

As the two rival spirits clashed in ritual rites,
a herd of bulls rushed in the ring till the earth shook
and the crowd quaked to see their sharp horns gleam in sun.
The lovely ladies of the court shook delicately
and on their backs and side-locks felt with secret joy
the bull's moist nostrils and the steaming odors rise,
but all the Mountain Maidens clashed their shields with rage
and stood erect like fortresses about the bride
who crouched with lily hands and screened her naked breasts.
Then on the funnel-shaped arena's edge appeared,
like doves with feathers puffed by an erotic swoon,
high priestess Diktena's obedient slaves of love.
Like rabbits, their small bosoms shook in the cool dew
and then uncurled with pleasure in the sun's first strokes,
and in their curly locks, new-washed with laurel oil,
a heifer's golden horns curved like the crescent moon.
Weaponless, but with gleaming thighs, they climbed the stairs,
and the lords laughed and winked, but the poor peasant boys,
smothering with lust, schemed how to work for many years,
amass great wealth, and sleep with them for just one night.
What use is their poor life, dear God, their desolate youth,
why spill their souls on the cold ground, small drop by drop?
Better to lose all in one night's compassionate arms!
Thus did the Holy Harlots unhinge the brains of man,
and when they met and clashed with the pure Mountain Maidens,
they raised their white arms high, their armpits smelled of musk,
and, as the rites decreed, both fought their verbal war:
"God swoops from mountain peaks to eat and play on earth;
we are his food and drink and even his sacred toys—
and learn, O sterile maids, we are his soft, sweet mates.
Let her now leave who fears to merge with her dread god!"
The scornful savage mouth of Krino flashed reply:
"We will not leave! We guard the innocent soul of man!
God is a spirit with pure white wings, a soul that sails,
light, disembodied, deep in our thoughts, without embrace.
It's we who keep the world in bloom with virgin souls!"
Diktena opened her much-kissed, much-bitten lips
as blooms in sun a double-blossomed, curled carnation:
"O sterile belly, marble earth unplowed, cursed womb!
God is a stud in heat that mounts the human herd,
nor does he ask you, Dame, what face he should assume.
At least he does not swoop down like a cleaving sword
but comes here like a guileless bull and plays with us."
Krino then stamped the ground with a chaste downy foot
never caressed by a man's thigh in lustful beds:
"The body is not a stable where God comes to browse!"

Diktena laughed with lips whose harvest has no ending:
"Flesh is an empty, worthless sheath without its knife."
But then the unblemished lady-archer flung her dart:
"Every free soul may choose that god who suits her best;
my god is a tall mountain summit filled with flowers."
"But my god is the flesh's deep, dark, groping roots!"
The silvery vestal voice cut in with speechless grief:
"This is the earth, the bloody arena of man's soul;
we fight our heavy god that, whether he will or not,
he may assume a face as full of light as ours."
The hoarse voice thundered then and all the firm earth shook!
"Forward! Unbar the doors! Smash every iron bolt!
O uncastrated guests of God, the wedding starts!
Your empty, seedless bodies that besiege the bride
keep her from God where she may blossom and bear fruit
and thus fulfill her sacred role on Mother Earth.
Lift up your tails with lust and flash your double-horns!"
The sun leapt up a sting's length in the sky, and soon
in olive trees the crickets chirred to earn their wages,
and the court ladies fanned themselves in the great heat.
Thus the pre-rituals ended, and the Bull-King signed
for all to rest before the somber rites resumed.
High up where the poor sat, the people quaked with fear:
they saw the soul stretched on the ground, a votive beast
beaten by the conflicting powers of light and dark,
and their minds shook, nor knew now what great god to choose,
for comfort's road dropped to the right, the rough ascent
rose to the left, and both roads seemed to lead to God,
while at the crossroads stood the human heart, and swayed.
The Holy Harlots leant above the lords, and laughed,
their bodies shimmering with a light and downy sweat
as shameless golden demons jangled in their hair.
A cunning archon fondled Diktena's soft knees:
"Your song is sweet, O decoy bird of earth, you spoke
with craft, and he who heard you lost his wits, forgot
we play but games here in this ring to amuse our minds.
All art is laughter to relieve us from life's griefs."
God's harlot laughed and seized the old man's thinning hair:
"Since you can't reach the grapes, you fox, you call them sour!"
Then the seductress slid like an eel toward the young men.
Slaves sweated in the palace meanwhile, ovens swelled,
cattle were slain, confusing shouts and orders rang.
To please the archons' gullets, the cooks toiled with skill,
and slaves stooped with their handmills and ground finest flour
sieved seven times, pure white, to bake the choicest bread.
A mother in a corner crouched and fanned her child

that, pale as wax, lay dying on the moldy ground;
she held her throat with one hand to choke back her sobs
and with the other flicked the death-flies from her son,
for they had smelled a corpse already and swarmed from flowers
to lay their eggs in his blue nostrils and sunken eyes.
But all at once a three-lashed whip whizzed on her back;
she bit her lips, then stumbled backward and blindly groped
to find her wretched handmill in the murky dark.
Day flung the courtyards open wide, and the great sun
poured through the light-wells gladly till the frescoes woke:
there partridges with brittle beaks kissed with their tongues
and flying fish with longing fluttered in white light;
amid a garden filled with crocus, a boy strolled;
on a wet pebbled shore, a plump sea-goddess sat,
held with one hand her breasts and with the other gave
thick poppies to nude men who came to adore her grace.
O sun, you force awake old ghosts on painted walls
then spiral downward toward the ritual threshing floor again!

The Bull-King gave the sign once more and three blacks seized
their conches, the crowd hushed, the palace dames fell silent.
Then seven bulls with tails erect leapt in the ring,
and their black nostrils dripped with sweat. They sniffed the air,
and from near fields where grain was winnowed, smelled the chaff,
then bucked with sighs and snorts and dashed back to return.
But from the shadows suddenly Mountain Maidens leapt,
balanced on tiptoe delicately with slender forms,
and gliding toward the fuming beasts with stealthy stride,
waved in the air red mantles to arouse their rage.
A lean black bull who still retained his sperm unspent,
for whom all earth still seemed a fat and greening pasture,
bellowed to see pale Krino stand erect before him.
The blood poured in his turbid brain and turned to mud,
and his admired body swayed like a lean bow
till all the palace ladies paled, sucked in their breath,
and watched their star-browed bull, their own enormous pet
who was the first to start the dance and charge to battle.
Light-footed Krino fixed her eyes on his, and waited,
but when his sharp horns touched her belly, hard as marble,
she quivered slightly, leapt in air and firmly grasped
his sword-sharp flashing horns in both her supple hands.
The young bull roared with rage and shook his neck with fury
to uproot those virile hands that forced his tossing head,
but Krino, with the onrush of the wild bull's strength,
swung herself forcefully, upside-down, her feet in air,
in a swift backflip, then stood upright on his shining rump.

She clapped her hands high in the air, kicked the beast hard
with naked feet, turned a full somersault, and fell
into the ready arms of a swift Mountain Maid.
Then Krino smiled and wiped the sweat from her pale body.
Meanwhile the other bulls played with the mountain girls;
sometimes they frisked and tussled sweetly, man and maid,
sometimes their hot blood swirled in storm, and their eyes rolled.
The crowd sucked in its breath, the palace dames stretched out
their perfumed necks in a deep thirst for human blood,
and the mind-archer marveled at the boundless grace,
the hidden, gnarled and twisted strength which bursts in joy
from the strong hands and feet, the faultless loins of man.
With steady, stiff-necked virtue, with firm stubborn hope
the flesh distills into the unconquerable pure spirit,
until it grows divine, turns into mind, and flaps its wings.
Ah, God, if only our strong souls were like our bodies,
to throw ourselves in difficult battles pitilessly
that bit by bit, with hardy love and wide-eyed patience,
we might pass on beyond the bounds of cowardly man!
Such longings blazed within the warrior's great mind;
the bull-ring seemed the head then of a monstrous man,
all bodies seemed like great thoughts filled with strength and grace
that could with delicate ease and playfulness throw down
and conquer musky demons and thick-headed gods.
The spinner of minds turned round and eyed his glowering friend,
but he sat huddled with his head pressed on his knees,
and as he scowled and brooded how the strength of man
is spilled on earth in vain to amuse the senile lords,
his mind began to butt his skull like a wild bull.
The Mountain Maidens still fought gently with the beasts:
at times they twined about their necks like asps; at times,
leaping upon their rumps, they swayed like upright spears;
some ran embraced in friendship with their virile foe,
their black locks loose and fluttering over the bulls' napes.
At the ring's rim, a gentle girl not yet fourteen
stood panting by a calf and stroked his neck until
the chaste beast sweetly moaned and raised his tail erect.
His head thrust deep in his bull-mask, the silent king
lusted for Helen's body glittering in the sun,
till his mind muddied as the beast's dark murky powers
poured from his panting mask into his withered loins
so that he longed for blood to flow and for the lewd erotic rites.

Noon now had balanced in the sky and blazed with heat.
A thresher dripped with sweat beside his wretched ox
that rested in the shade, freed from the threshing pole,

and soon his pale wife trudged along the dusty road
and brought him barley bread and a poor plate of food.
As they lay, hungry, by an olive tree's blessed shade,
the worker gazed on his lean wife, broken by toil,
on his thin ox amid the reeds, his wretched crops:
"Dear wife, the crop is small, our pains have gone for nothing."
But his meek lifelong mate, who at his side had fought
the two tormenting beasts, hunger and nakedness,
did not reply, although she longed to throw her head

on her man's sweating chest and break in loud lament,
but she held back her pain to keep his burdens light.
In the hot noon the palace ladies burned with heat
and fanned themselves with peacock plumes and pursed their lips:
"Ah, let them spill blood now so that the poor might leave,
and we begin the erotic rites of mystic night!"
In their lust's heat as they talked on, great pearly drops
of sweat and wild deer's musk dripped from their curly locks.
But the king tired, and signaled for the games to stop
that men and beasts might eat and rest beneath the shade.
Conch-grass and oats were fed the bulls till their troughs brimmed,
and as the Serpent Sisters stroked them with skilled hands,
their male wrath sweetened with the maids' caressing care.
The Mountain Maidens stretched out panting in the shade,
wiped off their muddy sweat, and then from the cool springs
sprinkled their burning eyes and suffocating brows
till in the shade they lightly steamed like scorching stones.
The Holy Harlots with slaked lips, with easy virtue,
scattered among the wealthy skippers, laughed with joy,
and on the archons' benches spilled their musk and wings.
Then slowly from the palace kitchens, black slaves brought
huge copper trays weighed down with even the milk of birds.
In the high tiers the people sat in beating sun
and gulped with greed their bread and olives, their crisp grapes.
The ring was hushed awhile, then suddenly in the fields
the crickets burst in song like needling, flaming rain,
and slave girls with long peacock fans fell on their knees
and beat the air that the court dames might eat with ease.
The palace slaves stopped for a while to munch some bread
and gather strength again for the hard work ahead;
the mother left her handmill, rushed to her sick child,
but in the infant's nostrils, lips, and hollow eyes,
the grim death-flies had poured their eggs, row after row.
As it lay stretched on the damp ground and clenched its fists,
its swollen belly shone with a dark poisonous green,
but as the mother clasped it tight and searched it well,
and found its body still quite warm, her sad eyes glowed,
and she began to rock it slowly and press its lips
against her sagging orphaned dugs, to give it suck.
She stooped and stroked it lovingly, cooed like a dove,
but all at once her wild eyes stared and her mind whirled.
As the slaves turned, they saw her clutch her bundle tight,
mount swiftly up the cellar stairs in a mute terror
and rush in the day's light to place her child in sun.
Thick, filled with buzzing sound, the blazing noon beat down,
and shadows gathered like black pitch in the tiled courts;

the bronze bulls dripped with sun, the burning stones still steamed,
crows cut through the pale sky and smelled with greed an earth
that lay supine now like a pale worm-eaten corpse;
and a small maiden, blond as wheat, moved slowly through
deep violet shades, and picked a golden-rayed sunflower,
then plucked each leaf and said, "He loves me, loves me not."
When the slave-mother saw her bloated child in sun,
she uttered a wild wail and fainted on the tiles,
but not one soul in all the bull-feast heard her cry,
for all were sunk in noise and laughter, food and drink.
Only the archer, hungry still, who watched the crowd
with swollen, seething mind, pricked up his subtle ears
as though he heard a cry pierce through the flaming light,
fierce and convulsed, that called his name with sharp despair.
He stretched his neck to hear who might be calling him
and reared his panoplied dark head like a roused snake.
The wind buzzed in the sun like an awakened hive
with cries and weeping till the ears of the keen man
gathered the scattered sounds like thick resounding shells,
and as he dropped them in his silent heart, they fell
deep in his loins where all burst in one cry: "Odysseus!"
—as though he were responsible for all man's pain,
as though there were no other savior on all earth.
His mind was suddenly seized with boundless joy and grief
until his shoulders held the world, and not his head.
He shook his mind till his thoughts fell in place once more.
O heavy hour! Crickets rasped, crows tore through air,
the sun at zenith stared on earth with savage eye,
and the slave-mother's cry was lost in the heat's roar.
The archer shut his eyes and held his quivering breath,
for high above his body he felt the noon descend
to his scorched brows, his throat, his guts, his hairy loins.
The arena buzzed, and a thick stench of rot steamed up
from the damp armpits, sweat-drenched hair, and fetid food.
Handmaidens knelt and lengthened their court ladies' eyes
with black Arabian paint in light and skillful strokes,
then swelled their breasts like roses with a secret salve.
Diktena held her breath, and with swift stealthy strides
slid through the crowd and plunged her crimson-painted nails
in the dazed archer's thick gray hair and curly beard,
and when he raised his head, he shuddered deep to see
the light-green, gleaming glance of her seductive eyes
that laughed and played like lustrous pools under the moon;
and then he heard her hoarse voice, choked with passion's heat:
"One night when you strode heavily in my father's halls,
I stood unspeaking by a column and watched you well;

before me sat the rotting king, his eunuched guards,
and the old senile skippers with their thick cosmetics
as with your glance you tore our palace to its roots
and gulped down bronze and gold like the hearth's serpent-god
till smoke rose spiraling from your blazing nostrils there.
You glowed like a wild bull, and the fragmented moon
hung down your flaming chest like a great talisman.
Many the rich shipmaster and world-famous lord,
white, yellow, or black slaves, whom I allowed to moor,
of my own will, at lustful midnight in my arms.
They shrieked in spasms, but I lay unmoved like earth.
Ah, when I marveled at your valor yesterday,
a great voice rose and cried within my pulsing heart:
'By the sweet lust that glues together man and maid,
I swear to choose this stranger, risen from azure waves,
to be my bull-god in the erotic holy rites.' "
And as she spoke the archer felt her odors grasp
his chest and loins and swiftly blunt his piercing eyes.
He smiled to feel the nets of life draw round him tight,
to feel the ancient thousand-year-old dragnet seize him,
then reached his hands and with a bitter yearning stroked
the harlot's much-kissed knees and finely molded calves.
Somewhere on ancient shores he'd seen the immortal gods
shining in chiseled rock, their sacred knees worn out
with too much kissing, smooth and lustrous like gold amber;
and now with his flesh-loving hands he seized and licked
the harlot's glossy thighs with greed and brimming joy,
then raised his head and plunged wide-eyed in the open net!
But the dour bronzesmith watched his friend with mounting wrath:
"For shame! Your bright eyes, great sea-eagle, have grown glazed!"
The headstrong man's gall rose as he rebuked the smith:
"I may now taste unfearing the most deadly joys,
the most seductive sweets, for these can't conquer now;
small sterile souls alone before great passion quake!"
His friend's unyielding eyes glared at him stubbornly:
"Master, I don't mince words; I was born in a roofless house:
the more a soul mounts toward its peak, so much the more
does a cruel, joyless, unembraceable duty bind it."
Then the quick-tempered athlete seized his snapping friend:
"O laughless bronzesmith, in a sun-drenched garden once
a twisting vine entwined a column like harsh rope
and climbed up, dry and withered, with no sprout or flower,
but when it reached and clutched the top, it branched and spread
and coiled about the capital with twists and turns,
then burst one morning in a cluster of wild roses.
Dry soul, when you too reach the top, you'll burst in bloom!"

He spoke, and stroked the damp curls on the harlot's nape.
Thus did the stubborn stoneheads clash, while in the ring
pale Krino, moved by longing, gleaned fair Helen's beauty.
Her hands and eyes could not be slaked to see and touch
the black-eyed beauty's famous honey-golden flesh,
and like a blind girl slowly groped at face and neck,
at breasts and yielding thighs, at smooth-skinned ivory feet,
till Helen tingled with the strokes of hungry hands.
"Never have I enjoyed such sweet caresses, Krino,
as now from your own virginal and virile palms!
When I was but a blossoming girl of seven years
a bearded gallant kissed me by the riverside.
Ah, Krino, my notorious body has not since known
such joy as that first kiss which now your kiss recalls!"
The maiden's lashes quivered and threw the world in shadow:
"Life on this earth, O Helen, is sweet, unbearably sweet!"
She hid her face between her knees and softly wept,
and Helen wept, then took the chaste form in her arms
till in the burning sun they both caressed and laughed with joy.

As the Bull-King gazed on his hated daughter, Krino,
who like a man clasped Helen tight in loving arms,
he growled and roared in his black mask like a wild beast.
The Negro slaves leapt up and pressed close to the throne,
listened entranced to the bull's head that hung above
and fumed and rumbled as it gave its dread commands
until their sallow eyes rolled in their heads, and glazed:
Diktena leapt with fear, flew headlong down the stairs
and gathered from the archons' knees her amorous swarm,
for she discerned how the black slaves approached with stealth
the fierce man-killer, the most savage bull of all,
and guessed the secret order of the jealous king.
"They've fed the bull the intoxicating savage drink.
Alas for vestal Krino! None can save her now!"
And Krino, that chaste maiden, slowly raised her eyes,
for suddenly in her bitter soul she felt her death.
The world now seemed to her like freedom's futile toy,
and life winked in her mind like a small lightning flash,
most short, most sweet, that quivers but to fade once more.
Quickly she buckled on her belt and hurriedly tensed
her lean and muscular arms, her strong and hardened calves,
wound thrice about her hair a crimson cloth for crown,
then fearless, stripped of hope, strode swiftly in Death's ring.
From the cool shade the Mountain Maidens leapt erect,
but the king's savage bull-mask roared with frantic rage:

"Keep back! Our vestal maid shall fight this bull alone!"
The people shuddered, but the palace ladies laughed,
for smell of virgin blood steamed in their nostrils now,
and then the savage mystic rites of lust to follow!
At this same hour on a far coast a fisher spread
his tattered dragnets and began to mend them slowly,
nor felt concerned for Helens, bullfights, or great kings,
for here his whole wealth was composed of sea, a boat,
and eyes that once roamed far but now were moored to land.
Life was a short run on the sea, a boat packed full
of dragnets, lobster traps, and octopus harpoons.
We load our nets on board, the sails are set at dawn,
a handful of smelts hooked, a bowl of fishstew sipped,
and there goes life, a shipwreck plunged to the sea's bottom.
The battered fisher sighed, then raised his salty eyes
and watched the sea for a long time that moved and swayed
till like a flying fish his heart, too, leapt on waves.
Meanwhile far off, life swelled and the court ladies glowed,
for by the riverside the black slaves pricked the bull
who stumbling, growling, turned his glazed and drunken eyes
on the packed massive crowd and roared with frantic rage.
The Mountain Maidens leapt and dashed into the ring,
fearing to leave poor Krino to the Bull-God's mercy,
but the king blew his sea-conch, roared, and the maids fled.
Slim as a switch, pale Krino stood in the shade and waited;
the wild bull danced and leapt about her, women screamed,
and cold and feverish tremors pulsed along their spines,
for the bull gleamed in sun, a mortal, a beast, a god.
From head to toe, like a lean spear, pale Krino swayed
and balanced her unbridled body high on tiptoe,
swinging it right or left to escape the touch of death.
Deep silence in the ring, hearts throbbed in every throat,
all turned to stone, and in the sun there steamed alone
a mortal and a bestial body, like two quivering flames.
The bull lunged swift as lightning, the dust swirled in clouds
as Krino lightly swerved, and the bull crashed to its knees,
but as it rose in fuming rage, the maiden leapt,
grasped both its horns, then balanced, somersaulted high,
and lightboned sat astride the brute beast's sweating nape.
The Bull-God stood stock-still, his hooves nailed to the ground,
like blazing firedogs his red eyes rolled in rage
seeking to find some place where he might smash her brains.
But she had tightly wedged her head between his horns
and glued her back to his, forming one compact body;
the blood throbbed in her veins, the bull's blood throbbed in rhythm,
both bodies merged in one immense heartthrob of death,

and the salt waters running down their hot thighs mingled.
But suddenly as the maiden raised her eyes to the sky,
her warm tears welled, then brimmed and tumbled down her cheeks
till all at once her heart dropped in the abyss, and vanished.
Her hands lost their firm grip, and her moist temples roared
—it was as though the bowstring snapped which held her spirit—
and as the maiden felt her end draw near, she broke
in bitter wild lament and on the bull's back swooned.
And the wild beast, as though it felt the maiden's swoon,
spread its hooves wide on earth, gathered its savage strength,
and ah, alas, tossed her lean body high in the air.
The crowd turned pale and their dry tongues stuck in their throats;
then, as a wild dove wounded in the sky falls tumbling,
crumpled and torn, so on the god's sharp double-ax
raised high on a marble column, Krino fell impaled,
and splattered the bronze cow with her warm brains and dripping blood.

At last as earth grew cool and the black shadows lengthened,
the twilight lay reposed in fields like a chaste bull,
and in the olive leaves the crickets hushed their song.
The thresher slowly gathered then his holy flock,
his two exhausted ox, his goats, his sheep, his dogs,
and all in sluggish kinship moved toward their poor hut.
His humble bedmate lit the oil-lamp in the hearth
then spread the low stool for their supper silently
and brought the lukewarm water to wash her husband's knees.
Mother by mother taught, their wives had knelt like slaves
to wash the hairy knees of their task-weary lords
who rested and rejoiced like gods in their own yards.
But as the plowman sat that night on his low wall
and watched his plucky wife kneel down to wash his feet,
he suddenly kicked the tub and sent the water splashing.
"Dear wife," he cried, "you're not a slave to kneel before me!
Know that from this time forth I'll wash my feet myself."
He spoke, and with his words slew an ancestral ghost.
Meanwhile long rows of shadows choked the festive palace,
but stooped slaves still ground flour, workers swarmed like ants,
and handmaids hurried in the setting sun to sort
with skill the sacred garments for the secret rites.
All's well on earth; even the poor slave-mother found
a tiny coffin made of clay for her small son;
the twisting octopus she painted on his brow
cast everywhere its tentacles, and clutched the tomb.
She stooped and wrapped her son with fresh vine leaves, then thrust
a cluster of ripe grapes in his pale hands and placed
on his unbreathing chest a toy bronze pair of scales;

on one small scale were painted worms wrapped in cocoons
as though wrapped in their shrouds, who slept the sleep of death,
but in the other scale had risen, transformed to butterflies.
The mother unbared her head and looked at her young son
wrapped tightly in his swaddling clothes like a cocoon,
and her heart, choked by death, now dreamt of sprouting wings.
One day a large all-golden butterfly would spring
from earth and slowly flutter on the springtime grass,
and as the mother passed through flowering fields, her son
would know her, and for a moment flit on her gray hair.
The sun had set now, and the Evening Star behind it,
star of that brainless public goddess, winked at earth;
all heavy hearts were lightened, the day breathed again,
and shadows fell compassionately and cooled the ground.
The serpent earth had shed its skin, ensheathed in stars;
the soul, too, changed its dress, and with its flashing tail
beat on its clay and sweating body cracked with heat.
"Earth smells like jasmine, and the paths of passion gleam;
rise up, pale body, eat and drink, for life is short!"
Thus cried the soul to its ripe flesh, as the Evening Star
fell on the naked thighs of women, the beards of men,
till bodies tingled in the erotic evening's hush,
and the king felt the quivering, rose and gave the sign
as three blacks blew their conches, and the games were ended.
The crowd rose from their tiers, the Serpent Sisters dashed
and with the sacred snakes coiled thrice about their arms
sprinkled the surging jostling crowd with holy water.
A slim brunette with a red necklace round her throat
shook basil dipped in holy water and cried aloud:
"My brethren, you were slaked and gladdened with God's presence!
He comes down like a shining bull to mount the earth
then plays at games and dancing with all mortal men.
He holds us gently on his horns, licks us with love,
and lets us wound his sacred flanks with our sharp goads,
but suddenly when he deigns to play with us no more,
he tosses his sharp horns and scatters all our brains!"
A tall stern maiden then, waving a long-stemmed lily,
with two green necklaces around her towering throat,
strode through the crowd and frightened all with her fierce cries:
"Brethren, you're filled with strength of our blood-drinking God!
The people's eyes are not permitted to see further!
Go quickly, Serpent Sisters, search amid the crowd,
chase away those not of God's breath or noble root.
The Bull-God calls into his Second Presence only
those free minds and thrice-noble forms of gentle blood."
Another, with three azure neck-rings, shook her snakes:

"God swoops down on the common people's heads like war,
but on the archons' heads he comes like a strong lover;
he'll come at last like a sweet dream and snatch our souls."
As the three holy maids strode through the tiers of stone,
the common crowd took fright and strove to leave the ring
until the archons' hearts felt light and free at last;
and as the Serpent Sisters sprinkled the court dames
with sweet rosewater to drive away the people's stench
and to perfume the world again, the full moon rose,
a pure gold honeycomb, and dripped its gold on earth.
Then sun-chapped lips grew sweet, stones spread with shadowy down,
the mountain-profile head of God sank down in calm
like a stone god that lay supine on the sea's bottom.
Motionless, stooped, thrust in the sharp quills of his brain,
the archer like a hedgehog crouched and watched the chosen
as giggling archons leant far back in their slaves' arms
and dressed themselves with various hides and bestial masks.
Some dressed themselves like monkeys, lions, or bearded goats,
each archon dragged up that one beast thrust deep inside
the dark stall of his breast and brought it out to browse.
The ladies, too, ensheathed themselves in thick-haired skins
of wildcats, nanny goats, she-lions and lustful cows
till now at ease at length each sank in her true body.
And as man's soul returned once more to a brute's hide,
it sprouted hairs and horns and claws, its clear eyes glazed,
till memory's holy treasure steamed like lumps of blood;
only two greasy passions could excite them still:
the soul had turned to womb and phallus, and sank in mud.
Oak-headed Hardihood leapt up, and on his cheek
the octopus spread its tentacles and gripped his neck:
"How shameful to pollute this night, a beast with beasts!
Dear honored master, let's leave this foul sty at once!"
But the unsated mind laughed and replied with calm:
"I like to hang on the cliff's verge of god or beast;
my mind can never be slaked with either good or evil."
"Diktena's body then has dulled your thorny brain."
"But Diktena's soft body, bronzesmith, shall be drawn
into my brain's deep forge and there be turned to flame.
My mind is not a gentle lamb that feeds on grass
but like a hawk hunts flesh and blood to sprout with wings.
But you still crawl on earth and have no right to speak."
Hardihood shook to see the slayer's upright brain
hissing like flame with flickering tongues in the moon's glow.
He closed his mouth, drew back, and fled far from the sacred feast.

A cool breeze blew, and earth sighed deeply like a cow,
sentries stood guard on every crossroads to prevent
all common eyes from sullying the secret rites.
The Serpent Sisters stooped and raised the holy bride
and slowly placed her in the heifer's brazen womb,
singing small wedding verses in a crooning voice:
"Where are you going, Lady Moon, to shed your roses,
where are you going, basil spray, to lose your fragrance,
where are you going, Soul, great lady of the world?"
Then from the echoing bronze the ecstatic bride replied:
"Sweet wine, sweet dizziness have swept my wits away;
I'm but a woman, a jug that thirsts; come fill me, Lord."
The Serpent Sisters then twined arms and swirled in dance
in a round ring as with their pulsing throats they shrilled:
"We can't bear all we know, nor lift our souls much longer!
We'll wear horns now and lose ourselves in the brute's passion."
They danced and sang as their feet leapt like partridges
that in the dewy daybreak come to strut on stones.
Then Helen's many-voyaged and man-nourished arms
rose from the heifer's brazen flanks and flashed in air
as the hoarse summons of the erotic rites resounded:
"O Bull, unpitying sweet horns, come wound me now!"
Odysseus seethed, dashed to his feet and watched the cow,
for he disdained to let the smallest poisoned drop
fall to the ground unless his dry heart lapped it all.
Meanwhile the Bull-King zoned the ring in twists and turns
until the ritual's round enclosures swiftly narrowed
as though the heifer were a swift stream's whirling eye
that to its dark alluring iris sucked the bull.
The Serpent Sisters laughed, unloosed their crimson belts,
a fragrant sweat broke like the dew at their hair's roots
till in the warm moon suddenly they smelled like beasts
and their words jangled on the tiles like wedding gifts:
"The wild sea at your wedding and your betrothal rites,
shall turn to sweet and peppery wine, the waves to mares
on which your brave goat-bearded in-laws come astride."
They sang, and when a shepherd's pipe trilled through the air,
stones, beasts, and waters tumbled down, and in-laws, too,
set forth on their white steeds and breached the holy ring.
When the Bull plunged, and the bronze flanks again resounded,
the Serpent Sisters laughed and hung their virgin belts
as wedding gifts on the bronze neck of the bridal cow,
then to the lords and ladies raised their hands and cried:
"O souls, sink into beasts, rejoice now, close your eyes:
each man becomes a bull, each maid a common cow!"
The stars began to jangle in the sky like bells,

the tittering sea lay on her back beneath the prows,
and the unguarded mind in sleep, that hunts for dreams,
sailed like a merchant on and on toward distant shores.
Over the multicolored, mud-drenched crust of earth
Death holds the keys, but woman holds the counter-keys,
and all take lover's lane, descend to the womb's pit
where soul is deathless nor dissolves in the cold ground.
Body and soul merge for a lightning flash, then fade,
and we all sigh most sweetly and are seized by haste;
a new-wed maiden opens her unsleeping eyes,
casts off her rich-embroidered sheets till the dark glows
—how all the knees of women gleam and glow at night!—
then steps on the cool terrace to breathe a little air.
The Serpent Sisters knelt about the brazen cow
and sang a lively song in the dew-laden night
to drown the liturgy's erotic shrilling cries.
But the profound man's skull roared and resounded still
as though the bride and bridegroom there fought lustfully,
as though their hands and feet there kicked and pounded hard
between both temples, right and left, of his thick skull.
In starlight, in his bloody entrails, the archer heard
his wild soul struggling to fly free from the brute beast;
he felt the unnumbered tongues of beasts that licked his loins,
a howling river filled with sharp horns, blood, and mire
that rushed to flood and drown the incandescent soul.
And as he planted his firm feet to buck the torrent,
the lords and ladies rushed the ring, a roaring burst,
and a bull crashed to earth like a cascade of stones.
All slowly formed in a slow dance about the cow,
grabbed red chunks of the new-slain bull and munched them raw—
some pulled the heart out, some tore out the slimy guts,
some smashed the bones and sucked the marrow's tender meat,
and nice court ladies, on their hands and knees like dogs,
lapped up the warm red blood with clacking flickering tongues.
How may such great unbearable and unspeakable love,
such joy, such grief, mix in the bull and tame all pain?
To drink his long-loved blood, dear God, and merge in one!
Odysseus watched, and mankind's murderous soul seemed deep,
bottomless, sunless, pummeled like earth's bloody crust.
Slowly he neared to snatch at hands and lips close by,
to keep in memory a deep final consolation
as all now scattered in twos and threes and crouched like beasts;
ungirdled night with open thighs stumbled on earth.
What joy you give to all males, O night-opened bosoms,
white crystal thighs, crisp breasts, slim arms and fragrant hair!
At the first kiss shame is forgotten, Death at the second,

and at the third, musk chokes the earth. The archer leapt,
and his neck artery throbbed and whipped his swelling throat:
"Ah, for my bow and a sharp arrow as tall as I!"
But suddenly as a warm hand closed his mouth, he felt
Diktena's body, clad in a soft tiger's skin,
throbbing and panting as she twined about him tightly.
"Stranger, you've not communed with god, your cheeks are pale,
your mind is still a wingless ant that grubs in garbage;
here, take these godly loins to eat for virile strength!"
She spoke, then stuffed his yielding mouth with the bull's loins,
spread out her tigerskin, laughed low, flung her arms wide
till in her warm embrace the archer held all Crete
filled with bronze armor, heady perfumes, murder, lust.
The godly island spread its thighs on the vast sea,
and on her savage breast he smelled the freshening brine.
Thus like a thief he rose and fell in her cool halls,
plucked fresh fruit in her groves and lost himself in lanes;
at times his heart was knifed, at times from branch to branch
it flew in gardens of those fabulous palace courts.
But suddenly both his temples creaked, the castle flamed,
the copper columns shook and swayed and the bull roared,
till bronze and gold poured tumbling like a blazing river.
Both had forgotten Death in their sweet lightning spasms,
but the sharp-taloned man unglued his mind from lime,
leapt swiftly to his feet and listened with great care.
Bridegroom and bride were silent now in their bronze cow,
the court dames sighed like nightbirds still on cooling stones,
and stars, unsullied and disdainful, passed above the earth.
Odysseus joyed in all things then with fearless lust,
for he felt god and beast merge fiercely in his loins,
clamped tight with sweet caresses like a man and maid.
Pale and serene, her breath like sweet carnation's breath,
her hands crossed lightly on her groin, Diktena slept.
She seemed like a sweet goddess who had just discharged
her heavy duty in sleepless war, and now reposed;
only her upright breasts, snow-capped and rosy-tipped,
kept vigil in the night like lofty twin night-sentries.
The archer reached his still unsated hands to touch them,
his fingers itching still with multiple desire,
but all at once he pitied the maid's sacred sleep
so that his avid hand hung hovering in the air
and a most sweet compassion slowly filled his heart.
The fate of woman suddenly seemed to him most cruel:
God, like a beast, mounts from the earth with muddy feet,
and woman, bowed and shuddering, her pale palms turned upward,
struggles, but can not, even *will* not resist the beast.

The warrior stooped and watched her valiant form with awe,
his humble faithful comrade in the earthen strife,
but as he stooped and reconciled the world's cross currents,
a harsh shriek tore apart the veil of the full moon
and in the dead green light slim Phida's form appeared,
rushed headlong from the palace gate in sudden storm
and shrieked as though an eagle perched upon her skull
and dug deep with its cutting claws and sucked her brains.
The lords and ladies poked out of their hides in fear,
then thrust their unrouged faces in their sweat-drenched hair.
Shrieking, the moon-crazed girl rushed headlong down the stairs,
and when she reached the arena's center, stooped and seized
Krino's blood-splattered spear and flung it with great force
against the cow's deep belly till its bronze flanks bellowed.
The demon-driven maiden laughed, screamed like a vulture,
flew to the column where Krino's broken body hung,
opened her desolate arms and speechlessly received
the thick coarse drops of blood within her thirsty palms.
The revelers then half-raised themselves and watched with terror
as Phida smeared her sallow face with the thick gore
and passed among the beast-faced men and women, cackling,
her green eyes glittering like a snake's in the moon's glow.
She grabbed the archer savagely with both her hands,
thrust back his thorny head within the moon's clear rays
then cast it from her suddenly with contemptuous scorn,
for on his beard and lips she smelled the stench of lust.
Ashamed, Odysseus leapt and rushed at Phida then
to seize her by her flowing hair, to cast her down
and plot the world's destruction, cross-legged, on the ground.
Meanwhile the king advanced from the bronze cow in wrath,
ordered the demon-driven girl chased out at spearpoint,
for now the time had come to spread the nuptial feast.
The court dames shrieked, spurred on the blacks who rushed with spears,
but Phida vanished, shrieking, in the twisting halls.
As he stepped past the entangled mass of men and maids,
the archer saw in starlight, on a white bull's hide,
arch-eyebrowed Helen braiding her disheveled hair,
and her throat shone, a pure-white swan's reclining neck.
The shriveled king knelt down, and round her golden throat
placed strands of pearls and fixed a gold crown on her hair
with lilies made of mother-of-pearl set with bright emeralds.
The archer stopped a moment to watch and etch with care
on the stone tablets of his mind the kneeling king
and Helen's throat, her naked arms, her shameless laughter,
because he knew well that one day he would heap up
these sorrows like dry kindling in his memory's blazing kiln.

Night skimmed on the vast sea with all her pitch-black sails,
small lanterns flickered on the beach, prows lightly slept,
somewhere a ship's dog barked, and somewhere long-oars splashed.
In a low harbor pub the five friends sipped their wine,
and the wine-seller, a tall Negro, poured their drinks
and sometimes raised his hand and snatched himself a word.
But all had their eyes fixed on two ships that prepared
to set sail soon at drop of midnight secretly:
hulls dug from huge tree trunks, crude sails of wild beast hides,
returning now to distant strands and fogbound coasts.

Then Captain Clam lowered his voice and hoarsely rasped:
"My troubles, lads, are vast, three mills can't grind them all.
We've chewed the rag to find what makes the world go round,
to find what pirate ship the soul of man might be.
I've bound myself with firm ties to those distant pirates
who'll ship tonight in secret from this harbor's claws.
They're blond-haired, they wield iron axes, dress in bearskins,
and two great gods laugh on their sails, the sun and moon,
and a thick cartwheel nailed with iron whirling hooks.
From their far shores the males once sniffed Crete's female scent
and came to spy the island out, to smell it, touch it,
to gulp it down and glut their cold blue eyes, and then,
still starved, turn back to their own land with the sweet news.
Aye, lads, they've filled their hold with samples of all kinds:
old wine, new grapes, lambs, goats, a brown-skinned girl, that when
they reach the dark cliffs of their native coasts, no one
can say that Crete was but the dream of a warm night.
They've stuffed all well within their minds—drydocks and walls,
lighthouses, guards, reefs, shallow waters, harbor gates;
then—to our health, boys!—they'll return with flaring torches!
I swear by the sea, our entrails are but tangled beasts,
and though you beat the octopus-heart, it won't grow soft."
Thus spoke bush-bearded Captain Clam; he pitied Crete,
pitied her great flotilla and her bursting holds,
and one small maid who yesterday had poured for him
the honey of oblivion on the shingled shore.
He stroked his beard, and all the leaves of his heart sighed:
"Man's heart, my brothers, is a heavy, heavy beast,"
and then he filled his cup again and drowned his cares.
But meanwhile in the cool yet bloody dancing ring
slaves ran to light the torches and to spread the feast
as the archons once more ate and drank, laughed and caroused,
the heavy beast-masks of their gods thrown down their backs;
Odysseus huddled low, his chin between his knees,
and filled his eyes with their lewd laughter, their loud talk,
and the wild tambourines which the tall Negroes clashed.
The Mountain Maidens by the river raised their cries,
wept for their virgin leader Krino, beat their breasts,
and their sweet keening dripped into the dewy night.
Meanwhile the prows at sea with sun and moon on sails
skimmed softly on the waves and vanished, crammed with news.
Souls of the dead flew past, a row of vagrant gulls,
widows sat by the shore, unbared their heads, and cried
to their drowned husbands to come ashore for a brief moment.
The thresher and his wife stretched on their humble cot
and slept with crossed hands, but their lips curved in a smile:

they dreamt their supper had been good, that their barns bulged,
and that they sank up to their thighs in golden grain.
And the slave-mother thrust her son in the damp ground,
tied a black kerchief round her hair and then recalled
what her child's laughter had been like, once long ago.
The solitary man sat silent, wrapped in night,
as still above him hung the thick and clustered stars,
and Scorpio lashed his tail, squirmed, slithered through the sky,
and with his bloody, fearless eyes allured the earth.
The mind, like Scorpio too, rejoiced to raise its tail
and lean on earth to count its dripping venom drop by drop.

And thus the bronzesmith found him as light broke, sunk deep
in speechless quiet, and crouched beside him, mute and sullen,
but as Odysseus turned and seized his comrade's hand,
the shrill and cackling laugh of Helen suddenly burst
amid the roused cocks' crowing like a partridge cry.
Squeezing his master's hand, the bronzesmith slowly spoke:
"Dear captain, do not sigh or claw your chest in vain,
I bring news in my fists held like a blazing torch."
The fiery man turned mutely toward his stolid friend,
then grabbed him by his savage knees, and ground his teeth,
until the bronzesmith growled but kept his pain in check.
"Don't break my knees now, friend! I'll tell you in good time.
That hour when you lay in the arms of those wide cows,
I prowled the zigzag halls and etched all in my mind:
the ins and outs, the sentries, tunnels, the blind alleys.
Mind-weaver, come, unlid my skull and you shall find
a heavy copper disk where like a twisting snail
the strong bull-palace squirms in many cunning coils.
I etched all crooked corridors in my bronze mind,
groped here and there, pushed open doors and listened long:
workers and slaves still rolled on tiles with revelry,
the blond-haired strangers with the sentry guards caroused
and captive slaves hung down in wells and groaned like bulls.
In a deep cellar I suddenly saw a lustrous flame
and groped my way down the dim stairs, holding my breath,
because I thought I heard an anvil struck with force
and a huge bellows rasping at the castle's root.
My mind shook with great joy, for I'd unearthed, I knew,
the secret workshop of the palace ironsmith.
They say the king has kept this foreign craftsman jailed
in the earth's roots, a dragon bound with chains of flame.
No soul has ever drawn near to see the new god's passion,
for guards have killed all daring spies sent by their kings
to ferret out and steal that holy secret skill.

By God, today I found that magic gate unguarded!"
Silent Odysseus still grasped Hardihood's hard knees
as in strong pincers, but his mind sailed far away.
"Holding my breath, I crawled to the hid forge with stealth
then slowly peered above the bronze-barred casement's sill
and my heart beat like a sledge hammer and cracked the walls.
First I made out the chaste eye of that great god, fire,
and a big-bellied slave who worked the monstrous bellows;
before him stood a blond-haired strapping man who beat
a fiery-white long sword and strove to pound it straight.
It was not formed of bronze, but of iron, great be its name!
He plunged it in cool water, pulled it out, deep-blue,
then thrust it in the fire to make its heart red-hot.
I gazed with bulging eyes and was amazed my heart
with its loud throbbing had not yet smashed the casement bars.
But my great joy was brief, for when on the dim stairs
I heard a woman hurrying, panting with heavy gasps,
I crouched in a dark corner, and saw Phida pass,
her wild face splattered with thick drops of blackened gore;
she leant and gasped against the door, then raised her fist
and pounded its bronze panels twice or thrice with force.
On hands and knees, I cast my glance in the secret shop
in time to see bold Phida grasp the blacksmith's hands
as the thick blood gleamed on her cheeks, her lips, her hair.
'Throw the slave out,' she whispered low, and blond-beard laughed,
but turned and roughly told the slave to leave, and he
abandoned the low flame, and fled in the dark night.
Though I could not see well now in the glimmering forge,
I could still clearly hear their tense and rasping talk
as flame-eyed Phida like a viper hissed in dark:
'You promised me your secret weapons for all the slaves
and the blond tribe, if I should sleep with you one night.
Blacksmith, that night has come. Give me your hands, and swear!'
The blacksmith's eyes lit up with flames, and his voice rang:
'I swear on this black iron, my god thrice plunged in fire!'
And then at once the maid replied with stifled voice:
'My virgin body's fruit shall be your spoil tonight!
The red god in my entrails shouts, and I obey!'
The blacksmith laughed, and swiftly with his calloused heels
stamped down the smoldering embers smooth, and spread a mat."
Then Hardihood fell silent and watched his master's eyes,
but he seemed not to hear the bloody news, and gazed
far off where mountain peaks were bathed in rosy down;
he watched that expert archer, the great sun, rise up
and kneel on mountain rims to brood on the king's halls;
he could discern already the warped palace roofs

where fluttering chicory blossomed and wild lettuce sprang,
where the old crenels gaped with feeble toothless gums.
He turned his gaze then sluggishly on the bull-ring
and there the women's happy throats had turned blood-red
in the first rays of dawn as though knives stabbed them through.
Then the mind-killer turned serenely to his rash friend:
"Bronzesmith, though each has taken his own road, we've both
worked well this holy night, both roads have led us through;
it's time we paid some care to our poor bodies now.
Don't get your gall up, lad; all shall distill in sleep."
He spoke, then set off with his heaving sailor's stride
and made for the bull-ring in the early morning light.
But the bronze-tamer took to heart his friend's indifference:
"You must have tired from playing with women all night long;
you're savage to the savage, friend, good to the good,
and yet a girl's lewd kiss can make you crash in ruin."
But the much-wounded athlete scowled at Hardihood
as he came stumbling after in his master's steps.
The orgies had now ended in a tumbled heap,
medley of women, men and dogs, till slaves appeared,
tall blond-haired stalwarts from the North, blacks from the South,
and from the tangled pack unglued their drunken masters.
The king was shaking his brain-withered moldy head;
long crimson streams of paint ran down his neck like ribbons;
then the strong blond-haired gardener, who the day before
like a small child had placed some grapes in Helen's hands,
loomed on the stairhead suddenly, gazed to right and left,
then quickly swooped and swept the bright bird in his arms,
and the man-lover, tickled by his thorny beard,
opened her eyes, laughed low, and clasped his lion's nape.
Odysseus paled and then stopped short, with neck outstretched,
and as he watched the barbarous body tightly twined
with the now shameless beauty, twitching with low laughter,
the palace suddenly shook and crashed in his wild head:
"I praise God, for he leads us well and is most cunning,
he masks, unmasks, gets staggering drunk, and now, behold,
he comes before me in the guise of drunken Helen!
Behind the woman's face I see his monstrous face!"
Meanwhile the slaves raised their drunk masters from the ring,
and lifted the carousers in the dawn's rose light
like wounded birds with gaudy and bedraggled wings.
"Open your eyes, bronzesmith, and in your memory etch
these drunken overlords, those naked shameless sluts,
and Krino in their midst impaled, a banner flying."
Hardihood turned, aimed well, and shot a piercing dart:
"Don't worry, slayer, all are engraved deep in my brain;

but shouldn't I etch our beauteous Helen also in bronze?
Was that her pallid form I saw in a stranger's arms?"
The man of seven bowstrings frowned, displeased, and said:
"Sit on the stone of patience, bronzesmith, speak no more!"
The smith rejoiced because he'd hit his captain hard:
"I'll get the largest sheet of bronze and etch with wrath
threshing floors, stairs, antheaps of crawling men and maids,
and in their midst, as mainmast with a crimson sail,
I'll raise poor Krino's brain-besplattered column high,
and in the foreground a huge man shall carry, laughing,
the limpid lady of silk eyebrows and rose breasts;
we two shall be shown crouched in ambush like two hungry crows."

As he was speaking, on the river's edge appeared
the virgin Mountain Maidens bearing jars of water
to wash poor Krino and sanctify the harlot earth.
But when they reached the arena's edge, they stood still, mute,
for Phida leapt before them with torn, ash-strewn hair
grimy with coal dust, filthy blood on her bared bosom.
And when she saw the maidens bearing the holy water,
singing slow hymns and spells for the polluted earth,
she thrust her hands upon her hips and shrilled with laughter:
"Hey, welcome, mountain ladies, you pure virgin mules,
lugging your jars of water to wash the harlot earth!
Root up the river with all its roots, go turn it off
its course, but there's no washing pure the whorish earth;
not water, but flaming blood will cleanse the sullied world!"
Hidden behind a column, the two friends admired
the viperish soul that hissed and thrashed with rage on earth.
Her thighs, her clothes, her hair were thickly smeared with coal dust,
a lion rolled in embers of a shepherd's fire.
She raised her hands, laughed harshly, and approached the maids:
"You think that with good hearts, virginity, and water
the lewd earth can be saved and not a knife stabbed through her!
Fire must fall from all four winds to save our souls!"
She spoke, and bitter froth now edged her scornful lips,
her eyes flung streams of fire that licked the palace walls,
her nostrils flared, but she grew calm and clapped her hands:
"I smell a honeyed fragrance till my bowels swoon!
I'm starved! All Crete roasts like a partridge on my hearth!"
She laughed, then dashed into the courtyards, spread her hands
and placed them on invisible forms, on shadowy dancers,
struck up a dance and stamped on earth with naked feet.
She leapt on stones as though God whipped her with his fire,
she was a green and frothing branch that squirmed in flame,
and her red hair burned in the courts in blazing streams.

High on the cornice eaves the crows began to caw
for they too smelled the stench and smoke of palace fire;
a newborn bullock raised its soft hooves high, and stumbled,
steadied its feet upon the ground, then turned with fear
and with its long-lashed eyes glanced sideways at the maid.
Then Phida's trusted troop rushed up, rebellious hordes,
dull-haired unwedded girls and mothers scorched by death,
wan workers stooped and warped with sunless daily toil,
brave hearts that longed for freedom but lacked every freedom—
all heard their leader shriek, foamed up from cellar vaults
and struck a swift dance in the courts, screaming like birds.
A mother first began her small and deathly song:
"All say they see their faces in a cup of wine,
but I see Death perched on my hunger-shriveled breasts,
I see my baby from my bosom slip and rot."
A widow snatched the threnody and hoarsely crowed:
"I stoop above well-water and see hanging gardens,
the gold court ladies laughing in the world's delights,
rejoiced with sun and moonlight, bread and bearded men.
Alas! I see my husband slaughtered in my lap!"
All spun with swirling spirals on the dance's verge
and Phida raised her slim neck, wrecked by many ghosts:
"Why do you whirl about me, sisters, wracked with pain,
as though I come from Tartarus now and firmly hold
your babes that fell and rotted, and your slaughtered men?
My sisters, I'm prepared to breach the lower world!
I stoop above the flames at midnight and watch my face,
I watch black Death who comes and holds a pomegranate
and he is followed by green dogs and blood-red hawks.
I greet him from far off and speak to him close by:
'Dear Death, you come to give me a cool pomegranate.'
'It's not a cooling pomegranate, my sweet maid,
in my clenched fists I hold your father's crimson head.' "
A sallow worker beat her calloused hands and shrieked:
"Sing, comrades, how our wooden clogs will clack and thud
when we sweep down the palace stairs with double-axes!"
All laughed and beat on the stone tiles with bony heels,
as though their reedy legs already rushed the palace.
The sallow worker laughed and closed her greedy eyes:
the brazen palace burned and her calm heart rejoiced,
for court dames shrieked, and honey, wine, and pure oil brimmed
and warmly laved her hairy limbs. Opening her eyes,
she flung her words out of her mouth like slinging stones:
"Oho! How bolts will crack and columns lean and sway,
how our dear mistresses will burn when gates fly wide
as with our brands held high we rush at dead of night!"

Odysseus then pricked up his spiraled ears and listened:
the black earth starved and shouted, its deep bowels gaped,
for the slaves cast all patience out and formed a pact
until the heart, the world's root, shook, and all life quailed.
With head erect, the man of swift mind felt hot blasts
of a far wind above him sweeping, stream on stream,
and starved battalions that swarmed down and zoned the castle
till nothing could be heard but wails, and here and there
the exhausted falling to grim earth with hollow thuds.
In sudden calm Odysseus heard the distant dead
and could restrain himself no longer, leapt to his feet,
and took the lead in dance and sang a savage tune:
"Many's the time I've danced on earth, many my dances,
but never have my eyes yet seen a dance like this!
I'll fling stones in my lap, raise kindling high, and bind
a red belt round my head to keep my brains from scattering!
Stamp, sisters, stamp on earth! It will eat us one fine day!
On the cold stone of patience, God, both day and night
I hone the sword of slaughter and leap the palace stairs,
rip all the rooftops open, choose both men and maids,
and then, astride the roof-beams, rub them on each other
and send them swiftly spinning till they burst in flame!
Stamp, sisters, stamp on earth! It will eat us one fine day!
Stamp on the earth before the starved worm grabs our heels!
I measured sea and land, but neither could hold my heart,
yet when I measured fire, it held my whole heart's pain!"
The Rebels shouted till their long hair streamed like fire
and Phida flung her arms to the bright sky and screamed:
"A female hawk sits high and awaits the coming sun . . ."
but her voice suddenly choked, and she fell down in spasms
for the brain-sucking god once more swooped low and struck her.
The Rebels ran and raised her head, closed ranks about her,
wrapped her in dirty rags as though to smother fire,
then grabbed her hurriedly, with stealth, and vanished underground.

But the great man of fire still tossed in the dawn's light
nor wished to sleep for fear his soul might flicker and die.
He took the river-course, crunched on the pebbled bank
and stumbled like a hawk who cannot tread the ground.
The bay leaves smelled of intoxicating bitter almonds,
insects at dawn were drying their dew-laden wings,
a falcon soared and knit swift wreaths against the sky.
The fiery man then plunged in the cool stream, his heart
and body grew serene, he placed a myrtle twig
between his teeth until his mind with fragrance brimmed,
then, cool and carefree, stretched on the hard pebbly bank.

With staring eyes he counted slowly, ruthlessly,
the palace's gold casements, its full vaults, its roofs,
he heard the dayguards' shrilling cries, the armor's clang,
the gold canaries wakening in their golden cages.
From the slaves' dungeons rose a gentle lullaby
like freedom's cry, and tore their lords' foundations down:
"O eagle sleep, who take our babes on your black wings
and nourish them with lion-brains on the high hills,
sweep down to our deep pit, pounce on my only child.
Here, take him, he's a small slave-child with a bronze chain;
break the bronze ring in sleep and cast it in the fire,
take slavery's anvil and revenge's pounding sledge,
then go, and in the morning bring my son back home
and let him hold the cooling sword of slaughter high!"
The suffering man heard all with greed, and shut his eyes,
as if he were himself the pale and suckling child
who listened to his mother's song and sank in sleep.
He sweetly merged with earth and slowly sank in soil
as the song rolled above him like a gurgling stream.
The women's quarter, like a red cage in his head,
sprang open, rushes swayed like people, rivers swelled
and wrapped around his mind as though they watered trees,
till slowly from the bitter bays and tufts of reeds
a sweet breeze fell, and gentle sleep possessed his long-lashed eyes.

Death came and stretched full length along the archer's side;
weary from wandering all night long, his lids were heavy,
and he, too, longed to sit and sleep awhile beside
his old friend near the river, by a willow's shade.
Throwing his bony arms across the archer's chest,
he and his boon companion slowly sank in sleep.
Death slept and dreamt that man indeed, perhaps, existed,
that houses rose on earth, perhaps, kingdoms and castles,
that even gardens rose and that beneath their shade
court ladies strolled in languor and handmaidens sang.
He dreamt there was a sun that rose, a moon that shone,
a wheel of earth that turned and every season brought,
perhaps, all kinds of fruit and flowers, cooling rain and snow,
and that it turned once more, perhaps, till earth renewed.
But Death smiled secretly in sleep for he knew well
this was but dream, a dappled wind, toy of his weary mind,
and unperturbed, allowed this evil dream to goad him.
But slowly life took courage, and the wheel whirled round,
earth gaped with hunger, sun and rain sank in her bowels,
unnumbered eggs hatched birds, the world was filled with worms,
until a packed battalion of beasts, men and thoughts

set out and pounced on sleeping Death to eat him whole.
A human pair crouched in his nostrils' heaving caves,
there lit and fed a fire, set up their house and cooked,
and from Death's upper lip hung down their new son's cradle.
Feeling his nostrils tingling and his pale lips tickled,
Death suddenly shook and tossed in sleep, and the dream vanished.
For a brief moment Death had fallen asleep and dreamt of life.

VII

To leeward on the sands the lily found its shelter;
olive leaves gleamed, for it had rained all night, and tears,
small joyous waterdrops, hung on the wind's long lashes.
Damp, stooped, the soul perched on the branches of old rain,
and white against the sky the clouds piled up like lamb's wool;
earth washed herself before the sun had risen, then shook
her wings at dawn like the drenched wagtail by the river.
Stars vanished, the translucent moon grew pale, then sank,
light leapt up like a rooster on all roofs, and crowed,
but still the archer sailed on the deep waters of sleep,
and as the first rays of the sun fell on his brow
a dream set out to unlatch the sealed doors of his brain.
It seems there was a lofty mountain peak, rose-lit,
whose stones he climbed in haste with his stout shepherd's crook;
down in the meadow marshes, hidden deep in mist,
like varied smoke of vertigo, the hamlets swayed,
and his old memories shook like fluttering handkerchiefs.
"Farewell, old tattered guises; like a knowing snake
I rise with my unused cool skin and climb in sun!"
He spoke, and a soft smile entwined him till he stopped,
then turned to his young hesitating heart, and said:
"Dear heart, dear bird, where are you flying with straw in beak
to build your nest on the moldy roof of our lord, Death,
do we start now, do we come now, daybreak or nightfall?
A sweet smile twines me round, but I can see no lips."
He had not yet stopped speaking in the murky fog
when two sharp narrow lips moved in a slight smile
as slowly from the thickening shadows, light, and air
the sweet face of a woman loomed, full as the moon.
Her brow rose like the sun, her smooth cheeks gently glowed,
her soft smile overbrimmed and lit the archer's brains
like mountain summits edged at dawn with rose-red light,
till his own flesh renewed, his graying hair turned black,
and adolescent down bedewed his apple cheeks.
He stretched his hand and longed to touch the miracle:
"Lady, is this the land of drunkenness and dream?

Lady, have I been hunting nothing but empty air?
Your smile's a heavy wine that sets my poor head spinning!"
But the pale lady of the sea-sands watched, nor spoke,
as the young man moved on and with his goldfinch heart
flew with a green leaf in his beak to build his nest.
She smiled again and drowned the young man with her smile.
"Lady, I'm off to distant shores, but I don't know the way,
my heart seethes like the savage sea, my mind brims over
with vast works not yet born, with lands I've never seen,
and like a fish's sack my bowels brim with eggs.
O Lady, move your merciful eyes! Show me the way!"
He spoke, and the air swayed, her throat and pale lips vanished,
and then the unbearded youth felt a strange hand rise high
and plunge three knives up to the hilt straight through his heart.
The young man's heart embraced the knives, then he set out,
and three springs welled within him, he cast three black shadows,
three black cares pierced and wounded him, and his pain swelled,
but in the waste he bit his lips in silence manfully.
Soon the hot day, that greedy tiger, licked and clawed him,
his brain became unhinged, his throat was parched with thirst,
until at dusk he tired and stretched on the cool sands.
For hours the sleepless youth felt life above him hover
like a new-breasted girl who fondled and revived him
until his flesh surrendered to her dark caresses
as midnight closed the eyes of his commanding mind.
He passed through valleys, wastelands, waters, and blue shores,
he saw himself dig in the sand, exhume a woman,
an ancient princess wrapped in myrrh and mummy-cloth,
and as he unwound her folds she opened like a rose,
her eyelids gently fluttered, lips and nostrils steamed,
until a heavy sigh rose from her swelling throat.
The young man licked his lips, drew near, then twined about her,
and all night long within his arms he held the cool,
small body filled with myrrh, and tasted all night long
her pomegranate in the hopeless fragrant hush.
A light breeze suddenly blew, and the frail body vanished.
Thus the strange princess vanished, and on spreading sands
only her small embroidered slippers gleamed like glass.
The young man in the wasteland moaned, cried to his love,
but in his burning anguish, his soul-killing pain,
he felt a gentle sweet relief and grasped his heart:
one knife had gone, and even the aching wound had healed.
The youth felt glad, and gentle breezes flicked his brows
as though the cooling winds of liberty caressed them.
He bent above the sands and hailed the silver slippers:
"Farewell! You have fulfilled your task on love's rough road."

He passed through seas and mountains till his hair turned gray
—what joy to fight on earth, to conquer and build towns,
to swoop with armies, battlecries and war, to hold
the keys of life in your brave hands and never surrender!
But as the archer proudly played with his bronze keys,
a small, small breeze passed by, and his tall city crashed;
he turned, and found grass grown already on the new-dug grave.
He leapt up, groaning, but faintly in his heart again
he felt a new relief, then laughed and gripped his chest—
the second knife had vanished, another wound had closed!
Again he took his withered staff, and his heart danced;
the wind of freedom played amid his whitened hair
as though buds of new wings sprang from his shoulder blades,
as though the sun would come to warm and sprout them soon.
Then as he lightly walked the earth, the world grew tall,
ghosts broke their husks asunder, flesh broke down its bolts,
and pallid princesses appeared and laughed in light,
all godly souls the dragon mind had cast in pits.
A miracle came and filled his hands like a tame dove.
Desolate wastes of sand stretched out once more, and far,
far off, he saw the smiling lady slowly pass.
"Lady, I've served two knives, the strife is ending now,
I've found life good and found death good! Well met, and welcome!"
He spoke, the third knife vanished, and the woman's breasts
dimmed in the sky like stars, rotted and fell away;
her smile still lingered for a while, then swirled like mist.
As the dazed archer placed his hand on his hot brow
and wondered whether he'd seen a dream or lost his wits,
a pelting rain began to fall, the rushes roared,
the women screamed, and the man-slayer leapt to his feet:
"By God, I must have fallen asleep! It seems I saw
the strangest of strange dreams, but I can't quite recall.
It must have held good omens, for my heart feels light!"
He spoke and rose; at once thick drops of warm rain stung
his forehead, hands, and neck so that he shook with joy
to feel the fragrant first rains strike his sun-cracked flesh.
The heavy rutting sky plunged like a black bull,
the clouds hung dripping down, and green-blue lightning bolts
licked at the stifled earth that stooped with rain-drenched hair.
Servants ran screaming in the yards and flung their aprons
about their faces to keep back the rain, and slaves
corralled the precious peacocks and the curly bullocks.
High in the upper casements the court ladies stooped
to smell the soaking earth, the drenched and steaming gardens,
and their thin nostrils sniffed and drank the world with greed.
Quickly Odysseus passed through the echoing courts and joyed

to feel the beating rain, to hear the bellowing palace
crash in the harsh downpour, to think that soon one day
the palace courts would roar, the casements clang, and flames
would leap in the four corners of his brain, and blaze.
He heard the women laughing, saw the palace sink
slowly in the unceasing rain, and odors rose from earth
as from a new-dug graveyard and refreshed his heart;
suddenly war and death, a woman's smile, all merged,
until his great mind glowed, and he recalled the dream.
He smiled, and in the lightning strokes his white teeth gleamed:
"All's well, whether the dream come true or the dream vanish.
I like to plunge knives in and out of my own bleeding heart!"

He slid with haste through crooked halls and drove straight on
to his deep narrow cell thrust between cedar columns.
Hardihood slept there, sprawled on tiles, flat on his back,
and the archer quietly stepped on tiptoe and reposed
on the stone chiseled throne, and from the narrow ledge
marveled and watched the heavy sky crash down on earth.
The fig leaves thundered, all the sun-scorched court-tiles steamed,
and the cracked earth, stretched out supine, embraced the storm.
Unmoving, mute, Odysseus sat on the low throne,
refreshed in the first rains; sometimes his female heart
opened her thighs, sometimes his mind, like a male lover,
came with its double-ax to ready earth and hung
its heavy, rain-soaked, curly locks above the loam.
In dusk the bronzesmith opened his eyes and mutely leant
against a cedar column, startled by his master's face
that seemed to hang above the earth, a bull or god.
Although the alert man spied his friend, he made no sign,
for still his hermit heart disdained to break its silence.
But soon the weather cleared, the white clouds rolled and swelled,
and in a deep blue sky the setting sun emerged.
The cedar columns gleamed, the new-washed stone tiles laughed,
and on the branches' tips the raindrops shone and trembled.
For a while he gloried in the freshness after rain,
but suddenly turned and growled to his mute friend: "I'm hungry!"
When Hardihood saw his master's opium dream had burst,
he dashed to the deep kitchens to fetch food and drink,
for he, too, felt his bowels sag from thirst and hunger.
Two slaves filled up a tray with overbrimming plates,
filled two bronze jars with wine and set out, weighed with food.
The first slave minced ahead, and on her upright head
balanced the laden tray and swaggered up the stairs;
the second followed with both jars, and on her feet,

coarsened and thick with mud, her brazen anklets jangled;
the bronzesmith followed last with bread beneath his arms.
Facing glad Hardihood, the hungry athlete knelt
on the rush mats, reached for the steaming plates, and then,
as one throws armfuls of dry brush to feed the fire,
he flung in his swelling entrails bread and wine and meat.
This hour at dusk the rich-embellished court dames rose
and set out for the public road to promenade,
their large eyes swept away by azure shadows still.
Munching his food with greed, Odysseus raised his eyes
and in the cool dusk saw the gold-adorned court dames
sauntering along the riverside, their long locks gleaming,
their small breasts shining naked in the darkling air.
Fragrance of musk and rose-oil from their armpits steamed,
the damp ravines resounded with their giggling talk,
shadows on waters lengthened, or drowned in myrtle shrubs.
In the aloof man's eyes and streams of his wild glance
the plump court ladies slowly passed or stopped a moment
as though entangled in the world-destroyer's lashes,
and then moved on, still saved to walk in the setting suns.
They looked like strange exotic sea-beasts who now sailed,
light and prismatic, on the smooth sea's tranquil surface.
Patient and stooped, a fisherman on shore, Odysseus
admired his catch before he dragged his nets ashore;
the bronzesmith near him glanced with wrath at the elite,
but kept his peace, still frightened by his master's look.
The slayer stretched, a glutted lion by a low wall,
but his friend passed the threshold, took the riverbank,
and like an earth-bull stooped and spied among the reeds.
Nobles strolled by and held small monkeys on their chests,
and ladies sauntered, pale, large-eyed, with curly hair,
and shone like summer lightning flashes after storm.
Hiding in ambush, Hardihood with his blue eyes
marked down, like a good hunter, all his quarries' paths,
their shameless wallowing sties and secret lurking-holes,
and when his mind had stalked and slain to its content,
he rose up, growled, and vanished in the castle's vaults.
For hours he spied on trap doors, battlements, and snares,
his wrathful mind still rampant with a secret thought:
"Oho, we're caught in a deep trap, God curse them all!"
When in the starlight he returned, he saw with fear
the archer sitting humped on his stone seat, and all
his heads, full seven stories high, glowed in the dark.
He took the oil-lamp from the wall, but had no heart
to light it, and in darkness mutely spread his mat.

He wished to tell his master where he had roamed and what
he had heard, but felt that spirit agonized and tossed
in silent terror like a tigress gripped by labor pains.

Three days the archer crouched and stretched on his stone seat
and only when they brought the food tray would he fall
and eat with a mute greed and stuff his body full.
Thoughts, castles, men and deeds piled in his mind like fruit
that fall in the night's quiet, lush and overripe.
The second night he muttered in his thick mustache:
"I cry out! Can't you hear? I'm lost! Come down to help me!"
The damp night gleamed, the stars hung down like fists of fire,
and on the wall the lioness shone in lilied fields.
He gripped the painted columns tightly with both hands
as though he suddenly longed to test his strength once more,
then like a lion he stretched on the ground and fell asleep.
On the third night he heard a rustling sound: "Odysseus!"
but did not turn, then held his breath to hear again,
and the cry echoed, with complaint and fear: "Odysseus!"
The suffering man then turned his savage head:
between the columns stood his god, his jaw hung loose
and chattered with numb fear, and his eyes glazed with tears.
He wore a sea-blue pointed cap, and in the dark
Odysseus thought he saw his own eyes, chest, and limbs
gleam there as though his own soul loomed and cried in night.
The rough-hewn athlete frowned with scorn and deep contempt
then on the columns beat his fists with rage, and screamed:
"Strengthen your knees, you fool, and stop your chattering, quick!
How have you dared to face me here without a knife?
Don't show yourself with such a mug before my friends!
Crawl in my guts once more! Stop crying! I'll save you, fool!"
He spoke; from his thick nostrils smoke like sulphur spewed,
but when the bronzesmith came at midnight he found him well,
standing erect, his cap askew, mocking and whistling,
and cast his arms about his master in joy, and thought:
"Our tigress, oho, has given birth, her belly's empty!"
The two gnarled souls began to dance then like wild flames
so that their minds might clear, their brimming strength distill.
The man of seven souls then sang a Cretan verse:
"Hey, I'm the lightning's only son, and the snow's grandson;
I cast the lightning when I wish, or I fling the snow!"
When they had tired of dancing, and their hearts had calmed,
they fell to earth, and the archer grasped his comrade's knees:
"I strained on tiptoe for three nights and cried to God:
'Come down, my Captain, they've thrown me in a dark jail!
Come down, you have no choice, for if I die, you die!

Let's put our shoulders to the door and smash it open!'
He wouldn't budge; deep in the earth I heard him growl
and hone his sharp teeth on the marble tombstones there,
but finally God came down today and stood before me!"
Hardihood fell on his friend's chest and cried with joy:
"Ah, master, tell me the whole truth, don't close your lips!
I see his huge face like a wildfire in your eyes!"
Odysseus thrust God's frightened face deep in his guts
that mankind's rabbit heart and weak knees might not buckle:
"Flame flashed between the columns, and the ceiling blazed;

our savage souls spoke mouth to mouth in lightning strokes."
The bronzesmith's eyes caught fire, he grabbed his master's knees:
"Ah, tell me what you said so that my mind may blaze!"
But then the sly man shut his heart and spoke with wrath:
"Blow up God's flame in your own mind, and ask no more."
He stooped and lit the two-mouthed hanging oil-lamp then
and joyed to see depicted on the crimson walls
the wild she-lion stretched on a white-lilied field.
He lay down by the proud beast's feet and watched the stars
leap in a boiling rage and strike on his wild head,
but soon his mind grew calm, sleep like a mistral came,
the white stars swayed like lilies, till his carefree soul
stretched like a lioness among them in a tranquil sleep.

Thus the long-suffering man reposed with myriad stars,
while Helen, by gold lamps and silken pillows, stooped
above her crystal sphere to watch her destined soul.
Like a foul canker crawling on a dazzling lily,
the old king placed his shriveled hands on her white breasts,
but Helen's mind was elsewhere—deep in her heart she smelled
a stallion's barbarous odor and two rugged flanks.
The full-lipped lady shut her eyes, recalled to mind
how they had passed through many lanes, how doors had gaped,
how with the lustful strapping man she'd plunged in vaults,
how both had lain on fragrant grain in perfect silence.
Amid the golden lamps she shook her head, and sighed,
then softly sank her face close to the crystal eye
and longed to see still further how her fate was formed.
But there the adornments only of her rich room gleamed:
tall slender lilies, spuming waters, gold-hoofed bulls,
and deeper, by her bed's green canopy, uncoiled
a monstrous eye with wings, and round it seven maids
with dazzling thighs whirled in a dance and swung their snakes.
Helen sighed, wounded by the world's great beauty then,
and from her open casement came the cool night dew;
under a waning moon the mountain slept in haze,
in olive trees the owl's lament dripped drop by drop;
this was the hour when the dead rose and bound their bones
tightly with thongs and ropes, not to disperse in air.
Sweet night and little moon, a morning's soft breeze blows
and the wild war on Trojan shores rages again.
The gallant youths are shades that rush to kill but shades,
their white lips form no breathing mist, their spears tear through
deep bloodless wounds, as though they tore through empty air.
A goddess with green eyes, a pure-white downy owl,
sits in a hollow trunk and with her hooting cry

counts one by one her phantom host, the passing night.
Thus swept far off, the marble-throated lady heard
solitude pass at moist midnight with softest feet
while glowworms and dread scorpions held her velvet train.
Then the dove-throated woman sighed, and sank her eyes
deep in the dew-cool hush and sailed upon the night.
Shades drifted in her brain, sweet voices, handsome heads,
far-distant emerald shores and passionate embracements
of brave lads who once swooned to smell her godly body.
Her heart ached then as with nostalgic pangs she thought
how many flowers and gardens she had not yet smelled,
and how her lips would rot on earth before, dear God,
she could drink up the whole world's joy from her small palms.
Her eyes turned once again to the magic crystal sphere:
thick herds of oxen, horses, sun-green grassy pastures,
mothers cross-legged on earth, giving their babies suck,
and others stooped to light the fire or stir the pot;
and blond men on the threshing floor who cast the quoit
or with sledge hammers beat on iron, their fiery god.
A tent of rags gapes suddenly and her loved lord comes
who in a white and fat-haired sheepskin holds their son
tight in his sunburnt arms, then tosses him in air,
but the small, suckling baby cries and flaps his hands
like fluttering downy wings to find his mother's arms.
Then from the tent the slender smiling lady comes
and claps her hands and gives her breast to her dear son.
Helen cried out, "My child," the sphere slipped from her hands
and on the patterned tiles smashed in a thousand fragments.
Meanwhile in sleep the senile king dreamt that his bride
had like the sun indeed sunk deep in earth, and vanished,
and that he ran behind her panting, lunging down
the vast stairs of the lower world as on his back
he carried his slain head, a huge and heavy hump.
But when he heard the crystal break, he started up
and from his golden-woven blanket poked his head
that like a turtle's shone with sweat, and from his dream
still trembled, wobbling over Helen's heaving breasts;
her starlit body shuddered and drew hastily back.
Thus night with all her snares passed through the upper world
and baited all heads sweetly, fed all foolish hopes,
for night can bring to men all shrewish day denies,
wrapped as a gift in the green leaves of opiate dream.
But when the bold cock rose and crowed, behold, night vanished,
the god of work then danced, and the fox-minded man
leapt up and, laughing, poked the bronzesmith with his feet:
"Ah, Hardihood, if I should not return today,

go to the harbor and tell our friends that I've been killed;
then, if you wish, do what your hearts dictate for vengeance,
not for my sake who, washed with wine, shall eat the dust,
but that your own still living throats may feel refreshed."
The acrid bronzesmith growled and grasped his leader's knees:
"Master, I'll never let you plunge to danger alone!"
For a long time they fought in silence round the room,
but all at once the smith felt awed, and his knees shook
as though indeed he fought with God in the dawn's light,
then stepped aside to let his master cross the sill.
For hours the bronzesmith cocked his ears, two conches coiled,
and heard the castle's uproar like a howling sea;
the palace bellowed like a galley swept by storm
as Hardihood still pressed his ear to earth and heard
his master's sailor stride amid that sounding vertigo.

Meanwhile Odysseus, many-faced, now smutched with must,
bore on his back a basket overbrimmed with grapes
and stooped to climb the stone steps to the women's rooms.
To right and left as frescoes bloomed, his greedy eyes
devoured the young men who with waists like wedding rings
brought golden rhytons to a bare, big-breasted goddess.
But when he reached the upper stairs and crossed the sill,
an eager hard hand grabbed him by his leathern belt
and a wild cackling laughter struck his startled head.
He turned his neck and shuddered to see Phida there
hanging above him like a hissing ravening fire.
"You suit me, for I think of God as sly, swift-eyed,
loaded with grapes of slaughter, striding through all thresholds!"
The sly man hid his mind in ashes like a torch,
then stooped, and mutely felt her flame sear through his hair.
"I seek a strong man! I can't fire the palace alone!"
The trickster hissed and flung his poison like a snake:
"When you danced yesterday, I saw your breasts besmirched;
go to the blond-haired ironsmith now for all your fires!"
But Phida screeched and dug her nails into the wall:
"The ironsmith's good for beating anvils with sledge hammers,
or, if you wish, for sleeping with fair maids on coal,
but I call God to swoop on earth like a strong man
who brims with brains and hopeless grit, ruthless as I!"
Her feverish eyes were clouded, and huge drops of sweat
rolled down her face and hung upon her pallid lips.
The shrewd man set his basket on the tiles, then gripped
her shoulders with his sharp and ruthless claws:
"Don't speak so much, girl! You have aimed your green eyes well;
now knit your knees and keep my secret hidden deep:

I am a god who's come to earth to play an hour!"
Then Phida, screeching like a crow, rushed in his arms,
but the dark-shadowed man thrust her aside and growled:
"God is not welcomed with open arms or a crow's croaking.
Souls stand erect and watch and wait for him to beckon."
He spoke, then raised the brimming basket on his head
and Phida strode before to smash all obstacles.
At the queen's doorway monstrous Negro guards advanced,
but Phida gave a signal, the fierce door-guards vanished,
and thus Odysseus, wrapped in vine leaves, crossed the sill.
Helen sat smiling on her golden throne, her maids
were painting her nails crimson and her eyebrows black
and sprinkling golden saffron on her new-washed hair.
Two stunted, short-assed court fools fanned her quietly
and from the open casements, gardens slowly strolled.
The swift-eyed lady turned, and her face shone with stealth,
for she discerned amid the thick vine leaves and grapes
two cunning snake-eyes gleam; she raised her regal hand
and her rose-fingered maids and hairless eunuchs vanished.
The pomegranate flower then opened and said gently:
"In vain, O son of lightning, do you hide in leaves
the rampant bonfire of your head, your blazing eyes;
you can do much, but still you cannot blot your soul."
Odysseus slowly smiled, then spoke up mockingly:
"All other souls don't have your cunning graces, Helen;
your soul can blot out calmly in a cow's bronze belly."
Helen half-closed her eyes and sighed with curling lips:
"You roam far from my mind and vanish now, Odysseus."
The great abductor shuddered; his powers had been shamed;
he felt her godly body slip from his dark hands,
and he recalled the barbarous stranger, laughter, hugs,
and how they'd fled with lustful haste to the deep vaults.
A meteor split him to his depths and fired his brain;
he dug his nails deep in his chest and cried with rage:
"You stable stallions in your world-notorious body!"
The dimpled lady coolly smiled and her voice rose
like a clear fountain on a lawn complainingly:
"If you're in truth that decoy soul that does not quake
even though it holds the joys and griefs of earth, then listen:
Deep in that sphere you gave me to behold my fate
I gazed on a tall blond-haired stranger at my right
standing beside a crimson tent, holding my son;
I gazed on a new land and sea, and you had vanished!"
She was still smiling, and from the golden casement ledge
looked far on fields and mountains, and her spirit soared.
The man of many sorrows clasped his swelling neck

to thrust down through his throat again the rising groan,
and in his guts he heard harsh laughter and a bull's roar:
"Archer, she has a proud soul, and I like her well!
She follows in your footsteps now, and sprints for freedom;
I am your god who gives her freely my full blessing!"
He listened to his god with wrath, fought savagely,
and sought to choke that voice within his star-burnt chest,
but God outmatched the black beast, and the archer sweetened:
"The god of freedom cries within me, and I obey.
O free soul, I rejoice when you sprout wings to fly
or open up new roads, or take a new virginity.
Helen, God in me cries: 'Farewell, and a good voyage!'
And yet, before we part, we have one duty more;
listen to what I've thought; O star-eyed, help me now!
Let's break down slavery's doors with axes or with wiles,
then both of us can say farewell on the warm embers."
But the sad decoy-bird with bitterness complained
that thus, dear God, she was abandoned ruthlessly
as though she'd lost already the form that maddened men;
and then, in spite, she shattered with her rosy palms
the ivory lily-charm that gleamed about her throat.
But the heart-reader with compassion read her pain,
approached her gently, softly touched her apple knees,
and counseled her to let her tears burst into light.
Helen rejoiced, and softly touched his graying hair:
"My dear friend, I shall always hold your dreadful glance
deep in my heart to feed me with undying fire,
for when one dares to break his bread and salt with you
a world-destructive fire forever eats his heart.
Now speak, confess, and tell me all your crafty plans,
for I too long to free myself from this vile bed."
With lowered voice the archer then approached her ears,
rose-shelled, and there unfolded his perfidious trap.
The king with all his slaves, his gods, his famous fleet,
whirled in a dance of scorpions in his fiery head,
their bracelets melted in his brain, their earrings dropped,
wildfire flared, the castle's old housekeeping crone,
and Helen, a baby at her breast, glowed in the fields.
The lady of lovely thighs listened in silent thought,
and when the pitiless killer stopped, she burst in tears
and ached for the doomed world as for her only son.
When noontime dripped on earth and shadows huddled close,
the archer passed beyond the castle's twisting halls,
the courts and the bronze towers, passed the outer gate,
and holding his mute heart sped swiftly toward the harbor town.

To right and left on mountain slopes the vineyards rose,
and vintage grapes leant on the earth like full-grown babes
that curly-haired and big-thighed women stooped to clasp;
the fragrance of the must-filled air, the vineyard's fire,
awakened the blind blood and secret ancient anguish;
thighs of young men and maidens smelled of lechery,
and as the dark dusk spread and coupling shadows mingled,
the burning lust grew savage, bitterness overflowed
as though the male god died and made all women widows.
But the world-wanderer quickly passed, sped down the road
and found his friends carousing in a humble tavern;
the harbor women sat astride their stony knees,
gleaming like pure-white pigeons by the river reeds,
and a tall Negro dragged his feet and served them wine.
Granite, that gallant woman-chasing tower, half-shut
his lashes, twisted his long raven-black mustache,
and thought once more of his old life until the wine
rose like a large flame-flickering snake and licked his brain.
"Fellows, I've never wanted more in this false world
than a good knife, a true, trustworthy, heartfelt friend,
and on my knees, astride, a wanton laughing girl."
Highlander Rocky heaved a sigh and then replied:
"I've tasted friendship, brother, buckled on my swords,
nourished my early youth on many a woman's breast,
but, O my brothers, the most precious treasure of all
is still the archer's talons when they crack my skull!"
Then Kentaur burst with laughter, thrust one hairy hand
around a wanton's hips, and seized and drained his cup:
"Don't break your heads, my lads! Everything has its place,
wine, women, song and faithful friends and shining weapons;
here in the upper world, the demon has matched things well,
they're all good, and by God, I never could choose between them!"
The piper sat astride the wine jars, played his pipe,
nor had a care for friends, nor headaches for young girls,
for with the wine's sweet dizziness his feathery brains
fluttered like moths and vanished in the holy light.
Like a lank worm who had completed death's full round,
his drunken soul had broken through the tomb of flesh
and lightly danced in wilderness to a song's grace.
Captain Clam wrung his wine-soaked beard, when all at once
a drunken vision struck him and his wits spun round:
"Quick with your hands, my friends, drink up! Give joy and take it!
Let all men's poisoned troubles sink to the sea's depths
like savage snake-green eels, and nevermore return,
for I've grown old with plundering lands and sailing seas,
sitting with my close-bosom friends, drinking sweet wine;

but never have I drunk, I swear, such wine as this
wherein I see a tall three-masted sea-cap sailing!"
His speech ran on till a dark shadow drenched the walls,
a great black shadow with a lofty sea-cap loomed
till all, with joy and laughter, leapt up toward the door.
The harbor girls took wing and fled, the Negro vanished,
and then Odysseus laughed and turned to his old cronies:
"Your good health, friends! I see you've fought the battle well!
No one, by God, can match us when we swing together,
for then we have the guts of lions, the eyes of asps;
but, as I've thought a thousand times, when you're alone,
you fall flat on your snouts and knees in harbor pubs,
sit on your asses all night long and forget God!"
Rocky alone grew crimson, stooped with heavy shame,
but his old friends burst out with laughter fearlessly
until the cross-eyed piper poked his head and chirped:
"All-knowing rogue, it's you who've taught us here on earth
to merge wine, death and kisses and to mix them well;
double is life, double our cups, and double our faces;
that's why my right eye glances left, my left eye right."
All the companions grinned, and the soul-snatcher joyed
to be received with glee, to find his friends untroubled,
waiting, with wine cups held aloft, his dreadful news.
With both hands then he grasped the wooden bowl they filled,
and as he gulped the Cretan wine, admired his face
that sailed, a fox or lion, deep in the sacred drink.
He burned, his mind whirled like a wind round wretched life,
and when he spoke, thick wine-drops dripped from his gray beard:
"Don't listen, friends, to what I've said! I've joked and teased!
I'm overjoyed to watch how you carouse and sing,
for all I see about me, women, wine, and meat,
pubs, crippled Negroes, and the sea's wild wind, shall rise
to gallant deeds within you when I give the sign.
As though you were my bodies, I caress you all,
for I rule seven bodies, I clasp seven souls.
We've eaten, drunk and kissed, until I think it's time
earth's other face should glow now to refresh our souls;
comrades, let's shut the tavern door and talk our hearts out."
Rocky leapt up and shut the door, the wine cups flowed,
and Kentaur passed out hunks of finely roasted rabbit.
Their leader's eyes flashed fire, and all with longing swarmed
thickly about his pregnant head and heard with care:
"Our God craves much and suffers much and hungers much!
Whoever said he pities man and stoops with care
for fear he'll crush man's soul that sprawls before his feet?
I've traced him step by step with care, now listen closely:

We both slipped slyly in the castle's crooked horns,
he sped before, I stalked behind, flames flared between us,
and as we hid behind the columns and clutched our hearts,
we both cried out, man's dreadful heart and God himself:
'They eat on golden plates, they vomit in silver bowls,
their full holds brim with fruit and grain, their thighs with women,
the time has come for earth to gape and grind them pure!' "
The dexterous man fell silent, but his snake eyes gleamed;
lusts, wars and hungers flared up in their wolf-pack's chests,
they drank until the mind, that laughless guard, shrank up,
they broke the boundaries of what coward man would dare,
and all their inner demons burst in song and dance.
Their bodies sprouted wings and flew, pure visions soared
when the old rusted hinges of their brains crashed open
till, on desire's bosom, truth and dream were merged.
The knowing man had waited for this holy hour,
and reaching out his hands, he drew their heads together:
"Eh, hunting hounds of God, how well you wag your tails,
how well your nostrils sniff the least faint trace in air!
Wine, kisses, god, and fire ascend in rows like loot;
now let each soul rise up and grab whatever it can:
each soul will show its rank by what it seeks to plunder."
The piper hiccuped then: "The strongest soul—excuse me—
scorns to grab even the most brilliant spoil of all!"
Odysseus swerved and pushed the tables until they shook:
"Look where you leap, or you'll fall flat on your face one day!"
The cowardly piper swallowed his tongue and quaked with fear,
but Kentaur pitied the fierce wolf-pack's warbling runt:
"This is your fate, deaf wretched nightingale, to drink
at dragon-wells and turn into a dragon's child."
But the man-killer poured the wine jugs in their cups
that their small hearts might broaden to receive his mind;
it was high time to put the unbridled brain in order:
"I'm not inexpert nor a novice; I've learned through pain
that fire is good when governed by man's inner light.
It's best to weigh things well before we plunge to deeds;
we'll scatter soon like strangers through the castle halls;
take heart, play dumb, we've never seen or known each other;
if they should get their wind up, not even one small grain,
dear glutton, will be found of your once greasy guts!
Only the arch-eyed beauty knows our secret, friends;
she'll aid and shield us sleeplessly with craft and wiles."
Granite lost patience then and cried in a harsh voice:
"All well and good, but quick now, friend, give us our tasks!"
The archer gazed on his proud slender hound and said:
"Granite, you'll stand guard at the inner gate and hold

the heavy keys that open and close our destiny;
Rocky, you'll scour the mountains with the wild game hunters
and track those shining bulls used in their wanton games.
Orpheus, dream-taken poet, you'll sit at the king's feet
and jest with him like a court's fool to calm his heart,
but you, my piper, with sweet flutes and magic tunes
shall lead him far astray and snare him in black pits.
Kentaur, you'll plunge to the dark vaults, as you like best,
and there divert the savage slavehands night and day,
feeding their pallid hearts so that the world won't vanish;
it pleases me to use your roistering good heart
like kindling wood for the destruction of all mankind.
You, Captain Clam, will stay in port and make new friends;
you'll find your task at first most sweet, and welcome, too,
but it may burst about you filled with death at last
and then it may be difficult, friend, to save your head."
Captain Clam laughed and seized the white top of his skull:
"I've only one head on this desolate earth. It's yours!"
The harsh man-killer smiled and grabbed his friend's white head
as though he thought to set up occupation there,
but sighed and rose, and all his wolf-pack leapt at once
till their small Mother Earth creaked to contain them all.
Laughing, they started then to share the world between them:
"My share," yelled Captain Clam, "will be the sea for wife;
our two beasts of the wood will share earth fifty-fifty,
the guzzler here will take the wine casks for his share,
and our unlaughing smith shall set his forge on fire
and melt down golden gods and bracelets to sharp swords!"
The piper found an opening and piped up once more:
"Brothers, you've shared the world between you. Health and joy!
But what about my cut? Am I the hairless fool?
And yet, of all of you, it's I who gain the most,
for with no wretched vineyards, farms, or business cares
I keep my head unhooked and play with all the world.
I sit enthroned on freedom's stone in a far corner,
and as I watch you all pass by, weighed down with cares,
I laugh, stretch my mind taut and shoot my darting words
straight to the mark, all claws and light, until you faint
and enter like pale shades into my lofty song;
this is my mind's great share, I want no other cut!"
The archer laughed and finally opened the tavern door:
"Good going, piper, you've grabbed the lion's share in truth!
But, friends, it's I who must complain, for where's my share?
Where do I best fit in so that my mind won't choke?
The sea won't hold me, honest earth now spews me forth,
and the vast sky is much too empty for man's spirit."

Then Rocky wrung his wine-soaked beard and spoke with pluck:
"Colossal man, you know the world can't hold you now,
and yet your proud soul scorns to take another prize."
And talking thus they scattered in the harbor din;
the stars were dewdrops on night's black-leaved marigold,
in their wine-groggy eyes the earth and heavens shook,
and from that earthquake the small toy of earth was smashed:
all workshops, towers and houses tumbled, walls crashed down,
and all the roofs of earth like drunken bonnets swayed,
for each friend turned to feathers, and earth sprouted seven wings!

That same night Phida crept to the seducer's threshold;
the moon was late in rising, and in flickering starlight
as her eyes glittered and her gap-teeth shone with greed,
Odysseus saw her laughing on the limestone tiles.
That night the bronzesmith and the ironsmith worked with stealth,
the palace noises round them thundered, laughter rang,
and drums of Negroes thumped in the lewd archons' rooms.
Sunburnt and lean, the thighs of Phida darkly gleamed
on the rough shining limestones, and between her knees
she wedged her chin, as square and grappling as a beast's.
Odysseus suddenly reached his hands and with his nails
dug deep in her hard skull and squeezed it silently
till Phida shuddered with the eagle's brute caress.
These two wild beasts had no great need for squandering words,
their souls merged mutely like two hungry wolves who prowled
a penfold's walls and spied the countryside around.
They crouched and growled in stealth, and in the misty dark
both pairs of eyes flashed flame, and their bold brains entwined
like two battalions that joined forces and closed ranks.
Phida stooped down and spoke to him of curious ships
with sun and moon on sails that on the salt sea skimmed
and to far-distant shores had brought the joyful news;
in a short time the blue sea would be filled with masts:
"Whatever you see, gods, walls, and flesh, will shake and fall
because the heart, too, shakes in man's dark hidden places."
"That's true," the archer cried, then beat the earth with his fists,
and said no more, but deep in the world's sluggish roots
he heard unnumbered hearts that brought the earthquake close.
The first white rooster crowed, and in the wakening courts
a blue-green radiance poured till suddenly in its light
the pallid king appeared surrounded by fat eunuchs;
he leant his groggy head against a cedar column,
then groaned, and retched till his rich food spilled on the tiles.
The eunuchs ran and brought him water in gold bowls,

soaked with rose-vinegar his pale and sweating brows,
then dragged him slowly up the stairs to the women's rooms.
The castle-wrecker spread his hands and gripped the walls:
"Thank you, O Unseen Leader! You have brimmed my eyes!
They're sated now this holy night, they want no more."
He spoke, and in the cooling dawn the two beasts slunk away.

Yesterday and Tomorrow, like two rampant lions,
stood back to back in the sun's flame-eyed disk and rolled
it gently down to earth to frisk and play with it.
The sun rolled on, and all earth's creatures changed their dress,
their emerald shirts grew faded, tore, and fell away,
the gaunt trees shed their leaves, the heavy rains came down,
cranes carried the young birds and then flew off like carters
of fierce swift-footed time, and soared on toward the sun.
Wine in the kegs distilled, cruel winter choked the fields,
the waters sizzled where the Pleiades sank ashore
like burning coals that in the frothing water smothered,
and shepherds set out for their green and wintering fields.
The plowman, with his yoked ox, held a pomegranate,
and flung it on the male plow-blade to increase his seed;
shaggy invisible demons trudged before his furrows.
Other clodhoppers had already sown their seed
and asked the empty sky with dumb unease for rain;
troubles were many and life hung on the wind's caprice.
From olive groves the olive-beaters marched and sang,
sorcerers shook their sistrums, dressed in sheepskin robes,
and all the workers' mouths gaped wide with roaring song.
Far off in Ithaca, where the dread forefathers slept,
the pale belovèd wife of the new fledgling king
awoke with fright at daybreak in the women's quarters.
She felt a sweet weight on her breast, a vertigo,
and when her husband lit the three-flamed lamp, distressed,
and soothed her with caresses and kind words, she wept,
felt close to fainting, and longed to eat a charcoal stick.
The young man laughed and recognized her pregnant wish,
knew that his son was now well-planted in her womb,
blew out the lamp, and hugged his holy bride with joy.
Meanwhile Odysseus, stalking about his golden cage,
twisted the palace round and round with unseen threads,
spied out and wrote down all in his mind's iron plates.
The daintily fed court dames beneath their canopies
drank warm concoctions of sage, mint, and dittany,
and gazed at black-eyed broadbeans to divine their fate.
Others stooped over bronze jugs filled with speechless water
wherein they cast red apples stippled with black cloves,

sang magic couplets that unveiled each other's fate
while a plump guileless youngster plunged his tender hand
and slowly drew for each her apple of destiny.
Young slaves perched on the window sills like birds and stitched
with golden fingers the dark sky with all its stars;
they stitched a flowering field their mistresses would wear
in springtime as they strolled along the blossomed streams.
A court girl sat beneath a covered balcony
on a gold-broidered pillow, mattress of soft down,
sunk deep in thought, and with red dye and a sharp reed
stooped over a smooth plaque of ivory-leaf and etched,
brimful of rain and sorrow, a small and bitter song:
"My heart was caught in the thick rain's entangling net,
the water lilies slept in pools, the crocus bloomed,
and earth, a pallid maid in love, crouched low and wept.
Dear God, my locks are stringy, my cosmetics blurred,
my fingers smart from wearing these thick golden rings,
the proud curves of my lips have fallen and lost their paint;
pallid and sad, I hang in rain like a plucked rose.
One day at dusk as a worker passed, and waters streamed
from his curled towering head, and his thighs gleamed with rain,
I winked at him most sweetly, shyly waved and smiled,
but he was awed by the rich necklace round my throat,
the golden crown I wear upon my heavy head,
and fell on the drenched ground and bowed with reverence.
The yard rejoiced, filled with his flesh, but my heart broke.
God, might I only lie with him on muddy earth!
My hair has fluttered loose, a sad complaint has swept me,
I bare my bosom to the winds and quake in rain
like a white rose whose petals fall and fade in wind."
After she wrote her dark grief on the ivory plaque,
she hung it by the window in the drizzling rain
and slowly her lament began to melt, to flow,
until it reddened her white harem wall like dripping blood.

And thus the palace roses paled and shed their petals
while the bold archer roamed the slavehands' sunless vaults
and Phida dashed before him like a panting hound.
The weaver's mind spun round, and in his wattled net
the cobwebbed palace like a golden scarab gleamed.
The dexterous man put on a pleasant face to fool
the king, and in the workshop of an old wood-carver
learned how to chisel demons out of fragrant wood
and joyed to see how the gods sprang to his fingertips,
how hands, legs, heads ascended to his mind's dictation.
The Cretan master craftsman bent to instruct his skilled

apprentice how to blow his soul in the lifeless wood:
"In every mountain stone, in every wood's gnarled log,
the huddled spirits smother and cry to skillful hands.
The one who cries is not God, demon, or the wind's sound,
for it's your own enslaved soul that cries out for freedom!
One night while sleeping in my workshop all alone
I heard a marble block cry out in the still night;
it was my own enslaved soul crying, choked in stone.
At once I leapt from sleep, seized all my sharpest tools

and in the lamp's dim light began to hew the block
and crash through the thick prison walls to free my soul,
till finally at dawn the godly head emerged,
cool and rejoiced, and deeply breathed the crystal air.
Slowly I freed its breast and shoulders, its lean loins,
and as it rose from stone to light, my own jailed head,
my shoulders, chest, and loins were also slowly freed;
and when my soul had from my hands wholly emerged
it raised its eyes to the sky and soared like a giddy bird!"
The Cretan laughed and seized Odysseus by his arms:
"I speak of birds and freedom, for slavery eats my heart!
For years I've fought and beaten my cage's golden bars;
I watch the sky, I watch huge wings pass high above me,
and in my hands I tightly grip my heart and cry:
'Don't hurry, child; I'm fitting you with secret wings!'
When we stop work, as night-birds brood and lamps are lit,
we sit on earth and then I soothe her with old myths:
'Dear heart, the North Wind on his mountain tower of ice
boasted with stormy lips one day he scorned even Death.
And South Wind slowly came and blew, then blew again,
till the dread tower melted down, and nothing stayed
but North Wind's crystal tears that flooded all the fields.
But don't think, heart, that the South Wind is God or Death:
he's but man's mind that slowly melts down towns and towers.' "
The apprentice watched the old man, fondled his skilled hands,
and longed to stoop and kiss those bulging shoulder blades
where curly though unseen wings sprouted, drenched in blood;
O might he have such eagle root and high descent!
In the gnarled master's glance whole flocks of free birds flashed
with wide wings, and men flew and earth plunged headlong down
as withers away and falls the cricket's muddy husk.
The Cretan followed with his eyes a snow-white dove
that spread its wings above the rain-soaked palace court,
flapped them with rapid strokes, balanced and swooped with speed,
then slid on the wet tiles and proudly closed its wings.
His ancient body tingled and his hands swayed gently
as though the earth beneath his feet had turned to air.
And when the holy bird amid the columns vanished,
the old man turned his glowing face, washed with cool wings:
"Freedom, my son, is two wings that man's hands have shaped!"
He spoke, then bent above a cedar block with care
and chiseled a sharp olive leaf with its dark fruit.
Within the murky hopeless rain of silent dusk,
that night when the bold archer turned to the damp vaults,
and God growled like a bull in sunless, deep foundations,
his seven souls replied with soft and secret lowing sounds.

As earth's wheel slowly turned, the days grew warm, time passed,
swallows flew by like arrows in a crisscross stream
and held thin many-colored threads to weave the weft
of water, sun, and lukewarm air, and with earth's warp
adorn the spring with dainty flowers and warm eggs.
The hornbeam sprouted and the ash gave shade to shepherds' haunts,
young grapevines budded with crab's eyes, maids yearned for love,
and lonely slave-girls in their cellars softly sobbed,
for their unkissed throats swelled and pulsed with secret pain.
Orpheus crouched by the old king and played his flute
to drug that opiate brain and slacken that limp soul
till the poor monarch's breath poured from the tiny flute.
One day when South Wind blew and swelled the trees, the king
stepped on the terrace and wept to feel earth's pungent smells
unstring his spine until it crumpled, bone by bone.
"I've never known before such a sweet fragrant spring
of birdsong, secret cries and smells—I'm filled with fear!
This is the last time I shall taste the world in flower."
Thus did the old king mumble in his room, and sigh.
As a girl gathered flowers and plucked a tall rose-bush
to match and send a full bouquet to her betrothed,
she spied the poor old king, and mocked him silently:
"The old thing rots away, he won't last out the spring."
In the closed gardens, almond trees were first to bloom,
motionless, hazed with fragrance in the whitening noon;
it was that scandalous month when maidens ran like does,
for they were chased by that invisible sweet lover
of spring with his moist quivering nostrils and curved horns.
Insects, too, donned their armor and foraged amid the grass,
lizards like courtly ladies dragged their slender trains
and with their sweet eyes softly glowed on scorching stones.
Within the crooked palace shy new-breasted maids
combed and uncombed the weight of their unbearable hair;
and on a low stool thickly rimmed with precious ivory,
Helen, the light-downed spoil of passion, sat enthroned.
The blood within her godly breasts had turned to milk,
a sweet weight overbrimmed her bosom and pale thighs
so that she leant to share it with an almond tree
that like a woman ready to beget her child
smiled in the light and also leant on Helen's shoulder.
For a long time both mothers rested, overjoyed
to feel their secret fruit maturing in warm sun.
"When my first birth-pangs come, O my white almond tree,
dear twin, I'll come to clasp you tight and bear my son
and twine one of your flowering sprays about my hair."
Thus Helen thought, and smiled, then stooped and once again

took up her golden cloth and with slow-moving fingers
began to stitch with flowers her new son's swaddling clothes.
She stooped, but her mind traveled on, her thoughts ran on
warbling like gurgling water through her pallid brow.
She bounces her new baby, plays, crawls like a bear,
he grows up with his father's blond and thorny beard:
"Mother, the steeds are snorting, Mother, I must leave soon!"
She wishes him good journey, then turns to hide her tears.
A white bloom from the almond tree dropped on her hair
and Helen shuddered, smiled, took up her needle again,
and once more stitched spring flowers on her baby's bonnet.
A slave with gray hair, once a prince's daughter, felt
her mistress's great sweetness, her nostalgic pain,
and fell before her lady's feet with throbbing heart
as her voice shook with flute-sounds in the sunny garden:
"Ah, mistress, when I see the dove fly, my heart burns,
and I feel curbed within my clothes, hedged in my house,
and raise my arms but find, alas, they are not wings!
In spring when earth thaws out and trees augment with leaves,
and caterpillars poke from soil and yearn for sun
and, yearning, suddenly sprout prismatic wings, and fly—
ah, mistress, if man's shoulders also could sprout wings!"
As the slave sang like a caged bird, in Helen's heart
her old life rose like a most faint and faded dream.
She could recall her husband dimly, radiant Paris,
and those brave youths who died at Troy for her sweet sake;
but neither joy, nor even sorrow, touched her heart,
for now she felt her baby ripening in the fruitful sun.

Night fell, sheep were penned up and cows were brought to stall,
the sweating steeds returned and whinnied in their stables,
stars hung like threatening swords above the heads of men,
and an old peasant spread his hands to the archer, filled
with gifts of the soft-skinned first-fruited almond tree,
and he ate of the slim fruit and joyed, feeling the freshness
of the green fuzzy almonds deep to his calloused heels.
Thus holding the green fruit he talked to slaves and workers:
"Perk up your ears my brothers, I bring you awesome news!
As I passed through the courts one day, I bent and wondered
how all slaves might sprout wings and poverty grow rich.
I heard a deep sigh suddenly, and a column swayed:
raising my eyes, I saw God stand by the cellar door
proudly erect, his slim waist strapped with a sharp ax,
and his beard streamed like fire and swept the cedar columns.
Just as a hunter calls his hounds, he whistled twice,
and my hair rose on end and flashed flame at the root;

he beat upon my ears as fists beat on a drum:
'Oho! I've waited day and night, my heart's a hide,
the time has come, the ships draw near, let the pig bleed!'
He spoke; I heard a clattering as of speeding steeds,
of snorting in the courtyards while fierce fires roared.
My brothers, look! these eyes still burn that saw him there!"
But a brusque worker mocked and beat his chest: "Our god
is woman, wine and food! There is no other god!"
The slavehands yelled, and workers snorted in their vaults,
their thick lips slavered with desire, their minds were smeared
with old wines, heaps of food, and wild resounding beds.
The lone man watched that midwife, mad Necessity,
and bit his bitter lips in secret brooding thought:
"These impious bodies have set out to free their god,
and like black beetles filled with phallus, belly, ass,
roll their foul spheres, the soul, and try to mount my peaks!"
A sudden thought swooped like a hawk on head and heart:
"They'll reach the peak, they'll eat, they'll drink with heavy minds,
their dull hearts will be twined with fat, their seed will choke,
and then, my God, another Archer will spring on earth!
Our stock is strong! Don't be distressed, God, we shall free you!
'How long will this game last?' you ask. To the world's end!"
The archer thus consoled his nail-sharp clawing mind,
gazed on the slaves more tenderly, and placed his hands
on their strong backs and solid thighs, then laughed and thought:
"God has dismounted from their masters' breathless husks
and rides astride the firm rumps of the workers now.
'Straight on!' he cries, and goads them to climb further still."
They talked and plotted closely at the castle's roots,
the archer thought one thing, the slaves another, but both
merged in this holy hour that pressed on toward destruction.
"Victory is our first duty, brothers!" the archer cried.
"God beckons, and the time has come to fire the castle.
Tonight we'll hand out iron weapons among our friends,
and all that mind has matched, our deeds will crown with victory!"

Meanwhile the king strolled slowly in the misty dawns
to watch the sun rise from his palace terraces
and to breathe free from his long-shadowed stifling nightmares.
Light dropped its petals like a rose, the river laughed,
but the disconsolate king kept his sad features turned
far toward the sacred mountain's head that spread reclined
like a dead prostrate king upon the fertile plain,
for heavy premonitions raged in his dark heart.
Nightlong, strange hands had moved and etched upon the walls

thick fires, black crows, blue eyes, red slaughtered heads,
and men with tall sea-caps who knelt and stretched their bows.
In the dawn's subtle light, the king had read with fear:
"King, I shall cast your white head to the black starved crows,
the blue-eyed blonds shall set your wealthy hall on fire,
and then a new sea-god shall raise his tents on earth."
On the same dawn of the holy feast, the coward king
with trembling fear read the same omen in his own head
and in despair stepped in the light to breathe some air.
Meanwhile, the archer walked the riverbank alone,
and his feet smelled of sage, his curly hair was damp
and slowly dripped with the fine frosty dew of dawn.
All night it had rained hard, but now earth shook and laughed
as myriad rainbows trembled in each dewdrop's globe;
butterflies froze on every bush with dew-drenched wings,
spry baby crickets, smeared with mud, hopped in the grass,
and birds dried their soaked feathers on the sunny tree-tops.
The archer's hard heart throbbed like that of a small child;
the first few fig leaves spilled a tart and acrid scent
until his nostrils quivered and his eyes brimmed full:
"How long will I still live to enjoy this world, dear God?
I plot manslaughter, conflagration, then all at once
the fragrance of a fresh fig leaf disarms my heart."
Within the cool ravines the slaves with their bronze scythes
cut rhododendron, rush, and myrtle boughs to deck
the bridegroom's house for his thrice-holy new betrothal.
Swift down the mountain slopes, descending with the hunters,
lean Rocky lunged, and dragged with lassoes of thick rope
the shining bull-calves to be slain for the night's feast.
Odysseus waved his hand to welcome the brave lad
and Rocky whistled to his master with two fingers
till all the mountain slope re-echoed that early dawn.
Hidden in myrtle boughs, only the sea-cap's top
with its blue tassel could be seen in the dawn's light,
and when an insect got entangled in his hairy chest
and swayed its fuzzy feelers toward the light with fear,
the pitiless killer picked it gently from those woods
then stooped and placed it on a myrtle bough with care.
Odysseus sauntered slowly thus with quiet eyes
as though he shouted to the upper world, "Farewell!"
for by his side he felt his final, old friend, Death,
whistling and walking there with his cool hands outstretched,
and when the hunched king saw the archer stroll in peace
his tongue clucked in his mouth, then drooped, thick-coated, dry:
"You've stuck your head out, buried viper! May you be cursed!"
For months he'd felt him glide about the castle walls,

counting all heads, taking the measure of all necks,
preparing to hang nooses from the tall roof-beams.
Under his golden blankets cowering all night long,
Idomeneus hid with fear in threatening dark
to avoid those crafty eyes whose glances pierced so deep,
and swore each morning to command his Negro slave
to bring him on a brazen tray that hated cunning head,
but every dawn his tongue stuck in his throat, and his heart shook.

Thus did the silent moons move on, sometimes like scythes,
sometimes like silver shields that dripped with poisoned drops,
until the trembling king saw his sly enemy stroll
carelessly through the shrubs toward the resounding sea.
He saw that sea-cap, and his dream leapt in his head.
His neck swelled in a tightened noose until he longed
to have that shameless head brought him on myrtle boughs,
but then his giggling eunuchs came, heaped high with all
the embroidered ritual garments to adorn the groom.
Heralds on every threshold stood and stretched their hands:
"The sea has raised her breasts, foam-flecked and washed with dew,
the springtime streams are fragrant as all river fishes
descend now to their salty seaweed beds to spawn.
Rise up, betrothed, to dress; rise up, O groom, to change;
put on your golden ring, put on your lofty plumes
and go down to the holy sea, its deep embracements;
the time has come now for the secret Cretan wedding!"
As the proud heralds cried, deep in a garden's shade
a butterfly strove to rise, but its great downy wings,
prismatic and mud-spattered, fluttered and fell to earth,
and a nude worm emerged and slowly sank in mud.
Then the king mutely stretched his arms to be adorned;
they decked him first with a gold mantle thick with shells
and rows of oyster-plaques that shone like silver scales,
tied two prow-pointed sandals on his withered feet,
then on his bony neck and chest hung starfish charms
carved out of crimson coral and deep turquoise stone.
The heralds raised their hands on high and cried aloud:
"This walking wonder is not sperm, nor mother's milk!
O God, this is a dolphin and the sea's great groom,
the billows are his in-laws and the waves his guests,
islands are sapphire-emerald neck-rings round his throat!"
Then beaming eunuchs with their plump hands silently
clamped on the king a pale fish-mask with coral eyes,
and last, placed on his thumb the holy mystic ring.
On this great ring the sea, a woman, sat enthroned
on shaggy rocks, and in her right hand held the sun,

and in her left the crescent moon, a straight-prowed ship,
and fertile phalli hung between her pregnant breasts.
Thus mantled and adorned, he leant on roselit columns
and in his shattered entrails felt his kingdom fall
on earth drop after drop and churn the soil to mud.
The lame-brained, wretched king then moved his vapid lips:
"My guts have rotted and rebel, my throat is worn,
I retch up all I've eaten, spew out all I've drunk:
high castles, women, wine and strong-knit downy boys.
Dear Mother Earth, I kiss your fragrant soil like bread,
ah, in what state begotten, in what state returned!"
Pain and lament swept through him till he burst in tears,
and the shocked eunuchs called for the court bards to come
with joyful instruments at once and soothe their king.
They brought lutes, zithers, sistrums, and poor Orpheus came
wearing the court fool's silver bells on his peaked head,
then sat cross-legged and stooped to play his sweet-tongued flute.
The king's mind swayed, and river rushes streamed in rows
and rustled round his blissful ears like dulcet flutes
until earth's heart unfolded and began to sing.
Water ran warbling, filled with joy, on the smooth stones
and streamed on toward the sea as the king's flowing mind
followed like foaming water down to the docile waves.
All life seemed like a dream, a fragrant jasmine bloom,
and as he held and smelled it, his heart in secret shook
as though he bent above the river and watched the world,
composed of light and water, rise and fall away,
till Death, too, seemed most light, shadow of a huge flower
that fell at evening on the heads of mortal men.
The spermless king then sighed and smilingly stooped down
and fondled with smooth hand the piper's supple fingers.
"Piper, you play, and the world becomes a flimsy veil
till fleets and galleys soar in air like butterflies
and I turn mist, and grass won't bend beneath my feet,
as though a disembodied soul leapt up and soared . . ."
And as he spoke, the tears ran down his golden sea-decked robes.

God dressed like a lean vulture then stalked stone by stone,
raised his bald neck aloft, hungry for carcasses,
and tagged behind the castle-wrecker along the river.
When the great murderer heard the vast dark wings of God
rise high and fall on earth and air, blood-splattered, torn,
he felt rejoiced like a fierce hunter with his lean hound.
A maiden, weighed with boughs of myrtle and rose-bay,
stopped by an old plane tree to get a moment's rest,
and when the archer gripped her with his blazing eyes

it was as though the maid's flushed face were rudely tickled
by hairy hands, until she smiled with roused desire
and felt a rank male odor brim about her thighs,
for the male mind like a river laved her myrtle boughs.
Beyond, he saw two children climb the green ravine,
their bodies like spry kids, their laughter like clear pools;
they scrambled up the flowery path in skips and jumps,
but when they met the stranger, they stood still, clasped arms,
and with untroubled glance watched that fierce face pass by.
But all at once the smallest, a girl, raised both her hands
and placed what flowers she had within those dreadful palms,
and then, like a grown maiden, dropped her eyes in shame.
The castle-wrecker crushed the flowers and swore wildly
because two children in the hour of dread destruction
had come to soften his heart with their unblemished smiles.
Raising his eyes and holding back his tears, he schemed
how he might spare the palace children, its sweet girls,
its fawns and lilies and its warbling tamed canaries.
But then the vulture's ruthless throat with harshness screeched,
and when Odysseus turned, he saw his God enthroned
high on the rocks, screaming at him with raging fury.
Then the fierce archer frowned and groped about his back,
unconsciously, as though to grasp his heavy bow,
and his gall-bitter lips twisted with scornful anger:
"Were you afraid, you fool, I'd pity a small child
and that your wretched belly would not fill with corpses?
That's how I like to hold my God, in either fist,
and keep him jittery: shall I loose him right or left?"
He spoke, then picked a stone and flung it at God's wings,
and the vulture rose and hovered in the azure air
to right and left and dumbly trailed his fuming master,
and thus the friends sloped downward toward the harbor silently.

Slim Captain Clam awaited him at the sea's rim.
Both stretched upon the foam-flecked sandy shore and held
the teasing sea embraced in joy, and heard close by
her gentle moaning in her deep and bubbling hollows.
When both were sated with the loved sea's undulations,
Captain Clam turned and tightly grasped his master's knees,
and the great pirate smiled in a serene response:
"Last night in sleep, my friend, two black swans hovered high
above my head and shone with crimson feet and beak.
The female danced and strutted round her mate, and swayed
her upright tail and slender neck erotically,
but the male swan stood still, held his beak high, and sang.

I have forgotten the words, my friend, but his strange song
feather by feather shed and fell on my raised head.
All night they danced and played and merged erotically
until at dawn there swooped a thousand-feathered flock
of eagles, water blackbirds, great horned owls till both
swans sang, and all in joy swept southward toward the sun."
Captain Clam's sea-stormed reedy head brimmed with wide wings
and swiftly voyaging mainsails in the South Wind's drift:
"Ahoy! You've sucked the castle in your whirlpool mind,
for emigrating birds already sweep your head!"
The castle-wrecker gently grasped his comrade's arms:
"Dear friend, I swear that this great hand of yours won't shake
when it shall thrust voracious flames in the ships' holds,
although you too may vanish, body and soul I love!
But I don't mind, I'll choke my pain, for I know well
that life is not man's highest or even his noblest good."
They rolled embraced in the rough sand, plunged in the sea,
gamboled and splashed in foam like sharks, tossed on the waves
as the sun struck their backs and bounced in flaming spheres.
The shore-nymphs saw them, and sea-sirens laughed and ran
to gaze on their well-modeled thighs and sunburnt loins.
Laughing and snorting, Captain Clam kicked back the waves,
and by his side the archer mutely spread his arms
and took the boiling, frothing sea straight on his chest.
When the two dolphins tired of water games at length,
they rolled with laughter on the coarse-grained sand once more.
The archer gazed long on his friend in mute farewell
and in his memory etched the rough-hewn, well-loved face,
the veins, the throat, the eyes, the white and reedy hair,
the beard, the temples, hairy ears and guileless mouth,
as though he fought with Charon in an airy ring
and strained to thrust all of his friend within his brain
so that not even his shadow might be left for Death.
Captain Clam felt his master's speechless farewell gaze
and with a sweet smile on his salty lips he said:
"Don't pity or caress my wretched body, comrade.
You know I count myself among Death's old, old friends,
we've shared black bread and salt together, knee to knee,
and I don't fear his swaggering gait, I like his odor!
To tell the truth, I've paid my duty to salt waves,
and it's a great reward for an old tar like me
to anchor in Death's harbor with a great armada.
But let's not leave our work in air; the sun's risen high,
people have packed the harbor, the wedding pomp descends.
You've said your fine farewell to Captain Clam. Let's go."
The cypress trees along the sea held up the sky,

and in their shade the pale king staggered with slow steps
to cast in waves his gold and mystical wedding ring.
His silver fish-scales glittered in the seashore's glare,
and as he stretched his hands above the waves he seemed
like a breast-plated crab with heavily armored claws.
For a long time the ring above the waters hung
as the sea's bosom swelled with quivering domed arcades,
and all her boundless feminine body moaned with lust.
Then the sperm suddenly fell, the deep womb gaped and closed,
the people roared, the exhausted king fell in a faint,
held up by waiting perfumed arms, his dim eyes glazed,
and his heart groaned like an old bull dragged to the slaughter-shed.

Life, brothers, is a crimson spangle on night's mantle.
Who is it, God, that sits in dark with dexterous hands
until embossed embroideries rise: blooms, cypress trees,
wild partridges with crimson claws, small sunburnt men?
Then all become unstitched and fall, rise new again
and open twisting paths of bordering cypress trees,
and thus the embroidery goes from cliff to cliff once more.
On greedy Death's soiled tablecloth there loomed in pride
a brimming palace three floors high that spread and shone,
and there coarse Kentaur in the palace courtyard stooped,
loaded to death with heap on heap of myrtle boughs
like a thick wooded peak, but swiftly was stripped bare
by slaves and slave-girls to adorn the votive halls.
The candelabrum stars lit up the walls and towers,
and in the fragrant dusk amid the springtime slopes
the palace gently swayed like deep, warm constellations.
High in their golden chambers the court ladies dressed,
and they too, like green earth in spring, wove belts of flowers,
stuck crickets in their hair, gold serpents round their arms,
and from their flesh an odor rose as of ripe quince.
They armed themselves with love's seductions, graceful joys
and sweet delights of flesh, then bravely sailed to battle
in single combat under the night's starry dome.
As the archer mutely leant against a cypress column,
the palace glittered in his eyes, a full-rigged ship,
slaves pulled the long oars, two by two, both men and maids,
and from the scorching hold the song of workers rose,
while on the deck above, the unbelted mates caroused,
and fate, that whore, that shameless naked siren, sat
on their wine-splattered knees, threw back her head, and laughed.
As the archer watched the window lights like strings of pearl,
the tables spread in the great courtyards strewn with bays,
his temples gushed with wind, a savage whirlwind rose,

and the whole palace with all its souls sank in his skull,
for as his mind had sucked up Captain Clam from Hades,
thus in the court, unmoving, mute, he fought with Death
to snatch from his red hands the moribund gold-plated halls.
He marked down every door and tower, each hanging garden,
dragged swiftly to his mind the proud bare-breasted maids,
the old decrepit lords, the infants in their cradles,
and his mind ripped, uprooted all, and swept them off.
He spied fat Kentaur hiding in his myrtle boughs,
and Rocky at the court's rim with blood-splattered arms
honing on sparkling whetstones his keen-bladed swords,
and Granite who stood guard before the palace gate.
Gliding up close to Rocky, the archer whispered low:
"Joy to those able hands that grab the wild bull's horns
and find unerringly the black neck's mortal spot!
If I were God, I'd set you loose on human herds!"
The gallant goatherd laughed, well pleased, and his teeth gleamed:
"That's a good thought, old youngster, I'll do all I can!
First I'll learn butchering on dumb beasts, to whet my strength,
and when you're God, by hook or crook, pass by, and signal!"
The crafty leader smiled in stealth and hurriedly passed
but suddenly felt a strong hand seize his shoulder blade,
and when he turned, he made out by a painted wall
the face of Phida glowing with great joy and fire.
She seized his savage hand and kissed it secretly,
but the wild castle-wrecker pushed her off, then dashed
with silent rage beyond the moon-struck girl, and vanished.
Reaching his cell, he stretched at the she-lion's feet
among the lilies, quietly, then cocked his ears
and heard night glide into the palace stealthily;
he heard lamps push her back, the watchdogs softly growl,
and as she gently slid from wall to wall on padded feet,
she darkened frescoes, smothered gods, and blunted knives;
she slunk like a black pantheress, and the archer's mind
prowled like a panther on the track of a new son.
Down by the seashore on the wings of night there moved
sharp-pointed ships, a blond tribe, women, children, dogs;
the sea smelled heavily of bears, coarse cries rang out,
neighing of horses, frothing waves that beat the night
like steeds, and all ascending swiftly toward the town.
That wild carnivorous beast, the archer's sly brain, pounced:
a maiden through the columns passed and tightly held
a flaming wax so that her ten translucent fingers
glowed, and her slim neck glittered with its dimpled chin;
she laughed and ran, and for a moment her face turned rose.
A sleepless peacock strutted by in glowering dark;

two bats flew by with muffled sound; on the far beach
the bittern's booming cry resounded in the reeds.
Low under the black funeral shards, at the rocks' roots,
long layers of bodies rotted and left beneath the mold
the pure-white deathless laughter of the gaping skulls.
Above, the living laughed unruffled, stamped their feet
and clapped their dying hands in the re-echoing pubs:
"Drink up, for Death's a legend, and red wine, my friends,
is deathless water! When we drink, our bare bones blossom!"
All tightly hugged young maidens to their hairy chests
and in a kiss's swoon forgot and mocked at Death:
"Heigh-ho! Let him swoop down at midnight with his scythe,
that rusted blade, and scare the toothless old men silly,
but we shall fight with a sweet kiss, and pin him down."
In the great palace, men and women swiftly massed
for the great orgy, and beyond the harbor's mouth
smooth waters soon began to heave and toss in stealth
as though beasts, fishes, and sharp prows approached in night.
Within the castle's marble hearths, the flames soared high
and the sparks prophesied the coming of a great guest.
The old crones fed the fire and cast their secret spells:
"If friend, then welcome, but if foe, then may he choke!"
And the Great Guest stood mutely by the castle gate;
his thick lips smiled with calm, his sharp eyes deeply sank,
his right hand clenched in a tight fist, his left hung down
palm open, with untroubled fingers in the cool breeze;
nor did the castle's fate torment his tranquil mind,
nor did his hungry heart seek food that holy hour;
for in deep silence, the night rang with all her stars,
the dark was sweet and smelled of musk, and his vast body
surrendered like a poplar leaf to the wind's blowing.
Long zigzag voyages, tears, poverty, and God
fluttered and played on his long lashes, slid like dreams,
until the contours of his face shone, purged and empty.
Thus did the archer's flesh rejoice in the calm evening,
while on stairs, cellars, terraces and royal courts,
on all the labyrinthine Cretan corridors,
the clogs of fate beat clattering like a good housekeeping crone.

VIII

Dear night, your star-stitched slippers need a golden rim,
they need a virgin maiden with ten slender fingers
to sit on the green ground and trim them with embroidery.
Stars rim the sky, and in the central palace court,
on the high summit of the royal palace dome,
a tiny night-bird lifts its scraggly bloodstained neck,
features of nightingale, harsh voice of the screech-owl:
"Eat and carouse until you burst, then sink in earth
with bellies big as drums, with necks of five-fold flesh,
that worms may swim delighted in your grimy grease!
Ah, your fine merging eyebrows and your curling lips,
your crisp and downy breasts, brimming with musk, my ladies!
When will your star-stitched slippers sweep them off, dear night?"
Thus did the good bird moan on the high palace dome,
but mankind's ears are filled with earth, they cannot hear,
and the good bird flew far away, fearing the scorching flames.

Night fell, the slaves returned from their fatiguing tasks,
night fell with deep blue down upon the heads of men,
and the small bird received the fearful news and turned
it to grim song deep in its bowels' magic flutes.
But as the archer slowly climbed the shadowed stairs
to relish the king's house once more in the night air,
he suddenly heard low wailing, and two slaves appeared
bearing the dead form of a small court dancing girl.
Then Orpheus, smeared with paints and dressed in monkey-hides,
the court fool's cap and silver bells still on his head,
fell sobbing to the ground and grasped his master's knees:
"Put fire to earth and burn it that my head may cool!
All day this dancing girl's bright smile was like the light
as she danced naked round the shameless archons' tables.
At dusk she leant against a column and softly sighed:
'I'm tired,' but the brute king laughed and ordered spread
a bull's hide on the terrace that the spiraling dance
of death might start until the dancer would fall dead.
Her tears ran burning down her cheeks, and full of fear

she started sobbing, like a small bird drowned in lime,
but the archons leant their hands on their exhausted chins
and watched the dancing girl all evening slowly fade
like a small flaming candle which a harsh wind blows.
I grasped their knees and begged them for a small compassion,
but they laughed scornfully and from her pallid lips,
like bittersweet old wine, sipped slow death drop by drop.
Master, I kiss your feet and claim no other god:
brandish the torch, don't pity the world, set it ablaze!"
His tears ran down till the cosmetics grooved his face,
but the strong man laughed bitterly and grabbed his brow:
"Hold tight your tender heart, you fool, if you've the strength;
don't burn the earth, O lame-brain, for a paltry maid!"
But Kentaur stooped with pity, raised the waxen body
high in his arms, climbed silently the darkened stairs,
and when he reached the court, strode toward the riverbank,
the slavehands following close behind with choked laments;
last came the stolid ironsmith with dazed blue eyes.
The lone man, with the dead girl on his mind, then spoke:
"Aye, ironsmith, you light the fires in the earth's pits,
but still your mind can't grasp what's happened on wide seas.
Now here's the secret news that Captain Clam just brought:
as far as the sea's rim, thick-strewn on all the waves,
there loom your own tribe's ships with sun and moon on sails;
this is the night we've longed for, midwife of fierce flames,
now is the time to pass the slaves your iron arms!"
Stroking his russet beard, the ironsmith heard with care,
and his blue eyes brimmed full of fires and pointed prows
and a fierce flaming girl who swiftly led the way.
The cunning man divined the girl and spoke with stealth,
his brain an iron herb that burst all bolted doors:
"When with our new god's iron strength the castle falls
and crumbles to the earth, burnt embers ground to ash
—give me your hand—I swear you'll take for your great share
the triple-flaming body of the king's first daughter."
He spoke, and red-beard growled and like a pincers squeezed
the archer's hand until his sturdy bone-joints creaked.
Meanwhile the funeral train approached the potter's field;
a tempest must have burst at night, for the ground gaped,
and tree-leaves drenched with tears hung downward toward the ground.
Under a humble almond tree with full bloom trembling,
shedding its petals speechlessly on the night air,
they gently stretched the fragile corpse of the young girl.
As friends entwined her castanets between her fingers
and crowned her pallid head with small bronze falcon-bells,
the castle-wrecker knelt beside the martyred feet

and kissed with reverence the pale toes destroyed by dance.
Seeing the piper digging like a dog close by,
howling with tears, he grabbed his nape and threw him flat
beside the dead girl's feet, her breasts, her lips, and cried:
"There, fool, fill up your eyes, your tongue, your nostrils, too!
Dig in your mind a body's length and plant this seed:
such, and the world beside, are what I hold within me!"
He spoke, and from the women's throats cries cut like knives,
a battle-song rose from the slavehands' savage chests,
and the brave girl, who'd fallen dancing on cruel earth,
glowed in her coffin like a warrior struck in battle.
Then swiftly smoothing the grave's soil with his hard heels,
as though in dance, Odysseus raised his battlecry:
"Some women fight on this vile earth with a sweet kiss
and slowly spread man's boundaries in the secret night,
others fight openly with children, husband, home,
and hold their tottering hearths together like firm pillars.
Each has her grace and worth, and both are gallant fighters,
but you, O small, small dancer with your supple feet,
with no son at your breast, no husband in your arms,
you served our dreadful god and died in his hard service.
May your ten martial toes be blessed forever and ever.
Your slender ankles shone on this black earth and cut
an open road for God, the unmerciful stern avenger!
O quivering flame that flickered in the desolate air,
dear sister, we won't let the ravening earth devour you;
you'll perch today on palace roofs like a tall flame
and sweetly sing, a small, small bird with burning plume;
you'll come to herald spring like a swift russet swallow."
He stooped, then planted in the ground an almond pit
so that one day the harbinger of spring might rise,
the almond tree, and in midwinter, armed with flowers,
drive out that ancient frost-haired nightmare from the ground
that liberty might braid her hair with scented almond blossoms.

As by the flowering tree they laid the dancing girl,
in the bedecked and spacious terraces above
the slaves fetched slaughtered votive beasts and flowered wreaths
to give their monarch's wedding a high noble grace.
In their gold chambers, archons armed themselves with paints,
the ladies curved their curly hair to hook the men,
and a sweet young court maiden who had just been wed
painted the last mole on the rim of her right eyebrow.
Within the royal courtyard facing the green hill,
the laden tables of the mystic wedding steamed,
and strong winds blew until the torches' flaming hair

swelled up and dropped thick resin on the flickering earth;
a buxom goddess, her full dugs empearled with dew,
squatted with open thighs on tables heaped with food;
she, too, was overladen with flesh, like man's own soul.
All the surrounding dry thorn-fence had bloomed that day,
passionate glowworms twinkled till their downy bellies,
brimming with blue-green flame, allured in the warm darkness.
In the great heat and the full moon, on desolate shores,
a young girl stripped by the sea's edge, and soft waves sighed,
and hairy salt-flaked demons pressed to gape and stare.
A young man, singing on the road to his betrothed,
suddenly stopped with anguish as in the full moon
he glimpsed the lonely almond tree, the wind's betrothed.
Far off, in distant forests, under the same moon,
wild beasts slunk down to quench their thirst in drowsy pools,
and monarch lion paused with stealth to hear their breathing.
As in his clear mind's crooked lanes he saw the tracks
of roe deer, wildcat, leopard, lynx, and plodding bear,
and the elephant's wide footprints sunk in rotted leaves,
his savage belly growled and at night's well-stocked table
he picked his game like a gourmand with tasteful care.
So in the palace halls the lion-minded man
stretched out his neck and watched while his strong body steamed
and slowly melted like a candle in his mind's flame.
But all at once he crouched and hid in a dark nook
for the great archons sallied through the middle doors,
led by that shepherd of great flocks, grim-visaged Death,
whose eyes were filled with loam, whose bones were painted red,
who held a small night-owl within his open hands;
he entered, bowed to right and left, but no one saw him.
Then came the captains of the seas, and on their heads
they wore tall azure plumes that swayed in air like masts;
their nostrils and damp armpits swarmed with small seed pearls,
the tiny eggs of wormy death, though still unhatched.
Then came the captains of the land with crimson plumes,
their old wounds, newly painted, grinned like a whore's lips.
They turned and bowed politely, but their drumlike bellies
grew suddenly green as though the spring grass covered them.
All kept their painted eyes fixed on the brazen doors,
and then the king appeared, a golden, cunning ape
with a long peacock train borne by four naked pages.
Death gestured with his hands and bade the king thrice welcome.
Behind came bath attendants, dream interpreters,
perfumers, lewd court jesters, eunuchs, buxom boys,
and at the train's long end the eyes of Orpheus gleamed.
Although the lion growled, still the fleet roe deer came,

their eyes filled with fresh waters and their heads with grass.
Only the lingering piper in the darkness smelled
the lion's odor, and his rabbit eyes twitched everywhere
but could not find the savage tracks, and scurried on.
Sitting on his high throne, the king smiled on his lords
and ordered the locked women's doors to be thrown open.
Like haughty frigates with sails billowing in strong winds,
bare-breasted, newly washed, the court dames swaggered in;
their rigging stretched and creaked, their sails were puffed with pride,
and as the flickering torchlight fell on their bare breasts
they shone like white-capped waves in the dawn's rosy light.
They dipped and swerved and scudded in the sea-drenched air
with merchandise of rich perfumes, and their holds brimmed
with kisses, cooling laughter, birds, and large-eyed nights
till Death, with pity, opened wide his harboring arms.
As the archer watched and stroked them all, bid all farewell,
his heart leapt like a lion's tongue and licked the earth:
"Farewell, O thick grape clusters, hair of blue musk-grapes!
Farewell, rich vines, for now the harvester has come!"
But all at once he seized a column and held tight,
for he saw moon-browed Helen swaying like a swan,
her pregnant form upheld by her old nurses gently,
her holy belly swollen, a mature ant-mother
who packed unnumbered swarms within her egg-filled loins.
Her apple cheeks had sunken, her eyes had grown huge,
her pale hands rested on her fruitful belly's prize
as, drowned in a sweet dream, she smiled on all from far.
Idomeneus rose, then grasped her supple wrist,
and full of pride and joy enthroned her by his side,
rejoiced to feel his son had formed in her firm womb.
But the all-knowing archer smiled, for he recalled
that a blond male ant grafted those notorious thighs
and planted a blond swarm deep in that ready womb.
Raising his hands, the king then prayed to his plump goddess:
"Mother of wheat and brain, O double dug of earth,
thrice welcome to our tables, bless our holy food,
let bread rise to our heads and be transformed to brain,
let meat sink in our loins and turn to a strong fortress,
let sweet wine tighten round our hearts like a red ribbon,
for mind, that keeper of keys, unlocks the holy flesh.
Welcome, O lords and ladies, to our wedding feast this night."

In gardens, night blooms opened in a honeyed hour,
stars gamboled in the sky and stealthily stooped down
to see how nobles eat on earth, how ladies laugh.
All lanterns were put out as ships approached the town

and swiftly leapt from wave to wave; all rowed in silence,
until at length the harbor light-towers came to view.
The workers pressed in gangways and perked up their ears,
slaves bound their heads with kerchiefs, massed their children close,
stretched out their scrawny necks and held their doors ajar,
but revelry and laughter rang above them still,
and an old crone, to keep her dear grandsons awake,
embellished ancient legends and created kings:
"My children, once upon a time a great king reigned . . ."
Just then Idomeneus raised his startled head,
for his gold winecup clattered from his frozen lips;
he leapt in haste, thrust to one side his Negro slaves
then slowly slid on tiptoe to a darkened column.
His eyes were filled with holocausts and secret signs,
and stretching out his hand, he slowly groped the column
with moist blind palms, as though his fingertips could read,
and fumbled on dark heads and eyes, on flames and crows,
and on a sea-god who crouched low and aimed his darts.
The old king shook and stumbled, dark froth edged his lips,
for his gold sandals had now touched the archer's heels.
Then Orpheus snatched a flute and played a rousing song
to turn aside the burdened soul of his tranced lord,
but he raised high his golden staff with rage, and struck,
till flute and piper's teeth rolled on the wine-drenched tiles.
Thick shadows swooped on the numb king, black lofty wings
darkened his mind, passed on, and others plunged behind,
as though black vessels sailed upon his darkened features.
It might have been the pirate sails that moored in secret
which struck his soul, it might have been brave Captain Clam's
dark shadow which that moment slowly stepped beyond
the great sea-gates that sealed the sea-king's famous fleet.
As Captain Clam slid stealthily with tranquil heart
and held the tools of conflagration tight, he thought
of his far wife and grandson, sighed with grief, but when
he heard near footsteps, wife and grandson fled at once,
and he crouched low against the wall and cocked his ears.
The old king stretched his neck and listened, filled with fear,
but his drunk archons mocked him with suppressed disdain,
and the curled ladies swayed amid a cooling breeze
with joy, as though they waved and played with distant lovers.
Midnight; the torches had burnt low with spluttering sound,
new shadows smothered everywhere, the warm air tingled,
and Helen's white and swanlike throat grew suddenly dark.
Slowly the death-condemned embellishments, the cups,
gold rings and frescoed walls, broke into wild lament,
and the stout columns quaked and tilted with great fear:

"Alas, a flame and two black eyes flare up on earth,
alas, if we could sprout wide wings and soar through air!"
An agile god of cedar wood, bound with coarse ropes
to a black column's shaft that he might not escape,
heard the shrill cries, strained at his cords with all his strength,
but the poor wretch could not break through the cramping nets.
A nightmare swooped into a pale canary's sleep
until it shrieked and woke with terror, flapped its wings
and pecked the bars of its gold gate with mounting dread.
A golden goblet with embossed wood-nymphs took wing
and fled from the numb fingers of its drunken lord,
but slavehands caught it quickly and returned it safe.
A snow-white feather swayed high on a fragrant head
and cried to the clear air to swoop and sweep it off
because a thin smoke rose, dear God, and it would choke!
It squirmed to flee the scented hair, swayed like a torch
with gallantry in peril, flapped with swelling joy
because it needed but one single gust to set it free,
but languidly a small white hand reached up and pinned it down.

Dear God, the snares of fate are made with faultless skill,
not one small wire snaps, not even one hinge rusts,
nor has fate need for bait with which to lure us on;
the rats are better off a hundred thousand times
that lick at least—how fortunate!—a crust of cheese.
In vain did souled and soulless creatures cry for help,
even hope at last was lost, all huddled in hushed dread,
for in the court there suddenly loomed, and blocked all doors
and roads, the flame-clawed incompassionate hounds of fate:
broad-buttocked Kentaur with an iron sword well hid,
mute Rocky with a red belt lashed about his head,
and reed-slim Granite by a doorpost hidden well
that his proud bearing might not scare the feasting lords.
The king's eyes glazed, and his mind split like a cracked jug:
"More torches! Light the courts!" he yelled, gasping for breath,
and as the hot flames lit their red and roistering flesh
the devious man grasped secretly his murderous heart:
"Brute forebear, clutch the columns firmly now, don't quake!"
He cried, then turned with calm; beside him, knee to knee,
his hungry god perched like a vulture and crouched close.
Then the man-slayer leapt and boldly drew his sword,
but his invisible god reached out, grabbed his red belt
and like a wineskin dashed him at the column's base
till the mute archer crouched beside his master's heels.
Hearing the tumult at the shadowed plinth, the king
stooped close, then stumbled back, for two still serpent-eyes

flashed in the dark and lured him helplessly toward earth.
He shrieked, like a small bird by vipers hypnotized,
and the man-killer turned and asked his crouching guide
whether the time had come to drop his sea-cap, raise his sword,
or to be patient still till laggard fate should come.
The Invisible arched his brows, and the killer understood,
jumped up, cried out to Orpheus to select a flute
and follow with a tune whatever song he sang.
The king sat on his throne, the senile skippers laughed,
and as Odysseus came and stood, tall as a column,
the sensual ladies of the court, the plump old dames,
turned toward him with coquetting eyes and pulsing hearts,
but arch-eyed Helen thrust her face behind her fan
and thought: "The time has come, his eyes are full of flame!"
then placed her hand on her full womb to guard her child.
His harsh voice like a vulture's struck and shook the walls:
"Eat, eat and drink my lords, and I shall sing a song;
I've roamed the earth, both East and West—may it be cursed!—
but still my heart has not been slaked, nor all the holes
of my hard head: eyes, nostrils, ears, and bottomless mouth.
Dear God, I've trudged the whole earth, knocked on every door,
slunk through unnumbered thresholds like a snarling cur
and crouched with every housedog under laden tables.
I've played the tumbling fool and joked that very hour
when my heart bit its brazen chains or barked in vain;
I've crossed my hands upon my chest, bowed low and said:
'King, may your reign and kingdom strike eternal roots!'
At the same time my hand dashed from my savage heart
and struck his palace columns and his lofty walls!
Lads, I can't sit much longer on the stone of patience,
for there's no greater virtue on all earth than fire!
Eat, eat and drink my lords! . . ." his voice choked suddenly,
his song hung hovering in the air, his laugh rang out
and clattered through the royal courts like tumbling stones,
for Hardihood loomed in the door and gave the sign!
A panting messenger ran up, knelt down and cried:
"Alas, great king, your arsenals have burst in flames!"
The skippers groaned, lurched up and tripped on drunken feet,
for they saw wildfire leap afar, the sparkling flames,
and as they wondered what to do or where to go,
the old king grasped his head between his shriveled hands,
groaned like a bull, for a bright flash swept through his brain,
and he turned quickly round and screamed with fright: "Odysseus!"
for he divined what dread hand rose in the thick smoke.
Then the swift archer gave the signal, cast his cap,
and as he sped there rose with him his tall, invisible god.

First Granite rushed with speed, seized all the blazing brands
and thrust them, flame-down, on the tiles to blot them out;
Kentaur, too, seized and thrust all lamps beneath his arms
and from the terrace slung them swiftly toward the river.
The drunken archons scattered toward the doors in fear
and shrieked as with one voice, the court dames swooned,
and the mute Negroes circled round their king like towers.
The unmerciful killer in the thickening darkness raised
the iron sword of slaughter, leapt upon the tables
and called on his old comrade, Death, to come and join them,
and Death at once leapt up, pitch-blind and iron-bearded.
O night, hear how your starry slippers strike the tiles!
Dust rose on the king's highways, heavy tread of feet,
until night stank with sweating armpits and bearskins
as the blond-haired barbarians rushed the castle gates.
Meanwhile bold Hardihood among the Negroes slashed
and cut a road through black flesh toward the cowering king,
but as he hacked and yelled, a monstrous Negro swerved
and leveled fiercely at his head with his bronze sword;
blood spurted like a crimson spring from his cracked skull
and spilled about his temples like a regal crown.
The Negro sentry snickered, but as he rolled his eyes
and raised to strike again, Rocky forestalled him, thrust
his long sword through his belly till his entrails spilled,
slimy and green, and slithered on the courtyard tiles.
The king fell on his knees in terror as there loomed
above him the tall sea-cap and the sea-drenched head,
but when the pitiless killer seized his shriveled nape
and raised him high with one hand, like a shivering dog,
Phida dashed up in time and grasped that dreaded arm:
"Man-killer, stop! This old man is my rightful share!"
As both fought for the king, an ax broke down the door,
and a large strapping man seized Helen with a great roar
and vanished, striding swiftly through the blood-drenched tables.
The archons dashed to flee through the wide-splintered door,
pursued by the enraged archer, while his comrades seized
torches and sowed flame-seeds throughout the women's rooms
as babies smothered in their cradles and young girls
clawed at their cheeks and shrieked to their Bull-God in vain.
The Rebels seized the stairs, clacked with their heavy clogs,
smashed all the storage jars, climbed to the upper floors,
piled high all silken pillows, golden robes, then shrieked
and thrust their torches in the heaps to feed the flames.
Groan after groan resounded, harsh and thin cries merged
with women's shrill lament and groans of murdered men.
The shivering king had run and clasped his Bull-God's neck,

thrust his despairing head between the towering horns
and hung there like a helpless votive beast for slaughter.
A woman's arms and double-ax flashed in the torch glare,
and Phida rose up frothing: on her breast and throat
her father's brains, warm, thick, and sticky, streamed in blood.
She opened her mouth wide to yell with frantic joy
but a tall Negro lunged full-bodied with a long lance
and pierced her through the back and entrails, thrusting past,
and as she fell, she clutched her father's bloody corpse.

Her green eyes fluttered swiftly twice or thrice, then glazed,
her mouth gaped open, bleating, then her jaws hung loose
and retched up all her soul in lumps of clotting blood.
When the fierce Negroes saw their slaughtered king, they froze,
and their poor useless weapons slid from their numb hands.
Yelling, the blond barbarians drenched the walls with oil;
tall tongues of swift flame rose and licked the battlements,
the heavy roof-beams cracked and buckled, the walls leaned,
all casements groaned, terraces creaked with shrilling cries,
and in the swirling smoke the plump court dames caught fire.
Then as the archer raised his eyes to admire the flames
—his slaves, his daughters—his amazed mind suddenly shook,
for through the smoke he saw a most strange fowl that spread
long novel wings and tottered in the reaching flames,
an awkward virgin-feathered bird on cliffs of air
that suddenly rose with swift momentum, creaking armor,
and calmly fled the flaming night down toward the sea.
"The old wood-carver!" the archer murmured in glad surprise.
"Good health and joy, O free mind, winged and sharp-clawed vulture!"
He waved his hands to wish the strange man-bird good speed,
but suddenly cast his flaming eyes down toward the town,
for highroads shook with uproar of tumultuous crowds;
quickly he told the bronzesmith to cut off the king's
pale head and plant it upright in the city square
enzoned by seven pirates bearing blazing torches.
"My friend, I've never taken back my word, I keep my vows;
this first land which we've reached I place as a bright crown
on your rough shaggy head; take care, don't let it throw you!"
He spoke, then grabbed the bloodstained hair of his old friend
and rubbed him like the upper grindstone of a handmill,
and the dark smith rejoiced as though he felt all Crete
perch on his bloody head with all her waters, towns, and beasts.

Day broke; the Morning Star laughed in the smoke-filled sky,
day stepped with her white feet upon the mountain peaks
and trembled, for smoke covered all her flaming cheeks.
The twisting palace creaked and kicked in roaring flames,
a blazing pine tree heaved a sigh and crashed in ruins,
and from the lofty mountain tops the vultures swooped,
mute, heavy-winged, as the archer raised his hands and yelled:
"Welcome, O guides and muleteers, carters of corpses,
be careful with your claws, no wineskins or fat sacks
of flour lie strewn here, but the regal heads of kings!"
Fresh, like a plump round boy, the sun leapt in the sky,
seized the white mountain summits till they turned rose-red,
spread out his fat small hands on grassy pasture lands,

found olive trees and fondled them, filled thorns with flowers,
then slowly groped until he found the plundered castle
and like a babe sucked at the conflagration's nipples.
Fed by the South Wind, flames devoured the palace walls;
that night the dogs and crows had their full share of meat,
the vultures stuffed themselves like cows and chewed their cud,
the flames collected their sharp tongues amid the stones
and calmed down till the comrades' raging entrails too
felt their own fires slowly dying and growing serene.
Man's sweetness tamed once more his rash improvident brain;
some in their hunger roasted lamb on the palace embers,
some with the court dames kissed on the still smoldering ashes;
body and brain got drunk, only the castle-wrecker
scorned to surrender his firm soul to headstrong joy
but like a lion climbed a salient rock, stretched out,
and with unsated eyes swept the whole town below.
The bloodstained sunset dyed all homes with crimson rays,
all doors were bolted hurriedly in narrow lanes,
and quivering bodies ran like ants on cobbled stones.
Silent, the castle-wrecker hung his head far down
the crag, and then his heavy jaw broke in a grin;
his eyes flashed fire until he felt his mind made one
with the hard walls of his burnt skull and burst in flame,
a lime-kiln where whole cities sank like kindling wood.
He sat down cross-legged then and spoke to his calm mind
as two old friends will talk astride their ambling steeds:
"Dear friend, I think we've earned our wages well today;
I marveled how you chose amid those craven mortals
and slew them calmly with no wrath or false compassion;
now here unstained with blood you came as from a wedding
and shone!—by God, it seems to me you even sang!"
His vulturous mind then laughed and croaked in a harsh voice:
"Your hands, ears, eyes, and nostrils shoot like a good archer
straight to the bull's eye of the flesh—how can I flee them?
It's true, I sang with joy an ancient rousing song:
'Dear God, if only earth had stairs, if sky had rings!
If I could climb those stairs and grasp those iron rings
I'd kick the earth away and shake the sky with quakes!' "
Although the castle-wrecker's heart with pity shook,
he gave no sign but challenged his bold mind with calm:
"You fool, don't think you'll make me sweat with your old threats!
Like it or not, I'll follow you, I'll push even further!"
But his mind laughed, then like a hedgehog spiked with grapes
from rolling in a vineyard, coiled in the archer's skull.
A youth from far spied him convulsed, crouched on the crag
like a young maid in childbirth, and with pity cried:

"Look, brothers, see, his bloodstained thoughts have not yet calmed!
I can't make out his features, yet I feel a heat-haze
sizzling about his temples like the sun's corona.
I fear his mind's grown wild and bristles with sharp thorns."
But his friends curled their glutted lips with cunning craft:
"Brother, how can the wildfire in his roused heart die
since after so much blood he's not yet kissed a woman?"
They spoke, then rounded up five crisp young girls, and drove
toward their great leader that the male in him might cool,
but he frowned wrathfully, until the young men roped
the girls like gaudy partridges and slowly went away.
In the sun's afterglow, Odysseus glimpsed the girls
like fuzzy peaches through the trees, and growled to think
how many times he'd shamed his mind with suchlike fruit.
His mind now barked beyond such women and such joys.
"Ah, Captain Clam," he moaned, "we never shall meet again;
all that we've said or done together, all that we've planned,
our tears, our joys, I clasp now to my chest like coals."
He suddenly saw in smoke, upon the highway's mound,
stooped messengers ascending slowly toward the castle,
then stretched on the tall crag and held them in his eyes.
Two young men trudged before and six old men behind,
barefooted, weaponless, roped tightly like low slaves.
"They've come to beg for mercy," mumbled the man-killer,
"hoping with tears and gifts of gold to touch my heart.
My gypsy heart may grow serene or spurt with flames
and finish off with scorn what wrath has left undone.
O lion-heart, I set you free, do what you want!"
They came within a stone's throw of the crag, then stopped
with hanging tongues, as though they sniffed a lion's stench.
The youths held disks of gold, the old men bread and salt,
and their bold leader held a bronze bare-breasted goddess
with a thick rope of rush wound thrice about her neck.
But as they walked in single file along the road
Odysseus sprang on his high rock and yelled out, "Eh!"
At once they hurriedly took to heel, scattered in fright,
then looking everywhere on high and seeing no one,
slowly took courage, gathered, and approached once more,
and the sly archer calmed his features and crouched low.
They laid their votive gifts on the earth, then raised their hands:
"If you are evil spirits, we'll slay five slaves for you,
our best and plump ones, that your bellies may eat well;
if you are good souls, then we'll sacrifice for you
frankincense, psalms, clean entrails, and good works;
but if you're men like us, here's women, wine, and bread."
The archer laughed, then to the messengers stretched his hands:

"Your jaws are chattering so, I can't tell what you're saying!
Glory to God, I'm not a spirit, but only flesh,
I'm made of thick brains and strong bones, and walk the earth!
Speak straight and clear! I only hear that manly prayer
which like a huge fist breaks my head against the stones."
A thin-haired elder fell then on his knees and cried:
"Here are the city keys, they're yours! Here's bread and salt
and our sweet goddess that you've roped with a slave's noose.
All these are yours, O master! Take them! Our souls are yours!
We ask but one thing only from your dread palms: Peace!"
Their backs broke out in sweat as the archer mocked in scorn:
"I'm not a god of comfort, friendship, or good cheer,
I hold no meat pot or winecup to cheer your hearts.
Who holds a sword is tempted, who has youth must play,
he who does not fear death on earth does not fear God.
Eh, ancient archon, stop your crying, don't lick my feet!
Peace is the daily food with which our holds brim over,
the stench of home, of honor, life, of farms and vineyards . . .
Oho! You make me sick! Pounce on them, leopard soul!"
The heralds heard his cry and scurried down the stones
and as they turned to look back, their eyes blinked with fear;
the old men saw a tall flame flickering on the crag
and the young men saw Death, barefooted, clothed in blazing light.

Odysseus burst out laughing, sat cross-legged again
with joyous and light heart, his tense throat now unlocked,
but suddenly felt deep hunger, clapped his hands with joy
and yelled out, laughing, for a loaf of dark wheat bread.
His friends were roasting lamb on the hot palace coals
and the sweet-blooded Holy Harlots with bare breasts
already had forgotten the pale palace youths.
Virginity blooms anew and new embracements open!
Three-deep, the Holy Harlots began their snaky dance
on the warm tiles that warped like dry leaves in the blaze,
and cackling Kentaur took the lead, waving a wineskin,
while at the tail-end stumbled the smoked, drunken piper,
a striped cat that had singed his fur close to the hearth.
But the musk-nourished dames, with torn disheveled hair,
hung stooped with fear on the blond strangers' hairy thighs,
and their tears mingled with their thick cosmetic paints.
Rocky leapt up, for he had heard his master's cry,
grabbed a huge chunk of bread, strode through the burning ruins,
laid it with care by his unmoving master's knees
then turned and left him to his wild seclusion there.
Odysseus turned his ears toward the far sea and heard
the tramp of myriad feet on harbor streets, storm clouds

of screeching maids and children thronged on crowded wharves
with their hands stretched to flee on the dark desolate waves,
and his mind gaped, unslaked, to hold their vast lament.
Feeling his hunger pangs, he reached his hand to eat,
but all at once his open fingers froze in air,
for a huge locust with taut feelers, fully armed,
had sunk his thorny feet deep in the bread's hard crust
and glared at the archer wrathfully with crystal eyes.
Then the man-killer felt his knee-joints snap with fear,
and gliding slowly off the rock, he crouched on earth.
The locust in the dim dusk seemed like a green Death
that swooped to take possession on his crust of bread.
"The bread's all yours! Devour it, take it, I don't want it!"
the archer yelled, then looked about him, light of heart.
For the first time he had felt fear, though seen by none.
Leaning his head on earth like stone, all unawares,
he fell asleep, and a dream swooped on his dazed mind:
It seemed he tightly grasped a black and shaggy flower,
a beast, an octopus that spread its tentacles
on fist, on fingers, then ascended slowly upward
and ravenously ate his hairy arm, dark flesh and bone.
"The Spirit!" he cried in terror, "the Spirit"; then leapt with fear,
and his right hand hung down his numb side, paralyzed.
He smiled, and knew that Death had beckoned him from far
and sent him as a gift that dark flesh-hungry flower.
"This scorpion, this black heavy flower suits me fine
to hang above my ear when the world sings my deeds!
Ah, good housekeeper Death, you think that my ant-mind
had sprouted wings with pride when this great castle fell
and send me this black messenger to keep me humble.
Ah, black mole, I too send a crow for messenger,
and a long letter, burnt in each of its four corners.
Death, castles do not fool me nor does plunder shake me,
my mind is firmly in the saddle and won't fall;
I've thrown the castle behind me now, and drive straight on!"
He spoke, then laughed as by coincidence he saw
at the same moment a black crow fly toward the south,
the messenger, you'd say, who seized his letter and flew on.
He shook his arm to make the blood flow in his veins,
then turned to find his friends, to touch mankind once more,
to eat bread, take a sip of wine, make his mind human again.

His friends had eaten, danced, and kissed, and now they lay
at ease to hear a ragged blond bard sing a song
accompanied by a horse-skull lyre hung with bells.
All demons of the earth and sea adorned its rim

and from its chords the blood of slaughter dripped, still warm.
The archer first seized bread and meat, began to crunch
his food like a wild bull to give his body strength,
then stretched out and rejoiced to feel the jolting song:
"Don't make too much of it, my lads, don't overboast
because you've spitted one poor castle like a quail
and think that you've subdued already man's proud heart.
Tigers have piled tall castles of bone, then stretched inside
like landlords, glutted to their ears with prey, while high
on the bone-towers both blond and black hair flapped in the wind.
The sea, too, has her calm, and though she spreads her arms
around earth's shores, they hold her, and she plays with sand;
even the swelling fire calms down when it has eaten;
but the heart of a strong man, my lads, can find no comfort.
A secret kiss can't tame it, wine can't make it drunk,
nor can a god fragment it with his lightning bolts,
for always it holds its tail erect and whips the earth.
Death looks upon it and his green eyes pop with fear,
he lifts his foot and stamps it deep in the damp earth,
but it pokes through the ground again and rears its neck.
It's not a snake to be attracted by sweet tunes,
for it's the heart that leaps on loam and strolls on cliffs,
then crouches, huddled deep in mankind's breast, and eats.
When God made earth's foundations and spread out the seas
and blew and raised the winds till the world came and went,
he called all living things. They came before him, trembling—
fish, birds, and savage beasts—and the Creator said:
'Ah, my brave gallants, I've shaped the upper world at last,
I've armed it with roofs, doors and roots, I've planted groves,
I've taken mud, and with my breath shaped mortal forms,
but now I've washed and sit enthroned to admire my work.
O slaves, your daily wage begins—before you scatter,
stop quaking, and bow low to my world-shaping hands!'
The tigers stooped and licked his knees, the eagles closed
their wings and sang like water blackbirds at his feet,
and elephants came and rolled and jigged like fat court jesters,
all creatures proffered him their grace with flattering wiles:
wings, furs, bright dappled tails, birdsong, tall horns, and musk,
the while their master, chuckling, sat and preened in sun.
Oho, my lads, how shameful this great world would be
if in that hour man's heart had not jumped up with pride!
The Old Man frothed, unfrothed, stamped with his stubborn heels,
but man's heart rose up mockingly and hissed in sun:
'I'll not bow or surrender, I don't like your world!'
The Old Man swooned, and his awed slaves ran to revive him:
'Cursed be that hour when I begot you on earth, O heart!

Why don't you like my world, you crack-brained crazy fool?'
The viperish heart puffed up but held his venom back;
the time would come when he would fling it at the sky
but now he held back, spoke not, and heard out the curse.
'This is my curse, you rebel: may you sink in earth,
may you lie sleepless and never say "I've had my fill,"
and may you strike with a small hammer night and day.
Build, if you can, a new and better world yourself!'
God had created man but now he bitterly repented
and raised an earthquake, rolled his eyes, and all beasts cowered;
but the heart rooted in a manly worker's chest
and hammered away with spite and love deep in his bowels.
The dreadful battle began, my lads, hammer and anvil!
Outside our chests the Old Man growls and strikes with terror;
whatever the heart has found by day he wrecks by night,
though we build bridges, he sends storms and knocks them down,
we raise frail butterflies of freedom in our minds
and the Old Man like a huge millstone grinds them fine;
then we create, for consolation on vile earth,
with sweat and tears, our shapely daughter, pure-eyed Virtue,
but he swoops down and drowns her in her tender years.
Brothers, to arms! for a great darkness chokes the earth;
I say that day will dawn—would I were still alive—
when both our gods—without, within—shall come to grips!
And then, my lads, joy to that man who'll still be here
to throw his cap high in the flaming air and give the signal!"

The man of seven souls leapt in the star-haired night
to hear the sounding minstrel call him secretly—
his inner God, too, called, and in a heavy shade
held two black frothing horses for an early start.
Earth shrank, and the man-slayer rose and longed to flee,
his eyes were crystal magic, and the cranes of fate
flew slowly by with dappled birds astride their wings.
"Rise, coward, for life flows on; rise up, the road is long!"
Thus raged the heart, and sharply spoke to the sated men:
"Dear friends, you've had your fill of food and kisses now;
great is that joy which treads upon a crumbled castle
and roasts it like a partridge on the hearth of freedom,
but it's a greater and more difficult good to plunge
to the near shore once more and hear the oars of flight
beat foaming in your mind like two enormous wings.
Rise up, man's heart, that the whole world may rise with you!"
Broad-buttocked Kentaur shook and tossed his wine-soaked head,
Orpheus heard the winds of freedom blow straight through
his flute and fill it and his hollow bones to bursting,

and the two mountain comrades raised their craggy heads.
Flames, wine, and heady kisses were sucked deeply down
in the dry well of memory, as all four drew close,
lighthearted, to the archer's loudly throbbing sea-breast;
Hardihood only squatted on the stones, unmoving.
Then the quick-tempered solitary raised his voice:
"Rise up, O bronzesmith, it's high time to rule your land.
Gird on the heavy keys of earth, like a good landlord,
wring your mind dry, confine with laws the unjust and just,
build stone walls round desires and fence all longings tight,
hew out broad virgin roads, my brother, that deeds may march.
The stubble of earth's been scorched, the land's been plowed with knives
and now awaits new seed to burst with flower and fruit!"
Hardihood leapt to his feet, and his blood-splattered head,
bound with tight thongs and hacked with wounds, now throbbed with rage:
"My friend, don't think I've overeaten and blotched my mind;
when you like a coiled snake digested king and castle,
I sent throughout this regal isle both horse and heralds
until the steeds with bleeding hooves spread the great news
that the king's tribe was rooted out, and a new god
and master planted in the fertile soil of Crete.
I'm not a dry leaf fluttering now in autumn's arms
but a great oak rooted in earth; no one can shake me!
Great spirit, the earth can't hold you, and all houses fear you,
you've done all you've set out to do, you've quenched your fires,
it's time you set sail now that the whole world may breathe!"
Odysseus' mind grew wings to watch bold Hardihood
wrench free from him at last and cut untrodden roads;
his seed had borne fruit in his friend, and he rejoiced
like God, who shaped the beasts and loosed them on the world.
Laughing, he touched his bosom-brother's broken head,
and as a lioness licks her cub with her rough tongue
when from her womb it drops with curly bloodstained fur,
so did the castle-wrecker caress his lion-child.
The bronzesmith's heart rejoiced, with the rude fondling soothed,
and all pressed close to see how two such savage beasts
caressed and said goodbye in sad departure's hour.
When he had wrapped his comrade's head with loving care,
the archer raised his hands as though to bless all men:
"May even this day be blessed in its entirety, friends.
Our wages were most bloody, but in our fists we hold
endeavor's strong reward: the ashes of dread injustice.
Alas for him who seeks salvation in good only!
Balanced on God's strong shoulders, Good and Evil flap
together like two mighty wings and lift him high.
The sweetest fruit of all that ripened on this day

is that one soul has found its freedom and cast me off!
But dusk has fallen; it's time we set night sentries round
so that our souls may stretch on earth and rest in sleep,
then at dawn, bronzesmith, O new mighty lord, come down
to the wild shore with your iron crown and see me off!"
He spoke, some stretched on the warm fields of spring to sleep,
the comrades lay, relieved, on the warped courtyard tiles
till dreams like gentle rivers came and drowned their minds.
But the much-suffering man lay in their midst unsleeping,
and all night long his brooding eyes flashed like the stars;
his mind, the unmoving North Star, stared in vigil all night long.

God dawned, the North Wind blew, thick clouds of dust rose high;
in the funereal courtyard, stretched in the pale sun,
two athletes lay, Phida and Captain Clam, that fearful pair.
The crowd pressed thickly round to say goodbye to both
great martyrs of high spirit before they were resigned
to hungry earth, that mute and fertile mother-worm.
The lone man stooped, gazed on his friend, a shriveled coal,
and blinked his lashes quickly to hold back his tears.
"Sit still a moment, friends; don't speak, let's see who's left us.
The better man has gone, the best, the master boatman,
our central mast has gone, my lads, our gold-flamed banner.
I thought to dance on your smooth gravestone, Captain Clam,
to order hautboys and nine pairs of lyres to play
and nine blind bards to sing in praise of the world's beauty,
but now, dear friend, the plan's gone crooked, the world's grown dark,
I don't want lyres or hautboys, no tune suits me now,
my pain drips in my heart like poison and eats me whole!"
The slayer's eyes welled up with tears, and his voice broke.
Hardihood threw on Captain Clam a handful of earth
and placed in Phida's arms a heavy pomegranate,
ordered a grave of double girth dug in the court
that both might sink to Hades like a loving pair,
then turned with arrogant eyes and faced his tearstained master:
"Why do you moan the dead? It's not for the first time
you've seen how gluttonous earth gapes wide and gulps us whole.
Yes, Captain Clam is dead, but with no further weeping
let's thrust his embers deep in loam like kindling wood
so that earth's black and spluttering hearth may blaze anew;
don't wait for the dead to bring you other aid or good."
But the much-suffering man abruptly answered back:
"The man of worth, O Hardihood, must still resist,
denying Death in death, his soul gripped in his teeth.
Nor like a woman do I weep my dead and beat the tomb
with stupid hope that he will rise, but it's my duty,

I think, to cast my unsubdued cry deep in earth
so the dark powers may learn that I defy their laws!"
Broad-buttocks burst in mocking laughter and hit back:
"These dark powers, as you call them, have no ears to hear us!"
Odysseus was rejoiced to see that even Kentaur
could hit back hard and twist from out his heavy yoke,
for they had eaten their leader's lion brains, and now
he marveled how they reared their heads round Captain Clam.
But still his eagle spirit with its sharp claws seized
their heads and fiercely dug into their hardened skulls:
"But we, O blockhead, with dogged spite and armored love
shall force those deaf dark powers to grow ears and hear us!
I know that God is earless, eyeless, and heartless too,
a brainless Dragon Worm that crawls on earth and hopes
in anguish and in secret that we'll give him soul,
for then he, too, may sprout ears, eyes, to match his growth,
but God is clay in my ten fingers, and I mold him!"
He spoke, and his ten fingers shaped the empty air.
The flame-swayed man still played his fingers in the light
when suddenly, like a flowering almond tree that decked
the earth, Helen appeared with pregnant heavy womb.
Her breasts, that bore both fruit and flower, glowed in sun,
behind her walked her blond-haired groom, hushed and subdued,
and when the archer saw them, his heart groaned with pain,
but calmly he continued his great thought, and said:
"Just as at night we search the yard when vipers fall,
and all our fingers flame and burn to find a knife,
so do I also grope in darkness to find my God.
For God is not a phantom formed by fear or hope
but the heart's only child, born of despair and courage."
From his great passion his head dripped with sweat, and when
he tired of shaping and unshaping the empty air,
he turned and seized the bronzesmith's head in both his hands
then loosed on its tall crown his flaming thought and power,
and the new king stood still and brimmed with brain and fire.
Slowly the archer unloosed his claws from that rude head:
"Bronzesmith, before I go, I'll give you my last counsel:
a crown is heavy and may crack a human skull,
so listen to my counsel and open your head wide:
When, Hardihood, you walk among your people, keep
to right and left two dreaded lions: force and patience;
govern your people, that dark beast, with merciless love;
portion the land with justice, free the slaves forever,
give virtue, power, and wealth a new virginity;
don't grow too proud or think to swallow the whole world;
accept the greatest good and say: 'It's not enough!'

and say to all of earth's disasters: 'I want still more!'
because a true man's heart will never say: 'Enough!' "
Then Hardihood grew bolder still and dared reply:
"On God's first castle gate a mute sign signals: 'Dare!'
and on God's second gate it reads: 'Dare once again!'
but on his last most secret gate God growls: 'No further!' "
The fierce abductor mocked and laughed, then shrugged and said:
"Who has not passed through the third gate has passed through none!"
He turned then to his comrades and his voice rang out:
"Men, Hardihood has settled on man's safe frontiers.
Here he surveys farms, vineyards, homes, and finds all his;
he looks on fire and drought and war, and quakes with fear.
Ah, king, here is my final and most daring word:
if the soul falls once more to belly, and your slaves
begin to groan, your lords to roister and carouse,
I'll swoop on this rich land to loot and kill again!"
He spoke, then slowly lowered in the gaping pit
his friend's burnt corpse, fearing that it might break in two,
and Phida's weeping Rebels raised her shattered form
and laid it like a sword by Captain Clam's right side.
They poured wine in the grave, and wedged a golden ship
in Captain Clam's tight fist that he might go to Hades
a skipper still, and at the maiden's feet they placed
close by her pomegranate, as a gift for Charon,
her father's head, then cast black earth, covered the grave,
and the much-suffering man stamped the ground smoothly down
with patience, like a brooding hen that sweeps the earth
with her fine wings, then lays her eggs and squats to hatch them.

When he had placed both warriors in the ruthless pit
Odysseus turned and gripped his crew in his sharp glance:
"Forward, my lads, our wages now in Crete have ended.
We're workers, lads, in God's wide vineyards, and a new
bright sun ascends, a new and better wage begins."
He spoke, then slowly cast a farewell glance about him:
his eyes would never see again these men and mountains,
the rivers and great sweetness of this noble land;
he'd passed by, cast a stone behind him, and the echo
rang in his mind like pebbles pitched down bottomless wells.
But as his piercing eyes in silence bid farewell,
his glance hung fondly once again on arch-eyed Helen
who stood beside her blond-haired man, drugged with desire,
like the moist earth that steams when the sun falls upon her.
"Helen!" he cried, and one of all his full hearts broke.
The indulgent lady raised her eyes then lazily,
half-smiled and said, "Farewell," and closed her lids again.

Stretching his arms toward sun-drenched Helen, the archer spoke:
"May God who plays with the earth and merges man and maid
grant you a son to balance well those two vast wings
that cut through mankind's boundaries with a double power:
the intoxicated barbarous heart, and the upright mind
that with clear head reins back upon the verge of chaos.
Helen, belovèd face of earth, these eyes of mine
shall never see you more, nor these rude hands caress you;
on my mind's peak you rose like glittering foam, and vanished."
He spoke, then turned his face, not to reveal his tears,
but the fruit-burdened lady only smiled and raised
her heavy hands from her full womb and waved farewell.
"The soul is also meat, it sticks, and won't unglue,"
thus thought the warrior, groaning, then he stopped awhile
to taste with bitterness how living men must part.
When he had drunk all bitterness, his mind grew calm,
and when he'd had his fill of farewells, he plunged down
the glen along the harbor road, nor once looked back.
The lean legs of the piper pigeon-toed ahead;
behind him, stumbling, panting, scattering dust and stones,
lunged his friend's splayfoot bulk, walking on air, dead-drunk;
clasped arm in arm, the two hill friends stepped briskly on;
and last, with cap askew, a screech-owl to his right,
the archer lunged down toward the sea and his mind pulsed
like a tall wave that rushed to merge with foam-flecked billows.
Diktena waited by the wharf on a huge rock,
her body shone in wind and burned in the hot sun,
and as the world-seducer raised his eyes and looked,
he thought he saw a siren singing by the bay
with upright tail, with female breasts and laughing nipples
that slowly swelled and dripped on waves their salty dew.
The suffering man smiled bitterly and his heart throbbed,
for in the twisting seashores of his mind there passed
like lightning those bright poisonous bodies with sweet cries
that lured ships slowly, sweetly to their bosoms' cleft,
the shores about them gleaming with bleached bones of men.
"Bind me with tight cords, lads, about the mizzenmast,
that I may hear their luring song yet have no fear
I might forget in dizzy kisses and sweet swoons
why I was born and where my mind now longs to go!"
Thus had he groaned with fear that he might lose his soul,
but his matured mind now could never lose its way;
he waved, and Diktena leapt up with joy and dashed
like a twined squirming snake and coiled about the prow.
Odysseus smiled, and spoke then to his gathered crew:
"Some leave their bones abandoned on the sands of love,

others go on, both blind and deaf to all earth's sweetness,
and others, bound to the mast, tied to some great idea,
harvest the tasteless dregs of honey with no fear;
but we, we abduct the siren, cast her in our ships,
and swiftly sail away together and merge them all:
danger and freedom and the lovely earth's consummate sweetness."

They rigged their sails and scudded free till shores were lost,
till the sea spread once more her crystal arms with love
and like a tossing treasure beckoned to her beloved.
The boatman sank his fists deep in her emerald hair:
"Coquetting sea, I know quite well the sun will rise
one day and freeze to see you beat my body blue
like an old empty corpse, and foam about it, laughing;
but I still love you, for your savage heart, like mine,
roams and disdains to settle down or even be true.
Prows pass above your heaving thighs yet leave no trace,
their wake froths for a moment, then your wide wound heals,
you spread your thighs again and call to other prows.
Oh, teach my heart to be like you, clothe it with brine,
take it and roll it on your waves, toss it with storm,
a spume in your wide wake, foam in your whirling winds."
Their full sails swelled and creaked, and the wide sea-flung hours
passed high above them like white gulls with hastening wings.
At dusk, spreading their meals upon the dancing deck,
all five sat cross-legged round the food in a closed ring,
then beckoned Diktena to share their bread and meat,
and she, with laughter, snuggled close, a downy fawn,
and in the twilight her knees shone like double stars.
When night fell and the sea's green hair of seaweed smelled,
the stars caught fire, flamed on high like burning coals
and cast down rare reflections on the fragrant waves.
Night passed, and once again the sun laughed in his cradle,
mounted to manhood slowly, burned with noonday heat,
and as the comrades rowed and talked, rolled down with flames
to his black-kerchiefed mother in the darkling west.
Broad-buttocked Kentaur laughed and his domed bellies shook:
"Now, by the vine, have I been dreaming, or is it true
that once upon an ancient time we plundered Crete?
For when I smell my beard, I smell the stench of smoke
and both my wretched palms steam of a woman's breasts,
and so decide that I've not dreamt—but then, who knows?—
I may be dreaming that my beard and palms still stink!"
He spoke, and Crete, like the sun's mistress, spread far right,
the backbone of a huge seabeast that pierced the waves.
But on the fourth cool dawn her holy ridges vanished,

and the friends' hearts, their brains and rigging, squeaked and swayed
in the North Wind's free breathing, drenched with salty dew.
"Where are we headed?" Orpheus cried, and quaked with fear.
"We've left all islands now, our native land has vanished."
But then Odysseus tossed his cap with fervent joy:
"There goes the navel cord, lads! Cut! We're free of mother!
Farewell, O Greece, with all your small sweet joys and griefs,
white towns and hamlets, azure mountains, heather, pine.
Farewell, O balanced virtues and housekeeping cares,
and mind, guardian of fruits, who raises tall stone walls
between the vineyards of God and man and chokes our hearts.
Earth spreads out southward, lads, and the mind plucks a rose,
then hangs it down his echoing ear and bursts in song!"
He spoke, and two bright dolphins gleamed far off and chased
each other like two golden gods in play, then sank
once more in foam and plunged within their emerald caves,
and in the archer's eyes the two plump dolphins shone,
a lustrous pair, as though thoughts flashed in the mind's eye.
Diktena in the sun next day unloosed her hair,
braided, unbraided, combed it, and sang a tender song;
but neither did she keen her wretched father's death
nor weep for her fair native land now wrecked by fire.
She smelled approaching Africa on the sweet breeze,
tall palm trees sprang like cooling fountains in her mind,
thick honey-filled bananas, pulpy prickly pears,
till in the maiden's velvet eyes there swiftly flashed
a stud-descended river-god with his blue beard.
Though but a virgin not quite twelve, a promised bride,
she'd gone to grant her flower to the rutting god.
Thus did the musk-maid sing, cross-legged upon the prow,
and five rough souls fell silent and perused her song:
"Wine is a beast that butts, god is a beast that kills,
the virgin too, dear God, is a beast when her time comes.
She beats her mother with hard words, her brother too,
nor at the bed's far edge or center seems at ease:
'Dear Mother, I can't sleep; I dread my sleepless nights.
I walk in gardens, Mother, and fragrance makes me faint,
I sit at my loom, Mother, and patterns come alive
till from the circling hem sea captains file in rows
and laugh and come alive, Mother, and sit in my lap
until I cry with pain and all the neighbors hear.'
Three years ago—today the fourth year starts—I wept
at my poor loom till Father's heart was stirred with pity:
'Your breasts are hurting, child, set sail for Africa,
the male god there will work his wonders on the sands;
with his great grace and strength, my child, you'll soon get well.'

They armed a pure-white frigate with a pitch-black mast,
they sat a shaggy god astride the splitting prow
and soon one night we slid in Africa's black embrace.
'Where's the seducing god? On whose door shall I knock?'
They laved me with strong balms, they dragged me to the river,
and my bare breasts and myrrh-washed tresses steamed with scent.
And when the storks had closed their wings and the sun sank,
I stepped down God's dark staircase, roamed his garden close
until the cool mute moon rose in the misty date trees
and I crouched naked in the ancient river's beard
and held a pomegranate and bit a myrtle twig,
and my nude belly glowed in dusk like virgin woods.
I crouched and heard the feet of men crunch on the sands,
night brimmed with scent, sprawled naked by the riverside
and sighed like a ripe maiden gnawed by solitude,
and I, too, sighed and felt her deep nostalgic pain.
With heavy-lidded eyes, I leant on flowering jasmine,
a breeze blew, veiled my belly with white blooms, and still
I waited for the god to mount me in a man's shape.
Sleep seized me for a moment, though it seemed like years:
I saw a mother writhe in childbirth on hot sands;
her bowels burst, she shrieked and, with the cry, cast up
a baby girl as though it were a prickly pear.
Then rain poured down, God fell in showers on mother and child,
and the poor mother sank in mud next day, and died,
and her small orphaned daughter screamed with hunger pains.
A tigress with full aching udders heard the child
and came each dusk and suckled her, and came each noon
and combed her russet hair with her long rasping tongue.
Twelve years the tigress-daughter grew on the hot sands,
and on her twelfth she felt her woman's strength at last.
Then she looked right, and yawned, looked left and soon began
to shout in the still desert and to scream in rain:
'I am a woman now, and my breasts rise like towers,
I can't hold back my strength much longer, I want war;
I raise my weapons and march forth, let men beware!
I am a woman now, a cooling well that floods
the sands till barren earth sprouts flowers and brims with men.
I am a woman now, I conquer death with kisses!'
The young girl shouted, loosed her hair and rouged her breasts
then came toward dawn on a great city with tall towers,
with strong bull-smelling youths and opulent old men.
In the cool shadows by the castle gate she stood;
all roads beneath her feet rolled down like tumbling streams
as from her echoing throat there brimmed the sweetest song.
Guides and their beasts stood still, all strong gatekeepers gaped,

the young men seized their weapons, the rich locked their shops,
all pregnant women heard and cast their sons too soon,
but still the unruffled girl sang on with lifted throat.
At dusk they spread for her the hides of snow-white bulls,
and when the young girl whirled in dance, with flowing hair,
men's curly locks caught fire, all castles burst in flame,
and caravans stopped far off and watched the leaping blaze:
'That's neither a castle burning nor a shepherd's fire,
a maiden must have stripped her breasts for a man's sake!'
Three nights she danced and burned, but when the third sun rose,
she moaned, then shrieked and fell down dead on the white hides.
And I, too, shrieked, leapt up in fright, and my dream vanished;
but straight above me, with his curly deep-blue beard
God smiled, and his sweet lightning bolts flashed in his hands.
Ah, both my breasts caught fire, my yielding thighs gave way,
and all night long I laughed and played deep in his arms
and then at dawn I bowed to his great marble phallus,
laved it with honeyed thyme, and as a necklace hung
my double golden breastplates and my crimson girdle,
and felt God kicking in my womb like a small child.
Set sail, my lads, our God has had my maidenhead;
haul high a red sail on my vessel's mizzenmast
that my dead father may rejoice to glimpse it from afar."

Diktena laughed and stopped her undulating song,
blinked her flirtatious eyes, and then her serpent tongue
flicked from her throat gone dry, and licked her scarlet lips.
Rocky glanced fiercely at the maid crouched by the prow,
but she had coiled on the archer's knees like a sly snake.
When stars at last had twined the sky with jasmine vines,
the comrades' minds grew calm, night spread upon the waves
like an erotic feast-day until the entire crew
sank in the flowering groves of sleep and in their arms
clasped Africa as though they clasped their virgin bride.
Meanwhile the archer, whose bold mind disdained mere dreams,
took Diktena at midnight in his arms with stealth,
and she, a virgin twelve years old, unskilled in play,
trembled in the man's arms, adored him like a god
as both twined round each other's limbs with joy, and merged
like twin sweet almonds nestling in their milky husk.
At daybreak the sly man detached himself, and laughed,
then turning to his crew's lust-laden eyes, he said:
"Good waking to you, men! Now tell me of *your* dreams.
I dreamt that I held Africa in my arms all night!"
But the crew felt that on his lustful lips a kiss
still padded like a savage beast, still rose and fell

on the dark cliffs and chasms of his hairy body;
they laughed, and scratched their thorny beards with upturned palms.
A strong gale gripped them from the north, and they stopped rowing;
the sea-horizon bent like a taut bow in which their ship,
arrow of some great hero, sped like a swift swallow.
The comrades talked about a hundred topics then;
one brought to mind his native town, one old desires,
and one let loose his mind far south and tried to guess
what they would see and do in Africa's hot suns.
Wind-spinning Orpheus spun tall tales of dragon lore:
"It's said the dragons know that all their monstrous strength
hangs by a small, small hair that crowns their massive heads,
but others feed between their eyebrows a red ant
whose death would cause their dragon souls to melt away.
Old tales, yet I believe them; water, stones, and air
hold mighty secrets, but how can man's grubbing soul
see them, since all day long it pokes in earth for food?"
The wretched mudlark sighed, and the spread-eagles laughed,
but then the lone man scolded his unfeeling crew:
"Don't poke fun at the piper's words, O lame-brained fools;
I see them like the spry cock-pheasant's gaudy wings:
they fly like man's prismatic, hollow fantasies,
but brothers, when the hunter catches them and plucks them,
he'll find firm flesh to eat, strong brains to knit his soul.
I have no red ant on my brow, no dragon's hair,
but in my heart I hold a secret, and that's my strength.
Listen, dear friends, and I'll reveal that secret now."
The salt tars stretched their hungry necks, their minds gaped wide,
and then their beast-emboldened master laughed with joy:
"Remember, comrades, that in dreams our shoulders sprout
with soaring wings, our hearts swell up with monstrous strength.
Though armies of our foes spring up, we hitch our belts,
leap over plunging chasms and dash on toward the fight,
one against thousands, in a fine contempt of death,
so long as our salvation's secret flares in sleep,
for all life is a pallid dream, an airy toy."
Then the mind-archer laughed, plunged his hand in the sea,
splashed all his crew companions with the salty spray
and shot the arrow of his double glance with skill:
"All life is a brief dream: I know that I shall wake
and all my deadly dangers and provoking pains,
so soon as the black cock shall crow, will fade in air."
Mutely his comrades raised his words in their hushed minds;
like a black cloud which swiftly spreads above a field
and covers all in a cool mantle of fine mist,
thus did his words drift over them and fog their souls;

but when they woke at daybreak, strengthened by strong sleep,
then Granite frowned and hit back with a bold reply:
"Last night you shot at us your light and poisoned arrows
nor even thought, man-killer, that our knees might buckle.
If life's a toy, a dream, how shameful then to strive
and lick the quarry's shadow on the ground, like dogs.
Better to raise our hands and tear the nets which sleep
the weaver weaves, and let our souls fly off like dreams."
The archer tied the sail-ropes first, and then replied:
"I like the dream, and I for one will raise no hand,
but if you want to know who made us drunk, then hear
my words, unpeel them if you can, eat and grow strong:
Learn that it's I who serve and also drink my blood,
it's I who hang about my mind the jester's bells,
and then, ahoy, I clap my hands, cackle and jig!"
But Granite closed his mouth, and Orpheus softly spoke:
"Lads, though I know quite well that life is but a myth,
I've not the strength to serve myself and get drunk too;
a great king pours me wine and I, his fool, get drunk."
Then the fat guzzler groaned and shook the mizzenmast:
"Faugh, but I'm dizzy! All words, wings, and no red meat!
I'm hungry! It's time to spread our humble victuals now,
and if our roast is shadow, Granite, as you've just said,
by God, I'd like to know one day what real meat's like!"
He spoke, and all fell greedily on red-blooded meat,
but Diktena curled tightly round the archer's knees,
and thought they spoke of dreams with brainless male bravado.
How they forgot the kiss, the only certain good!
But she said nothing, glad to tame her hunger now,
and munched her food in silence like a newborn calf
and waited patiently for sleep's alluring hours
that she might crawl in her man's arms and drain him like a leech.

On the next day the waves began to grow light-green,
and Rocky, as he fondled the sea-meadows, thought:
"The great god of this sea must be a kingly shepherd
who drives his flocks to pasture with his crooked staff."
And the world-wanderer opened wide his mind's deep pit
and welcomed the green waters with their mud and seaweed;
as rivers silt the earth, his mind filled up with shale.
Then at long last, toward sundown, coasts shone softly rose
and beaches swarmed with life, fishing boats crossed the waves,
and slim, bronze-plated warcraft, many-storied galleys
with tiers of rowing slaves who sang a worker's song.
A blue dusk fell, then night, and in the steaming haze

prows passed with strange erotic bowsprits, hawk-nosed gods,
and huge dung-beetles bearing suns on their black backs.
Unslaked Odysseus watched all with attentive eyes:
"Comrades, the earth is endless, like the soul of man.
Open your eyes and plunder all, stuff your chests full,
I see great order, blind obedience, antheaps of men,
for other gods—half men, half beasts—rule in this land;
open your skulls, my lads, let this world enter too!"
He spoke, and their bones creaked, their savage bosoms opened,
for the new partridge-snare spread now like drunkenness,
embroidered with blue skies, strange prows, and muddy loam.
Slender white storks flew swiftly through the violet air
and in their narrow beaks black water-serpents writhed;
two red flamingos paired, then smoothly rowed and flashed
like two enraptured thoughts and sailed on toward the sun.
The archer's restless heart for a brief moment calmed
and tightly merged with the upper world in brotherhood
for earth seemed now most pure, good for the heart of man.
At length they slid with slow oars on the sandy beach.
"Welcome, dark Africa! Lay up your oars, my lads,
for night has fallen; we'll breach the river's mouth at dawn."
The archer spoke, and was the first to leap ashore.
All scattered, gathered brushwood, built a blazing fire,
then cooked a fish stew, filled their gourds with heady wine
till their brains laughed and cackled like the seething drink.
But the mind-spinner, mute, unmoving, watched the shore,
as the broad river like a blood vein coursed his mind,
then heaved a sigh and spilled his wine cup on the sands:
"We've moored, friends, by the mightiest river on all earth.
Its wellhead, like God's own, is hidden, dark, untouched;
some think it springs from the sky and falls like cataracts,
others, that earth's own entrails burst to give it birth,
others descend it from the high snow-covered mountains;
no one has seen as yet its deathless swaddling clothes.
Three men once vowed to row their life long toward the south:
white-haired grandfather, sturdy son, and downy grandson.
After ten years, the grandfather died with oars in hand,
and his son thrust him deep in earth and seized the oars;
he passed through towns, waste valleys, rains, and scorching heat,
his hands froze at the oars, his hair turned snowy white,
but still the river flowed and seemed to have no end.
Then after forty years he sighed and crossed his oars:
'I'm dying, dear son, receive my blessing, take up my oars,
and don't give up these weapons, drink at the spring's root!'
The grandson cast his father in the stream and clawed
both oars, then all alone rowed on the deathless waters.

For forty years he rowed until his hands grew numb;
he went from stubbornness to spite, his mind forged on:
'Where will you take me? You've eaten father and grandfather too,
but I shall drink your deathless water one day, for spite!'
Long rows of years, like caravans, drifted down the banks,
the young man's mouth gaped toothless, his hair thinned and fell,
his legs grew crooked and his fingers stank with wounds,
but still the exhaustless endless stream poured from the south
and like a date leaf his prow sailed the infinite tide.
And when on the stooped grandson hopeless old age fell
and death approached, he crossed the oars on his thin knees
and brine flowed from his salty eyes and stained his cheeks.
'Alas, I've no hope left to find that deathless water.
Cursed be the brainless fool who in this world first tried
to track the deathless water's source, and died of thirst!'
But then a voice rose from the waters in sweet farewell:
'Blessed are those eyes that have seen more water than any man!
Blessed be that haughty mind that aimed at the greatest hope!
May you be blessed who rowed the current your life long
and now with dry unfreshened lips descend to Hades
to find the hidden deathless springs and slake your thirst!
My son, it's Death who keeps and pours the deathless water.' "
The man of many sighs stopped speaking, looked about him,
and his old comrades felt a shuddering down their spines
as in the dusk their bodies broke in deadly sweat.
"By God, your armpits drip with dew, your loins have fallen!"
the archer laughed, then portioned food to all his crew.
"But let's eat first that soul and body may knit well,
for that, I think, is mankind's oldest, dearest duty;
we'll fall to dreams then, that old craftsman sleep may come
to find out where our bark has leaked, and calk it well.
At dawn clear thoughts will rise in our sleep-nourished brains
and we shall see what purpose brought us to these sands."
He spoke, and then their armored jaws crunched into meat;
Diktena, too, ate slowly with the brawny troop
and in the fire her large eyes glittered like two beasts.
For a long time all hearts on the night sands were hushed,
but when they fixed themselves for sleep, Rocky approached
the world-wide roamer, looked at the young maid, and said:
"Against the stream in our great voyage of no return
what do we want with this wild maid, this rutting mare?
If she were forced to row, I'd pity her soft hands,
if she were used for kisses, I'd pity our drained youth,
and if unused at all, she'd eat our bread for nothing."
Odysseus answered his young friend with mocking voice:
"I, too, don't know where to enthrone the siren, friend!

Kentaur shall rig the sails and catch the veering winds,
Granite and you, for you're both strong, shall wield the oars,
Orpheus shall play his flute and firmly harmonize
our oar-blades and our minds with hopeless, gallant tunes,
and I shall hold the tiller toward Death's secret springs.
You're right, there seems to be no place for woman here;
but let this night pass, too, the gain's all to the good,
and when day breaks, what must be done shall then be done."
He spoke, all flipped the wine gourd for a last deep drink,
then yawned, stretched out in a long row, and sank to sleep,
but their sly leader drew soft Diktena aside
amid the tall green reeds, and sleepless all night long
with pitiless sorrow said goodbye to her forever.
Holding the girl's refreshing body in his arms,
he felt himself sail onward toward Death's mystic springs
to find the deathless water that his soul might live.
All life seemed like a water's murmuring that awakes
between two sleeps and lightly gurgles in the mind of man.

IX

Earth, like a fat and tranquil cow, bent down and chewed
her cud, and ground her somber jaws like two millstones.
The black soil thickly steamed, the sturdy rushes trembled,
and the cold summer-morning frost froze on the shrubs.
The river, a benevolent pasture-bearded god,
flowed on, caressing his voluptuous wife, the earth,
who, moist and passive, slowly spread her muddy thighs.
As the dew drenched his hair, the tall mind-spinner strode
along the sands with open and nostalgic heart;
he'd left the glutted girl asleep amid the reeds,
her body plowed and planted like the earth in spring,
and he climbed, light of heart, to reconnoiter high.
The torrid sun had not yet risen, but storks awoke
and with long silent wings sped toward the flowing stream;
on a dung-heap a fierce young cock challenged the sun
till the sky heard him, laughed, then slowly turned pale-white.
Holding the morning in his hands, a cool round fruit,
Odysseus looked, and seeing not a soul in sight,
freely allowed his tears to trickle down his cheeks.
For a long time he let the salty waters flow,
and felt refreshed; he had longed deeply for this hour.
Slowly he turned and watched the sea: her curling waves
swelled up erect to reach the sun, and turned rose-red;
he watched his palms, and they too calmed and turned to rose.
The rugged seaman smiled, and from his briny tears
curved rainbows gleamed in mid-air, snared in his long lashes.
Day broke, the Morning Star in azure melted slowly,
the great god woke and climbed the sky, thrust his gold horns
under the sea-horizon's roots, lifted the clouds,
and slowly freed from night his forehead, eyes, and mouth,
then balanced tranquilly among the heaving billows
and with great joy greeted the world like his own child.
Broad and rose-red, the river glowed, the gardens shone,
fishes upon the glittering waters leapt and played,
fishermen stretched and yawned, woke up, and seized their nets.
A bull-calf left his mother's udders, spread his legs,

stumbled with tail erect, and frisked in the moist pastures;
his mother felt the sun-bull pierce deep in her loins,
and sweetly mooed, unmoving, warm, bursting with milk.
All things seemed broad and gentle, earth a placid cow
that browsed on grass and gods, that ruminated men
and passed them slowly through her thousand-fold intestines
then cast them up in sun and munched them once again.
With no false hope or wrath, Odysseus clearly saw
his body like a crooked twig with its blue flower

trembling mid-air within the cow's Cimmerian mouth.
Calmly his brains began to shape, to unshape the world:
he felt that life and death were two milk-laden dugs
and that sometimes we glued our hungry lips to one,
and clung to the other at times until we fell asleep.
His mind, too, mounted with the sun, serene and calm,
and heard the pitch-black deathless waters roar within him
and listened to Death's hidden springs deep in his heart;
though wretched man's short life was not enough to reach them,
yet great joy to that man who passed through the most water!
The billows he had crossed plunged through his voyaged mind
but seemed too few, and his proud heart now sighed with shame.
Life passes, lost in mid-air, and all far-off shores
like sirens shout and spring above the teasing waves.
"Forward, my soul! So long as my hair blows in the wind
I shall not leave you unprotected, but hand in hand
—don't you complain—we'll stroll and saunter the wide world through!"
He spoke, and felt mute tenderness for his poor soul,
that wretched mud-winged glowworm crawling through his flesh;
quickening his pace, he longed to join his friends again
and start the hopeless rowing toward the plunging cliff.
When Aphrodite rose and the Pleiades sank to rest,
the friends together floundered from the nets of sleep
and plunged to cool their bodies in the emerald waves.
They snatched a bite of bread, then all together trudged
toward the port town to see new oven-loaves of men.
"You'd think God grabbed some clay, pummeled these dwarfish souls
with two large pitch-black coals beneath their arching brows
then placed them row on row to dry in the hot sun.
If a strong wind should blow, they'd crumble away to dust,
if it should rain they'd melt to mud, and phew! once more
God would seize mud and blood and pummel away for life!"
Thus spoke the cross-eyed piper, then spread his stork-lean legs;
behind him the two towering gallants crunched on sand,
and last trudged splayfoot, snorting like a panting boar,
opening wide wells in the soft sand with his thick feet.
The muddy hovels opened, and young girls appeared
with smooth tight buttocks, held their water pitchers high
on upright heads, and ambled toward the banks to fill them.
Kentaur devoured them with his eyes and rubbed his bellies:
"Ah, harbor breeze, how swiftly you mature breasts here!"
Thus did the huge hog-body grunt and wave to the girls,
but they slipped by with shapely thighs, and giggled shyly.
Long rows of ovens smoked already, babies wailed,
and old crones spread the russet corn on terraces;
against the sand-swept walls the grapevines smelled of musk

and their sweet-peppery fragrance merged with rank manure.
Old men fell on their knees and turned their faces east,
flooded with light, toward their great overlord, the Sun,
their prayers hovering softly on their trembling lips.
Still dazed with sleep, the young men set the cattle free,
and from the darkness the oxen ambled, shining, plump,
and plod on, stretching sadly toward the far-off fields
their long necks bruised by many heavy yokes, then lowed,
plowed on, and licked their nostrils with their rugged tongues.
Deep in his mountain-nourished heart sad Rocky sighed
and yearned for the land's sweetness, a clodhopper's cares.
How had he fallen in the sea-battler's briny hands
and followed this home-wrecker like a yelping dog?
Dear God, if only he could shake off free, plunge down
ravines, skirt mountain slopes, sit high on rocky crags,
eat wild hare once again, drink water from deep springs!
But as he brooded thus in secret, the boatman came
with rolling sailor's stride, with cap like a ship's prow,
holding on high a ripe and golden-rayed sunflower.
"This rich fat soil, I think, has drugged my heart with spells!
Brothers, my feet plunge roots, I'm friends with earth once more,
my nostrils smell manure, they flare with rank delight,
and a sweet sudden thought intoxicates my mind:
Comrades, let's rip the planking of our wayward ship
and with its deck beams, mizzenmast, and its deep hull
build us a house like others to stabilize our hearts!"
With a wry face, the piper stammered mockingly:
"May you rejoice in the fine stink of your new house,
and may you find a stout-assed maid, long-snouted sow,
who may beget you babes and pigs, may they live long!
May you become a staid town chief with lofty cap!"
But their snake-minded master looked in Rocky's eyes,
and the youth understood his gaze and bit his lips:
"Your hints don't make my heart recoil, lone-hearted man.
I set my mind completely free to yearn in secret,
to want what it has lost and long for what it hasn't;
learn that I hold the straining reins in both hands, tight,
but loose my horses fearlessly on high dream pastures!"
The brave lad braked his tongue, but still his mind raced on.
In his strong fingers Granite mutely broke his staff
and twitched and steamed as though to dash back toward the sea;
but the fat sot, who knew his master's tricks by heart,
picked up the piper like a suckling child and yelled:
"Let's go! He casts his bait to us old sharks in vain!
Hey, master, if we wanted marriage, joys, housekeeping cares,
would we set foot, do you think, on your death-plunging prow?"

The devious man then raised on high his heavy hands:
"By God, I've never deigned to cast you teasing bait!
My heart was suddenly caught by earth's seductive warmth;
I envied prudent virtue, mankind's simple joys,
but if you've scorned them once, I've scorned them all a thousand times!"

Day spurted like a honeybee, the meadows buzzed,
the sun beat down the harbor's sandy reach of shore,
men, ships, and cattle shook themselves and uttered cries
as though light suddenly had uncoiled their twisted minds.
Thickly, like melted gold, the sun poured on the waters,
the warm sea seethed and steamed with fishes, the boats tossed,
—tempestuous weather—and the magicians sat by wharves
and sold winds dearly by the dram to passing skippers.
At the port's mouth, where the two mighty waters met,
—light green of the wide river, blue of the open sea—
the friends were swigging in a humble fishers' tavern.
They gulped their barley-wine with greed, and their minds glowed
until the gaudy harbor gleamed in their dark eyes:
slender hard-almond bodies with their thickset skulls,
blacks with stout bison-loins who fetched wares to their masters
as they sat drinking sherbets in the heavy shade.
Deep voices, secret instincts in the archer's chest
rose up and fell like long-forgotten ancient sounds,
and his mind struggled to recall, his inner ear to listen.
Before his birth once, long ago, his eyes had seen,
his nostrils had once smelled this crowded port—but how,
and when? Although he asked, his heart gave no reply.
Dimly his blood recalled, his heart beat sluggishly:
a thousand grandfathers long ago, his forebears passed
this way with their pine dugouts and their tawdry goods
and suffered deeply for a kiss, a bite of bread,
for still their blood seethed blindly in their grandson's veins.
Dear God, how much more ancient is the heart's deep root,
and mind is but a last, last bloom of little memory!
The heart wants to recount what it has seen and suffered,
but stutters, mute, and cannot brim with a single word;
it hops round in our chests and shrills like a caged bird,
but the mind, whose life is shallow, who's seen and suffered little,
finds well-matched prudent words and flouts them with glib skill.
The deep-souled man turned to his friends and bared his thoughts:
"I've roamed all seas and lands, I've tramped a thousand roads,
I've suffered much and thought my mind had reached its goal,
but this earth always overreaches me, life cheats me
by changing face so often my mind can't grasp it all,
for memories surge in my heart's root that once, perhaps,

once long ago, with yet another boat and crew,
with yet another body I moored in this same harbor.
Ah, could we only know, friends, all that our hearts know!"
Glutton guffawed and mocked his master jokingly:
"Brother, just get me good and drunk, and then I'll spiel
where my mind roamed a thousand years before my birth!
Do you want names and places? As soon as my heart's drunk!
Drink up your barley-wine, my lads! Let deep springs spout!"
But as the guzzler drained his jug, an old blind bard
came close and huddled at his feet, stretched out his hands,
rocked his lean body and began a bitter song:
"I saw a rower pull his oars, and my heart ached.
He sighed, and his back throbbed, his loins fell out of joint,
he raised his head to gaze at and recall the sun
but a lean whip with sharp long nails swept round his neck.
'Row on! Let's get there fast to fetch our merchandise
that our old master may dress well and stroll the quays;
let's bring his old wife balms so she'll grow young again!'
Alas, some labor in the sun, some eat in shade;
I've seen the mud-drenched fellah drain the murky river
then sow his scant seed, harvest it, and yearn for bread.
'What is it you're remembering, child, that you sigh so?'
the timid mother asks her son, to plumb the riddle.
'Ah, wretched Mother, bread!' her hungry child replies.
The people stoop to earth and call to their god: 'Help us!'
but he sits buxom in the shade, well-greased with lard,
looks on the fields, grows glad, then looks on man, and fattens.
I saw the embalmer stinking as he drained his corpses,
his feet twined with intestines, his hands soaked in pus;
his bread smells of cadavers, and he dines on carcass,
he turns his poor wife's stomach when he wants to touch her.
I've seen the scrivener sit cross-legged in teeming streets,
bent over, listening, holding parchment and sharp reeds.
Mothers weep out their clamorous letters to their sons,
pale maidens sigh, bend down, and tumble out their pain:
'O scrivener, write him, tell him how my weak arms want him,
that I can't bear our separation, that I'll die soon!'
And old men write their grandsons: 'We're dying of hunger! Help us!'
The anguished scrivener, deep in the cisterns of his heart,
harvests the wormwood, hoards these poisons drop by drop:
'Each soul has its own pain, dear brothers, but I have all!'
Masters, my heart has emptied, all my song spills out,
only the last most bitter drop sticks to my lips:
I saw a blind bard singing, crouched on the damp ground;
he stretched his bony hands, but all passed by in haste,
and once again he drew his hungry hands back, empty."

He spoke, drew back his empty hands, and softly sighed,
till gluttonous Kentaur ached for him and stooped to fill
the hands of the blind bard with food, but his dark master
seized him by his strong arms and thrust them back again:
"Here where we've anchored, comrades, is earth's stricken voice;
it suffers, wails, and shouts to God; not a soul hears it.
Don't stuff its mouth—for shame!—with only a piece of meat!
The more I roam this earth and spread my claws, the more
I feel that the herald of my hunting god is Hunger.
Forward! It's time to cut the river's current, brothers,
for I divine before us much of God, much more of Hunger!"

The oars spread wings and the prow leapt, God opened wide
his bottomless mouth, thick, filled with mud, and sucked them in;
all day they bucked the current till their eyes were filled
with hot sun, birds, date trees, and gray mud-nourished towns,
and all that day dragged with it they walled up with joy
till in the noisy hush the piper clapped his hands:
"Oho! We've left poor Diktena asleep on shore!"
Then the four-storied ballast of the ship bawled out:
"Both earth and woman need the plow and want no rest;
we'd set our minds elsewhere, and our musk-girl was bored
to gaze on this lust-itching crew yet touch no man!"
The friends guffawed and teased their master with sly looks,
but the archer only shrugged his shoulders and licked his lips:
"I've placed her on the knees of the plump harbor-goddess
to sit on the stone phalli where all ships are tied
and watch the waves for merchants, with their money belts
filled full of sacred gold, and with their heavy coffers,
that she might open her white thighs for them to moor,
for isn't her beauty worth that yellow gold, my friends?"
He spoke, then roughly scratched his itching beard crosswise.
At that same hour by the swift-foaming harbor's bay
the young grass widow sat on rocks and watched the waves:
"I like these waters well, there's many a merchantman
borne by these ships, and many a downy lad for me;
God's cast me on a wealthy strand, blessed be his name!"
Thus spoke the lust-excited maid, waiting for men;
and as the naked mountains wait, deep in warm darkness,
for the great castle to be sacked, their peaks to blaze
so that the flaming news might spread from mount to mount,
so did her two white thighs wait now in azure shadow.
When the wind fell and the tall mizzenmast went slack,
the comrades pulled their oars and plowed against the stream;
the river stretched on the mud banks, a guileless grandsire
on whom the people, his unnumbered grandsons, swarmed.

Nude men bent down with leathern buckets and drew water
to irrigate the scrubby grain, dry and dust-beaten,
and others browsed their horses on the broad-thighed earth.
A heavy sun strode on the banks and cracked the mud,
thorn-pointed, thick-branched fig trees decked the riversides,
date trees raised tall unmoving hands in breathless air
as underneath them passed the desert's famous ships
like full-rigged bobbing camels, humped, flat-footed, mute.
A mother sat upon the bank and to her bosom clasped
her son who'd fallen asleep, his lips still wet with milk;
she sang low lullabies and fervently prayed to God
to nourish her belovèd well, to make him strong
that his gold wings might one day cover east and west;
but he, bent over his master's fields his whole life long,
hungry and tired, would one day curse his mother's milk.
Suddenly birds with crimson bellies and blue wings
perched on the topmost masts, lifted their emerald beaks
into the burning light and warbled a sweet song,
and the archer spoke then to encourage his weary crew:
"Row quickly on, lads, till we reach the holy city!
There was, yet was not—like a myth she comes and goes,
may she be blessed!—a famous lady, an arch-eyed beauty.
Some call her pure-white Swan and others call her Helen.
Her mouth's a pomegranate flower, her voice is honey,
and one dim twilight as we lay on the soft grass,
and a warm South Wind blew, these date trees, these far strands,
these wild aromas, loomed up in her brimming mind,
and her eyes glowed, her bosom sighed like rustling wings:
'You know the deepest roots of earth, world-wandering roamer,
you've prowled through every garden, yet one flower remains:
I know a hundred-petaled rose that blooms on sand,
fed by a sacred river, guarded by bestial gods,
and a great king, a honeybee, is throned in its heart.'
Her curly mouth then moved, flowing with sweetest sounds,
and spread voluptuous Egypt in my heart like veils:
sugar canes brimmed with honey, in the torrid sun
aromas melted from the claws of gaudy birds.
I looked on her swan-beauty, heard her speak, and thought:
'What do I want with unalluring dry-dugged truth?
Wonders and marvels only bloom and flourish now
on your carnation lips, in your curvaceous mouth.
I want no other fruit, my heart no other flower.'
But now, my friends, our eyes and nostrils have brimmed full,
it was no dream nor a red flower of her full lips;
we're close to that great rose, my lads—pull on your oars!"
He spoke, his friends took heart and dipped those bygone words

like withered roses in their minds where they rebloomed;
dusk gathered, and the river like a lean-striped tiger
became a crimson conflagration, foliage darkened,
and Rocky watched the date trees till his slender form
stretched up as though he strained to reach their topmost tips.
The hunched day-workers now returned to sunless huts,
the stars hung low above their heads, sharp-rayed and bright,
and their unseen forefathers crawled from gaping earth.
"Enough, my lads! The day's blessed work has turned out well!"
Thus did the boatman speak, and the crew crossed their oars.
They tied their skiff to a wild fig, with brushwood lit
a bonfire by the bank, and then sat down cross-legged,
weary with heat, grabbed bread and ate to knit their souls.
They held each other firmly by the shoulders then,
pushed hard, broke down the doors and breached the halls of sleep.
When their eyes closed, a thin wail like a mother's cry
that rises, falls, then comes again to pierce the heart,
groaned like a slow song from the chain-pumps drawing water,
but the old friends, dead-tired, and deaf to all men's sighs,
now sailed in sleep, untroubled, where dreams rolled and sped
above their flattened lashes like deep sluggish waterways.

Like dappled meadow-partridges on crimson feet
the days filed by the riverbanks, the friends pursued
like hunters, and time and the slow river flowed together.
Raising their eyes at noon one day, they saw in haze
a ghostly city steam in the sun's silent beams
with myriad lofty tombstones, with unnumbered demons.
The passionate voice of their unsated pilot rang:
"Put up your oars! We'll anchor here, this town will do.
I see the dead, and the stone gods, but no one living;
stay wide-awake, my lads, keep your wits keen, beware
of spells, we're entering magic in an open hour!"
He spoke, leapt on the burning bank, while his fast crew
drew up their pointed prow, beached it on sand, then spied
with stealth, their hot brains pulsing in the flaming desert.
That black snake, Death, digesting slowly, coiled on sands,
an Ancient Archon, Master Shepherd, long-tailed Dragon
with piles of golden wedding rings stacked in his guts;
softly, as though he dreamt, he hissed in scorching sun,
then reared and flicked his two-pronged tongue, with corpses gorged.
Supine beneath the ground, the dead with criss-crossed hands,
their chests stuffed full of spice and magic incantations,
with keys stuck in their teeth, awaited their soul's return.
The crew strolled through the tombs and trod on the long dead,
for earth held many heavy ghosts, the sun dripped fire,

and the dead city slowly seethed and steamed in light.
"The dead are sown in earth like seed, but they'll never sprout,"
the archer said, and marveled at man's patient hope,
brainless and gallant, that yet dared to strive with Death.
"They wear their charms like swords, they bind their chests with spells,
and armored thus they plunge in earth with flailing spears;
but slowly thrusting through the soil in the cool dark,
the Worm, that mute unconquered warrior, crawls and eats."
Rooted in sand, placed side by side, chiseled in stone,
gigantic gods loomed high and shone with bestial heads,
and Granite frowned and grimaced with severe disdain:
"How has man's spirit fallen in these mud-made towns,
to worship monsters and to lie with sacred beasts!
If we should ever shape our gods, we'll take for measure
our own proud spirit at its passion's highest peak!"
But the complex mind gazed on the new gods in silence
and thought how beasts were merged and grafted with man's heart,
how they had filled his belly, coiled about his loins,
and how that panting mongrel breed had turned to gods.
At times the beast's head smothers the dark soul of man,
at times man's reverent head springs from the beast's body
and fights for its salvation, filled with light and sweetness.
The archer's soul throbbed, for its dim divinings here
had stood in stone a thousand years, hacked in the sun.
Thus had these two great foes within him, beast and god,
fought fiercely in his bosom, head, and loins until
high in his mind they turned to friends from so much strife,
and forefather Beast thus met with grandson God within him.
"May you be blessed, entangled ghosts, for now I know
who cried within me and what my ultimate destination!"
Thus did the archer murmur, and his soul grew light.
But wind-brained Orpheus, meanwhile, sprawled on the tombs
and heard slow groans and muffled wailing, poignant cries
that rose from the soul's dungeons smothered deep in death.
Women and men cried hoarsely in a vast lament,
and with his ear pressed to the ground the piper heard
mankind's shrill wails amid that noisy realm of worms:
"May he be cursed on earth who gives his trust to virtue,
that bankrupt crone who takes our life's pure gold and gives
but bad receipts for payment in the lower world.
Ah, passers-by that stroll, travelers that come and go,
all that I had, I placed on virtue, and lost the game!"
The sands shook and fell silent, and then the piper heard
a thin, thin maiden's cry in dim and soft complaint:
"Virgins who tread above me, maidens, O you who hear,
take joy in your bright youth, my dears; may my curse bless you!

Barefooted pilgrims from the world's far corners sped
to gaze and bring me lilies, for they called me holy;
unkissed, untouched by man, I soiled life's lustrous fabric.
Ah, God, if only I could walk the earth for a brief hour!"
The whole earth sobbed until the piper jumped and felt
an indestructible swarm of mute worms lick his brains.
He scurried down the sands and moaned to his huge friend:
"Ah, Kentaur, help me! Demons and worms are chasing me!"
but as he ran, he blinked his eyes and shrilly yelled:
"I see a beast squatting on sand! Dear God, he'll eat me!"
A leprous demon's head loomed on the burning sands,
large-eyed and hopeless, pallid, carved from a huge rock,
and splayfoot rushed and raised his fallen air-brained friend:
"My lion-cub, your brain has curdled in all this heat.
Reach out your hand and see: this is no airy ghost
but only a carved stone that greets the sun each dawn."
Orpheus took courage then, his squinting eyes grew clear
and saw a monstrous form thrust to its neck in sand;
only its stubborn head still fought with proud despair
not to surrender its great soul to smothering sands.
"Splayfoot, my friend, I'll lose my mind! Support me now!"
Then glutton laughed, picked up and gently placed the fool
among his friends who huddled with parched, panting tongues
beneath the huge beast's lower jaw and gazed on the blank desert.

Odysseus rose in silence, for he yearned to stare
full in that head's vast eyes within the scorching heat.
Between the bounds of sleep and waking his mind blinked,
for somewhere in high dreams, where the soul lifts the flesh,
this sacred head had risen like the pallid moon,
desolate and forlorn; three knives had pierced his heart:
"Ah, Lady, open your lips," he'd cried, "show me the way!"
But she had twined him with a silent smile, and vanished.
Yet now, behold, her stone lips moved, a rasping rose
from the blank, burning sands like a slow serpent's hiss.
Odysseus leapt up on his toes, yelled open-eyed,
and the whole beast—wings, light, and flame—rose with him there.
Rushing to touch it, the archer groaned, "It's my true God!"
but the bright vision quivered, then burst in desert air.
Like a struck eagle, the mind-spinner fell to earth:
"How shameful that I, too, am but the sun-heat's toy!"
But as he turned and stooped in shade to find his friends,
his brain at once distilled and gleamed like deep lagoons;
he smiled and shut his eyes till in his heart there rose
the wings of eagles, claws of lions, the smiles of women,
until he felt rejoiced in his own soul on sand.

Then light of heart he strode ahead and found his friends
conversing gently with a spare-haired native elder.
They'd found him lying flat on sand, thrust in the Sphinx,
trying to free her chiseled neck with his bare nails.
He turned with mildness and explained the sacred signs:
"Each letter locks a soul within its holy bounds;
if on this rock you chisel birds that speed through air,
those wounded birds shall plummet from the sky and fall
into that magic snare, your hand, which cut the rock.
Hack out a beast, and he'll be walled in your strong trap,
entangled in your hieroglyph's entrancing nets;
pierce with a marble-cutter's tool a god in stone,
that sign becomes a shrine at once, God stoops and enters.
Look at these slender birds, these moons, these stars, these suns—
they've clung a thousand years on this choked neck and cried:
'Help us, our only son, free us from smothering sand!'
I heard and fell to earth and dug with my bare nails
to free God all I could, that my own soul might breathe."
Odysseus leapt, reached out with eager hands and groped
the thick marks on the rugged neck, half-choked in sand,
as though he groped the Great Word on his own hewn neck.
He rose then, wanting on this day no other fruit:
"It's close to sundown, friends, let's make for our ship now;
we've grabbed off and well earned our daily wage today."
But the old man reached out and touched him like a god:
"I ask one favor; strangers here are precious gods,
and we all prize that great day when they cross our sills
to eat our bread and share the joys of mortal man;
stranger, I kiss your hand, stoop to my humble hut."
The archer grabbed the old man's trembling hand with joy:
"Old man, you hold time's plenty, all that you say is true.
It may be we are gods indeed who have come here now
to bless your holy dwelling and to share your bread;
I'm sure these other four gods here will bear me out!"
Then laughter brimmed and gurgled from four hearty throats,
and the lone man's illustrious escort made for town
to clean up greedily at once the old man's fare.
The fallen day leant toward the west, tombstones turned red,
and far down toward the river, lamentations rose;
on a half-crescent boat a dead man lay supine
in an embellished coffin, and grief-stricken maids
sat upright round him, tore their hair, and shrilled like birds.
The old man turned and raised his hands in sad farewell
to the new dead now sown in earth to sprout in grain.
"Ah, what great joy when ears of corn rise in the light!"
The old man spoke, then nosed through tombstones like a jackal,

deciphering dead men's words: "If only, O passers-by,
I had sweet-flowing water to drink, apples to smell!"
Another dead man wept: "Ah, lads, please turn my face
toward the cool north to feel a freshening gust of wind."
Another moaned with thick twined symbols on his grave:
"I don't weep for my wife, she'll find another husband;
I don't weep for my children, for children soon forget;
but I do weep for sunlight, bread, and gentle talk."
Odysseus scorned, however, every cheating hope
and now recalled a sturdy peasant plowman's words.
One day as he sat crouched on oleandered shores
and spitted rows of fishes over glowing coals,
a passing worker boldly sat and shared his meal,
then from one topic to another, dwelt on Death.
The plowman scorned with condescension, mocked with jeers
those lame-brained fools who thought the dead would rise one day.
"My grandsire, a rich plowman, took me on his knees
but he disdained to stuff my brain with fairy tales,
and though he always talked of Death, he laughed at him:
'Grandson, I don't want charms or food laid in my grave;
I don't want wretched cattle slain for my soul's sake;
I know my future well, I haven't the slightest hope.
Listen, my son, and learn the grave's dread secret now:
when you pierce shallow soil, at the first gate of Hades,
a Negro swoops and grabs your soul's rich ornaments,
and she, poor tenderfoot, resists and cries in vain:
"Brothers and cousins, help me! They've snatched my golden crown!"
Go on and yell, for neither brothers nor cousins care!
On the next moldy stair the gate guard clasps her tight
and plunders all her charms and worthless talismans,
even plunders, alas, whatever good she's done in life
until the unhappy spirit sighs, her small voice quivers:
"Why do you strip me, slayer, why do you seize my weapons?"
At the third gate she's stricken dumb, then slowly, slowly,
earth chews up all her teeth, her ears, her nails, her eyes,
until six different kinds of worms devour her whole.' "
The archer now recalled the gnarled clodhopper's words
but held them back for fear of poisoning the kind elder's tongue.

They stepped in the old man's hut and filled it full of flesh.
In the cool hallway, his two daughters moved with joy,
set a low table, spread it with a fragrant cloth,
brought them their poor but tasty fare, a dewy jug,
then stood by shyly, with crossed hands, to serve the strangers.
The host then spoke with noble grace to his great guests:
"A stranger always bears the face of the unknown god;

strangers, thrice welcome to my humble hut today."
Peace brimmed on all their faces till the harsh sea-battlers
felt shamed to eat and breathe beneath that guileless roof.
The captain answered the old man in a soft voice:
"Many great virtues deck the steadfast heart of man:
to love the worthy friend and kill the hated foe,
to ache for wretched womankind, to fear no god,
but I don't think there's a more warm, sweet-blooded virtue
than to submit your home and heart to passing strangers."
Kentaur, unslaked with words, sat down and spread his legs,
then reached his greedy hands till the clay platters rattled.
All ate together in sweet friendship's freshening breeze,
and the two maidens sat cross-legged on woven rush,
placed shining zithers on their knees, caressed the strings
and slowly sang to gladden their noteworthy guests.
The older maiden first struck up a bitter song:
"Earth looks on fleeting man, looks long and sings with grief:
'Life is most short and death most long and there's no healing!
Smear perfumes on your body, paint your pale lips red,
enwreath your neck with flowers, your head with a gold crown,
then sit enthroned, king of an hour, and give commands.
Order stringed instruments to blow your griefs away
and place your kind hand gently on your loved one's knee
because astride your door the four pallbearers wait.' "
The girl sang like a nightingale and eyed the men,
then sighed, but felt ashamed before her father's gaze;
dear God, if only she could mount their sturdy knees
and, as the sweet song counseled, give and take of life!
But as she shook with anguish for fear her shame might show,
her younger sister throbbed, her soul with longing soared,
she lowered the fawn eyes her heart had overbrimmed,
then snatched the ballad from her sister's burning lips:
"A bird flies in the heavens with aromatic wings,
a young girl stands by the door's mouth with quivering breasts
because a sweet bird pecked them or a kiss aroused them.
'What are these crimson apples I hold on my cool bosom?
Where is the thief who will pass by and loot them, Lord?
Where is the mad North Wind to rise and fling them down?'
Then from the garden's depths an apple tree replied:
'Come quick, I've lowered my boughs to hold you both, beloved.
Call to your lover, quench his thirst, do what he bids you,
for I was born on earth to bear both flower and fruit,
and what I see or hear, I swear, shall never be told.' "
Both ceased, and round their features shone a quivering light;
the first girl gazed on the strong men and mutely pled,
the younger stooped, still fondled by invisible hands,

their thighs and loins enflamed, their small ears flushed with rose.
Then the bald piper swelled his chest, unsheathed his flute,
raised high his slender throat and sang an answering tune:
"Partridges wake at break of dawn, the green glens cackle,
the young son wakes at break of dawn to hunt with joy,
and Death wakes up at break of dawn and mounts his steed.
I also wake and hoist my sails and skirt the shores,
sometimes I laugh and sometimes weep or talk to winds:
'O master wind, blow on, blow on, my heart has swooned
because two maidens, cross-legged on a rush mat, sang,
and the earth shook like an apple tree and filled my lap.' "
Their father marveled, but his daughters spoke no word
yet trembled still like flickering flames that could not fade.
Odysseus then recalled old memories and encounters;
tall castles, women, seas, and caves rose in his mind
until he shook his head with force as though a cricket
had perched on his gray hair and rasped with deafening sound.
"Leave me alone, don't bother me, for I've loved much
those wretched apples that rot unplucked on the high boughs,
but they won't do, for a new hunger gleans my heart."
The stony-hearted man then choked his strong desires,
reached out his hands and gently touched the old man's knees:
"Good was the food: may your sweet home be ever blessed;
good was the song: it gleaned our hearts like a sharp scythe;
may your great god, the river, send strong men to frisk
in apple trees with both your girls and breed you grandsons.
But we must leave you now, for we have far to go,
and a home's honeyed bliss destroys a man's intent;
comfort and pleasure do not match with our dark god."
He spoke and rose, and all his comrades rose to leave.
The maids withdrew and sighed, then hung their zithers high
on the reed-covered walls among musk-smelling quince;
their heels flushed red like apples, they bent their slender forms
and from their dowries fetched their shining household goods,
unwrapped their flower-embroidered towels, still untouched,
and brought the holy strangers water to wash their hands.
Rocky stooped down and saw within the brimming bowl
the younger daughter's face, her eyes, her slender brows,
till the warm sweetness of her flesh made his heart swoon.
Life spread her nets with skill about his loins until
his eagle heart for a moment was trapped like a wild dove.
In his mind's eye he saw a river, a gleaming hut,
earth seared with panting tongue, the wilted wheat sun-scorched,
a cottage filled with sweetness, shade and fragrant quince
that hung down from the roofbeams, gleaming dulcimers,
a faithful wife who sat, in her calm cottage stooped,

and bared her glowing breasts to suckle her sweet son.
She suddenly sees her husband standing by the door,
her face lights up, and with her son still at her breast,
receives her man like a great king in his vast mansion.
And Rocky, a young plowman, spattered still with hay,
sits in the middle of his yard while his wife runs
to draw cold water from the well to cool his thirst. . . .
Feeling his mind grow faint, poor Rocky tossed his head,
and as the young maid gave him an embroidered towel,
her small hand shook with her desire's giddy need.
Rocky grew savage then, turned to his friend and growled:
"Captain, it's choking here! I'm off for a breath of air!"
As though Odysseus pitied even his own heart,
he wandered slowly about the house unhurriedly.
If only the soul of man had myriad forms to serve it,
he'd give one body to earth, build it a lovely home,
dress it with soft and shining clothes and marry it off!
Then it would entertain each night all passers-by,
and when they'd eaten, the soothed mind would rove in talk,
and hear tall tales of lands and seas and far-off men,
and though it sat unmoving, roam the entire world.
But alas, the soul is poor, it has one body only,
and he'd already cast his own with ruthless speed
headlong from wave to wave down toward the wild cascade.
Thus did he brood, and bowed with reverence to both hearths:
the one bedecked with flowers, the other hung with pots.
"I bow to the four corners of the upper world,
mind's four foundations: women, fire, wine, and bread.
Farewell! May God come to this house like a bright bridegroom!"
He gave his hand then to the old warm-hearted man
and to both girls who longed for children and had sung,
unshamed, their deep desire to every passing stranger.
The hand of one girl trembled in his heavy palm,
their fingers tangled then as though they could not part,
and the other girl's hand would not close, as cold as crystal.
But when they stepped out and the river's cool breeze blew,
their wagtail hearts grew firm, all magic spells dispersed,
and then the squint-eyed heckler teased his splayfoot friend:
"Kentaur, don't ask me why I laughed! I almost choked!
You looked so shy, my gluttonous sot, and lowered your eyes
like an old dame of noble stock with puckered eyes!"
God's fleshly ballast laughed until his tears rolled down:
"A crazy head can't change! I choke in honest homes!
My palms will grow hairs sooner than my head get brains!
I've no doubt prudent talk is good, virtues are good,
they, too, have their own sweet charms once in a great while—

to sit on fat behinds and gab with good homebodies;
but I'll be a woman-chaser until the day I die!"
The man of many wills walked last in brooding thought:
"I thank you, God, for these my nostrils, ears, and eyes,
my double kidneys, my hard thighs, my thorny thoughts,
but most of all for this insatiable vast heart
that loves all things on the bright earth yet sticks to none."
Midnight: amid the wealthy harbor's gold-prowed ships
their own poor vessel, dark and peeling, quaked with shame,
then danced with joy to see them come, and bobbed in welcome.

All the next day they rowed, rowed on and softly sang;
their hearts had never seemed so light, their souls so strong,
nor had they skimmed more smoothly on the foaming waves;
their ship was a swift gull that swept the river's stream.
They had no bread to eat, no wine to stanch their hearts,
so once again took up their thieving tricks to live.
In vain did landlords line the banks to moan and weep
for their fine flour, their lambs, their flasks of barley-wine—
the wolf-pack shared the plunder on the prow, unruffled.
Fat Kentaur played the host, sliced up the meat, and laughed:
"Poverty wants a good time, lads, pain wants a party,
and when our last hope's gone, let's get the tables ready,
twirl our mustaches, lads, until our brains twirl, too,
and all thorns turn to roses, stones to loaves of bread,
so that despair turns round about and leads the assault!"
Thus did good glutton chatter till all lost their wits;
and so with jokes and forays, manly talks and deeds,
the dawns climbed quickly up, the evenings scurried down.
Meanwhile that thirsty mother, Drought, scorched all the fields,
and wheat, man's firm foundation, died on its dry stalk
until the wretched people raised despairing hands
and beat their chests on the dry banks and groaned to God:
"Dear father, help or we'll go lost! Our wheat is dying!"
But God sank further in his muddy bed each day
and would not deign to rise and fructify the land.
The peasants groaned, beat on their drums, and their weak oxen
pushed to the riverbank and sniffed the dough-hard earth;
women and children straggled sadly to the dry banks
and farmers held as offering their last crumbs of bread.
When an old priest knelt by the bank and raised his hands,
the castle-battler stopped his skiff to hear the prayer:
"Almighty great grandfather and father of all Egypt,
great lord of grain, take pity: the earth's stricken womb
begets no longer till men and gods both faint with hunger.
Descend, pour your thick waters, cast your mighty strength

and swell the veins of earth so they may spout with milk.
Support the bottomless belly, the base of all creation
that spreads in darkness like manure, feeds all the roots
of heaven and earth, for if it dies the whole world dies!"
He spoke, then stopped and smeared his belly with rank mud.
Then the much-suffering man cried out, and the keel shook:
"Swell all the sails, for my heart aches! I'll hear no more!"
The crew was seized with a deep sadness till at dusk
the cowherd opened his wide mouth and mocked the world:
"God is a lucky shower, lads, rains where he wills,
forgets the widow's vineyard but recalls the king's,
gulps down your one but swells the king's three-thousandfold!
Ah, master, if you think you'll teach God anything,
then what a shame we left our feasts, our smacks and hugs,
far off on distant shores, for here we're thrashed by hunger:
a garlic grasped is worth three thousand birds on wing!"
The wrathful archer frowned and struck at his friend hard:
"Glutton, I'd gladly give three thousand spitted birds
to catch that one uncatchable bird which slips my mind!
This is man's noble task; if you don't like it, friend,
the road sprawls all behind you; take it now, and go!"
But Kentaur hung his head and swallowed his hard words:
"Oho! You put me on my honor! I've stuck my neck out!
May he who now turns tail go hang, and the way back, too!"
The brave blood-brothers laughed, pulled stoutly at their oars,
slept hungry on the deck that night, and then pushed on
once more at daybreak up the muddy steep ascent.
As waters grew more shallow, the stream slowly sank,
the tigress desert on her belly crawled and snarled,
and all the sparse grass crouched with terror on the sandy loam.

How the earth sped, a whirling quoit hurled down the sky!
One night they skimmed in the destroyed Sun City's port
then dragged their skiff ashore, found kindling wood and lit
a fire to eat their stolen and therefore tasty meat.
But as they ate among the ruins, they raised their heads:
the world was suddenly drenched in moonlight, on tall tombs
the moon's funereal kerchief spread with azure hem.
Supporting himself on his strong hands, Odysseus rose
and groped at the ruins stone by stone to feel the grooves
of great suns that with myriad hand-rays stroked in love
princes with narrow skulls and maidens almond-eyed.
Like a night lamp the moon climbed with unruffled calm,
the broken mouths on the stone ruins wanly smiled,
and crimson paint still glimmered on their chiseled rims.
A bitter anguish gripped the castle-battler's heart:

"Who knows what brains and bodies we tread on tonight!"
Thus did Odysseus cry, his mind boiled, his tholes cracked,
and Death dragged him in moonlight with a tightened noose.
His friends, meanwhile, had drowsed, for flesh had swept them off
and they had fallen to sleep like rain in thirsty sand.
A distance off, the archer smoothed a place to sleep,
but his blood seethed and sped like sleepless roaring streams.
For hours he fought off sleep in his clay threshing floor
because he had no wish to exchange his life for dreams
and longed to snatch more hours from tax-collecting Death,
but his mind dimmed and sank like setting stars at sea.
He drowned in sleep, and the ghost of the Sun City seized him
till like a frisking dwarf, a guileless snake, he drove
ahead like a dream-driven sleeper and slid in earth.
Not even a breast's light breathing nor the song of birds:
his soul like a slim flame flicked on his body's wick
until he felt his mind detach itself, then fade
and enter like a pilgrim in a marble-studded town.
The towers, tombs and homes shone dimly like dull pearls,
snakes drowsed in tangled coils, and slimy bloated worms
drooped over doorways in long rows and decked the yards.
Most gentle and compassionate now, with shriveled flames,
the sun hung over Hades like a flickering lamp;
it spread its beams, and each ray like a human hand
with five long fingers lovingly caressed the world
till seeds, worms, waters shuddered with intense delight
and dead men stood in their low doorways, raised their hands,
and the light pierced their hollow chests as though through glass.
Then as the dream-drowned man rejoiced in the night gardens,
a gleaming tomb before him opened like a white rose
and a nude regal pair, like green-gold wingless insects,
came out embraced, and sat in sun on their white tomb.
The man was pale and slim, nor could his shoulders bear
the full weight of his luminous and towering brow;
his chest, his flanks, his thighs were curved like a young girl's,
but his high forehead, ripening in the worshiped sun,
shone full of new gods, new seed, distant new desires.
Beside him lay the invincible queen of reed-slim fingers
who softly smiled with flaming lips and gave the king
a large gold-rayed sunflower with a deep-black heart.
Like insects after rain the two enraptured bodies
sunned themselves mutely on the tomb and sweetly merged,
but the king suddenly raised his downy, smothered eyes,
and as he gazed with calm on the night-roaming dreamer
and moved his sun-washed hands, the whole tomb gaped and swayed,
opened its arms and shouted with a speechless longing.

The great tomb-treader screamed and jumped among the ruins;
the sun had risen already a half-oar's length and turned
the waters crimson as the thick light licked the sands
and hungry herons lined the riverbanks and stooped
for minnows, motionless, without the slightest sound.
Like a black-seeded sunflower by the riverside
the heavy vision weighed in the archer's aching palm,
the wind played round him and his shoulders shook as though
a swarm of spirits touched him with their downy wings.
"Shades have bewitched me! That royal pair begged me in sleep
to lift them out of Tartarus into sun once more!
Ah, don't complain! May milk and honey calm your tomb!
I'll dig the earth at midnight, souls, and set you free!"
Thus did he brood that dawn, and weighed his firm decision well.

He turned back to the river where his friends, new-washed,
lay glittering on their backs on the sandbanks and ate
ripe stolen figs, soft skin and all, to cheat their hunger.
The sly contriver bid them a good day and said:
"Eat, make your loins strong, lads, I'll need you all at dusk.
Last night, my friends, my brains gave birth to a strange dream,
and I'll have need of six stout bodies to make it real."
The piper grimaced wryly, and his arms felt numb,
but since he did not dare to speak, he crouched on sand
and listened to his master spell his golden dream
and drip sweet honey drop by drop on their parched brains.
When the sleepwalker ceased, his hands with luster streamed
until the eyes of his crude crew lit up with gold.
Black ancient streams of blood awoke, long-smothered forebears
whose grandsons now grew wild, for ancient memory prowled
like dark wolves in their bowels until they burgled gardens
and stole sharp spades and crowbars for their long night's task.
When night fell, the sly thieves began to dig with speed,
conquered their terror, nor spoke for fear the graveyard ghosts
would snatch their voices; hope of gain kept them awake.
Their five spades flashed with toil, their armpits dripped with sweat,
and soon their minds grew groggy for it seemed they dug
heap on high heap of souls and bodies till they heard
heads groaning at their feet and rotted shoulders moving.
But when the ground rang hollow, they leapt in the deep pit,
groped swiftly, found a bronze ring in the soil embedded,
then wedged their crowbars, raised the lid, climbed down the tomb
and crawled half-bent and fumbling in long passageways.
The piper lit some brushwood to support his heart,
for round them, lo! old gods and kings awoke in joy,
sweetly imprisoned in cool multicolored paints.

Stooping through tunnels, soon in the torch glare the friends
perceived a small door gleam, and at the doorpost loomed
two Negro sentries keeping guard in chiseled stone.
Startled, they gasped and staggered back in swift recoil,
but the archer sharply strode beyond the cobwebbed sill
and the others followed and choked back loud cries of joy:
night gleamed like dawn from treasures piled in glittering heaps,
crowns and gold thrones and precious stones glowed in the dark
with two gold coffins thrust among them, wrought with emeralds.
Though terror seized them, they all held their breath, pried open
the rich-embellished lids, unwound the mummy-cloth,
then stooped with torches, and with startled eyes looked down
on a blessed royal pair in holy calm content.
Both on their bosoms held earth's heavy golden keys;
the king was slim, his head was curved like a thin gourd,
and in his hands he held a golden disk, the sun;
the queen beside him was tall-bodied, with broad thighs,
and held a golden-rayed sunflower with emerald heart.
First the all-knowing man cut open a small vein
to soothe the dark earth-demons and not be driven mad,
and sprinkled both the sacred heads and golden crowns.
Then the grave-robbers swiftly stripped the regal heads,
plucked golden necklaces, huge suns, and emerald rings,
the rich adornments of the dead, winecups and swords,
until their hands with amber, gold, and rubies brimmed,
and overladen thus, they climbed out toward the glimmering light.

Day broke; a flaming sky smeared all the ruins with blood,
flamingoes slowly passed in their pursuit for food,
their small skiff almost sank, with golden plunder heaped,
but when they opened sail and left the haunted sands,
the comrades gazed upon their laden ship with dread,
for now it seemed they sailed within a golden coffin.
They searched each other's face, but no joy lit their eyes,
for their mute souls were paralyzed and leaden-heavy.
Thus hours passed in silence, and no one thought of food,
each secretly planned how he might best enjoy his wealth,
and each man frowned and glowered in his turbid brain.
Each in his mind built rich town mansions, double-storied,
with laden tables, wild carousing night and day,
and with three sirens—women, drunkenness, and sloth—
who sang until the pale soul drowned in pleasure's sewers.
But all at once Odysseus rose, grabbed a gold crown,
stretched his arms wide and flung it in the river's stream,
silently filled and emptied his full fists once more,
and scooped up last of all a handful of red rubies,

flung them in shimmering showers toward the sun from where
they fell like clotted drops of blood on the red foam.
Then Granite sprang and grasped his loot in both his fists,
amber and emeralds, golden demons and flaxen cloth,
and Rocky kicked with wrath into the gaping stream
his golden-leafed sunflower and silver-hilted sword.
Broad-buttocked Kentaur sighed and turned to his sea-captain:
"By God, you bend us like a bow until the tight gut snaps!
If I surpass my coarse-grained nature unwillingly,
it's not because you've shamed me! It's just that I'm big-hearted!"
He spoke and fondled lovingly a golden goddess
he'd kept hid in his breast, then flung her with bad grace,
and his stone-studded heavy winecups and gold jars.
And Orpheus, who had plundered but an ivory flute,
gulped dryly with dismay and to his master cried:
"I've snatched up just one wretched flute! Please, please, dear master,
don't frown, please let me keep it for remembrance only!"
But the archer glanced with scorn at the still hungry waves
till from the blushing piper's hands the pale flute slipped
and vanished in muddy waters like a silver smelt.
All day they sailed the river without food or talk,
burdened with shame, nor looked into each other's eyes.
How thin the rind of honor and the crust of freedom!
We spin vast works in our proud minds, and with great toil
push up our muddy bodies to reach the godly peaks,
then flash! a moment's pleasure, and we're once more widowed!
Such thoughts seethed in the comrades' chests, but they kept mute,
and when cool evening fell, the wise man raised his voice:
"Brothers, you know how much I, too, hate poverty,
and yet today I suddenly felt our souls weighed down
with gold, unable to walk lightly, and I thought:
'Riches are good and they can buy the entire world,
but best is that proud hand that flings them to the winds';
and that, my lads, is when I flung my hands above the river!"

Though poverty pressed once more, they rowed with joy next day
and kept their minds sweet, brooding on their sacrifice
as freedom rose in their proud ship and swelled like sails.
With bitter litanies the landlords wept and wailed,
for their stone-hearted god, the river, still refused
to fling his fertile strength upon his wife, the earth;
and wheat, that stalwart athlete, lay in his furrow, dead,
as round him the poor peasants knelt in shrill lament.
Black-kerchiefed mothers by the dry bank's foaming lips
beat on the dust and called to their dead son, the wheat:
"O my sweet darling child, come toss your golden head,

scatter the soil, thrust through, cast off your stifling tomb!
Dear son, sprawl on the upper world, make the fields green!"
Thus did they weep their tiny yet almighty god,
and the crew-comrades pierced downstream through Egypt's soil,
while spite, like a black hawk, perched on their pointed prow.
The piper's brains one morning shone like a red rose,
for Helen's decoy breasts passed through his muddled mind.
But she, far off on the blue sea, on that great island,
lay stretched on pure-white bedsheets, and her gentle eyes
gazed proudly on her son asleep in a rush basket.
An old nurse bent above the newborn infant son,
filled him with strength and blessed him like a goodly fate.
She rubbed his scalp with salt to flavor his strong mind,
soaked him in wine that he might hold his own in drinking,
then roasted crabs, ground them to powder, and smeared his mouth
that he might grow new sets of teeth in his old age,
and spread his hands with scorpion ash that they might fling
fistfuls of knives on foes, kisses on faithful friends.
Then last of all she placed the child on a white he-goat
so that his loins might strengthen for the erotic wars,
and when the mystic armoring of the babe had ended,
she wrapped him in warm skins and gave him to his mother
to suckle sweetly her first drop of taintless milk
that he might pass untroubled then through earth's grim threshold.
"Iron-strong mother, may your dragon-son live long,
and may the world sing songs one day of his great deeds!"
The mother smiled, and when she bared her laden breasts,
casements and doors glowed suddenly, and far, far off
on Egypt's sun-scorched sands, the piper's brain blazed up
till his mind whirled with vertigo and his heart pulsed:
"Oho! A north wind blows, and Helen sweeps my mind!
What's happening, comrades, now, to her world-famous body?"
But his broad-bottomed friend rowed swiftly with deep sighs:
"Don't twist your neck off looking backward, my fine friend!
That arch-eyed form was a sweet dream, but the cock crowed,
ahoy! and the past has passed like billows and rolled away!
New dreams come smothering down, my startled ears perk up,
and my heart aches to hear these cries of hunger now.
Alas, I pity the poor children! They'll all starve!"
Then looking toward the sands, their knowing guide replied:
"Brothers, my heart breaks too, but mends as soon as broken.
Hunger's a mighty goddess; she, too, will lead us well.
She strides straight on with a black banner, her dugs hang down,
behind her crawls a horde of pallid children screaming,
but from their shrieks one day a brave new tune will rise.
If I could choose what gods to carry on all my ships,

I'd choose both War and Hunger, that fierce, fruitful pair!"
Thus did the strong man feed his crew with lion-brains,
and Granite winked at him and laughed to hear his words:
"Don't get all worked up, captain! Unless I'm sore mistaken
those two dread gods your heart desires sail with us now!"
The foxy-minded man then grinned and scratched his beard:
"Don't worry, friend, I know quite well they've crashed the hold—
that's why I've prinked and pranked them up with flattery so."
He spoke, then sat cross-legged and sank in brooding thought;
his mind bloomed like a thorny thistle on a cliff's edge,
ruthless, alone, with one untouched pure drop of honey
hid in its thorns, and he rejoiced in his great secret.
Days moved on sluggishly like wide banana leaves,
the nights stretched out beside them like cool Negresses,
the desert crawled on its starved belly, a fierce tiger,
and the crew shuddered, but the border-guard rejoiced,
for deep inside he felt cool wells, greenswards, and laughter,
and from his brain the mighty cloven river rolled
like a wide blood-vein round his temples, his thick neck,
his chest and thighs, and laved him and refreshed him wholly.

Like a huge lobster with red claws that seethed with wrath,
the sun boiled up next day, simmered on the hot sands
till date trees leapt in the red light like fountaining flame.
To give his weary oarsmen courage, their coxswain yelled:
"Take heart, my lads, the Holy City is not far off;
I smell huge highways, noble mansions, fragrant groves,
and there upon that distant hill, huge dragon-columns;
I prick my ears up and the crowded streets resound
as though a beehive dropped on this broad stream, and broke."
Then his crew rowed with courage till their small skiff shook,
but as the lone man gazed far off and his mind strolled
on desolate mountain peaks, the piper burst in song:
"Eh, scarabs, golden scarabs, watch us breach the rose!
Quick-tempered archer, keep your wits, don't start a brawl,
don't think you'll force the swerving earth to your own course,
don't put a spike in God's good plan, don't stick your oar in,
make of your heart a beehive now, plunder the flowers
—go to it, man!—distill their poison to pure honey!"
All day they rowed until at last, toward fall of day,
the monstrous city slowly loomed, a swollen rose
that in the slothful sunset swarmed on gleaming sands.
The crew then slid into the harbor's slim canals,
and as lights fell on the thick waters, the river smiled
as when the sky puts on its stars and then goes strolling.
Then they all cocked their ears to catch the slightest sound

but the poor piper's shriveled flanks began to shiver:
"Fellows, our stupid jokes, our filching, our fat words
will not pass current in this mighty city now;
my heart sniffs out great evil in this noisy fort."
But Orpheus suddenly ceased, swallowed his twaddling tongue,
and felt the killer's eyes above him eat him whole.
Odysseus sat in silence on his quiet prow
and listened to the half-choked tumult, shouts of men
distinct from women's giggling and the yelps of dogs,
then turned and spoke with quiet calm to his companions:
"Great ships are wrecked here; what then may a small skiff do?
If any of you now want to save your hides, then leave,
for my heart sniffs great evil in this monstrous fort."
The insulted friends felt as though knives had pierced their hearts,
and Granite, born of noble stock, as brave as he,
scorned now to let even a small fly light on his sword:
"We also are free souls, so don't insult us here!
He who sets out for sure possessions shames his soul!"
"Now here's a strong trap, lads," the glutton cried, "let's bite!
We'll need our wits and superwits to snatch that bait
with skill, then scurry off before the trap door slams down tight!"

While the brave pirates talked, within the city streets
night sauntered down and opened her refreshing arms,
shopkeepers tied their keys three times about their waists,
and young men swarmed down toward the river to promenade
where the kiss-workers and seductresses of love
spread out their thighs like sweet lime traps in the cool dusk.
Their Pharaoh stretched and yawned upon his golden sheets
and felt the full moon weighing on his fragile chest,
a marble tombstone that now crushed and pinned him down.
Sallow and sad, he sighed with boredom, reached his hand
and took his waxen tablets and his ivory reed
to etch a panegyric for his great grandsire:
how many castles he had wrecked, how many kings
he'd lassoed tightly noose by noose and then strung out
in straggling rows, tied to his horse's golden reins.
Ah, he still lived to haunt the palace and stalk through
his grandson's dreams and beat upon the palace doors!
The young king picked his reed to write a fitting song
and exorcise that evil, that great savage soul,
that it might flit from sign to sign and fade in air.
His sweet tongue strove to charm the snake out of its hole
and agonized to wrench his thought in proper words;
the letters danced in light like butterflies, then vanished,
and but one verse fell into place on the soft wax:

"I perch in your huge fist, grandsire, a small, small parrot . . ."
That night when the moon fell and stifled him with dread,
the grandson stooped, kept time, wrote and erased and mumbled:
"I perch in your huge fist, grandsire, a small, small parrot,
my wings are azure smoke, my belly a red rose . . ."
But soon his reed grew weary and his painted eyes
grew drowsy with their thick cosmetics, and the song faded.
Midnight: the golden prows skimmed on the glittering waves,
slim necks were raised up toward the sky, and the moon fell
like a white rose, full-blossomed, on the women's hair.
Odysseus groaned, for his clay body seemed too small:
"Ah, both my eyes are not enough, nor both my ears,
my nose and hands are few, too few, and both my lips,
to enjoy you fully, glittering-eyed, seductive lands!"
Fragrance of jasmine rose from the locks of rutting night,
like peacock tails the women strolled along the streets,
and almond eyes serenely swam in the moon's glow.
Behind thick lattices, shrill laughter leapt like springs,
the teeth of maidens gleamed, gold bracelets flashed and clinked,
and clogs beat on the narrow streets till the stones cackled.
Behind their master in the foreign city streets
the four friends walked and cast blue shadows in the moon.
One, in his hairy chest, thought long of poverty—
ah, how the grain rots uselessly, how small birds die!
Beside him, the light-headed songster took delight
in the rich-colored world, beguiling towers of air,
a huge cock-pheasant strutting slowly, late at night.
Behind them, hand in hand, the two slim comrades talked
of cold springs in the mountains, feasts on holy days
when they had danced so dashingly that girls had swooned.
"Life then was good, dear friend, most good, most true, and now
let Death come to our dance with his resounding lyre!"
Thus each one with his shadow passed through narrow lanes,
and thus the sun at daybreak found them, upright still.
"Ah, friends, bold nightbirds, see, the sun at dayspring brims,
it's time we lay now in our coffin-skiff to rest
that all we've seen this white night may distill to blood."
Thus spoke the knowing man, then stretched lengthwise on deck.
Pharaoh had also fallen asleep on his gold bed
but his unfinished song still straggled in his mind,
a honeybee's frail wing that flicked in wax, and stuck.
Exhausted roisterers and brothel dames turned home,
till night-moth love grew weary too, and shut his wings;
all the red lamps went out at last and in dawn's glow
the green moon swooned and fell into the desert's arms.
Sprawled on the deck, supine, the dragon-crew slept on,

and dreams like roguish pageboys softly came and brought
trays heaped with food, full wineskins, ovens of warm bread,
and as their jawbones clacked, they strengthened with dream-food.
But when they knew they dreamt, they woke and chased away
night's sweet chicanery, combed their straggling hair until
Odysseus turned to his wolf-pack with a wry smile:
"An ancient proverb says wolves are not fed with words
but set their savage scent against the traitorous wind,
then slowly padding on their paws, thrust in the fold.
This city's pen is fine, my friends, but hounds surround it
and myriad winds blow round us and snatch up our scent.
But cock your caps and seize your swords! We won't lack bread!"
Yet Rocky, who a thousand times had plundered flocks,
then pricked his booty toward his cave, unharmed and whole,
now tossed his olive locks and made a sour face:
"Here everything's in shipshape order, my fine friends!
Wherever you turn are guards and the harsh clang of keys.
Last night my eyes in vain sought everywhere to steal
but saw no door unlatched or a low wall to leap!"
Devious Odysseus placed his hand on the young blade:
"All true, light-footed thief, yet let's track down the prey!
Let each man forage for himself, let Craft and Hunger,
our two lean bloodhounds, aid us in our sacred chase."
He spoke, and then all five dispersed throughout the human hive.

What joy when twilight falls and the day's heat declines
and servants splash with water the still-burning sills
and doors are opened wide and girls come out to sit
and stitch by beds of marigold, and mothers gossip!
And you, new-washed, new-combed, without a single care,
your table strewn with food, your wine in the cool shade,
your dainty wife awaiting you with sweet submission,
stroll leisurely, as from your garden plot you hold
a jasmine flower, an apple from your apple tree.
And then your faithful friends pass by and hold your arm
and you exchange sagacious words, or joke or laugh
and with intriguing gossip's lure refresh your hearts.
Then your old sweethearts amble by, old loves long past,
and your heart whines no longer, for your mind is calm,
and sudden sweetness falls, as though you were already
a shade on the other shore, and flesh a dim remembrance.
The earth is good for those well born, the lords and ladies
with well-filled barrel bellies and gold money-belts;
but the poor famished crew dispersed in the rich town
and neither friends awaited them nor laden tables.
A thousand glances pierced them through, a thousand spears;

all hid in food like scarabs in manure, and chewed:
the big-wage earners sprawled in shade and drank cool drinks,
the stout big-buttocked gods choked in their own lard,
divinity grew coarse, and the soul drowned in meat.
As the two mountain lads slunk through the streets, they searched
with gripping glance to find unguarded food to steal,
poked here and there, got tired, and gave up hope at last:
"Brother, they've stowed their things so well that my brains spin!
The soul has here no sprinting ground to gather speed,
for all things, anger, wrath, or tears, are sold to measure.
Dear God, seize staid decorum here and shout it down!"
Thus Rocky spoke to his blood brother as night fell.
When the moon drenched the streets and the river blazed with lights,
the piper lingered by a crossroads, on his last legs,
and leant against a baker's shop to play his flute.
He played the sad and bitter tune of wretched hunger,
of orphanage and exile till even the branches shrank,
but the ant-swarm of scurrying men had other cares
nor turned their eyes to pity that poor shoddy trash,
and hunger, like a long-legged centipede, crawled through his guts.

At midnight when the silver-rinded moon had reached
mid-heaven, Kentaur found himself where three roads crossed,
where hoarse nightwalkers with their thick cosmetics roamed,
opened their arms and sweetly called to hastening men;
and there, in heavy darkness, a young maiden called:
"Come to my house, my sweet, and taste my cooling flesh."
Broad-buttocked Kentaur sighed and tried to laugh it off:
"Keep quiet, child, there's not a hungry bear can dance!"
With awe the young girl circled his three-storied rump
and all at once her soft heart pitied the shaggy beast:
"It's a great crime, my God, when such huge hairy flanks
as yours stay idle and don't join in dance with mine.
Come, follow me, my bear, and share my scanty bread."
At once the famished man's dull eyes lit up with flame:
"Lead on, my dear, my noble maid! All in your cupboard,
fish, wine, dry crusts of bread, I'll crush to a fine paste!
Don't scratch your dainty feet on these sharp stones, my love—
ahoy! I'll hoist you high! Don't tire yourself, my dear!"
He heaved the light bale on his back and with stout strides
his shadow stalked the narrow lanes, and the girl giggled.
Before a low door decked with shameless signs of lust,
they stopped, and Kentaur followed the dismounted girl
and rubbed his flabby half-drained bellies with delight.
When in her humble hut she lit her small oil-lamp,
some corn and onions glowed in corners, rags on pegs,

and a small pot of clay on a few dying embers,
and when she stooped to raise the pot, her bracelets smiled
so that poor glutton's hanging lips smiled in response.
Soon she had emptied her poor pot in a wood bowl,
Egyptian black-eyed beans with a few drops of oil,
and spread the dirt floor with a mat of woven rush.
Then glutton and the young girl squatted, face to face:
"The food is scant, my dragon, it'll only brush your teeth,
how could I ever know my guest would be like you?"
The maiden laughed, then struggled to insert her hand,
tender and small, between the dragon's gripping claws.
Two or three bites, and the bottom of the poor bowl shone!
The dragon cast his eyes about, searching for food,
then picked a few crumbs fallen on his twisted beard
and turned full-bodied toward the girl, his voice half-choked:
"I've roamed this whole rich town and not a single mouth
opened to say good day with sweetness or compassion;
only you pitied me, my dear, and fed me well.
May your lean body be forever blessed, my love,
may rich lads wait in droves outside your painted door,
may wealthy merchantmen dismount from laden camels
as you throw open your tall casements' crimson shutters:
'Be off, lads, I've no time now! The king lies in my arms!'
May your warped ceiling and these barren walls of mud
be studded full of golden nails from which shall hang
your fragrant garments, golden-woven, crimson, blue,
your silver slippers and your neck-rings, works of wonder.
And may I stand outside your door, zoned with your keys,
and hold in my coarse hands the delicate scales of love
to sell your famous kisses one by one for gold.
May rich lads wait in droves to fall at my crude feet:
'Open for us the Elysian fields, the young girl's thighs!
Ah, may we drink the deathless spring before we die!'
Then from the yard I'll mock and goad those wretched youths:
'Now scram, my lads! Go chase yourselves! You've chewed my ears!
Five kings and fifteen captains wait in line today!
Come back in forty days or so, and then we'll see!' "
The young whore listened, and her simple brain spun round
as in her black eyes, rimmed with blue, there flashed already
those precious gold-stitched garments on her reed-mud walls.
When she had perched at length on the sot's hairy thighs,
it seemed to her she'd climbed a great god's wooded knees,
and now, in truth, if rich lads knocked on her poor door,
dear God, she'd scorn to clamber down and open, the dear things!

At dawn the comrades gathered by the riverbank;
hunger, alas, breaks knees and wrecks the strongest castles,
and only lucky Kentaur rubbed his bellies now
and teased his friends and picked the food from his buck teeth.
Cunning Odysseus pierced him with a sidelong glance:
"You've swollen your potbellies till they mock and jeer!
A shameless man's flushed face is worth a pair of oxen!"
The piper dragged his weary feet, and his short sword
hung down between his legs like a dog's beaten tail;
he laughed to think now of that bakery where he'd begged:
"Does God want me to burn with thirst while wells brim over?
Three hours I stood before a bakery! Not a crumb, lads!"
Then the broad-shouldered guzzler teased his piping friend:
"Ah, you poor crumb, if only I knew some magic tricks
to make the murals come alive, give souls to paints,
I'd paint the deck for you with herds of hogs and ox
and flood the hold with wells and fountainheads of wine
that you might eat and float like a wineskin, you whiner!
I'd even dare to draw—now take this in good faith—
a buxom and obliging girl I once saw somewhere
and somewhere touched—ah, my crude paws still smell of her!"
He spoke, then rubbed his fist into the piper's face.
The tunester raised his thin voice in a sad complaint:
"Five friskers, five sneak chicken-thieves set out one day
with empty bellies over land and sea to hunt
the whole world, more or less, and eat it on a skewer!"
The quick-brained archer poked his hare-brained friend with scorn:
"Your feedbag's fallen flat and all your strength has spilled!
The soul you bragged about has burst like a windbag!"
Enraged by hunger, squint-eyes lashed out like a hook:
"Have you forgotten for what great goal, and why, we sailed?—
'Three men once vowed to row their life long toward the south . . .' "
But the archer cut the piper off with scornful jeers:
"Hey ho! The fly's puffed out his ass and shits the world!
I've never promised you wine, women, lard, or bread
but only Hunger, Thirst, and God—these three great joys!
I chose lone men that stank like beasts for my companions,
but now I see but pricked balloons and bleating bellies!"
The master's words hit Granite hard between the eyes:
"We, too, have worthy bodies hunger cannot break!
The river is long, and we'd be shamed now to dismount
our bodies even before the trek has well begun."
Odysseus laughed with scorn until his neck-veins swelled:
"Blockheads, you see but river! It never swipes your brain
our soul's the river, and that we mount but soul alone,

nor will the great road vanish if I dismount today!"
He spoke, but suddenly pitied his exhausted crew,
and chewed his lower lip and frowned in consternation.
Between his eyebrows the fine scales of his mind played:
"You know how much I love you, soul, but great flames eat me;
I must endanger you once more, forgive me, soul,
and yet, even though I wished to now, I can't turn back."
The beast within him growled, and he turned to his old friends:
"Farewell, my lads, I'll leave you for a few short days.
I see no cure as yet, but I shall go off now
till the soul slips from Death, as it is wont to do;
if we must die, let the sword strike, not hunger's fangs!
Wait my return, dear friends, do what you can meanwhile,
but if I don't return, then strew your heads with ashes,
shadow your eyes with pitch-black paint, take up your drums
and like the great Worm in the song, strike up your dirge:
'You've matched all well on earth, wine, women, bread and song,
but why, you Murderer, must you slay our children? Why?'
For I was but a small child when I lived on earth,
and died with a nude infant's knowledge of the world."
He spoke, and his harsh laughter shook the morning air,
but when his heart yelped in him like a snapping dog,
he held it tight with the mind's leash and drew it back.
In the dawn's light, seeing his pallid comrades melt,
Odysseus bit his lips with grief, for even the soul
must die for lack of bread as though it, too, were flesh.
"I ache for wretched man until my heart goes mad.
Sometimes he seems a god who grabs his clay and shapes
fistfuls of the mind's fancies, fistfuls of all desires;
he blows, clay turns to flesh and breath to soul, and then
to lowest of all low beasts, until I choke and spurn him!
Ah, had I steadfast feet, and friends with whom to fight,
I'd change all the heart's bitterness and the mind's wormwood
into a deathless water to drink and slake my thirst!"
He battled with his mind and felt his entrails battered,
yet he allowed but joy and light to flood his face,
then waved in sad farewell and vanished down the banks,
but in his pointed cap, my friends, the winds of freedom blew.

X

Like a fat votive beast, a ram with gilded horns,
the sun descended on the sands, a sturdy buck,
till all the granite statues laughed, their lips turned rose,
and their cupped fists were filled with golden spheres of light.
The sands and the scorched earth cooled off till red-haired day
picked up the swooning evening in his arms, and vanished.
How good, dear God, to sit reposed in this blessed hour
with faithful friends and chat awhile in a cool nook,
your cellars filled, your servants hastening up and down,
the scurrying ant-swarms at your door, while your slaves sing
and weave a precious flaxen cloth to cool your body.
Meanwhile you sit and talk of great responsibilities,
of whence we come and where we go and what the world,
word after word passed skillfully on a thin thread
embellishing the azure air of night with pearls;
to play with your old amber chaplet, worn with time,
and say with each one of its forty heavy beads:
"I've never stolen, I've not told lies, I've never killed,
I'm good, one day I'll stroll the Elysian fields with pride."
That day God's dream-diviners and soothsayers talked,
the exorcisers harvested the world's tall peaks,
ate well until their bodies swelled, perfumed their hair,
munched luscious fruits, sipped cool refreshing sherbets, walked
and talked of gods and virtue and of burning stars
in branching candlesticks that swayed through blazing air.
Down in the courtyards, slaves prepared the sacred feast
and dragged a fat young boar to slay as votive gift,
brought there by an old groom that God might grant him sons.
The butcher stuck the young boar cleanly through the throat
till blood, like water from a watermill's cascade,
splattered the granite calves of the great dragon-god.
They placed huge caldrons on the hearthstones, lit a fire,
and cast the boar in boiling water to scald him quickly.
Then a young slave jeered at the lack-brain votarist:
"He'd have no need of God if only he'd eat his boar!
Whang! After nine months' time his wife would bear twin sons!"

The butcher slyly laughed and threw his eyes toward heaven:
"The guy's got brains, my lad. He wants to be dead sure!
When these fat chattering priests have eaten well, by God,
if he should want *ten* sons, they'll all slink out one night,
filled with the boar-god's strength, and make him rows of sons!"
While the slaves gossiped thus, on the high terraces
the freshly shaven, triple-chinned old high priest sat
and boomed out thunderous praises to his bestial god.
The night before, after he'd eaten and drunk well,
his crocodile god with all its grace so moved his heart
that he had snatched his waxen plaque, and all night long
adorned his scaly master with a flattering hymn:
"O Lord Manure, bottomless belly, all-swallowing sewer,
you eat and drink to bursting, sprawl your limbs in slush,
then slowly shut your eyes, groggy with rich repast.
The whole world hangs between your teeth like rotted meat,
and then your harbingers, the blowflies, come and lug
the imagination's dappled filth for appetizers!
And you, a eunuch now without love's joys or frenzies,
nestle in muck with swollen belly, and softly fart
until your greasy, godly stench oils all the air.
You're good, you love the world, you give us dregs and slops,
small scraps of meat and drops of grease hang from your lips—
permit me, God, to pick and poke at your rich teeth!
Though you're a mighty crocodile, I but a worm,
I'm still flesh of your flesh, breath of your stinking breath.
Ah, help your tiny worm to be like you one day!"
The high priest dabbed the dripping sweat from his fat chins
and threw dark glances at the sluggish holy men
who on their swollen bellies crossed plump hands and sighed:
"Your psalm is good, my brother, and your skill is great;
when we have eaten the boar tonight, we'll praise him, too."
They stooped, half-shut their eyes, and watched the slaves below
who had laid out the lustrous boar and plucked its hair
until its white skin gleamed amid the gathering dusk.
They ripped his entrails out, and to the milling boys
threw the great scrotum, to be rolled in ashes first
then filled with dry corn seed and made a noisy rattle.
On the hot flaming hearth, to tease the appetite,
they roasted the fat testes, penis, the throat's apple,
while high above them the priests licked their lips with greed.
Then an obscene coarse priest with a hawk's nose spoke first:
"The boar's delicious, brothers; our blessings should bear fruit;
and may the stoutest here soon bring the bride God's grace!"
They were still laughing when a boy, a widow's son,
brought them the steaming tidbits in a warm clay pot

then stood among them watching, pale with hunger pangs.
The priests fell on the meat like vultures, gulped it down,
and the frail lad stood trembling, sniffing the fragrant meat,
until his empty entrails sagged and his heart fainted.
Then all at once he fell down dead at the god's feet.
As the slaves scooped him up and brought him to his mother,
the ancient high priest shook his solemn head with scorn:
"A slave's soul has no worth, my brothers; it lacks strength
to tread on this great earth with gallantry and freedom.
I pity the poor slaves, they're nought but airy mist,
a light breeze scatters them, a fragrance knocks them down;
it's only just they crawl on earth on hands and knees.
Today I'll write a hymn to God and pray for this great grace."

Thus the god-mockers roared with laughter, ate and drank,
while in the widow's hovel, savage wailing burst:
"Murderer God, enthroned on high, come down and hear me!
I look about me, Lord; where shall I place my child
to watch him always and not forget you, murderous God!
If in the ground, you'll tell the earth to eat him whole,
if in my heart, you'll come and rot my breast and lungs,
and if I fling him on your board, your slaves will run
and cover him with laurel leaves to shield your eyes!
I shall impale my son, you slayer, on a sharp spear
so that my pain may march ahead, my strength behind!
Smash in his head, my brothers! He is no true god!
Our children die of hunger and our mothers weep;
man's heart needs you no longer, God, and spews you forth!"
The mother wailed, beat on her breasts, then leapt the sill
and in the courtyards waved her son like a black banner.
Injustice cawed, then beat its wings and flew away.
Dear God, so many wretched poor, so many naked souls
and crooked bodies, pallid lips, blood-splattered feet!
The peasants seethed, and their breath steamed with hunger's stench.
Embalmers, carters, weavers, shriveled women marched
till in the burial glen the dust rose to their knees,
but as they turned into the dale, they stopped with fear:
was it a war drum or their own hearts thumping now,
or was it God who growled, a savage desert lion?
And as they trembled and gazed about to hide or flee
they saw a girl with streaming hair rush down the sands
and beat on a heavy drum, holding her head erect.
"It's Rala, Rala!" they cried, and yelled with hands outstretched.
A girl with flaming hair and a white kerchief beat
the drum, and her bright eyes were filled with starving men,
castles that tumbled, conflagrations, swords and steeds.

She beat until her virgin breasts burned in the sands
and all the burial glen roared like a hollow drum.
Deep in the entrails of the living, forebears moved,
nor was it dust that rose and choked the heaving throats,
for necks gulped down the dead and teeth crunched them like grit;
all ate death's bitter pomegranate filled with ash;
living and dead pressed close, and the wild ghost of Hunger,
their leader, rushed with bristling hair and bloodshot eyes.
"Now all together, the dead and living, let's burn the world!"
Thus Rala shrieked, then broke out in a whirling song.
The poor took heart, snatched up the tune till the tombs roared:
"Heigh-ho, full forty giants, forty brave young blades,
forty gaunt vultures flew and skimmed the castle round.
Heigh-ho, and Hunger met them at the king's gold door;
they gave her hearts to eat for tidbits, blood to drink,
and Hunger, lads, revived, flung high her handkerchief,
heigh-ho, flung high her jet-black kerchief dipped in blood!
Hunger flung high her kerchief, and the castle tumbled!
The sun rose and the earth shook; our forty-footed braves,
heigh-ho, were forty workingmen and forty workingmaids!"
The burrows of the dead resounded, the dead woke,
thick spirits harrowed the hot sands, all crossed hands broke
through stitches of the mummy-cloth till rotted ears
perked up, grew strong, and heard the workers' moaning cries;
one dead slave pushed the other till all rose in rows.
Could this be that dread summons which all await for eons
profoundly in earth's womb, could this be that dread trumpet
that blares sweet resurrection on the flowering earth?
Rala's long hair caught fire on her sweating shoulders,
she beat her drum and swiftly gathered quick and dead
before the priests could close the gates and seize their weapons.
All necks swelled suddenly then and choked the manly song,
knees shook with fear, for high on sharp-toothed battlements
the forty-footed gods stood in long rows on guard,
and all held in their mighty hands long twisted cords
to string the slaves from neck to neck like clustered grapes.
Hearing the rising tumult, priests rushed from their food
and struggled to discern, low in the darkling air,
the scurrying shades that yelled and swarmed on the hot sands.
They laughed to see the workers, slaves all skin and bone,
and Rala leading them with drum and streaming hair.
"Hunger has pinched them once again and driven them crazy!
They starve and want to eat God's grain, but it shall eat them!
Though we know well that God detests all needy poor,
yet I do pity them. Let's throw them loaves of bread."
Thus spoke a plump-cheeked heartless priest, then seized huge stones

and flung them with coarse jeers upon the starving crowd.
The people roared and rushed in frenzy toward the gates,
but when the high priest signaled, scalding-holes burst open
and bubbling boiling water poured on the packed crowd.
Their scorched and bony bodies simmered, their flesh steamed,
and a pale woman's glazed eyes spilled on the wet ground.
A flame-eyed maiden slid among the embellished columns,
reached boldly to the secret side door of the shrine,
drew back the heavy bolts, sprang in the street and shrieked:
"Rala, dear sister, the door's open! Follow me, comrades!"
Then Rala dashed, mustered the frightened workers, beat
her drum with frenzy till all breached the secret gate.
The temple flashed as hawk-gods spread their golden wings
above their doors and gazed on the ragged crowd with rage.
But Rala cried out fiercely to whip the workers' wrath:
"On with your torches! Their time's up, it's our turn now!
Brothers, strike out for freedom hard! It's now or never!"
Some rushed pellmell into the courtyard's brimming vaults.
"Murderers!" yelled the mother, raising her dead son high,
but then a crimson arrow pierced her sallow throat,
her hoarse cry choked and drowned amid her gurgling blood,
and with her child clutched to her breast, she reeled and fell.
Then as the workers billowed round the ponderous columns,
the temple gate swung slowly open and there loomed high
a monstrous crocodile with snapping crimson jaws,
and thunderous earthquakes rumbled in earth's dark foundations.
But Rala seized a torch and rushed to fire the shrine,
for crouched behind God's mask she saw man's treacherous face;
all the guards rushed to capture her alive, pressed close,
tore off her pure-white headband, wrenched her flowing hair,
forced back her hands and bound them with their belts—but then
Odysseus loomed up suddenly, snorting, in the central courtyard!

Following the uproar and stampede on burning sands,
the archer passed the burial glen, reached the god's shrine,
and in the torchglare saw young Rala fight with odds
as the fearstricken workers panicked in dismay.
A harsh voice rose within him as his new god groaned,
but the sly man scorned to reply, and bit his lips,
then once more heard the cry deep in his heart: "Odysseus!"
He gripped the columns tight and his mind lashed with rage:
"It's not right, fool! If I should die, you'll perish too!"
But still the cry rose in his stifling throat: "Odysseus!"
Then the enflamed man-killer swore, leapt from the columns,
clenched his firm teeth with rage, unsheathed his hungry sword,
and roared out with his stubborn and blood-bitten lips:

"Is this what you want, fool? Don't say I shrank from fear!"
He whipped his body on and with two long leaps reached
God's panting guards who struggled to bind Rala fast.
They heard a beast's loud bellowing, and the courtyard quaked,
limbs flashed amid the flickering torchglare, sharp knives gleamed,
and when pale Rala raised her black fawn-stricken eyes
she saw the image of her god amid the glowing tumult:
a man of strong limbs holding high an iron sword.
He clenched his lips, then raised his pitiless arm with rage,
hacked through the tangled mob and raised it high once more
as it dripped thick warm blood upon the ringing tiles.
Men's bodies in the seething struggle hissed like snakes
and slithered in the darkness, flashed once more in light
as their blood spouted, sizzling, on the courtyard tiles.
A hoarse cry suddenly tore through stricken Rala's throat
as the tall stranger crashed and fell, and from his skull
a bronze sword, deeply thrust, gleamed in the somber air.
At once the guards rushed on the wounded boar like dogs,
called out for torches, knelt and stared with marveling eyes.
He did not move, but his eyes blinked like smothering wells
and gazed a moment sweetly like a grieving snake's,
then he growled deeply, flung his hand up toward his head
and from his blood-drenched skull pulled out the deep-wedged blade
so that his spurting blood splashed Rala from head to heel.
She took the warm blood, quivering, then snatched up her headband,
soaked it in the black flow and cursed with bitterness:
"May I not die till on the temple's roof one day
I plant this blood-soaked kerchief as our freedom's flag!"
She spoke, then from her red lips licked the soft warm blood.
The guards then bound the wounded bodies tight with belts,
cast them upon their shields, and with swift, stealthy strides
sneaked into town along the riverbank at night.
Stars in the sky pulsed joyfully like throbbing hearts
and Rala kept her doe-eyes open all night long;
waters flowed past them, tall sharp-pointed date trees, ships,
high towers, hanging gardens, brazen castle gates,
and a damp dungeon finally, dim-lit smoldering lamps,
as three pale workers round her moved their calloused hands:
"Welcome, O comrade Rala, welcome bloodhound, fierce and brave!"

Thus the two eagles of rebellion now lay stretched
with blood-soaked wings within the castle dungeon's keep
while on the face of earth the mystic veils of life
continued to be woven with myriad skilled adornments,
with white moon-billowing threads upon a sandy warp.
The cry of the night raven dripped into night's entrails,

men, animals, and waters slept, earth crossed her hands,
and only Love and Death, those two nightwalkers, roamed.
Lord Charon bolts the doors until the neighbors shriek,
but the fierce butcher tightly belts his heavy keys,
drags off the lords unshackled, and the poor in chains.
Then Eros, Aphrodite's lad with wingèd feet,
clutches the magic iron herb that bursts all doors:
half-naked bosoms gleam, long painted fingers beckon,
sly lovers glide in courts, beds sing like nightingales,
and lo! again the cobwebbed thresholds brim with children!
In the mute courtyards of the king, in the full moonlight,
his grandsire glows in jet-black marble, monstrous, cruel;
about his stone base, groveling at his feet, carved slaves
are lassoed neck to neck, bend low and kiss his knees,
but he looks far off toward the desert, and on his head,
on his huge skull, he feels a stone hawk swoop with rage,
wrap him with binding wings, then plunge his brittle beak
and suck the brains and blood of the world-conquering king.
His crowns lie scattered now, his kingdom plunged in ruin,
for his weak wastrel grandson, that false poetaster,
shames his great race by wielding a sad, idle reed;
this was a tradesman, not a king; a wretched scrivener!
Midnight had passed, and on the headless vessel still
the comrades waited for their leader sleeplessly:
"The fox leaps once too often, and the trap snaps shut!"
thus thought the piper as a lean worm gnawed his heart.
Dawn broke at last; they climbed the bank and searched the streets;
ah, if his pointed cap would loom and the sea shine!
No one confessed to dark foreboding, though all trembled,
and pain coursed secretly through each like bleeding wounds.
Day rose and dragged toward evening, night pressed stifling down,
midnight weighed on them once again, a new dawn broke,
their eyes turned glassy from long gazing, the crew quaked;
three days went by, three nights, and still no captain came.
Then Granite mutely climbed the riverbank in stealth,
a faithful hound, and sniffed and poked through empty air,
but earth seemed lopped off, wrecked, no pointed cap appeared.
The mountain chieftain's eyes then blazed, for in his heart
he felt man's freedom like a secret shudder rise;
he gazed and broke in sweat, stared, broke in sweat once more,
despaired, then lightfoot took the mountain slopes, and vanished.
As Orpheus' choked lament broke on the anchored skiff,
Kentaur sat up and writhed till the poor vessel sloped:
"By God, if he's been harmed, I'll grab the columns here
by which this town rests on the waters, and root them up!
Oho, don't cry, you whiner! The heart is weak, it breaks!"

But the distressed crybaby whimpered, and soft sobs
quavered along the spring air like an orphaned hive.
Poor Rocky, struggling with his pain to find relief,
dragged bucketfuls of water and busily scrubbed the deck,
spliced all the ropes, wedged the tholes tight, and softly sang
a mountain song, but still he could not cheat his pain.
He suddenly buckled on his sword and tightened his belt:
"Don't pine away, my lads. To weep is a great shame.
That lone man taught us freedom; it's a good thing, curse it!
I'm off on a long trek, and if it's true the world
is a round floating disk, we're sure to meet one day."
He spoke, then clambered swiftly overboard, and vanished southward.

Meanwhile, far off, Odysseus manfully fought with death,
pale faces drifted round him, and from the narrow sill
a dim light dripped upon the old damp-smelling walls.
All day and night Rala had stooped and held his head,
mute comrades hovered near and tended him with care,
mixed him smooth pastes and smeared his heavy wounds with balm.
He tripped death up, for he'd been bred on magic herbs,
his flesh surged upward once again, his blood flowed on
until his heart once more resumed its daily task.
Only his mind, rebellious still, hovered in air;
his azure island drifted past like a pale cloud,
day broke, and then the star of dawn paled in the sky.
On a far mound he saw his son dash to the hunt,
then stand stock-still, for his lean hounds had sniffed a hare.
How fragrant the blue heather, how the fernbrake rustled,
how partridges awoke until the whole world cackled!
Then a thrice-noble woman walked the terraced roof
nor looked toward the dark waves, but on the mountain gazed
till her old nurse approached with puckered hands that brimmed
with dark and dew-drenched figs wrapped up in broad vine leaves,
and the queen turned and chose the ripest fig with joy:
"This is a good year, nurse, my lips will sweeten soon
with luscious figs and grapes, my breasts with sons and daughters."
She cooled her white throat with the honeyed fig, then laughed,
and the small island turned to mist, unraveled string
by string and slowly faded from the archer's mind.
At last on the sixth night Odysseus raised his eyes,
and when his cunning glance on Rala fell, he blinked,
then tried to recall her till his body broke in sweat:
tumult of voices, setting sun, mad surging workers,
a spacious courtyard and stone gods and glittering swords,
and this same girl sprawled at his feet, bloodstained and broken.
All flashed like lightning in the suffering man's dim mind

so that he placed his aching hand on the maid's head,
and she, who for six days and nights kept sleepless vigil,
cried as in birth-pangs, fell in an exhausted faint,
till kind flesh-healing sleep poured out and wrapped her round.
When she awoke she turned her large black eyes and saw
the three great hunters, whom she'd followed like a hound,
bending above the stranger's bed in whispered talk.
They asked him where he'd come from, for what secret goal,
and if ships followed after, filled with iron arms.
But Death's sly wrestler only smiled at them in silence;
earth's lukewarm odors slowly sank deep in his heart,
he heard with pleasure how his blood pulsed in his brow,
how men once more flowed in and out his staring eyes,
but he could not distinguish words nor his mind grasp them.
At length when his ears opened and his eyes worked well,
earth once more swayed like a tall tree, till joy and grief
fell once more lightly on his head like almond blossoms.
What were they murmuring over him, of what great goals?
He felt his huge bruised body come alive once more
with joy so great he felt his heart could never hold it.
Once more his flesh began to weave skies, shores, and gods,
the shuttle sped from head to heel in constant toil
to embellish all things seen, unseen, in the empty air,
to open new roads in the void, to set up signs,
to rise, to know where it might walk, what cliffs to take.
For the first time he spoke most gently to his body:
"You are the seas through which I've passed, you are the vessel,
you are my captain and the crew and the dread wind,
you hold the whole world like a mirror in your palm
and if you fall, it breaks, and heaven and earth die with you."
Then he felt weary and closed his eyes, his loud ears rang,
and he slid headlong in sleep's deep sea-weeded waters.
The guards shot back the bolts, cast the men hogwash, scraps,
dry brittle bones to lick and stone-hard bread to crunch.
The three companions crawled and shared food fit for dogs,
then spread their hardened hands on earth and said their prayer:
"Cursed be all those on land and sea who eat their fill,
cursed be all those who starve yet raise no hand in protest,
cursed be the bread, the wine, the meat which day by day
descends deep in the entrails of the exploited man
and turns not into freedom's cry, the murderer's ruthless knife!"

For three more nights Odysseus lay in silent thought
delighting deeply in the holy quiet, and calmly plucked
from the damp air and light his scattered reveries.
And as he struggled manfully with master Charon,

the river seethed with all its branches, rose with muck
to find his old wife, earth, and mount her with his slime.
Nor prayers nor tears had ever moved him, for God's ears
are arrogant, nor will they hear or pity mankind's hunger,
but simply snow had fallen twelve feet high on the far mountains
then melted in the Negroid sun's fierce glare. The river moved,
knocked down the mud-brick walls that frightened landlords raised
to mark their farmlands and protect them from encroachment,
but he claimed all and flowed in silence and smashed all walls.

He plodded like a ram and tupped the earth, his ewe,
and earth spread out her loins and thighs, her damp flesh creaked,
the sown seed moved deep in her guts, awoke and danced,
lambs frisked with joy on the moist ground, the date trees glowed,
and sterile women rolled themselves in the warm slime
so that their sandy hips might spread to cast a son.
Even the gods hung over earth and rubbed their bellies,
for wheat once more would swell now and the man-herds eat
and grain remain to ballast God's deep guts again.
But the deaf river mutely rolled his mud-green waters
nor gave a thought to men or beasts, nor pitied gods;
simply he squandered freely an overflowing strength.
Stretched on his bulrush mat, Odysseus heard no waters,
but munched the sodden bread of mud, and made it blood;
and as his flesh got well and his dim mind grew firm
he pushed against the ground and leant against the wall:
"It seems I'm not of male seed nor of woman born.
When I look back, I see my proud soul like a frigate
leaping from wave to wave, bypassing my own country.
I look ahead: gods squirm like scorpions, castles burn,
and these two fists of mine with ears and earrings brim."
Rala was startled, but caressed his feet with joy,
and his three jail-companions gathered near to talk.
Hawkeye, the leanest, seized the archer's savage hand
and writhed with wrath like torch-smoke struck by a wild wind:
"Fate is not all perverse, my friend! See, she has grabbed you
and cast you in our cave; welcome a thousand times!
Strike at the anvil, friend, and we shall feed the flame!
Earth brims with hunger and injustice; that day shall dawn
when our full hearts and lips shall brim with bread and love;
indeed, that day has dawned now in our herald hearts."
The castle-wrecker's soul then leapt and shook with joy:
"Rise, O my soul, you've fallen in a tiger's den!
These scorching flames must surely be your three lost brothers!"
Hawkeye still burned and flickered like a restless flame;
Scarab sat by himself apart, somber, like earth,
knelt on the ground and tried in silence to scratch through
the stranger, for his murky mind, that shifty peasant,
stung with suspicion, kicked its scales toward yes, toward no;
but Nile stood up, erect, and flashed against the wall
like smokeless light, unmoving in the thickening air.
Odysseus grasped his new companions in his glance
and weighed these souls that plowed and tilled at the world's roots.
The first held flame to scorch the sterile earth with wrath,
the second cut a furrow through the earth, his feet all mud,
the third and best held in his hand the seed for sowing,

and Rala fluttered like a glowworm, all flame and light
that flits and glows in darkness through the dew-drenched air
while God licks her refulgent belly, a blue-green flame.
The enduring man admired intently her black eyes,
her thin-boned body, her lean sword-sharp lips, and thought:
"How often have I not seen maids, like poor night-moths,
leap in the flames to burn when new fires sweep the world!
In that strong spiral they forget a woman's duty,
disdain to bear earth children, cut their right breasts off
to their milk roots to shoot their arrows unimpeded
and thus rush free into God's armies, bold, one-breasted."
Rala smiled gently and approached the wounded man:
"Stranger, you're tired and your eyes burn; sleep yet a while,
there's time for souls to know each other and flames to meet."
She placed her cooling hand then on his sea-swept brow
and his mind grew serene, his flaming eyelids closed,
though his lips quivered still, still hooked by brimming words,
but Rala tenderly placed her fingers on his lips,
and then he heard her murmur gently: "Be silent, child,"
and the ferocious killer shook before a woman's sweetness.
He shut his mind's five gates, trembled, and thought how even
the smallest virgin maiden cradles each grown man
tight in her arms like her own son, even though he were a god.

Meanwhile the three companions in a corner quarreled,
and Scarab, with a glowering face, put Hawkeye straight:
"Many's the time I've warned you, but to no good end,
for you've no patience, you make all our secrets plain.
I've often wondered how your scissor-tongue finds time
to blab of flames, loves, hungers, vengeances, and fleets!
I've always had my doubts about this stranger here;
he's not a worker, but a sly ship-owning thief
who sells and then resells the world like his cheap wares
nor cares a straw for vengeance or the starving poor.
I know this man's perverse and two-faced kind too well:
he moves so fast that in his hearth no ash may stay."
But Hawkeye grabbed his comrade by his ruthless knees:
"Brother, I feel this stranger has some mighty power,
he seems like a far-traveled man, a flame, a Cretan.
Let's let him cast his fire on earth with us a moment."
Nile burst out laughing till his bald head gleamed with sweat:
"Stop brawling, friends! I think that you've both spoken well.
He's a shipmaster, a great lord who plays with fire
and now drifts by this blaze we've fed on desert sands.
Let him be welcome with his torch, welcome his leaving!"
In silence Rala gazed on the strange vagrant's form,

his towering neck, his rough-hewn forehead, his gray beard,
his rugged adamantine chest bristling with hair.
Suddenly in his sleep his lips broke in a smile
and she, too, softly smiled and sighed unconsciously.
Not even in sleep was the great traveler idle now;
his mind was a swift ship, his sleep a long, long shore
where the nightwalker hauled his sails in dreamland's port.
Behold, he stood on a waste strand where the sea stretched
like boiling lead as the black-clouded, lowering heavens
thundered and flashed above it in a smothering rage,
and in the breathless air between dark heaven and earth
a slender trireme skimmed and foamed, a speeding arrow
with swollen sails, self-lighted like a lustrous star.
The suffering man stretched out his hands and cried, "My heart!"
and as his bitter lips spread in a gentle smile
in sleep, his tender smile was caught by Rala's eye
until her own lips dimly smiled in soft reflection.
On the next day Nile told the stranger secretly
how swarms of comrades worked like ant-heaps deep in earth,
how armored ships converged now from far-distant shores:
"It's time to set the world on fire, to free our hearts,
for who knows, friend, what man's despairing heart can do?"
The archer listened to this latest cry for freedom
and his heart swelled, his restless brain leapt once again—
how many colored wings will the strong mind still sprout,
how many wines must it still drink to change the world?
Always man's soul sprouts unexpected peaks of air!
Now as he heard the new cliff-plungers of the world
the archer tossed his head, brimful of ears and eyes,
and a sharp summit cut the air and raised his stature.
Nile watched him brood in silence as his forehead rose
and glowed, as he took time to choose his yes or no,
and marveled at that mind which cut new roads with care.
But Hawkeye shook with rage, his heart would not allow
the soul to weigh its yes or no in times of need,
and opened his mouth wide to vent his noisy wrath,
but Scarab clapped his huge hands on those fevered lips:
"Keep quiet! It's right the soul should judge before it yields."
Her large eyes filled with longing, anguished Rala gazed
on the archer's silent lips and prayed in secret thought:
"Dear God, let him say 'yes' that he may never leave me!"
Slowly Odysseus rose, and in his flashing eyes
a snake allured the watchers in the darkling cell:
"Brothers, my mind has taken measure, talked, begotten,
I've heard the wretched poor, I've heard the wealthy lords,
I've also heard a voice that threads them on one string

and hangs them like thick clusters high in empty air.
My memory slowly wakes, my bowels fill with earth,
I see I'm also a mother's son, of man's seed made,
but still I don't know if I love that beast called 'peasant'
or scorn to live much longer with the lords, their masters;
deep in my heart I hold a root not split in two.
Yet I know one thing well—I hear a monstrous cry:
it may be all the poor who starve, or my own mind;
it may be God, my brothers, dressed in tattered rags,
because it suits him, who now comes to oust the nobles;
it may be only a wind that blows and rasps the reeds.
Whatever it is, I like the voice, it wakes my blood,
and I don't ask if it's true or just, and I don't care,
I hear my heart alone and do what it commands.
Comrades, my heart cries out that I should join you now!"
He spoke, and the three friends kept silent a long time;
he seemed at once a good friend and a wide-eyed foe;
what tower could they entrust him with in the fierce struggle?
But then Nile seized his hand, and his mind brimmed with thought:
"You're welcome on your own terms to our just revolt,
whether from love or raging fury or search for God;
the task is huge, each soul will find much work to do,
and when it's done and each soul tastes its full revenge,
then at the two-forked road we'll part embraced, my brother.
You still will hunt your God, but we, stooped on the earth,
shall struggle on to bring the whole world justice, bread,
and as much freedom as we can to enslaved mankind."
But the archer heard the workers' chiefs no longer now;
weary of listening and of talking, his mind smiled
and sank serenely in the gardens of calm sleep
till dream, as though it lay in ambush on a high peak,
swooped downward like a sudden hawk and pierced his brain:
A streaming army flashed as toward a dreadful battle,
God like a somber general passed before each friend,
looked deeply in their eyes and chose without compassion,
but when God reached the archer, his mind plunged, yet hung
and weighed in a long silence both contrary eyes;
deep in those eyes he spied a fox, a fearless lion,
and a lean arrow-skiff which in the loom of air
wove and unwove gods swiftly with entangling threads.
The General seized and held the left-right-handed man:
"O flaming lion-fox, you won't fight on the right
with my illustrious host, for then your glance turns left,
nor will you strike left at the foe, for then your eyes
with swift and cunning claws swerve sharply toward my host.
What shall I do with you to keep your soul from waste?

Go freely back and forth, purveyor to both armies,
drive on, and bear supplies to both battalions then!"
God spoke, and double-faced Odysseus laughed in sleep;
his startled comrades stooped and caught the cunning grin
that like a snake uncoiled now from his lips to his thick ears.

When the sun left her, earth disburdened and cooled off,
birds thrust their noisy heads beneath their downy wings,
leaf after leaf embraced in shade, tree linked with tree,
and stars hooked in the hair of night and hung like earrings.
With heart-bled sadness, Orpheus spread on the clean deck
the salty bread of beggary on the planks of exile,
and Kentaur sighed until the whole ship came and went:
"When I was born nor 'oh' nor 'ah' had yet been born!
Orpheus, we've lost our golden crown, our wings are clipped,
the chief adornment of our skiff, our precious gear,
has gone, dear piper, vanished, and only we still stay;
brave gallantry has fled and only trash remains."
But skewer-head laughed awkwardly and swallowed hard:
"He'll wear out seven shrouds, I tell you; don't forget it!
He's skilled in myriad crafts and even can shoe a flea!
Come to your senses and stop wailing; I have, you know,
a brainy and divining worm between my brows
and see the future and foretell all that's to be:
I hear our songs again, see weapons, ships, and men,
we laugh and joke once more till our poor vessel creaks."
Glutton half-raised his triple-storied body then:
"Say it again, you balding fool; your brain drips honey!
He never was one to shuffle off, his mind's a hawk,
and Death will spit black blood before he gets him down!
Come on, let's eat and raise our spirits, you've made me hungry."
They ate, then sailed straight into sleep's huge open hands
which in their palms hold all we secretly desire.
Meanwhile the tender honey-wakened Pharaoh stretched
in his warm bath and listened languidly to slaves
who told him of a letter brought by Cypriote envoys.
Whatever the King of Cyprus deigned to write, passed through
the bathing youth's bored ears now as he stretched and yawned:
"Belovèd brother, good health, good wealth and stintless joy
to your unnumbered sons, your wives, your lords, your weapons!
May melted lead pour through your evil spirits' ears!
My flocks thrive and increase, even my hens lay eggs,
my slaves beget me males, my camels bear me females;
all things go well, and with my envoys now I send
twelve tall, unliftable bronze bars and five huge jugs
brimmed with my oldest wine to drink my health, dear brother!

But one gift begs another, so send weavers, please,
to teach my slaves how to adorn and weave fine flax.
I need an exorciser to drive off carrion crows,
and a great god to guard me from the evil eye.
I send rich gifts and wait for your rich gifts in turn."
The buxom eunuchs wrapped the written parchment scroll
then bowed and asked their king for his well-bred reply,
but the pale monarch shrugged, half-closed his languid eyes:
"I'm tired; go call my handsome pageboys to come now.
I'm very sad today, my lips drip poison still;
spread my gold garments to the stars, for I've been praised
to death, and like a tree diseased, my mind won't sprout
a single flower, nor will my bed or life bear fruit.
I'm faint with boredom. Bring me, before I choke with grief,
that insolent pair who raised their hands to burn my God.
I want to hear much weeping and refresh my weary mind."

He spoke, and his black slaves rushed to the dungeon cell
and pushed the pair with haste into the upper world.
Behind Odysseus, as he strode with silent strength,
came sharp-browed Rala with the glance of a wild fawn.
They passed the moon-blurred courtyards, shadowed garden plots,
they passed long rows of date palms twined with jasmine vines,
they passed the cool coiled corridors of the women's rooms
and gazed on opulent and rich adornments there.
Poor Rala snorted with contempt and swore with hate,
but the fierce glance of the intriguing man rejoiced,
for life was good, and fragrance good, and women's breath,
and thus he murmured to himself and hailed the earth:
"Farewell rich gardens, birds, and aromatic blooms,
farewell all languid eyelids and firm dexterous hands,
the king now has transfixed us with his murderous eyes!"
But when they neared the warming bath, his bold heart pulsed,
for on the bath's smooth marble slabs with his court fools
the painted, scented monarch of the world sat jesting.
He held his precious waxen plaque, his ivory reed,
and to the gathering read his song with haughty voice:
"I perch in your huge fist, Grandsire, a puny parrot,
my wings are azure smoke, my belly a red rose,
and on my head's high dome my crown is empty air.
I want to praise you, Sire, but you're a gaping cliff,
I want to chat with you at night before I sleep,
but you grow fierce at once and ask about your thrones,
what's happened to your armies, where your frontiers stand.
How should I know of frontiers or of charging armies?
This world, O Grandfather, is but feathers, wind and dust,

and I'm an azure parrot that flies in bluest air."
The court fools kicked their caps and bells to the high beams,
the plump pale pageboys giggled shyly, the slaves smiled,
and from a golden cage that hung beneath an arch
a tiny parrot awoke and cried out, "Grandpapa!"
The shriveled young king sighed and called his jesters close:
"Fools, art is a heavy task, more heavy than gold crowns;
it's far more difficult to match firm words than armies,
they're disciplined troops, unconquered, to be placed in rhythm,
the mind's most mighty foe, and not disperse in air.
I'd give, believe me, a whole land for one good song,
for I know well that only words, that words alone,
like the high mountains, have no fear of age or death."
Thus talked the scented youth, leant on his pillowed couch,
and sighed once more, then gently shut his tear-filled eyes.
Meanwhile the archer by the doorway did not move,
but his mind raced, and the world spun within his head;
perhaps this breathless, fragile seed of kings was right,
perhaps upon this brainless earth, this mad goldfinch,
a song may stand more firm in time than brain or bronze.
Ah, had he seven souls, he'd give one to a tender flute
and roam the desolate world and whistle to all winds,
but since he had but one poor soul, he'd never waste it!
Thought swept him up as though the North Wind drove the clouds;
the king forgot his cares, jumped up, looked toward the door,
recalled, and as his lips broke in a smile, he turned
toward Rala and with great elaboration mocked:
"Welcome, black eyes! Roses spring up to watch you pass!
O thick lips, eyes of burning coal, O hawk-hooked nose,
O vagabond and gypsy heart, O cursèd race
who soil the sacred soil of my revered ancestors!"
Then suddenly the young king shivered and crouched deep
into his swansdown silken cushions, softly sighed,
but soon took heart once more and twined his slender fingers:
"I don't want slaughters to besmirch my freshening bath,
I don't want warm blood splattered on a tender song.
My road's the road of milk and honey, I wish you well
and set you free! Whether you will or not, one day
you'll think of my great kindness and your mind will sweeten.
Ah, if the nations of the world would live in peace
under my hawk-grandfather's heavy widespread wings!
God has created some souls slaves and others free,
some were begotten from God's brain like sudden thoughts,
some from his biceps sprang, but you, O wretched slave,
you're but the black dust rising from his savage tread!"
Then the king wearied and fell back on his pillowed couch,

and flame-eyed Rala moved her flashing lips with wrath:
"I'm not your grandfather's biceps, nor his mind or dust,
and I acknowledge but one God—man's own free mind,
that small, coiled, poisonous scorpion with its threatening tail!"
The king turned pale, for her voice struck and pierced his heart:
"I understand full well your two-tongued snaky mind!
Seize her and bind her fast! She's cast a noose about my throat!"

Then from the doorway the sly man moved with great calm
and played with Death, a withered apple which he threw
within his mind toward the blue sky then swiftly caught,
and joyed because all his ten fingers smelled of apple.
The Pharaoh raised his weary eyes, and his face paled:
"Who are you, savage sea-cap, that approach in silence?
Your eyes are like dark prowling beasts in which I see
a dreadful message sent by many-tholed sea-demons."
Then the star-minded man, who would not deign as yet
to wall about his seething mind with clear-cut words,
grew light of heart on hearing what the young king guessed.
The seed fell in his mind, sprang to a fruitful tree,
for a new myth had sprouted in his fertile brain:
"I rush from frothing seas and bear disastrous news!
Our sons are countless, and our lands can't hold us now.
'Dear mother, wine!' the young men shout. 'Bread!' shout our daughters.
'Mother, let's swiftly go to the lord king of earth!'
With babies on our backs, with axes in our hands,
we mount the cold North Wind and knock on your bronze doors.
Master, give us your sacred head in place of alms!"
The king screeched like a bird and on his eunuchs leant:
"I've never killed, I've never stolen, I've not done evil!
My forefathers warred and slaughtered people ruthlessly
yet passed through earth most happy, swept toward Hades then,
and neither gods nor men spoke them a scurrilous word.
And I, who am good and preach of love throughout the world
and rule the earth not by the sword but a light feather,
must pay their ancient crimes! This is not just, my Lord!"
But the unsoftened archer felt no calm compassion:
surely the grandson now should pay the grandsire's crimes,
each leaf drinks from the same root of man's tribal tree,
and thus he cruelly blazoned his deceiving myth:
"I am a great newsbringer and proclaim my news:
On a far, famous island I saw castles blaze,
I saw, on high snow-covered mountains, blue-eyed dragons
who felled huge trees and swiftly set their full sails south.
I've seen by desert wells long camel caravans
and young men waiting upright under heaven's road

for the sharp crescent moon to rise that they might go.
I cry out in all towns and thunder in all cities:
'Eh, landlords, quickly double-bolt your cellar doors!
Hey, misers, thrust your moneybags deep in the earth!
I beat and pummel your dark doors in the wild night;
eat till you burst, go kiss your wives for the last time!'
I see a sword, O king, that swings above your head!"
He spoke, and from his bosom drew a lumpish dwarf,
gray hair and beard, blood-clotted eyes, huge ears and teeth,
which he had slowly shaped in jail with blood, salt sweat,
and green mold of the muddy bread cast them for food,
then placed it mutely on the monarch's trembling knees.
The sallow youth fell back on his soft couch with fright:
"Take back this sorcerer's spell, take back this evil dwarf!"
But then the unmerciful and cunning man said slowly:
"In my wild country, king, this is how war's declared!"
The pale king sighed and raised his hands toward heaven's dome:
"Blessèd be comfort, love and peace! We are brothers, all,
and all have earth for mother and the sun for father."
But the man-murderer's mouth broke in a mocking laugh
until the wan king felt his blood seep from his veins;
he saw the lone man slyly slink with a great ax,
a dragon with blood-clotted laugh and dark-green eyes.
"Go away!" he screamed. "Go where my eyes may never see you!"
and he began to sob and whine like a small child.
The harsh sea-battler's startled heart began to throb;
he longed to take the wretched youngster in his arms
and soothe him with caresses like a good grandfather.
Then he recalled the dream which one night hooked his brain,
the battle-god who marshaled his great host on earth,
and laughed to think what noble rank God gave him then:
"Ah, God was right to have no trust and weigh me well.
If only I could fight with both my friends and foes,
join in my heart God, anti-God, both yes and no,
like that round fruit which two lips make when they are kissing!"
His mind thus juggled, but his stern unyielding will
opened the road toward freedom with no double-talk,
and so the archer mutely turned, passed through the door,
the marble courtyards and dark gardens, the outer gate,
and swiftly, lightly strode into the wide free air.
Rala behind him followed like a sword-sharp flame,
then seized his ruthless hand and with great anguish spoke:
"There's no hope left for me on earth without you now . . ."
but her wild doe-eyes filled with tears and her voice choked.
The stars above them cast thick flames like shepherd-fires,
and Rala moved and burned on earth like a bright star,

yet she controlled her voice and calmed her pulsing heart:
"Let's hasten to our comrades' secret den at once;
messengers from the harbor may have come already."
Quickly they passed the boisterous city streets at night;
slaves bore their weary lords in rich-wrought sedan chairs,
and others rushed ahead, waving bright-colored lanterns.
Rala glanced sideways at the archer, mute, serene,
who swiftly stalked the narrow lanes while his rough hands,
his crafty eyes, his lofty sea-cap, flashed with fire.
Trembling, she reached and touched those world-creating fists:
"When you were talking and the king's bathed body paled,
your eyes brimmed full of islands then and harbors swayed,
and all on earth stretched out their necks to hear your words.
Even my eyes, I swear, saw in the blazing air
slim triremes with long oars set out full sail together,
and I heard camels, steeds, and swords resound on tiles."
The lion-minded man caressed her hair and laughed:
"Your crisp and flaming mouth has spoken truly, Rala.
As I talked on, I also felt my full strength ebb,
my wild mind falling to the ground, clump after clump."
Then Rala shivered long and glanced at his dark eyes:
"Myths tell that God created all this world with words.
He said, 'Let there be trees!' At once trees sprang from earth.
'Let there be birds!' and birds at once flew through the air.
He grabbed a lump of mud, shouted for man to rise,
his words fell on the clod, a man and a maid rose
as though seed, in a lightning flash, had sprung to fruit.
All of his words plunged thus on earth and swiftly spawned."
The sly man laughed, for he saw clearly in himself
the limits of his strength, alas, and fought with spite,
battling on earth daylong, nightlong to enlarge their scope.
It was a sweet and summery night when virtuous ladies
strolled on the mole and preened, dainty and prim in talk,
for Mistress Virtue sat enthroned between their thighs.
Gaiety, garden odors rose, tall date trees swayed,
and sated lords and ladies laughed by the cool river.
The sky shook like a mystic park, the river rolled
stars, trees, and houses toward the sea and drowned them all.
Ripe-bosomed girls sold jasmine to the new-bathed ladies
who wove them in their waved coiffures like scented stars,
but by the riverside mute mothers with dry dugs
leant over waters with their pale babes in their arms,
then once more plodded on, clutching their treasures tight.
Poor Rala wanted to cry out, but her throat choked,
and the sad archer felt his mind expanding swiftly
to taste new struggles and discern new kinds of pain.

"My God swells in me day by day and floods my heart,"
he murmured, as he brusquely wiped his brimming eyes.
Passing beyond the towered walls, they reached the fields
where a damp breeze was blowing on the wakening soil;
the early morning sky-cock rose and beat its wings
and Rala sniffed like a swift hound and led the way.
She double-tracked, leapt ditches, watchfully approached
a dark lone hut, then rapped upon it like a drum
and crowed three times like a night-raven with hoarse throat.
A low door opened slowly, and then a slender girl
threw herself suddenly with love in Rala's arms.
Deep in the lamp's dim light Odysseus could make out
a motley group who leapt to welcome them with joy:
poor native fellahs, dark-skinned slaves, slim blue-eyed youths,
and crisp-haired Negroes with deep brands between their brows.
They greeted Rala with great joy and told their news:
"At any hour now the shores will swell with ships,
last night our heralds told us all that we wished to hear—
that all the islands are up in arms and sail to help us!"
Then Rala danced within her comrades' arms and cried:
"The wind of freedom blows and swells the trees, my friends;
let's dash upon the dungeons, smash the brazen doors
and place our three chiefs in the forefront of the battle!
We who have sowed the seed of hope shall reap the flame!"
All hearts caught fire and swelled with overbrimming hope
but the much-suffering man disdained such easy joys
and rose to place firm order in their hearts and brains:
"Comrades, I've voyaged long and far on sea and soul,
my eyes have seen disease, gods, ghosts, and men, and yet
in no land have I seen a more false, murderous siren
than that wind-headed, babbling, blind bitch-hound called Hope!
Many of my dear friends have rotted on far shores
listening to her sweet song, gazing on her fair breasts.
Ah, shut your eyes, make your minds firm, don't hear her, friends!
Joy to that desperate man who still fights on although
all shores seem bare and his mind has nor gods nor hope!
Mix and weigh well your sturdy brains and your desires
and with a clear gaze search the treacherous shores with care:
how many ships? from where? what is their strength in arms
and what self-interest drives them swiftly to our aid?
No ship sets sail, I think, without some hope of gain,
no soul sets out on earth without some sure reward."
He spoke, his words hit home, all callow wings collapsed,
but all pressed closely round him with new-strengthened minds
and armed false cheating hope with action led by ripened thought.

The sun at length ransacked the earth, the city woke
as the much-suffering man approached his humble skiff
with haste, and his knees shook with his compressed desire.
Then his heart foundered like a fish and he stopped, startled:
the river rolled and boiled like thickening crimson blood
and licked with mud the holy date trees' topmost tips
and swept down, overbrimming, till the hamlets gleamed
like islands on the hilltops, zoned by swirling waters.
Glittering shoals of well-fed fishes swept in streams
plundered by many long-legged storks with gaping beaks,
and hungry crimson-winged flamingoes plunged and ate.
The archer shook with fear to gaze on the great strength
of that dread element with its thickened fertile flood,
but thought with pride of that other element, the mind:
"I'm only a small reed on the bank of that dark god
who overflows and mounts our mother, Earth, but yet
on the reed's thinnest point, on the pure flower of flesh,
all this great river like a dewdrop hangs and trembles."
As he trudged on, and his feet sank in the cool mud
and plunged deep roots, he thought his comrades must have fled
to quiet their wretched hearts and fill their hungry bellies,
but when he heard fat Kentaur's snores beat on the bank
like waves resounding hollowly in a domed cavern,
at once his captain's heart leapt like a glad kid
and he rushed toward his loved friend to refresh his soul.
Like a white gull that flutters its long wings and drinks,
his vessel lightly tossed upon the sun-washed waters,
and the much-suffering man grew calm, for sails, ropes, planks
nest tightly in the heart until there's no escaping.
Then he leapt lightly on the deck, ran toward the beast
who lay sprawled, snoring by the prow, and laughingly thrust
his longing hands on his friend's hairy shoulder blades.
Broad-buttocks stretched, half-opened his sleep-swollen eyes,
as though he glimpsed a good dream hovering above his head,
then shut his eyelids tight to keep the vision trapped.
"Wake up, O triple-buttocked body, rise, dull flesh,
I'm not a shadowy dream! I'm hungry! Let's build a fire!"
Then glutton's lips spread to his ears in a wide grin,
and when he reached and grasped lean flesh and bone, he roared,
and the skiff danced and tossed to their rude manly wrestling.
From the coiled rope at the stern's end, a pointed pate
poked out and all at once its dim brain swirled and twirled
for in the light one stood and laughed who seemed to be Odysseus.
From his great joy the piper lost his wits, he screamed
and came down tumbling on the deck like a hunched hedgehog
till breathless and worn out, he seized his master's knees,

while glutton grabbed the archer by his wounded head,
and plied him full of questions with wild throbbing heart.
But the much-suffering man laughed long and put them off:
"Let's eat a bit of bread first, that's our foremost duty,
and then, like fresh fruit for dessert, the words will come.
Piper, go light a fire, and you, my splayfoot friend,
tell me why our two mountain lads are not on board."
Then Orpheus knelt to light the fire and Kentaur spoke:
"Captain, you know quite well how when a gleaming ax
splits open a snake's head, its body squirms and throbs:
that's how we thrashed about, left orphaned on this shore.
Our mountain lads have taken wing and left no trace,
but we, your two burnt coals, have kept the smothering spark
of your far plan alive, and guarded this frail skiff.
I thought of footwork then to earn my wretched bread
and grabbed our wineskins and lugged water to all homes
and sang out like a nightingale in the hot streets;
and our poor piper piped at funerals and at weddings
and beat out sad or happy tunes, as fate would have it,
then hid among the feasting boards and plundered crumbs.
Hunger makes even the most noble man ignoble.
At evening we returned to our poor skiff, stretched out,
ate greedily, and passed the nights in talk, long talk
of distant voyages and joys and gallant deeds
until your pointed cap should gleam along the bank."
He spoke, then touched and gently stroked his master's knees,
but the unflattered mind shrank mutely in its skull:
"Both have adapted to the daily grind for food
and lick the licorice-root of sticky memory.
Those two are best who cast their yokes aside, and left."
While his fond comrades set him food and spread his bed,
he stooped and wondered how to set their minds aflame,
then ate and drank in silence, sprawled on the skiff's length
and called on sleep from waters with its freshening palms,
and sleep arose and stood beside him with a cool green fan.

He slept, and his wrecked body planted cornerstones,
while Granite, far away, trod on the roads until
all their black pebbles turned to gleaming sapphire stones.
With thoughts like crimson apples on a crystal stream,
his sunburnt body swiftly plunged down toward the sea
and an unfledged new song leapt from his haughty lips:
"O eaglet with your awkward wings and tender claws,
I know your joy now when you kick your nest away
nor bid your father goodbye nor leave a trace behind you.
It's good to listen to your betters with meek mind

and sharpen your claws silently on a great spirit;
but it's still better, ah, dear God, to stretch your wings
while boundless hopes and roadless winds spread out before you."
Thus Granite trudged and sang, shook his wide shoulder blades
like wings, and took deep pleasure in his savage freedom.
Meanwhile his bosom friend walked southward on tanned legs,
and stanched his tears, though his lips dripped with joy and grief:
good were the lion-heart's caresses, his harsh breath,
good his enormous shadow, good to stand beside him,
the heavy bow stretched tight, grasping the heavy oar,
never to say "I'm free!" never to say "I won't!"
never to allow yourself to judge or to ask questions,
only to follow faithfully in his steps and feel
that freedom is enslavement to one high above you.
Now that he'd gone and man's extended boundaries shrank
once more, and earth returned again to her low stall
like a swift mare who'd lost her daring cavalier,
ahoy! let's bind our headbands round our orphaned brows
and may that flame we stole from him keep burning, God!
Thus Rocky murmured to himself, tightening his waist,
kicking the sands behind him as his eyes gazed south.
Meanwhile Odysseus woke with a great start on deck
and thought he'd dreamt of those two lads of mountain grace
as though he'd seen two date trees, or two hawks in air,
but they slid mutely from his eyes like tears, and vanished.
He turned then to the two forms sunk in sleep close by,
woke them, and swiftly told them of his strange adventures:
his wounds, the dungeon, comrades of a wild new god,
and the new rage that roared now in his stormy head:
"The earth's as wide, my lads, as man's despairing soul!"
But the thin piper made a wry face and spoke boldly:
"You're always sprouting new arms like an octopus,
your destiny's accursed, for the whole world can't hold you.
We set out elsewhere once: to drink the deathless water,
but now again you long to search out devious roads
as when you feigned for ten years to be sailing homeward
but plundered shores, O crafty fox, or in cool caves
lay like a god in deathless arms, your land forgotten.
We sailed for secret springs, but now our soul-guide halts
and feels for the starved workers and their sniveling brats!"
But glutton touched his master's knees with happiness:
"The mountain snows have melted, rivers have swollen their banks,
new men have plunged upon you till your mind's a flood
that rolls through earth in a red stream filled full of seed.
These secret springs that flood you are good and holy too!
I'll also sail down your deep current like a frigate

nor, like the piper, ask you whither and why we go.
Heigh-ho! If I should live and sail a thousand years
I'll never have time to roam around your monstrous bulk!"
The devious man rejoiced to see that Orpheus perched
and boldly chirred on the lion's mane like a small cricket,
but then with youthful strength he seized good glutton's hand:
"I also, like a dolphin, follow the dark God's
swift bloody stream with joy nor ask toward what or why we go!"

The comrades talked and held their hearts within their hands
while that great weaver, the fierce sun, flung shuttles wide
and in the loom of air wove and unwove all men
until he hung the crimson tassels of his setting.
Far off, God's stream bore downward from the foggy north
a forest of slim skiffs in which blond bodies gleamed;
they dragged their dugouts on the banks, seized torches then,
set fire to rigging, sails, and their black keels and made
their vessels ashes to prevent all hoped return.
Good was this earth on which they'd moored, a tray of wheat,
good was this river and the many-winged clear air
and sweet dates melting in the mouth, fragrant as honey.
Their gods and dogs drove on ahead, trudged down the banks,
and men and women streamed behind till the earth rang;
they bound long hautboys round their waists, sharp double-axes,
and from their homeland carried fire in thick reeds.
They passed, and like a river drowned the earth and dragged
oxen and maids and horses till loud lamentation
arose and the king heard in fear and sent them envoys.
He chose his wiliest elders, his most crafty-tongued,
to drive those savage raiders from his sacred soil
with devious clever words, with their deceiving brains.
They held their speeches painted on long leathern scrolls
and searched their foxy minds, contriving clever tricks
to twine the barbarous blockheads in their brains' strong snares.
On two humped camels they brought two huge letter-packs;
like bird tracks on soft clay, the black inscriptions squirmed,
a swarm of ants on sheepskins, telling of ancient tales
and gallant deeds and what the soul in Hades suffers.
They came and stood like hoopoes on a mound of sand,
unrolled their scrolls, then through their noses with one voice
they shrilled like cackling hens who've spied a hovering hawk.
Thus they intoned and swayed their bodies back and forth;
at times their speech dragged on in lulling lullaby,
at times it roared and threatened like cascading stones,
at times they pointed to the sky, then to the camels
that stooped and chewed the grass, burdened with sacred scriptures.

They spoke, and the barbarians gaped with wondering gaze
and sniffed their new-washed garments, touched their crimson belts
and pulled the old men's ears to see their golden rings.
Some bent above the magic hides that babbled so,
then shrieked with laughter to see fires, necks, and heads,
as though they gazed at their own dens in heavy slaughter.
The old men read in one long stream, droning and chanting
of fearful ghouls or the sweet life that follows death.
They raised their hands on high and swore their gods were great

and would chastise all foes that trod upon their land
but that the strangers would rejoice on the road home.
"Ephemeral bodies made of clay, open your minds!
The gods cry out for your departure, and in your sleep
they'll give you handsome slaves, fat oxen in your dreams,
and when you die, they'll give you murals thick with paint
that shall depict the joys and goods of all mankind!"
The elders' haughty tongues were slaked, they rolled their scrolls
about their richly wrought, carved reeds, fell silent then,
and steaming, breathing heavily on their mound of sand,
twiddled their long thin thumbs and waited for reply.
But the bold raiders jeered, for their minds had no tongues,
and only few words rattled in their thickset skulls;
they growled like hungry beasts and gave no clear reply
Two young barbarians snatched the canny magic scrolls
and pressed them to their hairy ears, then stooped to listen
as though the scrolls were seashells where they hoped to hear
the distant myriad sounds the inscriptions had just made.
A bearded codger scowled and shook his threatening lance:
"Damned if we've understood your nasal sniffling drones!
You've puffed and heaved and sighed like newborn whining bear-cubs!"
Enraged to find their spells were all in vain, the elders
abandoned useless tricks and barked a few short words:
"The Monarch of the World awaits your quick reply!
What do you want of our gods? Why tread our sacred soil?"
But the barbarians laughed and shook their flaming reeds:
"We want your earth and women and your good rich food,
we want your beef and steeds, your daughters and your sons;
all that has feather, scale, or hair, old men, are ours!"
"But that's not just! Beware of our great gods in heaven!"
Then they whipped out their scrolls once more, and once more told
what's just, unjust, what's good, what's evil, what's yours, what's mine,
and of the twelve old elemental virtues of man.
But the barbarians, dizzied with the high talk, cried out:
"You've burst our brains with all that rant! Draw back, far back,
spread far and wide so that your land may hold us all!
Whatever we have to say we'll stamp in lively dance!
Go to it, lads! Uncork your minds in swirling steps!"
All bound their belts, unsheathed their iron swords, then howled
and swayed their torsos in a savage northern dance,
clashing their blades and raising high a virile song:
"The king gulps down his wine, he drinks it to get drunk,
he cocks his crown, hangs a carnation on his ear,
takes ten goatskins of mellow wine, twelve buxom maids
and twelve blind bards, then makes straight for his royal rooms.
He drinks, the king drinks wine until his mind grows wild,

he sees the fields where he has fought, he sees the slain,
he sees his black steed stand in blood up to its knees,
he sees, my lads, his god astride on his steed's rump!
He drinks, drinks all the wine until his chamber sways;
his friends and foes splatter his grain with flesh and blood,
his friends and foes manure his farms and vineyards well,
his heart is well manured and needs no other dung!
He drinks, drinks all his wine until his mind sprouts thorns,
he laughs, then flings his twelve plump women from the walls,
seizes the minstrels by their napes and casts them headlong,
then shouts for his dread god to come and carouse together!
Trembling magicians bring their god clasped in their arms,
then in his lap the king sets down the huge carved log
and slowly with an awl uproots the god's gold teeth,
pries out the beaded eyes with a sharp skewer slowly,
and the king drinks, he drinks his wine, drinks to get drunk,
and in the dawn they find his god strewn round the room
and the king sprawled and holding in his hands the god's
wild hollow skull from which he slowly sips his wine."
Thus the barbarians clashed their swords, danced, howled, and sang
and gave no other answer for the world's great king.
Till the sun set, the elders waited for reply,
but when night smothered all, they rolled their scripts once more
on their long reeds, climbed on their camels once again,
and like blind hairy caterpillars crawled homeward on the sands.

The river hamlets shook with fright at the dread news:
"Blond ghouls have anchored on our earth and smash our homes!
Their steeds have but to whinny and our mares get pregnant,
they sharpen their black swords afar, and our necks tingle,
they bring a god like fire, housed in thick round reeds!"
Magicians cast their incantations, chanted spells,
and stretched a crimson waxen cord from bank to bank
to bind the foe with magic and obstruct his way.
And when the sharp-jawed crocodile heard their heavy tread,
he rose from his thick mud, and seeing among the reeds
crisp blond-haired mouthfuls, opened wide his greedy chops
till from his gluttonous longing green saliva dripped;
he'd never tasted yet such plump red-buttocked bodies!
The granite grandsire moved, and all the palace shook.
War mounted his black steed until the stones flashed fire,
he knocked at night on taverns, knocked on doors at dawn,
till wives and mothers wept and sisters swooned, but he
grabbed young men by their hair and hung them from his saddle.
At midnight the jail's door was opened stealthily
and the three leaders secretly escaped, hugged walls,

slunk through deserted courts and melted in the dark.
Rala kept vigil all night long, tended the lamp,
waiting to hear their footsteps on the midnight road,
and huddled on her humble threshold like a dog.
She listened to her dark heart weeping in the night
then bit her fevered lips until she made them bleed:
"Cursed be those two oppressive beasts, a woman's breasts,
and three times cursed her spreading, always hungering, loins."
She leant her eyes on that old crone, seductive night,
until night slowly filled with children, and Rala trembled,
for she saw neither weeping workers, hungry flames,
nor young men in the slaughter-shed who groaned like bulls,
nor the three chiefs for whom that very night she waited—
she only saw babes in their cradles and a tall cap;
then swore, and with her nails tore at her heart in rage:
"Cursed be the crimson veins that spoil and turn to milk!"
She rose and felt her mute forefathers stir within her
and with full, bloated udders drag her down to earth:
"Sweet is a babe upon a woman's breast, O Rala,
and sweet a man's embrace within the dark night, Rala.
Don't fret for justice now, don't ache for the sad poor,
let men get frenzied, for they've nothing else to do,
but you were made a woman, Rala, above such cares
which on this earth split wasteful men apart like foes;
you have two breasts that sweetly join both friend and foe;
be patient, Rala, end your woman's duty now."
Thus ancient voices counseled in her heavy heart
and Rala wept with shame and cried in the wild night:
"Dear God, may I die twice before my high flame falls!"
She spoke, grew calm, and her mind flashed with sudden light,
for in her tender hands she held her savior, Death.
She smiled, for never had her heart felt such deep peace
as now when suddenly she knew that Death was freedom.
Hearing the crunch of graveled feet, she leapt to the door,
shot back the bolts and welcomed thrice the weary chiefs.
They met to plot in her low hut, and all three shared
like bread the great new danger on which they all fed.
Hawkeye would raise his shrill voice in the glooming shops:
"Brothers, refuse to bring supplies to the Egyptian army,
do not embalm the dead, my brothers—let them rot!
Refuse to bear arms, don't march to war's slaughter-shed!"
Scarab would rouse the starving peasants in fields and farms
to burn their masters that all slaves might share the earth:
"It's just that he who sows should reap, who works should eat!"
Nile would thrust slyly through the army, march to war
and open mutinous doors to freedom in all hearts.

But Rala heard in silence how the three shared all
the dangers as though only they were the true heirs,
and not one reached his hand to slake her hungry heart.
When Rala once more locked herself in her low hut,
she put her things in order, quickly lit a fire,
boiled water, mixed it with fresh laurel-berry scent,
twice barred her door again, and in the early dawn
began to bathe her virgin body like a corpse,
and her tears ran in silent fountains down her cheeks.
When she had washed, she opened her poor wooden chest
that held her wretched dowry, chose her finest dress
and decked herself like a new bride, though her heart broke:
"Alas, how shameful should they find my body in torn rags!"

Meanwhile the archer lay upon his deck supine
and marveled at the embellished sky, night's holy robe
hung with gold gleaming brooches and long silver charms.
The stars above him moved like letters, mystically,
some squirmed like scorpions on the sky's rim, others rose
like swords, eyes, vipers, ships, and flaming waterfalls.
Mutely the archer searched amid the sand-strewn stars,
and his bewitched mind quaked to hear their dread appeal:
"Help me, my only son, set free our souls from sand!"
The star-eyed archer rose and spoke to his two comrades:
"To all my questions, friends, two voices answer me.
The mind, that's prudent always, prudently replies:
'Now hold your frontiers well, build walls around your wealth,
don't starve for foreign hungers or ache for foreign pains,
erect your tower on desert sands, make solitude
your scornful fortress, guard her with her famished hounds.
Smash all my bridges, board my windows, lock my doors,
give me unbreachable stout walls and narrow slits!
I am the mind, earth's threshing-post! I stand and flail!'
Thus does my lone mind shout, roaming my castle's skull,
but my ungirdled, pitying heart leaps from my breast
and like a beggar runs and knocks from door to door:
'Brothers, dear brothers, give me your pain that I may share it!
Dear God, there's nothing yours or mine, nor friend's nor foe's,
I am the workers' heart of earth that cannot rest!' "
Then he fell silent, spied on his two faithful friends
and joyed to see his own face shining in their eyes;
they trembled at his words, but he spoke on and laughed:
"Don't pull such long sad faces, friends, for I know how
to keep my two bad neighbors from each other's throats:
like a great king I keep my dwarf-mind a court fool,
adorn his brow with feathers and his cap with bells

that with his jokes and tricks I may still bear earth's griefs
and mock at my poor heart at times to prick her pride.
And though I loose my heart to knock from door to door,
I hold her with invisible reins, as blue as air,
so that the falcon-hunting heart swoops back once more,
whether she wills or not, and brings the quarry home.
Thus have I trained those two beasts, jesting fool and falcon,
and slowly mount the burning desert paths of virtue."
As the much-suffering man spoke on, the dayspring smiled,
glutton got hungry and shared out fish, bread, and dates,
then gave the wine flask to the man of twin-peaked soul,
and he, with throat flung back, could hear the holy drink
rush gurgling down to fill the trenches of his brain.
He drank, then passed that cackling mistress back to Kentaur
who felt his veins swell in his flesh like thronging roots
as his vast body like a plane tree spread in sun.
When Orpheus sucked the sacred dug, he too grew bold:
"I've often pondered on the world, but my mind quakes!
The earth's so wide no man's embrace can hold her all,
but if we sip red water or eat a strip of meat,
earth nestles on our bosoms like a trembling maid.
If there's a God in truth, he's made of meat and wine!"
Odysseus, who had many brothers, now roared out:
"Ahoy! Rig all the sails! Let's make for the north soon!
At midnight yesterday my new companions said
that wine-red bearded War has moored among us here;
the slaves already have caught fire and send us signals."
In Orpheus' loins the wine grew strong and turned to blood:
"Ahoy, turn new, my flute, for a new tune begins,
a monstrous new song mounts the sky and knocks me down!
Only when I've drunk deep and my mind's blazing, archer,
do I know well toward what and where your onrush sweeps us!
I'd never seen before a freer, more stable soul;
we all drove toward the south because our own hearts wished
to hunt that still uncaught and blue-winged bird in air,
but as we dashed down toward the south, your spirit stopped,
free to plunge forward or to take the backward track.
Your hunting mind sets out at dawn and doesn't know
what wild game it will flush or shoot along the way.
You've said: 'Let's track the source of deathless water, lads,'
but when you started and the wide wind struck you, then
you stopped, for you heard new wells surging in man's heart,
and even I, with my dry wineless throat, could mock you:
'That great mind's now grown maudlin with the wretched poor
as though the final goal in life were mankind's comfort!'
But now I liken your full mind to those rich lords

who soon as they return from plundering, seek new roads,
take in their towers their armies with their families, too,
spread feasting boards for them to gorge on, fields to play,
then with great cunning cram them full of wine and food
that the brave lads might grow into lean meat for war
and make themselves a crow-god that will gnaw their guts."
Potbellied glutton laughed and grabbed the piper's nape:
"By God, not a drop of wine has reached your belly, it's all
leapt high to your bald pate and turned to brain and wisdom!
You've set all things in a neat row, in shipshape style,
but this is the main point: our heart-seducer here
takes all things in one ear then spouts them out the other!"
But the light-blooded songster's mind could not be changed:
"Now look who's talking! Our master perks up both his ears,
drags all he hears to his sly mind and makes them God—
thunderous flashes, hollow words, and the wind's whistling!"
As the friends talked, Odysseus mulled in silent thought:
"These two say 'God,' and their minds stop and go no further,
but I set secret sail and bear off on my ship
the newest siren, God, and sail on the waste seas."
The lone man stooped, untied the hawser and rigged sail:
"Words swarm like fishes in the sea, but learn, my brothers,
God is not shaped with meat or the air's false pregnancy
but with the savage daily sweat of wretched man."
They plied their oars then, and the sluggish river rolled
and spread its fertile mud upon the thirsting earth.
The sun leapt up, poured light on earth, the workers woke,
women and children wept, helped men prepare for war,
fetched cedar for returning, cornel boughs for strength,
and wives and husbands clasped as though they'd never part.
They all drank wine till their minds flushed, then the brave lads
set forth with red strings round their throats, and in the lead
King Sunless dashed, entwined in cobwebs, pale and sad.
Pharaoh turned hoarse with shouting at both gods and men,
then took his soft spear once again, his pointed reed,
smoothed his wax tablets with his hand, rubbed out his song
till from his slender backbone a new poem rose.
Now in his peril the whole world sprang in his breast
like the last light that plays on mountain peaks at dusk,
and all at once his slender reed took wing, and flew:
"Life is but air, mist, dream, a dew on the wet ground,
and War a flaming cloud with harsh hail impregnated,
an evening ship of air that sails with tranquil calm
on the tall heads of men and the round breasts of women.
And I'm but air, mist, dream, and the black sun shall come
and that black rooster, Death, shall crow, and I shall vanish too."

The sun, like a slain head, rolled slowly down the sands,
deep azure mists rose thickly by the river's edge,
and the light vanished sadly on the yellow banks.
The star-grains brimmed on the black fields, and the vast sky
like full-winged mills began to grind in the grim darkness.
Wild fawns slunk to their water-holes with quivering hearts,
the famished jackal dug among the poor men's tombs,
and night-gods calmly wrapped in fresh vine leaves all boys
who had just died, then crouched to eat them on the sands.
A beautiful Egyptian princess died that day
and lightly walked along the riverbank at night
and stooped to hide her rotted face from her dear friends;
Night with her aromatic armpits drifted past,
an immature most tender light bloomed on the fields,
till dawn, an awkward calf, came stumbling down the banks.
The three friends followed the rose-lidded river's flow,
white birds that shed a lustrous light passed over them,
the fishes in the waters frisked, and on the sands
villages crackled, burned, and maidens tore their hair.
The archer's brains breathed deeply the cool springtime breath
of Death with all its sweet and dizzying spells, unslaked,
as though he smelled night-jasmine in his gloaming garden.
His mind spun, all the boundaries of the world were lost
as though he'd gone amid his old acquaintances,
green fields and mountains, to hunt deer with his long bow
and all had suddenly changed, as in a drunken mist;
his murderous bow had budded like an oak-holm branch
and deer approached it without fear and browsed on its green leaves.

XI

How well, dear God, do young men sniff a woman's odor,
apples of strange lands, or a widowed country's pillow!
Mother, a warm breeze blows, and home can't hold me now,
dear Mother, birds with women's breasts fly from the south
and hold thin letters in their claws, and bring sweet news:
a widow, peppery widow bathes in a large river,
Mother, she stretches on hot sands and her joints creak,
she gazes on the wastes and sighs, looks on her breasts,
unsucked, like shriveled apples, and sends messengers,
Mother, of warming winds and birds and bitten apples.
Mother, my youth is smothering me, I'll wear my weapons—
sweet musk about my waist, and love songs on my lips,
and join that peppery widow with my body full of flames."

As bridegrooms round the queen bee buzz in clustering swarms,
cluster by cluster young men swarmed round widow Egypt.
Riverbanks shook with tumult, highways creaked and cracked,
the desert's loins caught fire and her thighs prepared
for strong erotic wrestling on her ready sands;
first skirmishes had now begun, the first lovebites,
the first, first wild caresses to arouse desire.
They pitched their tall tents on the plundered widow's lap
and her first cries rang out, quivering with fear and lust.
Slave girls were lined in the cool shade and shared by youths
who felt their breasts and loins, tested their teeth, then chose:
this one was good for fieldwork, that one for kneading bread,
this one for bed at night, that one for grinding grain.
With "I want this one" and "You take that," their blood soon raged
until they grabbed their swords, poured on the threshing floors,
and soon earth's entrails grew appeased, engorged with men.
Horsemen dashed by with conches, infantry marched with drums,
and gasping bleating flocks of men trotted like sheep;
house-roofs gaped open, triple-bellied brazen caldrons
seethed full of hogs and horses over fierce bonfires,
and the barbarians grabbed and gulped all, still unboiled,
until from their blond beards the grease dripped drop by drop.

The nostrils of the many-minded archer flared;
the poor had everywhere increased, war grew and swelled,
archons decayed, their roots hung loose in empty air,
till there remained but the mind's frail and shriveled flower
for it no longer sucked the gut's deep fertile dark.
A thousand welcomes to all youth and their firm buds!
God's cunning herald and his two most stanch defenders,
the double-buttocked athlete and the air-brained piper,
dashed in the battle's midst, blew on their shells and shrilled:
"Brothers, perk up your ears, hear what your heralds cry:
within our grasping hands we hold all Egypt now!
Who longs for hogs or horses, who for fecund maids,
who wants fistfuls of gold or towers of thick pearls,
ahoy, let him flail Egypt now! First come, first served!"
The blond braves heard the conches and leapt up, aroused,
their women gathered close with babes slung on their backs,
others rode naked on their steeds, some on young calves,
and their war-strengthened bodies gleamed in the hot sun.
Their barbarous youth struck at the archer's brain like wine:
lean codgers, hard-knit knees, coarse brains which had not been
as yet worm-eaten by knowledge nor licked clean by thought;
their guts were thick pine woods uneaten still by grubs.
O Earth, mother of swarming children, thick dense grove,
what have your eyes not seen or your clay ears not heard!
Wonders on wonders, lives on lives pass through you, Mother,
unnumbered wombs lie in your body, seeds in your loins,
and you beget great gods and beasts, just as you like,
and hatch your varied brood of eggs in the blank sun.
For hours he marveled at that spurting water, youth,
and when his eyes were slaked, from his deceiving mouth
his strong words struck the blond-haired youths from brow to brow:
"Why camp in ragged tents upon the desert, fools!
Jump on your horses, comrades, and gallop further down:
their three-floored cellars drown with grain, their gardens bloom,
their women sail like shapely frigates in the sun
and press their ears to earth, longing to hear your steeds
snorting with lust, your axes smashing down their doors!
Their males are drained and worthless, all their gods are senile!
Workers and wretched poor have sent me here to say
that all the archons' women and their plump curled boys,
all the bright gems they wear, the silver, the gold, are yours;
and when you're slaked with slaughter and lust, and your mind clears,
we'll share the spoils of earth together, half and half!"
He spoke, and the barbarians howled and clashed their shields:
"Yes, by our iron god, we swear: half yours, half ours!
Lead on, show us the way, great is our conquering god;

he sits enthroned in a thick reed and burns the world,
oho, he starves, and smells man's meat on every side!"
Their stalwart bodies swayed in air like blazing fires,
but that great mind, the archer, held the scales of fate
and harmonized the frenzied storm to ordered calm:
"Now let this holy night fall on our flesh and bones,
she knows all things, illuminates the thoughts of men,
and with his ax our god will cut new paths at dawn."
He spoke. Bold chiefs assembled of a strong nymph-race,
beastlike young men who smelled like shaggy buffaloes,
gigantic codgers tall as the snow-covered hills,
and all held council near the water's murmuring stream
and planned and plotted with great cunning till the dim stars rose.

Night shone and laughed with all her wealth, black-eyed and bright,
the South Wind blew, the date palms moaned and flapped their wings,
and the green glowing moon swam up the milky sky.
Between his two old friends Odysseus stood and gazed
with wonder at the crescent moon like a sharp scythe
that threshed the ripe heads swaying in the silver fields.
Glutton had eaten and drunk well with his new friends
and now a dark foreboding crushed his wine-soaked heart
till like a melancholy bull he groaned and sighed:
"The things I've loved most in this world are piebald studs,
women who bear their children well, a swift proud ship,
but best of all I've loved with an unsated pride
that downy gallant lad who buckles on his weapons;
good is the sperm of man, and blessed a woman's womb!"
He spoke, and tears without much cause streamed down his cheeks.
But then the piper sighed in mimicry and mocked him:
"The things I've loved most in this world are stout wine-kegs,
loin-laden sows with all their holy grease and pork,
and that fat downy stinking skunk we all call woman,
but best of all I love fat-ass when birth-pangs seize him!"
The king of cunning men then reached and seized both heads:
"Fellows, the thing I've loved best in this cozening world
is that most crafty myth, man's own deceiving mind
which ties a thin red string about the world's round reel
then with a kick unwinds and sets the great myth spinning!"
Broad-bottomed glutton wryly laughed and spun his yarn:
"Ah, fellows, once upon a time—and that's the low-down truth—
seven ripsnorters, seven roaring boys set out
but split apart in traveling, two by two paired off
till only three remained and glowed beneath the moon—
that is, till winds should blow and knock down two more men!"
Odysseus laughed and grabbed his old friend by the arm:

"Good going! Though your mills grind slow, they make fine flour!
It's clear to see you're right, for we shall part one day.
Don't fret! That's how things are. There is no cure on earth,
the Wheel spins on, and now not even God can stop it.
Forget it, splayfoot! Kick it behind you! Let it plunge!
Quit digging your brain so; it doesn't suit you, friend.
Hood both your eyes and blot all out, and a good waking!
Sleep is a god that heals the heart which waking wounds."
He spoke, and the two swiftly gave their souls to sleep
as through wide-open doors the dreams like peacocks strolled;
but that free bird, their master's mind, flew sleeplessly
because it seemed a heavy task to cleanse wild blood
or put some sense in the many-headed rushing storm.
But this task suited well his double-purposed soul;
he smiled, and thought that when he'd reach the lower world
and the black monarch of that land perhaps should ask him
what work he did in the upper world, what goal pursued,
his fleshless jaws would grin with laughter and croak out:
"Monarch of earth, I shall confess my secret craft:
I've always fought to purify wild flame to light,
and kindle whatever light I found to burst in flame."
Thus did he speak with dread Lord Death, Destroyer of Pain,
and then, unruffled, slowly passed sleep's dim frontier
and took the azure shadowy paths of plunging cliffs.
As he half-shut his eyes, that night-bird, the horned owl
with its effulgent spheres of orbed and golden light
was heard in sad lament along the moist South Wind:
"Bodies once more are heaped on earth, reapers once more
come casting man-seed to be ground in Hades' mills.
Oho, mole-miller, rise at dawn, start the great grinding!
There's much to grind, and the jaws of both millstones brim,
the blind mice at your feet now eat and dance with joy,
and seven rivers of worms roll toward the dark flour bins.
Alas for black-eyed maids who forget in a man's arms
and in nine months beget their sons on the mill's floor!
Alas for all small sisters and for wretched mothers;
I wait for dawn and hold five different kinds of poison,
the ravaging bitter rue and the dry chicory flower."
But their dull brains misheard that mournful voice in sleep
and thought a nightingale had perched on flowering boughs
and warbled in a most sweet voice till all, entranced,
heard love's song only and were borne to a moist, windless peace.

The crow sang like a nightingale to drowsy brains,
night softly passed swathed in a kerchief of deep black,
deep midnight crossed its zenith, and when stars grew dim

a crimson cockscomb, slowly rose from glowing sands.
At the day's spring the archer's mind leapt like a cock,
horses around him wakened, and tent flaps disgorged
unshorn barbaric men, young women with coarse braids;
fierce weapons clashed, fires blazed up and caldrons steamed.
The sun rose like a drunken lord, red-faced and flushed,
stumbling and staggering up the clouds, and his glazed eyes
rolled steaming round brave youths who challenged him to fight;
the night-bird hid in silence in a hollow tree.
"Our lord and master wakes now in deep pits of blood,"
murmured the suffering man, and gazed straight at the sun.
As with a faint smile on his lips he watched his mind
opening its tail once more within him like a peacock,
he hovered in indecision long and took great joy
in mankind's freedom as in a sweet secret thrill.
But as his soul frisked like a bird in the dawn's light,
he saw a hoof-worn weary stallion galloping near
on which tall Granite sat astride, urged it with haste,
and led thick herds of oxen, maidens, and young men.
With shining shield and spear and with tall waving plumes
he loomed by sunrise clouds and sang in a high voice,
but when he suddenly saw his eagle-eyed old master
tall on the bank, the lustrous sounds choked in his throat,
he checked his horse, leapt on the sand, and step by step
slowly approached and reached his hand to touch the dream.
The seven-souled man laughed and also reached his hand:
"Dear friend, I'm not a ghost. Here, grasp a flesh of clay,
place here your hand against my heart; it leaps for joy;
may God be praised, earth is so small we meet once more."
He laughed so that his sleeping comrades blinked their eyes,
and seeing Granite there, a sunshot stately column,
they cried, fell on his neck and smothered him with kisses.
Broad-buttocked glutton wiped his wet eyes secretly:
"To think that we've been mourning you as lost, and now—
good going!—you come with horses and a lord's high plumes!
Your freedom from the yoke, I see, has done you good."
The piper marveled at his towering body, his strong steed:
"I dreamt of a huge dragon, and my poor brains shook:
four-eared, six-footed, double-rumped, with musk-drenched tail!"
Granite ignored the laughter and toward his master turned:
"My heart was bitter when you left, I checked my pain,
trudged down the river alone and felt my shoulders ache;
by God, I swear they felt as though they'd burst with wings!
Lone man, you cast a heavy shadow; what great joy
to rise one morning and find the fearful lion gone!
I walked the earth and felt my heels had sprouted wings;

never in all my life had I felt such fierce joy,
for freedom also strikes a man's mind like strong wine.
One morning by the bank I chanced on my blood-brother,
Rocky, who also beat his fledgling wings with fear;
we gave our hearts a hitch, then parted to find out
if we, too, had some value in this world or were
but the oars, masts, and trapping of your ship, Odysseus!
Rocky chose to plunge south; I took a northern route
nor knew toward where I went nor did my mind once ask;
each morning I awoke and found a new creation
as though a new soul every day were born within me.
One evening as I roamed about the greening shores
I saw a forest of slim masts crowd the near banks;
strong bodies leapt the sands, and deep in muddy earth
plunged lances tipped with iron, as long as two tall men.
I liked their virile odor, longed for their wild breath,
and seized an iron lance until my mind blazed too."
The cunning fisher marveled and then cast his bait:
"O stout bellwether, you've opened paths that we shall tread!
Now that we've chanced here too, and our bright stars have met,
let's cleanse the world with flame, though we're but kindling wood!
Rutting blond-bristling herds now swarm the desert sands
but they lack that great shepherd, Mind, to lead them through;
let's join them, then, to give their dark desire eyes,
for they pursue a goal much higher than they know."
But Granite frowned and clashed against his master's will:
"I don't ask where I go, nor care for hidden goals.
Arch-cunning man, don't fire my fantasy, that whore
that makes my blood boil till I pour it in relief
and squander it without a care on any road!
Now if you love me, leave me, that I may not swerve
but follow my own footsteps and my native bent."
The archer joyed to see his friend raise his head high
like a free man and spread his long wide wings for flight.
He longed for the first thrust of freedom to tear through
the bosoms of his friends one day like eagle-claws
until they freed themselves from his hard yoke, and flew,
but now he turned and seized his bold friend's hastening wings:
"Granite, be patient yet awhile, for we must still
complete this task together with these barbarous hordes;
give in, sit on the ground and tell me the straight truth:
how many are they, what's their strength and what's their goal?"
Granite smiled wryly, sat on the ground cross-legged and said:
"Once more you seize and yoke me stealthily, you gadfly,
but I'll be patient, for it pleases me to please you;
I'll give you a crude account, dig out the fruit yourself.

They've sacked the towns and put all young men to the sword,
women they've dragged to slavery, cattle to slaughter-sheds,
nor left one small green spray in the luxuriant fields.
They're all in rut, they're weak with kisses, food, and drink,
some slay each other and share spoils at the sword's point,
their brimming strength destroys them, and soon that day will come
when their strong flesh will fatten the sterile sands in rows.
What pity this fierce blaze must swirl and fade in smoke!"
The devious archer listened to his friend in thought,
and when he'd heard and weighed all well, he curbed his voice:
"That's true, but the world's rotted and bears no other sprout;
I think all hope on earth now, brother, has gathered around
these barbarous loins and shaggy chests that swirl about us,
and thus God often wills, that broncobuster of men.
But they'll be crushed unless our minds can give them shape,
and we'll be crushed, for now it seems that we're all one."
He spoke, then rose and tightly squeezed gaunt Granite's hands:
"Forgive me if I still direct this holy task;
it's right that onlv one head rule in times of crisis."
Granite's hot blood rose like a siphon in his heart:
"When at your side I toil, I think that I'm still free,
and each command of yours seems but my own deep will;
yet what relief to tear the writ that binds me to you!"
The great soul-leader laughed and then caressed his friend:
"It's good for your own sake to stay with me awhile;
it does no good for a great soul to live and work
where still far greater souls than he don't live in constant strife."

And thus they spoke till daylight in the clanging din
that rose by the banksides from the disordered crowd.
Rala, new-washed, wearing the best of her poor robes,
a thick and glittering copper ring about one ankle,
sat in the middle of the public road, and waited.
All living creatures woke, storks fished in the dank mud,
small birds puffed up their breasts in light, their bellies breathed
with joy, filled full of eggs and strength and warbling song,
but flame-eyed Rala now recoiled with wrath, and thrust
beneath her headband two long locks the wind had blown.
She stooped, and on her headcloth the much-suffering man's
thick precious bloodstains glittered in the morning's light;
she'd sworn to plant it like a flag on the priests' roof
but wound it like a shroud now round her raven hair,
and her heart melted from her desperate threnody.
She leapt up suddenly, hearing the tramp of marching feet,
perked up her ears, and heard but blood beat in her brow,
for no soul walked the roads, and she sat down once more.

Ah, could she block the middle of the road, dear God,
when workers passed and staggered to the archons' whips,
and then scream out! What could she say? Turn back! Turn back!
Thus Rala stooped and wrung her heart, that black crow's nest,
and as her fierce heart whipped the earth, waiting in fear,
dust clouds rose suddenly in the sun, the banksides stirred—
tumult and shouts, brass weapons, sharp and whinnying sounds.
Rala dashed up, ecstatic, and opened her arms wide;
her nerveless limbs began to shake, her knees gave way,
she wished to utter a loud cry, but her throat choked,
she wished to cry out "Brothers!" but her tongue grew numb
and but one sound, a crow's cry, "Kraa!" tore at her throat.
The Egyptian army rolled up swiftly, horses neighed,
snorted, and steamed about her slender naked limbs,
and she reached out her hands, beckoned, and waved her arms.
Amid the dustclouds her arms gleamed for a brief flash,
her downy doe-eyes for a moment shook with fear
in the thick mass of horses' harness and bronze shields,
and then her pallid body suddenly sank in the stampede.
Seven black ravens swooped down in the smothering dusk
and, pecking hungrily everywhere for scraps of meat,
found but warm clots of blood, black strands of hair, and one
bronze anklet on a shattered bone that gleamed on the hot sands.

At that same hour, the archer watched the Egyptian troops
flooding the fields, wave after wave of black-haired heads
so numberless not even an apple could wedge between.
Although he frowned, he felt no chill run down his spine,
his hairy armpits were still cool, unsweated, dry,
but all his comrades shuddered, and the piper's pate,
pallid with fear, poured with salt sweat in swift cascades:
"Their troops are endless, comrades! I can't even count them!
If they should reach their hands to heaven, they'd blot the sun,
if all should spit together, a river would roll and drown us!"
He spoke, and his drenched clothes dripped with his salt sweat.
His vulture-minded chief caressed the wind-struck head:
"Comrades, the battle's lost, there's no salvation here,
but let's choose freely, before swords clash, what road we want:
that one which leads toward death, or that which leads toward life;
let our four heads, that brim with brains, rise up to judge."
But Granite, with an eagle's stance, swiped at his master:
"Since when has the great archer asked us our opinion
when Death, the horseman, loomed up suddenly in our path?
And though he asks us now, he scorns our wretched honor."
Then Orpheus gulped and raised a bold opposing head:
"I may be sickly, but I've not feared Death, God curse him!

Though I'm a seven-months' child, that's what my heart says too!
I've always stood prepared to give my flesh to earth
or let my slim flute-playing fingers rot and fall.
Thus with no shame or hindrance, I'll also have my say:
Let's fly! for he who spins great schemes is duty-bound
to hold his life in rich esteem and cast it off
only when his strong corpse will tilt the scales of fate;
but here we'll die in vain for scraps of empty honor."
Then double-buttocked Kentaur rose to speak his heart:
"Fellows, I know we'll perish here in a skunk-trap!
You all know how I crave this slut, sweet-breasted life,
yet what can I do, alas? I'd blush to turn tail now!"
He glanced at his loved master and shyly dropped his eyes,
but he had cocked his cap askew, a sign of death:
"I too can't quench my thirst for life, I love the light,
but I've seen much on earth, spanned all and measured all,
and found one thing to love and wear like a true charm:
I've always found that men who hold great goals on earth
squander their lives each daring moment heedlessly.
I see no hope—that's why my heart cries out: 'Don't fly!'
Not that I feel ashamed or value stupid honor,
but in extreme despair some beast within me laughs."
Then he fell silent, his eye lost in inner worlds,
but yet he always kept some back door of escape:
"Danger is good and suits me, but that opinion's good
that holds the scales of fate and weighs each danger well.
See what my female brain has given birth to, friends:
We shall not wait for the foe to fall on us in sun,
but we ourselves shall pounce on their drowsy troops at night,
for patience, brothers, does not suit the desperate heart."
He spoke, then swiftly strode toward the barbarian chiefs,
and his companions marveled at his lurching gait
as though earth were a ship's deck tossed by surging storm.
"Now is the time to plant good words, like crimson plumes,
on the chiefs' heads to give their minds courageous airs,"
thus thought the sly man, striding through the motley tents.
Those soon to die ate on the run, some bounced their sons,
and some were giving last commands to their dear mates
while Death stood over them and listened, though stone-deaf.
The archer thrust claw-footed Death aside, then passed
and at each chieftain cast sharp glances hung with hooks,
hung with much precious bait, and every hook a fish.
He seized the shoulders of a tribe-chief with forked beard,
with pure-white peacock feathers on his lion's head:
"I envy your white hair, grandsire, and your fine plumes.
Bold gallant deeds adorn, I see, your towering form;

but chief, your eyes have not yet seen a war like this,
for on its holy head wings of fierce eagles shine."
The old man sighed and then confessed to his new friend:
"Many foot soldiers and much neighing have filled the fields."
But then the archer burst out laughing and slyly winked:
"Don't go pretending you don't know the secret, chief—
a savage mob of slaves and workers await our sign
to fall on the foe's flank and rout it utterly.
Their bull-faced gods will wallow then in their own blood!"
Thus the arch-cunning man enflamed their desperate breasts
for he knew well that hearts have always fed on air.
When he caught sight of a young blade, a virile bull,
the crafty man stood still and called that all might hear:
"One night on a wild mountain peak I saw a lion
stand still, red-haired and gorged, watching the far-off fields,
and I, crouched on low ground, with admiration gazed.
Young man, I quake, for you recall that mighty lion."
The youth kept silent, but from his wild groin and thighs,
from his firm loins, strength rose like waves into his heart
and all his downy features flushed to hear such praise.
The many-willed man marveled at man's godly body
that stands so proudly balanced on the cliff's dark edge.
He looked on sun-bronzed feet firm-rooted in the earth,
the shaggy lion-thighs which in their savage shade
covered the godly phallus with its deathless flame,
the chest that in bronze bars guarded the tiger soul,
and on the topmost peak, high on a towering neck,
the head, that savage hearth, walled thickly on all sides,
and in the head a world-destroying, world-creating spark.

Night fell, low candlesticks burnt bright in the black air,
and the companions felt that when their chief had gone
hunger rose without hindrance in their guts, and yowled.
Granite leapt up and chose a fat beast from that herd
which he had stolen the night before from the sandhills,
slew it, gouged out its entrails, smeared it with thick clay,
then lowered it, thick hide and all, in a fiery pit;
and when they'd packed it close with burning ash and stones,
the piper raised his proud wind-swollen head like wings:
"An old, old song is smothering my poor mind like fog,
so let this sad wretch sing it, friends, to find relief:
Ah, Death once wed the Earth and built him a tall tower,
he hewed young men for floors, old men for cornerstones,
he hewed small children to make doors and window-frames . . ."
But Kentaur stopped the piper's mouth with his huge hand:
"For God's sake, bite your tongue, you've made my blood turn sour,

now don't go conjuring wretched Death, may he be cursed!
Brother, I shan't mind when my bones disperse like stones,
but I shall weep to leave behind so many winecups,
so many lambs, so many girls who must sleep alone."
He spoke and sighed, then bent down with his shaggy arms,
quickly unearthed the pit until the fragrance poured
from the flushed lamb till all their famished bowels shook.
At that same moment their lion-master's shadow loomed:
"I see you toil at good and tasty tasks, my friends.
I'm mother-in-law's delight, I come at lunchtime always!
Let's fall to eating so our teeth won't spill on earth;
they say there's no more tasty food than the last lamb."
They raised the roast lamb, skinned it to its tender flesh
and ate their fill; then Granite, wise in shepherd's lore,
scraped clean the lamb's translucent shoulder-bone,
raised it against the light and pondered its dark signs:
"I see clear marks of evil on this beast's bare bone:
a crimson river, tombs that gape in long, long rows,
and four deep yawning pits that lie in wait for meat."
Then feather-brains grew numb, groped at the gaping tombs,
and when he felt grooved lines strung out in a long row
his flute-enraptured, pallid fingers shook with fright.
Bold Kentaur laughed and threw the bone into the flames:
"Our fate lies not in a sheep's bone but on our backs!"
Then the deep-minded man pressed his lips tight and thought:
"Not on a sheep's bone, and not even on our backs;
fate writes on water, a wind blows, and all things vanish."
He cast his glance about and harrowed each loved form
that sat and ate in shadow or on fine sands played;
the young men armed themselves, the women polished weapons,
and babies woke and thrashed their feet and bawled for milk.
Though all his friends talked on of Death, he kept his peace
and watched with pleasure how his ankle-vein swelled up,
like a fierce pulsing spring that thrust through the rich soil.
A rough beast roared and reared in the man-killer's breast,
but light is an unpitying whip that tames all beasts,
and the mind rose in mockery and reproved the heart:
"For shame, bereaved and bitter heart! Still, still inured
to this ignoble, bloody game on the green wold?
Man, like the dew, lies on the grass, then melts away."
He gazed on stars; night hung at zenith, thousand-eyed:
"A scurvy dog lives on, my lads, so don't you fear!
Belt on your arms, it's shameful now to talk of death;
let's pass through these brief hours together, arm in arm."
All felt ashamed and leapt up till their bone-joints creaked;
the pointed head rose proudly with swashbuckling dreams:

"Boys, let me take my flute and play you my last tune.
You'll see, the catch will burst with joy and goad Death on."
But the archer thought it now unfitting to mock fate:
"Hadn't you better change your reed for a sword, piper?
You've plenty of time to warble after the gory battle,
if you've still got your lips, that is, and we our ears.
Here's to our meeting, friends, and may Fate's will be done."
Then the conch blared, and Death, the horseman, charged at once.
Bold Granite grasped his iron arms, but they grasped him
before he grasped them tight, shook him before he shook them,
and like a hound he harried the troops and roused the youths.
Lightfooted as a night-beast, while his armor blazed
with savage streaks of blue in the star-glittering night,
the castle-wrecker with his chiefs dashed to the fray.
Kentaur rolled like a stream in the army's straggling rear
while at his side the piper hopped, a long-legged stork;
and last of all Death stalked with crooked shepherd's staff
pelting his votive lambs with stones, whistling, goading them on.

At midnight, sentries caught the tramp of hurrying feet,
turbid, tempestuous on the sands, and the reeds shook;
but as they opened their mouths wide to sound the alarm,
gaunt Granite fell upon them with his naked blade
and cut their throats till neck and voice both spilled on sand.
Tall flaring torches fluttered everywhere, tents shook,
all seized their weapons hurriedly, the darkness shrieked,
and foes and friends entwined and hissed like tangled snakes.
Odysseus strode among the troops with raging heart,
his hands burned and flashed flame, his glittering double-ax
fell mightily, broke bones and clove whole backs in two.
Spear crashed on spear in heavy fight, sword clashed on shield,
the great mass smashed the small and pressed hard on its heels,
till in the slaughter's tumult Granite's thin voice cried:
"Archer, goodbye! Comrades, I plunge to Hades now!
If ever a bitter word escaped my lips, forgive me, friends!"
Whirling his sharp ax like a windmill, the archer yelled:
"Granite, grasp your soul tight between your teeth! Be brave!"
These words had barely left his lips when his brains flared:
a whistling arrow flicked his ear, pierced through his cheek,
and black blood filled his mouth and brimmed his lips with poison.
Granite rushed up to catch his friend in his weak arms
but the strong thrust of a spear crashed him to his knees.
The enemy roared with rage and rushed with savage spears:
"Now all together, strike them hard! These two are beasts!"
and both those famous forms had vanished from earth forever
had Kentaur with his buffalo bulk not breached the attack

and suffered five sword-thusts from which five rivers ran,
for when he heard his master's groans in the vast din,
he rushed, though steeped in blood, to live or die together.
Blond and black bodies rolled in the thick mud entwined,
clasped arm to arm and breast to breast with groans and roars;
their hot brains spilled and steamed, sticky with hair and blood.
Hawkeye was tumbled down and rolled along the bank
as five tall bodies dragged him, pummeled, kicked, and struck,
but when he saw five workers in the dim light, he yelled:
"Comrades, I'm on your side! I fight for freedom too!"
But, ah, alas, Death would not hear, and the five struck him
until his fountaining voice of freedom choked in blood.
Scarab had heard his comrade's cry in the fierce din
and rushed to help him, but a strong hand grasped his nape,
flung him to earth and rubbed his face in grimy dust,
but when in the dawn's smile he saw the small beast-eyes
of a dry shriveled peasant-slave enflamed with rage,
then Scarab's words came tumbling in a swift cascade:
"Friend, I'm a peasant too and fight that all may share
the land . . ." but his voice stopped as a sharp lance plunged down
and made a mash of his rebellious plowman's brains.
Dawn's light began to whiten as the stars grew dim,
torn bodies, sprawled in pits of blood, turned red as roses,
and seven flocks of hungry crows swooped through the air.
Kentaur looked up with fear and his hair stood on end;
he groaned and tried to move, but his loins screamed with pain
and his heart's hollows filled with thickening clots of blood,
until, in one last try, the dragon cried: "Odysseus!"
and cocked his ear, although his jawbones shook with fright.
Was he still living? Had the earth gulped their beacon light?
A thousand years swept by him in a lightning flash
but all at once that good beast heard a feeble voice
and paid no heed to his cracked loins or hollowed heart,
for through the reeds he recognized his captain's voice.
Another well-loved voice rose in the battle's din
as Granite's lips broke through their clotted blood and cried:
"Death shall not take our souls, my friends! Hold them clenched tight!"
Upon the branch-tip of a date palm a bird hopped
then raised its neck toward heaven and sang a happy song,
and on its pulsing throat the sun hung like a charm.
At once all life took heart, grim Death became a tune,
and from the bird's small throat the whole world breathed again.
Poor Kentaur gathered up his gutted bellies, groaning,
but a light fainting-spell blacked out his brains until
it seemed the amber cluster of a grapevine grew
in shade close by and gleamed and hovered above his head.

A slender blackbird with a yellow beak drew near
and pecked at the globed fruit while its swift-darting eyes
glanced trembling at that monstrous bulk enthroned in shade.
But Kentaur's mind dwelt now no longer on the grapes:
he saw a girl who swung with vigor through the vines
and her limbs played in light and shade, and her hips swayed,
until his own brains swayed and the field sank and vanished.
He tried to rise then, but the earth shook, and he fell back,
opened his eyes, gazed on the sands, his flowing blood,
till his mind cleared, remembered, and his heart grew bitter:
"Mushheads and lamebrains such as mine should crack and spill!
We chucked away grapes, girls, and food's great joy, to die
for foreign scraps and to kill men we've never known!
Shove off, O doddering heart! Quit leading me astray!"
Then suddenly he thought of his close friend, and sighed:
"Lads, I don't hear the piper, and my poor heart breaks!"
The wretched songster tried to open his bruised mouth,
and struggled, but from his lean larynx no sound came,
for a sword's double stroke had pierced and slit his speech.
Time passed, the sun hung in mid-sky, a melting bronze,
and dripped on the heaped bodies of corpse-hoarding Death;
flesh had begun to rot and smell, the crows swarmed near,
fat blowflies swooped and poked in nostrils turning blue,
and all—sun, birds, and soil—began to work with haste
and turn those bodies back to the earth's sunless forge.
At high noon, the king's herald, in red sandals shod,
passed by and swiftly turned the heads of all the wounded,
then to his followers barked commands in a shrill voice:
"Choose all the chiefs and lave them with our soothing balms,
for in the sacred rites to his great fathers, the king
wishes himself to slay those heads that rose against him."
And when that dying fox, Odysseus, heard those orders,
unlooked-for hope flashed through his mind; he raised his eyes
and saw slaves lift the heavily decked barbarian chiefs,
drag Granite's forty-times-slashed body with great awe;
but seven staggering slaves raised glutton's monstrous bulk,
panted, and dumped him lengthwise in a low ox-cart.
The herald looked about, then kicked the wounded men
that now were turning blue in the sun's dripping blaze.
"Drive on! I think we've gathered all the plume-decked heads;
I see no other haughty pate that breathes or moves—
throw sand on the remaining bodies, thrust them deep."
But as the cartwheels crunched upon the moldering flesh
on the way back, a hoarse voice rose among the dead:
"Water!" the cunning archer groaned, and raised his head.
Then the slaves turned, and when they saw the pointed cap,

they burst in cackling laughs and clapped their dark-skinned palms:
"The greatest chief of all would have escaped our king!"
Four slaves rushed up and raised him high with buckling knees:
"This man has wrecked world upon world! He mustn't escape!"
But when with his hooked glance the archer spied the piper,
he raised shrewd hands and cried out to his humble friend:
"Great chief, here's to our meeting soon in the deep earth!"
The herald with the crimson sandals turned and saw
a pale pate, quivering like a rabbit, rise with fear
as black blood streamed in fountains down its grimy neck,
and the red-sandaled slave burst in loud laughs and kicked him:
"Pick up this sallow broken-down great chief of theirs!
O, how our king will laugh when with his golden feet
he tramples on this dry cracked flask and grinds it fine!"
He spoke, they flung poor Orpheus by the archer's side,
and on that wretch Odysseus placed his heavy paw
like an old lion who mutely guards his toddling newborn cub.

Thus War, the horseman, turned back to his crimson courts
and dragged brave gallants by their belts, girls by their braids,
and hung small children from his saddle-horns in clusters.
Behind him the blind followed, stumbling with long staffs,
and some way back the cripples, the armless, the half-wits,
and mothers in long rows who walked alive toward Hades.
Full-glutted crows strolled by the riverbank, digesting,
crocodiles sweetly shut their lidded eyes, and yawned,
for the blond meat had been quite good, and in slow rains
new flesh would sprout once more and then be munched anew.
Suns passed and sank in sands until the full moon bloomed
like a white rose of silence and perfumed the night;
boughs of the almond withered in spring's giddy spell
and cast its flowers and downy almonds and green leaves;
trees flowered and bore fruit, time slowly passed, and still
the chiefs in the king's dungeons stretched and groaned.
But Nile lay calm in a far nook, plotting with craft
how to pierce through the thickset walls and walk once more
in sun to heal poor mankind's fallen, orphaned heart.
To all his comrades, tillers of earth, toilers in shops,
he sent precise dispatches through the dungeon's grapevine:
"Brothers, don't weep, don't cry; your pain will soon be healed."
But round him the barbarians' eyes were sore with weeping,
and the four friends groped their own bodies with hard hands
to search their savage wounds and count their injuries,
how many teeth had been pushed in and firm ribs crushed.
Granite's gaunt body was a sieve, nor could he bring
his loose jaws yet in line to grind his scanty food.

Orpheus had lost his teeth, and his once babbling mouth
was locked and could not spout as yet with human speech.
Kentaur stooped low and marveled at the sweeping wounds
on his huge paunch, then laughed to think they'd not swept lower:
"Oho! Girls would have called me grandma then, not grandpa!"
The archer, with his shattered head wound in waxed cloth,
sat cross-legged on the ground and gave ironic comfort:
"Patience! Don't weep, my gallant lads; three moons have passed,
and the fourth moon, most red of all, shall rise up soon
and like a curly red carnation cleave our throats.
And when all four of us lie stretched in the cold ground
our teeth shall fall far right, our jaws shall spill far left,
our brains, our flesh, our souls, our dreams shall be worms' food."
Cold shivers shook their spines, yet they all smiled, and smeared
their wounds with a flesh-healing balm to stop gangrene.
But the blond-bearded chieftains stalked like raging lions,
rapped on the walls and probed them, climbed to the light-wells,
until their nails broke out in blood, their hair dripped sweat.
In the adjoining dungeons all night long the slaves
wove cloth in closely woven strands, gold-stitched velours,
and their sad dirges licked along the humid walls.
The desperate friends stretched out their necks and cocked their ears
and took the women's songs for curse and blessing both:
"My mind and my loom break in forty fragments now;
may your head, master, break in forty fragments too!
My sons sit on the thrones of patience and wind the spools,
my daughters wash their long black braids with scalding water,
my shuttle is made of fingernails, my loom of bones,
I sit and weave with a black kerchief round my head,
and terrors are my warp and curses my dark woof
until my heart swirls swiftly round on a red reel.
Spin on, spin on, O heart! Finish your master's shroud,
adorn it with tall cypress trees, sequins and swords,
hang all your pain for tassels and all your joy for fringe,
make it of coarse thick wool which no soft tears may pierce!
Descend you weary-laden, descend in the dark earth,
help me to finish swiftly my dread master's shroud,
let each hem hold my pain, each corner hide a crow,
a lean voracious crow to peck his heart out bit by bit."

The dark heart of the archer pitied his poor friends;
longing to find some toy that would divert their minds,
he took twelve slender sticks and hacked and whittled out
twelve cross-eyed earless gods in matched pairs, two by two,
then through their swollen bellies passed a crimson thread,
and laughed, for when he pulled the string the poor gods danced,

kicked up their feet and hands, wagged their lugubrious heads,
and a thin cry, "I'm hungry!" sprang from their bare guts.
His comrades roared with laughter, and the chiefs pressed close,
played with the red string, laughed, and passed their time away
until their minds grew bold with battling gods and air.
Then the poor piper blabbered with his toothless gums:
"I've heard it said that when the octopus is starving
and chews one of its arms, another sprouts up soon.
Aye, octopus, I see you've enjoyed renewal now!"
But Nile stood up and shook his bald resourceful head:
"What pity, archer, to waste your strength on games and laughs,
to squander it thus on hidden and quite useless rage.
You too once labored for an hour, struck out for freedom,
but now your mind once more stoops under ancient yokes,
because the soul that mocks at God is God's slave still."
But the archer snorted like a stud and would not answer;
with shattered head erect, he murmured in his heart:
"Their god is just and good, he holds his scales aloft
and portions bread and brains to all in equal shares;
but my god smothers in my chest, no justice holds him,
nor these old-lady virtues nor man's mortal joys."
Thus in his mind he mutely spoke and carved the walls
with secret signs of manly thoughts stamped on his brain:
a pointed upward-speeding arrow, a hungry flame.
Night fell, and when the glitter of the light-well dimmed,
the archer watched in the lamp's light how his old friends
were calmed by that old crone, sweet numbing need for sleep:
like long, long rows of caravans with jangling bells
dreams passed along the desert sands and reached their minds
where they unpacked their camels in the brain's cool cells,
bringing to one his babe, his mountains to another,
and to still others, buxom women, wine, and food.
The archer leant against the wall and fell asleep
until his sleepless soul soared from the flesh's yoke
on wings scraped clean of mud, eyes freed of blindman's bluff,
and the strong body, that dark middle wall, crashed down
until the mystery of the world shone clear as water.
Then the sleep-struggler slid in a dark stumbling dream
groped by pale slimy tentacles and grasped by tails;
wings, throats, and bosoms roared, thick jaws like millstones ground;
only a dancing flute's dim sound was heard far off.
Odysseus longed to bow with awe toward earth and cry:
"Mother, I've plunged deep in your bowels! Mother, I've come!"
but his voice broke in sobs and stuck in his dry throat.
He choked, and flung his arms out wide to grasp some air
but as he raised his eyes he saw the sky rear up

then like a silent millstone start to grind the earth.
Between them both, the scared beasts on their bellies crawled,
and as the archer shook for fear the world would choke
he saw a dragon—man or beast—crawl on its hands and knees,
face down, and strive to raise the sky on its arched back.
It stumbled, buckled at the knees as its bones creaked,
and when it turned its anguished face, Odysseus paled
to see its eyes drip blood, its lips wrench with sharp pain
as from its mouth's black cave a voice cried out for help.
An earthquake rent the earth in two: snakes, scorpions, ants
poured down like turbid rivers; all the wild beasts dashed
screaming from the dense jungled woods; oxen and steeds,
hearing their master's cry, strove with their heavy yoke;
great apes ran howling, thrushes, storks, blackbirds and hawks,
even the tiny sparrow, sped with their armatures
and strove with gasps to raise the sky but a hair's breadth.
All heaved in close formation and plowed up the ground
till earth's great Son took courage, knit his splintered bones,
bucked up his hands against the ground, braked with his knees,
and hair by hair unglued the azure dome from earth
till with deep groans he raised the sky on his broad back.
He stooped to get his breath, and blood poured from his ears;
life breathed once more and moved in freedom, monkeys rose
on their proud hindlegs and began to screech with joy,
and two worms sprouted wings and flapped in blazing sun.
"Father!" the suffering archer cried, "Father, enough now! Rest!"
But the dragon dug in earth and strove in a new task:
to raise the huge sky like a head on his bent shoulders!
The archer flushed with shame, then with the savage beasts,
insects and flying fowl of the air he rushed to wedge
his chest against that foe, the sky, which strove to crush them.
Thus all night long, filled with huge horns and wings and claws,
he strove to help that athlete in his fearful task,
then stopped for breath at daybreak and half-opened his eyes,
but still the dream poured through his brain like swirling mist.
He looked on high and his heart lightened, for dawn smiled,
raw and rose-green and tender, from the round light-well.
For a long time he could not rise, his wild mind pulsed,
the tears that he had shed at night still drenched his beard,
and when his comrades pressed him round and questioned him
he looked for hours in their dark eyes but could not speak.
Poor glutton probed his friend with fear and cried, "Odysseus!"
Then the night warrior shook free from his dreadful dream
and, filled with welling joy, seized his friends' heads and cried:
"I've seen him!" but his smothered throat could make no further sound.

Crouched mutely in a corner, all day long he hacked a block
of wood while surging waves reared in his blood and struck
his brains with rage as at moss-covered rocks, to smash them.
He rounded out the skull, strove to recall that dragon
who'd fought the sky like Death to save poor Mother Earth,
dug out the eyes, carved the mustache in high relief,
and branched two veins like horns between the glowering eyebrows.
But when the work lay finished in his hands at night
he flung it to the ground with raging bloodshot eyes
for his own cunning features gaped from the hewn wood.
He grabbed a new block then and slowly carved all night,
striving to drag up from his entrails that great warrior;
in his wild mind he still recalled those eyes and brows,
that dread, that stubbornness and grit, but his numb hands
could not impress them on the wood to free his heart.
For three long days he toiled and fought, but his thick fingers
formed fiery cunning eyes and mocking grinning lips,
coarse curly beards and pointed caps and old sea-wolves;
he carved his own soul still, whether he willed or not,
and the great athlete still lay hid deep in his heart.
For three long days God strove to see his own dark face,
and at the lone man's failures Nile smiled mockingly:
"You're flinging stones in sun! What shame to waste such strength,
stumbling on ghosts and scarecrows, trying to find God!"
But the dark struggler kept his silence until he tossed
his many-storied head and spoke to his close friends:
"Many here think man's soul is slaked by bread alone
and gab lifelong of rich and poor, of bread and food;
those savage flames which speed like arrows from the brain
they turn into a poor housekeeper's humble hearth
where old crones place their pots, old men their spindly legs.
I hate all virtues based on food and bloated bellies;
though food and drink are good, I'm better slaked and fed
by that inhuman flame which burns in our black bowels.
I like to name that flame which burns within me God!"
Nile turned with arrogance and mocked at the heart-battler,
but he dashed up like a wild beast with flaring eyes:
"I've fought with men and gods, I've weighed them well and found
the sea more firm than earth, the air more firm than sea,
and man's impalpable soul still yet more firm than air!"
Thus in the earth's foundations those two fought with words
as from the glorious crust of the carousing earth,
with hooves of painted crocus-color and bright red,
black steeds returned their archons from wild merrymaking.
Within the heavy air of midnight crammed with ghosts
magicians sank up to their necks and swam in silence;

foul witches milked their snow-white ewes under the moon
and cast the milk to the air-troughs from whence it flowed
like a calm river down to earth and breached all homes.
The archer, too, with open breast received the moon
that from the dungeon's skylight dripped in pure-white drops,
a cool intoxicating milk that slaked man's heart.
At dawn Odysseus woke from sleep, cool and refreshed;
he'd passed the empty night without one dream, and now
his mind woke early like a cock with swollen breast.
In the first glimmer of dawn, he started patiently
with steady hands to whittle deep on a dark log.
His mind blew over him in a fair wind, chips flew,
the eyes became deep wells, the great skull a hard flint,
the brows a rock-strewn cliff, the mouth a deep dark cave,
and the wrenched lips hung loose and yowled like a wild beast's.
Then the creator slit his vein, smeared God's lips red,
smudged him with bloody fingerprints, carved out two eyebrows
and plugged the deep wells of his eyes with lumps of earth.
He felt relieved, and his breast cleared, his mind grew calm,
and then he gazed and marveled at his mighty son,
his son and lord, his grandsire and his entrail's root.
Gibberish sounds and savage tunes sprang from his throat,
words poured at times like a crow's caws or the sweet carol
of a small bird that soars and quivers in azure sky.
It was as though Death screamed, as though our little life
flashed for a moment in the light, a gay goldfinch
from whose bright beak all its erotic rapture flowed.
Hearing the cry, the comrades raised their eyes and screeched
to see the dark contorted mask hung on the wall,
cackling insanely in the dawn with blood and mire.
"It's War!" they cried, and reached their longing hands with greed,
but the barbarians yelled "It's God!" and staggered back.
Deep in the palace pits, deep in the dungeon's mold,
all hearts shaped and unshaped their savage savior's face,
but Nile kept silent and shook his bald head with wrath,
and the archer thrust his wood-carved mask at the mute worker:
"Comrade, make up your mind. Here, bear him without trembling,
here is your dreadful worker, your great God of Vengeful Wrath!"

Day shriveled in the upper world, the dry soil cooled,
and from the sands, like a mute ghost that stood and stared
before it moved on toward the roofs, the dead moon rose.
Dogs stretched their scrawny necks and wept, the jackals howled,
and their blue shadows scurried swiftly through the tombs.
The king's rich-laden tables choked the starving poor
for this was his forefathers' feast day when the dead

swarmed from the earth like honeybees till the boughs shook.
Lean, lily-footed dancers doffed their crimson sandals,
unbound their scented sashes, hung them on full boughs
until the tall trees gleamed as though a thousand snakes,
bright-plumaged birds, and the moon's silvered phantoms perched there.
Groping the ground with their tall staffs, their heads held high,
seven blind minstrels stumbled in the rich rose-gardens
and held their ancient well-versed lyres in tight embrace.
On joy's rich feasting boards the archons placed a coffin
as grim reminder to carouse till the world darkened,
till a gaunt mummy in their orgies loomed and beckoned.
One blind bard pressed his ear against his somber lyre,
plucked at the chords and heard a song as yet unborn
that kicked within his heart to erupt and please the king.
"Great God, who once gouged out my eyes, stuff up my ears,
thrust a large lump of mud into my greedy mouth
and tear my soul out as one tears a fish's gills!
Dear God, I'm weary of singing now to thankless kings!"
Then memory, like a jackal, scratched in the bard's skull,
his heart was coiled with venomous snakes, and his mind hung,
a blind thrush in its bony mew, and sang of Death.
The blind bard listened to the grim song in his heart
and shuddered, for he thought his voice this day would be
most sweet to hearten the dead and living among the trees;
alas, his mind swooped on the king's feast like a black crow.
Meanwhile, as sweat poured down his sallow cheeks, far down
in the earth's cellars, slaves spread out Death's final feast
with tray on tray of luscious food and cooling wines;
bare-breasted girls brought roses and rich fragrances
that those about to die might taste all earth could give.
Nile's savage forehead glittered like a shaft of light,
the blond sea-captains sat among the bare-thighed girls,
and at the table's head, with all his friends about him,
the tall head of the castle-wrecker leapt like flame.
High on a nail the muddy and blood-splattered mask
of his wild god hung down, and the wall dripped with blood.
The old friends ate and drank and held their souls tight-reined
for fear they'd break out in great sobs and savage groans,
and then the piper drew his seven-reeded pipe
and played a scoffing, taunting tune to mock at Death,
but when the lone man turned and scowled, the piper stopped
and listened to the sage man's noble calm advice:
"Man's soul may seek for Death in many varied ways:
some wail, some laugh with fear, and some with boastful words
call manfully on the dark slayer to come and fight,
and some stretch out their necks like meek, obedient lambs.

We shall receive him like great lords, my friends, erect
on our two feet, and not with laughs and shameful cries,
but like great kings late risen from the world's bright banquet
who, having eaten and drunk well, retire to sleep."
Then glutton groaned and drained his winecup in one gulp:
"By God now, if I weren't so shamed, I'd start to wail!
Ah, if I'd only known, how I'd have reveled in life!
But now, when I look backward, fellows, at what I've done,
it seems to me I've never drunk or loved or eaten
nor sailed the seas under your heavy shade, Odysseus.
When Death shall seize and hoist me on his steed's dark rump
he'll question me over and over again on my spent life:
'Have you seen women, flowers, seas?' 'I've not seen anything!'
'And small birds warbling in the dawn?' 'I've not heard anything!'
'And wine and bread and meat?' 'I've tasted nothing, nothing!
Life passed like a brief dream and now, Death, that I've wakened,
alas, you come and drag me by the hair to the cold ground!' "
Thus Kentaur stuttered, muttering incoherent words,
until the lone man seized his hands compassionately:
"Friends, I forgot to tell you: some receive Lord Death
with no esteem, with blathering tongue, stewed to the gills!"
Glutton jumped up in wrath and the words welled from his heart:
"All life with you is hard, and death with you still harder!"
But Granite was not frightened and proudly tossed his head:
"Am I not free to do whatever I like, my friends?
Fellows, I've got a feeling I'd like to burst in song,
but not of friends or drinking, nor of upper worlds:
hardhearted man, it's to your much-loved head I'll sing!"
The mountain lad then leant his head in his cupped hand
and with a firm clear voice began an old brave tune:
"The forty-footed man lies dying on quaking earth,
skies flash with lightning, thunders roar, all Hades sways,
the tombstones shake to think of lidding his eagle wings.
No human house could shelter him, no cave could hold him,
he threw isle after isle in seas and stalked across them,
holding an oar in one hand, the North Star in the other."
The archer spread his hands and spoke with quivering voice:
"Farewell, North Star and oar! Farewell, O gaudy world!
Good was the voyage, my bowels have brimmed with sea and brine."
Midnight approached, jasmine had rotted in the girls'
warm hair, and the barbarian chiefs began to groan
like buffaloes dragged before the slaughter-shed's grim gates.
Nile struck his fist on the feasting boards and cried in wrath:
"What shame for soldiers to welcome Death with drink and dirge!"
The lone man struck back at the venomous-minded worker:
"My friend, they're right to bid the world farewell in tears,

for come, admit it, life's most sweet, may she be cursed!"
But Nile's dry sword-sharp lips muttered in mulleined wrath:
"I bring Death no great gifts of joy or sweet delight
but the death-offering of a child who died of hunger."
Then the world-wanderer shuddered deep to think how hard
a heart could grow, scorched by a cruel, unlaughing love,
and turned serenely to that stern black-mantled soul:
"The earth is good and of great grace and outstrips man's
acrid, most wrinkle-bellied and parsimonious brain;
sorrows and joys, falsehoods and truths, masters and slaves,
bottomless bellies that eat on, children that starve:
joy to that brain that holds all these and does not faint."
But the great worker struck back with still stubborn head:
"The world, with brains like yours, grows wild, unpruned, unclipped,
but we don't spoil the earth with fondling, for we fight her,
and water all good things she bears, and kill all evil.
Earth has no heart, mind, ears, or eyes, but we, the leaders,
a mere fistful of souls, have heart, mind, ears, and eyes,
and one day earth will take our hearts for her example."
The lone man murmured with great calm, his eyes far off:
"Joy to that brain that holds all things and does not faint!
God spreads the enormous wing of good from his right side,
the wing of evil from his left, then springs and soars.
If only we could be like God, to fly with wayward wings!"

Thus in the earth's deep roots the two souls fought with Death
while on the traveler earth's aristocratic face,
in her deep gardens, slender-fingered dancers leapt
and the blind minstrels raised their throats to sing of light.
Even the master minstrel found a novel song,
crisp and delightful, to refresh his monarch's mind,
and thus forgot the dread tune which his heart would sing.
But the king bit his venomed lips, for in his head
at night a heavy-shadowed nightmare had hit hard;
alas, deep in his sleep he'd seen a man's black corpse
with a huge bell about its neck, swaying in air,
touching the sleeping roofs with its low scraping toes,
and its black eyes dripped clot by clot on the dark earth.
All night he'd held it like a kite on a thin thread
and watched it sway and hover, watched that rotting corpse
drip worms upon him one by one in a slow knell.
"Ah, when shall daybreak come to exorcise that carcass
that I may breathe pure air again and hail the sun!"
And as the Pharaoh longed for light, he saw the head
of a huge forty-footed man climb up the sands
and cackle with a mouth of black teeth drenched in blood.

His dream diviners were struck dumb, his court fools cringed,
lady-loves spread their arms, dulcimers shook with song,
but still the poison swelled on the king's bloated lips.
A wily steward bowed at the king's holy feet:
"O long-lived monarch, now command your famous lords
to calm your mind with tales of their great deeds and joys."
Old men retold their voyages, the strands they'd passed,
the many-thousand-plumaged birds, strange tribes of men,
the many speeding ships their two deep eyes had seen.
A leching stalwart laughed, told of the girls he'd had:
black ones who smelled of corn, and slant-eyed yellow ones,
brown ones like wheaten bread and others white as snow
whose thighs had kept their coolness even in scorching heat.
A great magician dug up mankind's ancient roots
that move in beasts and clamber down to roots of trees:
"Earth is a tree on which men hang and sway like leaves,
on which kings climb to the top peaks and burst in bloom
then knit to sweet fruit, filled with seed, the world's salvation."
But the king grew wild, stamped his foot and yelled: "Be still!
The more you talk, the more my fierce dream chokes my heart!
All of you hold worm-eaten bodies like torn flags
and wave them proudly in the damp and slimy air!"
He spoke and glared with rage on the high steward who shook
with fear and lost his wit and ready craft that once
brought laughter, that frail bird, to perch on the king's tree;
but all at once he smeared his crafty mind with birdlime
then bowed out backward toward the garden close, and vanished.
In the low dungeons the barbarians still fought on
to bid the earth farewell, some with pure wine and some with women;
the lone man's gallant friends talked quietly of Death
with undimmed eyes as though it were some foreign land
made of translucent veils, most fabulous, to which,
whenever a fair wind blows, the voyager sets his sails:
then Death draws near like an unwelcome friend, a hunter
who spies life drinking by the stream like a shy fawn
and suddenly with his vulturous shade obscures the spring.
The archer, too, rejoiced to stoop with thirst and drink
Death's shadow and his deathless water in one gulp.
He felt all his past life sweep in a lightning flash,
waters rose in his mind, eyes, voices, lips and hair,
and Rala swept by suddenly, flashed like a star, and fell.
He smiled serenely and recalled how one day he
and Rala had roamed the burial glen to goad the embalmers.
Cadavers peeled and crumbled about their living feet,
the earth grew fat with too much food in her vast entrails
so that the archer stuffed his nose to bear the stench.

Wading and stooped in stagnant waters, the wretched craftsmen
gutted the dead, scooped out their brains, and with black pitch
and healing aromatic herbs stuffed each cadaver.
Others adorned a dead man's face with rouge and paints,
and thrust into his pitch-filled guts old magic spells:
"I've never lied or killed, I've never had my fill,
I've never stolen water or disobeyed my master
but groveled at his feet and trembled in his shadow."
Others amid the tombs, adorned with bridal pomp
the immortal dwelling of the soul now wed to Death,

and drew the furnishings most dear to the earth, the mind,
the sea, that it might lack not even a green twig.
Thus from the slaves' black fingertips the drawings flowed
with skillful craft, filling the walls with pleasing shapes;
life sprang like jetting water from the hand's five flutes.
Down in the lowest strip, broad rivers flowed through grass,
reeds gently, freshly swayed like bodies of young girls,
and flaming flowers rose on the waves' glitter, fish
sped swiftly and danced gaily with bright upright tails.
Along the second strip the black earth spread, new-plowed,
and mud-soaked farmhands stooped down low and sowed the seed;
close by, within a new-dug ditch, a pair embraced
that earth and seed might thus unite and sprout in wheat.
In the third strip their masters fatly sat in shade
rejoicing with large eyes to watch their dancing slaves
and their blind bards sing in the sun with earth-filled eyes;
nude slender slave-girls came and proffered the great lords
bright flowers and cooling sherbets served on silver trays.
Slim hieroglyphs like swift birds flew and soared in air:
"Life is most good, and drink is good, and song is good."
As the much-traveled man climbed all life step by step
painted upon the rich-wrought walls, his heavy flesh
grew lighter step by step until he breathed pure air.
On the fourth strip the Immortals shone like flaming birds
while at their feet the spirit like a nude worm crawled;
aye, Dame Soul quaked and held in her hands her open heart:
"Dear heart, it's I who've fed you even with the milk of birds,
dear heart, it's I who've never denied you anything,
and now I ask you for one favor: O heart, confess not!"
The highest strip of all, still blank, enzoned the tomb,
and the far-sighted man longed to see what great shapes
more lustrous than the Immortals would adorn it now.
His temples gently throbbed when he saw an old slave
climb up the scaffold, stand erect, and with both hands
scatter upon the blank strip blue and crimson paint,
and the archer shook to see tall flames, wild famished tongues,
clutching and streaming swiftly from mountain peak to peak.
Gone were the waters, wheat, and gods; pure flame remained,
virgin and uninhabited, man's ultimate heir,
and the tormented archer smiled to see how flame,
his secret fear, rolled now unruffled, beauty's hem,
an ancient ornament that could no longer fright man's mind.
The sun rolled and fell heavily on the streaming sands
and the stone gods received him in their radiant arms
as their one only son, their faces turned toward light.
A conjurer stood upon the ladder's topmost rung

and blessed a monstrous hawk-faced god hewn out of granite
by blowing upon his face old magic incantations:
"I blow on your vast eyes that you may see the world
and all your faithful who bow low with well-filled palms;
I blow in your vast ears that you may hear earth's roar,
our greasy hymns of praise and our fat flattering words;
I blow on your vast nose that you may smell far off
the turning spit that roasts the meat of votive offering;
I blow on your unsated beak and your hooked claws
that they may clutch the skulls of men and eat their flesh
yet leave for us, their high priests, some rich scraps of food."
The archer heard man blowing with his puny breath
to bring to life that brainless, silent, granite god
with all the passions of unjust, unsated mortals,
and the man-killer yelled to God till his mind shook:
"I blow on your vast hands! Raise them and smash the world!"
His breast caught fire and seven crimson suns danced up
in the sand-smothered sky till earth, in his thought's pyre,
turned red-hot like an iron sphere and climbed his mind.
The lone man suddenly feared the world might go to wrack,
then reached his huge hand hurriedly to grasp with joy
and sweetness Rala's cool full-rounded breasts until
his mind stood still, with the poor world then reconciled.
And thus in that last hour he took for recompense
and joy the full round shadow of a woman's breast,
and as he closed his eyes to enjoy this last farewell
he felt this was not now a maid's cool flesh but that
he held the whole world in his palm and said farewell.
His hands thus brimming with but azure quivering shade,
the wages of his strife, the great world-wanderer waited
to vanish like a thunderbolt in the gaping earth;
life was a tranquil lightning flash where the swift eye
barely had time to blink and watch foes, women, friends,
green shores and azure seas and a sweet thousand showers;
all earth in his ten fingers seemed like a lovely toy.
As he caressed that rich wage in his empty palms,
the dungeon doors burst open, the steward advanced with pomp,
and the barbarians crouched on earth and groaned like bulls,
the comrades rose and slowly tightened their lean waists,
but the sly eunuch raised his shriveled hands and said:
"A heavy dream has struck our king until sweet wine
and tender kisses turn to poison on his pale lips
and all his gentle heart-leaves shrivel in his breast.
Aye, strangers who've profaned our holy land with war,
whom dark exotic lands have bred in the far North,
who of you know of magic and ghost-binding spells

to exorcise our Pharaoh's incoherent dream?
Let him rise now! I promise full reprieve of life!"
But no one spoke, all hung their mute heads toward the ground,
till the resourceful man arose, who still in Death's
enclosing pincers struggled to take wing and flee.
Quickly he tore his clothes and smeared his eyes with mud
to fight Death with the cunning both of fox and lion:
"I've studied all the crafts that bind or unbind man,
magic enchantments, witch-herbs, and six-pointed stars.
I shall decode the dream and fling it in empty air;
but that the gods may fall upon me and move my brains
I shall dance first and utter frantic raging cries
until my fierce head flames beyond man's mortal powers."
He spoke, then from the wall took down God's savage mask,
threw it across his back and strode out through the dungeon door.

Earth smelled of lily and jasmine, naked maidens stooped
and proffered court dames roses and their lords old wine,
slim dancers stopped by trees that dripped with the moon's beams,
and cooling scented sweat frosted their weary bodies.
Odysseus smelled the fragrant world, and his mind spun,
his nostrils quivered, his eyes blinked and his ears rang,
for all life flickered like a tongue between his brows;
dear God, if only he could make her stay forever!
A dizzy craving swept along his breast and thighs
until a tremulous fumbling dance flowed through his flesh;
he turned right and bowed low, then stooping left with anguish
fell at the king's feet, quivering, like a beast of prey.
The dance sprang in him suddenly, his bone-joints tingled,
his mind like a swift siphon sucked up feast and lords
till all his disembodied longing poised in air.
He shuffled through the first steps of the sacred dance
holding his hands outstretched as though he begged for bread,
then slowly passed with mournful glance from lord to lord.
A strident whining bubbled in his quivering throat
as though small orphans wept with far, convulsive sobs,
and his mud-tattered rags flapped in the scented air.
The smiling archons marveled at the stranger's skill
in aping the uncaressed small orphans softly sobbing,
the sickly tramp who went from door to door and begged.
Then like a tiger crouched to spring, he clenched his fists,
raised one foot high in air like a curved twisted paw,
and as his neck grew taut and his teeth flashed in darkness,
the carved mask of his god thumped on his back and groaned.
His feet leapt as in rage and drummed on the hard ground,
his savage hands pulled tightly at invisible bows

and unseen arrows whizzed with speed in the moon's glow.
This was no simple dance: war sprang in the rose shrubs,
black crows perched on the feasting boards and hoarsely cawed,
and the king gasped and leapt, by shadowy arrows struck.
The archer's rage calmed down, his throat relaxed, and sobs
pierced through the night like wailing maids who tore their hair.
The slow dance dragged and crawled, and now lean cripples roamed
and limped upon the earth, for the cruel war had stopped,
and blind men fiercely groped the ground with their bent staffs.
The lords laughed unabashed; in their mind's eye they saw
their maimed slaves coming from the slaughter, stooped with spoils;
only amid moon-shadows, far in the dense grove,
a girl recalled her lover and softly began to weep.
The lone man fell and bowed down low at the king's feet
then slowly, slowly mounted like the ascending sun
so that when the court dames and revelers finally saw him
they shrieked out, terror-struck, for on the archer's face
was tightly wedged his grinning god's fierce, hideous mask!
The king screamed and reeled backward in his archons' arms:
"Ah! That's the seven-times-reborn sun-demon's face
that struck me in my sleep! Help me or I'll go mad!"
But when the steward charged with wrath to seize the dancer,
the quailing king shrieked out again and stopped him short,
for as Odysseus fixed God's mask on his fierce brow
six pairs of flames leaped from his arm-joints, head, and feet.
Then all minds crashed, veins swelled with fear, the whole world shook,
and the man-killer, seizing his black-hilted sword,
leapt in a frothing dance about the monarch's tables.
A wide-eyed, tall intoxication blazed in his head
as his feet whirled him on beyond both life and death
where he no longer whined, or fought, or wept, or begged
but touched the black soil like a god till the stones smoked.
Then all at once he stood stock-still before the king,
broke in harsh laughter and fixed him with his mud-filled eyes.
The startled youth, conceived in orgy, reached his hands,
but with a thundering cavern-roar the sly man yelled:
"Good is the quail, the blackbird, and the turtle-dove,
but of all birds I like the eagle, the cross-eagle, best,
and most of all when it holds a king's head in its claws!"
The king, more dead than living, spoke with quivering lips:
"O evil spirit, choose those you want, but leave my land,
pass quickly through the boundaries of my soil and soul!
May you be cursed! May my breath dissolve you in all winds!"
And then the king spat thrice so that his curse might hold.
Turning to his cowed courtiers he gave swift commands:
"Give him enough supplies to last at least two moons,

let trusted guards conduct him to our far frontiers,
then cast him far out from our holy land to cleanse our kingdom!"

With slow firm strides Odysseus passed through night's dance-ring,
plunged down the dungeons, opened the long tunnel's door,
and his scared comrades milled about his sweating body.
He stood erect among them and his thick lips steamed,
then he stamped on the earth, threw out his arms, and laughed,
for once more life had not abandoned him, his mind
was whole, his nostrils smelled the heady stench of men.
All pressed him round with questions, striving to find out
whether within his hands he held their life or death.
Then Kentaur shouted, as new seas came flooding round him:
"Captain, do we cast anchor deep in the earth's grave
or shall we see our foaming prow scud in the wind?
If only the road to deathless waters were still unending,
still to be passed, and still no end to that great passage!"
As the lone man groped at his comrades' heads and backs,
he choked with joy to feel man's warmth and life's good stench,
for new joys and new loves rose in his heart and swayed
as though he had just then been born, a full-grown man,
and stood on the earth's threshold, filled with stupefaction.
He then recalled the newborn cricket far away
that hatched on an old olive tree and shook to see
the brilliance of the world spread out, all sun and trees;
he too, now, like that cricket, brimmed with glowing strength.
Then when he'd had his fill of fondling, he found his voice
and told how he had danced, how his bold god had rushed
and opened wide his ponderous jaws and gulped them all:
"Eh, comrades, calm down now, for I've a somber speech:
I've just been born this hour, I've just returned from Hades!
A pity on all the years I've wasted! My life was shameful,
for like a craven slave I've tread in man's old footsteps—
were I to die today, I should have lost the game!"
His eyes flashed and cast sparks in the dark dungeon;
cold and hot waters tumbled down the glutton's spine
to see them, and the wretched piper shook with fright,
but the blue-eyed barbarians glowed and yelled as though
they dashed on horseback through their far snow-covered plains.
The flame-eyed archer bound his waist with a strong belt,
tied his strong sandals, cleansed his eyes of the thick mud,
then turned to all his troops, medley of blond and black:
"God is no song that darts and fades in empty air
but a warm throbbing throat that brims with flesh and blood;
he's called us, spoken his dread word, and rushed ahead.
Forward, my friends, let's tread in our forerunner's steps,

plunge southward, lads, in Africa, in the sun's heat!
There at the utmost rim of all, at the world's end,
where wheat grows tall as trees, and weeds to a man's height,
and the pig-thistle springs beyond a horse's rump,
there we shall build new castles and a brand-new city,
there we shall raise new hopes and virtues, joys and sorrows,
there our strong arms will finish what the proud heart orders.
Push on! We'll give this old whore earth a new virginity!"
All the barbarians roared, and joining arm to arm
raised the flushed archer high till the whole dungeon shook.
The piper buckled on his flute like a slim sword
—who knows, dear God, what tune the wretched reed will spout?—
and with his cricket-shanks stalked to the dungeon door,
but flatfoot flung him horseback on his nape and yelled:
"Hold on, my fine friend! What's your rush, my sparking lion?"
And Granite zoned and zoned himself with his red sash,
for all his yearning mind flew far off, far away,
deep down in Africa's hot wastes, and his heart danced:
"Ah, for the desert's clear pure air, for spreading roads
where the proud crane, that swift road-guide, may surge ahead
till at the road's far end my Rocky looms and shines!"
As Granite yearned and zoned himself for the new road,
workingman Nile approached and spoke to the town-builder:
"Good luck to your air-castles, O rebellious soul.
You clutch air in your hands and we but a lump of earth;
give me the liberty to come with you awhile
for my life still may bear some fruit on this poor earth.
But we shall part before you pass our frontiers, friend,
for on this land where I have suffered I must one day
reap the great harvest of revenge with workers' scythes."
Day broke, the skylight wanly smiled like a weak sun
and the mind-reader pushed the door as his friends passed,
wing-footed hunters with wide eyes that flashed with fire,
and gazed on the endless road as their ancestral home.
Their leader smiled serenely and then with his swift glance
spied on his wild new friends and to his quick heart said:
"Rise up and lead, O double-lightning, double-ax,
for this bare earth grows bold and thorns press round to choke us.
Strike, O lean lightning, right and left! Open our bloodstained way!"

XII

Boys, never mourn the warrior! What though he miss the mark?
Though he err once or twice, he'll swoop to arms once more,
sling a carnation on his ear, then cock his cap,
and once more friends will throng about his groaning boards.
His friends feast in his courtyards, eat and drink with joy,
then strike up rousing songs until their hearts catch fire.
Brandish the torches now, push on, our horses neigh,
this whole world's grown too narrow, and I choke for air!
Out of rams' horns, I make curved bows, swift ships from trees,
I gulp down birds and beasts, drink undiluted wine,
and wake at dawn to find the meat has climbed my head
and burst in gallant flame that spies and hails the world.
I grab an ax, hack out a god, bow down and worship,
but then I see him one clear dawn and raise my ax:
'Blockhead, dry log, my heart has no more room for you,
nor can you hold my strength, and I shall knock you down!'
Then I hack God to kindling, throw him in the hearth,
and in the darkness stretch my still-unsated hands,
grab women like soft clay and with them mold more men,
then set them loose on earth that they may dry in sun:
'Ahoy, my lads, let's see where this great world will end,
how far the soul will stretch without the bowstring snapping,
but if it snaps, my friends, don't mind, it soon will mend
and once again the arrow will rise in light and strike the sun!' "

Thus did gaunt Granite sing as the youths beat their drums
and a riffraff of motley men pushed on behind,
all those the roaming guide had chosen for his troops.
By God, how had he found the top cream of the crop?
He must have culled the land's best buds for his bouquet,
each sour-apple's pip, each walnut tree's hard nut!
What gallant cutthroats, what knife-slingers, what low crooks,
what roughnecks, rakehells, were not found in his wolf-pack!
Ripsnorters of the rope and rod, whoremongering pimps,
long-fingered fleecers, pirates even of empty air,
free hearts that had no fear of demon, man, or god.

With these came stout horse-wenches, lumbering monkey-sluts,
harridans, sirens, gypsies, and homebreaking tarts,
brazen and flaunting whores, frail sisters big with child,
and troop on straggling troop of demon-seeded bastards.
Their guide had skimmed the land and gathered all the scum!
All stooped to earth and cast a stone behind their backs:
"Cursed be your fertile fatty soil, rotted with lords,
may the black plague and snake-coiled curses eat you whole,
may all the poisons you've made us drink become your wounds!"
They screamed and raised high heaps of stones on the frontiers,
and when the king's troops finally left them and turned back,
Odysseus blew his conch, and Kentaur raised his voice
into a thunderous blast until from all sides round
the motley mob pressed close to make its final choice.
Then the death-archer rose in the packed crowd and took
God's mask from his broad back and held it high, aloft,
turning it round in sun, full of black blood and mire,
and when the crowd had hugged the fear deep in its heart,
the man-decoyer's voice rang in the desert sands:
"O heart, don't quake! My people, come, bind your brains tight!
Look well now on your dread God's eyes, his teeth, his lips:
this was the mouth that growled and struck the pale king dumb,
these were the bloodshot eyes that rolled and gulped their gods,
this is the black ram that will lead us in the grim desert!
Bind your brains thrice, and then, O brothers, say farewell
to your loved homelands and to all good times forever;
gone are the wines and pots, the good terms with your lords,
gone are the flattering hopes, gone your consoling gods,
gone is the right to raise your head or to turn back.
And if you ask me what good things this god will vow
to trusting hearts that follow him, then cock your ears:
hunger and thirst are what he holds in his black pouch!
This is the cruel truth, lads! Don't you come whining when
in the dry wilderness you wander ragged and hungry!
Here on the sands I cut a line with my iron sword:
behind lies slavery and our fat grain-mother earth,
before lies liberty and hunger. Weigh both well.
He who has never killed or stolen or not betrayed
or murdered in his mind, let him now rise and leave!
Who in his heart of hearts still whispers, 'I like this earth,
and spacious is man's head to hold me'—let him leave!
We in the wilderness shall shape a rutting god
stifling with liberty and hunger, blood and brains.
Place your hearts well within the scales and search your loins:
we too won't bear that man who can't bear God's grim face!"
The hardened roughnecks listened without fear, nor moved,

for each soul weighed itself and found it was not wanting—
untamed desires, murders, thefts and manly deeds
seethed in their daring hearts and boiled up in their brains
till memory roared in all their heads with mud and gore.
As the great archer watched his mob, his churlish roughs,
he suddenly turned giddy with love, pity, and pride:
"O men, warm bodies, hearts who are Death's roaring flutes,
O holy dust, air, water, fire and brain, my children,
forward! Let's tighten our belts firmly and start the climb,
but now, before we move, let's bathe in the cool river
and wash away dishonor's crust and slavery's mire;
our God now seeks to pierce new flesh and lie ensheathed."
He spoke, and all leapt laughing in the azure river's stream.

But Granite with his gallants heard a roaring sound
and saw far off a herd of bison line the sands.
"Out with your swords! God's passing by in a buck's shape!
Our road starts well, for meat's a good foundation stone."
Thus Granite yelled, and his men charged the sacred beasts.
Soon, as the motley crowd climbed up the banks, new-washed,
and gazed upon the wastelands with their fresh-cooled eyes,
they saw great Granite with his wild-game hunters come
and drag two monstrous bison on their bloodstained backs.
The archer's words still seethed within the people's minds,
their savage god hung like a sharp ax from their belts,
like fire from their eyes, and gazed on the sands, laughing.
But as they looked on the dark beasts and the sharp horns
a monstrous and unbearable hunger pierced their guts,
and even before the hunters could unskin the beasts,
all, men and women, yelled and grabbed at the raw meat
and with their teeth, their dog-teeth, tore it all to shreds.
The beasts were minced to pieces in a flash, devoured,
and the mob, smeared with blood, became wild buffaloes;
their heads, like dens of cavemen, roared with savage cries.
The many-faced man felt his great mind twist and whirl
till the proud veins between his eyebrows spread like horns:
he rushed into the bison-sated crowd and nailed
his iron lance deep in the sand and on its tip
hung the mud-splattered, awesome mask of his dread god:
"Hold me, my lads, don't let me fall! God stalks and groans!"
Granite was startled to see the dark drunken state,
the savage bison-stare of his enraptured master:
"For shame! Our leader's glance is glazed, and his mind shakes,
a wild wine strikes him, evil winds now whip his soul!"
He spoke to Kentaur who stooped low and moaned with fear
for he, too, felt the spirit coursing along his spine.

The demon-driven man leapt high and grabbed the mask,
stumbled, as though he had no strength to hold it high,
then lashed it thrice about his head with a thick thong
and swept into a swirling dance with his dread god.
He felt God's spirit pour within him like thick flesh,
his mind dashed down from crag to crag till on the last
stark cliff his brain was freed from trance and his voice cleared:
"Ah, the spread-eagle has soared away, and the dance stops!
Friends, when I held God's mask lashed to my giddy skull
I saw our secret goal and where our road must lead:
earth's fate shone clearly in my heart, all roads sprang open,
till now I hold the future etched in my lined palms.
I stoop and see wild beasts and wars, sorrows and joys,
and a huge city dangling from my slender thumb.
But it's most shameful to unlid or tell with words
the secret will of God or what man's heart can do;
we shall unwind the yarn of fate as we march on!
Rapture was good, a heavy flaming bird that passed
and filled our guide, the antlike mind, with flashing wings,
but now our dread task starts on earth with no bright wings."
He spoke, then split his troops according to their kind:
"Let's cut apart our army, lads, into three columns:
Granite shall lead the first brave group of gallant youths
and the one-breasted girls who have not yet known men;
Kentaur shall follow with his crowd of feeble crones,
for he's soft-spoken and his heart pains like a mother's;
I shall come last with comrades in the prime of life,
mature men who have reaped the fruit of topmost strength;
our piper, Orpheus, with his drum and dulcet flute
shall scamper freely where our God shall choose to blow him
for, being a songster, he claims the free air for friend.
Thus our three ranks shall march in order, row on row.
Forward, my lads! If our stud-god wants his own good
he'll march with us on our rough desert road and share our fate."

He spoke, and the three columns swayed, the army moved,
and the wild god stalked on ahead like a black ram,
while high above, the hot sun ground them like ripe grain.
Mutely the ancient river rolled and tagged the troops,
the date trees moved their honeyed hands to welcome them,
and famished crows from far off swarmed and spied to see
how long these creatures would stand straight and move their limbs.
Like heavy winking eyelids, nights and days blinked by,
and the hot days walked in and out and beat their clogs
on the resounding river-stones and the coarse sand.
The nights adorned their black throats with resplendent stars

and like ferocious Negro widows roamed the banks
and jangled joyously their star-embellished bracelets.
When sad nostalgia seethed within the piper's breast
his new tune danced upon the sands like a moonstruck
and downy deer until all throats poured forth their flutes.
Once more the long days rose sand-spattered on the earth,
rough scaly crocodiles slid through the tepid waters,
strong snakes coiled in spasmodic twists and flicked their tongues
while their small glittering eyes flashed sweetly like a girl's.
Soon, far off they discerned a village of mud huts
and each seemed like a towering pile of dead men's skulls;
nude women scrambled screaming to their terrace roofs,
and old men, trembling, placed at Granite's sturdy feet
trustworthy signs of love and friendship: dates, salt, water.
One day in some dry bushes the world-wanderer saw
an old man crouched, transported with ecstatic joy,
striking a bow's gutstring with his small fingernail.
Like a bee-swarm's light murmur or wing's gentle hum
the bowstring's tremolo slowly vanished in thin air
and the enraptured codger cocked his ear and listened.
He heard all of the wilderness, the river and woods,
his small and humble hut, his sweet and gentle grandson,
his god who stood on guard before the sacred village gate.
He heard his desolate spirit quivering through the chord,
his youth, all girls he'd ever enjoyed, men he had slain,
for life was a blue well, his soul a honeybee
that flicked the water slowly with its wings, and drank.
The archer turned back softly, and feared to scare away
that frail-winged insect, the parched soul that drinks but sound.
With panting and protruding tongue, the sweltering noon
crouched on the earth like a bitch dog with pure-white paws;
all throats were parched with thirst, and the ragged stifling troops
sprawled by the shady river-slopes to escape the blast;
the upright sunrays lanced all motionless sluggish things,
and heads flashed in the scorching light like gourds of wine.
As in a dream within the fiery haze, the troops
watched lean giraffes descend, spread out their spindly shanks
and stoop with their snake-slender necks to drink the stream.
Odysseus walked, and memory like an army followed;
the sterile burning sands billowed and steamed in stripes,
far-distant yet familiar voices welcomed him,
souls rose and gleamed in the roof-gutters of his mind
and he rejoiced as though he'd come to his first homeland,
for like sweet wells his soul sprang up in every step.
One day amid dry branches in the desert sands
he chanced upon a man's bleached skull that brimmed with bees

who'd picked it for their hive and filled it full of honey.
He laughed and turned to the awl-headed, panting piper:
"Ah, songster, may your fate grant that your head one day
may hang down, filled with honey, from dry desert boughs
that all who pass might say, 'This was a great bard, surely;
his songs have turned to honey and his thoughts to bees
that even now—behold!—glean life from desert blooms.'
Let glutton's skull become a wine-gourd, that brave lads,
drinking his health in future times, may thus invoke him:
'Who could that dragon have been who left this monstrous skull?
This is no cup, my brothers, this is a bottomless jug:
one small sip strikes you blind; two, and the world goes lost;
three, and the earth grows new and like a daughter spreads
her freshening hands and strokes your dark beard drenched with wine.'
Let young men nail our Granite's savage skull high up
on a tall cedar for a mark, then take their bows
and on gay holidays contend to bring it down.
But may an eagle seize my skull and soar to earth's
top crag that it may see the world for the last time,
then may the eagle suddenly spread its bloody claws
and drop my head to the stone earth and dash my brains out!"
The piper listened without speaking, his glazed eyes
saw how the desert smoked and slouched like a rough beast;
the soft soles of his feet were scorched, he hopped on sand
like crooked crabs who scuttle on the sizzling hearth.
Odysseus smiled with kindness and touched his friend's arms:
"Poor sparrow, I'm to blame for leading you astray."
The puny fledgling sighed, then touched with fear, as though
he touched a cliff, the killer's dark abysmal palm:
"Forgive me, slayer, because at times my mind grows frightened,
but don't be angry, for I revive and bravely step
once more in your deep footprints with my spindly legs."

Slowly they breached and thrust deep in the desert's throat,
the scorched grass curled with heat, the road was a parched hide;
the sun, a round bronze disk, brimming with burning coals,
rose, spilled its flaming brands, and then was quenched in dusk.
The hot earth slowly cooled, all living creatures breathed,
God once more sprouted sweetly in men's smoldering hearts,
a thousand heads poked out, a thousand bright eyes gleamed
amid dry boughs, in coarse-grained sand, deep in mud pools.
Camels fell down like crumbling towers in the wastelands
and slowly ground their teeth, chewing their cud of twigs;
like an old camel, too, the desert lay and chewed
its cud, as fires were lit and women fed the flames.
Fishermen brought their fish and hunters their wild game,

all three troops met, new life was launched on a sandspit,
but in the dawn all scattered, and the disburthened sands
appeared as though no prattle of men had passed above them.
Broad-buttocked glutton stumbled in a heavy sweat,
a well-fed and well-sodden shaggy god with thighs
of long coarse hair that shone in the bonfire's blaze.
"I've turned to a nanny with old hags and bawling babes!
See how my breasts have bulged to suckle these small beasts!
Relieve me, if you love me, friend, or I'll squirt milk!"
With sour complaints he plied his leader every night
who only marveled at his monstrous bulk, and laughed:
"Kentaur, I like it fine to watch you stretched on sand
while infants crawl about you and children mount your back!
Now if the saying's true that we're each part of God,
I swear then, fat-ass, you must be his monstrous belly!"
They ate, and blond and black beards squatted by the fire;
sometimes they cracked coarse jokes to ease their hearts awhile,
and sometimes from their memories fished out hoary tales
or, looking back, told anecdotes of childhood days.
And when they lay in a vast sleep, they felt the night
stroll on the earth like a dark legend filled with sounds.
But black days crushed, the wheels of fate began to creak;
soon their scarce food gave out, they hungered, their guts shrank,
their hunters turned back empty-handed to starved troops,
and though they searched all day for some sweet fruit to eat,
all fruit trees had now vanished, not one leaf remained,
and only thorn-sharp shriveled boughs curled in the sun
like swollen-throated snakes that spit their deadly venom;
and ravens cawed with eagerness, and circled low.
Somewhere upon the sand's frontiers the archer saw
a small fresh leaf that swayed its green blade in the air,
and the great leader lowered his now humble hands
and tenderly caressed the small green border-guard,
the last last leaf of all, and spoke to it in stealth:
"O glorious and despairing warrior, small green blade
who cast your spear against these fierce sands fearlessly,
you are the only comrade in the world I have."
Thus spoke flame-eyed Odysseus as he stalked the sands.
At noon a hunter spied in the mud-murky river
a tree-huge crocodile digesting in the sun
with myriad birds that darted through his jaws and ate;
he seized his ax, knelt on the earth and warmly prayed:
"Great God, with your fat meat and all your oozing lard,
pity your loving people here who die of hunger;
stand still, don't move, take pity, let me kill you now!"
He spoke, crawled close with stealth, then suddenly like a flash

thrust his two-pointed ax deep in the gaping jaws.
The beast-god roared, but when he champed his chops with rage,
the twin peaks pierced his brain, and the huge dragon fell.
The hunter knelt and bowed to the great beast with awe:
"Our thanks, compassionate God, who of your kindness deigned
to give your people your own flesh and save their souls."
All rushed and ripped the beast to shreds, and the young girls
tore out the musk from his dark loins and smeared their flesh
to arouse the young men when they lay on midnight sands.
They heaped stones, lit huge fires, and gave way to joy;
they ate their god and their hearts healed, their legs grew strong
and swirled in a wild dance when evening shadows fell:
"Captain, forgive us if we've said a word too much.
Don't listen to our grumbling. Lead us night and day.
In Charon's ancient tavern we're all drunken sots."
Fat words! They went in one ear and came out the other!
The lone man knew too well how well-fed men can boast;
when food's at hand, their minds at once soar to the skies,
but if no fat game's near, then hunger shrinks their valor.
It's only the new-eaten meat that speaks so boldly.
Meanwhile the proud troops flew on wings and swirled in dance
then cast their eyes to the red West and hailed the sun:
"Light of our eyes, celestial drum with crimson hide,
beat quickly till we reach the castle of our Lord South.
His fortresses are dampening fogs, his roofs are clouds,
he sits enthroned amid his guests, the three wild winds;
some call him a pale prince, some the consumptive South,
a small bird sits on his red roof and calls him Death:
'Dear Death, full forty brave lads march the desert sands,
dear Death, your palace melts and all your roofs are tears,
why in their hands is the great sun a crimson drum?' "
Thus all the slaked mouths sang in the descending sun
but in the violet dusk their quick-eyed leader spied
huge rocks that loomed like dragons in the desert sands
and ran off softly from his troops to touch those ghosts.
But when he reached their monstrous shadows, his heart leapt,
for carved on the huge rocks he saw strong rutting rams
amid whose curved and lofty horns the great sun rose,
and each ray was a ripe and bearded stalk of wheat.
Elsewhere slim maidens danced about a tranquil boy
who played a slender flute while a thin crescent moon
hung like a sacred charm from the sky's hollow chest.
Their tresses fluttered in the wind like twining snakes,
their upright throats were lifted to the morning breeze,
and still the red cosmetics gleamed on their curved lips.
The archer stretched his yearning hands and stroked the stones:

"How joyfully you played in ancient times on these
dry sands, dear God, and passed full cycle, trees, beasts, men,
till Death's sands suddenly smothered you and left no trace!
At times the heart can't bear this tragic game, O God,
for what is doomed to die, had better not have lived at all!"

Foodless days passed once more, shrunk bellies once more gaped,
skin-and-bone Hunger hove in sight and hailed the troops
then took the lead, a captain dressed in filthy rags.
One day the blistering sun leapt down and beat the earth,
the conch blared for departure, but the squadrons groaned
and milled about their leader with black-eyed despair:
"You took us on your wing, man-slayer, pumped us with hope,
but what do we care for freedom if we have no meat?
Slavery with meat-pots is a thousand times preferred!
Let's turn back to our sacred mother who tends her poor,
for he who fills our bellies is our one true God!"
The lone man leapt from crag to crag of frenzied fate
and on its gulf grasped and ungrasped the reins with joy:
"I'm not a shepherd who'll lead men to fat green pastures,
I don't want either their strong stench or their rich milk,
pity won't make me swoon, nor will their hot tears touch me,
for I was born to hunt alone and to eat alone!"
Thus thought the heavy-hearted man and watched his troops
till Granite rose and shook his bloodstained spear with wrath:
"When you ate well, our God then seemed to you almighty,
and you all longed for liberty and its great cares;
now that your empty guts have shrunk, your hearts shrink too,
and like deflated pricked balloons your souls break wind!"
He turned his flaming face toward dark Odysseus then:
"What are you weighing, captain, now in your dark brain?
There's no fine weighing here: we plod through tragic wastes.
Lower your eyebrows, archer, frown, give me the sign,
let few and chosen live to breathe the earth's thin air."
But the open-minded leader knew that exhausted men
yearn for and reach their god, and then fall back once more.
"Hunger sometimes betrays the pass, but sometimes virtue,
that two-tongued shepherd, leads them on to prudent fields:
do well and you'll be paid well, give me and then I'll give you,
don't boast or overspeak, keep silent, worship power,
don't eat too much, don't think too much, nothing too much,
and keep your virtue, your world and god to your own measure.
With suchlike virtues man's tall reach is cut to size!"
Life hung a moment on a spider-web's frail thread
but all at once the slayer pitied their drained hearts:
"Friends, listen to my faultless heart that always knows,

much sooner than my eyes or mind, where fate must go:
Far off I see God smile and stoop to feed the flames
beneath long rows of boiling caldrons brimmed with meat.
Forward, my lads, let's get there quick, for the smell chokes me!"
The archer's large eyes overflowed with flames, food, trees,
until they filled with courage the troops' hollow bones;
once more all took the desert road in the sun's thorns
and sent ahead as guide that false air-pregnant bitch-hound, Hope.

At noon they passed through sun-scorched wastes with fevered strides
until, as their souls swayed and fluttered in the heat-haze,
they saw cool pools and sheep that browsed on greenest grass
and date trees quivering in the sun in a white town.
With eyes refreshed and hearts that throbbed like singing birds
they rushed with longing to embrace those emerald groves,
but these flew further off and swayed in flaming light
until they shed like roses in the sky, and vanished.
A dumb dread choked the mob: could this be but a ghost,
a plaything of their cunning god who grinned and mocked
their hunger now and flipped them in his bloodstained claws?
They gaped a moment, blank-eyed, at the empty light,
then all at once their knees gave way and they fell prone
on the hot sands and stretched their necks like calves, and groaned.
Gaunt Granite in a frenzied rage raised his spear high
and kicked them with great wrath to make them rise and march,
but they, like beasts with necks outstretched in slaughter-sheds,
huddled with chattering teeth and quaked the whole night through.
At dawn it seemed as though the sun had cracked their heads
for all broke into tears and shouts, leapt to their feet
and cried to the great archer now to give them cause.
When seven-souled Odysseus heard them, his heart flared,
the cap on his gray head stood up from his great rage:
"Who of you want to turn back now? Get up and leave!
Let all be winnowed here and the chaff flung to the winds!
But if you want grim war, push on, for my palms itch!"
He signaled to the piper then who seized his drum
and beat a war-tattoo; Granite swept on with his own group;
maids who had not borne children but had kept their strength
still pure, reared from the desert sands like savage vipers.
With a swift glance Odysseus calmed his trusted friends
who rose and gleamed about him then like brazen walls,
but mothers shrilled and slaves threw up their hands and screamed:
"Alas, we don't want war! Allow us to leave in peace!
Cursed be this long-drawn task, this endless sea of sand,
O slayer, that has no ending and will drown us all!"

Their flame-eyed leader turned; between his eyebrows throbbed
the large vein of his savage strength like a curled whip:
"By God, then leave your bodies here for wolves to eat!
No one has ever passed these sands who had no spirit;
if you had spirit, even your hunger would change its course
and turn to a proud rage and to unyielding spite."
He spoke, the people turned to stone, and their hearts sank;
the sun beat savagely in the sky, a poisoned fruit,
the sand's thighs steamed, the dry stones broiled with haze and heat,
till a wind suddenly blew all traces from the sands
and the slaves shook with terror and raised their gaunt hands high:
"We'd die before our time if you should leave us now!
Have pity, murderer! May the wind take all you've said!"
A wild beast roared and reared up in the slayer's chest:
"My heart's a thick bronze plate, my mind's an iron claw,
I've never scratched my words upon the brainless winds.
I want your stench no more, for I hear clamoring wings,
and in my brains my brothers rise, the famished crows!"
The people growled and muttered, mothers tore their hair,
till glutton's heart was wrung and he leapt up with rage,
snorting among them, and spoke boldly for all to hear:
"Dragon, your strength's grown out of hand! Draw back its reins!
These are still men, take pity! O sky, stand still and judge!"
But his hard master's ruthless voice thrashed out at once:
"I told you from the start: our god is a ruthless god,
his mind's a pitiless sieve that winnows chaff from grain."
"Pity the blameless children then. Don't leave them here."
"I pity them all, but nurses are a burden now."
Then glutton growled and all his bellies tossed and heaved,
his eyes filled suddenly with tears and he moaned softly:
"Slayer, you've swallowed mankind whole in your cruel chest
till in your entrails' root only a wild beast moves."
"That's true, you rattle-brained dumb fool! Do what you want!"
Good-hearted Kentaur sighed yet dared to speak once more:
"Though I'm a blockhead, slayer, I've still a human heart.
Women and children first, by God! I tell you, master,
I won't leave them to death, with or without your leave!"
The archer's eyes flashed fire like a savage beast's:
"Aye, nanny, I see that your fat udders drip with milk!
Shove off, you fool! Go hang your head. These are not souls,
only green empty entrails, corpses that soon will rot,
but if you pity them in truth, then a good journey!"
He spoke, touched Granite's arm, then signaled to the piper;
the drum beat for departure, and the chosen friends
began a swift song of the road and lunged through sand.
Kentaur stood in their midst, his great heart torn in two;

whether he tacked or hauled up sail, his ship was lost—
how might this clashing pair find place in his fat bulk?
But when a baby's cry was heard on a dry breast,
all his vast body, like a mother's, groaned and sighed:
"A fig, you murderer, for your spite! With or without
your courage, if I can, I'll save these orphaned kids.
We, too, I think, have souls. Don't ride your high horse now!"
He spurred his bulky body then and turned his face,
and as they took the rough road back, a mother swerved
to gaze for the last time on youths who steamed in heat,
but all at once she shrieked in fright and closed her eyes,
for the man-killer with his high cap plodded last
and on his black burnt back the savage mask hung down;
there the man-sucking god grinned in the torrid sun
and blood dropped clump by clump upon the spreading crimson sands.

The days lit flickering fires over their bare heads
and nights like chilling waters coursed along their backs;
young girls grew pale and thin, their eyes were ringed with blue,
and young men further tightened their lean hollow waists.
A great magician with the army once crouched low
and scratched on rocks wild game and birds to trap their souls,
but birds flew by in dazzling blaze and beasts loped off
and left the sad magician with but useless snares.
The sun rose from its oven like a round breadloaf
and scorched their famished bellies, wild game stalked their minds
like chubby gods who in their paws held man's salvation,
but, merciless and silent, they would not draw near
nor sacrifice their flesh to save the human herd.
Around the fire at night Odysseus told his cares,
slowly unwound his snake-coiled voyages with skill
to cheat with words his comrades' hunger and hot thirst.
One night, as all sat cross-legged on the sands, he felt
the young men press their knees against the young girls' thighs,
and spun an ancient myth of how young men and maids
first met on earth and how the erotic fountain sprang.
He stroked his gray beard, and his thick lips dripped with honey:
"Blessed be the earth and water, and blessed be fire and air
that shape and join the soul and body of mortal man,
and blessed that master-craftsman who so planned all things
that some are stalwart men and some sweet-bedded maids.
My friends, now listen to an old myth as night calms down.
When, as folks say, the sky lived lovingly with earth,
fifty young women roamed the land, fifty young maids,
and fifty brave unmated young men roamed the wastes;
all still were fresh young shoots, new-sprung from Mother Earth,

and on their backs still bore fresh loam and greenest leaves.
The maidens drove on toward the North, the young men South,
the maidens opened their eyes wide, their wild hearts pulsed
with longing, their minds poured in long cascades and asked:
'Green grass, tall tree, who may your father and mother be?'
'The earth,' thus murmured the green grass and the tall tree.
But still desire could not find rest in the maids' hearts:
'O earth, who was your mother, who can your father be?'
Earth roared then from her caves with a hoarse voice, 'I live!'
nor did her mud-brain know how else she might reply.
At night the stars lit trailing fires in the dark sky
and young maids lay with sleepless eyes and heavy breasts:
'Dear stars, who was it lit you first in the desolate sky?'
But the stars burned so far away, they could not hear.
The maids called day and night, but still no answer came.
One day when earth had filled with flowers and fields turned green,
the maids ran down in the fierce heat to the cool spring,
the youths converged in the fierce heat and ran to drink,
but when the young maids saw the youths, their wild hearts throbbed:
'You there, you naked forms, what kind of beast are you?'
And the brave lads with their cracked youthful voices cawed:
'We boast that we are men. And you, with rearing breasts?'
'We bear the name of women, and we've no need of men!'
The stalwart youths laughed mockingly and crossed the grass:
'As men, we shall drink first. Make way, bare-breasted beasts!'
'We shall drink first!' the maidens cried, and rushed the pool.
Thus from this proud word-battle, body on body clashed
so that from dawn till sunset the wild skirmish raged
as the young men fought fiercely for their loot of brides.
When the sun fell once more, a stalwart youth cried out:
'Lads, seize them by their breasts and then they'll lose their strength!'
Night fell, and soon the stars leapt to adorn the sky,
the lions roared in their dark caves, the lovebirds sighed,
until at midnight the stars set, dawn broke in rose,
a small bird slowly flew and sang by the cool spring:
'Dear God, the young men can't remember, and the maids forget!
They ran to drink, but the kiss came, that fearful beast,
and stood before the spring till now there's no unkissing!'
Full fifty sons were seeded in full fifty brides,
they gave me fifty cups to drink at the wedding feast,
but ah, alas, the wine but wet my thick mustache,
it never reached my lips nor even sweetened them.
All was a traceless dream, my lads; I woke, but see—
fifty young men and maids now clack their knees together!"
The sly man stopped, then laughed; the maids and lads laughed too,
but yet he never disclosed the heaviest word of all:

from that time on when maid meets man by the cool spring
they never question earth again nor gaze on stars,
but deep in earth they dig a fertile pit to breed and spawn.

Night passed, until at dawn the great disk-thrower cast
the sun like a vermilion quoit on the sky's rim;
the drums resounded, and the young men leapt from sleep,
tossed from their heads the sweet seductions of the night
and once more plodded on the day's coarse endless sands.
Granite first took the lead, and glittered like a star
with streaming banners, a lean-boned and noble form;
behind him swept like flames his hand-picked glowing youths,
and the pale piper hopped close by with his huge drum,
his neck embraced by wounds like coral crimson rings;
last came the silent archer, looking behind and after,
a porter who lugged his heavy god on his burnt back
and in the desert's fiery glitter held his heart
like a refreshing water-gourd to slake his thirst.
A choking flame-ferocious wind sucked up the sands,
the sun grew dim as though eclipsed, the young men vanished,
and Granite's tall shape in the sandstorm vanished too.
Then the man-killer stopped, a black flash crossed his mind:
old deadly battles and his memory's ancient cries,
as though with other troops and in another life
where all drank wine and the mind crowed and his brave lads
had mounted their white steeds and dashed into the desert
with their black twisted headbands, with their drums and weapons
to fight the fiery whirlwind with their gleaming spears.
As they thrust deep in the sand's furnace, all at once
a huge wind rose and the sand-mountains heaved like waves,
rose and swelled slowly, then once more came settling down,
but ah, alas, what had become of the brave youths?
Odysseus thus recalled his once sand-smothered boys
and silently watched his youths on the sea-sands until
it seemed to him they dashed once more to the assault.
But as he looked before and after, he spied a girl
some distance from the troops who bent her body low
and with cupped hands spilled water on the sterile sands
as though she nourished some small plant in slow farewell.
Swept by a frenzied rage, he dashed on the young maid
who in her place of sleep had found a small blue flower,
transplanted it with care, and now in watering it
was trembling in her heart nor wished to leave the desert.
The fiery guide of God reaching out his flaming hands,
entwined them in her hair three times with mounting wrath
and three times shook her like a sack and dashed her down:

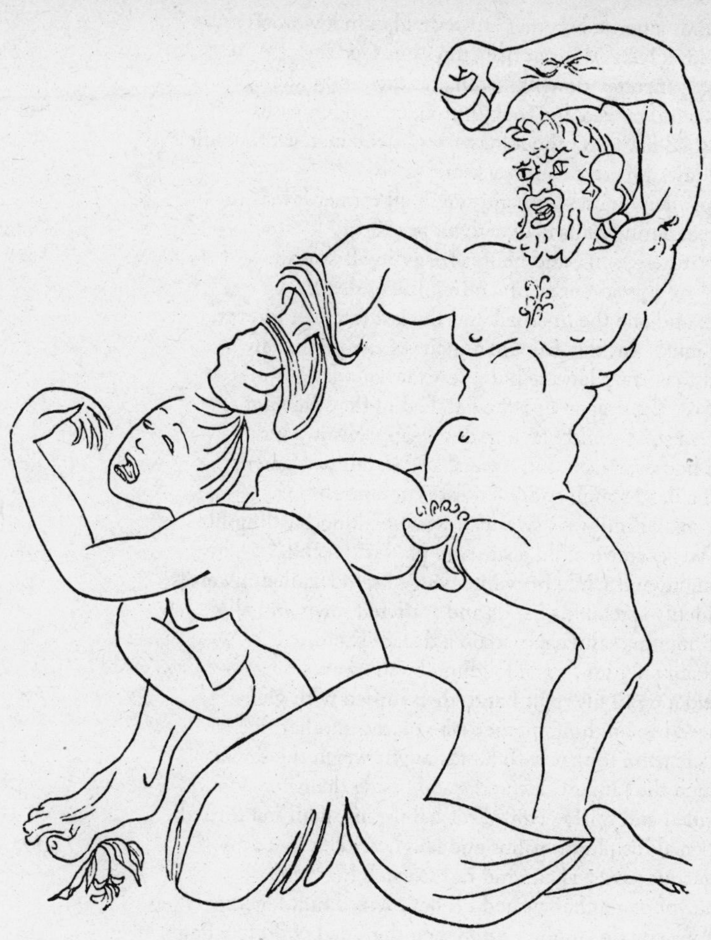

"I've said I won't have flowers, not even one green blade,
planted in this wild waste nor on the roads we pass,
for then the heart takes root and never again will leave!"
He stamped on the frail flower then with his bare feet
and ground it wrathfully in the sand as the girl moaned.
At night when all fell down with hunger, limp and drained,
he stood erect by the huge drum, beat it and cried:
"Friends, I repeat what I've once said, and make it law:
so long as this road lasts and our goal's still to seek,
no soul shall plant not one green leaf in these dry sands.
Who plants a tree becomes a tree and roots in land,

who builds a house becomes a threshold, window, roof,
who holds a baby in his arms betrays our God!"
He spoke, then lay down brooding on the sands, alone,
and his mind moved and took untrodden hidden paths
and pushed his secret thoughts toward steep man-eating cliffs:
"To all laws I'll erect contrary secret laws
that must deny with scorn and smash all former laws;
only great daring souls may with all perils play
and plant trees, sons, and houses freely in all lands
because for them, root or uprooting, life or death,
are one, and one the first hail and the last farewell forever.
Now I must beat the drum to announce the public law
and trust contrary laws to but a few rare minds."
Such were the dragon eggs he hatched in the still calm,
and like a small child playing, dug deep wells in sand,
shaped houses, streets and towers, and in tall battlements
erected a dead scarab-god, then cast ant-hordes
till the small sand-ways swarmed with seething bustling life.
"Ah, I've become a child again and play with sand,"
he thought, and while his white-winged mind smiled inwardly
he suddenly spread his hands and scattered town and all.
Far off on a smooth beach, upon a distant shore,
a small, an only son, came toddling by the waves
and held a fig in his right hand, then turned with glee
and faced his laughing mother who placed another fig
in his left palm so that both hands might weigh the same.
But when the father came and stood beside the gate
and smiled and softly clapped his hands, his small son turned
and opened his plump palms and laughed like a sun's ray.
Telemachus gave a shout and ran to catch his child
and the young mother rushed till both seized him together;
the happy couple laughed, and when the small child touched
her crystal shoulder tenderly, the young bride's breasts,
brimming with milk, pulsed with a fragrant warmth and life:
"I fear he grows more like his grandfather day by day.
Look at his spite, his glance, the way he holds the figs;
alas, I see the traits of your dread father here.
Where can he be, dear God, where in this holy hour?"
At the same hour, far off, the wandering grandfather raised
his burning feet and crushed the frail toy town of sand:
"For shame! I'm not a child! New toys consume me now."
He laid his head, that thick beehive, on the smooth sand
so that his thoughts might close their wings like honeybees,
content that this day, too, the poisoned wastes had been well gleaned.

The sun exploded, and the piper cried with joy:
"My eye keeps twitching, I foresee some great good coming!
I dreamt of our broad-buttocked friend; they brought him dead
with bagpipes and with drums until the earth roared back,
for funerals, lads, in my home town, look much like weddings."
But his companions turned their backs and plowed ahead;
they could not joke, for hunger roped their choking throats.
The features of the seven-souled enflamed man darkened,
but still the piper on his cricket-legs hopped close,
slitted his small squint-eyes and threw out taunts and gibes:
"You aimed and shot yourself! You fell in your own trap!
In vain your murderous heart digs pits, in vain digs deep,
for it still mourns the women and children you sent to die!"
But the archer turned away and mocked the air-brained fool:
"Our cock-eyed fisher casts his bait, let come what may!
I don't think twice for such as the earth breeds in swarms,
but ah, broad-buttocked Kentaur's pain tears at my heart."
He spoke, then hurried ahead to hide his brimming eyes,
but as he rushed, he suddenly stopped and held his breath
as though he'd heard the vanguard leader's joyous cry.
Then he sped swiftly, stopped again, and cupped his ears
till he heard Granite clearly shout, "A town! A town!"
and watched his youths and maidens fly with feathered feet,
for in the middle of the desert a green grove swelled
and in the sunlight thatched huts gleamed, row after row,
and sheep with bells about their necks browsed on green grass.
The friends fell prone at once to hide all living trace
from the town's sentries, who stood upright on tall stands,
but the mind-spinner watched in silence and knit his heart
for fear they once more saw but the mind's vain mirage.
Closing his eyes, he pressed his ears against the earth
and heard dogs barking and bells ringing and cries of men,
then flung himself upon the ground with his lean scouts.
The friends clashed in opinion as they watched the town;
first Granite spread out swiftly a bold plan of attack:
"Let's fall upon them now before they get their wind up,
and plunder their deep holds and fall on their fat flocks;
behind us cliffs of famine lie, and a feast before us."
But the more prudent thought of sly, more peaceful means,
and the foxy-minded man dug in his brains for tricks—
how like a passing beggar he might case the town,
mark down its ins and outs, the entrances, the exits,
and snare the houses with no trace at dead of night.
Crouched on the sand, the pirates mulled through all these plans
while the town's sentry, high upon his scorching stand,

spied on the earth around him with round hawklike eyes.
The day was tranquil as a beast in heavy sleep,
the meadows steamed, the cows upon the greensward gleamed,
the chief's bean gardens and his cornfields swelled with fruit,
farmhands and spindly children drew up from the wells
cool gurgling water, then stooped above their fertile plots.
The eye looked and rejoiced at all the good things round
like a great king who sits on high and rules his land.
The sentry could no longer hold himself, and leapt for joy,
all he could see was his, held tight in his possession:
that bride who led her flock to the cool spring, she too
was his, his eye reached out and seized her like an arm.
He looked on melon-plots far off, and his throat cooled,
he watched bee-gardens on the banks and licked his lips
and gulped his sweet saliva with unsated greed.
A white cow gently mooed with her distended dugs,
and her full udders fell into his thirsty lips
as he threw back his head and sucked the flowing milk.
Ah God, what great joy when the eyelids open wide
and fill with women, beasts, and fields, and all, all yours!
He could not bear such bursting joy—he'd draw a knife
and cut into his swelling veins to find relief,
but as he grasped his blade, and the dogs suddenly howled,
he turned and saw the far grass move in rippling waves:
heads gleamed and vanished in the light, shields rose and flashed,
until he cried "To arms!" and beat his drum and yelled.
The whole town rose as one, the women hid and quaked,
the young braves seized their weapons, the earth shook, and soon
nude brass-ringed bodies gleamed before the village gates.
Then the man-killer grabbed his iron sword and cried:
"Comrades, it's no use quarreling now what road to choose
for fate has taken the lead and chosen without our leave!"
As the black braves foamed through the gates, their archers dashed
wave on black wave that billowed high in a great wind,
and on a lance in the vanguard their dread god flashed,
a stuffed and ponderous jackal that in grinding jaws
still held and licked the dry bones of a human skull.
Behind it flashed strong stalwarts smeared with gleaming fat
who held shields made of the scaled shells of water-turtles,
and on each shield, with secret signs in flaming paints,
the dread ancestral god of every tribe was stamped.
A black stud-dragon swooped down till his heels plowed up
huge dust-clouds in the road, and the earth heaved and tossed,
but when he came within a bow-shot's furthest reach,
Granite knelt down and with a lethal arrow pierced
his scaly neck and sent him crashing like a bull.

Roaring, the dragon-brood then seized their bows of horn,
and though the arrows barely bruised two of the troop,
both rolled upon the sands convulsed, their wounds turned green,
and soon they breathed their last with empty and glazed eyes.
The archer turned, looked at the two, then leapt with rage:
"Comrades, they've smeared their arrowheads with deadly poison!
Onward! Draw your short swords! Let's fight them close at hand!"
He lashed his god's mask with strong thongs about his chest
to keep it firm in the great clash, all drew their swords,
the battle flashed on earth like a great fire, and passed.
All who were saved that day still quailed when they recalled
black glistening bodies, pointed teeth, wild bristling hair
and flailing swords that rose and flashed in the hot sun.
Their brains were dazed in the noon's heat, from every shield
the red paint thundered, all the tribal gods leapt out,
lions and crocodiles and snakes, and dashed to eat
those creatures who so suddenly surged with a new god.
Through flaming clouds of dust the swift-eyed archer saw
his god burst through the sturdy thongs, leap to the right
and laugh until his myriad teeth flashed in the sun.
Granite saw all his troop about him fall like trees
and cried to his tall captain in a piercing voice:
"We're lost unless you find some new trick, dexterous man!
This jumble of men, gods and beasts will blot us out!"
But the much-suffering man roared out as his god's tears
and wails flowed and resounded with his mingling blood:
"Comrade, the time is past for tricks! Rise up and strike!"
His proud words echoed still when a belovèd voice
thundered amid loud trampling feet on the scuffed sands:
"Courage, we're here! Courage, we've kept our souls intact!"
and then a broad-rumped shadow fell on all those clashing heads.

When Kentaur had resolved to save the orphaned troop
he turned to the scared women and the famished children:
"Take heart, my dears, we're not meat yet for the lean crows,
nor will we drop down dead because our captain's left us;
we, too, hold castles full of hearts that won't crack soon,
we, too, can be more stubborn than our stubborn friends."
He spoke, and all took heart, their souls crept in their breasts,
and, tightening their lean waists, they pushed on with their great
good god, their stubborn, ponderous and broad-rumped friend.
"Ahoy, my dears! I've got a big speech now! Don't laugh!
Hunger will harvest that one first who has no faith,
for he who fears, stinks to high heaven like a skunk
and when Death sniffs him out then there's no saving him.
By God, in this whole world I don't know a more sly,

more cunning, useful virtue than sheer dizzy pluck!"
But the soft-hearted sot did not neglect to free
as many men as he could spare to hunt for game.
One day they found a native hunter, bound him fast,
then forced him with fierce threats to lead them somewhere close
where they might find wild game to eat, a place to sleep.
He led them through far sandhills; they killed game and ate,
their souls took flesh, their feeble forms grew strong, and then
they spied a town amidst the trees, fierce uproar on the sands,
and saw their friends scream and fall headlong on the earth.
They felt the danger and rejoiced deep in their bones
for now they had a chance to shame the proud young braves.
Like a huge bison Kentaur fell on the twined mob
and it was then his thunderous voice swooped on their heads:
"Courage, we're here! Courage, we've kept our souls intact!"
The blacks howled and drew back, their knees gave way with fear,
and all their tribal gods, snakes, crocodiles, and lions
climbed back with fear and crouched upon their turtle shields,
for they had seen a more dread god fall from the sun.
Blood-drenched Odysseus then leapt up with open arms:
"A thousand, thousand welcomes, friend! Give us a hand!"
Fat Kentaur only grinned with his wide innocent mouth
and did not speak, for his fat neck had swelled with joy,
but he fell to, and hacked about him to find relief.
The blacks threw down their weapons, raised their arms on high,
and the proud hunter yelled to all his savage hounds:
"Lads, they've thrown down their arms! Stop the wild slaughter now!
The snares of pity and friendship serve our interest here!"
Then arm in arm they zoned the cowering blacks about,
picked up their weapons and then climbed to the strong town
that spread and shone in rose-rays of the setting sun.
By the closed village gates nine sweating slaves stooped down
under the weight of thick beams spread with lion skins
where like a hippopotamus their old chief sat enthroned.
His hair and shaggy bellies steamed with a rank sweat
and slaves ran up to help him raise his lumpish arms
as a high eunuch's voice squeaked from his greasy throat:
"Welcome, O white-winged birds who come from distant shores,
the hungry gods are slaked now and will eat no more,
the gods were thirsty, but now they want to drink no more;
we bowed down to their will most gallantly, but now
it's time that we, ant-heaps of earth, should eat and drink;
but first let's bury our sharp swords and kiss like friends."
He spoke, then his eyes filled with glutton's bulky form,
—surely their chief, since the most fat—and spread his arms:
"Great chief, when we have eaten and our hearts have wined,

let's form firm blood-ties; take my peerless daughter then,
sought by all chiefs, a hippopotamus of fat!"
Greedy-guts laughed and stroked the plump sides of the chief:
"Let's eat first, king, and then we'll look into the wedding.
Well said! The gods are slaked, they've eaten heaps of men:
let's lard our own guts, too, with oxen and fat sheep,
then let your daughter come and sit on my fat knees—
I've got a curly huge carnation for her, too!"
The chieftain planted three sharp arrows in the earth
and the huge groom rammed a long sword into the pit
and planted a green basil spray sprinkled with honey.
Thus both sides buried war and planted friendship there;
then the town gates were flung wide open, and the king spread
his pitch-black sweating hands with their rank he-goat smell:
"Break down my house doors, groom! Enter with all your train,
let blood turn to sweet wine and skulls to drinking-cups!"
The nine king-carriers and the groom dashed through the gates
and on swift feet the famished friends pressed close behind;
the streets were all deserted, frightened doors were locked,
and in their rooms the women shrilled and tore their hair,
but when all reached the dragon's den and his huge court,
the slaves set their king-dragon down on tender twigs
and the friends sat cross-legged about him on swept ground
and waited for great friendship's swirling dance to start,
the heaped round trays, the wedding banquet's larded feast.
The haughty sun broke down, long shadows cooled the lanes,
in pairs the wounded dragged themselves by pools to wash
their wounds, happy that Death had skipped them by a hair,
then all sat still and sweetly smelled the roasting meat.
Orpheus had not a word to say, a tight noose choked him,
his heart shook like a reed, for on an old oak tree
he saw huge clusters of white skulls that hung and swayed.
With fear he nudged his master and hissed in his sharp ears:
"Look there at Death's huge apple tree weighed down with fruit!
Alas, our fate has cast us with man-eating beasts—
these are the dread dog-headed blacks told of in myths,
all sweet speech till they turn to snarling, biting dogs;
these are those double-dealing beasts who'll eat us all!"
But the heart-battler hid his shuddering fear and said:
"Songster, be still! Do not forget your carefree craft;
you pass the world's ache through your dulcet flute where pains
turn magically to memory and memory into song."
Before the singer's pallid lips could say a word,
huge slaves appeared with tall trays weighed with steaming meat,
breadloaves and foaming date wine and bright jugs of bronze.
The stars appeared, torches were lit, jaws ground away,

all fell upon their food and drink with hasty greed,
and as they ate, night the hyena with soft paws
crept in and cast her shadow on the courtyard stones.
The fetid chief sat silent on his bloodstained throne
and leant his hands on shining bones of his old foes;
as sweating slaves knelt down to fill his gaping mouth
with lumps of meat, the grease ran down his triple chins,
he snorted, and the trembling slaves ran up to fan him.
The archer then signed secretly with his swift eyes:
"Comrades, there's too much fondling and attention here;
keep a sharp lookout, don't drink much, hold your swords ready."
Meanwhile some slaves ran bringing from the battlefield
the blood-soaked heads of the white troops on brazen trays;
they bathed them in the murky stream, then smeared with balm
and thickened myrtle-oil their nostrils, hair, and eyes,
and filled their purple mouths with wine and roasted meat.
When they had decked the heads like grooms and fed them full,
they knelt, bowed low, and prayed with fervor to each head:
"Alas, don't curse us, brothers, because we slashed your necks!
Such are the wheels of chance, the written twists of fate,
but arrows are loaned things and spears but boomerangs:
that day will come when our heads, too, will hang from trees.
We stoop and fill your lips with meat and mellow wine;
ah, rest, my brothers, rest, and merge with the dark loam,
hold the earth's entrails tight, don't turn to vengeful ghosts,
for we, too, soon shall lie in earth with equal rage."
Thus they bowed low and tried to appease the mighty souls
not to turn vampires, praying to the new-slain heads,
but in night's coolness, under the full laden trees,
the living flaming heads, unruffled, ate and drank.
Granite climbed swiftly on the plunging cliffs of thought,
for the wine's spirit, the wine-barrel's cunning goblin,
secretly poured him whole wine-bowls of griefs and growls
until he sighed with longing and his winecup cracked:
"Rocky, I see you in my cup, a shriveled rose;
though I drink wine, yet I drink poison too, my friend,
I drink your pain, I beat upon the ground and shout:
'Rocky, get up and come, let's drink together awhile,
let's swap two heartfelt words to ease our heavy pain.'
But don't come like a ghost without your breath or body;
I want to squeeze you by the hand, to hear your voice;
and when the rooster crows at dawn, don't leave me, friend,
stay, and let's kill a cock and drink to your good health."
Thus friendship's true-love stuttered with his wine-ghost friend.
Kentaur stretched out in the chief's yard like an oak tree
on whose green boughs the pallid piper hung and shook:

"Hey now, don't sigh, my songster! I like that tree of skulls
hanging with heavy luscious fruit; look at it well!
I swear it's a fine tree and bursts with pomegranates!"
Slowly the piper's giddy mind swirled with the wine
till all the world became a vineyard, his friends grapes,
and his head hung like a grape-cluster filled with song
till the grape-harvest swelled and dark grape-treaders came.
Only the archer was not trapped, but cleansed his mind
with vigilant eyes, his brain snake-coiled and his ears cocked;
he sat on thorns, distrusting the obsequious care,
the flowing wine, the fragrant scents and the low whispered talk.

Night bloomed upon the humid earth like a black rose,
the stars rained with a thin dew on the downy dark,
and in night's innermost heart a light breeze gently blew.
In the dim torchglow the archer saw a Negro troop
who sat cross-legged upon the ground and held strange gear
of music on their knees, in bird or jackal shape,
and each began to blare with its own singular sound.
But all at once the wedding conch boomed loud and long
and flatfoot turned to marvel at his comely bride.
Slowly the wedding pomp passed by with jackal shrieks:
first came full-breasted, naked Negro dancing-girls
streaked with bright yellow paint like long-striped tigresses
who beat the dowry with wheat stalks, or held tall drums,
and slowly dipped into the wedding-bond's slow dance.
They reached out quivering toes and groped the magic ground
but trembled and drew back, as though their feet would wake
unknown dark powers that still slept on beneath the soil;
but slowly their dark flesh took wing, their eyes turned white
and flashed like lightning, their crisp breasts leapt up and swelled,
and musk aromas from their humid armpits steamed.
The orgiastic dancers ground their bellies, shrieked
with gleaming teeth, then fell in the aroused men's arms,
but the archer rose erect and leant against a tree,
for savage atavistic memories stormed his skull
and the bronze hinges of his mind's gate burst in two.
He bent his shaggy eyebrows into ruthless bows
and spoke to that still sleepless forge, his lucid mind:
"Ah, master-craftsman, now let's see what you can do:
fetch up the sperm from the roused loins to the clear head
and make it soul!" A warm wind blew, white orchids steamed
on the dark women's crinkly hair, fat widows danced
and bore about their necks their husbands' whitened skulls,
and then the bride snaked in like a wild hunted beast
to spy the land, lust-laden, painted to the gills,

her stout and buxom body smeared with gleaming grease.
An old witch doctor slunk about the growling groom
then threw upon his shaggy back a wedding robe
close-woven, scaled with yellow-gold canary wings,
and the roused bridegroom rushed through the rank sweating dark
to grab the shining bulky flesh of his fat bride.
Thus in the sacred chase both bride and bridegroom played;
the white shells jangled in her hair, their hot breaths steamed,
the guests all laughed and danced, and the young singers ran
screeching about the courtyards like wild fowl in heat.
Exhausted Kentaur gasped to catch his slippery bride,
then suddenly with a wide sweep of his greedy paws
pounced on her greasy back as with a wildcat's claws
and dragged her to an upright phallus hewn from stone
that in a far-off darkened corner sweetly glowed.
The bride no longer laughed but moved her hands with awe
and, murmuring softly, laved the sacred stone with fat,
stooped low and worshiped, took her bridegroom by the hand
and led him to the sacred oak's ancestral heads.
The king placed in his grandsire's skull a hutch of wheat,
and then the bride stretched out her arms with joy and cried:
"Grandfather, wake, come to your vine-fields once again,
they have grown wild with weeds, they need your lustful blade!
Grandfather, wake, strap on your manly weapons now,
rise from the earth and in my entrails knit your flesh,
harvest my youth and tear my womb, appear once more
as a male child and in your cradle laugh and play!
Here is the man, grandfather, who'll burst my lock for you!"
She spoke, then with her heavy lips licked up the wheat
from her ancestor's snow-white skull and chewed it slowly.
The suffering man beheld the rites with silent joy;
man's sluggish wheel moved slowly in his secret brain—
he climbs the soil a babe, then in old age slumps down,
then once more, as the earth's dark jaws grind fine, he leaps
from the dark womb and issues, weeping, to blazing light.
The mystic wheel whirled in his mind with flashing sparks,
all generations in his mind rose, sank, and fell,
then once more swarmed within him, seethed and hatched their eggs.
The pace of life now seemed to him to move so slow
that it could never match the throbs in his wild breast.
As the spread-eagle soars on high to spy the ground,
thus the great archer blinked his eyes and scanned the courts;
the night reeked like a Negress in a heavy sweat,
the erotic chase had ended, and the groom now bore
the bride slung down his back, a votive beast new-slain.
Like night-black gleaming leopards, the dark dancers pounced

on the aroused friends who in lust threw off their weapons;
then the black songsters with snake-flickering eyes crept near
the white girls of the troop, grabbed them in greedy arms,
then screeching like wild birds, thrust through the undergrowth.
Unmoving in night's silence, grim Odysseus heard
his women laugh and his young stalwarts roar like bulls,
but kept his untouched body free for other tasks.
As the blacks slowly crawled and snatched the cast-off weapons,
and snuffed the torches out until the stars hung low,
he saw the fat king rise with stealth and make a sign.
A thunderbolt abruptly crashed in the slayer's brain
to see the two-faced jackal tricks of his black host;
he leapt at once into the yard, lashed to his face
the fearful and brain-splattered mask of his dread god,
then moved with ponderous steps about the stricken king
who gaped in silent fear until his whole flesh quaked
and his teeth chattered, for a new god crushed his heart;
he gasped and tried to cry out, but his jaws hung loose
and his throat gurgled like an overturned wine-gourd.
The archer seized his conch and blew a long hard blast;
his friends who lay on Negroid breasts in a deep daze
heard the dread blast that signaled of approaching peril
and sluggishly tried to rise from the flesh-woven nets,
but black arms twined like serpents, loins still seethed with lust,
and the drugged lovers sank once more in dark embrace,
enwrapped once more in the thick coil of glistening thighs,
and all lay quivering in the erotic noose of arms.
There white girls, in the deep warm stench of Negro flesh,
smothered like honeybees drowned in a rich black honey.
Then the clear-headed leader blew once more in rage
to assemble all the faithful round him in closed ranks,
for now the cunning snares of Death were spreading tight.
First to rush out was Granite, buckling on his arms
—women are cooling water to drink and cast away—
and, snorting, took his place beside his furious chief.
The blast shook all the trees and dragged sleep by the hair,
eyes once more opened in black arms, and nostrils quivered:
alas, embracements were most sweet, and rough the road,
for in lust's sticky kisses all still swooned and trembled.
Groggy with lust, broad splayfoot stumbled out from shade
with swollen lips and golden wedding mantle gleaming,
his beard and shaggy armpits dripping with thick musk,
for, like a bee, he'd thrust in a black rose, and now
buzzed out, his savage bellies, wings, and furry feet
thick-splattered with gold pollen from the plundered flower.
Behind him floundered the scuffed piper on wobbly knees;

by God, he too had lingered long amid black blooms,
playing with apples, sniffing at a few last grapes,
and when the first conch blew, he deadened his deaf ears,
climbed a sweet apple tree and wedged among the boughs.
"Oho, don't shout so, archer! I can't hear a thing!"
But when he couldn't bear his captain's second blast,
he crashed down from the leaves, bruised here and there, and came
with his blade hung between his thighs like a whipped dog.
"Cursed be the female tribe that trips us with its snares!
They stick to us like leeches, then sting us like crampfish
and bind us in their lime-twigs, lads, until there's no escaping!"

The black sky had turned milky, stars flicked here and there,
and when the black chief and his slaves saw the armed troop,
both men and women, swarming swiftly from the grove,
they huddled close in trembling fear and speechless watched
the ruthless strangers plunder all their stores and flocks.
"Fellows," fat glutton shouted, ravaging through the barns,
"come on, there's plenty of booty here! I'll set up house!
Don't feel bad, Father-in-law, I'll only take my dowry!"
Odysseus stood erect and gleamed in the dawn's light:
"This savage nightwork, too, has ended well, my lads;
hunger and rage and war, fat arms, good food and drink:
behold, earth's wheel has come full round and drags us with it.
May God thus whirl our fate about like the swift stars!
Now onward! The earth spreads with further joys and griefs.
May all who wish to stay behind wake to a sweet dawn,
we winnow as we plod and cast all chaff to the winds."
Tall horse-legged Granite pushed on first with all his braves,
and broad-rumped Kentaur stalked in stately pomp behind,
his gold-canary shoulders glistening like the sun,
but his bride tore her hair and clung to his broad hips:
"Don't go, my dashing horseman! Don't leave me, my sweet mate!"
The guileless groom looked backward and his pure heart trembled
for his mind gaped with a babe's awe in his thick head:
"What mystery's this? How can two strangers meet and bed
until there's no ungluing them in hands or feet?"
He scratched his head and sighed, "How can a head like mine,
and that a blockhead, solve the world's obscure enigmas?"
Turning, he beckoned to his bride, but when he spied
his cliff-guide's pointed cap, he hastily dropped his hand
and played the innocent child, then swiftly took the road.
"He'll give me a tongue-lashing now, and he'd be right,
for I did overdo it and took my own sweet time!"
Thus splayfoot mumbled as he sped to escape his master.
Odysseus ran and lashed God's mask to his dark chest

with sturdy thongs and felt it gnaw deep at his heart
the way a child will bite and suck his mother's breasts,
and his god's bloodshot eyes, his nostrils, ears, and jaws
opened and closed on his wild chest and gaped with hunger.
Day broke, the sun roared in the sky, a bursting sphere
that beat down and rebounded from earth's drum-taut hide.
All heads once more were scorched by flame till their heads blazed,
God's face changed and grew savage once again; the world,
flaming and desolate now, spread like sand-blasted wastes.
Like a good shepherd, Kentaur counted with his eyes
how many had been winnowed out in the ruthless trek,
how many had turned back and died in scorching sands,
how many had anchored in a woman's harboring breasts,
and God, how many girls had stayed, in black arms locked.
He counted over and over again, and his spine shook,
for he felt God above them winnowing hearts and souls
with a fine sieve, picking and choosing ruthlessly,
till glutton's mind could bear no more, and his thick lips,
bride-bitten, quarreled profoundly now with God's caprice:
"God, you've sure muffed your job! Your world's a stinking crime!
If *I* were God, I wouldn't change myself one bit,
I'd cut up wild on earth once more, I'd chase the girls,
I'd take a ship, I'd sail, I'd once more choose the archer
to make all my decisions, take on the world's headaches,
while I sprawled on my back and quaffed life like a lord!
I'd fling my heart wide open to the four wild winds
like a paternal home and welcome good and evil both.
I'd play no favorites, all are my babes, I like them all,
and if at times they tire and fall on earth to rest,
I fetch them into light again to gaze on the sun.
But this god that Odysseus lugs on his burnt back
strikes ruthlessly at earth and kills without regret.
You're two of a kind! To think that such as you now rule the world!"

Their heads grew ripe in the hot sun like hanging fruit;
as shadows lengthened and night fell, they lit campfires,
turned on their shoulders slowly, stretched on sand, and slept,
a bevy of birds which sleep the hunter strings together.
The people slept, but by the fire their chiefs kept vigil,
and the archer, sitting in their midst, feeding the blaze,
rejoiced to see that flames, the more they eat the more
they flick their greedy tongues as though to eat still more:
"I bow in reverence to your hunger, my great brothers,"
he murmured, then turned to his fellow-travelers gently,
for all that day his bursting heart had seethed and boiled,

he'd kept his lips and brains unlaughing, locked up tight,
for in his heart joy had expanded and pain increased.
He watched his sleeping troop, rejoiced, and wished them well:
"While the world sleeps, leaders must always keep the watch
and speak of good and evil done, then take full measure
and cut the future's cloth true to the mind's desire,
for the strong spirit holds the world like wax and molds it.
This seemed to me like a good day, my faithful friends,
behind us the green town, before us seas of sand,
and we, between them, join in one God's double face.
I see it clearly now, the desert's my true land;
I thrust more deeply in myself the more I pierce her.
Heat, hunger, wild beasts, trees which hang with skulls for fruit—
these are mosaics with which man's heart and the earth are built.
Thrust these few words deep in your minds and lash them tight:
the more our journey widens and new roads unwind,
the more God widens and unwinds on this vast earth.
It's we who feed him, friends; all that we see, he eats,
all that we hear or touch, all that thrusts through our minds,
he takes for his adornment and his strutting wings.
Soon as we see these savage thorn trees on the sands
he too sprouts thorns and stings us with ferocious rage,
and when we hear the wild beasts prowl, he too grows wild,
growls savagely and scares poor man out of his wits.
In our own land he wears white linen cloth with grace,
but here in Africa he grows ferocious, wears bronze rings
in his wide ears and nostrils, tall plumes on his head,
sweats like a Negro, and like a Negress stinks with musk.
God is the monstrous shadow of death-grappling man."
But as the archer spoke and fed the flames with boughs
and his eyes sailed upon them as on crimson seas,
he burst out suddenly in a startling cackling laugh:
"Now by the sword I wear, I sometimes lose my wits;
it's true that he may need us, that we two are one,
it may be he's our master and on desert sands
heaps high at times a tray of bison, water, bread,
and not because he loves us—drive that from your thoughts—
but to keep living the flesh on which he rides through life!"
Granite arose and cast huge handfuls of dry thorns
upon the dying flames till they leapt up like lions;
his smothered heart could bear no more, and he spoke out:
"On the day I left my craggy native land, there blew
deep in my heart full fifty winds and fierce typhoons.
Passions ate at my heart, nor could I free them then,
but now at length all things distill within me clearly;
now I know why and for what cause I'd give my life.

As we pierce through the desert sands, two great commands
are etched deep in my mind, the voice of our dread God."
"What great commands?" his leader cried, and his heart throbbed.
His friend, as though confessing, said in a low voice:
"This is the first which from on high spoke to my heart:
'May he be cursed for whom both sorrow or joy suffice,
may he be cursed who smothers not in mankind's virtues;
open your arms, my brothers, that the world may grow!'
Then softly, softly, when great hunger stabbed our guts,
the second great command pierced my illumined mind:
'Only great hunger feeds my god, and great thirst slakes him.' "
But then the piper shrilled out with his murky brain:
"As I trudged on I shouted in my slanting mind:
'Where are you going, fool? Will you never stop? Behold,
I see roads heaped with the bleached bones of crazy travelers!
Though I seek deathless water, alas, I sink to Hades!' "
In some of his friends' minds the lone man's words struck home:
"You're off the track, my piper, for you think you speed
to find deep wells of deathless water to slake your thirst,
but Granite here has hunted down and caught my secret:
to climb and hunger, Orpheus: this is my God's feast,
to thirst in the desert, Orpheus: these are my God's wells."
As Granite gazed on the low flames, his bright eyes dimmed
as though he felt ashamed now of that day's confession,
and he rose swiftly, grabbed and flung some thorny brush
in the low fire until it blazed with sputtering tongues
and cast reflected crimson stripes on all their faces.
Then Granite tried with stealth to shift the dangerous talk:
"I've loved and never had enough of two live things:
to watch flames lick their tongues, and animals at play."
But the soul-snatcher laughed and caught his comrade's arm:
"One day, my friend, I'll carve on every skull and stone,
and on all tree trunks, the commands of our dread god.
I shall engrave them on all flesh with flaming iron
that I might march with open eyes straight on toward Death."
A river-bearded ancient archon shook his head,
with deep sword-slashes on his bones, with crumbling teeth:
"You gab too much of God and pass him through too fine
a sieve until there's nothing left of him to eat.
I hear but one cry only, more than enough for me:
'Never ask why, but follow a soul greater than yours!' "
All then fell silent, and the archer's backbone shook
as though a thousand souls had hung about his neck
while he drove on and chose salvation's road alone,
salvation's and destruction's, for the two were one,
and both pursued one goal, a two-tongued hungry flame.

Midnight: the fire crackled swiftly, danced and ate,
and the archer's brains, too, crackled like dry burning thorns;
the owl's mournful voice dripped on the moonlit sands
and the flame-flickering leader touched slim Granite's knees:
"Don't speak, my brother, for a majestic city looms
on my heart's mountain summits and my mind's plateaus.
Flames leap and sway in my dark head and lick their tongues,
they build tall towers and castle gates and battlements,
they build long rows of homes where mothers laugh and work,
young men stroll by with spears, and girls with water-jugs,
old crones beneath the flowering pear trees weave their shrouds,
and I hear wedding songs, laments and lullabies,
and smell full ovens in the yards, wine-must in kegs,
and women who have laved their locks with jasmine oil.
The Laws sit round the castle walls like hungry beasts
with gaping greedy jaws and eat and drink and growl."
As the dreamer talked, the piper raised his reedy flute
and soon began to play a swift and rousing tune,
but the archer, deeply ravished by his castle dreams,
heard no flute sounds, not even glutton's mocking laugh,
for when he stopped, broad-bottom burst in cavern roars:
"Air-building master-craftsman, with your flames for trowel,
confess now: if you lacked the piper's dulcet flute,
you never could complete alone your tall dream castle!
He's your hod carrier lugging clay with a thrush-feather!"
The many-minded man grew angry and stamped his foot:
"Not even miracles can pierce your hide, my friend,
for with a cuckoo's cry and a flame's flickering tongue,
with the empty hollow wind-toys of the playful mind
I shape my tall dream castles swiftly in my head.
That day will come when my thin shadow will turn to meat,
my inner flames to outer stone, when my mind's visions
will swoop to earth down from my head's tall hidden peaks.
See, I strike stone, grab earth, and seize your arm—
just as my fists have filled now, so one day, I swear,
I'll build my tall dream city with stones, beams, and gods.
This is how cities are first planted in firm ground!"
And then Odysseus smiled and would not speak a word;
his bright eyes swiftly labored with the toiling flames,
stars in the heavens shone like clusters of thick nests,
great thoughts shone upright in his dark and savage head,
but his mind held the flute of silent thought, and played serenely.

XIII

A vulture balanced his wide wings on the air's peak,
he saw the desert and rejoiced, he saw stuffed wells,
he saw long rows of skeletons bleached in the sun,
he saw ant-swarms of men plod on the stubborn sands.
Fixing his piercing eyes upon the ant-swarm there
he circled lower, waiting for the maimed to fall
that he might once more swoop and feed on man's fat brains.
When the archer saw the vulture high above his head
he opened his arms wide and hailed him like a friend:
"A thousand, thousand welcomes, vulture! Swoop down low
that I might cling to your proud neck and grasp your breast.
Come take my measure that your belly might contain me;
coffin, I like it when you hover above my head!"
But the far vulture did not hear, it beat its wings
and vanished southward toward snow-covered mountain peaks.
At that same hour Rocky cut through the dense woods
and, seeing the bird, lifted his slim arms and cried:
"Vulture, if only I had your wings and your lithe grace,
I'd soar high up, balance myself and look about me!
O holy bird, swoop down and take me on your strong back
that I might see my friends and dine with them a moment,
then bring me back to wilderness and forest beasts,
for I love liberty, though burdened by great pains."
Thus Rocky begged and prayed, flapping his arms in vain;
his slender body was parched dry like hides or shells,
his skull was full of wounds and scaled like turtle-shells,
his flesh was gashed by wild-boar tusks and lion claws,
cut up with poisoned arrows, stung with scorpion bites.
The mountain summits swooned in pallid dusk, the woods
choked with blue shadows as Rocky cut into a clearing,
a slender sword unsheathed, and bent like a lean twig.
He lay down tired on the grass and caught his breath:
"Your health, O heart of man, wild fate-devouring beast!
Where have you cast me, you soul-juggler, on what great wheel,
for now that the soul has ventured, who dares stop or check it?"
He closed his eyes and the last cliff gaped in his mind:

They'd set him bait like a wild beast, caught him in snares,
then whittled wooden spits and built huge fires round him,
rubbed him with pungent spices, smeared him with fat grease
and pressed about him, screeching for a tasty meal.
Suddenly, as he gazed on death with scorn, he heard
a voice, perceived a pointed cap high in the air,
and his mind leapt but measured all with cunning stealth:
"My soul, take for example now the archer's soul.
It's good to stand erect in flames, unmoving, proud,
and burn like a tall torch that flares in a wild blaze,
but better still to seize the mind's unburnished weapons
and fight to the last ditch and leap the mounting flames.
O spirit, vulture-clawed and sly, descend and seize me!"
As Rocky yelled, the spirit seemed to hear his voice,
for the long road of freedom flashed within his mind;
he jumped up and began to dance on the green turf;
his lean feet leapt so swiftly that he almost plunged
deep into Hades like a lustrous falling star.
Two wings sprang from his temples, two from his slim heels,
his feet and brains took flight, the stones about him sparked,
his handsome body hissed like flame, fell like a star,
yet kept on dancing boldly on a sword's thin edge.
The flames went out, the cannibals forgot their hunger,
a pregnant maiden whinnied in the pangs of birth,
and all the old men raised their hands and softly spoke:
"It'd be a great crime, God, if earth should lose such feet.
It's good to sit with grandsons round you in your yard
and eat the tasty meat of that erect pig, man,
but there's no greater joy on earth than a fine dance;
it conquers thirst and hunger, joins both foes and friends.
We'll spare your life so dance won't vanish from the earth!"
Rocky took to his heels and came to that dark wood
where now he sprawled serenely in luxuriant grass,
a snake who'd shed his skin, then shakes in the cold wind.
At dusk when shadows lengthened and hunger flailed him hard,
he rose, passed through the wood's few straggling trees,
holding a crooked shepherd's staff of ilex wood,
and tried to find a place to sleep and light a fire.
As in his mind he spun man's dark and daily needs
he suddenly fell to earth and thrust in tangled shrubs,
for far off in a gulch he saw a village gleam.
His nostrils smelled the stench of that dread monster, man,
and crawling on his belly like a snake, he slid
from stone to stone, then spied from the edge of a huge rock:
the town spread gleaming white between two mountain slopes
and round it rose tall walls built out of earth and reed

on which black banners waved and sparkling fires glowed;
in the dead center shone a king's house of tree trunks
with rows of bleached men's skulls about the hanging eaves.
But no soul moved in that deserted, haunted town,
no naked women screamed, no children laughed at play,
no tranquil smoke of evening rose from the rooftops;
fear crushed all rooms, and only the low sound
of drums unseen was heard in slow funereal beat.
Poor Rocky stooped and shuddered as he thought with awe:
"Perhaps the town's bewitched, or killed by deadly plague,
perhaps a vengeful ghost has turned the place to stone,
yet I'll go down to see, and let fate's will be done."
About his waist he wound a strong tough vine, then seized
his sturdy staff and like a shepherd lunged down toward his flock.

Door after door was tightly shut and double-barred,
all fires were stamped out and all dogs were gagged and leashed,
women and men crouched on the floors in silent dread
for on this day their king was bidding the world farewell.
Seed was imperiled in the whole town, the pregnant girls
ceased to bear males, nor would the oxen drop their calves,
grain withered in the fields and all the wells had dried,
for the king's soul had shriveled, and on this day three huge
black harbingers of their dread god set out to slay him
that a new rutting ram might lead the human flock
and the earth spread new loins to catch the fertile seed.
Flat on their faces, the people prayed for ghosts to come
from the high hills with their white hair and savage bolts:
"Grandfathers, take your flocks, the lowering clouds, and come!
We're killing our old king to exorcise the curse,
bring us a strong new king and build us strong new fires!"
Thus men and women on the terraces begged and prayed
then opened their hearts wide to hold the miracle.
Meanwhile the ancient chieftain with his crimson sandals
dragged himself through the streets, bidding the world farewell.
Feeble and sallow-faced, with a white straggling beard,
he stumbled on the stones, and his eyes filled with tears,
for his own kin and friends denied him, streets were bare,
and only his ancient dog, wounded and gashed by age,
limped after him on tattered paws and licked his feet.
The old man roamed in circles through the empty streets
as though he twined a crimson thread about his throat;
his eyes brimmed and the earth grew dim, it suddenly seemed
as though clouds crashed from the high peaks and wound him round;
were these his grandfathers, cold white shrouds, or lethal thoughts
that spun and wound him tight in an unceasing whirl?

"Ah, to escape, dear God, and hide in the deep woods
where none could find me—even to live but one day more!"
He threshed his eyes around, and seeing all streets bare,
the dying man's mind spun, again he gazed with fear,
saw not one soul, then swiftly ran to flee from death;
but as he stretched his shriveled hands toward the town's gate,
he suddenly screamed, drew back, and his words choked his throat,
for on the sill was spread the hide of a black bull
and on it gleamed the sacred skull of his own father,
his people's token that he must join his sire soon.
The king's knees buckled under, he crashed down to earth,
and his old dog drew back with fright and barked for help,
but no soul came to ease their pain, and the king rose
and grasped his father's white skull tight in his black hands.
At once his eyes flashed fire, he swiftly raised his neck,
knowing not even God could grant him one day more,
conquered all hope, then tossed with pride his whitened head
and turned back toward his throne to await his death with courage.
At once from three town gates three sorcerers set out
and each held in his hand a long and glistening knife.
In evening's dusk the bloodstained palace softly glowed
with the white skulls that laughed with gleaming sharpened teeth.
In a dread hush, the king passed through dark passageways;
on the first stairs his womenfolk crouched low, and screamed,
black, naked, young and old, who'd come to say goodbye;
upon the second stairs his friends and faithful slaves
kissed his thin hands and feet and cried in sad farewell;
on the third stairs his old dog crouched and softly wept.
The old man stopped because his weak knees shook with fright
and he recalled sweet life once more, and lost his pride:
"Alas, my kingdom's gone like mist, my life like air!"
he murmured, crawling up his high throne's seven steps,
and cold sweat dripped from his dark armpits, eyes, and ears.
He huddled on his throne and clapped his sweating palms
till slowly from the wall a hundred-year-old bard
appeared and held a thousand-year-old ivory flute,
and the king spoke with open arms and quivering voice:
"Old man, you've made me happy; sing me my last song,
play that my fallen soul may turn serene and strong."
The minstrel stooped and soon the sonorous flute was heard
as though he listened to a seashell's roaring sound
of waves that like white horses plunged and tumbled down,
mounted by savage winds in infinite assault.
As the bard listened to his old sea-battered flute
his voice was suddenly heard in a most gentle sigh:
"Once there was not, or was . . . not even the rose remembers . . .

a great and happy king who held a sword aloft;
he was a curled carnation that would wilt at dusk,
a golden-rimmed and gleaming cloud that passed at dawn
and changed to a thousand faces in the squandering air.
I kiss your memory and bow low to your great grace
O cloud, O smoke, O red carnation, my great gracious king!"

The ancient minstrel sang, while fate's three harbingers
flattened and slid against the walls, slunk door by door,
but on their necks and ankles bells shook clangingly
and on their grimy rags their bronze wind-sucking gods,
their whistles, irons, keys and chains, jangled and jarred
as though three herds of bison, goats, and sheep dashed by.
When the bright Evening Star beamed in that holy hour
and they had almost reached the gaping palace door,
and all together raised their feet to cross the sill,
the Negro prophets suddenly stopped with half-raised heels,
stared hard with yellow goggling eyes and shook with fright,
for Rocky loomed up suddenly with his savage staff.
All three fell to the ground and howled like votive drums,
then slowly raised their heads and spoke with reverent awe:
"O most pure spirit, fallen from stars in a good hour,
welcome, celestial vulture with your golden crown!"
The handsome youth brandished his shepherd's staff and scowled,
for he had been well schooled in a great fox's court,
and spoke to the three blacks with kingly arrogance:
"My greetings, small black crows with azure-painted nails!
As in the guise of a white eagle I cut the sky
and spied your wretched huts, I thought them buxom hares
and swooped to eat them, honing my long pointed claws."
He spoke, then crossed the palace threshold with swift strides.
Cunning directed his quick mind like a keen guide;
a limpid, light intoxication swelled his strength
as though he slept and a sweet dream unlocked a host
of wealthy master-chambers in his lordly breast;
proudly he paced from door to door with tranquil joy.
Preceded by the three blacks with their myriad bells
he passed through courtyards, kitchens, musk-drenched women's rooms
in a deep breathless silence through deserted halls
and cut the night behind him sharply like a sword.
The king had painted his dark eyes, his cheeks, his lips,
his faded ancient wounds and eyebrows of thin hair;
he'd donned the dreadful armor of a hopeless struggle,
placed round his throat a necklace of his foes' filed teeth,
wore glittering earrings, stuck long feathers on his head,
then seized his ax to wait for death before his throne.

The mournful song had strengthened his exhausted knees,
and as he stood stiff, speechless, at grim Hades' gate,
to plunge down like a great chief to his dread forefathers,
three pairs of ruthless eyes gleamed at the bottom stairs;
the old man longed to raise his pitch-black banner high
and like an army march erect to meet his dark ancestors.
Night hooted among the chambers like a mournful owl,
waters within the courtyards leapt like gurgling streams,
and Rocky dimly made out huddled shapes that fought
with silent rage amid the jangling bells, but no
grim slayer's growl or choked voice of the slain was heard,
only a dim contorted form fell from the throne,
rolled down the seven steps, then sprawled on the straw mats.
At once a naked glowing pair leapt from the dark,
a still unmounted girl and well-knit virgin boy;
according to their sex, they held soft sticks and hard,
crouched on the ground and rubbed the sacred pair together.
Their black arms glowed like snakes, and from the holy wood
an ancient god rose in the dark and sweetly laughed;
a spark leapt up and the fire caught, the kindling flashed
like newlyweds who with the body's strokes and strife
blaze up until their joyous son leaps in the dark.
The lamps cast a great light and licked the palace roofs,
the conch now of salvation blared, doors were unbarred,
and six black heavy hands placed into Rocky's palms
the king's head like a wine-bowl brimmed with fragrant spice:
"The pale old sun has set, a new sun mounts the sky,
the father falls in the dark earth, and the son sprouts!
A thousand welcomes, king! Plant roots in our good soil,
sprout up with goodly grain to eat, sweet blooms to smell,
make savage fire spring that all our poor may cook,
and when your strength's exhausted and your loins are drained
then we shall meet, O short-lived king, in the deep dark!"
They spoke, then raised and placed proud Rocky on the blood-soaked throne.

The great sun with his laughter and his heavy breath
came down to the king's court to grant his proud esteem;
behind him gleamed and waddled the corpulent great chiefs
carting their gifts of slain lambs, boar-tusks, and plump boys;
the new king's humble subjects fell down prone, and bowed.
Blind minstrels lifted to the king their throbbing throats,
nude palace dancing-girls gleamed in the break of dawn,
but Rocky gazed far toward the woods and softly sighed:
"Where are my friends to see me now, where do they sail?
Where are you, deep and cunning soul, to smile at me?
I'm only worthy to be a grape in your grape-cluster."

Leaning upon his sill, the new king raised his nose
like a lean hunting-hound who sniffs his master's scent,
as though in truth he'd flushed some trace in the empty air,
for that same dawn the archer had crossed the desert sands
and thrust in Rocky's jungle of luxuriant woods.
With heavy axes, Granite and a few brave youths
stooped low, drove on ahead and slashed at twisting vines
and cut a path through bloated leaves of monstrous trees.
Smothered in putrid mold, Kentaur could hardly breathe:
"Again God changes face and tries to scare our souls
with garments of rank mud, mildew and stinking slime;
when will he ever turn into a generous friend
and loom up in our path to give us friendly greeting?
When will he stand in the wild wastes one day and wave
his hands and bring us gifts of women, wine, and bread:
'Hello, my lads, greetings to all! Welcome, black eyes!
Come on now, sprawl in my cool shade, eat of my bread,
I am your ancient great-grandfather whom all name God!'
But no such luck! He casts us down from crag to crag,
for though we've fled from sterile drought, here God takes on
his other face of leeching slime to rot us all.
Ah, what a feast all life would be had God my heart!"
Odysseus smiled with wryness but would not reply.
Days passed by, damp and dark, as the sun strove in vain
to pierce through thickset leaves and dry the septic stench.
Earth's orgiastic juices soaked the tepid soil,
vine-twisted trees sprang lushly with damp hollowed trunks,
thick snakes swam in the marshes and small scorpions dashed
with joy to ripen their soft stings in moldy humus.
The chicken-hearted piper lagged behind with dread
and pressed his flute-trained ear against the rotting earth:
"Dear God, a ground-war rages, I hear moldering wings,
throats groan in their last gasps, jaws champ and grind away;
alas! our Mother Earth's gone mad and eats her own!"
While his clairvoyant buzzing brain harked at the earth,
he heard a clamor of hoarse caws and myriad wings
as parrots passed on high like gold-embellished clouds,
and the light gleamed, a feather-woven multicolored stole.
Like a gold parrot, too, his mind leapt in his skull
till he forgot the moldy grinding earth, and cawed:
"Oho, I choke, I crawl on the earth, I shout with pain,
but when a small bird flutters by with crimson wings
all of my pain becomes that bird and my mind sings."
The sun plunged downward and was lost, and the full moon,
like night's white breast, brimmed with a pale and frothing milk,
streams shone like Nereids, lions' manes dripped silver dew,

and rough-skinned gleaming tongues licked at the milky air.
The jackal's wail rose in a piercing lamentation
and the hyena's mocking screech made the night quake;
trees thundered, branch struck frenzied branch, huge elephants
now plunged through moonglow, bathed and played in jungle wastes.
Night with its thousand eyes prowled earth like a wild beast,
thirsted, then went with fear to drink at water holes;
animals stretched their necks to drink, but their knees shook,
their lips strained one way and their eyes, their ears, another.
Odysseus hid his fear and listened to the night;
within the sodden stifling heat and tainted air
his sleepless mind uncoiled and spoke in the wild wastes:
"Steady your weak knees, archer; don't let fear destroy you!
This fetid forest is your own God's ruthless heart
swarming with insects, snakes, and beasts, flowers and stench;
Hunger and Love are here a pair of lecherous lions
that crawl in its black ditches with blood-splattered paws.
Prowl in that heart, my heart, like a small lion cub."
Apes screeched amid the trees and swung down low to see
how those white creatures walked on earth, a new ape-race,
erect and tailless, balanced on two straight hind legs.
Broad-bottom roared with laughter and to the piper cried:
"What shall we call these—gods, or beasts, or dumbstruck men?
They look like my old forebears! When I wake in woods
a monstrous monkey leaps within my jungle guts,
strives to recall, and stares as on his native land!"
But the light-headed piper sighed in choked reply:
"I look on these dark woods as on dark tombs, and tremble!
I can't turn back, and I'm afraid to push ahead;
I'm caught between two millstones here: the archer's hands."
Coarse-bellied Kentaur chuckled, then caressed his friend:
"Ho! Even he's convulsed between his god's huge fists!
Who knows what monstrous millstones grind even mighty Zeus?"
Granite kept silent meanwhile as he thrust ahead,
nor was aware of dark forefathers nor thought of God,
but as he swung his ax and cut a path through woods
his haughty fevered mind and thoughts flew far away:
"Ah, Rocky, pounce now like a lion here, and roar
and bellow till your gold mane gleams in the night dew!"

But Rocky sat upon his throne while the old chiefs
taught him with wisdom all a king's responsible craft:
how to speak mildly like a lord, laugh like the sun,
and how to hold his feather aloft, a mystic sword.
Three shining maidens stretched for him on a soft bed,
three mighty Nereids of the hunt, the wheat, the well,

and held him tight to bear him sons that all might teem—
beasts of the mountains, holy grain, wells of the field—
and Rocky threw himself into a fat and regal lust
like a starved honeybee who dips its wings in honey.
Sometimes he played with life and mocked it like a dream,
but sometimes huge desires and cares burned in his breast
to seize his weapons, and lead his people in swift assault,
and like a dashing horseman breach the African forts,
string young men neck to neck like hanging partridges
and dangle young girls neck to neck on his steed's saddle.
And who knows, for the earth is small, he might one day
upon his swift return meet with the archer's troops:
"Well met, and thousand welcomes, friends! Draw back a bit,
my head is dizzy, lads, I can't quite make you out—
is it great Granite's shape that dazzles my dim sight?"
Far from each other, both lads secretly longed to meet,
but each performed that duty which his fate decreed.
One day as Granite found among some thickset shrubs
a suckling leopard cub sunk in a sated sleep,
he dashed and seized her in his arms, then with soft strokes
calmed down her striped and bristling back and her white belly.
The clumsy suckling struck out with her still soft claws,
opened her frothing mouth until her milk teeth shone.
"Now here's a fitting gift for the cantankerous man;
such is his savage heart, I think, but a bit larger!"
Thus Granite thought and smiled, then with great joy rushed up
and wedged the handsome beast into his master's arms.
The archer stroked the cub as though it were his daughter
and felt it beating like a deep heart in his breast:
"Friend, I recall you said one night by the campfire:
'I've loved and never had enough of two live things:
to watch flames lick their tongues, and animals at play.'
But you forgot to mention man's own heart, my friend.
Now I rejoice, for in my fists I hold your gift
as a three-headed good: beast, fire, and gallant heart."
He spoke, and his loud laughter fell like rain on leaves.
They strove for two moons to tear through the forest's nets,
and every morning, with his chin locked in his knees,
the archer crouched and listened to his crackling head
as though new powers were ripening in his savage skull.
Two contrary and diverging crossroads forked his chest:
his patience and his plodding mind showed him one way
but his unbridled warring heart climbed up another,
and he rejoiced, because both ways seemed equally good.
When the new moon at last cut through an evening's dusk,
they left the last enormous trees, cut through the wood,

and night flew off with yellow eyes, passed like an owl,
until the sun's red rose climbed up the sky and bloomed,
and the troop yelled with joy, rolled down and kissed the stones
that turned pale gold and glimmering in the slanting rays.
Broad-bottom dripped with moisture like a wet plane tree,
his beard had gathered moss, and plants grew from his sides:
"Now by the Almighty Sun, I'm musty and smell of mold!"
His dislocated bone-joints creaked, his bellies steamed,
and near him the green piper yawned, for his hot head
buzzed like a beehive from the feverish jungle heats;
the young men also stretched and shivered like wet dogs.
With pale and sunken cheeks then slender Granite gazed
at the far deathless mountains, and his glad heart throbbed;
the wandering man beside him sunned himself and heard
the pelting sun fall on his head, his neck, his sides,
gripping and fumbling at his flanks as its bright rays
caressed him whole, from top to toe, with loving hands.
The tranquil heart, too, like a rain-drenched butterfly
spread out its brilliant wings to dry in the hot sun
and felt that God was also drying his wet wings.
Twelve bright tattooed star-clusters shone about his waist
as the sun passed and with its flaming hands caressed
the mystic symbols of his fate graved round his loins:
twelve sacred zodiac stars, twelve axes through whose holes
the archer with his bow of light had shot gold shafts.
When finally his nostrils dried and his bones warmed,
Odysseus stretched on the hard earth, then shut his eyes,
and in his memory's tail the woods became a feather.
The leopard cub played at the silent archer's feet,
whetting her virgin talons on his savage flesh;
the two friends played and howled in a dread solitude
nor did the cub or lone man think of men or woods.
As Granite watched his leader play, he gently smiled:
"Master, you've dried your flesh like a wet sword so that
its cutting side might not be dulled, its blunt side rust;
I marvel how we saved ourselves from that foul marsh;
where is your gripping eye now marching off to, archer?"
He who could talk to beasts heard, but did not reply,
for he had voyaged far—how could he open his mouth
and give an answer to the voice of mind or friend?
He jumped up, blew the conch, and the whole army moved.
Together with the sun, the strength of man awoke
until the fiery wick of his long backbone burned.
Slowly the fields turned crimson as they reached tilled land
and saw their first men—naked blacks who dug the soil
and in their flaring nostrils wore long copper rings.

Their gleaming faces were carved deep with zigzag cuts;
one could walk up their jutting jaws to the hung lips
then up their flat coarse snouts into their bleary eyes,
climb up their slanting monkey-brows and soon be lost
in the mudholes and lice-pits of their mangy brush.
The happy comrades yelled with joy as though they'd found
their long-lost brothers in an unknown sun-washed land.
The blacks were bending, opening pits and planting seed,
while young girls danced to help them so the wheat might sprout
with heavy beards on thick strong stalks like their long hair,
but when they saw the white men, they all screeched and ran:
"The dead have wakened! Phantoms swoop down to haunt our town!"
they shrieked and moaned, clambering the mountain slopes with fear.
Granite ran on ahead, then shouted with great joy:
"There's a large town in the glen! The oven fires are lit!
Come on, let's get there quickly, lads, before night falls!"
But their arch-cunning master yelled and stopped his troop:
"It's shameful when the belly rules and hunger sways!
Tonight we'll sleep in open fields with empty guts
and not fall in a trap by breaching towns at night;
let's see what the mind says at dawn when the earth's bright."
Without a word the troop stretched out amid the stones
with empty bellies till that sly mind-tamer, sleep,
came down like mountain mist and covered them with dreams.
Each dreamt that his dark troubles had a thousand faces,
and the heart-battler saw a black worm in his dream
that writhed and thrashed with violence on the murky ground;
immense dark undulating rays lanced through its skin,
the earth flashed luridly, the dry air flicked with flame
till the tormented man cried out with grief, "It's God!"
then stooped and gathered it with care in his crude palms,
and there the black worm lay serenely in man's warmth.
As with his flaming breath the lone man thawed the worm,
the small beast slowly shuddered, shivered, then bit by bit
its thin skin cracked, its body opened, its entrails burst,
and in the sweet infusing warmth of man there sprang
and burst to right and left two thousand-eyed wide wings
till a bright butterfly suddenly filled the lone man's palms.
The sentries yelled, and the archer leapt from his sweet dream;
three trembling blacks with feathers on their heads ran up,
fell prone upon the earth, bowed to the troop with awe,
then slowly, as their hearts grew bolder, raised their hands:
"O great white spirits, birds who snatch our souls and fly
far off to the other shore, dread carriers of the dead,
a lethal and black-taloned plague has swooped and struck us,
torn out our rotted guts and sucked our sickly souls!

O great white eagles of the sky, heal us and save us!"
But the sharp-witted man stamped on the earth with wrath:
"How does the wretched race of black man dare to come
to their white dreaded gods and beg with empty hands?
For whom do you think you browse your sheep or grow your corn?
The Immortals hunger, they want bison and flour to eat,
for only when they're sated will they cock their ears
to black man's supplications or the dark earth's pain."
The Negroes shook with fear, scattered like smoke, and soon
far on the sloping mountainsides their swift heels gleamed,
and the friends burst with laughter, but kind glutton scowled:
"Have you no heart, fierce beast? Didn't you see their pain
and how their poor jaws chattered and their armpits steamed?
I, too, am hungry, but yet I'd give them a kind word."
The seven-souled man stroked his leopard cub serenely:
"You won't do for a god, you pity men too much.
But never mind, we'll heal these blacks for your sweet sake.
Piper, get up! I've hatched a way to stop your fevers
and perk you up by making you their town's great savior."
But the poor piper raised his flushed and fevered face:
"Oho, my ears roar of the sea, and my throat's parched,
I've not the lips to laugh with now or strength to rise."
Then the swift-handed man thumped him until he shook:
"Courage, my blear-eyed friend; with raucous jokes and cries
we'll hack out an almighty god to trap fool man.
Bring me a thick block, lads; let's carve a blockhead god!"
The comrades laughed and dragged out a huge half-burnt log
then hacked away until the piper, too, took heart,
forgot his fevers, seized an ax, and hewed away
while the flame-minded man egged on his lion-brood:
"We've got a thick log, fellows, a sharp-cutting ax,
a mocking mind, enough and more than enough, I swear,
to make a miracle-working god and the world's savior!"
The piper then grew bold and measured the block thrice:
"It's big enough for a drum-gut, air-pregnant god!"
His feather-brains caught fire till he began with rage
to hack a bloated belly edged with shaggy hair
then drew the sacred rites upon it with thick paints:
bread, food, and huge wine-casks, and under the domed belly,
within a fistful of pig-thistles, wedged a goat-bell fast.
God stood revealed then to the piper's marveling gaze;
his friends applauded, but then mocked the god-creator:
"Good work! Huge is his worship, and his belly's huge,
but haven't you lost his godly head in all your haste?"
The wretched piper blushed and bit his wagtail tongue:
"The bitch from too much haste, they say, bears bowlegged pups.

I'll just cut off a bit of belly to make his head."
He raised his ax, but the god-mocker seized his hands:
"Leave him alone! This great god has no need of heads!
Hitch up your heart, my piper, fling God over your back,
climb up to town and trade him, then send camel-loads
of heaped-up food, goatskins of wine, for we're starved, brother!
Songster, we've run you down and called you worthless. Rise!
Rise now, strap on your wrangling pipe and shame us all,
teach us that a good song is worth a thousand hands.
Now listen closely: each word is a mighty seed,
so sweeten all your words with no false shame or fear,
then, lad, let your unbridled mind go plunging down,
thrash with your flailing hands and neck, foam at the lips,
and if you can—and here's the trick—when the need rises,
fall on the earth and swoon, but keep on your guard, for if
you suddenly burst out laughing, wretch, we'll all go lost!
You'll see: the blacks will jump for joy, their eyes will bulge,
and, who knows, even a miracle can happen then,
for the soul flares up quickly and the body melts.
But hold on tightly to your head, don't lose your wits,
and if the insane get well, and blind men suddenly see,
and jungle fevers hiss and steam from burning mouths,
then whisper to yourself, and keep your thoughts a secret:
'Everything's smoke, air, brains, a fancy falsely pregnant!' "
Orpheus heard all this good advice but swallowed none:
"You've raved amuck on purpose just to drive me mad!"
Then the all-knowing man laughed wryly and thumped his back:
"Don't dig too deeply in the soul or you'll go daft.
I'll trust you now with only this, treasure it safe:
the heart's a hidden magic flower called bright-blaze
that flames in dark and turns all it touches to pure gold."
The cross-eyed piper's mind could not digest these words;
he shook, glanced at his master and then at the far town,
but the sly archer pushed him on without compassion:
"Orpheus, get out from under my yoke, unglue yourself;
now, for the general good, march off with your own weapons
and stop those wagging evil tongues, dear friend, who say
that songsters are not worth the daily bread they eat."
He spoke, and honor blazed within the piper's breast;
he seized the new god, cast it manfully down his back
where the drum-swollen belly shone, the goat-bell rang,
and his two fluted shanks soon vanished up the rocky slope.

Then Kentaur twirled his fat mustache and had his say:
"Shave both my whiskers, friends, if I turn out a liar:
our friend forementioned may be a punk, but he's all there.

Mark what I say—he'll beat us all, and then some, too."
Meanwhile the piper, wailing his fate, stumbled on stones,
and when with a strained sweating back he'd puffed and reached
the hilltop and spied below the town's sun-beaten huts,
he dropped his holy burden under an oak tree's shade
and wiped the sweat that poured down from his narrow brows.
It was high noon, the stones steamed in the fearful blaze
and the sun leapt on terraces and sang in fields
like a coarse peasant who returns from his work drunk
with a red wine-soaked kerchief round his burning nape.
Then in the savage heat, as wings sprang from his back,
spindle-shanks raced through town, screeching to hide his fear,
and when he saw skulls hanging from the trees like fruit,
the bolted doors blood-drenched and wreathed with swarms of snakes,
he almost died of fear, but tossed his head with pride:
"If you can't get your breath back now, don't be a piper!
Now cock your cap, this is a dream, and you'll wake soon!"
The town was roused and leapt with life, doors banged and clanged,
all saw a lean white bird that swooped to seize their souls,
and though the piper blenched with sickly fear, he yelled:
"Run, friends, God has dismounted in the oak tree's shade,
your hills have filled with haunting ghosts—open your cellars,
bring them good wine to drink, fat sheep and bread to eat,
for gift brings gift, and when they've eaten, you'll all rejoice,
for with a small small breath they'll blow your ills away."
The rooms filled with commotion, all the arched doors opened
and swarms of women, children, and men rushed screeching out
and held their holy offerings high, bread, meat, and dates;
mothers came bearing their sick babes, girls their clay hearts,
and young men on their backs bore off their wretched parents.
Wails, shouts and cries of joy rose with thick clouds of dust
led by the piper's pointed head that shrilled in trance,
but when they reached the oak, all shuddered and shook with fear,
and Orpheus, paralyzed with dread, sank on his knees.
"Onward, my lads!" he groaned to bolster his own heart,
but the mob crouched and sucked its breath, for the oak growled,
leaf shook with leaf, branch clashed on branch in jabbering talk.
His hair on end, the tranced man crawled to God's old oak,
saw in the deep blue shade the monstrous belly blazing,
and tried to grin obsequiously, but his jaw sloped,
and when he stooped and tried to raise the flaming block,
the goat-bell bellowed, his knees gave way, and he fell prone;
but taking heart once more, poor cross-eyes bowed and cried:
"Great God, all that I've mocked now comes to scourge my soul!"
Boldly he grabbed his god and rushed out to a clearing,
and as the mob fell on its face, groveling and shaking,

cross-eyes enthroned his god on a tall sun-washed stone.
The trembling mob took courage, raised its eyes with stealth
and blinked with awe upon the god's round bulging drum;
some saw a pitch-black head with three deep flaming eyes
and some a monstrous mouth that chewed an infant child.
When Orpheus found his senses, he smiled secretly
and mocked his monkey-heart with its fool's cap and bells:
"Come on, my monkey-heart, let's break in dance! Take care,
don't stumble to the dance tune of my tambourine!
Look now, the festival swells high, don't shame me now."
He spoke, let loose his fettered heart and clapped his hands:
"Brothers, our god is hungry, open your cellar doors,
white birds have swooped and flung this god like a white egg
beneath your holy oak to hatch in blazing light!
Listen, for his dread voice bursts from my mouth in flood!"
He deepened his thin voice until a rattlesnake
crawled up each trembling ear and licked it hungrily:
"Black men, the sun's my throne, I grasp a double ax,
I've listened to your pains, my kind soul aches for you,
and now I've swooped to earth to choke the throat of illness.
I'll give back eyes to all the blind, legs to the maimed,
I'll give male-bearing herbs to every sterile maid,
but first bring my reward, give me and I shall give you!"
The piper's brains now blazed till his head shook and swayed,
his words bounced back from the hot ground and hit him hard;
though he struck terror, terror grabbed his crooked knees;
he sowed false hopes and his own bald pate sprang with grass
for his words burst to life and coiled him round like snakes.
An old man, blind from birth, screeched "I can see!" and wept,
a lame man sprang up suddenly on the stones and danced,
a young girl, wrung with passion, saw her lover stand
in the empty light, and reached her hands with seething heart,
and as the piper stood in the thick crowd, all pressed
him close, confessed their pain, and their pain shrank and died.
The sun set, twilight fell and sank all eyes in shade,
fires were lit, the people danced, and sterile maids
knelt down and played with the bell's clapper till fields rang
and the proud piper sang the praise of his god's grace:
"If heavy lust should seize you, it'll turn to buxom girls
who'll come clap-clapping up your stairs on wooden clogs;
if hunger flails you, God himself will fall at your feet
like a wild hare, strip his own skin and stretch on coals.
Each herb on earth to his clear eyesight stands revealed,
antidotes to all evils, nostrums to all ills.
Come all infirm and suffering, I am the well of health,
I hold balms, medications, laxatives, injections,

balsams for all fevers, charms for the evil eye,
and babies for your womenfolk. Come one, come all!"
The piper shrilled till his tongue burst, all night and day
bartering and selling his great god, marveling with awe
what fearful powers a man holds in his wormy guts.
All things on earth, disease and joys, are the mind's fancies:
it blows, they take on flesh; it blows again, they vanish.
But slowly the mob's warmth and the air's ululation
dizzied the feathery brains of the air-seeded fool.
At midnight in god's wooden womb he heard a light
rustle of wings, like the soft sound of fumbling bats,
and felt a dense and fluttering swarm of hissing souls.
He leapt to touch and see, but then recalled his words
and laughter when he'd held the ax and hewed this god,
but as he drew near now, his mind turned mud and mist,
the oak in darkness filled with ghosts and bloomed with stars.
One night the piper could bear no more and raised his ax,
but as the black log roared and echoed with shrill cries,
his pigeon brains gave way, his spindly limbs grew numb,
because, from the oak's heavy shade, in the thick dark,
he saw a wild flame blaze and heard a great voice cry:
"Piper!" then all at once from the oak's root there burst
hoarse cackling laughs like waters in a wild cascade.
With his own eyes he had seen Death, God's spirit whipped him,
gibberish sounds foamed at his mouth, and then he fell down fainting.

Thus on the hilltop the poor piper fought with air
while in the fields his glad friends seized row after row
of camel caravans weighed with rich and lavish food.
"Fellows, our bellies are filled, the soul's come back to its place!
Blessed be the piper, each bite we take is his forgiveness;
bravo, he's got the blacks now eating out of his hand."
For thus did marveling glutton sing his old friend's praise:
"He's sold that wooden belly dear, each dram a camel!
God is good merchandise, my friends, sales without end!"
But the archer's heart grew heavy as he watched the slope,
until on the fifth day he grasped his bow of horn
and climbed up toward the twisting hilltop, murmuring:
"His brain is much too small and the trick much too great,
a thousand dark doubts tyrannize my decoy mind."
He found the piper with the blacks prone on the ground
adoring the block with babbling and bombastic praise,
then seized his famous bow with rage while his wild heart
swelled like a viper in his chest and hissed with scorn.
Gliding light-footed toward his friend, he kicked him hard,
but Orpheus crouched, gazed sullenly and twitched his ass

until the lone man grasped him by his grimy nape,
raised him high toward the sun, then dashed him down to earth:
"Piper, wake up, an evil dream has poisoned your brain!
What shame to worship wood! Open your cross-eyes, see,
this is that same domed belly you hacked but yesterday.
Quit kicking, raise your bleary eyes, give me an answer!"
But the pale head kept mute and only hissed and squirmed
as the unpitying archer shook it like a wineskin.
"That's what you've come to then, the world's butt and buffoon!
Sometimes my heart boils, but at times I burst out laughing;
I've no more patience now and call for the last time:
Get up, cast off this vertigo, this passing dream,
I promise not to tell a soul nor even to blame you;
Orpheus, think well on man's nobility, his freedom!"
But Orpheus stared with a dull gaze on his roused master,
threw himself huddling on the earth and grasped with fear
his blockhead god in the thick shade of the old oak.
The archer's blood rushed to his head, he clenched his fists,
and all his limbs felt tired as though he'd killed a man;
slowly he tamed his wrath, then dashed down the descent,
and his eyes brimmed with tears, he sighed and chid his mind:
"Haven't I told you more than once or twice, you fool,
to use your hard hand gently, for men break in two,
but you still stubbornly think the world can reach your height."
He spread his legs with wrath and swiftly lunged through stones
till in his passing the whole mountain shook and roared.
When finally he reached his troop he raised his hand:
"Push on, my lords who squat in shade like dogs on dung,
soon, I've no doubt, you'll want to pitch your tents here too;
it's time again to wring our guts and raise our hearts."
When the cub saw her friend, she leapt on his strong shoulders
and licked his sweating temples with her rasping tongue,
and he caressed her fondly like a favorite child.
All shook to hear their angry master's rousing cry,
and when they turned and saw his face in the clear light,
they quailed, for snakes crawled coiling round his beard and hair
and four eyes gleamed with yellow rage on his dark brow.
A cold and deadly wind blew on the glutton's chest
so that he turned to Granite and slowly began to wail:
"I loved him like my own two eyes, we never parted,
his sprightly songs would often rouse my drooping heart,
but now we'll never see our chirping friend again.
Look, the man-killer's eyes have sunk now in deep wells!"
Eagle-eyed Granite frowned and thought of Rocky then,
yet kept his mouth closed, for he longed to hold his pain
wholly unsquandered like a secret consolation;

but guileless glutton blabbed on to relieve his heart:
"The more his ship is tossed the more he casts off ballast.
In Crete he flung two comrades off to ease the hull;
one was still living, with a bloody regal crown,
and one he held in ruthless hands like a burnt torch;
then Rocky vanished, our bright sun, light of our eyes,
and now that mouth is gagged which once adorned our prow.
Only we two still stagger by the gunwale now,
but friend, don't preen yourself, for soon that time draws close,
I see it even now, and welcome, when our turn will come."

As they talked on, Rocky far off strolled through his town
and all his people knelt and worshiped his white feet
while twelve bronze-armored blacks trailed in a long row,
their white eyes rolling and alert for fear he'd vanish;
behind them, waving his long trunk and silver bells,
plodded an old white elephant with a golden tower.
Meanwhile the comrades clambered to a high-pitched knoll
where fresh winds cooled their temples, and their flanks rejoiced,
sunburnt and firm, to tread on a more sturdy ground.
Poisonous cacti crawled with thorns among the stones
and struck stark fear, though somewhere in their thorns there smiled,
—who would have thought it?—virginal flowers filled with honey.
Lavishly colored serpents sunned themselves in hollows,
opened their sluggish eyes in narrow slits, and then
thrust still more deeply in the sun's sweet dizziness.
Gazing on holy earth, the archer's brains spread wide,
his dark eyes filled again with a more human glance,
and when at night he stretched to sleep with his small cub
he felt an azure flower in his thorny chest
bloom with a drop of honey in the untrodden calm.
He felt the gods grow lushly on the savage earth,
uncoiling their leaves quickly like the bloated leaves
of the banana trees that cast their fruit, then fall.
Within his flesh the lone man felt his heart and mind
and all the deep dark roots of his refulgent powers
thrive in luxuriant, monstrous growth like plants or beasts.
Earth and man's soul rose up like trees within his mind,
the sky too rose, a flowering tree in the calm nights,
and he a quivering leaf—ah, might that day come soon
when he'd become a flower, a ripe fruit filled with seed,
then let the strong winds blow to sweep him far and wide!
Thus slowly in the forest solitude his mind
grew ripe and his heart sweetened with much brooding thought
until one night, when fires were lit and all stretched out
and like a loving father he'd portioned food to all,

poor Kentaur seized his courage, found his tongue, and said:
"Master, sad words float on my lips all night and day
but no one dares to tell you now of his heart's pain."
The lone man heard and his gall rose; he turned his head:
"It's true! Your eyes shall never again look on his face!"
Startled, the guileless man then left that savage shade
who played with his wild leopard cub nor ate nor drank
but lay apart and watched the sky till his mind creaked.
It seemed the stars had changed the course that fate had set;
where were his old acquaintances of night, the stars,
which his night-wandering mind had taken for sure signs?
Gone was the Bull, the Eagle, and the Eagle's Tail,
the Charioteer had set, and the Seven Sisters vanished,
the vast star-river had plunged into a dark abyss,
and the Yoked Seven Brothers plowed the sky's foundation;
even the unshaken keystone of all stars, that led all ships,
seemed also to have changed its course and turned toward setting;
a strange new sky had suddenly burst above his head.
He turned to earth once more and fondled his wild cub,
her bow-taut and lean body, her fuzzy belly, her flanks,
her small yet sharp milk teeth which glittered in red gums,
until the handsome beast growled sweetly, stretched her claws
and lightly scratched his bitter chest with playful strokes.
Odysseus gazed on his own face in the leopard's eyes:
"No son of mine has ever so sweetly sacked my heart;
only with you, my cub, have I felt my fatherhood;
in your sharp claws, your tumblings, and your eyes' fierce sparks,
daughter, you hold the seed of my dread race immortal!"
At dawn they found them both immersed in a deep sleep,
and the small leopard had her strong and downy paws
softly entwined about her sleeping master's pulsing throat.

Panting, they slowly pushed through a tree-packed ravine
until one morning swirling clouds hung heavily
on windswept peaks and covered the low brooding sky.
Lightning bolts zoned the earth, branches of trees lit up,
the zigzag fire chopped the trees with thundering sound;
beasts ran in terror, all the tumultuous forest howled,
the lion's roar resounded and the jackal's wail,
monkeys shrieked in the swaying boughs and huddled tight,
and the troop crouched in silence in old hollowed trunks.
Then all at once the wind fell and the wild storm raged;
a warm rain filled with fragrance struck and whipped the trees,
parched leaves and thick coarse blossoms gaped and smelled of musk
and all earth opened to gulp water deep in her bowels.
Then broad-rumped Kentaur, dripping like a river-beast,

his armpits hung with tangling vines and crinky moss,
sat stooped upon a moldy trunk and shook his head:
"Oho, my lads, we're all bogged down! What a great shame
to go to Hades now like frogs, mudsoaked and smirched;
how those deadheads will burst with laughter to see our plight!"
But huddled in a tree's old hulk, the lone man felt
an inexpressible joy, breathing the damp and mold
and the strong stench of beasts that in the cloudburst steamed.
He brooded on the lizards, geckoes, newts, and snakes
that, glued to earth, now listened to the world's quick pulse
throbbing with fear like a vast heart deep in the ground.
His mind sank like a nude worm in the great downpour;
but bit by bit the weather cleared, the world grew light,
clouds drifted by in fleecy tufts, and wet leaves laughed
sun-washed on earth by all the raindrops' seven hues.
The troop once more pushed down the road and sank in mud,
bright parrots whistled through the air and flashed their wings,
small beasts poked out and licked and dried themselves in sun,
and every backbone on earth laughed, refreshed by rain.
The lone man's breast, too, laughed as though it were the wood's
parched heart where it had rained and where the sun now shone,
his nostrils quivered with the smells of moistened earth,
and when they'd lit their fires at night and stretched to eat
he asked both of his friends with brotherly affection
to share a fat wild kid he'd killed along the way.
When they had licked it to the bone, the sated archer
slowly and with no joy or pain disclosed his thoughts:
"Aye, friends, I look upon the world and see two paths,
but still my mind has not resolved what road to take;
I'm thinking of the piper, lads, and of man's heart."
He stopped and stroked his cub until his mind grew calm
then told his friends about the piper's wretched downfall;
sometimes he burst out laughing, but at times he stooped
and poked the fire to choke the hidden sighs that rose:
"When will the heart, that clinging burr, come to her senses?
She sets lime-twigs on earth to catch some birds, then goes
wool-gathering and gets caught herself, and starts to sing."
Pot-bellied Kentaur deeply sighed and rose to leave:
"All of us, bone and soul, all push on toward our ruin.
To meet your doom by women's kisses, wine, or sword
is not a heavy shame and suits the worthy man,
but to hack out a log and shape a rotten belly
and then, O nitwit, to forget without much cause
and worship your hand's plaything as a god indeed—
ah, the heart's leaves are four, and two of mine are ashes!"
But the stone-hearted man lay with his cub on earth,

listened to his soft-hearted friend sob in the trees,
then laughed, and in his bronze head steadied his mind firmly:
"I love each handsome hour, all twelve dappled pairs,
brothers and sisters, white and black, and stroke them all,
but I love best that one great queen in each full round
from whose waist hang the heavy keys, who holds an ax
and, full of eyes, keeps standing watch in my heart's core.
She watches how my friends walk, how their feet proceed,
nor will forgive a wrong step taken, nor give odds.
Alas, you stumbled, piper, and the sentry saw you!"
The lone man rooted up his friend, pruned his hard heart,
cast off those doomed to ruin, kept but useful friends,
for earth was not a sickbed, it was a field of battle!
He suddenly turned and longed to play with his wild cub,
but she, with bristling hair, with shaggy and cocked ears,
was listening to the far ravine, sniffing and trembling
as though she'd heard the sweet growl of a passing leopard
that called to his small sister's long-lost grieving heart.
The lone man's daughter then unsheathed her hidden claws
and honed them on a tree, growling with roused desire.
Odysseus struck her on the back with a small stone
and she snarled savagely until her milk teeth gleamed
and a small, small drop of blood moved in her flushed eyes;
but then she crouched and slowly clenched her strong front paws,
uncoiled them, slouched, and sluggishly approached her master:
"Daughter, I see you've cut new teeth, your strength has swelled;
greetings to my god's fangs that now shine in your gums!"
The lone man spoke, then man and beast embraced and sank in sleep.

The night dreamt of the sun and broke into soft smiles,
women and men awoke at cockcrow and moved on,
and waters moved, the whole world moved with tail raised high.
In early dawn a slaked and strutting lion stalked
along the mountain slopes to drink at the wellhead;
he'd eaten a fat prey, for his chops dripped with blood.
Hearing the troop's loud tramping in the woods, he stopped,
and as he looked on men serenely, his huge head
rose like the royal sun and shone in russet dawn.
Passing before him silently, the shuddering troop
glanced on the haughty monarch with a stifling fear,
and when they passed, the lion gently growled and yawned
then slouched off sluggishly, for he'd recalled his pool.
As they cut past the woods, the sun shot shafts on earth,
a light breeze gently breathed upon the treeless fields,
and as they scattered in the plain to search for roads
they suddenly saw a large town wedged in a deep gulch.

At once both joy and fear surged through their famished guts,
the town now seemed like a ripe fruit to their starved eyes,
and all sat silently on earth to plan the plucking.
While they were weighing ways of cunning or of force
they heard drums beating in the gulch, whistling in trees,
and suddenly, even before they could unsling their bows,
they saw nude demon-driven blacks scatter and run:
their hair, in cockscomb tufts, flapped in the wind like wings,
long painted phalli gleamed about their grimy necks,
lean crimson flames in thick paints danced about their loins,
and when they saw white bodies, they fell prone with fear.
But when the archer smiled, they lost their sudden dread,
slowly approached and groped at the white forms of air,
suddenly screeched like birds as their brains flashed, and then,
to keep from stifling with the joy that crushed their breasts,
they caught each other's shoulders and broke in swirling dance.
They were black braves who had not yet enjoyed the taste
of a girl's body and who in wastelands strove with dance
to rape the ripe maid of their roused imaginations.
They shrieked and growled like rutting beasts, their filed teeth gleamed,
they swayed their lean arms like the black swan's supple neck
and stroked invisible forms with their red-painted palms.
When their roused bodies wearied and their minds calmed down,
the youths sat cross-legged on the ground and with cracked cries
told how they'd lived alone for months in the dark woods.
Their loins had ripened, their black cheeks had bloomed with down,
and now before they'd enter manhood and know woman
they hailed their savage virgin youth with dance and laughter.
In the next moon they'd dash to town with shouts and drums
and swirl in warlike dance about their holy oak,
and then when maids approached them with their supple thighs
they'd rush upon them in the holy heat of dance
and thrust their seed deep in that flood of swooning flesh.
Smiling, the much-tormented man rejoiced to see
animals, men, and birds that with wings, song, and musk
decked themselves out for nuptial rites each gaudy spring.
The seed adorns itself with crimson and green wings
like a prodigious bird that flits from tree to tree,
a brightly plumaged chieftain with a red-tipped spear.
But though the archer watched the seed decked like a groom,
he still remembered their bare stomachs, and asked for food.
A young brave smiled with glee and slapped him on the back:
"Don't worry, your sunk bellies will rise as round as drums,
for we've changed masters in our town, a new king's come,
a pure white spirit, and the glad people still carouse."
Odysseus calmed, and when the blacks spread through the woods

he turned to his exhausted wolf-pack and consoled them:
"Be patient yet awhile, my lads; tighten your belts,
and in dawn's light I'll thrust through town to reconnoiter;
my eyes are twitching, comrades, and my palms are itching."
Hope calmed and slaked their empty guts, all sank to sleep,
and when God dawned, the lone man woke and gave commands:
Kentaur was to remain in charge of all the troop
while he and Granite scoured the town for food and drink.
"I thrust my hand in fire, and fate will cook us meat;
all things go well, my friends, so keep your trust in earth."
He spoke, then lightly touched strong Granite's iron shoulder
and both like two dumb beasts lunged downward toward the town.

Trees woke and slowly drew apart, the town walls moved,
the sun leapt like a cock and crowed on all the roofs,
the blacks awoke and from their rooms peeped secretly
to watch the two beasts stalk with vigor through the town,
and maidens smeared their slippery bodies with date oil.
Rocky, clad in his golden plumes, roamed sleeplessly
about his palace decked with skulls, pallid and sad,
and twelve black executioners trailed the votive beast.
He felt souls hang and weep about his pulsing throat
till pity suddenly smothered his once ruthless brain:
ah, could he only cast a bit of light about him
and cleanse the conflagration of dark Africa!
The sun leapt to the ground and struck the palace walls
till the two columns in the doorway woke and shone.
About them climbed the creatures both of heaven and earth:
a turtle straddled the low base, and on her back
a pure white elephant knelt with ivory tusks raised high
on whom a fiery lion crouched with blood-soaked mane;
a golden-feathered cock-god crowed on the fierce lion,
and on the cock a human pair lay tightly clasped;
between them sprang a tall bronze spear that tossed in light
and on its tip, like a smoke wraith, there slowly flapped
a long blood-clotted strand of hair of the slain king.
Rocky stood still and marveled at the emblazoned shafts;
his turn had come to let his raven hair grow long
that it too might one ritual day be nailed, pure white,
on the bronze spear to flutter in the indifferent wind.
He smiled with cunning to himself, then clapped his hands
and the doors opened to admit his eunuch slaves
who came to dress their chieftain with a festive robe
coarse-woven and hung with crimson feathers, nests, and eggs,
for their great conjurer was to bless their king today.
Suddenly through the doorway two vast shadows swayed

and deeply darkened the red-painted, savage sill.
"Brother, I like these monstrous palace pillars well!
Thus have I often carved man's true shape in my mind:
treading the earth firmly, he mounts every step,
cleansing from godhead slowly, turning indeed to man,
till on the topmost step Death's banner looms and flaps."
Thus did the sage man speak as he strode past the door,
but suddenly all the sentries screeched from the tall towers
and the black chieftains stretched on the earth and stripped their backs,
while their great sorcerer stumbled upon them, as though dead drunk,
laden with jangling bells, horns, feathers, and strong charms.
Possessed by a dread god, he staggered and seized the king:
"O short-lived chief, O passing bird of dead man's realm,
I bless your hands, I bless your feet, your chest, your neck,
I bless your piercing eyes, but at your hair I stop
for I can't see your black locks fluttering high in air!"
He stopped, and sweat dripped down his body like dark mud.
The king caressed him, but he struck his hands with force:
"The black locks of your head will never mount and wave,
dripping with blood, upon our sacred pillar's top;
you stand on a burnt castle like a blazing torch!"
He howled, then fell down frothing on the chieftains' backs.
"Through that great uproar, Granite, it seems to me I heard
the sound of a loved voice, or has my mind gone daft?"
But Granite had already heard, pushed past the guards,
then crossed the courtyard with great strides, sped up the stairs
with pounding heart, while the archer followed with swift strides.
Motionless in his crimson plumes on his high throne
the king with haughty glances watched his chiefs adore
his bright green sandals and his shadow of azure hue.
When Granite saw him shining in the flickering light
he yelled and hardly touched the ground from his great joy;
Rocky screeched like a hungry vulture, and the black slaves scattered.

For a long time both wept together in close embrace
until the archer came and fondled the broad back
and the long, regal hair of his now famous friend.
"My brothers, stop at length your fondling and your tears,
it's time for the dust clouds to settle! Let's see the light!"
But the tall mountain bodies wept and sometimes laughed
nor would they deign to place a halter round their hearts.
Yet all good things on earth draw but a short breath,
so doors were shut and all three friends sat down to feast,
and ate and drank like dragons while the black slaves scurried.
They sent a messenger then to play a joke on glutton:
"Comrade, kick up the dust and come, even though you're eating!

Blacks have attacked us! Hurry! Let's die together at least!"
Then their great leader filled a wine-bowl up to the brim
and drained it to the good health of his new-wreathed friend:
"Comrades, our god is lucky, fearless, and most great,
and yet most honored, for great souls like us support him.
Remember, friends, how he set forth with filthy rags,
how hunger flailed his entrails, how fear shook his mind,
how all the beasts in the wild lands once rushed to eat him,
and now see how he looms with all his regal feathers!
Rocky, don't tell us yet how you climbed this high throne,
I like to cup the marvel mute now in both hands."
But Granite poked the knees of his long-wished-for friend:
"Don't listen to that sly dissembling head that now
pretends his hard heart does not long to hear you speak;
dear friend, desire kicks him hard, and he's all humbug!"
Then Rocky laughed and gazed long in the archer's eyes:
"The wine you've fed us with, lone man, has gone to our heads.
When you once left us on the bank, I rose in spite,
tightened my belt and brains, then took the road due south,
and as I passed through deserts, hungry, and beasts dashed
to eat my sun-scorched body and to drink my soul,
your strong shade always stood close by and gave me comfort.
'Onward, my soul!' I yelled, 'this is the road to freedom!' "
He was still speaking when a shadow crushed the feast
and glutton panted past the threshold, fiercely armed,
but when he saw feasts and not fights, he laughed and roared:
"Mocker of God, you've fooled me! Phew, I'm out of breath!
What's this? A three-course dinner and a well-spread feast?"
Then Rocky's laughing voice greeted his long-lost friend:
"A thousand welcomes, fat ass, to my lordly suite!"
Greedy-guts heard and lost his wits, he leapt the table,
and when he saw proud Rocky high on his lion throne,
he moaned and grabbed his much-loved friend in his fat arms:
"Fellows, I think this life's gone daft and turned to myth!
Five or six hoodlums once upon a time set sail;
some were bewitched, some died mid-journey, but one tramp
cut off all by himself in a good hour, and now
behold him, a great King of Blacks at the world's end!
I'm afraid, my lads, that we'll awake one day and find
we're still in Ithaca's bay, dead drunk on its far beach,
still gazing on the spreading sea with brimming eyes,
and that this famous voyage of ours was but a wine-dream."
Then well-mouth fell upon the food and licked it clean,
and when he'd finished, he recalled his friend and sighed:
"Ah, that poor scrawny eagle's egg, may it fare well!
If only he were here to play his pipe now, lads!"

He murmured sadly and his popeyes brimmed with tears.
"I swore by the great sun I'd never betray him, lads,
not even when birds should build their nests within my skull."
As he was speaking, the witch doctor shook in sleep
and filled the air with the harsh sound of jangling bells.
"Awake, great conjurer!" shouted Rocky's regal mouth.
"They say your mind's as sharp as swords that cut through air,
it cleaves the hills like mist and scatters all the woods,
and in their open baskets Time and Place, your slaves,
bring us the past and future like refreshing fruits.
Throw magic in our eyes to see him we desire."
The king then rose and raised the old man from his bench,
but he sprawled on the ground where all his strength poured out
like undiluted wine until the wolf-pack's brains grew dim.
As Rocky turned and beckoned then to his old friends,
the tables disappeared like mist and the walls vanished,
a swirling blaze unwrung the temples of each man,
and lo, the piper, dressed in a bird's yellow plumes,
and smeared with grease, hopped far off on a distant road
and with an incense burner smoked his woodblock god.
Two girls with jugs poised on their heads were passing by,
but when they saw him from afar they fell to the ground
and he with closed eyes spit three times to exorcise them;
his narrow back hunched heavily in the burning sun,
and then the piper vanished in thick clouds of dust.
The palace walls sprang up once more, the feast took shape,
the three friends still held winecups to their trembling lips,
but greedy-guts felt stifled and rose to breathe clear air:
"Everything seems dissolved in mist! By God, I'm drunk!
Brothers, I'm off to the high hills to stretch on stones."
Then the much-suffering man mocked at his own proud mind:
"For shame! You swagger like a turkey, bite like ticks,
swell like an evil blister and deform the soul;
you long for flesh and ships and seas, for bread and meat
to work your miracles, to perform your gallant deeds,
but, O my mind, can you stand still in empty air
without ship, body, god, or any earthly aid
and blow on ships and flesh and scatter them all like mist?"
Thus did he rub and pummel his mind's haughty face
and for an hour he envied those exotic powers
with which the old man ruled and marshaled all the winds.
But the proud man grew calm again, turned to the feast,
seated drunk glutton to his right and filled his bowl:
"Here's to your health, you sot!" "And here's to yours, you grasping hawk!"

They ate and drank for three whole days, talked three whole nights,
but on the fourth dawn the world-wanderer raised his hand:
"We've had a giddy shindig, lads, a rousing, bang-up time,
but such a life is only fit for brainless gods
and scorned by the heart-battling soul of mortal man.
Aye, Rocky, arrogant body, eagle-feathered soul,
it's time to free yourself from joy. Cast off your crown!"
But the cross-eagle honed his claws and scratched the boards:
"You know that I don't care for joys or thrones and that
a sword-cut suits my skull much better than gold crowns,
and yet the dangers here and the spoils both are good.
My mind has grabbed all Africa in its eagle claws;
I shall make war, string captive gods in hanging clumps,
and when I've watered all my fields and fed my trees
with thick and fruitful blood, then I shall spread my wings
above my people with great peace and hatch man's virtues.
To these poor blacks I shall bring friendship, freedom, light,
and thus fulfill man's highest duty before I die:
to leave life taller by a head to all my sons."
Majestic Rocky stopped, although his mind still seethed,
then reached his firm hand and caressed his master's knee:
"Forgive me, captain, I but follow in your own steps;
I want, with your own blessing, to go far beyond
your own twelve exploits and your own twelve arrowed axes."
But Kentaur scowled and grabbed his brimming bowl with rage,
then set it down again with stubbornness and cried:
"What rant! There's not a thirteenth ax in all this world!"
The proud king sighed and with a heavy voice replied:
"The mind can string a thousand axes on earth still
and only Death would be the final bloodstained ax."
But glutton was not appeased and sharply probed his friend:
"By God, I'm struck dumb that our chief's most trusted spear,
you, who rejoiced to fight once mutely in his shade,
have grown so bold and rear your head with your own banner!"
But Rocky laughed and fondled his friend's shaggy back:
"You've found it, friend! I raise the flag of freedom high
exactly because I *am* our chief's most trusted hound!
Hasn't he often cried, 'Comrades, break free of me!'
Archer, I've studied your words well. Good health! Goodbye!"
Deep in his heart the bold bellwether felt his soul
being torn apart as though a viper was giving birth,
but in his friend's last feast he raised his cup with calm:
"When I was born, they say, it was not day or night
but that the black and the white hours both gaped wide,
and that's why I've a wind-chart in my breast for heart,

why each new step I take is a new road each moment,
and why my every thought is a splendid star that pours
and flashes with green-azure flames in the vast dark.
Rocky, I watch you fluttering your new wings to flee,
and all new roads within me fall supine and beckon.
I can still grab you by your loins and cast you down,
or I can see you off, unruffled, with great calm,
or like a grandfather I can place my heavy hands
on your black locks and bless the holy strength of youth;
my heartbeats are proud peacocks that spread haughty tails."
The archer ceased, then stretched his eyebrows like curved bows
and his three friends stood motionless for him to shoot.
Then Rocky's tranquil and unquivering voice was heard:
"I wait for all things calmly and I welcome all,
nor do I know, I swear, whether my wide heart longs
for strife or peace or your grave blessing. All are welcome!"
The seven-souled man smiled profoundly, spread his hands,
and grasped his friend's black locks in both his fists:
"Blessed be the bold, audacious daring of your youth,
steady your knees, my friend, don't let my blessing throw you:
Now may that winnower God, who scatters age like chaff,
grant you the power to cast the disk of earth much further!
Dear God, how many foaming seas, how much green earth,
how many multicolored birds and sweet desires
I'll never have time enough to taste before I croak
like a poor beggar with outstretched and greedy palms!
May you reach that far land I've aimed at since my birth
and, if you can, load my large flowering tree with fruit."
He spoke, then bowed his own gray head and begged his friend
to grasp it with both hands and bless him in return,
but startled Rocky flung his hands out wide and cried:
"Lone man, it's not for me to stretch my hands and bless you!"
But the soul-seizer then replied with a wry smile:
"It's not on Rocky that I call, but on all youth,
on all disdainful youth to care for me in my old age."
Then Rocky seized the lone man's graying head with fear
and moaned as though he held the world's head in his hands:
"Great head, unsated mouth and towering heart, O father,
you are the earth's green fertile vineyards, we the grapes,
you are the endless sea and we the ephemeral foam,
you are the tree of life and we the boughs and leaves
where we strive ceaselessly, O lord, to hang both fruit
and flower on your high summits and your deep embrace.
I give my mind brave counsel and I goad my heart,
but all in vain—I've longed for one thing all my life:
never to flee from out your dark and dreadful shade!"

He spoke and his eyes brimmed, but he could not release
that heavy curly head he'd seized with such great fear,
and sentimental Kentaur brimmed the bowls with wine:
"You've got me bawling, friends, both of you spoke so fine,
but the sun's mounted high and calls us to take the road;
archer, you've winnowed well, and only two remain.
Your health, King of the Wilds, and your good hour, master;
may fate, that lamia, fix it so we'll meet one day
in a small boat, once more stripped down to rag and bone,
with a wind blowing, and the piper sweetly playing."

Then the soul-snatcher's black eyes shone with tranquil light
and he stood straight and drained his brimming cup of wine:
"One night on a small island at the world's far end
I bid my son farewell; it was no dream, and I
recall it hurt, for it's most difficult here on earth,
where bodies lie in tight embrace and need each other,
to part forever from son, parents, wife, or wealth.
But new farewells and strong new pains accost us now;
brave youth, here's to our meeting in the earth's embrace!
So long as you live, breathe, and tread this earth, defend
with bravery that one pass entrusted you by fate!"
He spoke, then seized firm Rocky's shoulders in both hands,
and the great king accompanied them to the town's edge
and held in silence Granite's hand tight in his own.
But when he roamed his flaming streets alone at noon,
tagged by his twelve tall Negro guards with swords in hand
who dogged his every step and rolled their yellow eyes,
he quaked, and his heart quailed a moment, but at once
he paled with shame and felt the archer grip his arm
until all life hung like a bow and dangled down his back.

Once more the troop trudged down the road to start the trek
in lands without man's trace, or water, or bird's wing;
green serpents once more reared their heads and puffed their necks
and hissed with frenzied rage as the white travelers passed.
Nine days and nights went slowly by till their striped souls
became tree-snakes that coiled and pounced on every prey,
and then the archer beat hard on his brother-stones
and hailed the jagged mountain peaks that touched the sky:
"Well met, O native land, hard shell of my tough mind;
for years my heavy heart, long exiled in green lands,
has yearned to lay its eggs in your stone eagle-nests."
One day as he tagged behind, and longed with ruthless pride
to sharpen his dull troop for years on stones like these,
he suddenly heard advancing Granite shout with joy:
"The sea!" and the sharp man was startled, for it seemed
as though the sun-dried mountains round him laughed like shores,
and he stood trembling on his toes with neck outstretched.
As he stood listening, he heard thundering waters crash,
and huge waves beat against his temples row on row.
The sharp sea-battler moaned, clambered up rough-strewn rocks,
and suddenly through bare boulders on a plunging cliff
—the suffering man's brains foamed and roared like a cascade—
an endless blue-green shore lay stretched below his feet.
Broad-bottom hugged his comrades as his tears gushed out

and tumbled down his cheeks and his disheveled beard:
"Fellows, by God, I think we've reached the world's far end!
The earth ends here, there is no more! Here on the edge
of the cliff's rim we'll build our freedom's city now!"
But the much-suffering man cried out with shaking voice:
"Brothers, draw in the reins of your unbridled hearts,
I fear your minds make flesh of air, your eyes run wild.
Don't turn your joy loose yet, let's first descend and dip
our undeceiving hands in that alluring sea
before we let our hearts laugh shamelessly with joy."
He spoke, and his mind's blade pierced through each hoping heart;
then all dashed silently down the slope on feet of air
but kept their eyes fixed on the sea to hold it tight.
Behold, as the day mounted, fields grew dark and fogged,
the mountains disappeared like clouds and the sea vanished.
The troop ran panting, and the lone man rushed ahead
and put his heavy heart in order with good advice
to take both yes and no and make them both bear fruit.
As his eyes fluttered, all at once the dark clouds scattered,
the unmelted snows gleamed once again, and from the crags
of the blue shore thundering waterfalls foamed and fell.
The waters flew in huge fistfuls, dashed down the rocks,
and the archer rushed down toward the sea to touch it first,
but as he plunged his hands in water and wet his lips
he cried out in surprise and his heart leapt with joy,
for this was not salt water nor the sea's salt spume—
his hands now cupped the sacred river's reverent wells!
He braced his body on a mossed rock in an awed silence:
at last he held the sweet fruit of his longed-for goal;
the deathless waters leapt with joy and licked him now
like that old faithful dog who saw his long-lost master.
Broad-bottom in the glittering waters hopped and splashed:
"Drink of the deathless waters, lads, set your minds free!
All that we've seen and suffered were but dreams of air,
thirst never parched us, hunger never stripped our bones,
nor did we ever quarrel on the bare desert sands.
Our piper, bless him, stretched once by the riverbank,
took up his reed and made our brains sway in the breeze,
and thus with his sweet piping strains our journey's ended."
The friends all laughed and in their water-mother swam
until their flesh and souls were cooled, their pains forgotten,
and when they stretched, replete, the many-willed man rose,
his eyes rimmed with new anguish, his lips pale as mist,
as though the wells were now behind him, dry, depleted,
and he climbed up toward unappeasable new thirsts.
He cocked his cap askew on his gray head, and spoke:

"Lads, though we've come to our first cliff and our first duty,
I now discern a cliff that beckons further still;
but let's cajole our flesh awhile—it, too, is a god,
warm and short-lived, to which a daily worship suits.
Set up lean-tos of branches, fix hearth-rings of stone,
plant slanting tented boughs and set the caldrons boiling,
then when you've eaten, stretch on beaches, pair by pair,
because too many loved friends dropped along the road
and it's time, lads, to breed again and save our stock.
But I shall climb alone to this high mountain's peak,
for I have much to say to my old lion-heart,
and as all wedded pairs shape sons in the dark night,
so shall we shape our holy city in these wilds
with guardian laws and battlements of our firm hearts.
When it has well formed in my mind and straddles space,
I shall descend, and we shall seize both trees and stones,
and all that hovers in air, and plant it firm in earth.
Farewell! I shall return when seven days and nights have passed!"
He spoke, then leapt from rock to rock on agile toes
and like a young man scrambled toward the rose-lit peak
while his friends at the mountain's root in silence watched
him wedging through the mountain's dense and twisted paths
as his long shadow fell along the morning slopes.
"Dear God, help him to bear his savage solitude,"
his people murmured anxiously, and wished him well,
and glutton wiped his eyes in stealth that none might see him weep.

As the archer climbed, and the arena of his eyes spread wide,
solitude struck him like a sea and cooled his mind:
"A thousand welcomes, Solitude, O large-eyed mother
of all disdainful, proud young men, you with your small,
small wreath of wormwood on your snake-coiled, pure-white hair!"
He spoke, then heard a scurrying sound, and turned his head;
the leopard cub with tail erect and panting tongue
rushed up his knees and scrambled to the lone man's shoulders.
Odysseus laughed and fondled her white belly slowly:
"How kind of you to come, O Lady Heart, with your new teeth!"

XIV

What joy to climb the mountain's holy solitude
alone, in its clear air, a bay leaf in your teeth,
to hear the blood pound in your veins up from your heels
and speed on past your knees and loins to reach your throat
and there spread like a river to wash your mind's roots!
Never to say, "I'll go to the right," "I'll go to the left,"
but let the four winds range the crossroads of your mind,
and as you mount to hear God breathing everywhere,
laughing beside you, walking, kicking at sticks and stones;
to turn, and like a hunter out for grouse at dawn,
see not a single soul, not even a wing in air,
though all the mountain slopes about you chirp and caw.
What joy, when earth shakes like a flag in the dawn's mist,
and your soul sits astride a steed sword-sharp and strong,
your head a castle of great power, while from your chest
the sun and moon hang down like gold and silver charms!
To hunt for that uncatchable high bird, to leave behind
your mind, and jangling life, and joy, that faithless whore;
to say farewell to virtue, to all-numbing love,
to leave behind the moldy and worm-eaten earth
the way new cobras shed their flimsy skins on thorns.
The lackwits laugh in taverns and the girls grow pale,
the landlords shake their velvet caps with threatening looks;
they envy your red apples, soul, but dread the cliff,
but you strike up a gallant tune and like a bridegroom
walk straight toward solitude with bridal gifts in hand.
Lone man, you know that God avoids the herd and takes
the desert paths alone nor casts a shadow there;
you've learned all crafts; most wily man, and neither God's
own traces nor man's tracks can make you change your road;
you know the forest clearings where dark demons eat,
the wells which water the dread phantoms of the breast;
you hold all weapons in your mind, seize what you want:
ambush, bewitching spells, harehounds, or feathery shafts.
That day as you climbed up at dawn and walked with light,
both of your rude palms itched, your cunning eyes cast flames

and beat among the bushes everywhere to flush
that savage bird, your wild waste's god, with its rich plumes.
Light-footed on the mountains, the cool hours passed
and leapt like kids among the crags with their bronze bells;
the sun paused in mid-heaven, the day cast off its yoke,
and twilight slowly settled on cool, azure mists
till with his friend, the light, the archer also stopped
on a sharp barren mountain peak with clawing crags,
precipitous and parched, no water and no grass,
wild nest well suited to his eagle-grappling mind.
At length the first star fluttered in the darkling air,
a golden housefly caught in the night's spidery web
which slowly, slowly caught still more till the black dome
in marble traceries spread like webs after a rain.
"O night, I love your darkness, for it's filled with stars,"
the archer murmured, as he hailed the astral flocks.
His mind, a carefree star, hung high in the black night
a moment, then plunged to earth once more, with flesh concerned:
"O drayhorse body, tomorrow morning your great task starts;
eat well, sleep deep, build up your strength, for if you knew
what I've in mind for you, your hair would stand on end."
He spoke, then the sly master opened his wool sack
and with delight took out roast partridge, bread, and wine
and fed his hungry body to conserve its strength.
He licked the partridge to the bone, turned up his flask,
bent his head back and gulped the date wine till he felt
its strength spread like an octopus through all his veins.
The cub lay at his feet and chewed a mountain hare
which she had stalked and caught amid the beetling mountain crags.

As night increased and fires faded, the troop stretched out
along the dark foothills and tried in vain to sleep;
some heard the waters beating on their minds' long shore
and had no heart then to surrender and sink in sleep;
others recalled the archer and quaked to think what he
might bring within his murderous palms on his return.
When he had eaten, he rose and sought a place to sleep,
and when he saw a cave's low mouth in the stars' light,
he wedged his body through, a sword in its dark sheath,
until the furry bat of sleep spread its black velvet wings.
He slept and dead men rose and swayed, the ghosts awoke,
the mountain's bowels gaped, and phantoms, black and white,
slid silently along the plunging mountain crags:
"Who has an iron belt or marble hands, my lads,
or heart of pregnant tigress, let him take to arms!
The time is ripe, the archer sleeps, his mind is hushed;

who'll cast a spell on his coiled brain before he eats us?"
Their voices leapt from peak to peak through the ravines,
but all ghosts of deserted wilds crouched in their caves.
As dark night crumbled, the rough tongue of savage day
licked at the breast, the throat and head of the lone man
till he awoke and hailed his mistress silently.
Throughout the earth cocks rose and crowed with swelling chests,
delighted birds among tree branches pecked the sun,
and Kentaur yawned and looked up toward the looming peak:
"Light strikes the summit, the lone man must be awake,"
he thought, then raised his head and like a faithful hound
sniffed for his master's trace amid the scented air.
But the lone man still joyed to watch the flimsy light
pierce through the cave like slanting arrows and wake the walls.
"O sun, great sun, my brain's high peak, my crimson flag,"
he murmured, and his banner-bearing mind rejoiced.
But as he gazed on the rock walls, his heart leapt up,
for all about him in thick paints a wild hunt burst:
striped tigers, bears and buffaloes and monstrous beasts
pounced frenziedly, with paws against their bellies pressed,
and a nude man, lean as an ant, with a huge bow
flung arrow after arrow on their quivering backs.
"Greetings, O my blood brother; hail, my ancient flesh!"
the lone man yelled as he leapt up to greet his friend,
then with glad heart he crawled into the feathery light of day.

Like bees who suddenly smell one early dawn that spring
had come in the warm night and filled their fields with flowers,
the thoughts of the world-wanderer buzzed with sweetest sounds.
Ah, what great joy to free the mind like a roebuck
and roam the fields with downy flanks and savage horns,
to take delight in the whole earth, its bridal doe!
If life were only an erotic toy, death but a myth,
our memory an unmounted virgin in our hearts
desirous of the past no more, wanting no future,
loving no other moment but the deathless present!
"I give you leave to play today, O flesh and mind,
to suck the cliff's wild honey and the wild waste's milk
until the shrunk skin peels and the hair falls to expose
the crimson apple of virginity newborn!"
Thus did the traveler talk now to that armorous pair,
his flesh and mind, who in their passion had given him birth.
His staff struck stones as he climbed toward the eagle crags;
that day he had no cares or friends, no lordly airs,
his chest laughed, his heart danced, his mind beat brilliant wings,
and his coarse bones played like far-distant dulcet flutes.

Amid green slopes he sang all day, a cuckoo bird
that summons the cool spring with wings still wet with dew;
stones sprang with grass to hear him, pear trees burst in bloom,
yellow-green lizards came to sun themselves on rocks
and the sage man lay down with them like their big brother,
like a huge, holy crocodile that guards his people.
Perhaps sleep took him for a moment and shook his brain,
the firm frontiers had fallen, truth and falsehood merged,
and raven earth adorned itself with peacock wings.
Stones bloomed with red carnations, reptiles swelled in size,
the sun descended like a lord dressed in gold robes,
holding his earth-wife in his arms dressed with the moon,
and passed out wings to worms, and flowers to the wild weeds.
Then his most secret wish came like a virgin maid,
smiling and full of light, lay by the archer's side,
and like a partridge blinked her black eyes, sweet and wild.
But as the proud man stretched his arms to fondle her
a small, small naked worm crawled up his hairy chest
until he suddenly shuddered and sprang up in fright.
The setting sun had sunk in the field's dusky shades,
and though he had not eaten, the full-sated man
returned to his wild den and slept like a small child
with drops of milk still lingering on its frothy lips,
laden with dreams within the deep and ringing cave.
At midnight a wood dryad, Nereid of the night,
sniffed that great virile form and stood at the cave's mouth;
her hair was made of moon rays and her breasts of dew,
and as she slid into the cave and saw the mortal
she knew him for that heart-seducer, that world-swindler
who neither goddesses esteemed nor dread gods feared.
She suddenly screamed with fright and scattered all his sleep.
"A moonbeam must have struck my head and pierced my sleep
for in that very hour I dreamt of star-eyed Helen!"
He spoke, then swiftly turned on his left side to catch,
dear God, that dream with the large eyes before it flew away.

But in the dawn the lone man rose with empty arms
and only his gray beard still lightly smelled of musk;
the highest peaks were flushed with rose, the top crags smiled,
the seven-souled man's head, armored with sun, flashed fire
until his mind beat at his inner doors and yelled:
"To arms, forebears and grandsons both, the war begins!
May all the souls and hearts that crouch in my egg-swarms
come out in sun, for Mind, the King, calls all to council."
Then he sat down cross-legged upon a monstrous rock,
scowled fiercely, and addressed his mind with sober speech:

"You shall sit crouched on this huge rock, O blind, black worm,
nor shall you raise your head—do you hear?—before you sprout
salvation's wings to right and left of your bare back."
Then he turned sweetly to his heart and begged with warmth:
"O heart, O decoy of God's bird on the earth's boughs,
summon that male wing, Lady, to descend on earth!"
Day climbed, and thistles on the sharp crags bloomed with light,
earth woke, stretched out and yawned, then moved her sluggish thighs,
gazelles returned to their dark haunts, hares to their burrows,
the glutted lions licked their manes and thought of pools,
and far away a bird upon a fir tree's topmost tip,
or the mind's peak—for who could tell the difference now?—
began with lustrous head to sing a gallant song,
and the sun gleamed like golden down on its warm breast.
In silence the archer felt the sun like honey pour
along his naked hairy chest, his sturdy thighs,
and as he sat cross-legged and planned the war's assault,
a tart smell struck his nostrils till, at the rock's roots,
seeing a fuzzy flower bloom like a sea-crab,
he stooped and filled his hands with its fat fragrant flesh.
He shut his eyes, and as he sniffed, his heart crashed down:
darkness and odors, old, old joys, and clanging doors—
he was a babe once more bounced on his nurse's knees,
he stooped above her cloven breasts, those hidden clefts,
and sniffed the damp and earthen smell of female flesh
till with voluptuousness he paled, and his eyes glazed,
so that the nurse cried out and dashed him with rose water.
One other time had his brains gaped and filled with scent:
a bearded man had hugged him in his rough embrace
in the loud harbor—he was not quite two years old—
ah, how the rude sea laughed, how heady musk smells rose
of tar and cordage, rotting fruit and salty brine,
how all the hinges of his tender mind creaked wide
to admit for the first time the sea and its tall masts!
He slid from the man's chest and rushed to the loud shore
until his entrails turned to waves and filled with foam
through which white seagulls darted and the shingles roared.
Raising his small fist boldly in the empty light,
he cried to the vast sea: "O God, make me a god!"
then waited for reply a moment with clenched fist
and once again commanded: "God, make me a god!"
The great sea rose in wrath and rushed to gulp him down
but he seized stones and pebbles, pelted her with rage,
until the startled waves turned back and groaned with fear.
For the first time he had touched the world's three elements;
now in this hairy aromatic bloom he smelled

once more the musky odor of sea, woman, and god.
The heavy wheel of earth turned back and memory rose
with her large eyes, her white and undulating hair,
till the archer in his entrails felt the suckling child
sprouting up swiftly in his mind's reviving breath.
He drank cool water and turned cool, ate bread and turned
to bread, a drop of honey made his heart a hive;
his grandfather gave him mellow wine and his mind turned
to wine vats filled with hairy demons and rank lust.
His knees and loins grew firm, his cheeks sprang with soft down
until one dawn he hauled his crimson sail on high,
a beardless adolescent still, to steal a bride.
Eggs hatched in every nest till the trees filled with beaks,
hares frisked in the wood clearings, fawns on meadow grass,
and his wife danced within her husband's nuptial arms
till their son came in nine months' time, and the world glowed.
But with his son there came one night in his black ship
that pirateer, grim War, and snatched him to far lands.
The archer's temples creaked, his lips broke in a smile,
his voyage darted from the sea's resplendent bow
and passed through all the twelve gods like twelve sea-gull isles.
Ah, how man's deep unsated entrails ate and ate!
The grim man-slayer shut his eyes, his temples pulsed,
all things rose in his bowel's dusky pod once more
and his head brimmed with joy and rage, seashore and fruit.
Memories and hopes dashed up like waves, their ebb and flow
at times drowned his deep entrails and at times exposed
snakes, scorpions, slimy leeches crawling through their depths.
He flung the fleshly orchid over the plunging cliff
then tossed his brimming head on high to keep from stifling.
Shaking with fear at his mud-roots, the lone man cried:
"I'm not pure, I'm not strong, I cannot love, I'm afraid!
I'm choked with mud and shame, I fight but fight in vain
with cries and gaudy wings, with voyages and wiles
to choke that quivering mouth within me that cries 'Help!'
A thin, thin crust of laughter, mockery, voices, tears,
a lying false façade—all this is called Odysseus!
What shame to build my castle on this fake foundation."
For solace then, he called his daughter, his fierce cub,
and when their bold eyes met, two wild beasts reconciled,
the unmoving archer watched within those yellow orbs
the dreadful, deep commencement of his mastering mind.
He watched the first Odysseus on the crust of earth
dash from a cavern's mouth and rush out toward the sun.
In his left hand he held a firm high-breasted girl
and in his right a sharp brain-blooded double ax

with which he'd killed his fierce grandfather, stolen wives,
and now was chased by blood-kin, women, men, and dogs,
and ran on, frothing, blood-drenched, through the coiled ravines.
In the archer's veins wild memories seethed, he growled and scowled,
then sped to the high crags, for voices pressed him hard,
and cruel hates, shameless longings, hissed within his heart.
"How shall I ever be saved, alas, or raise my head
above these muddy guts so that my soul won't drown?"
The seven-souled man wearied as the sun declined
and sought to set, his eyes grew sweet, and from great hunger
his entrails hung like blue grape-clusters pecked by birds.
A spark gleamed opposite his cave in laughing strides,
belle Aphrodite, whom he recognized and hailed,
his old seductive mistress, welcomed a thousand times.
Thus with this eye-coquetting star in her black hair
night came and stood before the lone man's cavern door,
and as he raised his eyes toward the sky's flaming river
he felt himself drowned in that astral cataclysm,
his heart but a small drop of light that fought the flood
and swam with stubbornness against the swift night-wandering stream.

Stretched on his rock, the archer slept like a calm river
and his outstretched and flaming palms had brimmed with stars.
His bosom leapt like two deep springs, howled like two souls
as though a man and woman there, the heart and mind,
were fiercely quarreling like an ancient married couple.
The suffering man smiled long to hear that wrangling pair
tearing his bowels apart, plowing his heart in two,
and chirruped like a peasant who yoked his stubborn ox:
"Push on, lean Gray and Starry Brow, unlock the soil;
although my farm is small, I'll fill it full of seed
that all may eat until they burst, cattle and men!
Push on till welcome Death comes to unyoke us all!"
Thus did the plowman goad his two most faithful beasts
in the deep-furrowed and well-seeded fields of sleep,
but his heart ever fought the yoke and kicked the plow:
"I'm choking, no frontiers can hold me! I'll smash the yoke,
I scorn to plod the threshing floor of patience now
or like the calf be yoked to winnow chaff from wheat;
beyond firm earth and bread I yearn for the dread abyss!"
But in its head's coiled tentacles the sly mind laughed:
"O poor but haughty heart, for shame! When will you build
your castle on this earth with gallantry and grace?
You march off as though haunted chaos were far shores,
as though God were a gaudy bird that flies through air;
heart, don't you know that God and cliffs are your own fancies?

Bend to the yoke, be patient, plow your own fate's road!"
But like a vulture the heart screamed and clawed its breast:
"I will not bend to yokes, I smother in your good soil;
far off, beyond all boundaries, I hear monstrous wings,
I hear sweet cries and weeping, but a thick wall parts us;
I want to smash that wall and perish all together!"
Thus the heart fiercely screamed and seethed in pits of blood
till it was suddenly pierced by a dread outcry: "Help me!"
The mind like a scared rabbit scurried in its lair,
but the heart cried with joy, a deep and gaping wound:
"I pour my blood! Let all dark forebears come and drink!"
As the heart yelled within the archer's deep dark cells,
earth's bowels shook with fright and all the tombstones burst.
Ah, how the dead rushed up to drink man's warming blood,
and the man-slayer shook to watch ancestral ghosts,
his old and long-lost friends, the shades he once had loved,
throng round his veins to suck his blood and take new life.
The phantoms howled and dashed against his breast like waves,
they grasped and kissed his knees and hung about his loins,
and the most bold perched on his skull and screeched like hawks:
"Give us your blood to drink, set us on earth once more
that we may sip a drop of water, eat sweet bread,
and once more touch a woman's warming flesh at night!"
But in his heart's deep pit he chose with ruthless right
and thrust the shades aside with his long shepherd's staff:
"Plunge down to Tartarus and be damned! Never come back!
What a hard life you've chosen—water, women, bread!"
His father came and mutely stretched his trembling lips,
but the son thrust him with his heels out of his heart:
"Father, you've earned your holy wages well on earth,
you've lived and shaped a son better than you. Enough!"
All his ancestral kin rushed up with lapping tongues,
but the bold sentry with his goad plunged them to Hades:
"Earth has no need of you, the past does not return,
earth has surpassed the dark grandsire with champing jaws,
and now it's shameful to squander your bold grandson's blood
to help his ape-forefathers rise from the cold ground."
But his heart suddenly throbbed, his lion mind grew pale,
for he saw Captain Clam approach with gasping mouth
and drag himself to his heart's pit to drink his blood:
"Dear Captain Clam!" he cried, and spread his yearning arms;
the pallid face stared at his friend with a wry smile
and strove to speak but failed, for its throat turned to ash,
then dragged itself to the heart's pit to be revived.
The archer's eyes then brimmed, but still he raised his staff:
"Dear friend, the need is great, and there's but little blood.

You know how much I love you, but you know it's vain
to govern this doom-driven, plunging world with love.
I beg you, Captain Clam, don't drink my heart's warm blood,
for you've fulfilled your duty on this earth with honor
and you've no other greater good to give the world.
Return to the cold ground and let your betters drink!"
He spoke, and quivering Captain Clam grew wan and vanished.
Then the tormented man sighed long and wiped his eyes;
his pain was heavy but no tears must dull those eyes
that watched with ruthlessness and chose among the shades.
Then the phantoms scrambled mutely to his forehead's roots
like black sheep, and his mind with ancient longings swarmed;
in his excited memory shone old moons and suns,
poisonous fruits and women, castles, children, steeds,
rousing good revels and long distant voyages.
As the tormented man gazed deep in memory's well,
he suddenly saw a heavy shade on the rim's edge
stand mutely with a sword-gash on its bloody skull.
"Hardihood," cried the archer in pain, "unlaughing friend,
have they already seized your crown? Has your sun set?"
But that rhinoceros, Hardihood, nosed through the soil
and strode to reach the heart and drink a drop of blood
as though he'd just been slain and still kept all his strength,
and as he kicked and fiercely thrust the ghosts aside,
he suddenly staggered back and vanished like a frog in mud.

But when Odysseus saw his three ancestral Fates,
forty foot high, plunge in his bloody pit with wrath,
his heart at once gave up its steaming brimming blood.
Their three tongues lapped and clacked and their throats swelled until,
drained empty, the pale archer hung above the pit.
Then Tantalus, that unappeased, unsated soul,
leapt up with lips more pallid, parched and thirsty still:
"Who set his heart for trap and called my name? I thirst!
Before I touched it, it went dry and suddenly vanished!
Thanks for the miserly drop you spilled to heal my heart;
I see betrayal in your eyes—you want to plunge roots now!"
Odysseus seethed with wrath, opened his mouth to speak,
but his great forebear shook his head with scornful pride,
stamped thunderously till earthquakes gaped and gulped him whole.
Then the Great Athlete rose, but his once massive form
had been devoured by must and mold to skin and bone,
and plump white worms crawled slowly up his shriveled shanks.
The archer brimmed with tears to see his great forebear:
"Heracles, sacred spite, man's great daemonic soul,
hard-working man's clenched fist that pummels ruthlessly

the tough dough of our flesh to pound it into spirit,
proud grandsire, crowned with twelve great constellations now,
I thought to see you spring from earth on your black steed
with Death's own bloody head swung from your saddle horns,
but see, your teeth are chattering and your knees show rot,
for that great octopus, grim Death, has seized and sucked you.
Don't weep, lean on my own firm flesh, don't be afraid."
Then in the musty air an earth-filled voice replied:
"Ascetic grandson, you who fight under my shadow,
archer who've strung your own twelve axes row on row,
see how the worms now crawl on my world-famous body!"
He spoke, then leant on the archer's arm to keep from falling,
but when he felt the warming blood course through his veins,
his bone joints creaked, his bosom swelled, and once again
the lion's skull rose high and covered his blond head.
He gazed deep in his comrade's eyes and hailed him then:
"Grandson, I find you well on earth with your warm fists!
Ah, if my knees have rotted, the green world is vast
with flowing water and fresh clay to shape new forms,
and plenty of sun to dry them, winds to knock them down.
Forward, don't brood, my grandson, for all things go well!
I've battled both on land and sea, I've longed to be
a deathless god on earth, but my strength broke, and now
I've raised two topless pillars in mid-road for signs
that you may see how far I've gone, and go still further.
The final labor still remains—kneel, aim, and shoot!"
The racked man shuddered to hear his great forefather speak,
to feel his agitation flooding his own flesh:
"Grandsire, I thought to see a vast joy light your form,
for, wrapped in flame, you once attained to virtue's peak,
but now you groan and push me on to newer tasks.
Lord of our race, give me your blessing! What is my task?"
But the much-wounded form with hopeless grief replied:
"Ah, I can't quite make out what the last labor is;
I feel it glowing mutely in the downy dark;
at times it seems a gentle god, then a wild beast,
at times a very ancient, thousand-year-old heart.
Ah, take me with you to the final task of all!"
He spoke and dashed with yearning in the archer's arms;
and as the lone man hugged the shade and clasped but mist,
he felt his entrails fill and thrash with anguished pain.
The lion's skull rose high and covered his own head,
old rotting wounds coiled round his flesh like tentacles
until he shrieked as both forms joined and merged in one.
The archer leapt from sleep; the sun had shot up two
whole spear-lengths in the sky, the world had calmed,

phantoms had scattered in thin air, gates closed once more,
and memory like a sucking lamia sank and drowned.
Then the shade-smothered man unloosed the leopard cub's
paws lightly from his stifling throat, and deeply breathed,
for in him battering waves still beat in ebb and flow.
But as the lone man suddenly looked below, he shook
with fear, for his huge shadow lengthened with a lion's crown.

Splattered with light, he went from mountain peak to peak,
a light veil spread in flowers above his burning mind,
and as numb ghosts unraveled slowly in his heart
Odysseus watched without the slightest fear but joyed
to feel he carried in his heart's core that dread race.
His memory stretched in light, opened its eyes in sun
(the more that memory's neck is wrung the more it shouts),
and those brave deeds and joys his ghosts longed for in vain
woke in their grandson now, made monstrous by such sleep.
"I'm not left hanging in the sun, hovering in air,
for deep roots bind me to the earth and my veins climb
like tangled ivy out of ruins and hug my soul.
I speak not for myself alone, my mouth is not
a narrow honey-cell where one bee comes and goes,
but a great beehive where unnumbered workers toil.
This body which I hold and lug on toward the grave
is not one body but battalions which for years
set out from distant shores to plunder the whole world.
My dead now do not lie in earth or rot in grass:
all are crew comrades in the trireme of my soul!
'Hold the soul well upon the seas!' my own dead cry,
'Live well that we may live, drink well that we may drink,
enjoy those girls and towns we've not had time to breach;
our blessing, grandson, forward, put an end to passion,
we'll kiss with you those lips you kiss, hug those you hug;
why do you think we've shaped you from our heart and blood?
That you might end what we've begun and be the heir
of passion's hollow winds to give it flesh and bone!
We are the earth's deep mother roots, you are the flower!' "
As all his famished forebears shouted, the archer felt
them mount from his deep entrails, reach his reeling brain
and spread like ancient wine along his thirsty veins.
He carried in his bowels and led like a black ram
all his far-distant native land, vineyards and fields,
and all his dead with their white bones and hollow eyes.
A sweet pain webbed his tranquil mind, and his heart gaped,
filled with all the unborn, the alive, the entirely dead.
In the gold lightning flash of thought his brain struck sparks,

the deep dark walls came tumbling down, death merged with life,
and as he leant against a rock the lone man strove
to place his sudden vision in a clear cold light:
"The black seas lie unharvested, the mountains sweat,
my body is a ship weighed down with myriad souls,
and I, the captain, sail toward death with rapturous joy.
Astern, the dead push like north winds till the planks creak,
abaft, my grandsons gambol like white gulls on waves,
and at the prow my tribe's own spirit flaps its wings.
I stoop and gaze at my own entrails, my deep hold:
hoarse voices, starving beasts, and fiercely rowing souls,
and pile on pile of wine kegs, food casks, and dark slaves!
Push on, O parents and grandsons both, I hold the tiller,
pull at the oars, a north wind blows, the port's in sight!"
Thus did the man of many souls talk to himself
as he bent low and joyed to see how his dark roots
thrust through the muddy earth, long-lived and many-branched.
"I'm free at last of my own shade, of my own flesh!
O three-peaked deathless tree of my great race, thrice welcome!"

He raised his lashes, and his lighthouse mind spied all
the vast world with the eyes of all his race,
and as he brooded deeply on the plunging gorge,
an eagle from the crags loomed in the heart of light
and whirled in widening rings to warm its frozen wings.
But as the unsated heart rejoiced in the dawn's calm
he suddenly felt on the rose-wounded peak a deep
and smothered sigh tear through the air from the earth's pit.
Turning, he saw Prometheus nailed to a huge rock,
and from his writhing lips the archer's own blood streamed.
Black iron pincers nailed him to the boulder's root
and his immense brows gleamed like tall snow-covered peaks.
"Father!" His eagle-mind swooped on the giant's breast.
"Who calls? I hear the sea's roar and a harsh wind blowing."
"Father of flame and brain, I grasp you by the knees;
I'm but the smallest of your small waves, I kiss your feet."
Then the torch-bearing dragon's voice was heard in joy:
"Deep in the depths of blackest night I dreamt of suns,
I dreamt the boulders to my right and left were wings
and that I swooped in the dawn's light, a great cross-eagle.
Who are you, Son, for when you called me, my dream vanished?"
"I am that much-resourceful mind, cunning Odysseus.
Now, Father, that I've lightly touched your holy feet,
my own desires have vanished like once childish cares,
my voyages seem of little worth, my loot, my life!"
The mountains shook like wings and the slopes filled with mist:

"A thousand welcomes, brave mind of god-battling man!"
But the great grandson raised his hands to his forefather
as trembling palms are stretched to feel a warming fire:
"I bow and hail with awe the hard flint of the mind.
You are that soul who raised my low brow toward the sun
and planted earth firm at my feet like my own home.
At my ten fingertips you lit flame's piercing eye
till men and beasts all pressed about me to pay homage;
I bow and worship your great grace, old lord of hope.
You tamed the dewlappèd bull and bent it to the yoke,
you furrowed the dark earth and taught me how to plant
all seed like flesh and wait with patience the gold grain;
even that muddy worm, the wingless heavy heart,
you filled with wings and hope and flung it toward the sun.
I sailed with your great blessing, but as boundaries spread,
I still held fate's unrighteous yoke like wings aloft
nor trembled at the sky nor feared its thunderbolts,
for as I walked the earth, Grandfather, you held my hand!"
But the great dragon's frown eclipsed the blazing sun:
"I've not illumined or saved the world! My life went lost!
God's lightning flash turned into brain, and the brain rose;
I, too, rushed up like God, seized clay, made men,
licked them with flame, thrust in their brains a spark of light,
placed knives within their fists and hopes within their hearts
then spread my deep arms wide and loosed them on the earth:
'Children of earth and fire, belovèd clay, push on!'
But all my troops forsook me and my sons betrayed me,
now see to what I've come, O Grandson, where spite cast me:
I'm nailed to memory's sleepless rock and shout in pain.
Alas, I could not finish life's most glorious task!"
The fierce man's choking voice fell at the giant's feet:
"Grandfather, entrust the final task to my strong shoulders."
But that unbridled wild heart had not heard, and muttered:
"I've not illumined or saved the world! My life went lost!
I did not kill that lawless God nor make my peace
with him so that man's suffering heart might find repose;
that's why I hang mid-air between the earth and sky."
The seven-souled man touched his lord's lit fingertips:
"I feel your suffering and I bear your burdens, too.
I know it's right to thrust impossible tasks aside:
'War!' cries the mind, 'but don't cross man's ordained frontiers!'
Yet a hoarse cry springs from the center of my heart
and in my earthen breast stands straight and fights with Death!"
But the refulgent rebel bitterly shook his head:
"Beyond all flame and light, beyond even Death, my son,
the final labor, the last ax, still gleams with blood."

Then all the summit smoked as the great body groaned
and, like a strong oak split by lightning, burned and glowed
till the man-slayer reached and grasped the lord of light:
"Grandfather, speak the final word, give me your blessing!"
But the rough mountaintop stood bare, only its peak
resounded still with a great nailed and heavy sigh.
As the long-suffering man strove to pierce through the light
a fierce spasmodic voice clove through the torn air, "Help me!"
"Who called?" the tortured man cried out, stretched on his rock,
but no soul answered, though he felt his giddy breast
quivering like the rough mountaintop and crying, "Help me!"
The heart of man had turned to a fierce cry that tore the air.

The archer leapt in silence, his mind glowed and spun,
he jumped from crag to crag, the stones rolled at his feet
as though a dense battalion tramped the mountain slopes.
"I need companions! Men, come now from land or sea!"
He yelled in the rough-breasted mountain, the rude clefts,
and his wild cry of freedom leapt and struck the towns,
struck every head, then swiftly passed and howled through wastes.
His savage chest was locked and barred, and the sun struck,
cajoling it with patience for a long time to open;
the sown seeds of laborious man woke in the soil,
all idle hands branched out to work, eyes fluttered wide,
and babes cried in their cradles for their mothers' milk.
Massed troops of workers armed themselves, each with its tools,
and set out for the holy war to earn their bread;
girls every dawn with cooling water wet their eyes
to wipe away the sweet and shameful flush of dreams.
All mankind's races woke then in the sufferer's breast;
all sons of mother earth, the sallow, blond and black,
laughed, sighed, and hugged the lone man's savage chest
and he stooped down and blessed in him that deathless pair,
woman and man, who strove to plant their god on earth.
"O dark-lashed wingless love for earth, with both your wild
and muddy feet sunk deep within the first spring rains,
you fill my heart and make my breast a bridegroom's suite.
My throat chokes, my heart throbs—if only I could speak!
Dear God, if only I could clasp and cry 'My brothers!'
Each soul's a fading will-o'-the-wisp, one syllable
drowned in the sea's immense and ever-moving song;
if only we could free our heads from the wide waves
to watch and sail upon the entire sacred song
so long as our hearts hold in light and the sweet air,
that we might all merge tightly, word with word, and find
the secret meaning of the voyage, and the bright port!

Rise, archer, stand erect on your head's tallest crown
to see and to rejoice in man's first murky dawns!"
The ancient warrior spoke with fervor and stretched the world
till boundaries moved and swayed, till crowded herds of man
rose in the archer's entrails as his mute forebears
stepped back with fear to admit the races of all men.
How small his native land then seemed, how thin the soil
that rose from the small brains and brawn of his weak tribe!
Races of men seethed in his bowels, battalions moved,
the soul spread everywhere, plunged deep, struck deeper roots:
"It's not I or my forebears who set out within me,
for in my bowels I feel white, yellow, and black hands
that sway above the abyss and cry to me for help."
Then the archer struck his chest and cried with piercing joy:
"I've found the steadfast rock on which to build my deathless castle!"

The hot sun fell behind the ridges, the stones cooled,
and twilight stretched upon the fields, a wounded fawn
with large black eyes on which the smothering night had fallen.
The birds fell silent, night came down like a black wing
and the archer suddenly longed to hear a gentle voice;
he stretched and pressed his ear to earth, his brains refreshed,
and from the soil a weak complaining sound arose:
"My son, it's a hard task to shoot that bow, your mind,
far further than the boundaries of the human race
and reach that highest peak of all, goodness and grace!"
The captain then of the wind-battered heart replied:
"Aye, old crone mother, you forget how tight I claw
life's sorrows and injustice, nor will I let them go!
Ah, granite memory, O beloved uncrumbling stone,
huge deeply graven block on my mind's lintel top,
I raise my eyes and see that fate is shores and seas,
that the twelve fat and shameless crows who rule the sky,
the haughty youths within my house, the arrogant lords,
wanted not love or peace, only the bloodstained ax!"
Once more the far wan words of Mother Earth were heard:
"The time draws near, my son, to pass beyond all need.
Now make your peace with beasts and trees, pity all men,
they're all my children, pummeled from my earthen guts;
son who last sucked my breast, my hopes all hang on you!
Joy inexpressible, great pain, great longing, dreams,
tear at my heart and daze my mind—it's you, my son,
must tell me all I've longed for, do what I'd want to do!"
Pressing his ear to earth, the archer listened still
to the far-distant grieving voice of hid desire,
then turned and scolded that fierce tigress, his cruel heart:

"Esteem mankind who from the beast disjoined and fled,
don't hone your claws, you witch, but look on him with love:
he walks earth freely without claws, or horns, or tusks,
unarmored, naked as the frog, but in his head
the lightning sits enthroned and spies on all the world.
I shout to God who nailed my grandfather to a rock
and raise my fists against him—let him fling his bolts:
'Slayer, you hurled man down to hunger and disease,
placed but a pallid woman at his side, no fire,
but when that human pair tilled and manured your mind
like oxen yoked and stooped to plow the barren earth,
whether you willed or not, in your black pits they strove
to thrust the seed of freedom like huge dragon teeth.
The time has come, brave heart, to raise our banner too!' "

Then he turned back and stretched before his cavern's mouth;
his beard burned all night long as with an astral fire,
and like the lion's cubs who whet their nails on rocks,
dreams came and clawed his stony temples ruthlessly.
It was not only his own voice that tore his heart,
it was not only his own greedy tough-skinned race,
nor only human cries that seethed within his guts,
for grunts, growls, bird song, caterwauling, chirps and yowls
leapt from his loins like fistfuls of cascading spray
and earth poured through his blood with all her horns and wings.
His veins then moved like sluggish snakes, like monstrous worms,
and the world's muddy mother-roots rose up toward light.
He felt himself at length freed from the snare of race,
he felt his roots plunge deeper than man's puny brood
and guessed he now drew close to his most ancient forebear
who like a water-bison roared in his bowels and rose
whenever heavy rage or dreams or a woman's kiss
still ravaged his heart's roots and stormed amid its ruins.
The archer quaffed the heavy wine of the moon's light,
he heard the insects rasp with sweet erotic cries,
he heard night rustling through cascades and swaying boughs,
he heard his angry leopard cub growl near his cave
and gaze far down the mountains, sniff the wild wastelands,
and as she smelled male sweat, deep musk, and hidden breaths,
she flashed her master slanting glares of yellow wrath.
But the heart-reader smiled, he guessed her pain, recalled
his own fresh youth when he had glared at his own father
on hearing a girl's cool and distant laughter ring.
A fat and female scorpion squirmed through leaves and stones,
for she had drained the empty skull of her male mate,
and now she tossed and rolled and licked it savagely

then flung it suddenly down a cliff and quickly dashed
with her wide belly full of eggs, and dug in soil.
The male had sown his seed, then died, his duty done,
and the she-scorpion took his dread hopes in her thighs
and thrust in soil with joy so that her sons one day
might move and eat her guts, then leap in the bright sun
that she, too, might descend to Hades tranquilly.
"Ah, who thrusts us to die with such great sweetness, God?"
the archer sighed, rejoiced, and stretched on a huge rock,
and felt birds, male and female scorpions, insects, beasts,
throughout all earth, in the dense trees, in the deep air.
He cast his few poor rags aside and longed to touch
the earth through all his length, like a nude snake, and merge
with those huge muddy dugs which pour man's milky sleep.

Thus did the two great bodies sleep, nude, merged in one,
and in a long sweet dream it seemed to him night smiled
as though she also dreamt of light, a golden egg
that in her brooding darkness hatched the sun to spring
like a great cock with crimson crest and beat its wings
while the serene earth cackled like a dappled hen.
And as the sighing archer smiled with night's sweet dream,
it seemed that daybreak burst, that the sun stood before him
and that he rose, then sat and gazed about him calmly
as though he felt deep breathing, myriad souls and eyes.
Behold, in the first glimmering streaks of blond-haired day
he saw that all the fabled cave walls had gone blank
as though black hunters and red beasts had all been freed
from their enchanted snares and moved in the light now.
A swirling and erotic dance, nude maids and men
who for a thousand years had whirled entrapped in paints,
slid freed now from the walls till only the hung flute
of the young shepherd lad who led the dance still stayed.
Thick shades and airy phantoms rustled everywhere
and wound the great soul-snatcher like the moon's corona.
"These are my true forebears," he murmured. "Bow with homage!"
But as he turned his firm head toward the shadowy throng
he felt a thousand fragile heads swirl round and round
as though two magic mirrors glittered in the cave,
and a warm beaded sweat dripped from each pallid brow.
"Shades choke me, wings spring from my shoulders right and left,"
the lone man cried, and shook his hairy arms with force
till all the cave with tear-stained eyes and bodies brimmed.
"I'm not one person now, huge armies surge behind me,
black, yellow, and white men, and I run on ahead
while a fierce bird with crimson claws stabs through my brain."

Thus thought the many-minded man as his skull swelled
and his throat strove to cry out sweetly, "Brothers, brothers!"
but he was suddenly startled and stepped back with fear,
for the cave's azure darkness flashed with streaks of flame,
with many-colored wings, moist nostrils, sword-sharp horns,
and his cowed leopard cub crouched at her master's feet;
all quivering beasts crawled speechlessly and shook with fright
as by a mute invisible hunter pushed and probed.
They longed to speak a brotherly word, but their thick brains
turned mud and tumbled in their crude impounded skulls.
Never had the much-suffering man felt such huge sorrow,
for the beasts' groans were heavy in the azure air;
he opened his arms wide and cried, "Welcome, my brothers!"
He rose, and all at once a warbling joy swept through him,
his brain turned to dense forests, his veins to swift streams,
and all his skull brimmed over with horns, tails, and wings.
The coral coils of his head swirled, the world rushed on,
and like a wealthy lord who in his tower, erect,
receives his ancient warriors and his faithful friends,
thus did the wandering man hail all the beasts with awe:
"Welcome to my dark head, to my tall brazen tower,
fierce fighters, comrades, kings of earth! Make way! Make way!
Leviathan now, our great primeval forefather comes
with his stooped heavy head a mass of mud and brains.
O great grandfather, I stretch to kiss your rough rude knees.
Tall fortress, mountain undefiled, I hear you thrash
like a wild sea beneath your cracked and wrinkled hide.
O tall tomb, wrathful horns, hides, flesh, and rank manure,
you trample on the newborn soul's wet fledgling wings
that smother and strive hopelessly to lift your weight.
I am your fortunate soul that from your heavy thighs,
your deep dark castle doors, dashed into light to play.
Look at my brows and eyes, Grandfather—don't you know me?
Night-prowling ancient ghost, deaf ears, glazed eyes, mute mouth,
you stoop to earth and you don't know your grandson still!
Make way for him to see! May his dim memory blaze!"
Odysseus cried, stepped back for his great grandfather to leave,
then opened his arms wide, stooped low and hailed his father:
"Hail to our king, O Ape with future golden crown,
with your vermilion fat behind, a king's red robes!
Joy to that father who sees his son and thinks in secret:
'I'm but a beast. What shame to walk or talk with him!
My mind's a lump of blood and fur—what can I say?
I'll gape at him from the dark woods as he goes by.'
Father, behind the trees, deep in the hollow trunks,
I see your much-tormented and much-honored face.

Ah, father, raise your head on high, don't be ashamed,
upon this savage earth you have fulfilled your old
parental strife with patience, hunger, groans and fears;
now raise your sad eyes proudly, marvel at your great son:
I am that dream which clove like lightning your dark brain."
He spoke, and the poor ape, with coarse and furrowed nails
clawed at his shaggy head and his eyes glazed as though
he struggled to recall, to hear and see his son.
Then Mother Earth's last great accomplishment turned round
to greet with joyous homage his most humble forebears:
"I greet that great ascetic, the low black-browed beetle.
O sacred, seven-souled, and stubborn drudge of God,
you slave all day and roll your lump of dung on earth,
you fall, then rise and grasp it tightly, fall again,
rise up, grasp it once more and start the steep ascent.
Back! Let him pass, my brothers! He, too, is a great god!
Thus, I suppose, a monstrous scarab shoves with grit
the green dung-sphere of earth and rolls it up the sky
and to that muddy ball entrusts her sacred eggs.
Welcome a thousand times, mute brother, faithful drudge!
Welcome, O handsome weasel, fur-skinned civet cat,
welcome, O hedgehog, marten, squirrel, and faithful dog.
And welcome, ox, sacred to earth, with your large eyes,
your hooves still muddy from the heavy toil of day,
your nape still bloody from the rough yoke's stooping weight;
you wake at daybreak, plod to your dark stable door,
and like a husband watching his still pregnant wife
you gaze on the far fields with holy patient strength
and in the fat coils of your muddy brains declare:
'There's still much work to do. Master, awake, it's dawn!'
Slowly you stretch your scabbed, scruffed neck to moo,
and the young master, waking, turns to embrace his wife:
'My ox have woken, sweet; it's dawn, and I must leave you.'
Swiftly he leaps and comes to your warm fragrant stall,
gropes at your hooves and belly with fast-beating heart
for fear the evil eye has pierced or gadfly stung you,
but when he listens to your heart, his fears calm down.
He fills your empty trough with feed and gossips on,
chatting about his work, his orders, his advice,
and you, my brother, listen and slowly chew your cud
without a sound; you know how much these upright beasts
like to talk on and on, although they wield the goad;
you slowly turn and mutely watch the sleeping world,
your eyes filled only with untilled or furrowed fields.
Brother, stoop down, enter my brain, shake off the yoke,
the ripe fields of your master's mind are but green air,

your yoke's an azure shade, your plowman is but smoke,
welcome a thousand times to my head's warming stall!
Welcome to wolves and sheep, to lions and shying fawns;
brothers, there's no more enmity in my mind. Be friends!
It's time for all to merge now in this holy fold."
He spoke, then grouped his shaggy brothers row on row,
and when he'd finished welcoming his myriad beasts,
the many-souled man turned and hailed the feathery fowl:
"Welcome to all warm flying forms, the thoughts of air!
Dear God, when I lie stretched on earth and gaze on high
I feel the blue sky's holy dome like a vast skull
through which cross-eagles soar, crimson and gold birds dart,
and when at times their beaks drip blood or their throats pour
with sweet lamenting tunes, then my heart floods with love.
Brothers, I'm like you also, for I have hidden wings,
I grow with the wild hawks and dance with the swift gulls,
the wild North Wind's the goatherd of my airy flocks
and dashing South Wind is my faithful shepherd's dog.
But night has fallen, the aery chase has ended now,
so welcome, brothers, to my parental sheltering roof.
Welcome to wasp and hornet, cricket, flea, and fly!
Welcome, O thousand-egged, much-pregnant Lady Ant;
you drag yourself like a Great Dame, wingless and full,
your belly brimming with unnumbered seething eggs.
Good was the sudden fluttering in the warming air,
your body small and swelling, your wings opening wide,
your bridegrooms fast behind you with their stings raised high.
Some rolled expiring on the earth, and some held back
their strength, nor would expend it, God, but soared and watched
your glowing belly shine in the high blinding light.
I am the bridegroom ant, the bride, and the blue sky!
It lasted but a lightning flash in your dark loins,
and wingless now, you crawl on earth, remembering nothing,
but I still fly and couple in my brain immutably,
my bridal wings still shed, still spread upon the earth,
nor does time pass but that I take him for my groom.
Ah, my poor heart is torn, my entrails gape and shut,
and I submit my body to God's quartering winds,
a flowering almond branch plundered by honeybees.
Come all my long-lost exiled brothers, beasts and birds,
the middle wall falls crashing, the heart opens, welcome!"
Thus did the suffering man hold all earth in his hands
but could not bear the pain or joy, and his eyes brimmed.
O tears, O cool, most guileless good of solitude!
He felt the full warm breast of life touch his own breast,
he felt her heavy breath, her sweetness, her deep musk:

"O Lord, beast that I chase with longing, bird I hunt,
how may I lodge you in that cave, my mind, for I
have no swift ship to fetch you through the stormy seas
nor a white horse to bring you galloping down the fields,
your long hair washed with dew and smelling of wild thyme.
I hold no taut bow in my hands to shoot you now
but place my heart on the green grass, huge honey-drop
that slowly melts in your great heat and calmly waits.
Come buzzing down, O Honeybee, come drain me dry!"
The hunter shouted loudly through his mind's ravines,
an unexpected sweetness calmed his weary heart
and he leant on night's cornerstone, the rock of dream.
He felt the beasts breathe in his breast, huge herds that pressed
with longing round his heart and licked his open palms
as though he held a white lump in his hands and fed them salt.

Night passed with all her marvels, slowly, endlessly,
earth filled with scent and coolness, tranquil drops of rain
splattered her flaming face, the stones laughed low and long,
and azure lightning flashes lit the mountaintops.
A plowman stretched his hands over his fields with joy,
in the world's dark foundations the dead glowed like roots,
and seeds kicked deep in Mother Earth like embryos.
The erotic spring rains steamed, earth trembled and cracked open,
the river fishes swam toward the salt sea to spawn
and others swam to find sweet water to lay their eggs.
In Crete the wine casks were prepared for the wine's must,
were washed, rewashed, splashed with warm water to close the seams,
and the South Wind got drunk from smelling the rank must.
In far-off temples, stern ascetics robed in yellow
shuddered when the first raindrops fell, then in their courts
all raised their trembling hands to the frenetic clouds
with wailing cries and groaned out all their sins and crimes.
Within his sleep the suffering man then dreamt of cranes,
and as his broad lips stretched into a tranquil smile,
his mind rose like a stork and stood in its dark nest.
The pelting night rain fell and clattered on the stones,
the waters branched in rills and dashed from crag to crag,
the sky sank glowering on the earth, and clouds like hair
hung down caressing her with long and wormy strands.
In the black cave small insects quivered, wild beasts growled,
birds gathered their wet wings, and all together crawled
in the dream-voyaged body of their soul-guiding master.
They thrust in his deep armpits, twined in his gray beard,
until in sleep his flesh turned mist, like clouds, absorbed
huge flocks of birds and insects as he turned all wing.

Like a cave's arched deep entrance, his great forehead gaped
and there all rain-drenched creatures crouched in fellowship,
sweet rubies nestling in the mind's huge pomegranate.
Sleep had refreshed the lone man, dreams had healed his wound,
good were the night's seductions, good the cool night rains,
and when he woke his wild lips dripped with honey still.
Day broke, he jumped up and stood still by his cave's door;
clusters of tepid raindrops struck with slanting force
his brows, his hands, his neck till, shivering, he rejoiced
to feel the fragrant first rains on his sun-scorched flesh.
His thirsty leopard cub was licking the drenched stones,
her yellow eyes gleamed as she watched her lustrous friend
stand by the tranquil entrance watching on far peaks
how God's huge body spread to slake its heavy thirst.
God's feet had sunk in mud, his beard had turned to streams
and rolled in foam down deep ravines, his wide mouth steamed,
and turtles, snails, and insects ran with quivering haste
and thrust themselves into his armpits and dank hair.
"Ah, you've enjoyed the cloudburst on your body, God!"
the lone man cried in rapture as his heart grew sweet.
Slowly the weather cleared, the sun appeared and smiled
till on God's watery lashes raindrops laughed, a huge
bright rainbow stretched and zoned his glittering hair
so that he sank serenely in a mute unuttered joy.
Then in the heavy silence, secret coupling cries
of a sad man and lustful woman shook his breast
until he stooped and listened to his female heart:
"I looked for you to come on lightning wings, my love,
to smash my door at midnight and to sweep me off
that I might fall down trembling at your holy feet.
But you, dear God, are calm and sweet like a man's flesh,
and blue waves and green meadows play within your eyes.
Earth's fragrance almost choked me when you came, my Love,
and my black entrails blazed up like a mortal's hearth;
now I entrust my trembling palm to your kind hands
for you are good, like a mere man, and quake, like me."
A heavy voice was heard then like a bellowing beast's:
"Who wakes me from my sleep and lifts me from the ground?
I slept well, motionless, amid the roots of trees,
I enjoyed the downy darkness in the loins of beasts;
who called and lit my turbid dream so that it vanished?"
"It's I who called, man's female heart! Come out, my love!
I'm but a river reed and call you like a throat,
I can become a roof, or rot in desolation.
Ah, glean me, Lord! Make me a flute on your sweet lips!"
"O clay heart, deep jug of a deathless bitter water!"

"Love, do you weep? I never hoped for such great joy."
Then like a flute the voice sang bitterly in the breast:
"I'm not that god who like a bridegroom breaks the bolt
and enters lightly in his loved one's house at midnight.
I only know a blood-drenched and beast-breathing love
that eats my entrails like a black and famished crow.
Don't call me! I pity your virginity, my child!"
But her breast's open rose allured the lover still:
"My own, come rest your body gently on my knees.
We two shall shape the world with love and stubbornness,
a new bride's piercing pain threshes my tender breast."
Thus did the heart tremble, beat the ground and call on God
till earth with spring rains burst and in the sun there sprang
a firm-fleshed gallant youth, covered with mud and wounds,
so that the woman cried and spread her smoldering arms:
"O manly body, sturdy, lean, with firm round grapes,
my trembling knees have melted sweetly in your shade."
"O mortal heart, you called! I've sprung from the dark soil!
Our humble hut is ready and awaits us now.
Come, for the holy smoke will rise from our hut's roof,
our trough will brim with bread, our cradle with plump babes.
O heart, Death has no fears for me since first you called!"
The woman's deathless tune was heard in warbling song:
"I shall be with you, Love, in wars, in joys, in cares.
At noontime as you till the field I'll bring your food,
your jug of cooling water, under the plane tree's shade;
at dusk you'll find our oil lamp glowing on the hearth
and all of night's sweet hopes upon my fruitful breast."
The young man's muddy chest resounded with delight:
"Dear wife, my brooding heart blooms like a tree again,
one couple on the earth alone renews the world!
Leaves fall like people, empty flowers droop and die,
but the tall tree of life casts deep gigantic roots
and in bad seasons one bloom still adorns its tip,
fights off the powers of the worm, the wind, the storm,
and won't give up the fruit it holds clenched in its teeth.
Hold fast, O heart, dear wife, for I've no other hope!"
The hour hung heavily and was slow to fall to earth;
Odysseus heard both cries, as though from the world's rim,
then leant his chest above the abyss and shuddered deeply
to hear how someone climbed his guts with stubborn groans,
something both beast and man that trod a bloodstained road.
"Who are you, virile voice? Pirate, what is your name?"
"I am that dark beast, God, who mounts eternally."
"Though I stoop low in darkness, I can't discern your face.
You seem a savage centaur with broad shaggy rumps,

I see your hands held high in light, your knees in mud,
you stretch your loins like a longbow, and then squirm through
your crushing body's weight, your soul clenched in your teeth!
What hunter so pursues you that you gasp and groan?"
"I climb my own dark body, Son, to keep from stifling.
Trees and beasts smother me, and your flesh chokes me, too;
I fight to flee you, not even your soul can hold me now.
Help me, my son, that from your mute and muddy flesh,
from your constraining soul, I might at length fly free.
Ah, what if I'm now too late and perish with you on earth?"
"I won't have God, my warrior, trembling in my heart!"
"But I'm afraid! I see no end to this dark climb!
I plod, I stumble and stagger in all flesh, I shout!
Each lovely body is a lime twig—I can't get free!
Each soul is a dark forest where beasts eat me whole!
Help me, my son! I'm caught in your dark loins! I groan!"
"Don't groan, it's shameful, and the timid souls may hear;
whisper your fears to me alone in the dark of night;
we two shall hide between us the world's jeopardy.
I like despair and stubbornness, I scorn my flesh,
and like a fisherman who grabs an oyster shell
and with his twisting knife unseals the solid pearl,
thus with my sword I'll free you from grim Death, my Lord!"
He spoke, then seized his bow and arrows to hunt for game;
it wouldn't do to have his entrails shake with hunger,
for God had need now of firm flesh to clutch and keep from falling.

The wheel of earth within him turned, and his god glowed
nor seemed a mighty beast now nor almighty foe
to break a lance with on the earthen threshing floor,
nor yet a bridegroom to merge sweetly with man's heart.
All bodies and all souls cried out, "We're lost!" Two hands,
the hands of God, stretched toward the light and shook with fear.
Then the much-suffering man felt thirsty, grabbed some fruit,
but as he opened his mouth, his mind suddenly shook,
for in the fleshly fruit he saw the seed crouch low,
clutch at the rind and shout with fear that it might fall.
The lone man smiled and bit into the juicy flesh,
and when his body had rejoiced and his throat cooled,
he thrust the seed, that hidden god, deep in the soil,
then plunged down toward the dark ravine, spied all the land,
and as wild pigeons passed, or hares, or full-fleshed fawns,
he shot his deadly arrows happily everywhere
till his hands filled with pulsing forms, with bloodstained wings;
he lit a fire in mid-gulch then, roasted his game,
and hurriedly fed his feeble body like a beast.

"Forgive me, God; I know you dwell in birds and trees,
crouched low, your chin wedged tight between your knees,
your heavy shinbones glued to your subservient back,
and spread your small hands now toward light and call for help.
Yet like a hungry octopus you thresh my entrails,
chew your own tentacles, then sprout new ones to eat!
Roast these birds quickly, flames! O heart, rise up and eat!"
Then his heart rose and ate until his mind rejoiced,
his earthen flesh was sated and his knees grew strong:
"Birds, fruit, and water have all become Odysseus now,"
he said, then stood erect on a high rock, and laughed.
He lived through all his journeys; what he wished, he kept;
he held like fruit in both his hands his hybrid god
who also strove on earth like man to seek salvation.
Much-suffering man, you heard God's anguished cry and climbed
man's steep ascent from crag to crag to its high peak.
First, in the small tent of your puny flesh, you warred
with longings, stubbornness and cares, passions and profits,
but your soul longed for further peaks, and you set forth
to wield your weapons in a greater, higher ring.
You pitched your tent in your own race till hearts, hands, brains,
filled your great body, and you marched like a vast army
with three high tiers of dead, unborn, and living troops.
At once all races moved until the sacred hosts
of poor hand-battling mankind marched within your heart
and war spread through the twisted mazes of your mind.
Then all at once the flocks of water, earth, and air
dashed as supply troops at the tail end of your army,
comrades-in-arms, to aid you in the bloody battle.
All those who once had fought alone, without a mate,
you paired off in your lambent breast till all foes merged
in your embrace into an only armored love.
A great erotic whirlwind blows on earth above,
birds swoop on giddy wings and mate in the dazed air,
all silver insects and all shaggy bodies whirl,
and dizzy hearts in sharp birthpangs give birth to God.
A crimson-feather vulture swoops to pierce the flesh;
some call it Love, some call it God and Death, and some
have called it Outcry that leaps from flesh to flesh and shouts:
"I stifle in all bodies and I don't want the soul!"
The archer felt the Outcry flick its tongues of flame
on his skull's crown as though it longed to fly away,
and then he bit his bitter lips and thought with pride:
"I know the soul's the wick and you're the flame, my God,
but I won't let you fade in air thus aimlessly;
the song clove through my brain, I know now what I want:

I'll build a towering castle on earth to guard you well!"
He spoke and his brains shook till in his head there rose
a city tall and glittering, walls, gates, battlements
zoned by ten great commandments, pierced by sleepless towers.
Already in his deep mind gardens and homes grew,
and young men threw the quoit, babes sucked their mothers' breasts,
stone laws sat down enthroned like old men on the walls,
some holding scales and swords, some the green myrtle bough,
till the much-suffering man rejoiced to see what he so longed for.

He jumped from rock to rock, his lion shadow leapt,
the sun resounded like a gold war-shield held high,
animals moved, trees rustled, and the waters chirped—
the whole world like an army marched, and the archer led
and felt that he'd become all earth from his loins down.
God seemed then like a faithful friend, a chieftain torn
with wounds who grasped him if he stretched his hands,
who answered quickly if he ever cried for help.
A huge and warlike army camp spread through his mind,
and as he climbed the ridge a sudden longing seized him
to burst out with a happy tune in those wild lands:
"If God were to remake me, I should want to be
a slender, golden-feathered cock to fetch in day;
but then again, if he disdained to re-create me,
all's well and good, long may he reign, I ask no favors.
Blow all you want, you windbag, stretch my crimson sails,
for when you rage you fill my sails and swell my heart!
Ahoy, lads, God's a whirlwind and there's no returning!"
As the archer sang in the wild wastes, his heart grew light,
his castle grew immense and firm, devoured the air,
drew down the sun into its boughs like a tall tree,
and as his city flowered and knit, the lone man felt
like a ripe seed that burst in bloom to be disburdened.
But all at once he leant against a rock and felt
God gasp and plod at his right side, stumbling on stones,
and the archer turned to greet him like a gentle host,
but his hand hung in air and his eyes stared with fright
for God changed many forms and leapt in the evening air.
His forebear now passed by with greedy hands outstretched;
starving, he reached for fruit, but the tall trees grew taller;
thirsting, he reached for water, but all streams went dry;
tiring, he leant against an oak, but the oak vanished.
The old man sighed and cursed, then once more plodded on,
but his face suddenly changed again, for now there passed
the myriad-wounded athlete with his lion's skull,
tagged by that savage and three-headed bulldog, Death.

But as the tall mind-spinner tried to shout with joy,
the mighty champion sped and vanished in thin air.
Then the sublime white-bearded lord of the mind passed
with his fierce eagle, holding tightly in his embrace
the holy infant flame, glittering from top to toe,
until the rocks at his great passing flashed like flint.
Thus all three shepherds of the human race passed by,
and as Odysseus roamed the ridge, the gaunt rocks rang,
tumult and tramp of feet encircled the mountain's rim,
horsemen and infantry dashed by, battalions climbed,
raised banners fluttered in the air, and lances gleamed.
The archer drew back swiftly to let the armies pass,
but armies in the gloaming there were none, all youths
had vanished, only an old bent vagabond passed by
stumbling on stones and slowly munching a dry bun.
The much-tormented archer shuddered, his eyes glazed,
bitterness, rage, contempt, and fear swept through his mind;
he raised his hands to the old tramp and the gorge rang:
"Old man, are you my fearful God? Stop, speak to me!"
But the old man slowly turned his face and bit his lips;
and the unsweetened archer shook to see the pallid hue,
the savage bitterness, the spite, the unfathomed eyes,
the flickering flames that glittered in his eyes like snakes,
the bloodstained endless upward road he climbed with grief.
The rebel's heart ached like a woman's to see him thus,
and tender words sprang to his lips and trembled there—
ah, how he longed to fall in his arms and ease his pain!
But since he felt ashamed to show such tenderness,
not knowing what else to do to hide his shock, he hung
his bloodstained bow on his left arm and whistled softly.
As the sun set behind his back, the full round moon
before him rose in gold till both their beams commingled;
both stars glowed lovingly and smiled, like man and wife,
then parted; the sun vanished down the mountain's rim,
and the moon paled and softly hovered in the afterglow.
The summits laughed, then grew serene, rocks hung in air
and swayed like clouds in the unworldly azure light;
far off in distant seas all sails were sunk in silver,
and towns with all their houses drowned in the sweet flood.
All minds shook secretly and in the full moon's light
went strolling till old memories in that stillness woke,
voices long lost and souls long dead, loves that became
white ghosts and drifted lightly on pale moonlit roads.
Then moonstruck memory leapt and woke, a death-scorched mother
on whose unsweetened lips words tottered as if to fall,
but only blurred sounds poured in dismal lamentation.

On Negro villages the sun-filled moonlight dripped,
far-distant hamlets drowned in silver, the troughs brimmed,
and all the narrow cobbled lanes flowed like rich streams of milk.

At the far foothills fires leapt, the thatched huts smoked,
the young men danced, and Granite like a cypress swayed
and soon forgot his captain, who might never return—
ahoy, good voyage! the earth could do without even him!
On the lake's edge he'd build a town with his brave youths
and cast deep roots like Rocky's on the Negroid earth;

the soul preens like an eagle and has no need of masters.
But Kentaur gazed at the full moon and heaved a sigh:
"Oho, the world has lost its peak, our oak tree's blasted,
I've lost my greedy lust for food, I don't want wine,
what shall I do now with my strength, how shall I spend it,
for what fine purpose put on flesh and fill my sides,
on whose ship shall I stretch as bulk and ballast now?
Ah, when will mountain peaks turn rose and leap with flame
because you tread on them, lone man, with burning feet?"
Kentaur then fixed his eyes on the high barren peak
with anguish, waiting for his chief in the moon's glow.
But he, far in his cave, slept like a household snake,
sated and slaked, with heart rejoiced and belly braced,
till he had merged his body's length with earth and sea.
He slept and dreamt of fir trees, that he climbed a steep
rough mountain where the fir cones gleamed with resinous glue,
and as he climbed, the mountain's hoarfrost slowly cracked,
his heart grew clear as crystal ice, his fir-peaked mind
lanced through the vast light of the sky with needling thorns.
But when the Morning Star rose up and struck, he leapt
on rocks, his heels grew wings, a red carnation flicked
his ears, a goldfinch on his mind's dome preened and sang.
Then the bow-lover burst in light, and his heart danced:
"I take delight in all the earth, and I touch God;
we both set out at daybreak, our minds drenched with dew,
and when I turn and see God at my side on his black horse
he bites his pallid lips and greets me silently,
then whips his horse with wrath, speeds on, and the day starts."
But as the archer's proud words flashed between his teeth
a slender serpent reared up in his mind and hissed:
"You dunce, you nitwit, I'm surprised! You sunstruck fool,
that crimson bird, the Outcry, must have burst your brains!
Master, you're building mansions in the air, you've made
your fantasy a hound to fetch what game you please,
but I want wood, stones, trowels, men and clay, for dreams
won't knit or souls be born in any other way.
You think that you've caught God, your quarry, and swell with pride,
but you've but wound the winds with your air-pregnant mind.
Border-guard, pass all mankind's exploits now, return
from whence you came, that holy darkness filled with light,
and build your mansions with blood, water, sweat, and tears.
You mounted high, war spread his massive tentacles;
dead, living, and the unborn, like ornaments, passed through
the smooth and empty crystal of your hawk-swift eyes
till you saw good and evil, foes and friend alike,
all comrades in the troops of your all-swallowing god.

Your dry-thorn brains caught fire, you flicked and faded fast
in that hot whirlwind your mind shaped from empty air.
Enough! Come down to earth! Let's see what you are worth!"
Stooped low, the archer heard the serpent scold, but spoke
no word, and when the harsh voice hushed and coiled in rings,
he gathered clay and pebbles, mixed a thick rank mud
and swiftly shaped on earth what his swift mind had spun:
A sentry-tower first, grouped round by homes, all zoned
by sharp-toothed battlements and tower-breasted walls.
He raised a tall tent then to house his mighty Lord,
to merge in manly friendliness his God and man
and bring a proud new bridegroom down to widowed earth.
Thus to the soil he bent to sow his fancy's forms,
and when he'd finished planting, his mind felt relieved,
the soft clay sprang to life, rooms brimmed with shouting men,
the pebbles turned to mothers suckling their infant sons,
the small stones shone like naked youths who threw the quoit,
and God rose from the roofs in banners of blue smoke.
The archer's heart caught fire, he leapt up from the ground
and felt his yet unborn great city's battlements
encircle his gray head like a king's golden crown.
The mountain slopes smiled gently, all wings woke and flew,
the female scorpion coiled on earth and warmed her eggs,
and orchids in the sun's blaze steamed, black-fleshed and firm.
"Farewell," the archer shouted, "farewell, O rocks and trees,"
for he had gleaned the wasteland's honeycomb, and now
he wore God close against his skin, a sweet cool flame.
As he lunged down the mountain slopes, they lunged along,
his lion-shadow, too, rushed headlong down the crags
till all the rocks and trees raised their green hands and yelled:
"Pity us, master, we're fading! Look at us now! Turn back!
Plant us in some great work's foundation! Use us! Save us!"
The seven-souled man joyed to feel that nature now
was his co-worker and, like an eagle who breaks boughs
to build its nest, he spied stout trees and cornerstones:
"Brothers, be still! All of us, beasts and stones and trees,
shall be wedged tightly with firm layers in God's body.
We're all in the same army, comrades; the human troops
march on ahead, and you, birds, beasts, and trees, bring up the rear.
It's only right that your warm flesh should feed the mind.
A dreadful war's begun! To arms, my gallant troops!"
Thus did he speak with earth profoundly, drafted workers,
planed rough trees with his mind, clove rocks into stone blocks,
until his vision spread its peacock tail, tall in the sun.

When the heart calmed and the mind filled, proud solitude
gave of its ripest, dearest fruit, fierce liberty.
The inner holocaust then turned to light which soared
to man's precipitous desolate brows and like a flag
waved there, struck by the sixteen haughty winds of freedom.
The black storm swelled with rage until in the thick darkness
light soared with gallant bravery and proclaimed fierce war.
Dreams yearned for bodies, virgin maidens longed for sons,
and in all heads the unkissed and shrunk ideas wept;
the soul at last had reached its ultimate task, the Act.
Like a sharp ax in the dense forests of the heart,
the Act struck right and left, cut down a ruthless road
and breached the narrow brain to break the ancient siege.
The archer gazed profoundly at the world and felt
it was not now eye's sweet mirage, no bridegroom's cloak
which God once donned to make love to the female soul,
nor gaudy middle-wall to hide us from grim Death,
adorned with sun-shot spangles by compassionate hands,
most sweet, most luring spangles to efface the grave—
life is a fierce assault in which the lustrous powers
struggle to tear the darkness in a grim ascent
in search of deathlessness and freedom on this earth.
Two great contrary windstorms, male and female blasts,
once clashed within the arenas of the earth and mind,
and in one delicately balanced moment this world was born;
let's ride that male wind too, and vanish down the blast!
It is not man's most fruitful nor most difficult duty
to find out in the abstract high reaches of his mind
with what pulse God walks gasping on this earth with pain;
he, too, should now come down to earth and walk with God,
for only thus may mortal man become immortal.
On the mind's death-scorched rock, narrow, ephemeral,
struck by all times and spaces, thrashed by all the gods,
the daring Act hews down the woods, builds sturdy ships
and strives to cross the abyss like a dark sea, to save
its precious cargo, its much-wounded, bleeding God.
On this abyss the Act and God, lone shipmates, talk
with fear, pale, hungry, broken, gazing on far seas,
age now on hopeless age, and with great longing strive
to raise the nonexistent shores from endless waves.
Deep in his heart the archer heard a savage voice
that summoned him to take up arms and to fight on:
"Rise, O great Archer of the Mind, hitch up your loins,
pummel the earth like dough, stoop down to earth and blow
the murky brain away, that trees and beast may rise

and that the dark inhuman powers may change to God.
When in your wars and victories you subdue wild chaos
into firm laws, you do not only free a god,
but make a god, who like a glowworm crawls on earth.
Why have you played and fought for ages in your mind
till all seemed tricks of the imagination, ghosts,
wings of the intoxicated head, parrots of speech
that with harsh jabbering shrieks darted through men's brains?—
that you might free yourself from the game's joy, Odysseus,
that you might fall to your great task, stoop down and dig,
a worker in the untilled vast vineyards of your Lord!
We want no idlers here on earth, no roaming tramps,
but diggers of the earth who free the soil like souls!"
Thus spoke the voice, and the archer hailed it with great joy:
"Welcome a thousand times, child-bearing Lady Act!
The time has come to stretch blue-eyed Idea down
on earth like a chaste bride and fill her full of seed!
Stones, waters, trees, you're welcome all to our great wedding!"
The bridegroom spoke, then slung an orchid down his ear,
bound osier strands about his waist, cocked his tall cap,
and, singing wedding couplets of erotic passion,
leapt down from rock to rock and took the road's return:
"Open all doors and windows now, break all the locks,
O bride, receive the bridegroom, shepherd of all flocks!"
"Mother, the groom has come now, riding his red roan,
give him your blessing, Mother, he's snatched your girl from home!"
"Today the sky and the day glow with love, my Love,
today in blazing light are wed the eagle and the dove!"

The spirit of love now flamed from his ten fingertips,
he held time in his hands like a red bitten apple
and brought it to his bride for an engagement ring.
Brides gathered larch-tree leaves to dye their wedding gowns,
the trembling newborn light slid slowly through the fields,
and the bare-bosomed sea smelled fragrantly like all
white breasts in all the world at dawn that suckled sons.
The earth and sky were new, Death was an open rose,
the mind was a huge sunkissed rock within whose clefts
only wild pigeons and stone-swallows built their nests.
The archer shrilled like a tall crane, chirped like a swallow,
and like a puffed-up russet pigeon spread his wings;
all's well, the heart is sated, the green world is vast
and dashes now toward men from the man-hating summits.
What joy to lunge down from the peaks while at your heels
the world trots like a faithful dog and wags his tail,

to come back like a savage hunter who wrecked the woods,
though not to say, "I heard the partridge sing in the glens,
I heard her, yet I could not see a single wing!"—
but in your fists to hold the palpable partridge warm and slain!

XV

A slender maid at evening lay by the lake's rim;
her throat choked in the stifling air and her blood swelled
like curly red carnations at a new bride's door.
Half shutting her black-painted eyes, fated for kisses,
she flung her fancy's shuttle and began to weave
deep in her heart a baby's rich-wrought swaddling clothes.
Deep in her happy heart she stitched seas, fish, and ships;
deep in her fertile heart she stitched earth's flowering trees;
deep in her faithless heart she stitched her husband hanged;
deep in her leching heart she stitched her true love coming.
As Granite passed and spied her on the lake shore's rim,
gall rose and dimmed his eyes, he uttered a loud cry,
for he recalled her husband, his once precious friend
whom they had found at dawn, alas, hanged from a tree,
and his blood seethed until he came to grim decision:
"They've killed my dearest friend and I cry out for vengeance:
Let seven maids be slain at dawn on his dark grave,
and first to lead the dance shall be his black-eyed wife!"
At the lake's margin Kentaur was building a lean-to
but when the sun's blaze struck him and he longed for shade
where his great buffalo's bulk might feel refreshed and cooled,
he heard gaunt Granite's order and he roared with wrath:
"It's a great crime to spill such innocent blood on earth!
If by all means you must have vengeance for his death,
sow seven sons to bring your friend back sevenfold!"
But the rough mountain lad turned round and laughed with scorn:
"Shame on your monstrous body, shame on your tough teats,
for all their manly blood has spoiled and squirts out milk!
Who asked you to speak up? Who asked for your advice?"
Great glutton growled and did not speak to vent his rage
but all night long his blood boiled as there swarmed about him
hornets of men and maids who stung his guileless heart.
Not far off, heavy-hearted Granite with his youths
caroused and picked out seven maids to slay at dawn,
then ate wild boar till their mustaches dripped with fat.
At daybreak sleepless glutton roamed about the woods

till in a clearing he met Granite and cried out:
"Brother, it's shameful we should quarrel, it pains my heart,
for then the unbridled mob will howl with evil joy
to see their chiefs at loggerheads, with butting horns.
And then I've also thought, and my knees shook with fear,
that seven days and nights have passed this day, and soon
—don't get your gall up, lad—one better than us will come,
and then how shall we dare to meet his fearful glance?"
But Granite raged to have his master used for scarecrow:
"You ass, do you think I fear the shadow his cap casts?
I think myself a man, I nourish a strong soul,
I listen only to the dictates of my heart and do
whatever I like; that skittish whore has killed my friend!
I'll have his blood back sevenfold! Who dares to stop me?"
But every speech has its own bitter counterspeech:
"Measure your words well, Granite! All the shame is yours!
It's better to swallow hard than say a shameful word."
But haughty Granite stroked his slender black mustache:
"Sipping may suit the sot, but boasting suits me fine!
I've never opened my mouth unless I had just cause.
Don't call me Granite if I don't do what I say!"
The monster's fat neck swelled, but he gulped down his wrath:
"I know that you are nobly born, shoot of a great tribe,
and I crude ballast in your ship, a coarse splayfoot,
but my soul's also free, I do whatever it tells me.
Not many of us survived the wilds, and while I live
I won't have souls die just to please your stubborn spite!"
The mountain archon laughed with scorn and pricked his friend:
"Let's fight each other in the sight of all the troop
and let the seven women await their destiny:
if you should win, they're yours; if I, they're mine to slay!"
Glutton's good heart sighed deeply, choked by what was right:
"Brother, then let your will be done; such is our curse.
Let's give our word, however, not to fight to death,
there's much work to be done on earth, much dread ahead;
it's only just we seek our deaths at greater heights."
Gaunt Granite shook with laughter, but he reached his hand:
"Very well, then, our lion-strife will stop at death;
I, too, prefer to keep my soul, that wild bloodhound,
safe in my savage chest for a more glorious hunt."
They spoke, and parted with great wrath, their bodies steamed,
and then at evening, when day's kiln was flickering low,
they smeared their limbs with slippery wild boar's fat and cleared
a wide arena in the woods for fighting space.
The seven maids, the bridal loot, set up their wails,
while in their midst the widow stitched her swaddling clothes.

The troop, too, parted in two seething hostile camps;
some prompted Kentaur how to spread his legs out wide
then how to seize that slender form and smash it down
and thus strike terror in all souls that trod on justice;
and others pressed round Granite's fire and sang rousing songs.

Enflamed and smeared with blood on the sky's rim, the moon
loomed speechless in the night, a slaughtered soldier's head,
and on all waxen faces cast its bloodstained beams.
The drums beat, the huge bodies in the arena gleamed,
but first they roused each other's wrath with gibes and jeers:
"Come on, potbellied sot, I'll tear your guts apart
then dig in with a harbor dredge to drain you dry!"
But like a turkey, glutton swelled and gave no quarter
for black rage seized him and he spoke with bursting sides:
"Go on, you scrawny cock, you windbag of hot air,
think of that time you almost pissed your fool head off,
for if I hadn't swooped in time, by God, today
you'd be bare bones and through your ribs the carrion flies
would buzz in swarms and the black crabs go scurrying!"
By now gaunt Granite's blood was seething, words were vain
and choked him, so he lunged and seized fat glutton's sides,
but he dug both huge feet like columns firm in earth:
"Strike all you want, foam at the mouth, but you won't budge me!"
They fought, and the earth shook; they lunged, and the woods rang;
there where broad-buttocks stamped his feet, the arena sank,
there where the hill-chief stamped, cisterns of black blood gaped,
their eyes turned bestial and their black-bruised bodies swelled.
Suddenly, like a vulture, Granite swooped and seized
glutton's fat nape till its veins swelled, his face turned green.
Both foes and friends pressed close with fear and held their breath:
an eagle and a bison thrashed on bloodstained earth,
and as the eagle dug its claws in the beast's nape,
it spread its wings about the dazed and bloodshot eyes
and struck between the horns to suck the bison's brains.
The women shrieked with grief because from Kentaur's throat
they heard his heart's commotion break in rattling gasps.
But with a choked cry suddenly Granite's body sagged,
and broad-backed Kentaur seized his comrade by the waist
and groped to find where that proud body might be maimed,
till his whole soul from his ten fingers poured with fear,
and when he felt poor Granite's left arm hanging limp,
soft-hearted glutton burst into a loud lament:
"Forgive me, friend, my crude hands yet don't know their strength."
Then filled with joy unhoped for, the seven women screamed
and rushed to kiss their savior's limp and bloodstained hands,

but he turned, grabbed their hair and knocked their heads together:
"You whores, you're all worth less than Granite's little nail!
If I'd known what I'd do, I'd rather have slain you all!"
Thus did he growl, then turned to dress his comrade's wound,
but Granite bit his lip and thrust splayfoot aside,
and the good-natured man cried out, to soothe his friend:
"Aye, don't take it to heart, it's clear as clear can be
this wasn't a serious fight but only a fool joke,
for how can this potbelly of mine be matched against you?"
He plunged in the lake water then at night to cleanse
his bison-body from its thick sweat and clotting blood,
and smutched the crystal lake about him for nine spans.
Swaggering out then, light of heart, his bellies swayed,
his new-washed flesh in layers laughed with clotted grease,
and when he saw his wounded friend stretched on the grass
attended by his troop who smeared him with soft salves,
he slyly smiled and swaggered like a cock inside:
"Aye, though his arm should heal, the shame will sting him still,
for wounds don't heal within the mind, but swell and rot,
and though you throttle memory, curse her, she still shouts."
With these conceited thoughts fat glutton plodded on
to stretch his weary shanks now on his new-built bed.
A gentle and cool breeze blew by and dried his limbs,
far off a maiden sang with longing as she knelt
and milked her pregnant cow and filled her milkpail full;
her virgin breasts hung heavily now and swelled with pain,
she also longed to be a mother, to swell with milk,
until a strong and greedy son should milk her too.
Fat glutton's mind flew off down Africa's wide fields,
plowed up the river's current, down to sandy shores,
and like a fat fish-eating gull swept out to sea,
skimmed wave on wave and perched upon a Cretan rock.
"Look at those shores and seas, by God, those men and maids,
look at what food and wine I've gulped, and I'm still starved!
Oho, you've overdone it, heart, you're overbrimming,
and one day soon, there's no escaping it, you'll burst!"
Thus splayfoot muttered to himself, then suddenly leapt,
for somehow the quaint notion struck him in a flash
to wear his gold canary-feathered nuptial cloak.
All life seemed good, the wrestling in the ring seemed good,
and God, how good the spitted lamb shanks smelled that day!
"I might as well snatch me a maid to cool my eyes.
My jaws are sturdy millstones still and grind to pulp;
push on, great glutton, let's go feed our windmill's guts!"
He spoke, then steered his bulging prow straight toward the spitted meat.

When the maids saw him with his gold canary cloak
he seemed a great bird-hunting god come from the chase;
they smiled and spread fresh leaves for him to sit and eat.
Nightingales sang, the night was warm, and the moon rose
like a round holy charm to exorcise the dark.
Earth is so vast that man's poor arms cannot embrace her,
but greedy-guts embraced his troop and joyed to see
women and children eating, growing, young lads dancing,
his brave youths cleaning weapons with the wild boar's fat.
"Eat, drink, and kick your heels, for there's no other life,
we're but a fistful of thin soil, a gust of air."
He spoke, and strutted by the fire, admired by all;
nine youths then raised him and enthroned him on a rock,
drums beat and howled, resounding to the emerald moon,
and seven maids, placing their hands on their wide hips,
began to dance and sing a song in glutton's praise:
"Blackness has fallen, monstrous thunder strikes the gorge!
Is it the Earth Bull mounting, lads, or Death come down,
dear God, to gulp the river dry with all its stones?
Raise high your brave hearts, lads, fling wide your brazen doors,
run to the rooftops, maids, and wave your handkerchiefs,
for it's not Earth Bull mounting nor dread Death come down,
it's broad-rump wrestling on the marble threshing floor.
See, full of joy and sweat, he's plunged for a long swim;
in his left nostril ovens blaze, and in his right
horses are stalled, two couples sleep on his broad back;
he goes to drink the stream but pities the poor fields,
he goes to raise his hand but pities the poor mothers,
softly he walks on tiptoe so the world won't sink!
Friends, on a feast day, as he lunged from the high peaks,
Death climbed the mountainside and smelled good human flesh,
he saw the feast-boards strewn on two-and-forty trestles,
he saw our brave men dancing in a twelvefold ring,
and the great uninvited cannibal cocked his cap
on his curled locks and set off for the laden feast.
When the two giants met in dustclouds by two peaks,
great glutton reached his hand and stopped Death in his tracks:
'Friend, aren't you gorged by now, hasn't your heart turned red
from eating man's most virile parts and women's breasts?
Go toddling home to mama now, or I'll swipe you dead!'
But the housebreaker growled, stung by such brazen words:
'Oho, where will you hide from me when your day comes?
The lower world will fill with fat, where worms shall sail!'
But glutton, our great monster, laughed, his bone-joints creaked:
'I know it, and you're welcome, slayer, to all I've got,
but when I woke this morning, stretched my arms and yawned,

and felt my great bones creak, I took a solemn oath:
aye, Death, my lad, you shan't go to our feast today!'
The two huge monsters shook their spears, roared and replied,
but when their word-war ceased, they grabbed each other's waists
and fought from dawn's light on. At length the red sun set,
the Evening Star appeared and beckoned, the songs ended,
all placed their wineskins in wool sacks, tucked up their lyres,
the young maids tied their kerchiefs, young men bound their belts,
loaded their mules with crimson rugs, and the roads flashed:
'We've had a good time, lads, and Death did not appear!' "
Enthroned on rock, great glutton laughed with swaggering pride
and his sweat trickled in the folds of his fat flesh,
but when he thought of Death he scowled and clapped his hands:
"Strike up the dance, my girls! Swirl on! May damn Death croak!
But while I live, the earth shall stand, and while I breathe
we'll joy in bread, wine, love! Let Death come, if he dares!
The dance lasts long—he's welcome to all dregs and crumbs!"
When Granite's comrades heard the song, they seized their bows,
for rage is blind, and rushed to choke the singing throats:
"Dogs, you know well our friend lies wounded in great pain,
yet here you go carousing with your drunken sot!
Oho, sharp arrows, take up now their song's refrain!"
The women screamed and scattered, and the young men raged,
but glutton jumped up, stumbling, and his voice roared out:
"By God, you're sticking in my throat! So far, no further!
Out with your black swords, lads! Let Death fall where he may!"
The bright full-bodied moon sailed to the sky's peak
at drop of midnight, shadows clutched like tangled hair
and toward the lake shore mutely rolled in pallid light
as knife blades rose and fell and flashed in the moon's silver glow.

But all at once a great cry rang, the pebbles creaked,
and a long shadow spread on earth with lion's head.
As Kentaur swerved and looked, he suddenly crouched with fear
like a sheep dog who by the penfold meets a lion,
and shadows shaped like shooting bows fled through the woods.
High up, the full moon's bitter face turned soft and sweet
and the great shadow swiftly knelt on a high knoll,
the bowstring tightened, stretched, and reached to the right breast,
and then the sheep dog's shadow slowly unwound and stood
upright within the moon's full light to take the shot,
and a hoarse cave-resounding voice boomed on the earth:
"Shoot, I'm ashamed to face you! Have no pity, master!
I'm still not fit to live in your shade or eat your bread."
The monstrous shadow rose and its long bow grew short:
"Cursed be my lion's marrow that you've fed on, fool!

I thought you'd sprout wide wings and follow in my steps,
ayee, you cow's dung, scram, go hang your head, be off."
After he'd trounced him well, he turned and roared for Granite,
and when the gaunt man heard, he bit his waxen lips
but sprang up fearless from the ground, strode through the grass,
and came out in the moon's light with his broken arm.
The archer turned, approached him with his leopard cub,
and all at once his mocking voice rang in the moonglow:
"Oho, what shame! Great Granite smells of slavery too!
One day of freedom struck him, and he lost his wits!
And I, you fools, come bearing from the mountain peaks
a flaming city with four gates and towering walls!"
He spoke, and his new eyes of yellow flame struck sparks,
and his sharp teeth within the stillness ground with rage.
Speechless, alone, he roamed the forest for three days;
his heart was sown with bristling thorns, his wavering mind
at times longed for man's herd, at times for the pure desert.
At times the fierce thought struck him to clamber on high rocks
and stretch his long bow taut, as once before, and pierce
those thickset skulls that squandered God's wealth shamefully;
at times he bit his lips and swore that whether they would
or not, he'd build his God with human souls and turn
them all to stones and trees to find salvation with him!
Darkly he groped at both great roads, and longed to see
which, in this forking moment now, his mind would choose.
Gaunt Granite mutely followed his great master's strife
and waited with his upright soul for yes or no;
he'd never beg him on his knees, he'd never exchange
his haughty pride for all the mind's or the earth's loot.
But Kentaur, sad and fasting, followed at his heels
and trembled lest he leave and sink their souls in peril:
"Granite, our fate hangs by a hair at the cliff's edge.
If only we could grasp our two-willed master's knees,
perhaps his friendship would return, his black rage calm."
Thus glutton blabbered to his old friend, starved for talk,
but Granite wrapped his broken arm in fresh green leaves,
scowled with disdain, then turned and talked to Pride alone:
"Mother, who sits in wilderness and feeds all beasts,
O rock-strewn and unlaughing peak of arrogant man,
Mother, if all the great good things of earth should leave me,
gallant deeds, friends, immortals, then I'd cock my cap,
for at despair's far verge you sit, I know, and beckon.
Your clenched fists do not hold a blossomed laurel bough,
nor food for farmers, a large stalk of fruitful wheat,
neither an air-blown rose nor a seductive grape;
Mother, you bid me welcome with a long sharp whip!"

Thus did the two friends talk and scourge their souls, while all
the calm troops cooked their food, nor did the slightest sound
of these wild breaking waves pierce through their thick-skinned skulls.

The third day, on a high plateau, the two-willed man
saw a wild twisted pear tree blossomed in the sun;
all year she'd fought the elements with gallant spite,
the rain, the frost, the whirlwinds and the cankering worm,
yet in her bark had slowly spun her pears with patience
until she trembled like a bride and broke in flower.
Joy filled the tear-drenched mind of the quick-tempered man,
and for long hours, until the evening shadows fell,
he admired his far victorious sister wedged in rock
who took what fate had given, water, soil, and stone,
and stubbornly in sun turned all to subtle flower.
The archer also felt his twisting body knit
and thrust its flaming head toward light as fruitful flower,
and as the tree deep in its bark rejoiced in pears,
he also felt with joy how deeds swarmed in his soul.
His nostrils played and sniffed at the full-blossomed tree,
and when his hungry mind gaped wide and filled with scent,
he felt he swallowed the whole tree, both flower and fruit.
Smiling, he seized the tree and felt its rugged bark;
it was no ghost or thought, only a blossomed log,
and as he shook the boughs, it showered his head with flowers.
When he released the pear, he heard a wing's light swish,
then turned and saw the gaping mouth of a dark cave
where a gold-feathered bird with puffed and blood-red breast
opened its brilliant wings and vanished in the dark.
The catcher of birds rejoiced that God, as he was wont,
sent him for herald a small bird with colored wings,
and then he crossed the cave's dark mouth, threshold of fate.
Much had his deep eyes seen, but never a cave like this;
he lit a torch, and hours passed, and still he walked;
glittering columns hung from high marmoreal domes,
and from the earth black phalli rose hewn out of rock
formed from small drops that slowly dripped dark age on age,
and maidenhair about these pillars tightly twined.
Beneath the earth a mighty river swiftly rolled
with roaring sound of the invisible water's rush;
rock-swallows built their nests within the noisy clefts
and from the domes in tangled clusters hung the bats.
Now parched with thirst, Odysseus fell on a scooped rock
and to his heels rejoiced in God's refreshing coolness
for his bones creaked and blossomed like the jasmine vine,
and as he slowly nestled in a throne-hewn rock,

he bent and heard the sacred river's lion-roar,
and as he listened, time dripped down and turned his mind
to stone till God's voice spoke within the heart of man.
Ah, what great joy in the wilderness to feel God fall
drop after drop and turn to phallus deep within you!
To feel his holy hand within the freshening dark
groping to find your hand and clasp with a friend's grip!
For hours the lone man listened to the mystic voice,
and when his heart had brimmed and his full mind was slaked,
he rose from his high throne and tossed his flashing head:
"All of God strives in greatest peril in every breast.
Great King, you've ordered all things well, all shall go well,
nor shall those passes in my trust be ever betrayed!"
He spoke, retraced his tracks, then stepped in the moon's glow.
He made his mind up calmly, then called his two friends
and stretched with them by the campfire, laughed and ate,
though no one spoke a word, not even his fellow runners;
this was the day, they guessed, when he would aim and shoot.
When they had eaten, the arch-cunning man reached out
and grabbed his comrades by their curly faithful heads:
"Fellows, at noon today, on my God's rocks, I saw
a tough and twisted pear tree blossoming in the sun;
its leaves and flowers shook, then sang with human voice:
'How long shall I deign to guide you, fool? No matter how
you boast, disdainful man, or strive to shake your yoke,
you'll still plod, shackled, round and round man's threshing floor.
Accept your fate with no false shame, and you'll surpass her!
What else did you expect from the rank herd of men?
Their hearts are airskins, their brains mud, their loins manure,
but yet I love them and I like the stench of earth;
I know well how the spirit blooms, how God is shaped,
what filth my black roots browse on in the darkest gloom.
See how I milk the rock, suck up manure, and turn
all into flowers with patience, with despair, with love,
and now I stand firm in your path, a blossomed pear;
behold me, take me for your model, start your work!' "
Then the much-knowing man stooped low and raked the fire,
and Granite heard the lash swish through his mind with pain
but took his punishment, nor moved, a just reward;
and Captain Glutton would not raise his eyes in shame
for fear his tears might then be seen in the fire's light.
The lone man threw some boughs until the flames reared high
and for a long time watched their flickering tongues in thought.
The flames danced in his eyes and turned his beard bright red:
"We'll plant our town's foundations, then, at break of day;
deep in my brain its seed shines like a small, small flame

and from my brain will leap to earth and spread its roots,
sprout leaves of babes and women, blossoms of brave youths,
and at its tip my God shall burst as the flame's fruit!"
With his sharp knife he drew a circle around the hearth,
raked well the fire with a lit torch, quartered it well,
raised in the center a tall heap of burning coals
then thrust in its hot heart his tall black-hilted knife:
"Open your brains, my brothers, this is our town's seed,
and God stands on its peak with burning brands about him,
women and strong men at their prime, youth in their bloom,
and fresh twigs at the left, children not yet enflamed,
and burnt-out embers further off, the black old men,
while round our city loom the tower-breasted walls."
He spoke, and his two comrades, stooped in night's black pitch,
watched marveling how their city shone for hours on earth;
and when they had well sown her in their furrowed minds,
the archer swiftly scattered the fierce flames and stamped her out.

Day broke, and God smiled like a sun in the pale sky,
the people woke, swarmed festively, and splayfoot led
the herd while his voice roared along the wooded beach:
"Your health and joy! Perk up your ears, I've got great news!
We'll cast the deep foundations of God's city here;
the past is past, now kiss it all a dead goodbye;
brothers, we'll plant here a new iron-headed earth!"
The conch blared as the archer opened the new road,
and at the mouth of the black cave the pear tree glowed
at rose-red break of day like a sweet conflagration.
The city-builder turned and seized his famous bow:
"Brothers, I shall cut walls of air with my swift arrows!
O sun, rise at this hour and let our earthbound souls,
and let the crawling worm sprout upright soaring wings!
Black demons, run and hide, for I shall shoot my shafts!"
He spoke, looked to the North, then stretched his heavy bow:
"Oho, quick-tempered North Wind, hear me out, don't growl!
Fetch us a race of white men, wheat, and buxom sheep,
send us your swifting swallows with flowers in their bills,
and if you bring us news of our native land on wing,
it's welcome, let it fall on us like the sweet dew!
All, native lands and exile, in our minds are one;
our native land is where God is, all earth is ours!
Descend, O North Wind, come, we'll take your measure now,
dash like a horseman through our city's northern gate!"
He blessed himself, shot his swift whistling arrow north,
then turning southward once more stretched his bowstring taut
and cut the quiet air with a new conjuring spell:

"You too, O gallant South Wind, with your downy cheeks,
bring us your crinkly black-skinned men, your clouds, your rain,
your precious ivory tusks, your hides, your heavy gold.
Enter our castle like the prince of fabulous tales,
dark-skinned, with wet and sweating hair, with slender hands,
followed by long, long rows of camels and bronze bells.
Prince South Wind, here's your castle gate with silver knockers!
O East Wind, from whose golden egg the day is hatched,
and you, West Wind, whose keys unlock all doors at night,
O my great brothers, I shall build you towering gates
that your proud necks and handsome bodies may not stoop
when with twelve princesses you come at dawn or dusk
to stroll amid our narrow lanes with silver sandals!"
These conjurations the gate-sower cried aloud
as he shot fiercely at the four foundational winds,
and chosen gallants dashed along the arrowy paths
to find the swift bronze wings and set up boundary stones.
When fate's full circle had been finished and bound firm,
all marched with axes, spades, and hoes to dig foundations,
and when four corners reached the depth of two tall men,
the archer exorcised the cornerstones with blood.
At first he slew six cocks, then six fat hens, those twelve
great gods which once upon a time on azure shores
he'd worshiped with both fear and joy, to his great shame;
but now he cut their throats to bless new battlements
and longed for a new guide, called on another god:
"I slay you twelve slaves, Lord! O, crush them with your feet!
May these twelve ancient thoughts of mine, my brain's old toys,
crow in your spacious courts each dawn and lay their eggs!"
When he had slain his twelve old gods, he longed for a still
more glorious votive gift to bless his city walls,
and slit his left hand's regal vein and poured his blood:
"Good are the springs of Mother Earth, and good her milk,
good is wine also, and the strutting peacock, too,
who spreads his tail and strolls in the Cimmerian skull;
and man's and woman's sweat is also holy, good,
miraculous, and falls like heavy seed on earth
to fructify her sweetly and to wreathe with pearls
the sacred brow of virtue; but that huge red rose,
that mystic flaming beast, the blood of a proud man,
I hold to be the greatest spell of all to bless
and found gods, castles, or great thoughts. I pour my blood
to root your city firm, to raise a bristling camp,
tall towers for you to lean on, and a hard stone head
to guard your stubborn mind! O heavily wounded Soul,
O Bird, I spread you food and drink: come down to perch!"

He spoke, leapt from the pit, and portioned out each task:
one gang of workers hewed the stones, one cut down trees,
one great group built the walls, another chased wild game,
old women fought the ovens, maidens kneaded bread,
and all sang workers' songs to lighten their new tasks.
Men's voices rang and clashed, but like sweet silver bells
or gurgling water ran the women's warbling tunes
till glutton thought of old times with a sighing heart:
"Alas, if only you were here to play, dear piper,
the stones would mount up by themselves, one on the other,
and our whole town would rise without one armpit's sweat;
but now, where can you be, my dear, what roads devour you?"
But to his moaning sigh no soul replied, for all
were twittering like the happy birds of spring, entranced
with love, who built their nests in which to lay their god
like a huge egg that he might hatch them sons and daughters soon.

Time passed as swiftly as a bird's bright honeymoon,
trowels and cleavers flashed, the smell of new-cut wood
rose as the town climbed like a tree and filled the air
while souls soared with it like ecstatic singing birds.
When they stopped work at sunset and pressed round their fires,
the archer strove with patience to etch his dread god
deep in the hard flint minds of his most simple people:
"Now hear me, brothers, and cock your minds, for I shall speak:
God does not sit enthroned on clouds nor in black Hades,
nor flits like empty shades through man's imagination,
but he, too, walks the barren earth and struggles with us.
At times he turns into a plowman after the spring
rains fall, or to a boatman tossed by foaming seas,
at times into a soldier who grafts his blood with ours.
Now he's become a master-mason for whom we fetch
stones, wood, mud, souls, and as he works with joy, he sings.
When the day's work was done last night, I saw him stand
to watch what had been built and munch a crust of bread;
his long beard in the sunset gleamed like burning thorns,
and as he smiled he murmured happily, 'Well done!' "
The people listened, and at dawn when all hacked wood
or fetched mud hurriedly, or built their walls, all felt
they hewed and built their god's great body on firm earth.
Slowly the town took form in sun and filled with sound,
crenels and ramparts rose, the four broad town gates shone
till streets and lanes with all their tributaries rolled
like streams with still unfinished homes on the far banks.
"Ah, how the great thoughts of a full man spread their roots
upon the ground and then take shape with sticks and stones,"

the lone man murmured as he watched his craftsmen toil.
He judged each soul in action, marked deep in his brain
each strength, each bodily movement, and each grace of mind;
he'd picked already what great workers were most firm
with their sharp tools of trade for earth, or sea, or air,
yet placed above them the sharp-spoken and cruel lancers
who held the keys of manliness, the seal of honor,
but highest, the mind-battlers, the full fruit of strife.
The town formed like a body in the archer's mind;
all rushed to the same goal obediently and worked
toward their full-rigged, invisible monarch in their hearts.
At night, when all cooked by the fire's submissive flames,
the master-craftsman counseled his hard workers well:
"God wants no separate hearths or double-bolted doors;
who in his croft corrals his children, wife, and beasts
walls up all virtues, makes them idle, chokes his god,
till the whole world's confined within his private gate.
Within God's city is no separate husbandry;
let the young man in rut seize what girl fills his eye
and thrust deep in the woods to enjoy the lightning bolt
then part again at dawn before the sweet flash fades.
But let old crones and codgers, mankind's useless trash,
die quickly and return once more to the good loam
that their tribe's roots may eat and drink and bloom in grandsons.
Let all youths grow to manhood in wide courts apart,
far from their parents' heavy shadows, free of heart,
for this town, brothers, is the town of all brave sons
who shall surpass their fathers and set their prow for God!"
He spoke and showed the palpable, apparent walls,
the body of his God, that each day inched from earth;
but when the great-eyed man remained alone at night,
his town's invisible ramparts creaked and rose in flames
and purple smoke from the four walls of his great head.
Blue, secret castle doors where Death might come and go,
laws and injunctions, hopes and orders rose and swelled,
but all were pale smoke spiraling in his mind's great fire
nor yet would condescend to be enfleshed in words or law.

One day as he was spinning in his mind with care
on what great fertile law, custodian of all virtue,
he might make fast a town that strained beyond man's reach,
he heard a whirring sound as of a thousand wings,
stood still and saw tall earthen columns, cracked and dry,
from which dense clouds of winged ants burst like swirling smoke
until the sky was blackened and the sun eclipsed.
The great lawmaker thrilled to see the wedding stream

soar to create in light the mighty destined groom,
and as his mind spun round the mystery of the world
the cloud fell down on earth and heaps of gray-ashed ants
swarmed on the ground and floundered with bedraggled wings.
The deadly and fierce wedding had ended in bright air,
and those who held God in their guts and reached the bride
had filled her body with battalion-forming seed,
but heaps of wretched flagging grooms expired on earth,
for the all-sucking god had now no need of them.
A fundamental hawk-eyed goal flashed through his mind:
"This is the sign I've yearned for, this is my great law!"
he muttered as he rushed to see the great soul-strife;
but birds had smelled the loot already and swooped down,
mute serpents slid and gulped, gold-beetles, scorpions frisked
and chewed the soft, exhausted grooms with greedy haste.
Earth shook with sweet reverberations as beasts filled
their bellies while man's mind browsed over all, refreshed,
and with unsleeping eyes gazed on the just, fierce law.
"Whatever blind Worm-Mother Earth does with no brains
we should accept as just, with our whole mind, wide-eyed;
if you would rule the world, model yourself on God."
Thus did he think, then swiftly to his building turned,
but held all laws etched in the tablets of his mind.
Finding broad-rump befouled with mud from top to toe,
as he helped finish first the old men's wretched homes,
the exasperated archer flung sharp, taunting words:
"Quit mollycoddling the old men, softhearted fool!
By God, at times my demon tempts me to round up
all useless codgers on the cliffs and shove them off!"
Such cruel words pricked the heart of the compassionate man:
"Ah, murderer, you don't even ache for your own father!
Mark me, one day you'll be cast down from age's cliff!"
The archer's claw-sharp mind reared up, his temples throbbed:
"By God, when my mind rots and my flesh wastes away,
I'll climb to a high peak and cast myself to death!
And when my soul at length gives birth to our town's laws,
then know that I shall scorn to turn toward the cruel Archer
to help his interests or find ways to flatter him.
God is the warrior worm of which I am the head;
on me let triple pain and triple malice fall!"
The lone man drew apart and in his mind there rose
a rugged old man's rock before the city's gates
from which he'd push off all the senile patriarchs.
He formed stern laws within his heart, then on the slope
sat down and grasped a huge smooth slab to carve his granite laws.

At night as all sat cross-legged by the fire in talk
and drank a bit too much, the archer teased poor glutton:
"Potbelly, we've worked hard today, and now at night
let's solve a little riddle for joke and recompense:
what would you say is the greatest good on all this earth?"
Big-bellied glutton with a sigh exposed his heart:
"To sit bathed by the seaside after a long trip;
to eat and drink with friends, while from the garden close
you hear your shuttered women laugh and chatter on;
to sit at dusk as a breeze blows and wafts the sea's
salt brine, mixed with the fragrance of lean, spitted lamb."
But the archer cut in sharply with a scowling face:
"To march to battle with brave friends at break of day
and find a sea of foes that billows down the field,
then suddenly, as you turn, to see God at your right,
mounted on his black steed, but pale, trembling with fright,
and then to stretch your arms and give his heart support!"
Kentaur spoke not a word but broke in a cold sweat;
he should have had another, more carousing master
who'd keep a feast spread day and night beneath the trees
and like a woman nibble life away in shade
nor give a damn about dream-towns, nor wish, dear God,
—what nerve!—to re-create the very world God shaped!
Since it was glutton's fate to fall in savage hands,
alas, he might as well kick up his heels, and sing!
Thus did God's bulky ballast brood deep in his heart
nor dared to open his mouth or speak his heart's desire
because the lone man sat in darkness and flashed with fire.
In truth the archer felt a flame gnaw at his heart
and longed for that dread hour when he might strew the flame
on all, and let who could withstand the terror survive.
Next day a heavy downpour burst, and heaving clouds
tossed like frenetic dragons in the lowering sky;
some from the black lake mounted and seized all the air
while zigzag lightning flashes crashed in the dark woods.
The drenched town-builders scurried laughing into caves,
their bodies steamed, their eyes sparked in the lightning bolts,
and the resourceful man, like a huge octopus,
admired their glistening forms, his mighty tentacles.
"These can now bear the ruthless secret on their backs,"
he thought with pride, and turned with joy to speak to all,
but as he pondered in what way to slant his words,
the downpour ceased, earth laughed and wrung her dripping hair,
the rainbow hung on high amid cool waterdrops
and craftsmen clambered up their scaffolds eagerly.

The archer stooped and stepped out of the cave, alone,
and on his lips his silent secret hung and trembled still.

Moons came and went, the wheel of earth rolled slowly on,
the rainy season stopped, a pale light winter passed
until the still-unbearded wheat stirred in its seed.
Earth grew her hair, the mountains swelled, the ground awoke,
the cuckoo bird perched on a bough with brooding thought,
and as it spun spring's sweetness in its breast, it heard
the sun-adoring god deep in its heart, "Coo-coo!"
and all at once its black eyes glowed and filled with flowers.
"Coo-coo!" its straight throat echoed, and through all the fields
evergreen oak shrubs budded in the quickening breeze.
The flag and sword-grass broke in bloom, wild lettuce laughed,
and the first sprouts pierced through the bark till the trees cracked.
Together with all plants, the blood of all youth bloomed,
a giddy sweetness swept their brows, their knees gave way,
until their knowing master smiled and called a halt
to work for three whole days and nights of holiday.
He sent a youthful herald with apple cheeks of fuzz,
his naked body decked with flowers, to shout through town:
"Young blades who flaunt a thin mist on your upper lip,
young girls whose breasts have suddenly risen high and firm,
now listen to our master craftsman's proclamation:
All trees have swelled with sap, birds pair off on the boughs,
God walks the earth like a green lad or breasted girl,
and all earth seethes with life, and all hearts burst in bloom.
Forward! Let brides and grooms of God adorn themselves,
let girls new-washed and lads with their carnation stalks
arm themselves now for war to cast each other down!
For three nights let them fight embraced in the cool cave!"
Thus did the bloom-decked boy scatter the happy news
and the lawmaker joyed to know that soon with bliss
the unbearable sweet swoon of flesh would knit to sons.
Slow in his heart he turned the wheel of earth and life
until he planned to dedicate four fetes each year:
one for unmustached youths, one for all full-grown men,
one for the bones of age, one for the rotting dead.
How else might the crude crowd, if not with giddy dance
and fetes, forget the salt sweat of its daily toil—
and in those ways it could—with song, with wine, with dance,
and with the body's tight embrace, mount step by step
to reach that mighty warrior, that great lover, God?
All this the lone man spun in his mind as the night passed
and the sun rose, a drum stretched tight with lion pelts

that boomed in the high heavens and startled the young maids.
They wove wild lettuce flowers about their virgin brows,
the young men wore the sword-grass bloom, and both linked arms
while that good dame, their Mother Earth, looked on with pride
to see her youths roll toward the cave in full cascades.
They held their glowing torches high, their laughter rang,
and their nude bodies glistened in the humid cave.
But a young couple suddenly stopped and clutched each other,
for in a shallow water-pit two skeletons gleamed,
a man's and woman's bones entwined and nestling there.
A long, long time ago a young man chased his girl
deep in the cave till they got lost in the dark maze
and wandered shouting day and night as all hope died;
then the young girl embraced the young man shamelessly
and both fell in a shuddering blaze of love to Hades.
Now their white skeletons were twined in tight embrace
and sweetly shone within the eyes of each young pair.
The lone man turned and fixed two torches in the ground;
how beautiful, dear God, the new-washed bodies shone—
the young men gleamed like swords, the girls like empty sheaths.
His shadow in the torch-glare danced like a huge lion:
"Perk up your ears, my lads, I bring you sweetest news:
I've seen God walk the earth in many different shapes,
I've fondled him as infant, pitied him as crone,
but never does my heart rejoice so much as when
he walks earth dressed as a young man or a young girl.
I watch him as he twirls his thin mustache with pride
and glances sideways at the girls and sweetly moans.
The maids crouch near their mothers but hear sounds in air:
'Come, let me clasp you tight that you may never die!
Come, leave your mother and become a mother too!'
And then again I watch him as a downy girl
who walks earth boldly as her strong and supple thighs
stride through the grass like slender hounds that stalk their prey.
She passes by with fragrant breasts and gleaming hair
till every youth thinks she has beckoned him, and sighs:
'Ah, could I plant my son there, God, and never die!'
Open your earthen eyelids, lads, come close and see:
each youth holds one of God's two wings in his dark loins
and each girl holds the other wing deep in her womb;
now in the cave's dark heart, in an erotic siege,
join God's two wings, O youth, and set him free to soar
like every daring son or fledgling bird that sings."
He spoke, and all uncoupled wings pulsed in the dark;
the young men shyly glanced at girls and made their choice
of lover, pale and silent, till their two stars met.

But in their midst the traveler stood with throat erect
as though he listened to bees swarming in spring air,
as though on distant azure waves he still could hear
the forty-two winged oars which had set out one day,
when he was still a beardless youth, and fetched his bride.
He stooped, then walked out, sighing, from the cave of youth.
The three love nights passed swiftly like lean lightning bolts,
and God, that crimson wild dove with the flaming eyes,
flew in the cave three days and nights with double wings;
but on the fourth dawn brides and bridegrooms slowly rose,
serene and sated, and with rapturous joy marched out
to finish with joint labor now their children's home.
They built and sang like birds, they shaped a high peaked roof
and raised red swaddling clothes in air for a bold banner.
Then birds came, too, and built their nests, and small eggs gleamed;
the cool days passed, the ripe eggs hatched, and summer came
with her warm slender feet, her long and curly locks;
snakes coiled, uncoiled in rows, the Rutting God appeared,
males honed their claws, musk spilled its fragrance everywhere,
and in a quivering silence females stood and waited.
Though black night smothered down, the earth still steamed with heat,
and when the archer tightly clasped his leopard cub,
the haughty virgin growled, switched earth with her long tail,
and as she opened her red jaws and flashed her teeth
her older brother fondled her and begged her warmly:
"Dearly beloved, never before has my heart merged
so tightly with a living form as now with yours;
but I see that your womb sighs, and that you long to go."
Thus did he speak and stroke the cub to heal her ache,
but with erotic pain she sniffed the dry red hills,
for all the russet soil reeked of a leopard's musk;
at times she turned back to her master with a fierce glare,
at times she arched her back until her wild fur sparked.
The churlish man's heart sweetened as he felt her pain:
"What shame to squander all your fate for my sake, virgin!
God in a leopard's form now growls and stalks the woods;
merge with him now, be filled with seed, increase your kind,
for leopards, too, are bright adornments here on earth."
He spoke, then set his loved cub loose within the rutting wood.

A peasant with his huge feet steeped in heavy mud,
day woke each dawn and went to work on the great town
as step by step it rose tall-columned in the light.
As ramparts rose with laws like high ferocious towers,
God talked and gave his orders to the leader's mind,
and he strove slowly to distill the hid commands

deep in the black pit of his heart and make them song.
One day God sprang on earth with iron weapons armed
and struck Odysseus with his foot till he sprang up
and marshaled his loose wits, as cries of love and war
rang out and ruthless great commandments throbbed in light:
"I am your own dread God, your Chief of Staff in War!
You're not my slave, you're now no plaything in my hands,
nor yet a trusted friend, nor yet a favorite son,
but comrade and co-worker in the stubborn strife!
Manfully hold the pass entrusted you in war;
learn to obey—only that soul may be called free
who follows and takes joy in goals greater than he.
Learn to command, only that soul on earth who knows
how to give harsh commands can be my mouth or fist.
What is my road? A rough, rude, limitless ascent!
To say: No one but I can save the whole wide world!
Where are we going? Shall we win? Don't ask! Fight on!"
Thus did dread God command within the lone man's breast,
and the lawmaker's mind grew light, the air grew mute,
and he sped swiftly toward his city with great joy
to find smooth slabs of upright stones on which to carve
the great and difficult laws entrusted him by God.
As he walked on and thought how he might raise a troop
to aid that God who always mounted earth with groans,
he saw beside the town's south gate a monstrous stream
of blind black ants that swarmed with a devouring greed.
A baby camel had been caught in that fierce charge
and only its white bones now gleamed on the black ground;
the frightened people stopped their work and fled like leaves
but in the rush a baby fell from its mother's arms,
laughingly sank within that dread cascade of ants
and in a flash only its bare thin bones remained.
The largest of the black ants, with thick solid jaws,
scurried like leaders up and down the frenzied troops,
bit, barked commands, and brought the stream to ordered flow.
The suffering man stooped low and watched the mystic powers,
greedy and blind, that welled from the ground's guts, and knew
that earth's crust at his feet was but a thin trap door.
When the dark plunderers suddenly swerved and disappeared,
the people turned to building with unruffled song,
and Death's grim raid became the cause of laughs and jokes.
Memory soon forgot all it had seen and feared
and covered horror with a colored cloak, as always;
when pots were set above the hearths that very night,
then Death, the Ant, became the fancy's glittering toy.
But the compassionate man's frenetic heart was wrung,

his black-robed memory stooped and loosed her matted hair,
held up the stream of ants for mirror, wept and wailed.
Silent, and sickened with all food, Odysseus lay
in the wild moonlight by the lake and called on sleep
till that old sunless codger came with all his brood.
The lone man dreamt that on his body blind ants swarmed
and ate him to the bone, that his flesh knit once more,
but that the ants swarmed once again and ate him whole.
All night his quivering flesh would fade and knit in waves
until in the dawn's light he felt these were not ants
but the dark stars that crawled above him silently and ate him.

One night God leapt full-armored in the archer's brain,
and as he felt the dread command, he jumped from sleep,
blew on his conch and marshaled all his troop with haste:
"Let all work stop this day! Let a great feast be spread!
Flowers have wilted and fruit knit, let all our bodies
that also have borne fruit, play for a moment now;
I here pronounce a mystic feast of fruits in summer."
Fathers and mothers dropped their working tools at once,
plunged in the lake to bathe, and then with heavy paints
of blue and red adorned their bosoms and firm limbs;
all that the soul longed for in secret they drew now
on their strong bodies: women, gallant deeds, and dance.
As mute Odysseus crouched in dark and watched them cross
his God's cool threshold, he rejoiced to see the cave
become a session of bright stars, a croft of flames.
He locked his lips, his people held their breath in fear,
and from the bowels of the earth a heavy roar
thundered as though a monstrous black bull bellowed there,
then the ground shook with earthquake, and once more stood still.
For fear that man might lose what little strength he had,
the archer shunted off his hovering savage thoughts:
"Brothers, strike up the dance and give your minds a spin
till in your breasts God's fountains leap like five deep springs,
and then, my lads, I'll speak and tell you a great secret!"
All whirled on the dark cliffs of dance, and their brains spun,
bodies forgot their destinies and flew like birds,
a light intoxication zoned their brows like wings,
and when Odysseus felt they had all reached their peak,
he raised his hands, stopped the mad dance and spoke with care:
"I'll tell you a great secret, don't be heavy-hearted!"
But then a curly-bearded stalwart raised his hand:
"In the swift giddiness of dance, hearts fear no death!
Cast us your words! We'll wear them on our ears like roses."
The lone man arched his brows in scorn of such bold praise,

turned to his troop and darkly cast his heavy words:
"Brothers, God trembles in our breasts and cries for help!"
The startled stalwarts took alarm and grasped their swords,
all mothers were struck dumb and tightly clutched their sons,
a youth, but newly wed, embraced his trembling bride
for fear the son he'd planted in her womb might die.
But Granite's scornful lips broke in a mocking smile;
he also longed for such an anguished God on earth
who rushed with his brave men to battle, nor from pride
even thought of victory as his just and true reward:
"I'll die a thousand deaths, but let me fall from high!"
Upright, the archer shot his shafts in the cool cave:
"He's not Almighty, brothers! Blood pours from his veins,
he stumbles on the earth with Death close at his heels!"
Painfully wounded, his friends groaned to hear him speak,
a newly wed young maiden clasped her child and said:
"I don't want such a God who can't even save my child!"
But the archer's lightning-shivered mind struck in reply:
"My god is made of fire, water, soul, and sweat!
He's not a vast immortal thought, or bird of air;
he's only mortal flesh, like us, a flickering brain,
a restless stubborn heart that trembles like man's own
nor knows from where he started nor toward what he goes.
Whoever of you can bear him, comrades, let him stay,
but he who seeks a deathless and compassionate god,
let him leave now at once with all his goods and kin,
and let the last cruel sifting start this holy day!"
He spoke, and sulphur spilled in the resounding air;
all lost their joy, and blond, black generations swarmed
about his heavy words and buzzed all day like bees
who feel a bear's paw treading on their fruitful hive.
Broad-bottom wandered through the town as though new eyes
and ears had sprouted in his boar-hide's roaring head,
as though the taste of water had changed, as though bread rose
like martial ramparts where God crouched in quaking fear
and strongly fortified himself to war with Death.
"Oho, his hand is heavy, for good or evil both.
You thirst, and crash! he falls on you like a cascade;
you hunger for a slice of easy-come-by bread
and he sends ovens-full for you to turn to spirit;
you hold within you a small spark of soul, but he
blows till you burst in conflagration and turn to ash!
Our bodies are the threshing floors where God fights Death,
and ah, joy flies away, sweet sleep no longer stays,
for deep within our guts we hear his soul at strife."
That night toward sunset Kentaur spoke to his cruel master:

"A life like that is so inhuman, it'll knock me down!
As I roamed restlessly today with savage heart,
I fondled trees and oxen, the small girls and boys,
and tears rose and hung heavily on my lashes' rim,
for we all flow like rivers lost in a vast sea!"
But the all-knowing man caressed his comrade's back:
"Don't rush yourself, O glutton, and your sides will knit,
the cleavage of your soul will turn to wild war songs;
cling to my weighty words and they will turn to wing."
But Granite laughed until his eagle-glances flashed:
"Such is the god I've longed for, such a Chief of War!
Only thus may the soul fight proudly on this earth
for it knows well that its great strife may be in vain.
As I came by now, God rushed past on his black steed;
oho, he looked like Rocky with his wedge-shaped beard,
his haughty and sharp stature, the glance of his fierce eyes!
'Aye, friend, rein in your black steed now, let's talk a while,'
and he reined in his frothing steed, reached out his arm,
so that for hours we rode in silence, hand in hand,
and all at once earth seemed an endless upward road
and all life seemed like two warm hands that tightly twined as one."

Thus by the fire the three companions shaped their god.
Meanwhile earth ripened ceaselessly, the grass turned sere,
winds blew and cast the shriveled leaves in swirling heaps,
fruit rotted on the trees and flung its fertile seed
till autumn like a wounded lion stretched on earth.
Since daybreak, in the hallway of an old man's house,
an ancient chief lay dying with grandsons and great-grandsons,
the archer's faithful friend, who one night by the fire,
when all the comrades held high talk of God and Fate,
had suddenly raised his savage head and heavy voice:
"I've always heard one cry, more than enough for me:
'Follow with stubborn faith a soul greater than you!' "
Now like a lion the ancient warrior stretched to die;
in vain his sons at midnight spread his clothes and weapons
to the high stars to exorcise all evil spells,
in vain the sorcerers from his lips and nostrils hung
long sharp-toothed hooks to catch the soul and hold it firm,
for the old battler laughed and swept the charms away:
"My soul needs now no magic spells or charms, my sons,
I'm glutted with the whole world's joys and seek to leave;
bring me my armor, bring my gold, my gems, my robes,
bring me thick crimson paints that I may dress for Death,
then set me down on the good earth for a good start."
At the old man's commands, his grandsons laid him down,

and then he sat up straight and seized his brazen shield,
laid it across his knees, gazed on his pallid face
then dyed and swelled his ancient scars with carmine paint,
adorned his head with plumes, and then with swaggering pride
tied round his neck a necklace of his foes' dog teeth.
When the great rite had ended, he stretched out his hands
in silence, and all kissed them, each in proper rank,
his sons, brides, sons-in-law, his grandsons and great-grandsons.
When night had fallen and the last great-grandson passed,
he turned his eyes to the far East, closed them, and died.
The lone man buried him beneath the pear tree's shade
so that God's roots might eat and sprout in great-great-grandsons;
all beat the grave into a threshing floor and there
their ruthless leader led the dance and called that soul:
"Grandsire, you're useless here; revive in the rich loam!
You came to earth, you ate and drank, you clasped young girls,
you rushed to battle and passed through the whole wheel's round
till now, drained dry of duty and all sperm, you sink
in our dark native land, the earth, but soon you'll sprout
as a plump great-great-grandson on a woman's breast.
Here are some somber counsels, lads, to emblazon Death:
It's only right we sing with joy the old man's death;
he'd lost his use and strength, he ate our bread in vain,
let his foul flesh descend to earth's great workshop now
where he'll be poured in a new mold and take new shape.
But when a childless young man dies, strike up a dirge
on his bare tomb, for a great soul descends to earth
not to return, and God's forever shorn of a sharp spear."
Thus did the lone man strive to give Death shape and plan;
noon hung above the world's head like a dangling sword,
and far off on a distant shore, on a high mound,
the bones of his forefathers stretched in camomile;
a sweet sun warmed the fattened soil, and the worms ate.
Under the shade of a young olive tree, which once
the lone man planted on his father's grave to suck
his flesh, a bronzed plump boy lay sleeping quietly.
A moist autumnal breeze blew round his curly locks,
a gentle smile in sleep played on his chubby lips,
and his young mother-queen with her firm husband came
and slowly bent to admire their one belovèd son.
He dreamt that he was hunting bright-blue butterflies,
and as he leapt through grass, he tripped on a red apple,
and from that fruit his loved, lost grandfather sprang and held
a small ship fully rigged, and smiled on him most gently.
"Grandpa!" the young boy cried, and suddenly opened his eyes,
but his fear-stricken mother seized and clasped him tight,

and the king turned his yearning eyes on his young son
to exorcise that heavy shade which choked his dreams.
Was it his dreaded father who now had come in sleep
to kidnap his belovèd son on his swift ship?
How could he guard his son, what sentries plant to keep
his father from swooping down and snatching his one child?
The young king shook but said no word, and calmed his trembling wife.

Approaching winter flecked the mountain peaks with snow,
jackals put on their heavy hair, wildcat and fox
dressed with their fattest fur upon the mountain slopes
till God shook, filled with anguish, even in the nude worm.
There is a time for earth to bloom, for fruit to knit,
a time for wintry death to blow trees, gods, and men
flat to the ground until the new wheel turn once more.
Man-loving life at evening sighs, leans on her door,
an unplowed feverish widow watching the long road:
"I've plucked the petals of my heart out one by one—
will my man come or not, will my son come or not?"
Her cellars overflow, her great hearth glows like gold,
within her sunken vaults her stooped slaves weave, unweave,
she decks her body with branched velvet, silver cloth,
but her voluptuous flesh grows withered like dry flowers
on which no sun shines and no water pours, dear God.
She smells, a long way off, the world's far realms, and weeps.
Ah, once upon a time upon this desolate road
a towering stalwart man with thick mustaches strolled;
his blond flesh smelled like a wild boar's, and on his limbs,
his thighs, his loins, his shoulders, swift ships sailed tattooed
with thickset suns, half-moons and stars, while his warm blood
leapt in his chest like a red flaming beast in rut.
But now her loved man had grown old, useless in bed,
God also had grown white and old and lay on the ground
where snakes and lizards coiled, where bats swooped at his side:
"Winter has come, grandfather, we're drowsy, let us thrust
in your dark hollows and white hair to sleep in warmth;
O, bless us now that we in time may greet the sun."
The old man heard, spread out his hands and blessed the beasts,
Odysseus also heard, and sighed, for at his feet
he felt rain fall that would revive his fathers that day.
"When it rains hard, the dead file out from earth like snails,
their white bones creak, their lips are filled with mud, they weep,
but they fall down once more in mire and sucking soil;
the dead deserve a feast day in the heart of winter—
when shall my town be built and all things take their place?"
He pondered how to bring a new uncommon scope,

beyond man's reach, to weddings, births, and even death.
Slowly the rain stopped drizzling, and the archer stooped
to smell the odor of moist earth till his mind filled
with thick and poisonous mists that brimmed with ghosts and sounds;
Rala rose suddenly in the evening's humid dusk
with her bronze flashing anklet, and her swollen lips
moved like a wound within the mist and closed again.
"Rala," her sighing leader cried with wide-flung arms,
but pelting rain began to fall, the earth grew dim,
till Rala like a hollow bubble sank in earth.
"Alas, the dead lie far too heavily on my chest,"
the archer murmured, as he clawed his wounded heart.
Deep in dark humid Tartarus, the earth ground its dead,
the sun spun on and then plunged down the foggy fields,
and the archer mutely strove to break free from the dead.
His people in God's cave began their winter's night work.
God was the only master of all, of earth and tools;
walls between souls were tumbled down, what's yours, what's mine,
all worked like brothers and like brothers shared all things.
Some built and carved out cradles, some hewed wooden yokes,
some chiseled charms for which Odysseus sketched a face
to copy out and hang round their protected throats:
a small, small dwarf filled with unsated eyes and ears,
with yearning, flaring nostrils, gaping, greedy lips,
on whose nude body mystic symbols cried aloud:
"Look, listen, smell, taste, touch all things with all your heart!"
As the resourceful planner roamed about the cave
he took delight in watching his troops work and play
till legend, rain, and God all merged within his heart
and the night work rose calmly in his mind and shone
like secret warlike eves before a battle dawns
when all the savage armor glows and flesh is honed.
All cradles shone like shields, all spindles gleamed like spears,
and the work-tools of women, fishermen, and farmers
hung in the archer's drafted mind like tools of war.
The dead had fed him poison, he could bear no more
and longed to raise all humble work to a high plane:
"Brothers, our fingertips flash fire like God's own;
when our hands touch the world, the world's face is transformed,
the stone is saved if we but pick it from the road
and wedge it in our homes or in the slingshot's cradle
or on it carve the symbols of our hearts with skill;
all seed is saved if sown with patience in the soil
for its jail opens and God sprouts like a green shoot.
Each soul holds round itself its special threshing floor
of passions, dreams, and thoughts, of mortals, beasts, and trees.

Forward, my brothers, free them and you free your souls!
If you're a worker, plow the earth, help her to bear;
if you're a soldier, throw the sharp spear ruthlessly
for it's your task to kill, though others may show pity.
God smothers in the foe, he chokes and cries out, 'Help!
O, kill this body, Son, that I may climb still further!"
If you're a woman, choose your mate with extreme care,
yoke tight the strongest man like a great ox with smiles
and tears to sow you children in your fecund womb;
the female God within you chooses him, not you!
When to your bosom you clasp a son to give him suck,
say then: 'This son is God, may he drink all my milk!' "
Thus in the deep night work the suffering man unwound
and proudly lifted high the fate of man and maid;
all souls now moved and fluttered on the chasm's lips,
his words fell whole in every heart, but each heart hatched
that mighty Word, the egg of God, in its own special way.

Midwinter, in those ten days holy to all birds,
the gulls begged God to let the sun appear, to calm
the furious winds and soothe the seas that they might find
time on some sunny stretch of shore to hatch their eggs.
The Old Man heard, smiled on the earth and sent the sun
till seashores shone with warmth of birds hatching their eggs.
When the archer saw the sun, he seized his chiseling tools
and walked about his city walls to carve new laws;
loud voices and commands tormented his dark head
until he let them loose on rock to free his mind.
Sparks flew until his tools and slabs of stone caught fire,
his beard and hair filled with blue smoke and flying chips,
but he bent low and hewed his God to bind him tight
in thick and mystic snares that he might never flee.
He carved flames, blood-drenched roads that rose in zigzag curves,
he carved trees, beasts, and hearts, a swift and slender ship,
and that small bird, frail freedom, with a wounded breast.
He chiseled ten dark slabs of rock with ten commands:
"God groans, he writhes within my heart and cries for help."
"God chokes within the ground and leaps from every grave."
"God stifles in all living things, kicks them, and soars."
"All living things to right or left are his co-fighters."
"Love wretched man at length, for he is you, my son."
"Love plants and beasts at length, for you were they, and now
they follow you in war like faithful friends and slaves."
"Love the entire earth, its waters, soil, and stones;
on these I cling to live, for I've no other steed."
"Each day deny your joys, your wealth, your victories, all."

"The greatest virtue on earth is not to become free
but to seek freedom in a ruthless, sleepless strife."
He seized the last rock then and carved an upright arrow
speeding high toward the sun with pointed thirsty beak;
the last command leapt mutely on the empty stone
to the archer's joy, as though he'd shot his soul into the sun.

They planned to inaugurate their town at the full moon
because its four wings now rose toward the sun, its thick
strong bulwarks and its massive high watchtowers.

Kentaur could not stay on the plain from his great joy
but climbed to a tall cliff and watched all seethe below;
he heard far women's laughter, children's wails and shouts,
and saw smoke hover in the tranquil evening air.
Broad-bottom's mind shook when he thought how man's seed falls
to earth and there takes shape and grows to monstrous size.
A nude much-suffering couple came to a cool spring,
bent down and tasted water, crumbled the soft soil:
"Dear wife, unload, we'll strike our roots in this good place."
Deep in the woods he raised his ax while his wife knelt,
set up her simple hearth and lit her fire there;
they hacked down trees, gathered and hewed thick cornerstones,
then hurriedly set to building their son's sacred hut.
Lizards came quietly on rocks and watched, the dog
roamed round his master's property to guard it well
and mark its boundaries on the earth with barks and growls.
Thrust in the flames between two hearthstones, God swirled high
and gazed upon all things on earth, future and past;
if he but wished, he could leap out, snatch off the roof
and swallow in one gulp the couple's sacred toil,
but out of pity he sat serenely and held his strength:
he watched the woman kneel to cook her simple food,
and he delighted to keep vigilant watch at night
and warm the two nude bodies nestling in the wilds.
Thus did man's myth begin on earth, thus do sons come
and set the bobbin whirling round with a new speed
and spin life's crimson thread to still more greater heights.
In Kentaur's mind, God, the sweet water, flames and dog,
the man, his wife, his son, were bound in a tight noose,
enwrapped in crimson thread until they gasped for breath.
"Ah, fellows, if I only knew in this strange world
for whom we wind the thread or warp the yarn, and who
sits at the loom and weaves, unweaves this strange design
with the bright woof of life and the dark warp of death!"
Tall on the cliff, he closed his eyes, shut out the town,
but it still proudly gleamed in the sun's blazing rays:
"Man's life, dear God, is but the blinking of an eye."
Then he smiled wryly, stretched until his bone-joints creaked,
and lunged down toward the glen to gather myrtle boughs
and deck the four town gates with greens so that at dawn
the town might glow within God's loving arms, a virgin bride.

Meanwhile Odysseus swiftly climbed the high watchtower
which he had raised with fir boughs on the mountain slope
that in pure solitude he might commune with God.
The air grew more ethereal, smelled of mountain musk,

and like a woman finally freed, who holds her son
tight in her arms, a high achievement toughly earned,
thus did the archer clasp his town tight in his soul.
"What is this life, dear God! How tightly merged in one
with our own souls are women, air, the light, the sea!
Ah, Earth, dear wife, might we but march eternally
each by the other's side through pelting rain and storm
till, O sweet comrade, our hearts brim with joy and pain;
to watch you in the lightning flash and place my hand
on your curved belly, your white shoulders, your warm throat!"
The lone man's full heart danced, his spreading city gleamed,
white and untouched, like a bull-calf just born that lifts
its large eyes slowly on the world for the first time.
When in his brain he'd hatched it like an egg, he had
not thought such a bright, wide-winged hawk would burst in air—
always the soul casts up high, unexpected peaks!
The archer's eyelids fluttered with great happiness:
"O my bright city, shield of God, my body's thought,
you rise on earth in three tiers like my mounting heart:
your feet are rock and clay set in huge cornerstones,
your ruthless chest is made of hewn commands of laws,
your tall peak vanishes in air like a great cry!"
A heavy heat and stifling clouds rolled down, rocks broiled,
the lead sky slowly melted in thick sweating drops
and not a single tree leaf rustled or wing moved.
Then through the thickening light the archer slowly moved
and gasped until he reached his dark ascetic hut,
and when he stooped and crossed the doorway, his eyes calmed
to gaze on his lean bow that from a column hung
and made his heart leap like a child who longs to play.
His joy so overwhelmed him that it could not stay
within his motionless hot body, cribbed, confined,
for his town glowed deep in his palm, a crimson apple.
He reached and grasped his world-renowned ancestral bow,
but as he squeezed it tight, it crumbled in his hands
and vanished as a white smoke rose in the blue light.
He scowled, shot piercing glances round, then slowly rubbed
his bow's thin bark between his flaming fingertips
and sagged against the column as his wild heart seethed;
but as he rubbed it, the new tree trunk creaked, then hung
and hovered like a white ghost, scattered in swirling smoke,
and as the roof crumbled to earth, the whole hut vanished.
His gray hair stood on end, he leapt through clouds of dust,
glared fiercely round, growled like a beast, and his jaws shook,
but mastering his dumb terror, he stopped his teeth from chattering,
steadied his dreaded spirit till his bone-joints knit,

then felt ashamed, grew bold once more and kicked the dust:
"By God, who's master here? I knock! Come out and face me!"
But as he kicked the dust dregs of his crumbled hut
he saw swarms of ash-colored ants thrust in the ground,
and his mind cleared with understanding, but his heart
hung heavy still as he took the road back, depressed.
The earth still simmered, the sun rolled in heavy blood
and the whole glimmering town was splattered with fine flame.
The windless waters of the lake boiled from their depths,
the crunch of stones was heard far off as though beasts ran,
trees suddenly creaked, then all at once remained quite still.
"Hold tight, my soul, I think earth's crust will split in two!"
Swallows flew off in flocks, but crashed in the false dusk,
ducks winged toward far-off waters with their necks outstretched,
and as the archer ran, he heard a clamorous roar.
Turning, he saw thick droves of rats dash down the rocks
from the high summit, screeching as they leapt in fright,
and laughed to see their hairy snouts trembling with fear:
"Oho, see how their gallant whiskers bristle now!"
the god-moved archer yelled, then stopped to watch his town.
Crowds swarmed the streets and decked them with fresh myrtle boughs
that God might come as bridegroom and take full possession.
For a long time he looked with pride and fainting heart:
"O city, iron castle and high tent of hope,
God, who once roamed all roads, a tramp with bloody feet,
will like a good grandfather now be walled to rock
his grandsons; and that drunken, wide-winged fantasy,
that once chased air, will fly down to your fields with wings
clipped now, and like a housewife glean her fruitful grain.
I like to grasp the mind's slow turtle in my claws
and lift it toward the sun-shot peaks of air, to God,
that it, too, may rejoice in the whole rhythmic round
for a brief flash before it sinks to its humble lot.
City, I want to hunt no longer now, I long
to bind my harehound mind to your strong virgin walls;
the time has come, my heart is full, my claws are slaked."
Sweetly his sated lips moved in the gathering dusk:
"Much does my mind plan for you, city, like a father
who feels his son stand in earth's heart with all roads open."
Then the great lord of towns stopped speaking, his heart choked,
and once more, panting, he lunged down the mountain slope,
but in the rough rocks suddenly saw a coupling pair
so clasped in the sweet giddiness of love they could
not hear his tread nor even an earthquake's heaving roar;
it seemed as though an azure smoke hung over them.
"They've both caught fire, and burn," the flame-brained archer thought.

"May God be with them, may their seed grow tall and strong!"
and then he tiptoed softly from that holy place.
At the town gate he met broad-buttocks, mounted high,
decking the town with laurel berries and myrtle boughs,
and Crete's flame-crimson castle flashed within his mind
where once broad Kentaur decked it like a votive beast;
nor did he speak for fear he'd raise the evil-omened bird.

The bride-wreathed streets and byways smelled of flowering boughs,
and noisy child-filled courtyards chirped like poplar trees
that, as the sun sets, sing with nests and fluttering wings.
In all the women's quarter, new-baked wheaten bread
swelled in the ovens and filled all hearts with fragrant scent;
a plump maid, who would soon give birth, heaved a deep sigh,
and all girls swiftly brought her bits of fresh-baked bread
that she might not untimely drop her child from greed.
A mother's crooning lullaby arose far off
and it, too, scattered everywhere in dusk like smoke:
"My son, my eagle, when with sharp birth-pangs I bore you,
why did I not sprout golden wings and soar in sun,
why was the earth not dazed to flower in winter snow,
why did the swallows not return with song, my son?
If there's a God, he lies here in my cradle now!"
The archon's proud eyes filled with tears of brimming joy:
"Give birth, increase on earth, lie in each other's arms
so that the blind ants may not eat us and choke God;
all my deep hopes now lie in you, child-bearing maid."
He murmured, then stopped in joy before a curly boy
who swaggered proudly by in the conceit of youth,
his bold eyes slashed by inexpressible deep dreams.
The young man swung by like a cock, and every lane
burst into bloom, the cobbles shone like precious stones,
the rooftops sprang with banners, young girls cast their musk,
and even the humble hungry hen plumed like a peacock;
Death held a crimson rose and waved it in his hand.
Meanwhile hot lightning bolts like snakes slid through the lake
and parrots suddenly rose in green and azure clouds,
cawed raucously and sped north past the sultry town.
"It's a good omen, lads! They passed by on the right,"
broad-bottom yelled, but all at once his thick voice choked,
feeling the man-destroyer's eyes devour him whole.
"Hold on, by God! Once more a demon mounts him, hooved
and clawed, and once again smoke swirls from his dark head,"
he groaned, then searched the woods to cut more myrtle boughs.
But the man-murderer deplored his own harsh glance
and his heart longed to brim, to clasp his friend, to say,

"Forgive me, friend, I love you, but my throat feels choked,
earth and God crush me with oppressive weight today,"
but his mind screamed in mockery till he stopped with shame.
He saw the Evening Star that throbbed in mist on high
as on the moon's dim face a moldy shadow fell
and crawled up bit by bit, covered the pallid chin,
spread past the mouth, then swiftly rushed to blind the eyes.
All light on earth had swooned away, trees shook with fright,
the birds and beasts began to screech, and wrought-up youths
shot flame-tailed arrows at the sky with reckless pride;
unmarried maidens bared their breasts, and wedded maids
lit bonfires by their doorsteps to inspirit the moon.
The suffering man watched how the leprous shadow ate
the full moon's cool refreshing face that rose with calm
till only the white brow remained like a lean scythe.
Night swooped on earth with greedy lips, stars burst to view,
and silent flashes flickered at the sky's dark rim.
"I'm stifling," a pale woman shouted, big with child,
and on her burdened belly placed her trembling hands;
the archer of the winds sighed deeply, and sped on:
"To keep your son from stifling, maid, I'd lift the lowering sky!"

He crossed the town gate hurriedly, pierced through the woods,
then raised his eyes and searched the sky with raging glance
as though a hunter had from ambush flushed his quarry.
"Each soul in its own station may save the entire war;
I'll stand here in my body's tower and fight with rage!"
But as the proud oath still rang in the warrior's brain,
a roar burst from the earth's foundations, the woods shook,
until the headstrong archer raised his fist and yelled:
"What are you bellowing for? Who do you think you're scaring?
Rise up, smash in my skull, spill on the steaming stones
this stubborn brain that made you God! Heave up your wrath!
If it were not for me—don't you forget it, fool—
the black ants, beasts, and snakes would have devoured you whole!
Rains would have fallen, rank weeds clutched and drowned you deep
in your mud-cradle even before you raised your head!
Now that I've saved and bred you like a lion, you dolt,
you open your mouth to eat me, O ungrateful wretch!"
The lone man yelled and thick smoke rolled above his head.
He lay down in the breathless woods: not a beast stirred,
the shriveled tree leaves curled and coiled in the dead hush,
his fingertips itched as with ants, his lips flashed flame,
the storm still plunged from far away and pricked his flesh,
both town and lake shore flickered in the lightning's lunge
like a black ship submerged and swiped by savage storms.

Then as his mind heaved in his skull like the tossed town,
he heard the heavy tread of feet, hot gasping breath,
turned swiftly and saw tusks that gleamed in lightning flares
till a white elephant plunged in moonlight, drenched with sweat.
On its rough nape a strapping man seemed to lie stretched,
and in a lightning's flash the archer saw a long-loved head:
he dashed, and the whole forest shook with his loud roar:
"Aye, Rocky, faithful lion, you've come in a good hour!"
The elephant stopped and blared, then cocked its flapping ears,
and Rocky fell down mutely on the archer's chest.
They flung their arms out wide and clasped each other tight
and when their joy was sated and their heads had cleared,
the eagle-battling mountain lad turned round and gasped:
"Master, I've run all day and night through woods and wilds,
nor closed my eyes, nor do I think I ate or drank,
that I might come in time to stand close by your side.
Prophetic phantoms struck me, my heart deeply roared
that on a sword's sharp edge you lay in deadly peril.
I've come to fight here at your side! We'll die together!"
The suffering man was touched, for he had never known
such pure integrity, such manliness, such love;
ah, when it turned out well, how good man's seed could be!
Odysseus clasped the curly and unconquered head
in tight embrace and stroked it long with silent love;
but hearing a deep sigh behind them, they jumped back
and saw that the groaning elephant had stretched full length
on the soft ground and dug a deep pit with its tusks.
It smelled the earth and growled, then thrust its wrinkled head
slowly into the pit with heaving gasps and groans.
Poor Rocky fell upon the beast, clung to its neck,
caressed it tenderly and spoke soft, calming words,
but its hide quivered, its eyes glazed, and its long ears
hung loosely down its bald-smooth back till all at once
it spouted water from its trunk so that the pit
became a grave of mud where the white grandfather lay
and, in expiring, slowly smeared his twitching hide,
his white back, monstrous bellies, and huge rump with mud;
slowly he settled, huddling in the pit, and sank.
Rocky caressed the huge grandfather, and burst in tears,
his hands and chest were smirched with mud, the grandson's face
rolled in the grave's foul mire, smeared with smutty death.
Odysseus watched his friend's young form and shook with rage
to feel that earth and worms already had stuffed his mouth.
"Never shall I forgive and bend down to that vain,
that senseless dark which blots the holy light of man!"
Then he thrashed out with rage against his ruthless god:

"You fool, how in your greatest need can you abandon
most glorious man who lives and fights to give you shape?
You fill our hearts with cries and vehement desires,
then sink your ears in silence and refuse to listen;
but man's soul will fight on, you coward, without your help!"
His heart leapt high, spurned Death, and in the black air cut
a thousand roads to fly through on a thousand wings,
then, screeching like a hawk, strove to unwind what fate had woven.

XVI

Three birds perched high on the day-sentry's castle tower,
one gazed far off to sea, another at the far fields,
the third and best leapt down into the bowels of man,
fluttered its crimson wings and raised its swelling throat:
"I'm not a crow that hunts for corpses on the plains,
nor a white gull that dips in the sea's waves to cool—
I am that bird who sings within a cage of flames!
Some call me God, some the great seed of crafty man,
the pallid call me Bird of Death, and their souls quake,
but I'm that still uncaught and burning bird, your heart."
Thus did the small bird sing on the day-sentry's tower;
bulls in their caverns heard and champed to break their ropes,
two camels tightly pressed their young and licked their throats,
parrots took wing, rats screeched and scurried up the slopes
to the high eagle-crags and thrust deep in the stones,
newts, lizards, scorpions, hedgehogs, huddled on the ground,
gathered their brood and goods and suddenly disappeared.
Only the herds of men were deaf, for the bird's song
could not pierce through the thick-skinned shield of their soft brains;
the young men buckled on their arms, girls combed their hair,
mothers, who'd given birth to sons, adorned their breasts,
for so the day decreed; all wreathed their throats with flowers
and set off for God's cave, their mammoth dancing ring.
When day broke and the sun-cock rose on the world's peak
and Aphrodite's star dissolved in dawn's light gently,
Odysseus grasped the mask of his god, Monarch of Men,
and tried within the cave to lash it round his head,
but it leapt like a savage bird and tried to flee.
The seven-souled man lashed it tightly thrice with thongs,
staggered, grabbed at a rock, and both his temples roared
as though an eagle dug its claws deep in his brains:
"Is this the day to eat me, fool, on your feast day?"
the suffering man yelled out, and bit his lips with rage.
A small bird heard, and sang high on the sentry tower;
never before had he heard such sweet birdsong soar,
as though the heart of man looked on his town, and wept.

At the cave's mouth, with dread suspicion, the archer cocked
his ears and heard a far sweet wail, a mocking laugh,
and the air whistled as though brushwood had caught fire:
"Keep quiet, my heart! I know, but hold on tight! Don't shout!"
Thus he advised his lion heart, but his limbs trembled.
Meanwhile the youths, lovely as girls, came swaggering up,
the young girls walked with swaying hips, alluringly,
and Kentaur's gold canary-cloak gleamed like the sun.
In the cave's darkness the two slender mountain lads
shone arm in arm, and Granite fondled his dear friend,
unslaked still with the sweetness of unhoped return.
The sun, mud-splattered, sank and drowned in murky fog,
dogs in the courtyards howled, and waves far off were heard
seething on the lake's surface, though in windless calm.
On the hot hearthstones seven votive lambs were roasted,
youths shouted for their god to come and stroll through town,
and the young girls whirled into dance till the cave flashed;
teeth gleamed, and serpent eyes bewitched the enchanted crowd,
songs leapt from mouth to mouth, caught fire and burst in blaze:
"Mother, I love the sun, earth's fragrance drives me mad!
What pride the mountains hold, dear God! They don't fear death!
What pride the unmarried hold who clasp a son in mind,
what pride the new-weds hold who clutch babes to their breasts!
Descend, male God, and in my lap I'll fetch you soon
red apples, crimson rose-tree blooms to make you blush;
I'll bring you a small cradle, also, to rock your son.
The blue sky's good, but not so lovely as the earth
that does contain both man and God, both beasts and trees,
and even my most small, most secretly pregnant heart.
Mother, I love the earth, I even love its pain!"
The young men leapt and danced apart in hoarse reply:
"Good is this earth, and good your apples, glittering girls!
We hold for you red curled carnations—come and see!—
large flasks of poison and black-hilted blades of love.
Come now, let's merge our wealth, let's barter merchandise;
earth is a gaudy fair, give me and I shall give you!"
The two wild dances merged, the dancers held hands tight,
and the young men's mustaches flicked the maidens' hair:
"Welcome to earth, come eat and kiss and drink, dear God!"
Then all fell silent and stooped low for his reply
and heard a bellowing roar that made the cavern reel;
but even before thought could break in and cleave their hearts
the lone man leapt from the thick shade with his god's mask:
"I've come and find you well on earth! I like your town!
I like the bulls you've sacrificed, I like your maids
and your lean youths who hold the earth so it won't fall.

Your earth has sprouted in my heart and spread wide roots,
and when I look at you, man is my only hope."
His words still rang in the choked air when a green flash,
glance of a wild beast, blazed through all the quaking cave,
and a bull's bellow roared in the deep bowels of earth.
The air-brained people leapt in joy because they thought
their heavy god had heard the summons of frail man,
but the archer now no longer held brain-sucking hopes
and from the cave dashed like a hound to sniff the breathless air.

Tenuous clouds of dust rose and obscured the day,
no tree leaf moved, a scorching heat-haze choked all breath,
no insect rasped, no bird sang, not a beast was heard,
only from the new-matted roofs there swayed and hung
a deep-blue smoke, banner of man the weather vane.
Like a blind thing, the soul of the night-walker touched
the lake, the trees, the dogs, questioning with groping palms,
but all drew cowering back and gazed with silent fear.
Raging, Odysseus called on all dark powers to shout
whatever dreadful news they wanted him to know.
His heart seethed and his veins deployed like worms that twined
about his body as though to gulp it down alive,
then his mind suddenly howled, smelling the dreadful news.
He choked, flung his ferocious mask across his back
and with black bursting temples rushed toward the town walls,
raised up his flaming eyes to the high mountain peak
from whence thick puffs of smoke swirled as the earth shook,
then leant against the north town gate, and his breast raged:
"Frail body, O great soul, hold firm, yield not to shame!"
A great roar burst from the earth that heaved and tossed like waves
till towering dust clouds rose and wrapped the smothered sun.
As time ran out, the hopeless man dashed down the streets;
he saw two curly-headed children play with joy,
he saw a boy and girl embraced in a dim nook
where the youth whispered sweet persuasive words of love
slowly, alas, as though he had a world of time.
Odysseus' hard heart brimmed with tears, he seized them both:
"Hurry, enjoy your bodies, join your longing lips;
dear girl, cast off all shame; my children, time runs short!"
Two old men, quarreling further on, begged him to judge,
but with his bitter lips he broke in mocking laughs:
"Go straight to Hades, fools, don't ask for justice here;
only one judge, the dread earthquake, shall part you now!"
A youthful mother stooped to suckle her dear son
and from full-slaked desire her glazed eyes rolled back,
her mouth hung open, gaping, and with prostrate hands

in the hot dusk she enjoyed her own son like a lover.
Odysseus leant against a wall to keep from falling,
then slowly and tenderly caressed the unfledged babe:
"Ah, what great pity—that soft head and those blue eyes,
that curved and milk-fed mouth, that body's tender flesh
shall not have time to ripen and rejoice in sun."
Thus did he wail, then softly spoke to the poor maid:
"Why aren't you at our city's celebration, mother?"
She laughed, and a small mole shone near her smiling lips,
she bounced her baby on her knees and kissed the mole
that gleamed near his own lips, and hung about his chest
a small bronze hand to guard him from the evil eye.
The lone man knit his knees, then pushed off from the wall,
lunged down the street, and in his heart's tumultuous depths
broke into clashing strife with his devouring god:
"If you had any shame you'd honor mankind's sweat!
This poor world issued from your hands dishonest, sick,
child of old parents, brainless, smutched, an outcast tramp,
until we came to perfect what you so badly shaped!
You shaped the boundless sea, but we the cleaving ship,
you shaped the raging river, and we the steadfast bridge,
you shaped the savage horse, and we the rein and bit.
You shaped coquetting and unbridled womankind,
that dark high-buttocked beast, and we shaped sacred love;
you let Death loose on earth—but fool, what can he do?—
we shape our sons, you murderer, and they sack his strength!
Smash us with flames and thunderbolts, we'll find some cure,
and if your blade pierce to the bone, it'll not go further!"
Thus did he mutter to himself as his heart raged,
and when he came to the dark cave he watched with grief
the dance and laughter, then glanced at his three old friends.
All three ate and caroused, wine-swept on the cliff's edge,
and on Chief Rocky's breast there still hung, like a charm,
a regal flute made of an eagle's narrow shinbone
on which he played with such sweet rapture that sad song
the old bards taught him, that he glazed the minds of men;
but seeing the soul-grabber, they leapt up confused,
for a dark heavy cloud hung smoking over his head:
"Here comes the toll-collector right in our joy's midst,"
broad-bottom groaned dejectedly, and his joy fled,
and when they stepped out of the cave, their master mocked:
"Joy to the harehounds that I called to help me hunt!
You fools, haven't your nostrils flared or your hearts quaked?
The whole world smells of sulphur, the peak belches smoke!"
All cast their eyes to the high peak, and their lips blenched:
smoke-tufts rose swirling from the pitch-black rocks as though

the kiln of earth had cracked and all the pipes had burst.
But Granite shrugged his shoulders, nor did his eyes dim:
"Welcome to Death! He's welcome, but our souls are tough!
He'll find they clutch tight to our bones and love the flesh."
But as he spoke, a hollow thundering made them reel
and as all four clutched at each other to keep from falling,
the man of seven souls laughed low and fiercely growled:
"Ho, that's how he replies to weak man's holy mind!"
But Rocky manfully opposed his master's wrath:
"We'll give that coward much more than we shall take, my friends,
stiff spite for stubborn spite, and if we're now to die
we'll sink into the ground bolt upright, fully armed!"
The suffering man caressed his comrade's haughty head:
"Well spoken, gallant youth! If earth should gape to gulp us,
we'll sink erect in the whirlpool! We want no other joy!
Forward! Let's share between us the roads where Death will pass:
I'll swiftly take the cave to soothe the frantic crowd
then marshal all, that no one may get lost in storm,
and march them out in light to fight Death in closed ranks.
Kentaur, take women and small children for your share
and swiftly open a straight road to the north at once,
for yesterday I saw that beasts were rushing northward.
Granite, keep a stern rearguard watch with your brave youths
and gather what you can of goods, of beasts, of food.
I've placed all hope in the seed of death-grappling man!
Rocky, stand sleepless guard high on the north town gate
and with your vigilant conch give notice what safe roads
to take, whether toward the low woods or the high peaks;
watch the whole round arena, set us on our true course.
Forgive me, Rocky, for giving you now the heaviest task:
Do you recall I promised on the shores of Crete
I'd not forget you, but would take your soul one day?
The time has come for you to show your pride and breed."
Rocky's heart pounded and his temples pulsed to feel
that bright immortal wreath, Death's fresh green laurel bough:
"Master, from you I've always longed for one great joy:
that you would ask me for much more than I could give."
Thus they spoke manfully and shared Death longingly
while the tempestuous smoke spread like a monstrous pine
and swelled in storming waves until it wrapped the sun.
The mountain thundered, flaming columns leapt on high,
and suddenly thick hot drops of mud began to fall.
The comrades felt that their last day on earth had come,
and the four clasped each other tight without a word
as from the burning darkness Kentaur's groans were heard;

but first to break away was the lone man who tossed
his head as each one took his destined way with no look back.

As they ran on, the darkness thickened, crisscrossed stones
whizzed through the air like hail in flaming, burning lumps.
Then the great wailing burst, earth's bowels shook and roared,
and mothers with their babes fell shrieking to the ground;
young girls held their adornments to their breasts, and ran,
and children stifled with their toys clutched in their arms.
In green-blue lightning flares, herds of stampeding men
blazed briefly and then plunged to dark in the striped night;
at times amid the women Kentaur's body gleamed,
at times gaunt Granite's body glowed as he rushed swiftly
to lead the young men north or kick old men aside,
and sometimes Rocky's voice was heard choked in the din.
The rent earth shook and staggered as Odysseus dashed
to find the children's nursery home and save the young;
his features swirled in smoke and his gray beard was singed.
Suddenly boiling waters streamed on the town from high,
the cavern heaved and burst, the dead leapt from their graves,
and the archer, too, leapt in the azure flames and dashed
toward the ruined threshold of the children's shaking home.
In his wide arms he snatched the young boys, two by two,
and flung them in the street, then called splayfoot to come
at once with speed and herd the children swiftly north.
But that pure animal would not budge or leave his side:
"The earth sinks! I won't leave you to face Death alone!"
He spoke, then rushed to seize his master's arms by force,
but the archer reached his hands and pushed him back with rage.
Kentaur's eyes brimmed with tears, he opened his arms wide,
but the earth shook again and cracked, the lintel bulged,
and rocks hung hovering loosely above the archer's head.
At once broad Kentaur stooped and placed his monstrous back
like a broad column beneath the trembling cornerstones.
The man of seven souls growled like a tiger and sprang
clear to the street, but when he turned to find his friend
in the thick dark, he heard the creaking lintel crash,
and a bull's bellow roared amid the tumbling stones.
"Flare up, O lightning flame, that I may see my friend!"
the archer roared, and dashed into the smoking ruins.
As the flames' zigzag slashed like a red snake on earth,
it lit up Kentaur's dreadful and most guileless head
in scattered fragments on the stone, sinking in mud.
Odysseus dashed without a word but gripped his mouth
to keep his jaws from chattering, then fixed bulging eyes,

dry and unmoving, on the splattered, steaming brains,
and as he looked, his hair turned white in the grim dark.
He drew back, walked earth heavily, and in the ruins
heard women groaning with their babes, calling on God.
A mother stood erect, her son clutched tight, and screamed;
first her black hair caught fire, then her clothes blazed up,
until she stood erect, an upright torch that fired the road.

At break of day the town sank, and the mountain's mouth
closed tight and swallowed its full-sated tongues of flame;

the sun shone laughingly upon the flaming clouds,
and light spread like a rose upon the ruined land.
A mother sat upon a tree's scorched root and clutched
her son, burnt to a cinder; round his neck still hung
a small bronze hand, thrice-holy charm against the evil eye.
She slowly rocked her son and cursed in lamentation:
"Foul God, may you be damned by all my twenty nails,
may beasts devour you in the woods, worms in the fields,
and may not one warm heart be found to give you shelter!
May you be cursed, foul God, who burnt my only son!"
Amid the wretched crowd that groaned and staggered by,
pale Granite mingled with scorched hair, and with great pain
caressed the men's and women's hair and their burnt backs,
struggling to give their quivering breasts new heart again:
"By God, if only two were saved on earth, a man
and maid, they'd fill the earth with sons and daughters soon!
God shouts, and we too shout until one shouts no more!"
A youth, who yesterday had seen his sweetheart burned,
jumped up with wrath and cursed the sky to ease his pain:
"May you rot, foul old man, may evil Death engulf you!"
But useless curses now were not to Granite's liking:
"Friend, I believe in man; whatever on this foul earth
resists us, I'll call God, and fight him to the end!
But onward, lads! I hate superfluous words! They're cheap!
Northward in wealthy Africa a new road cleaves;
we'll plant man's virtue there in a new plot of ground;
the past is finished, gone, my mind's forgot it all,
I see new seed before me and a new race of men."
He spoke, and once again their shriveled hearts grew bold.
They took the dark road forward, their sharp pain grew numb,
and the mind soothed the heart with all its ancient tricks.
Dear God, don't give man's soul all it can truly bear!
But Granite's soul stood upright and disdained to die;
that biting dog, his memory, snarled within his heart
nor would adapt, nor would forgive, nor shut its eyes.
Night fell; they lit a string of fires and slept in woods,
but haughty Granite could not close an eye in sleep
for his three friends stood mutely on his heart's abyss.
He mumbled as his eyes glowed wildly by the fire:
"It's not for you I seethe, master; I know you'll cut
a cunning tunnel through all ruins and then emerge
astride black Charon with your pointed cap held high;
I shake for fear the flames have eaten Kentaur's body.
Rocky, you stood erect on ramparts, zoned by flames,
you blew your vigilant conch to set us our true course,
but when with tears I begged you to descend for fear

the town wall should crash down and crush you, ah, dear friend,
you sadly shook your head and waved a bold farewell."
Then his eyes welled, and since he could not bear his pain,
jumped up at midnight, faced the leaping seething stars,
and sped on winged feet southward, cutting through the woods.
Forlorn and secret hopes blew through his mind and sailed:
perhaps he'd meet his friend's firm body on the road
and both would cry with joy till the world bloomed again:
"Friend, I don't care now if a thousand towns should fall;
we'll place our staffs upon our shoulders and set out
like shepherds who have lost their sheep and search the slopes
yet play their pipes unruffled. Farms and flocks are good,
I know, but friendship is greater still and conquers all."
Thus did poor Granite speak with his wind-battered mind
and passed through the dark wood until at dawn he saw
the waters of the lake shine calmly like red roses.
The waves played on the pebbles with a rustling swish,
vultures in flocks like heavy sheep hopped on the crags
and crows with sated bellies strolled and preened like haughty lords.

Granite searched for the town, but no town could be seen;
he bit his lips until his blood ran bubbling out,
and as he stood mute on the chasm's rim and saw
the north town gate still standing upright, black and scorched,
a heavy groan of indignation shook his breast:
"From now on Death and God are one! May they be cursed!"
God seemed to him a crocodile in the sea's midst
that shuts its cunning black eyes and pretends to sleep;
then brainless man takes courage, climbs its scaly back,
grabs trowel, clay, and stone and builds his tall dream-town,
then couples on the savage scales and fills his cradles;
but when the brainless monster suddenly flicks its back,
all, souls and rocks and swaddling clothes, roll in the waves.
Gaunt Granite stuttered, and his feet grew numb with fear
as though they trod upon a crocodile's rough scales.
Stepping with care on the rim's edge, he sank in mud
still warm, then reached the town gate at the chasm's lip
and there, as he revived his loved friend in his heart,
and felt the world once more rebuilt within his breast,
he heard slow steps behind him, a faint crunch on stones,
and without turning guessed it was the long-lived man.
A fierce spite wrung his lips—somehow he knew that only
this cunning man still lived, that Rocky was now dead.
He turned his eyes and saw a ghostly shadow fall
on the burnt, tumbled rubble and mount the scattered stones,
but no tall cap or lion's skull encased its head—

its hair seemed like long wings that beat the fluttering air.
As it approached and stood still by the castle gate
a choked cry split gaunt Granite's breast in two,
for curly beard and hair and mustache waved pure white,
and two grooves, like sword cuts, were gouged on its dark brow.
It held a stout staff tied with a long pointed stone
and lashed with fury on a heavy column made of earth
that like a man stood upright by the creneled wall.
It struck and struck again, biting its bloody lips;
Granite wished to cry out, but fearing the wild eyes
and the white ghostly hair, looked on with speechless dread.
The column peeled and tilted, its soil slowly crumbled,
and as the lone man like a famished jackal growled,
a bronze shield suddenly gleamed as a man's slender corpse
came slowly into view, burnt to a pitch-black cinder,
its shield upon its shoulder, holding its spear erect,
biting the sea-conch still between its tight-clenched teeth.
Granite drew back, then groaned and fell in a dead faint;
yet the lone man heard nothing and rushed to clasp the corpse,
but as he stretched his hands, the cinderous body fell
in heaps of bones and ashes at the white ghost's feet.
Then the much-suffering man drew back and clutched his throat,
his bloodshot eyes bulged from their sockets, dull and glazed,
as though he gave the world his last farewell, but then
with his right foot he suddenly kicked the sooty bones
down the black chasm, and with his burnt feet swiftly smoothed
a wide arena about the ruined ground and stood
proudly erect, flapping his naked arms like wings.
For a long time he gazed on the sun's East, then turned,
gazed West, and groaning turned once more, gazed North and South,
the while his head remained the hub of four wild winds.
He sat down cross-legged on the clay, then crossed
his hands, and his white hair like dandelion fluff
was plucked and swept in silence in the sun and wind.
Granite took courage, swiftly crossed the sooty mud,
but as he reached the white-haired mind, he stooped and yearned
to shout the choked cry in his heart: "Great Captain, rise!
The earth is good, don't leave her now, take up your arms,
become your people's guide once more and cleave new roads!"
These words surged up and hung on Granite's trembling lips
but his voice choked in his tight throat, he staggered back,
for the lone man turned slowly, speared him with dark eyes
as his mind marched beyond all sorrow, joy, or love
—desolate, lone, without a god—and followed there
deep secret cries that passed beyond even hope or freedom.
Granite drew back in silence; as he crossed the ruins

his blood beat in his brows as though his heart had burst;
he took the road to knead his troop once more like yeast
and raise a new town somewhere that the seed of man might live.

Untamed Odysseus then raised his head high and hung
above the chasm and sank into the terror of thought.
The contours of his brain glittered like mountain peaks,
the whole earth shone, the darkness like a spool unwound,
his eyes sank inward, his white head swayed sluggishly,
his soul cut cleanly from the worm, became all silk,
and slowly wove its fine cocoon in the empty air.
As the fierce sun grew dim, his memory grew more sweet,
leopards passed by like sighs, and the world's holy myth
like an enchanted prince was drowned in the swift stream.
The inner rose burst into bloom and sucked his heart,
his mind grew light, and the starved flesh turned into spirit;
light formed a scorching ring about him, the woods shook,
as in the center, moveless, hopeless, the archer crouched;
the woods wrapped round him like green flesh, his mind flung leaves;
when dewdrops gleamed on boughs, Odysseus also gleamed,
for his whole body in the dewdrops swam and glowed.
Ants scurried in thick swarms with insects, eggs, and seed,
and he too strove and fetched and hid his treasures deep;
he watched snakes coil and sun themselves on stones and knew
the sleep of poisonous snakes was holy as a child's;
he fondled grass as though it were a loved one's hair,
his snake-mind gently slid and coiled on warming stones,
and in that nestling sweetness he heard words of love:
"A white black-headed worm deep in the forest bores
through a sweet apple, and I crouch on stones and wail
because a white black-headed worm gnaws at my brain.
In damp tree-hollows coupling scorpions, newly wed,
keep motionless, nor eat nor drink, dizzy with lust;
the males watch death approaching in the females' eyes,
the females watch small scorpions playing in male eyes,
and ah, deep down, both in their male and female orbs
I watch my own face fill with death and deathlessness."
He pressed his ear to earth and heard the small seeds toil
flat on their backs, fighting the soil courageously,
thrusting through stifling stones, groaning for life and freedom.
"I am a small seed, too! I strive to lift the earth!
I hear the roots of trees grope mutely in the dark
like long blind worms that softly suck, I hear my veins
spill on the ground and suckle softly too, I hear
the birds of air, I hear the insects of the earth
opening their wings in close embrace, and my head gapes

that all might enter, warm their eggs, and hatch them soon.
Now the great forest sups and clacks its tongue with greed,
varied sweet fruit perch on its palate, slowly melt,
and on its bitter lips bees drip their pure wild honey."
Far off a pomegranate softly burst and flung its fruit
and the archer's breast was filled with pomegranate seed.
His nostrils quivered as he smelled deeply in woods
fragrance of rotted leaves, waters, and steaming soil,
white hidden jasmine sprays that blossomed in dark wells,
until the great ascetic's eyes brimmed full of tears

and his brains smelled of laurel, thyme, and golden furze,
his fingers dripped with the thick musk of too much love.
Though motionless, he grabbed with greed at the whole grove,
his body cooled, his palms were filled with herbs and plants,
and round his neck a spiraling ivy slowly curled.
His flowing feet like rivers ran, his chest flung grass,
and like hushed pools of jet-black water his eyes gleamed
behind the morning-glory blooms that twined his beard.
He turned his head right, and the forest, too, turned right,
he turned his head left, and the forest, too, turned left,
he yelled "I!" in his heart, and the whole forest quivered.
For the first time he felt he lived and had a soul.
Odysseus brimmed with waters, trees, fruit, beasts, and snakes
and all trees, waters, beasts and fruit brimmed with Odysseus.

As days and nights plucked off their hours like daisy petals,
Odysseus questioned all like a great lover in pain
and then rejoiced in their reply, in the great "Yes!"
One morning as his body glowed rose-red in sun,
and all his senses, his five bronze-etched weapons, shone,
he fondled his lean sides, his loins, his armored head,
and his hide shuddered to recall all it had borne
and joyed in—suns, rain, sea-drift, women, wounds—until
he suddenly felt a tender love for his maligned,
most faithful body, raised his hands and blessed it wholly,
beginning with its black and much-experienced eyes:
"O eyes, sheer magic crystals, the mind's fiery tears,
O sun-washed flowers of the soil's most high desire,
you saw and yet escaped all gaudy partridge snares
earth offers, slowly fondled all rich colors, joyed
in all the games which the bright spider webs of flesh
spin on the earth with skill; you saw strange seas and men,
fluttered like butterflies on all earth's varied blooms
and slowly sipped their honey, sucked their poisoned drops.
Now like an eaglet you perch high on the mind's crags
till earth seems much too narrow, outer wealth too poor,
and you turn back to inner jungles, O orbed flame!
My dear unslaked, unsated eyes, may you be blessed!
And you, shells of a secret beach, cast on the sands
of our resounding world by mystic swirling storms,
O ears, O serpent spirals, caves of the rattler's peal
of many copper bells, remember how you reared
upright like savage flame to hear what the world rang!
Ah, sweet, sweet sounds reposing to the wagtail flesh,
battle cries, wails of slaughter, and in holy dawn
the cool and dizzy twittering on the topmost boughs!

When we remained alone and all sounds huddled low,
O, how you trembled, downy ears, and heard the hush
as of wings' distant rustling or a bowstring's twang,
and stretched along the earth full length to hear far off
the slow and stealthy footsteps of your great foe, Death.
My dear unslaked, unsated shells, may you be blessed!
And you, O flowering wound, carnation-curled and crisp,
O crimson lips that kissed—and still the kiss remains—
intoxicating honey, fuzzy peach and mellow wine,
how much I love you that with myriad veins and thin
transparent skin kissed all the world full on the mouth.
How ardently in all this world you tasted fruit,
dark bread and meat, the five-times dizzying wine, and cast
them down your funneling entrails to become pure spirit!
Then pallid woman rose and in great hunger pressed
her strong and lickerish lips on yours till both your mouths
became one honeyed fruit—you ate and longed for more!
My dear unslaked, unsated lips, may you be blessed!
And you, my rabbit, sniffing at the ghostly air,
coming and going, sleepless, silent, at your master's door,
taking your choice of smells, betraying the foul stench—
thank you for such great pleasure in this odorous world.
Ah, heavy-scented flowers I've smelled, brine of the sea,
earth's breathing after rain, the sour scent of sweat
from the deep armpits of friends who row in sun together,
and the sweet milky fragrance of a woman's breasts!
Neither the ears nor eyes, not even the full lips,
can pierce the heart of mystery with such nakedness.
Smell, you're a thick memory—when you wake, dear God,
you plunge down silently and plunder the head's castle.
To you the world's a lump of musk to sniff and probe!
My dear unslaked, unsated nose, may you be blessed!
Blind mother, with your fingertips' unnumbered eyes,
O deaf, mute nurse, who grope your grandson, the rough world,
I stoop and shudder when I feel your greedy hands
fumbling my feet and chest slowly both day and night,
squeezing against my throat until you reach my brain!
Before eyes, ears, or nose were born, or the head bloomed,
you crawled on damp creation with your myriad feet
and touched all things your body's length, merged with the soul,
while all things yet unborn seethed in your brimming belly!
The flesh filled with your gifts so that for centuries
nude feet rejoiced to walk on the coarse sands or climb
the plunging mountain crags or tender meadow lawns.
And when I plunged deep in the sea or the sun's blaze,
how my dark body bloomed in all its million pores!

What do I want with the mind's hollow satisfactions,
why should I seek gods in the clouds, grandsons on earth?
O thick wide net that spreads throughout the sensual skin,
O baited fishing line with your unnumbered hooks,
keep well, plunge in the sea, we need no other joy!
Mother, you know I love you, for I'm not pure soul
but filled with sucking pores like you, with flesh, like you.
My dear unslaked, unsated touch, may you be blessed!"
When the mind-battler had finished blessing his five senses
he sank in the deep joy of silence, and his eyes
turned inward like smooth mammoth boulders in the ocean's depths.

As in the evening's buoyant breeze there lightly sails
the jasmine's stifling and seductive scent, so does
the fragrance of sweet holiness come winging by.
It flies past harbor waters, spreads along the plains
where the old plowman breathes it till his whole life steams
like stagnant pools of leeches, and he sadly sighs,
forgets to unyoke his oxen, drops his plow at once
and slowly takes the road to follow the sweet scent.
A pallid woman stood and leant against her door,
turned her face southward, sniffed, and her mind seethed:
"A great ascetic must have come, for the woods smell
with heavy musk like a strong rutting beast in spring:
I'll fill my bucket to the brim with milk and honey,
a goodly gift, then kneel before that mystic lion
and be made worthy of his grace to bear a son."
The scent spread on the waves and struck a fisherman:
"How the deceiving earth smells, lads, God curse her hide!
A fragrance strikes as of musk-deer or a maid's thighs;
a great ascetic has come and changed the taste of air!
Row quick, let's come in time to exchange our merchandise—
he'll give us blessings, we a pan of mullet fried;
it's best to keep on the good side of hidden demons."
Thus spoke the cunning fisher as his oars flung foam.
An orphan girl sat silent in her desolate yard,
shucking gold ears of corn, but her mind drifted far
to her dead parents' bodies not yet decomposed,
and her sad bosom tingled, by the grave's soil spattered.
She suddenly raised her head, and her wide nostrils flared:
dear God, how the aroused air smelled of her betrothed!
Her apron brimming with the flaming seeds of corn,
the young girl rose, half opened the door, and like a hound
sniffed in the air for traces of the strong erotic deer.

Thus many souls set out, bearing their votive gifts,
and the alluring lone man sat on stone, unmoving;
soft moss crept up his feet, grass sprang from his green sides,
and his white hair and beard gleamed like snow-covered shrubs.
A slender cypress tree, the mighty athlete struck
deep roots in earth and ate up mountains, rose to heights
in the empty air with no branch, flower, fruit, or shade.
Only the five swords of his flesh swayed in the hush
and clashed in disembodied strife and stubbornness
to push at length beyond their fate and burst in wings.
One night an erring nightingale perched on his head,
and as with throat raised high it warbled its sweet song
the windswept man could bear no more and softly wept,
for, ah, a small bird's caroling unwound his heart;
and as he listened to the bird sing to the wind
his sentry mind forgot and left its gate wide open
so that Telemachus, well nourished, sweet, appeared
and clasped his own dear child, and thus began to scold:
"When, Father, will your heart grow sweet and satisfied?
Man's feet were first created but to walk the earth,
his hands to pull the oarblades or to grasp the hoe;
God did not make men wings, Father, to cut the air;
but you strive to surpass man's holy measurement
and turn your hands and feet to wings till the earth flares
and fades like lightning bolts in your inhuman brain.
At times like scorpions you spout flames in burning hearths,
at times you freeze up like a winter snake, but never
rejoice in the serene and sacred warmth of man."
As his son scolded, in his wretched crown there rose
his world's far memories like huge dappled butterflies;
the somber brain-filled elders of his island came,
and all his musk-grapes, his ripe figs, his straight-prowed ships,
his dulcet flute held by his mountain shepherd lad,
till his brains filled with women's laughter and female clogs.
The great ascetic watched his longing's flimsy veil
wave lightly above his head in streams of varied hue
while like the spider's subtle web his memories stitched
the air, then gleamed and beckoned like alluring sirens.
The dead rose from their graves on distant shores, and fought;
fair women rose within their caves, unbound their hair,
and their small breasts leapt like twin flaming lion cubs.
Fond memory with her curly belly rose from waves
like a much-traveled leprous mermaid at the prow
and beckoned with salt-eaten hands for a long time.
The lone man laughed, but when the sentry in his head

leapt up, desire vanished like fine azure smoke;
he kicked the earth and called upon his first forebear:
"Aye, great forefather, bottomless heart, O hopeless need,
climb up on earth, look proudly on your freed grandson.
We're saved, we have no castle now, we have no tent,
our soul has not a place to stand, the heart is pierced
and drained, nor does the mind know where to lay its head.
Ah, grandsire, I've surpassed your pride: you thirst because
you've never drunk, hunger because you've never eaten,
but hunger itself has sated me and thirst unslaked me."
He spoke, then once more turned his black eyes inwardly
until his head began to rise and swell like yeasted bread.

In dark or flaming flashes, days and nights passed by,
his old life like a rotted hull sank in his eyes
and his stout body writhed to change its withered flesh;
even the stones groaned "Ah!" and "Ah!" and strove to blossom.
The bright arena in his head spread far and wide,
and his thoughts widened, spilled, and flooded all the fields;
in his mind's furrows, towns were sown and sprang like nude
tall women who with bites and kisses, fears and tears,
surrendered wholly to a man's caressing hands.
Men rose up swiftly on the earth like swarms of ants,
labored and laughed, wept, kissed, then once again plunged down
swiftly into the earth and sowed their heads in furrows.
All, in earth's brief green lightning flash, run toward the grave.
Our faces dart like wings and gleam in the bright sun,
mothers most gently watch their daughters raise their necks
and try to see their sons behind a man's broad back.
All without pity fix their bright eyes straight ahead
and run to catch the sweet red apple of the world,
but the pit suddenly yawns and the holy apple falls.
Man rises from the soil like the luxuriant grass
then sinks in soil once more like grass, and earth grows fat
munching with greedy haste her children's well-fed corpses.
We sail upon a roaring, black, tempestuous sea,
and we've entrusted, lads, our parents and our sons
to a small flimsy walnut-shell that sinks us all!
The waves are thick black drops of blood which loom and fall,
foam glitters on their crests a moment, then disappears,
only the sound of slashed and gurgling throats is heard.
The great ascetic cocked his ears and stooped to hear
a buzzing whir that rose from soils black, white, and red.
Earth spread around him, an enormous threshing floor,
where men like nude worms crawled and worked their greedy jaws

while he leant over them and slowly fed them full:
"Eat on," he thought, "eat on, pass through your cycle, worms,
then sprout with wings like souls to free yourselves, and flee!"
He clasped life like a maid and tenderly caressed her,
he held earth's children to his breast and gave them suck,
he laughed and wailed like a small infant in its cradle,
he was earth's father, mother, son, and her beloved.
When the sun rose, the gates of mankind opened wide,
crews swarmed upon their ships and workers filled the fields;
when the sun sank, the gates of mankind shut down tight
and human brains sank in the Tartarus of their dreams;
his bare breast shut and opened like swift silent gates.
A maiden sat by her broad loom and sped her shuttle;
fragrance of curly basil filled her window sill,
cool water-jugs stood in their niches, towels hung
on walls, and her black-kerchiefed mother scanned the fields
for herbs, but the maid stayed at home and sped her shuttle
because grief for a shepherd boy gnawed at her heart.
The speeding whistling of the reel, the pedal's beat,
the slender maiden's song, passed by far fields and streams
and struck tall men in taverns, lads on distant farms,
then struck a rustic shepherd boy who played his flute:
"Dear God, was that the nightingale? Did the world sigh?
Or did the maiden raise her throat to sing of love?"
Then the young shepherd turned, looked at the window sill,
looked at the curly basil, and his heart caught fire;
the great ascetic also turned to look, and smiled,
for the slim warbling maid, the youth who played his flute,
nestled within his mind like two twin-pitted almonds.
But soon he frowned severely and bit his lips. Black news!
Dread war broke out, doors clanged, and married couples clasped
each other tight as though they'd never part; far off
bronze weapons glittered on the mountains, fields turned red,
Death sat enthroned on his black steed and from his head
thick blood dripped down and plucked-out hair and gouged-out eyes.
Night fell and the full pallid moon rose in the sky,
the wounded groaned amid the fragrance of cut hay,
black buzzards heard them, swooped and ate, and the groans ceased.
Slowly in the moon's sweetness the mind-archer's brows
and his tempestuous eyebrows straightened and grew calm.
In his right hand he held a city high that burst
like pomegranates filled with seed, or a sweet beehive;
his head turned right, and the whole city, too, turned right,
his head turned left, and the whole city, too, turned left,
he shouted "I!" to himself and the whole city yelled

as though it now first felt it lived and had a soul.
Odysseus brimmed with warriors, lovers, women, lands,
and armies, castles, women, men, brimmed with Odysseus.

The archer walked the cliffs of his precipitous mind,
and Negro heralds rose and stalked among the glens:
"A great ascetic has come and sanctifies our forests!
Forward, let all with bodily pains, the deaf, the blind,
the halt, come with their brimming gifts! All shall be cured!
Let those whose souls hide secret sins come with their crimes,
let them confess them to his grace, and their pains will scatter.
The holy herb comes dear, my lads—first come, first healed!"
Such glad news shook the country like an earthquake's blast,
the straw huts trembled with the clash and bang of doors,
cripples hopped down the roads, the sterile women screamed,
some tried hard to withstand the spell and clung to trees,
but a bewitching power drew them and they stumbled on
like drunkards sucked down in the great ascetic's gyre.
Snakes slithered close and sunned themselves on his stone knees,
snails strung themselves in slimy neckrings round his throat,
a pair of swallows by mistake built their first nest
within his tangled thorny hair, and all life twined
like a wild honeysuckle round his star-scorched body.
As the days passed and pilgrims came with gifts in hand
and fell down prostrate at his feet, the deep dark eyes,
the black wells of the mute ascetic swallowed all.
The first to come was an obese and grease-smeared whore
whose savage nails and crinkly hair dripped fragrant musk.
A black, flame-scorched wild pear tree raised its sooty arms
like a maimed maiden above the ascetic's reverent head,
and there on a dry branch the whore, with twitching ass,
hung a gold heart for votive gift, and hoarsely cried:
"O great ascetic, pity me! Last night I found
the first white cursèd hair among my crow-black locks;
ah, raise your hand, chase it away, or it will wreck me!"
The brooding lone man gazed on her, earth gently quaked,
and the fat startled whore tripped assward in the shade.
Next came a sighing hermit perched on green fir boughs,
a hunchbacked fistful, borne by two stooped men who fetched
and placed him gently at the archer's placid feet.
The seedy hermit's whining, wheedling voice was heard:
"Ah, my dear brother, God's black blaze has burned me, too.
I've not known any joys, I've never yet touched woman,
I've never laughed, I've never traveled or got drunk,
that I might die full worthy of the immortal crown.
We'll go to heaven together, brother, arm in arm!"

But the archer burst in laughter and with his hard heels
sent the poor hermit tumbling in the dirt and soot.
A king appeared then, wearing earrings of wrought gold,
followed by a great troop of men and chattering women
who in their black fists held thick lumps of kneaded mud
fetched from their yards and family graves, mixed thoroughly
with their salt tears, their murky sweat, and their warm blood.
These they heaped high about the ascetic's holy feet
and the king bowed in worship in the bloodstained tracks:
"Ah, save my people! They bring their tears, their sweat, their blood
kneaded at night to dark dough with our sacred soil;
life is most heavy, death most heavy, the world's a trap—
shape us a god that we might bear the wild waste's road!"
The sun-mind placed a heavy hand on the black mud:
"I pity man, whom the great winds will sweep away;
what skills the wretch has thought of to withstand grim Death!"
he thought, and set his mind adrift on deep dark waters.
Meanwhile the trembling peasants hung their votive gifts
on the wild pear until the shriveled branches bloomed
with oxen of thin metal, and feet, hands, heads of clay.
The pilgrims' stench reached to far-distant villages,
gardeners smelled the profits and set out and beached
on the lake's sandy shore in boats piled high with food.
Tumblers and jugglers with their gear and monkey tricks,
minstrels with their resounding chords and lilting lyres
sniffed from afar and ran to grab whatever they could—
even a swig of wine or bite of meat would do!
The lone man gazed unmoving, then with feverish hands
grabbed the dark lumps of mud and warmed them in his palms;
he felt the futile efforts, the black bitter toil
of man's dark fate on earth, and his heart swelled with grief;
at times he rang with laughter till the branches broke,
at times his tears swirled round him like a rainbow's arch.
One dawn a whirlwind swept within his brimming heart,
his blood surged through his veins in cycles, his mind seethed,
and his arms spun like wheels to plunder the dark clay.
His hands could not keep up with his swift mind, the mud
whistled like flames with maddening faces, monstrous forms.
This was no longer mud or flame, no longer woman
who groaned beneath the pummeling, merged with the male mind—
thus in the first damp dark must God have seized the clay
and cast it full of fertile seed to shape a mother.
In the sun's blaze, the ascetic dressed, undressed the earth,
his mind burned, his hands whirled, his body poured with sweat,
and his swift eyes were swept by wild intoxication;
thoughts dug deep furrows in his wide and flaming brows.

The herds of men crouched trembling, and at times discerned
huge monsters hurtling through the clay, or now and then
caught glimpses of dark bristling backs or bloodstained gaping jaws.

The wings of day sped by like flaming lightning bolts,
the lone man's temples creaked, his thoughts spread far and wide,
his memory grew more savage, leapt on birds, seized beasts,
and as he barked and bellowed, sang and hissed on stones,
his mighty mind, that ancient river, rose from mud,
a guileless grandsire whose beard streamed through fields and farms.
The lone man smiled and felt a tickling as eggs hatched
within his bushy hair in spring and mothers chirped;
the fledgling swallows in the eaves of his white head
hopped but hung trembling, fearful of his plunging cliffs.
Shutting his eyes, he listened to his blood course deep,
and as Earth rose within his mind, he shook to see
an endless worm that thrashed its body in the sun;
Earth then recalled her sufferings, her deep memory swelled,
she looked back fiercely and relived the dreadful trek.
Cries scorched her as she stumbled in the desert, screaming,
but soon the conflagrations mellowed, her womb cooled,
rocks softly crumbled, and her bowels slowly yawned
and sprouted a moist quivering blade of greenest grass.
When the grass tasted light, it wailed like a small child
and called the world's four nurses quick to suckle it:
first Mother Earth, then sun, then rain, then the air's breasts.
The great ascetic plunged his eyes in inner wealth,
followed his entrails' roots, bent down and then recalled
how arm in arm with Mother Earth he once had climbed
the dark ascent, passed flames, trees, beasts, until both took
from the mind's tiny light-well one small drop of air.
Earth's last-born son with sweetness opened his eyes wide,
the herds of men grew weary, their eyes glazed, and all
rolled huddling down to earth and merged with mud and dung.
Like the full silent moon who with great hauteur casts
her beams on sleeping earth, thus the sage man kept vigil
with mute, self-lighted head erect in the thick darkness.
One day at dawn a naked Negro boy crawled close;
his teeth gleamed by the cliff, his palms emitted musk,
he slid like a snake on his black belly and hissed on stones:
"Alas, your flesh is leprous now, your body is bone,
your shanks are cricket-thin, your belly is like a frog's,
your bones hang down in splinters like an unroofed hut!
Even the still unbowed high castle of your head
rattles like a sapped beehive rotting in the rain.
Beetles have taken you for dung, and the horned owl

for an old hollow trunk; storks, grosbeaks, hoopoe, cranes
have plucked your white beard to its roots to build their nests.
You've coughed all winter long, or like a turtle wheezed,
all summer long you've huddled on the stones and hissed,
and now you sit here hungry while your giddy mind
with eagle glance sees the unseen, grips in its claws
all souls, but cannot see that your great bow has crumbled."
Then the mind-battler raged and bellowed like a beast,
but the black dwarf laughed loud and stretched his gleaming neck:
"What a great crime, lone man, that in your troubled cares
and pains you still can't quell your pride and wrath.
You hold the sky and earth in your sharp claws, but still
you can't choke down that most sweet, most great foe, the Archer!"
Hissing, the black snake flicked and thrust deep in the ground.
The proud ascetic's face grew clouded with dark shame:
"This sharp seductive voice rose from the earth to mock me;
I see a final superhuman struggle shine
deep in my mind," the lone man murmured sadly, drenched with sweat.

A cuckoo perched on a dry branch and scanned the fields,
and then before a cock could crow or the day smile,
within the lone man's lightless bowels a huge eye
sprang like a sun and watched him, hopeless, calm, and stern,
till the mind-archer leapt and spoke with quaking fear:
"Who are you? When you look at me I feel ashamed!"
He heard a voice deep in the curved leaves of his heart:
"I am that eye, that vigilant beast that stalks your mind;
whether you will or not, I stalk you ruthlessly
in your salvation, vice, your shame, your gallant deeds."
The lone man leapt with indignation, his mind flared:
"I'm made of spirit, fire, earth, and air, I rack
myself in these wild wastes, I want no eye to watch me!"
"But I don't ask you. I mount your mind and gallop on!
It's only I who live and rule—you're but a toy,
a glowworm crawling on damp earth with fading light."
"Who are you? My heart throbs and flutters painfully."
"Do you still ask, lone man? We've lived together long."
The sad yet mocking voice then faded from his heart.
O flaming Eye of tigress Life that shines in darkness!
Then the mind-traveled man leant on the wild pear's trunk;
the pilgrims still lay, wearied, on the ground about him,
and in the shedding petals of dawn's rose he saw
his whole life like a legend walk toward the bright sun.
He spread his hands and blessed his mind and all his life:
"May you be blessed, my life, the bitter laurel's brief
and scented garland still upon your snow-white hair!

I kiss your slender ankles and your wounded feet;
how did you ever breach the pass or cross the great
main road, O most tormented life, one-breasted soul?
When I was young I held the earth like a huge sphere
nor feared life's kiss nor quaked before the dreaded gods.
I scorned to feel compassion, my full powers seethed,
I brimmed with poison like the scorpion's stinging tail,
and like a scorpion I'd have writhed upon my mind's
hot coals had not a small maid come to touch my heart.
Ah, how she calmed my mind, made sweet my lips until
all earthquakes turned to flowers and you and I both fused
till in life's deep sea-lairs we two were merged in one.
Then my heart's double-bolted gates swung open wide
and a small boy with dappled wings led me through lanes
of colored flowers gently to cool garden plots
within that maiden's soul, and smiled on me. Dear God,
in just one night my heart had widened with a sweet kiss,
and my stern mind sailed long on strange seductive shores
in the deep body's frigate with a loot of women.
May you be blessed, my life, who passed the heaviest trial
of all and with the light breath of a spring's cool breeze
knocked down the fortress of my own unpitying ego!
Then slowly as I grew more gentle, I longed to pass
even beyond sweet large-eyed Love and in my arms
clasp tight all of my native land like a maid's body.
O glittering harbors, sand-smooth beaches, tossing boats,
mountains with crystal waters and the pungent thyme,
old crones who spin their wool, maidens with fertile wombs,
brave gallant lads who fight the earth or foaming sea,
stones, bodies, souls, how could my mind contain you all?
Then pains for hurts not mine brimmed through my darkened heart
and all the joys of my luxuriant race poured out
as though a dam had burst and drenched my mind completely.
The soul's a thousand times more tasty than good meat,
and like a lion that once has tasted human flesh
and then disdains nor longer wants a humbler prey,
so I, too, wanted nothing less than human souls.
My native land seemed cribbed, for past its shores I felt
other bewitching lands and other lean-fleshed souls,
brothers and sisters, myriad forms of joys and sorrows
that stood on their far shores and longed for me to come.
May you be blessed, my life, for you disdained to stay
faithful to but one marriage, like a silly girl;
the bread of travel is sweet, and foreign lands are honey;
for a brief moment you rejoiced in each new love,
but stifled soon and bade farewell to each fond lover.

My soul, your voyages have been your native land!
With tears and smiles you've climbed and followed faithfully
the world's most fruitful virtue—holy false unfaithfulness!"

The sun had mounted as the archer blessed his life,
and then the pilgrims slowly stretched, rose from the ground,
and dreams took wing like parakeets and flew away.
In the lake's crystal pool the soaring mountains hung
like lofty sunken thoughts, like roses petal-plucked;
the day grew mild, the holy athlete turned serene
till in the mud he dipped ten fingertips with joy
and shaped things tenderly as though he fondled flesh.
Forms briefly rose and gleamed in sun, then once again
were plunged in pummeled mud, and other forms took shape.
"The great ascetic has grown meek, for see, his hands
mold monsters now no longer, but only tranquil men!
Take courage, lads, draw near, let's tell him all our pain."
Thus did the pilgrims speak to give each other heart,
but as the dreadful lone man raised enraptured eyes,
all huddled on the earth once more and shook with fear.
The world-creator cooled himself in the fierce blaze
by raising all trees' rustling in his memory's glens:
the oak tree's mystic murmur and the poplar's swish,
the olive's downy hush, the pine tree's whistling whir,
the gallant plane tree's cooling warbling melody;
he held all foliage in his mind like a green fan
and waved it slowly now to cool his blazing brow.
A maid at length took heart, drew close, and with great fear
tied colored rags about his ankle-bone as though
he were a holy tree, to make her prayers come true.
She moved her thick and night-kissed lips beseechingly,
but when the ascetic gave no sign of hope, the maid
sank in the bottomless mute wells of his dark eyes.
A king took courage then, opened his mouth and cried:
"Pity my people, Father! If the time has come
for you to sink in the earth's grave, then take our crimes
like a black necklace round your throat to vanish with you."
The lone man only laughed, then shook his head with wrath;
the time had not yet come to sink in earth, for still
he climbed and still the sun stood on his heart's high peak.
In the sun's distant icebound realms he saw his bones
wrapped round with seaweed, battered by the frothing waves,
and on his skull a fat black raven perched, the Soul.
Before he'd reach those realms, he'd many a bun to chew!
Then the sun set and the first darkness crushed the earth;
all souls sank down in sleep, the craftsman's hands grew calm,

and the wheel stopped which shaped, unshaped the forms of men
till ghosts, washed with the dew of night, appeared and danced
in the great threshing floor of the ascetic's fancy.
It was as though he'd tired of men, thrust them in mud
and longed to pass the hours with his mind's fantasies,
for his great brain was sated now, and chose with finer care.

At midnight, when the dark mind blooms, Odysseus sat
in moonlight by the wild pear's root and softly called
on souls alluringly and gave them flesh and bone.
The mystic weaver drifted through the sky and wove,
and in that waning moon's thin web the phantoms swam
with azure eyes like pale cerulean flowers of night;
mounted on forty waves, the young shore-naiads leapt
till all the enchanted lakeside sighed from rim to rim;
and the black bark of tree trunks cracked and flung with force
the cool green hamadryads with nude feet and breasts:
Almond and Apple-Blossom, Spider-Web, Caresse,
and good Dame Comely, noble source of all the nymphs;
sweet peas and mossy violets sprang wherever they danced.
No one might dare imagine such fresh souls, such limbs
so firm and lean as burst from the black bark of trees.
The nymphs of woods and wilderness all swarmed and smiled:
the twelve prince charmings reared upon their dappled steeds
and laughed and flung the sun for discus all year long;
the brain's lean vampires and the heart's dark sea-snakes rose,
the midnight werewolves, wandering ghouls, and donkey-trolls;
it was high time for myths and legends to walk the earth
once more like men and women and warm-blooded beasts.
A forty-footed one-toothed crone spread her thighs wide,
fat grease-drops oozed from her gray hair, her udders hung
brimming with fertile milk that dripped on the moist ground;
as her blue lips uncurled, she waved to the lone man,
and the wind-shepherd smiled and played his dulcet flute;
his airy flocks with their mild silver bells rolled down
from the brain's crags and the corrals of silent calm,
but still he could not see their black bellwether, God.
He seized the mudballs then and in the heart of night
shaped and reshaped the clay with both his whirling hands;
in the hot night his brains hissed like erotic snakes
and his strong incantations danced on the bare stones
and fell on every house-roof like a cackling rain.
He dug a small pit with his nails, poured his black blood,
then called on the great phantom, God, to loom before him,
and in a thunderous roar and lightning flash God sprang
full-clad in armor, a vain, bearded, swaggering dwarf.

Odysseus laughed and groped the form from head to toe:
"A thousand welcomes to my hearth, O firm-fleshed crab;
I'm hungry, and I like your claws with their lean meat."
He spoke, then seized God's chin to crunch the jaws,
and the ghosts shrieked and scattered, all God's sirens wailed:
"Pity our god, revere him, see how he sweats with fear,
see how his tears and sacred rouge stream down his face!"
But the god-battler stamped upon the earth with rage:
"I've no compassion for his sweat or even my soul,
and I disdain all toys, nor do joys lure me. Enough!
I've passed beyond the bounds of virtue or of hope."
He spoke, and God took fright, leapt up, changed many faces,
besmeared himself with paints and soot, turned somersaults,
drew swords and swallowed them, cast ropes in air and climbed,
chewed burning coals, puffed smoke from his flat ears, then twitched
his fat ass like a clown and jigged with bumps and grinds.
But the god-slayer raised his fist in loathing scorn
and God began to bellow like a monstrous bull
who wails with neck outstretched before the butcher's ax.
A mermaid damned Odysseus with her tear-filled eyes:
"Cursed be the heart of man that knows no reverence,
cursed be his mind that snatches the resplendent veil
to spy his father's nudeness without fear or shame!"
The ghouls and vampires burst in tears, the Nereids screamed,
for none could bear God's pain much longer now, but still
ruthless Odysseus mocked and arched his eyebrows taut:
"Oho, look at that bawling babe, that scabby tramp!
He's all set now to cast his last bait in our hearts,
wandering from town to town, knocking on every door:
'I've come to earth for you alone, for you I starve!
Open your souls and purses, give me alms, take pity!' "
God fell flat on his face and grabbed the mocker's knees:
"I stoop and bow low to your grace, don't kill me, son!"
But the god-battler mocked and pricked God ruthlessly:
"You were a brilliant feather once that wildly leapt
like a gay spangle on my crown whenever I danced;
but then I set you up as scarecrow in my fields
to fright the wretched mob from nibbling at my grapes,
dressed you in gaudy rags, gave you a rusty ax,
and hung the sun and moon about your chest for charms.
By God, I made you with such craft, such cunning wiles
that for a time, like Orpheus, I was almost fooled!
But I was born in a charmed hour, great freedom's son,
and raised my fist before you had time to gulp me whole."
He spoke, then with swift strokes ground God's face in the dirt.
First he uprooted the gay feathers from God's crown

who screeched as though he were a peahen plucked alive,
then slowly fleeced him of his charms, his bronze gewgaws,
his false sword-cuts, his necklaces, his crimson rags,
until, stripped bare, God rolled in dirt like a nude hen.
And when God fell to earth, the mind of man leapt up
within his head like a broad-breasted cock, and crowed;
it seemed day broke, sweet light flowed down the mountain slopes
and the god-slayer's heart grew warm, his black chest opened,
till like a bridegroom with curled locks, smelling of thyme,
he drew the bolts and let the world stroll in his heart.
The nightingale appeared once more, perched on his head
as though the heart were an unruffled bird that sang
with no unsolved enigmas now on green earth's highest bough.

But as the sage rejoiced in liberty's light breeze,
a deep voice suddenly filled his breast and cried, "Odysseus!"
and as the appeal resounded and the lake reeds raged,
the phantoms disappeared like crickets or small newts.
The lone man stooped, and in his mind now heard "Odysseus!"
"Dear heart, what dread voice calls me? Answer me, dear heart!"
For the third time the voice rang in his ears—"Odysseus!"
Then the heart-reader knew the voice and spread his arms:
"Great Athlete, with twelve constellations round your loins,
I recognized your harsh and bitter voice, my dear.
O Flame, distilled to pure light from your constant strife,
body that bent like a stout bow and shot your shaft,
the sharpened soul, and with it slashed the world's frontiers,
Father, it's you I call both in despair and joy!"
The secret voice still struck the ascetic ruthlessly:
"My only son, who strive and search for freedom still,
who quiver like a quartered snake on desert sands,
raise your head high, my dear, recall your gallant youth:
slim as a bow you knelt before my bloodstained knees
with your mind's quiver flashing full of two-barbed shafts
and looked straight in my eyes and roared unpityingly:
'I like this old man's head, it's full of wine and brains,
I'll fall in its deep hold and plunder all its loot!'
I smiled, stooped low and fed you my brains tenderly,
taught you to shoot the bow with skill and cunning craft,
to pass beyond small passions, how to reach the great,
yet search still further, urged by virtue's stern appeal.
Once, I recall, as I, too, walked through mountain passes,
I saw a small wild blackbird hop at break of day,
perch at the feet of a gray-templed ancient thrush
and listen with his head held high to that old bird;
thus have you too, wild blackbird, looted all my brain!

At times you listened to my counsel like spring rain,
at times my words would split your heart like lightning bolts
until you shook like a nude chick in the air's clamor.
But I rejoiced in the wild heartbeat of your youth
and thrust you ruthlessly, most cruelly, toward the cliff;
I called on you to choose between two armed camps there:
one was pitched high on the mind's peak, all light and flame,
the other was plunged low in dark and muddy flesh,
and then I called on you, my only son, to swear
by your mind's peak to fight those muddy pits forever
and always speak disdainfully to your groveling flesh:
'My body, do you long to sleep? Then all night long
I'll keep you upright like pale wax the flames melt down.
To eat? I'll feed your belly with empty air, like wings.
Tired? Then stand straight on the toes of one foot only
and whirl round like a weathercock on the world's roof!'
And you, my brave heart's wing-clawed son, you seized my words
and swiftly made them deeds, but deeds were not enough,
so that I threw red apple's virtue further still.
My song rang out like freedom's savage battlecry
and gods bent down to earth to hear my stern advice:
'When you have finally trod your flesh and freed yourself,
then split your soul in two armed camps with one sword stroke:
in one the gods shall stand with multicolored rags,
with secret hopes, with virtues that hang like slack dugs;
man's mind shall whirl in the other like a weather-crow.'
You rolled your eyes with fear then, I recall, and clung
tight to my knees to keep from plunging down my mind.
I seized you by your arms and cried out bitterly:
'Man's mind can never shoot the arrow further still!'
Alas, now that I lie with worms in the cold ground
I cry in anguish to see the greatest task of all."
Though the god-slayer strained to hear, the groaning stopped,
and then with hands outstretched to earth, he called the dark:
"Grandfather, fling the final task down on my head!"
Then from the other shore the dreadful voice was heard:
"When you have purified your heart of gods and demons,
of virtues great and small, of sorrows and of joys,
and only Death's great lighthouse stays, the glowing mind,
then rise, my heir, and sternly cleave your mind in two:
below will lie your last great foe, rotten-thighed Hope,
above, the savage Flame, no light, no air, no fire,
scornful and superhuman in man's hopeless skull."
He spoke, and like two heavy wings, the entrails closed.
Calmly the lone man shut his eyes to taste, full-slaked,
the silence in his loins that thrust his soul so high

that it leapt motionless in a great flaming kiln,
a fire no thorns could feed, where no wind ever blew;
upright, it stood on strife's high peak, stripped of desire.
The lone man gently smiled and hailed his haughty heart:
"Dear heart, you've flown beyond the final labor, Hope.
You've grown serene, all storms have merged within your depths,
sorrows have piled so high that now they form your joys.
Where shall you turn, dear heart? Whom shall you speak to now?
Slowly, in a great hush, you glide in dark like a wild hawk."

He stood straight on the cliff as though his feet would dance,
all his ten fingers tingled, his slim arches burned,
his body flicked like tongues of flame, and his brain whirled.
The pilgrims slept, dreams passed above them like white swans
whose red feet glittered and who sang with open beak
a strange marauding tune as from another world.
They leapt up from their sleep and seeing with great fear
in dawn's rose light the dread ascetic standing straight
close to the cliffside, flapping his bare arms like wings,
they shook, and in their hearts all felt some bitter news.
But their flame-swollen leader looked upon the crowd
and neither pity nor compassion filled his heart;
he stood unmoving, listening to his fingers dance:
"There is no master now on earth, the heart is free!
At dawn from my right temple the sun leaps in flame,
sweeps through the great dome of my head all day, then falls
at dusk in my left temple, swollen with crimson blood;
stars blaze now in my mind, and men, ideas, beasts
browse in the ephemeral green meadows of my head;
laughter and tears throng in my black eyes' irises,
dreams flood my brains, and phantoms drown my heart, but when
the mind snuffs out like a thief's lantern, all things vanish.
I kindle fires in fog, I plant bell buoys on waves,
I cut roads through the air and build all things from chaos;
my five slave-weavers at the loom of my swift mind
weave and unweave all life on air's firm-fibered cloth
until I cover the whole abyss with a strong net.
On this I stitch my house, give birth to all my sons,
entrust the seed of future wheat, hitch up my horse,
and found my life on mist for a brief lightning flash.
And when I blow, all vanish, but my heart speeds on
shorn of all condescension, anger, hope, or pain,
a small and dapple-feathered flash that lanced the night.
Forebear, who crouch on the other shore and shoot your shafts,
with your own blessing I've surpassed you and return
singing at dusk from the mind's glen and drag with me

the slain fawn, Hope, with her large weeping eyes now glazed.
I cock my cap awry, stride singing through the earth,
and holocausts mount up my hair, a flaming crown!"
Although the lone man ceased, his blazing body burned
like bonfires on the mountain's rim where the stones flashed,
and his mind, armored like the scorpion, strolled on coals.
The crowd took fright and cupped their hands against the blaze,
for on the cliff once more the alluring voice rang out:
"By the three-hundred-and-sixty-five joints knit to flesh,
by the three-hundred-and-sixty-five snakes round the soul,
no master-god exists, no virtue, no just law,
no punishment in Hades and no reward in Heaven!"
The lone man burst in cooling laughter like a wild spring
that suddenly splits the ground and leaps high toward the sun.
The pilgrims shut their ears and tried hard not to hear
freedom's wild voice, or the cool spring that splits the grave,
for his eyes rolled and glazed as though he'd lost his wits.
Some laughed with jutting jaws awry, some burst in tears,
some rushed with stones and staffs, roaring with rage to kill
at once this herald of a sacred, proud new earth.
But like a flaming iron that glows to a white heat
and singes poor man's lashes, thus the lone man glowed
on the cliff's edge so that the crowd drew back in fright;
unnumbered flaming sword-sharp hands flailed round his body
and seven crimson heads in tiers flashed in the air.
When the blaze finally calmed and all the myriad hands
and seven tiers of heads plunged in the lone man's mind
and his bare body seemed its normal self once more,
he turned and looked around him, but not a soul remained.
Somewhere on the far plains he saw huge dustclouds rise,
on the lake's waters gasping oarblades rose and fell,
and in their panic the crowd left behind tall piles
of hatchets, wooden clogs, caps, slippers, flasks and belts.
The foxy-minded man looked at his loot, and laughed:
"By God, you'd think that freedom was a plague that killed!
In former days my preening heart would have grown bitter
if left thus nude on earth without gewgaws or wings.
Well-met now, desolate wastes! Welcome to both your eyes!
A thousand welcomes now to savage freedom's freezing breath!"

Through his free heart there blew a chaste immaculate wind;
he stepped on the high peaks of both despair and strength
and on his mind's rim broke in dance like a wild eagle.
The great cry of a grasping bird tore at his breast,
the ancient wounds upon his shoulders burst in wings
and his mind swooped and soared within a whirlwind dance;

nor souls nor stones were told apart in that mad whirl
till the Earth and the Archer's flesh were merged like man and maid.
A lustful hot wind blew, his downy belly glowed,
the arteries of his body rushed and twined around
earth's crust to keep it firm from crumbling down the abyss.
His Soul hung over the cliff, all phallus and all womb,
starved for a kiss and cried for males, craved for a kiss
and moaned for female ghosts to come, then carved on air
meaningless mystic signs filled full of light, and played
but with no purpose, from sheer strength and without joy
because it knew the voice must turn back wretchedly
to lips that called. His breast's cave groaned with echoing sounds:
"I rise high on the shores of time, I shape, reshape
with water, blood, and sand the adventures of all man;
as thoughts leap from my brows and fall to earth, they turn
at once to men and maids and merge in tight embrace.
Like the smooth tusks of elephants the face of earth
shines on in sun and rain, and I stoop slowly down
and fondle it with speechless tenderness, and muse:
What shall we carve on this belovèd ivory face?
A murderer's knife, an eating bowl, or a fine comb
to gleam on a girl's raven hair within the abyss?
On all ten fingertips strength leaps in sweetest flesh,
and as in his deep gardens a king slowly picks
what maid to throw his kerchief to from all his harem,
so do I gaze on all desires, and curb my strength.
My solitude is cruel today, the air's too warm,
I'm weary of being alone, I fear that I shall faint,
and this swift terrifying dance unlocks my wits.
I yearn to see and to be seen, to touch, be touched,
my heart throbs like a new god's heart, I pity man,
I pity him so, I'll nail wings on his wingless brains
and cast down all those wicked walls that jail his soul.
O trees, get drunk and burst in bloom; girls, swell your breasts;
and you, brave youths, hatch in your minds all your desires—
life's but a lightning flash, my lads, and death is endless!
I gaze on earth and love her, I don't want to die!
I gaze on a man's and a maid's body, and I shout:
'Fill it with joys and sorrows, daring dreams and deeds,
raise high the crimson sun and the mind's soaring kite,
light up the high head's magic lantern till it glows!'
I love to stroll and watch maids at their window sills,
to see the fragrant smoke arise at dusk from roofs,
to hear beds creak and crack at midnight in the dark.
I pass by towns and lands, bless them and shout in air:
'O mankind, joys and tears, warm bodies, O my children!'

I once saw pallid monks, in the first bloom of youth,
dressed in black cassocks, who as lustful maids passed by
and made all earth they stepped on smell of jasmine flowers,
gather their frocks about them, lower their eyes, and spit
to ward off every evil eye, and curse the earth—
I raised my fist on high and roared, 'May you be cursed!'
I laugh, give birth, rejoice, gaze on the earth and say:
'This whirlpool earth's my trusted wife, I love her well!
Sometimes I turn to cloudbursts in the wild spring rains,
sometimes to hot midsummer suns, at times again
to strong male souls and mount her like a bull at dawn.'
On! Let the heavy beasts awake in memory's cave,
let the black forest of the heart growl as dusk falls;
I dance, and all the tight coils of my head unwind!"
As the archer leapt and yelled, the earth could not keep up
with his swift dancing till it dwindled and cast sparks
like a shy bride surrendering in a man's wild arms.
The soul leapt like a fiery tongue, with longing licked
the small dark body of the earth that nestled close
and swooned with sweet caresses like a maiden kissed.
Earth was swept up, then sprouted in his brain like seed,
and all she strove, unnumbered years, in old night's womb
to turn to root, leaf, flower and fruit, swelled now with leaves,
bloomed and bore fruit in his wild head, then all at once
vanished like lightning. Ah, time is bitter and space confined;
the lone man's dance shall overbrim, then fall from time
like an illumined star and vanish in the world's dark night.

But as he danced, he held the human short-lived soul
clenched tight between his teeth for fear the winds might take it.
When the great dancer had danced his fill, he shrank like fire,
the burning stones calmed down, the world stood still once more,
and as he panted, the brain-sucking man could hear
his blood leap frothing through his flesh from head to toe.
Like the lithe snake who in wide circles twists and coils,
delighting in the world from head to tail, just so
the archer wished to merge in one from head to foot.
He bent and fiercely bit his heel till his lips filled
with warm salt blood, and thus his fearful body drank
communion as he sipped his blood, refreshed, till all
his strength flowed round his body in full, steadfast rings.
Man, woman, god, and beast all merged within his blood,
turned to blood brothers, vanished in swift freedom's wheel:
"I've no more children, comrades, dogs, or gods on earth.
May they speed well and prosper, may winds fill their sails!

Enough! I want their breaths and their sweet swoons no more,
for I'm all ships, all seas, all storms, all foreign strands,
I'm both the brain-begotten god and the anti-god,
I'm the warm womb that gives me birth, the grave that eats me!
The circle is now complete, the snake has bit its tail."
At length Odysseus leapt erect, he cut new roads,
his heart grew light, his white beard gleamed like grapes in sun,
and his mind shone like mountain summits after rain.
As the full-bodied moon stepped lightly up the sky
and the sun plunged in waters silently to cool,
the freed mind of the great god-slayer stood between them;
he felt he tossed the sun and moon in both his hands
and flung them in the sky like falcons trained so well
they came when called again, bound with fine golden chains.
The honey of evening slowly dripped on the cool ground,
the heart grew tranquil in calm truce with sovereign Death,
till for the lone man freedom was a saddened power
that crossed her hands and watched all things on earth with tears,
and wore a wreath of cliff-weeds in her russet hair.
He passed beyond pride's arrogance, the drunken rage
of plunder, each man's secret week of sin, until
the savior, saved from his salvation, bent with awe
and kissed his mother, Earth, with sweet humility
and the due homage of a son long prodigal.
He wandered round her knees and reached to clasp her breasts:
"Mother, with your large dugs that hang above the abyss,
I've quenched that thirst, I don't want your right, sacred breast;
your pure white milk was good, but now I want the black:
Mother, I reach my hungry hand to clasp your left breast too!"

XVII

The pure white rose of silence bloomed, night lost her wits,
and the great victor brooded in the moonlight's glare;
his eyes spread out until they covered all his skull,
his hands and swift feet multiplied and whirled in light,
a mystic wheel that gathered speed and could not stop.
Both life and death were twin and two-edged blades that shone
and tossed in his black fists, shot high in the moon's glow
then crossed in air and swiftly plunged like lightning bolts.
The walls of his head opened and the world seemed narrow,
his mind grew claws to a span's length, his wings grew huge,
he changed to man, maid, god, together and apart,
joy merged with sorrow, good and evil made their peace
till all within his mid-brows took their ordered place.
The mind like a black beetle thrust in the earth's rose
but held its brains tight, not to faint with fragrances,
and kept its wings high, not to sink in thickening honey,
then gleaned each drop completely, emptied all the rose,
and when it finished, its feet, neck, and belly gleamed
in light, gold-spattered with the flaming pollen's dust.
The evening dripped with mild moonbeams, and the night smelled
with the strong peppery scent of blossomed medlar trees;
the grasses quivered, and in tree-leaves, lightly swayed
by breezes, eyes of birds bloomed like star-clustered lights.
Phantoms and men had vanished, leaving as much trace
as birds leave in the air or ships leave on the sea,
and every moment in the darkness was heard falling
like honey from an unseen hive that swells in the heart.
The mighty athlete also drank each drop of honey,
distilled from varied poisonous flowers, thoughts, and fears
into a quintessential, thick, pain-killing scent,
each drop immortal, no beginning and no end,
where past and future, savage time's two-sided wings,
were folded motionless and sank in heavy honey.
"Time has been conquered now and rests in my warm heart,
trapped like the lovelorn nightingale on flowering thorns,"
murmured the white-haired victor as in his heart's depths

he felt his dreadful strife had turned to amorous song.
Though the world had not quaked or the mind roared, the earth
changed calmly in his eyes, creation was dislodged,
and night blazed up like an alluring wild-dove's throat.
The lone man's heart was suddenly filled with lilting love
as though enmarbled snow had melted on high peaks:
"Go on, my heart, let's burst in song, this night is good,
for I was born today, and my small mother, Earth,
gives of her first milk to her darling first-born son.
Yes, by the twelve fine plumes in the stork's sacred tail,
new eyes have raised their lashes, a new spring has come,
new virtues with strong claws have blossomed in my blood.
May sterile memory, that most evil stingy witch,
plunge down to Hades, and may life turn chaste once more!
I bow to my much-traveled blind forefather, sleep,
and kiss his hands that fumble till they reach my crown
to give their blessing: 'You, my grandson, are the light
of which I've always dreamed. Bud now, that I may bloom!'
O gypsy Life, with sun-braids, with coquetting eyes,
for years I've stumbled in your light, your holy haunts,
for years been put to shame, hunting your empty shade,
thrashing my arms with rage, tearing the wild wind's hair!
Sometimes you seemed like Beauty, passion-quelling Helen,
a shadow's coolness, smell of musk, or the sea's air,
seductive dancer paid in the ecstasy of drink
to please our eyes with your adroit erotic tricks;
at times, when earth embittered me in my full youth,
you seemed, O Life, like the grass-widow Virtue, sad,
unlaughing, and I seized my spear to guard you well,
as though you ever cared, O luring siren-song,
for justice or injustice or the joys of men!
One dawn as I gleaned the mind's loneliness in vain,
I heard the seas, the heart, the earth call me for help;
God called in greatest peril, and I rushed to build
a head for him to hide in, town in which to sleep.
Forgive me, Life, if I've so stupidly pursued
such gaudy plumes as whence we come and where we go;
I've squandered years in hunting what I thought firm flesh,
your three great shadows: Beauty, guileless Virtue, Truth;
but may these wanderings, too, be blessed that in good time
brought me to your nude body cool as warbling water.
If I were young, I'd bind a kerchief round my head
to keep my brains from spilling after too much love;
if I were old, I'd weep in silence as I reached
my hands to fumble at your firm crisp breasts, O Life;
but now we're met beyond old age or lustful youth,

beyond all tears or kisses, time or space, within
the ephemeral deathless throbbing of the human heart.
Well met, integral Freedom! We are both well met!
Naked, stripped bare of gods and plumes, with the cool dew
on my mind's cockscomb, I lunged down from mountain strife
and you rose high from billows, glittering in the sun,
the salt stars quivering on the fringes of your hair,
till we both merged within the moment's deathless shore.
All dark partitions crumbled then, those ghosts, those thoughts,
those sterile virtues which disjoined our amorous flesh,
till in thick heat I fell and lapped you like cool water,
and you, too, sucked my stinging blood with yearning gasps.
We rolled on the wet beach, tight-clasped and drunk with love,
lips glued to lips, eyes staring in each other's eyes,
till we both climbed intoxication's four tall steps:
wine's ecstasy, God, love, and star-eyed liberty.
On the sheer crags of brimming strength and full despair,
on the high peak of drunkenness and laughter's bloom,
arise, O Life, and play! Earth's a good threshing floor!
My guts are filled with souls, my mind is filled with flesh.
What would you like—a wedding pomp on mountain slopes
that Orpheus leads, or armies with torn flags that fight
and slay each other for our sake in the sun's blaze?
Or would you like a large town spread amid the plains
where blue smoke puffs from roofs, where doors open and close,
where children scream and women laugh, dogs bark, and all
the crazy hubbub of the city spills in sunlight?
All bodies are but ghosts of dew which the mind swells,
they meet, they clasp, they part, they raise tall clouds of dust,
then all at once the mind grows bored, and the world clears.
Rise up, Dame Life, give me the sign and choose your toy!"
Midnight and heavy solitude: a leaf would now
and then detach itself in silence, slowly drop to earth,
like a dead falling star, a disembodied heart,
a cricket that on stones stopped chirring when it found
its sweet companion and rejoiced in all it longed for.
The full round moon at zenith poured upon the beard
and the white-haired, well-sated chest of the god-slayer;
had gypsies seen him then, they would have seized a sledge,
mistaken him for tin and pounded him to bits;
had shepherds seen him then, they would have spit three times
to exorcise and drive away a ghostly ghoul;
and had girls come, they would have screamed in the moon's glow
to see the old god Priapus lure them on with wiles,
and each in dream would suddenly clasp her lover in her arms.

The ascetic smiled, and three slim maids sprang from his lips:
"Ah, Pearl, Caresse, here's an ascetic by the cliff!
He sits cross-legged, he beats on stones and shouts in air."
"Ascetic? Where? I see but sticks in the moon's glow.
Sisters, let's set these twigs on fire and save their souls,
for in moist logs the fire smothers, wails, and shouts:
'Ah, Pearl, I'm choked in these black logs! Ah, set me free!' "
"I see two eyes that gleam beneath a pear tree's shade,
amorous and despairing. They lure me and shout, 'Come!'
Sisters, farewell! Is this a jar or child I hold?
No water-well exists, no mother, father, home,
for all have sunk deep down and drowned in those black eyes."
Then the wing-shepherd called, and an old wizened man
fell from his mind to the hard ground like a dry leaf:
"Who called? A strong voice seized my nape with gripping hands,
pummeled me heavily on the ground and blocked my way.
I swear I've given birth, I've built, I've tilled my fields,
I've filled my yards with sons, gods, grain, domestic beasts,
plowed land and women well. I'm tired now, let me be!
There's no oil left in these old eyes, my lamp's gone out.
Who holds me back? I hear a voice, and grope with fear.
Ah, here's a heap of bones that wails on the cliff's edge."
The great mind-reveler sighed, his longing filled with flesh,
and the slim dancer in his mind sprang on the earth:
"I see a marble threshing floor and a tall spear
with gold canary wings and lofty rooster plumes,
and on its tip a woman's blond hair flaps in sunlight.
I washed, dressed in my finery, donned my golden breastplates
to guard my bosom well, then rushed to find my king.
What king? Within my mind a great voice cried out, 'Dance!'
What shall I dance? There's flaming air above my head
and flaming air beneath my feet; if I but slip
I'll plunge headlong to Hades like a falling star.
Some call me woman, others call me dance and war;
I'm that unmoving mind between the earth and stars
that loves to play and think up women, dance, and war!"
Then the proud victor scowled with rage and knit his brows
till great battalions fell to earth and weapons clashed:
"We've moored by a great castle, lads, where banners flap
in crimson, black, and yellow on high battlements!
Push on, lads! Cast your scaling-ladders, seize your arms!
Both life and death are good! Grab what comes first to hand!
What joy to toss life like an apple high, and play!"
The heart-seducer blinked then with his cunning eyes
and a lass, kissed in secret, slid from her low hut:
"Belovèd, when I hear your rustling in the reeds,

I lose my wits as though a young man touched my knees,
and now they leap in the moon's glow like man and maid;
my eyes have never seen a sweeter night, my dear,
nor is there bird can sing so sweet as now my heart;
my maidenhead longs to be plucked like a ripe apple."
When the sly merchant thought of gold, long caravans
like subtle shadows skimmed on sands before cockcrow.
Dear God, what spiced aromas, what bright birds and slaves
sprang from his heavy head and spilled along the ground!
"Hey, push on there! Why do the camels stop midway?"
"I won't push on! Before me lie huge castle gates.
Horsemen dash by full-armed, serfs plod with heavy loads,
here blind and maimed and leprous beggars shove and shout.
Brothers, we've come to a great city, rich, unknown;
spread out your wares upon the ground, let the world gape,
strip the slaves naked for the market, wash their hair,
let heralds scatter, beat on every door and shout:
'Ladies and landlords, rise! The caravan's come, be quick!
Put gold now in your palms, bring all your lambs to market,
select your spotless daughters quick and sell them dear!
Lucky the eyes that see us, the feet that come in time!' "
Then a white elephant sprang from the ascetic's mind
and from its broad arched nape a slave's voice leapt and cried:
"Bold, long-lived king, how dare I say it? I'm afraid!
I've pled with our white elephant, I've stroked him gently,
I've raised my whip and flogged him, but he still won't budge;
he flaps his ears and twitches his fat wrinkled hide,
for a huge conflagration, king, blocks all the road!"
"Fetch water, fall upon it, put it out, I say!"
"All your three-hundred-and-sixty-five most trusted slaves,
master, have fought in vain to blot it out since dawn,
but water only soaks and kindles it like oil;
it sparks with human speech, I don't know what it says!
It laughs like a gay dream when touched, but it won't burn,
yet when you try to pass, it rears like a mad snake.
It must be an ascetic who dwells in flesh of flame!"
"It must be an ascetic who cools his soul in flame.
O faithful servant, hold my beast, let me descend
to bow with humble awe and worship his great grace."
The ascetic's mind then flapped its wings like a proud cock
till the air filled with brides and grooms, in-laws and lambs:
"I see boards strewn with sheep and wine and brimming bowls,
old nurses fan the flushed bride in the nuptial room,
next door the fat groom puffs and pants, and his thighs sweat,
brothers and cousins fetch full trays of fragrant meat,
aunts fill the jugs with wine, dilute them secretly,

and young men cock their caps awry and maidens swoon;
then the doors open, the bards come and strike their lyres
till all toes start to jig upon the straw-strewn floor.
This is a good time, brothers, to unsheathe your flutes;
strike hard the tambourines, let the drums take the lead,
let the white bear cub dance on the wide threshing floor.
The groom looks affluent, lads, we'll fill our bellies soon!
Get up, thrush-pregnant minstrel, swell your throbbing throat,
marshal your homeless mind from the high mountain peaks,
make of your fantasy a flame and start the song!
The bride's thin braids are like a mouse's scanty tail,
her hands are pestles, she's pig-snouted and popeyed,
but you, O mythic minstrel, rise, give her new birth!
Make her a tall cypress tree, slim as a switch,
plant curly basil leaves on her bald pate, raise high
your hands to the sky and then bring down the sun, bring down
the full moon too—ah, don't be stingy, friend—and hang
them round the new bride's shriveled throat until the groom
grows giddy, spills his wits and opens his purse wide!
Dream-poet, sing her charms, don't be ashamed, we're starved!
Tell her: 'At your great wedding, O thrice-noble maid,
may mountains turn to oxen, snows to finest flour,
the seas to sweet white wine, all ships to drinking bowls,
and waves to swift racehorses which your in-laws mount and ride!' "

As men and women sprang from soil to hear the spells
that echoed from the mind-ravines of the soul-snatcher,
an inexpressible love and secret pity seized him:
"The blade of my despairing mind plowed in a flash
through earth, and the soil filled with souls, and bodies moved
in new-plowed furrows like white, black, and crimson worms.
O my dear people, frail blue smoke, toys of my brain,
green quivering phosphorescence in moist river glens,
warm bodies, smiles and tears born of the mind, my children!"
The contours of his features shone and pulsed with light,
the night was sweet, fragrant the silver-woven air,
and as he watched their hands, their feet, and their weak bodies
that toiled all day with the hard soil, all night in bed,
a profound pity filled his mind; he shut his eyes
and gently stroked within his arms his daughter earth
till a great longing rose high in his throat and lips
to cast them simple, satisfying words, like meat.
A tender and sweet voice was suddenly heard: "My children!"
Within the full moon's webs, the souls in anguish tossed
like night-moths to escape those nets of gossamer,
and the ascetic's eyebrows squirmed like snakes that hissed

and coiled on the rims of his dark eyes' sunken wells.
The phantoms staggered back in fright and clung to rocks,
paralyzed, gaping, watching in the moonlight's glow
how the great body blazed now like a burning rock.
Its myriad faces rose and fell and flicked in air;
at times proud stalwart men or ancient codgers flashed,
at times fierce leopards reared their tails and licked their lips,
then suddenly all the faces vanished and a voice
rang out in light, most bitter and most sweet: "My children!"
Slowly the neck turned flesh once more, the mouth took shape,
and the lone man distilled again from the world's ends.
The phantoms scattered terrified, the camels vanished,
the old white elephant grew savage and pushed back,
Pearl and Caresse melted like mist, the peddling thieves
scooped up their merchandise and scuttled off like hares;
only the dancer stayed and leant her heavy locks
above the chasm until the whole cliff glowed with light;
beside her stood an old king with his golden ring,
a forty-footed warrior, a young singing prince,
and a robust slave smelling of the stable's stench.
The many-faced man spread his hands most tenderly
and felt his five dream-mortals formed on the firm ground
as though he'd brought five plowmen to plow up the earth,
five dappled oxen yoked to pull his daring dream.
He laughed profoundly till his sword-lips reached his ears,
then slowly to his mouth set his funereal flute,
a human shinbone which an ancient hermit once
had placed into his hands as votive farewell gift,
and played a plaintive lullaby, a luring song,
and the five mortals stretched on earth and lost their wits,
the hinges of their minds creaked, double doors burst wide,
and thoughts walked into ancient gardens, deep and dark.
Voices have bodies, too, and words have flesh; it's true
that laughter, tears, and sighs, movements of every kind,
are male and female, all, and merge in empty air.
A flute, made of a dead man's bone, makes all things drunk;
the wine-bowl of the holy night spilled at the brim
and the five heads filled full and splashed on the wet ground.
Then the pale maiden sighed, and as she raised her head
and shut her eyes, she blushed and mused in secret thought:
"Your words, ascetic, seemed to me a gallant youth
who smears himself with fragrant oil after his bath,
then strolls at dusk with a red rose hung on his ear
as pale maids from behind closed shutters spy on him
and their hearts break: 'Ah, might I only bear his child!' "
The dancer sighed that night and yearned thus for a son;

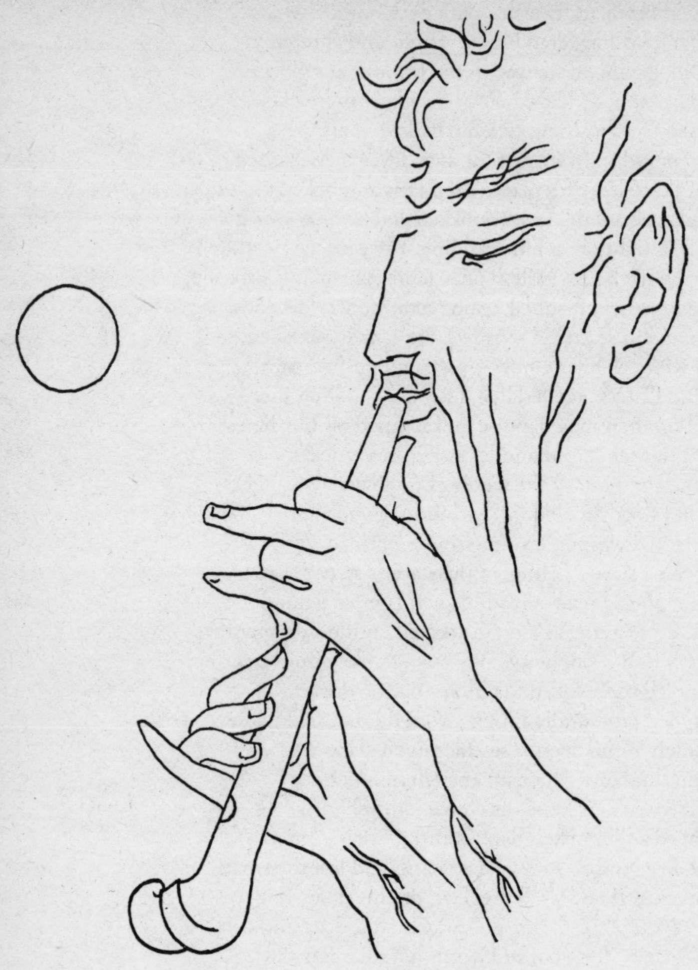

it seemed that the young singer heard her yearning sigh
deep in dream's flowering gardens, and his sad heart bled.
Dear God, to lie for a brief hour, before he died,
in his beloved's lap! Then let the world go hang!
The young man brooded on the maid and softly sighed
till dewy heavens like a vine hung in his head.
The old man glued his eyes on the moon's brilliant blaze,
recalled in silence his lost youth, his empty life,
how he had heaped his virtue's tower with silver and gold

although his nights lacked love and his days gallant deeds.
As he leant toward the grave, he cursed at virtue now,
that scandalmongering hag with her untouched shrunk dugs!
Dear God, if he could be a wretched youth once more!
The stalwart warrior lay on earth, a sated lion,
beside him the slave sighed and quarreled with God because
he loved the archons only and held slaves in scorn
nor cast them a brief kiss or crust of bread for comfort.
Their eyes and brains thus fluttered breathlessly
as on the cliffs of sleep they muttered to themselves
while the soft luring sound flowed from the lone man's flute
and softly, slowly filled their ravished ears with song.
For the first time Death seemed to them a tranquil sleep
and life a blossomed honeysuckle hung in chaos
where the dreams perched at dawn; thrice-welcome nightingales
entwined in honeysuckle spray, and poured their warbling song.

PRINCE: "Ah, Mother, I can't sleep, my bed won't hold me now!
Dear Mother, shut the windows, close the shutters tight,
I've never known a night so sweet, for my heart melts.
A nightingale is singing in a flowering shrub
and my throat chokes with blossomed trees and thorn-hedge smells.
Ah, might I only die and my brains sink in soil!
But ah, the earth is good, I want to live, though not
alone, dear God, within this closed and fragrant garden."
OLD KING: "Alas, my life has been unfruitful, sickly, weak.
When I was young I bragged and spun deeds in my head,
earth seemed so small and narrow it couldn't hold my heart,
and I would stroke my long mustache and chirp with song:
'If earth, lads, were my steed, the moon my talisman,
I'd spur my steed until I reached great God himself:
"Your health and joy, man-killer!" "Welcome, my brave lad!
Sit at my table, eat and drink, sit down and sing!"
"But I've not come to heaven to eat and drink with you.
My hands are earth, my heart's a flame, my mind's a sword!
I've come astride my youth to give you battle, Lord!"
"Take off your clothes, my brave young man, throw down your arms,
pull out your fingernails, your teeth, your eyes, your tongue,
then cross your hands, my lad, that I may take your soul."
"I won't take off my clothes, I won't throw down my arms,
and I won't cross my hands that you may take my soul!
I have a soul, Lord, just like yours, we're both brave men,
take up your arms, come down, fight on earth's threshing floor!"'
That's how I bravely challenged God and fought him hard.
I longed to outfit mighty armies and swift ships,
my mind dreamt of far countries, women, shores of pearls,

and all my bosom, stooped to earth, sought deathlessness.
But now? I look back and see bitter shames and passions,
armies that cut and scattered, worthless friendships, loves,
good food, good drink, a well-arranged household routine
where the empty heart plods back and forth and chews her cud.
O murdering God, I'll cross my hands now! Take my soul!
My daring youth's armada forged into the wind
but sank and vanished in a household washing-trough!
Today when nightingales sing sweet and the trees bud,
I wander in the sad moon's light and long for youth."
WARRIOR: "Always a sweet light drunkenness impels my heart.
I've passed through mountains, countries, seas, I've conquered towns,
I've juggled women's heads and breasts high in the air,
and through my open fingertips blood-rubies flow,
but still my heart's not gorged, nor are my hands replete.
I always think I've touched a girl for the first time,
climbed up a castle for the first time or held it tight
like a red apple, cooled my hand for the first time.
My heart strains like a ship's sail and my body creaks,
black women wave from beaches with white lotuses,
sharp odors strike my nostrils, corals build their isles,
and rocks are crammed with eggs and naked fledgling gulls.
I shout, greet all the shores and seas, and then pass on,
for in deep caverns I've seen lonely Freedom shine
as in the dark she washed and combed her hair with stars,
and when she moved her azure eyes and saw my shadow
she sang a most sweet song there high on the cliff's edge.
'Ah, Lady Lure,' I cried, 'in truth I do adore
your sweet though acrid song, and your blond floating hair,
but I can't stay, I loot your song and then pass on,
for still the voyage is long, my dear, and life's a drop.' "
SLAVE: "My master lies upon his golden bed and sleeps,
the ox are chewing by their troughs, the moon has risen,
and day has ended—ah, may it, also, go to the crows!
Cursed be this life, and cursed all those who long for life!
The rich from too much food and women and red wine
fumble from wall to wall, vomit, then feast again,
but we're forbidden the sweet flesh, and starve and thirst.
Oho, it's a foul shame that God won't heal our hurt,
or is he also an archon, lads, romps like a scamp
and from too much of a good time has lost his wits?
My heart's grown wormy now from questions, pains, and tears,
I want to wail in a loud screech, but fear my master,
I want to hide in the wild woods, but fear the beasts,
I want to draw my naked blade, but fear my god;
fear is a deep dark well in which I've plunged headfirst.

O pallid moon who watch me sitting here in tears,
pity me, close your eyes, give me your consolation,
give me rich myriad dreams, or give me women, food;
pity me, spendthrift lavish sleep, open your purse,
it gives the worm great joy to dream at times of soaring wings."

At daybreak between sleep and waking their minds tossed,
they squirmed and stretched on the flat stones but found no rest
till the soul-snatcher lowered his flute's alluring sound
and the tune's sweetness poured in their light-sleeping ears
like the far-distant tinkling of sheep-bells at night.
Then sleep broke softly from the tree of night and hung,
a ripe full-seeded male fig, in their unripe shadow,
and as the eyes of their flesh closed, their inner eyes
burst open, till to the cadence of a dead man's bone
the five souls were untwined and twined through one another.
The maid was first to lead the dance in dreamland's ring,
and as with fear and joy she smelled the men, she cried:
MAID: "Four men are here! I am the only maid! Alas,
what if they now should sniff the scent of a girl's breast?
Ah, like the nightingale, I too shall hide in thorns;
come close, wild grapevine, sister, twine me tight; come close,
O nightingale, sing loud, conceal my trembling heart;
rise up, O sighs, for the clear moon is hid in mist.
May no man's eyes now see me or his cruel hands touch me;
my maidenhead is a sweet apple, Lord, protect it!
Oho, if they should seize me I'll claw out their eyes;
welcome is death a thousand times than the world's scorn!
If the prince seized me, though, and swore he wished me well,
I'd not cry out, for his pale face is very sweet;
I'd rock him gently like a son between my breasts.
But if the warrior rushed and grasped me tight, alas,
how could I ever guard my virgin body, Lord?
He treads the earth like a bull; it groans, and his teeth shine;
I see his hairy arms, and my breasts hurt me! Ah,
if he should squeeze me in his hands I'd break in two,
yet no girl's come to harm, just squeezed in a man's arms!
But best of all is to be gleaned by the old king's hand.
He'd heap my doorway with a pile of towering gold,
he'd arm me handsomely with pearls and golden coins
and on my wedding finger he'd place the wedding ring;
alas, he's a thin shadow lost in the moon's glow.
Only the slave's left now, he stalks like a wild boar;
how can a girl sleep, Mother, on his shaggy chest?
Ah, in the road there leaps and steams a strapping man
with crooked cap aslant, with the asp's wily eyes,

and a slim leopard stalks before him with tail held high;
his hands are empty, but they glow like flashing knives,
on his broad back he bears the heavens and earth like two
small goats, smiles like a shepherd, locks them in their pens,
and in his fists he holds and plays with my pale soul!"
The bone-flute suddenly stopped, and all the five night-prowlers
stood still within the dream at once with hovering feet
until the heart-seducer smiled in pity for all man
and raised his hands above the black-doomed ghosts that death
might let them find fulfillment in the sun awhile.
His thoughts then rose like smoke in the night's windlessness:
Odysseus: "Ah, five warm bodies shrivel here, five wretched souls
like caterpillars crawl, mud-soaked, and gasp for air.
Ah, how I pity them! I'll fall on them and nail
flames to the right and left of their soft backs like wings.
The sun falls on the ground and rims it with pure gold,
it shows no special love or hate, and its great eye
looks on all cities, men, and worms with the same joy;
and thus my eyes shall make earth sprout with wings of flame.
Open the mind's deep hold and let them eat and glow,
let the worm stretch in sun and take whatever it can!"
Thus did the soul-seducing pirate think, then placed
his flute of dead man's bone against his sucking lips
and, as the first sounds fell, five spirits turned their heads
in fear and looked at him, stooped on the cliffs of sleep:
Maid: "In the unripe moonlight his eyes flash with emerald sparks.
Alas, he stalks through earth with rage, he spreads his hands,
he opens his mouth and speaks, but I can't hear a word."
Odysseus: "Like fragments of a windmill rotted from old age
their five warm bodies lie unmatched on the strewn ground,
a wheel, an axle here, a wing, a tower there,
the two millstones disjoined, the gold grain poured to earth.
But in my memory I still keep that splendid shape,
and in this wilderness, in the moon's spread, I'll raise
a windmill sonorous and intact, and feed it grain
and set its great wings whirling with my mind's four winds.
Ah, you five tentacles of all my passion, stay!"
Maid: "We stay! If only we could run far, far away!"
Odysseus: "What shall I do with you, now that you're in my claws?
Your tears and laughter are deep cisterns in your breasts,
I like both fountainheads—which shall I open first?
I hold five hearts tight in my hands, five tangled skeins,
a windmill's five white wings; now when the wind shall blow
how shall I cast my willful mind on those torn wings?
Shall they grind slowly, gently, a fine household flour,
or shall I blow so fiercely that sails, millstones, grain,

explode once more and vanish in my whirlwind mind?
Far better not to ask! Whatever comes is welcome!
I blow them my own spirit to open their clay eyes,
I blow them my own spirit to open their brows wide.
O children, an erotic South Wind blows, the hills
are moved, the world is a plucked rose, a dwindling fragrance."
MAID: "Dear God, a sweet breeze blows upon my curly brows;
earth moves, my brain whirls round, a mighty forest looms,
dusk falls, and azure cooling shadows spread on earth;
far far away I hear small silver bells that weep—
ah, ah, I now hear mournful sounds deep in the darkling air."

OLD KING: "Faithful slave, stop! My heart feels something evil here!
With my gold carriage which you drive, and its four steeds,
entrusted slave, we're dashing pellmell straight toward death!
See how the parrots perch now on the topmost boughs,
see how the blackbirds jeer and mock us with shrill cries,
see how the wild goats, fawns, gazelles, and all wild things
gaze with no fear as though we were but empty shades!
Apes climb the pomegranate trees, pelt us with rinds
and stick out their behinds with no respect or shame;
O faithful slave, shout loudly, let all creatures hear
and flee with fear: 'The King of Africa goes by!' "
SLAVE: "Master, I'm hoarse with shouting at the birds and beasts,
'The King goes by! Now hide from his great face in shame!'
They eat on shamelessly, befoul themselves, pair off,
whistle and jeer before you, king, and show no awe;
but you're a good man, pity them, don't wish them ill."
OLD KING: "These are not birds or beasts but phantoms of the woods."
SLAVE: "I'm but a slave, I've not been given the grace to see
such souls, but only bellies, feet, and birdshit, master.
They say the spirits live further off, there at the root
of a high slender date tree with infertile boughs.
They say that a lightheaded warrior passed one night
and saw them dancing in a moonlit forest grove,
but I think, master, they were male and female hares."
OLD KING: "I beg of you, dear slave, don't laugh—it seems I dreamt
a great ascetic sought for grace in this dark wood.
Which date tree? My old eyes have blurred, the world's grown dim."
SLAVE: "There at the cliff's rim, upon that hanging rock."
OLD KING: "Lower your eyes and hands with holy reverence, slave!
Well met, O fearful tree, on this cliff's murky depths,
thrice holy date tree, without shade or fruit or hope!
For forty years a great ascetic groaned and fought
here at your roots and sanctified all earth around,
east, west, north, south, a thousand miles, and lured all souls.

When I was young and hunted tigers in these woods
I lost my way and stumbled on this holy ring
one night and peered with fright amid some blossomed boughs.
A sweet most beautiful spirit, dancer of azure skies,
knelt nude before the great ascetic sunk in thought
and held in her slim hands and swayed a feathered fan
to cool his creaking temples in the fevered dark.
Her lily fingers shone like ivory, finely shaped,
her raven hair protected her sweet nakedness,
and I, who fought with tigers and pursued wild lions,
took fright at her nude sacred body and turned back,
but a bough creaked, she slowly turned, laughed, and was lost
in air like a faint rainbow made of the moon's beams.
Slave, shut your scoffing lips and exorcise your laughter!"
SLAVE: "Forgive me, master, if I also say my say:
May this sky-spirit you speak of stay with us forever!
It seems the great ascetic once had made a masterpiece;
she must have had the soul you spoke of, king, and still
a wee, wee bit of flesh. It may be that one night,
as the great athlete toppled from his lofty thoughts,
he tripped and found himself glued on her suddenly,
and then from too much squirming, a wee stroke too much,
in nine months' time, it seems, the spirit—forgive me, God!—
began to bellyache like any other simple maid."
OLD KING: "Slave, stubborn mule, don't mock, don't add to all your sins;
on this vile earth the spirits live like men or maids
made pregnant with no kisses, watered without water."
SLAVE: "I'm but a slave and do not understand souls well,
but I've heard say they love ascetics wondrously
and whoop it up in women's bodies in dark caves
and that the son conceived is deemed to be God's son."
OLD KING: "Slave, O most scurrilous soul, your lips move secretly;
retch all your filthy words out now and cleanse your mind!"
SLAVE: "It's said—forgive me, king!—that the ascetic's daughter
bursts into beauteous bloom far from the eyes of man,
that she, too, hungers, strives, and groans beside her father
until the spirit descends and shades her like a man;
I don't know how, my master—it seems the soul descends
with breasts to holy men, with beards to female saints."
OLD KING: "O slave, O murky heart, your eyes are blocked with mud,
you can't see the unseen as yet or touch the untouched.
At times I deign to cross with you some simple words
and cast in your mud-furrows seeds of simple speech,
but all the seed lies fallow in your sterile head.
You've ears, but you can't hear, you've eyes, but can't see God,
yet a blind power always urges that I choose you

to guide my golden chariot in a difficult hour,
for my heart loves you, O dull-witted shaggy beast."
SLAVE: "Master, far better than your nobles, those musk-rats,
or eunuch slaves, those gelded cocks and faithful dogs,
shall I flush out and find your son in these dark woods,
for I don't yet believe in spirits or stifling ghosts;
I brush all pallid shades aside, hunt down the meat
and cut a faultless road straight through this sterile earth."
OLD KING: "The spirits of the wilds must have misled my son;
how can you ever find the road to bring him back?
Turn the gold reins, dear slave, drive to the palace now;
we've turned the forest inside out in vain since dawn;
the sun has set, and with it every hope I've had.
As he was hunting mountain game or forest deer,
a cunning spirit must have donned the downy shape
of a musk doe and led my darling boy astray
from cliff to cliff, from stream to stream until, dear God,
they both descended deep to Hades, step by step.
Ah, faithful slave, I'll deck your head with splendid plumes,
I'll give you precious amulets that all your life
you may be safe from scorpions or seductive maids,
I'll hang a noble's golden seal about your neck,
and ask but one thing in return: find me my son!
Why do you laugh? Bow down, you fool, and hear my words."
SLAVE: "Ah, I'm not laughing: plumes and seals and amulets
have made me lose my wits. What road shall I choose now?
Master, rise from your pillows, the forest forks in two:
shall we go right or left? Both roads seem good to me,
but you're the king and hold all roads within your hands.
Make up your mind, command me, don't ask my advice."
OLD KING: "The bold heart trembles now nor knows what road to take.
A deep voice in my wasted entrails cries aloud:
'Aye, king, in this dark hour you hold your destiny.
Your whole life hangs on a thin thread in hovering plight:
if you should take one road, life like a warbling stream
shall flow in chaste delight to water fields and flowers,
to run fresh watermills, to bring down teeming fish,
as on its banks a rout of red-cheeked children play;
but if you take the other road, you'll find your fate
rearing in ambush like a flickering conflagration,
until your mind catch fire, your castle burst in flame,
and your whole country disappear in smoke and ash.'
These are the bitter words the voice shouts in my mind,
and in deep groans I raise my hands and fiercely plead:
'Ah, where, to right or left? Save me from the wrong road!'
But only ruthless laughter in my heart replies."

SLAVE: "Master, the night has fallen and darkened both great roads.
Raise your hand high; command! Shall I go left or right?"
OLD KING: "What's right, what's left? Guide my gold chariot where
you please!
All crooked roads at length lead to the same dark cliff."
SLAVE: "Then with your blessing, my lord king, I'll take the right!"

The bone-flute stopped, the lone man wiped his neck of sweat,
master and slave were suddenly dazed, the horses neighed
and reared on crimson-painted hooves that broke in blood,
a baby parrot fell and squirmed on earth, confused,
for all had heard the sweet flute play, that now had ceased.
As the god-killer wiped his sweat, a mocking laugh
tore the sheer-woven veil upon the loom of dream
and a glad voice was heard in watchful sleeplessness:
ODYSSEUS: "Man's written fate swells up and stinks like rotting wounds.
O golden chariot, I, too, thought you should turn right;
earth's a great gyre, the heart's a whirlpool and gulps all.
Slaves, steeds, and masters met; I blew, and off they went!
It's time I gathered now, and in the vortex cast
those two rose-petals that, clasped on the cliffs of youth
and flaming date tree's root, now kiss so tenderly.
But first I'll crouch down low and press my ears to earth,
for their words scatter sweetly down the chasm's lips;
before my full mind puffs and the world drowns, I take
much joy in hearing how my phantom creatures talk of love."

PRINCE: "I hold you on my knees, my dear, and clasp you tight,
I stroke your hair, your breasts, your shoulders, your soft knees
and shake for fear you'll vanish when the black cock crows.
I've never felt the spirit so sweet or warm before,
as though it, too, were fragrant flesh and firm embrace.
Alack, I pluck your apples, but I fear the cliff,
for your great father was a mighty man of magic
and this firm form I hold, these godly sounds I hear
will vanish like a thought of my deluded mind."
MAID: "My dearest love, I'm a real body and a real soul;
I'm the ascetic's child who loves you, smells your musk
and twines your stalwart body like a wild-grape vine.
Dear God, I never dreamt that flesh could be so sweet!
I don't believe in spirits now, my mind rejects them,
all spirits together are not worth man's holy body;
it's you I've waited for, warm flesh, to be so blessed!
From a sweet apple tree we'll hew our fragrant bed
and our son's cradle from a lasting old oak tree,
and if some logs remain, then in the sweet nighttime,

sitting before the fire, we'll carve our household gods;
you'll hew from oak a male god with an unkempt beard,
and I from apple a plump maid who holds her child
and smiles with gentle patience on our smoking hearth."
PRINCE: "Dear wife, your bones emit sweet musk and cinnamon!
Take this red pomegranate, burst it at my door
that sons and grandsons may soon scatter through our courts."
MAID: "I ripened like an apple on the tree's top bough,
and now I tremble, for I feel my landlord's hand
searching amid the boughs to find and pluck me! Ah!"
PRINCE: "It was no unicorn, it was no small musk doe;
my fate leapt through the woods with a beast's lovely grace
and I rushed after it, as suns and moons burned bright,
to hunt down an uncatchable and godly fawn.
But suddenly then, with downcast eyes it beckoned gently
and vanished, and I saw you, love, nude on the ground.
My wits were dazed, I thought creation was reborn,
for round me all streams warbled, all trees burst in bloom,
the full moon like a page-girl strolled on the green earth
with large white poppies in her hair, parted the trees,
till I could see you clearly at the date tree's bole
kneeling before your father's corpse that smelled of musk.
I threw my bow on the grass then, and you and I
washed his still warm though pallid head and decked it well.
You raised your calm eyes then nor asked me who I was."
MAID: "I did not fear or ask, I felt salvation near;
the soul's a sky-kissed lady, but she longs for flesh."
PRINCE: "Ah, the night-vigil near the stream and your cool body!
How all stars hung down naked in the trees, how sweet
the nightbirds sighed in mountains and the beasts in woods!
Suddenly then a goldfinch swooped from the tall trees,
perched with delight upon your father's flowered hair
and puffed its saffron breast and warbled all night long.
Ah, our veins swelled and throbbed, our throats choked with desire,
we'd never before enjoyed such rapturous melody,
and our two bodies merged on earth and soared like souls."
MAID: "Be still, my love, for in the breath of night I hear
wheels rolling close and the soft sigh of steeds, I hear
an old man's mournful voice and a crude man's reply."
PRINCE: "Ah, that's my father's voice, dear love, I hear his weeping."
MAID: "Alas, the soul is a dream, too, and fades like flesh.
Ah, have I clasped warm flesh or but a snatch of air?
Your father's come, my love, to sunder us forever!"
PRINCE: "Don't weep! For love of you I shall renounce my father!
Don't fear him, love, but tell him that your father died
and that you've lost your way within this ghost-filled wood.

His face is ruthless, but his heart shakes like a child's,
he'll pity your all-holy youth, he'll stoop and raise
the daughter of our great ascetic from the ground
and, filled with joy, enthrone you in the golden room
of our rich palace for the love he bears your father;
from that time on our lives shall roll on soft gold beds.
Don't weep, my moon-cheeked love, I'll wait within the cave;
see how his golden chariot shines already through the trees."

SLAVE: "O master, I smell musk, as though musk-deer were coupling!
Earth gleams, and on all foliage pour the moon's mild beams.
Has the translucent moon rolled down to earth, O king,
or is the ascetic's daughter sitting there in tears?
Ah master, don't grow pale, don't be afraid, dismount,
it's not a lion or conflagration, it's not a ghost,
it's not your fate, my master, it's only a young maid.
Alas, my king, your gracious face is pale as wax."
OLD KING: "I hear a deep voice, faithful slave, and my heart quakes;
turn back the golden reins at once or we'll go lost!"
SLAVE: "Master, she's raised her face; the dawn breaks on her lips!
Be still that we may hear the girl, hold firm your knees!"
OLD KING: "O slave, I see a cliff ahead, our steeds stampede!"
MAID: "Ah great king, pity me, love and revere all souls.
The great ascetic, my loved father, has sunk in soil
and his last wish was that I fall at your great feet
and beg from you a simple gown, a humble hut.
Behold, O long-lived monarch, how his soul has whipped
your haughty steeds and brought you to my poor retreat.
I want to cast myself before your holy feet
but ah, I fear my hair won't guard my nakedness."
SLAVE: "The maid has risen, and all light rose with her rising!
Ah, how she feared to rise and show her nakedness,
but now she walks erect in light and her pale flesh
glows like translucent water plunging down a cliff.
Ah, I have studied women well, I know their tricks!"
OLD KING: "Draw back your hands, O naked form, don't touch my knees!"
SLAVE: "Forgive him, lady; all day long he's scoured the world
to find his darling son, love whips his tattered soul;
don't weep, his guardian angel's loony, pain has made him daft."
MAID: "Ah, master, raise your eyes, look kindly on me now,
I'm nothing to be scorned, I come of noble stock,
my father, too, was monarch of all the spirits of air
and a crown glowed invisibly on his white hair.
He walked on water as on earth, he swam through land,
and when strong foes besieged your castle, O great king,
my father puffed his cheeks and they all flew like mist.

His daughter now stoops low and pleads for a small boon.
Take me into your carriage, throw me a rag, I'm cold!
Then cast me at your castle door that I may beg
with lepers and blind men; I'll be no burden, king.
My lord, your eyes are brimming and they flow with tears!"
SLAVE: "Your naked form illumines much, but blinds mankind;
allow me, maid, to speak to him for your sweet sake.
Dear master, it's grown dark, we'll lose the ready road;
what shame the pure ascetic's famous branch should plead
and you not turn your head to speak a gentle word!
They say that when from body the strong soul is freed
it swoops through air and soars with even greater strength;
her father's soul, O king, lies coiled within the cave
like a great serpent, flickers its forked tongue, and listens.
Command me, king, to place this orphan in your chariot."
OLD KING: "Lady, forgive me; my heart's mossed and dazed with grief.
O daughter of the earth and sky, O rare blessed spirit
of the wild wastes, it's I should fall at your slim feet!
I burned with love and reverence for your lustrous father,
his thoughts like an unconquered army zoned my walls,
my ewes gave birth to females and my slaves to males
for in his holy palm we lived in tranquil peace;
and now that fate has made me worthy to find his child,
I bow down and adore, O maid of the holy wilds,
I bow and lift you from the ground, O regal crown!"
MAID: "Great king, your gentle words have slaked my thirsty heart
and like a golden cloak enwrapped my naked form;
now dressed like a great queen in your immaculate words,
I'll slowly come from shade once more and loose my hair.
Ah, let my fingertips but touch your holy knees."
SLAVE: "Oho, a woman's hair is like a sharp sword-thrust!"
OLD KING: "O faithful slave, my eyes have blurred, lean me against
the tree and throw my steed's warm golden saddle-cloth
on the nymph's nakedness whose dazzle makes me blind!
Alas, esteem my white beard, God, don't shame me now!"
SLAVE: "Lady, blot out your nakedness in this gold cloth,
perch on my hands and let me lift you on the couch;
there like a sated tigress stretch or sit like flame."
MAID: "Slave, what strong arms and brawny back you have! I laugh
because you lift me like a feather, and I shake
for fear you'll break my thin bones in your sturdy arms.
Ah, if the old man were not here, how we'd both laugh!"
As in the golden chariot the gold-glowing maid
enthroned herself enwrapped in her gold cloak, the steeds
snorted, the holy date tree sprouted flame for fruit,
and the ascetic's soul hissed like a household serpent god.

Then the flute's tune grew wilder and fate's speed increased,
the lone man rose on tiptoe and laughed long with pride
to see how all things took their place in his mid-brows.
He saw the forest glinting with the maid's reflection,
he saw the old man cracking on the cliffs of passion,
he saw far castles burn, he saw a comely maid
braiding her cool thighs in a gorgon's knot with men.
ODYSSEUS: "All's well! Go to it, flute, speed up your melody!
Child-bearing flame, how bright you glow in the gold couch;
the soul's a date tree on a cliff, and fire's her fruit!
A secret passion burns your quivering lips, O king!
Forward! Be light of heart, old man! Reveal your pain!"

OLD KING: "My faithful slave, rein in the steeds, help me descend;
I long to cling to rock, I've cracked from too much weeping."
SLAVE: "Master, the stars are blotted out and clouds crush down,
sharp sulphur stings my nostrils, soon the storm will burst."
OLD KING: "Patience! Rein in the steeds, and I shall soon return.
I see a moss-grown altar on that shaded path
where I shall go to talk in quiet with God awhile;
O faithful slave, the spirits choke my heavy heart."
MAID: "Stretch out your black arms, slave, and lower me to earth;
now that the old man's hobbled off and we're alone
I long for a red flower I saw on the grass there."
SLAVE: "The old man looks up at the sky to be consoled,
our lickerish maiden looks at earth and longs for flowers,
and I, straight in the middle, see not earth or sky!
Lady, why do you laugh and cuddle against my chest?"
MAID: "Ah, slave, your dark beard tickles me with its sharp thorns."
OLD KING: "Why have you given me this flame to fetch home, Lord?
Pity the heart that loves you, Lord, revere old age!
Haven't I always been your faithful slave, the clean
and cutting sword you held, a feather in your wings?"
MAID: "Ah, ah, a shower of thick raindrops struck my lips!
Dark clouds have crushed the peaks! I'm scared of lightning bolts!"
SLAVE: "Let's run into this stable, lady, out of the rain."
MAID: "Ah, how the stable smells! I like its pungent warmth!
Ah, ah, the lightning strikes!" SLAVE: "It was my eyes that flashed."
MAID: "I've never seen on earth before so strong a man!
My father always bent in wind like a slim reed;
if he but munched a single date, he'd break in sweat,
but you are stronger, slave, than even the greatest spirit."
OLD KING: "I was a fountain once of nobleness and honor,
but now the garden's vanished and the fountain's dried,
my heart swells like a wound now and will burst like boils
to expose the shameless worms that fill my rotting guts.

Until today, I drowned them and drowned with them, Lord,
but you raised high your hand, and struck! I've no hope now.
You don't reward fair virtue, Lord, or keep your word."
SLAVE: "Lady, you laugh, and like a viper lick your lips."
MAID: "So long as in this pungent stable we're alone,
I'm tickled and well pleased, although it flash and thunder.
Ah, but your face has grown deformed, and your teeth gleam!
Respect the ascetic's holy child! Don't touch me, slave!"
SLAVE: "I'm no old man to think the flesh untouchable soul.
You're not a sky-soul, lady, nor a wing of air,
but soft sweet-bedded flesh, an upright downy sheath
that's had a lifelong hankering for black-hilted swords!"
MAID: "I can't see well in this thick dark, all seem the same;
a kiss's giddiness makes slaves and masters gods.
Slave, squeeze me in your strong arms, break me like a toy!"
They rolled in warm manure and coupled in cattle-dung;
the slave growled like a buffalo, and the maid chirped
like a small early-morning bird struck by the sun's first beam.

The mind blew like the North Wind, and earth shed its leaves,
the slave had had enough of kissing, the king of praying,
and the mill swelled its groaning wings and ground again.
The golden chariot moved and the whip chirped all night,
the golden town gates gaped, and as the maiden placed
her rosy-ankled foot on the pale ivory sill,
the palace's foundations creaked and the walls cracked.
It was as though fate's thralls had made a mystic pact,
as though they'd waited for the kiss's secret sign
to march their armies from afar and zone the castle.
Thoughtful and foiled, the old king sat enthroned and clicked
his virtues one by one on holy amber beads:
"Dear God, I haven't killed, or thieved, or shamed my bed,
I have not touched the ascetic's child, though my heart breaks;
why do I dread your wrath or fear to face you, Lord?"
Then to God's mocking laughter all the palace rang:
"They think to hunt the tiger, Me, with wiles! What shame!
They think they'll catch me if they set good deeds for traps,
but I'm a tiger, not a ghost; I'm starved for meat!"
God roared with laughter, plunged, and joined the other camp.
Moons bloomed and withered hot suns rose and fell, and still
a cruel invisible murderer pushed the frenzied hosts
and made them strive with fierce assaults to breach the walls;
but the king's only son, wilting in shade away,
tightened his stubborn lips and at his father glared:
"May you be cursed, old man, who keep my loved one locked
nor let me see her, till my mind's forever numbed.

May your skull burst to bits and your walls crash to dust!"
The king kept silent, wearing on his hoary head
his virtue's bitter olive wreath with pride; the slave
hung all his hopes on balsam Time that heals all wounds
nor knew that old man Time himself has his own master.
Odysseus wiped his flute, then leant against a rock
and watched his five slack dancers tottering on their feet
as once again the mills grew weary and fate ground slow.
Then the swift-minded man leapt from the rock, erect:
ODYSSEUS: "I brace myself and kick the Wheel of Fate! Whirl on!
Let old men drool, and let the dead be patient still;
we have no time, our hearts beat with sledge-hammer blows,
the iron is white-hot now, and life is brief, most brief!
Let generations flick in sun like lightning streaks,
let all trees flower and rot in a brief flash on earth,
let kingdoms in one day rise like the sun at dawn,
climb swiftly to mid-heavens and finally fade at dusk.
Let life's wheel also whirl as swiftly as my heart,
let the young man cry out and the maid rise in sun,
let me cast love with her red ankles down to earth,
let wretched people fall like brushwood in the hearth,
let all that take long years to bloom last not one hour!
Come forward, faithful slave, appear, come bring the dreadful news!"

SLAVE: "O king!" OLD KING: "Don't spare me, slave! Speak bold and clear!
This heavy heart no longer aches; give it no thought.
I know my army has turned tail and scurries back."
SLAVE: "O king!" OLD KING: "Don't hurry, slave, my heart has turned to stone."
SLAVE: "O king, your army's lost! It's faded away like mist!"
OLD KING: "Don't moan. An ax can't cleave what fate has foreordained.
Thank you, my God! Ah, you've repaid my service well!"
SLAVE: "Master, I've never feared, but my heart trembles now.
Their fierce king falls on us with his vermilion feet
and treads our skulls as the grape-treader treads his grapes.
When their steeds dashed at daybreak and the highways roared . . ."
OLD KING: "O faithful slave, be still, I wish to hear no more.
Sages, be still! See how I've thrived on your advice:
the holocaust is my red crown, and grief my harvest;
a hard hand rules our fate, and to resist is shameful;
hide from before my face, I'm weary of this world,
it's rotted like a fruit in sun, it's filled with worms,
and only you remain, my only son. Come near me now.
O God, hear my complaint, my one unbearable shame:
you've given me an only son, who won't—for shame!—

take up his arms to fight the foe and save his race!"
PRINCE: "I've sworn not to take arms or to protect the town
until you smash your jail and give me my belovèd.
Stretch out your hands, old man, and choose! Write down your fate:
I hold your kingdom in one fist, the maid in the other!"
OLD KING: "I fling my arms to heaven and swear a mighty oath:
I'll not draw back the bolts, you'll never take the maid!
I hold a soul as grieved as yours! Fate's will be done!"
PRINCE: "O wild winds, blow, scatter his castle's ashes far,
may his white beard be steeped in blood, may all his wealth
be blown to the world's ends, and may his kingdom fade!"
SLAVE: "Master, the field's aflame, battalions press us close,
the foe has zoned the city, and the frenzied crowd
rush to burn down the palace with red flaming brands!"
OLD KING: "In your dread hands, O Lord, I see a wreath of flames.
O slave, what do the people want of my red crown?"
SLAVE: "Master, the people charge you with a heavy crime
because you hold our dread ascetic's only daughter
deep in a dungeon's pit unjustly, with no cause,
and now the ascetic's soul has risen and cracked our walls.
Set her free, master, loose this sorceress on the foe,
she's stronger far than armies for with her white hands
and her caresses she can kill the foe's fierce king.
The crowds complain you smite them out of stubbornness;
do what they wish, don't let one soul destroy them now."
OLD KING: "The moment every man's conceived, a worm is born
and crawls on past all fields and peaks to eat him whole!
The same thing happens when a town or a whole world's
conceived, and now that our own city's worm crawls close
here on this plain, not even God can change our fate."
SLAVE: "Master, I hear the dungeon's bronze bolts crash and fall!"
OLD KING: "I hear the flesh fall from my soul, and mist from mind . . ."
SLAVE: "Master, they've smashed the bolts, they've pulled the dungeon
down
and brought to light, unshackled, the great ascetic's child!"
OLD KING: "All things are smokes, shames, fancies of the burning
mind.
Run swiftly, slave, bring me the maid, for fate speeds on.
Make keys and counter-keys, O heart, bolt yourself well
and say this was a lustrous dream, that the cock crowed,
that life stripped off its golden clothes and turned to air."
SLAVE: "Master, here at your feet I place the slender maid;
she can bewitch the cycling sun, cast down the moon,
and bring the foe to utter ruin in just one night;
open your eyes and mind, command your sacred wish."
OLD KING: "Life's a red lightning flash; I walk in its bright glow,

I've seen all things, I've no more hope or fear, I'm free!
Death is a long, long feather that I hold aloft."
PRINCE: "Welcome, midwinter sun, O welcome, bright new moon,
a thousand welcomes with your cool arms, maid I love!"
OLD KING: "Ho, seize my son and cast him in the iron pit!
Alas, maid kissed in stealth and stealthily made pregnant,
undress yourself and glow on earth, unbind your hair,
kneel at the date tree's holy root once more, and weep.
I quiver in your lime-twigs, bitch; your spells have crazed me,
but I am old and graceless—go to the fierce king,
tell him that you're once more alone, that you fear beasts,
and when within his tent you clasp him in your arms,
here, take this poisonous knife and stab him through the heart."
MAID: "Dear God, time has its twists, and now my turn has come.
My body is my security, my breasts are shields,
and I shall bring you in my pouch the fierce king's head;
your castle trembles, and one kiss will make it firm,
but I, too, seek a costly recompense, O king."
OLD KING: "Speak up, maid kissed in stealth and stealthily made pregnant,
but weigh your words well, don't ask what my heart can't give."
MAID: "I stretch my white arms at your castle gate and beg:
master, come out, give me for alms your only son."
SLAVE: "Wake from your nightmare, master, exorcise these spells;
a murky darkness, monarch, chokes your lustrous soul,
but don't forget that you are king, and the world's crown."
OLD KING: "Oho, this whore and her beast-womb long for no less
than our one son, our throne, the earth, our head and crown!
The body is a ship that scuds with full-rigged sails
on deep dark waters frenziedly to find its doom;
the soul of man is a lightning flash, a gust of wind."
SLAVE: "O master, give her what she wants! It's our last hope!"
OLD KING: "Lady, I've rooted up my heart! Take joy of him!
I rip the regal crown from off my whitened hair
and place it like a coal of fire about your head.
We crawl from fire to fire on earth, and thus proceed;
between two towering, blazing pyres we dance and weep,
nor does death pity us, nor does life want us now."
SLAVE: "Master, don't weep; no matter what it says, the soul
can bear all the world's worse, most bitter decadence;
the whore heals all shames swiftly and grows young again."
The old king mounted silently the day's watchtower
and saw streets burst in bloom where the young maiden passed;
a strong and fair wind blew and swelled her crimson gown
and flowing tresses like a pirate ship full sail;
a spark set out, increased, and swiftly sped across the plain.

Then the god-slayer raced his tune till his flute danced,
for he, too, saw the maid walk with seductive step,
and blessed her from his heart and gave her his advice:
ODYSSEUS: "Don't be ashamed now, paint your lips and shake your hips,
you're not just any common girl, no harbor whore,
you are unhaltered fate speeding with silver sandals!
Don't ever condescend to say, 'I pity man,
leave pity to slaves, and fainting spells to ugly maids.
O Fate, flame speaks now in our breasts with her long tongue!
Our soul contemns compassion, justice, goodness, truth,
nor cares for virtues or ideas, men or gods,
they're all good kindling-wood, and hunger gleans our soul;
go with my blessing, pay your whole debt with a kiss."
He spoke, and the proud maiden blazed, lit all the plain,
looked on the troops as kindling-wood, looked on their king
and coiled thrice like a viper, like a small, small bird
in his deep armpits and his heart's audacious core.
The twilight sauntered past, the mountains crawled in darkness,
all fountain sources moved, beasts thirsted, the earth smelled,
and as the warrior-king tossed in his lustful bed
dawn broke and all wings woke, trees laughed with rose-red smiles,
the sun first struck upon a sparrow's flinty head,
and when the king raised his dark lashes, his bed glowed.
A woman's words in bed have great world-shaking power,
and the mind-archer smiled, tamed his delirious flute,
then placed his whorled ear close against the bedside's rim.

WARRIOR: "May the cock never crow, may daylight never break!
Lady, I'll gather nutmeg pods to pelt you with;
never before have I known flesh so poisonous sweet;
I wake, but honey drips still from my thorny beard,
I live and hold you on my chest as in a dream;
lady, why didn't you raise your hand to kill me then?"
MAID: "Sleep took you gently on my breast at break of day;
there you smiled meekly like a babe with curly hair
and mumbled softly as your bare chest rose and fell,
as though a childhood dream were fluttering in your mind.
You are a mighty warrior smeared with hair and blood,
your muddy knees and your black fists still smell, still reek
with women's sour embracements in a slaughter's din,
but when I marveled at your sleeping like a babe,
for the first time I felt a mother's palpitations."
WARRIOR: "And I smiled secretly and kept a sleepless watch;
I knew that if I slept you'd slay me in my bed—
I found your poisonous blade hid in your crimson sash,

and also your wide pouch where you would thrust my head.
When by the tree I saw you nude, coiled like a snake,
your slant and beckoning eyes, your thighs that steamed with lust,
I sniffed the assassination well, but unperturbed
I took and laid you on my bed of lion-pelts.
I know all snares of life, and plunge with open eyes!
Then I began to kiss you sweetly, and God flashed.
As thieving sleep took me a moment on your breast,
I dreamt I burned in cinnamon and laurel boughs,
drenched with rose-oils, and flared up in a roaring blaze
till on your fragrant bosom, lady, I turned to ash.
But see, I've wakened and still live, you still rejoice
in my thick nostrils, in my hairy hands and feet."
MAID: "A woman's breast is like a drunkard's country, filled
with wings and demons which the hunter hunts at dawn.
When from the tree you raised me, my eyes throbbed with fear,
I'd never seen such rough, repellent ugliness,
but when you smiled, a chasm suddenly filled with flowers.
As though we two were old and trusted friends, you told
me all your joys and sorrows, opened all your heart,
nor asked me whence I'd come nor what I sought of you.
Belovèd, dawn has broken; I worship this great day,
for you shall spring full-armed and crush the castle! Rise!"
WARRIOR: "You are my falcon, lady, with vermilion claws;
I don't want now to take their castle with my troops;
let them but give me your sweet hand like a red rose."
MAID: "You smile, and in your eyes I see the cunning noose;
come, place a new-slain head in my wide pouch that all
their narrow castle gates may gape to let me through,
and when in jubilee they've emptied all their walls,
fall on their battlements, my dear, like a starved lion."
WARRIOR: "Within a drunkard's land, upon a woman's breast,
I've hunted many times at night before dawn broke,
but never before have I rejoiced so much or feared
as now when in my hands I hold such flaming prey.
I kiss your hands, your feet, my dear, your crisp cool breasts.
Behold, your pouch shall brim with a new-slaughtered head:
I see your lily feet already blooming in crimson blood!"

ODYSSEUS: "Ah, I no longer want to watch cock-pheasant man
with shriveled brains, with flimsy plumes stuck on his head,
crowned with a dappled cap! I blow, and fate speeds on!
They've decked their town with laurel boughs, burst all the kegs
till wine spills out like blood and dulls their languid eyes;
the wretched king sits on his throne and lifts his hands."
OLD KING: "Thank you, all-holy God, your soul aches for this world;

you filled my cup with bitterness to test my love,
my soul distills to pure gold in your blazing kiln.
Forgive my sins, Almighty, that for a brief hour
my heart grew faint and mouthed most bitter words, while you,
all-knowing Father, held my salvation in your hands."
ODYSSEUS: "Of what salvation do you dream, on what God shout?
Earth hangs, and light coils like a noose about her neck.
Lift up your eyes, the whole plain moves now toward your town,
your stables weep their horses, and your palace weeps
its kings, your golden garments weep your flesh and bones;
your trusted slave, bowed low before your foe's red feet,
surrenders the town's silver keys on a gold tray.
Enough, my grinding's done, and my millwheel has stopped;
the smell of deadly camomile intoxicates the air."

SLAVE: "O dread, O long-lived king, here are the castle keys!
His palace smokes in ashes, his streets sail in blood,
for with no spirited resistance or complaint
our old king stretched his tender neck, and here I hold
his white head in your pouch. Shackled in dungeon irons,
his only son was burned in the town's conflagration,
and here's the small, small heap of ash his body left."
WARRIOR: "God holds each soul, weighs each dram well in careful
scales,
nor does he love, or feel compassion, or need friends,
for God entrusts his fate to the most strong alone
with stern commands to rule the world without compassion.
Where's that untamed sweet beast with female breasts who spread
her lily hands with love and gave me king and castle?
Let conflagrations blaze of scented wood, cast huge
piles of rose-bay and laurel boughs, of clove and nard,
and pour great jars of rose-oil that the flames may soar.
Then place her body on a bronze war-shield, and paint
her lips, her brows, her upright breasts, that she may rise
with a great warrior's holy honors in a tall blaze;
she used her body like a shield in gallant strife
and killed men with her strong embracements, two beds cracked;
the cycle now has come full round, her woman's task is done!"

In the soft luster of the moon Odysseus laid
his flute of dead man's bone on the dark knees of night
and soon his dream with its curled russet tresses ceased.
On a stone pillow, on refreshing cool cliff-weeds,
the great mind-looter leant his white and wearied head
so softly that the five souls round him did not wake
and still rejoiced a while in fates more great than theirs.

Then the ascetic, that soul-snatcher, shut his eyes
and raised his hands to the arch-cunning juggler, mind:
"O Mind, Great Steward, secret Father of all Time,
the heart is but a slice of fat, a chunk of meat,
and clings and will not part from sons or fecund soil;
my virtue blooms on piles of dunghill infamies!
O Mind, all women wept and smothered in my breast;
earth was a narrow bed, how could she hold them all?
Strong virile men would stifle and choke in my roused loins
until thick smokes of passion rose and my head reeled.
Seeds shouted in my loins and raised their sharp-hooked stalks:
'Father, give us a body too, we're cold, we're starved,
give us a name that we may live, a brain to thrive;
we, too, want to become both male and female spores
that we may pair off on the earth in a glad coupling.
We won't live in your brain's coils any longer now;
like a full harem's virgins, shriveled and unkissed,
we listen at the lattices and horde the wealth
of our firm thighs, man's lust, the noises of the street;
Father, break down our bars that we may flee and live!
If only earthen arms would clasp us, that with love,
begetting, dying, we also may rejoice in earth!
Break open, head, and sow us in a sun-washed land!'
All unborn children yelled within me, stifled me,
my manly blood was grafted with deep, dark desires,
the soberest thoughts got drunk and decked themselves with wings,
most modest words like shameless parrots flew and cawed,
my soul became dark Africa's barbaric revelry.
Black demons zoned me, Death turned lawless and distraught,
till you came, Savior Mind, gave order to disorder,
made firm the shaken laws of this most futile game
till longing wrapped you like a roaring holocaust
and azure smoke leapt from the fiercely burning brain:
'This is not joy or sorrow, this is not compassion
filled with new yearning men and trembling soil,' you groaned,
'these are but smoke rings rising now in open air.'
You spoke, then to that crossways dashed where five roads meet,
our five short-lived delights, the eye, the ear, the tongue,
the lady of high birth who sniffs, the crone who gropes;
you leapt and danced, changed full protean shapes, then sat
on deep insanity's dark shore and played your games.
You took and pummeled sand, then said, 'Now you are meat,'
and swiftly it began to love and weep and shout,
as though it were firm flesh indeed that brimmed with soul.
My entrails emptied and grew light, all my desires
were dressed in bodies, leapt in light and danced with joy,

freed finally from every pain and every need.
They call you Spirit, Lord, for you beget proud flesh,
they call you Flesh, O Lord, for you beget all souls;
O Mind, you master sound, cut down the sun to size,
deceive the ears and eyes and bring the heart's desire!
And when sad lamentation sweeps the untouched maid
she opens wide her empty arms and broods in thought:
'I see and hear, I taste, touch, smell, but all in vain,
my senses watch the sky and shout like greedy beaks.'
And then one night, O Lord, you mount her like a bull
until at dawn the maid with sated senses leaps
on the sun-terraces and hails the dawning world:
'Life is most good, kisses are good, and bread, and meat!'
And when the young man feels his brows have weighed him down,
then you become a great thought, you descend in deeds
till the young man grows glad as though he held his son
and were son, father, mother, all—three heads in one.
You change and play, Lord, and rejoice in savage power;
there's no one on this earth you love or even hate,
you've run away from father, mother, and left your sons
but houseless vagabonds that knock from door to door.
Nor hopes nor troubles fool you now, your hollow bones
whistle like flutes in an invisible shepherd's hands.
Like a black cloud you pass on high above men's heads
and good housekeepers raise their eyes and greet you thus:
'They say it'll rain, that earth will cool, that seed will sprout,'
but you pass on in waterless and windless void.
You blow, raise towns and countries till whole armies march,
but quickly bored, you blow once more and make all vanish.
A lightning flash thus tore the bowels of the abyss
and showed the reverent body of our Mother Earth
hung in the dark blue chasm of immortal Death.
The lightning flash went out, and all things once more thrust
in the dry unflowering rind of dark Necessity.
Once more the swelling oak trees crouched in acorn husks,
and earth, that precious lustrous peacock, closed its tail
and pecks now at the dung heap like a famished hen.
All things from heady drunkenness returned ashamed,
trees, waters, men, and gods, and once more thrust themselves
in grease-smirched working clothes, in humble daily tasks.
All was a visionary dream, a dancer's mist,
the mind but turned the wheel of love a bit more swiftly,
then all at once, in one breath, the five weather-cocks,
the imagination's five creations, loved, died, rotted.
O Mind, last born of demons, pregnant head like that
broad mare the castle-wreckers raised before Troy's walls,

O pure unpitying eye, O lash of light that whips
the brainless night and flogs her flesh with lightning bolts,
thank you for scattering my great pain in a sweet game!
The man most virile holds the dreadful keys of life,
locks and unlocks with no sure hope, disjoins but air,
groans not with blows, nor trembles, but with courage thrusts
into desire's nonexistent palace built on air
and gladly girds himself with the great Keys of Nothingness."

The sun was still unborn, the day-star laughed long still
under the sky's profound and gold-smoked wings, and still
the archer blessed and praised his playful, juggling mind.
Now sated, slaked, his heart played on the chasm's edge
and in great calmness waited for the sun to rise.
Slowly the boundless sunlight spread, the day-star shrank,
dawn bound her golden kerchief, all the leaves turned rose,
and the lone man's white hair turned red by the cliff's edge
till his heart filled with mountains, morning stars, and wings.
He leapt and seized that gold-rimmed heavy wheel, the sun,
which had bogged down in the mind's mud, and set it free.
He moved, and mountains swayed like roses in the light,
he zoned his waist with tender vines, then cut himself
a flowering staff, serenely walked from rock to rock
and joyed to feel the dawn's fuzz on his newborn skin.
As he lunged down the blossomed slopes in joy that dawn
with a small laurel spray that filled his mouth with scent,
the dawn's light burst within his heart till his head swayed
and leapt like disembodied fire in lucid air.
He laughed until his wide smile stretched from ear to ear:
"Now that my brain has cleared and sees that earth and sea
and sky are but the eye's creations, the fierce beast
that guards the well is slain, the deathless water flows,
smashes the dams of memory and the brain's thick walls,
pours fiercely down from the high mountains of man's head
and sweeps into the plains with ships, fish, stars, and trees,
moves all the windmills of the mind and the heart's wheels,
streams on, hails all, then plunges laughing down the abyss.
Brothers, so long as our lives last, heigh ho!, let's brim
that earthen cup, our bottomless and thirsty heart,
and drink the deathless warbling water, its cool sound!"
An unexpected sweetness seized him as he spoke,
for in his heart the brothers, Mind and War, embraced,
and he stood still to enjoy the world's conciliation.
Deep in that silence then he heard his bones break out
in warbling song like rows of flaming flutes in sun,
as though a wealthy wedding pomp set off from far

and swiftly poured down mountain slopes to find the bride.
The archer's knees gave way, he knelt on the rough ground,
bowed low with reverence, kissed his Mother Earth like bread,
and as he touched her body, a dream slowly spread,
an ancient myth, and on his quivering lashes hung.
He saw Earth lean her dugs against her monstrous rocks,
then reach her trembling hands amid the soil's warm smell
and blindly stroke with love her two most mighty sons.
The sons grew savage, rose, and envy coiled and twined
in their dark loins like a green asp with coal-hot eyes:
"Dear Mother, hold me on your knees, give me your lap,
for I am War, the first-born son of your strong bowels;
and by my birthright all your wealth is justly mine."
The smallest flicked his hissing voice like a sharp fang:
"Dear Mother, take me on your knees, give me your lap,
I am your pet, your handsome youngest son, the Mind;
blind Mother, I'm the light that cuts new roads for you."
Their mother spread her hands and fondled both young heads:
"My boys, set out together, circle round my globe,
and he who first returns shall mount my lap, a king."
The first-born jumped upon his russet mare, and sped;
the youngest pressed his ears against the earth and heard
the hooves beat in the distance swiftly as stones sparked,
then circled and adored his mother's body thrice
and slowly mounted up her vast beloved knees.
When frothing War returned from the world's distant ends,
a fuming passion seized him and he yelled in wrath:
"Mother, why do you hold him on your knees? While I
roamed these long years, he wasted all his life nor left
your loving side, nor helped his friends, nor fought his foes,
but stooped and idle, with pale hands, played on his flute!"
Mother Earth fondled in the dark her youngest child:
"My son, you circled once earth's outer rind, but he
flashed thrice like lightning round his central core, the Mother.
I'll cut a spray of the wild olive tree to wreathe his head."

Prone on the earth, the archer listened to both sounds
deep in his entrails, and rejoiced, and asked himself
which one was he—the first son, War, or darling Mind,
then laughed, knowing that this was but an ancient myth,
and that both Mind and War, frail thought or sturdy deed,
feather of peacock, or the war's unpitying blade,
changed places freely in his juggling hands, just as he pleased.

XVIII

Life hangs like a Queen Bee on the earth's flowering branch,
and the four winds, all bridegrooms, clasp her secretly
and feel her fuzzy belly gently brim with dreams,
with future joys and distant wings; but the brave mind
can only for a lightning flash, one breath of air,
fight with black Death or stroll through chaos and there beget
great gods and thoughts, imagination's flights, and give
nobility and breed to the earth's puckered hide.
The archer, highest blossom which the world can sprout
after most fearful strife with phantoms and with gods,
walked on the earth with dry nostalgic eyes and said
farewell caressingly to all the living world,
until the flowers filled with teardrops and the leaves with dew.
He passed through many roads and cut through many woods;
how the world shone! as though made virgin, like his soul;
rocks laughed as though the sun had pierced into their hearts
and the dry white-thorn laughed and wept with crystal dew.
He held his heart and mind now like a double-ax,
and numberless sweet-throated memories soared and perched
in the great tower of his mind like cooing doves;
women within him cried like seething, chattering towns
and hamlets laid their passion-smothered bosoms bare;
the flesh got drunk and sprouted souls, and the mind, too,
the famished son of need, got drunk and burst in song.
A giddy sparrow, that thickheaded bird, flew high
and gazed upon the archer with black beady eyes,
then twittered round him full of joy and wished him well.
The sly bird-catcher waved his hand and hailed the bird:
"Good morning, my dear sparrow, my most darling flute.
Ah, how I love your soft small body, your warm belly
filled full of tiny eggs and seeds of grain and song.
If only the soul of man—what luck!—were like you too!"
For the first time the wanderer felt the world his home,
as though he smelled grass or saw trees for the first time;
he reached his hand and cut a spray of flowering sage
and the scent rose till his brains smelled like mountain slopes.

For the first time he raised his eyes and saw birds fly
and felt their bodies' holy warmth cupped in his hands.
Like an old hen that sprouts a crest and hoarsely crows,
day rose on terraces, and as the lone man walked,
the distant hamlets woke and chimneys belched with smoke.
A new-wed Negro rose at dawn before doors opened,
stumbled, and woke his bride, then both knelt on straw mats,
placed iron spheres before them, smeared them with fat grease
and the man raised his pleading voice in the dim hut:
"O precious dowry of my wife, I bow and worship.
Don't let us die of hunger, O strong god of iron!
Deign now to fall into our fire, soften a bit,
become a slashing double-ax and guard us well.
O fallow deer, gazelles, wild boars, I call you, come!
Stay firmly in my hands now, ax! Don't shake! Strike hard!"
He spoke, then lit a fire, and his young, faithful wife
knelt down and blew it with a reed and fed the flames
till in the hearth the spheres began to redden slowly.
In Africa's deep heart the human herds awoke,
the sluggish river woke, the caïques tossed and swerved,
and a grim plowman hunched his back and clove the soil.
He had no other comrades in his wretched life,
dear God, than his two faithful ox with steaming snouts,
and thus he turned to them and told them all his pain:
"Giddap, my Russet, giddap, Gray, even this shall pass.
The Master, high in the far heavens, lifts his goad
and pricks our wretched backs, for he's in a great rush;
and here, the master of the earth sits in the shade
and he, too, pricks our backs in turn till the blood flows.
Patience, O brethren ox, the world's a heavy yoke,
the earth's a hard and stony field, hunger wrecks all;
wherever he is, my brothers, day by day Death comes,
fetching cool water in his palms, hay in his lap,
and sweet black wheaten bread, and he'll unyoke us soon.
Giddap, my Russet, giddap, Gray, salvation's close at hand!"
As thus the plowman talked with his stooped lowing ox,
the sun fell on their backs until their foreheads glowed
as though it were a gold sphere wedged between their horns.
Day ripened and rose high on earth like a white sail,
crews rose with the red sun to start their daily tasks,
the earth, a three-tiered galley sailed in the bright air
and the archer, her old sea-wolf, stepped from rock to rock
on balanced tiptoe, till his glad heart swelled with winds
and like a holy compass showed the surest way.
At noon a cricket clung to his right shoulder blade
with gleaming, thin, smoke-silver wings and sparkling eyes,

and as its quivering body brimmed with rasping song,
together the two friends lunged down the mountain slope.
The mighty archon of the mind then hailed his friend:
"Welcome, small cricket, for you perch on Death's own hair
with three all-crimson regal rubies in your head!
Wee athlete, I admire your pluck and stubbornness;
you do not live on the sky's dew and empty air
for your intestines seek firm food that they may sing.
Cling to the Tree of Death and drill it full of holes
until it spouts with honey and you're fit to burst;
be quick, I don't think we've much time, for soon at night
the great green Locust will swoop down and slash our necks!
Let's be in time, my friend, to fling a lustrous song
and a shrill voice from branch to branch in night's dark tree."
Thus did the lone man talk and reached to touch his friend
but it leapt up with rasping wrath, thrust in his hair,
and there, as in white-thorn, its high thin voice began
to saw its master's brains in two with shrill delight.
The demon-battered peak of earth began to shake:
"I think that somewhere, as I plunged toward a blue beach,
while at my back the smoke of a new-plundered town
still swirled, a famished crow perched on my shoulder blade
with beak still bloody from a king's disboweled guts;
but now a tender cricket clings, its silver mouth
full-fed and slaked with song and a rare drop of honey.
All things at length are harmonized with the soul's cares!"
He spoke thus with his cricket and his wealthy mind,
then crossed the mountain, goading his air-flock before him,
his flowered shepherd's crook slung straight across his back.
Nor did he think of hunger now that flailed his bowels,
nor did he longer bear his old crew's heavy corpse,
but in his mind the earth and sky beat like two brilliant wings.

The pine rejoices in the rain, the fir in snow,
and the good man rejoices as he walks the earth
with but a cricket in his hair, no dogs, no gods!
The sun reclined at the ascetic's left-hand temple,
and earth grew light and cool as soon as the sun set;
to the far ends of Africa all live things breathed,
men plunged in the cool rivers to refresh themselves
then beat their drums and bellowed, swirled in dance until
the Evening Star struck all with sweet intoxication.
Blue shadows spread like plots of violets, the night spilled
like a sweet-peppery wine that made brains reel with drink,
and life and death were joined, widows and dead men merged,
a pyre was raised high in the woods as the sun fell

and in the afterglow the last farewells began.
The widows wailed and clawed their cheeks, the trusted slaves
shrilled as they laid a fat corpse on a tall pyre's peak,
then poured oil on the wood, set it afire till flame
leapt up and licked and clasped with joy the prostrate meat.
A stout witch doctor raised his plump hands toward the pyre:
"Push off! The flames now swell your sails! Good voyage, friend!
We've given you many orders; don't forget them, mind!
Tell our forebears that if they want to eat slain men
cast in high heaps in pits, and drink deep jugs of blood,
they, too, must dash to help us when the war drums beat.
Yesterday not one poked his nose out! Let them starve!
We've not one slave for them to eat as votive gift.
Tell them to move their feet fast if they want to eat,
to gird their swords, nor haunt us with their hungry whines.
You're starving? Then come down to help us! Stop your twiddling!
Tell them that here the world is poor and the meat little.
Push off, O herald; take our pains to the underworld!"
Thus in the shades of evening, in the night's embrace,
sorrows and joys changed places often, black-white spots
on the sunburnt and dappled leopard hide of earth.
Odysseus, hungry athlete, stood at the steep edge
of a dusk-smothered deep ravine and sought to find
a smoking hut far down the plain where man and wife
stooped low and poked the fire to cook their holy meal.
He heard a slight commotion in the brush, then turned
his eyes, but did not move, and saw a scrawny wolf
slink through the shadows slyly, slowly cutting down
against the wind that sheep dogs might not find his scent.
But when the starved beast sniffed man's odor, he stood still,
and his great brother smiled as their two glances crossed;
one in his black brain mused if he should pounce upon
that upright form, or slink away with draggled tail;
the other in his sunwashed mind thought of a truce:
"Dear Brother Wolf, abandon your sly crooked paths;
don't seek in fright to veer from winds—sheepfolds await you,
and the rough sheep dogs wag their shaggy tails with love
and wait your coming, O great prince of shepherds, Wolf!
The shepherd gives the shepherd lad strict orders now:
'My son, it's time to rise and push into the woods;
stand with esteem before the Wolf's great lodge and say:
"The shepherd of unnumbered sheep and fierce watchdogs
sends greetings to the famished chieftain of the woods;
his dogs are tied, his sheepfold's gates gape all night long,
he has no work to do, his buxom lambs increase,
both wolf and shepherd are old fellow-traveling friends,

and both set out together, famished, to find lambs.
Master, it's time to stop our quarreling. Let's be friends.
May my fat croft become your noble household also.
Welcome, O Chieftain Wolf, let the feast boards be spread!
Behold, the sheep have smelled you out and bow their heads,
the shepherd welcomes you like a loved king who year
on year in dark and wretched exile fought his foes
and now returns at length to his chief town with joy."'"
Thus quarrels and friendships merged within the lone man's mind
and the wolf bent his savage head serenely, thrust
his tail between his legs and slunk along the shadowed shrubs.

Meanwhile, as black night mounted like a monstrous castle,
the mighty warrior huddled by an oak tree's root
and called on sleep, his faithful slave, to start his task.
In the moist air a female glowworm silently,
with her pert belly glowing, mistook the lone man's beard
for a bright flowering bush, chose it for her night's rest
and with blue brilliance called on the male grooms to come;
as the god-battler shut his eyes, the glowworms swarmed,
and all night long his bright beard shone with dazzling blue.
The ascetic's sleep was thick and sweet, filled full of wonders;
as a sea-diver spurts from waves and holds in hand
a heavy precious coral, the god-battler woke,
his entrails cool and glowing still amid the coral.
Again he raised his staff, plunged southward and passed on
but saw no fruit to eat, nor slightest trace of man;
the sun shone through his body, thinned by hunger pangs,
and as his eyes grew dazed, he heard a buzzing sound
as Death like a great sea-fly or a black night-moth
opened his downy wings and hovered in azure air
till the archer raised his hand and spoke with a full heart:
"Welcome, O mighty landlord, welcome, final haven,
welcome, O tail-end of the dance, wasp-sting of life!
Welcome, cup-bearer with your deep wine-bowl in hand,
give us to drink till we get drunk, let minstrels come
—all kinds of men and trees and seas and dreams and thoughts—
to sing in all the streets before the grand return!"
A butterfly came and perched upon the rain-drenched soil,
then closed its wings, and lo, once more turned to a worm.
Odysseus then half-closed his eyes and shook with laughter
for he knew well the dazzling tricks of cunning Time
that with swift sleight-of-hand grasps shadows, light and air,
then shapes, reshapes in play the wonders of the world;
it casts the dry stones of date trees in burning sand,
broods on them like a hen and hatches them like eggs.

Dear God, who'd ever think to find so tightly locked
in those dry stones, such soaring date trees, such long leaves,
such honeyed dates that burst in clustered rows in light?
In his frail famished throat the archer tasted all
the date trees' sweetness longingly, then stood beneath
the flowering branches of a date palm, faint with hunger.
In a half-daze he heard a scuffle on scorched stones
and saw a peacock and a viper thrashing fiercely;
the poisonous serpent hissed and flicked its two-pronged fang

and strove in frenzy to pierce through the feathered plate;
fluttering in wrath above it with full-swollen wings,
the handsome bird struck with its beak as with an ax
and then with sharp claws tore the viper on the stones
and gulped it greedily chunk by chunk to nourish well
its godly gold-flecked feathers and its turquoise breast.
And the god-slayer smiled in his faint daze, well-slaked,
as though the viper's meat had plunged in his own bowels
and gold-flecked wings had sprouted from his pulsing brows.
The handsome glutted bird wiped his red beak on stones,
uttered a harsh glad cry, then leapt from branch to branch
of a huge cedar tree, and perched like golden fruit
until the lustrous lone man fell in an exhausted swoon.

Night smothered down with stars and her seductive wiles;
like the gray foaming waves his mind roared hollowly,
gulls flew deep in remembrance, memory smelled of brine,
and as he raised his eyes he thought he lay beneath
a plane tree whose burs glittered in the night's sky-well.
"Old friend, we'll sleep tonight clasped in each other's arms,"
he said, then as he leant his head upon the tree's
dark wooded breast, its spirit rose, and a green-haired,
slim dryad sweetly clasped the lonely white-haired sage
till in his brains there opened huge and hidden orbs.
Cluster by cluster, downy beehives hung in sun,
cranes flew back, fetching swallows, white-thorns burst in bloom,
air buckled on its wings aloft and crowed like cocks.
Slowly the barks of trees cracked open, the wells brimmed
till all their hidden phantoms leapt, the plane trees swayed,
and each tree turned into a spirit with mudstained feet;
small hairy demons danced with horse-tails stiffly straight
and beautiful brown-haired Nereids reeled in flowering fields.
Two girls with heads thrust back in rapture beat their drums,
an old potbellied satyr dragged a lean he-ass
with cackling cries, a wineskin slung across his back.
A shaggy youth danced in the lead and held aloft
a fertile phallus, that full-weaponed head of hope;
bare-bosomed maenads danced, and flaming apples clashed
and clashed again in apple trees and glowed in night.
A red-haired maiden loosed her hair till flames rushed down
her back, another spread a leopard hide and placed
her virgin thighs as offering to the lurid sky.
The wedding pomp passed through the glen like a swift stream
till youthful Greece's azure seashores gleamed and glowed
as gentle light dripped softly on old olive trees
and all the bare and billowing mountains smelled of thyme.

Then the far-exiled dreamer blinked enchanted eyes
and all the pomp sank in the waves, dissolved like foam,
the sea's roar spread and boiled in a waste wilderness
and a slim skiff like a man's body, a carved bier,
leapt in the frothing waves and sped on toward the South.
The sea grew savage, leapt astride the stern and bow,
but the unruffled coffin sailed from wave to wave
and cut a path, although with torn and screeching sails.
The vision dripped with honey in Odysseus' heart,
and azure Greece, blown in his mind like a cool wind
and filled with fragrance of wild thyme and dew-wet pines,
swept through his brain and breathless body all night long.
He'd never felt his native land so sweet before,
and when he rose at dawn and shook his whitened hair
it seemed as though blue butterflies had perched on snow.
"My native land's too shy to come in the day's light
and like a harehound waits in hiding till night falls;
sleep is a good and great temptation—may it be blessed!"
He rose, and his knees shook from want of food and drink;
he felt the earth beneath his feet like a thin trap,
and as he moved and saw smoke rise in sun far off
he thought he heard mild lowing, as of cows that grazed,
and the strong odor of a village smote his mind.
He tripped and stumbled giddily, his knees gave way,
his white head nodded till he fainted and fell prone.
Far down the dusty road there soon appeared a slim
and sway-hipped maiden hurrying on with hasty steps
to bring her husband's supper at their distant farm—
a pitcher of cool water, rice-milk and warm bread.
Brass anklets jangled on her feet; she'd just been wed,
and yearned to reach her husband soon, unyoke the oxen,
spread cool leaves on the ground, lay out their humble meal,
eat well, then lie on grass and play like newlyweds.
But when she saw the lone man on the ground, her heart
swelled like a mother's and ached for that exhausted form;
kneeling, she gently raised the white-haired head with care
for fear his fragile limbs might crumble in her hands.
The soul of the much-suffering man twitched in her arms,
for the warm smell of woman smote his waxen nostrils;
he raised his eyes, then shut them with a gentle trust
and knew that life had clasped him in her arms once more.
The newly wed young Negress held the dreadful head
and slowly fed it like a child with milk and rice;
his dizziness distilled to calm, his nostrils smelled
milk brimming and a female body's soothing warmth
till visages of all maids he had loved on earth

merged, changed, and glittered in this maiden's kindly face.
From a cave deep as the heart, upon a gleaming beach,
a bitter sigh was heard, a blond-haired goddess rose,
swayed palely in a dark cave's mouth, then disappeared.
Other fair maids flashed in his mind, and their tears flowed,
apple on swaying apple which the fall rains beat.
Then the long-wandering man reached out his hands and stroked
her sunburnt shoulders and dark hair, her lips, her throat,
and the slim maiden blushed, uttered a cry, and laid
him gently on the earth as though he were her son.
He shut his burning eyes that she might not take fright:
"Ah, mother, my small mother, how shall I bless you, dear?
May your womb bear a child much greater far than I;
alas, I swear I have no better gift to give you."
He spoke, then rose and hailed the date tree's cooling shade,
the full-green, foliaged, warbling plane tree of his dream,
then said farewell to the goodhearted maid, and still
a drop of milk hung from his lips as from a baby's mouth.

Once more, with firm knees now, he took his lonely way;
a woman's odor, sweet rice-milk, and fostering dreams
swirled swiftly down his entrails' funnel and became
strong flesh and regulating mind and gentle breath.
The shadows lengthened, all birds crowded in their nests,
and the sky's candles flared in rows as the great traveler
leant on a lightning-blasted oak to let night pass.
As his mind filled with eyes like the long peacock's tail,
he stretched on earth, hailed all creation had ordained,
listened to the light chat of birds, the trees' soft sighs,
and heard the nude worms strive in soil to burst in bloom,
to sprout with myriad eyes and wings and soar in sun.
"Child-teeming Mother Earth, O thick wood grove through whom
wonders on wonders pass, entrails on entrails gape,
O deep nest filled with varied eggs that hatch in sun!"
He spoke, and with his calloused hands caressed the soil;
he heard the wide earth sitting on the steps of space
and weeping like a woman gripped with labor pains.
"The birds and trees cry out, the worms cry out, and all
creations of the proud mind shout in the wild wastes.
With wind and rain and snow, with bread and wine and meat
we all work silently together, stooped in dark,
shaping the world's salvation with our painful strife,
and when a son is born one dawn, how the world breathes,
how all dogs wag their happy tails, how fish and birds
and muddy worms and hopeless brains sprout brilliant wings,
how all gods scatter through the air like startled crows

to see the pale cadaver leap and stretch his bow!"
Leaning against the lightning-blasted old oak tree
the lone man brooded in the wilderness, rejoiced
in his mind's myriad eyes that sweetly glowed on earth
like constellations; all his life in memory passed
like melodies, his bones became a proud pipe's reeds,
and all the storms and cares that struck him his life long
passed through his body's flute and turned triumphant song.
That night in the cool mistral and the rare star's light
he felt the holy taste left in his mind by nights
when he had stretched on earth, rejoiced to gaze at stars,
and each night had its own most sweet, most bitter scent.
Far in his native island, at the world's ends now,
night smelled of musk like a new-blossomed almond tree;
in Crete night slowly passed like a great archoness
laden with pearls, wearing the moon for amulet,
and a nude Negro page held up her flaming train
gold-edged and spangled with the glowworm Pleiades.
In Africa, night growled like a tall virgin forest
where stars in darkness mutely glowed with dreadful eyes
as though fierce lions, leopards, tigers lay in wait
while Scorpio coiled and dripped its venom on the world.
Sometimes night seemed like a black rose that drove men wild,
and Death like a small honeydrop lodged in its heart;
at times she seemed a heavy-breasted mother weighed
with too much milk, poured for relief through the vast sky
drop by white drop, or in a silent river's flow.
Then the god-slayer's lips brimmed with the bittersweet
memories of all his nights, until his heart was filled
with precious gold of honeys, poisons, thick perfumes
that fluted in his mind like distant warbling sounds
till from his astral contemplation his huge brow
with light and sweetness filled, shone like a smokeless flame
as though it were a full moon freed from life's desires
and held its light as final loot in brooding thought.
At midnight, black Temptation saw the sacred flame
shine like a golden egg in a tree's hollow trunk:
"The earth has hatched the flame of freedom much too quickly;
I'll rise and smother it with clouds of heavy dust!"
It spoke, and a small Negro boy sprang from the ground
with carmine-painted nails and gold bells round his throat,
who crawled toward the tree's bole and held in his plump hands
some heavy dust to cast on the lone man's soaring flame.
But the unsleeping eyes shone sweetly in the dark
and the black startled Tempter slowly backed away
while his soft flattering voice came floating through the air:

"O brimming, deep, and three-decked vessel of salvation,
you've roamed all earth's most wealthy shores, you've taken all
for your rich merchandise: joys, troubles, gods, and hopes,
all man's enormous sacred tears of pearl, and now
you open tranquil sails, a fresh wind gently blows,
your midmast sprouts with grape-hung vines, and a small bird
sits on its topmost tip, your heart's a small, small bird,
and friends and foes are dolphins now that bid farewell:
'Good voyage, brimming vessel of salvation! Go!
The poor ports of our wretched earth can't hold you now;
and do not deign, O Free Heart, ever to return—
it's sweet to scatter in the dream of nonexistence.' "
The full-rigged mind then turned and sweetly smiled in shade,
and the Black Tempter, thus emboldened, crawled close by,
twitched his behind like a court fool, with bumps and grinds,
then boldly stroked the lone man's limbs with probing hands,
and his soft words wove through the air in cunning snares:
"Master, my mind is dazed! I count, then count again,
and find all thirty-two of the earth-savior's signs
still glittering on your laboring and much-suffering flesh.
Look! On the holy arches of your feet, fate's wheels
speed on and drag the cart of joy, the savior's spoils;
on your unmoving legs all towns and cities whirl;
your thighs with freedom shine, undazed by kisses now;
your quiet phallus grows serene, drained of all passion;
your navel has forgotten Mother and closed its wound;
the twelve great labors' constellations gird your loins;
your breasts are double trap doors where you've sealed up tight
all phantoms found in water, earth, or air, or mind;
your heart beats heavily with great calm as though it strikes
to cut the hawser that still moors the earth to God;
your shoulders twitch and sprout with soft and fuzzy wings;
the demon of light laughs on your right shoulder blade
and that of darkness on your left; both strive and tug
like two strong balanced wings that cut new roads together;
your brawny arms embrace the earth like a bridegroom;
your two wide palms are flooded with the mystic signs,
with eagles, scorpions, lilies, streams, and a large plume
that mounts your fingers' clefts and plunges down their cliffs;
your flashing fingers meet and part, then swiftly clasp
like five wed couples playing life's most holy game;
your firm throat hammers out the laughter's thunderbolt;
your teeth, those two and thirty beasts that gorged on flesh,
have been tamed now and meekly crouch in their dark den;
your lips, a sharp and two-edged sword, guard all your thoughts
nor will permit a hollow, useless word to pass;

your smile reflects a secret conflagration's blaze;
and like a salty sea your breath cools all the ground;
your tongue's a savage flame that leaps and licks all heads
and their great thoughts until they turn to ash at once;
the deepest silence in your ears now turns to song;
in your white hollowed temples the light drips in wells
like water in hollows of old rocks, slow drop by drop;
your eyes laugh like a viper's and allure the cliffs;
your eyebrows like a fine scale slowly weigh all deeds
and keep them neither overbold nor overprudent;
between them looms the third, rare, superhuman eye,
a rapturous yet hopeless moon, until earth's crust
flutters like a most flimsy dream-embroidered veil;
your brow's a lofty flint which when the hammer strikes
sparkles with thoughts that pour like stars in the dark night;
your veins flow on like rivers in your holy head,
water the gardens of your brain, turn your mind's mills
and bring down mud to nourish our salvation's seed;
your tall crown shines, a temple filled with clustered lights;
your face is water plunging down the cliffs of death,
it flicks with myriad features, laughs, then sweeps to chaos;
your voice is deeper than the lair of a slaked lion;
and in the mighty lighthouse of your head's high peak
the guard of sleepless silence shines like a gold casque.
O border-guard, I thrust my temples in your skull;
in greatest vertigo, deep in the whirlpool's heart,
I feel the savior's final and most mighty sign:
your great mind does not move but knows that all things move!"
Salvation's leader heard the Tempter, but kept silent;
he felt the black hands grope him stealthily, he heard
laughter and bitter wails, voices that rose from earth,
huge hidden wings and souls and tongues that licked him clean.
Flinging his black hands wide with fear, the Tempter cried:
"The savior's two-and-thirty signs glow on your flesh,
and as the crescent moon holds in its shining keel
and lightly licks the dark remains of its old form,
so in your cupped hands I discern the old black world.
Serenely now, with no desire, or grief, or hope,
draw back the bolts of nonexistence, and escape!
You are earth's first-born son, you were the first to drink
of freedom's deathless water till you quenched all thirst;
life has no higher peak, no greater bloom to grant."
Thus did the cunning Tempter speak, and when he rose,
the lofty pointed cap with its star-tassel shone.
The border-guard turned sleepless eyes and rested mouth
on the black Tempter, and the great woods also turned:

"Ah, old arch-cunning comrade, my mind's ancient cloak,
you've not dared to expose the deepest brand of all;
my mind has climbed earth's highest peak and knows this truth:
'I am the savior, and no salvation on earth exists!' "
The playful Morning Star of freedom laughed, the ground
hissed like a snake, and the Tempter suddenly disappeared.
The warrior, stripped of all hope now, smiled on his mind:
"Your great impatience scattered the black lord of guile
before his ears took in the greatest final task:
erect on freedom's highest summit Laughter leaps!"
He spoke, then closed his eyes, folded his soul like wings,
opened his arms to the low stars, and sank in tranquil sleep.

The cooling flame of freedom wrapped him like a cloak,
life and death sweetly merged as though he gently held
jasmine and April roses till their fragrance mingled.
He gleaned within him double joys of man and god;
in the same luscious meadow, dreams and firm flesh browsed,
his hands rejoiced in fondling all the upper world
and yet his mind rejoiced to scatter it far and wide.
His backbone then began to play like a long flute:
"My house is azure atmosphere, the stones are clouds,
my two town gates are sun and moon, the rafters dreams,
and in my mind's green pastures all thoughts graze like flocks;
my slaves, the gods, stoop low and fetch me fantasies
and in my fingers glow the castle's keys, the flame!
Freedom ascends like smoke and holds up the whole world,
my children are the lightning's flash, the winds, the seas,
and death is a bitten apple, an infolded rose
which I press to my chest till my mind faints with fragrance.
The hornet has lost his pain-packed sting, his yellow goad,
and flies on my white-flowered head, a downy moth;
joys, glories, virtues, griefs are freed from venom now
and drift like springtime clouds above my hoary head.
All in my brains distill to quintessential pith,
a puff of blue-green smoke, the secret of the world."
Thus did his dream play through his long bone-flute, and all
which in his waking hours he strove with toil to gain,
played in his sleep like sound and passed like lilting song.
The suffering athlete's soul and his mud-rooted flesh
were drenched at night with dreams and fructified with sleep,
and when the great sun struck and woke the world, he smiled
in secret softly now with sweetly rested eyes,
played joyously in the azure downy air-frontiers
that part deep sleep from waking, and then lightly swing
with no enigmas on the clear mind's topmost bough.

Gently and sweetly the dream merged with cool new sounds
that rose from the green mountain slopes and swept his brain.
Was it a shepherd who led lambs till the slopes swayed
or were more dreams arriving with their myriad bells?
For hours, with lashes closed, enraptured, he rejoiced
in the bell-jangling waters tumbling down his brain,
and when he slightly raised his eyes toward the great din
vast elephants came plodding through his dream-brimmed orbs
with multicolored lanterns round their necks, bronze bells,
tall golden towers on their backs with giggling girls,
nude men that gleamed in light and mounted up the slope.
Then flaming, regal, yellow banners flapped in air
and in their midst there loomed an old white elephant
with tiny golden gods that danced and jangled round its neck.

A bitter prince had come with his rich caravan,
laden with incense, feathers, slaves, and fruit, to climb
the sacred mountain slope at break of dawn and fall
prone at the ascetic's holy feet to heal his soul.
A ghoul had mounted him, an evil wind had struck him,
his heart was coils of deadly snakes, his mind was caged
like a blind thrush within his skull and sang of Death.
He quailed to see black Death in hovering air above him
and scorned to live much longer in such shameful fear;
winecups of gold and maids in bed he left untouched,
his great ring cut his finger like an unhealed wound,
women danced naked round him with their tambourines,
his blind bards sang like nightingales to ease his heart,
and through his open doors his fragrant gardens strolled.
God gave him many gifts but left his mind a wound,
till all at once the prince cried out with anguished pain
for in deep-shadowed air he saw rose flesh decay,
dancing-girls turn to skeletons and clack on tiles,
lipless and throatless blind bards stare and gape in sun!
All of the multicolored bridal veil of flesh
turned to torn rags and vanished in thin air until
only the coarse white bones and the plump worms remained.
He cupped his face within his hands and softly sighed:
"I won't look on the sun's face much longer, God;
I'll take a thin, thin silken thread and slash my throat!"
But then his faithful slave knelt down and raised his hands:
"O prince, a great ascetic broods on a high peak
and holds within his hands all gods and all disease,
he also holds that secret dwarf who wounds your heart.
All night he blazes on the mountain cliffs like fire
and all day in his holy hands he plays with clay,

shapes gods, then blows and scatters them, shapes men,
blows once and gives them soul, blows twice and knocks them down.
Thus does the lone man spend his time, and laughs because
he has surpassed the mist of groveling cares or frowns
and now stands upright in the mountain sun, and plays.
Great prince, I've sent three envoys on swift feet to bring
the great ascetic here with pleas and precious gifts;
the lord of your salvation, prince, should soon be here."
Then hope like gentle dawn poured in the prince's heart
and he armed precious caravans to meet the saint:
"It's only right that pilgrim-princes fall with musk
and wail at the ascetic's feet and kiss his knees
for he's the decoy-bird of spirits, the king of air;
I'm king of muddy loam and he of azure sky—
prepare my caravan that I may soon adore him!"
Three days they crossed field after field, three nights they stretched
beneath the stars with their exhausted elephants,
and when they reached the foothills, an aroma poured
from the sweat-streaming hermit like a rutting beast's.
The prince glanced at the mountain peak and his heart failed;
it seemed to him a blazing iron struck by the sun,
that sparks streamed down its rugged slopes, that the air shook.
The king's son signaled to his servants without a word
and then the caravan stopped at once, the maids jumped down,
and the slaves cleared a space and pitched his golden tent.
"It's only right before we gain the holy peak
to wash our hands and feet and to refresh our minds;
let the great spirit strike, we shall be pure and washed."
He mumbled with his bitter lips, then called aloud
for his old faithful slave who'd held him in his arms
since infancy, and the old man bowed in the gold tent:
"Ah, faithful slave," the young prince sighed, then burst in tears,
and the slave touched his master's knees with trembling hands:
"O Prince Motherth, you've reached the holy mount, don't fear!
The earth has changed, the sun's grown mild, the elephants dance,
white birds swoop to my right, and my unerring heart
feels that all time has bloomed, that your salvation's ripe,
and that oblivion with her torpid poppies comes—
ah, there's no greater good on earth than to forget."
But the prince raged and stamped on earth with his slim feet:
"Let slaves drown in oblivion's muddy brains with fear,
but a great prince confronts all things both night and day
without a slave's low fear until his mind matures.
Motherth, don't shirk a prince's great responsibilities
but weigh all things on earth with clear, unfearing eyes.
Hold well in mind those three almighty messengers

who've blocked your golden elephant's victorious road.
Gaze always on that sallow man who froths in spasms!
Gaze on that rotting old man's corpse that fouls the soil
and drips its eyes, ears, mouth to earth like pus. Alas,
he marched through life like a bold youth—behold his end!
Clasp like a scarecrow in your brain that youth's pale head
supine on a white pillow, drowned in stifling flowers,
whom four pallbearers quickly whisk away in dread.
Blessed be that dreadful day when I first saw these three!
Life is a huge unfolding flower, and Death its fruit.
A prince must always raise the dreadful secret close
to his clear eyes and hold it like a mirror there
and in his own face gaze upon the whole world's face.
The body is a lustrous thing and smells of musk,
its holy head is made of ivory, precious, proud,
with myrrh-washed curly locks, with carmine-painted lips,
and there the foul worms crawl and munch! O faithful slave,
come close and answer me: Will not one soul be saved?
Will these large lustrous eyes turn into lumps of mud?"
The poor slave shook to see his master's doe eyes brim
with tears and slowly streak his newly painted face:
"O long-lived prince, it's a most monstrous crime to lift
the holy veil of Mother Earth and spy her shame.
It's only just that we should spring at break of day
like wheat stalks, with no cry or curse, and then toward noon
sprout with a gold head full of seed until at dusk
we softly fall once more on the clay threshing floor.
Not one soul can be saved from the worm's fragile mouth!
It's proper that a prince should understand this law,
accept it proudly with no stumbling steps and march
with head held high, a leader, toward the lower world;
let all his people spawn to save the seed from rot."
But then the sad youth shook his pale head bitterly:
"Why should it live? Why should the seed of man be saved?
Why should we breed our children for Death's bottomless mouth?
O slave, who bend your wheaten head to the sharp scythe,
now raise your eyes and look in mine, give me reply:
How shall we ever conquer that black butcher, Death?"
The faithful slave raised his head high and his eyes shone:
"By spawning swarms on swarms of children, long-lived lord!
When the exhausted father falls to earth and rots,
let sons and daughters hang behind him in thick clusters;
first flood your courts with grandsons and great-grandsons, prince,
then only may you draw Life's flimsy bolt, and leave.
Mankind's deep bowels are not easily emptied, prince,
for like the fish's entrails, filled with eggs and milt,

all our own bellies, hearts, our armpits, breasts, and sides
and our dark heads brim full of daughters and strong sons;
only in this way, prince, may mortals vanquish Death."
But the exhausted prince of earth cried out with grief:
"Deep in my loins I hear babes kicking to leap out,
to eat and drink and turn to good lean cuts for Death.
We are but fodder sent to earth for the worm's food.
Dear slave, it's time for mankind's heart to find repose,
for earth's grim slaughterhouse to crumble, where they herd us
like votive beasts and deck our throats with crimson ribbons.
O true slave, do you weep? Don't kiss my rotting hands!
Behold, for on my weary head Death is my golden crown!"

The gold tent gaped abruptly and a guard rushed in:
"Prince, our first envoy has arrived, and gasps for breath!
He holds the great ascetic's face carved out of wood!"
Then the old herald fell prone at his master's feet:
"Prince, in my hands I hold the secret of the world!
Your heart shall now grow gay, your soul shall find its balm!
I saw the great ascetic play by a cliff's edge
with all the gods as though they were a baby's rattle.
Then I stooped low and marveled, seized a block of wood
and carved out the ascetic's laughing baby's face;
now, prince, I place the infant in your holy palms."
The king's son seized the sacred mask with pallid hands
but as he gazed on its gay features, his mind whirled:
"This can't be the ascetic! I see a giggling babe,
its tender new-cut teeth still drip with mother's milk
and a crisp red carnation dangles from its ear!"
Then the old herald kissed the prince's feet and cried:
"For days and days I fixed my eyes in light, and watched—
he crawled on all fours like a babe on the cliff's edge,
clasped by his ancient wet-nurse, Earth, the thousand-dugged.
I longed to approach and tell him of your great request,
but though I strove three days, I could not take one step."
The gold tent opened and the guard once more rushed in:
"Master, the second herald's come and gasps for breath!"
A stalwart man fell, shuddering, on the golden mats:
"I give God thanks that I've escaped and come in time!
I saw him, master, on the cliff, and my heart stopped:
his armpits steamed, his black beard glowed, and when he spread
his arms, I thought the wheel of the vast world had rasped.
Three days he buckled on his arms, but to no end!
On his left side he seemed to weep, but on his right
to brood, and seen full-face he laughed till stones crashed down.
I perched on a high boulder, grabbed wild ilex wood

to hack out that impalpable ghost, to catch in wood
that soul which blows and disappears, and which our mind
can't grasp; now, prince, I place it in your holy hands!"
The prince broke in cold sweat, then seized the hardy log:
"Dear God, this is not an ascetic's nor a man's face;
I hold a crimson-bearded dragon, grim-faced War!"
The gold tent opened and again the guard rushed in:
"Prince, your third envoy has returned, and gasps for breath!"
A gallant youth fell prone before the prince, and cried:
"I saw him! Like an old forebear he sunned himself
on a great cliff, vines twined him round, and nightingales
built in his hair, beasts walked his flesh, and his white beard
poured down the cliff like an old hoary river-god;
a red rose hung behind his ear, a setting sun.
I climbed a tree and yelled, 'Grandfather, our prince calls!'
but my own echo struck and felled me like a stone.
Stubbornness seized me then—with trembling hands I grabbed
a knife and carved his face from an old olive trunk;
now prince, I place the ascetic's face within your hands!"
The ruin-hearted prince then stooped toward earth and cried:
"O dreadful spirit, O mighty three-yolked egg of air!"

When the three messengers had left the golden tent
the ravished prince then raised his tear-stained eyes and saw
his faithful slave alone in a far corner, weeping.
"O faithful slave, don't weep! Look in my eyes, reply:
What happens to a man's body when it stays a month,
what happens when it stays a full year in the grave?"
"O long-lived master, I beseech you, don't, don't ask!"
"Slave, my request is my command! Answer at once!"
"O prince, six kinds of fat worms, six invading troops,
six waves of famished worms rush swiftly toward the corpse;
each wave first towers high, swoops down, eats all it can
with leisure, then rolls off, makes way for other waves,
all in good order, prince, and not one bickering quarrel!
Before the body well expires, the good news sweeps
the air and the dung-flies with their huge bellies swarm
from gardens, dung-heaps, stables, cow barns, filthy lanes,
and perch on the still-striving, dying man's pale lips,
on his blue nostrils, the deep pits of his dark eyes,
and quickly lay their eggs in clusters, heap on heap.
At once, when the man dies, the blowflies swoop down, prince,
the savage meat flies, too, with their fat fuzzy bellies,
and heap on the warm corpse their white and welling eggs.
Then four pallbearers come, open and close the tomb,
and in the first nights slowly the corpse softens, swells,

the chest turns blue, the head becomes soft yellow wax,
the belly bloats up like a wineskin and turns green.
Then eggs hatch everywhere, on nostrils, eyes, and ears—
and all at once an army of blind silent worms
march, mount, possess the body, and begin to eat.
In time the fingernails drop off, the belly cracks,
the human corpse becomes a hogskin of fat lard,
O long-lived prince, till finally a new white wave
of worms appears, like cheese grubs, and begins to eat.
The flesh becomes black broth and pours out in soft slush,
and then the third great wave leaps up and swells until
tall heaps of maggots sink into the broth, and eat.
Slowly the corpse becomes a tough dry hide, and then
a deep invisible host of larvae hatch and gnaw
what filaments still stick about the bones and skull.
Close on their heels the fifth most greedy wave mounts up
of strong-jawed worms and maggots that begin to saw
and munch away the nerves, the brains, the shroud, the nails.
At length, in three years' time the final wave mounts high,
the final table guests arrive deep from the earth
and squat about the corpse to eat what scraps remain.
Nothing at length is left of man's once mighty body
or his almighty soul, O scion of great kings,
but his white, naked bones strewn underground until
within his empty head, the bulwark once of God,
only a soft damp mold distills, a flabby dough.
But don't think, prince, that this is man's once holy brain—
this is not brain, but dross, dregs, filth and sediment,
the myriad droppings of the waves of worms that passed!"
The slave fell silent then and shut his lips with fear,
but the weak seed of kings, death-stifled, spoke no word,
and heard his slave's voice for a long time, saw the worms
still rise and fall within his mind in six huge waves.
But then he suddenly shook his head, his eyes shot flames,
his voice for the first time rose in a gallant cry:
"I've never heard before such a strong martial air!"
He spoke, then sank his head upon his chest in thought;
his black-veiled memory stooped above his giddy mind's
resounding threshold where she combed, uncombed her hair
and held the stream of worms for mirror, and softly wept.
As his soul sank within destruction's dazzling mist,
drums suddenly resounded, loud rejoicing shouts
struck at the young man's worm-enraptured brains and ears
and an old archon knelt and bowed before his lord:
"King's son, your race is firm now, for your seed's been blessed,
and your great throne spreads roots in earth like a stout oak;

I bring you happy news and this ripe pomegranate:
a son was born to you last night, the world's grown firm!"
But the new father flung his hands on high with dread:
"Ah, help me, God! New chains now tie me to wretched earth!
I strike against life's fetters and shout in empty air!"
The faithful slave in tears then clasped the prince's knees:
"Hold your heart firm like a strong king, don't shake with dread;
joy also is an urgent beast that drinks man's blood,
but what great shame if your soul now can't bear that too!
Behold, your twelve slim dancing-girls have come, your twelve
blind minstrels with their zithers raise their throats and sing
the golden-crimson birthday of your first-born son."
He spoke, then placed the pomegranate in the youth's hands:
"O princely father, may your courts and your gold floors
brim like this fertile fruit with daughters and strong sons!"
The prince seized savagely the shameless seeded fruit,
and his eyes brimmed with tears, and his throat tore in two:
"Thus may my seed and the great seed of all the world
scatter and spill on earth to rot, almighty God!"
He spoke, then raised the seeded fruit to smash it on the ground.

But a strong hand reached out and held the raised arm tight,
and when the king's son turned to see what mortal dared
to stop the onrush of his sacred arm, he saw
the ascetic stand before him with a gentle smile.
The dancing-girls like swift chameleons disappeared,
the blind bards shut their babbling mouths, the slaves backed out,
and the prince clasped the knees of the sage man with fear:
"O dreadful spirit, great three-bodied egg of air!"
The white-haired athlete spread his battlemented hands
and with great sweetness fondled the youth's raven locks
until the prince's mind stood still, his speech grew firm:
"Though I rule towns and lands, I still don't rule my heart;
all day and all night long I see Death loom in air,
I stoop to drink and see his face float in the bowl.
I take some bread to eat, and my hands fill with worms,
and when I clasp a maid I break in loud lament
for in my arms I feel the loved corpse putrefy.
Many-souled saint, plumb line between our life and death,
I fall a pilgrim at your feet, and in your court
pile all the spice and treasures of my caravan,
but give my soul some medicament, my mind some drug.
They say at drop of midnight you pluck heaven's herbs—
pity me then, give me the magic herb of health
that I may not discern earth's worms or Death in air."
But the soul-snatcher played with a tree leaf and smiled

to watch it twirl within the sun's prismatic light
till his small flame-reflecting eyes began to flash.
The death-lured prince stood waiting for reply, but still
the great ghost-dragger of the dual mind's wide wings,
one light, one dark, smiled to himself, sunk in his game,
till the prince touched his shoulder and cried in a choked voice:
"What do you see in that green leaf and do not speak?"
Like gurgling water then the lone man's words gushed up
and fell from walls of silence and the mind's high crags:
"I see, O pale king's son, a mighty city rise
like a flesh-eating scabby leper, mount the stem
and slowly spread its tentacles on this fresh leaf.
I see the noise-resounding streets flash in its veins:
bent workers walk in sun together with their kings,
frail women stroll and clasp their babes like infant gods
and youthful horsemen dash from the wide city gates.
Then I hear sounds and weeping, laughter, groans, and wings,
till on the leaf's edge slowly leprosy is healed
as the great city sinks and its din dwindles far.
This is the secret herb I hold that cures all hearts!"
He spoke, then placed it laughingly in the youth's palm
and he, with joy and fear together, slung the leaf
above his ear like a red rose and cried aloud:
"Guardian of earth, your words are joy and a great solace!
O sage, you gaze on Death while monarchs, cities, towns,
countries and peoples twist like leaves and fall to earth."
Then the death-battler felt his mind brim full of love
for the unripe and shriveled youth who shrank before him;
he cast his calm gaze on that waxen face until
the youth stepped back in fear, for in those somber orbs
the heavens and earth gleamed like a desert, and above them
he saw his own face sinking like the waning moon.
"Guardian of earth, you too hold Death within your eyes!"
Then the god-slayer slowly stroked the youth's black locks:
"My son, I too watch Death before me night and day;
the proudest joy which now unites us here on earth
is that we've emptied both our hearts of gods and hope,
yet you sink nerveless to the ground, for loneliness
has driven you wild, and freedom cleaves your head in two.
But I hold Death like a black banner and march on!
When I drink water my mind cools to its deep roots,
for I know joy is fleeting and does not return;
I munch bread and rejoice to know that I cast crumbs
in my frail body's furnace that my soul may blaze;
I take my joy of woman till the whole earth laughs
and nestles sweetly in my arms, in haste to feel

before I die, my sacred heir stir in her womb.
Death is the salt that gives to life its tasty sting!"
The proud carouser laughed until the gold tent shook
and the youth's mind was pacified, his voice relaxed:
"I hold your knees, ascetic, and I feel your strength
course through my feeble arms and spread throughout my heart;
like a fir's tip that upright leaps in mountain frost,
the many-branched vast tree of man takes joy of you.
With you I feel the eagle-loved high peaks of air.
Ah, father, fold your lofty wings, perch by my side
that I may see and hear you till my mind grows tall."
The sage man laughed, then seized the pomegranate fruit,
smashed it in two so that its cooling rubies glowed,
and as they ate it calmly like two newlyweds
the mind's blaze like a pomegranate tree leapt into bloom.

The day passed by like lightning but the pallid youth
still cocked his head or raised it high like a small bird
who listens, fluttering, to an old blackbird's advice.
When night turned into honey in the full moon's blaze
the caravan broke camp, rimmed everywhere with light,
and the first elephant-guide then turned his face toward town.
But the ghost-haunted prince screamed in his golden tent,
for bitter pain slashed at his arms, his pale flesh swelled,
his veins swarmed through his body like swift streams of worms.
The faithful slave stooped and discerned in the youth's arm
a small hole deeply gaping, like the greedy mouth
of some invisible worm that munched the frothy flesh,
and he drew back in fright and bit his tongue, for now
he saw his master's heirs already on the march.
But the great athlete only smiled, pushed back the slave,
placed on his lips his flute made of a dead man's bone
and slowly played a sweet, persuasive lullaby,
a mystic charm that might bewitch and lure the worm.
The greedy mouth stopped munching, and the white head rose,
as though transported, from the slender body's flesh,
and twined about the prince's limbs like a silk thread.
The young man fell asleep to the flute's sweet allure
and felt he rose in dream disburdened, like a mist,
and scattered, soul and body, in the dew-drenched air.
When he awoke, his arm reposed on his calm chest
and like a satiated viper the flute stretched
on the stone knees of the much-knowing sorcerer.
The king's son laughed and to the fortuneteller said:
"My heart was an unflowered thorn which at your touch
swelled to a crimson rose and brought my breast relief;

you hold the magic plant that opens every door."
The mind-magician with his many tricks replied:
"I know no magic tricks nor hold the magic plant;
within a haunted palace, as the legends tell,
there rages a fierce monster who awaits that kiss
which will again transform him to his handsome shape.
Such is the evil of this world—our soul's the kiss!"
But the prince smiled and to the fortuneteller said:
"Such is our life in this vile world, and Death's the kiss!"
He spoke, then gave commands that his white elephant,
his old grandsire, be brought, and the return begun.
Night and her black eyes smiled and gleamed with all her stars,
waterdrops laughed and wept upon the dew-wet leaves,
and all the prince's retinue began to move;
its silver bells were waters tumbling down the glens,
the women's laughter from the golden towers fell
and tinkled on the stones like fistfuls of small pearls.
All of night's heart unfolded, a black-blossomed rose
on which the caravan like a monstrous caterpillar,
crawled in the moon's light, to the bells' tinkling sound,
both men and beasts shut their eyes sweetly, road on road.
If passers-by had seen the pale procession pass
like dreams in the moon's daze, they would have clutched the trees
and uttered shrill, sharp cries of fear to break the spell;
if Death had chanced to spy them in their nightly trek
he would have raised his hand with joy to welcome them;
but neither Death nor a stray traveler crossed their path,
and when the caravan rose from night and crawled to dawn,
slim tails, coarse rumps, and flabby ears dripped with the dew;
the men's uncombed hair curled like curving fingertips.
Within their midst marched the white regal elephant
and in its golden tower sat the ancient youth;
again grim Death, the octopus, sucked all his flesh,
again it gleaned and gathered his still green desires.
Slowly to his old faithful slave he poured his pain:
"O faithful slave, I could not shut my eyes all night;
the ascetic is a lightning bolt that sears my heart;
I see both flowers and coils of worms in the abyss
and pass in fear between both flowers and writhing worms;
his seed has fallen upon my head, the stitches creak!"
The slave kept still, for in his coarse and rustic heart
he could not feel a monarch's noble obligations.
How could one have all good things—women, son and crown—
and not sprout wings or keep the heart from joy unriven?
In early dawn, on a huge elephant astride,
the hardy athlete held the light like a long lance

and pierced the trees, the birds, the wide and misted plains,
and with the bells' light sounds and fluffy shades he shaped
the warm belovèd body of the living world.
His claw-sharp mind, that holy hawk of freedom's flight,
swooped through the air and gamboled in swift turns and loops:
"Forward! Saved now from the heart's passions, the mind's ills,
we freely hang upon this crackling flaming air
all mankind's joys, and write his burning history there!
Some crackpots search for God, thinking perhaps he lurks
somewhere amid the branches of the flesh and mind;
some squander precious life, chasing the empty air;
some, still more pigeon-brained, think they've already found him
and work on his compassion with their begging whines
till their minds break from too much joy or too much pain.
But others, great brain-archers, know the secret well:
by God is meant to hunt God through the empty air!
These tread the highest peak, these hunger satiates;
such border-guards fight bravely on despair's sharp edge,
but yet I think my claws clutch at a higher peak."
High on his elephant his mind thus lanced the air
while his head waved in the sun's light like a great flag
and heralds passed through villages and cried aloud:
"The mighty savior, brothers, with his secret wings,
the great ascetic with his brain's abundant herbs
cuts through the light astride a pure white elephant.
Open your hearts and roads, my brothers; let him pass!
He wants no lovely maid, he wants no gold or food,
he's passed beyond all joys, replete, he walks the wastes
and with fine freedom's feather beats our bodies on."
When the near hamlets heard, they woke, doors banged and clanged,
the old town elders donned clean clothes and grabbed their staffs,
the young men buckled on their arms, maids washed their hair,
twined them with sunflowers, drenched their armpits with sweet musk,
then swayed like palms and lined the roads to watch the ascetic pass.

World-famous Margaro with her unnumbered pearls
walked in her flowering gardens all day long, alone,
with her gold peacocks and her reed-slim pure-white hounds.
Rich merchants moored their precious caravans and placed
at her all-sacred feet with their vermilion nails
musk, ivories, lion pelts, for but one night of love.
A golden bird with woman's breast and bloody claws
perched on her garden's topmost tip and all night sang:
"Men, leave your women, wheedling what they want in bed;
come, old men, life is short, night falls, come fill your palms
with gold and lustrous pearls to buy my precious kiss;

young men in rut, come, listen to your youth and take
the primrose path and knock upon my crimson door.
My lips are of carnelian flame, my bosom leaps.
I've lips and breasts for sale! Who'll buy? Come soon, come soon!"
As when wild war sweeps past and smashes every door,
thus in this blast of love all honest houses shook;
its blare flew past the lofty mountains, shook the ports
and stopped all ships at mid-sea in an idle daze:
"Coxswain, release your rudder, sailors, leave your oars,
let the ship go to wrack, it's Margaro who calls!"
It was at drop of noon that Margaro attuned
her shell-like rosy ears hung with small golden bells:
"Dear God, I hear the caravans, my lovers come
in hordes, huge elephants pass by and gold bells ring;
I must adorn and paint myself, then lie in bed."
But her black nurse rushed naked through the flowering trees:
"Lady, the great ascetic comes, the world is blessed!"
Then Margaro leapt up and called for her perfumes:
"Nurses, bring Africa's most precious scented balms,
bring me my peacock mantle, my embellished pride,
so that my youth may shine for him like a sweet star.
I pass a heavy imperiled moment! Slaves, adorn me,
for the great lover comes who soon will loot my body!"
She smeared her lovely hands with crimson, her teats red,
painted the eyelids of her almond eyes dark blue,
joined her two eyebrows with a mole, bound golden shoes
on her pale feet and sailed out through her crimson door.
The stones were startled, every street with roses bloomed,
mothers shut all their windows, old men stooped and sighed,
her heels laughed as they passed and wrecked all honest homes.
Proudly she left green youths behind and reached the crossroads
and there stood like an almond tree and spread her flowers
then shut her eyes as tinkling bells approached, earth shook,
and mountains smelled of musk, but opened them again
as the white elephant passed by, then humbly spread
her dainty scented hands and at the crossroads begged:
"O decoy master, who in wild wastes lures all souls,
my gardens wait for you, my tables are heaped high
that you might eat and rest refreshed, that I might clasp
your good word then, ascetic, like my suckling son.
Much-knowing lover of earth, descend and clasp me tight!"
White-haired Odysseus smiled as the seductress stroked
the elephant's hard knees and its gold talisman;
then the heart-wrecker spoke with deep resounding voice:
"Beloved fellow-warrior of my dreadful strife,
I saw you somewhere as I fought with shadows once;

I thirsted, you scooped water in your slender palms
and I knelt down like a shy fawn and drank until
I sprouted many-branched and manly horns from joy;
my dear, I shall descend to eat in your cool garden shades."

As the sun dripped on earth like a lush honeyed fig,
the mortal wedding pomp stopped at an arched door
with shameless and erotic signs on its red lintel,
and the old athlete leapt like a youth in the whore's court,
but the frail prince leant weakly on his old slave's arms
and tottered to the garden like a wounded fawn.
Under the flowering trees weighed down with honeybees
the lone man stretched in scented shade like an old lion
as naked slaves dashed to and fro and quickly fetched
sweet fruit, refreshing crystal drinks, while their swift heels
flashed crimson like ripe apples in the shaded lawns.
Then Margaro crouched at his feet, coiled like a snake,
and her sweet-bitten and seductive body smiled
to taste in silence novel and most secret joys.
Her silk-thread eyebrows arched coquettishly, her eyes
rejoiced to watch the white-haired saint beneath her trees
drinking the crystal sherbets slowly drop by drop
and tasting the rich food like an immortal god.
When he was satisfied, he washed his hands, then turned,
and Margaro's notorious body flushed and swayed:
"O spring of great desire, O well of deathless water,
a woman is an empty jug; stoop, fill it now!"
But the heart-knower smiled, and all the shadowed gardens
with their resplendent peacocks, waters, trees, and fruit
glowed softly, quietly in the afternoon, rejoiced
like heads that suddenly have begotten brilliant thoughts.
His lustrous hand slid slowly on her new-washed hair
then softly licked her temples, ears, her lips, her cheeks,
lingered upon her fluttering lashes, then once more
ascended slowly, smoothly to her fragrant hair
till all at once her lovely face grew thin and faded
as though the unsated fingers ate without compassion.
The strong soul-snatcher looked at her with pain, then raised
his flesh-devouring hovering hand above her head:
"Salvation may be sought by seven secret paths,
and you, O much-kissed body, are the most occult.
May the soft mattress of your labors be thrice blessed,
for in your deep refreshing gardens' azure shades
your worldly-wise, forbearing body all night long
draws back the bolts of our salvation with caresses.
Some bring the earth salvation with the mind's bright toys,

some with the fruitful drudging goodness of the heart
or with a high proud silence and child-bearing deeds,
some with that sacred single breast, manly despair,
or with that gray-haired horseman, war the murderer.
But you take lover's lane, open your door with stealth,
clench myrtle sprays between your teeth, place Lethe's flower,
a blue bloom on the cliff, within your bosom's cleft.
You merge all bodies into one, break down frontiers,
and strong men, clasping you in the cool shadows, moan:
'Ah, there's no you or I, for Life and Death are one!'
And souls that I have held upon my knees cry out:
'Ah, there's no you or I, for Life and Death are one!' "
The lone man spoke, and Margaro's glad heart sped swiftly
like a white gleaming hound that with great joy and pride
has flushed a hare and calls her master to the kill.
She spoke then to her bosom's precious scented cleft:
"For my own soul's salvation, the love-path is good."
Then like a thirsty fawn, the weak dream-taken prince
approached the athlete's brimming well and placed his lips
on the wide rim to drink each cooling word that rose.
Servants stood, gazing longingly amid the trees,
their black eyes burning in the cooling shadows there,
and slaves plucked heavy flowers to deck the sage and prince.
Earth's mighty Honey Drone fell silent and rejoiced
in the earth's gentle buzzing, in the flowering trees,
in the stooped woman quivering like a flaming bride
who waited for his words as for her dear betrothed.
He placed his hands upon her bright hair's gleaming part:
"Ascetic fellow-toiler with your loosened girdle,
blessed be your fingers with their henna-painted nails
that hold the golden keys and open Charon's door,
where the locks drip with scent, the threshold smells of musk;
I, too, clasp the gold keys that open salvation's door!
Blessed be your thick curled hair that smells of a green wood
sanctified to its root because a saint dwells there;
at midnight you unbraid and braid the stifling youths
as I, too, braid and then unbraid all mighty thoughts
with the great comb of silence and thus loot all men.
O Lady, thrice, thrice blessèd be your crimson mouth;
like a sweet fruit that nestles on lips still unslaked,
the holy kiss distills, full-flavored, joyous, cool;
my mouth, too, is a lime-twig smeared with sweetest words
that to their wounding thorns allure the singing birds.
O joyful mighty martyr, well-versed amazon,
I reach out begging hands: O Lady, give me alms,
place in my hands, that I may touch it and rejoice,

the cool and downy fruit of your erotic strife."
Much-fondled Margaro first quivered and then laughed:
"O Master Drone, who hold the earth in your holy arms,
I place my meager daily wages in your hands.
When from afar I see the man I love approach
and my heart beats with passion, my knees melt, I say:
'In all this wretched world but you and I exist!' "
The strong brain-pirate seized the woman's words and said:
"Compassionate and sweet is your love-strife's first fruit,
my hand grows joyous, Lady, and my throat grows cool;
give me the fruit now of your great devotions."
"When on my knees I hold the man I love, I cry:
'Beloved, I feel at length that we two are but one!'
This is the second fruit of my erotic strife.
Ah, I, at least, could never pluck a higher fruit."
The unsated warrior clenched his hand and spoke no word;
his ruthless mouth was warbling like a mighty bow,
he felt his strength grow to a vast inhuman size,
he pitied all weak souls a moment, then rose to leave,
but turned and saw the prince who with his large eyes shut,
his pale head tilted sideways, trembled for his reply,
so that he opened then his holy mouth and spoke:
"Reach out your tongue-kissed hands spread with a lime-twig snare
where I shall place the heaviest, sweetest fruit of strife:
'Even this One, O Margaro, this One is empty air!' "
The black-eyed maiden shrieked and fell prone to the ground:
"This dreadful word you give us, saint, destroys us all!"
But the worm-taken prince leapt up with cloudless joy:
"My heart throbs and my mind glows! I hold freedom's keys!"
His black locks fluttered down his back, a lion's mane,
his youthful body in the twilight gleamed erect
like a tall sword which an unseen hand sweeps through air.
"My saintly savior, give us the good word again!"
Slowly and sweetly in the withering shades of dusk
fell life's and the ascetic's highest, most fearful fruit:
"Even this One, O prince, even this One is empty air!"

The prince's sallow cheeks grew flushed, his eyes grew clear,
his empty and sick entrails healed with inner peace:
"Freedom, herb of forgetfulness that blooms on cliffs,
most precious antidote and balm of poisonous life,
home-wrecking Liberty, well met! Your good health, worms!
Seven well-hidden paths lead to salvation's grace
and I shall take the straitest road of black despair
and empty my full heart of sorrows, passions, joys.
Motherth, abjure your eyes, your ears, your nose, your tongue,

forswear, Motherth, all virtues, glories, deeds, and minds!
Forswear all earth's creations, they're but fantasies,
for we chase shadows, mounted on swift shadowy steeds;
Death is a shadow, too, that hunts the shadow, Life;
O Motherth, shut your eyes, your ears, your nose, your mouth:
for even this One—do you hear?—this One is empty air!"
Bitterness stung the god-destroyer's blossomed mouth:
"O immature soft soul, you can't as yet support
freedom's most dreadful bloom, and kneel like a low slave.
Forward! Though life's an empty shade, I'll cram it full
of earth and air, of virtue, joy, and bitterness!
So long as I walk on earth shall earth walk at my side!
When butterflies flit by, I thrust them in my mind
and hold them tight with their bright dress to keep them safe
until I die and we both rot in loam together;
thrust the earth like butterflies into your mind, my son."
The youth's mind smothered like a burnt-out candlewick:
"I won't accept strong wine before the butcher's door
so that in stupor I may not know toward what I go;
I'll stretch my neck to the sharp ax with clean clear eyes!
Your great good word, by scattering me, has made me firm.
The ax and my neck both are but frail azure shadows."
Then Margaro clasped tight the world-destroyer's knees:
"Master, alas, I can't bear now your bitter word.
My heart has shriveled, my soft arms have lost their strength;
dear God, how can I now embrace but shadowy forms,
I, who love sturdy bodies and even their strong stench?"
The lone man of the double-ax but gently smiled
then placed his right hand on the hair of the black-eyed,
his left hand on the young man's handsome, luckless head:
"How sweet and full of flattery blows the cooling breeze!
I see that shadows have grown long as the sun set,
I feel between my eyebrows the great Evening Star
and two warm bodies floundering in my hands at dusk.
If I could raise them on my wings to see Death whole,
to see the muddy spotted crust of the whole earth
that freedom's cry might burst and scatter all things wide!
But our seductress hangs upon the cliff and weeps
and longs deep in her heart for an immortal love;
our prince stands upright on the cliff, denies all things,
but can't find strength to soar with wings above the grave.
I know a man on earth with two long grasping hands,
and if he hungers for warm bread, he dines on dirt,
and if he thirsts for water, he drinks the savage brine,
and if he longs for a cool chat as evening falls
then he and Death, like two good neighbors, laugh all night:

'Welcome, good neighbor Charon, O great shepherd, come
and let your muddy-headed human herds go hang!
Let's sit like lean wolf-chiefs tonight and chat awhile.'
They laugh and talk of grain and vineyards like two lords,
they prate of massacres and voyages and war,
and like green youth in rut they gab of firm-fleshed girls,
of Lenio's flouncing breasts, of Rala's flashing thighs.
'Ah, Death, man's heart, that crazy flapping flag, is good!'
They sit on the low walls of joy, eat well, drink deep,
then clash their drinking-cups at dawn like brazen shields.
Man's mind, erect and clear, takes long deep drafts of Death
as of a white full-flowered rose warmed by the sun,
but Charon stammers and can't bear the heavy weight
of the mind's laughter and the free heart's conversation:
'Dear friend, this wine is much too strong! I must leave now!'
He stumbles, lurches down the court, trips on the sill,
the wild wine makes him sick and heaves at his mouth's door
till he spews all he ate and drank, befouls the tiles,
and I, his neighbor, mock and hoot at him with glee:
'Ah, Charon, wine and the mind's laughter are both good,
so is man's friendship, but it needs bold, brave companions!' "
As the archer talked, he stroked his hoary beard which fell
down his broad bosom like a river and flowed in night,
while his snake eyes with sweetness lured pale Margaro.
Now by the sun-washed wine of his proud words entranced,
she felt groves opening in her heart where gallant youths
of a new race walked proudly through her lofty trees
bearing huge curling poppies thrust into their belts
and knocked upon her crimson door and sought her kiss:
"Ah, Margaro, come quick, for Death yelps at our heels!"
The tender-hearted whore rushed out to welcome them:
"Quaff all my kisses, lads, before your red lips rot,
eat my seductive eyes, lads, for earth swallows all,
come cling, though for a moment, lads, to my warm flesh!"
While thus Odysseus talked, in Margaro's white breast
salvation's path with shadows, flowers, and fragrance bloomed,
and with her coral lips she kissed the ascetic's hands:
"The wound you gave me blooms in me like a red rose!"
But in the ruined bosom of the sallow prince
a naked chasm gaped on freedom's peak, stripped bare
on the wing-bladed air of comrades, shade, or flowers.
The sickly prince leapt up and tossed his hands like wings:
"Aye, Motherth, doff this worthless golden shroud you wear,
cut off your raven locks, scented with laurel oil,
cast in the mud your bracelets and your golden sandals,
abandon your dear wife, your son, your eyes, your ears,

until stripped naked, with no virtues, wings, or robes,
wave your pale hands and bid these thick shades disappear."
He spoke, then clapped his hands and called his faithful slaves:
"Run to my palace, slaves, with my white elephant
and tether him, bare, orphaned, in my marble courts;
fall down with low obeisance to my ancient sire,
then take my golden crown and cast it in the river,
give all my golden garments to my wife that she
may stand decked by her door and take a new betrothed.
Body of man, awake! O soul, fly from your sheath!
Dear slaves, I see wings fluttering on your shoulder blades!
O landlords, fling your cellar keys down deepest wells
and free yourselves of food and drink, of women too,
come free yourselves of brain and God, of fear and hope,
and save the fragile soul from flesh that it may soar and flee!"

But the great athlete slowly rose and blessed the trees,
cool water, bread, and the small downy body, too,
of Margaro that gleamed amid star-blossomed boughs:
"All things have cooled the mind and fed the body well,
and may fate grant you time, O Margaro, to wedge
in tighter armor these bright shades that hedge you round—
trees, golden garments, sweethearts, and most envied youth.
Never to say: 'I will not kiss these empty shades!'
but to fling wide your hungry arms, embrace the shades
and say most sweetly, as they suck oblivion's milk:
'O shades, great shades, my travelers, come to haven here!'
I place my old hands, Margaro, on your black locks—
bear the war well, my gallant sister, never leave me!"
He turned then to the seedless youth who had stripped bare:
"Ah, if I only had your youth, your curly flower!
Like a new bridegroom first uncovering his shy bride
I'd strip earth naked and cry out with lust and joy.
But you—shame on your raven locks, your bridegroom's face!—
abandon the earth, your lovely bride, and spurn the game.
I've heard it said that in old times two bosom friends
were cast in a dark slave-ship to be killed at dusk;
the first lost heart at once and his eyes sank in pits,
but his friend's sturdy spirit stood erect and gazed
on the blue sea and mountains, smelled the briny air,
tasted a cup of wine, possessed a lovely lass,
and moments passed like sated years as he caressed
the earth and life with his deep palm and said farewell.
Aye, king's son, both were souls, but who is worth your love?
Who can we say is a free soul, and who a slave?

Come, cast your judgment, prince! We're both in a slave-ship!"
But the transported youth crouched mutely on the ground,
folded his golden robes, tore off his regal gems
from his curled locks, the sacred and great ring of state,
that poisonous and golden wound, from his pale hands,
then heaped them with contempt and called his faithful slave:
"Dear friend, behold, my butterfly and gaudy wings
I've stripped off one by one till I'm earth's worm once more.
Most faithful friend, I touch your knees with reverence.
If ever you have heard me call you slave, dear brother,
I beg your great forgiveness in this fearful hour.
I thought I was perhaps immortal, a gold bird,
and you the dust that rose and vanished at my heels.
Now in Death's lightning flash I recognize you, friend,
for slaves and masters are all kin at the worm's feast.
I beg you, do not weep; I've freed myself from shades.
Greet for me one by one my much-loved skein of shadows,
my father, mother, my newborn son, my sweetest wife,
and tell them that I'll hide in woods, I'll free the earth,
that though I shall not move, I'll set the mind's strength loose
to fly ahead and melt the North's cold crystal ice,
to turn South, right and left, toward sun, away from sun,
to reach the crimson East and the all-swooning West,
to slash across the heavens with no love or rage
and smash at last the innocent and brilliant powers,
then plunge to Tartarus and harvest those dark roots
that flow like crimson veins and water all the soul.
It's time for the five shameless elements to part:
air, water, fire, earth, and man's most fertile brain."

As the soul-snatcher crossed the young whore's garden plot
he stood upon the threshold with resounding heart
and dragged all things in his eyes' nets for the last time:
the fragrant body of the maid, the downy youth,
the faithful slave who lay prone on the earth and wailed,
and the slim handmaids running with swift rosy heels.
For a brief flash his eyes grew glazed, he pitied man,
and once more struck and scolded his still shallow mind:
"In truth, you're very strong, for many times I've felt
you smash my skull and break through like a heavy beast,
but yet you lack the greatest and most noble power,
O mind, to hold your full strength back with a strong bit."
But then the lone man tossed his head with pride, and smiled:
"All's well! Let the word loose—it's not pure gold to keep
hid in deep coffers for your son's inheritance;
plant it like a great seed, free it like a fierce beast!

Behold how here, in Margaro's wide courts, my word
leapt up like fire, a pomegranate tree whose boughs
hang heavily down with seven different kinds of fruit;
the sensual whore strains hard to pluck the one most sweet,
but the sad prince would choose with pride the bitter fruit,
and other hungry birds will come to peck and bite.
But soon that day will come when freedom and despair,
wild brother, savage sister, will meet beneath my word
as though from the same belly, fed with the same milk,
and seven varied fruits will merge in one whole fruit."
Dark smothered all the gardens, and unnumbered suns
hung dancing in a male row on the thighs of night;
low in the scented courtyards, in the azure dark,
the maiden's thousand-kissed soft features glittered still,
the prince's golden garments and his new-shorn locks
lay gleaming on the tiles like funeral ornaments.
But as the white-haired athlete crossed the threshold where
so many feet had trod, he tripped in the vast night
so that the pale prince raised at once his star-washed face—
his eyes and bare breast shone, his eager lips at length
sucked at the sterile teats of the wild wilderness.
Seeing the great ascetic trip in the dense dark,
he thrust a burning brand in his gold clothes to light
the traveler's way, till in the gardens the flames leapt,
flared on the laughing nurses, on the weeping slaves,
on Margaro who stooped and followed with mute awe
earth's white-haired old bellwether with his silent bell.
The lone man's shoulders also glowed in the gold flames,
and Margaro stood still and marveled in the wilderness.

Slowly he crossed the streets, passed through the city gate,
thrust in a wood, stopped by an open clearing then
and stroked his beard, rejoiced in the starry solitude.
He was once more alone, and turned his white-haired head,
nor did his feet know now what road to take, nor did
his mind, that great road-pointer, know what to command;
his soul spread like an open sea, and roads ran everywhere.

XIX

As fog rolled down the mountains and mist drowned the fields,
the wild hare trembled, eagles gathered high in air
and hovered with long-voyaged wings and hoarsely cawed:
"Alas, great darkness falls and drowns the floating earth."
"Brothers, this is no downpour, nor a smothering pall,
I see a dragon in the sky with thrashing tail,
he swoops with open mouth to swallow sun and all!"
"That is no dragon, friends, that is no raging storm,
I see Death dash across the fields on his black steed!"
Thus did the eagles quarrel on air's tumultuous peak
while down below on flimsy earth's worm-eaten crust
Odysseus stood erect in the fresh dawn and watched.
Slowly he turned, looked right and left, before, behind,
perceived his shadow spread like a black-petaled rose,
and his mind flashed and saw at once all his new road.
He had no God or master now: the four winds blew,
and in his chest his compass-heart led on toward Death.
The lone man's mind grew vast, he took a new road then,
hung a carnation on his ear and bit his lips
as life flared up and faded on his salty gills
and Death perched like a cricket on his shoulder blade.
Petal by petal fell the full-blown rose on earth
till but the stamen stood, rough, filled with fertile seed,
and sped erect with joy to burst down the abyss.
Odysseus spread his hand serenely in the cool dawn
and like a beggar calmly stood for alms to fall
when suddenly two huge drops of warm rain pelted down
into his thirsty palm like two enormous pearls.
He smiled and closed his fist as his whole body cooled,
then bent his now redeemed and double-minded head:
"My fist is slaked with charity and wants no more."
Huge drops began to fall upon the sun-scorched soil,
leaves flashed, the fragrant plants filled all the air with scent,
and as the sun sailed through the mists and the stones smiled,
the North Wind rose and blew until the storm dispersed.
Woodcutters meanwhile entered the wet woods with fear

and lightly stepped on tiptoe not to scare the spirits
that had assembled in trees and shook their bony limbs
or knocked their heads in furious winds until they merged,
stood straight like mighty pillars, and supported God.
Like puny ants, the lumberjacks swarmed round the roots
with axes at their waists, held honey in their palms
to soothe the spirits of the trees, those dread forefathers.
Passing through groves of fir and pine, they reached the oaks
and raised their eyes with mute awe to the huge forebears,
then hid their axes fearfully behind their backs
and stepped on tiptoe close, with honeyed hands outspread:
"Forgive us, grandfather oak, bear us no evil now,
we want to raise our children here, plant roots in soil
so that our souls won't fade from earth, our seed in wind;
but master, we've no wood with which to build our homes.
Come, grandsire, give us a good roof, become our house;
come, grandsire, be our plow that we may sow and eat;
become our son's stout cradle and our wife's strong loom;
come cast within our blazing hearths your final flower,
the crimson bud of flame, to keep us warm and dry!"
Thus did they try to supplicate the great old oak,
then slowly raised their axes in the shade with fear.
Light had been stifled with the shower, the damp woods steamed,
the frothy soil smelled sweetly like a new-dug grave
so that earth's odor rose into the archer's brains
as though it were an acrid wine and shook his brows
until his skull roared in the woods like crashing rocks,
like a great flint, and flung sparks in the burning air.
A lightning flash coiled in his hair like a blue viper,
earth flared and danced like a bright star, cast roots like seed,
a tree sprang up and swelled, flung flowers and fruit, and then
a sudden cry of "Fire!" rang in the wild woods
and all things turned to flimsy azure smoke, and vanished.
Like eggs that burst with hollow sound in a great fire,
the archer heard earth crack deep in his head's hearth,
but as he sang and stretched his mind's great inner bow
his eyes grew suddenly dark and his ears buzzed as though
a twanging chord had snapped in two in his mid-brow.
His face turned to a pallid blue, his sharp eyes glazed,
and his mouth twisted as he tried to shout, but choked,
by demons whipped, then spread his arms to keep from falling;
but the ground shook with sudden fury and knocked him down.
Then the deep woods resounded and the wild beasts raised
their tails with fear, the foxes stiffly cocked their ears,
earth shook again, storms raged, dark brows and temples gaped,
but slowly mountains calmed and the soul raised its head.

Odysseus took a deep breath then and looked about—
what joy! the forest blazed, deserted—not a soul
of man or beast had seen the athlete's sorry fall.
He leant against a tree, then slowly stood erect
in sun and felt Death's fingers on his shoulders still.
The sunlight fell in a white blaze and struck the ground,
and eagles spread their wings on the white fluffy clouds;
his brain reared like a king snake in the brilliant light
and swayed its undulating head to thaw in sun.
"Death laid his fingers lightly on my shoulders then!
Deep in my heart I heard him calling me to come.
Oho! My end at last approaches, the ground gapes!"
He spoke, and his brains seethed, his tholes ripped wide, but as
he mused on his sad words, his mind broke into bloom,
his forehead slowly cracked, and softly in the sun
between his eyebrows rose, unseen, the great third eye.
A deep joy drenched his soul and body through and through,
he felt this was his famous body's final flower;
and as through a clear emerald the sharp eye discerns
far things, and sweetness inexpressible laps the world,
and the sun loses all its poison, the air its sting,
so did the third clear emerald eye stand over the world.
He saw and hailed all virgin things for the first time,
looked on all things for the last time and cried farewell.
Each moment Time is wound, then springs like a fierce tiger
within whose mind past, present, future flare and die;
end and beginning close the circle spun by fate
and in that sweetest union the third eye arose
in the god-slayer's brow like a pure precious stone.
Turning, he saw his boon companion, old man Death,
standing with his lean sword beneath a fig tree's shade
while seven crimson dogs with green eyes yelped in rage.
But the brain-archer gazed on old man Death and smiled:
"Ah, friend, you wait for me in shadow astride your horse,
you hold the reins of my gray steed with your one hand
and with your other shade your eyes and search the road.
Push on toward the blue sea, O slayer! I'll greet you there!"
The sea rose in his loins and flooded all his mind,
then on his sulphurous nostrils dashed her salty spray.
He raised his white-haired head and smelled the briny air,
then like an elephant who sniffs Death's odor nigh
and to the light soil stoops serenely his old head,
recalling dimly the far haunts of his own kind,
the dark woods he had roamed, the streams where he first bathed,
and from the foreign and confining glen makes straight
for the dim cradle of his birth to perish there,

thus did Odysseus push on toward his mother, the dark sea.
He drove on southward, smelling from the world's far ends
the cool sea-spray so that his soul spread swelling sails
and Death, too, turned and whistled till the ground twigs cracked
as horses, dogs, and hunter dashed through empty light.
The archer followed close behind, pushed through the glen,
holding an oleander blossom, Death, between his teeth;
a rough song of the open road rose in his mind,
and all his retinue before him, steeds, dogs, Death,
heard the resounding tune and ran, his faithful hounds.
Like the white elephant's round ancient eye, he passed
slowly through plants and grass and bade the world farewell;
his mind broke the hooked barb of life, shook itself free,
and breathed in deeply the cold, savage brine of Death.

He marched all day, well sated, without food or drink:
"Farewell, tall silent hills that have no fear of death,
farewell, O short-lived trees, and you, my brother beasts,
we've played a lovely game, but all things have an end."
Then mighty autumn blew until the wounded leaves
lay dead on the damp earth like birds of varied hue,
and as he crunched them on his way, Odysseus shuddered.
All turned to mirrors where the soul now watched her face;
the lone man was a tree with trees, a stone with stones,
he woke with birds and all his inner wings would shake;
the elements that formed him threw their arms out wide,
air, water, earth, and fire that once had shaped his soul,
until he merged in kind with the world's elements.
His mystic and invisible body, azure-hued,
flickered about his flesh and cast ray-tentacles
that twined about earth's brawny bones and clasped them tight.
All flesh had turned to spirit now, all soul to flesh,
all to swift dance and counter-dance led by the mind
until he trod on earth no more but like the wraith
of a dead saint danced without wings above his head.
Man's boundaries stumbled, and mud-walls came tumbling down;
at dusk in a dark forest a striped tiger leapt
and stood before him as its lean tail flailed the earth
and its chest glowed with hunger like a sneak thief's lantern.
The freed mind watched his brother with unmoving calm
while from his bowels brimmed a deep forbearing love,
and both stared in each other's eyes as the man's flesh
melted and slowly turned to food for the starved tiger
until the beast accepted love in place of flesh.
Their mystical communion lingered for many hours
until the mind became frail flesh in the thick air

and the tamed tiger gently growled, stepped back with tail
held high, and sated, full of joy, leapt in the wood.
As the moon rose like a lean prow in bluest air
and slowly dragged its round and sunless hull down toward
the dark West in a sky of flickering starry flames,
the death-consenting man recalled the golden ships
he once rejoiced to watch on the Nile's fertile stream
as they sailed slowly on with cargoes of dead kings.
When the night shadows fell, the lustrous border-guard
stretched out supine on the roots of a wing-stormed date
and watched the careless stars amid the poignant leaves,
and watched the heavens slowly turn like a huge wheel
on which man's wretched mind turned also, bound with law.
Ah, with what ruthless silence do stars sail the sky,
and we, shipwrecked within a deep black well, drag out
a savage shriek in vain, in vain cry out for help,
for no star ever swerved toward earth to save one soul.
Only the third eye watched the heavens hopelessly
nor deigned to weep, nor asked for shelter, but between
the ruthless eyebrows of the freed man slowly whirled
the world around and ground it calmly like gold grain,
for all things live and die in its one wink alone.
Odysseus stooped and shuddered to feel the mind's strength;
earth fell and sprang like seed in his brain's furrowed coils,
and what for eons had striven in night's womb to sprout
in shoots, fruit, flower, now in the holy lone man's brain
sprang in a flash with fruit and flower, then swirled in smoke.
But suddenly as his brain wove and unwove the world,
he felt black fingers touch his shoulders once again
till his delirium worsened like a wound so that he clutched
the date tree not to fall, and as he pierced the dark,
he saw Death standing to the left of the date palm
with all his seven flaming bloodhounds panting there.
Then the old athlete wanly smiled and waved his hand:
"Why such great haste, dear friend? Why not consult me too?
Don't lick your chops with your dry tongue; I'm still strong bone;
I'll let you gnaw my bones one day, but now I need them,
for the soul clasps the body tight until it rots.
Come close, that hunter and the hunted may agree;
I wish now slowly to descend toward the far waves
where I may hew tall trees once more and build my last
most slender, arrowy skiff, most slender, narrow bier,
so that with my strong chin thrust tight between my knees,
my hard palms gripping my world-wandering weary soles,
(as once I huddled tightly in my mother's womb),
I may once more return to the sea, to that vast womb.

Until then, Death, whether you will or not, be patient!"
He spoke, then like an archon slowly walked and stretched
his left hand toward the savage shadow, wrapped in fear:
"Keep seven steps behind me, Death; I'll call at need."
Death stopped and paced back seven paces, stepping slow,
while his red hounds rolled their green eyes in savage rage,
and the great athlete, by this lustrous army tagged,
burst out with laughter, thundering in the cave of night:
"By God, when my flesh lies dispersed in the damp ground,
my throat shall turn to a red cock to rise and crow,
and if worms poke into my nose, strong snakes shall rise,
coil round the well and gulp the fairy princess down;
my mind shall turn to a blackamoor, descend to Hades,
and browse on gold it won, and guide its property
of gods and ghosts and dreams and fragrant harbor towns!"
He spoke, and as firm clumps of grapes hang on a vine,
the bright star-clusters rose and dangled in his glittering brain.

His mind like a clear crystal crossed the night until
the light came dancing in the dawn like a spry kid,
leapt on his shoulder blades, then stretched in his strong lap.
When he arose, he joyed in rose-cheeked earth that came
and stood before him like a nude firm-throated girl:
"Death has revived my appetite, I'll rise and eat!"
the lone man shouted, laughing, and his nose and ears,
his eyes, searched everywhere for stilts to prop his hunger.
Hearing a rustling skirmish in a large oak tree,
the famished athlete stealthily approached tiptoe
and saw a small bear cub that stretched its shaggy paws
and reached for a gold beehive gleaming through the boughs.
It licked its pointed snout, with sticky honey daubed,
knocked down the honeycomb, looted its liquid gold,
and the god-slayer sat on earth and like a lord
accepted the divine thick nectar his slave proffered:
"Your health, my good co-worker, O my sweet bear cub!
It's only right that men and beasts should work for me,
it's right that a tree's toiling roots should feed its flower,
for only thus may the savior fruit of freedom ripen.
What freedom? To stare in the black eyes of the abyss
with gallantry and joy as on one's native land!"
He spoke, then set out southward with the dawning light.
His soul stretched out and sweetened, his eyes, ears, and hands
caressed the world insatiably and stroked it smooth
till slowly his gnarled heart turned to a ripening fruit.
He watched the young tree-nymphs with locks of maidenhair
swinging themselves in sun high on the supple boughs;

he hailed the ancient silent trees, their dread grandsires,
then sat cross-legged at night on their humped roots and talked
with their green spirits, their moss-haired ancestral crones.
He saw in sun the phantoms of the invisible world,
he saw at night the downy shades that sauntered past,
and he strolled with them too, a ghost among the ghosts.
Sometime toward dusk he heard the crimson setting sun
groan like a young bull dragged to slaughter in the dark West.
He heard the scarab, stretched supine upon the ground,
breathing his last with joy, for he had done his duty
and thrust his holy seed in his mate's fertile womb,
stored dung in the deep burrows for his sons to eat,
and now, like a meek saint, stretched out his claws to die.
One day the three-eyed man saw noontime walk the earth's
sun-stricken road like a king's son who held and waved
aloft a tall-stemmed yellow flower while thick round drops
of pearly sweat dripped from his hair, but when he saw
the lone man from afar, he climbed on a white rock.
As the lone wanderer slowly passed and looked on high,
he saw no king's son there, but only a tall sunflower
that hung its heavy head and watched the traveler pass.
Another day he saw a snow-white peacock leap
on a cliff's edge and open there its silver tail,
squandering its beauty in the wilds without reward.
"Ah, beautiful, abundant wealth, I'll take two plumes
for the two oars of the last skiff I have in mind."
He smiled, and toward that silver treasure stretched his hand,
but the white peacock scooped its bright cascade in wrath
and swiftly vanished in the trees like the pale moon.
The lone man's eyes flashed flame as he recalled the two
good things which always calmed and lit his darkened heart:
the warm white rose that steams within the blazing sun,
the windless sand that strews a beach like fine white flour,
and now their third white brother that strolled past with spreading tail.

As the swift-dying man walked on, he sweetly joyed
in the firm world reflected in his ancient eyes
and in the emerald unseen world of mystic eyes.
One flaming evening he discerned in a deep hollow
a town that gleamed amid the trees and riverbanks,
and heard the bark of drums and dogs, the talk in rooms;
and as the sun set and the burning houses cooled,
the young men crowed like cocks, girls chirped like newborn chicks,
and mothers, like milk-fountains, fed their suckling babes.
Songs of the cradle, of the grave, of the nuptial bed
rose from the town in tangled skeins and choked the air,

and the bellwether cocked his ear and heard the songs
pour in his mind like festive, sad, immortal tunes.
He turned to the rocks and sought a sheltered place to sleep,
then saw amid the boulders a lean snakelike path,
and in the twilight's plucked and vaporous rose discerned
tall trees that loomed to right and left, carved skillfully,
for each tree on its trunk depicted a new face
so that serene, sad, savage masks glowed in the dusk.
Odysseus walked the lane and fondled tenderly
the carved deserted gods, the passions of the soul:
on one tree, bony Hunger cackled in dim light,
and on another, blond-haired Thirst with sunken eyes;
still further down, black Lechery grinned with myriad teeth
and plaguy Sickness with a fat frog's bloated cheeks;
on an old plane tree Madness held her sides and laughed.
Each tree embodied an old different human passion,
and as the archer calmly passed and stroked each trunk
he shuddered deeply as though plunged in man's dark soul:
"I've flushed a wild beast's lane that leads to an ascetic;
I know these passions well, my old acquaintances,
for I've thus carved the trees of all my inner groves;
now as I pass they also stroll with me like dreams."
But as he mused on these starved beasts that eat man's mind,
he dimly saw a tomb cut in a giant rock:
"This must be the hard turtle shell of the wild hermit;
I'd like to see what beast torments his riven heart,
what god has smashed the hinges of his frenzied mind,"
he mumbled mockingly and crossed the shaded sill.
In the cave's midst, within a hollowed tree, there glowed
the coarse bones of a skeleton with gaping jaws;
its foes' teeth in a necklace hung about its throat,
on one side greenly glowed a slim time-rusted sword.
As the god-slayer fumbled in the dim-lit cave,
he made out in one corner jars of cooling water,
drills, chisels, augers, tools of every kind, bunched herbs,
fresh fruits, and crumbs of dry black bread in a rough hearth,
and small wood-carven gods strewn on the cave's floor.
The lone man kicked them with his feet, then laughed and mewed:
"Oho, the old cat's here, with droves of rat-faced gods!"
As though in his own home, he ate some bread and fruit,
poured water down his thirsty throat from a cool jug
then wiped his beard and cast his eyes about the cave:
"The dead man lives in this old tomb as though alive!
Ah, if he'd only rise at night to welcome me,
to light the fire and roast the underworld's wild game,
the fat shades of the partridge and the dead gazelle,

and fill my airy beaker with a phantom wine,
I'd even taste those shadowy feasts and welcome them!"
He spoke, then stretched contented by the dead man's bones
and called upon his old slave Sleep to come in haste
whether as downy wings or like a heavy quilt,
whether with naked feet or with soft lulling bells;
and Sleep spread like a honeycomb on his mid-brow
and dripped its heavy honey in his brains the whole night through.

At dawn Odysseus heard a whirring sound, and woke;
the tomb still smothered dimly, a Cimmerian mouth,
and a small honeybee buzzed round a curly flower,
which had uncaring spread its beauty on the tomb's dome,
till all the grave buzzed like a honey-haunted hive.
Light slowly drifted in until the tomb turned rose,
the smooth walls woke, the paintings on the cave-rocks swayed
and spoke of the three great concerns of earth's first man:
wild game, a woman's fertile heavy hips and rump,
a god who in a corner stood with ax in hand.
"Good health and joy, ascetic, to your skillful hands;
you've matched well man's three monsters: hunger, love, and God,
but you've forgotten my own face, the Unbidden Guest!"
He leapt up lightly and stood straight by the cave's mouth
and watched the mountain tops turn rose, the snake-paths gleam,
as down below in the dim village the doors gaped.
Seven bright blackbirds perched in the old oak that loomed,
a huge and many-branched grandsire, at the tomb's mouth,
where like goodhearted spirits the seven burst in song
till the old oak grandfather swayed and joined the tune.
The archer then recalled his own ancestral oak
and how, long since, he'd danced amid his sacred tombs
and given the shades to drink from a bronze jug of blood.
The old Odysseus walked on a far riverbank,
shade of a slaughtered monster, a thought formed of air,
until his mind distilled and sweet serenity
settled upon the mountain rims of his stone skull.
His calm was not a soundless void or a deep hush
but a harsh jangling caravan in his mind's court;
things past and things to come conjoined with each heartthrob,
the moments clashed like shields, like castles tumbled down,
or perched like blackbirds in his mind and burst in song.
For a long time he roamed the cave or with calm hands
fondled the tree-masks as he whistled through the grove,
until he suddenly hungered and turned back once more
to share his meal in peace with the tomb's long-dead master.
But when he came to the cave's mouth, his heart fanned open;

a hundred-year-old man crouched like a heap of bones,
blind, with no hair or lashes, yet with scrawny hands
carved swiftly out of olive wood an old man's head.
"Your health! Well met, old codger; master craftsman, hail!
You grab dry logs of wood, blow with your ancient breath,
and they melt down like wax, slaves to your every mood,
leaping like demons, gods, or nude girls, as you wish.
Thus did I once, too, hold the dry log of the world."
The startled codger raised his shaggy arms and cried:
"Ah, ah, if you're the great ascetic, fold your wings,
for when the heralds cried your coming throughout the land
I seized my hermit's staff and beat about the woods
for three whole nights, pursuing that false wagtail, Hope!"
The lone man laughed as dappled light played on his face:
"I am, and am not wings; I cast my shade and go;
I am, and am not throats; I cast my song and go;
the shades I see, turn meat; the shades I don't see, fade;
I'm the great savior of the world where no salvation lies."
The huge brow of the ancient hermit rose in shade
until the dark sill flashed and the whole cave was lit:
"I've chased that dreadful bird through woods my whole life long,
I've never rejoiced in sleep or bread or woman's body;
alone, led on by smell, armed with my spirit only,
I've hunted that dread bird, salvation, through dark woods;
now that I hold you I smell sulphur on your hair—
such is the savior's odor, all old legends say!
Lower your head, my lord, that I may reach my hands
to grope your features, touch your hair, that this poor hand
of mine, a shriveled twig, may burst with fruit and flower."
The mighty athlete mutely crouched by the old man
who reached a fumbling hand and slowly groped with fear
to feel the lone man's sunburnt face with its deep grooves,
and his dry fingers clutched the rough contours as though
they dug up thorny shrubs, as though they skirted cliffs;
but when his palm had gorged itself, it gaped in sun
and like a slim moon held the holy skull unseen.
"I'll find a well-veined precious oak with netted grains
to carve in firmest wood this dread head I now hold,
and when I've done, I'll cross my hands upon my chest,
for I'll have touched my greatest hope, and need no more!"
He spoke, then leapt into the cave and thrust his mouth
within the dead man's rotted skull and cried with joy:
"Father, he's come, the Savior's come, arise, he's come!"
Three times he yelled into the skull, took three long breaths,
and thus disburdened, turned to the light again, crouched low,
and slowly tears began to fall in streams and poured

from the night-smothered burning pits of his blind eyes
and ran along his cheeks, his lips, dripped down his chin,
until his ancient ivory features glowed with joy
like gleaming rocks that laugh when struck by sun after a rain.

For hours he spoke not, laughed in his god-carving mind,
and his whole life became all tears and drowned his soul,
and his whole heart spilled on the earth with gurgling sound.
Hours passed, the two old archons of the wilds spoke not
while all about them in the threatening woods life sank
her hoary hands and sprawling feet in blood and mire.
Even the beasts in sun took fright as though they'd seen
a lion's shadow, and ran, striking the earth with claws;
a monstrous serpent through the water twined and curled,
then coiled in silence threefold round a crocodile
that idly basked within the river's cooling stream.
The thrashing waters foamed and churned with crunch of bones
as the poor crocodile screeched loudly with sharp pain
and flailed the waters with its tail, but the snake wound
it tight in slimy joy as with a woman's arms.
The wretched beast strove to slip through the strong embrace,
but the erotic limbs poured round it in new waves
till in the white noon, in the tranquil sun-shot waters,
a hopeless dry crack rang, as though a beam had broken.
As the old hermit listened to the forest's din,
and rivers foamed and wild beasts roared within his heart,
he felt he knew each outcry of their wounded lives.
Then he reached out, groped slowly with his stiffened hand
and firmly gripped the stone knees of the silent guide;
"O dreadful bird whom all my life I've chased through woods,
I've learned all there's to know of crafts, my brains set out
and soon traversed the mind's lone lanes to their far ends,
but all roads led to plunging cliffs, and I turned back.
I know the tongues with which the birds and beasts converse,
sometimes I chirp like crickets, at times I roar like lions;
I sit on the olive boughs and sing to the fig trees,
at night I turn to water and join its gurgling talk,
and when elves dance at noon's most sacred upright hour
I place a lyre with bells on my old knees, and play,
dear God, the cares and the cravings of dream-taken man.
All ghosts and fates roost in my eyeballs' sightless pits,
I know the secrets of all herbs and how to heal
those hopeless pilgrims who ascend to seek my grace;
I call, and phantoms rush like greedy birds who've heard
the birdman's sly halloo, and flap their eager wings.
I carve high heaps of gods to solace wretched men

who dash and cling to my lush fantasy's creations
till all their pains take wing and fly away like birds.
Only I writhe, forlorn, and shout in the wilderness.
Why were we born? Toward what do men and beasts proceed?
For years I've groaned in rain and the sun's ruthless blaze
until my eyes spilled coarsely on the ground in tears.
All spirits have slaved for me, all men held me in fear,
but still my empty hands stretched out and begged for alms
till, as I sat by my cave's entrance yesterday
and wailed my tree so full of flowers yet not one fruit,
a small bird whistled like a spirit unrestrained
as it flew southward past my head, and cawed in glee:
'Old grandfather, raise your head on high, the Savior has come!'
I jumped up trembling then and cried to the small soul:
'O bird, come down! Here is some grain! Say it again!'
But the bird bore such flaming good news in its bill,
it sped to scatter it with song throughout the world.
I rushed into the forest then and listened: the ground swayed,
animals poured like rivers, the insects massed in force,
deep waters from their channels swerved and forked in sand,
and a small sacred snake wound round my loins and hissed:
'Push on, grandfather! It's time we also flowed to sea,
the fairy tale has turned to myth, the Savior has come!' "
Then the old man fell silent, and his tears ran down
a face that smiled like rich-wrought rainbows in the sun;
he stretched his hands out taut like hungry tentacles:
"O dreadful bird, with a spirit's bloody breast and throat,
now that I die unfruitful, you pity my poor life
and fold your brilliant wings and cling to my dry tree;
a thousand welcomes, fruit, although my branches break!"
Then the freed athlete laughed and smiled on the old man:
"Well met, untamed and heavy heart of the wild wastes!
You arm and deck yourself with dappled darts, you stand
here in the wild lands where I pass, you block my way
and like a chattering beggar fling your questioning hand
and ask with trembling gasps: 'But why? And where? And whence?'
You fetch the Savior a deep sack of searching tongues!"
Then the starved athlete laughed and strode into the cave,
cut bread, chose the best apple from a stone-slab shelf,
drank cooling water to quench his thirst, then wiped his beard
and once more sat serenely by the ascetic's side;
but the old man stretched empty palms with greed and cried:
"If you're the Savior, then reply, though you would not."
The man whose mind blew four ways liked this rude retort:
"Grandsire, I like your words, they ring true in my ears,
they tumble down and knock on my great heart, but still

your mind rolls on the ground, stuffed with leaves, dirt, and hair;
you'll find my words as yet too hard to understand,
if understood, much harder still to keep recalled,
and if recalled, their weight will surely crush your mind.
Now shut the palm of beggary and the mouth of pain
and press your ears against the earth to hear, for thus
I also wept and questioned till I pressed my ears to earth."

In a sun-stricken clearing, on a scanty tree,
the few leaves slowly danced and bid the light farewell;
two yellow flowers drooped and pined away for fear
the sun would vanish soon and leave them unprotected;
all other souls on earth like yellow flowers too
turned toward the sun and trailed its light till sudden sorrow
fell on them all like darkness as they shook and withered,
remembering wretched death and the appalling dust,
for with the sun, souls also bloom and shut like flowers.
Shrill cries were heard in the deep woods where monkeys dashed
from branch to branch and breached the garden plots, and then
from a great distance rose the shrill hyena's wail.
The old man hung his heavy head, but his heart danced:
"It's true, no virtue can surpass what patience finds.
My sword, I've honed you on the stone of patience long
and hold the uncaught and lean-fleshed bird of victory now."
Although he bragged, the old man's heart was heavy still:
"Savior, stoop down, for my mind swells and brims with thought:
there's much we have to say, we two, and mouth to mouth."
The sun set thickly where the village's round huts
with open doors and windows gaped amid the fields
in clouds of dust and looked like heaps of dead men's skulls.
A Negro boy came clambering up the stony path,
approached, and placed with trembling at the hermit's feet
some bread, a ring of dried figs, and a jug of water,
then sped back to his village without word or sound.
The old man sighed in bitter and complaining whine:
"Ah, could I only start my life's road once again!"
When the black boy reached home, he clasped his mother tight:
"Mother, a fiery lion sits by our ancient's cave!
Mother, the old man crouches at its feet, and weeps!"
The village doors resounded as the news stalked through
each threshold like a lion, and prowled the dusk until
it came and stood at night by a poor mason's door.
A few days since, the master had fallen from a tall scaffold
and now lay dying in a dim hall, and called his son:
"Come now, my only son, that in this last dark hour
I may bequeath to you my trade's few honest tools;

I've had these weapons from my father and he from his,
passed down through many generations. Arm yourself, son!
First take the trowel to shape the clay, the straight plumb line
to find what's upright, then the trusty water-level,
the squared right-angle and toothed chisel, crowbar and awl,
strong holy weapons that I entrust you with, my son,
that you in turn may give them to your own first-born.
To some were given spears or swords to slaughter men,
to some the mighty thoughts by which the world is ruled,
but fate has given us in trust the mason's tools.
Each soul has its own grace. I worship and bow low,
O faithful, true co-workers, old ancestral tools
who've helped even me to earn my bread on earth, and now
in my son's hands begin a new day's work and wage.
O trowel, aid my son; O plumb line, hang down straight;
dear water-level, please forgive his awkward hands,
but they'll mature, you'll see, and even surpass me soon;
go with my blessing, holy tools, to my son's hands."
The father spoke, subdued his pains, then stood erect
like his old forebears when they, too, bequeathed their tools,
and as from his dear father's quivering hands the son
took the old weapons, they turned young in youthful hands.
He stooped and kissed the honest tools in salutation:
"Welcome, grandsires! May I deserve your blessings too!"
Thus did the father entrust his craft's new destiny
to his son's hands, when all at once a voice rang out:
"At the cave's mouth a lion threatens our saint! To arms!"
The son rushed through his yard, flung wide his outer door
on a deep night where flickering lanterns swayed in courts,
where yelping dogs in fear thrust through their masters' legs,
and old crones cast and shook dry beans in sieves
to find out if a lion or fierce god stalked the cave.
Two elders with a kerchief tightly bound their heads:
"Give us our cudgels, grandsons, we shall climb the cave.
Ah lads, we've heard such dark news that our old hearts bleed."
All the youths felt ashamed and buckled on their arms,
and the young mason's son cried to his sister then:
"A lion may be stalking our old hermit's cave!
Don't weep, dear sister; help me gird my weapons well,
for I'm ashamed to leave the old men to their peril."
Meanwhile the ancient hermit once more sighed and groaned:
"Ah, could I only start my life's road once again!"
But the world-roamer, silent and unmoving, held
his greenly glinting eyes wide open in the dark,
and his heart slowly cracked to hear the futile sighs;
he found their taste so bitter that he locked his lips

as his mind flowed, a far-off mist, and rolled to sea,
but he unlocked his lips in pain for the old man:
"Health to your hands, grandfather, which all woods obey!
Take up your tools and carve a god, who'll give you youth
that you may spring from earth reborn and take new roads."
But the old man smiled bitterly with lips awry:
"Now that I've shrunk, the gods perform no miracles;
when I was a strong man and carved from wood, they say
the gods became strong men in turn and smashed the world;
but now that my sides ache and all my loins have shrunk,
the gods' loins also rot and their sides throb with pain;

great Savior, I can't find my own salvation now."
He ceased, then suddenly raised his ten thin fingers high:
"These are the only ten almighty gods I have!"
Again he deeply sighed and made the tomb resound:
"Ah, were I young, I'd gird my weapons round my waist
and set out with my friends as though all life were ours.
I'd never spread again my begging hands toward heaven,
but I'd become a great king, taste all wines and meat,
spill blood, then go to my good wife when war was done.
I would be handsome, just, and good; in my great court
my kindliness would stand like a luxurious cow
and sweetly moo for all poor folk to come and milk her.
I'd ask no questions then, but laughing, loving, weeping
with all mankind, I'd plumb the secret of the world.
I know your lion's odor now, and my life's changed!"
As though the heart-seducer fed him with youth's herb,
the old man's loins grew strong, his joints knit once again,
he cocked his cap and felt his hunting mind fly off
to foreign lands in chase of wider wings; he leapt
from cliff to cliff as a cool wind assailed his brow,
and round his mighty head, where tossed his raven locks,
a bloody twisted cord wound in a crimson crown.
Like a young warrior stepping then in his bronze armor,
the old man softly glowed and slowly, slowly stepped in sleep.

"Brother, fear not! Let all the faithful raise their swords!"
The brazen mountains seethed and smoked in the sun's blaze,
and the sea licked the seashore with her rasping tongue.
Armies of giants leapt, and their bronze armor gleamed,
the young men lit tall crimson candles and green lamps,
and mothers screamed until the earth cracked wide to hear.
Death's mother clasped her lethal son and begged in tears:
"Son, pity the poor mothers, pity the young girls;
son, don't you hear their weeping and their wild lament
and the small children laughing, and the sweet soft talk
that young pairs whisper secretly at dead of night?
Let pain subside awhile and let the bright sun laugh."
Death hung a rose above his ear, twirled his mustache:
"Mother, this is no wedding feast I'm going to!
The iron-hearted king has sent his heralds here,
the greedy raven, the black jackal, the blind worm,
and ordered me to sack all towns, to smash all doors,
so plug your ears with wax, Mother, to drown their groans."
He spoke, then spurred his steed and disappeared in dust.
At that same hour a king leapt in his brazen armor
and mounted his white mare as mountain ranges shook

and trees raced backward swiftly till the stones struck sparks,
and in that mighty onrush all men shrank to ants.
At dusk at length the young king stopped and wiped the sweat
from his flushed face with a gold handkerchief, then stooped
and in a glittering river rimmed with willow trees
glanced at his noble laughing face, his gleaming teeth
and the red ribbon woven round his hair with kisses;
he gazed on castles he had burned, towns he had wrecked,
young children he had orphaned, all the souls he'd snatched,
and Death beside him with a rose hung from his ear.
His heart was suddenly moved and his mind sweetly dawned:
"Run off to your old mother, O foul butcher, Death,
for now I pity men and want this dread war stopped;
I want songs now in every room, the hum of looms,
and mothers cradling their young babes at evening's door.
Death, I too am a newlywed, my mind drips honey;
I'll cast my brazen armor off and dress in silks,
I'll stroll through grass in gold-embroidered, limber cloaks,
I'll fight my Lady now with bows of flowering bay,
and with red roses tip my shafts to stain our bed,
and all shall come and clash their shields of happiness.
Dear Death, you've served me well; take for remembrance now
my pearl-stitched waistcoat and my golden-hilted sword,
and fare you well, for evil times have gone forever."
He spoke, and grim Death vanished from the water's glaze
and only frail rose petals drifted down the flowering stream.

In fields the branches blossomed with the first red shoots
and in the marble palace court the slim queen sighed
and two fawns followed tamely her long velvet train.
Stooping, she asked the marble lions that rimmed the well:
"Dear lions, have you seen my loved king in the meadows?
He rides a white mare, eagles dart in his blue eyes,
his long hair is adorned with a red twisted cord
which my own hands have woven and my own blood dyed.
Dear lions, if you see him, tell him to return."
The waters leapt and fell upon the lions' manes
as through the wrought gold gate the horseman dashed, and reined.
In the dark gardens, pomegranate fires bloomed
and all the pictured carvings woke on painted walls:
the gods spread out their hands as though to bless the earth,
ancestors laughed in rows with their marmoreal lips,
the horses smelled their master and neighed stone on stone,
and a small worm crawled in the court and burst with wings—
for the king held his sweetheart in his arms all night.
Next morning at her window, with her jet-black eyes

drowsy for want of sleep, and through her golden grille,
the slim queen envied men that walked the roads below.
Then like a bride in whom the seed has caught, her heart
hankered for curious dishes and for strange desires:
"O passers-by, my heart beats so, I long to come
and tread your earthen streets and walk in mud awhile;
I can't bear more, O passers-by, and I shall weep!"
She watched a hobbling hag walk barefoot in the mire
until she also longed to sink her feet in mud.
Then the king ordered hundredweights of clove and spice,
and hundredweights of nutmeg, cinnamon, and mint,
and hundredweights of ginger root in mortars ground
and heaped high in the court and drenched with oil of rose
to form a clay mass that the queen with her white feet
might in the dawn descend and walk on fragrant mire.
The king's heart sprouted wings as though to soar with joy
for from earth's tree he'd plucked all sweet fruits, one by one,
till no desires or joys remained, and the world wasted
before his heart could fully taste its brimming strength;
but still the king was not aware he'd reached the abyss.
He crossed his city and his streets with marveling joy,
held high the scales of justice, with his people shared
possessions of the earth and sea, and the heart's graces.
He heard the slim maid's loom, the mother's lullaby,
and from the palace terraces at dusk he saw
glad women hang in clusters, clustering children play.
Rich heralds from the world's far corners came and fetched
humped camels weighed with heavy gold, round rings of slaves,
bright trees of coral, precious ostrich plumes, until
the marble lions gaped and laughed and the king twirled
his jet-black hooked mustache and like a tiger stalked
his spacious marble courts, his golden corridors.
But one dark night alone amid his flowering trees
he drank a sharp wing-voyaged wine, and his heart swelled,
his life rose like a lotus in his memory's pool
and he sighed deeply till his dim eyes filled with tears.
The world lay wholly at his feet and swarmed with wealth,
his body was an ivory tower where women perched
like nightingales at dusk with fluttering wings, and sang,
but his heart suddenly sighed with sadness, his proud hands
spread like a beggar's in the night with greedy palms.
He screamed and burst in tears until the palace cracked,
and the dream-sages huddled, exorcisers mouthed,
heart-healers rushed with charms, old men with magic herbs,
and all the palace's disease-wise quacks dashed up
with their long beards and cunning eyes and clacking tongues.

They babbled of their nostrums with most subtle guile,
puffed hard to blow the evil away, smeared magic salves,
brought healing snake-balms and a honeyed sweetroot soup,
but the king wailed on unconsoled, his heart felt choked,
and laughter, that uncaught bird, never more returned.
Then his dwarf jester cocked his cap and bells awry:
"Give way, I'll make the unlaughing king cackle and caw!"
He mewed, crawled on all fours on earth, crowed like a cock,
cackled and cawed like partridges, like vultures screeched,
and his protean throat broke in a goldfinch song.
But the unlaughing king in nausea plugged his ears:
"I will not hear that fool who shames all mankind thus!
Cast him in iron cages with the monkey tribe!"
A slim maid stretched in bed and dimmed the sun's own face:
"It's I who'll make the unlaughing king cackle and caw!"
She wore the heavens on her breast, the sun and moon,
she placed gold scorpions in her hair, pinks at her ear,
then swaggered toward the palace gates with swaying hips.
An old man sinned to see her, a child gaped with awe,
two burghers met her and their purse-strings snapped in two
so that their gold coins rolled and gurgled on the ground,
and the young sentries of the palace flushed and glowed:
"It must be dawn! The palace pillars burst in flame!"
"The evening air in afterglow is filled with scent!"
And the third sentry shouted "Fire!" and raised the sign,
a crimson flag of flame, so that the whole town seethed.
The Negro hangman who stood still by the king's side
turned and unsheathed his shining sword and loudly yelled:
"Great king, through your wide threshold a slim maiden sways!"
The sun and moon on her firm breast gleamed and approached,
she stripped bare, the gold scorpions stirred, and the pinks fell,
then silently she placed her head on the king's knees.
But deep within the woman's eyes the king discerned
an infant that spread chubby hands to clasp him tight,
and he jumped up, turned in despair, and called his slave:
"Her bosom seeks a child! I loathe it! I don't want it!
Take her, my slave, sleep with her, cram her belly full!"
An ancient sage then stroked his snow-white hair with pride:
"It's I who'll make the unlaughing king cackle and caw."
He crouched on a low stool at the king's feet and wove
for seven days and nights the world's grim chronicles:
for seven days and nights his knowing mind unwound
the wars, disasters, lusts, and wiles of all mankind,
but on the seventh dawn at length the king cried out:
"Man's history is a heavy shame of wars and tears,
the earth's a blood-soaked slaughterhouse, there is no truth,

nor joy, nor virtue, nor reward, nor saving hope."
He huddled on his throne and ordered his black slave:
"Cut off the wise man's tongue, he's poisoned the whole world!"
At last toward midnight a blind minstrel came and raised
his darkened eyeballs high to the unpitying heavens
then broke into tormenting wails, a proud lament,
and though the king stooped low, he heard no lucid words,
but his mind flashed, he reached his hand and cried, "It's true!"
Then he flung off his crimson sandals, his tall crown,
his gold two-headed eagles and his golden seal,
and two by two lunged swiftly down the palace stairs.
His father in the courtyard reached his hands to stop him:
"I am your ancient father, son!" "I never was born!"
His son forestalled him by the gate and blocked his way:
"I am your son, don't leave me now!" "I have no children!"
His wife opposed him in the public road and clasped him tight:
"I am your wife, have pity!" "I want no children born!"
The king traversed the road, passed through the city gate,
crossed through his fields and vineyards, climbed the low foothills,
stopped for a while to listen, and then rushed on again:
behind the trees he heard the far sea's bitter roar,
behind the rocks he heard the far sea's bitter roar,
behind his lustrous forehead broke the thundering waves.
"My kingdom's but an island and the sea's its noose!"
Hungry, he seized a crust of bread to rouse his soul,
but still he heard the mocking sea behind the bread
and flung it on the stones, nor wished to eat again.
The king took to his heels once more, crossed road on road,
and lo! a dragon with nine pairs of heads leapt down
between two lofty mountain peaks and blocked his way:
"The mind to conquer me, great king, has not been born!
I am the Law, father of virtue, thorny hedge
that guards man's ordered way, the sacred boundary line
behind which spreads the desert with no hope or god!"
But the unlaughing king still heard behind the Law's
blood-splattered heads the thundering of the distant sea,
and the earth gaped and his mind suddenly gulped the dragon.
The young king crossed road after road, the mountains swayed,
and a bold god with flashing lightning bolts in hand
leapt high in the hushed darkness of a cave and cried:
"Where to, unlaughing king? I'm God, the world's last limits!
There aren't more roads for you to pass or straits to cross,
I am the end of sky, of earth, and of man's soul!"
But still behind God's back the king heard the sea's roar
and God sank suddenly in the gaping mind of man
till the mind leapt on the king's laughless head and cried:

"I only, man's great mind, exist on earth and sky!"
But still behind these words the sea mocked on in foam
and the mind shuddered and clamped tight its shameless mouth.
Once more he took the road, dashed through the mountain straits,
trees met and parted, rocks split wide, then merged again,
and all about him the stones broke in whirling dance.
One morning his exhausted nostrils smelled salt air,
an endless empty sea roared at the faint king's feet,
opened her frothing mouth and crunched the sandy shore
like a bitch-dog till Mother Earth shrank back in fear.
The poor king clutched his anguished heart to keep it whole
then grasped a log and hewed a new Unlaughing Man,
planted him like a bellbuoy on the foaming wave
then dashed in silence round the shore and swore an oath
never to stop until he'd circled all his land.
He ran around his wretched kingdom shore by shore
as days and nights passed by and emptied, full moons waned,
but still the unlaughing king ran shore by shore and wailed:
"I'm snared in a round trap! Alas, I rule an island!"
Cold winter came and went, the summer strolled and passed,
the snows fell once again, and one night the king's feet
tripped on a sodden log so that he fell down prone
and in the morning saw he held the uprooted buoy,
for he had come full circle, and the noose closed tight.
The sea had mounted and begun to eat it whole,
its wooden knees had rotted, seaweed wrapped its feet,
and the white slimy sea-worms crawled and licked its soggy thighs.

The unlaughing king then flung his wooden mask far out
to sea and struck inland again with calm despair.
He suddenly came to a mountain heap of dead men's skulls,
and shuddered, for he guessed he saw his own old masks,
the soul's deep ancient sheaths, deep ancient ships in which
his mind had often sailed on deep oblivion's sea.
His whole life was a pile of bones, and junkman Death
cackled through every mouth and wailed in every eye.
Groaning, he clambered up the heap on hands and knees
as the bleached skulls with gaping jaws rolled clacking down,
and when the brine-bleached bones turned red toward set of sun,
the panting king at length climbed up the silent peak,
sat down cross-legged, then gazed about him with great fear:
the sea roared everywhere and rushed to gulp his kingdom!
His pale mind shook, and smoke rose from his head until
in lightning-like recall he plunged in the serene
and azure sea of deep oblivion, then sprang up,
clutching cool-dripping rubies, turquoise, coral boughs

entwined with salts and seaweeds of his ancient lives.
He'd been a monstrous armored lobster thrust in rocks,
a weightless flying fish that longed to mount the air,
a hawk that pierced the clouds, a mole at the earth's roots,
till skulls of myriad birds and beasts had wrapped his soul.
He'd growled a thousand years, he'd talked a thousand years,
at times he'd been a blood-smeared hunter, a rude rustic lad,
a rough clodhopper sowing and reaping the year through,
a sly and wealthy merchant and a fierce sea-wolf
who scoured the shores, tall at the prow, with ax in hand,
till his much-wandering blood had calmed for the last time
and turned to an unlaughing king's transparent soul.
But now, behold, the warrior sat on his old shields,
well-sheathed within the various skulls he had once worn,
and his mind cast the last beams of its afterglow:
"At last I've found the secret, and my heart grows light:
the mind's a lamp with little oil—blow, it goes out,
and all go with it, heavens and earth and the blue sea."
Struck by this sudden thought, the king began to laugh;
he laughed, and mountains swayed, he laughed, and the world shook,
he laughed and the skulls gaped and broke in cackling cries.
But all at once, dear God, a sharp knife swiped his throat,
and he smelled Death approaching like a cooling breeze;
his laughter stopped and he grabbed earth in both his arms:
"Mother, let me still live a moment, an hour still!
Mother, don't let me die now with still open gaping palms!"

The wet dawn slowly turned to rose and climbed the land,
and the light-archer, lying on his stony bed,
silently watched for hours the hermit's forehead toss
with quivering billows in the squalls of heaving sleep.
"He deeply dreams what he desires, he's born anew,
for sleep, that great magician, blows, and the dark body
drops like a black crust till the soul sprouts upright wings
and freely flies and sips the honey of each desire."
Thus did Odysseus muse upon the dream-drowned wretch,
but all at once the old man's lashes filled with tears
and he screamed, "Mother!" and flailed his hands the whole night through.
"Mother!" His cry rang clearly like an infant's wail;
but the heart-battler gazed on the old man in silence
nor spread his hands to exorcise the savage dream.
"The old man's living now the life he wished to live,
for dreams can cure the deepest wounds of waking day;
let him dream on, that his whole life might not go lost."
The two town-elders, meanwhile, climbed the rocks with gasps
while armed young men behind them followed stealthily,

until at break of dawn the old men quaked to see
long flickering tongues of flame that lit up all the cave,
and they heard bronze shields clash as though two armies met.
But when it had well dawned, their hearts leapt up with joy
for the great cave-rock shone and swayed in a white blaze,
a mountain of bright quivering wings and gleaming eggs,
till the first elder raised aloft his shriveled arms:
"The rock glows as with myriad wings to soar in flight,
the dread ascetics talk of God at break of day!"
He spoke, both climbed, light-footed, one behind the other,
and slowly neared with trembling the now rose-red tomb
till in dim azure light they saw the crystal beard
of the unknown ascetic flow like a pure stream.
He held the open hand of their ascetic high
as though he read man's fate within its gaping palm,
then raised his flaming eagle eyes and gently smiled
to give the pale men heart, and signed them to come close.
They crept up step by step with buckling knees, but when
they saw their hermit's body in the peace of death,
all wept and tore their hair: "Alas, our light has gone,
for our good ghost, our grandfather, plunges deep in Hades!"
Then the much-knowing athlete rose, and his eyes shone:
"Your great ascetic longed to return to his first home
but on his hand his soul clings like a beggar still
and stretches gaping toward your town and begs for alms—
my children, fill it with rich gifts, or it will eat you!"
The young men joined their shields and the old men their staffs,
then both raised high the holy corpse, climbed slowly down
the slope, and placed it underneath the town's great oak.
All good souls quickly came to kiss the holy corpse,
but its hand still stretched open, warm and gaping still.
Odysseus loomed above the crowd and ruled their fears:
"This dead man wants no tears, his still unsated hand
will not close till it clasps the dearest thing you have."
The dazed crowd shook and fell upon the gaping hand:
town elders cast their golden coins, young men their weapons,
chieftains the heavy bronze keys of the famous castle,
then mothers brimmed its gaping pit with their salt tears,
young maidens filled the palm with kisses, carnal musk,
and a small child hung on its fingers all his toys,
but the hand gaped with hunger still and cursed them all.
Keen wailing rose as the avid hand reached out to pull
down with it into earth the town and all its souls!
Ah, what gift now could slake that dreadful hunger's greed?
Odysseus felt the people's pain, pitied their souls,
then stooped, dug with his nails, approached the avid hand,

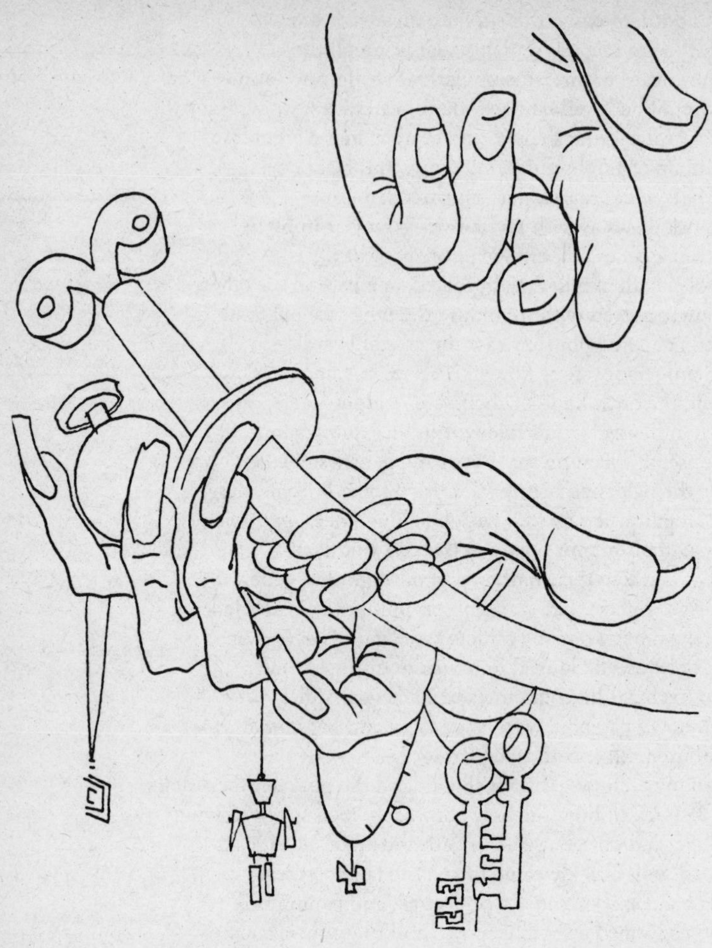

silently filled the bottomless palm with earth, and then
at once the shriveled fingers closed, full satisfied.
The elders fell and worshiped at their Savior's feet,
young maidens clasped his knees, widows his hands, and begged
him to remain as the town's guardian, their soul's shepherd,
but the lone man pushed through the crowd and took his way,
proud to deny his wealth, his joys, his gains each hour.
He passed the arched town gate and crossed through wealthy fields:
"What shall I do with this complaining life of ours
that sometimes makes me laugh and sometimes makes me sigh?

I rub it with my fingers like a laurel leaf
until my flesh and mind both smell of laurel leaves."
Thus freed of man at length, the soul of the saved master
whistled a lonely shepherd's song in the sweet wilderness.

Once more alone, he raised the wretched dust of earth,
once more the forest like a shaggy beast arose
and dragged behind the ascetic with a furry tail.
His new companions leapt like flying fishes high
in his mind's waves and followed him to the far sea:
the young death-smothered prince with his large eyes
who with no hope took the most brave, despairing path;
the much-kissed, much-washed body of sweet Margaro
that followed in a peacock blaze the lanes of love;
and now this old man, this unsated brain that asked:
"What is our life, and whence, and where?" this rampant hand
that sought reply from heaven and earth, that begged one word,
to which but one fistful of earth rose to reply.
"Just as a traveler bends to earth and watches ants
struggling amid the threshing floor and lugging chaff,
then suddenly lifts his heel and grinds them into nothing,
thus does the human ant-heap strive on this poor earth;
but no great mind regards us, no heart mocks us even,
only above us a foot hovers and stamps us out!
Heigh ho! with our great troubles and our gallant songs
let's jump down the abyss, clasped in each other's arms!"
The lone man marched all day as he recalled with grief
those hopeful youths who rose to assault the empty air,
and the air gently blew and smashed them on the sands.
"But we, my comrades, we know the secret well, and with
no hope at all we mount our steeds and fight the air!"
Thus did he mutter to himself as the earth's rose
dipped, and at dusk a river's small cool-singing branch
flowed through a sheath of rhododendron blooms and willows.
Rejoiced to find a friend with whom to march toward sea,
the lone man bared his feet to greet his comrade well,
but as he bent above the stream, his backbone thrilled
to see thick shoals of bride and bridegroom eels that swam
to sea, turned silver by love's fire, enflamed by passion,
all darting swiftly now to mate in the briny depths,
leaping and playing gaily, gleaming in sun and shade
like tangled snakes and rushing to entrust their seed
that eels, too, might not vanish on the impoverished earth.
Walking the bankside with the wedding pomp, he mused:
"If only in Death's briny depths we too could hatch
the inexhaustible new eggs warmed in our minds!"

After three days had come and gone, he reached a town
so wrung by pain that no smoke rose from the rooftops,
for foes had passed and put to sword all virile men,
all small male children, all the lusty stalwart youths,
and left but the immature and flowerless small girls,
the withered widows, baggy-breasted dying crones,
who huddled now in their bare yards and wailed with grief
because man's sperm had perished from the town, destroyed.
Only a small male child had crawled into a pot
and thus survived the slaughter, and now mothers passed him
from lap to lap and gave him suck with tender care,
for all hope of their sacred race's flickering flame,
their forebear's memory and their own homes' ancient roots
distilled and hung now from his small and hairless worm.
Pallid and weak, the boy wailed in the women's arms,
and his gold bonnet gleamed with myriad silver bells.
The many-souled man swiftly passed the wretched lanes
where the poor women wept and wailed within their rooms,
while in the empty yards, deep in blood-splattered grass,
delivered she-goats stood and suckled their spry kids
and gasped with joy to feel their bursting udders flow.
At the town's rim the suffering man stood on a knoll
and gazed upon the widowed roofs that spread below
and the gold bonnet gleaming in the female flock,
then raised his hands on high and blessed the young male shoot:
"May man's great seed not spill on earth and disappear,
may new men spring in time from earth, and in warm air
raise futile wings and towers to make their hearts rejoice!
The earth is only shadow, yet the glad heart clasps it tight."

The lone man now no longer counted days and nights;
each moment was the mother-well of deathless youth
so that he followed happily his compass heart,
knowing that all roads led unerringly down to sea.
One dawn, upon the highest trees, those great forebears,
he spied some gaudy-colored rags tied to the boughs
as secret prayers to the dread spirits that cure all ills;
further on, tall and monstrous rocks with chiseled suns
shone in an open clearing heaped with votive gifts
of clay plates, honey, milk and dates that steamed in sun.
"Here's Fear and Hope, the two great parents of all gods;
by this I guess there's a large village not far off,"
the lone man said, nor hastened nor relaxed his pace.
Then soon one day he heard drums beating everywhere
in the wood's darkest depths, and others beat reply,
as though ghosts hidden in the trees proclaimed his coming.

The sounds woke ancient mystic terrors in the blood
—thick forests, dangerous hunting, women, swarming beasts—
and the mind stooped and shuddered over a black pit.
What thousand-year-old savage life had passed this wood
with bloodstained ax of stone held tight in iron hands?
Memory, too, was a deep cave where wild beasts crouched,
and when they moved, the head creaked like a trap door sprung.
The sun turned shadow-ward and birds perched on their boughs
as the much-wandering pilgrim crossed with longing hope
the noisy village gate of a child-swarming town.
His black eyes then grew tranquil as the night sea-wind,
fragrant with scent of women's armpits and ripe fruit,
washed all his sunburnt dusty body with cool waves.
In the blue shadows, the streets swarmed with many souls,
wizened old men sat cross-legged on straw mats and wore
green turbans or white lofty bonnets on their heads,
and a young maiden passed, her hair new-washed and combed,
each thin lock braided with a pearl thick as a bean,
while on her nude breasts jangled amulets of bronze.
She passed with swaying steps, rang like a rattling snake,
shook her young hips most sweetly, smelled like a musk beast,
and glanced so piercingly with childlike painted eyes
that the great old ascetic blushed and lowered his own.
He sniffed the tented long bazaar where slender boys
bent down and in stone mortars pounded spice and herb,
where old men ground in silence magic paints and rouge
and yearning girls in darkness bought them secretly.
The wide-sleeved chieftains with their gold seal-rings rode by
mounted upon their wavy-humped and black-eyed camels,
and in their silken sashes new-cut roses gleamed.
Young women strolled with golden slippers, and all dripped
so with perfume, like savage birds flown from the woods,
that the old burghers paled with lust and shut their eyes,
fearing to shame their lives, dear God, in their old age.
A frenzied hermit held a heavy incense cup,
knocked on all doors, cast fumes to drive the demons off,
and a rich funeral slowly followed with slain heads
of a dead chieftain's slaves so that in the dark grave
they still might serve him well, bake bread, and wash his clothes.
All the onlookers hissed and yelled, old merchantmen
seized their long staffs and chased the dead man mockingly.
Amid the hired lamenters and the screeching crones
a maid like a musk-tigress passed in rut until
the funeral turned to wedding pomp, the dead men's sons
stopped in their tracks, forgot their father's fate, and sighed.
The wandering man then sweetly shut his dazzled eyes.

One day by a large stream he'd seen a black-skinned girl,
stripped naked on the bank, who lay and watched the waves;
in her left hand she held an apple and in her right
a brilliant small canary with clipped yellow wings
that in her black palm raised its throat and sweetly sang;
the village stretched now like that girl by the stream's bank.
But as he held his vision still in cleansing eyes,
he heard a lyre with silver bells ring at his feet,
and then with clear eyes saw a bard lustrous in shade
who knelt and played upon a monstrous throbbing lyre
with leaping fingers dancing on all seven chords,
and flames ascended from his flowing curly hair.
All the crowd clustered round and hung upon his lips,
the old men gathered up their wares and left their shops,
the young men left their pestles, the young maids drew close,
and chieftains spread embroidered rugs and sat cross-legged.
With glutted longing, steaming in the evening shade,
the whole town raised its ear to grasp the latest tune,
and two sly blackbirds on an olive tree stooped low
to steal the song and sing it to the trees in spring.
Then the black minstrel raised his ancient glowing head,
puffed up his chest and throat, and through his open mouth
the new song soared and hovered like an eagle in the sun:

"Oho, my lads, perk up your ears, set your minds spinning,
we're but a black fistful of earth, yet our throats sing,
and if one falls for the worm's food, don't pity him, lads,
for he had time to raise his voice in the wilderness,
and though his dust turn to black dust, his song remains;
I too shall sing my song before my own throat rots!
Far on a distant shore, at the world's utter end,
for two moons on a bear-hide, on a bloodstained bed,
an old king fought with Death, nor would resign his soul.
The king's son stood by the gold pillows and begged Death:
'Dear Death, I ask one favor only: raise your sword,
seize my old father by his hair, give me the crown!
I've grown old, raised my children and grandchildren too,
but still the old king won't give up the world's gold keys.
O Curse, rise if you're sitting! If you're standing, run!'
The old king heard his son's cruel words and heaved a sigh:
'O Prince Elias, aye, don't hurry, you won't wear
my crown until you hear cocks crow with human speech.'
When the prince heard these words, his flashing eyes grew dark,
he leapt up, buckled on his sword, wound round his head
tightly a crimson kerchief thrice to hold his brains,
and a black viper with three flaming poisons stung

his heart as his hot fists flared up and flailed the air:
'Dear God, send me to war, divert my frantic mind
that my exhausted hands may not kill my own father!'
God heard his pain and raised a war; at once the prince
plunged deep, slashed row on row of throats, and toward the end
dragged lengthy necklaces of stooped slaves tightly noosed
until at dusk his palms had brimmed, his wrath had shrunk,
but his dark soul still seethed, unslaked, unsatisfied.
His friends caroused on terraces with food and drink,
but the lone mountain tree is beaten by all winds,
and the prince passed down streets until he gained the woods.
Oho, my lads, perk up your ears, they're still unrotted,
for a small bird, a small, small bird shall come to sing.
Then the cock-pheasant saw the prince and flapped its wings
and on a tall black cypress sang with human speech:
'O Prince Elias, don't be sad, don't be downhearted,
you'll never wear a regal crown or crimson shoes
or ride a pure white elephant with golden studs.'
The prince stood still and listened to the dappled wings
as the sun sank and the stars flooded the dark air
and a thin tailless viper reared in his burning heart:
'Cock-pheasant, aye, my father shall descend to dust;
cock-pheasant, aye, although my lands fall to the crows
my soul burns upright in my breast and will not fade;
whether fate wills or not, I'll wear the golden crown!'
The embellished feathers fluttered and the cypress swayed:
'O Prince Elias, heavy heart, your boast is great;
loosen your crimson kerchief, kick the world goodbye,
hang a carnation from your ear and seize a lyre.
All flow on toward the sea and drown in that dark stream,
great towns and all their souls submerge, all women rot,
all gold crowns rot, and even gods rot like the trees;
don't cling to them, O Prince, they fade like whirling smoke,
the only deathless flame is man's own gallant song!
O Prince Elias, aye, if you're a brave man truly
then choose the loftiest crown of all for your gray hair.'
The king's son laughed, turned toward the town with muttering heart,
nor knew on what to cling nor where to go, but roamed
from village door to door, then chose one at long length
and knocked upon the master craftsman's workshop door:
'Aye, master craftsman, make me an intrepid lyre
worked skillfully with seven chords to hold my pain.'
The master craftsman chose his woods and carved a lyre;
he made the body of linden and the lid of lime,
he made the pegs of ivory and the scrolls of rosewood,
he made the bridge of gold hung with a maiden's tress.

Then Prince Elias seized the lyre and plunged in woods:
'I'll crouch amid the tall trees of the wilderness
and play my lyre, dear God, to tame my savage heart.'
Seven times with his hand he struck the holy lyre
and seven times the strings stayed mute and the song vanished,
nor did his heavy heart find rest or his pain dwindle.
The king's son raged, kicked at the earth, and his mind shook:
'I'll rise in wrath and kill the master craftsman now
for he forgot to string good chords and give them voice!'
But two long many-colored wings flew over his head:
'Ah, Prince Elias, songs are paid for dearly, lad,
the lyre won't speak or sing because it thirsts for blood;
your lyre thirsts to drink the blood of seven heads
so that its seven chords may leap and roar in song.'
The king's son laughed with scorn and stroked his dark mustache:
'Cock-pheasant, aye, that's easily done! I'll seize my bow
and soak my lyre with seventeen, not seven, heads,
for the earth's choked with bodies and my quiver is full!'
But the wings hung so heavily that the cypress stooped:
'O Prince Elias, aye, don't boast, don't stroke your beard,
your lyre longs to taste the blood of your seven sons!'
Then Prince Elias groaned, plucked at his thorny beard,
grabbed his sword frenziedly and thrust it in his calf,
then slowly walked, knocked on his door, stood in his court,
and raised a cry and called his seven sons before him:
'Aye, lads, grim War has raised his head! I'll seize my weapons,
and you, my first-born son, rise up! Only we two,
father and son, shall wade through our foes' blood that all
our grandsons and our great-grandsons may tell one day
how two, father and son, cut down two thousand foes.'
His son leapt up and thrust his sharp sword in his belt,
both spurred their steeds and dashed straight to the battlefield;
the son slashed left and gleaned the earth, the father right,
and his mute lyre heaved and tossed on his broad back.
Dawn rose and mounted toward high noon, the sun sank low,
until at dusk the son, drowned in his blood, cried out:
'Father, I'm dying! Greet my children! Ah, farewell!'
Then Prince Elias roared, scattered his foes before him,
flung his dead son, his first-born son, on his strong back,
and his tears muddied earth from battlefield to town.
His lyre then plunged in his son's lion blood and drank,
and as it drank, it swelled and creaked, tossed on his back
till a chord slowly stretched a gutstring through its heart.
He cast his son in his court heavily, slaves pressed close,
washed and rewashed their master, but no washing helped.
He took his lyre drenched in blood, plunged in the woods,

and when he was certain that no soul could watch his shame,
he rolled on earth and struck himself till the trees cracked
and the cock-pheasant passed and flapped its dappled wings:
'Don't weep, my dear, for all things fall to earth and rot;
some fall like leaves of the plane tree, and kingdoms fall,
even my lustrous wings shall fall and my throat rot,
but the song, Prince Elias, the song shall never fade!
Rise up, there's work to do, for six sons still remain!'
Then Prince Elias rose and stumbled down the road,
dug in the earth, buried his son and barred the door
of the cool tomb, lay down and seized his lyre, then stooped
and struck it with his heavy hand as his heart groaned—
but the lyre lowed like a sick cow and would not sing,
nor would the heavy heart of the stunned king grow light.
He shouted in his courtyard then, called his six sons,
then groaned, reached out his hand and chose the second youth:
'Rise up, my son, take up your sword, we march to war!
My hot fist throbs with flaming strife and will not cool.'
Father and son clove heads in war's red slaughterhouse;
dawn rose, then mounted toward high noon, but when dusk fell
the great son crashed to earth and moaned like a slain bull:
'Father, I'm dying! Greet my loving wife! Farewell!'
Again in the moon's glow he raised him on his back;
again the lyre swelled, the second blood-drenched chord
drank deep, then spread and twined about the twisted pegs.
Oho, my lads, perk up your ears, let your hearts break!
For seven dawns two horsemen dashed through the town's gates
and though both father and son returned all seven times,
the father fetched upon his back a headless son.
The anguished prince then tripped and staggered on the stones,
the laneways brimmed with blood, the wretched courts with tombs,
and the lyre licked its lips, sated with precious blood,
till seven voices, seven chords, roared in its heart.
Old men then broke in wild lament, the women keened,
and in his soul's great pain the old king heard their wails,
sat upright on his pillows, spread his hands and cried:
'Ah, Prince Elias, may you be cursed with a father's curse!'
But Prince Elias mutely gazed on his shrunk father,
looked on the wretched courtyard tombs, on all the world,
and heard a curse crow like a cock within his breast:
'Father, may you be cursed, and cursed the seed you sowed,
and cursed all sons and sweetest life and golden crowns!'
He spoke, and joyed to feel his entrails rip like rags.
Flinging the seven-chorded lyre on his bent back,
he bound his waist with rushes, let his hair float free
that had in seven days and seven nights grown white,

nor sighed nor groaned, but opened wide the palace door
and with great strides passed through his old ancestral town,
passed through his castle, hamlets, rivers, and strode on;
his blood flowed till the dust beneath his feet turned clay,
seven swords pierced his heart, he cast full seven shadows.
He passed through fields and mountains, crossed the sea, strode on,
until one dawn I saw him hanging on a high cliff.
Like seven bonfires, seven rose trees blazed about him
and seven twittering swallows in the sunlight played;
cock-pheasants flew by silently, the clouds sailed on,
a leopard leapt with joy, and a small cricket clung
to the old childless hermit's white and bloodstained hair.
Slowly he sat on earth cross-legged, caressed a flower,
hung it above his hairy ear through thickened blood
then swiftly shook his shoulders in the laughing light,
two wings that longed to flee, took down his clotted lyre,
laid it upon his knees, and the deep chasm glowed.
Touched by his fingertips, before his hand could strike,
the lyre like a living heart throbbed on his knees;
its wood sang like a thrush, its seven sated chords
leapt like man's sometime laughing sometime weeping heart,
and the song soared like deathless water through clear air.
He sang and his heart lightened, his dark mind grew cool,
his sons flew past like swallows, bloomed like singing flames,
and his old father sank low like the setting sun.
Memory perched on freedom's highest branch and sang
without a single care, with joy, a mother finch
who watched her small eggs gleaming in the azure sky.
When the lyre stopped and the earth grew mute, the lyrist rose
and set off southward, followed by the faithful earth;
he talked with kings and then passed on, he talked with women,
he stooped and listened to their gossip, sweet as water,
he talked with ghosts, with beasts, he sank in realms of sleep,
in that cool coal-black river where he swam all night,
then clutched and drank from earth's two udders, Life and Death.
Ah, Prince Elias, aye, god-slayer, turtle decoy-dove,
you stalk like an ascetic in your spotted rags,
with snow-white hair and savage eyes, with flaming lips.
Gulls dart above you swiftly, worms crawl at your feet,
and all, three stories high, flow swiftly on to sea;
O Prince, I've no more need of you! Good voyage now!
One dark night as I huddled in some ilex shrubs
watching your fingers strike as your lips gaped in song,
I plundered all your singing tricks and picked your brains;
now may the fishes eat you, may your larynx rot,
don't think that we, too, Prince, have no sweet throat to sing!"

The bard then bit his lips and the song suddenly stopped,
he wiped his sweat, then laughed, and opened his wool-sack:
"Heigh ho! my throat's sung well, but hunger chokes it now.
By God, although a song's immortal, it's a beast
and needs lean meat to strengthen, wine to spout and roar.
All are the belly's woof, my lads, and bread's the warp,
the body is a whirring loom that never rests,
and now that my song's ended, here's the secret, lads:
I'm starved! Stuff bread in my wool-sack, don't let me croak!"
He took his empty wool-sack then and went the rounds,
and all pressed close to give him gifts: one gave him bread,
another dates and flasks of wine, another meat,
ladies gave cinnamon flowers, widows threw him roses,
maidens cast quince and apples, boys cast honeyed sweets,
and as he felt his sack grow heavy, he laughed and said:
"Farewell, my sack's grown pregnant and my heart swells so
you'd think, by God, that both of them were belly-brothers!
Besides, what do you think a song is made of, lads?
It's made—I swear it!—of old wine and lean goat's meat!"
He spoke, maids gazed and marveled, and householders laughed,
but though he seemed half-witted, eagles filled his eyes,
and though he touched no maiden, he enjoyed them all
and slept with all at midnight in the open fields.
But he was wed now to the four winds, and flung his lyre
beside his bloated wool-sack, then trudged on to fetch it
to other towns, a still unslaked, unsated beast.
When the crowd left, the great ascetic like a ghost
rose from the shades and reached his calm hand toward the bard:
"Aye, lustrous bird of fancy, fold your flapping wings,
I want to cast a precious word in your wool-sack."
The savage singer in the darkness scowled and raised
his eyebrows at this sudden lordly man who spoke,
a four-eyed mind that like a glittering basilisk
drew near as cunning words flicked from his flaming lips:
"Aye, feather of a peacock brain, lightheaded brother,
now that we're all alone at dusk on this long road
and not a soul can hear us, tell me the real truth.
I'm that ascetic you saw crouched on the cliff's edge;
I held no roaring lyre upon my knees, no flames
blazed round my head, nor did I raise my throat in song.
On my fate's spindle then I spun another life!"
But the hoarse cock of song then slowly shrugged his shoulders:
"What do I care about your life, ascetic archer?
What do I care what's false or true, what's yours, what's mine?
It may well be, you fool, I've sung my own pain only!"
But the god-slayer accepted the wild words with calm:

"May you fare well, my son; I like you. Flap your wings!
The paths of life are seven, and with your song, my dear,
you've chosen the most cool, and fly from me forever.
My son, did not a chart of winds spread through my heart,
I'd seize an echoing lyre, too, and stalk beside you."
But the disdainful, headstrong bard replied with pride:
"Take your own road, ascetic, I've no need of you.
See, I've good comrades as I tread on mother earth,
for Death jeers at my right, the heart weeps at my left."
The mighty athlete locked his lips, but his heart throbbed;
he longed for a brief moment to spread gripping hands
and tightly clasp that haughty lyrist as dear friend,
but stood unmoving in the lanes of night and watched
with tranquil admiration as the bard turned dim
and disappeared, a deep star-cluster in the azure night.

XX

Captain Sole's weapons wailed in heavy threnody,
his battered shield turned round and bawled to his blunt sword:
"Alas, how can I ever go to war or face a spear?
Bedbugs have eaten me, the filth of flies has shamed me,
mice do not fear me, and my belly's but a sieve.
Ah, raise me, lads, that I may stand, or set me down,
and you, dear sword, don't lean against me, go far off,
for if I see your cutting edge, alas, I'll faint!"
The sword but sighed against the wall, and its sides cracked:
"Alas, I've rusted, brothers, my voice has grown hoarse.
Sharp side and dull are one, my blade is full of nicks,
I try to rouse my wrath, but can't; my loins have shrunk,
my rusted studs drop out, I shake like a thin reed.
Dear God, I want now no man's evil, I shun wars,
I only want to lie in a soft velvet sheath
all night and day and dream that we are all good friends."
The slender spear leapt upright in their midst and cried:
"Ah, don't weep, shriveled brothers, rouse your hearts, march on!
Hold me and I shall hold you, clutch each other tight!
Last night I dreamt a dreadful dream, and from great fear
my one and only tooth shook so, it soon will fall!
I dreamt of war, my lads, I dreamt of flashing spears,
oho, I dreamt our master stroked his black mustache!"
The helmet with its thousand holes then gaped and yelled:
"Alas, I've studied well our master's air-brained skull:
it bellows like an empty gourd with not one seed.
If he goes off his bean, my lads, and takes a shine
to war, and comes to unhook us from our cobwebbed nails,
then farewell bedbugs, idle comforts, beds of dust,
for no soul shall escape our master, Captain Lackwits!"
The battered shield once more poked out its timid head
to urge with gallant speech that all withstand their lord,
when like a turtle's head it suddenly shrank with fear
for their still drowsy master stood by the door's mouth.
He was lean, gangly, gawky, his head flat as a pie,
his hair was matted and his ancient scars were dyed;

upon his waterlogged and sallow chest was drawn
a burning heart that cast its scorching flames and flicked
its tongues round painted signs of burning battle cries.
He raised his reed-thin arms and to his weapons cried:
"Brave lads, the time has come to let your hearts rejoice,
for night and day, most manfully, you've wept and wailed:
'Ah, Captain, you've forgotten us! Remember war!
What shame to rot on our dull walls and hear outside
tumults of savage fighting and the slaughter's din!
Pity our youth that goes to waste in idle ease,
let's kick our heels in dance once more, let the world flash!'
Comrades, I've listened to your pains! To arms, brave lads!
O sword who long to thrust and parry, to cut deep;
and you, my shield, tall tower, ironbound and strong,
before whom dragons fall and whom no host may pierce;
and you, bronze helmet with your always upright plume,
forward, let's march to war, for enslaved freedom calls!
Earth rots and goes to waste; let's plant a new brave world!
I can no longer sleep, for I hear cries and pleas
of slaves that crawl in cells and widows who cry out:
'Pity us, Captain Sole, raise high your slashing sword,
they've dragged our men to jail, they've slain our orphaned sons:
you are the world's one comfort and our only hope!'
Hand-laborers that toil on land, and crews at sea
who work all day and starve with no sure recompense
call stealthily at midnight till I leap to hear:
'Aye, Captain Sole, we're wasting! Make up your mind! Arise!'
I take upon myself the whole earth's pain, for I,
as her most stalwart son, must give my stern account.
Forward, O shield and spear! Cast flames! Thunder and roar!"
He spoke, and then unhooked his thousand-wounded blade,
bound his pale shield with string to keep it all one piece,
wedged on his hollow head his towering casque of bronze
through whose rent studless cracks the whistling winds could rage,
then grasped his spear that bent and quivered like a reed
and all marched off together to a ruined stall
where in the sun a bony ancient camel wheezed.
"Lightning, rise up, we're off to war! Let the world flash!
Hold on, don't let your youth run loose, hold back your strength
until I snatch the great ascetic to a safe place!
They say that he, too, once set out to save the world,
but he knows nothing of arms now, he wields no sword;
ah, what great shame if our dog-foes should eat him up!
Pity him, Lightning, fetch him on your double rump!"
But the old camel's face turned green, and her knees buckled:
"Alas, you're off to die, dear master, and I with you!"

Then his poor mother came and stood by the door's arch:
"Where are you marching off to, Son, to what war now?
Where to, with your old weapons, your decrepit beast,
with no gold in your purse, no army at your side,
with your white hair and beard? We're all a laughing stock!
Turn back! The world is evil, Son. They'll smirch your name!"
"Mother, the heart can't question; it but loves and cries!
Mother, I pity mankind and I hate injustice,
I'm off to bring bread, love and freedom to all men."
He gave a hop and a jump, plumped on his camel's back,
then swayed and preened himself, passed through his ruined yard,
and conflagrations flapped above his burning head.
Doors were flung wide as he passed through the village lanes,
the young men whistled, the girls laughed, the old men winked,
and children scoffed and jeered, then pelted him with stones,
but he, unbending, filled with pride, with spear erect,
looked on the hungry widows, looked on their wretched huts,
looked on the scraggly babes, and swore to wage fierce battle
till freedom glowed and all should find their place in sun.
As he turned slowly and his bones creaked, he raised his hands
and looked upon his shameless town that mocked him so:
"Don't wail, my town, I know full well your sad complaints.
Don't run behind me weeping, I'll do all I can."
His bony camel shook and stumbled step by step
amid dark pointed stones and hellebore in bloom
and poisonous ripe poppies thrust in thorny brush.
When slim snakes flickered through the stones, the old beast shook,
her tongue stuck in her throat and she whined, pale with fear:
"Alas, you're off to die, dear master, and I with you!"
But he still flailed his rusty sword in the wilderness
then cupped his eyes against the sun and strained to see
whether the foe or white sheep gleamed on the mountain's ridge.
He perked his ears and gaped, yet could not quite make out
whether he heard the clash of arms or a flock's bleating,
but when he saw black clouds roll down the mountain peak,
his craze burst like a falling star, and he spurred his beast:
"Follow me, lads, attack! Cut them to shreds! Assault!
Lightning, take wing, let's reach that manly threshing floor!"
But his old camel reared, then fell flat on her face,
and the bold rider tumbled, stumbled, sprained his ankle,
and bit his lips to feel the pain, limped and cried out:
"What joy! Freedom, I'm wounded in my fight for you!
Where are you, Mother? Look on me with boastful pride!
Mother, I wonder you don't sprout wide wings for joy!"
He twirled his curved mustache, then hopped with limping gait
and clambered up his camel's back with gasps and groans

till the poor beast turned round and once more wheezed and whined:
"Alas, you're off to die, dear master, and I with you!"
But now he scorned to listen to the mind's poor cares
or the earth's humble voices, and toward the black clouds
spurred wretched Lightning as he slashed both right and left.
He hungered, and stones steamed like bread in the wild wastes,
he thirsted, and snakes in the heat-haze flowed like streams;
pain ripped his twisted bowels, but his towering plume
flapped like a vanguard flame or banner on his battered casque.

That very hour the great ascetic climbed the rocks
rejoicing in the wastes as in a leopardess;
with pleasure he recalled his gardens, brooks, tall grass
and towns that hummed at dusk, but these bare mountain rocks
were his true gardens where his naked mind might stroll.
He stooped to earth and grasped a stone, and the stone leapt
and floundered in his fist, a bird that strove to fly,
till the disk-throwing athlete laughed and flung the stone
so that it hurtled down the cliff, full-winged and free.
The freed heart plays with pebbles like a carefree child,
rides horseback on a reed that bucks like a true steed,
laughs with all ghosts and phantoms, jokes and plays with spirits,
then thrusts at night its small fist in star-bins of pearls
like a fat miller who thrusts his hand in grain and flour.
He plays horse with his great thoughts as with slender reeds,
jigs with them till they snap, then picks still other reeds
and shapes them into flutes and plays what tune he wills
till the whole wasteland brims with his wild cackling cries.
As he looked round him, a strong joy rose in his mind
till, glad among all ruins, his heart throbbed and cried:
"When earth at length flicks from its hide this lice of men,
thus shall all stones glow, bare and free, in the hot sun,
thus do my guts already seem to flash and laugh."
But suddenly, as he basked in solitude, he heard
laughter and voices, tramp of feet in the deep glen,
then stretched full length on earth and hung over a cliff.
Black armed men scattered here and there on scorching rocks,
shouting and laughing as their slaves, bound with bronze chains,
picked brushwood and lit fires to roast the spitted meat.
An old man in their midst stood straight, bound hand and foot,
a crown of shavings on his proud and narrow skull;
he groaned, then cried with toothless gums to the wild waste:
"Freedom, for you I die! Others shall come behind me,
a host of sons and grandsons, and they'll set you free!
Lady, don't cry, I'll come back from the dead to save you!"
Odysseus pitied this long-faced old man, and thought:

"By God, we're well met in these wilds; here's a new friend!
The spits are ready, the flames leap, but he stands straight
and dies in a denial of death, and shouts on freedom!
Aye, gnarled old man, your madness is a mate to mine;
I'll rise and yell and snatch you from the jaws of death,
for we are few, nor must our kind fade from the earth."
The blacks then heard a mighty host that shook the cliff,
snorting of frenzied horses, clash of rock on rock,
but when they raised their heads they saw, white-haired, serene,
the old ascetic stumbling down with flapping rags.
Frightened, all ran behind their fires for barricade:
"Ah, that's the great ascetic, lads, the dreadful lion
that roams the earth half-starved and bites all trembling souls.
Careful! Don't rouse him! He wields the dread thunderbolt!"
Thus did they mutter as they crouched behind their fires.
When the old codger saw the ascetic, he strained his hands
to break the cords, to free his arms and clasp him tight:
"Welcome, O equal friend, you come in a good hour!
We two shall now march on and save the entire world!
I shall march first with sword in hand and slash new roads;
I'll smash the chains of slavery, knock down castle walls,
and you shall plod behind and set all things in order.
I'm Freedom's true right hand, armed with the flashing sword,
and you're her left heart-hand that pains for all the world.
Forward, the time has come! Follow your leader! March!"
Odysseus smiled and looked with pride on the old man
who strove with his bound hands to clasp him in embrace:
"Friend, you deny what's near your nose, and sing in flame!
Here's to your health! Though you're a slave, bound hand and foot,
your mind soars with the wings of fancy, the heart's rage;
you draw your sword wherever slaves are weaponless!
But raise your eyes and look: the blacks have hewn your spit,
you've no time now to save the savior of the world!"
But Captain Sole laughed slyly and consoled his friend:
"Come, place your hand here on my heart—that's where I am!
Fear is a beast that we must also kill, my brother.
These are not flames you see, that's not a pointed spit;
don't weep, these are but crimson wings, an archon's staff;
hold onto patience for a while, your mind will spin!
I am that deathless bird who, when it turns to ash,
leaps from the ash in joy, for the devouring flames
turn into wings as long as oars and mount toward God!"
As the black chieftain's heart grew bold, he poked his nose,
raised the spit high and laughed, then turned to Captain Sole:
"Aye, brave old man, I know an ancient fable too!
Forgive me, great ascetic, if I tell my tale:

Once long ago, they say, a female ape came down
to men to learn their crafts and all their subtle wiles;
she learned how to walk upright, how to cook in hearths,
to dress her shameful parts with gaudy crimson robes,
and to bow down before a painted log for God.
One day she sighed and pitied her unlucky tribe
that without God crawled on all fours like naked beasts;
thus, with an anguished heart, she thought to make beasts men.
Then she roamed rivers, woods, and caves and shrilly cried:
'O brother beasts, come close to hear my words! For years
I've lived with those erect pigs that reside in homes,
and now I've come to teach you all their secret craft.
Elephants, tigers, lions, wolves, come out and hear!
Come, bring your children to my school! I'll make them men!'
Next day the cave of the ape-teacher was crammed full
with screeching schoolkids whom the schoolmarm shaped to men:
she taught them to walk upright and to cook raw meat,
to hide their hairy shameful parts with plantain leaves,
to wear a cap and flip it in polite salute.
She held a switch, and as she whipped, her mind grew bolder.
One morning, when the lion cub forgot his breeches,
the ape schoolmarm in anger switched him on the nose
but the cub opened playfully his gaping mouth
and with one bite gulped down the foolish marm, kerplunk!
Let all who have ears, hear! Let all who have minds, think!
Old man, my fable is ended. Now may yours begin!"
But Captain Sole tossed his proud head and laughed with scorn:
"Good riddance to that ape, she should have known her strength!
But if the lion should ever wish to enslave the beasts,
he need not fear: no greater jaw than his could eat him!"
He spoke, and the blacks laughed, then with great hunger seized
the spit and pressed round Captain Sole to run him through,
but the great archer cast his flaming glance within
the black men's yellow eyes till they stepped slowly back,
then he drew near his brainless friend, caressed his hair,
unbound his holy hands and his pale bony feet
and in the fire cast the cords and flung his noose:
"Aye, you black crinkly heads, listen to what I say!
I've left no stone unturned, I've roamed all lands and seas
to meet this world-renowned chief of the imagination,
that he might give me that bright feather God had not.
The same nurse gave us suck, the same milk made us strong,
but our roads parted in this world nor met again,
for I took all the scoffing sea for my full share
and he soared high and took the empty air for kingdom;
but now the two milk-brothers meet, and the crowns merge."

He threw small smelt for bait, and caught full shoals of fish.
The black men snarled like dogs from whom the meat's been snatched,
but the sly trickster laughed and grabbed the old man's limbs:
"Look, he's all skin and bone! From too much brooding thought
he can't make flesh enough for one good decent bite!
Chief, let him go; I swear he'll come to his wits soon,
he'll go with prudence to his tower, he'll eat, he'll drink,
he won't give thought to strangers' cares, his mind will dim,
till like a glutted hog his flesh will swell with fat.
Fellows, hold back your spit—where can the poor pig go?"
The black chief then made a wry face and bit his tongue:
"Better an egg in mouth than hens in my neighbor's yard,
but since I fear your great curse, I'll withdraw the spit;
it's a good thing earth feeds us with more fattening fodder.
Now with your blessing, grandpap, we'll strike camp elsewhere."
He spoke, then blew his conch and ordered his black troop
to drive the slaves ahead, to set up hearths elsewhere.
But Captain Sole screeched loudly and poked his prudent friend:
"For God's sake, look! They're dragging off the slaves! Up, friend,
raise your mind high, for Freedom calls, and my palms itch!"
But the archer grabbed him forcefully and set him down:
"Hold on! Where do you get such strength, such dizzy rage?
You're a disarmed old fool! Let well enough alone."
But the old codger raged, his dreamy eyes flashed fire:
"I'm not disarmed! Justice is my protective shield!
Earth issued from the hands of God imperfect, foul,
and it's my duty to perfect it, I, alone!
So long as slavery, fear, injustice rack the world,
I've sworn, my friend, never to let my sharp sword rest.
Follow me, all ye faithful! Be bold, lads! Don't fear!"
He spoke, then dashed ahead, alone, with sword in hand,
toward the dark pass of the ravine where the slaves trudged.
The silver-lined air smelled of musk in the mild night,
the lizards slithered in their holes, and from far off
was heard the whining yowl of hungry jackals prowling.
With awe the archer hailed the wild ghost of the flesh:
"May you thrive well, rebellious heart of air-brained man!
You've fortified yourself with dream, nor wish to leave,
nor, O spread-eagle, deign to walk on earth again.
Stifled with fear and sense, the mind is yoked to need,
but you, O heart, keep two doors, and when sorrow strikes,
fling wide imagination's golden gate and send
bold Freedom strutting like a peacock through the streets.
Virtue, you first descend here in deceiving dreams
to an unkneeling lonely heart that plows but air.
You know that you will burn and fade in flame one day

but you assault the deep abyss, turn flame to wing!
Good luck to you, my friend, may your mind know no better—
for you are the earth's crimson wing, the only one she has!"

Mountains and rocks turned rose-red in the dawning light,
and the sun-drunken skylark with its tasseled mind,
confused by drinking too much light, burst into song—
heart, brainless soaring bird of air, wounded with light!
The more it sang the more it raged till the sun seemed
a pomegranate tree weighed down with fruit and flower
on which it hopped from bough to bough and pecked and sang.
A tangled skein of song and wing, it pierced the light
and vanished, but its melodies in a light shower
still fell and cooled the scorching throat of flaming air.
Dear God, with the bird's song the earth forgot grim Death,
even Death forgot his scythe, and in enchanted dream
sat on a high rock listening to the skylark's pain.
Wiping his lashless burning eyes, he sighed and moaned:
"Cursed be my wretched fate! If only I one day
might also lie on the green grass to hear the birds!"
But Death had not ceased speaking when at his shrunk feet
the crazy songster tumbled like a lump of earth
and a small drop of black blood hung from its red beak.
The lone man trudged from cliff to cliff all morning long
till in a glen he saw a village built of cow-dung
where pigs and children rolled in the mud lanes with joy
and a thick stench rose from the village filth and slops.
In a drugged yard old men and young with gaping mouths
lay stretched and breathed the smoke of secret, mystic herbs;
with sunken ashen cheeks and dry cracked lips they sucked
the dark and slowly moving dream of happiness;
this was their one joy and escape from wretched life.
Hunger and filth, man-eating foul hyenas, prowled
their homes, Death like a scorpion raised his stinging tail,
and as the lone man passed, green poisons splattered him:
"Life's but a trap where the mind falls, all doors are traps
which we fling open with our dreams or our strong thoughts;
the more our freedom grows the deeper down we sink.
Man's whole submission to all great necessities,
alas, may be the only outlet Freedom has."
Thus did Odysseus muse, passing through stench and filth
to crystal meadow air wiped clean of human breath;
but when he saw a calf roped near a slaughter-shed,
a black sleek calf with a white spot stamped on its brow,
the cruel god-slayer stopped to admire it silently.
It leapt and danced with joy because for the first time,

freed of its mother, it sniffed and gazed at the wide world;
how the light soil heaved gladly to its tossing hooves,
how its moist nostrils still smelled of sweet hay and milk!
But all at once a red door opened, and the gay calf vanished.

At last the stone-bare mountain ended, and there stretched,
far off, a sodden plain of black-green flowering marsh
within whose midst a green lake gleamed with a lone isle
where an old tower loomed, besieged by twining ivy.
The sun saw it but rarely, the wind barely lapped it,
sunk in foul stagnant waters, drowned in warm quagmires.
"How can the soul of man live in such vile morass?"
the lone man mused, and longed to meet the tower's lord,
to see what human souls become in flowering bogs.
As slowly he approached the lake through tangled weeds,
a skiff skimmed from the island and shrill voices called:
"Renowned ascetic, greetings from our castle's lord!
He begs that you will condescend to sup with him
and chat awhile with peace in the night's nobleness."
Odysseus leapt and sat upon the velvet prow
and then the rowers slowly beat the turbid waters;
a froglike people croaked, knee-deep in muddy marsh;
in the far reeds a sluggish hippopotamus
opened its dark jaws wide and yawned with lazy scope.
Two spotted watersnakes raised their entwined heads high
and still without uncoupling watched the sky and hissed
even though an ash-black hawk cut slashing circles round them.
As the black oarsmen rowed, the skiff slit through the reeds,
plowed slowly through thick turtles in the sluggish waters,
then wedged between gorged flesh-leaved lotuses that hung
their milk-white long-necked flowers like tall erotic swans
and marveled at their faces in the murky stream.
All year the female blossoms sail on the lake's surface
while in the deep unmoving waters the male blooms
sleep and suck sluggishly the mud with long white roots.
Then in midsummer suddenly the thick warm waters move,
Love's vehement South Wind sweeps through all their secret lanes
and to deep mud-sunk waters brings the great command
till the impetuous male blooms break from their thick stems,
cut free from life and swoop up toward the sun to meet
the females and die sweetly as they fling their seed.
When the great traveler reached to touch a monstrous bloom,
Helen rose like a lotus in his memory's pool,
and bloodstained battlements gleamed in the muddy lake;
his old friends rolled supine like shriveled leaves, and all,
countries, embracements, cares, sailed on Love's drifting waves.

"Life is a wedding, Death a funeral, and we're the grooms,"
thus the soul-leader mused, then laughed, and leapt ashore.
With regal mien, fat-bosomed, dressed in golden robes,
the great lord of the tower sat to greet his guest;
two slaves stood upright, cooled him with long peacock fans
as with plump fingers he serenely played with beads
of a frail amber rosary that rejoiced his soul;
but when he saw the border-guard cut through the reeds
he tried with sluggish effort to rise and bid him welcome:
"Well met, O great ascetic, fancy's brilliant bird!
Like a white swan you pass through our black stagnant bogs
and our eyes glow to see you and our hands to touch you;
surely our minds will also glow to hear your words."
He spoke, laughed cunningly, then with politeness ceased,
and the much-traveled man caressed the buxom arms:
"Well met, O female-swollen lotus, thick and fat!
You sit enthroned by turbid pools, root deep in pleasure,
then send your calm and seedless mind to bloom in sun;
I've longed to see how souls may thrive in mud and mire."
The fat lord glanced obliquely at the great heart-snatcher
and did not speak but beckoned to his slaves who brought
a thick-haired lion pelt on which the lone man sat.
As night fell, rosy mists rose on the nacreous lake,
somewhere an azure fish, playing in twilight, leapt
in air with yearning eyes and flashing silver scales,
but then with gasping gills sank in the mud once more.
Like a hooked fish the Evening Star throbbed through the mists,
and man's frail soul lamented in the nets of night.
Slowly the soft voice of the fresh-bathed lord then rose:
"The world's news drifts above my tower like feathery clouds:
somewhere a new and mighty king appears, somewhere
a flock of wild ducks rise and hunters rush with bows,
somewhere a maid begets a babe with horns and tail,
somewhere a heavy hailstorm blasts trees in their bloom.
Thus did the great news of your coming pass our tower:
'A great ascetic treads the earth, and mountains glow!
Joyous those eyes so worthy as to see his face,
thrice joyous that mind which stands beside his own great mind!'
Thus did the good birds chirp above my tower's roof,
and now I see and hear you, and my mind grows calm;
your coming gives me such great joy, my tower shall raise
its yellow banner aloft with its long azure snake."
He spoke, ordered his nation's yellow banner raised,
commanded that two fighting cocks be brought at once
to amuse the weary mind and give the heart delight
before the feasting boards were spread or talk begun:

"Forgive me, great ascetic, but I like toward dusk
to watch cocks fight with fury and fall to breathless death;
they seem to me no different from great gods or men."
Deep in his silent heart, the man of many minds
weighed sadly this great lord with his benumbing lips
and brilliant brain who in his gold cage cunningly
had locked tight various gods and thoughts and mocked them all:
"All turn to night within his brain and cast blue shadows,
joys cannot make him drunk nor sorrows crush his soul
for life has withered in his heart, may he be cursed!"
Meanwhile the two cocks faced each other, breast to breast,
beat their clipped wings with fury, stretched their scrawny necks,
circled the ring, scraped at the earth with sharpened claws,
tall, lean, shorn of their crests, their eyes hot burning coals.
They crawled close slyly, stalked each other with great craft,
then suddenly leapt like lightning, slashed and stabbed in air
till the ground filled with feathers, and then beak to beak,
unmoving, silent, baleful, held their rage in leash,
but swiftly leapt once more as wings and talons clashed.
Both thin necks streamed with blood; the eye of the small cock
spilled on the ground, and he rolled steaming, his wing broken,
but once more leapt with dauntless rage and clutched his foe
who struck at his head fiercely with his bloody beak
in swift sharp hammer strokes as though to drink his brains.
The small cock's other eye spilled out, his brains gaped bare,
but still he fought on blindly, neck erect, and stabbed
in darkness till with hoarse choked cries he fell to earth.
Facing the yard, the victor swelled his breast with pride,
crowed thrice with shrill harsh cries to announce his victory,
and when in lust he heard the excited cackling hens
respond, he strutted, limping, toward the chicken coop.
The great lord of the tower laughed and clapped his hands:
"It's only right the strong should kill and the weak die;
it pleased me, O great guest, that you gazed motionless
nor raised a hand to part these two contending lives.
I always goad my cocks to fight when strangers come
and watch them stealthily and weigh their souls with craft:
some break into applause with joy, some burst in tears,
some rush indignantly to part the peerless birds,
but you bent down and gazed with no joy, wrath, or tears."
The man of free mind smiled and made his secret plain:
"Between the two eyes in my brow a third eye looms
that grinds together castles, mortals, gods, and birds.
When I watched your fierce cocks, my lord, I watched all men,
I watched both Life and Death in a grim strife on earth,
and my third eye remained unmoved, yet my twin eyes,

my lord, fought like your cocks with anger, joy, and tears;
but your mind's a thick lotus—how can it understand?"
The tower lord gazed on the stranger with great unease
but once again a smile gleamed on his placid lips:
"It's time that we, like the immortals who, they say,
set infant man loose on the earth to fight like cocks,
should stretch at ease with appetite by feasting-boards;
and when we've eaten and drunk well, wise words will come
and give the final spice to bread, the wine, the night."
He spoke, then signaled to his slaves to serve the food.

Amid the honeysuckle vines the tables glowed
and the two masters slowly stretched their noble hands
and satisfied their hearts' desires for a long time;
good was the breast of partridge, good the rabbit roast,
and like a hidden beast the old wine stalked their brains.
When they were gorged and their eyes gleamed, the tower lord
raised his full cup to toast the precious stranger's health:
"That unconcerned great mind seems best that like a bee
gleans drops of honey from all things and then flies on;
thus with light wing I've also passed through women, wine,
food, arms, and from their poison gleaned a drop of honey.
Joy to that mind that sits on high and rules the heart!
When great souls pass my tower, I invite them all,
and when they spread their wings like dappled birds, I like
to crawl and pluck with stealth their one most precious feather.
O godly peacock of the mind, spread wide your tail,
they say your golden feathers glow with myriad eyes."
The savage traveler paused and searched his mind a moment;
a double, triple, brilliant blossom smiled before him
with neither fragrance, roots, nor seed in murky air;
this man nor loved nor hated, all great passions passed
and were refined to nothing in his barren heart;
he was earth's final shriveled bloom, the sterile chaff.
Odysseus filled his wine bowl and spoke solemnly:
"Many birds passed me in my zigzag voyages,
many wings molted, many souls rejoiced my soul;
thousands of dead I saw on land, thousands on sea,
until my eyes grew glazed to look on Death so long,
but slowly in my heart, fear, joy, and God's desire
became a gallant outcry and a wing of fire.
The sentry of the mind shouts 'Fire!' and the gods quake,
the sentry of the heart shouts 'Fire!' and all hopes molt,
the sentry of despair shouts last, 'My soul, don't fear,
only you walk the wilds and set all things aflame.' "
The plump lord of the tower laughed and slyly winked:
"Unless my eyes have not well pierced your subtle mind,
nor senseless longings nor great gods have fooled you either;
sleeping and waking both are shameful, life is a game,
and still more shameful is our free and haughty mind
that gives in trust to life its wealth and expectations.
I also am the sea-mind's sterile old sea-wolf,
I perch on the high masts, I spy to the world's ends:
one night, O soul, you'll sink in the great whirlpool too,
in Death's grand cataract, you and the whole wide world."
The tower lord stopped speaking, but his plump lips gleamed;
he gazed on all the earth and smiled at the pale sun

that sank in the warm lake like an accursèd ghost.
Once more his voice hissed in the flowering garden close:
"Why should we weep or cry, why should our minds despair?
Great joy to him who roams the whole world through and leaps
from flower to flower until the worms devour his flesh;
life bursts a moment in the brain, then disappears!
You too, I think, have seen the secret and winked at me;
give me your hand, O secret brother, smile on me now!"
But the stern mind replied to the frog-bloated man:
"One day I met a great striped tiger in a glen
and my heart leapt with joy so that I shouted, 'Brother!'
I dash into the arms of all that on this earth
laugh, love, or weep, that I may laugh or weep with them,
but you, O quagmire lord, my mind rejects you whole!
Both of us know the secret, but you in great exhaustion
play with both Life and Death with sluggish mocking heart;
I rush, clasp in my arms the smallest worm, and shout:
'Dear brother, I'm your companion both in life and death!' "
Then the great lover listened to his barking memory
and like a diver dragged up dripping coral words:
"One day on a far isle I saw a windmill creak
its wings with sluggish weariness in windless calm,
and as its millstones crumbled with no grain to grind,
the whole isle sighed and gasped as in the throes of death,
as though the tattered windmill were its very heart.
I almost choked with wrath and yelled to my wolf-pack:
'Forward, my lads, haul up the sails, give life a shove,
I can't bear now to hear my loved earth's dying gasps!'
Such is your mind, O tower ghost! I must leave now."
The buxom eunuch smiled; only the rosary's sound
of clicking bead on bead was heard in the damp air,
and the soft echo of the fragrant amber kept
harmonious time with the reposed lord's laggard heart.
He spoke then with a weary, slightly mocking voice:
"What at this moment does your heart long for, my brother?
Dancers or mellow wine, battles or sweetest song?
You are a strong-winged vulture, you must not leave now."
The proud spread-eagle calmed his darkly beating heart;
jasmine perfumed the coolness, stars hung low and swelled,
for night had come, exposed her bosom and bared the moon.
Odysseus' white hair glittered as he rose to leave:
"I'm very fond of dancers, battles, and old wine,
but while you're at my side I don't want to rejoice
in all this holy deathless wealth that flares and fades.
Time is a clinging shirt of flame that wraps my soul;
for you it's but a cooling muck in which you sink

slowly with piglike pleasure till all joy is smirched;
aye, lord of mud, farewell, my slim flame says goodbye."
The seedless man then puckered up his glutted mouth:
"Farewell! You've made my holy freedom poison here!
Only that mind was wholly free, I've thought till now,
that could strip off the veil from life and see her nude,
then taste all things indifferently with mocking skill;
but as I hear you speak, new whirlwinds gape within me
and toss those quiet waters where my swan-mind sails.
Aye, slaves, run quickly, bring the skiff, ply fast your oars
and swiftly land this stranger far on the other shore!
O dread still-beating heart that longs to eat the world,
farewell! Death will come soon and glut your mouth with earth."
He spoke, and the sun-dancer beat his feet like wings,
strode through the fragrant gardens, reached the reedy shore,
as the plump eunuch clicked his amber beads behind,
unburdened and serene once more, and moved his lips:
"O grasping bird, how bright you gleam and flap in sun!
Sometimes it seems as though all wings shone round your head,
sometimes you seem to glitter nude as a plucked hen.
I'm glad my mind touched you awhile; I've had enough,
and now I'm glad to see you go, not to return."
The mind that tamed all flame and made it pure as light,
then turned light back to fire and played with light and flame,
faced the great lord and with no joy or sorrow said:
"One dawn Death touched me lightly on my shoulder blade
and all at once my body shrank and my mind reared;
you are Death's fingers on the shoulder blades of earth."
Then the soul-snatcher ceased to speak; deep in his chest
he felt his shaken heart pulse as though zoned with cares,
as though he'd seen the last excrescence of the world;
when earth would grow diseased and strength disperse like smoke
such sallow shriveled souls would slowly molt in loam.
"Good luck to you, new forms, new joys of the upper world
that once by far Eurotas, by green river reeds,
naked and glittering, fought till Death himself stood still
and from his heart swore wrathfully at his black fate.
O man's firm body, our virtue, nobleness, our pride,
that like strong shining bronze, with your lean narrow shins
and with your shapely flanks, your hips, and your broad chest
raise like a column all our hopes on this good earth,
you're not a sheath that longs for God to fill it full!
Body of man, you are a sword with two sharp sides
for whom flesh, brain, and the whole earth are your great sheath.
So long as you can stand on snowpeaks and gleam in sun,
all ghosts are your familiars, all gods are your fools,

and I place all my hopes on the earth that grows such flowers!"
The wandering man spoke to himself as in his mind
he spun old and still future hopes and tightly held
man's holy pomegranate filled with babes and seed.
Thus with his precious treasure the sun-minded man
strode through the marshes with their mud-formed lotuses
and for the last time turned to watch the weed-filled tower
that, drowned in heavy-shadowed ivy, darkly glowed
in mist like an old windmill stripped of all its arms,
like bodies that soon rot when stripped of wings and souls.
Then the god-slayer sadly smiled and spoke with wrath:
"Aye, septic lotus, you have freed yourself from seed
and now your earthless roots hang in the hollow air.
Your fat loins fester, your mind rots, your heart's a frog,
but I, crammed full of earth and blood, dripping cool dew,
still love and ache for Mother Earth and fight with Death.
I gaze deep in man's entrails, on a woman's breast,
and long for them to brim with joys and dream and seed,
to burst in flame and burn like deathless pyres in chaos!
I tread old men to dust, I merge young men and maids
with love that all night long they may reshape earth's face.
I watch the seedless soul that fades and mocks the flame,
then rush behind it to light again whatever fades;
I sit by wells where it once passed and once more pluck
the gallant youths and maidens that had fled in fear
and draw them sweetly to the woods to merge in darkness.
I open homes it closed, till thresholds fill with children,
till ovens blaze once more and slender maidens sit
at the earth's loom with joy, their heart a piercing arrow.
I love to roam through lands and towns where I can feel
the stalwart men at work, the mothers giving suck,
for thus are children born, thus is the world tilled,
thus does the soul I love rejoice and play on earth.
Summer and winter long the soil reeks in my heart,
the cuckoo sits upon my highest branch and sings.
Aye, tower lord, you weigh all poisons, mock the world,
but I don't fear you, for new winds blow through my mind,
because each dawn the earth and man's bold heart are born anew!"

Odysseus sauntered thus in the moon's pulsing glow
and heard with joy the wild beasts thrusting through the shrubs
as their blue shadows slid with stealth amid the paths.
The wild hares danced in moonlight, the wild asses brayed,
the waters fell asleep at midnight, but the mind of man
kept vigil like a lion prowling the dark earth.
Softly a red she-fox emerged from thorny shrubs,

sniffed at the air to right and left with her moist snout,
then cocked her ears to part the sounds of solitude;
she held one paw curved high before she stepped, and when
she had well sifted all the scents and sounds of night,
she raised her tufted tail and slunk into the woods.
A dense gorge darkly glowed within whose towering trees
and plunging shadows the flame-minded man was lost,
for his heart seethed and held its dark commotion still.
His mind still held the swooning face of Mother Earth,
thoughts of the leech-filled tower lord passed like a ghoul,
like an unerring forecast of man's final fate.
"His soul is a ghost of light with not one drop of blood,
without one root in earth to drink those holy mothers,
Joy, Sorrow, Patience, and full-breasted, fertile Hope;
his nerves like dodder tendrils flap in empty light."
The archer pushed on, struggling to dispel that ghost
and take some consolation from the beast-eyed night;
about him he saw, heard, and smelled Hunger and Lust
that prowled the dark in silence and aroused all loins
until the lone man's heart rejoiced in its mud roots.
A thick-necked wolf passed through the windless woods and stooped
with empty belly and red eyes to sniff the ground
and find sheep droppings somewhere or a trace of hare.
The trees shook suddenly, uproar swept the trembling woods,
and monkeys shrilled and clambered to the topmost boughs
where with cupped eyes they watched until their hair stood upright.
Odysseus fell flat on the ground and hid in leaves;
his temples pulsed as though their hinges had come loose,
as though swift drunkenness had struck his kindled brain.
The hot night filled with bodies, her black armpits reeked,
and all the night-woods steamed with musk and heavy sweat;
insatiably the lone man peered amid the leaves
and like a startled rabbit cocked his ears to find
if evil nightmares crushed him or from too much moon
night's visionary brain had turned to watery gruel.
Black naked women ran, their loins wrapped round with leaves,
and an old towering chief led them and rushed ahead
as blood dripped from his sharpened ax and his white beard.
Long necklaces of bloody ears flapped round their necks,
and as the gasping women reached a clearing, they fell prone,
and their old leader wildly rolled his bloodstained eyes
and shouted hoarsely in the windless calm of night:
"O God, I shout, but you don't hear! I stamp on earth!
Rise from the ground and grab your ax, stand by my side!
Can't you see I've grown old, you fool? My savage son
rushed with his ax to grab my females from my court

and I with great fatigue struck twice before I killed him!
Women, don't scatter now, and don't let your loins seethe
like those broad-buttocked mares who hear the stallions snort!
Shout to my God as I, until your throats grow sore!
Oho, you beast, rise from the earth! Rise up, my Lord,
I'll string a necklace of twelve heads about your throat!
Ascend and eat my twelve sons in the moldy earth.
I'll deck you with red wings so that your mind may soar,
and—do you hear?—I'll pay you well: three buxom maids!
It's I, the Old Chief, calling! Rise! Rise from the earth!
Now that their thighs and loins are strong, my greedy sons
hunt me to grab my women slaves! Rise up and slay!
Ah, decoys of our ripe male god, fling your arms wide,
yowl, tigresses in rut, till the great tiger comes,
raise your black breasts for bait so that his brains may crack!
Oho, deep armpits, cast your reeking musk and stifle God!"

Odysseus peered from leaves and thickets, raised his face
and watched the young maids scream and break in a swift dance
then raise their shining black breasts high and call on God
until God, like a strong man, loomed in the moon's glow.
The old chief bellowed then and clapped his withered palms:
"Oho, a dread Lord smeared with blood and fat ascends
from the profound dark depths of earth and shakes the world!
I like you! Thus did I also glow in youth, like you!
Ah, I've grown young again, my two dogteeth grow fierce;
come quick, roll up your sleeves; help me, I need you now.
But let's come to an agreement first so we won't quarrel
about the plunder and come to loggerheads once more.
What payment do you want? Don't stamp your heels! Draw near!"
The dark god cackled and spoke boldly to the old chief:
"I want all of your female slaves; their black breasts please me."
"They please me too! Look at me well, don't reach your hands!
Mothers still give my children suck on their black breasts,
my hands can still flash flame to knock your daring down;
don't set my teeth on edge; hold your reins tight, my Lord.
I, as the leading ram, shall give you three good ewes:
this old crone of a slave shall light your hearthstone fires;
this middle-aged housekeeper with her skillful hands
shall comb your grimy hair and smear you smooth with grease;
this young well-bedded maid will glut you with her lust."
"Make way, and shut your mouth! I'll choose whatever I please!"
"Then choose, you slayer! Glut your belly's hollow cave,
but don't dare set your grasping hand on this young maid;
I swear by my sharp ax, you slayer, you shall not have her!"
"Shut up, you shriveled fool! I'll cram your mouth with dirt!

I stretch my hand above your flock and choose this girl."
"You can't have her! Don't growl, I'm not afraid of you."
"Oho, the old wreck shakes his hatchet and grows bold!
With two of my forked fingers, fool, I'll break your pate."
"Alas, you've quashed my skull, you've cracked my temples wide!"
"I want the prettiest girl you've got. Bring her, be quick!"
"It's I who raised you from the earth, gave you an ax,
armed you with phallus, loins and brain. Is this my reward?"
"Fool, what reward? I'm God! No greater thief exists!
I pass by, grab whatever I please, and Death's my purse;
I open it and pay in full with worms and loam.
Don't curse, but press your ears to earth and listen well."
"I hear my eleven remaining sons hemming me in,
and Death, the harehound, leads the way and sniffs my tracks;
stand by my side and help me, slayer; I'll pay you well."
"But first I want to see my recompense. Slay the girl now!"
"You've not a drop of shame or pity, you grind fine;
you've caught me in my need and scorn man's ancient soul,
but my day will come too, when the wheel spins full round,
and then you'll spew out all I've crammed you with, you fool.
Here, at your feet, I groan yet slay her with my ax,
but swear first that you'll help me kill my defiant sons."
"I swear, old man. Don't weep, my word's an iron noose."
The old chief seized the maiden, his eyes filled with tears,
then twisting her long tresses hard, he flung her down, and struck.

Flat on his face on earth, hidden among the leaves,
the archer heard the two beasts quarrel and held his breath
as in the moonlight's azure brilliance he discerned
the cutting ax flash high above the maiden's neck.
Then the gigantic chieftain waved his hands in air:
"Great God, I smear your knees, your breast, your loins with blood
until you laugh from top to toe, and steam, and glow!
I've kept my promise, Lord, now it's your turn to pay;
come, stretch your gaping mouth and swallow all my sons!
Why do you mock with jeering laughs and flap your hands?"
"I laugh, you fool, because you've trusted in God's word;
I'm God, you can't get round me! I swear, and then unswear!"
"What shame! Not only do you break your word, but boast!"
"I don't want you, now that you're old. Your heart's a husk.
Now that you've slain your maid for me, you burst in tears,
but I pelt you with stones, and laugh! You're useless, fool!
I like your bold brash sons, I'll eat and drink with them."
"You'll have no time to revel! I'll thrust you back in earth!"
The old chief growled, then grabbed his bloodstained double-ax
tight in both fists and like a woodsman hacked away

and hacked on madly till his god was strewn on earth,
till the great demon fell in heaps and smeared the ground
with paints, hides, crimson feathers, bells and straw.
Then the chief broke in cackling laughs and clapped his hands:
"Aha, it's not the first time that I've killed such demons!
Blessed be my calloused hands that seize a senseless log,
hack it away and carve a head, shape hands and feet,
paint it with saffron, blood, and lime till a god leaps,
a dog to tag my heels in chase and flush wild game.
Each time God scorns to help, I seize him by his feet
and dash his brains out, like a bird's, on the sharp stones."
But as he roared and his feet sparked in flashing dance,
he suddenly stopped with hovering heels and gaping mouth,
for God with clamorous tumult roared above his head:
"O pigeon-brained, pigheaded fool, well met in death!
I'm not one to be bound in wood or paints or vows
for I'm a monstrous heavy heartthrob, a great voice;
I kick old men aside, rush on, and seek out youth!"
The old chief raised his head, then clenched and shook his fists:
"Where will you hide, you slayer? I'll bind you fast with flesh
and nail you with the greatest spell of all, the brain!"
Then a maid screamed in fright and touched the chieftain's arm:
"Alas, I saw a sharp-clawed vulture flying south,
and in his claws, my lord, he held your hoary head!"
An ancient sorceress tightly clasped his knees and cried:
"Master, your old knees shake and knock, your eyes are mud,
for God, that dreadful fire, has gone, and left you ash."
But the old dragon raised his fist and struck the crone:
"Be still! I'm a fierce hound, my knuckles are hard stone!
Fetch me my heavy ax and a huge block of stone,
then scatter swiftly, hide, for if my sons should come
and find us unprotected here, they'll kill us all.
If only I had time to carve God from a mountain!
Go, women, cut your locks, then pound the crimson paints."
He spoke, then seized the stone and hacked it breast to breast;
he growled to frighten God, struck hard to bring him out,
but God like an unbridled horse neighed in the stone.
A woman past her prime then grasped his hands in pity:
"Master, you miss your aim, an evil spirit strikes you,
stop beating that black stone or it will knock you down."
Sorrow and anger swept through the old chief, he yelled:
"Though sparks fly from my eyes, my arms cease to obey me,
and I've no longer strength to wield my double-ax;
when I strike left, it knocks me down in a foul ditch,
when I strike right, it thumps my shoulder like a beast;
I've no strength or endurance left—fetch me a log,

my loins are weak, I can no longer strive with stone."
Three maidens cut a log, three others brought it close,
and the old sorceress pounded many secret herbs;
the youngest maiden clasped the old man's weary knees:
"Don't tremble, grandfather, I hear voices, keep your wits."
A maid in rut climbed up a wild oak tree and yelled:
"Welcome, brave youths! Your dogs cut through the clearing now!"
But the chief hacked the knotty wood with frantic rage,
splinters stuck in his beard, flames leapt from his fierce eyes,
the ax's blue sparks vanished in his shaggy chest:
"Women, keep still, God leaps within my flaming fists!
I glue my lips on your thick lips, come take my breath;
I glue my breast on your hard breast, come take my strength;
I blow my spells in your huge mouth, rise up and live!
O flame, coil like a viper round his heartless heart!
O ax, wedge in his fists and give them strength and power!
Aye, you man-slayer, you vicious hound, leap from your tomb!"
But the maids clasped him tight and broke in loud lament:
"Master, what god is this that leaps out of your hands?
Look, it's a dead man's skull, no hair, no eyes, no teeth!"
The old chief stared, then flung the log to earth and cursed:
"I call on God, and Death replies! May both be cursed!
Death, the great shepherd hisses from the ground and flings
his staff to trip my feet and drag me toward his fold,
but I am the great chief! I'll not give up my soul!
Women, fetch me the holy skull of Death to wear
with its red feathers and its thick blood-clotted beard;
I, with my heavy ax, my warm and heaving breath,
I am great God himself and sit on rocks enthroned, like Death!"

The old chief moaned and decked himself in Death's fine robes,
then sat cross-legged and grim upon a towering rock;
suddenly through the leaves the wolf-pack's eyes and teeth
glittered as all the eleven youths broke in the clearing.
The women steamed with shameless rut and dropped their leaves,
and the archer watched them crouch in shrubs in the moon's rays
while the cowed sons spoke low and donned fierce masks for fear
their father's spirit would see them when they slew his body.
Odysseus cocked his ears and spied with careful stealth
on the dark youths who muttered and crawled slowly close,
mumbling to one another in low quivering tones:
"See how the Old Chief sits cross-legged, wearing the black
and flaming armor of Death; the maids cling to his waist."
"He sees us now, and beckons! He'll soon throw the noose
and rope us tight like bulls dragged to the slaughter-shed."
"A voice roars in my entrails, 'Kill the Old Chief now!' "

A harelipped youth slunk in an open moonlit space
and then his quivering crawling voice flicked through the night:
"Rise, father, choose yourself a maid, run for your life!
Your time has come, our eyes have turned blood-red with lust,
we, too, want sons and grandsons to renew our race,
for you've grown old, your blunted blade can plow no more."
One lean and blear-eyed youth, who bit his fingernails
with terror, whispered hoarsely to the savage men:
"Brothers, revere dread God, that flesh which gave us birth."
But then a club-nosed, horse-legged stalwart growled with greed:
"Father, I long to drink your blood and to grow strong;
it's time you sank in earth, crammed full of stones and spells,
your hands tied at your back so you won't block our way."
Then all the sons took heart and tried to press him close,
but the old man leapt and cackled as his jangling bells
tossed wildly on his heavy thighs and scrawny neck,
and his shrill mocking voice goaded his lustful sons.
"If I yell 'Hoot!' these rams in rut will run like hares!
Be bold, take heart, come closer, choose a buxom ewe!
Come, my thorn-bearded son, come take the youngest maid,
come close and bite her, for her flesh is good and cool."
The sons held back the beckoned one with hushed advice:
"Brother, don't go, she's meat cast in a trap for bait:
see how he's slyly raised his ax behind his back."
But lustful thorny-hair stuck out his savage neck:
"Swear by your god, old man, that you won't rush to kill me."
"I swear by my great god that I won't touch a hair!
Don't spurn your luck, you fool; the girl's in rampant heat,
see how she whinnies like a mare, how her thighs glow;
stretch out your hands and grab her, son, with health and joy!"
Ah, how the brains of the young groom splashed on the stones!
The old chief laughed, raised his ax soaked with blood and brains
and wiped it on his burning temples and shrunk arms,
and his sons howled with frothing lips that writhed with wrath:
"Old man, you broke your oath! Vipers shall sting you now!"
But the chief howled with mocking laughs and from his fists
licked two or three thick drops from his son's splattered brain.
"I take my cue from God and break my vows! I, too,
freed from all virtue now, shall do whatever I please!
Women, don't move, cling tightly to my hanging pelts,
I'll strew ten more black beasts for you on crimson grass."
A long-thighed maiden rushed to rouse the shrinking men:
"Shame on your youth! Don't fear him, brothers, kill him now!
He has no nails to scratch with; blow, and he'll tumble down."
One horselike vixen reared her rigid breasts and shrieked:
"Brothers, that youth who strikes him first I'll gorge with lust

and fill his yard with herds of sons, twin after twin!"
They heard, their eyes flamed till the one most lustful cried:
"O arch-browed maid, crawl close and seize him by the knees
that I may cast my noose and break his scrawny neck in two!"

Odysseus raised his dark and grasping eyes, then clung
tight to a rock to keep himself from dashing out
as the son flung his horse's lasso with great strength
and it fell whistling round the old man's neck; a great
bellow shook all the earth as though an oak tree crashed.
With their fierce masks, the sons rushed out and held aloft
bright axes in their father-slaying, trembling hands
as the maids danced and twitched their shameless hips and rumps:
"Come forward, grooms, our hearts grow light, new nights begin!
Ah, how we lust to clasp young men on the green grass!"
Then the strong sons bent with their blades above their father,
pushed all the women back and yelled to them in wrath
to draw away nor watch the fearful murder done.
The snow-haired archer, deeply hid in the thorn shrubs,
felt his heart leaping, lassoed to the jutting rock,
and knew profoundly man's dark longing need to slay
the ancient father and sleep safe in mother's arms.
His heart rose in his breast and cried with pity then:
"O mind, all my desires rebound from yes and no,
at times I turn all phallus, then to that tower-lord;
come harmonize at length man's double, monstrous wings."
Odysseus then half-opened his eyes and found them brimmed
with moons and lewdly dancing shades and steaming mouths
so that he thrust his face in shrubs once more, and spied.
The sons had bound their father tight to the huge rock,
then grasped each other's shoulders in a savage dance;
their warlike cries rose like a crawling threnody
as in fierce song they portioned out their father's might:
"Ah, father, mighty chief, great woman-violator,
you tensed your mighty loins and spawned thick tribes of men,
you filled the fields with females and the caves with males,
you ate and drank, gave birth to swarms, ruled all the land,
but now it's time you lay down with the myriad dead
that we, too, may know women's arms and see God's face.
Father, before you sink in earth, give us your strength,
don't let snakes eat it or the tree roots drink it dry,
leave us for heritage your eyes, your loins, your brains.
Brothers, advance, let's swiftly share this ancient boar."
The youths danced wildly then about the dragon's corpse,
and each son lowered his black fist and struck that part
of his strong father's body which he most desired.

The harelipped son stooped first and struck the heavy head:
"I'll smash his skull in two and drink his wily brains;
when foes besiege me, like my father then I'll cut
with craft, with the brain's ax, a safe door of escape.
I'll set lime twigs for spirits, snares for the wild beasts,
and when foes chase me I'll turn green and hide in leaves,
I'll turn gray rock amid wild rocks, or smoke in air.
I want the old man's thick fat brains for my full share!"
"I'll snatch his slender throbbing larynx for my share
then sit at evening on smooth rocks and sing so sweet
that yearning maids will hear and cackle like roused hens,
that youths will set their weapons down to cool their minds,
that black Death will forget on which door he should knock."
"I'll take for my full share his arms and his sharp ax,
that when I raise my hand above a neck or tree
the deep dark woods will shudder, knees will shake and quake,
and men and trees will yell 'The Old Chief!' when I come near."
"I'll take his flashing feet for my spoils' slender portion;
ah, when the Old Chief danced on the round threshing floor
how his hair swirled, how loud he roared and glared at women!
Earth must not eat his feet, nor must his brave dance spill
from his ten toes like water and vanish forever in earth."
"Ah, I want only his hawk eyes for my full share!
O eagle-eyed, you pierced the hare in the fern-brake!
When from high crags you spied, earth spread below your feet
supine with all her waters, mountains, beasts, and men,
like a young girl who strips to show her beauties bare.
Ah, I shall never let such eyes spill on the ground."
"Father, I long to clasp your ears against my temples!
When you pressed them to earth, it buzzed like a wasp's hive;
you could detect the lion's tread and the fawn's drift,
the heartbeat of the hare, and the foes' secret number;
not even water escaped you as it dripped in caves
where you would lead your tribe to drink and cool their loins.
Father, give me your ears, or they'll grow deaf in earth."
"I choose your virile bullock-loins for my full share!
You grabbed all females by the hair, dragged them to caves,
you mounted the world's women like so many mares!
Although Death gleaned, you sowed, and once again our dead
sprang up in double crops, and the world bloomed again.
I want your pointed plow-blade, God, so it won't rust!"
"Brothers, I want his heart, that hammer of hard bronze
that beat with frantic rage to smash the entire world.
My heart is weak and girlish, wedded to far things;
I watch men kill each other, and my mind flies far,
and when I see maids writhe in pangs of birth, I weep.

Ah, I shall eat his heart to get me a beast's heart!"
"By God, my brothers, where did his proud mien reside,
his speech as ponderous as an ax, his lion's breath—
within his breast, his gobbling tongue, or his stout loins,
or was it wind I might sniff out and pluck from air?"
"Father, when you felled giant trees and built a boat,
then leapt within it, plied the oars till the waves foamed,
ah, Father, how I yearned, how my heart burned with lust
to see you killed some day that I might seize your hands,
that I, too, might hack giant trunks and mount the waves!
Forward, O regal heirs, let's share our father! Hack and slay!"

The dance stopped and the ten sons raised their axes high
but the light-archer clapped his hands before his eyes
and heard hoarse yells and laughter, arms that rose and fell,
the crunch of bones, the dreadful bellow of a beast
as warm thick drops of blood splattered his trembling arms.
Because he could not bear this secret of the world
he felt ashamed and raised his eyes that throbbed with fright:
like screaming vultures that swoop down and rip a corpse,
and one soars off and holds the feet tight in its claws,
and one sits heavily with the guts hung round its neck,
and the most bold grips in its claws the bloody head,
thus did the sons rush at the wake to eat their father.
The hour was sweet, and scented earth spread her night-flowers,
the waters swayed in thirsty nostrils of wild beasts
and the moon lay stretched on the field like a dead boy;
young men now wandered in far towns, dew on their hair,
the scent of the belovèd still steamed on their chests,
and new-wed mothers woke at midnight, vexed with cares,
and smiled to hear their sons at play within their cradles.
The ten heirs screamed and rolled their bloodshot eyes with joy
then slowly licked their bloody lips with their coarse tongues
and once more broke in a wild dance till their brains swirled,
their head-plumes leapt and thrashed, flames tossed within their eyes
until their father leapt in their bowels with ax in hand.
Each son became his fearful father, danced and sang:
"Brothers, let's drown our memories now and wash our hands;
ah, we've not killed our father, for he lives and reigns
complete within the sated entrails of each son!"
"Oho, my neck's grown thick and strong, my hair's turned white,
I've no beginning or end, I've lived a thousand years!"
"My eyes have grown to monstrous size, the world's grown small,
whatever I see is mine, I've grabbed the Old Chief's eyes!"
"I've grabbed his ears, all speaking beasts or birds are mine!"
"I've grabbed his heavy phallus, all fat maids are mine!"

"I've grabbed the Old Chief's daring heart, I fear no man!"
"I'm the Old Chief himself, look at his arms, his hair!
Heap in the center of our court our flocks, our pelts,
our weapons, children, maids, then raise your axes high
and let the strongest son who kills the rest be chief!
My eyes brim blood, my father roars in my guts, 'Strike!' "
Odysseus rose then to his knees with goggling eyes,
and as the brothers roared and fought, the maidens seized
the youths and with shrill cries tried to prevent the slaughter.
One maid tore at her hair and in delirium screamed:
"The Old Chief comes as vampire! See, his frothing ghost
has driven his sons insane and laps their spouting blood!
Old crone, O white-haired witch, drive it away with magic spells!"

An ancient sorceress, with a yellow spirit's mask
hung on her sagging dugs, rushed out and clapped her hands,
stamped slowly on the ground as though she drove a stake,
then swirled into a magic dance until the youths
stood still with fright, their axes raised above their heads.
Beating her hands, the ancient hag hissed like a turtle:
"Scat, evil spirit, scat! I blow to right and left!
If you're a small flame, fade! If you're a small dog, die!
If you're a thought hid in a head, flow into feet
and there turn to delirious dance and drown in earth!
Dance, my lads, dance! Stamp the Old Chief deep down in stones!
Brave youths, throw down your weapons, wake from the grim curse,
I hold in both my hands my dark and quivering thighs,
I hold my dugs from which two streams of black milk flow,
and in my loins and womb I hear a voice command.
Brave youths, a great god in me looms and cries, 'Don't kill!' "
The father-slaying sons were dazed by this new law
that issued from the frothing entrails of the witch,
but a roused youth, strong as a bull, mocked at the hag:
"Who then will snatch his women? Deep in my bowels I hear
the Old Chief hop in rage, alive, and shout, 'My son,
raise your ax high and be the last remaining male!' "
The women's bosoms heaved, the young men growled, and as
the yellow mask of fear leapt on the old hag's breast,
the second great new law seethed from her frothing mouth:
"Brothers, a mighty god within me shouts, 'Don't touch
your father's women who matured in his deep caves!'
Your moldy ancient father roars with ax in hand
in each one of his women's loins and spies with wrath,
and as your seeds pour in each womb, he kills them all!
Quick, brothers, scatter all your mothers, sisters, maids
to other courtyards in far distant and strange lands

and barter them for many foreign and sweet wives.
I rise on tiptoe and spy out far distant towns,
I see maids fresh as crystal water or wheat bread,
others are sunburnt, their deep bowels seethe with eggs,
and all are yours in barter, that your seed may sprout.
I swear by our Mother Moon, there is no greater joy
than to delight in watching how a strange girl eats;
her dancing is most novel, strange her smell and smile,
and strange the way she gives her kiss or takes it back."
The ancient sorceress clapped her hands and stamped on earth
until her soul, as shrilling as a cricket's rasp,
allured the savage sons to a great blaze of lust.
Behold, the tough-skinned brain with all its greasy fat
flew off to foreign places, passed through foreign towns
and mutely crouched on a tall peak to spy the wondrous land.

Dear God, what wells of cooling water, what sweet chat,
what heavy painted water-jugs, what female backs
that burn bronze in the sun, white, yellow, brown and black!
The women stroll in forest clearings, chirp like birds
and sway their hips till the earth sways, and youths go wild
and leap like cocks with golden feathers high in air
and mount the maids, those hens that hatch within their minds,
then swell their chests with cocky pride, and crow in triumph.
Leaping in thought these distant forms, the sons lost track
of time, and their thick hands, their lips, their thighs got lost
in distant foreign lands, on fragrant foreign breasts
till they no longer yearned for their cruel father's women.
Parrots awoke in treetops, the air shone and rang
with upright feathers like the first dream of a bride;
the early morning dew glowed on the lion's mane,
and a huge multibranching honeysuckle, drenched
with musk, twined round the strong horns of a rutting buck.
The hearts of the black sons grew calm, their minds grew sweet
until they cast their masks away, and in the first
pale beams of dawn that lit their faces, now turned mild,
all understood their brotherhood, and in dim light
once more entwined their arms and broke in a swift dance:
"Farewell, for the wind blew, and a strange spirit swooped,
until our arms turned into masts, and far lands called.
We've seen maids that we liked, we'll take for merchandise
our own maids with their hawser hair and milk-pail hands,
we'll sell our sisters and mothers with their swelling rumps!
Our hungry kisses leap like goats from crag to crag,
swoop down to foreign strands and knock on women's doors.
Oho, my lads, we buy and sell well-seeded flesh!"

The trees about them creaked till apes rushed out and stooped
to marvel at their upright brothers who at dawn
danced as their thick mustaches dripped with drops of blood.
Behind them huddled, row on row, with upright tails,
the wood-squirrels, leopards, martens, fawns and civet cats,
all the embellished, tassel-tailed furs of the forest,
and further back there swooped and perched upon a dark
fir's top the great starved archon of the corpse, the crow.
Amid the shaggy beasts, the jungle's brilliant wings,
the groaning sons strove with delirious flesh and soul
to shape a dance that they might understand the great
new laws, and their red rolling eyes were filled with future wings.

Hidden among the trees, the wings, and the wild beasts,
Odysseus shook to see that from his fingers dripped
the warm blood which had splattered him from the chief's slaughter.
His temples gaped like smashed gates of a plundered castle;
what if his inner jails had cracked and from the bars
of time the ancient savage captives had broken loose?
"Somewhere in dreams or in the slaughter's vertigo
I hid in this dark wood, I saw these dragon-sons
and with them slew our father, and with them broke in dance.
Time gapes unhinged, my mind is soiled, and I've turned backward!
Ah, I can't bear them! When I rise, they'll scatter and fade!"
He took two strides, stood upright in the bloodstained ring
and pierced the savage dancers with his ruthless eyes
so that they suddenly stopped, and their feet hung mid-air.
"The Spirit!" they shrieked and stuttered with fright. Their knees gave way,
their sturdy loins crashed down before flesh-eating eyes,
and their firm flanks began to quiver like fine mist.
Then the light-archer slit them with his arrowed glance
and pierced their dark brains, necks, and chests until their bold
audacious bodies rose disburdened on the mind's
high peaks and soared through air like the autumnal clouds.
The first-born son then opened his mouth wide and strove
to voice his fear, and to crawl close to the dread Spirit,
but his thick jaws slipped crookedly, he gasped and stopped,
for the earth came and went beneath his stumbling feet.
Both men and women screamed and fell flat on the stones
as in the circling trees the ape-ancestors thronged
screaming, and scratched their testicles with filthy nails.
The great ascetic stood stock-still and felt his brain
swirl like a shooting star that casts red-azure flames,
and heard his Mother Earth in the deep silence scream,
and then caress his ripe head with its precious gold:

"Help me, my first-born son, pity my laden womb,
it's filled with vipers, beasts, and gods; I eat and eat
but there's no eating them, for they spew out like springs!
The Spirit, that lustful white bull, mounts me night and day;
rise up, blow hard, my last-born hope, that all may die!"
Earth cried out for salvation to her son, the mind,
and he in pity for his mother, held back his strength
till in the dawning light he saw blood-clotted beards,
blue lips that never bit a woman's holy flesh,
and arms that longed to clasp, amid foul filth and milk,
a spadeful of lean meat, a son, and give him suck.
He did not hurry as he groped real limbs and flesh,
no dream had spilled on earth and bred but fantasies,
these were not demons who had burst his chest's bronze bars
but his own blood-kin made of phallus, womb, and brain.
A soul-complaining voice then burst from Mother Earth:
"Pity them, dreadful Spirit, for these, too, are men,
but they've just parted from the beast, their brains are still
dull and coarse-grained, filled with mud, pebbles and thick blood.
They strive to rise on their hind feet, to conquer weight,
and when they see the earth, they seize sharp stones and try
to rip my womb apart and to entrust their seed;
when they see maids, they grab them by the hair and thrust
them down to the hard ground to shape new men and maids,
and all the demons watch and break in a cold sweat.
Pale Spirit, you smile, but they don't fear you, O dread Death;
if only you won't rush them, they'll find time to sow
both earth and women to produce sons, daughters, seed!
Give them a little time; they'll scorn to ask you more."
But the lone hurried athlete shook his ruthless head,
for though that spendthrift, his proud mind, would grant all things,
it would not give that greatest good of all things, Time.
Time was no mountain peak or thousand-year-old oak;
the head is a bright bubble, a teardrop filled with air,
above it the earth and heaven, lights and shadows play,
and when a light breeze blows, the head scatters and fades.
Flat on their faces by the archer's feet, the sons
awaited the great gift of Time from the strong hands
of the dread sage who held the rusty keys of earth,
but when the lone man laughed and held his fists clenched tight,
the blacks in startled terror rose and raised their axes:
"Brothers, it seems that all our prayers have been in vain,
that's the man-eating Spirit, the killer, the Old Chief;
strike, brothers, rope him swiftly or he'll eat us all!"
But then the youngest son clasped a tall rock and moaned:
"Brothers, let's cling to this stone phallus arm in arm,

for the ground cracks, alas, and our feet sink in the earth."
Then the maids saw their full breasts rot, and screeched with fear:
"Help us, dear brothers, hold us tight; we see dark wells
where we plunge headlong with our hands crossed on our breasts!
Death, let us live! Boughs, hold us up, don't let us fall!"
"Alas, dear sisters, this is no well, may it be cursed!
The Spirit stands here, silent, still. It gulps us all!"
Their feet and hands bound tight with azure air, they fought
and struck at empty light, their minds threshed in a dream,
their fingernails dropped out, their flesh swelled and turned green
and worms crawled from the earth and gnawed their moldy brains.
They groveled on the ground and fought to catch their breaths,
but their white teeth fell to the earth like ears of corn,
and as the sun at daybreak sucks mists from the grass,
thus did the lone man's blazing eyes gulp down the huge
dark ghosts that rose from the damp earth to haunt his soul.
Then the earth cleared and the mind calmed, once more the pitch-
black portals of the bowels closed, and the dread demons
crouched growling in the sunless cellars of the mind
till the glad archer wiped his sweating chest in sweet relief.

The battle had been fierce, for many savage heads
had reared, rebellious in his mind to knock him down:
old recollections of dark caves, memory's harsh cries,
old monsters, the mind's phantoms, time's appalling frights.
But his bull-fighting mind had raised its flaming lash
so that all monsters knew their master, bowed their heads,
thrust their long tails between their legs, then yowled and stooped
beneath the sun's bright yoke to till the fertile dark.
The lone man pulled the tangled reins and brought the world
to its true course once more and fixed Time's wobbling wheels.
Then the night-roamer stooped and in a crystal pool
of water cooled his eyes, his ears, his kindled brain
until the earth, too, cooled with him, and the sun laughed.
A small, small bird with yellow breast and crimson crown
raised its full throat in the clear sky and burst in song,
and the plump squirrels in branches, drenched with warming sun,
gnawed gently at the new-leaved twigs with sweet delight
as their two eyes, like drops of water, mirrored all
the world about them—the green trees and the small nests.
The archer, gently smiling, rose from the great feast
of savage memory, that old hag, and to the sun
spread his benumbed bow-loving hands to keep them warm,
and joyed to see the newly thickened drops of blood
turn slowly, gently, on his fingernails, to drops of dew.

XXI

Time slowly passed and the wheel turned, moons rose and fell,
earth stretched out like a fawn before the archer's feet
and he stooped down and stroked it with a mute caress.
At times he passed by sluggish streets, or flowering fields,
or yellow sands that like a tiger flicked in light.
Varied aromas, birds, and tongues of strange men changed,
flutes, dances, and streets changed, and different kinds of masks
covered the ancient gods and aroused the eternal fears.
Stones rasped like crickets in the burning day, till night
fell like a sudden sword and split the world in two;
then beasts, freed from the yoke of the flame-archer sun,
prowled from their secret lairs in hunger, silently,
and the celestial candelabrum blazed with light.
White-haired Odysseus walked and bid the world farewell,
but did not hasten, for he loved earth still and spread
his hands, his eyes, his ears and slowly said goodbye.
His leopard cub with her striped back loomed in his mind
so that he wondered where, in what deep grass she lay,
stretched on her back or playing with her spotted cubs,
and the archer sighed to think he'd faded from the heart
of his old friend who had dissolved like windless mist.
He walked in rampant suns and stood in vapid moons,
his shadows swung about him like a windmill's wings,
and in his heart he carried all his precious friends,
memory's wings, mute shades, dogs of the lower world.
Like a snow avalanche that falls from a high peak
and gathers new snow as it sweeps the mountain's slope,
then crashes, groaning, a snow-mountain of dread size,
the lofty man's mind rolled and swept all things before it.
His throat gulped down the dead, and his teeth filled with grit
as though he'd tasted Death's grim pomegranate filled
with ash, and he rejoiced because deep in his heart
and inner tombs he still held his dear friends intact.
"Don't worry, lads, no soul shall die while I still live;
when waters swell and houses sink and the earth drowns,
climb on my shoulders, comrades, cling about my neck,

and, swimming all together, we'll reach the other shore.
What shore, alas? That cobwebbed coast, that anchoring shoal,
our secret native land that brims with fragrance, Death!"
He spoke thus with his friends and walked with their dim shades:
one was all bone and held a flute, one had splay feet,
two were like supple lances, two like savage wolves;
and some, tall sirens shod in golden sandals, sped
on tiptoe and pursued their leader like lean hounds.
In Hades the rose-cheeked turn pale, the white turn black,
but living hearts have magic herbs and resurrect
all those they love, and thus the freed mind walked as all
his gold-belled wedding caravan of memory tagged
behind him with no molted wing, with not one shriveled leaf.

Time passed and brought the rains, it passed again and brought
the sun into the lone man's hands like very hot
wheat bread, till one bright dawn he closed his eyes, and wept.
Ah, what was this good thing that suddenly drenched his mind?
His curly hair revived like sated tentacles
and his blood cooled and danced down to his very toes
as his mind rose erect and beat its azure wings.
Then the great-chested man spread his hands toward the East:
"A thousand times well met, O cool belovèd brine!"
He stooped and dipped his hands deep in a flowing brook,
then like a bridegroom washed himself till his face shone
that he might not go to his loved one soiled, uncombed.
He spied the land from a high rock, felt the salt air,
and then his old crew crowded close, his swift ship creaked,
the billows drowned his heart, the world bobbed up and down,
and his mind clove the sea-waves like a breasting gull.
Then the world-wanderer strode ahead on bloody feet,
forgot their weariness in joy, grew cool and pushed
far down while old shades danced about him as he rushed
to lead his crew who now smelled brine and leapt from earth.
Hungry, he thought of fish stews they had gulped in coves
as some poured wine and others fed the fire and all
the evening air was drenched with rhododendron bloom:
they hungered and ate well, then cast themselves in sleep
like fish, and floated all night long with tails erect.
And when their eyelids opened in the seaside air
their ship hung on their lashes like the morning dew;
it too had slept and dreamt its hull had swelled, its prow
had turned into a porpoise, its long oars to fins,
the crew to baby dolphins riding its arched back
as all sped out to sea and raced the swifting gulls,
and when it woke, it saw the crew lined on the beach.

Then Rocky swam and climbed aboard and stood erect
like a green branch, a slender-bodied god of bronze
whom mothers in the dark with supplication stroked
that he might come in dream and fill their wombs with sons.
Granite thrashed through the waters like a lean swordfish,
and he, too, was a god of Love and rampant youth;
but Orpheus seemed like an ill-shaped, pale weathercock,
like the last seed of an old father who could bequeath
his son no bones or meat but only froth and air.
As Kentaur spread his limbs supine upon the waves
and blew and churned the whitening waters into foam,
he seemed like a sea-demon who with ponderous weight
swooped down and mounted the shore-sirens and the waves.
High on a rock alone, the dreadful lone man stretched
like a huge octopus whose tentacles were all
his friends that now played, lashed, and spread on waves, on sand,
as he through many souls and bodies sucked at life.
Their ship watched them for a long time and softly smiled
and swayed with blandishment and wished them a good day.
The holy voyage once more foamed in the archer's mind,
and as he watched the emerald wash in the ship's wake,
his vanished voyages once more gleamed on the waves.
"O heart, resounding lyre, now rise and strike new tunes;
your singing strings are made of sturdy tiger gut,
your twisting pegs are tight, you've reveled and caroused
completely in life's sun-feasts of the mind and flesh.
All the desires danced about you like trained apes,
seductive songs rose from the wine, creation hung
a red carnation on its ear for your dear sake,
and now, O heart, within the desert's blazing kiln
a salt breeze blows and the sea leaps, that blue-eyed witch!"
He spoke, then climbed on a high rock to spy the land
and his eyes brimmed with water as waves leapt and laughed;
the curving seashores everywhere smiled happily
and fleets of jet-black fishing-boats tossed on the waves.
The white-haired athlete smiled, took up the road once more,
and as he dashed down toward the sea, his mother's breast,
he met a yellow-skinned and slant-eyed maiden there
who on her shoulder carried a long sea-ravaged oar.
"Maiden, where are you taking that great winnowing van?"
As though she felt coarse tickling hands, the maiden laughed:
"Oho, it seems you've never swum or seen the sea
nor seen or touched an oar by which all ships are rowed!"
The cunning man stretched out his hand and stroked the blade:
"Your health, O my long sea-hand and the mind's sharp sword,
I bow and worship man's swift wing of liberty!"

He spoke, then pressed his mouth against the salt-bleached wood,
and the maid, startled, broke and ran down the long beach in fright.

Odysseus swiftly walked along the flowered fields
and with wide eyes and secret loathing gazed on all
the last remaining muddy seeds of mankind's race.
They hopped and screeched like apes with eyes of slanting flame,
and a thin cutting smile gleamed on their hairless lips.
"They're from another dough, another baker's oven!
Ah, had I many years to squander, I would sit at ease
and play and weep beside a yellow woman's breast
and thus learn all the deep hid secrets of this race;
it seems that man's soul grazes here on a rich pasture."
He spoke, then entered a domed flowered lane of trees
through whose twined boughs a warm spring shower softly fell
as flowers quivered in the mingling sun and rain.
Women with white clogs and embroidered kerchiefs ran
with chattering laughter down the path of happiness
to worship their fat smiling god amid the blooms.
He sat cross-legged enclosed by branches bridal-decked,
with double rolling bellies, triple flowing chins,
with half-closed sluggish eyes that winked and gazed on all
his worshipers who came from the world's distant lands
to find, perhaps, cure for their pains, hope for despair;
but he burst in loud laughter as his bellies shook
and his hands played with rosaries made of human skulls.
Before him the world-wanderer stood in silent awe;
the stone was a translucent green, as clear as water,
sunrays passed through the body, lit the pulsing heart,
and through the deep neck laughter could be seen ascending.
The emerald marvel laughed at the world-roaming tramp,
and as pale lights and shadows flicked, and thick coarse drops
like those of sweat and tears fell from his lofty brows
and slowly dripped within his black and long-lashed eyes,
he laughed, for he knew well these were but drops of rain.
"This god is free," Odysseus thought with sudden joy.
"We're well met, Lone Man, here on laughter's highest peak!"
The archer gazed, then plunged into the god's deep heart,
a swimmer in green waters on a moonlit night,
and his harsh body cleansed and shone, his mind felt free,
floating on waves of nonexistence, a huge fish,
a wave composed of fragile dream and azure air.
For a long time he swam in the vast emerald's sheen
and felt great joy, disburdened, melting like a lump
of salt in the dark endless brine of turquoise sea,
and when he'd had enough, he took the road once more.

As he walked on, the air turned cool and stung with salt,
the billows broke in cackling and applauding sounds
until the sea's great bridegroom broke in a quick run.
Soon he saw fishers mending their torn nets on sand:
"Good fishing, lads!" Odysseus yelled in a loud voice,
but a great wind swept up and dashed it down the coast.
The billows rattled on the pebbles, plashed and played
like a leashed dog who sniffs his master's scent, and barks,
until the sea's great archon hailed his dearest friend:
"Well met before my house, O faithful ancient dog,
O sea, who bark your welcome in remembrance still!"
He dashed down to the shore, caressed the frothing mane,
recalled that other faithful dog, dark eons past,
who in his sullied courtyard wagged its hairless tail
and in defiance of the suitors dashed to greet him.
"Argus!" he cried out in his mind, and the dog leapt
from his far grave, besmirched with mud, and wagged his tail.
Shadows of memories multiplied and thronged the beach
in curling petals round the lone man who in joy
played with the waves, cast a flat stone in ducks and drakes
that hopped the waters swiftly seven times, then sank.
He played and shouted with the waves for a long time;
not a soul saw him rolling on that foreign strand
till filled with seaweed and salt flakes he stretched on shells
as seagrass lapped and twined about his whitened head
that like a hairy rock, uncombed, gleamed on the shore.
He shut his eyes and on the shingle stretched full length
and his mind spread like long sea-fennel down the beach;
if ghosts or gulls had seen him, they'd have gulped him whole
and waves would have crashed down and crammed him full of salt.
"What can man's troubles be, that vanish like the foam?
Did these feet tread earth's thousand roads, bloodstained and sore,
did these eyes weep, did these ears hear a sad lament?
I've never wept, I've not felt pain, I've sailed the seas
like the curved nautilus, erect, and laughed like foam!
O sea, O untamed heart, joy of despairing man,
all, all are yours, my meat, my bones—lick them like mermaids,
turn them to slippery stones, to amber sleek and smooth,
turn my white skull to ivory through which fish may glide
and females lay their eggs and the males squirt their milt."
He kept his eyes shut tight, and then the mute sea-hours
folded their wings like placid and well-sated gulls;
perhaps he slept by the sea's foam for many hours,
perhaps his sleepless thoughts like arrowy shuttles sped
from East to West and wove the embroideries he desired,
perhaps he stood by the blue shore but a brief moment;

then hurriedly the border-guard strode toward the noisy port.
The city like a gorgon raised its prow on earth,
heavily painted, tower-breasted, with wide eyes
of lust that on the sea gazed like a harbor whore.
Night fell, and many-colored lanterns flared in rows
along the quay, the dappled wind with sweetness hissed
and smelled of flowers, spices, and the sweat of men.
Roads branched off everywhere like rivers, and clogs clacked
and zithers sighed as laughter seethed through lattices,
till the archer stood and listened to the sigh of love:
"Ah, dear God, pity me—how can I sleep alone
again on such a night, a night with a long tail,
the strong cock-pheasant's long and lustrous tail?"
The lone man listened, startled, to the maid's desire;
had he a thousand bodies, he'd have set them loose,
masked with the face of him each maid longed for in dream,
to jump into the beds of those that slept alone.
A sweet compassion filled him for the lonely maid
and he slid past her yard to knock upon her door
that she might not weep all alone in bed that night,
but there he saw men's sandals heaped high on the sill;
young men and old, rich men and poor passed through that door
in their bare feet as though to wade through a wide river,
and now they sailed on the maid's body in deep bliss.
The lone man laughed, then took his road once more in peace.
What joy! Odysseus whistled like a whirling wind;
if only he had time, dear God, to enjoy the town
before the wind blew, and bazaars, men, laughter, vanished!
Good was this multicolored structure of the air
in which the archer took delight like a box kite
that soared through dark with a lit lantern at its head.
His mind kept plundering as he passed road after road
till, tired at length, he reached the harbor's noisy shore.
In the hot night the smell of tar and the sea's brine
merged with the stifling stench of workers' armpits drenched
in sweat, as harbor girls, the sailors' consolation,
strolled on the wharf with naked and decoying breasts,
with flesh-seducing musk, with crisped and curly locks,
with henna-painted nails and azure languid eyes;
they swayed and primped, stood at the crossroads and made signs.
Startled, the lone man gleaned this new crop in his mind:
"These are not men," he thought with arrogant disdain;
"they gnaw like mice through rubbish, braid their hair in queues,
until I retch as though I've touched their slimy bellies."
But as these cruel disdainful words rose in his mind
he saw a bent old man sit cross-legged on the wharf

then gaze far out at sea upon the frothing waves
and sing to the wild winds a bitter lullaby.
He could not catch the garbled words, nor had he need,
for the lone man knew well that all man's bitter pain
rose up and scattered from this throat in helplessness.
"What can this wonder be? Who took clay, wing, and air
and dared create that bright goldfinch, man's fevered heart?
We are all one, we shout by every shore, we weep;
our deepest outcries are bread, women, God, and Death,
and this, my brother, burns in the same kiln with me!"
Odysseus longed to fall into those yellow arms
and call that strange man brother, with deep tears and laughter,
but felt ashamed to act the child in his old age.
Slowly he left his yellow ancient brother there,
walked down the shore, breathed deep the odor of the ships
that skimmed in and skimmed out like silent hunting bats
with sails of pelts and mats of straw, while on their prows
bronze dragons crouched and chewed young captains newly drowned.
"Your good health, brothers," the archer murmured as he hailed
these souls that on their prows hung Death for talisman.
Toward gaudy ships that moored with precious merchandise,
haggard old spinstresses with battered sandals went
to greet the wandering groom who never will come back.
Year after year these wretched hags asked every crew:
"O sailors, have you seen my love on foreign shores?
He wears a golden ring, a cap I knit, he took
my lock for good-luck charm, and my dear maidenhead."
The sailors tell them tales, mock them behind their backs,
and the old hags turn home and double-bar their doors
for fear the neighbors would find out and burst in laughing jeers.

The seashore dives blazed with loud laughs and rowdy noise,
and the white archer sat between two strong sea-wolves
whom he had met that day, and now they drank like friends.
Unmoving, silent, sad, his white beard stained with wine,
he slowly bid the earth and its deep joys farewell;
he watched the crews sip at their wine about the fires
with eggs of octopus, sea-urchins, and soft crabs;
he watched the skippers in the seaside taverns drink,
bare-chested, tousle-haired, till with wine's dizzy spell
their trips came sailing in the taverns like tall legends.
His mind swelled as he listened in the fishers' pubs
to skippers tell of lily-wonders that turned all
their native snowlands into crystals and snow-flowers.
One had thick reeking thongs that bound his oaken calves,
his slanting black eyes flashed with fire, and round his neck

he wore, for god and good-luck charm, a silver bear.
He talked, and shoals of shimmering fish came tumbling down,
mountains of seabirds rose, and their cracked eggshells tossed
beside the seashore foam like pure-white lotus blooms;
reindeer sped swiftly with their pearl-encrusted horns
that glittered in the nacreous mists of frozen fields;
seven curved necklaces of rainbows arched the skies,
snows glimmered with a thousand hues, and fingernails
and hands dripped with green, red, and azure precious stones.
As the world-wanderer listened, his mind burst in flame:
"I shall not drown in waves, nor shall I sink in earth
before these rainbows come to shroud my living form;
I've seen the peacock's azure, green, and golden plumes,
and now I long to see earth's snow-white gleaming tail!"
As the snow's captain talked, in the hushed pub there strolled
a plump god dressed in bearhides, thickly smeared with grease,
and all threw fat lumps in the fire to warm him, fed
him seals and hung smoked fishes round his grimy neck
as he munched lard with greed and reeked like a white bear.
Then the world-wanderer laughed, for speech was a swift ship
with bursting holds on whose curved prow there sat an old,
old hag with clacking tongue who screeched like a plucked hen,
and on whose deck the lone man sat to roam the world.
The second, slender, red-skinned captain laughed and brimmed
the brazen bowls with wine, and his long painted nails
cast rosy sweet reflections on the glittering cups.
"By God, at times the whole world seems like a strange myth,
the mind like a bewitched and pallid prince who flings
the hundred gold gates of a haunted palace wide,
all doors adorned with different knockers, varied signs,
but the mind holds key-clusters, opens and walks through.
Now, Captain, you've flung wide the white snow-covered door
with all its dazzling flakes and bears, its wild reindeer,
and the mind entered, that charmed prince, and cried with joy,
for it had never dared divine such deathless lilies!
But I was born in flame-drenched lands, on sun-scorched shores,
unlocked a crimson door, walked through a thousand gardens
of flowering pomegranate trees where flames are roses,
where all our seashores gleam with crimson-painted prows.
Our god's a cunning merchantman who roams all shores,
sells gods and goddesses with tiers of naked dugs,
sells magic charms, seductive paints, and healing herbs.
He's very rich; strong scent drips from his curly beard;
his fingers, ears, and nostrils gleam with garish gold,
his fleets roam all the coasts, and we're his cocky crew,
his sailors, boatmen, cabin boys and merchantmen,

and when we die, we spread our memories wide before him:
'Master, here's what we've sold, our profits and our loss;
cast your accounts and pay us what you owe us now.'
We don't talk with entreaties or with prayers at all
but only with 'I work, you pay,' 'Give me, I'll give you!'
Hades is a great shipyard where we build our boats,
splice ropes, calk gaping seams, patch up our tattered sails,
study the weather, then set sail for the living world."
The red-skinned cunning captain was still talking when
the light sweet clink of copper rings rang from the door,
and when the sea-wolves turned they saw in smoking dark
two round plump Negro breasts that shone like brazen shields,
and a girl's giggling laughter merged with their rude talk.
Then the snow-skipper swiftly leapt and seized the girl
who laughed and waddled close to cuddle in his hides,
and all forgot the gods, veered off to earth once more,
and momently the archer, too, reached in the dark,
slowly caressed in silent awe the warm black breasts
and then with tranquil calm withdrew his sated hand.
The dark-skinned merchant laughed and slyly winked his eye:
"Say the word, brother! If you like such harbor pets
I'll fetch you from the shore a shoal of black-skinned flirts
who've vowed themselves to God for man's sole consolation."
But proud Odysseus did not speak, his mind soared far:
"Let this be my last fondling of a woman's flesh!
How good to feel my palm now brim with a black breast
that covers all the white breasts I've enjoyed in life;
my hand's prepared to grasp tight now earth's earthen breast!"
He softly smiled and fondled the earth within his mind.
When the snow-captain took his fill of the girl's hugs,
he placed about her ankle a bronze ring for thanks,
and the girl, tinkling, laughing, vanished down the mole.
He brimmed the bowls once more, then to the sly man turned:
"Each to this table fetched his country and his god,
till—by the sea!—it seems here in my waking dream
that wine and kisses both have taken a new flavor;
but we have waited still in vain for you, my friend,
to tell from whence your tall cap comes, what jig you dance."
For a long time Odysseus watched his face in wine
flickering and running like a phantom down the beach
until it vanished gulp by gulp along his thirsty throat,
and when he spoke he felt he pulled his tongue with hooks:
"When on my land I glean my fields and store my grain,
when I have trod my purple grapes till the must brims
and my cheese makers come with their best season's cheese,
I spread my feasting-boards in my four spacious courts

and then invite all mighty lords to come and dine.
I stand straight at my door as all my guests ride up,
dismount, bow at my feet, and greet me with esteem:
'May you live long to enjoy your wealth, great tower-lord!'
When I return from wars and my deep holds are heaped
with piles on piles of precious slaves, of bronze, of gold,
and all my people crowd the shores, loud cries explode:
'A thousand welcomes, O great king with your vast plunder!'
But when I sit cross-legged on earth in silent pall
and will no longer deign to touch food, flesh, or drink,
ah, when my flesh turns into soul and sizzling flame,
then all the mighty kings of earth, of sea, of air,
fall at my feet in fear and shrill with stuttering tongues:
'O dread ascetic, pity us, look gently now!'
Even the gods fall at my feet and cry in fear:
'Don't blow and scatter us like mist, almighty mind!'
But when I sit on earth, alone, and bend my head,
gaze at my hands and knees, hear both my temples creak,
crumble a lump of loam and smell the pungent soil,
then a small voice drifts up from my heart's inner core:
'You worm, that crawl on earth and often change your wings,
fly from my sight! I'll raise my foot and crush you flat!' "
The seven-souled man stopped, his eyes in darkness shone
like an ascetic's, a great king's, a monstrous worm's.
The two sea-captains watched their friend in great alarm
for he had swept them off to distant shores, wide courts
and haunted towers from which they found no sure return;
like the Dog Star that shimmers in the sky and turns
to turquoise, emerald, sapphire lights and ruby glows,
the lone man in the tavern's dusk changed many hues.
The red-faced pirate opened his mouth wide to speak
but all at once his voice stuck in his throat, for all
the harbor buzzed, and torches flared in a great blaze.
Odysseus dashed with haste and looked out of the door,
but the dark pirate laughed and seized him by the waist:
"Don't spoil our feast, my friend, don't leave the savage wine;
the crack-brained crowd are worshiping their latest god.
Two years ago a Cretan ship smashed on these rocks,
and when the crew were landed safe, they kissed the earth
and raised an altar to that god they thought had saved them;
I happened to be docked beside them on the mole,
and as I like to probe in things—because I know
that learning is rich merchandise and dearly sold—
I asked the Cretans what great god they lugged abroad.
All swiftly flapped and waved their hands, all spoke at once
of an immense sea-demon that had stormed their coast

and smashed all wealthy Crete on one full-flowered night,
but now they lugged him in their hold and with his blessing
sailed to far-distant shores to found new city-states.
They've fetched their god here with his tall sea-cap, and all
the frantic Negroes listen to that cunning crew
and slay sheep to his grace till miracles come tumbling,
and now, today, his feast-day bursts on this old mole.
The soul's a weathercock upon the roof of flesh,
struck by a thousand winds that turn her where they please."
Then the sun-archer sank his lips into a smile,
sad and profound, and slowly to the pirate said:
"I think I've also seen him in my trips somewhere,
but I can't now recall his face or even his name;
gods are like countless birds that pass above our heads
and the mind soon confuses their harsh cries and wings."
The red-skinned skipper laughed and clapped the lone man's back:
"I sell gods, too, with other wares, along this coast,
I barter hollow spirits for ivory and gold grain
and thus learn to distinguish different sorts of gods.
I well recall that Cretan demon of the sea
with all his visible attributes and secret name:
A sea-cap like an upright prow, a flaming beard,
a curved bow in his huge hands as he stoops to kneel;
some in their prayers call him 'Savior,' and some 'Slayer,'
but in their secret hymns the priests cry out 'Odysseus!' "
The archer frowned and bit his tongue, that from his lips
his savage mocking laughter might not burst in peals,
but yet he pitied wretched man, that craven dog
that wags its tail and fawns upon the hand that beats it.
Meanwhile the hymns grew louder, blazing brands approached,
and the procession like a brimming river flowed;
nude Negroes leapt and yowled as with curved swords they struck
their limbs and features savagely till the blood flowed;
nude children, wreathed with seaweed, led the liturgy,
and in their tender and small hands white seagulls shone.
The varied souls of the new god marched slowly past:
the first soul that passed by was Fire in bronze bowls
held up by seven boys and fed by seven girls
who flung it fragrant cinnamon and scented oils;
the second soul glowed in the hands of a fierce youth:
an upright Bow with silver bells, made of stag horn
where on each end the eyes of two bright rubies gleamed;
the third soul passed, held in the arms of full-grown men:
a Ship with golden prow and full three-masted wings
and a tall sea-cap perched upon the topmost mast;
the fourth soul in the hands of ancient archons passed

and gently flickered, fluttering in the warm night air:
the Feather of a pure white peacock, lean and light;
then the last soul of the dread all-knowing demon passed:
the unmoving Star, the Pole Star, stuck on a white skull.
Black priests in sea-blue robes and flaming headdress tossed
their incense-burners wide and sprinkled the tall ships
and the frenetic dancing crews with the sea's brine
the while they slowly chanted strange hermetic hymns:
"O fearful flame, descend into our pitch-black hearts;

shoot, heavy bow of the sharp mind, shatter our brains;
ship, take us on your prow to far-off foreign strands;
O feather, deathless spirit, lift us high in air,
behold, the unmoving Pole Star points toward the dark cliff!"
As the redeemed great athlete watched the black-skinned mob,
the ardent mouths that moaned, the swollen beaten breasts,
a speechless rage and sorrow rose and choked his throat
although he smiled with sorrow and his white beard gleamed:
"I've been reduced to a god and walk the earth like myth!
O wretched soul of man, you can't stand free on earth
or walk upright unless you walk with fear or hope!
Ah, when will comrade souls like mine come down to earth?"
The double-willed man's heart then cracked and broke in two,
but mended in a lightning-flash again, and the wound closed.

At dawn the sea found him asleep on her wet shore
and dashed him with her foam again, and again asked:
"Mother, what can this monster be that sleeps on stones?
I lick it soft and lap it low, flood it with foam,
and yet it's not a dead swordfish or rotted hull
nor a white-bearded rock that blooms in a deep cave;
it must be an old sea-wolf shipwrecked on my shore."
Odysseus opened his eyes wide and laughed to watch
how the sea rose like Helen with flirtatious eyes
and sunned herself nude on the stones, rolled on the sand
and dug deep hollows on the beach with her small hands.
She stretched out prone and watched with longing her old love
who had remembered her and turned away from land,
that sowlike, dull housekeeper, and now brought her gifts
of his sea-urchin mind, his toughened bones, his flesh.
She watched him sweetly, murmured secret words amid
his thick and hairy thighs, his heels, his white-haired head,
and licked and lapped him with her soft and foaming lips
till the smooth pebbles rattled down her shingled shore.
Odysseus slowly slid his feet up to his knees
in the cool waves, then launched his body like a boat
and with a long swift leap plunged, prow and deck and stern,
and sank in the cool lap of his long-lost belovèd
till his world-wandering loins became refreshed and light.
He spread his hands out wide and floated on his back—
what a long time he'd yearned for just this salt embrace!
Now like a sponge he opened and closed his thirsty flesh
and drank salt water deep, but could not quench his thirst.
What are those withered roses that have lost their scent,
but when they're dipped in water, swell and bloom once more?
Rose of the lone man's body curled on the blue wave!

A breeze swept in from land and puffed, waves turned deep blue,
and in the spreading sea the border-guard's white head
bobbed like a gourd-buoy gently in the morning light.
The sun rose, laughed, and fell upon his nut-brown body,
and the hours dripped like honey on his golden head.
At noon, at length, he waded out, rolled on the beach
till his beard filled with sand, his lips with salty flakes,
and with his briny hands he played with shells and pebbles.
"I'm thirsty! Ah, for a sip of water to cool my heart!"
As he sighed softly thus, two honey-colored calves
moved stumbling down the flowering mountain slopes, and made
straight for the seashore, mooing, dug their snouts in sand,
and when sweet water brimmed the shallow pits, they stretched
with yearning their long gleaming necks and slowly drank.
Odysseus leapt and with his nails dug in the sand
till slowly sweet, clear water bubbled round the rocks
and he, too, fell before the bullocks longingly
and lapped it swiftly with his tongue and filled his bones:
"How beautiful the world!" he cried, and his eyes brimmed;
"Ah, how can the delighted soul decide to leave it ever?"

He turned his head then toward the harbor town with hunger
and set off to find bread, to beg from door to door,
and he recalled himself as a great king when walls
crashed down and castles rocked though he but stretched his hand;
and he recalled a dazzling beach, an emerald cave
where he had seized a goddess by her long blond hair
with his coarse hands and laid her mutely on the ground;
and he recalled how he had stretched his hand one dawn
and launched his ship and left his native land forever
with all its ancient tombs, and vanished down the waves.
His full fist had enjoyed much, brimmed with satiation,
but never had it felt such joy as at this hour;
how good to stand now at a laboring man's low door,
silent and proud, and stretch out a poor beggar's hand!
Day glowed and tinkled like a dancer in all yards
as the world-wanderer, a clay bowl clutched in his hand,
knocked on the village doors adorned with birds and dragons.
Close by, an orchard bloomed where an old gardener stooped
and stroked with tenderness the mane of a bent pine
and pulled it gently down that it might fall with grace
like a large peacock's emerald tail and deck the ground;
with an unpitying love, with gentle stubbornness,
the old man swerved and tamed the wild pine's destiny
until Odysseus marveled at the mystic strife:
"If only by such fondling I could turn the course

of Death!" the lone man thought, watching the old man
battle the dreadful powers with patience and mute joy.
Just such a skillful, pitiless, erotic hand,
he thought, fights with our hearts, and some men call it God,
some Fate and humbly bow, but I call it man's soul
that now has freed itself and takes what shape it wills.
He spoke thus to his mind, breathed deep the heavy scent
of blossomed plots, passed through the district wall by wall
till mocking fate, as though it followed with sharp eyes,
cast him in crooked and expensive lanes of lust.
The sun had set, and rutting males came down in droves
like strong cocks puffing out their glistening feathered chests,
and giggling women waited, row on naked row.
Like shiphead gorgons covered with bright heavy paints,
each stood firm-breasted by her door and laughed as sweat
ran down and thick rouge cracked on their wet cheeks, and dripped.
"Well met, my painted sisters! Your good health and joy!"
Odysseus shouted, right and left, with a wide grin,
but the young hens played shamelessly with his white hair
and the whole district clacked with goading jeers and laughs:
"Welcome to grandpap! Hail to his empty saddle-bags!"
The laughter rolled along the lanes like tumbling stones,
and lone Odysseus felt ashamed, sought where to flee,
like a rhinoceros pecked by myriad goldfinch flocks.
An ancient hag with sagging dugs stood by her door
and held two bursting pomegranates in her hands,
an old, old warrior of love who still could fight
with gallant strife on her worn mattress, old Dame Goody;
and now she ran to help the archer escape the jeers:
"Forgive them, they're still young, old man; youth knows no pity;
here, take these pomegranates to refresh your soul."
Odysseus grasped the fruits as though they were two breasts,
then through the laughter of lust's sacred district swiftly passed.

He walked through virtuous neighborhoods and tossed his hair
to drive away the butterflies that filled his head,
then strolled along the beggar's road with bowl in hand.
A young maid saw him pass and barred her door with haste,
three Negresses pressed by the wall to let him pass,
and he, a monstrous beggar, cast eyes right and left
and chose a house with a low newly whitewashed door
adorned with bridal fetishes in crimson dyes,
on whose stone lintel the fresh wedding wreaths still bloomed.
He leant on the doorjamb and knocked; then clogs were heard,
the joyous tinkling of bronze bracelets filled the yard,
the humble door was slightly opened, and a shrill voice

rang out as the new bride stepped back with fear to see
a tall flame seize her house and lick the buckling roof;
she wanted to cry out again, but the flame lowered
and a calm lion seemed to watch her house benignly.
But as the wretched woman's brains reeled with surprise,
the great beast vanished in the light and an old man
stood in the doorway with his beggar's hand outstretched.
Then the young woman sadly spread her arms and said:
"We haven't cooked today, forgive us; we're poor peasants;
may the good god of beggars show you mercy, grandpap."
But he smiled cunningly and wooed her with mild words:
"Three kinds of charity, small sister, bloom on earth:
the humblest, the most modest, that gives little, are deeds,
for these can nourish flesh and soul but a short time—
they last an hour or two, then from the memory fade.
More hard, more noble is that holy charity
we give, dear sister, when a beggar in our yard
stretches his hand, and a deep voice within us cries:
'Ah, this is I who stand at my own door and beg;
God stands outside my door and cries for charity!'
And though you give no crust of bread nor move your hand,
the beggar is well fed, his heart grows strong, he bows
to worship your kind hand, then knocks on other doors."
The new bride felt afraid and bowed her head toward earth
as her round bosom sweetly ached with new-formed milk,
and her lips, gorged with kisses, quivered in the dark:
"Father, there's but one word I have to give you now:
'God stands outside my door and cries for charity.' "
"Ah, my dear daughter, I'm still hungry; raise your eyes,
my fevered fist is empty still, my cheeks are hollow,
only the third great charity may fill my hunger.
It grabs and brims life full, it goes beyond death even,
it pities and feeds the entire body, it feeds our soul,
it pities and feeds the demons, it even feeds the gods,
for thirst and hunger, bread and water merge in One."
The new bride shrieked with fear and raised her hands on high:
"Grandfather, my knees tremble; leave me now, I beg you,
go to some wealthy house and give your blessing there;
pity me, I've just wed and love my husband only,
and my whole bosom longs to feel my first son's lips."
Flaming Odysseus softly sighed and waved his hands:
"I pity you, maid, that's why I've chosen your low door
and lean against your bridal house to tear it down;
in both my fists I hold and fling into your yard,
like burning coals, the third great charity!"
The woman shrieked with a dread cry, then bared her breasts,

and her words clove her female heart like a sharp sword:
"Take me, ascetic! Neither home nor deeds can hold me;
nor words, nor son I've waited for are now enough;
I'll stand in the sun's blaze erect and hold my long
black hair for fan and with it cool you, my dear love."
The great bread-seeker sighed and squatted on the ground,
looked with compassion on the new-wed bride, and mused:
"My words have struck too deeply, I must take them back."
He made his eyes serene then, hid the holy flame,
looked at the bride with tranquil calm and gently smiled
so that she felt her heart fill with both fruit and flower
until her lips grew sweet again, her slant eyes flashed:
"Grandfather, O my wits went wild as though sun-struck!
I passed through savage lands without one man or water,
without a son or husband clasped tight in my arms;
now I've returned from foreign lands, saved by your grace,
and find my husband's odor, my own home again.
Sit for a moment on my steps; instead of alms
I'll bring you food from Mother's house to brace your soul
for you have saved me from most bitter dread, grandfather."
She spoke, and the god-slayer closed his eyes and heard
her wood clogs on the cobbled street, the tinkle once
again of her bronze bridal rings against his ears
like laughing shingles of the playful sea, like fading thoughts.

Well-fed, toward dusk at length he turned to the dark glen,
passed through a forest of wild cypress trees and pine
about whose trunks and boughs were twined long snakelike vines.
Within a grove a naked maid had given birth
to triple children there, and now with hair unbound
rubbed herself on the trees and danced about their trunks
to make them fertile till they bore a thousand fruits.
Bound to a locust tree, a cow mooed piteously
because they'd taken her new calf, and all the field
lamented with the aching mother's lowing pain;
and as Odysseus saw an old man stroke the cow
he, too, caressed her gently, took a lump of salt
which the young bride had given him, and as the cow
licked it she grew serene and soon forgot her son.
The old man laughed and to the stranger said with scorn:
"What pity to waste good salt! Let her moan all she wants!
So did I also wail the son God snatched away
but, weighed with other cares, I soon forgot him too."
"Old man, another salt consoled you, we're all one,"
the lone man murmured, and then made for the seashore.
The weather cooled as gathering storm clouds brimmed with tears

and lightning flashes flicked on the god-slayer's flesh;
he heard the cocks still crowing on the roofs far off,
frogs croaked amid the marshes and small sparrows turned
and sped home, startled, perching on the swaying boughs;
all smelled a change of weather, a wild rush of rain.
Odysseus stopped and breathed the moist plant-fragrant air,
the autumn wind that plucked the leaves and stripped the trees
till like a spear-thrust he received the first swift drops.
Earth's body cooled profoundly, a blue haze filled the fields,
the smell of soil and rain seeped in his furrowed head
till like a whirlpool he rejoiced for the last time
to feel the tall tree of his body allure the clouds
as shriveled leaves soon tangled in his beard and hair
and his eyes sweetly felt the first rain fall like tears.
But his heart suddenly leapt as a loud cry rang out:
"What do you stand and wait for on the scented soil?
For you no other autumn or first rains shall fall!"
He felt ashamed before the chiding voice, and vowed
to hack down trees at dawn and build his last new ship,
then crawled like an old octopus in a shore cave,
huddled in silence, supperless, and passed the night
with no deceiving dreams to soften his wild mind.
At dawn he went into the woods to choose with skill
his ship's wood, pine and oak and the wild cypress tree.
The tall trunks creaked and groaned like masts in a swift wind,
the clouds hung down like sails, and all the rigging shrieked,
earth turned into a tossing frigate, north winds blew,
and the archer stood straight on the gunwale deck and felt
winds blow from his tall temples as from mountain crags.
Odysseus paced on the slant deck of the whole world
and foreign wares and distant strands rose in his mind—
earth was a trireme brimmed with women, wine, and fish,
with honeybee's soft wax to fill a dead man's lips,
and a black crow flapped on the prow to lead the way.
White swans with ruby eyes rose slowly in his mind,
warm downy reindeer, towering snow, and old man Death
like a white shuffling elephant in the cold night
that lures us on with his small, sweet, and saddened eyes.
Once more the voice rang out, like Death's alluring song,
like a sad crawling cry that rose from icy wastes:
"What do you stand and wait for on the scented soil?
For you no other autumn or first rains shall fall!"
The snowbound athlete swiftly shouldered his sharp ax,
and as he searched the woods and chose from tree to tree,
they all cried out and beckoned with their topmost tips,
for all longed to escape at last and turn to masts:

"Aye, Captain Wind, take us and hew us into masts,
we're bored with patience now, with happiness, with faith,
we long to crash down toward the shore and change our fate!"
The captain heard, but chose the strongest trunks nor showed
the slightest favor, for with ruthless mind he longed
to build a coffin, stout and strong, not an erotic bed.
On the drenched leaves the drops of rain both wept and laughed
and in each drop of rain the sun, too, laughed and wept.
The lone man stopped before the trunk of a huge pine
and saw upon its topmost tip a lean and hungry crow
that perched and shrieked as though it wished to chase away
the lone woodcutter who had raised his shining ax.
"I like this dragon pine and its black fruit of crow,"
the lone man murmured, as he raised his stalwart arms,
but the whole woods resounded as the great pine shook,
and the black fruit on the high boughs yelled furiously:
"Murderous water-ghoul, don't strike! You'll wreck my nest!
If you hack out a cradle, cursed be the son you rock,
if you hack out a plow, cursed be the seed you sow,
if you hack out a ship, may it sink in windless calm
and toss you toward a coast where the sharp reefs shall eat you!
You fool, all trees have souls, and even crows feel pain!"
The crow wailed on, but the ax roared and drowned its shrieks;
at the first wound he gave, the lone man knelt with awe
and slowly sipped the fragrant blood of the old pine
that he might thus become blood-brother with the tree's good ghost.

He hacked away three days to pile wood for his ship,
and the blue sea washed in and out and drowned his mind.
Dear God, to build one's coffin, to heap high the logs,
to come close swiftly to your tomb with each ax-cut,
to carol like a bridegroom blithely, to sink down
together with the sun and swim in the cool sea!
He thought how on sun-haired Calypso's distant isle
he had once swiftly built a ship to reach his home;
how sadly then the goddess sang, sweet, but in vain,
to keep him in her nets, in a god's deathless splendor,
and now, just so, he strove to leave the green-haired earth.
At dusk he caught sea-urchins, fished, and with forked sticks
dug out the fleshy oysters that browsed in the dark weeds;
he roamed along the shores in search of the sea's food,
laid sun-broiled fish in rows in hollows of sea-salt,
uprooted fresh sea-fennel, sat on the dry sand,
an old white elephant, and munched the fat-leaved herbs.
"Sea-urchins, mussels, oysters, help me, O my comrades,"
the lone man shouted as he cast his reed-harpoons.

When he sat cross-legged in the dusk at length, well fed,
then like a dragon-bird with bloody flame-smeared breast
the fiery soul perched on his head and shrieked and sang,
shrieked on and sang intemperately, a springtime finch
that sees her small eggs flashing in the sky's blue depths.
It sang, and all the birds of earth and the mind's passions
kept still to listen with erect enchanted throats;
and Death, who in that hour of dusk came riding out,
heard that untamed and crimson bird, reined in his steed,
and his soul listened for a moment, lost in song.
On other evenings, when his full day's work was done
and the rich fish stew bubbled by the hearthstone fire,
the lone man stretched on weeds and softly hummed a song,
a mocking flutelike tune that wandering gypsies sing
to tease their monkeys into dance at festive fairs.
His memory listened to the hissing tune, and leapt,
a shameless monkey with a red bell-jangling cap,
and danced on its hind legs and mocked the listening gods
while its swart master watched with pride and clapped his hands:
"Whirl on, you old mad hag with painted crimson nails,
mock all you've seen and done, let loose all you remember,
blue, white, and crimson bubbling balls that burst in air!
O heart, I was born yesterday and I shall die today!"

With work, with memory and with mocking, laughing songs
the white sea-eagle passed his days high in his nest
and the beasts came to sniff his traces and to spy;
they crowded close and their eyes shone in the wet leaves,
the monkeys rushed about him screeching, aped his ways,
and when he bent his body and his ax struck hard,
they bent their bodies, too, and helped the old man work.
One day a black lightheaded traveler passed that way,
thrust secretly amid the leaves, and watched with fear
how monkeys, leopards, elephants and weasels ran,
assisting sons, to fetch the old man water, tools,
to open paths and to drag down the heavy logs;
even a bird with crimson wings flew through the sky
and fetched divine flame in its claws, the lightning bolt.
The crack-brained traveler rushed with haste pellmell to town
and told of the great miracle, and all minds shook.
The seashore filled with ghosts and demons; all who passed
closed their pale lips for fear of chewing the shrill sounds,
for they heard laughter and choked wails and piping songs
and the ax striking joyously to trim the craft.
All who passed by at night discerned the ascetic bent
and listening to the murmuring of the frothing surf

as spirits played about him and gleamed as white as foam.
With quivering startled eyes the night beachcombers saw
men, beasts, and spirits toil together to build the ship
as though the whole world suddenly had turned to friends.
The brains of men are always filled with wings and air,
nourished on bubbles always, and well fed with smoke:
alas, no spirits ached for the old man, and beasts
but snarled and left him all alone to fight the woods
with but an ax for comrade, and no other help;
the two alone hacked down the trees and planed them smooth,
the two alone stooped down and roughly hewed the hull
and gave shape to great freedom's final savage wing.
He looked not like a bridegroom but a worm that swayed
its white head right and left, its feet, its hands, its arms,
measured and spun its white cocoon, measured and spun,
until its shroud drained from its heart and twined it tight.
A brave young man took courage once and sidled close:
"They say that beasts and birds with fire at night have helped
you build your holy ship—may all its nails be gold!—
and that ghost-craftsmen rise to aid you from the sea.
They say that water, earth, and air are your familiars
and that you sit enthroned in flames and give commands."
He spoke, then stretched his trembling neck to catch each word,
but the deceiver answered with full brimming throat:
"They say that once Odysseus lived on this frail earth,
they say that once earth, sea, and air existed, too,
they say that Death once came and wiped the whole earth clean!"
The lone man spoke, then laughed until the seashore rang
so that the wretched youth took fright, and his jaws shook,
but as he ran, the slayer's laughter pierced so deep
that the youth's jaw and his teeth slipped his whole life long.
Then in great fear, the black town-dwellers fetched fine gifts
of votive offerings, cool fresh fruit and slaughtered game
to soothe the dragon who had beached upon their shores.
Each morning the pine tree that shaded the sea-cave
glittered with offerings hung each night by secret hands,
and the man-slayer laughed and plucked the tree all day.
Mothers crept close and laid their babies in his tracks
to give them strength, and hunters thrust their bows in sand
that his old feet might tread them till the azure beads
that hung on either end might blaze like piercing eyes
and guide their faultless aim till the prey dropped and died.
As all passed, stooped, along the ascetic's shore and felt
the secret silent powers flow through them in streams,
a hidden joy and trembling coursed along their spines.
One day a fisherman came close with his reed rod,

opened and closed his pale lips thrice, took heart and cried:
"Ascetic, I've a word to say, but don't get angry!
For sixty years I've thrashed and ached on the sea's brine,
my hands are stiff and slashed, my mind's a lump of salt,
I've seen triremes and freighters, arrowy skiffs and rafts;
some seemed like broad sea-turtles, some like sharp swordfish,
some sailed like nautili, and some like dolphins leapt,
but never have I seen a skiff like this you build:
I see a pitch-black coffin rising from its ribs!"
The flame-eyed boatman then with a calm gesture shook
the curled wood shavings from his beard and white mustache
and in the light his sad yet teasing voice was heard:
"Old man, I took a rule and measured my old body,
old man, I took a rule and measured my heart and mind,
I measured earth and sky, I measured fear and love,
the greatest happiness of all, the greatest pain,
and from my measurements, old man, this coffin came."
The fisherman then lowered his brine-eaten face
and shuffled off without a word, trudged down the beach
and searched among the rocks for bait, plucked insects, flies,
and a long slimy worm with which to tempt the eels,
then stooping in a windless cove he cast his bait
and his long line far out to sea, but his mind fished
the ghost-ascetic, his strange words, his bitter laugh.
He felt a mute invisible fisher stooping down
above us all, called Death by some and God by others,
who casts his net and drags us all to his far shore.
His wicker basket is brimmed full of varied bait,
and to each one he casts that lure which each desires—
the mullet longs for urchins, the sea-wolf for herring,
the parrot perch for its own kind, the smelts for flies,
and the male cuttlefish swoons at the female's glow.
We, too, like fishes puff and snap our greedy mouths,
nibble at the sweet bait of women, wine, and wealth,
then flounder with glazed eyes and rush down into Hades.
But as the fisher shook his head, he suddenly leapt,
for his reed shook—a huge fish must have gulped the bait—
and all his dark thoughts sank at once, his sorrows vanished,
his heart pulsed like his line, and his hand reached and tossed
as a red mullet, fat with spawn, writhed in the sun.
Ah, life was very good, his sons would eat that day,
and all the ascetic's flaming words were mouthfuls of hot air.

Toward set of sun the next day as Odysseus stooped
above a hollowed rock and stirred the melted pitch

to smear his hollow hull, trimmed to a coffin's shape,
he suddenly heard broad Kentaur's steps along the sand
and saw him striding down the shore, holding his bellies,
while thick canary feathers flapped upon his back
as he rushed longingly and sniffed at the tar-pit.
His captain spied on Kentaur with a sidelong glance,
then made his voice serene to keep from frightening him:
"Welcome, broad-bottom, welcome greedy-guts, most welcome!
Heigh ho, your nose sniffed out the aromatic tar,
you've cast off earth from your pale chest, worms from your throat,
and rush to pull my oars again and to taste brine!
Dear comrade, my heart shakes and yearns for you, and yet
on this last trip, I can't take even your memory—
I beg you, dear old comrade, don't reach out your hands!"
He spoke with a sad ruthless voice, then raised his eyes:
there on the beach, in a long row, like wounded gulls
with shattered ashen wings, his old companions perched
and gazed at him with small and beady glittering eyes.
But the wild waste's strong lover filled his fists with sand
and flung it fanwise where the brooding shadows sat:
"Scatter, my brothers, vanish from my mind, I beg you!"
But like a squirrel the piper leapt on the ship's prow
and set an airy flute to his pale cobwebbed lips,
then all his friends jumped on the deck and grabbed their oars,
long narrow shadows, till the vessel sailed through air.
Odysseus shut his eyes and felt with longing all
the waves strike at his flesh and beat like throbbing breasts
as in the night air a shrill mournful song arose,
the dark voice of the sea, that great bewitching tune
that cleaves the soul from flesh, crowns it with salt seaweed,
then slowly, gently, draws it toward the sky-blue gardens.
"It's time that the head broke and the world drowned in waves,"
the archer thought, and shuddered, then at once felt sad
that he would soon no longer see or touch, nor plunge
to cool himself within the sea's vast blossomed rose.
He pitied his shrunk body, the earth's great miracle,
on which he'd worked so many years that it might throw
love's five long tentacles around the world, but now
that he had learned to smell, touch, taste, and see, the time
had come for this great wonder to disperse in air.
He clasped his hands about his knees, then cast his eyes
upon the sand and sea like a long grasping net,
and his mind glowed, a rain-drenched mountain peak in sun.
His narrowing glance scooped up a small and spiraled shell
that gleamed on sand like a man's convoluted ear.
Slowly he reached his hand, picked up the little hutch

and marveled at that serpentine frail sheath for hours—
work of a secret love and patience, year on year,
that shaped it gently in the depths of the dark sea.
Ah, how it glowed like mother-of-pearl, like the brain's coils
that gathered every holy sound and strained to hear
a crab or lobster scurry past, a storm that burst
high in the water's infinite ship-battered blaze.
And now, behold, like so much trash the heavy breath
of the strong tide had spewed indifferently on sands
this wondrous seashell wrought with endless toil and care.
The archer pressed the empty shell against his chest
as though he clasped a son, and suddenly, dear God,
a flood poured from the shell and drowned his heart and mind.
Once more the mighty athlete pitied his old body,
pitied his calloused palms, his stiffened wobbly knees,
his feet that roamed the world, his lips that once had kissed,
and his eyes brimmed unwillingly, his dry throat swelled,
for his heart throbbed with pain that day and smelled the grave:
"O heart, erotic bed, where all day, all night long,
that loving couple, Life and Death, clasp tight, and kiss!"
He spoke, then dipped his white head in the sea to cool;
his mind, that great wreathed athlete, cooled then and distilled;
once more he stretched upon the shore and slowly talked
as though both old and new companions swarmed the sands:
"By God, lads, what a thing is man's remembering heart!
Now that dark shades have crushed my lustrous mind
I well recall that white coast where my boat was wrecked
and my crew's corpses sailed supine on waves, and I
was cast headlong upon the rocks and burst in wails:
'I don't want to live now in pain, let the waves eat me;
my heart is crushed with battling both great gods and man—
let me now cross my hands, dear God, and drown in waves!'
Then as I sobbed in my despair for Death to come,
a small, small bird with crimson bill flapped in the sun,
hovered, and perched on a black boulder, wagged its tail,
trilled twice or thrice with mocking glee, then flew away—
O bird, O soaring heart, who fetch a small grain-seed!
At once my exhausted heart leapt up with fortitude,
my entrails brimmed with blood and my bones filled with brain,
I saw the sea before me, the whole earth behind me,
and there, between them, man's soul sang with mocking glee
and on a dry black boulder hopped with blissful joy!"
Thus did the man of whirlpool mind speak to himself,
then rose, without awaiting words or counterwords
and, like the sinking sun, plunged headlong in the sea.
When black night fell at length and wrapped the drowsy world,

the lone man fell asleep, disburdened, cool of heart,
and hung like a grape-cluster high on the tall cliffs of sleep.

Odysseus dreamt that, followed by his leopard cub
as hunting hound, he stalked the woods to track some deer;
the earth grew wider at each step, the world's face changed,
cypress trees bloomed with roses, cedars sprang with lilies,
and all black stones were twined with fragrant jasmine locks.
Animals strolled through woods like hermits, two by two,
birds like pure harmless spirits soared and talked in light
and the hawk stopped and beckoned to the blackbird till
both perched on a fruit-laden vine and pecked at grapes;
the golden sun sat on a green sunflower's stalk
and gazed, love-stricken, at the earth with a coy smile.
When the game-hunter suddenly saw a roe-buck move
amid the shrubs, he knelt and drew his deadly bow
then sank his feathery shaft deep in the downy neck.
The deer sighed like a man, then knelt with buckling knees,
but as the archer rushed and grabbed the long-branched horns,
the wounded animal uplifted his large eyes
that ran with tears like fountains on a shriveled earth
and gazed into the slayer's eyes with mute reproach.
The mighty hunter shuddered and his mind leapt high
like a struck roe-buck that a secret arrow pierced,
and the two brothers gazed and wept in silence long:
"Alas, my arrow missed its aim and struck my heart!"
But as his bitter thoughts still dripped within his heart,
a savage leopard pounced on the stag's steaming flesh
and all at once fierce hunger rose in the archer's mind.
He leapt, and from the leopard's sharp teeth swiftly seized
the deer's fat thigh, then quickly cast it on the hearth
and sat cross-legged on earth and ate it to the bone.
Then as he wiped his beard and thick mustache, he said:
"A great and mighty tiger rules the living world,
I've never chewed before such lean and tasty meat."
He laughed, uprooted then the roe-buck's branching horns
and slowly all things vanished in his toiling mind
till in the black and devastated night alone
two fists shone as they shaped a new, most murderous bow.
When the sun sprang and struck the hunter's laden eyes,
he leapt erect and all his mind's taut bowstring twanged
as though he still held an unseen death-battling bow.
All day the great god-slayer chased the swifting stag
with its large horns that sprouted high within his dreams,
and then returned at dusk with empty hands, and slept,
supperless, but the stag rose in his dreams once more

and slowly, with proud steps, approached the hunter, bent
its neck and with its rough tongue licked the cruel crossed hands.
The archer felt the deer above him, its warm breath,
and did not move his hands for fear the startled stag
would flee once more to sleep's impassable forest crags.
Only his mind still muttered secretly, and pled:
"If you're a demon, help me in my hunt at dawn,
if you're a ghost-filled haunting dream, then scatter far,
for I won't soil my brain with phantoms made of air;
but if, my friend, you're a live deer, I beg you, stay,
don't flee, I need your horns to make a stout new bow—
come, let's embrace like brothers in each other's arms."
He spoke, opened his eyes, but that most sacred stag
vanished, and as he watched the dawning light and mused
where he might go to flush the mighty stag, he glanced
at the great pine where every dawn the people hung
their gifts, and there discerned a giant stag's sharp horns.
He rushed with rage for fear they'd disappear again
like ghosts, but his fists grabbed and filled with longed-for horns
that dripped with thick blood still and splattered lumps of brain.
The archer leapt with joy, for this sure sign that came
from the deep seashores of his dreams seemed a good omen;
then he sat cross-legged on the sand, and with strong hands
toiled hard and wrought with patient skill to shape a firm new bow.

As he worked on he heard a sea-chant close at hand,
and when he turned his eyes he saw bronzed fishermen
hauling their nets along the beach, gleaming in sun,
lightening their toil and troubles with their rhythmic song.
They grasped each knot and slowly dragged the net ashore,
strove on until their rousing song turned to a sigh,
and the old athlete felt a deep ache in his chest
as though he, too, were dragging the long net from far.
The fish-scales flashed like silver, the net dripped with foam,
and fishes floundered in the sun with goggling eyes
till the shore smelled and the poor fishers, hungry, tired,
lay down or built a fire and strung the fish on reeds,
then rubbed their hands and laughed to see their work well paid,
for seven souls had toiled and seven homes would eat.
A slender virgin-lad with flaming fawnlike eyes
raised his slim-fingered hands toward the clear sky and said:
"Blessed be the grace of God, our one eternal Father!
It's He who from His love created fish and sea,
it's He who brims our nets and fills our hearts with joy;
O comrades, raise your hands on high and cry, 'Our Father!' "
They raised their calloused hands that still dripped with the sea

and sweetest exclamations chimed on warbling shores.
A deep and tranquil joy poured in the young lad's face:
"Dear brothers, all our hearts grow sweet, and the earth's changed.
Our bodies now feed well on a dry crust of bread;
one good word said, and all our pains fade far away;
the black earth changes her grim face; like a large nest
it hatches in the sun serenely, shines at night
as small unnumbered bird-beaks open round its rim
with hunger, point up toward the sky and call their Father.
Earth is our path, and the blue sky our destined home
which we've set out to reach like brothers by nightfall.
Courage, my brothers, I feel the sky will open soon!"
But a fierce stalwart fisherman with a square chin
frowned with frenetic brows and clenched his angry fists:
"On this earth, brothers, black injustice still rules all,
the good still starve on whorish earth, the evil thrive;
at night when I can't sleep I step in my dark yard
and the stars seem like flames that burn within my head:
'Ah, sword-sharp spirits,' I moan, 'it's time you came to earth!' "
Then the sweet voice of the lad who fished for souls arose:
"The spirits indeed have come, my brother, and walk the earth
but carry no flame in heart, no flashing sword in hand;
they open their arms wide, kind words sail on their lips,
for only thus, with love, shall earth merge with the sky."
But the young man's impetuous heart still raced and seethed:
"Words without weapons, friend, can never dare to fight
the two-edged sword of cruel injustice, and win through.
I also like kind words, but with sharp sword in hand!"
Once more the quiet voice was heard in sad reproach:
"Though we've lived long together, you don't know me, friend."
He ceased, then laid his young head sadly on the sand,
and an old fisher tried to reconcile both sides:
"Brothers, I think no soul may step in our Lord's house
unless he holds his good deeds like a cutting sword;
knock on the mighty landlord's door with your good blade
and he must rise to open, whether he would or not!"
But once again the sweet voice rose as the waves hushed:
"I'll tell you in a myth of my heart's pain, my brothers,
for though the strongest thoughts may fade and kingdoms vanish,
the myth can never fade or vanish from men's minds.
One day a mighty hermit died within his cave
and fiercely rose toward heaven, grasping in his hand
the good deeds of his holy life like a long sword
and, like an owner, banged upon his Father's door.
'Who knocks with so much boldness on my castle door?'
'Open! It's I, the great ascetic, that pounds your door!'

'What beneficial acts or good deeds have you done
that you come pounding on my door with your long sword?'
'I've followed your strait path, obeyed all your commands,
I've never sinned with wicked word or evil deed,
I've fed the hungry, cast my wealth to those in want,
I've not touched wine or women, all night long I've raised
my hands high to your holy heaven and cried, "My Father!"
My good deeds now are this long sword with which I knock.'
But the locked castle rang with mocking laughs and gibes:
'O foolish saint, all your good charities and deeds
can never pay me back for those two lustrous eyes
I deigned to give you once to gaze on the green world.
If you should cross the flashing threshold of my door,
you'll owe it to my holy grace and my good nature!' "
The pale lips smiled, and then in sadness shut again,
but the impetuous youth struck back with bitterness:
"Well, lads, let's cut our hands off then, they're of no use!
Our good and evil deeds are both of no account!
Rudderless, pilotless, we're tossed on a wild sea.
No, God is not a father, he's a fierce sea-wolf,
and we're his crew! Woe to the hands that don't know how
to rig the difficult sails with skill or pull the oars!"
He was still talking when a shadow crossed the sand
as the freed athlete quickly stalked to the sea's rim,
his newly relished bow slung on his shoulder still.
His ship gleamed on the waters as a smooth wind rose
and he rushed down to hoist the sail, for in his teeth
he held the earth like a green leaf and said farewell.
Among the fishermen he saw the slim lad glow
like a black swan who sings with upright saddened throat:
"Your word's a bitter knife, my friend, that wounds my heart.
Woe to that man who clings to earth, who dares to judge
injustice, hunger, cares, with but the brains of man!
Don't place your trust in your dull mud-created eyes;
neither slave galleys, chains, nor hunger, nor cruel swords
can touch one soul that stands erect and looks toward heaven;
let our flesh rot and fade, but let our souls be saved,
let our feet mold in earth that they may dance forever."
Disturbed by this strange answer, the fierce youth replied:
"If an unjust and lawless man should strike me hard
on my right cheek, what is my duty then, O fool?"
"O then, my brother, turn your other cheek, and smile."
The archer listened, and his heart with terror shook;
he'd never heard on earth before so sweet a voice,
but his mind mocked, denied those gentle words, and mused:
"His lips are skillful artisans that weave words well,

but if I raise my hand, he too will leap with wrath
and raise his small hand to revenge his pain and shame,
and all his cloying words will vanish down the wind."
He crept behind the youth, then raised his hand and struck
the unsuspecting lad hard on his tingling cheek
as all the friends jumped to their feet with growling rage—
but the young fisher smiled and turned his other cheek:
"O white-haired brother, strike again to ease your heart!"
But the sun-archer's shriveled hand hung down with shame:
"Forgive me, friend, I longed to measure your strange mind,
to cast my plumb line and find out what depths you sail.
The seas you sail are fathomless! O pilot, hail!"
He spoke, then deeply moved, sat by the black swan's side in silence.

The old sun drowned at length in the blood-splattered sea
and the great sower stalked the sky and cast fistfuls
of stars in night's black furrows, and all sprouted, bloomed,
till light at daybreak came and swiftly gleaned them all.
The two still sat upon the beach, sunk deep in thought;
the boy forgot his mother who wept for him at home,
and the old man his ship and the fair wind that blew
and listened to the world's last voice with deep repose.
The Morning Star pulsed in the heavens, a flaming heart,
the ground was flecked with crystal flakes, the weeds with frost,
but slowly the sun strengthened as its light poured down
from tall crags like a river and drowned all the plains
till the sea raised her hands toward her first ancient love.
Odysseus placed his hand upon the young lad's shoulder
with a light touch, as though he feared to crush his bones:
"To think I hastened with swift pace to leave the world!
Time passes now, the North Wind blows, my swift ship leaps,
but yet I keep my passion reined and can't drink deep
enough of your strange words that herald love and peace.
I fought on earth, the zigzag path I took was drenched
in blood, I conquered till my backbone glowed with light,
and now I hoist red sails to keep my tryst with Death,
for he who still has hope puts his great soul to shame;
yet I rejoice that suddenly a nightingale
saw me traverse this shore and sang to say farewell."
The young lad sadly leant on the god-slayer's breast:
"The words you utter, brother, are most sad, most proud;
how can one man alone save his soul here on earth
unless all souls are saved together in all the world?
If one babe starves on earth, all of us die of hunger;
if one at the world's ends should raise his hands to slay,
we have all raised our hands, and we're all slayers too;

we're all twined in one root, we blossom in one soul.
Forgive me, brother, if my words now form a myth."
With gentleness the archer clasped the god-struck boy:
"Tell me your myth that the whole world may turn to myth."
The young boy smiled and with his sweet voice softly said:
"They say that once when a great king gave up his ghost
and his soul rose, he knocked on the Immortal's door.
'Who pounds my door?' God shouted. 'I,' the king replied.
'There is no room in Paradise for two,' God growled.
The king returned to earth once more where year on year
he lived like an ascetic, strove to save his soul,
then rose to heaven once more and beat upon God's door.
'Who pounds my door?' God cried. 'It's I,' the old king yelled.
'Descend to earth,' the voice roared, 'here is no room for two!'
He plunged to earth once more, strove for ten thousand years,
moaned 'Ah!' and 'Ah!' for the hard stone to blossom too,
then once again the old king took the sky's blue slope,
stood quivering by the sacred door, and softly knocked.
'Who knocks?' 'Father, it's You who knock on your own door.'
At once God's door gaped wide and the two merged in One!"
The archer for a moment stood in silent thought;
though the boy's voice was sweet, it could not dull his mind,
for his thought flashed on Margaro's most fragrant plot
and he recalled the cruel word he had planted there,
then gazed without compassion on the warbling mouth:
"And this last One, this One is also empty air."
But unperturbed, the tender fisher softly smiled:
"Body and mind, both land and sea, are smoke and air,
only this final One still lives and reigns as God,
as the pure soul that broods on the world's sacred egg."
Odysseus cast his glance on the god-taken eyes,
large, waveless, without depth, certain of victory,
and felt they might one day, after much ardent rage,
after much singing strength, force chaos to assume
the tender face of God and rise up toward the sun.
But he still liked to goad the new soul like a tempter:
"Man has his body only, a flask filled with sweat
that glows like phosphorus softly in the endless night;
I bow to its great grace, it flames and fades like lightning."
Startled, the gentle boy then touched the old man's knees:
"The body's but a bridge for souls to pass through chaos;
dear friend, do not blaspheme, do not think thoughts of sin;
worms, when they love the rose, change into butterflies."
The archer ceased, and gazed into the boy's large eyes
as his mind tossed like sails struck by opposing winds;
he then caressed the virgin hair and slender back:

"How may a heart that never loved seductive flesh
speak of the spirit or dare to judge the chastened soul?"
The boy felt shamed and dropped his head, but his voice rose:
"Only he who has never touched the bait of flesh
may speak of spirit, brother, or rule the chastened soul,
for then his heart fears not the earth's seductive wiles."
Then that despairing form, that freed mind, that strong heart,
the bold death-archer, jumped to his feet and touched the youth:
"You've made my last hours here on earth both blessed and good;
your song is good, my friend, and it's refreshed my mind,
but I've no time to stand and listen to your tunes
for the fair wind of last farewell looms now, and blows.
May you fare well! Let us each take his own road now;
good are your words of love, but my mind walks the earth
with a bold stride, alone, and has no need of balms,
a wasteful wax that burns and lights not one man's path!"
Then the boy's gentle voice was heard with a sweet sadness:
"I pity souls that live and die far from their God."
"And I, too, pity both the soul and flesh of man,
and all the earth, our wretched mother, and God the father;
I pity them all and sing, I pass, and they pass with me.
My brains have filled with knowledge, my wide hands with deeds,
and to this day my heart's remained bold, joyous, warm,
and loves all things, both life and death, but with no trust.
The festival has ended now, the feast is over,
the wind but etched my name on sand in passing haste
and left but one fruit in my hands as my life's loot—
open your hands, my brother, take it for parting gift."
The young lad cupped his hands and stooped, as though he bent
to fill his palms with water from a cooling brook,
and the old man stooped and laughed, then proudly cast his word:
"That man is free who strives on earth with not one hope!"
He ceased awhile, as though he'd sunk in a dark fog,
but raised his head again, and his mind filled with sun:
"I've seen and loved much on this earth, I've gleaned sweet hopes,
and sorrows, too, I've harvested the mighty gods;
the frigate of my heart brims full and hoists its sails!"
He spoke, then raised his hand and said his last farewell:
"You love that giddy golden finch, the soul of man,
that's caught in the lime twigs of flesh and flaps its wings
high toward the empty air-brained sky and strives to flee,
but I love man's sad flesh, his mind, his stench, his teeth,
the mud-soaked loam I tread upon, the sweat I spout,
but best of all that dreadful hush when war has ceased.
Farewell! Our meeting was most good, and good your words,
but better still this parting which will last forever."

The young lad clasped the old man, and his downy eyes
streamed with tears down his cheeks like a new-wounded fawn:
"God is compassionate and great, and he can save
at the last hour that soul that does not want salvation."
He spoke, then bent his head and slowly dwindled down the shore.

Then the slaked white-haired athlete seized in his strong arms
his small skiff like a girl and thrust it in the waves;
he slung his bow across his back, hung round his neck
his tinder and his precious double flints for fire,
then plundered the great pine of all its useful gifts.
As he braced strongly with his feet to launch from earth,
he suddenly heard a swift crunch on the sands behind him
and, turning, saw an old hag, painted to the gills,
running, her apron filled with pomegranate fruit.
His heart rejoiced to see Dame Goody, that old whore,
stand laughing by his side, opening her fruit-filled apron
to give him pomegranates in a last farewell.
Odysseus seized the crimson fruit with deep desire
until his cool fists felt refreshed and his eyes brimmed:
"Ah, dear Dame Goody, I never hoped for such good treasure!"
The dame of night-doors smiled with mirth and her eyes glowed:
"One day I heard you shouting by yourself, alone,
talking with spirits, and my soul pained for you then;
my dear, I've plucked my garden bare of fruit for you!"
Profoundly in his mind Odysseus laughed and thought:
"Ah, how I love this last gift which earth hands me now!"
He gently touched the thin knees of the much-kissed whore:
"Dame Goody, if a god exists to pay a man's good deeds,
he'll sit you throned on high beside his greatest warriors,
for from the casement loopholes of your sentry-box
you've cast long looks like spears and wounded passers-by
who stood alone and brooded on their many cares,
how life is short and fades, nevermore to return;
and when they had well weighed all things outside your door,
they knocked, and drowned with your soft arms in Lethe's flower,
while you, in your wide holy bed, held gallantly
the tough ramparts entrusted you in this great war.
O limping, white-haired, one-toothed, gallant warrior,
you've fought in the great fight and come close to your goal.
Your health, dear friend! The fruit is good! Hail and farewell!"
The old recruit of kisses heard her praises told,
and her loins filled with joy, her sagging dugs grew firm,
her long life glittered like a pomegranate tree,
her bed clashed like a war-shield in the strife of love,
like a young girl she danced among her garden blooms

and all the contours of her face glowed with love's flame.
Odysseus leapt into his skiff, a youth renewed,
cast in his hold the pomegranates like old friends,
gripped all the landscape with his reaching glance, then loosed
his mind's five tentacles and fondled all the earth.
An octopus in rut who flings a tentacle
on his unmoving mate with slowly sucking pores,
then draws it softly back and casts another arm
and strokes her mutely in the depths for hour on hour—
thus did the dying man's long mind reach out to stroke
the earth with all his smell, his touch, his taste, to clasp
her tightly in his arms and speak his last farewell.
The sun sank, and the face of widowed earth grew dark
as though she wept because her lover was now leaving;
the shore sank, and the wounded light fought gallantly
on the tall peaks until it fell to night's assault.
The archer of the sun watched the world slowly fade,
and after many moons had passed above his head
and he was sailing through the world's vast hopeless snows,
he quite forgot that earth had passed from his glazed eyes,
and but one scene remained deep in his memory's pit:
once when he had skimmed close along some looming cliffs,
it darkened, all the silver-smoking waters dulled,
and as he looked high at the crags with head upturned
he suddenly felt thick drops of honey strike his lips.
He licked his mouth, then cupped his hands against his eyes,
for high in a deep hollow by some wild fig trees
he saw an ungleaned honeycomb of monstrous size
that hung above the waste sea, slowly melting drop
by drop, hushed, useless, fading in the dark abyss of night.

XXII

O Virtue, precious and light-sleeping daughter of man,
how you rejoice when, all alone, biting your lips,
poor, persecuted, thrust into the desolate wastes,
you find no friend on whom to cling, no straw to clutch,
for there no souls crowd round to marvel at your grace,
no gods are there for whose dear sake you fling your lance,
yet upright, silent, you fight in the wild wastes and know
you'll never win, but battle only for your own sake.
Rise high, O Virtue, gaze now on that white-haired head
with its despairing brilliant brain that sails and plays
its gleaming tentacles like a frail nautilus.
Joy, sorrow, life and death blow through his tossing heart
like four swift winds and drive his flesh and mind down toward
the plunging cliff, two lovers clasped in tight embrace.
He's harvested the sea and all the joys of earth,
he's plucked their flower whose honeyed poisons choke the heart
and hung it on his ear, then sung and strolled toward Death.
If earth had mind, it would rejoice, if fate had eyes
it would embrace this old and mighty warrior, touch
with fear and admiration his deep wounds and clutch
him tight so that it, too, might not descend to Hades.
All stones would burst in threnody, all trees would wail,
all beasts would snarl and raise their paws to pounce on Death,
and the most lustrous maids would strip their bodies bare
to lure Death on so that upon the downy daze
of their sweet breasts he might forget that holy head.
But earth is stupid and fate purblind; both have sent
that mighty lighthouse, that great sleepless brain to die
unwept and unprotected in the frozen wastes.
The sun like a gold quoit sped down the heaven's road,
and the round silver moon rose like a dead man's mask
and covered the pale tranquil face of the brain-archer.
He sailed in his light coffin all day, all night long,
and the whole sky and sea stretched taut like a curved bow
against his hoary-haired swift-dying chest until
he felt his skiff between them speed like a swift arrow.

Above his white head seagulls slowly rowed and sailed
a day or two, but then grew tired and swerved back;
a lean sea-eagle wove him wreaths in air all day,
perched like a sleepless ship's boy on his mast all night,
but on the seventh day it, too, grew weary and flew away.
Two sharp-nosed frothing sharks followed like hungry dogs,
opened and closed their gleaming teeth with longing greed,
but when they lost all hope of food, they plunged away.
"Farewell! Turn to your prey, I'm not yet food for sharks,"
the boatman mocked, and cast off fish and birds like old
soiled clothes, and breathed the crystal solitude, stripped bare.
At times birds passed above him, smeared with sweetest scent,
and their sharp claw-tips dripped with musk and the air flashed
like a cock-pheasant's feathers, gold and crimson wings.
At times a feather fell upon his foam-washed deck,
but the quick-handed man flung it upon the waves:
"Farewell, O wings and fragrances, ideas, dreams,
farewell O multicolored precious filigrees of air!"

His lone heart played and beat profoundly, his eyes flashed,
his mind flew back and forth in the vast solitude
like a swift eagle, and space sank, and time was conquered,
and all his oldest joys shone in an instant flash
until his heaving and unheaving heart could not
recall such great untrammeled joy, such lofty flight.
Sweet, very sweet had been his dread on that first night
when in the dark he'd laid his hand on a maid's body;
how like a hawk he'd shrieked, how all the world had sighed
when in his arms he'd held a son for the first time!
And then that third dread shriek when on a distant plain
he'd held on high his foe's slain head for the first time!—
but no past joy could match the joy that filled him here!
Astride his coffin now he dashed toward his great host,
grim Death and his spread feast, and in his hand he held
as gift, wrapped in fresh grapevine leaves, his own white head.
In that black whirlpool hour of parting when the soul
clutches the body in great fear and won't let go,
the lone man's savage heart quailed not, his mind shook not,
but in the just scales of his inner pride he weighed
his soul well, wing and claw, and found it was not wanting.
His mind between his temples swelled like a red rose
brimming with drops of crystal dew and honeybees,
and now he rode toward the Unknown's great portal, there
to lean his large and sated brow and call that huge
and black-striped yellow wasp to plunder all his honey.
An old, old marriage song now tingled on his lips

that his old nurse had sung thousands of years ago
when as a lad he'd broken spears with clay toy gods;
now it returned and took new strength within his mind:
"One day a brave young man set out to get engaged
but neither did he change his clothes nor zone his belt,
and left his sword deserted on the wall to rust;
nor did he turn to Starbrow, his swift-footed mare,
to stroke her long and silky mane and say goodbye.
His mother stood on her worn threshold and cried out:
'My son, put on your wedding cloak and zone your belt,
don't startle your new bride, don't shame your father-in-law,
go fill your purse with gold and give alms to the poor.'
'There where I go to get engaged, now, Mother dear,
no one will ask about my clothes or crimson belts,
the poor there do not long for gold, for all are lords,
their wine is an abyss, their sheep unnumbered stones,
the bride lies in her bridal bed and has no eyes.' "
Thus did the old betrothed man sing, and sailed his skiff
upon a thick and desolate sea that slowly seethed
and smelled of fragrance like white-blossomed almond trees.
About a rock toward evening in the open sea
he saw a swarm of sharks cut through the frothing waves
tumultuously with gaping jaws and saw-sharp teeth.
The dying bridegroom laughed and hailed his savage friends:
"Welcome, thrice welcome, bidden guests with your large teeth;
I'll strew fine food on foam for you to gobble soon!"
But all at once he uttered a hoarse cry, for all
the sharks were dashing through love's ring for their own joy:
nine bridegrooms there were chasing one lone bride, nine jaws
gaped frenziedly and churned the waves with frothing blood,
but the white bride, indifferent and alone, swam on,
awaiting the strong conqueror to make her deathless.
The lone man stooped and watched the foam-washed wedding pomp:
the silent bridegrooms fought to death in roaring waters
till all the waves were rimmed with hems of frothing blood;
the lead shark suddenly swerved, trailing long streams of blood,
then others swerved with gaping wounds, and plunged away,
till only the last, strongest, remained, with tail erect.
Watching the conqueror come, the female spread her fins,
approached, then brushed his belly with a light caress,
skimmed off, and swerved close once again to arouse the male
who floundered still amid the blood to cleanse his wounds.
"Your health, my brother! You've paid well for female wiles!
O bridegroom, may the blue sea grant that not one drop
of sperm from your male savage sack may lose its strength,

and may these blood-drenched waters brim with baby sharks;
thus in my own swift passing may I leave my savage sperm!"

The lone man spoke, then as the North Wind gently blew,
he seized the tiller, raised his head and saw night fall
and pour down in a black mist while the scattered stars
shone like far burning castles in the sweep of night.
Luminous flashing skates and phosphorescent fish
flame-quivered in the waves as all night long there rolled
the two profound vast rivers which surround the world:
the lecherous and night-wandering sky with its fish-swarms
that in deep silence pastures its unnumbered smelt,
and the vast sea with clustered stars of sperm and milt.
The waters gleamed with silver scales, all of night's heart
was fragrant as a nutmeg tree the dew had drenched,
and every dawn the armored sun slashed the horizon
like an impassioned warrior with great force, then rose
and climbed the desolate sky, gazed on the desolate waves
like a lead ram that plods on though its flock is lost.
One dawn Odysseus leapt erect and cocked his ears
for he had heard a most sweet sound rise, deep and choked,
from the profoundly green sea's dark and tranquil depths;
he leant his ear against the deck and heard his skiff
and the waves quivering like a lyre's impassioned strings,
and then he closed his eyes, and his mind spilled in waves,
for he had never heard so sweet a siren before,
as though the sea were a ripe maid who on stone shores
sat weaving for her lover, singing old love songs
while her cool arms, that in the wastes sighed uncaressed,
swayed upright till they turned rose at their fingertips.
The skiff seethed suddenly and tossed, a great roar rose,
and as the archer leapt erect he turned and saw
a rushing, tumbling river of fish that swept the sea.
The frothing waters boiled like caldrons of fish stew,
and the mute fish, streaming together in thick swarms,
rubbed silver scale on scale till sweet sounds filled the air,
and as the lone man heard the fish's threnody
he shook to his heart's root with overflowing joy:
"I've said, and say again—I've no quarrel with the world,
and if the mind, at my last breath, grow suddenly weak
and start to curse, don't listen, Life, the wretch is mad;
may you be blessed with all your laughter, all your tears!
Ah, could I mount in sun a thousand, thousand times,
I'd start the pitiless ascent once more, O Life,
the wails, the wars with wily gods and stupid men.

I'd wait for the love-pointing star to shine, I'd start
once more the night-embracements on the dewy grass.
I turn and gaze on all I've done or joyed on earth:
O Life, your sweetness is so great that if but one
drop more should fall, I'd lose my pride and burst in tears!"
The lone man thus, with no vain boasts or weak reproach,
sped swiftly toward the South to keep his tryst with Death,
and his desires fell mutely on the waves and drowned
like lovesick girls for whom the world seems too confined.
The sea grew more serene and spread like mother-of-pearl
which dolphins ripped through now and then, but still it healed
and thickly poured with graceful tints of oyster shell.
One day at afterglow when the waves rolled serene,
rose-leaved and violet-misted in the cooling dusk,
the sharp world-wandering man's unfailing eyes caught sight
of some low-spreading rose isles made of coral stone.
No huts rose on the shore, no smoke rose through the trees
as the skiff drifted unconcerned toward those round disks
of the waste sea with their coarse sand and brackish water.
A few scant date trees darkly gleamed in the afterglow
with amber light, long-leaved amid their sword-sharp boughs,
and from the clefts of coral rock that steamed with heat
thick shaggy crabs and sluggish turtles rose and fell.
As the archer rowed by slowly down the shores, he saw
old sunken ruined cities, mortar-bound huge blocks,
and armor of a moss-green, rust-corroded bronze.
In row on row still stood, or fallen flat, the old
blind hulking gods hewn roughly from huge ancient logs,
within whose monstrous ears at night the bats gave suck
to their small fuzzy babes, and coarse-haired spiders hung
in empty nostrils and the eyes' black moldering pits.
Cracked and in ruins, the deathless lepers stood by waves
as vines twined round their thighs and rotted their black knees;
their eyes had fallen, their teeth had spilled on coral sand,
and now they spread their fingerless and crippled hands
in hopes a passing ship might see them and give alms.
But the god-slayer shook his head and curled his lips
and without pity passed the humped and leprous gods:
"Dark demons, we have suffered much in your vast hands
but now our turn has come to glean our glad revenge.
Smite without pity, soul! O hammer on anvil, strike!"
He spoke, and his harsh laughter shook the seas as from
the deep heart of a dazzling mist the full moon rose,
a huge and lustrous pearl wedged in its oyster shell,
and the wreathed athlete slowly slid within a glittering fog.

The days passed by and stroked the sea with downy touch,
their plucked and gaudy feathers fell upon the waves
as they stripped off their golden bracelets and red cloaks
and drifted by in long straight rows like pallid crones.
Musk-scents evaporated, waters turned opaque,
the melancholy sun hung in a boundless mist,
cloud forms of air sailed swiftly in a whitening dome
and a swift secret shivering swept the sea and sky.
The mists slide stealthily within our own hearts, too,
which are not made of stone, alas, but of soft flesh
more tender than our lips, and ache as soon as touched,
and stifle if a shade but falls, and break in tears.
The archer's heart in those wild wastes began to shake,
he sat unmoving by the rudder, clenched his teeth,
and grimly chased away his memories and sweet joys
for fear they'd find the secret gate to his hid heart.
His mind raked up a thousand tricks to see him through,
and once when the low sun spilled on the waves like wine
in that sad twilit hour when even God recoils,
a song of his old life leapt in his heart until
the archer's pride rose with its manly yet sad song:
"Our fishing boat, that tramp, sails one day here, one there,
and I shall sing a gallant song, my rowers all,
until your arms sprout boughs, until your minds turn oak!
A mighty king sat high within his seashore tower
and wore a golden crown; he drank and heard his heart
laughing like shingles of the sea in his glad breast
till his gold crown fell in the waves and disappeared.
Then the king's laughter ceased, for cobwebs filled his heart,
and he sent heralds through the world on horse and foot:
'Listen, all lands and seas, these are the king's commands:
He who will plunge in the sea's depths and fetch my crown
shall wed my only daughter as his high reward
and be my only heir, and king of all the world!'
The king cried out, and lands and seas roared in acclaim
for a brave youth rose up to take the deep sea plunge
and slowly stripped till he stood nude on a high rock.
Neither a golden crown nor a sweet princess shone
within his manly mind that scorned to seek reward,
and as he bid the world farewell, a voice rang out:
'Why do you plunge toward death, brave youth? Open your eyes!
You'll not rejoice in a girl's arms or golden crown!'
'I know that in the sea's dark depths I shall not find
a crown, a king or a king's daughter, not one god
to marvel at my pure and disinterested deed;
souls may be sure of golden crowns only in death;

but even so, if rewards were there, I swear that I
would never take the plunge toward death with such great joy.
Farewell, O earth, for you were worthy to bring forth
souls brave enough to do great deeds with no false bait!' "
As the archer sang in the wastelands, his heart grew bold;
ah, had he but a thousand lives, a thousand crowns,
he'd throw them all into the sea, then strip and dive!
He sped down swiftly through the waters, holding Death
like a curled rose, and deeply smelled its bittersweet,
intoxicating fragrance as his moved mind swooned with joy.

One night a strong wind blew, the clouds piled in great heaps,
the sea and sky merged into one, and the keel sighed.
Unsleeping all night long, the lone man fought the winds
until at dawn he barely saw through frenzied storm
two dragons loom before him, two rough roaring peaks
whose ridges he felt quake and crack as he drew close.
He gripped his tiller proudly, and his brave chest swelled,
for he knew these were Yes and No, Death's mountain peaks
that loomed at the world's end, that gaped and closed and smashed
all ships which dared to pass beyond the world's last bounds.
He heard shrill cries, spirits that croaked like greedy birds
and had a hawk's cruel claws and scabrous female dugs.
Kneeling, he seized the tiller tight in his right hand,
pulled at the sail's rough rope with his left hand and fought
with silent courage, open-eyed, to reach and pass
safely at this dread moment mankind's last confines.
He heard one shrieking mountain rage and roar out "No!"
but "Yes!" the other answered in a tranquil hush.
At last he skimmed his craft along a windless peak,
and as his red sail passed beneath rough hanging crags
the mountains swayed with massive flocks of swirling birds.
The wild-game hunter laughed until the waves resounded:
"Oho! the dread scarecrow that guards man's last confines
is but a tranquil mountain of white eggs and birds!"
He pushed and slid his coffin in a pearly cave,
tied it with a rough hawser, climbed the craggy rocks
and took with him his piercing arrows and long bow,
for the birds swooped and shrieked till the rocks seemed to shake.
Climbing on high with back bent low, he joyed to hear
the mountain slopes resound and flutter right and left
as though his shoulders sprouted with tumultuous wings;
eggs glittered in black hollows, the rocks smiled serenely,
and all the promontory moaned like lovesick doves.
The white-haired archer mounted still with bloody feet,
and when he reached a barren peak and turned eyes south,

his heart like a sea-eagle flapped its wings and shrieked:
before him spread an endless, mastless, sterile sea.
A freezing fierce wind blew, the sun hung in a mist,
and the great athlete's jaws began to shake with cold;
but as he searched for twigs to build a warming fire,
thick hail burst on the crags with a tumultuous roar
till his unbridled and rebellious head rang out
like a rough boulder in the harsh and pelting hail;
but he stood upright, growled, and mocked his barren head:
"Hey, white pate, blockhead, how much longer in this world
will the rains drench you, the snows freeze you, the suns scorch you?
You've turned thick hide and stone! Haven't you had enough?"
When the huge hailstones ceased, the sun once more appeared,
and the quick-handed archer built a fire, stretched his bow,
brought down thick flights of birds, strung them along his hearth,
and when he'd eaten, he stuffed his apron full of eggs,
then clambered down the crags, stretched on his coffin, crossed
his hands, and gave himself to a light death, to sleep.
When he awoke toward dawn and saw the maidenhair,
the swift rock-swallows cooing lovingly with joy,
the pale cool light and honeyed sweetness all about him,
he shook to think he'd sailed into the land of myth.
His thoughts had fluttered far off to Calypso's cave,
and hour by hour he waited for that sun-blond head,
that firm immortal form to flash deep in the shade,
but her bright head seemed long in coming, and his thoughts thrust
in other deep cool caves, on other azure shores,
like a sea-bug that crawls and fumbles in rock clefts.
Slowly his brain distilled, his thoughts fell into place,
and then the lone man yelled with joy amid the rocks
for now he knew he liked much better than all joys,
than even the act of love, to roam at the world's end,
to light huge fires upon the guardian dragon's peak
and gather eggs on its man-eating dark abyss.
When the cool weather cleared, the archer rigged his sail,
loaded his coffin with the loot of birds and eggs,
then laughed with joy and cried farewell to the world's last frontiers.

He left behind bounds of the possible, all joys
of man, and thrust into a virgin sea where no
ship passed, no pilot soul had crossed her shoulder blades.
Ash-colored seabirds swirled and cawed about his mast
to marvel at this new swordfish with double fins
and the red upright wing that swelled in the cold wind.
At night in the man-murdering soul of the wild wastes,
as the blind boatman spread his pincers gropingly

on the dark waves, he felt the touch of shaggy claws.
"The sure reward of him who finds new roads is death!
My soul, don't cast your eyes about, don't cock your ears,
don't seek companions now, you've cut off from the herd;
cling tight, O soul, to the pure breath of solitude."
As the black current strengthened and the pointed prow
skimmed swiftly, frothing southward with no oars or wind,
Odysseus shuddered one cold dawn, for in his mind
the swift thought flashed: this was no current or plain sea
but an unleashed mute whirlpool that now swirled toward death.
"Ahoy, my gallant soul; don't whimper, swift-eyed girl;
life's but a song, sing it before your throat is cut!"
The pallid sun-cock rose with plucked and molted wings,
and as it slowly crawled and limped on the sky's rim
the archer gazed at his old friend with grief and mocked:
"One day amid my flocks I saw my stalwart ram
tup row on row of buxom ewes and then, drained dry,
crawl quivering with shrunk bags beneath a fig tree's shade.
O sun, you've also tupped a thousand shores and seas
and now stand shivering in the shadows with shorn hide!"
But all at once his laughter ceased, he cocked his ears,
for a deep bellow crushed the tempest-churning waves,
and the swift-dying man leapt up and thought he'd reached
the sacred pit of doom at last, the killer's mouth.
He cupped his hand against the sun and saw the waves
far off flash silver as they swelled and seethed with foam
while all about them flocks of savage seabirds swirled.
"Dear God, the wonders of the world are without end!"
He had not finished speaking, held in wonder still,
when a swift whirlwind of fish seethed and spun him round
so that his skiff plunged wildly as he dashed to seize
both sail and oar and push clear of the wrecking tide.
The sea turned stone as a thick hurricane of fish
with roe-filled bellies and white scales flashed swiftly by
while birds plunged greedily and gulped shoal after shoal.
The suffering man strove to head off the perilous flood
but stopped with gaping mouth and let his rudder kick
on seeing a huge beast astride the fish cascade.
Its mouth glowed darkly in the light like a sea cave
in whose vast pit swift shoals of little fishes plunged.
From the beast's nape a gushing spout of water sprang
in a rich gaudy rainbow scattering in the sun,
a water-mast on an exotic frigate's deck.
When in the tumult at long last the roar was lost,
the lone man clasped the marvel in his inner sea,
happy that in this final hour, before his eyes

would shut forever, his mind had seen this fierce assault.
He shut his eyes and smiled, for recollections crossed
his memory's dark ravines and drowned him in their flood:
the blind and silent river flowed of that ant-swarm
that once poured round his city like a swallowing death;
the blind moles who had sniffed the earthquake scurried past,
and stars fell which he dreamt one night had crawled like worms
and eaten all the last leaves of his sleeping heart.
The archer still with secret admiration mused
on his white head, that buzzing slanting wasp's nest filled
with stings and honey, that gleaned fields and shores in flight.
"What is this life, what secret yearning governs it?
There was a time I called its lavish longing God,
and talked and laughed and wept and battled by his side
and thought that he, too, laughed and wept and strove beside me,
but now I suddenly feel I've talked to my own shadow!
God is a labyrinthine quest deep in our heads;
weak slaves think he's the isle of freedom, and moor close,
all the incompetent cross their oars, then cross their hands,
laugh wearily and say, 'The Quest does not exist!'
But I know better in my heart, and rig my sails:
God is wide waterways that branch throughout man's heart."
Thus spoke the voyager's untrammeled heart and mind
as the rough sea grew greener, wild with smothering mists,
and the North Wind grew sharper as with chilling breath
it blew and on the tiller froze the lone man's hands.
Clouds dragged like sluggish smoke along the sea's expanse,
drenched and corroded every bone and swelled each joint
till the soul huddled like a chattering, naked bird.
One dawn upon the waves he saw the first ice floes,
thick lumps of bobbing human heads that rose and sank,
that lightly tossed and touched his prow, then skimmed far off;
at the sky's rim the sun now rose at drop of noon,
rolled through the mists, exhausted, then sank once again,
unable now to mount the earth like a fierce bull.
But one damp dusk the lone man gaped with startled eyes:
the sun had sunk, but a white-yellow banner spread
and softly fluttered in the sky with silver fringe;
slowly a rich-wrought fabric rolled, ribbons unwound,
rubies and emeralds glowed and pulsing sapphires streamed
till at its top a saffron tempest burst in gold.
As the god-treading athlete skimmed through the sky's blaze,
myriad rainbows dangled from his crystal beard
and all his glittering coffin brimmed with precious stones;
when he spread out his hands, his fingers dripped with pearls.
It was as though the banner longed to seize the sky,

assault dark Tartarus, too, and take possession there.
Long vines of flame spread their curved tendrils through the air,
hung with grape-clusters of thick light, then slowly swayed
as though rocked gently by a warm erotic wind.
"I never dared to think I'd wear this lustrous crown,"
he mused, and skimmed through fields of Death adorned with roses.
He hung his new stag-bow across his sunburnt back,
and both his black flints lightly scratched his crystal chest
as regal wreaths passed ring on ring above his head:
"Thus, when a mighty king returns from a great battle,
a dome is raised of myrtles, laurels, and red roses
beneath whose arch his hacked and reverent head may pass;
I've come from a great war, and all the arches bloom—
a thousand times well met, ancestral, lethal castle!"
He spoke, then spread his hands to greet his gathered people there.

That same night as Odysseus bent above his tiller,
exhausted, his mind wandering in a drowsy daze,
the night moonlit and starry, the sea smooth as milk,
a silent shrouded phantom suddenly loomed beside him,
and then before his hands could grasp the trailing oars,
his keel smashed gently, mutely on hard crystal ice.
Then the much-suffering man leapt to escape his fate
and fight grim Death by swimming in the open sea,
hoping to find some sudden rock on which to cling.
Like a cracked shard the green moon floated through the sky
close to the break of day as the unconquered man
struggled to find some land which his blue nails might clutch.
For hours he fought Death stubbornly and still held high,
nor would surrender to the sea, his bloodstained head.
"Sun, my old friend, appear! Give me some light to fight by!
If I'm to die now, let it be in your warm light!"
He spoke, and the compassionate sun in sadness rose,
and as its fragrant light fell on the desolate wastes,
Odysseus cried with joy and swam toward a near crag.
His frozen fingers clutched with frenzy at the rock
till the death-battler slowly dragged his body up,
and then fell, blue and bloodstained, on the whetted claws.
A sweet and lethal sleep rushed down to wrap him round
as though his regal veins had cracked and all his blood
and all the world poured out and drained his body dry.
But still his vigilant mind kept guard in his hard skull
and yelled until the sleep-drowned beast leapt up with fear.
He jumped to his feet once more, but the cold cut his flesh,
his pallid lips refused to close, and his teeth chattered,
though still his heart stood firm and struck like a strong hammer.

Where was the blazing sun, alas, the yellow sands,
the fragrant rhododendrons and the girls at play?
What joy to have your ship wrecked on a sunlit coast
where sea-nymphs with free-flowing hair, when you awoke,
took you at dusk along the beach to a gold palace!
But then he plugged his memory, mutely tossed his head,
and with blue body slashed with wounds, limped on the rocks.
Ice wastes spread everywhere, not even a crow's cry
was heard, snows loomed like frozen castles or turned tame
and stretched in long smooth sheets, deep azure in the shade.
No breath of man, no fragrant smoke rose from man's hearths,
no beast's damp nostril misted the cold crystal air.
Frightened by the inhuman silence of the snows,
Odysseus then recalled mute noons and speechless nights,
the haughty palaces he'd burned, the hush that spread
at dusk and wrapped the ashes when the flames had ceased;
he then recalled the dead that lay in the cool grass
with their blue silent lips, their ears plugged from all sound,
though always one worm slowly bored its way, and this
was one small solace in the speechless solitude—
but not one comfort could be found in this white hush.
The lone man shuddered, opened his mouth wide to shout,
but though he strove, he could not utter a crow's croak,
then clutched his throat in fear and closed his dangling jaw:
"It may be I'm already in Death's crystal realm,
that soon like a white elephant with crimson eyes
the host will come amid these snows and bid me welcome."
Thus did he speak to his numbed mind and cast his eyes
fearlessly round to fight the holy beast with awe.
The sallow sun crawled in vast whiteness tinged with rose,
the azure-emerald moon still dripped with poisoned dew,
and the bird-hunter perked his ears and thought he heard
the crying of wild birds and swish of flapping wings.
His knees grew strong again, his blue lips wanly smiled:
"I hear wings fluttering now; Death has a thousand shapes,
and he may choose to come as a white monstrous swan
and lure me here on earth with his sweet ruby eyes.
Don't fear, my soul! Let come what may, evil or good!"
He spoke, then clutched his bow and strode across the snows,
and as he turned a mountain's rim, his heart grew calm,
for on a rock plateau a spouting geyser sprang,
boiling and roaring with thick steam and scalding water;
the snows around had melted, thick shrubs darkly glowed,
and flocks of birds now huddled in its warm embrace.
Hot breezes wafted round the seven-souled man's face,
and his eyes brimmed with tears, he opened his stiff lips:

"Beloved mother, O great warmth, sweet breath of earth!"
His mind grew supple then, the cold fled from his veins,
and hurriedly he gathered twigs and heaped them high
in a small cave beside the spout, then seized his bow,
and the rocks echoed with the leap of startled wings
as on wild thickets plummeted the plump seabirds.
Quickly he took down from his chest the two sharp flints,
gathered an armful of dry twigs and sweetly said:
"Come cast into my ready hearth your final bloom,
the crimson bud of fire, grandfather, to warm us both."
He struck sparks then, and the blood leapt within his veins
as in the hearth he cast the birds, sat down cross-legged,
clasped himself round his waist with love, his legs, his knees,
groped at his chest, and then caressed his white-haired head:
"O seven-souled, you've stood up well, you won't die yet:
limbs, bow, and fire and mind—all weapons are in their place;
perhaps for a whole month, perhaps for two or three,
perhaps for even four, you'll still hold out on earth!"
He smiled, stretched in the cave with sated belly, plunged
like a dolphin to deep sleep, and when the sun arose
it found him upright with pursed lips, plotting his icy way.

The pearly day glowed like a tunny's silver belly,
thick flocks of white birds screamed and fished among the waves,
and far away a bear raised high its shining snout
and growled with joy as though it sniffed at human flesh.
The lone man crossed through snows and climbed as his brains shook;
rocks stretched in rows like ancient dragons turned to stone,
needle-sharp barren summits rose, ice-covered slopes,
a flaming mouth that once had yelled, though not a soul
had heard, then clenched its teeth with scorn in a vast hush.
The lone man felt the silence seep deep in his heart;
he, too, like that burst mountain once had roared and shook
and now would freeze to ice in a vast silent spell.
On a tall barren boulder he discerned blurred marks,
approached, then clearly traced wild vine and laurel leaves
and a sharp-pointed date-tree branch deeply incised
in the old bony memory of primordial rock.
His heart throbbed, and he hailed the leaves like long-lost brothers:
"I bow and worship the sun's sweet and flaming cries,
O my belovèd comrades, laurel, date, and vine!"
The untamed hermit then caressed the traces there
of a far passion vanished in oblivion now,
but joyed to think that, eons after, one lone man
had passed by and caressed life's long-dead graven bones.
As thus the lone man mused, the snows had turned dark blue,

and fear swept through his mind to think how soon the sun
now sank before it had well climbed the crystal peaks.
The days crouched low, and the renowned sunflower shrank;
life stood on its hind legs like a white polar bear,
danced slowly in the dusk, played with its cub, the sun,
and licked its face so that it dwindled day by day.
The archer gazed on the snow-covered threshing floors,
but when a strong wind swept and froze the flesh and mind,
he turned back, shivering, to his windless cave once more.
A heap of dark leaves waited for the burning spark,
ashes glowed wanly still for man's brief consolation,
and when Odysseus saw his traces, his heart pulsed
as though he'd crossed the sill of his ancestral home,
and his frostbitten lips moved in a mumbling sigh:
"How long shall I change houses and betray my hearths?
How many times have I rolled on far shores, alone,
with a land breeze for covering, pebbles for my bed,
and not one crumb of dry bread even to feed my heart?
Life, you've a thousand faces, and I love them all!"
He spoke, then squatted, lit the fire, filled the hearth
with plump seabirds that he might eat and warm his soul.
He munched and gazed on the fierce fire, his savage friend;
the two of them could softly chat for endless nights
in mute recall of all they'd done and burnt on earth,
but from his toil exhausted, the lone man stretched out
beside his flame-eyed stalwart friend and sank to sleep.
He had not seen his mother in his dreams for years,
as though the earth with gaping mouth had gulped her whole;
nor had her sorrowing sacred smile appeared again
to sweeten her belovèd son's tumultuous dreams,
and of all this the archer secretly complained.
That night at last he dreamt of her as though he were
in his old father's palace when the stars shone bright
and she lay dying in her royal bed, as pale as wax.
He saw himself kneel by her side and hold her hand
and listen to the thin blood thickening in her veins
as slowly the sweet misted warmth of life dissolved.
All night he stroked and fondled her white sweating hair,
then, as his lower jawbone trembled, he stooped, pale,
and kissed her deeply sunken eyes, now turned to glass.
"Mother, don't fear, you'll wake soon from this ugly dream
and in your courtyards call your slaves to gird themselves
and start again their ancient, daily household tasks.
Mother, now here's a secret to rejoice your heart:
last night your daughter-in-law woke up in a great fright
for in her fruitful womb she'd felt a painful throb;

Mother, your pallid hands shall hold a grandson soon!"
As her son talked, the unmoving mother sweetly drank
the happy news along her heavy body's length
like Mother Earth absorbing the slow, drenching rain.
Her son stooped low and kissed her eyes, then talked once more
that silence might not cut, alas, the thread of joy:
"Mother, it's almost break of day, the cock will crow,
and the bad dream that struck you will disperse in wind;
at morning when you rise with your brain clear as light
you'll call us all and laughingly expound your dream:
'Death means a good and blessèd wedding in all dreams;
only, I saw it with such starkness, my heart froze;
but may my son be blessed who has so well consoled me.'
Mother, do you hear? Ah, there, you smile and move your eyes!"
All night the son cried out and fought invisible hands
and held his mother tightly clasped to keep her warm,
but that great Octopus, grim Death, had gripped her feet,
now numb with cold, and mutely spread his tentacles
to her old bony ankles, her shrunk thighs, her waist,
and her afflicted son stooped low and watched them rise
till they should touch her warm heart, and his mother die.
He held her thus embraced in his dream all night long,
and when he woke at dawn his heart had turned to stone;
he could not lift his arms, as though he still clasped tight
his frozen mother's heavy though invisible corpse.
By crawling slowly, he massed twigs, then lit a fire,
stretched out his blue-black deadened body near the flames,
and as it warmed and new life once more flapped its wings,
he quickly roasted heaps of birds on the hot hearth
then hung them thickly round his waist and mutely took
the hopeless upward slope of the snow-covered wastes.
When he first stepped in light, the sun's beams dazed his eyes,
and for a moment his mind spun with myriad suns
that danced flame-red, gold, azure in his blackened sight
till all at length distilled and only the sun's head
remained like a pale phantom on the sky's low rim
and rolled on the iced mountain peaks, sad and forlorn.
As the death-hunter stumbled on with bloodstained feet,
light followed him on all four paws, a frozen dog,
climbed quivering up the hills, then vanished in the snows.
Stars lit their myriad candles in the sparkling air,
icicles glittered in straight rows, and slowly night
poured like a blue-green river in a ruined world.
Sliding and tumbling on the ice, rising again,
Death's stalwart pilgrim was besmirched with blood and snow,
and as he lurched toward a white doom with bloodstained beard,

and heavy crystal ice hung down his hoary head,
he gently raised his eyes and saw low at the sky's rim
a flaming brilliance leap and darkly flash with gold
as the mute pallid prince of night rose in the sky.
The ice-fields laughed and gleamed, snows with reflection glowed,
until the lone man's footprints shone with silver rims.
"O white musk siren-wine distilled from the moon's vineyards,
neither a maid's embracements nor sleep's downy clasp
can ever surpass your softness or your tender touch."
Then his mind gently hovered in a sweet caress:
"O moon, O snow-white peacock, O ice-crystal sun,
O blooming pale moonflower in death's garden plot,
bleak silver mirror where I mutely watch my face!"
As he still welcomed and caressed the precious moon
he saw a lofty hill in its seductive glow,
climbed to the summit on all fours, spied like a hawk,
then cried out—either his eyes played tricks or a town flashed
with round huts made of ice blocks that in starlight gleamed.
He cocked his ears, and when he heard the bark of dogs,
sweet tears ran down his cheeks, and his lips wanly smiled:
"Lady Life stretches out her snow-white hands and wants me still!"

The dogs had smelled him from afar and rushed up growling,
but stout Odysseus raised his freezing arms in rage
and mutely stood prepared to shoot with tautened bow
as from the ice blocks tall men-seeming shadows leapt
and shrilled with fear when in a lightning bolt they saw
a snow-white god advance with a horned bow stretched taut.
Oil lamps with quivering wicks were fetched, and old men cried:
"The Great Ancestor, the Great Spirit has left his shores!
He must have frozen in Hades, thrashed by mighty Hunger,
and now with chattering teeth runs toward the warmth of man!"
An old man, fat as a seal, rolled at the archer's feet:
"Grandfather, O Good Spirit, welcome! I kiss your heels!
I am the great witch doctor whom the stars have told
that you were coming, hungry, that you'd left your ice,
and would soon deign to stay awhile by our poor hearths.
Enter, there's fire to warm you, and blubber to make you fat."
Without a word, the great death-archer stooped and crossed
the old man's sill, enthroned himself like a great lord
before a burning stone-lamp, then stretched out his hands.
He warmed himself and ate while the witch doctor sang
charms of his holy coming, smeared him with warm grease,
then spread a snow-bench with fat hides for him to sleep.
The suffering man then shut his eyes and smiled with joy;
the blubber of the seal seemed good, and good the warmth,

and his coquetting luck seemed good as flickering fire,
so that he crossed his hands and sank in a white sleep.
Odysseus slept, and felt the family round him sleep
and meekly breathe like gentle cows in steaming stalls,
and the flame's hearth burned in their midst, a sleepless gold.
O Fire, how you flicked in darkness like the heart
of man, a holy, sleepless, pure and large-eyed love!
In other lands where the sun's blazing kiln shoots down
with savage spears, you jig like a gay dancer, call
like decoy-birds, nude, shameless, with your jangling bells,
but in Death's snow-frost here, in icy solitude,
you willingly keep vigil, Fire, a small sister
who all night long keeps watch above her ailing brothers.
O Fire, you are a mother's knees, a cousin's laugh,
the honeyed sweetness of our youngest, smallest sister.
The lone man's body warmed and brimmed from head to toe
with loving kindness and deep joy; if only, God,
he could embrace the fire tightly like a young maid!
When he awoke in the dim dawn, he fixed his eyes
in silence on the flames for a long time and heard
them lick and lap his brains like a belovèd hound.
Through a thin opening in the roof of snow and ice,
pale beams of light crawled slowly in the mewed-up hut
where men and dogs, twined in close mounds, were still asleep,
and crawling flames caressed their sallow swollen faces.
Stifling, the archer raised the pelt that hid the entrance,
to breathe fresh air and to revive his smothered lungs,
but stepped back, startled, as sharp needles pricked his face,
and blew upon his hands with joy in the warm stench.
A maiden woke and screamed with fright to see him there,
but the old couple slowly rose without a word
and filled the lamp with lumps of grease to feed the fire
so that the brazen pot above it might soon boil
with the fat larded remnants of the slaughtered seal.
An old crone struggled with the pot and lowly tasks
and the witch doctor knelt beneath a small round hole
where a rare drop of light dripped slowly, raised his hands,
busied himself with higher worship till his choked
and pleading voice was heard in fear: "Don't kill us, God!"
and the god-slayer shuddered, feeling the man's dread.
Man-eating God was drops of light in these night lands;
he struck man heartlessly, then stood with ax in hand
beside a home's dark door, killed all who dared to pass,
and man, poor ruined wretch, raised high his pallid hands
and begged, not for good comforts or one drop of joy,
nor even for one bright plume to stick into his mind,

but only for one precious grace: not to be slain!
When the witch doctor dropped his arms, his face turned calm,
and he bowed low and dumbly at the archer's feet;
meanwhile the food had boiled, and all with greedy haste
sat round the brilliant fire, women, dogs, and men.
Odysseus ached to see such stark submissive fear,
and with distended nostrils deeply breathed in all
these pale new comrades who had chanced on his fate's road.
What crops of body-battling men swarm on the earth,
and everywhere the same salt burning tears run down,
whether on white or yellow cheeks, or on black jaws!
Earth had now filled with these dark grease-smeared swarms of men,
and the great wanderer wanly smiled and reached his hand
to touch the maiden's hair, but like a mare she neighed
with frothing lips and drew back toward the steaming pot,
spread out the meal as all grabbed at seal-lumps and gulped
them down till the lard flowed, encrusting chins and necks.
When all had eaten and wrapped themselves in warming pelts,
the snow-tent's heavy door-hide opened with slow stealth
and the town elders humbly came with precious gifts
for the Great Spirit who had moored in their poor haunts:
lard, hides and hounds, so that the Spirit might feed well
and wrap itself in good warm pelts when hunting seals.
The wandering man received the gifts without a word,
ate of the blubber, took the dogs, thrust in the hides,
and the town chief rejoiced that God now dressed like man
and like a man ate of their fat and blessed their dogs.
They stepped back through the door and disappeared in mist.
The archer rose to bid the failing light farewell:
"O daily marvel, flaming fellow-countryman,
O Sun, we've both here lost our way in this dark dungeon;
our claws, O eagle, have turned to ice, our wings have molted.
Where are the azure seashores of our sun-shot Greece
where we both swam on seas and the world leapt on waves
like a red apple we each strove to seize and keep?
O Sun, now we're both trapped in the snows here like bears!"
He spoke, the sun turned deathly pale and its eyes glazed
as huge white silent stars appeared and dripped like wax
in a mute wake all night on the dead shrouded earth.
"Now Mother Earth has died, her feet have turned to ice,"
the lone man murmured, and recalled his dream and crouched
without a word, like a strong beast caught in entangling snares.

When the light vanished, the maid chewed on a seal's pelt
to soften and to sew it for her bridal dress;
she'd given her word, and now she stooped, awaiting the sun

to come in spring, when she might wed, if all went well.
She chewed with joy, laughed in her flowering thoughts, for all
things would go well, the sun would shine, the grass would spring,
and soon on the earth she'd spread her hairy wedding pelt.
The lone man's mind beside her coiled like a dazed snake
and only three cares came and came again and fell
in smothering pall: to keep warm, to sleep well, to eat.
He mused: "Thus must the beasts live all their stifled lives,
thus must the trees wait for their water, manure, and sun—
ah, who can cut the thread to escape and to breathe free?"
Man's fate here wore an ugly mask, an ugly doom,
for other small and deathless gods ruled in these snows:
the Seal, that greasy goddess with a boar's mustache,
almighty Lady Fire who perched in the hot hearth,
and great King Sunless, that dark lord with frosted beard
who like a rutting roe-buck with vermilion horns
plows straight through every village, smashes down all doors,
but sometimes only tinkles like sweet distant bells.
Wrapped in his double bear-hides, the world-wanderer strove
quickly to stir once more his frozen mind with thoughts.
Meanwhile the old witch doctor bent by the fire and carved
a god weighed down with fat, his daughter's precious dowry;
he stooped and carved all day and night, and his heart trembled,
for on his sorcerer's shoulders lay the whole town's cares:
all hungered, seals had now grown scarce, lamps spluttered low,
and all the fault was his, for not one of his spells
had brought them God in a seal's shape to kill and eat.
Trembling, he turned to the lone man with a sad smile:
"Good Spirit, deadly fears are crushing the whole town,
our strongest hunters have all gone to hunt in Hades
and left us here defenseless while starvation prowls.
I sink in snow, I sing and strive to lure the seal,
I cry to the musk-elks, invite the reindeer sweetly,
I rush and beat the frost-filled air with my harpoon,
and though it once returned weighed down with meat, alas,
it falls to earth now, bloodless, and our race will perish!
Good Spirit, pity us all, gird yourself well with weapons
and rush out hunting on the ice, shout till the seals,
those buxom dames, come waddling out to fill our pots.
The Spirit's in duty bound to feed its starving people!"
Then the old man fell silent, the stooped maid got tired
of chewing, her throat swelled, and in the filthy air
she longed for kisses and began to sing of spring:
"Mother, I'm weary now of chewing the seal's pelt,
a sickness smothers my small breasts and makes them numb,

they swell in the wild night till I can't bear their ache.
Mother, my limbs grow wild, my dress can't hold me back,
I'm stifling, Mother, I'll knock down our hut, I'll flee!
A maid who smells her marriage has great strength, they say,
for spring comes when she calls, and the good sun appears;
she lays her small breasts on the snows, and with their warmth
the waters thaw and flow, the fish rush down the streams,
and she-bears lick their fur in stealth while their warm eyes,
glazed with delight, brim sweetly with white fuzzy cubs."
As the maid sang, and the old mother with hoarse voice
kept time, the cracked and quivering voice of the old man
rose from the hearth behind the two, dulled with complaint:
"We fear the dreadful god, and our hearts break in two,
we yearn to beg him for a beast to save our souls,
stumble on snow and yell, but our own shouts return
whizzing about us like sharp stones and break our heads;
he only lets but incensed songs approach him now!
I've heard it said that men on other shores are bold
and dare address him face to face and ask for favors.
One day a bone-thin Negro fell on our white snows,
then shook his fists and shamefully roared at the cold sky:
'Fool God, you've portioned all things wrong, you've lost your wits!
You've sent earth too much water—give us a little meat!'
I heard and trembled, and thought the world's roof would fall
because of mankind's babbling mouth and shameless mind."
The rock-rough murderer laughed and teased the old witch doctor:
"I've heard it said that on far isles, on azure shores,
the sun walks like a wealthy archon hand in hand
with earth, his lovely wife, clad in an emerald cloak;
God limps behind them like a beggar, knocks on doors,
and plays a thousand sleight-of-hands, a thousand tricks
to please their hearts a bit and earn a crust of bread,
but all the mortals laugh and cast him crumbs and slops—
such was the land that gave me birth, such my buffoons!"
The lone man laughed, then stretched his long legs toward the fire
and the witch doctor shivered and looked round in fear:
"Lock your mouth tight! What if he hears us? We'll all die!
This whole white world is ruled by one god only: Fear!
We've neither faith nor love, O grandfather, only Fear;
we fear the earth, the sea, the sky, disease and pain,
we fear the dead and living, all the beasts we eat,
we fear our minds, our hearts, our memories and our dreams,
we fear all careless laughter, our wild myths, our songs!
The thick air round us is crammed full of evil ghosts
and everywhere in darkness their teeth, claws, and their horns gleam!"

When the witch doctor ceased, he shook to his heart's core,
and the archer pitied deeply mankind's fallen state,
how its great soul had shriveled, lost its brilliant hues
as though it, too, were but a rose plucked by the snows.
Quickly he tossed his head on high to scatter fear:
"Ahoy!" he roared abruptly, and seized the old man's arms,
but as he opened his mouth wide to ease his heart,
the pelt-flap of the snow-hut moved, and there trooped in
the settlement's stout elders wrapped in their fat hides.
They kissed the feet of the much-suffering man, and wailed;

their oil was dwindling fast, their hounds were growing fierce,
though hunters had roamed far they'd seen not one moist snout
but only ghosts that leapt about them with hoarse jeers.
Last night a woman had gone mad from wretched hunger,
the dogs were getting rabid, evil was gathering head
and like a plague would spread to beasts and men, to gods!
"Good Spirit, pity the wretched town, go out to hunt,
the seals will spy you and come close for very shame."
The suffering man spoke not because his heart was heavy,
and his great brow grew dark, without day's dawning light,
for life now seemed to him a helpless ruthless game.
He seized a wizened spermless codger tight, who wailed
like a slain seal, and shouted in his deafened ear:
"Grandpap, you've lived unnumbered years in these cold snows
and now that your eyes brim with reindeer, seals, and stars,
I, the Great Spirit, want from you the entire truth:
Old Man, why were you born, what was your goal in life?"
The startled codger tossed his shriveled hands on high;
the mighty question rose in his mind for the first time,
his small eyes suddenly gleamed, and he yelled out: "To eat!"
Deep sadness struck the lone man, pity and high scorn;
life strove for generations in these wretched breasts
and met one virtue only in all the world: to eat!
The great seductive tempter wished to shout with joy:
"Sun, song, sea, God, a woman in your arms all night!"
but he kept silent, in pity for man's dreary fate,
then spread his hands above the sickly heads and said:
"Once as I crossed a blazing desert, Death dashed on
ahead astride his mare, the burning sands, and laughed;
wherever he stopped, the earth was scorched and the wells dried.
And I ran on behind him fiercely, held my heart
like a small hogskin of cool water and spread my hand
and silently caressed the earth's last gallant grass
that raised its pale but proud head high on Death's frontiers.
'Your health and joy, O comrade sentry,' I called proudly,
'I, too, have come to die here or to be saved with you!'
Now on the edge of this abyss, earth's frozen heel,
I find your snows are like those sands, your souls like grass,
and once again I spread my hands with love and shout:
'Your health and joy, O comrade sentry, we are well met!'
Forward, seize your harpoons, let's rush to the great hunt,
it's only just that the Spirit turn to flesh and feed mankind!"

The moonlight's silver fringes hang down far as earth,
the pale mind hovers softly, drifting toward the moon,
and a most sad yet most sweet song, like a seal's wail,

drifts up from our deep hearts and quivers above the snows.
Thus will the light shine downily, and thinly lick
the desolate and rugged earth when the sun shrinks
and flocks of stars browse on her snowfields unrestrained.
As the world-wanderer heard his heart in his warm hides,
it seemed to him like a sweet bell that drivers hang
on the lead-reindeer's neck to help from getting lost.
He led his troop in the great hunt, and crunched on ice;
in the dull nacreous glow the snows loomed like huge beasts,
like frozen waddling seals, like pure-white elephants,
like snow-enmarbled dogs and hunters in long rows;
stars hung like brittle icicles, frost-spirits played
on the smooth snow-strewn stretches like bear cubs newborn;
the sea spread, crystalline and green, in a hushed calm;
sometimes a falling star burst mutely overhead
and the dogs barked, but soon the hunters pitched their camp,
hid in the snowbanks, held their breath, and longed for seals.
For hours the hunters crouched unmoving with eyes fixed
to spot the slight warm breath break through the ice when seals
poke up their whiskered snouts to get a breath of air,
but their feet froze like glue, their hands grew stiff and numb,
and though the old witch doctor's spells rose high, they fell
on the snows, empty, and rang hollow in hungry hearts.
"O eyes of our dead parents, O almighty stars,
O Mother Moon who broods until they hatch in skies,
and you, O good fat spirits who command the seals,
O forebears, listen to our cries: we die of hunger!
We don't dare speak to God of our great pain,
for he has never starved—how can he feel man's pangs?
Forefathers, come, for you have all spit blood on earth,
pity our grandsons, choose a plump old man among you,
dress him with hides, weigh him with meat, then let him come
in a seal's form on these cold snows to feed us now.
He will do well to come again to his own town
and plunge in his tribe's entrails, then rise high in lamps,
that his great ancient race may once again take heart."
As the witch doctor sang to allure the stars, he looked
stealthily round in starlight to spot azure smoke,
but no seal's misted breath was seen, not a star fell.
Then in that endless silence, dead for countless years,
the old magician lost his wits and his brains flared;
a thousand stars poured through him, his forefathers swooped,
till he began to hurl his dread harpoon with force
and it sped back and seemed to drip with clotted blood
so that the old man shouted, frothing, and his thickened tears
suddenly turned to icedrops on his frozen cheeks.

"I've cast dread spells on hunger! Push on, friends, don't fear!
The whole night waddles like fat seals crammed full of meat!
Eat, for our great forefathers come weighed down with fat!"
He sang, then swiftly danced and brandished his harpoon;
the dark god of insanity beat on his loud drums,
the freezing archer shivered in the shrouding ice
and all minds watched with fear for the great miracle.
If only he could turn to seal, fall on harpoons
and feed the whole town with his entrails lined with lard!
For the first time he felt the body's full delight
when as a sacred votive beast it feeds man's soul,
but the seal-miracle, alas, was late in coming.
He gazed on mute stars only now that swarmed like ants
and sometimes fell along the cheeks of night like tears
and sometimes gazed on man disdainfully and spurned him.
The hunters tried to allure the miracle in vain,
but in the stillness suddenly distant janglings burst
as though a hundred sleds swept by with silver bells.
"The blizzard!" all screamed, and ran pellmell to flee the blast,
rushed down the path they'd cut through snow, while at their backs
the bells swept like a roaring sea, and sharp snow-spears
swirled in a needling siphon as the hunters screamed
and stumbled in their haste to escape the blinding blast;
the archer tagged at the tail-end and his soul strove
to hold tight to his startled mind and keep it calm.
Far off on islands of the blest, flat on her back,
the blue sea laughed with Master Sun, the vineyards smiled,
the heat scorched all the fields, but a cool sea-wind blew
as gleaners stretched in the sweet shade and their limbs smelled
of acrid must, their chests and armpits steamed with sweat.
When the grape harvest ended, the feast days would start,
their lord would fling his courtyards wide for man and maid
to eat and drink with the gay god of curly locks.
Then all their toil would turn to smoke, mount to the sun
and play in wreathèd rings within the wine's dim dazzle
in the far-distant vine-clad islands of the blest.
Basil and marjoram, the sea's strong summer winds,
coquetting wagtail waves, islands that sailed through air,
and small sweet clouds of springtime with their changing shapes—
dear God, Odysseus felt his brains would burst with longing!
He sighed with sadness, then cast his eyes about in stealth:
perhaps that sun was but a sweet seductive dream,
or were these shrouding snows here but a stifling nightmare?
The lean exhausted dogs barked as with burning eyes
they watched their wretched masters weeping by their hearths;
the mothers portioned the last fat among their children

as the stone lamps went out and the snow-huts grew dark
and the old women, men, and children shrilled with fear:
"Light all the lamps, for the stag-elk with flaming eyes
will see the darkness and swoop down to eat us all!"
Then the old men grabbed the last fat with hardened heart
from even the infants' lips to feed the failing lamps;
they felt the lean stag-elk approach with stealthy steps,
knock on each door, and where it found a hut in darkness,
wedge its sharp horns tight in the walls to send them tumbling down.

The old witch doctor danced the dead to their ice graves,
then, wild with hunger, huddled round his frozen hearth,
for he had seen that drunken god, who grabs men's wits,
dance on the crackling snow with an insane delight.
One day, returning from his brother's grave, he'd seen
God striding through the town lopping the roofs off homes,
followed by frenzied hags who broke in a wild dance
then dug in snow and swallowed heavy chunks of ice
and yelled that earth, for love of them, had turned to seals.
He held God's face tight in his mind, then grabbed a log,
strove silently to wedge him firmly in the wood
with hands bound to his back, then plant him firm on earth
that he might leap no shoulders to gnaw at a man's brain.
His daughter sat beside him chewing the seal's pelt
and munched in haste to shape and sew her wedding dress,
for soon the sun and the fat seals would come again,
the musk-deer with their precious horns, the downy ducks,
to line their guts once more with lard, to swell their brains;
then all would pile in the snow-sleds, in-laws and friends,
and she and her betrothed would cut through snowways first
to reach the frozen ice, before the snows could melt,
and pitch their tents on the firm rocks of the spring's thaw.
There on the topmost rock their bridal tent would rise
surrounded by green long-haired willows and thick reeds
as from their rooftops the bride's crimson banner waved.
Within would stand their holy furnishings, new-hewn,
the well-remembered cradle, the unblackened pots,
their new stone lamps, their still unused and hooked harpoons,
and her resounding loom on which to weave firm cloth
so that her son might find his armature complete.
When they remained alone with their new furnishings,
like lusty landlords they would pull their tent-flap tight,
kneel down before that god who holds man's germ of life
and sweetly merge on a musk-deer's embroidered hide.
The maiden chewed before the fire, half-closed her eyes,
then smiled in patience, for the sun already rose

in her small bridal heart and spread to her loins warmly.
Her mother huddled by her side, shriveled and thin,
with withered empty cheeks, with bones that pierced her flesh,
nor spoke nor swayed, but sank in a narcotic daze
till in her dreams her forebears came with beckoning signs
and fed her with roast hare, gave her sweet wine to drink,
till the old lady smiled in sleep and swallowed hard.
The lone man gazed on the low fire and smiled, for soon,
whether it willed or not, the sun would come, and he
would leave in a small skiff they'd built him of sealskin,
and when the waters thawed, he'd raise his one long oar
and vanish southward toward the sun, not to return.
"Blessed also be this earth that with its savage ruth
has fed us with the crystal poisons of her heart,
charitable jellyfish that stings us till we freeze
and set sail, with the mind's consent, to the white further shore."

As the world-roamer stooped in thought and fed his mind,
the old witch doctor screamed, the log slipped from his hands,
and he dropped nerveless on the hides with a deep sigh.
His daughter quickly stopped her chewing, raised her eyes,
clasped her dear father tightly, rocked him like a babe,
and he, as in a dazed dream, heard his daughter sing
the dead man's song, as though he had already crossed
the ashy river at the earth's foundation roots.
"Father, do you recall how you returned at night
with empty hooks and empty fishnets, and damned life:
'May life be cursed that smashes in our hungry mouths!' "
As from another, misty shore, his voice replied:
"Yes, daughter, I recall, but life, alas, is sweet!"
"Father, do you recall your sighs when the hearth died
and your intestines drooped and you cried out to Death:
'O Death, O tasty reindeer full of fat and meat,
come, I can't bear my hunger! Feed me, or I'll starve!' "
"Yes, daughter, I recall, but life, alas, is sweet!"
"Father, do you recall when you clasped your dead child
and shouted to the sun that set and stars that rose:
'What in this world are children but morsels for grim Death?
Cursed be that couple that gives birth and feeds the Slayer!' "
"Yes, daughter, I recall, but life, alas, is sweet!"
Thus father and daughter keened, each from two different shores,
and when she opened her arms wide, a river flowed
and foamed between them, ashy, dark, and stained with blood.
Hearing the deadly song beat on her ears in dream
and shake her mind, the mother opened her eyes slowly
and saw the old man pant supine with rattling gasps

as the maid clasped him tight and keened the songs of death.
"My husband has set sail to eat with his forefathers,"
his old wife said with envy, shut her eyes, and dozed,
but then the old man seized his daughter's virgin hips,
his loins grew firm and warm, he climbed to earth once more,
and life smiled on his quivering lashes like salt tears.
The maid once more began to chew the seal's tough hide,
her mind flew off once more to her loud wedding pomp
and the ice within her once more melted, the sun shone.
The wind of madness blew now in a dull red storm,
brains echoed like resounding drums, and dogs, gods, men
moaned in great hunger from a bottomless cold darkness;
they drank snow and ate snow and clasped snow tight in sleep,
and even Death approached like snow with snow-white dogs.
Old men and women huddled round the sorcerer's lamp
and brought their last thin shreds of fat to warm themselves
till the witch doctor's decoy-heart, beside the fire,
opened its beak and sang a sad and dragging dirge
that swept man's heart far off from hunger and from love:
"What are these joys and sorrows, God, this life on earth,
roots moored in pitch-black waters, ceaseless tears that flow,
hands that clasp tight against the world's vast solitude?
The heart is a black tigress stalking through the night,
which one day may growl fiercely and swallow the whole world—
then a low song will suddenly smash our world in two."
As the witch doctor sang, unbearable tumult surged
in their emboldened shriveled hearts, their bodies cracked,
their secret shames were conquered till their naked souls
sprang up in the song's sweetness, drenched with blood and mire.
Like cobras that had heard the magic flute's sweet song,
they locked their poisons in their fangs and reared in light
with honeyed eyes, allured from the heart's deepest pits.
Then in the filthy snow-huts men and women swayed
with frothing lips, till with swift gasps, beyond their will,
all there began confessing their dark crimes and sins:
some told of savage murders, some of petty thefts,
some of their sleeping with their neighbors' easy wives,
and one told of perverted thoughts that weighed him down
to fall upon the town and put all men to sword
till he remained alone with cattle and plump girls.
All, swept away by the unbearable sweet song,
poured out their laden hearts until, disburdened, they began
to weep and kiss before the dying man's low hearth
till all entwined in one fraternal knot of love.
Odysseus jumped erect and leant against the pole

in the hut's center, silently, and held his heart
to keep it firm from falling in the coiled crowd shamelessly.

Thus with confession's cliffs and famine's massacres
the baneful hours crawled through snows like evil ghosts
as the stone lanterns flickered low and Death rode by
on his red stag-elk, beckoning, and swept men away.
Once a white bear, out of compassion and deep love,
fell in a pit that youths had dug by the iced shore,
and they seized her with awe, dressed her in queenly robes,
then beat their drums and brought her to their huts with pomp.
The elders bowed in worship and the maids embraced her:
"Forgive us, noble lady, hold no grudge against us,
your role on earth is to be killed, to fill our bellies
so that man's seed and mothers' breasts may grow and swell.
Welcome! Our bosoms surge with honey and sweet milk!"
As soon as he smelled meat, the sorcerer revived
and donned his holy ritual robes and his fierce mask,
thus to mislead the noble she-bear's sacred eyes
that she might not stalk through his sleep and swiftly climb
the foliage of his dreams with her thick crooked paws.
He bowed and worshiped humbly with sly, flattering signs:
"O tasty and well-muscled goddess, hear our prayers:
descend to our shrunk entrails, line them well with meat,
then come again to earth that we may once more eat you;
the mills of life are strong and good—birds, beasts, men, gods
turn and once more return between their savage stones.
Enter and feed the millstones well, start the jaws working,
let the thick bones begin to crack in the great grinding
till our holds fill with meat, our bellies' funnels burst
and the mind's flapping mill-sails swell and whirl anew!
O firm-fleshed spirit, Mother Bear, forgive me, though
against my will I raise my ax on your plump neck,
for all my people long to merge with you as one."
The old man spoke with fear then raised his glittering ax,
and his brains burned, his arms bulged with a dragon's strength,
and the snows round him reddened full three fathoms wide.
At the first stroke the she-bear roared, and the old man
roared in reply, and the whole gathered town roared too;
then at the second stroke the great beast's holy neck
rolled like a newborn sun on earth and all eyes shone
and all dry throats were watered well and deeply quenched;
at the third stroke bear, men, and blood were merged in one
and Death leapt on his stag and rode to other settlements.

Thus did the human herd live on, from hand to mouth,
as under the snow-shroud, amid the torpid roots,
spring moved her stiffened limbs with stealth in the deep dark.
Rotating Time whirls round, and insects, birds, and beasts
once more rise into light, bound tight to its huge wheel;
when flaring nostrils smell the spring, eyes blaze with joy,
snows creak and crack, the stars grow pallid with sweet light,
and day will wake with crystal bracelets, stretch and yawn.
Low willows then will cast their shade on harbor shores,
the fuzzy and green lichen, too, will crawl on rocks
and the warmed earth forget the savage pain she bore.
Brides with completed dowries then will open doors,
look toward the East and long for days to smile with warmth
till the dark sky blush red, the hanging crystals smash,
and snow-sleds speed once more in the year's wedding pomps.
Deep in the earth the snakes begin to squirm, the worms to crawl,
and the old stag-elks hear deep rumbling in the snows
and gather their thinned herds to trek down toward the shore.
The old men too, like ancient elks, stand on their sills,
sniff with distended nostrils, bend their listening ears
and weigh what hour would now be best for their departure
before the thin ice thaw and swallow the whole town.
On the sky's rim a pallid dawn began to tremble
and all eyes laughed and glowed, fixed warmly on the East
where the sun rocked in the sky, an infant in its cradle.
With a gold bonnet, swaddling clothes of azure smoke,
it rose up, stumbled to its feet, but once more fell,
wobbling and whimpering in the arms of Mother Night.
Then the witch doctor yelped, broke in a whirling dance
and donned his springtime's magic mantle, richly wrought
with myriad clustered eggshells, dappled plumes of birds,
and cast his witching spells to advise the infant sun:
"Welcome, ah welcome, Sun, our dear belovèd pet!
Open your arms wide, lads, unlock your drowsy eyes,
unsheathe your sleeping swords, set loose your hunting hounds,
for the earth's caught in labor pains, her belly aches,
and her son staggers in her womb and kicks her belly!
Come out on rocks, O Sun, leap downward toward the shore,
take up your ancient crafts once more and your old roads!
O Sun, who like a peddler roam with your gold sacks,
stay in our village for a while, spread out your goods,
and we'll press round and buy all the good things you've brought.
You bring us grass and musk-deer and the blue-furred fox,
you bring us fishes in your nets, eggs in your lap,
you bring the bridegroom and the babe to the maid's breast.
Break into dance and sing, toss your heads high, my lads,

cock-a-doodle-do, I cry, and flap my morning wings!"
He crowed then like a cock with a hoarse voice, and maids
like decoy-birds broke in a bold dance round the youths
who, as their ancient custom rites prescribed, began
the double chant of spring, and to the maidens sang:
"Ah, there's no greater good on earth than your sweet kisses!
The snows have melted, fish swim free in the warm waters,
earth sprouts with greening hair, thorns bloom and black rocks smile,
our souls flood from our loins and seek another body;
ah, maid with playful eyes, how sweet your kiss, your lips!"
Then the maids clapped their hands in tune and bared their throats:
"Your kiss is good, but better still the wedding ring!"
Again the young men took the tune as their veins swelled:
"See what we've brought you, maids, two spheres of fragrant musk!
Here are gold bells for your small ears, and ivory combs,
and crimson coral neckrings for your unkissed throats.
Give us a kiss, sweet maids, and take these precious gifts."
But the maids laughed with playful eyes to arouse the youths:
"We'd love to enjoy the fragrant spheres you bring as gifts,
but we've two singing birds locked in a golden cage.
Give us our rings, then break the cage and catch our birds!"
For two days youths and maidens danced in mock word-war
as the youths sought the kiss and maids the wedding ring,
till on the third day dowries and agreements closed.
Thus wretched man rejoiced in one brief hour of kindness,
but in the unpitying sky God called his messengers
who had just then returned from earth with startling news:
"We saw a young pair sit alone and sweetly kiss
and speak such tender words, we thought for a brief hour,
—and caught our breaths—that the black earth had turned all sky!"
"Oho, rush down, my heralds, swiftly kill them both!"
"We saw a young man sit under a willow's shade
then stoop and clasp in his hard palms his flaming head;
and in his mind, that gazed on the world's decadence
around him, he shaped dreams to open straight new roads
and bring to earth all exiled virtues, justice, peace."
"Oho, rush down, my heralds, swiftly kill him too!"
"On the bank of a large river when the blizzard broke
we saw a small and humble hut shine on a cliff,
and when we peeked through its low windows we could see
about the hearth four blond-haired children laugh and play
as the glad mother gazed with pride and forgot God."
"Oho, rush down, my heralds, swiftly kill them too!"
Last came a pure-white herald, his wings weighed with snow:
"Rebellious spring has returned to earth, may she be cursed!
The peaks have thawed, and once again the shameless heads

of grass and worm and idiot man thrust through to light
till at earth's edge, although the ice has not well thawed,
men mass in troops to trek down to their summer camps.
They load their infants on their backs, their goods in carts,
and a betrothed young couple hastes with joy to reach
its goal, to pitch its tent on earth and sleep embraced!"
The sallow Old Man stooped and to his heralds hummed
as slimy and green poisons dripped from his pale lips
and his last cruel command hissed at his slavish troop:
"Oho, rush down to earth, my heralds, swiftly kill them all!"

Deathless Assassin, as with your faithful gang you talked,
waters on earth below moved sluggishly, earth slowly stirred,
and the witch doctor dreamt and gave the sign to leave,
for in deep sleep he'd heard the icelands crack and thaw.
As light grew bolder and the day raised tender eyes,
Odysseus donned his threefold hides and fox-fur cap,
thrust quickly through his leathern belt his two-edged ax,
then seized his sealskinned kyak like a pointed spear,
cast his glance softly round, browsed on the herds of men,
then stood amid the bare snow-huts and cried farewell:
"May every bite of fat you've fed me turn to children,
and may as many ancestral souls climb on these snows;
may all your women fill as many jugs with milk
to raise strong sons as jugs of water I've drunk here;
and may as many swords flash for your sakes in air
as fires have blazed within your huts to keep me warm!
Now I, the Good White Spirit, spread my sacred arms
to guard your seed, my grandsons, and to bless your heads
and stand as roof and aid above the dark abyss.
Children, farewell! My grace be with you night and day!"
He spoke, then trudged on toward the shore, and in his arms
he clasped his new skiff like a long shark smeared with fat,
eager to launch it like an arrow on free waters.
Meanwhile the yelping dogs were yoked to the snow-sleds
and all climbed in and strove to see somewhere on land
spring sitting sunnily on the infrequent grass
wearing the green wreath of a pallid willow branch.
Flocks of pure white and azure birds streamed through the air,
screeched hoarsely with shrill joy and fetched upon their wings
the fragrant and warm breath of land, grass in their bills,
all led by that wild dove, teasing and warm-eyed Love.
The whole town followed in a white unbroken row;
the gallant youths in their swift snow-sleds rushed ahead,
mothers and babies, old men, grandsons, rode behind,
and middle-aged men, at their prime, brought up the rear.

Their greasy bodies gently thawed in the thick hides
and the sun shone and glittered in each separate beam
until the brave emboldened youths broke into song:
"Ahoy, my lads, we're saved, the sun once more leaps high,
the heart of the wastelands has thawed, our hearts have thawed!
My left hand clasps my love, my right hand my harpoon,
the sniffing dogs rush on ahead, and hung on high
like a groom's golden lamp, the sun shows us the way!"
As the much-wandering man pushed on, he saw on snows
his shadow tightly twined with his skiff's shadow there.
The smooth ice gleamed in the sun's rays, the snows turned rose,
and the earth tingled, quivering, as the boatsman strode
to reach the waters that glimmered green to the far sky.
In the first snow-sled, the witch doctor's buxom daughter,
wearing with swaggering pride the brand-new bridal dress
she'd chewed all winter long to soften, touched her groom:
"We'll pitch our tent upon the highest peak, my love,
so the old men won't come to part our merging bodies;
they say there's no more forceful joy on this sad earth
than to lie by your loved one's side in the warm sun."
The bridegroom's slanting eyes flashed with enchanted light:
"Words of our great forefathers, love, are never wrong:
good are the sun and fire, tasty and good are seals,
and good a woman's body to hold in tight embrace,
but better than all these, they say, is the first son!"
The maiden blushed but laughed, and the young groom, grown bold,
looked swiftly round behind him at the long row of sleds
where titillated youths and maidens laughed and sped,
where women and gay children screeched with giddy joy,
and the witch doctor, his father-in-law, rode by their side.
What joy, for not one soul was watching the young groom!
He reached his hand to that quince-garden, his love's breasts,
and when with his right hand he grasped the firm round fruit,
the brains of both for a long time swooned in a daze.
As the green waters glimmered and the ice-sheets cracked,
Odysseus thrust himself into his sealskin skiff
until his boat and body tightly merged in one.
He gleamed like a sea-centaur then, half-boat, half-man,
with knowledge brimming from a great god's snow-white head,
and a man's heart between them throbbing, mortal, warm.
The lone man plied his oar and his heart swelled with joy
as like an arrow or swift gull his kyak sped:
"Thus from my mother's womb should we have been well matched,
O final form: god's head, man's heart, and a ship's keel!"
He spoke, then cocked his ears and heard the women's songs
as in the azure shade they hailed the unflowered spring.

"If I had blessings I'd give all to those poor souls
who now ascend the ice and speed on toward the grass;
I've ached much for the world this sterile winter here."
As the world-wanderer talked thus to himself, he raised
his hand to greet his friends on the ice for the last time;
like bear cubs in their furs, the children laughed and played,
and others in deep sheaths upon their mothers' backs
poked out their copper-green and slant-eyed heads with joy
and watched their parents, the swift dogs, the rosy sun.
The old witch doctor flapped his eggshells, and with care
brandished his long staff like a sword to guide his flock;
still in his hand the young groom held his loved one's breast
and ached with joy in its warm touch and in the kiss's swoon.

When they drew close to the foothills of a sharp peak
and the dogs pulled with panting gasps, and youths and maids
rushed on ahead to pluck the love-herb from green earth,
the old witch doctor suddenly stopped, and his knees shook,
for deep in the bowels of earth he heard a roaring blast;
the ground shook, his legs staggered, he fell flat on ice
and yelled for the snow-sleds to stop, but the gay songs
and the glad shouts of children drowned his feeble cries.
Odysseus heard with fear the earth's foundations roar
as the ice shook deep to its roots and foothills swayed,
and when he gazed far back he saw in the sun's blaze
the sleds, still unaware of danger, rushing headlong.
It was the bride who first cried out and lunged to seize
the reins and stop the snow-sled on the plunging cliff,
but the frenetic lead-dogs leapt in gaping waters
as the groom seized his love, then leapt to save her, too,
but both had only time to plunge, tight-clasped, to Hades.
Behind them rushed young couples filled with joy and song,
their minds dazed deeply with the honeyed breath of spring,
nor heard the old witch doctor's cries, nor spied black Death,
but rushed on as the ice-fields cracked and waters leaped—
till they clutched vainly at earth's edge by the mountain's rim
and dogs and men and maids were plunged in lurching waters.
Before the pale witch doctor could move his nerveless feet,
or his numb throat break in a piercing, wailing cry,
all dogs and all men drowned together in churning foam.
The archer gazed with horror in that dreadful hour:
a soft swish as of tree leaves or of scurrying beasts
moved for a honeyed moment in the springtime breeze
as though men once inhabited these wastes of white,
then the earth suddenly gaped and whiteness spread once more;
the name of wretched man was writ on ice and snow,

then the sun rose, thawed it to water and sucked it dry.
Odysseus bit his lips and held back blasphemies,
for joy within him had turned to savage pain, flowed free,
and as he watched the laughing sun flinging its roses
on snows, on waters, till the summits bloomed with bliss,
he choked the rising sobs in his dry throat with rage
then raised his hands and hailed the great world-sovereign disk:
"O Sun, who gaze and shine on all this teeming world,
who with no preference cast your rays on Life and Death,
nor pity man's misfortune nor his rectitude,
would that I had your eyes to cast their light on earth,
on sea, on sky, on wretched fate indifferently!"
Thus did the boatman speak, then clutched his whirling head,
tore fiercely at his chest and to his soul cried out:
"What shall I call you, O man's soul, how shall I limn you?
Sometimes you seem like a lean ship that swiftly sails
on the dark waters of despair, Death at your helm!
You know well there's no sea, there's no safe haven home,
but a black cataract has clutched and whirled you round,
and though you fiercely fight to row back, O my soul,
and deeply feel at length that no salvation comes,
how I adore you when you cross your oars like hands
and upright on despair's edge, with no hope or fear,
break out in the wild wastes with a gay gallant song!
O soul, you stretch your bottomless, your unslaked palms
to quench your endless thirst with that immortal water, Death!"

XXIII

Great Sun, O Father, Mother, Son, three-masted Good,
you sleep with our pure women on the fertile earth,
for if you do not thrust your seed deep in their flesh,
man's sperm is void and sterile, each drop lacks its son.
You are our mother, too, firm breast that brims with milk,
and all our open mouths await you, all lips gape
to grasp your light at break of day and suck it sweetly.
Great Sun, you cast your warm wings on the nested eggs,
peck with your golden beak upon their fragile shells
until the callow bills within peck in response
and the thin middle wall falls slowly, the shell cracks,
and fledglings drop into your lap and chirp for food.
You are our son, you splash in water, roll on grass,
cling to our breasts when hungry, turn blood into milk,
and when, my son, you wake at dawn and turn rose-red,
a thousand birds wake in our breasts, a thousand cradles.
O Sun, Great Son, profound joy of our earthen eyes,
hold us forever in your palm, hatch us, dear God,
turn all our feet to wings and all the earth to air.
Take the old archer, Sun, in your caressing arms,
don't leave him here alone, for see, the worms have come,
their hidden jaws are munching at his entrails now!
Great Sun, flood down into his bowels, turn all the worms
to thousands of huge crimson-golden butterflies!
In a great blaze of wings and light, in salt embrace,
make Death come riding down astride a gallant thought!
Let Death come down to slavish souls and craven heads
with his sharp scythe and barren bones, but let him come
to this lone man like a great lord to knock with shame
on his five famous castle doors, and with great awe
plunder whatever dregs that in the ceaseless strife
of his staunch body have not found time as yet to turn
from flesh and bone into pure spirit, lightning, deeds, and joy.
The Archer has fooled you, Death, he's squandered all your goods,
melted down all the rusts and rots of his foul flesh

till they escaped you in pure spirit, and when you come,
you'll find but trampled fires, embers, ash, and fleshly dross.

Old archon Time passed by and a small worm crawled up
and sat aloft on his white head, herald of doom,
then opened his frail jaws and swallowed all the world:
"By God, what lands I've swallowed, what great towns I've smashed!
I've just returned from the ice-fields and gorged myself
with brides and bridegrooms, lusty grandsons and old men;
I've swept the snows so well that not one soul remains.
But what's this shameless skiff I see that leaps the waves?
Dear God, the fearful white-haired head glows in the poop
that year on year I've longed for on all lands and seas!
It strikes deep roots like a stanch oak or sturdy rock,
I stoop and hear strong demons thrash their swords within it;
alas, how can I lay it siege or pierce its bones?
I'll take a deep breath first and buckle on my arms."
The sun broke into wild lament, gazed on the sea
and saw the rosy worm gird on its arms and twist
and turn high on the head of swift-approaching Time.
It stooped and gazed, broke into tears, nor wished to set:
"My heart shall break now if I wash and rest in waves
and leave you in the dark alone to fall in Hades,
for on your brow already I see the first worm crawling!
Alas, there where you long to go, where now you cross,
there is no sea to cool you, no swift ship to sail,
there are no men whom you may juggle like dull stones
or flip on high with heads or tails, just as you please,
nor gods where like a scorpion's tail your brain might rear
and cast its fearful sting in their blue hearts of air.
Alas, there where you long to go they'll snatch your weapons,
your ears, your hands, your lips, your still unsated eyes,
and fling your mind, dust of all dust, on their dim shores!
Who was it once saw sails on seas, or foam on waves,
or the winged passage of a hawk in azure air?
Who has seen trace of the world-traveler on earth and sea?
It was blue smoke that vanished, fire that disappeared,
the rustle of tree leaves at noon, heat-haze on rocks,
red lightning flash on a wild singer's darkened brows!
Alas, at our black parting now my eyes grow glazed,
I can't distinguish joys from sorrows, truths from lies;
the myth falls headlong like a star in the vast night
and leaves a smothering trail of sulphur and of jasmine!
Sun of an inner sky and sea, peak of an inner world,
O Mind, I rose and sank in your world-famous head,

roamed round your walls and thus encircled the whole world,
but now I'll vanish with you, too, and drown in waves!"
Thus did the sun lament and veil its pallid face
with a sad tender cloud until the whole world shriveled,
then on the humble coffin it slid its pallid hands
and softly stroked the white head of the death-doomed man.
But as the seven-souled man watched the sun, yet heard
no words, it seemed to him his friend was drenched in tears,
and he raised high his calloused hands to comfort him:
"Dear Sun, I've sailed days without end on these cold seas,
I've been abandoned by all men and the heart's passions,
my heaving breast has emptied, ebbed away and dried,
the gleaming pebbles have grown dull, the nymphs have fled,
for all have smelled the dark abyss, sought other seas,
and only you still follow, O red faithful hound.
Go back! The hunt is ended! No wild game remains!"
But the sun melted the thin cloud, marshaled its light,
then cast it longingly on that ripe distant head
and held it softly, sleeplessly, in lustrous hands,
and the archer raised his eyes and scolded tenderly:
"O Sun, your light obstructs the myriad stars about you;
go off to your good-fated mother now for she
has strewn you tables of rich food, soft beds for sleep;
unyoke your snow-white steeds at last to browse on waves.
Don't weep to watch me disappear; I've cocked my cap,
for soon the lyres will ring, and my white bride will come.
Sink in your waves, don't see her, or your heart will break."
But still the sun refused to listen, and roamed in rings,
spun the white head with light, wove and unwove with rays
tall candles for the dead, and flaming silent wreaths.
The slim skiff gleamed and quivered in the unsetting sun,
tall icebergs broke off, far away, without a sound,
and slowly, slowly sailed, rose-red, on the green waters.
Somewhere the fins of sharks flashed by, and the sea shuddered,
somewhere the black seals barked and wailed like weeping babes,
somewhere resounding clouds of birds swept on white wings.
But as the lone man raised his head, his brains were filled
with the shrill cries of air, warm bellies, and white wings,
then spread his arms and on the wild birds' passing necks
hung messages and salutations for the living world.

As moments passed like sated years, he bid farewell
to earth and life and fondled them with aching palms.
A great gold ship of air loomed on the sky's sea-lanes;
high in the upper airways blasts of wind blew by
and the cloud swelled and puffed, changed many shapes until

it piled up high like weightless cotton and shed its wings
as the Old Man watched its myriad gambols silently.
Sometimes it seemed like a thick smoke that would soon scatter,
revealing, as far as the eye could see, the burning castle;
sometimes it floated on blue shores like a huge town
with towers, walls, and fishing boats, but winds blew by
and the town molted and hung down in straggling threads.
"Hail, O small airship, little sister, land of cloud,
winds blew and shaped us, winds shall blow and we shall fade."
The lone man spoke and waved his hand to the upper land
but it had scattered down the sky and left no trace.
Meanwhile the sun leapt up, full-armed, and shrieked aloud
like an unsleeping guard who watched a town besieged;
he'd seen the danger and cried out, but neither god
nor man, not one soul in the inhuman hush replied,
and the worm buckled on its arms, took a deep breath,
crawled slowly up the dying archer's body, coiled
between his eyebrows till he shuddered, raised his eyes,
and saw a Shadow sitting on his foaming prow,
coiling, uncoiling silently, flickering in light,
swift-spinning like a top, changing both form and face.
Sometimes it turned to a lean crow that honed its beak,
at times to a fierce ship's dog yelping round the prow,
at times to a black peacock with wide-spreading tail.
The sealskinned skiff sped like an arrow through the waves
and an erotic jet-black swan gleamed on its bow
with ruby eyes that in the pale sun sweetly burned.
Slowly the shade distilled into a stooped old man
with snow-white bushy hair, a beard like a swift stream,
and a warm cap of blue fox-fur perched on his head.
In his deep sockets flashed a pair of small black eyes,
and slowly with his bony arms and narrow hands
he pushed his shadowy oar with sluggish weariness,
and the swift-minded archer wanly smiled and guessed
who now had seized his oar and sat on his sharp prow;
his old ribs opened and his thin bones faintly creaked
to make room for his long-expected mighty guest.
For a long time he neither spoke nor moved, but as
he watched his old friend, sweet compassion moved his heart
so that he opened his blue lips and bid him welcome:
"Ah, Death, how old you've grown, my dear, how white your hair,
how much misfortunes and black cares have maimed your flesh!
Your face, like mine, bears the same slash in the same place,
wherever my flesh is scarred, your flesh is wounded too,
and there between your eyebrows a small worm lies coiled.
I bend my face above the water and see your face.

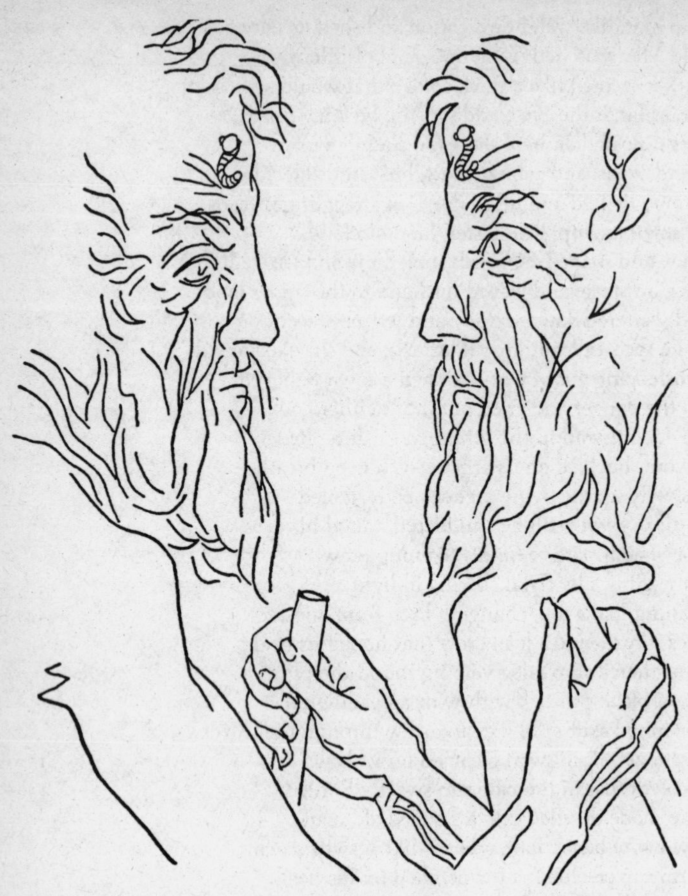

O Death, great Temple Sacristan, O faithful hound,
you've zoned my shadow like a shadow my life long,
rushed forward like a king, or lagged like a low slave;
how much you've suffered and grown old on earth with me!
Welcome, dear friend, lie down that we may rest together."
Death in reply but sweetly smiled and fixed his eyes
on the calm darkened eyes of the fox-minded man,
and the two gazed together silently for hours
and gently rowed on the smooth pearly threshing floor.
The sleepless sun caressed the two old heads until
their white and stubbly beards burned like a brushwood fire,
then it hung down like a gold tassel from their fox-fur caps.

The heart filled and could take no more, hands overbrimmed,
the mind's full flower turned to seed and scattered wide
with joy on the salt waves of the ancestral plain.
The lone man's mind burst open and his memories poured
like cascades down his temples in the vast solitude.
Behind him the Wheel softly, mutely turned, his brows
creaked, and Time, an ancient python, opened its mouth
and spewed all it had swallowed till they gleamed once more.
Odysseus shook with joy—he had not lost one drop
of memory, and rejoiced in all his myriad heads
that glittered in long rows, snow-white, jet-black, or gray.
An old man, white with years, stood in the sun, thick-boned,
and a mature man that scaled castles and clasped women,
or plundered sea-lanes by himself in rotting hulls;
on a high threshing floor a youth hurled a stone quoit,
his mind a rosebud still, with savage virgin leaves
as yet unfurled, and held his famous voyages
and his far-distant future deeds in leaves immured.
Still further back, the lone man watched his body fling
small boats upon the waves, in shape of a lone child
whose spirit like a fearless captain rode them all.
Then, as a suckling child, he seized his mother's breast,
bit its rose nipple deeply with a ruthless greed,
and as she laughed and wept, she felt this son of hers
would one day seize life's holy breasts and suck them dry.
The suffering man could trace himself no further back:
within his parents' bodies he had seethed like fever,
strolled in his father's loins past the betrothed one's door,
and as his virgin mother stooped with trembling fear,
she felt her son's feet kicking in her untouched womb.
His mother by her window sewed her bridal clothes,
and when she stooped, her locks fell on her working hands
as her swift fingers flew and the embroideries rose
from her small heart and spread and soared until they wrapped
her secret dreams with yellow and with crimson wool.
She stitched blue seas and ships and oars, black dwarfish men,
and her tall son, their captain, zoned with a red belt,
till her young maiden mind like water poured and flowed.
Thousands of years before all parents saw the sun,
he'd flashed like foam on water or like flame in caves,
or twined about a plane tree like a cunning snake.
He'd learned with patient stubbornness, with his great Mothers,
Silence and Earth and Sea, how he might mount at last
on loam one day in a man's form and live his life.
"Brothers, together now, let each one gird his arms,"
cried Death's antagonist to all his myriad forms;

"one of you take a child's toys, one a young man's youth,
another a man's lustful craze and two-edged sword,
and let the last one mount that pure-white steed, the soul,
and plunge to Hades like a proud slain conqueror;
my lads, it seems to me that Death has come full cycle now!"

He gathered all his memories, held Time in his hands
like a thick ball of musk and smelled it in the wastes
with flaring nostrils till his mind was drenched with scent.
Time melted in the lone man's fingers till his nails
dripped with aromas like the birds of inner Asia
flown from rich woods of nutmeg blooms and pepper root.
He was drained pure till life turned to immaculate myth,
and into tranquil princesses his fearful thoughts,
for in his mind dread God distilled like oil of roses.
And as Odysseus smelled the ripe and flaming fruit,
a sweet swoon seized him, all his entrails came unstitched
and his veins opened with unutterable relief
and all his body's armored net which once he cast
to snare the world—nerves, bone, and flesh—became disjoined.
The five tumultuous elements, that strove for years
to forge the famous form of the world-wandering man
shifted and parted now and slowly said farewell—
earth, water, fire, air, and the mind, keeper of keys.
Like five old friends who have caroused the whole night through
then stand at dawn by crossroads, for the talk is good,
and make half-hearted stray attempts to part at dawn
but find still more to say and stand with door ajar
and still hold hands and twine their fingers, lingering still—
thus like these five old friends who had caroused all night,
the archer's five strong elements, his five proud friends,
stood at the crossroads of his brain and could not part.
The mighty athlete then caressed his white-haired head.
"O nacreous, pearl-lined jewel-box, O brimming head,
in you the seeds of the whole world became one kin,
for trees, birds, beasts, and man's own gaudy generations
all rushed to sprout within you, not to plunge to Hades,
but now that they've all sweetly met and merged like brothers,
it's time, dear head, that you were smashed! Fall down, and break!"
The lone man spoke thus to himself and with sad love
gazed on his elder brother who still lightly sat
enthroned on the dark prow, deep-scarred with ancient wounds.
How many ancient memories, what sweet conversations
strolled slowly through his mind, sailed on his speechless mouth!
The many-faced man smiled, and the same gentle smile
spread on his old friend's lips and turned to a wide grin

while his small flaming eyes gleamed like a black swan's.
The hunting mind of the god-slayer dashed in the fogged
and distant woods of memory and flushed out his pains
till his misfortunes cawed and scattered like fat quails,
and in remembrance his life's voyage burst and blazed
in his white head like a blood-trailing falling star.
He plunged and clutched from cliff to cliff, but once again
his fate's wheel flung him to another deeper gulf:
"O Tantalus, O great Forefather, blessed curse,
O bottomless mouth, O hoping yet despairing heart,
O hunger by strewn tables, thirst by cooling streams,"
he cried, and greeted hunger like satiety,
and his old grief like joys, when once he'd roamed the world.
"All gods and all my ships have rotted in my hands;
nothing remains of my proud friends but a small tuft
of gray hair in my fists, memories, and fragrant dust.
I clutched at trees to keep from plunging down the gulf,
but trees broke from their roots and left in my bruised hands
a slender quivering grass blade, a faint drifting scent.
As a last refuge, then, I clung to my only son,
but my son pitched me off unpityingly and rushed
to cast his parent in mid-road and reign sole lord.
With force and rage I rushed to leap man's narrow walls
and at a large-eyed vast idea clutched with pride,
but it climbed up my body's tree like a spry ape
and played with my head's apple, gently chewed and munched
till it had eaten all, then leapt to another tree
and plucked another's head and sucked another's brain.
I raised a great god on earth, but one blazing dusk
he sank like a large town in earthquake and thick smoke.
My hands shone in this world like tall fruit-laden trees
filled with great joy and gallant pride still unconsoled,
but now I bring them to wry Death filled with air only!"
As the great archer spoke thus, he caressed his hands,
his feet, his thighs, his white-haired chest, his sturdy loins,
and his most precious, thousand-wounded, martial head.
Raising his eyes, he saw on the bowsprit before him
his old friend watching with a sweet yet bitter smile,
and as their eyes met in the icy wastes, they gleamed
like scorpions at their honeymoon, like streams, like snakes.
The emerald waters, drenched with light, reflected both
the white old men, a pair of silver swans that sailed
unsinging, though their slim necks overflowed with mute
and sad songs of departure till the waters glazed.
As both friends drifted in the sun on turbid waters,
the multivoyaged man recalled a flaming rose

he'd seen one day weeping in rain on a cliff's edge;
full-blossomed, fallen down supine, with open heart,
despairing, hushed, unmoving in the darkening dusk,
its petals shed and fell drop after drop like blood.
This rose now blossomed on his memory's darkening cliff,
its tears still glittered and its bloodstained leaves still fell
slowly within his memory, his remembering heart.
Even a rose could make the archer's heart still sigh,
but he felt shamed once more, raised his eyes toward the prow,
and as Death smiled and swayed, canaries flock on flock
sprang from his armpits and the hollows of his palms
till the town-battler stared, the rose dispersed in air,
and from the open cage of his cracked memory flocks
of gold canaries flew and covered his black prow.
A thousand years ago, on Crete's blood-splattered shores
one noon, his friends had smashed the castle's brazen gates
and massacre raged through courtyards, and the women wailed,
yet he could now recall not one old man or maid
who seized his ruthless knees or stretched their necks to die,
but only massed canaries in golden cages high
in air that shrieked and smothered in the turbid smoke.
At that time, as he'd sunk in slaughter's swooning daze,
he'd neither moved his lids nor raised his eyes aloft
to pity the gold birds that in the blazing flames
vanished, though guiltless, with their high-born mistresses,
but now, dear God, they'd sprung to life, and from those far
most wretched shores had flown and perched on his brain's boughs
until his white head warbled like Death's iron cage.
As the lone man rejoiced in their despairing song
he saw a deep-blue butterfly that hovered close
above Death's white-haired head, landed with fluttering steps,
then got entangled, floundering, in his long mustache.
But old Death, tickled by the downy wing's caress,
alas, sneezed on the prow with sonorous relief
so that the lone man laughed and wished him health and joy.
But the poor startled butterfly with fluttering wing
flew quivering past the castle-wrecker's shoulder blade.
How did this fragile soul, dear God, find itself here
in this white wretched bitterness, the sea's last rim?
The archer shrank back mutely as the butterfly
perched on his mossed mid-brow, and memory leapt within
his heart like a dark beast and slowly chewed her cud
as an old harvest-month returned, for once more Crete
shone in the sea's midst, crisp and warm, with curving shores.
Her haughty summits glowed rose-red that hour in light,
and all her virgin thorny mountain-ridges laughed;

amid the esteemed great continental Mothers, Crete
shone like a playful gold-haired siren who with joy
now stretched on azure waves and sunned her naked form.
And once upon a time, on a small tiny fold
of her strong body, curly-haired girl-gleaners laughed
and sang the ancient love laments of vintage time:
"Alas, you were not made to lie in the cold ground,
for you were made, my dear, to lie in a maid's arms
in sweet May gardens the night through, while in your lap
ripe apples tumbled, almond blooms rained on your hair,
and red carnations hung in rings around your neck."
But no maid's mind was on the sad thought of the words,
for doves, caresses, kisses swirled to the wild tune,
and flocks of waggish lovebirds laughed on all the vines.
The learned young men who carried grapes to the wine press
stripped off the bitter pod of song and in its heart
found and exposed the sweet fruit of its double breasts,
then tossed their curly hair, seized swiftly the sad tune
and to the maidens' wails replied with love refrains.
Within their master's courts, the many-voiced wine-vats,
brimming with vintage grapes, groaned with resounding din.
Blond, naked, strapping men hopped in the vats and jigged,
for all were drunk and dazed with the grapes' acrid wrath;
their hanging thick mustaches dripped with the wine's must,
grape-stems got tangled in their armpits and long beards
and must poured thickly from the troughs into huge tubs.
The archer's old friends drank in taverns, stretched on sands,
and fate still hovered round the rich-wrought castle gates,
but when their master passed and beckoned, then flames roared
and the whole castle writhed and swirled like autumn leaves.
Glad in the thickening smoke to find his duty done,
he would repose at evening like a working man,
or slowly like a sated household snake digest
his plunder, golden rings, plump gods, and wealthy kings.
But on the ground he suddenly saw in its last gasps
a quivering and blind butterfly with tattered wings,
and his eyes brimmed with tears, the heartless man's heart cracked
till with his nails he dug the soil and thrust it deep
as though he buried his belovèd daughter there;
of all the world-renowned and sacred Cretan town
only one deathless quivering butterfly remained.
Ah, all things merge in kinship in our final hour;
the down of a small wing is balanced in the mind
and weighs as much as the most glorious realm on earth.
What joy! No man is paid for life's fatiguing trek;
he counts, recounts his wages in his heart but finds

two or three rose-leaf drops, but two or three small wings.
"All, gods and sons and wars and thoughts, all, all were grass,
frail grass on which I browsed like a strong elephant,
but now, an old man with white hair and whiter brains,
with no cruel master in the sky, no cares in Hades,
I'm launched and slide in the close-fitting gaping ground.
To whom shall I shout now, 'Well met!' to whom 'Farewell!'?
Not one soul bears me company, not one soul greets me here."

As he was speaking, mourners from his memory rose,
groups of lamenting women whose entranced eyes shone
like black, green, sea-blue stars within the ruined air,
each one with an entreaty on her firm-locked lips.
His heart remembered and rejoiced, took back its words,
for in the world he'd known a horde of wing-clawed men
who had drunk much, fought side by side, shared bread and salt,
yoked themselves many times like ox to plow this earth,
but their souls never once had joined or merged in one.
It seemed as though male bodies were hard shields that rose
between men and prevented the nude soul's embrace,
that with maids only might full nudeness be enjoyed.
All good, all progress which his mind had known on earth
he owed to maids alone, for they tore down all flesh!
Only they felt his pain or took him by the hand
and stepped down to the holy body's secret groves
where both plucked the most flaming flower of all flowers.
Bodies of varied tribes, immortal and mortal arms
had, each one, led him sweetly to most secret rooms,
each to a town unknown, shores seen for the first time,
forests filled with aromas, deep refreshing streams
where he kicked off his sandals and took the cool plunge.
And if he knew how the great gods lived in their sky
and how their huge hearts throbbed or how their vast minds worked,
he owed it to one bed-seducing star-eyed goddess;
if joy had ever spread into his softened heart,
if castle gates that parted souls had ever opened,
blessed be those lily-fingers dripping musk and myrrh
that held the keys of life and opened to let him in.
Splendid are the mind's blazing lamps and the soul's flames,
wondrous the heart that battles with all azure shades
and pours out all its blood on earth to rise in spirit,
but all—gods, demons, laughter, tears and giddy thoughts—
swirl swiftly like a whirlwind, merge in one, then sink
and drown in the curved womb that lies supine and beckons;
it only is real, all else on earth are gaudy wings.

"O thousand-faced pellucid good, nude womankind,
no one, although he live on earth a thousand years,
can quench his thirst if once he drinks your deathless waters;
for now, a hundred-year-old man, I've cast my thoughts
and giddy glories far away like patched-up rags,
nor do I want my son, nor call my home to mind;
ah, could I only arm death-battling ships once more
that you might stretch upon my stern, immortal maid,
that my old comrades might come, too—I like their stench!—
and push off to new voyages on Death's vast seas!"
The lone man turned his head and looked back toward the world
as though, dear God, he sought to find his hastening friends
or a long host of women looming deep in light.
Sweetly swept off by love, he felt compassion now
for his tormented body scarred by many wounds:
"Like the fierce lion who returns to his deep lair
alone, but filled with memory, without mate or cubs;
like a pure airy spirit whose mane drips with dew
then gleams on the dark threshold like a funeral pyre,
and vanishes, thus have I seen you stand, O body,
at Death's own door, brimmed full of memories and desires.
O faithful body, let most sweet compassion fall
like honey in your sated heart before you die,
for see, you turn your rough-hewn face, consumed by storms,
and slowly watch the light-filled world for the last time.
All's well! I gaze with cheerful calm on all my roads
through earth and sea, on all my roads through every heart,
and if the fire and water that first shaped me merged
once more on earth, a second, third, or a tenth time,
I'd take the same roads once again, the same sharp arrow
would twang unsatisfied from my right breast forever.
I'd drink all bitterness again, I'd glean all joys,
but from the start I'd strive each time to go still further,
to cross and pass all roads with swifter, greater strides,
for the soul has no ending, nor can thirst be quenched.
Heigh-ho, in my old age I long to summon all
kingdoms and towns to council by Death's door, and shout:
'Come, you old elephants, come, rag-and-bone old men,
come, ancient worms, you secret councilors of earth,
gather about me without fear; great cares have struck me;
let's form an old man's council, brothers, let's find out
from whence we come, my lads, and where it is we go.' "
His words still moved upon his tongue, his thoughts still held,
but gaunt Odysseus, life's stanch warrior, that old crane,
felt tired now and dropped his head, immured in sleep,

and as Death watched him opposite with wordless greed,
like an old brother a much younger come from far,
the seven-souled man wanly smiled and slowly sank to sleep.

Far off rains fell and seized the world in their wide nets,
seeds stretched their roots in sleep, swelled up and filled with milk,
the dead lay naked in the loam and bulged with rot.
In sleep, earth is transparent and all rocks are crystal,
and the much-suffering man stooped low, gazed on the dead,
gazed on his father, and his heart broke, for not once
in life had he said one sweet word to him, and now
at the world's end, in sleep, he thought of him, and wept.
Slowly the rain stopped dripping as Odysseus bent
and sniffed the savage smells of earth till his mind brimmed
with a thick poisonous tumult filled with ghosts and shouts.
Phantoms plunged in his entrails, the dead woke and rose,
the holy tree of sleep swelled with a rustling sound,
and from its downy branches hung thick-blossomed dreams.
Leaning against the tiller, the mind-roamer slept,
but his mind still kept vigil back of his dark lids.
Like an old archon or a mighty king who greets
his faithful lords, his servants, and his next of kin,
the great mind greeted graciously the noble spirits
and opened wide his swelling chest to hold them all:
"Open my spacious courts, O slaves, my doors, my gates,
rip off the heavy roof, that all my guests may come,
for I hear birds and spirits, and all my doors are jammed!"
The kingly mind thus cried and hailed the holy heralds.
His roof gaped wide till, tightly locked in their warm wings,
the quivering birds descended softly, slowly there,
and stooped down, twittering mournfully, to say farewell.
The grosbeak and the chaffinch came, blackbird and hawk,
vulture and partridge, jackdaw, eagle, all at peace,
their sharp claws sheathed, their blackest passions now wiped clean;
in that great evening all the sated peaceful birds
perched in his myriad-nested head to pass the night.
This was the very first winged hour of holy night.
Next came the beasts, the hairy brothers of our hearts,
and like a heavy river licked the lone man's feet;
with sated teeth at length, their savage eyes grown mild,
brooding like thoughtful men, they trooped in, two by two,
jackals and foxes, lions, bisons, wolves and lambs;
some silent, some in tears, their tails between their legs,
all stooped and said farewell to the mind's shepherd-king.
Their claws turned into idle ornaments, their horns
turned soft and hung like two long locks on tranquil brows;

the hares no longer trembled, fawns with leopards walked,
snakes, tigers, scorpions, bears, played with disburdened heart
in the dark forests of a mind serenely dying.
That was the second, shaggy hour of holy night.
Then to his faithful flocks the shepherd said farewell:
"Goodbye, you have toiled well, and in the savage strife
you have well given your tasty meat, your furs, your hides
to help imperiled man in his first sentry hours;
don't weep, another master will come soon, you'll all
rejoice to spend your strength on one greater than you."
He spoke, then raised his glowing face toward the vast sky;
deep from the darkness the stars armed themselves and came—
some dripped like blood, some raged as in a drunken fire,
some swept through darkness, yellow as a leopard's eyes,
some laughed and showered down with joy's erotic orbs.
Like wings, fires, waterdrops, enormous battlements,
like funeral candles for the lone man's dying mind,
like large warm tears that slowly dropped on his white head,
the stars passed by in silence, sinking down the West.
At last the trembling stars dissolved, the full moon sank,
and the whole dome of heaven plunged between his brows.
That was the third and star-eyed hour of holy night.
Then as the stars like a long necklace decked his throat
and the mind wrapped itself in shrouds, lean horsemen dashed
in furious gallop on pure-white moon-breasted steeds
across the plundered and deflowered sky of night.
Unripe youths shone and dashed ahead, and old men followed,
old warriors with deep sword-cuts on their sunburnt chests;
these were great thoughts that dashed on steeds to find and greet
their father, Mind, who now passed through man's last frontier.
Wars had enflamed them year on year, discords had wracked them,
some stooped to earth and toiled with patience and with craft
to free enslaved man's heavy soul from fear and darkness;
some screeched and cut like vultures through the blazing sky
and dared to bring back in their beaks the godly fire;
and others smashed the earth's foundations ruthlessly.
But all great thoughts set out at length, foe merged with friend,
the night crushed down, earth reeked, the stallions stamped and neighed,
the brothers rushed together swiftly on white steeds
and all swept through the archer's temples with swift pomp
as the great archon hailed his mighty sons with joy:
"A thousand welcomes, O brave lads, my giant sons!
I'm sailing toward the lower world, but you're still firm!
Go mount each sturdy brain you find, mount each bold heart!"
He spoke, and the thoughts scattered and took myriad roads;
they'd met in their brave father briefly, and then parted,

and some rushed down to earth once more, some swept the seas,
but the most daring pierced the sky to loot the stars.
This was the fourth outriding hour of holy night.
Now with hermetic rituals the dark spirits passed
mutely, with folded wings, to bid the mind farewell;
all dark and lustrous powers passed by arm in arm,
night ghosts and demons, angels, gnomes, elves, trolls and fates
entwined their shaggy bony arms and golden wings
and felt for the first time, in the great dying mind,
friendship's and freedom's sweet unutterable joys.
The evil spirits held in their sly hands fine gifts
of crimson and refreshing fruit, wine, women, towns;
and the good spirits spread their empty lily hands
and sang, though silently, great freedom's massive dirge.
As all ghosts sang and faded in a quivering mist,
and all the varied beasts and birds, the thoughts and stars
sank, scattered, fled like smoke until the world grew light,
the seven-souled man smiled and his mind winked and played
as though a good dream drifted past his snow-white beard:
"Those were not gods, nor beasts, nor trees, those were not men,
those were not sorrows, loves, or joys, that was no heart
that throbbed within me like a sea and stormed the world;
they were brief lightning flames in which I shone and vanished!"
That was the deepest light-winged hour of holy night;
downy and warm, it meekly bent its silent head,
crouched, wrapped in tender wings, a lump of earth, and slept
caressed by the great mind of the death-traveler now
who also shut his weary wings and huddled close
like a dark eagle settling slowly by his mate's warm side.

His mind slept wrapped in wings, and far away in woods
roamed the blood-splattered beasts as ticklish day awoke
naked in light at break of day with giggling smiles;
and as the first soft beams of dawn licked at the stones,
the startled peacocks woke, the shameless monkeys leapt,
the slim and spotted vipers poked through sand and raised
their bloated throats to drink the light like tiger lilies.
The daughters of the sun passed by with their warm feet
till on all heads the upright noon hung like a sword,
and at the wild abysm's rim, the earth's cold claws,
the tranquil archer slowly was unsheathed from sleep
and felt rejoiced to see his old friend at the prow
like a black-feathered and death-smothered savage swan
that raised its silent neck serene to sing in air.
Still down his whitened temples poured the ghostly dreams,
for stars, beasts, birds and thoughts still streamed along his head

as though dark phosphorescent lights licked at his bones:
"Death falls like a black sun on our soul's flowering groves,"
he thought, and slowly raised his eyes to laugh at Death,
but ah, the prow plowed empty through the shattered sea!
Old Death had vanished without trace, his mighty guest,
and left the lone man orphaned, one heart now, not two,
that pounded with profound throbs and strong double strokes.
Feeling the miracle draw close, the dying man
then crossed his oar and heavy hands, crossed his mind too,
and let his death-boat drift upon the sweeping tide.
He stretched his feet and scanned the length of his small craft:
his measurements were true, his coffin fitted well,
and coffin, sea, and body tightly merged in one
as Death blew like the sweetest and most fragile breeze:
"O Death, the soul is a dry branch! Blow, make it bloom!"
The thousand-eyed sun ached still for its precious friend
and with warm tentacles caressed in gentle strokes
his hoary hair, his chest, his knees, his feet, his hands,
and as the hopeless warrior felt the sun's warm palms
and their smooth tenderness, he shook, his coffin swayed,
and both world-wanderers slowly, deeply said farewell:
"Aye, I'm departing, Captain Sun; take courage, friend,
don't weep, all pain's forgotten soon in forty days!
Strengthen your heavy heart and to your sad mind say:
'The sunlit game of life flashed well on earth and sea
and on the lambent air! Enough now, fare you well!' "
But the sun stroked the hard-burnt body speechlessly
and in its dulled mind sadly said farewell, and wept;
but the swift-minded man, guessing his friend's ache, cried:
"Dear Sun, a couplet in my throat coils like a snake
and I must shout it out, O Sun, or it will choke me:
'Sun, let's pretend I've never seen you! Ah doom, O doubt,
I've held a slender burning candle, and it's gone out!' "
As in the narrow coffin the two leopards played
they suddenly saw in the rose mists, erect on waves,
a tall broad-breasted mountainous snow-castle loom
and drift by, mute, despairing, the dead's sacred isle,
a soul transformed to a pale ghost that sought to breathe.
The ancient athlete did not speak, but bit his lips,
and with bent head gazed on his lonely bloodstained soul
as it sailed silently and swam on the green waters.
When the ice-mountain dwindled in the drifting mist
and vanished like a phantom in the sun's pale beams,
the lone man shivered secretly and his eyes glazed:
"This must be Death who passed by, sad and pale," he thought,
"fumbling the sea like a blind man in vain to find me;

this must be that white elephant I soon must mount!
O mind, since all your wiles and tricks won't work here now,
turn dread Necessity to pride here, if you can,
and with no swoons or false bravuras bravely mount
that pure-white elephant that passed, and let it take
me where it will without vain protest or surprise
as though I had myself selected the same road."
He spoke, then tightly bound his ax about his waist,
slung his curved bow of stag-horn down his shoulder blade
and round his shriveled neck hung his two precious flints;
although he knew well that no weapons now could aid him,
he wished to scatter to the winds full-armed, erect, and proud.

He shut his eyes serenely like a full-fed babe
who drops his mother's nipple and on her warm breasts
fumbles and cuddles close, then sweetly falls asleep.
As his great lashes fell and covered the whole world,
from his deep bowel's threefold pod, dear God, there sprang
and quivered on his mind's full-shadowed sill his frail
untouched rose-baby body and his bubbling laughter.
Time and space met and merged like fruit in his brain's rind,
all distant things drew close, the wheel turned once again,
the past shone in his fist like deep translucent water
wherein the dying man in silence watched his face:
"Ah night, O flashing flint upon the nuptial bed
where my strong father merged first with my virgin mother!
O great soul-seizing sperm, filled with all light and mud,
in which I leapt invisibly once, soul, body, and bow,
in which I swept toward the dark earth, a blazing star!
In her ninth month my mother walked the sounding shore
to play with her handmaidens, to refresh her mind,
and to breathe free of the dark fruit that filled her womb.
Labor pains gripped an earth who'd slept with myriad men,
and she crouched low on stones amid her maids and yelled
till creatures of the mud and brain rushed up with fear
to help her as wind, soul, and bread, and noble thoughts
stood by like faithful midwives to await the child.
And as my mother calmly walked on the blue shore
she felt as though long wings within her launched and soared
as her son kicked her womb, that bolted castle door;
all seemed to her deep dreams, the air a turbid sea
through which with sweet fatigue she thrashed her arms to pass.
She saw an ancient fisher plod, weighed down with nets,
and a young hunter far away with a stretched bow,
and high aloft on a shore rock she saw a god

clutch to his breast a babe and gaze far out at sea:
'Your health, begetting mother, eagle-nest that gapes!'
Then the young mother laughed and with the pebbles played
as the waves washed her feet and cooled her naked knees
till a great swordfish swam close by and ripped her womb.
A tall black ship then drifted by with a red mast
from which a robust sea-chant rang, and as the mother
stretched out her cool and snow-white neck to hear with joy,
her belly grew serene and her son listened also.
Then as the pallid mother followed the red sail
and all her soul like a red sheet flapped in the wind,
pains gripped her suddenly, and before her maids could come,
her son rolled out on shore like a hot burning coal
entwined with seaweed, splattered with salt blood and sand."
Thus in his ancient coffin on the edge of space
and time, the ancient athlete through closed lashes watched
with pride the raw babe wailing on the distant shore
as the maids rushed with fear to save it from the sea.
All earth felt light again, the waves like dolphins leapt,
far off ill-fated castles trembled and maids laughed,
whole fleets cracked in mid-seas, a great and noble island
with a bull's golden horns bellowed with fear and rage,
and twelve gods who had swooped on mankind's rotting corpse
raised their crammed guts with fear and scattered like black crows.
The archer then remembered his soft sprouting body
that played amid his parents' gardens, thrust in mint
and in curled basil leaves which reached high as his shoulders.
One day his father had fed him honey in fig leaves,
and all, brains and soft head, became a honeycomb;
if he ate grapes, then his mind filled with vineyard fruit,
if figs, he turned to fig, to wells if he sipped water,
for his mind, like soft wax, took all the world's impression.
Now he'd returned to his dread mother, the vast sea,
and brought her back his battered, once rose-misted flesh.
A chilling mistral suddenly blew, and his frail body
flapped like a tilting vessel's sail which a light breeze
wheedled and gently coaxed to rise and leave, for now
the red sail would be rigged and the world float away.
He fumbled at his rocky knees, his ancient shins,
played and tried out his rusty joints, stretched out his arms,
slowly caressed the sun's twelve labors round his loins,
the twelve bright constellations which enwrapped him round,
opened his eyes and watched how the sad sun caressed him,
then stood up straight and felt it time now to tear down
life's holy toy made of earth, water, fire, air, and thought.

Odysseus spread his hands and blessed his famous body,
his five night-long carousing friends, and said farewell:
"O Loam, thick prudent dowry of mud-mother earth,
O strong hutch of the homeless mind that like a tramp
roams far and rots in sun and rain, by ghosts devoured,
O Loam, who open your arms wide to take him in,
I feel you like mute heavy ballast in my bowels,
gripping with strong foundations so the mind won't wreck me.
You wrap my heart with fat, stick to my shanks like mud,
drag me to earth that I may not fly off and vanish!
You grip tight like a peasant in my entrail roots,
stoop down and plow my riches, count what strength I have,
sell your goods slyly, cheat your spendthrift neighbors short,
slowly enlarge your fields and farms, increase your wealth,
then at the crossroads sit enthroned like a great landlord.
The heart runs on ahead and whips you to take wing,
and sings to give the narrow earth more breadth and scope,
but you, O elemental loam, tag flame on foot
nor haste with longing, for you know toward where you go
and even rejoice when your feet sink in earth's warm mud.
You hear the mad heart flap its wings and long to fly,
but you plod on, speak with coarse words and mock the bird:
'What shame, you dolt, to long for skies when earth's at hand!
What a great crime if now my hard heels sprout with wings,
for the green earth is sweet, and I have heard it said
that even in the Elysian Fields souls weep for earth.
My belly, my coarse hands, my feet adore the earth,
nor do wild wings torment me nor far gods enchant me,
for if our eyes are made of clay, they shine like stars!'
Dear friend, you speak with your thick head, you open roads,
and bent with patience to the yoke, a sluggish ox,
you pull at the mind's brilliant blade and chew your cud;
but dusk approaches now and your day's work is done,
it's time to drop your yoke, to lie stretched in your stall,
O father, loam, and faithful ox, and the mind's earthen rind!"

Then the mind-archer ceased and his sad heart felt light
as though his ballast of mud, stones, and heavy earth
had suddenly sunk and his freed body had sprung in stature!
He stretched his hands and blessed his second element:
"O Water, wandering female source of life, I cup
your flux to give you a firm face and say farewell.
You warble swiftly, vanish, fluctuate and slide,
you turn all the mind's mills and all its fantasies,
nor condescend to faith, nor know what pity is.

You pierce through the black earth with rage, play with the sun,
you make the rainbows and the water-kingdoms bloom
then blot them out once more and play with other toys.
You are no peasant to strike earth's roots in my heart
but a swift-vesseled sailor who's squandered all his wealth,
glad to set sail at daybreak in a walnut shell
and leave behind all certain good, his home, his son,
virtues and feasts and comforts, all his useful gods,
and roam nude through stark foreign strands, a weathercock.
'I'm neither flesh nor mind,' you roar, 'I pass and flow
like laughter after rain, the seven-stringed sky's bow!
The mud-brained peasant lifts his startled eyes and shouts
to see my yellow, crimson or green zones foretell
his golden grain, his red wine, his green fragrant oil,
then licks his lips with greed and welcomes me with joy,
yet I'm but the rain's toy and one of the sun's smiles.
I'm not Landlady Earth, I don't sit all day long,
faithful beside my honest hearth, to await my husband,
for I sport night and day with all the sixteen winds,
and though I pluck virginity's crimson thorn-filled rose
it blossoms once again nor ever shrinks or fades.
Some call me sea, and when a ship plows through my waves,
I close its blue wake, and my honor once more blooms;
some with due reverence call me soul, an inner sea,
and deck me like a bride with breastless and dry virtues.
They call me deathless, pure, without one lump of earth,
they say I long to flee from the frail body's shame,
and though I listen to their words, I clasp flesh tight
the way a fierce girl clasps her sweetheart in the dark.
I'm not a shriveled spinster, I'm not pure, unkissed,
and I'm not chaste, nor came on earth to live a saint,
and once I clutch a body, it can't shake me off,
for never have I yearned for skies or longed for gods.
Archer, I've loved you much, and now that you must go
nor leave me either your strong hands or virile thighs,
don't sigh, my tight-twined love, our time has been well spent!' "
Thus did the deep voice murmur in the archer's heart,
and when it ceased and the wave closed his bleeding wound,
the deeply bitter voice of the flesh-wrecker rang:
"O my heart's female element, O washing wave
that waters me, you draw me with you night and day,
but now we've reached that parting where embracements end."
He spoke, bent down and scooped some water in both palms
then joyed to watch it falling from his fingertips
drop by slow drop, sad, multicolored, in the sun-washed sea.

When his palms emptied, he turned then to his third friend,
to his third inner element, and said farewell:
"O greedy greyhound, O my leopard heart, O Fire,
you who disdain both earth and water, who lick cliffs
then leap to the twin peaks of my despair and strength,
hear me, O Fire, mother, daughter, hear and obey!
My ancient bones are empty now and hiss like reeds,
my backbone spills into the sea drop by slow drop,
earth's left me with indifference, turned to loam once more,
and roguish faithless water once more flows to sea;
you only have stayed faithful in my middle brow
O Fire, O noble dancer, dance-adoring flame
who seek new kindling always so the world won't fade!
To scrape joy from their joyless hours and loveless goods,
the prudent landlords of the earth with their fat brains
gossip with poison-nosed, sharp virtue stealthily
or hold the keys of power and let loose every shame
or fondle some seductive girl on a soft bed,
but I choose only you, O Fire, with your tall cap!
Ah, leopard-spotted, we've played well together, pierced
through castles, stormed through hearts and cast fierce sparks
till all—stones, wood, and hearts—gave up their final bloom!
O Fire, you know the secret that has burned my heart:
'I don't love man, I only love the flame that eats him!'
When as a lion I prowled through the low homes of men,
I did not rush to save a single body or soul
for my mind scorns the ash and dross you leave behind you
and with dread fear hunts only you, O mystic flame!
You flapped above my bold head like a tattered flag,
you shouted and I shouted too, and your tongues leapt;
earth's and the heart's foundations tumbled down and left
but warm ash slowly smoking in my hollow hands.
You did not stoop to earth to heap up peasant wealth,
nor felt a sluggish joy in the wave's yes and no,
but rushed ahead and knew well where you aimed your shaft:
to burn down towns and hearts, to burn your master too.
You scorched and cleansed the earth to cut new furrowed fields
till better sowers come and the soul bloom once more.
O Fire, the wolf's your shepherd, the fox guards your vineyards,
you scatter wealth to the four winds and shout to all:
'Come, I'm the landlord, seize my wealth and goods, eat, drink,
for all's mine, towns and brains, and I want none, I choke!'
That's why I've loved you, leopard, with your upright tail!
Well have we played and burned together our lives long
when your claws made my body bleed or cracked my mind,
when all night in my sleep I heard your cackling tongues

lick my hands clean of skin and strip my brains of meat.
I walked in rains and sun-blasts of the wretched earth
alone, with no dog, children, friends, no gods, no hopes,
and strove with you alone, O Fire, to outstrip you only;
but you leapt over the head's ferocious battlements
and fixed me firmly with your famished flaming eyes
for you knew well how tasty a master's flesh can be.
Rise, eat your father, Fire, that we may die together!
Wrath and compassion choke my heart, I won't play now,
my soul leaps like a fiery breath from bough to bough,
clutches and claws head after head at night and shouts:
'O Fire, wipe out whore-mongering earth, my sons have shamed me,
my daughters have shamed me too, and I shall blot them out!'
I watch the crimson thread that slowly mounts the earth,
the bloody turbid phosphor of glowworms that crawl
and squirm with lust and couple in the mud, then fade
within the rain-drenched ruts of man's imagination;
I watch, and scorn to play here on this whorish earth!
Soul, country, men and earth, gods, sorrows, joys and thoughts
are phantoms made of water, loam, and the mind's froth,
good only for those quivering hearts that hope and fear
and those air-pregnant brains that belch their sons to birth.
Our trembling bowels groan: 'From whence, and why, and where?'
our heads groan too, resounding in the boundless night,
and now a voice within me leaps in bold reply:
'Fire will surely come one day to cleanse the earth,
fire will surely come one day to make mind ash,
fate is a fiery tongue that eats up earth and sky!'
The womb of life is fire, and fire the last tomb,
and there between two lofty flames we dance and weep;
in this blue lightning flash of mine where my life burns,
all time and all space disappear, and the mind sinks,
and all—hearts, birds, beasts, brain and loam—break into dance,
though it's no dance now, for they blaze up, fade, and spin,
are suddenly freed to exist no more, nor have they ever lived!"

The spark lives in the body, roars, and both our lungs
feed it like bellows till our bowels burst in flame,
and the archer hailed the conflagration like a dew
then turned with calm to say farewell to his fourth friend:
"O Air, who gently rest on conflagration's dome,
who hold light like a mystic task, flame's final fruit,
invisible, secret stature high above our heads,
descend, amass yourself in the head's crown, then vanish!
You hold the cool pure light, you conjure smoke away,
for as the lily stares on its mud-roots in earth,

you look down on the smoking flame and rise up purely.
You take the ash that drifts, still warm, in my coarse hands
and scatter it like a good plowman who sows his seed
till ash turns wheat once more and the world once more sprouts.
You smash the body's dungeon till all passions merge,
sing like a carter, pass from flesh to mystic flesh,
jump past abysms and fetch secret news and breaths
to hospitable hearts that bloom and brains that bear.
I felt you blow in my sad heart like a strong wind,
you were the sun's unseen corona, virgin down
about my rough and ruthless head and my cruel words.
You sprang from my deep entrails like a bridegroom bee,
like a proud drone in springtime when the heather blooms
till the chaste honeyed queen-bee with her fragrant body
secretly sighs, within her regal cells constrained,
and spreads and tries her wings, then licks her body well,
for honey-cells have brimmed and all await her spawn.
Then the drone dons his armor, arrays himself in sun
and wraps himself in love's most sacred panoply.
His eyes dilate like a gold cap, spread round his head,
then swiftly sweep, though motionless, through the sky's dome
and spy on the whole azure globe to catch the bride.
His small ears open wide, and if a feather fall,
he hears the whole wood ring as if a tree had crashed,
he hears how the queen dresses and adorns herself,
he hears how her whole working army buzz about her,
rasp secret counsels in her ear, then see her off.
His taste augments and plunders fields like honeycombs,
his tongue flicks even about the sun like harvest knives,
his nostrils swell till in the springtime air he feels
the bridal body soaring in the wedding pomp
as honeyed premonitions burgeon through his body.
Earth is a buzzing beehive grove, the dripping sun
a golden honeycomb he gleans until he feels
about his sticky feet and fuzzy happy belly
her regal body merge with his and fill with seed.
Aye, honey-drone, good was the wedding, good the game,
old Honey-Mother Earth brimmed with transplendent seed,
nor now has need of you but rushes to give birth,
and all your empty guts hang from her sated thighs.
O honey-drone Odysseus, air, light, unseen form,
I raise my eyes on high and see with trembling joy
Death riding the most violent nuptial lightning bolt!"
For hours the dying man watched the sun's lonely wheel
graze the sky's level rim, nor rise nor sink in waves
as a continuous dawn poured in the pearly sea.

Without once touching the smooth waters, the sun turned,
pale, hopeless, weaponless, about the archer's snow-white head.

In his skull's secret lair, the suffering man approached
with calm the fearful scorpion with its sting raised high:
"O Mind, great master-craftsman of the homeless air,
like an ascetic in his cave you sit cross-legged
deep in the skull, a sacred athlete, a great martyr;
your thoughts leap like trained falcons in the sky, and shriek,
pretending to be gripped by hunger, to hunt game.
In empty air's blue ring you marched earth's brilliant troops
well-decked with flesh and soul, with fantasy and truth;
you leapt to earth and danced, pleased with its fragile toys,
you often changed forms, wings, plans, names, rolled carelessly
like a small child on savage shores of a black sea,
scooped up wet sand, then pummeled it with haste and cried:
'I'll make clay men, I'll set thick armies on the march,
I'll blow into their nostrils, fill them full of soul,
for I won't play alone on the world's haunted shores!'
At once the poor sand trembled and began to move
till trees, beasts, birds, stark-naked dwarfish men sprang up,
seductive maids who decked themselves, bold fighting braves,
and white immortal souls that strutted down the beach
like swaggering pigeons as they flapped and tried their wings.
Now blow, O Mind, and turn them into sand once more!
Animals shout, the waters roar, trees burst in bloom,
birds and dark demons rush on me like harbingers
to see how with untrembling hand, of my free will,
I've dared to open the earthen door to let Death in;
but I still smile and fight black-eyed Necessity
with pride that won't be put to shame, but sees and loves her.
The heart beats, passions churn the swelling seas to foam
till the mind looms within the flood, a monstrous rock
down which the quiet waters plunge in cataracts.
O Mind, your four steeds, water, fire, earth and light
strain at the bit and leap, but you hold the reins firmly
and temper savage strength with the brain's prudent thoughts.
Though your steeds snort and fly with wingèd hooves to reach
those fat stalls which they think await them at road's end,
and though you know the secret well, for your eyes brim
with chasms and despair and death and gallant deeds,
your hand is firm, you spur the swiftly dying steeds,
you feed them well, caress them, deck them handsomely,
then all together, road, steeds, chariot, charioteer,
plunge swiftly headlong tumbling down the bottomless gulf!
I love you, Mind, for fearlessly, with open eyes,

you dash with pride straight for the naked cliff, and plunge!
In the fine scales of your mid-brow you weigh all things,
and in your every sorrow, every joy, you temper all
with your wise thinking—water, fire, earth, or air—
for you know well that life is but a game of scales.
If a grain more of earth should fall, man's mind grows heavy,
the poor soul's caught in the lime-twigs of mud, and drowns;
if a drop more of water falls, man's firm face breaks,
its dough sags, it can't grip, it spills, and flows, and rolls,
it tastes with no sure memory, clasps with no real arms;
if a flick more of flame falls in fate's kneading trough,
alas then to the immoderate heart, for the whole world
burns down, and life turns ash within our palms once more;
if in our ripe heads boundless light should overblaze,
then pallid and pellucid life, that star-stitched veil,
flutters and plays above us like a drifting cloud;
but our strong fists will never deign to be deceived
or rise to grasp air-phantoms like the firmest flesh,
and life will fade in air like a soft shadowy dream.
O Mind, great charioteer, you hold the myriad reins
of sacred virtue and of shame, of fear, of hope
in your strong hands and drive on toward the plunging cliff;
I thank you, for you've ended your hard duty well;
now that the cliff looms close, O Guide, let loose your steeds
to plunge with chariot and charioteer in the dark gulf,
for we've arrived with luck at length at our long journey's end!"

Then the great athlete slowly crossed his workman's hands,
a light but paralyzing swoon poured through his body
until, deep in the shadow of the flesh, his mind,
that huntsman, and his heart, that faithful hunting hound,
lay down fatigued and burdened with their slaughtered prey.
The lone man closed his eyes till like a serpent-god
sleep wound in heavy coils within his head's dark cave;
black lightning bolts tore through his brain, the deep earth gaped
with its dread trap doors as in the damp swarming dark
God stood above his earthen troughs with heavy hands
and pummeled clay till from his armpits the sweat poured.
His monkey-daughters and his red-assed servant-sons
dug earth and sieved it fine, then broke in cackling cries:
"The Old Man's gone berserk, lads, childish, addle-brained,
he sweats, unsweats, till with blood, tears and sweat he shapes
erect nude pigs and makes them stand on their hind legs,
sets them to bake in sun, but the soft showers fall
and the clay melts to mud, the Old Man weeps and wails:
'Alas, my latest children have turned to mud again!'

But now, they say, he's shaped a two-legged upright pig
with pointed cap on his tall noodle, a strong bow,
and hung two flashing flints in his mind's tinder box.
Come on, let's see what this new pig amounts to, lads!"
But as the monkeys jabbered in the world's deep womb
and jeered at the old codger with his dripping armpits,
an ape-hag suddenly staggered in with frothing teeth:
"Red-buttocked brothers, help me, hold me or I'll fall!
The Old Man's mad, he wants to burn the entire world
and bake his latest child so that his soul won't fade!
He's running to thrust it in his blazing oven now!
Frog-God of Rain, rise up and cast your spells once more,
call down the clouds, let the rains fall, make the world mud!
We're lost if this last son's successful and well-baked!"
The monkey mob screamed shrilly, rushed to come in time
before the Old Man thrust his clay dwarf in the hearth,
leapt swiftly, then stood still with horrified dismay
and watched God enter the hot flames as the world swayed.
"We're lost," the poor beasts moaned. "Here's a new master born!"
The earth shook seven times, as though by birth-pangs seized,
and slowly God walked from the fire and his arms clasped
a curly-haired small man baked black as wheaten bread,
and when God bent above it, blew, and in its ear
entrusted his great word, at once its azure cap's
long tassel stood erect and stiff in the bright air.
The frightened Frog-God fell flat on his paunch on earth
and tried in a choked voice, with gurgling river sounds,
to allure the cackling rain that perched in the damp trees.
The sky, in full concordance with the fearful beasts,
blackened with clouds till rains began to erode the world,
to strike the trees till the leaves fell, to melt the earth,
to beat and blind the sun till in the rain-drenched dark
God moaned, "My child!" and bent above his earthen son.
But his son flourished and grew bold, he cocked his cap;
his eyes, his chest, his belly gleamed in rain; he twirled
his black mustache, then laughed and kicked the Old Man hard:
"Go pack, you doddering fool! Make way for me to pass!"
Then from his belt he drew an iron sword on whose
broad blade there flashed the sharp-etched threat: "God, I shall slay you!"
Poor God grew pale and staggered back with buckling knees:
"Alas, I shouldn't have shaped such a dread beast! I'm lost!
I'll run and hide in the vast sky, for the earth's his!"
His red-assed servants ran, his monkeys held him up
and dashed him with rose water to revive his wits,
but his eyes glazed with staring on his last-born son
who with cocked cap and tassel bright as the pole star

flung to the light a gallant and defying song
with words first heard on earth that made the Old Man quake:
he sang of joy, revolt, of freedom, and of bold new roads!

Odysseus slept and sank into the world's foundations,
he plunged in sacred roots and like an infant clasped
the great dark Mothers and with unslaked passion sank
his thirsty mouth with greed into their earthen dugs.
As his mind melted on his brows and poured like sweat,
his ears were plugged, the song died at the earth's roots,
and ancient Mother Silence spread her brooding wings
on the world's wastes as she had done before Life rose,
till the great archer with crossed empty hands, with trust,
surrendered to the crooked tide of nonexistence.
Then with shut eyes he saw, with empty ears he heard
a huge snow-mountain with a thousand silver bells
sing in the still unsetting sun with joy and slide
on the smooth waters like a bridegroom's snowy sled.
As his mind dropped its reins, he tossed his head and watched
with silent fearless wonder that pure crystal isle,
that snow-white peacock, that white elephant of Death,
that hundred-petaled, heavy-scented rose of white.
In silent greeting then he moved his waxen lips:
"Welcome to all I've loved most in the living world:
that proud white peacock, the mind's lightning; life's white rose;
that pure-white elephant with whom I'll plunge to Hades!"
His thought's reflections rustled sweetly and still held,
his entrails quivered like a bowstring's tremolo
when suddenly thunder burst within the iceberg's heart
and the snow-mountain cracked and clove, its top crashed down,
then split in two and bared its pure hard crystal heart.
But the unyielding proud man jumped, his mind burned clear,
his heart leapt up and poured into his regal veins,
and the last soul the seven-souled man held in store
rushed to his aid and held his swooning flesh upright.
"Rise now, don't cast your weapons off, uncross your hands,
how shameful, fool, to plunge to Hades headlong, blind!"
Pushed on beyond its will, his body tossed and cursed,
squirmed from the skiff, leapt out, then strove with stubbornness
to cling with hands and feet to the white mountain's slope.
His nails clutched grippingly and clawed the sliding ice,
but he fell down and rolled, ice zoned him everywhere,
and his despairing body once more clutched and gripped.
But the snow-mountain, like a ghost with cloven heart,
immaculate and mute, slid slowly from the grasp

of the tormented man till on the water's edge
alone, thick blood-drops gleamed, and shreds of white hairs shone.
But all at once the seven-souled man's mind flashed fire,
he grabbed the ax that hung down from his leathern belt,
struck at the ice and cracked it, clutched and gripped the clefts
with his ten nails, then on all fours crawled up the slope.
His white beard reddened with thick drops of dripping blood,
but like a horseman he gripped tight his crystal steed
then mustered all his strength to shout with a hoarse cry
and call up swiftly from all Hades, lands, and seas
his faithful comrades, his old crew, his sunburnt troops,
that all might plunge to Death together, sail and oar;
but the cry choked in his cracked heart, and his throat foamed.
Joy was a silent hopeless waste, and the sea poured
like frozen honey in a dream where ancient souls,
old outcries, old immense battalions, insect hordes,
huge honey-yearning molted wings, all Life's assault,
unmoving, mute, in one great mass now slowly drowned.
Only at times a flying fish with coral eyes,
rebellious soul that still remembered life in dream,
leapt from the thickened waves to see the upper world—
the sea erupted for a lightning flash, the bright air gleamed,
but once again the waters hushed and the game vanished.

Life swayed like a sunflower, dark with too much light,
and turned its brooding face toward the black sun, toward Death.
Stars seethed behind the light till night's great cypress tree
with its black-leaved unfruitful boughs burst into flame;
the birds awoke from sleep and stumbled with scorched wings,
moths gathered like gay in-laws, worms like wedding guests,
the mole rushed like a harbinger with upraised flag
and Death paced like a bridegroom with a viper-ring
to wed the archer's rich aristocratic soul.
He asked a hundred mills for dowry, souls for grain,
half of the mills to grind with tears, and half with blood,
and one mill to be turned with the deep sighs of men.
Then the redeemed shipmaster on his fleet of ice
and with his snow-white bloodstained beard, with his smashed nails,
opened his black eyes wide and watched the bridegroom come.
His blue hands froze, his feet became as hard as bone,
slowly his brains became benumbed with drowsy sleep,
and his mind hovered like cold breath and passed like mist
or a frail empty phantom on the foaming waves.
The coward ax dropped from his waist and on the ice
left its old master weaponless in that dread hour;

his faithful heavy bow slipped from his shoulder blade
and left its Archer undefended, stark, alone;
and the thread snapped that bound the sacred chips of flint
till they rushed headlong to escape the grip of Death.
The North Wind passed and laughed to see him, stretched its arms,
snatched off the hairy pelt that fenced his flesh and bones,
and left him stripped and blue-lipped on the seething sea
till all the spirits of the air pressed round and burst
with bells to jeer and taunt him with their silvery sounds.
White seabirds dipped, enormous seagulls swooped and wound
the pale death-stricken man in swirling loops and rounds,
and their swift nooses tightly bound and choked his throat.
Then the great wailing, death's high threnody, began,
and the pale sun drew close and burst in lamentation:
"Alas, alack, the mind's great eye is setting now!
I took great joy to light the world, to watch at leasc
one free soul that still loved and understood my light,
but now, O upright wing, you molt, and I molt with you!"
The sea, too, heard and rose, and to her loved one called:
"Where are you going, beloved? Don't leave me widowed here!
With whom shall I play now at dawn or quarrel at night,
who's worth the trouble now to toss with smashing storms,
to batter his strong loins or cleave his hull in two?
Aye, Captain, take me with you, I shall miss our games;
let Hades brim with our embracements, our fierce fights!"
The birds heard also, swooped and shed their downy breasts
in a sad twittering threnody, then the seals came,
compassionate plump sirens who began to weep
like mournful women, circling round the crystal tomb.
More seals converged with tears from the world's distant ends
—gods, countries, sweetest exiles, passions and ideas—
till the vast sea resounded with their plaintive dirge.
Then nine lean crows appeared and honed their dreadful claws:
"Oho, my lads, we've hunted him nine times nine years,
and though we've grown old with white wings and bleary eyes,
he still stands proudly on his feet and fights with fate.
When his death rattle rose, we smelled his scent far off,
and from a small and thin-boned island zoned with vines
and olive trees, we left his mighty death-gorged oak,
and came here, brother birds, all nine, to lick him clean!
Make way, O gulls, his body has been ours since birth!"
Then the gray-templed ravens of his island cawed
and huddled round the feet of the swift-dying man,
but as the sea-wolf heard them in his thickening daze
he slowly raised his hand, and the corpse-eaters vanished.

The sea again heaved with its dirge, the seals swam round
once more with their thin hung mustaches, their maid's breasts;
his seven faithful souls appeared like mist on waves,
rowing a small cloud slowly, with translucent oars,
and when they saw their captain clutching the cold ice,
then seven hoarse cries shrilled from seven splintered throats:
"Aye, Captain, your tramp vessel on its final trip
takes the cool dew for tiller, the black clouds for sheets
and spreads the flute's sound for a sea on which to sail—
the time has come now, raise your throat and give the sign!"
But their great captain's loins like a tall castle crashed,
he longed to raise his hand, to utter a loud cry
and welcome his dear comrades, his old faithful crew,
the seven dreadful and deep souls his body bore,
but sweet sleep poured like honey down his sunken brains
and his mind's final flame assembled, flickering, faint,
on his long backbone's topmost and despairing wick.
Then the great maggot rose, that fat prophetic worm,
its rosy body clad in armor, opened its jaws wide,
took the first bite in secret, munched, then gave the sign.
But the death-traveling boatman watched with open eyes
as his deep entrails melted, his flesh swayed like mist,
and water, earth, air, fire and mind all slowly snapped
and severed till each took the great road back once more.
His cords and nooses broke till the whole world was freed,
all pleasures soared and disappeared, pain found repose,
and the cadaverous sun leaned down to drown in waves.
Love only still twined tightly in his moldy heart
and threw a quick look backward till its lashes brimmed:
the past still blossomed and bore fruit, no soul or flesh
was lost in the earth's maw, and stubborn memory, too,
that tombstone slab, burst into bits and cast its dead.
If only the small early moments of dawn, dear God,
would rise and blow their breath on the mind's windmills now!
Ah, clasp the body tight, O soul, until it rots!
The mighty athlete clenched his teeth, dredged up his strength
for fear that red-black bird, his soul, might flee her cage,
needing her still a moment to utter his last cry.
As a low lantern's flame flicks in its final blaze
then leaps above its shriveled wick and mounts aloft,
brimming with light, and soars toward Death with dazzling joy,
so did his fierce soul leap before it vanished in air.
The fire of memory blazed and flung long tongues of flame,
and each flame formed a face, each took a voice and called
till all life gathered in his throat and staved off Death;

then the hush roared, the soul leapt for a flash in light,
bodiless, naked, weaponless, and dashed to clasp
the dread souls it had loved when it once lived on earth:

"O faithful and beloved, O dead and living comrades, come!"

XXIV

A thousand welcomes to those giant breezy lords,
the four great winds who storm the crossroads of the mind!
The North Wind's door burst open and like a starved town
the master's great brow fell, smashed down like a frontier;
the North Wind's door burst open and trees marched in rows,
slim sharp-leaved date trees, honeyed and young apple trees;
all fresh and cooling fruit set out, figs, grape and quince,
all seeds and herbs of all kinds, a green monstrous tree,
plunged down his ample brain, sweet savory left the fields,
green mint the gardens, wild thyme flew the mountain slopes,
all rushed to sweep into the lone man's hollow skull.
"Let's plant our roots in his mind, lads, and we won't die!"
Back of his skull, the South Wind's door burst open wide
till beasts and birds swooped happily, for musk deer leapt,
spread-eagles plunged down from the sky, ants swarmed from soil,
green glowworms lit their bellies, he-goats steamed with lust,
slim sacred snakes uncoiled and licked the sizzling air,
all rushed in at the South Wind's door to save their souls.
Huge vans of reindeer, camels, elephants and bears
swiftly set out and vanished in his head's huge dome,
and Pan, that goat-hooved forest demon, that earth-dragon,
stood by the brain's dark entrance and spurred on his flocks:
"Make haste, my brother creatures; hurry, birds, worms, beasts,
our best most precious grandson with his wide-spread wings,
with his strong twisted horns, the holy brain, is dying!
The savior has stretched his hand, he's opened the underworld,
the funeral's started, our green brothers all have come,
be quick on your feet, beasts, be quick on your wings, birds,
let's hail the savior of the world for the last time!"
With her cool rosy fingers, daybreak gently woke
the right-hand snow-white temple of the great god-slayer
till the sun's double doors burst with bird song and wings
and all the invisible ghosts set out, all the mind's hosts,
all apparitions leapt like dew-washed does and deer,
the spirits of green earth and sea and air dashed down
with all their tiny silver bells, their golden veils,

till the brain's furrows laughed and shone like gleaming shores;
then step by step upon the mounting air there swept
all the imagination's strutting rich-wrought birds,
gods, thoughts, dreams, mists, and perched on the mind's barren boughs.
As the sun set upon the quivering crimson waters,
its last beams opened the archer's left-hand snow-white brow
and brimmed its ancient hollows full of frothing blood.
The door burst open, smothered deep in azure shades,
and rows of pilgrims, leaning on their crooked staffs,
swooped down into his brain, plunged in his memory's wells,
laughing and weeping, with strange cries, in sheepskins dressed,
some wrapped in date leaves or in brilliant ostrich plumes,
some nude as crystal water, men of every kind and breed.

All four great castle doors burst open, and all guests,
trees, phantoms, beasts and men, all wearing festive robes,
massed in the streets and courtyards of his spacious brain;
but still the funeral had not started, light still stayed,
the great soul-strife still held, and a fierce voice rang out:
"Don't seize my hair, O Death, I won't give up my soul
before my dear companions reach my ship of snow;
the stitches of my skull have opened, the whole world
is crammed inside, but I don't see my long-loved crew."
Deep from his bowel's darkest cave the answer came:
"Archer, I hold your cobweb-wrapped and renowned crew
on my hard granite knees and grind them fine in earth;
don't be so proud, you slayer, I've got you here alone!"
But in the mind's vast courts and memory's grooves once more
the seven-souled man's death-destroying voice rang out:
"All faithful forms I've loved, all hearts and all souls, come!
Broad-buttocked Kentaur, come, pick up your bones and come!"
Broad-buttocked Kentaur squirmed, his bones knit once again,
his bellies bulged once more, his heart with murmurs stirred,
his coarse hands sprouted hair, his thick beard sprang to life,
he shook and kicked, then leapt up toward the upper world
and poked out like a mud-soaked beetle who thrusts through
a dung-pit where he'd long caroused, reeking with muck:
"Ahoy, my friends, a strong wind blows, the brine descends,
my nostrils now grow warm once more, my strong bones creak,
I hear a voice high in that wretched upper world.
Is it perhaps the cuckoo bird or are young men
casting the discus on my tomb with shouts and laughter?
I hear wide white sails flapping, I hear the sea's roar;
push on, let's rise and leave, I hear our captain call!"
Bowed down before the oak, the piper shook his nude
and pointed pate like a scared rabbit, his tears flowed:

"Where are you now, dear master, where are you roaming now?
By what seas does your tall cap sail, by what strange men
does your mind browse, that dread unsated elephant?
I turn a backward look and gaze on my past years:
alas, blue waves and islands, women and great towns,
hungers that thrashed our guts and wild carousing times—
all these I spurned and then betrayed, O wretched fool!
Ah, if the wind-sails of our life unwound once more
and the earth's myth began once more to twist and turn,
I'd never leave you, master, I'd stay to the dark end!"
He sighed and turned his rabbit's head to right and left;
below, in sun and rain, the Negroes' round huts gleamed,
the sky's rich rainbow-belt spread through the moistened fields
and a young maid came slowly to the old oak tree
and placed near the witch doctor's knees a tub of milk:
"Pity me, master, my son's sick and the dogs bark,
Death roams my neighborhood, and I've no other son."
But the sad piper's thoughts had sailed on distant waves,
and when the mother's pleas cut through his dazzling trip,
he frowned and with great wrath kicked at the proffered tub,
spilled all the milk on earth and cast a grievous spell:
"May you be cursed! The first-born son of earth and sea
now dies at the world's end! May the crows eat your son!"
He spoke, and his flute-dreaming ears brimmed full of sound,
long billows rose on earth, the stones burst into storm
and his thin temples sprouted oars and roared with winds.
At last when his sharp body's prow set sail and foamed,
a voice roared "Orpheus!" high, aloft, and the wretch crouched,
but a huge dragon's paw grabbed him by his bald pate
as though an eagle clutched a hare in its sharp claws.
Thus screeching, his whole body dangling, he was soon swept
to a long promontory struck by sharp sea winds,
and beat his pallid hands and roused his manly heart:
"Once more my nostrils flare, once more they drip with brine,
and my old throat once more perks up with fluting sounds.
Dear God, how good to launch on journeys in old age;
already I can smell the breath of our proud captain!"
He shrieked, but his old cricket's voice was suddenly cut
when he saw triple buttocks and double shadows fall
and heard a loved and long-lost voice boom like a cave:
"By God, dear piper, you've crouched at the old oak's root
and I've scorched earth's four corners, lad, to flush you out!"
Broad-buttocks roared with laughter and his throat grew firm,
his hands grew strong, he snatched his friend's pale form and tossed
and juggled with it on the distant foaming cape.
But cross-eyes smelled the moldy loam, and his eyes brimmed.

"Don't weep, my whimpering friend, I don't smell of the grave,
though worms drip from my eyebrows still and from my hair;
I rolled out on the new-washed soil from my great joy,
for when I heard my master's voice, my wits went wild!"
The sighing piper blinked his quivering bleary eyes:
"Dear friend, you're eaten by damp earth, you smell of death,
your flesh hangs down in tatters from your greening sides
and I see camomile and grass in your thick nostrils."
But glutton stopped the piper's mouth with his huge hand:
"Friend, why do you prattle so of death, why prate of tombs?
Filthy old gold erodes and stinking silver melts,
but the strong soul of a good man can never rot.
Here, place your hand, my brother, deep in my left side."
The piper's shriveled body shook as with pale hand
he groped in rotted entrails of his friend, their deep blue wounds:
"Here is no heart, dear brother! I grasp a lump of mud!"
But glutton wiped his mouth and flung down two small worms:
"Ah, don't distort things, friend, don't wail, I'm not yet dead!
Come, raise your feeble arms and grasp me by my loins;
for all we know, we're both dead, or perhaps we dream
we're darting over lands and seas like swifting birds
because we heard from far our dying master's cry;
friend, don't get lost, don't question, follow your dream only."

Death rattles shook poor Captain Sole, he swooned toward Death,
and all the village gallants laughed, decked him to die,
took down his armor slowly that it might not crumble,
and an old woman pounded paints in pumpkin shells
to color his pale lips, his shriveled hollow cheeks,
and make his dreadful old wounds blossom like red roses.
The female mourners crouched in rows on earth like crows,
tore out their hair by handfuls, beat their sterile breasts,
and wailed out all he'd seen and done, all his brave deeds,
and how Death seized him now to drag him down to earth.
As in his darkest depths he heard them, his brains roared,
the frozen sweat dripped from his body drop by drop,
but deep in memory he rejoiced—he'd done his duty,
defended justice with his weapons as best he could,
fed all the hungry poor and freed the wretched slaves.
In truth, he'd left behind him many bitter cares,
but others would take down his still unrotted weapons,
for he now placed his hopes on youth, his gallant heirs;
great hopes still blossomed in his heart, and his brains swelled.
Deep in his daze he felt them smear him with fat paints,
and he recalled old spear-thrusts, coughed with proud conceit,
and the youths' laughter seemed to him like bitter wails:

"Don't weep, my lads! Come, dry your tears, the world's not lost,
another hero will come, perhaps one greater than I,
and he'll complete all that I've left undone on earth."
He spread his trembling hands to bless the callow youths
but suddenly shook with speechless awe, sat up in bed,
and his taut ear-chords broke, far billows smashed his brains,
and his heart tossed like fishing boats, tugged at its ropes,
as from far shores a voice cried out, "Captain Sole, help me!"
Then Captain Sole jumped from his bed, strapped on his belt,
forgot, from his great haste, to seize his rusted sword,
dashed swiftly through the door and dashed into the street.
Ah, how the earth had changed, how wings sprang from his feet,
how like a spirit he leapt from form to form and fled!
He heard the village laughter, and his heart rejoiced;
like a frail cloud he swept through air and sat on streams,
perched on the tops of trees, rushed on ecstatically,
passed waters, woods and rocks, and drove on toward the south;
then all at once he smelled the sea and his chest swelled—
from deep within blue waves he heard a loved voice call
and he dashed forward like a starving gull to reach the cry.

But as he raised his empty and dream-woven wings
he saw a tall foot-traveler running down the beach
whose russet head was cloven with a deep sword-thrust.
"Oho, that's a great king with a sword-thrust for crown;
he, too, is a great world-captain full of wounds and scars.
Since he runs swiftly south on the same road as I,
I'll stop here to defend him now for pity's sake."
Captain Sole stopped benignly by the seashore's rim,
grasped tightly his long empty sheath with his left hand
and placed his right hand on his chest to show esteem.
As surly Hardihood drew near with crunching steps,
pebbles resounded down the beach, smoke dimmed his mane,
and from his mind his seething thoughts swept up like flames:
"If it's true, murderer, that you called, and that I leapt
out of my grave, I'll seize my sword once more and stand
at your right side to burn that famous town once more!
I've learned much in my first life! Now in my new life,
I'll know, friend, how to wield the sword, how to twist brains
and mount the people firmly, that dumb surly ox;
my soul still flames, nor will earth ever put it out!"
He roared, and in his hand still held his shattered sword,
and a fat worm still hung from his dark eyebrow's ledge.
Captain Sole turned with grace and hailed him like a king:
"Well met, O fearless lord! I see they press you hard!
Take heart, brave youth, I'll don my armor and dash out;

if you've a thousand foes, I'll scorn them; if three thousand,
I'll turn for a brief lightning flash and slay them all!"
But surly Hardihood glared at the old codger
who naked, heavily painted, bowed and waved his hands;
then he wrung wrathfully his poisonous lips and scowled:
"Scat, you old fool! What shame to see old age so drunk!"
With a rude hand he thrust aside the tottering captain,
and the poor wretch turned stone and burst in loud lament:
"I fight for his own good, talk to him from my heart,
bow down to earth before him, yet he shames me, God!"
He wailed, but when the voice called out his name once more,
he gathered strength and sped toward the far cry with speed.
Hardihood frowned with wrath until the fat worm fell:
"God and my soul! That drunkard's taking the same road!
Archer, what shame! Haven't your years brought you some sense?
Whatever cheap wind-driven trash still blows your way
you pick up and entrust with oars and shame your ship!
If only now I had no need of you, I'd turn back quick!"

The air smelled of sweet musk, and velvet slippers raised
red tulips on the greening earth and grass on stones
as two bright laughing women with their naked bosoms
ran flying down the roads and cut through azure air.
The old one held thick pomegranates to her breast,
dew-washed and bursting, gleaming crimson in the sun,
that with reflection reddened her pale sleepless face:
"I know he loves this fruit, and what great joy it'll bring,
so I've once more gleaned all my orchard for his sake;
ah, dear Love, give me wings that I may come in time!"
The young one stooped and strove to shake off cobwebbed films
and sticky loam from her grass-filled mud-splattered throat;
she flung her black death-kerchief off, and down her back
there fell cascading her still-fragrant raven locks,
and her most sweet yet saddened voice rose through the air:
"Dame Goody, ah, if only this were not a dream
of walking earth in the warm sun and fluttering breeze!
If only life's erotic drunkenness would burst
once more, and our maids paint us in our garden close
and the young merchants beat upon our doors once more
to bring us gifts of perfume, ivory, gold and plumes.
Dame Goody, I'm afraid we'll wake, our joys will vanish."
But the obliging Dame, mistress of all love's arts,
now pitied the young maid, caressed her shoulder, smiled,
and her hoarse voice rose kindly from new-painted lips:
"By the sweet dread I felt when I first slept with men,
I swear a great oath, Margaro—we're truly walking,

this is in truth the old cool wind, the gallant sun,
and here I hold cool pomegranates tightly clasped!
This is no phantom of our minds, so don't be sad,
but listen how my warm throat bursts with sweetest joy!
Our great Belovèd called and we leapt from our graves
and now rush swiftly to adore his bloody feet;
then with his blessing we'll return to bloomless groves
once more and bare our bosoms to console the world
like cool springs in mid-road for passers-by to drink."
Margaro smiled, then stopped, and once more shook the loam
from her yoked painted eyebrows and her pallid thighs,
and old Dame Goody thought of life, and her heart brimmed,
her teeth in her shrunk gums once more like jasmine gleamed,
her hanging udders once more slowly rose and swelled.
They passed through a dark wood where varied birds soared past,
trees bloomed, swayed silently and cast their colored flowers,
and two robust and lordly cocks with lifted crest
stopped in the fields to admire the two lustrous maids.
Dame Goody laughed, rejoicing in the golden cocks
as though they were rich merchants with their precious wares:
"Ah, lovers seldom seen, come, welcome to our doors,
your wallets on your chests, your red caps on your heads!
I hold musk in my hands to feed you with, my lads."
The proud cocks gazed with admiration, swelled their chests,
their stiffened combs grew scarlet, they crowed loud and long
as though to summon the late sun at break of day.
Thus the two women swiftly passed with heads held high
and old age slowly fell from them like fetid moss
until they looked like sweet new honey or old wine.
Dame Goody laughed and winked, then cried to her old friend:
"How many kinds of men passed through my bed, my dear!
Now that I walk in dawn and my flesh blooms once more
and my breasts once more climb my bosom like small rabbits,
all in my arms revive and fondle all my limbs.
Margaro, seven different kinds of men have loved me,
seven most different waves have washed through my cool body!
Those robust animals, whose blood boils in their thighs,
caught sight of the red lantern by my door, then laughed,
kicked in the door, rushed in my yard, and smashed my bed.
On eves of holidays, rich landlords zoned their keys
about their waists, then knocked upon my door at dawn;
they stood within my courtyard, held their lust in leash,
and for long hours bargained slowly in a low voice,
for they had learned, you see, to spend, but to gain more,
to sow their seed, but harvest a rich croft of sons,
for merchants, though they sell mud, want pure gold returned.

Others, who could not bear their shrews or household cares,
tapped softly on my door caressingly at night,
hoping they might forget their sad lives in my arms,
and I'd console them as a mother does her child
and in their wine cast with compassion Lethe's herb
till all their souls poured out like honey through my thighs.
Some crawled with fear and lust, weeping for me to open,
for all at once they felt life wane and death come soon,
they saw their strong loins shrinking, their teeth falling fast,
that armless, deaf and blind, they'd pass through earth and die
without their hearts once soaring for a lightning flash.
'Let's go to lovely Goody, lads, to ease our hearts.'
They held gifts in their hands and perfumes round their waists,
got drunk, though with no wine, fed well, though with no food,
and though they'd not yet touched my cooling breasts, were freed!
They stood outside my door and their minds shook like reeds:
'Before we're swallowed by dark earth, let the door open!'
At times I looked out through my grille and shook with fear:
young gallants knocked with glittering armor, hair unshorn,
and all my scented house resounded with hard blows,
my faithful dog growled fiercely, my canaries trembled,
and I dashed swiftly, donned my armor, decked myself,
rose water on my breasts, black paint on eyes and brows,
a curved mole on my ear, a small mole on my cheek,
then dashed down to the court, threw back the musk-drenched bolts:
'Thrice welcome to the balsam archons, the rose dragons,
welcome to the fierce males who come to slay my heart!'
And when I watched them leave as day broke much too soon,
I sighed and leant against my casement, pale and wan.
Dear God, I still can't glut myself with this sweet world!
When in the evening pools grew dim and the stars blossomed,
when maids returned from wells and nightingales rang out,
when night had not yet grown jet-black but swayed with blue,
then beardless lustful youths from shade to shadow slid
and their raw youthful bodies trembled, their throats choked—
they dared for the first time to fall in a maid's arms.
With trembling knees, they knocked upon my door in stealth,
and I cast off my pumps, slipped off my copper rings
to make no jangling sound as I drew back the bolt,
or fright the youths with clanging bells, for they had fled
often to hear me come arrayed in my full armor.
At other times earth's sweetest heartless gallants came,
twisting their thorny beards, their hands upon their hips,
and beat upon my door and laughed with rousing shouts;
they did not come like beasts to sleep and kiss with greed,
nor like fat landlords to glean sons for fruit, then leave,

nor did they come soon to recall and soon forget,
nor did they shake like virgin boys or weep at dawn—
no, these strode armored through my courtyard silently,
the stairs creaked as I huddled in my pillows, pale,
nor do I know if joy or pain tore through my loins,
yet I praised God because he gave me breasts and womb.
Aye, Margaro, I've studied love in this world well,
there's much on earth I've suffered, yet I don't repent,
and now that life's come back, I'll take the same road twice!"
Dame Goody talked and ran with longing on light soil,
her pomegranates burst in her love-glutted arms,
and Margaro once more bound up her raven hair
in her death-kerchief, slowly covered up her breasts,
and the world's vertigo seemed like the frailest dream;
young men and old who passed upon her tented bed
seemed like shy shadows, shameless, happy, brave or sad,
and life rolled gently on like distant and deep waves;
Death, too, rolled gently like deep waves within her head
and the maid laughed, because she knew the secret well.
Ah, when would she fall at the ascetic's feet and cry:
"Your mighty word has made me fruitful, swelled my life
like the good apple tree that bends with too much fruit,
but a wind blew, O master, the firm apples fell,
rolled on the earth and rotted, but I still don't care,
I know that life's a lightning flash which I've gleaned well.
As you advised, all in my arms merged into One.
How I rejoiced in and caressed that One, dear God,
for I knew the great secret—even that One is empty air!"

The black-eyed maidens finally ceased, drowned in their dream,
their red heels glittered and then dwindled down the earth
as from some trees a pure-white elephant thrust through,
old and benign, with golden trappings and moon-charms,
on whom slim Rocky sat, holding a crimson spear
and fondling cockily his black and glistening beard.
Deeply he breathed the fragrant air and sang with joy:
"Ahoy, a warm breeze blows, the shriveled logs have bloomed,
pale seeds revive, burst in the earth, mount toward the sun!
Forward, my lads, the wheel's turned right side up again,
our nostrils fill once more with scent, our loins with blood,
and the hawk-heart has come and perched within our breasts.
Boys, I must sing a couplet now or I shall burst:
'Life, I can bear your pain no more, I'll turn to ghost,
I'll slip one night through your small keyhole and snatch you off!' "
Thus sang the handsome youth, although he made no sound;
behind him, on the elephant's spreading rump, clasped tight,

sat two Egyptian maidens in a glittering joy,
who once—do you remember, lads?—when the sun reigned,
after the supper's sweetness in their humble hut,
sang with their zithers of a virgin's aching pain.
Sitting astride now on the snow-white elephant
with the brave handsome youth they'd longed for one warm night,
they laughed, for passion found its outlet in their dream.
With painted fingernails they held their zithers still,
two pomegranate blooms thrust through their breasts like wounds,
earth quivered like a cobweb decked with men and flowers,
and the birds shrilled like children in exotic nights.
As the two sisters listened, they shook rapturously,
and as they sniffed strong Rocky's smell, their nostrils flared:
"O gallant youth, your black locks smell of frankincense,
your voice is hoarse and your thin body clacks like bones;
come, turn your face, my dear, and smile on us awhile."
Then the youth turned his waxen face toward the young maids
and lumps of loam still straggled down his curly beard;
he smiled, and the maids shrank with fright at his green lips
as his strong moldy breath poured on their breathless throats.
"O stalwart youth, we're frightened, for the fat worms fall
from your pale swollen lips and from your rotting throat;
hear what the birds are chanting us with human voice:
'This is no elephant, but only the whistling wind
with a dead man and two live maids astride its back!' "
The young man laughed, and his white teeth fell to the ground:
"They're only birds, my dears, poor stupid birds! Don't listen!
I keep world-famous youth clutched tightly in my teeth.
Take heart; don't fear, my loves; clasp me with all your might!"
Then the maids laughed, took heart, spread out their longing arms
and tightly clasped the dead youth till their nipples rose
like the hard beaks of birds that drink after long thirst:
"O my belovèd, your breath no longer smells of mold,
your hairy armpits brim with sweat and drip with musk;
do you recall sweet apple trees that bloomed far off
in our sad heavy song, within our father's house?
Our apple trees now swell again and burst with bloom,
a warm breeze blows and two firm fruits fall in our laps;
oho, we like your apples and we love your shade—
rein in your elephant, my dear, and let's lie clasped!"
But Rocky's seagull mind longed for far-distant seas
because his master's voice blared like a heavy conch
or like a black ram's bell that summoned all his flock.
Raising his crimson spear, he gently pricked and spurred
his wise white elephant and longed with all his heart
to fall in Hades soon, clasped in his master's arms.

Although the girls' caresses had enflamed his heart
and earth's sweet breath had mounted in his muddy nostrils,
he feared to turn and frighten them, but softly said:
"Aye, maids, do you recall how one warm night you sat
cross-legged on rush-reed mats and with your zithers sang
till the low house-post shook like a tree and cast its flower?
Long years have passed, kingdoms have drowned and stars have fallen,
but in my mind that deathless post still stands and blooms;
aye, maidens, take your zithers and console me now
for in your song a flowering apple tree conversed."
The youngest maiden laughed, her reddened fingernails
moved in the dusk, struck at the rusted chords, and then
she raised her throat and her voice leapt and cooled the world:
"A bird soared through the sky with fragrant lustrous wings
and a young maid stood by her door with quivering breasts . . ."
But then her song choked in her throat, for bells rang out,
the brave youth yelled with joy, leapt lightly to the ground
and dashed into the shaded trees with open arms:
"Granite, the earth can give me now no greater joy!
Dear God, has a dream struck, or do I clasp you tight?"
His friend with long white hair and flapping gaudy plumes
gleamed in the shadows like a great Egyptian king;
behind him trudged long caravans of elephants,
and camels crawled in the warm evening like blue smoke;
aromas filled the air with musk, gold cages gleamed,
canaries sang, and hoarse-voiced parrots shrilled and cawed;
in fresh reed-baskets melons and grape-clusters glowed,
and slaves with flowing hair and jangling copper rings
rose laughing on gold saddle-cloths like wedding guests
who brought rich regal gifts to ease the archer's heart.
"Rocky, I clasp you in my arms, but my brain reels;
alas, life cannot ever give such great joy, friend—
I fear we've met in Tartarus or the streets of dream."
Thus tightly clasped, the two friends swiftly, lightly passed
with their long manly strides, their bodies' slender sway,
and skimmed the azure seashore, trod on foaming waves,
while on the elephant the maidens shrieked to watch
the two slim bodies vanish in the distant sea
and leave them, wretched and alone, on the long ruined road.

Far by a cooling river's rhododendron blooms
the body of arch-eyebrowed Helen now lay dying
at dusk, her lily feet stretched toward the warbling stream.
Her daughters, sons, and great-grandsons, a siren's brood,
wove her white hair, then with rose water washed her face
that her long lids might open, her throat breathe awhile,

to say a few good words and give them all her blessing.
Two days and nights she breathed upon the sands in pain
nor would earth eat her or the sky sweep her aloft,
but like a white spring cloud she hung midway in air.
Then from her heavy coffers of carved cedar wood
they lifted her funereal veil, her rich-embroidered shroud
which the old lover of fine clothes, bent by her loom,
had woven skillfully with myriad rich adornments:
a deep green field spread in the midst with scarlet tents,
around the hem a blue sea broke with foaming fringe,
and upright in four corners four tall towers burned.
Gently above her body, blond granddaughters stooped
and washed her with rose-vinegar and cooling scents,
and bared her neck, her much-kissed but now fallen breasts,
sails which no soft erotic wind might swell with love.
She opened almond eyes, which now crow's feet had trod,
and watched the gurgling waters mutely through the reeds
as they flowed swiftly, joyously, to meet the sea.
She strained her ears and heard the river running deep,
she heard her life like warbling water dwindling far
and her mind running down the waves like a frail mist
or muffled rustle that now swept in murmuring wash
all the brave lads slain for her sake, the burning towers
and the swift ships that sailed and sank in her black eyes.
All hung on her thick lashes now for the last time,
all earth's embracements, its glad sorrows, its bitter joys;
ah, in the living world she'd finished her hard duty!
But suddenly, as she brought to mind far-distant seas
and said farewell to all old archons in her mind,
she shrieked, and her notorious body broke in sweat,
for she had seen the archer's savage cap, his beard,
his slightly smiling lips that softly cried out, "Helen!"
Her lily cheeks flushed red, her bosom rose and swelled;
dear God, if only she could wreck her home once more,
stand upright on the prow, be blown by all four winds,
close her sweet eyes and let fate take what course it would!
As by the flowering riverbank she lay expiring,
her mind with a soft flutter cast its last faint rays,
and a young girl but twelve years old, with swinging braids,
rushed to Eurotas's green bank, cut a fresh reed,
then rode it like a horse and ran along the sands.
Her virgin girdle flapped like an embattled flag,
her body was a field where the white lilies bloomed,
and in her large black eyes the whole world sailed and drowned.
For a brief moment the old hermit in his grave
smelled the girl pass above him and tossed off his tombstone,

then hatched out like a crow, leapt on the ground once more,
though in his hand he still held tight a lump of earth.
Although the burning sun had set, the earth still boiled
and the old man leant against his cave to keep from falling,
gazed on the girl, then sighed as his throat brimmed with sound:
"Where are you going, O cool body, O twelve-year maid?
Tell me, O deathless water, and I shall come with you!"
When Helen turned and laughed, the earth swayed like a rose,
the old man broke in a swift dance, the earth's dust swirled,
her girlish laughter seethed like mad waves in his heart,
till, mounting his oak staff, he hopped along her side.
As the two forms ran side by side, spurred by desire,
a bitter yearning brimmed within the old man's heart:
Dear God, if only he could take earth's lanes once more,
he'd not chase kingdoms then nor empty ghosts of air,
for these are empty smoke that fades and leaves no trace—
he'd found a simple home, a cool and humble hut,
he'd be but a poor worker, an unbearded youth;
and this blithe maiden, mounted on her supple reed,
with her twin towering breasts that ripened on the cliffs,
he'd choose for his small wife to breed him stalwart sons,
for she, dear God, was all ghosts, all earth's burning towns.
The maiden glanced at the old man and slyly smiled:
"You seem like a great magician, the watchdog of Fate!
Bend down and read my palm, reveal my written doom;
ah, could I only know my fate, what man I'll marry!"
But as the old ascetic seized her lily hand
and touched her firm-fleshed body, he sank in a deep sea
and his mind leapt from wave to wave and disappeared.
As the coquetting wanton laughed, her hand sprang up
like cooling water in the ascetic's shriveled fist:
"It's no use scowling so, old man, I'm not afraid.
Fate blossoms on my bosom like a double rose."
Bent over the open hand he held, the shrunk old man
felt a sweet dizziness and fragrance strike his brain;
in her small palm he could discern huge suns and moons,
tall lilies filled with honeybees, and a deep hull
that sailed up rivers, floating through the lily-blooms.
"Dear girl, your life will flow serenely like calm water,
you'll stand like a pure lily in your husband's home,
your womb shall breed a horde of babes and clustered stars."
But the girl fingered her small lips with stubbornness:
"Old man, I don't want hordes of children, household cares,
untouched pure lilies, wretched husbands, peaceful hearths;
I'll cut another road, my heart seeks other skies!"
She spoke, then beat her horse-reed, dashed down toward the waves

and her shrill laughter swept the bank like gurgling water.
The old man sighed, stooped down, and let his dark tears fall
like downy eyes, warm, thick, and blurred, on the hard stones,
but the girl rushed ahead astride her lucky reed
and her braids flapped in the fresh breeze like leaping flames.
All things, both Life and Death, blew like a strong wind,
and the old ascetic leant toward earth in soft complaint:
"Aye, archer, cruel ascetic, you've still not left me alone
but clasp me in your brain so I can't rot in earth;
once more, as the sun warms and my bones burst in bloom,
you send me here, alas, a decoy girl to tempt me!
Dear God, when shall I ever find repose in the deep ground?"

Good are the crimson apples on the apple tree,
good the clasped couples kissing all their bodies' length,
but like good sisters strolling in each other's arms
earth has no greater or much sweeter joy to give:
they swept by swiftly arm in arm with rippling laughter,
flowing like fresh cool springs where travelers quench their thirst.
Oho, see how the grave's loam reconciles all foes
and wipes away all wretched cares and tames all hearts,
for Diktena, that easy whore with skillful hands,
clasped her snow-virgin sister, Krino, longingly.
Mounted astride a jet-black bull with flaming eyes,
they swiftly plunged and rushed on toward the azure waves;
their black and curly locks were twined with jasmine flowers
to hide the moldy stench of their half-rotted flesh,
and a small bit of mold lay on their nostrils still;
but both their minds were fixed now on each other's love,
and they rushed on, nor saw the mold nor death's white worms.
Krino bent down and gently stroked the frenzied bull
that once on the earth's face, within a sun-drenched ring,
had tossed his horns in furious rage and snatched her life;
now she'd forgotten all her pain, lost all her wrath,
made friends with foes, and to her sister turned and said:
"If we in truth shall ever return to flowering earth,
I'll take another road, find other joys in youth,
for if I had firm arms and thighs once more, dear sister,
I, too, should love to clasp a cluster of young lads
and take my fill of kisses and of night assaults
so that my flesh won't sink to earth still unconsoled.
Dear God, I've lost my youth, my apple tree bore flowers
but not one single fruit, I've seen not one red apple!"
Then Diktena of the much-kissed and glutted breasts,
of the curved mouth, a golden ring that dripped with honey,
clasped tenderly her sister's body, still unkissed:

"Ah, don't lament, dear sister, for life is not enough,
nor are earth's cooling springs enough to quench our thirst;
dear God, a maid's small body is a bottomless well,
no matter how much we kiss on earth, our lips want more,
and only Death, my dear, will ever glut our mouths.
I know this now at last: all roads on earth are good,
but ah, we're given time to take but one with haste,
then yearn for others vainly, and no cure exists!
If I, dear sister, could return to flowering earth,
I'd long to take, O Krino, your own virgin road.
Ah, I'd shine proudly with great scorn, glow like a star,
no man's breath ever would soil the lily of my heart,
I'd hunt wild mountain game, then in arenas fall
and fight with bulls, my thighs still cool with mountain frost,
my twin breasts towering and untouched, like the sharp double-ax!"

Thus did the two curled Cretan sisters sigh and speak,
mounted upon the bull, clasped in each other's arms,
while far behind them, two war comrades who had lain
in loam together, walked the earth but cast no shade:
old Captain Clam, that sea-wolf with his folded sea-cap,
and that lean, still untamed and raggèd princess, Phida.
They'd heard together the choked cry of their great leader,
together tossed their tombstones off, tore from their shrouds,
picked up their fallen teeth, gathered their molding flesh,
and rushed together swiftly as their bare bones clacked.
When Captain Clam first sniffed a salty seaside breeze,
he placed both hands above his eyes, but saw no sea,
yet his broad nostrils flared and played like Venus' shells:
"Comrade, can this be the sea's brine and the sea's wind?
Will the waves rise in truth to wash me with their spray?"
His mind was parched with thirst like a wide-nostriled sponge,
a worthless fish left by the fishermen on shore,
expiring and convulsed, but now, God, suddenly
his gills were filled with water and his mind with salt.
He turned his guileless head then to his slender friend:
"Phida, I count again and again, and my wits spin—
wasn't it we who died on the dark shores of Crete?
But even now my black breath smells of burning wood,
I see a sharp lance piercing through your bosom's cleft!
Phida, was that a dream which vanished when we woke,
and now that our great master's called, has dawn set out,
will the vast light, the true light, leap out of the tomb?
What joy, dear friend! We've wakened now, the waves will come,
the sails will rise on the blue sea and fill the air!
Don't weep, I swear to you I've never felt my heart

pulse with such joy on earth or my feet leap so lightly!"
Captain Clam broke in smiles and strode over the earth
scattering his Cretan ashes right and left in wind,
and sea-chants sailed like vessels in his stormy brain,
large fishes tore through his blue mind, triremes set sail,
and his burnt hands beat through the air like flashing oars:
"Phida, I think our captain has built a new flagship
then tossed his cap on high and yelled for us to come;
his crew will rush at once and spread from stern to prow,
step up the masts, haul up the sails, grab at the oars,
and a strong wind will blow us wherever Death directs.
I feel that my burnt chest already swells like sails."
But pallid Phida groaned and with great terror strove
to wipe her father's sticky blood from her red hands:
"Ah, Captain Clam, will the sea ever cleanse this blood?
Since dawn when we set out I've stopped at every spring,
washed and rewashed my hands but still the blood remains!"
The sea-wolf's pitying heart ached for the girl; he placed
on her rough shoulder blade a burnt and gentle hand:
"The vast sea blots out all, it sweeps and cleanses all
our sullied bodies till like foam they leap on waves
and all our memories fade and melt like lumps of salt.
When at long length our eyes catch sight of our great captain
standing erect in the sea's midst, waving his cap,
ah, Phida, we'll be stripped of souls and bodies both!"
The snake-haired maiden sighed, washed and rewashed the blood,
but other thick blood clots sprang up like monstrous eyes
and glowered at her darkly, scarlet, moveless, mute.
"Ah, Captain Clam, will the sea ever cleanse this blood?"
Then the old sailor scowled and scolded the poor maid:
"What shame that now in such a gallant soul as yours
the blood we spilled once long ago should rear its head;
have you forgotten we fought for freedom in the world?"
Phida turned fierce at once, her regal blood veins swelled:
"Yes, Captain Clam, I know it, but I'm killed by pain!
If we had brought bold freedom to the trampled slaves,
bread to the starved, then let the black crows take my father!
We fought for freedom in the world and plunged toward Hades,
but now I see slaves stooped to the hard yoke again
and bowing to their lords, and all our strife in vain!
Ah, though I've spilled my father's blood, where's freedom now?"
Captain Clam sighed in secret, but he spoke with force:
"Phida, don't worry whether your dear blood and care
bore fruit to a rich earth or died in sterile ground;
now that my earthen brains are cleansed of heavy fog
I know well what our captain meant when once he said:

'I fight and ache for freedom, but I scorn rewards!' "
A bitter green foam stained the patricide's thin mouth:
"All women love to feel their wombs heavy with fruit;
the heart's a woman, too, and longs to achieve her passion."
Then the old sea-wolf stooped, cut a fresh blade of grass
and hung it from his pale lips like an emerald sword,
and his voice stopped, his words piled up behind his teeth.
Deep in his wretched heart old Captain Clam knew well
there's nothing sweeter in all earth than to sit down
at dusk by your own door, a common worker drenched
with the day's sweat, the hard day's wage held in your hand.
A strong soul can't be fed with shadows, it wants meat,
it's a lean wolf, its hunger can't be fed with hope.
Captain Clam brooded long, then in a sudden glow
his grandson flashed within his mind, leant on his chest,
but the waves crashed once more, his master's mounting roar
drowned his loved grandson, swept him like a fish to sea;
then the fierce sea-wolf cocked his cap against his ear
and rushed along the azure seashore's husky susurration.

The far-off guests all reached the cooling sea at last,
merged with the foam and sailed, flew with the seaward gulls,
and when the shores had emptied, a lean wrinkled dog
rushed up with longing yelps and sniffed the seaside air.
He had set out from the far shores of his cool isle
where his old bones had rotted long in pits of dung,
for when he'd heard his master's cry and mighty need
he'd leapt up, wagged his tail, and rushed along the air.
His pale neck was still bloody where his master's nails
had seized him ruthlessly so that his joyous barks
might not forewarn the reveling youths of his lord's coming.
His bleary eyes had recognized his master well,
he'd crawled and quivered, rushed with whimpering whines, then twined
and tangled with his master's feet, licked at his heels,
but the dread hunter, forcing his tears back with stealth,
had quickly seized the grimy neck that throbbed with joy
and squeezed until the faithful hound rolled over, dead,
though his tail's naked tip still quivered with delight.
The finger marks had turned to coral, his neck's pride,
now studded with his master's tears transformed to pearls;
he'd flung the tombstone from his grave, yelped frantically,
and now his quivering and moist nostrils sniffed the air.
From Hades he'd heard whistling, swift belovèd steps
that filled the earth and atmosphere and choked the shore;
his bald tail sprouted hair, his white teeth gleamed once more,
and he rushed toward the sea: "What joy! In his great need

my master did not call his father, nor his great son,
but from his island chose and called to me alone!
Either my master is getting married or fights with Death!
Forward, we'll feast and revel if his boards are spread,
but if he's giving up his ghost, I'll spread my legs
and stretch out like a rough-hewn pillow at his feet."
Then the old hound, still trembling on his moldy legs,
sniffed at the air about him, barked, and dashed toward the far south.

When the dread outcry leapt from the cold mount of snow
and flicked like flame, the memory of the lone man flashed
and hung like a rainbow in the sun before it vanished,
and the last blue-green stars with a soft blur lit up
a lofty temple drowned in thick banana trees.
Stone, sated lions, demons pure of heart kept guard
by rich-wrought doors, held upright their long twisted tails,
and laughed in a long row with gaping crimson jaws.
Down on the sluggish river blazing vessels brought
pilgrims and holy offerings, while on the curved prows
great conches blared and heralds with loud cries proclaimed:
"Our mighty Athlete, great Motherth, completes his task;
empty, disburdened, turned all light, he moves through air
and sits on the high summits and slowly fades away.
O men, O wingless worms who yearn for wingèd plumes,
push forward, leave your homes, give all your goods away,
come swiftly, come in time before the Ascetic leaves!
Joy to those eyes and ears that see and hear him now
for they, too, swiftly will sprout wings and fade in sun."
The conches on the river blared, the heralds cried,
and the wreathed athlete of the mind, with fainting heart,
sat cross-legged by a leafless, fruitless, blooming tree.
Like the slim silkworm, he had eaten all earth's leaves,
the mulberry's fresh green, and turned them all to silk;
now round about him swarmed companions old and new,
man-seeming monkeys, savage beasts, fowls of the air,
and stared to watch how the great god of earth and air,
the guide of the clear mind and guileless heart, would die.
They saw how his pale hands had shrunk, his feet dissolved,
his face become a snow-white veil that flapped in light
and how Death's odor drifted through the air like musk.
Behold, some riding savage cranes, some on fierce lions,
some on full-blossomed lotuses and some on clouds,
the sowers of his seed came clad in yellow robes
and raised their throats in funeral psalms to mock at Death:
"Salvation's Word is an imperishable, ruthless fire!
Brothers, we were not sent to earth to found our homes

with souls and stones, or to plant trees, or sons, or thoughts;
fire is our only wine, our bread, fire is our home,
our plow is a famished fire, and we have fallen on earth
to plow and sow the sterile ground with burning coals."
A lean old man whose flesh the greedy soul had eaten
sat cross-legged on the ground and clapped his wrinkled palms:
"I've found salvation, I've left my ancient parents both,
I've left my weeping children and all my weeping gods,
I've freed myself from joy and grief, I've cleansed my heart,
I laugh and clap my hands, blot out my mind and shout:
'I do not see or hear or taste or touch or smell!' "
A sweet disciple danced and waved a gaudy fan
made of wild parrot plumes, red, azure, green and gold:
"I do not love or hate, or want, or fear, or hope;
I wave my colored fan and all my passions fade!"
The great Ascetic smiled, and his bright hallowed head
illumined all like a lit lamp, and the psalms ceased;
he stooped, and his ten fingers wove, unwove in air,
or stretched out motionless like birdlime boughs where perched
all spirits, all blue thoughts, his inner butterflies.
A faint smile glimmered on his pale translucent flesh
and his voice rose like magic spells and hailed the world:
"I bend my face and watch it flowing down the stream,
I see the South Wind swiftly write my name on waves;
may my long voyage fare well, comrades; farewell, friends.
Like the blind fish that struggle in the ocean's depths
till their flesh melts to light and blazes through the dark,
thus did I rage on earth to turn all meat to light;
but now that little flesh remains, one drop of mud,
I'll summon my great servant, Death, to take it all,
I'll raise my hand in silence, and the world shall fade!"
But as he raised his glowing hand to summon Death,
an old man stooped with awe, kissed his frail feet and cried:
"Master, before you die, grant us your wisest word!"
Then the serene face shone with a faint smile that poured
on the dark earth around him like dusk's afterglow,
but he spoke not, his words perched in his heart like birds,
hawks, nightingales, larks, storks and cranes with bloody claws.
"Monstrous canary, yellow wing that skirts the cliff,
sing us your final song to free our trammeled souls!"
But then the Ascetic frowned and earth shook to its roots:
"Aye, hermits, open your ears wide, make firm your minds;
five roads run through my mind, five wings rise up to fly,
I weigh all and rejoice, I'm free to take all roads.
Shall I cry out with certainty, 'Here's to our meeting!'
or shall I say that we shall never meet again?

Shall my words fall like a serene and spreading stream
to water deeply man's dream-driven fantasies?
Or shall an eagle plunge and seize the heart till both
make love on desert sands and play for a brief hour?
Or shall I tell you the whole truth and crush your hearts?
Frail hope, despair, or beauty, or a sweet game, or truth—
I've passed all these five paths, I've opened a new road,
I've gone beyond the Word, cut through thought's foolish nets,
and fling you, for profound reply, a wordless smile."
He spoke, and his smile spread through all his glowing flesh
like the full desert moon's light-drenched and sweet caress,
and in his answer his disciples' brains were lost
as all their aching shoulders suddenly sprang with yellow wings.

Emboldened Death at last approached with reverence;
the afterglow with girdling golden-silver rim
like a distraught farewell poured out and wound the world;
earth was relieved of the sun's golden weight, the hour
was sweet, the stars had not yet come, and earth and sky
hung in a trembling mantle of pale violet mist.
The mighty Keeper of Keys then wished to signal Death
who had stood waiting, trembling like a humble slave,
but as he raised his finger quietly to give the sign,
two well-knit men approached, dressed in a foreign garb
and well-bound hair, a silver cricket on each shoulder;
the holy hand hung in mid-air, and Death drew back.
The two companions were engaged in rapid talk:
"Dear friend, I think we've reached our journey's final port;
my loud heart bids me anchor by this holy river.
We've passed great mountain peaks that shone clear and serene,
great cities and translucent waters, gaudy birds,
heavy barbaric treasures that rejoiced our eyes,
traveling for many moons now at the world's far ends.
Brother, I never knew that earth had such long wings;
you may for years plod on beyond the walls of Greece
and pass through mountains, seas and plains while all the sky's
foundations still unfold and earth spreads new wings still."
The young man fondled his strong comrade's sunburnt back:
"And I, too, brother, never dreamt so many roads
led through world-wandering beauty and the heart of man;
as soon as I return, with luck, to my loved country,
I'll step into my workshop, paint Athena's lips
bright crimson, once so savage and unkissed; I'll hang
clusters of playful curls upon her manly brows;
I'll carve celestial Aphrodite like a wench
with firm round buttocks and in her soft hands I'll place

two slender feathers like two oars to rule the port;
a garish Eastern peacock struts within my brain."
But the robust man with his sloping wedge-shaped beard
turned round and seized his youthful friend's stone-battling arms:
"Speak softly, brother, a bright gathering gleams before us;
old men and young sit grieving round a bloomless tree,
and there a naked great ascetic lifts his hand
and looks on the world's tumult with a tranquil smile."
The young man stooped and his cheeks burned with crimson flame:
"My heart frisks like a kid, my friend; I must speak out:
that god glows here whom year on year we've sought together,
and now at length we'll hold him wholly in our embrace.
See how his sacred arms shine like a falcon's wings
that hover in the blue air's highest peaks of light;
see how his myriad-featured face flares like a spirit!
I fear to speak, yet I can't keep this secret now:
that bronze Apollo, whom I've brought as distant gift
from lustrous Hellas, trembles in my breast with fear!"
The young man was still speaking when an elder rose
on tiptoe from the assembled group and raised his hands:
"The great Ascetic hails the world for the last time!
O strangers, don't approach, don't soil his sacred hush."
But the strong, bearded man replied with haughty words.
"We've journeyed far on purpose to exchange two words
and seek advice from this new archon of the mind;
they say his every word is a precious heavy pearl,
and now that we've flushed out our godly quarry here,
your hands, old man, must not hold back our bold desire."
The elder shaded his dim eyes and softly said:
"Far-traveled man, what soil may be your native land?"
Then the wedge-bearded man replied with a proud mien:
"Old man, we boast that from an earth with azure shores
we set out on this pilgrimage to see your god
who sorts, they say, the interests and the brains of man;
we carry bronze to etch his wise words one by one."
The old man shook his head and spoke with a soft smile:
"God, countries, laws and shores are smokes that fill your heads."
The elder comrade turned then to his youthful friend:
"We must have reached, my friend, the lotus-eaters' land.
They've tasted of the fruit and they've forgotten all;
they've reached the pure-white cypress tree before their death;
they've drunk the stream of Lethe till their heart's a sieve,
a cracked jug from whose slits the whole world drains away;
but I shall answer them and steady their dim brains.
Forgetful man, that burning tower was no mere dream
which our world-famous parents sacked one holy night;

and when on conflagration's peak their hands raised high
the flower of all Greece, rose-breasted Helen's body,
that was no mist, but a warm woman's giddy flesh."
The old man smiled, then to his silent comrades turned:
"Brothers, these are the imagination's famous lads,
the fish that flounder in the fishermen's thick nets
although they think they still skip free in boundless seas.
Their history is mind's vertigo, a traceless dream,
poor barren fields and azure seas, nude bodies, songs,
and nonexistent ghosts. Once, in their scattered wits,
they manned armadas, rigged their masts, sailed for a span,
scowled in the sun, then on some land discerned black signs:
'The foe, ahoy!' they yelled. 'There's the great town of Troy!'
then rushed at once pellmell along the phantom shores,
merged, parted, merged again with shades on empty sands.
Unhappy wretches, don't you know all these are games
of that sly god who sits on high and plays with men,
who builds his famous castles out of dew and light?
Your Helen passed like fleshless shadow, a loot of air!"
Repressing nobly his great anger, the youth replied:
"If Helen was but empty shade, may she be blessed!
It's for this empty shade we fought with widening minds;
when old at length we turned back to our longed-for land,
our minds crammed with adventures and with manly deeds,
our ships, like heavy-laden caldrons, brimmed and spilled
with oriental honeyed maids and golden shields.
The world, O great ascetic, is a fresh-bathed Helen;
she wears veils stitched with castles, foreign strands and seas,
she guards her breasts with both hands, weeps with happiness
and follows the most stalwart youths, yet as she walks,
her small, small steps, like those of Victory's, glow with blood.
Black bread, clear water, and blue air are good and real,
they sink deep in man's entrails, give him flesh and soul,
till slowly with great strife all shadows turn to meat.
You sit with crossed and idle hands, sunk deep in thought:
'There is no Helen; all on earth are shade and mist!'
But 'Helen' means, old man, to live and fight for Helen!"
Yet still the ascetic shook his shaven head with pity:
"For how long, like male scorpions, will you squirm in Earth's
erotic honeyed claws, that fearful female scorpion?
A pity for your eagle eyes, your lofty brows!
Awake at last, uproot your wants, abjure your nightmares,
smother your hearts and your thick brains so they won't shout,
perk up your ears, for mountains, trees and waters roar:
'Come, come and merge as one with earth, with mother roots,
merge into one with sacred winds and the good showers!' "

The ascetic's voice allured with sweet intoxication
until the man with wedge-shaped beard embraced the youth:
"Don't answer him, his brains are waterlogged and drowned;
let me now cast him strong round words like whirling quoits:
Aye, old ascetic, your eyes lure like snakes in vain,
we're bound by other laws and ruled by other gods;
they're nude, they're lightly smeared with balms, their nostrils steam,
they sit at our own tables, drink, leap in our beds,
make sweet love with our wives, and we in turn with theirs,
until our warm bloods mix, the sons of men grow fierce,
and the gods' strength grows sweet, grafted with female ways.
We've conquered fear by planting on the abysm's edge
the pure and tranquil features of man's virtuous deeds;
we work with futile thoughts as though they were firm bronze
and now, behold, we've brought our Victory's statue here,
rich gift from Hellas for your lotus-eating saint!
Make way, old man, make way now, don't obstruct the light,
I love to talk with gods alone, and face to face."
He spoke, then with no reverence pushed the sage aside,
took two bold steps within the dazzling light-drenched ring,
then spread deed-loving hands and hailed the holy saint:
"O clear yet subtle thought who balance with great skill
the soul's immense conflicting wings, both Yes and No,
for love of you we've come from the earth's inner heart.
We, too, adore immortals, found and build great towns,
fight in our rings on feast days, carve on slabs of stone
our thoughts and deeds of gods and men so they won't fade,
but inbred civil discord wrecks our homes and towns,
brothers in unfraternal strife that dooms our race.
Rise, sage, and give us, if you can, new laws of love!
Our great ancestors proudly came from plundering raids
and brought deceitful Victory in their bloody hands;
help us cut Victory's wings so she won't fly away!
Let order rule anarchic rage, let the Word reign,
let's give the glowering demons a soft smile of light,
let Death merge peacefully with Life deep in our hearts.
Your comrades round you stutter, trip, and can't recall;
make firm our minds to stand guard on the black abyss,
help us to turn our mutterings to integral thought!"
The warrior was still speaking when Motherth turned slowly
and flashed his eyes till the two bodies wholly glowed
and hovered in his smile like playthings made of light.
The young man writhed, then rushed to fall into the net,
but the mature man seized his friend and held him tight:
"Brother, hold lustrous Hellas firmly in your mind!"
But the young man drew close to the smile's magic well:

"A soft smile bubbles from his mind, serene, profound,
pours on his flesh like honey, spreads on all the earth,
and in the dusk his face's contours flick with light.
Ah, could I snatch his smile and bring it like bright plunder,
more brilliant than the mind, to intellectual Greece!"
His startled friend gazed on the young man's pallid face:
"Alas, you've tasted the lotus's forgetful fruit!
Your eyes are burning, honeyed poison brims your lips,
let's leave before our native land fades from your mind!"
But the dream-taken youth glowed with a soft smile:
"This is our native land, dear friend, this is the rock
on which great God is carved with faint forgetfulness and air."

His comrade clasped the waist of the still trembling youth
then calmly turned to the unflowered tree that smiled
and had now cast one overripe sage fruit to earth.
"Speechless Ascetic, who on strife's peak sit enthroned,
we've brought our words like heralds, and we seek reply."
But the old man once more spread his compassionate arms:
"O brothers, wash your mouths in deep oblivion's stream,
our great Ascetic smiled and all your flesh dissolved—
this is the mighty answer, friends, the total Word."
The seedless unillusioned brain, translucent head,
leant gently on the unflowered tree, and its soft smile
allured both heralds closer like a fisher's net,
though they clung tightly, arm in arm, to keep from falling.
The moment of full freedom loomed, the pale flame hissed
and gathered strength to leap far from the sputtering wick
as the translucent Saint now smiled and beckoned Death.
But as he shut his eyes and his back touched the tree,
its branches brimmed with pure white bloom, a warm breeze blew
and the white flowers slowly fell, mute tufts of snow,
and covered all his body, his shoulders, feet, and head.
"It's Death!" some awed disciples cried in loud lament,
but others laughed, broke into dance and clapped their hands;
behold, salvation's door had smashed and gaped for all!
The beasts and birds cried out, and from a lowering cloud
the gods stooped low to find a worthy paradigm
of how the soul is freed, to free themselves one day.
Then the wedge-bearded man turned to his youthful friend:
"Why do these strange barbarians dance and laugh and weep
like God's fanatics who tread snakes or burning coals?
They soil the reverent face of holy Mother Earth."
But the youth sighed as his mind raced beyond the earth:
"This Sage, my friend, seems like a greater Dionysus;
sober amid earth's wine-vats now, ruthless and sweet,

he treads on man's heads as on clumps of purple grapes.
Blood splatters, rises to his knees, his loins, his chest,
then floods his brain like wine but cannot make it drunk,
for blood within him turns to soul and lucid light.
Now I'm ashamed I've brought our god as talisman,
as though this Sage would condescend to fear the abyss!
Greece is a small and dwindling thought within his brain."
The elder spread his arms to guide the enraptured troop:
"Don't weep or wail, my brothers, and don't dance, keep calm;
our great Ascetic strides now past Death's sacred door,
his hands and feet grow bright, his body glows with joy,
the victor treads his native land, and the great walls
of mind and flesh fall silently that he may pass.
Flesh dances, and mind dances! Death is a swift dance!"
Both young and old, unmoving, marveled at the great
soul-warrior sinking now serenely deep in the earth;
the sun had hid himself, drops fell from lowering clouds,
long lightning flashes swept across the southern plains.
Earth, like a woman who had given birth and looks
at her first son with joy amid the rain, now crossed
her hands serene in silent happiness, and died.
But as Motherth was sinking in the cellared ground
he suddenly heard a dread cry tear the sky above him,
a swift noose seized and hung him for a moment high,
his soul and body hovered in the darkling air,
the faithful shrieked, and when they raised their eyes they saw
a dread spread-eagle soaring, screeching, through the sky,
and their great Sage hung dangling in the grip of savage claws.

It soared on southward, lost amid the twilight's flames,
and pallid Rala raised her worm-enraptured eyes
and hailed the flashing, fleeting bird with longing heart:
"Eagle, if only I had your wings or the great joy
to hang thus from your savage claws, to tear the sky
and reach my love at once to find out why he wants me!
From his hoarse cry, dread bird, I fear his life's in danger."
She bound her blood-soaked kerchief then to hide the mud,
bit hard her pallid lips to make them red as flame,
then, stooping low to stagnant waters, watched her face.
Ah, she'd grown ugly, lean, her eyebrows had thinned out,
only her downy eyes still moved with beauty's grace,
like jet-black water lilies in a deadly marsh.
How good to be returned to the warm breath of earth!
Once she'd betrayed her destiny, but never again!
Ah, she'd repented squandering her rich life in vain
for future joys and glories, to revenge the poor,

nor ever plucked the ripe fruit of a woman's tree.
What joy! Now that she'd scooped her flesh from muddy earth,
and copper anklets jangled on her sun-bronzed legs,
now that the proud two-headed beast leapt on her bosom,
she rushed toward her belovèd's voice and longed to fall
within his virile arms to bear him sons one day!
But now she stooped above the stagnant waters, fixed her hair,
and cried with lips that brimmed with cobwebs and complaints:
"They call me the Great Martyr, virgin with beast's eyes,
raise statues to my memory, altars to my name,
and worship my virginity, that cobwebbed gate!
I've squandered all my body for a great idea!
Ah, if I'd only known how heavy my breasts hung!
All I could not fulfill in flesh I strive to enjoy
as statue now, and glut myself with marble kisses.
Quickly, to be on time before the temple gates
burst open, I paint my lips and nails, I bare my breasts,
smear unguents on my limbs, twine roses through my hair,
and when the sun leaps and the panting faithful come,
then as the rites prescribe, unmoving, mute, I give
myself to warm embracements and to savage love;
but ah, the stone takes all the joy and gives me none!
But see, the statue's come alive now, the flesh flames,
so farewell, farmers, workers, here's my new path now;
I'm not a man to brood upon the world's good works,
for I was born a maid, and a maid's duty is love;
I rush to meet my loved one, for I've heard his call."
But as she looked in leech-filled waters, Rala saw
a thin shade hovering close that slowly raised its hands,
and all at once she knew, as though it were a dream,
what handsome youth stood at her side and gently smiled.
She bit her lips till the blood flowed, she seethed with rage;
so he'd come too, with baby faith and fleshless good!
She raised her face and ran on south, but the young man
slid calmly by her side and sought her company,
for night had fallen, he feared to walk in dark alone,
and a good word at the right time consoles the mind.
Lightly they sped on swift tiptoe from grass to grass
as on day-broken meadows the frail rolling mist;
the slim young fisher held his net slung down his back
and his illumined features shone with quiet joy
as though the waves had washed them or the sea had drowned them,
and his voice rustled like the sigh of blossomed trees:
"Rala, what joy to live with someone at your side
and to return home in such peaceful dusk as this,
slow and serene, your working tools clasped in your hands,

while God roams through the streets like a soft lullaby
and drifts through courtyards where shy virgins hear his song,
satisfied, mute, nor long for a man's lawless kiss;
to pass through the still night, to hear breasts rise and fall
like fluttering fledglings in their warm and downy nests!
Rala, the earth's a nest in the warm palms of God!"
But the unsquandering body with its flaming kerchief,
in whom desire for men at last had burst and swelled,
now swerved with wrath, and both her dust-grimed cheeks turned red:
"Ah, if there were a god in Heaven or deep in Hades
or even on this wretched earth, I'd stand before him
with a honed ax and curse him in a screeching voice!"
The startled fisher boy closed tight his ink-black eyes,
his sigh whiffed through green rushes like a fledgling's cry,
a fragile soul that swept through leaves when the wind blows.
But Rala pricked the squeamish lad with mocking jeers:
"Go pack, you fool! Your tasteless soup of camomile
does not refresh my sacred heat or heal my pain!
Scat! Vanish in your skies! I don't want chastities!
Your pure-white lilies make me retch, your sweetness cloys,
I hold my breasts in both my hands and rush toward love!"
But suddenly, as the young maid mocked and hissed like snakes,
she heard a crunching sound in the fresh reeds, and turned:
behold, a female leopard with great wrath dashed out,
then reared her head, sniffed at the air, and raised her tail
as though she smelled a leopard's sweat in the South Wind.
Rala spread out her hand and stroked that stormy back:
"Thrice welcome, O twin sister, welcome, O twin eyes,
a thousand welcomes to the starved unsated flame!
I love you when you wag your tail and strike the world,
for you're starved always, and you long for human flesh;
let's run, dear sister, our great leopard shouts far out at sea!"

Thus like a stream the shadowy caravan rushed and swelled
as two by two all sped and merged on sea, air, land;
old comrades met and merged nor parted ever again,
Phida and Rala twined as friends, pale Krino dashed
from her black bull and fell in Helen's girlish arms,
sweet Margaro and Diktena strolled arm in arm,
all lightly swayed from peak to peak at the wind's bidding.
The Cretan mistress, happy in her youth, turned first:
"Dear friend, we're walking now toward the unsetting sun,
its holy light drips on our flesh and flows like honey;
now close your eyes to enjoy the warm hands of our god."
Margaro turned, shut her long lashes, and then smiled
as on the air she smelled the archer's sulphurous breath:

"Ah, hold me on earth forever in your warm embrace!"
Her full lips slowly ceased to flutter their red wings
and her words vanished like sweet bees in flowers lost;
then the two bodies, vowed to arts of love, walked down
the azure shores, light-heeled and silent, sun-caressed.
The sun took fright as the earth darkened, showers whirred,
and all the wedding guests, that sweet parade of shadows,
nude breasts and crimson lips and hairy arms and thighs,
cooled weary feet at length on the dark waves and raised
pellucid hands on high to scan the distant sea:
"Where is our captain now, dear God? Who called for help?
There spreads a waste and desolate sea, and no tall cap's in sight!"

In a deep daze beyond them, on the other shore,
their captain stood, straight, silent, on his mount of snow,
his white beard hung with crystal ice, his lips dark blue,
and gazed far out at sea as his heart called for help.
The leader's flesh dissolved and poured in gaping earth,
but his deep yearning tore through mountains, plunged to Hades,
then seized the loved damp clay till flesh once more congealed,
till that wild bird, the soul, soared free and once more built
its nest in the sun's beams with flesh and blood and dreams.
His comrades yelled from shores, in haste to seize once more
at oars, love, war, their old tasks in the savage world,
and their great leader felt their haste, his heart leapt high;
he saw the caravan coming, heard the joyous bells
and smelled the myriad fragrances that Granite brought;
he saw broad-buttocks, decked in his canary cloak,
bearing the piper on his shoulders like a kid
that once had wandered from the flock and now returns;
his nostrils flared and sniffed the sweet and downy maids
like bitter rhododendrons in cold crystal air.
Turning, he saw old Captain Clam, and hailed his friend:
"Thrice welcome! Health and joy! Welcome! There are no ports,
there's no more parting, Captain Clam, to scorch our hearts!
What were our voyages till now on mud-drenched earth
whose shores constrained us always and whose vile stench choked us?
With Death for pilot here we sail on shoreless seas,
in our strong ship of flesh we sail the deathless waves,
and all we've longed for on vile earth sits on our mast
and warbles to our minds, a golden male canary.
A thousand welcomes to my crew, my dolphin swarm!
All's well! I count and count again, not one soul's missing!
Quick with your hands! Unload the great king's golden camels,
for I smell figs and grapes, my lads, my memory brims
and welcomes fruit I've loved. Don't let one small grape fall,

hang all upon our masts until our hearts revive.
You've twined a spray of basil on my snow-white head.
I see a blood-soaked lyre that sails the crystal air,
our Prince Elias' armor, and I'll pluck its chords
and play Life's great refrains to keep Death entertained.
Forward, belovèd forms, small branches of my soul,
O mind's starved tentacles, cling to the mizzenmast,
a strong wind blows once more and our hearts swell like sails!"
Then their old captain stooped and all his friends rushed up;
some clutched his heavy hands and clambered swift aboard,
some gripped the icy slope and climbed up step by step,
some sat in a closed ring and plied their shadowy oars.
Rocky enthroned his elephant on the icy prow,
Krino embraced her bull and pushed him tenderly
to step on the snow-ship that both might never part;
on the cold crystal Helen sat, slim-throated swan,
and Rala fell at the clear body's frosted feet
and clasped them with her bloody and mud-splattered hands.
The seven-souled man then stood upright, hailed his troop,
caressed the women's hair, pale Rala's savage lips,
the yet still virgin and crisp throat of the child, Helen,
then softly touched their shoulders, stroked their moldering backs,
and welcomed his dear comrades in his ample brain
as though they were huge silent thoughts that wrapped him round.
He heard hoarse battle cries in his dream-taken mind,
cool laughter burst and flaming banners flapped in air,
hands groped to find his hands in sun and to hold tight.
As his dog, Argus, licked his feet and warmed his legs,
earth's hot breath rose and mounted till it reached his heart,
and as he stretched his empty hands to stroke his dog,
his crystal frigate shook and swerved in the cold foam.
He raised his eyes and joyed to see his three great forebears
tread stanchly on his frozen deck and plant themselves
in a straight row of three aloft, his ship's tall masts.
He wished to speak, but the maids felt his deep desire
and wreathed the limbs, beards, chests of the three living masts
with necklaces of pomegranates, grapes and figs
until the death-ship like a hanging garden glowed.
The cricket who had perched one dawn on his right shoulder
as the two chatted and lunged down the road together
now smelled the figs and grapes, then spread its silver wings,
clung to the lone man's beard and burst in rasping song.
The three great forebears dipped and swayed, the three masts creaked,
winds blew from all the world's four corners, the ship moved,
and as the dying man's mind swayed, the whole world swayed,
but the old captain stood erect on his white prow

and cupped his hands above his eyes, scanned all the sea,
and his heart yearned for his most faithful final friend:
"I shall not leave until you come with your gold cap,
your playthings in your hands, and climb this icy deck;
our voyage is most long and the mind wants to play."
As thus he murmured, casting far his sun-glad glance,
a warm soft body suddenly crouched beside his feet,
and when the great death-archer looked he saw entwined
and panting there a curly-haired sly Negro boy;
sweat from his armpits dripped, and in his palms he held
seeds of all kind: birds, beasts, trees, sorrows, joys and men;
he also held the mind's huge eggs: dread gods and myths,
great thoughts and virtues, freedoms, loves, and gallant deeds.
The seven-souled man saw the Tempter and laughed slyly,
their cunning glances crossed and juggled in the air,
their laughter spread to their ears' roots, and their long locks,
the white, the black, caught fire and leapt in crystal air.
Thus the two comrades talked in silence, eye to eye,
and as the Negro lad and the mind-spinner laughed,
both turned and caught in their eyes' nets the crew, the ship,
the destitute and emerald sea, the mournful sun,
all end and all beginning, present, future, past.
They played with the earth's and the mind's seeds at odd and even,
sometimes they merged and turned to a forked flame in sun,
sometimes the great world-mockers parted and laughed slyly.
At length the myth grew drowsy, curled by the hearth asleep,
and the world folded its vast wings and dropped its head;
then the great hybrid mind cast tongues of flame and light,
soared high and plunged, rushed through the crossroads of the flesh,
and sat, almighty, on the body's fivefold roads.
Its glance encircled the whole world, it laughed and thought:
"I shall create men, towns, and gods, I shall rig ships,
I shall seize clay and wings and air to shape a world,
I shall seize clay and wings and air to shape all thoughts,
we'll play in sunlight a brief hour and then push on."
His mind now danced and cackled on the green-haired earth;
glutted with loam, he scorned it, soared on high serenely
and blew to scatter life's toy down the hollow winds.
"I'll strip beasts of their armor, I'll smash gods and men,
I'll turn all thoughts once more to mud and wings and air,
I'll flip my hands, and all great towns shall tumble down;
good was the game we've played on the world's emerald grass!"
Slowly the curly-headed black boy closed his eyes
and dropped his head upon his chest, then clasped his knees
and like a weary fledgling wrapped his wings for sleep.
In pity for the lad, the great ascetic stooped

and fondled the thick lips and the drenched curly hair,
and then the Negro boy, that cunning charming spirit,
opened his dark eyes slightly, glanced at his old friend,
then shuddered as he saw the world-destroyer's orbs.
They whirled like deep dark funnels where the whole world spun,
within them all earth's creatures danced, his comrades yelled,
and the snow-flagship with a roar hauled up its sails.
The mighty athlete slowly fondled his sly spirit,
and his dark palms ate up its airy flesh with stealth;
its dark cheeks sank, its black sun-nourished eyes dropped out,
its thick lips rotted, still unslaked, its ears disjoined,
its cold skull glittered, bald and smooth in the afterglow.
The frontier guard then smiled and hung the Negro boy
on the mid-mast as scarecrow for the lower world.
Slowly his glance caressed all things for the last time;
the hour had come to fling his laughter in farewell,
and his throat rose and laughed, his frigate leapt erect,
figs and grape-clusters swayed on his ancestral masts,
the sailors seized their oars, the billows boomed and roared,
and all the women sang farewell to the lost world.
The piper sat astride the prow and placed the mind's
shade-smothered flute with skill against his breathless lips
till a faint tune rose distantly like a night shower
pelting with cackling laughter on a lover's roof.
Erect by his mid-mast amid the clustered grapes,
the prodigal son now heard the song of all return
and his eyes cleansed and emptied, his full heart grew light,
for Life and Death were songs, his mind the singing bird.
He cast his eyes about him, slowly clenched his teeth,
then thrust his hands in pomegranates, figs, and grapes
until the twelve gods round his dark loins were refreshed.
All the great body of the world-roamer turned to mist,
and slowly his snow-ship, his memory, fruit, and friends
drifted like fog far down the sea, vanished like dew.
Then flesh dissolved, glances congealed, the heart's pulse stopped,
and the great mind leapt to the peak of its holy freedom,
fluttered with empty wings, then upright through the air
soared high and freed itself from its last cage, its freedom.
All things like frail mist scattered till but one brave cry
for a brief moment hung in the calm benighted waters:

"Forward, my lads, sail on, for Death's breeze blows in a fair wind!"

Epilogue

O Sun, great Eastern Prince, your eyes have brimmed with tears,
for all the world has darkened, all life swirls and spins,
and now you've plunged down to your mother's watery cellars.
She's yearned for you for a long time, stood by her door
with wine for you to drink, a lamp to light your way:
"Dear Son, the table's spread, eat and rejoice your heart;
here's forty loaves of bread and forty jugs of wine
and forty girls who drowned to light your way like lanterns;
your pillows are made of violets and your bed of roses,
night after night I've longed for you, my darling son!"
But her black son upset the tables in great wrath,
poured all the wine into the sea, cast bread on waves,
and all the green-haired girls sank in the weeds, and drowned.
Then the earth vanished, the sea dimmed, all flesh dissolved,
the body turned to fragile spirit and spirit to air,
till the air moved and sighed as in the hollow hush
was heard the ultimate and despairing cry of Earth,
the sun's lament, but with no throat or mouth or voice:
"Mother, enjoy the food you've cooked, the wine you hold,
Mother, if you've a rose-bed, rest your weary bones,
Mother, I don't want wine to drink or bread to eat—
today I've seen my loved one vanish like a dwindling thought."

THE END

SYNOPSIS OF THE ODYSSEY

Originally I had thought of preceding each book of the poem with a short "argument," as in Milton's *Paradise Lost* and *Paradise Regained,* but I feared that the reader might eventually come to think of these not as the translator's but as the poet's original synopsis. Inevitably, especially in the later and more philosophical books, even the slightest exposition of events involves much individual interpretation, and though I have often discussed every aspect of the poem with the author, I have thought it best to relegate the synopsis to this Appendix where it may be acknowledged clearly as the translator's and thus freer scope be given for those sections of the poem which will always remain open for philosophical or symbolical speculation. This synopsis is meant to assist the reader in obtaining a clearer perspective of the action, especially if he glances at the argument for each book before reading the book itself, and to help him systematize the philosophical thought entwined with a richness of episode, metaphor, and parable. He will often find incidents described in such a way as to include an interpretation. This synopsis, however, is in no way to be thought of even as an abstract substitute for the poem itself, especially in those parts where the symbols and allegories take on varied significance for each reader, and where the thought is instinctively and inseparably part of the poetic texture. Perhaps this précis may also be of some use later to scholars who might wish to make the necessary exhaustive comparative studies or to research into derivative sources.

PROLOGUE

The poem, appropriately, both opens and closes with an invocation to the sun, for the imagery of fire and light dominates the poem and bathes it iridescently with symbolic meaning. The central theme is boldly announced:

O Sun, my quick coquetting eye, my red-haired hound,
sniff out all quarries that I love, give them swift chase,
tell me all that you've seen on earth, all that you've heard,
and I shall pass them through my entrails' secret forge
till slowly, with profound caresses, play and laughter,
stones, water, fire, and earth shall be transformed to spirit,
and the mud-winged and heavy soul, freed of its flesh,
shall like a flame serene ascend and fade in sun.

The sun symbolizes godhead, the ultimate purified spirit, for the central theme is the unceasing struggle which rages in animate and inanimate matter to burn away and cast off more and more of its dross until the rarefied spirit is gradually liberated and ascends toward its symbolical goal. Concomitant and contrapuntal themes are also announced: the laughter and joy that rise through and above tragedy; the freedom from all shackles which prudence and the comfortable virtues dictate, from all philosophical, ethical, and racial ties; the certainty that for each individual the phenomena of the universe are but the mind's creations. And from the beginning the poet strikes the tone which he maintains throughout: that of adventurous and dangerous exploration of both physical and spiritual worlds; a heroic, serious, yet ironic and playful braggadocio in the face of annihilation; the accents and the rhythms of folk song, the tall tale, fable and myth; the passionate yet laughing play of the poet's imagination with his material as he casts off from all sure anchorage like a restless mariner and launches into a shoreless sea of no destination: "Ahoy, cast wretched sorrow off, prick up your ears—/I sing the sufferings and the torments of renowned Odysseus!"

BOOK I

Odysseus subdues a revolt in Ithaca. In Book XXII of Homer's *Odyssey,* after Odysseus has killed the suitors of his wife with the aid of his son, Telemachus, his old nurse finds him amid the corpses "splattered with blood and filth, like a lion when he comes from feeding on some farmer's bullock . . . a fearsome spectacle." He forces twelve unfaithful maidservants to clean up the gory evidence of the massacre, then orders them strung up and hanged in the portico of the central courtyard. It is here that Kazantzakis has cut away Homer's last two books and grafted the opening of his sequel, for his own first book begins abruptly with an "And," as though he were continuing a previous sentence in Homer where Odysseus strides to his bath to cleanse his bloodstained body. Some incidents from Homer's last two books, as the tender recognition and reconciliation scene with his wife, Penelope, are entirely omitted; other incidents are reshaped, as the recapitulation of his adventures, the first meeting with his father, and the angry uprising of his own people. As the new *Odyssey* unfolds, still other incidents in Homer are reshaped or given another interpretation.

The savage aspect of Odysseus terrifies Penelope, and he in turn feels nothing of the anticipated joy on beholding her. The widows of the men killed at Troy, and the fathers of the slain suitors, accompanied by the shades of the dead men, arouse the people to revolt and rush with torches toward the palace to burn it. Odysseus summons his son to help him put them down, speaks with contempt of both rabble and arrogant archons, and insists on the right of autocratic rule. But to Telemachus, a mild-mannered youth who wants nothing more than to follow in traditional and conciliatory paths, his father now seems a stranger, harsh, cruel, and murderous. He wishes that this "savage butcher" had never returned from Troy. As they go to face the mob, Odysseus tells Telemachus of his meeting with Nausicaä and how he longed for her to become his son's bride. He then confronts the mob, and by pretending to think his people have rushed up to welcome him, subdues them craftily with specious promises, then cows them until they kiss his hand and follow him obsequiously to the palace. There he dismisses them, then joins frightened Penelope in bed. Telemachus dreams that his father, in the form of an eagle, seizes him by the skull, soars with him into the sky to test and strengthen his daring, then drops him headlong.

Early next morning Odysseus explores his palace, taking an inventory of what the rapacious suitors have left, and nostalgically recalls some of his old adventures. He confers with his farmers about his fields, his cattle, his slaves, portions out jobs, sets his realm in order, then announces a great feast in honor of his return. Filling a jug with the suitors' blood, he climbs a mountain to his ancestral graveyard, pours out a libation that his forefathers may drink and revive, dances with them on their graves, then climbs to the mountain top and views his island lovingly. On his descent, he stops by a humble basket-weaver to beg some food. Though he does not reveal who he is, he tells the old man that Odysseus has returned, but the basket-weaver is uninterested in the fate of kings, and concerns himself only with the simple needs of daily living, deplores ambition, and praises the common life, the proven verities, compliance to Death and Mother Earth. With arrogance, Odysseus upholds the life of individuality, revolt, and cunning, yet concedes that all life is vanity and that all roads are equally good.

Odysseus' father, Laertes, who all his life has been as much a farmer and landsman as his son has been a sailor and adventurer, crawls out to his beloved fields and calls out to Mother Earth to take him at last. At dusk all gather to the great feast of their king. Among the revelers is Kentaur, a glutton and great drinker, broad-buttocked, barrel-bellied, splay-footed, a mountain of meat, sentimental, softhearted, affectionate. His particular friend is Orpheus, a poetaster and piper, cricket-shanked, scraggly, cross-eyed, dream-taken and timid. When the feast begins and all wait for their long-lost master to pour a libation to the gods, Odysseus shocks them by proposing a toast to man's dauntless mind. As the revelry progresses, the chief minstrel rises and sings of the three Fates which had blessed Odysseus in his cradle: Tantalus who bequeathed him his own forever unsatisfied heart, Prometheus who gave him the mind's blazing brilliance, and Heracles who bathed him in the fire of the spirit's laborious struggle toward purification. Reminded of these bequests, Odysseus in fury lashes out at himself for wishing to settle down safely and seek no further paths to knowledge and exploration. He knows he has a more primitive atavistic ancestor in his blood. His confession frightens his people, and Telemachus once more curses a father who seems to be all that is contradictory, restless, and unappeased, revolutionary yet autocratic, atavistic and savage. Odysseus calms his heart by walking down the seashore at night.

BOOK II

Odysseus leaves Ithaca forever. By the fireside the following night, Odysseus tells his father, his wife, and his son that on his voyages Death had approached him in three deadly guises. (1) With Calypso life had seemed a dream, and he had been tempted to accept her gift of immortal youth, but an oar cast up by the sea recalled him to life once more. He built a ship and sailed away, but when he came in sight of his native land, a storm swept him off, and in delirium he visited the gods on

Olympus, who crowded about him to admire his mortal and aging body. (2) Shipwrecked on Circe's island, he was tempted to turn beast for love of her, to forget virtue and the spirit, and to wallow in fleshly delights, but one day the sight of some fishermen, a mother and her baby enjoying the simple comforts of food and drink, recalled him to life, its duties and delights. (3) Again he built a vessel, and again he was shipwrecked, but with Nausicaä he was tempted to lead a normal, unassuming life, the sweetest of all the masks of death. Although he abandoned Nausicaä also, he was determined to fetch her one day to be his son's bride that she might breed him grandsons. When Odysseus finishes his tale, he realizes suddenly that his own native land is the most lethal mask of death, a confining prison with an aging wife and a prudent son.

Soon after, his father, Laertes, feeling the approach of death, crawls with his old nurse at daybreak to his orchard, bids his trees, his birds and beasts farewell, sows grain, then falls to earth himself like seed, and dies. Odysseus buries his father, then sends a ship with a great dowry to fetch Nausicaä for his son. His island seems to him a strange place now, for a new generation flourishes, and the town elders, with whom he had longed to confer, seem rotting, senile, timid. Odysseus decides to leave Ithaca forever. Several months later, in autumn, he finds Captain Clam, a grizzly and trustworthy old sea-wolf, and persuades him to leave also. Next he visits the bronzesmith, Hardihood, a red-haired, burly man from the mountains, sullen, secluded, with a stain like that of an octopus on his right cheek, and enlists his aid by promising to lead him to the god Iron, a superior new metal. A few days later, he finds Kentaur drunk in the middle of a road, and takes him also. Working by day and carousing by night, the four companions begin to build their vessel. Orpheus is attracted by their food and revelry, and Odysseus takes him on as a crew member to comfort them at times with song. The townspeople, fearing that all five men are demon-driven, persuade sorceresses to make a manikin in the shape of Odysseus, hammer it with nails and then cast it in the sea, but when Odysseus finds it, he laughs and throws it in the campfire for kindling. One day a stranger joins them, Granite, a brooding young man of noble bearing, a mountaineer of good family, who had killed his younger brother over a woman and now roams restlessly, burdened with guilt.

Meanwhile, the various women with whom Odysseus had slept on his voyages hear of his return and send him all his bastard sons and daughters. He puts them to work, deeply moved by one of them only, his daughter by Calypso. Telemachus and a representative of his people, a man who had lost his arms at Troy, plot to kill Odysseus. In the summer, Nausicaä comes at last in her bridal ship, and the wedding with Telemachus is celebrated. A minstrel sings of Crete and of her cruel, military god, most suited to Odysseus' temperament. During the wedding feast, Odysseus discerns preparations made to kill him, confronts his son at once, yet rejoices to see in him such manliness and revolt. He promises to leave Ithaca the next morning, and that night, with his companions, loots his own palace of food and weapons, then leaves at dawn without saying goodbye to his son or wife. The friends launch their ship and set sail for unknown destinations.

BOOK III

Odysseus goes to Sparta. To while away the time as they row and sail, Orpheus tells a story of a male and female worm, representative of man's stubborn spirit, who find ways of overcoming God's attempts to kill them by fire, hunger, flood, and death. At the same time that Helen, in Sparta, is filled with ennui and longs to be abducted once more, Odysseus dreams of her calling him for help, her armpits dripping with blood. He wakes up, startled, and directs his crew to make for Sparta. Completing the story of the two worms, he recounts how they had settled in a far northern village which God had partly destroyed by a meteor, and how one day the male worm had smelted the ore, discovered iron, then matched his iron sword with the copper sword of God and had slain that old decrepit man in heaven. Thus, Odysseus implies, will the lowly barbarians with their new iron weapons conquer the decadent bronze civilizations. The companions now sight land, stop for food and water, then after three more days disembark near Sparta. As a present for Helen, Odysseus chooses a magic crystal ball given him by Calypso, takes Kentaur with him, steals a chariot and horses, and makes for the capital. He considers how Helen has never been for him a carnal temptation, but has always inspired him to the high valor of the mind. As they ride along the Eurotas at harvest time, they encounter members of the barbaric blond Doric tribe who have been descending into Greece from the far north, and who symbolize for Kazantzakis the new savage blood which is to revive the now decadent Greek civilizations, first by destruction and then by intermarriage. Odysseus rejoices that he was born in a time of upheaval and transition between shifting cultures and new worlds.

As they sight Mt. Taigetus, the five-fingered mountain which looms above Sparta, Odysseus suddenly realizes that he has come here with the hope of convincing Helen to run off with him on new adventures. Stopping by a roadway shrine to Aphrodite, he prays that his wish may be granted. When they arrive by nightfall at Menelaus' castle, they find the hungry peasants in revolt because their king has been confiscating most of their harvest, but as they are about to attack, Odysseus suddenly leaps before them and frightens them into storing all their harvest in the castle by telling them that they are in danger of attack by the blond Doric barbarians. When Menelaus has at last guessed who this stranger must be, he cannot find him, for Odysseus has penetrated into the dark halls of the castle to seek Helen. When they meet, both are deeply moved, and recall the past glories of the Trojan war. At supper that evening, Odysseus is scornful of Menelaus' soft life, and warns him that the barbarians will find him an easy prey, but Menelaus defends the comforts of old age. Odysseus speaks of the new god, barbarous and savage, who is rising now to replace the civilized gods of Mount Olympus, and feels himself disturbedly in sympathy with the destruction this new god symbolizes. When they part for the night, he presents Helen with the crystal ball.

Unable to sleep, Odysseus roams the palace and bids farewell to vested wealth and comfort. An obscure reaction has been fermenting within him against his own aristocratic class, and an awakening sympathy with the hungry workers, the Doric barbarians (symbolic of periodic primitive powers that destroy decadence and sow the seeds for other cultures). Kentaur explains to the slaves that by the new god Odysseus means the new metal, iron, which the barbarians have brought with them and which will soon destroy the old gods and civilizations based on bronze. After Odysseus helps drunken Kentaur to bed, he feels a sudden love and compassion for all mankind, and envisages the earth slowly distilling all phenomena to the pure honey of the spirit.

BOOK IV

The second abduction of Helen. Menelaus dreams that he is riding with Odysseus through scenes of contentment, but that his friend proffers him the sword of contention. On awakening, Menelaus rides out with Odysseus to show off his lands and wealth, assures the villagers that they are safe from attack by the barbarians, and orders the young men to prepare games of skill with which to entertain their guest that evening. They pass through summer harvests, watch straggling tribes of blond barbarians gleaning what poor scraps remain, and rest in olive groves where for the last time Odysseus tries to persuade Menelaus to accompany him on new adventures; but when he sees that his friend is concerned only with the comfortable virtues, with profit and loss, he fiercely decides to abduct Helen. They continue their ride to the upland pastures of Mt. Taïgetus where Odysseus admires the brave young shepherd, Rocky, who has climbed the high mountain crags to kill the marauding eagles that have been stealing his lambs. Odysseus requests and receives the shepherd lad as the sixth and last member of his crew, though Rocky goes with him reluctantly. Menelaus believes that a man should follow whatever fate has ordained for him, but Odysseus replies that it is man's duty to fight his fate, surpass his doom, and even his god. Meanwhile Helen, with her retinue of Trojan slaves, laments the destruction of Troy, and in her crystal ball sees a preview of her flight with Odysseus, and a glimpse of Knossos.

The two friends return with Rocky to the castle, and as Menelaus bathes, Helen tells Odysseus that she has resolved to leave with him. They plan to steal off together the next morning. That evening the aristocratic youths, the workers' sons, and the bastards spawned on the Spartan women by the blond barbarians, dance in the palestra to entertain their guest. The workers' sons perform a dance of harvesting which is wrathfully stopped by Menelaus as it quickly turns into a rebellious hacking for freedom. The young men of the aristocracy dance with a harmonious restraint and proportion admired by Menelaus, but scorned by Odysseus who sees them lacking in tragic awareness of the spirit's and body's strife. Then the bastard sons rush into the arena in a mock battle which swiftly turns real until blood flows. Menelaus stops them in rage, and rises to present the wild olive wreath to the youths of the nobility, but Odysseus snatches the spray and presents it to the bastards, indicating thus his contempt both for the ineffective poor and the elegant rich, and his preference for the outlaw virtues, the illegitimate and lawless, that which destroys traditions and smashes frontiers. He declares that only the strong have the right to rule. At the castle gate, representatives of the blond barbarians request permission from Menelaus to settle in his land, and when Menelaus grants their request in fear, Odysseus with scorn sees that this is the inevitable conquest of decadence by virility. At the farewell feast that night, although he is planning to betray his friend by stealing his wife, Odysseus—half in genuine sorrow and half in cunning—speaks of his great love for Menelaus and of his sorrow at parting, and Menelaus, sentimentally moved, gives his friend a gold statue of Zeus, the god of friendship. Odysseus vows eternal friendship, but when his friend falls into a drunken sleep, offers Helen new adventurous paths of danger and strife, and rejoices when Helen, though afraid of his cunning and savagery, accepts freely. Meanwhile, Kentaur advises Rocky like a good friend, consoles him and warns him of the dangerous yet alluring life all lead who follow the unpredictable archer. In a dream that night, Odysseus has a vision of Zeus as a wrathful god of friendship betrayed, but dismisses all the Olympian gods as figments of men's hearts and fears. When day breaks, the three friends steal a chariot and make off with Helen.

BOOK V

Arrival in Crete. At nightfall of that same day, they reach the rest of the crew, and swiftly set sail, though toward no certain destination, inspired by Helen's presence. A fierce storm blows for three days and finally smashes their rudder. Concerned for Helen only, Odysseus curses a baleful and murderous god. In cowardly fear, Orpheus whines that God is demanding a sacrifice in expiation for the abduction of Helen, but though Hardihood approaches to cast her into the waves, he finds that he cannot, overwhelmed by her beauty. Odysseus rejoices at his manliness and declares that he will make Hardihood king of the first land they sight. Almost immediately, the storm subsides, and Crete is sighted, a land of great wealth, but now in its decadence.

They land in the harbor near Knossos, fall into a tired sleep, then wake next day at noon. Odysseus sells the golden god of friendship for food and clothing, the crew members scatter throughout the colorful port, and Helen and Odysseus meet a peddler who tells them they have arrived on a holy feast day when their senile king, Idomeneus, Odysseus' old companion at Troy, is climbing holy Mt. Dicte to commune in a cave with the priestess of the Bull-God and thus regain his virility that his people and land might once more become fertile. (Throughout his poem, Kazantzakis has taken many incidents and symbols from Frazer's *The Golden Bough,* as here the fertility rites and rituals of primitive peoples.) The peddler sells Odysseus an ivory god of seven heads: the first is bestial, the second is savagely martial, the third voluptuous, the fourth represents the flowering mind, the fifth tragic sorrow, the sixth a serenity beyond joy and sorrow, and the seventh the ethereal soul. For the first time, Odysseus is deeply moved by the prescience of the gradual purification his vision of God must undergo, from the pure beast to the pure spirit.

Leaving Captain Clam, Kentaur, Granite, Rocky, and Orpheus in the harbor to repair their ship and to keep watch, Odysseus joins a stream of pilgrims and mounts toward Knossos with Helen and Hardihood in a hired cart. Their waggoner tells them of the bull rituals soon to be celebrated. The blond barbarian gardener, who gives Helen a drink of water on their way up, is the one who will later become her husband, symbolizing the merging of archaic and savage blood to produce the new coming "classic" race. They reach the palace and find it being decked with lilies and palms by the Serpent Sisters, priestesses of Mother Earth. Amid leopards and her three Negro lovers, Diktena appears for a moment, the second daughter of the king, the priestess of the holy temple harlots. As Odysseus goes to announce their arrival, confident of an immediate welcome, the blond gardener suddenly appears and silently offers Helen a cluster of grapes, then vanishes. Odysseus returns, furious at his repulsion by the palace guards, and all three sleep with the other pilgrims on the courtyard tiles.

Early next dawn, the Serpent Sisters supplicate Mother Earth in dance to fructify their king, and thus all of Crete, but their dance is suddenly interrupted by Phida, the eldest daughter of the king, who hates her father's decadent realm and plans an uprising with the slaves and her group of dedicated women, the Rebels. She falls screaming in an epileptic seizure, but when Odysseus rushes to her aid, the palace eunuchs suddenly rush out and take her away.

Meanwhile, old King Idomeneus has crawled into the holy stalactitic cavern on Mt. Dicte where priestesses masked like cows surround him, as from a hollow bronze bull the high priestess of the Mother Goddess arises, and the sham ritual begins. King and priestess come to an understanding whereby he gives her property and gold in exchange for a nine-year blessing of fertility and strength. The news is blazoned by beacons from mountain peak to peak until it reaches the palace and town where the people spread their garments on the streets that their king may pass upon them and impart to them his new virility. When on his return Idomeneus is told that his youngest and virgin daughter, Krino, has not been caught to be his incestuous bride in the bull ritual, he orders that the men sent to catch her should be put to death. Krino is the leader of a virgin band of Mountain Maidens who in the sacred ritual oppose the Holy Harlots led by Diktena.

After being made to wait ignominiously, Odysseus and Helen are admitted to the king's presence and his decadent inner court. Idomeneus resolves to make Helen his ritual bride and to kill Odysseus, because his presence anywhere always spells disaster, but when Helen refuses unless Odysseus is spared, the king consents, though forebodingly, then commands the Serpent Sisters to prepare his bride in seven days and nights for the holy bull ritual.

BOOK VI

The bull rituals at Knossos. Seven days later, at cock crow, the Serpent Sisters entreat their Bull-God to descend and fertilize the earth and their people. The bull arena quickly fills, the common people crowd in the upper tiers, the painted lords and ladies of the court sit below. Though Odysseus gazes on all with loathing, he still marvels at any manifestation of mysterious and brief life. When the sun rises, the King appears wearing the mask of a black bull with golden horns, mounts his throne, and signals for the games to start. In the center of the arena, on a white bull's hide, Helen lies, naked, beside a hollow bronze cow. As a herd of trained bulls is let loose in the arena, Helen calls out, in ritual, to be saved from the Bull-God, but Diktena and her Holy Harlots exhort her to submit. Krino defends the body as a chaste and pure instrument of God, and Diktena as flesh to be offered him in sacrificial and lustful rites.

As the pre-rituals end, and the Holy Harlots scatter amorously amid the archons, we are given glimpes of the hard lot of the slaves in contrast to the lustful decadence of the court. The King signals again, seven bulls are loosed in the arena, and the famous acrobatic dancing and somersaulting begin, led by Krino. Further scenes of poverty and oppression in Crete are shown; at noon, as a thresher and his wife eat their scant food in the fields, the King orders the games stopped and the feast spread. The slaves scurry to prepare and serve the meals; a slave mother rushes with her baby into the sunlit court from her dark dungeon, and finds that it is dead—only Odysseus hears her scream, and feels that he is responsible for all the pain on earth, as if he were earth's only savior. Gradually in Odysseus an almost Christian consciousness of the world's suffering is being awakened, and a sense of responsibility toward pain and oppression. He is dazed by the rot and stench of the civilization around him. At this moment, Diktena claims him for her partner in the orgies to be held that night, and Odysseus resolves, to Hardihood's disgust, not to spare himself anything of degradation, knowing that a strong soul cannot be soiled.

Meanwhile, in the arena, Krino has been strangely drawn by Helen's beauty; the two women kiss and caress each other in the burning sun until Idomeneus, enraged by jealousy, orders Krino to play with the fiercest bull of all, who has secretly been fed irritating and intoxicating herbs. Although she knows that she is going to her death, Krino plays acrobatically with the bull, is suddenly gored, tossed high in the air, then falls impaled on the double-ax standard of the Bull-God. It is now twilight. The thresher and his wife have gone home, the slave mother buries her child, and the Serpent Sisters escort the common people out of the arena so that the orgiastic secret rituals of the nobility may begin.

At the full moon, the lords and ladies of the court don the hides and masks of various animals, the Serpent Sisters raise Helen and place her in the hollow bronze cow, and as the King slowly approaches, a bull is slain, and all fall upon it and eat it raw. As Idomeneus steps into the bronze cow, the lords and ladies engage in orgiastic lust throughout the arena, Diktena stuffs Odysseus' mouth with the bull's loins, and both fall into an erotic embrace. Suddenly Phida appears, shrieking, flies to where Krino lies impaled, and receives the dripping blood on her outstretched arms until her enraged father orders her driven out of the arena at spear's point.

Meanwhile, the five crew members have been drinking in a harbor tavern where Captain Clam tells them of secret arrangements he has made with the blond barbarians who are now setting sail for their native land to bring reinforcements. As the decadent nobility feast through the night, Hardihood comes and reports to Odysseus that in his wanderings through the labyrinthine palace cellars he had discovered a secret forge where a captive barbarian was forging weapons of iron for Idomeneus. Phida had suddenly appeared and given herself to the ironsmith in exchange for iron weapons promised her and her Rebels.

At early dawn, the slaves come to gather their drunken lords and ladies, and the blond gardener again appears suddenly and makes off with Helen. As the Mountain Maidens wash and bury Krino, Phida and her troop of Rebels sing and dance songs of poverty, oppression, and revenge until Odysseus, deeply moved by all he has seen and done, joins her in a dance and song of slaughter and rebellion. Phida falls into a paralytic swoon, and her Rebels take her away. Unable to sleep, Odysseus lies by the riverbank and listens to a slave singing of freedom. Finally, as he drowses and falls asleep, his old companion, Death, makes the first of his many appearances, lies beside him in comradely embrace, and the two sleep together. For a brief moment Death, also, falls asleep and dreams of life.

BOOK VII

The conspiracy to destroy Knossos. In his sleep, Odysseus dreams of Fate in the form of a woman who stabs him with three knives, with three great experiences and adventures in life: woman in youth, war and glory in manhood, and death in old age. At sunset Hardihood and Odysseus watch the decadent lords and ladies strolling by the riverbank, and mark them down for slaughter. For three days and nights Odysseus broods in agonized silence on the projected destruction and massacre of Knossos, and calls on his God for help, but the god that finally appears is a tearful and frightened likeness of Odysseus himself. Odysseus' image of God is to change, gradually, from a timid god to a god of battle. Realizing that it is God, not he, who needs assistance, Odysseus dismisses him in scorn, but tells Hardihood that he has had a vision of a savage and flaming god of heroic proportions.

As she lies beside the senile King, Helen reminisces of her Trojan days, recalls her escapade with the blond gardener, then gazes into her crystal ball and sees herself married to the gardener and living with their son in tents. Odysseus disguises himself, and assisted by Phida, who urges him to join her revolt, visits Helen in the women's quarters. He mocks Helen for her affair with the gardener, but when she asserts her free will to choose her own destiny, Odysseus rejoices, as always, when anyone shows a will equal to his and takes another road. He unfolds to Helen his plan for the sacking of Knossos, enlists her aid, then leaves for the harbor town. There he finds his friends carousing in a tavern, and tells them of a new god he has seen who is not compassionate, but wrathful and unsated. He then assigns to each his role in the uprising, and informs Captain Clam that he is to remain in the port to assist the incoming barbarians and to fire the arsenal.

As summer passes, Odysseus consults with Phida, Hardihood helps the blond ironsmith forge weapons, and the barbarian ships sail for Crete from the far north. Winter passes, the plot progresses. Odysseus works with a slave, a skilled wood-carver (much like Daedalus) who studies the flights of birds and longs for freedom. When spring comes, Idomeneus has a premonition of his death. Helen, pregnant with the gardener's child, has forgotten Sparta and Troy, stitches her baby's swaddling clothes, and dreams of her son. Odysseus tries to rouse the slaves by lying, once more, about his vision of a flaming god, a fierce warrior and ruthless hunter. Although he longs now to help the workers, he is under no illusion, for he knows that slaves want that which their lords already have; yet he feels that God is now working out his liberation through the medium of these oppressed bodies, and that this is the next step toward the purification of spirit in an endless strife to the world's end.

After a sleepless night before the day of a great holy festival, Idomeneus paces restlessly at dawn, filled with nightmares and premonitions of destruction. Odysseus and his friends are preparing the massacre. Dressed in a mantle adorned with marine figures, the King is symbolically wed in a spring ritual with the sea. As Odysseus walks along the river toward the harbor and a young boy and girl proffer him flowers, he is seized with pity that even such innocents must perish in the general massacre, but when he sees his god hovering near him in the form of a pitiless vulture, he steels his heart. He learns that in the holocaust of old values, many who are innocent and blameless, or simply victims of circumstance, of heredity and environment, must also perish. He plays with Captain Clam on the beach and in the sea, for both feel that the old sea-wolf is fated to perish when he fires the arsenal. Idomeneus is wedded to the sea, and faints. The palace is decorated for the festival, all the conspirators take their allotted stations, the barbarian ships secretly approach the harbor, and the plotters prepare for the massacre.

BOOK VIII

The destruction of Knossos. That night a slave girl, whom the archons had forced to dance until she died, is buried by Odysseus and his friends. Even Orpheus is moved to vows of vengeance. Odysseus tells the iron-smith that the night has come to distribute the iron weapons. In the palace amid great feasting, Idomeneus looks on pregnant Helen with pride, thinking she is bearing his son. Odysseus and his vulture god crouch in darkness by a column and observe the feast at the exact moment when Captain Clam is creeping into the arsenal to set it on fire. Idomeneus, and even the palace walls and adornments, sense with terror the coming destruction. At midnight, when his god nods approval, Odysseus suddenly rises and, to the fluting of Orpheus, sings of unslaked fierceness, of cunning deception, until a messenger enters in haste and shouts that the arsenal is on fire. Odysseus then gives the signal, and the massacre begins. Just as Odysseus is about to slay Idomeneus, Phida intervenes and beheads her father with a double ax, but is in turn killed by one of the Negro guards, and falls on her father's corpse. Phida's Rebels and the barbarians sack the palace and set it on fire; the blond gardener makes off with Helen. Through the smoke and flames, Odysseus catches sight of the wood-carver flying away on constructed wings.

After the massacre and the burning, Odysseus proclaims Hardihood King of Crete, as he had promised during the storm. At dawn, as the vultures, crows, and dogs eat the corpses, the victors broil meat on the embers of the still-smoldering palace, and fall to carousing, but Odysseus withdraws to a high rock and spurns both food and women. Toward sunset, a delegation of townsmen come with gifts to plead for mercy and peace, but Odysseus again scorns all the virtues that appertain to peace and comfort and instead proclaims war and death. When at last he takes some bread to eat, he spies a green locust perched upon it like a green Death, and for the first time feels fear. He falls asleep and dreams of the ravenous Spirit, eating him whole like an octopus, consuming the flesh in order to live, making man ever discontent and humble before greater deeds to be done. He then joins his companions and tells them they have accomplished nothing. He tells them a fable of how God created the world and all living creatures, then called on all to bow in reverence, but how the human heart refused to bow or surrender its freedom. Ever since then, a war has raged between what God destroys and what the unsated human heart rebuilds. Odysseus dashes to his feet, eager to follow his heart at once to further and higher adventure. He advises Hardihood to begin his rule, but when Hardihood says that he has already sent runners throughout the land, Odysseus rejoices to see that another spirit has proclaimed its freedom from him and formed its own independence. "The sweetest fruit of all that ripened on this day/is that one soul has found its freedom and cast me off!"

Next morning all gather to bury Captain Clam and Phida side by side. Odysseus declares that God is a blind dark power seeking to evolve through nature till human beings give him senses and a soul. Helen then appears with her gardener, and Odysseus begins his farewell. He advises Hardihood to rule with merciless love, with force and patience, to free the slaves, to portion out the land, to be forever unsatisfied, and to break through what may seem to be impossible frontiers, for he fears that Hardihood, like most men, will freeze into the forms of comfortable virtues once he settles down and cultivates his own possessions. He bids Helen farewell, then leaves without looking back.

Taking Diktena with them, the comrades now sail southward, and on the fourth day, as Crete disappears and Odysseus bids Greece farewell forever, he rejoices to leave behind all sureties and to sail toward unknown creations and freedom. Diktena sings of how she had been sent as a twelve-year-old girl to give of her virginity to an unknown Egyptian god. Odysseus tells his crew that he derives his strength and courage from the knowledge that all life is a brief dream, a toy, and when Granite replies that it would be best then to commit suicide, Odysseus retorts that he is the creator of his own dreams, that he both serves and drinks his own blood, that he accepts necessity with joy. At dusk one day, they moor near the mouth of the Nile, and Odysseus tells his crew a fable about a grandfather, a son, and a grandson who rowed all their lives long to find the still unknown source of the Nile, the fountain source that would bequeath immortality, though all died on the way. Odysseus then declares that "Blessed are those eyes that have seen more water than any man," that the hidden deathless sources may be found in Death only. Rocky objects that the presence of Diktena among them is distracting, that she is useless, and Odysseus agrees to leave her behind.

BOOK IX

The decadent empire of the Egyptians. Next morning the friends all walk down to the harbor town, delighting in a strange new race of men. As they drink in a harbor tavern, Odysseus feels dark, atavistic roots, as though he had sailed these waters in another life long past. An old blind bard sings to them of pain and poverty, but Odysseus refuses him food because he feels that in this land Hunger is the herald that will lead him to his new god, and that to feed one mouth is to feed none. The friends abandon Diktena to her willing fate on the harbor's docks, and sail down the Nile.

Odysseus urges his crew to row toward Thebes, about which Helen had once spoken. After many days, they anchor by a ghost town of ruins, tombstones, and gods with animal heads. Odysseus realizes that beast and god have always warred in man, as the spirit sought to evolve into light through dark atavistic roots. He knows now that his ultimate destination is to free God as far as possible from the beast, toward more and more salvation. One day the friends find a huge stone Sphinx, and an old Egyptian trying to free it from the encroaching sand. Accepting the old man's invitation, they go to his house for a humble meal and are served by his two young daughters who sing to them of love, yearning, a home and children. All feel the strong attraction of hearth and home, Rocky most of all, but they all reject it for the insatiable and faithless heart.

As they continue to sail down the Nile, they plunder and steal in order to live, for everywhere they find drought, hunger, and extreme poverty. One night they anchor in the ruined Sun City, Heliopolis, where Odysseus dreams of a tomb and of a king and queen (Ikhnaton and Nefertiti) who beg him to unearth them. They dig at midnight, find a tomb of a king and queen laden with treasure, strip it, then load their skiff until it almost sinks with gold and jewels, and continue their journey. But their hearts are heavily laden, for now all long to settle down in comfort and pleasure, until Odysseus suddenly grasps fistfuls of the treasure and begins to fling it overboard. All follow suit until not even Orpheus' ivory flute is spared.

They sail now with free hearts, but hear everywhere laments of hunger and starvation. As Orpheus wonders how Helen is faring, we see her in Crete, maternal and content with her newborn son. Kentaur pities the starving Egyptians, especially the children, but Odysseus replies that Hunger and War are two powerful drives which force men to push further on in their exploration of the world's limits: "If I could choose what gods to carry on all my ships, I'd choose both War and Hunger, that fierce, fruitful pair!" After many days, they anchor toward nightfall at Thebes, a bustling crowded fortress smelling of evil. The Pharaoh is a world-weary, timid youth overshadowed by the remembrance of his grandfather, a great warrior. He has no other ambition than to finish a lyric which he writes and rewrites laboriously. The friends roam the streets all night, gazing on the pampered lords and the seductive ladies until at dawn they fall asleep on their deck and dream of food. When they awake, they all disperse to seek food, but only Kentaur succeeds somewhat, for he finds a young whore who invites him to share her scanty meal. Next dawn, when they are all still hungry, Odysseus reminds them that he had never promised them either women or food, "but only Hunger, Thirst, and God, these three great joys." Then he tells his comrades that he will leave by himself to seek some kind of solution, and that if he does not return in three days, they are to shift for themselves.

BOOK X

Rebellion in Egypt. Led by Rala, a young Jewess, the people rise in revolt against the decadent priests and their crocodile god and storm the temple. Odysseus, swept by the onrush, tries to save Rala, but suffers a severe head wound. They are both thrown in Pharaoh's dungeon, and there Rala and three other revolutionaries—Scarab, Nile, and Hawkeye—tend him anxiously for three days. (Meanwhile, Rocky and Granite have abandoned their skiff, Rocky going south and Granite north, but Kentaur and Orpheus remain.) In a coma, Odysseus sees his son, Telemachus, out hunting, and Nausicaä on her terrace eating figs. After six days he finally opens his eyes, and Rala faints from weariness. The three revolutionaries try to question him, but when they elicit no information, curse the exploited man who will not rise in revolt. Hawkeye is lean and volatile, as restless as fire; Scarab is somber, suspicious, a peasant close to earth; Nile is intelligent and reasonable, like smokeless light. Hawkeye invites Odysseus to join them in their revolt against hunger and exploitation. Odysseus recognizes in Rala the type of dedicated idealist who sacrifices dreams of husband and home for an abstract cause. Then the three revolutionaries quarrel about Odysseus; Scarab believes he is an opportunist, a cunning shipowner who longs for profits only; Hawkeye believes he is a Cretan of hidden powers; and Nile believes they are both right, that Odysseus is probably one who comes from the upper classes but who likes to play with fire, and advises his two comrades to accept him for what he is.

Next day Nile reveals to Odysseus how the workers in Egypt have been organized, and how they are all awaiting reinforcements by ship from the armed barbarians, the Dorians. Odysseus replies that he does not know whether he loves the bestial peasant or whether he simply no longer wants to side with the decadent nobles, but that a cry in his heart urges him to join the revolutionaries. This he will do, although he deeply feels that he belongs to neither side. His ambivalence disturbs the revolutionary leaders, but Nile tells him they will accept him on his own terms, no matter if he joins "from love or raging fury or search for God." Odysseus then dreams of God as a general recruiting an army, who, when he recognizes the dangerous ambivalence, the double-faced betrayal of Odysseus, advises him to act as purveyor for both sides.

Pharaoh, laboriously composing his lyric at his bath, commands that Rala and Odysseus are to be brought before him for amusement, then mocks Rala as a representative of a cursed race, whines that he is a man of peace who simply wants to keep the status quo, and that God has created some rich and others poor, but Rala declares she acknowledges one God only: man's free mind. Odysseus warns Pharaoh that a new race of barbarians is inundating his land, announces the doom of Egypt's ruling classes, then as a sign of war places on the king's knee a dwarfish god he had shaped in prison out of bread, blood, and sweat. This is now Odysseus' image of God, the god born of Hunger and Oppression. In terror, Pharaoh directs that Rala and Odysseus be set free.

Rala takes Odysseus to a secret meeting of revolutionaries where they hear news of approaching barbarian reinforcements. Rala advises an immediate attack, but Odysseus cautions against hope and says that he fights best who fights without either gods or hope. Returning to his skiff, Odysseus finds Kentaur and Orpheus still awaiting him, but he admires Rocky and Granite who have asserted their freedom and gone off to shape their own fates. When he tells his friends of his adventures and of his desire now to join the revolutionaries, Orpheus mocks him for sentimentally swerving from his determination to find the source of the Nile.

Meanwhile, the barbarians have landed and begun to plunder the land. Pharaoh sends them emissaries who try ineffectually to frighten them off with words, magic, and their bestial gods, but the barbarians answer with a savage dance and song about a king who gets drunk, smashes an image of God, and then drinks from the hollow skull. The three leaders escape from jail, and Rala, tormented by her love for Odysseus because she feels she has thus betrayed her cause, bathes, puts on her best garment, then waits by the crossroads where the Egyptian army is to pass, determined to commit suicide. Odysseus tells his two crew companions that his mind and heart are opposed, for his mind wants to build an ivory tower of retreat, and his heart wants to knock on every door and share in every suffering; he prevents them from killing each other by making his mind a court fool to mock his heart, and by giving his heart the restrained freedom of a falcon. This ambivalance and tension in Odysseus between two opposites is the central key to his character.

BOOK XI

Revolution and defeat in Egypt. Both sides prepare tumultuously for war on Egypt's sands. On the morning of the battle, Granite appears with some barbarian hordes whom he had joined as they landed in Egypt, but he tells Odysseus they have been weakened by excessive plundering and carousing. Odysseus sees in the barbarians the new blood that will revive the rotted culture of the Egyptians, and he knows now that his purpose is to give direction to their savage onrush. As the Egyptian army passes, Rala hurls herself before the horses and is trampled to death. When Odysseus sees the endless Egyptian host, he realizes that there is no hope of winning, but elects to fight exactly because of this.

The barbarians and revolutionaries attack at midnight, but before dawn they are entirely routed, and the four friends lie on the battlefield, seriously wounded. At noon the king's herald passes among the dead and wounded to fetch the mightiest chiefs for the king's amusement and sacrifice, and by several ruses Odysseus manages to have all his friends carted away. They lie in dungeons till past springtime. To amuse his friends, Odysseus carves out the twelve Olympian gods into marionettes pulled by strings. Nile retorts that the mind which mocks at gods is a god's slave still. But Odysseus has slowly been creating a new image of God, one who has nothing to do with justice or virtue, but is best represented by a hungry flame, an arrow constantly mounting upward. He dreams of a shape, either man or beast, which slowly tries to raise the pressing sky from earth, helped by animals, birds, insects, and by himself. For three days and nights he tries to carve out the features of his new god, but to his disgust carves only a replica of his own features, for God is always created in the present image and evolutionary development of man. Nile mocks, but Odysseus declares against those who seek economic comforts only, and declares that he serves an inhuman flame which burns within him and which he has named God. After a third dreamless night, Odysseus carves a savage mask of his new god which his friends immediately recognize as War and the barbarians as their own fierce god. Odysseus names him the God of Vengeance.

Pharaoh resolves to kill the rebel chiefs on his ancestor's great feast day as sacrifice, and when he allows them a last orgy, the friends confront death with varied emotions. But Pharaoh is in the grip of a nightmare he had seen the previous night, of a savage and monstrous head that rose above the horizon, a dangling corpse. No pleasure can console him, no dream interpreter ease him. Meanwhile, in his dungeon, Odysseus recalls a visit he had made with Rala to the embalmers, and rejoices to remember that on the walls of the tombs they had painted a devouring flame that flashed beyond all comforts of life and nature, even beyond the gods. Recalling how a conjurer once tried to blow spirit into the mouth of a hawk-faced god, Odysseus knows that it is man who gives life to gods. Pharaoh's chief steward visits the prisoners and offers reprieve to anyone who can exorcise the king's evil dream. Odysseus offers to interpret the king's dream in dance. With the mask of his newly carved god dangling down his back, he dances of beggary, of war, of the maimed and wounded, then suddenly clamps the mask on his face. Pharaoh shrieks with terror, recognizing the terrifying face of his nightmare, then commands his guards to escort Odysseus and his troop out of the land. Odysseus returns to the dungeon, tells his troop of the glad news, eager now to leave Egypt, to lead his people to a new land and there build a city and civilization based on his new vision of God. Nile offers to follow them to the frontier, but declares that he will remain in his native land to foment rebellion.

BOOK XII

The flight out of Egypt. Odysseus' troops are composed of the despairing, the criminal, the riffraff of life, that disruptive element which most often breaks down old values and treks toward new frontiers. When they reach the frontier, he holds up the mask of his god and asks all to choose between the poor comforts of their slavish existence and this new god who offers only thirst, hunger, and freedom. He wants only the unregenerated, the restless, the unappeased to come with him. In a dance of delirium, Odysseus declares that God has revealed to him the new road and the new city they must build, then divides the group into three troops. Orpheus precedes with his flute, Granite leads the youths and the amazon-like maidens, Kentaur the old and the children, and Odysseus men in the prime of life.

For three days they follow the Nile amid crocodiles, snakes, and mud villages till they reach the desert sands. As they penetrate further and further into the desert's throat, they pass a human skull filled with bees, a last blade of green grass, huge carved rocks of a past sand-smothered civilization until, weak with hunger and thirst, they clamor to return, even though to slavery and poverty. Granite is ruthless, but Odysseus understands man's frailties and urges his people to plod further to where he tells them he envisages food. Their despair is increased when an oasis to which they hasten proves to be a mirage, but Odysseus reminds them that he had promised only a pitiless god of thirst, hunger and war. Obscurely moved by the ruthless laws of survival and necessity, he determines to abandon all who do not have the strength to follow him, but tender-hearted Kentaur, enraged at his master's seeming inhumanity, refuses to leave the old and the children to their death, and stays behind to lead them.

Odysseus and his remaining troops plod on; he tells them fables to cheat their hunger, refuses to let them water even a flower for fear their hearts, also, might cast roots, and keeps them pitilessly on the march. (In Ithaca, meanwhile, Telemachus and Nausicaä play with their small son tenderly but are dismayed to note in him many characteristics of his fierce grandfather.) At length one day the troops sight a Negro village, but before they can decide how to proceed, they are attacked by a fierce Negro band which almost annihilates them. Kentaur and his group, who had captured a Negro hunter and forced him to lead them to where food might be found, appear suddenly and turn the tide to victory. They make peace with the Negroes and are welcomed by the village chieftain, a monster of fat, who mistakes Kentaur for their leader because of his own monstrous bulk, and proposes to marry him to his daughter, "a hippopotamus of fat." A great feast is prepared in a courtyard under an oak tree hung with the skulls of enemies. Odysseus, suspecting that the Negro chief will try to surfeit them with food, drink, and women, warns his men to be on the alert. In an orgiastic dance and ritual, Kentaur and his fat bride are wed, and all disappear to couple in the shadows, but as Odysseus keeps vigil and notices the Negroes stealthily gathering the weapons, he blows on his conch in warning, and with difficulty disentangles his friends from black erotic embraces. They plunder the village of food, leave behind those who refuse to continue, and plod on.

Kentaur broods on the ruthless god of Odysseus who sieves out his followers so cruelly, according to survival, and plays no favorites. Odysseus tells his troops that all adventures and all experience lead to further revelations of God, that God grows as man grows, changes with man's environment and culture, for it is man who feeds him: "God is the monstrous shadow of death-grappling man." God needs us, not out of love, but because we are the flesh through which he lives and grows. Granite declares he now knows for what two causes he'd give his life: for that which scorns man's comfortable virtues and restlessly seeks to find further horizons, and for that which declares that hunger and thirst are what impel men to explore and to seek. Odysseus agrees, and carries this thought still further: that salvation and destruction are one, for only by the dissolution of what has been accomplished can man enlarge his spirit and reach his only salvation. He tells Granite of his vision of a city based on this new vision of God, and tells Kentaur that cities must be created out of vision before they can be turned into deeds.

BOOK XIII

Through dark Africa to the source of the Nile. In his travels, meanwhile, Rocky stumbles on a seemingly deserted village at a time when the old king is being assassinated, according to traditional ritual, by three witch doctors to make way for a young fertile chief. The people hail Rocky as one sent them by their white-haired gods, and make him chief. Odysseus and his troops, meanwhile, have been pushing through a jungle of damp mold, of monstrous trees, entangling vines, and savage animals; here God has taken the mask of a frightening and fetid forest, of rapine and lust. Rocky is taught his duties as a chieftain of the Negroes, and plans wars and conquests. One day Granite captures a female leopard cub and presents her to Odysseus; they become inseparable companions. Finally the troops cut through the jungle and soon spy some Negroes tilling their fields, but these run away in fright at the approach of white men. Granite sights their village and wants to press on immediately, but Odysseus counsels waiting until the following day. At dawn three Negro envoys greet the white men as though they were gods, tell them of a plague which is devastating their village, and ask for help, but Odysseus speaks to them so fiercely in a demand for food as recompense, that the Negroes scatter in fright. The friends help Orpheus hew out a savage headless god from a block of wood, then Odysseus tells him to take this to the village, fall into a seeming trance, proclaim that this god will heal all ills, and then trade it for food; but he warns Orpheus that he must not be deceived by a few miracles that might indeed happen. Orpheus, however, is swept away by his own self-induced ecstasy and when, indeed, the crippled walk and the blind see, believes in the artifact of his own hands, falls down and worships the god he had created, and though he sends food to his friends, refuses to return, not even when Odysseus comes to take him.

After a storm one day, Odysseus scornfully tells his friends what had befallen Orpheus. They spy a town in a deep gulch, and in a forest find some Negro boys undergoing a ritualist sexual spring rite before descending into the village to possess their brides. Leaving Kentaur with the troops, Granite and Odysseus descend to the village and there with great joy are reunited with Rocky. Kentaur joins them for a great feast, and a sorcerer conjures up a vision of Orpheus dressed as a witch doctor, prostrate before his new god. After three days and nights of feasting, Odysseus bids Rocky cast off his new crown and join them once more, but when Rocky reminds him that, in line with his own teaching, a pupil must cast off his teacher and become a leader of men in turn, to shoot beyond the twelve axes Odysseus once strung with his arrow, Odysseus rejoices, blesses Rocky, and asks for the blessing of the youth in return.

The friends leave Rocky, and after nine days of marching through stony wilderness, they sight some mountains and begin to climb them. One day Granite yells out, "The Sea!" and all, through a cleft, glimpse an endless blue-green shore. When they reach the waters, plunge into them with joy and find them sweet, they realize that they have come to the end of their journey, the lake source of the Nile where they plan to build their ideal city. Odysseus directs his troops to erect temporary shelters on the shore while he climbs the adjacent mountain to commune for seven days and nights with God in order that he may thus formulate the new laws and plans for the ideal city. Accompanied by his leopard cub at dawn, he begins his ascent.

BOOK XIV

Odysseus communes with God. It is in this book that Kazantzakis develops the core of his ascetic philosophy, further amplified and more clearly systematized in his small book *Spiritual Exercises: Salvatores Dei.*

First Day (1-84). Odysseus climbs the mountain all day until at night he finds a cave in which to sleep where neither ghosts nor demons dare attack him.

Second Day (85-161). In the light of dawn, Odysseus sees that the walls of his cave are painted with primitive drawings of a hunt, and hails his blood brother, the first archer. He dedicates this day to song and joyful embracement of life, then daydreams of his most secret wish, the possibility of deathlessness, but a small worm climbs up his chest to remind him of his mortality. At night he sleeps once more in the cave.

Third Day (162-443). Odysseus sits on a huge rock, calls the bird of god to descend, then sinks into silent contemplation. He recalls his first experience with the three elements, woman, sea, and God: how as an infant he had almost fainted when he first smelled a woman's breasts, and how at the age of two he had pelted the sea with stones and yelled: "O God, make me a God!" He ate and became the things he ate, grew to adolescence, wedded, had a son, then went off to war. Choked with memories, he acknowledges that mysterious primitive forces within him have stifled much in his heart that cried out for liberation. He looks in the yellow eyes of his leopard cub and sees himself as mankind's prototype, a caveman. Atavistic memories seethe within him, cruel hates and shameless longings in which his soul lies smothered; he becomes aware of man's fathomless line of evolutionary development from inanimate nature to all forms of animate nature, to man, to spirit. At sunset he sleeps on the rock and dreams that his heart and mind quarrel like an old married couple. The female heart is dissatisfied with the boundaries of law and order which the timid mind is constantly erecting; she wishes to break through routine, cast off the yoke, smash down the middle wall of phenomena and plunge through into the other world, down into the abyss, into God; but the male mind scolds and tells her to be content with what is visible and at hand.

When the eternal Outcry in man shouts for help, the mind scurries away, but the heart pours out her blood in order that the phantom forefathers may drink and revive. An individual, however, must choose whom of his forefathers he wishes to revive, what of heritage and history he wants to retain. Odysseus thrusts away those who wish to live for material values only; he denies his father, Laertes, because a father must always give way to his son; he denies his family ancestors, for earth has now produced sons better then they; he denies even his dear friend Captain Clam because the world must be ruled not by love alone but by more ruthless principles of what is most needed. Only when his three great Fates approach does Odysseus give them of his blood to drink. Tantalus drinks, and then accuses Odysseus of planning to build a city and to settle down, of betraying the unappeasable heart, the restless search. Heracles drinks, and Odysseus hails him as that hero who in twelve labors pummeled man's flesh into a refinement of spirit, and weeps to see him now emaciated by death. Heracles urges Odysseus to complete the task he himself had left unfinished, to push on to the thirteenth and final labor (immortality), though he cannot discern what it may be.

Fourth Day (444-736). When he awakens, Odysseus becomes aware of all the phantoms he carries in his bloodstream. He knows now that he is the product of all these phantoms have done and what they still long to do. He, like all men, is a bridge between past and future, holding within himself the dead, the living, the unborn. The realization that he carries infinite depths within himself frees Odysseus from a concern with his own Ego so that he knows now that he must go beyond the I to his own racial ancestors. But now he sees his third Fate, Prometheus, nailed to a rock, and addresses him as father of flame and brain, as the "brave mind of god-battling man," as one who stabilized man on earth and yet impelled man's mind toward the sun. Prometheus laments that he has failed, forsaken and betrayed by man whom he had created, and that he could not finish "life's most glorious task," that he neither made his peace with God nor killed him, that "Beyond all flame and light, beyond even Death, my son,/the final labor, the last ax, still gleams with blood." He vanishes, and the Outcry is heard shouting for help once more.

Odysseus now plunges beyond his particular race and into a feeling of brotherhood for all races, realizing that he and all men are units in the evolutionary stream of all mankind. But now the voice of Mother Earth within him bids him push on beyond the boundaries of the human race itself to make his peace with all of nature, with beasts and trees, to direct her now and tell her what to do (as if, in the scale of evolution, man can now go beyond necessity and himself direct the life-process). In dreams that night, he feels himself a part of all animate and inanimate nature, of birds, beasts, insects, rocks and sea, until he touches the most atavistic and primordial sources of the universe, the inscrutable and uncompassionate rhythms where life and death cannot be differentiated one from the other.

Fifth Day (737-950). At dawn next day it seems to Odysseus that the men and beasts on the cave walls have come to life and swirl in dance about him. Soon he feels himself close-pressed by the phantoms of primordial life until they all make way for Leviathan, the most primeval ancestor of all, the great mass of somnolent life in which the soul had just begun to flutter its wings. After Leviathan passes, Odysseus opens his arms to welcome man's immediate ancestor, the Ape, and addresses him with homage and affection. He turns then to all other creatures from which man is descended, even the humble dung-beetle and the ox. In his brain all become friends, the lion and the fawn. He welcomes the birds and the insects until his identification with living creatures is complete, so that in the spring rains that night all creatures seek shelter in his body and his brain.

Sixth Day (951-1246). Amid the rain-drenched earth at dawn, Odysseus listens to a male and female voice within his breast. The female heart, with love and tenderness, calls to the Spirit (to God), that is still submerged in mud roots and animal flesh, and longs to make it more human, to further it in its evolutionary ascent. The Spirit warns that it is savage and bloody, but when the heart still calls with love, it springs up as the heart would wish it, in form of a gallant youth. Odysseus now hears the

Spirit (or God) groaning within himself, ever climbing a bloodstained road through inanimate and animate nature, and finally even through man. Trees and beasts smother God, even man's soul cannot contain his ever-upward reach, and he begs Odysseus to help him fight free. God is filled with fear, for he sees no end to the dark climb as he stumbles and struggles upward. Odysseus vows to dedicate himself to the liberation of this Spirit which in him cries out for help, and he now sees this vital impulse in all things, in the fruit he eats, in the seed he plants. All is one cyclical nourishment: "Birds, fruit, and water have all become Odysseus now!" He comes to the realization that it is God who is eternally crying out in man to be liberated.

The poet now addresses Odysseus to tell him that he has gone beyond the restrictions of his ego, his race, all mankind, and even all animate and inanimate things, until he has heard and understood the Outcry that stifles not only in all bodies but even in all souls, and struggles to mount further still. This insistent struggle toward purer and purer refinement some call Love, some God, some Death, and some an Outcry. The soul now seems to Odysseus but a wick which the flaming Spirit consumes as it yearns for other kindling, that it might burn with a more rarefied light. He vows to build an ideal city that will embody his vision forever. Singing with joy, Odysseus suddenly sees a vision of God undergoing many forms: as Tantalus, as Heracles, as Prometheus, as charging armies that symbolize the military campaign of the spirit, and finally as an old vagabond, an outcast constantly scorned and persecuted, in whom may be seen "the savage bitterness, the spite, the unfathomed eyes,/the flickering flames that glittered in his eyes like snakes,/the bloodstained endless upward road he climbed with grief." Odysseus is wrung with compassion, and then filled with serenity as the setting sun and the full moon glow simultaneously on opposite sides of the horizon.

Seventh Day (1247-1410). An inner voice mocks Odysseus that his air-castles are of no worth unless realized in actual practice and works, in acts and deeds. With pebbles, clay and mud, he builds a model of his proposed new city, then plunges down the mountain slope. He knows that the world was made when two antithetical forces clashed, one male and the other female, in the arenas of phenomena and the mind. The Act hews forests, builds ships, and with its precious cargo, God, who is wounded and bleeding, crosses the fearful abyss in a constant strife, age on hopeless age, "to raise the nonexistent shores from endless waves." A voice in Odysseus urges him to use all the powers of his mind and imagination in order to shape nature and life in their image, for then man not only frees a god, but even makes a god. Odysseus embraces Lady Act as a bridegroom his fecund bride, then hurries to his fulfillment, to the building of his ideal city.

BOOK XV

They build the ideal city. On his return Odysseus finds that his followers have split into two antagonistic camps led by Granite and Kentaur. In disappointment and rage, feeling that man cannot ever attain those heights which their leaders envisage for them, he roams the forest for three days, and on the third day contemplates a wild pear tree that had split through a rock, twisted into growth, and finally burst in bloom. It seems to him a gnarled symbol of the spirit's vitality, taking whatever fate has given of soil and stone, and flowering stubbornly in the sun. Nearby, he finds an immense cave, then calls Granite and Kentaur, makes his peace with them, and decides that, like the pear tree, he must accept given conditions and work with the recalcitrant herd of mankind.

Next dawn the foundations of the new city are laid. Six cocks and six hens are slain as symbols of the passing of the twelve Olympian gods. The people are separated into three groups of ascending rank: the craftsmen, the warriors, the intellectuals, and a socialist state is created (from various elements in Plato's *Republic,* St. Augustine's *The City of God,* and More's *Utopia*). Marriage is outlawed, children are to be held in common and educated away from their parents, old and useless persons are to be allowed to die. But Odysseus could not find the foundational law of his thought until one day he saw a flock of termites mating in the air. He saw that as soon as the bridegrooms had performed their one function, they fell expiring to earth, gobbled up immediately by birds, beetles, scorpions and snakes. With fierce joy, Odysseus embraces this as a ruthless law of necessity and survival in nature: "Whatever blind worm-mother Earth does with no brains/we should accept as just with our whole mind, wide-eyed./If you would rule the earth, model yourself on God!" Kentaur is appalled by what he considers his master's heartlessness. Odysseus longs to tell his people of his new god, but he postpones doing so, fearing they are not prepared to accept so cruel, ruthless, and selective a god.

In the spring, after many months have passed, Odysseus declares a fiesta of three days for the mating of young men and women, and also sets his leopard cub free to find her own mate in the mountains. Again he sees a vision of God as Commander in Chief, of all men as co-workers in the great battle where man must learn both to obey and to command. Each must act as though the entire salvation of the world depended on himself alone, but as though it did not matter whether he won or lost, for all that mattered was the struggle itself. One day he sees with horror a troop of blind black ants devour a baby camel, and then a human infant, and forever after keeps this vision before his mind's eye as the grinding destructive power behind all nature and human endeavor, the gaping gulp that awaits us all. He is overwhelmed by the tragic necessity of life. At last one day he tells his people of the dread law of survival and existence, and that the new God they are to worship is not a protective and almighty god, but no weaker and no stronger than they themselves.

Indeed, God needs their support, for not even he knows from whence he comes nor toward what he goes. All but Granite are dismayed by a god who cannot help them by supernatural means, who cannot be separated from themselves as struggling mortals. Kentaur exclaims in despair, "Our bodies are the threshing floor where God fights Death."

Summer passes, and in autumn Odysseus declares the dying of a great chief as an occasion of joy, for this man had fulfilled his duty on earth; tragic would have been the passing of someone still young. (In Ithaca, his grandson dreams that his grandfather had given him a toy ship, and both Nausicaä and Telemachus are filled with fright.) When winter comes, all work at their various crafts in the huge cave. Odysseus carves the Ten Commandments of his god on stone, and each law revolves about the idea of God as a struggling evolutionary growth of the spirit throughout all phenomena. This tragic, necessary vision must be embraced with joy, for "The greatest virtue on earth is not to become free/but to seek freedom in a ruthless, sleepless strife." The last commandment is a symbol of the ascending struggle: "an upright arrow/speeding toward the sun with pointed thirsty beak." When the time comes to inaugurate the town, there are many foreboding incidents. The air is hot and stifling, termites disintegrate Odysseus' hut and bow, rats flee down the mountain, screeching. As the people deck their houses and streets with palms, Odysseus looks with pride on his city where he believes the good life may finally be attained. An unnatural darkness falls, the moon becomes leprous, the earth shakes, and Odysseus, subconsciously aware of what is happening, rages against his betraying God. Rocky appears astride a white elephant, for he has sensed the danger from afar and has come to fight by his captain's side.

BOOK XVI

Odysseus becomes a renowned ascetic. Although ominous omens appear, only Odysseus seems to heed them. All throng next dawn in the great cave to celebrate the inauguration, but as Odysseus dances, the earth shakes and roars. Odysseus rushes out and sees the mountain belching smoke and lava. He rages against a god who made the world so imperfect that man is forced into an attempt to perfect it, then assigns various tasks to his friends and himself rushes to save the young children in the town. As the nursery begins to buckle, Kentaur suddenly appears and props the doorway; Odysseus leaps free, but Kentaur is crushed in the ruins. Soon the entire city, all but the North Gate from which Rocky had directed the fleeing troops, is swallowed in a gaping chasm.

Granite had begun to lead a troop northward, but returns and finds Odysseus, his hair turned white, clawing at a column of earth that soon reveals Rocky's cinderous body. It disintegrates, and in tragic fury Odysseus kicks the dust and bones into the chasm. Granite tries to comfort Odysseus, but "his mind marched beyond all sorrow, joy, or love,/desolate, lone, without a god and followed there/deep secret cries that passed beyond even hope or freedom." Granite leaves Odysseus forever and leads his group toward another life. Odysseus now falls into the "terror of thought," an inner contemplation which blazes with light, and identifies himself with all of nature, the snakes and the grass, the ruthless laws of death and destruction, the seeds struggling toward light. He enters into a mystic communion with insects, fruits, and all growing things, with streams and stones. His feet flow like rivers, grass grows on his chest, morning-glories twine about his beard: "Odysseus brimmed with waters, trees, fruit, beasts, and snakes,/and all trees, waters, beasts and fruit brimmed with Odysseus." He comes to a tragic acceptance of life as it is, but transcends it with joy, and then blesses his five senses for their omnivorous and unslaked desire to know the entire universe, because only through them may a man apprehend nature directly.

For many months he remains in ascetic contemplation on the rim of the abyss, and as his fame spreads throughout Africa, pilgrims come to worship him and to seek his healing powers. Telemachus appears to him in a vision and tells him not to push beyond man's possible attainments, but Odysseus calls to his first forefather, Tantalus, and cries: "Ah, grandsire, I've surpassed your pride; you thirst/because you've never drunken, hunger because you've never eaten,/but hunger itself has sated me and thirst unslaked me!" He identifies himself with all persons, with all human races in their brief lightning flash toward death. Pilgrims of every sort bring him gifts and hang them on the branches of the wild pear tree. A black chieftain gives him lumps of mud taken from his people's graves and kneaded with their tears, sweat, and blood, that the great ascetic might mold them a god to bear their pain, but Odysseus looks with compassion on man's futile efforts to escape suffering, and molds but maddening faces, monstrous forms of primitive terrors.

One day Temptation appears in the form of a snakelike Negro boy to mock Odysseus and to tell him that he has become decrepit, that his mind has disintegrated, that he is still filled with the pride and wrath of his ego. But Odysseus envisages a struggle of the mind that may push on even beyond man's physical limitations. A third inner eye of the life-stream itself now rises within him, and Odysseus blesses all his life as he recalls his daring youth, the sweetening influence of women on his character, how he longed to embrace his native land at first but then longed to travel further. He blesses his restless search, his soul which has been faithful to no one thing: "My soul, your voyages have been your native land. With tears and smiles you've climbed and followed faithfully/the world's most fruitful virtue—holy false unfaithfulness!"

Odysseus now turns to the playful creation of the mind, first with the lumps of mud given him by the Negro chief, and then with his flute. He sees a brief vision of his death amid icebound seas. He creates various fantasies of his mind—nymphs, the twelve months, werewolves, creatures of myth and legend, and finally an image of God as a vain, bearded, swaggering dwarf. When Odysseus turns to destroy him, God changes many protean forms and begs for his life, but Odysseus declares that even God is a creation of the mind, that like Orpheus he had almost believed in his own artifact. He destroys the image and rejoices in his freedom. Up to this point in his quest, Odysseus has tried to purify his concept of God, but now he turns away from even a monistic and anthropomorphic conception to a humanistic and evolutionary concept of nature, to representative types of men on earth for pattern, and extols man's mind as the Creator—for man himself, at least—of all phenomena. Death, not God, becomes his constant companion.

A voice now cries out thrice within him, and Odysseus recognizes Heracles, his great forefather who had struggled through twelve labors to purify his spirit through flame into light, who taught him to pass beyond all small passions, to aim at the great, and to strive still further, all in terms of actual deeds performed. Now, in death, Heracles sees that man may reach even further than the twelfth ax. He looks upon Odysseus as his heir, begs him to purify his mind of gods, demons, virtues, sorrows, joys, and the final and greatest foe, Hope, until there remains only the essence of flame, scornful and superhuman, a fire no thorns can feed. Odysseus realizes that he has now unbound himself from the final chain, that of Hope in an anthropomorphic God no matter how purified, and in complete freedom realizes that all phenomena, as an individual sees them, are the creations of each particular mind. The sun rises at his right temple and sets at his left, and "when/the mind snuffs out like a thieves' lantern, all things vanish." With the aid of his senses, man weaves the fabric of his life over a bottomless abyss, over Nothing, over Death. Odysseus now exclaims: "No master-god exists, no virtue, no just law,/no punishment in Hades and no reward in Heaven." He has ascended the seven tiers of heads which he had bought from the peddler in Crete.

Frightened by his ecstasy and the blazing light of his freedom from God, the pilgrims had fled in terror. Now on the rim of the abyss, Odysseus dances ecstatically in affirmation of life with all its antinomies. He bites his heel and drinks his blood in a symbol of complete communion and acceptance. He has passed beyond arrogance and pride, the drunken rage of plundering and possession and guilt, until he who had striven to be the savior of the world finds that he is saved even from the need of salvation. Stooping with humility and homage, he kisses Mother Earth and accepts the universe in all its aspects, both evil and good.

BOOK XVII

Divertissement: The drama of life. Odysseus remains in an ecstatic contemplation where past and future seem enveloped in an everlasting present. Life seemed, at times, the pursuit of women, beauty and pleasure; at times, the pursuit of virtue and justice; at times, the necessity of assisting an endangered God and embodying him in an ideal city. But now all these seem shadows, and Odysseus turns to embrace the nude body of life, stripped of all illusions; he bids her rise on the crags of strength and despair, on the peaks of both drunkenness and laughter, and there, according to the mind's playful desires, create whatever it wishes—a wedding pomp, a war, the normal life of a city. Odysseus smiles, and three maids are born. He calls, and an old man falls to the ground. He sighs, and a slim dancing girl springs up. He scowls, and battalions besiege a city. He contemplates gold, and a bazaar seethes with merchants and commerce. Odysseus is seized by an inexpressible love and compassion for these creations of his brain who rush through their roles as if they were real.

Slowly, as he comes out of his trance, his creations vanish until there remain only an old king, his son the prince, his faithful slave, a fierce warrior-king, and a maiden. Taking up a flute made of a dead man's bone, Odysseus plays till the characters come to life and live their roles; when he stops playing, they freeze in arrested postures. A drama unfolds among them, depicting the eternal passions of life: love, lust, jealousy, war, betrayal, the survival of the strongest. The maiden, daughter of a famous ascetic, lies in a forest beneath a tree where her father has just died. The king, in a gold chariot driven by his slave, searches throughout the forest for his son. The prince has found the maiden, declared his love for her, yet fears that she is not flesh, but spirit purely. Hearing the king approaching, and fearing that his father will part them, the prince urges the maiden to cast herself on the king's mercy, then hides himself in a cave. When the old king sees the maiden, he is terrified by her nakedness, senses evil and wants to withdraw, but because he has esteemed her father, he bids his slave clothe her and place her in the chariot. As the slave lifts the maiden, she admires his animal strength and wishes they were alone. Odysseus stops playing his flute and laughs to see life spinning its old rounds: the king cracking with desire; the temptress, which is woman, burning towns and castles in the offing. When a storm threatens, the old king stops by a roadside altar to pray, the maiden and the slave take shelter in a stable and fall to lust on a bed of manure and dung.

After the three reach the palace, the old king, tormented by jealousy and guilt, imprisons the maiden to keep her from the prince. Soon the warrior-king besieges the palace, the prince refuses to lead the army unless his father will free the maiden, but the king refuses and casts him in prison also. Then the slave prevails on the king to send the maiden to the warrior in order that she may seduce him and then behead him in his sleep. The maiden agrees on condition that the king will give her his son on her successful return, and the king finally, in disgust and despair, agrees. Odysseus again stops his flute and urges the maiden to fulfill her role, one that scorns compassion, justice, goodness, truth, and has no care for virtues, ideas, men, or gods. Toward dawn, after the warrior and the maiden have passed a night of love together, he asks her why she had not beheaded him, as he suspected she would, and she replies that when he had laid his head, replete, against her bosom, she had felt a mother's compassion for her child. Now she urges him to fill her pouch with another's head that she may fool the old king and thus betray him into the warrior's hands. The old king thinks his kingdom has been saved, but his slave treacherously beheads him and presents the head and the keys of the city to the warrior-king, announcing at the same time that the prince has perished in the burning prison. The warrior-king declares that God is not concerned with love or compassion or friendship, that he cares for the strong only and supports those most fitted to survive who rule without compassion. He commands that the maiden be burned on a scented pyre with the honors of a great warrior.

Odysseus now stops playing, and the five actors sleep on. He addresses the Mind as the creator of all that lies fallow and shouts to be born, and to which the Mind gives form on the shores of insanity, which is life. There the Mind sits and plays the game of life, creates and destroys. Some have called the Mind Spirit and declared that it begat the flesh; some have called it Flesh and declared that it begat the Spirit; but it is something beyond both, and it plays in the abyss of the Universe. Man, with the free play of his mind, locks and unlocks the chambers of life, though he hopes for nothing; he does not complain under life's blows, but strides through the nonexistent palace of his desires as though it were real, holding the keys of Nothingness, for he knows that at bottom all is a dark abyss and an oblivion.

When day breaks, Odysseus continues his journey toward the southern tip of Africa. He sees that through his mind and senses now all the creative impulse flows and plunges, laughing, down the abyss: an image of a deathless flowing stream. Within him War (the ceaseless strife of evolutionary creativity) and Mind (that which gives the stream direction, order, body, shape) embrace in a creative strife.

BOOK XVIII

The prince and the prostitute. Amid common scenes of daily life, Odysseus continues what he knows is his last journey and begins his last long farewell to the world, rejoicing in life as though he were looking on all things for the first time. At noon, as a cricket perches on his right shoulder and bursts into song, Odysseus recalls how at Knossos a crow had perched on his shoulder, its beak still splattered with the blood of kings, and a profound spiritual change in him is thus symbolized. At night in a forest a black chieftain, slain in war, is burned on a pyre. Odysseus meets a hungry wolf, but greets him like a brother. Himself weak with hunger, he welcomes death, and when he sees a peacock attack and devour a viper, another image of the grim struggle in life, of beauty fed by slaughter, he falls in a faint and dreams of pagan, bacchanalian Greece.

Next dawn as he continues his journey, he again falls fainting with hunger and is fed by a passing Negress bringing food to her husband in the fields. That night Temptation visits him again in the shape of a Negro boy and informs Odysseus that he now bears all the thirty-two signs of the perfect man, that he has therefore attained his salvation and should now scatter into non-existence, but Odysseus replies that the Tempter has not named the greatest sign of all: "I am the savior, and no salvation on earth exists." When the Tempter disappears, Odysseus regrets that he had not named for him a still greater sign: that embracing ecstasy (as in Yeats' *Lapis Lazuli*) which transcends all tragedy, for "Erect on freedom's highest summit, Laughter leaps."

On awakening next day, he sees approaching the elephant-caravan of Prince Motherth (the representative type of the Buddha). This Prince had once seen three fearful signs of man's decay—a diseased man, an old man, a beautiful youth dead in his prime—and now roams the world in anguish, seeking to find the answers to evil, death, and decay. Hearing from a faithful slave of the great ascetic in Africa, the Prince had journeyed far to consult him, had pitched his camp close to his retreat, then sent three envoys to make their report. Each envoy returned with a different account of what he had seen: the first, an old man, had seen a baby; the second, a mature man, had seen War; and the third, a young man, had seen an ancient grandfather. When the Prince asked his slave to tell him what happens to a man's body when it dies, and the slave replied that it is eaten by six waves of worms, the Prince wept, unable to accept the horrors of death.

Odysseus suddenly appears, and Prince Motherth begs to be given some medicine that will prevent him from seeing the face of Death in all things. Odysseus replies that both he and the Prince have looked beyond the gods and all hope into the face of Death, but that though the Prince sinks nerveless to the ground in terror, he holds Death before him like a black banner and marches on, for "Death is the salt that gives to life its tasty sting." Unable to accept Odysseus' heroic affirmation, the Prince nevertheless accompanies the ascetic on his journey south, hoping to find a more palatable answer to his despair.

The ascetic's fame has spread throughout Africa, and all throng to watch him pass. Among these is the famous courtesan, Margaro, who invites Odysseus and Motherth to dine with her. Odysseus tells her that the secret paths to salvation are seven: the play of the mind, the fruitful drudging goodness of the heart, proud and lofty silence, fecund activity, manly despair, war, and love, and that she has taken the last and most occult, that which strives to merge antitheses as represented by male and female, that which breaks down the barriers of flesh in ecstasy until the lover shouts, "Ah, there's no you or I, for Life and Death are One!" This is the very answer which the ascetic gives, and Odysseus calls Margaro his "ascetic fellow-toiler," the martyr of joy, then asks her in turn for the distillation of all her experience. Margaro replies that she tells her lovers, "In all this wretched world, but you and I exist," and then, "Beloved, I feel at length that we two are but One." Odysseus replies that there is a third synthesis: "Even this One, O Margaro, even this One is empty air."

Motherth rejoices because he understands Odysseus to mean that not even Death has meaning, that it, too, is empty air, and decides to reject life in all its aspects and come to complete negation, to the *via negativa*. But Odysseus rejects both Motherth's nihilism and Margaro's affirmation of hope, and merges both views in a declaration that only by facing the hopeless and annihilating abyss of Death may a strong man then affirm life fully and raise the structure of his life on the rim of chaos, giving it himself meaning, beauty, worth, value, even though he knows that this is only an illusion: "Though life's an empty shade, I'll cram it full/of earth and air, of virtue, joy, and bitterness." Margaro cannot soar above the flesh, nor Motherth lift himself above the grave. Odysseus says that the truly free man not only plays with death as with one other element in the vital passing stream of the universe, but that he is even exhilarated by it; this proves too heady a wine even for Death himself, who vomits all he has swallowed. Margaro begins to see a glimmering of Odysseus' meaning, but Motherth, fully persuaded in negation now, abandons his kingdom, his wife, his newly-born son, and wishes to free himself completely from all the trammels of flesh. But Odysseus again affirms the tragic joy in all of life, and as he says farewell to the prince and the prostitute and goes to cross the threshold, he stumbles, and Motherth burns his golden garments to light the ascetic's way.

BOOK XIX

The hermit's avid hand. As Odysseus is traveling through a forest, Death touches him on the shoulder and knocks him to the ground. "He had no god or master now: The four winds blew,/and in his chest his compass-heart led on toward Death." Within him a third, an inner eye, gazes on the world as for the first time, where no past, no present, and no future exist. He spies Death in the form of an old companion awaiting him under the shadow of a fig tree, but begs him to wait a bit more until they reach the sea, and when he continues his journey, Death follows at a proper distance as Odysseus bids the world farewell in a mystic trance where all opposites are joined in love. Again Death fells him, but Odysseus begs him to follow seven paces behind him until he can reach the edge of the continent and there build himself a skiff in a shape of a coffin, that he may return once more to the sea as to the womb. One day as he eats honey plundered by a bear to keep himself alive and to strive for freedom, he asks and replies: "What freedom? To stare in the black eyes of the abyss/with gallantry and joy as on one's native land."

One day, Odysseus comes upon a blind hermit who asks him if he is the savior and ascetic renowned throughout Africa, but Odysseus replies that he is the savior of the world where no salvation exists. As in the woods about them the grim struggle for survival persists, the hermit confesses that all his life he has pursued answers to the eternal questions: "Why were we born and toward what goal?" yet has found nothing but a fearful abyss which he cannot interpret. He begs the ascetic for the final truth, but Odysseus replies that if he were to give the true answer and his answer were understood, it would crush the hermit's mind, and advises him only to press his ear against Mother Earth and to listen with care. By this Odysseus means that man must accept the earth's, or nature's, laws of necessitous strife, survival of the fittest, and ultimate annihilation, before he can hope to build bravely on the abyss. The hermit now regrets his abstemious life, his search for God, and wishes he might have lived like a mighty king replete with the joys of life, dispensing justice and goodness, asking no questions about life's purpose. As he falls asleep, he dreams of what he would have liked to have been.

He dreams of a great king replete with all the joys of peace and home who suddenly turns melancholy; nothing can give him pleasure, neither jesters nor women nor wise men. He hears a minstrel's song, but understands only that it is a lament, and crying out, "It's true!" casts away his crown and tries to escape from his kingdom, but finds that he cannot, for it is an island bounded everywhere by the roaring sea, by the abyss. Then a monster, the Law, attempts to constrain him within its confines, but the king's mind swallows the monster. God then tries to stop him, at the last limits of the world beyond which man cannot go, but behind God the king hears the sea still roaring, a further eternity, until God also sinks in the mind of man. Then the Mind itself rises and declares, "I only, man's great mind, exist on earth and sky," but even behind man's mind the annihilating sea roars and mocks, and the mind quakes. Reaching the sea at length, the king hews an image of himself as a tragic unlaughing man, sets it up as a sign, and speeds on his search, but one day, when he trips over his own image, he realizes that man is forever caught in the round trap of his own existence, his world, his mind, his given limitations. He strikes inland, climbs to the peak of a mountain of human skulls, and contemplates his long evolution from the sea and various forms of life to his present eminence as the Tragic Man. He cries out that the universe for each man is valid only in so far as a man is there to apprehend it, yet when he sniffs Death approaching, he suddenly stretches out a still-unsated hand and clutches his mother, Earth.

At this moment in his dream, the hermit cries out "Mother!" and dies with his hand stretched out, avid and unsatisfied. When the nearby villagers try to bury him, they find they cannot close the outstretched hand, and Odysseus tells them that it will not close until they have filled it with their dearest treasure. The elders cast their gold into the hand, the youths their weapons, the chieftains the bronze keys of the city, the mothers their tears, the maidens their kisses, a child its toys, but the hand still gapes, unsatisfied. Then Odysseus stoops and fills the avid hand with earth, and the hand closes, sated at last. Acceptance of Earth's necessitous law of annihilation is the bitter answer.

Odysseus continues his journey south and broods on the hermit's dilemma, knowing that some invisible force stamps us out the way a man's foot stamps out an ant heap. He travels amid scenes of massacre and destruction until he comes to a jostling village of oriental color and zest for living where even a passing girl will distract sons from their father's funeral. There he hears a minstrel singing about a Prince Elias whose father seemed as if he would never die or give up the crown. When a cock-pheasant sings to Prince Elias in a human voice that only through song, the loftiest crown of all endeavor, may he hope to become glorious and immortal, the prince orders a lyre made with seven chords, but it remains silent whenever he strikes the strings. The cock-pheasant then informs Prince Elias that songs are paid for dearly, that each chord must be baptized in the blood of each of his seven sons. One by one Prince Elias takes his sons to battle, and one by one, as they are slain, he drenches each chord with their blood until the lyre bursts into ecstatic song. Cursed by his father, Prince Elias in turn curses all of life, flings his lyre across his back, and roams throughout the world. The minstrel declares that one day he saw Prince Elias sitting by a cliff's edge playing his lyre as the chords leapt "like man's sometime laughing sometime weeping heart." In this book Kazantzakis has contrasted the useless cyclical pursuit of the hermit with the answer given to one who listens closely to the earth's annihilating response. A man is imprisoned in the kingdom of his earth and in his own identity; behind man's attempts to control phenomena by Law, by concepts of God, by the encompassing mind, the eternal sea of annihilation roars. With his works, nevertheless, with a song sung joyfully and gallantly above this abyss, a man may hope to keep his "deathless flame" burning a while longer. Thus the tragic affirmation of life in joy is once more symbolized.

BOOK XX

The impractical idealist, the hedonist, and the primitive man. Captain Sole (the type of Don Quixote) takes up his rusted armor once more and sets out on his decrepit camel, Lightning, to save the world from slavery and injustice. Captured by cannibals, he is bound to a stake by their slaves and prepared for cooking, but Odysseus spies him and runs to his rescue. The cannibals, in fear of the renowned white ascetic, set Captain Sole free, but the black chieftain tells a fable to indicate that savage mankind can never be taught civilized ways, but will simply devour its idealistic saviors. Nevertheless, as soon as Captain Sole is freed, he dashes in frenzy once more to free the slaves, and though Odysseus admires this rash and rebellious heart, the imagination that dares to leap beyond the possible, he spurns it because it dwells far from reality, in wish-fulfillment and fancy only. Odysseus wishes Captain Sole well, and plods on. Passing villagers drugged with hashish, he broods: "Man's whole submission to all great necessities/alas, may be the only outlet Freedom has!"

Continuing his journey, he comes to great marshlands and an island with an ivy-wreathed tower set amidst turbid waters. He is taken to the

Lord of the Tower, a fat and sluggish hedonist who has longed to converse with the famous ascetic, and has prepared him a gourmand's feast, but first entertains his guest with a cockfight. He marvels that Odysseus, unlike his other guests, gazes on the cruel battle with neither pleasure nor disgust, and Odysseus replies that his real eyes are indeed moved with joy and anguish at the death-struggle on earth, but that he also gazes on all things with an inner, a Third Eye, which remains serenely unmoved. The Lord of the Tower replies that best is the unconcerned mind which gleans its honey from every flower of experience but is never itself involved. Odysseus understands that this is a man who has never loved or hated, who mocks all spiritual values, the last dregs of a decadent and hedonistic existence. He then tells the Lord of the Tower that he had himself looked long on Death until he transformed all fear, joy and God into a spiritual flame, but the Lord misunderstands Odysseus to mean that life is without value, that the free mind keeps sterilely aloof. (The Lord of the Tower, Prince Motherth, and Odysseus have all confronted Death and the Abyss, but in different ways: the Lord with ironic and mocking indifference, concerned only to reap what passing pleasure he can; Motherth with negation and withdrawal; Odysseus with agony and the transforming joy which are both part of the onrushing creative drive.) Odysseus replies: "Both of us know the secret, but you in great exhaustion/play with both life and death with sluggish mocking heart;/I rush, clasp in my arms the smallest worm, and shout: /'Dear brother, I'm your companion in both life and death!' " As Odysseus leaves, he recalls the bastard youths in Sparta who had fought with such vitality, and praises all striving, violent, evolving life.

In the woods one midnight, he watches the eleven sons of a black chieftain (who had previously killed one of his twelve sons) hunt down their old and sterile father in order to kill him according to traditional ritual, and then to possess his wives and kingdom. After they have slain him and each son has eaten in communion that portion of his father which contains the strength he covets, they resolve to fight among themselves until but one remains to possess both kingdom and wives. An ancient sorceress, however, proclaims the laws of a more civilized procedure: "Don't kill!" "Don't touch your father's wives," and bids them take their women from other tribes. As Odysseus watches, he feels that he, too, in distant ages long past, had evolved from such primitive origins and had once killed his own father. (The poet here deliberately contrasts the highly sophisticated and decadent Lord of the Tower with the ever-present atavistic primitivism in man.) Odysseus now hears Mother Earth crying for help to be freed from her primordial origins.

BOOK XXI

The gentle Negro fisher-lad. After several months, Odysseus sights the ocean, and as he hurries toward the shore, he passes a yellow and slant-eyed race which he has never seen before, and a god with a huge emerald belly squatting cross-legged with half-closed sluggish eyes. When Odysseus reaches the shore, he plunges into the waves joyfully and plays with them for a long time, as with his faithful dog, Argus, then proceeds at night to the bustling harbor town and enters a tavern where sturdy sea captains are depicting their native lands. One, from the far South, tells of the snowlands; a red-skinned captain tells of a flame-drenched land of gardens and merchantmen; and Odysseus in turn tells them nostalgically of Greece. At this moment all rush to the door to watch a passing procession, and Odysseus is told that some shipwrecked Cretans, who have settled here, are celebrating their new god, whom some call Slayer, some Savior, but whom the priests in their secret rituals name Odysseus. In ironic mockery, Odysseus realizes that he has now been reduced to the stature of a god: "I've been reduced to a god and walk the earth like myth!/O wrteched soul of man, you can't stand free on earth /or walk upright unless you walk with fear or hope./Ah, when will comrade souls like mine come down to earth?" The symbols of the new god are fire, a bow, a full-rigged ship, the feather of a white peacock, and the Pole Star stuck on a white skull.

Next morning, after playing with the sea again, he walks through the town with a begging bowl, rejoiced to be brought to this state of essential simplicity, he who once had made love to the goddess Calypso and been offered immortal youth. As he stops to watch an old gardener forcing and training a dwarf pine into shape, he considers that just such a skill-ful, pitiless, erotic hand "fights with our hearts, and some men call it God, /some Fate and humbly bow, but I call it man's soul/that now has freed itself and takes what shape it wills." As the young whores in the red-light district mock his aging body and his white hair, an old prostitute, Dame Goody, takes pity on him and gives him some pomegranates. He then knocks on the door of a newly-wed couple, and when the young bride opens, tells her that there are three kinds of charities: the first and most modest gives only in terms of deeds done, the second identifies itself with the beggar until he is well fed, but the third and greatest feeds souls and gods till all merge into One, then abandons hearth and husband in a ruthless quest.

At dawn one day Odysseus fells some trees to build his last skiff. Rumors spread that he is assisted by spirits; the townspeople bring him food and votive gifts; and when a fisherman observes that his vessel resembles a coffin, Odysseus replies that he has measured his body, his heart, his mind, all earth, sky, fear, love, happiness and pain, and that this coffin-skiff is the result of all his measurements. His old crew comrades crowd round him now in the form of ghosts, but he refuses to take them with him on his last voyage, even in memory. Contemplation of an intricately wrought seashell evokes for him the slow evolutionary progress of the universe. In dream he shoots a roe-buck with his arrow and then feels that he has pierced his own heart, but nevertheless he eats the meat with relish, for "A great and mighty tigress rules the living world." Although next day he fails to hunt down a stag in order to shape his last bow from its horns, he does find some stag-horns amid the votive gifts left by the townspeople, and with them shapes his bow.

One day amid some fishermen he hears a young Negro fisher-lad speak of One Eternal Father who is Love, of the earth as a path that leads into the sky. Another young fisherman opposes this as an unrealistic view of life, insisting that injustice rules the world and that evil thrives. An old man replies that only with good deeds may one enter the Lord's gates, but the fisher-lad answers that man will enter heaven only by God's grace. When he says softly that if someone were to strike him on one cheek he would turn the other, Odysseus hits him hard, confident that even this sickly boy will rise to defend himself, but when the lad does indeed turn his other cheek meekly, Odysseus shakes with terror at such a revolutionary view of the world. The two converse by the sea all night long, Odysseus upholding the path of war and strife, and the Negro lad (the type of Christ) upholding the path of love and peace, of selflessness, of an ultimate realm where man and God merge into One. Odysseus replies that even this One is empty air, but the lad insists that only this final One is real, "as the pure soul that broods on the world's sacred egg." Odysseus accuses the boy of loving only man's soul, whereas he loves man's flesh also, his stench, the earth, and even death, denying that the soul has value apart from the flesh, for it must evolve and purify itself in and through the flesh. When they part affectionately at dawn, Odysseus takes as his only weapons his bow, two flints, an ax, and whatever the townspeople had left him for food, then launches his skiff. Dame Goody runs up with a last gift of pomegranates. Leaping into his boat, Odysseus bids the earth a last farewell, tasting it slowly like a drop of dripping honey.

BOOK XXII

Odysseus sails toward the South Pole. The poet invokes Virtue, most joyful when most persecuted, that struggles for the sake of the battle alone. As Odysseus sails and landmarks disappear, he recalls three tensions in his life: when he first held a woman's body, when he first grasped his son, when he had slain his first enemy. But now he faces the greatest of all: Death. He sees a shoal of sharks where the males contend bloodily for the female. A tumultuous rush of fish reminds him of the ecstatic flow of life, which he now blesses with all its wars, its cunning gods, its stupid men, its tears and its laughter. When he passes by coral islands with huge wooden statues of primitive gods, with sunken cities in their shallow waters, he exclaims, "Dark demons, we have suffered much at your vast hands!" He now approaches the last antithetical limits of the world, the huge clashing mountains of Yes and No, but on coming close finds them to be serene peaks inhabited by flocks of birds. Climbing one of the peaks, he sees before him an endless sterile sea from which cold winds blow. After eating, he cuts into that virgin and cold sea.

The sun has been turning more and more pallid, hovering closer and closer to the horizon. He sees a whale swallowing a fleeing shoal of fish, recalls the black ants that ate the infant camel and the human child, and exclaims that there was a time when he named the lavish longing and fierce assault of life "God," but concludes that "God is a labyrinthine quest deep in our heads;/weak slaves think he's the isle of freedom and moor close,/all the incompetent cross their oars, then cross their hands, /laugh wearily and say, 'The Quest does not exist!'/But I know better in my heart and rig my sails: /God is wide waterways that branch throughout man's heart." The first ice floes drift by.

One day after sunset he sees the aurora australis like a lustrous crown of death above his head, and that same night he crashes into an iceberg, is flung into the sea, and at sunrise climbs, exhausted, on a crag. As he plods over the snowfields and ice, he finds a hot geyser surrounded with shrubs and birds, eats and sleeps, then next day discerns on a boulder the fossilized marks of a primordial hot climate. After many days of plodding he spies a human settlement of igloos, and is welcomed by the inhabitants as the Great Ancestor, the Great Spirit. He lives in the igloo of the witch doctor, shares their life, and discovers that here man asks not even for comfort or joy, but only not to be slain, for Fear and Hunger are the only gods. The pallid sun disappears, and through the long Antarctic night Odysseus watches many die of starvation as all wait for spring to come and the ice to thaw; yet even here he blesses life.

When spring finally comes, all prepare joyously for their journey to their summer sites, and as they speed in their sleds, singing, Odysseus bids them farewell and once more embarks, alone, in his new seal-skin kyak. But suddenly the earth roars, the ground shakes, the ice gapes, and all—men, dogs, and sleighs—are plunged into an abyss of roaring, freezing waters. Once more the poet reminds us, and for the last time, of the yawning darkness which surrounds the universe and man's puny endeavors. As Odysseus watches in horror, he restrains his blasphemies, nor does he curse as when his city had also been swallowed by the abyss, but simply says: "O Sun, who gaze and shine on all this teeming world,/who without preference cast your rays on Life and Death/nor pity man's misfortunes nor his rectitude,/would that I had your eyes to cast their light on earth, /on sea, on sky, on wretched fate indifferently." He speaks to man's soul that sails on the dark waters of despair with Death at the helm, knowing there is no safe haven home, only the black cataract of death that whirls its ships onward. Odysseus worships the soul most when, knowing there is no salvation, it crosses its hands on the cliffs of despair, without hope or fear, and welcomes Death, singing.

BOOK XXIII

Odysseus blesses life and bids it farewell. The poet invokes the Sun, the source of heat and life. As the worm of Death arms itself to devour the archer, the sun laments that now it, too, will disappear, for it has existed only in the archer's mind. When the worm crawls on Odysseus' forehead, he shudders, and then sees a shadowy form on the prow of his boat which, after turning into many shapes, distills into the form of his old companion, Death, whose features are identical in every way with his own, for we each carry Death in our decaying bodies and nourish him as we grow. Odysseus welcomes Death as a long-expected guest. He recalls his past, tracing his life backward from old age even to the embryo and the rhythms of the universe. As he feels the five elements of his body disjoining, he summons Tantalus to tell him that he, too, has given up one security after another and now meets his end completely disburdened, until Death will find in him nothing to plunder but dregs. Vividly he recalls three images of his life: a rose on a cliff's edge shedding its petals into the abyss, the canaries that sang in the holocaust of Crete, a butterfly scorched in the sack of Knossos. He invokes and praises woman in his life, for only with love are the barriers of flesh demolished and the source of life penetrated.

He falls asleep and dreams of his ancestral dead and of his father,

Laertes. All phenomena pour into his head to say farewell: the birds with sheathed claws, the tamed beasts, the stars and moon, great thoughts that strove to free men from fear and darkness, good and evil powers now reconciled. He awakes and rejoices to see his old friend still at the prow, but as Death suddenly vanishes, Odysseus knows that his end is drawing near, and he grasps his bow, his flints, and his ax that he may die armed. He recalls even his conception, and then his birth on a seashore when far-off visions of burning Troy and Knossos also rose concomitantly with his birth, and the twelve Olympian gods scattered in fear. Odysseus then blesses the five fundamental elements of his body: Earth, the ballast that keeps the ship on an even keel; Water, the restless, ever-flowing flux, the unsated voyager; Fire, that consumes all flesh and phenomena and turns them into spirit; Air, the final fruit of flame, the light, the drone that fructifies the queen bee, earth; Mind, the regulator and creator of all things, the charioteer of the other four elements which it drives headlong down the abyss with fearless joy. He dreams of God creating man to the terror of birds and beasts who sense that their master is being born, of man growing in pride and power until finally, in revolt and freedom, he chases God out of earth and into the sky.

As Odysseus sinks deep in the earth's roots, into Mother Silence, surrendering to the tide of non-existence, he hears an iceberg approaching, and as it looms before him, a mountain of ice, and crashes into his boat, he jumps up, flings himself on the slippery wall of ice, clings to it with bloody fingers, and tries to call to his old comrades for help, but the cry chokes in his throat. The ax slips from his waist, the bow falls from his shoulders, the flints drop from round his throat, the North Wind strips him bare, and all of nature bursts into lamentation. The seven lean crows who have followed him since his birth now huddle round his feet, and his seven souls come rowing on a cloud. His mind's final flame flickers on the wick of his backbone, and the worm takes its first bite as the five elements of his body snap and disjoin and the sun prepares to drown. Only Love and Memory remain as they cast up their dead in a last effort. Odysseus' spirit, his consciousness, leaps like a flame from its wick, and for an eternal moment glows disembodied in the air before it vanishes forever: "As a low lantern's flame flicks in its final blaze/then leaps above its shriveled wick and mounts aloft,/brimming with light, and soars toward death with dazzling joy,/so did his fierce soul leap before it vanished in air." It is in this eternal moment that the entire action of the twenty-fourth and final book takes place. The fire of memory blazes, clasps all souls it has loved on earth, and calls them to its assistance: "O faithful and beloved, O dead and living comrades, come!"

BOOK XXIV

The death of Odysseus. The four winds smash open the four gates of Odysseus' head. Through the north gate all plants rush into his head to strike deep roots; through the south gate animals, birds, and insects rush in to save their souls; through the east gate thoughts, dreams, and creations of the imagination rush pellmell; and through the west gate troop men of every race and kind. All mass in the streets and courtyards of the archer's spacious brain to live on in his memory.

But Odysseus cries out that he will not give up his soul before his dead companions come. Kentaur hears his master call and leaps out of his grave, gathering his moldering bellies, and joins Orpheus, who has been weeping because he had betrayed his master. Together they rush through the air to join their dying friend. Captain Sole is lying on his deathbed when he hears the cry, and as he rushes along the beach to come to his friend's aid, he meets Hardihood, his head cloven in two. Captain Sole runs up to offer his assistance and put Hardihood's enemies to rout, but Hardihood only wonders with contempt where Odysseus had picked up such an evident fool. Dame Goody, her hands filled with pomegranates, hurries with Margaro who laments the passing of love and lust, but Dame Goody, to console her friend, recounts the seven types of men to whom her body had given some consolation. She declares that she would take the same road in life again, but Margaro wants to tell the great ascetic that she has learned her lesson well, that though all in her arms had merged into One, that One was but empty air. Rocky hurries by on his white elephant, accompanied by the two Egyptian girls at whose home he had eaten, but when he meets Granite at the head of a great caravan laden with fruit and spices, he joins his friend with joy and leaves the two girls behind. Helen, her hair white with age, lies dying by a riverbank in Knossos, surrounded by her children and grandchildren, but when she hears Odysseus' call, she longs again to wreck her home, to take to sea, driven by fate. As she dies, she turns into a twelve-year-old girl on the banks of the Eurotas in Sparta, and as she rides a reed over the hermit's grave, he leaps out, rides his oaken staff with her, and longs for a home and hearth with just such a girl for wife. Diktena and Krino come riding the black bull which had killed the mountain maiden. Krino sighs and says that, could she only live her life once more, she would, like Diktena, enjoy the bodies of young men; but Diktena, in turn, longs to experience the pure joys of virginity. Captain Clam hurries by with Phida. He is anxious to join his captain on their last deathbound voyage, and Phida laments that she can never wash her father's blood from her hands, that decadent Knossos had been destroyed in vain, for the slaves had once more turned abjectly to their slavery. Argus leaps out of his grave in Ithaca, joyous and proud because of all in his native island Odysseus has chosen neither his wife, nor his son, nor his father, nor his mother, but his dog only.

Under a tree in the Orient, Prince Motherth lies dying surrounded by his yellow-robed disciples, and when they ask for his final word, offers them only a faint smile. When they insist, he says that the roads toward salvation are five: through love, despair, beauty, play, and truth, but that beyond all these, beyond the Word, lies only a wordless smile. As he prepares again to die, two men arrive from Greece, for they have heard of the great Oriental sage and have come to reap his wisdom. They debate with his disciples on the relative merits of the East and the West, the Orientals insisting that all is illusion and dream, the Greeks upholding the anthropomorphic conception of gods, denying the abyss, and placing emphasis on virtuous deeds, on the Apollonian view of harmony and balance. The older man addresses Motherth directly and speaks of philosophy, of how order must rule anarchic rage, of how the Word and not the Smile must reign supreme, but when Motherth simply smiles in answer, the younger man rushes to embrace what now seems to him more lustrous than the mind, and proclaims Motherth to be a greater Dionysus. But as Motherth is sinking into death, Odysseus' cry for help tears the sky, and an eagle swoops down and carries off the great sage in its claws.

Rala hurries to fall into the arms of the man she loves, regretting that she had ever espoused an abstract cause or denied herself husband and children, scornful that she is now worshiped on earth as a virgin martyr. She is joined by the Negro fisher-lad who had preached of love and peace, but Rala rages against him in contempt, finding his philosophy pallid, cowardly, chaste, and of a cloying sweetness. When the leopard cub leaps out of some bushes, Rala welcomes her as a twin sister.

Thus, all those whom Odysseus has kept alive with love in his memory rush to help their master in his last moment. Rala and Phida embrace as friends, Krino falls into Helen's arms, Margaro and Diktena join hands. Odysseus spies them from afar, welcomes them to his white ship of death, and begs them to hang the masts with the figs and grapes he has loved so much. He sees Captain Elias' blood-soaked lyre and longs to "pluck its chords/and play Life's great refrains to keep Death entertained." All rush and crowd the icy ship of death, Rocky on his elephant, Krino with her black bull, while Argus licks his master's feet. Now the three great forefathers come, the three Fates—Tantalus, Heracles, Prometheus—and plant themselves on the deck like three towering masts from which the women hang pomegranates, figs, and grapes, until the death-ship glows like a garden. The cricket that had once perched on Odysseus' shoulder comes again, hides in his beard, and bursts into rasping song. Then finally Temptation, that small Negro boy, crouches at Odysseus' feet, and as the two look laughingly into each other's eyes, they play with all of life until the universe merges into a forked flame and the mind soars like fire and longs to burn all away into nothingness once more. As the Negro boy falls asleep, Odysseus fondles him, and when the boy awakes and looks up again, he shudders to see the whole world swirling in dance within the world-destroyer's eyes. When the boy falls asleep again, Odysseus hangs him like a scarecrow on one of the masts. Now that the time has come for final farewell, Odysseus laughs, thrusts his hands into the pomegranates, figs, and grapes, and all suddenly vanish. Then his mind leaps, soars, and frees itself from its last cage, that of its freedom.

EPILOGUE

The poet invokes the sun who in great sorrow has sunk beneath the horizon but refuses the food and drink prepared him by his mother. He upsets the tables, pours the wine into the sea, and laments that his beloved one has vanished like a dwindling thought. Thus the poem begins and ends with the sun, itself a long metaphor of the transmutation of all matter into flame, into light, into spirit.

AN ADDITIONAL NOTE ON PROSODY

Ancient Greek meter was based, as in Homer, on a quantitative measure; that is, syllables were counted long or short according to the *length of time* each took to pronounce. This distinction has long since disappeared from the Greek language, and syllables are now considered long or short according to whether or not they are stressed in pronunciation, exactly as in English: a long syllable is a stressed one, a short syllable is an unstressed one. There is, however, one basic and most important difference between all inflected languages, such as the Greek, and an analytical language, such as English. An inflected language, because nouns, verbs, and adjectives must show case and tense by the addition of extra syllables to the root stems, has almost no monosyllables of any importance. The metrical accents, therefore (keeping the beat with secondary as well as with primary accents), almost always coincide with the rhetorical stress. Take, for example, the opening line of Book I of the *Odyssey:* Σαν πια ποθερισε τους γαυρους νιους μες στις φαρδιες αυλες του. The marks below the line indicate the metrical accents. The marks above the line indicate how the lines would be stressed by most persons in declamation. It will be noticed that there is coincidence of metrical accent and rhetorical stress in every syllable except the last syllable of ποθερισε and the monosyllable στις. This is the only variety possible, in so far as beat is concerned, in an inflected language; that is, it is possible *not* to stress in recitation a syllable which receives a strong or long metrical accent, but to give it an emphasis sufficient only to keep the underlying beat. This is what I would call a light syncopation or counterpoint (the word preferred by Hopkins), and I use these terms to indicate a variance, a disagreement, a cross-ruff between metrical accent and rhetorical stress. But it is almost never possible to stress emphatically in recitation a syllable which receives a *weak* or *short* accent in the meter. This is because in Greek (other than the weak monosyllables found in articles and pronouns), monosyllables of any importance can almost be counted on the fingers of one hand. In every line the metrical count will be eight, but the rhetorical stresses may vary from a hypothetical one (in actual practice, four) to a possible eight when there is exact coincidence between every metrically accented and every rhetorically stressed syllable.

Now take the sixth line of the same opening: και μαυρα σταζαν αιματα πηχτα κι απο τις δυο του φουχτες. Again, it will be noticed that there is exact coincidence between metrical accent and rhetorical stress in every syllable except the last syllable of αιματα and the last syllable of απο. I have translated this line thus: and thick black blood dripped down from both his mur der ous palms. It will be noted that though every metrically accented syllable has a corresponding rhetorical stress, the unaccented syllables "black" and "dripped" also receive a strong syncopation or counterpoint, for here the meter is wrenched from its position and an opposing crosscurrent is set up. There is more than enough coincidence between metrical accent and rhetorical stress on "thick," "blood," "down," "both," "murderous," and "palms" to keep the prevailing beat which the strong rhetorical stresses on "black" and "dripped" attempt to vary or destroy. Such a strong syncopation is possible *only* with monosyllables, in which the English language is extremely rich, and in this variation, I am convinced, lies the true beauty, music, and variety of traditional English verse. A good reader of traditional English poetry must keep these two counterpointing measures in balanced harmony, keeping the steady underlying beat, as a pianist keeps his, but varying it with the full-flowing cadences of the rhetorical or interpretative stress. It is my belief that a comparable counterpointing occurred in ancient Greek verse between the quantitative accental beat of long and short syllables and the rhetorical stress of the words as they were pronounced regardless of quantity.

In every line of my hexameter, the metrical count will always be six, but the rhetorical stress can vary from a hypothetical one (in actual practice, four) to a possible twelve. Let us take some new examples. Here is line 947 from Book VI: the hon ey of ob liv ion on the shin gled shore. This has only four rhetorical stresses, and only weak syncopation, that is, on the syllables "of" and "on." Line 446 of Book VII also has four rhetorical stresses: like a clear foun tain on a lawn com plain ing ly; but although it, too, has a weak syncopation on the syllables "a," "on," and the last syllable of "complainingly," it has a strong syncopation on the syllable "clear." An example of a line that has five rhetorical stresses (with strong syncopation on "God" and "deep") is line 414, Book XX: God is a lab y rin thine quest deep in our hearts. Line 511, Book XVIII, has six rhetorical stresses which coincide exactly with its six metrical stresses: E rect on free dom's high est sum mit, Laugh ter leaps; but though line

904 in Book XVIII also has as many rhetorical stresses as it has metrical accents (that is, six of each), the relationship between the two is syncopated or counterpointed: But I hold Death like a black ban ner, and march on! Line 425 of Book XIV shows seven rhetorical stresses: The fi nal la bor still re mains—kneel, aim, and shoot! I have rarely gone beyond the eight rhetorical stresses shown by line 6 of Book I, and which I have already quoted, or by line 925 of Book XXIII: Soul, coun try, men and earth, gods, sor rows, joys and thoughts. A reader may recite line 795 of the same book with nine stresses if he chooses to stress the adjectives as well as the nouns of the last half of the line: Night-prowl ing an cient ghosts, deaf ears, glazed eyes, mute mouth. Theoretically, it is possible to have as many as twelve rhetorical stresses, as in a line, for example, which contained a packed catalogue of animals, all monosyllables: cat, dog, ox, lamb, goat, bull, horse, bear, fox, lynx, ram, ewe.

The metrical accents in all these lines are always six, though at times a certain unit, or foot, of a line may be inverted for the sake of a minimum variety, or augmented by the occasional use of anapests. The rhetorical stresses, on the contrary, are always free, and vary from a theoretical one to a possible twelve, though their placement and their number often depend on how an individual reader may wish to stress the meaning or the emotion involved. Though all metrical accents have the same mechanical emphasis and weight, the rhetorical stresses are of different weights and intensities and range considerably in pitch. Oftentimes a syllable is not so much stressed as held on a level tone, either because it carries less emphasis than the one preceding or following, or because there is a great difference in duration between syllables, as in the last line quoted, between "ing" of "prowling," "eyes," and "glazed." In line 1003 of Book IX, for instance: I'd choose both War and Hun ger, that fierce, fruit ful pair! the syllables range in duration from "and" to "fierce"; each stressed syllable would receive different intensities according to the interpretation of the reader, and "both" might be held, if not stressed, in order to bring out the proper meaning. In: God is the mon strous sha dow of death-grap pling man (Book XII, line 1209), the first syllable of "grappling," for instance, would be held and not stressed by most readers. It will be noted that the semantic meaning (qualitatively) and the prevalence of consonants (quantitatively) in a word or syllable determine to a great degree the long or short duration with which it is pronounced.

This by no means exhausts the prosodic complications of a line, but I have thought it necessary to make clear at least the relationship between metrical accent and rhetorical stress because the two are still often confused in academic and creative circles. In a traditionally metrical line, many readers still confuse stresses and accents when they attempt to scan a line. Metrists have often been led astray by the metrical system of inflected languages, and have imposed this system on English, unaware of the great role Anglo-Saxon monosyllables play in the English metrical system, not only giving English poetry its peculiar beauty but also forcing on the language the creation of a meter indigenous only to a tongue which is based on stress and contains a plethora of monosyllables. Because a monosyllable can never be *mispronounced* in terms of stress, it may be placed in a weak part of the foot or in the accentual meter, and yet receive a strong stress in the rhetorical reading. The various groupings into which the rhetorical stresses or the unstressed syllables fall, whether iamb, trochee, amphibrach, dactyl, etc., should not be confused with the metrical scansion which may only be found among the metrical accents—unless, of course, a regular pattern is set up and then repeated among the stresses, in which case another problem is involved.

What I have written holds true only for the traditional meters of English, and not for such a syllabic system as that of Marianne Moore, the sprung rhythms of a Gerard Manley Hopkins or his adaptors, or the various complications of free verse. An unjustly neglected book which contains the best analysis I know of the relationship between metrical accent and rhetorical stress (though it is inadequate in a consideration of more modern measures) is *Pattern and Variation in Poetry* by Chard Powers Smith (Scribners).

A word about the difference in syllabic count between English and Greek lines: Because of the uninflected and monosyllabic character of the English language, the majority of verses written in that language end on a strong or "masculine" accent, and the lines therefore are counted in *even* numbers; but because the Greek language, in common with all inflected tongues, is polysyllabic, and because the accent falls frequently on the syllable before the last, the lines are counted in uneven syllables, and are predominantly weak or "feminine" in their endings. Typical English lines are ones of six, eight, ten or twelve syllables; typical Greek lines are ones of nine, eleven, thirteen or fifteen syllables.

NOTES

Following are a few brief notes, primarily about modern Greek folk songs, tales, legends, sayings and beliefs. Although Kazantzakis made some conscious use of anachronism, and although the action of the poem really takes place in the timeless realm of myth, he had a deep conviction that many of the customs and rituals among the Greek peasantry were also prevalent in archaic and classical times. Anyone who is familiar with the persistence of pagan rites in the ritual of the Greek Orthodox Church today, is easily persuaded. Those folk songs, sayings, or beliefs where the text needs but brief exposition or is self-explanatory, I have grouped together for easier comparative reference.

BOOK I

251: The princess is Nausicaä. See Homer's *Odyssey,* Book XVI, 360.
306: The owl is one of the attributes of the goddess Athena, protectress of Odysseus.
604: Camomile and cypress trees are planted in Greek cemeteries and are symbols of death. See I, 640, 949; XI, 704-05; XXIV, 135, 1190-91.
633-34: The fig tree, a soft wood, is symbolic of woman; the oak tree, a hard wood, of man. See II, 1261-63; XIII, 232-35; XVII, 683-85.
691: See note to II, 603.
1199: See note to XIV, 414.
1235: According to folk tales, the black cock crows when it is still night, the red cock just before dawn, and the white cock when dawn breaks. See II, 1448; VII, 722; VIII, 1179; XVII, 665; XIX, 229.
1268: The apple is an erotic symbol in all Greek folk songs, legends, and tradition. When a girl favors a young man, she gives him a bitten apple; if he wishes to accept her favors, he eats it. See II, 1170, 1321-22; III, 238-39, 711; VII, 771-75; IX, 579-89, 610-18; XI, 10; XII, 1091-95; XIV, 1391-93; XVI, 61, 68, 671-73; XVII, 178, 435, 668, 689-91; XVIII, 264-65, 323-24; XIX, 1152, 1392; XXIII, 372-76; XXIV, 375-79, 432-39, 595-96, 623-24.

BOOK II

603: The pomegranate is a symbol of fertility in marriage. As a bride crosses the threshold of her new home, she casts a pomegranate to the ground, and the marriage guests wish her as many children as the scattered fruit has seeds. See especially II, 1251-57; also I, 691; VI, 1176-82; XVII, 687-88; XVIII, 818-21, 832-39; XX, 643-45.
1134: Made of fine butter and spices for holidays (especially Easter) and marriages.
1136: Red is a symbol of joy.
1170: See note to I, 1268.
1211: Maidens braid seashells and charms in their hair to ward off the evil eye.
1220: The boy who performs this ritual must not be an orphan.
1221-23: This is still observed in Crete, for the reasons given.
1225-27: In Crete the moon is a symbol of the female, the sun a symbol of the male.
1231: During the marriage cere-

mony, wreaths made of white wax flowers are interchanged by the best man on the heads of the bride and bridegroom. These are later framed and hung in the bedroom or parlor.

1236: The bride must enter her house with her right foot first in order to bring it good luck. See also note to V, 1292-93.

1243-50, 1261-71: A bride must make her obeisance to the water of her household well and to the fire of her hearth.

1251-57: See note to II, 603.

1261-63: See note to I, 633-34.

1282-84: On the night before her wedding, when the bride goes to the well to fetch the water with which she is to wash herself, she must not speak either going or coming. See also note to VII, 771-75.

1321-22: See note to I, 1268.

1448: See note to I, 1235.

BOOK III

238-39, 711: See note to I, 1268.

670-75: Kazantzakis replied to a critic who could not understand why Odysseus does not possess Helen erotically: "You do not see the obvious: Helen's abduction by Odysseus was not an erotic one. Helen was stifling in Sparta, and she longed to leave; Odysseus wanted to take her with him as a new Trojan horse, to lean her against the disintegrating civilization of Knossos in order to destroy it. The same episode is capable of another interpretation: Helen is the Achaean beauty who by merging with the Doric barbarians creates the new Greek civilization. As soon as his plan was realized (that is, when he saw her in the arms of the barbarian gardener), Odysseus departed, leaving Helen to fulfill her mission, to transubstantiate in her womb the barbaric seed and to give birth to her son, Hellene. But naturally Odysseus does not part from Helen so serenely . . . he leaves with the incurable sorrow a man always feels when he sees a beautiful woman in the arms of another, even though he never desired to possess her. Helen was warm flesh, not a disembodied idea, and Odysseus could not part from her forever without being deeply troubled. However, he had to leave, and he did so. What could he do with her? It was not his only purpose to contribute to the creation of the new Greek civilization by uniting Achaeans and barbarians. Helen was but one stage on his onward journey." See VIII, 903-18.

836-39: See note to IV, 1091-1119.

BOOK IV

66: According to Greek folk belief, when a person is born, the worm of his death is also born and sets out to meet him and to devour him. See especially XVII, 977-81; also XXIII, 38-58, 136-45, 1284-86.

182: Folk saying. Also IX, 286, 1057, 1144, 1278, 1282, 1305; X, 288, 489, of a man who travels much; 604, 611, 618, 632, 852, of extremely prissy women who are easily hurt; 888, 1174; XI, 341, 454, 486; XII, 30, 682, 691; XIII, 538, 645-46; XVI, 303, 1239; XXIV, 730-31.

286-92: Folk lore and beliefs. Also V, 1-3, 144; IX, 884-85; X, 106, for a flag of revolution; XI, 117-19, 367, 1190-91; XIII, 568-69, 651; XV, 1143; XVII, 1315-44; XXIII, 827-30.

456-57: From folk songs. Also V, 330-31; VI, 1173-76; VIII, 490-91, 569, 793-94; IX, 60, 67, 1115; X, 1174; XI, 1-2, 440-42, 499-500, 696, 1322-23; XII, 1-4: XV, 196-98, 232, 651; XVI, 1-4, 705; XVII, 1068; XIX, 791, 1187; XXII, 85-98, 596, 1450-51; XXIII, 668-69.

1091-1119: According to Stesichorus, Helen was not really carried off to Troy by Paris. Instead, she was carried to Egypt and kept there by the king, Proteus, till her husband could claim her; it was a phantom that accompanied Paris to Troy. This version was adopted by Euripides in his *Helen* and *Electra.* See also III, 836-39.

BOOK V

97-100: When Paris and Helen ran away from Sparta, they stopped for a while on an island near the mouth of the Eurotas.
1105: Zeus was hidden in a huge stalactitic cave on Mt. Dikte in Crete by his mother, Rhea, to prevent his father, Cronos, from swallowing him. The cave, a place of religious worship since ancient days, may still be visited. It was in this cave that King Idomeneus invoked the Mother Goddess in Book V.
1158: If the bride is a virgin, the bridegroom gives her a black-hilted sword for a present.
1292-93: An evil-footed man is one who brings evil into the house he enters. The first person who enters one's house on New Year's Day brings with him either good or evil for the ensuing year, according to his character. See also note to II, 1236.

BOOK VI

386: The "milk of birds," like Coleridge's "milk of Paradise," is an imaginary food, a heavenly nectar.
636: Grapes, oranges, or honey are placed in the hands of the dead as a present for Cerberus in Hades.
723: See I, 1235.
734-39: Small poems such as these, usually in couplet form, are sung to the bride and bridegroom before and after their marriage.
768-69: A bride dedicates her girdle to Aphrodite.
1176-82: See note to II, 603.

BOOK VII

255-57: Cretan distich.
366: The body of a dead man is often washed with wine.
722: See note to I, 1235.
761: A common longing among pregnant women of the Greek peasantry.

771-75: On June 24, St. John's Day, girls throw their individually marked apples in a large jug or tub of "speechless water." As one of the girls recites a prophetic distich, a young boy pulls out an apple which indicates to whom the distich applies. The poems are often very bawdy. See also note to I, 1268, and to II, 1261-63.
1327: Earthen jars are often broken and cast into the grave to denote death.
1332-33: Deathless water, equivalent to the Fountain of Youth or Eternal Life, is death itself, or may be found only in death. See especially VIII, 1253-59; also IX, 1260-1350; XII, 1238-48; XIII, 1346-51; XIV, 990; XVII, 1295, 1303; XVIII, 1117; XIX, 1354; XXII, 1465-76; XXIV, 543, 1255-56.
1343-46: If his fire blazes to a great height, a Greek peasant believes that he will soon be visited by an important guest.

BOOK VIII

66: In Greek legends, a magic herb exists which opens all doors.
266-69: Statues of gods were often bound with rope so that they might not abscond to other villages or countries. See also VIII, 531-32; XXII, 1063-66.
623: A letter burnt in each of its four corners is often sent as a challenge or insult.

1179: See note to I, 1235.
1253-95: See note to VII, 1332-33.
1262-95: An abbreviated form of a story in Herodotus.
1290: Taken from an Egyptian hieroglyph.

BOOK IX

120: There is a folk belief that short-buttocked women bear children best.
579-89: See note to I, 1268.
610-18: See note to I, 1268.
761: Ancient Heliopolis, near the site of modern Cairo.
803-20, 875-83: Ikhnaton (known also as Amenophis or Amenhotep IV), 1375-38 B.C., sought to make Aton, the solar disk, the one supreme god of Egypt. His wife was Nefertiti.

1026: Ancient Thebes, near modern Quena. See 1026 ff.
1260, 1350: See note to VII, 1332-33.

BOOK X

613: A brainy worm, in folk tales, comes when cattle are dying and coils between their eyebrows. See also note to IV, 66.
552-55: See the vision Odysseus had of a vagabond god in XIV, 1179-96.

624-41: Kazantzakis has taken this from an actual letter written by a king of Cyprus to a king of Egypt.
647: Garments were exposed to the stars to exorcise them of evil.
1359-60: From folk tales. Young men going off to war are thought of as having an invisible crimson string about their throats. See XIII, 123; XV, 1204-09; XVIII, 691-93; XXIII, 920.

1361: There are many versions of the Prince or King Sunless in Greek folk legends, but all agree that he was so named because he would die if the sun but looked upon him. One legend says that he lived in an underground palace by a river which he would cross every night to visit his mistress, Lady Irene. Noticing that he always left much before dawn, she resolved to keep him longer one night, and ordered all the roosters in her land slain. He started out later than he thought, and just as he reached the river, the sun rose, struck him, and killed him. See XXII, 822.

BOOK XI

10: See note to I, 1268.
704-05: See note to I, 604.
1088-90: Part of the Negative Confession from Chapter CXXV of the Egyptian *Book of the Dead*. Before the forty-two gods in the Hall of the Double Maāti, the deceased must recite a prescribed negative statement of the sins he did not commit.

BOOK XII

574-76: Many folk tales end with this formula, as though all were a dream, like a wine barely tasted.

1091-95: See note to I, 1268.
1238-48: See note to VII, 1332-33.

BOOK XIII

123: See note to X, 1359-60.
232-35: See note to I, 633-34.
997: In folk legends, an eye fluttering means that a friend is coming, and a palm itching means that it will either strike someone or be filled with gold. See XIV, 36.
1346-51: See note to VII, 1332-33.

BOOK XIV

36: See note to XIII, 997.
414, 441, 452: In his first labor, Heracles killed the Nemean lion and clothed himself with its skin. See I, 1199; XIV, 1171.
423: Gibraltar, called by the ancient Greeks "The Pillars of Heracles."
428-29: On Mt. Cithaeron occurred what is known as the "Choice of Heracles." As he was meditating on the course his life should take, two women, Pleasure and Virtue, appeared before him, one offering a life of enjoyment and the other a life of toil and glory. He chose the latter. In Kazantzakis, the twelve labors of Heracles represent the arduous battle with material things which a hero must undergo in order to purify his spirit. The death of Heracles is also symbolic of this interpretation. His wife unwittingly gave him a robe steeped in poisoned blood. It clung to him and caused him such fearful suffering that he had himself carried to the summit of Mt. Oeta and burned on a pyre. He was taken to Mt. Olympus by the gods and there became a demigod. See XVI, 1118-21.
565, 581: The twelve axes are those which Odysseus strung with his bow in Homer's *Odyssey,* Book XXI, just before he killed the suitors. In Kazantzakis' *Odyssey,* these are equated with the twelve labors of Heracles. According to Kazantzakis, man has the illusion that the thirteenth and final ax or labor is that of immortality. In his *Zorba the Greek* (Simon and Schuster, 1953), Kazantzakis asks: "Does our unquenchable desire for immortality spring, not from the fact that we are immortal, but from the fact that during the short span of our lives we are in the service of something immortal?"
990: See note to VII, 1332-33.
1094-95: This was the hybrid fruit of his voyages, child of two parents, one of the flesh and the other of the spirit.
1171: See note to XIV, 414.
1179-96: See X, 552-55.
1385-90: Cretan distichs.
1391-93: See note to I, 1268.

BOOK XV

190: From folk legends. The Earth Bull is a heavy beast, like the hippopotamus, that growls in the bowels of the earth.
600-03: In *Zorba the Greek,* Kazantzakis asks: "Who was the sage who tried to teach his disciples to do voluntarily what the law orders should be done? To say 'yes' to necessity and to change the inevitable into something done of their own free will? This is perhaps the only human way to deliverance. It is a pitiable way, but there is no other."
1204-09: See note to X, 1359-60.
1370-71: A Turkish folk tradition.

BOOK XVI

61, 68: See note to I, 1268.
204-05: See V, 691-703.
278: In Greece the sign of the evil eye is made by thrusting the outstretched fingers of a hand at a man's face, in a contemptuous gesture.
671-73: See note to I, 1268.
985-87: Part of African tribe ritual.
1118-21: See note to XIV, 428-29.

BOOK XVII

178, 435, 668, 689-91: See note to I, 1268.
195-97: The slave is talking to the Old King, who is also on the elephant's back.
240-44: A wedding song.
665: See note to I, 1235.
683-85: See note to I, 633-34.
687-88: See note to II, 603.
892-93: Very popular among the Greek peasantry is the *komboloï*, a kind of secular rosary with which a man often plays by clicking bead on bead as he walks or converses. The best are made of amber. See XX, 407-08, 579-82.
977-81: See note to IV, 66.
1294-95: In Greek folk tales a dragon coils about a well and eats all the maidens who come to draw water. He is often killed by St. George. See XIX, 230-31.
1295, 1303: See note to VII, 1332-33.

BOOK XVIII

102-05: This happened in Knossos.

264-65, 323-24: See note to I, 1268.

427-83: There is a Buddhistic belief that the thirty-two signs of the perfect man, of the savior of the world, were schematized on the sole of Buddha's foot.
498-99: The Tempter is part of Odysseus himself, and now merges with him once more.
639-46: Many incidents such as these in the life of Prince Motherth are taken from the life of Buddha. Kazantzakis has written a poetic drama entitled *Buddha*.
691-93: See note to X, 1359-60.
696-749: In a Byzantine legend, the three Magi visit the Christ child; to the first, he seemed like an old man with a white beard; to the second, like a man in the prime of life with a black mustache; and to the third, like a babe suckling its mother's breast.
818-21, 832-39: See note to II, 603.
1117: See note to VII, 1332-33.
1208: In answer to several newspaper articles on "The Metaphysics of the *Odyssey*" by Miss Elli Lambridi, Kazantzakis wrote the authoress: "There are four stages through which, in my opinion, a man may pass: (1) good and evil are enemies; (2) good and evil are co-workers; (3) good and evil are one; (4) this one does not exist. In the first stage live all men of action; in the second, many men of theory (if these want to interfere in action, they will be forced, if their action is to bear fruit, to return to the first stage); the third stage is common to all the mystics of Europe and the East; the fourth, only to those of the East. . . . A few men, by continuing their onward march, may reach this abominable, inhuman—or divine—stage and live it beyond the objections of reason. . . . After many years of patient struggle Odysseus reached this lightning flash of vision. Thus his Odyssey, that is, his onward journey, was suddenly enlightened. What is meant by enlightenment? It blazed up and vanished in a lightning flash."

BOOK XIX

99-106, 139-40: Buddha says that we must look upon the world as if we were seeing it for the first and last time; this he calls the "elephant's eye."
229: See note to I, 1235.
230-31: See note to XVII, 1294-95.
232: In folk tales, a blackamoor often guards treasure hidden in the earth.
668: In folk legends, these are magical aids.

670-75: In folk tales, Death's mother often loves men and tries to protect them from her son.
1143-44: A custom in Egypt, that dead men might not harm the living with the evil eye.
1152, 1392: See note to I, 1268.
1354: See note to VII, 1332-33.

BOOK XX

407-08, 579-82: See note to XVII, 892-93.
629-32: Odysseus remembers the bastard sons of the Doric barbarians and the Spartan women. See IV, 743-98.

643-45: See note to II, 603.

BOOK XXI

761: A cross made of wax is placed between the lips of a dead man that vampires may not transform him also into a vampire.

BOOK XXII

278-82: According to folk legends, the Kingdom of Death begins here.
822: See note to X, 1361.
1063-66: See note to VIII, 532-34.

1078: In some Grecian villages on the night after the wedding, it is customary for the bridegroom to display on the balcony of his home his bride's bloodstained bedsheet as proof of her virginity.
1421: According to Greek folk legend this herb will arouse love in the woman to whom it is given.
1465-76: See note to VII, 1332-33.

BOOK XXIII

38-58, 136-45, 1284-86: See note to IV, 66.
372-76: See note to I, 1268.
920: See note to X, 1359-60.
1260: See I, 634.

BOOK XXIV

8: A monstrous mythical tree which is all trees in one.
135: See note to I, 604.
375-79, 432-39, 595-96, 623-24: See note to I, 1268.
543: See note to VII, 1332-33.
746-48: In his poetic drama, *Odysseus,* Kazantzakis describes how Odysseus chokes to death his faithful dog, Argus, to prevent him from betraying his master to the suitors by his joyous barks of welcome.
940: In ancient Orphic beliefs, the River Lethe in Hades flows from the roots of a white cypress tree. A dead man finds the tree with the help of an amulet he wears, and is guided to the Elysian fields.
1052: That is, Prince Motherth.
1087: That is, Apollo, the Greek god most opposed to oriental mysticism.

1190-91: See note to I, 640.
1255-56: See note to VII, 1332-33.

1302-05: See XVIII, 81-114.
1363: That is, the Tempter, to whom Odysseus himself had given birth. See note to XVIII, 498-99.

About the Author

NIKOS KAZANTZAKIS *has been acclaimed by Albert Schweitzer and Thomas Mann as one of the great writers of modern Europe. He was born in Crete in 1883 and studied at the University of Athens, where he received his Doctor of Law degree. Later he studied in Paris under the philosopher Henri Bergson, and he completed his studies in literature and art during four other years in Germany and Italy. Before World War II he spent a great deal of his time on the island of Aegina, where he devoted himself to his philosophical and literary work. For a short while in 1945 he was Greek Minister of Education. He was president of the Greek Society of Men of Letters, but spent most of the later years of his life in France.*

He is best known in the United States and England as the author of three enthusiastically acclaimed novels, Zorba the Greek, The Greek Passion, *and* Freedom or Death, *but he was also a dramatist, translator, poet, and travel writer.* The Odyssey: A Modern Sequel, *which he worked on over a period of twelve years, is considered to be his crowning achievement. He died in October 1957.*

For a full account of Kazantzakis' life and work, and of The Odyssey *in particular, see the Introduction to this volume.*

About the Translator

KIMON FRIAR *is an American scholar, poet, and translator of Greek descent. He has taught at Adelphi and Amherst colleges and at the State University of Iowa, New York University, and the University of Minnesota. From 1943 to 1947 he was director of the Y.M. and Y.W.H.A. Poetry Center in New York, and in 1951-1952 he was director of presentations at New York's Circle-in-the-Square theater. His translations, poetry, and criticism have appeared in a number of anthologies and in the* Atlantic, Poetry *Magazine, the* New Republic, Saturday Review, *and other magazines. He is the co-editor (with John Malcolm Brinnin) of an outstanding anthology,* Modern Poetry: American and British.

He met Nikos Kazantzakis in Florence in 1951, and the two men sensed an immediate affinity for each other's work and aims. In 1954, with the aid of a Fulbright Research Fellowship in Modern Greek Literature at the University of Athens, Kimon Friar began his monumental translation of The Odyssey: A Modern Sequel. *His four years of con-*

tinuous work on the translation have carried him on what now seems another Odyssey, for he has worked on it in the American midwest, in New York, Antibes, Yugoslavia, Athens, throughout most of Greece and the Greek islands, and in much of South America.

About the Illustrator

GHIKA (NICHOLAS HADJI-KYRIACO GHIKA) *is probably the most distinguished of contemporary Greek artists. Painter, draftsman, and stage designer, he was born in Athens in 1906, studied in Paris, and had his first one-man show there in 1927. In addition to subsequent shows in Paris, his work has been seen in one-man or group exhibitions in London, Venice, Brussels, Athens, and other European cities. His first American show was held at the Alexandre Iolas Gallery in New York in 1958.*